THE NEW ANNOTATED

SHERLOCK HOLMES

VOLUME II

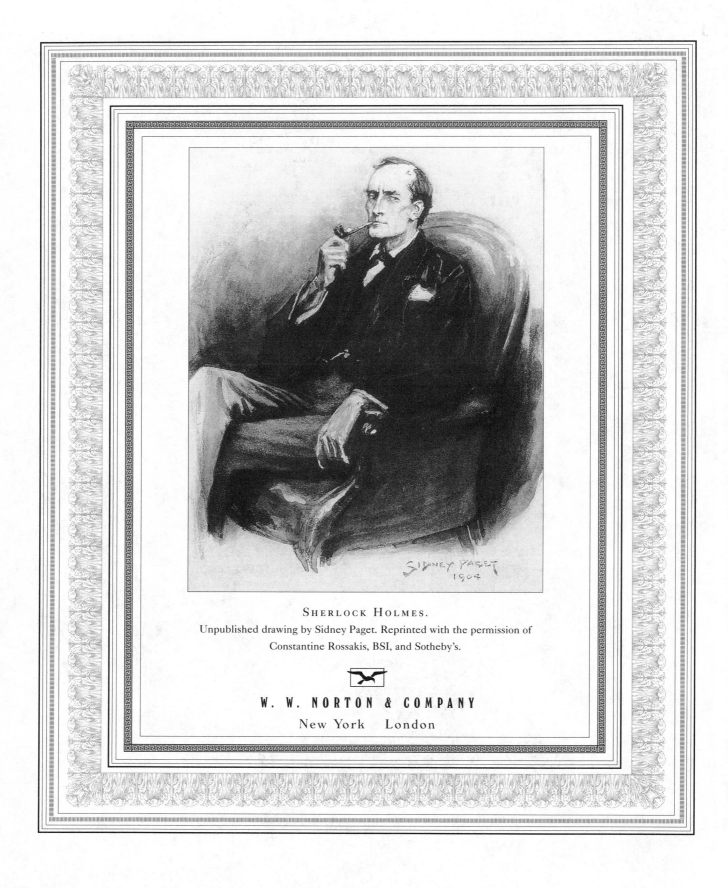

SHERLOCK HOLMES.
Unpublished drawing by Sidney Paget. Reprinted with the permission of
Constantine Rossakis, BSI, and Sotheby's.

W. W. NORTON & COMPANY
New York   London

SHERLOCK HOLMES

VOLUME II

The Return of Sherlock Holmes
His Last Bow
The Case-Book of Sherlock Holmes

Sir Arthur Conan Doyle

Edited with Notes by LESLIE S. KLINGER

with Additional Research by PATRICIA J. CHUI

Book design by JAM design
Production managers: Andrew Marasia and Julia Druskin

Doyle, Arthur Conan, Sir, 1859–1930.
The new annotated Sherlock Holmes / by Sir Arthur Conan Doyle ; edited, with a foreword
and notes by Leslie S. Klinger ; introduction by John le Carré ;
with additional research by Patricia J. Chui.

Includes bibliographical references.

ISBN 0-7394-5376-9

W. W. Norton & Company, Inc., 500 Fifth Avenue, New York, N.Y. 10110

W. W. Norton & Company Ltd., Castle House, 75/76 Wells Street, London W1T 3QT

CONTENTS

THE NEW ANNOTATED

SHERLOCK HOLMES

VOLUME II

Arthur Conan Doyle.

THE RETURN OF

SHERLOCK HOLMES [1]

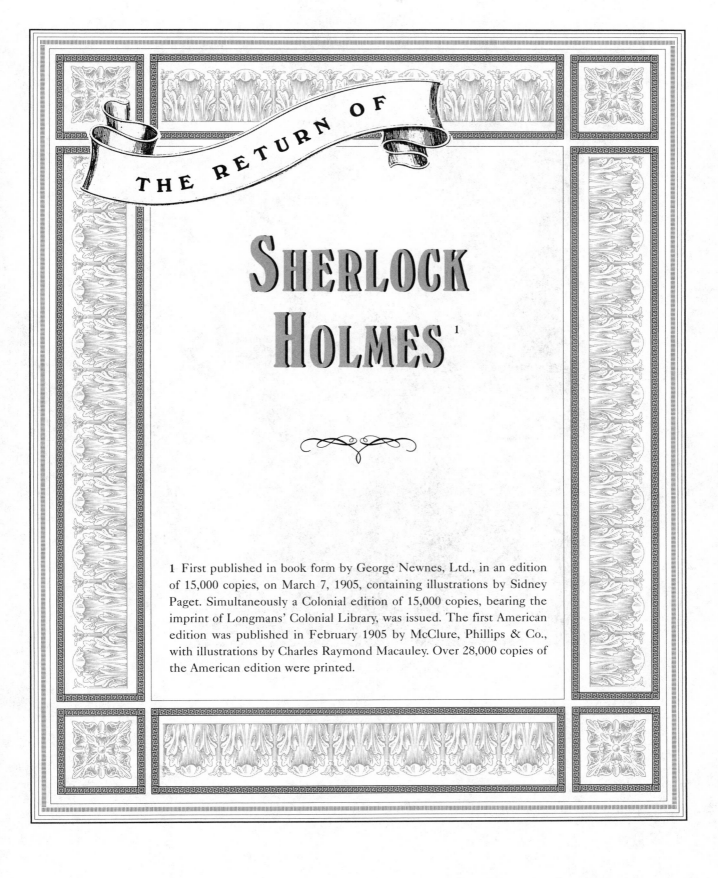

1 First published in book form by George Newnes, Ltd., in an edition of 15,000 copies, on March 7, 1905, containing illustrations by Sidney Paget. Simultaneously a Colonial edition of 15,000 copies, bearing the imprint of Longmans' Colonial Library, was issued. The first American edition was published in February 1905 by McClure, Phillips & Co., with illustrations by Charles Raymond Macauley. Over 28,000 copies of the American edition were printed.

Frederick Dorr Steele, *Collier's* 1903.

The Adventure of
the Empty House[1]

"The Empty House" may be the most widely hailed story of the entire Canon. When it was published in the Strand Magazine's *October 1903 issue, ten years after the public was informed of Holmes's death (in "The Final Problem"), the magazine made no pretence of that issue's contents: bold letters at the top of the cover trumpeted "Sherlock Holmes," with the story title in smaller letters below, and the first page of the story declared "The Return of Sherlock Holmes" in large letters above the title. In September 1903, the* Strand *had announced: "Fortunately, the news of [Holmes's] death, though based on circumstantial evidence which at the time seemed conclusive, turns out to be erroneous." While many read the story for the highly emotional scene of Holmes and Watson's reunion, there are scholarly issues as well: The murder of Ronald Adair seems impossible as described, unless Moran were on top of a passing bus. Another puzzle is why Moran escaped the gallows for his crime. Finally, there are clues to the location of the "real" 221 Baker Street provided by the description of the "empty house" across the street.*

IT WAS IN the spring of the year 1894 that all London was interested, and the fashionable world dismayed, by the murder of the Honourable[2] Ronald[3] Adair under most unusual and inexplicable circumstances. The public has already learned those particulars of the crime which came out in the police investigation; but a good deal was suppressed upon that occasion, since the case for the prosecution was so overwhelmingly strong that it was not necessary to bring forward all the facts. Only now, at the end of nearly ten years,[4] am I allowed to supply those missing links which make up the whole of that remarkable chain. The crime was of interest in itself, but that interest was as nothing to me compared to the inconceivable sequel, which afforded me the greatest shock and surprise of any event in my adventurous life. Even now, after this long interval, I find myself thrilling as I think of it, and feeling once more that sudden flood of joy, amazement, and incredulity which utterly submerged my mind. Let me say to that public,

1 "The Empty House" was published in *Collier's Weekly* on September 26, 1903, and in the *Strand Magazine* in October 1903.

2 As Christopher Morley explains, Ronald Adair earns the title "The Honourable" by virtue of being the son of a peer—in this particular case, an earl. For more on the peerage, see "The Noble Bachelor," note 16. Morley goes on to clarify that while the title could be used by either sex (his sister would also be an Honourable), it was not transferable by marriage; therefore, had Adair married, he and his wife "would have been announced by the butler as The Honourable Ronald Adair and Mrs. Adair."

3 "Robert" in the original manuscript (corrected) and in the first English edition; the

Strand Magazine and *Collier's Weekly* versions, as well as the American editions, use "Ronald."

4 Publication of "The Empty House" occurred almost immediately following Holmes's retirement. See "The Second Stain," note 5. From 1894 to 1903, Watson had supposedly been prohibited from revealing the news of Holmes's return from the dead to the public, and yet there is a plethora of evidence that Holmes was actively pursuing cases during that time. Edgar W. Smith finds it "difficult to believe" that the news was a shock "to the hundreds of people who had come in contact with the Master in the course of the dozens of cases he had handled since his tardily acknowledged resurrection, or to the many thousands of others who had heard of these cases, and, inevitably, of him." Smith does not suggest what story, if any, Holmes bothered to tell his new clients and old friends.

5 The exact date is not stated. "One would have thought," remarks June Thomson, in *Holmes and Watson*, "that, even if [Watson] were not keeping a journal at the time, the day of his reunion with Holmes would have been etched in figures of fire in his memory."

6 In visiting his various patients, muses Christopher Morley, Watson would likely have to utilise the services of a hired carriage, as it's unlikely he would be earning enough to maintain his own. Furthermore, Morley chides, despite his apparent dedication to his work, "The fact that he kept thinking about the Adair case rather than his patients suggests his heart was not in his profession."

7 See "The Boscombe Valley Mystery," note 14.

8 An address on the mansion-heavy Park Lane, alongside the eastern edge of Hyde

which has shown some interest in those glimpses which I have occasionally given them of the thoughts and actions of a very remarkable man, that they are not to blame me if I have not shared my knowledge with them, for I should have considered it my first duty to have done so, had I not been barred by a positive prohibition from his own lips, which was only withdrawn upon the third of last month.

It can be imagined that my close intimacy with Sherlock Holmes had interested me deeply in crime, and that after his disappearance I never failed to read with care the various problems which came before the public, and I even attempted, more than once, for my own private satisfaction, to employ his methods in their solution, though with indifferent success. There was none, however, which appealed to me like this tragedy of Ronald Adair. As I read the evidence at the inquest, which led up to a verdict of wilful murder against some person or persons unknown, I realized more clearly than I had ever done the loss which the community had sustained by the death of Sherlock Holmes. There were points about this strange business which would, I was sure, have specially appealed to him, and the efforts of the police would have been supplemented, or more probably anticipated, by the trained observation and the alert mind of the first criminal agent in Europe. All day[5] as I drove upon my round I turned over the case in my mind[6] and found no explanation which appeared to me to be adequate. At the risk of telling a twice-told tale, I will recapitulate the facts as they were known to the public at the conclusion of the inquest.

The Honourable Ronald Adair was the second son of the Earl of Maynooth, at that time Governor of one of the Australian Colonies.[7] Adair's mother had returned from Australia to undergo the operation for cataract, and she, her son Ronald, and her daughter Hilda were living together at 427 Park Lane.[8] The youth moved in the best society, had, so far as was known, no enemies, and no particular vices. He had been engaged to Miss Edith Woodley, of Carstairs, but the engagement had been broken off by mutual consent some months before, and there was no sign that it had left any very profound feeling behind it. For the rest, the man's life moved in a narrow and conventional circle, for his habits were quiet and his nature unemotional. Yet it was upon this easy-going young aristocrat

Park Lane near Marble Arch.
Victorian and Edwardian London

Park, signified a stature of high status and considerable wealth. In William Makepeace Thackeray's novel of social climbing *Vanity Fair* (1848), for example, a clear-eyed student at Miss Pinkerton's academy for young ladies is described as being "attached" to a desirable gentleman named Frederick Augustus Bullock not out of any great love for him, but because her mind is "fixed,—as that of a well-bred young woman should be,—upon a house in Park Lane, a country house at Wimbledon, a handsome chariot, and two prodigious tall horses and footmen, and a fourth of the annual profits of the eminent firm of Hulker & Bullock, all of which advantages were represented in the person of Frederick Augustus."

9 Gaming clubs, started mostly by veteran gamblers, proliferated in the West End sometime around 1891, as Ralph Nevill details in his *London Clubs: Their History and Treasures* (1911). Given his apparent fondness for gambling, Adair was fortunate to escape any great financial catastrophe; Nevill writes, "Such clubs were in reality little but miniature casinos, and the main, if not the sole, qualification for membership lay in being possessed of ample funds and a tendency to part with them easily." Perhaps Adair was wise in limiting his appearances to an establishment like the Baldwin, a club for card players that, according to Nevill, "admits no strangers . . . [and] which opens at two o'clock in the afternoon. The stakes here are very small."

10 See "The Red-Headed League," note 56.

11 We have seen references to Lord Balmoral before in the Canon: He is the unseen father of Lord Robert St. Simon ("The Noble Bachelor"), and his horse ran in the "Wessex Cup" ("Silver Blaze").

Balmoral Castle was the royal summer and hunting estate in the Scottish highlands,

that death came, in most strange and unexpected form, between the hours of ten and eleven-twenty on the night of March 30, 1894.

Ronald Adair was fond of cards—playing continually, but never for such stakes as would hurt him. He was a member of the Baldwin, the Cavendish, and the Bagatelle card clubs.[9] It was shown that, after dinner on the day of his death, he had played a rubber of whist[10] at the latter club. He had also played there in the afternoon. The evidence of those who had played with him—Mr. Murray, Sir John Hardy, and Colonel Moran—showed that the game was whist, and that there was a fairly equal fall of the cards. Adair might have lost five pounds, but not more. His fortune was a considerable one, and such a loss could not in any way affect him. He had played nearly every day at one club or other, but he was a cautious player, and usually rose a winner. It came out in evidence that, in partnership with Colonel Moran, he had actually won as much £420 in a sitting, some weeks before, from Godfrey Milner and Lord Balmoral.[11] So much for his recent history as it came out at the inquest.

On the evening of the crime, he returned from the club exactly at ten. His mother and sister were out spending the evening with a relation. The servant deposed that she heard him enter the front room on the second floor,[12] generally used

leased by Queen Victoria in 1848 and bought for her by Prince Albert in 1852. Philip Weller reports that Victoria occasionally used the name Balmoral as an alias (presenting herself as "the Duchess of Balmoral" when travelling incognito), and he suggests that Lord Balmoral may thus be a concealed reference to the Prince of Wales's involvement in the great 1890 "Baccarat" or "Tranby Croft" card scandal. In 1890, the prince's friend Sir William Gordon-Cumming was accused of cheating in a private game of baccarat (cards) in which the prince was a player. The prince extracted a written agreement from Gordon-Cumming that in exchange for the silence of everyone present, Gordon-Cumming would never play cards again. The affair resulted in a serious embarrassment to the Crown, when an action for libel was brought by Gordon-Cumming in 1891. The prince was called as a witness, and vicious cross-examination laid bare seamy aspects of the prince's private life. Rumours even spread that Gordon-Cumming had been forced to "take the fall" for the prince's wrongdoing.

12 In American numbering, the third floor.

13 In the manuscript, this is a "bullet of an expanding character"; in *Collier's Weekly* and American editions, an "expanded revolver bullet." Also known as a "dumdum" bullet, the expanding bullet was once primarily used in game hunting; the exposed lead nose (or "soft nose," for lead is a soft metal) distorts the body of the bullet upon impact, creating a larger wound. These bullets were first made in the town of Dum Dum, a suburb of Calcutta, and the headquarters of the Bengal artillery until 1853. In 1899, the use of dumdum bullets in warfare was banned at the Hague Convention, and that ban was agreed to by Great Britain in 1905—not that the ban would have saved Ronald Adair.

as his sitting-room. She had lit a fire there, and as it smoked she had opened the window. No sound was heard from the room until eleven-twenty, the hour of the return of Lady Maynooth and her daughter. Desiring to say good-night, she had attempted to enter her son's room. The door was locked on the inside, and no answer could be got to their cries and knocking. Help was obtained, and the door forced. The unfortunate young man was found lying near the table. His head had been horribly mutilated by an expanding revolver bullet,[13] but no weapon of any sort was to be found in the room. On the table

The unfortunate young man was found lying near the table.
G. A. Dowling, *Portland Oregonian*, July 9, 1911

lay two bank-notes for £10 each and £10 17s. in silver and gold, the money arranged in little piles of varying amount. There were some figures also upon a sheet of paper, with the names of some club friends opposite to them, from which it was conjectured that before his death he was endeavouring to make out his losses or winnings at cards.

A minute examination of the circumstances served only to make the case more complex. In the first place, no reason could be given why the young man should have fastened the door upon the inside. There was the possibility that the murderer had done this, and had afterwards escaped by the window. The drop was at least twenty feet, however, and a bed of crocuses in full bloom lay beneath. Neither the flowers nor the earth showed any sign of having been disturbed, nor were there any marks upon the narrow strip of grass which separated the house from the road. Apparently, therefore, it was the young man himself who had fastened the door. But how did he come by his death? No one could have climbed up to the window without leaving traces. Suppose a man had fired through the window, it[14] would indeed be a remarkable shot who could with a revolver inflict so deadly a wound. Again, Park Lane is a frequented thoroughfare, and there is a cab-stand within a hundred yards of the house. No one had heard a shot. And yet there was the dead man, and there the revolver bullet, which had mushroomed out, as soft-nosed bullets will, and so inflicted a wound which must have caused instantaneous death. Such were the circumstances of the Park Lane Mystery, which were further complicated by entire absence of motive, since, as I have said, young Adair was not known to have any enemy, and no attempt had been made to remove the money or valuables in the room.

All day I turned these facts over in my mind, endeavouring to hit upon some theory which could reconcile them all, and to find that line of least resistance which my poor friend had declared to be the starting-point of every investigation. I confess that I made little progress. In the evening I strolled across the Park, and found myself about six o'clock at the Oxford Street end of Park Lane. A group of loafers upon the pavements, all staring up at a particular window, directed me to the house which I had come to see. A tall, thin man with coloured glasses,[15] whom I strongly suspected of being a plain-clothes

14 "He" in American editions.

15 S. E. Dahlinger, in "The Adventures of a Hated Rival," suggests that this is Barker, Holmes's "hated rival upon the Surrey shore," described in "The Retired Colourman" as "[a] tall, dark, heavily-moustached man . . . with grey-tinted sun-glasses." D. Martin Dakin comes to the same conclusion. See "The Retired Colourman," note 17.

16 There is no book in English, apparently, called *The Origin of Tree Worship*; S. Tupper Bigelow notes that the closest match is James Ferguson's 1868 book *Tree and Serpent Worship*, with the handful of a subtitle, *illustrations of mythology and art in India in the first and fourth centuries after Christ from the sculptures of the Buddhist Topes at Sanchi and Amravati prepared under the authority of the Secretary of State for India in Council with Introductory Essays and descriptions of the plates*. Unfortunately, this appears unlikely to be the book so handily carried by the old "bibliophile," for it weighs over eleven pounds!

"I knocked down several books which he was carrying."
Sidney Paget, *Strand Magazine*, 1903

detective, was pointing out some theory of his own, while the others crowded round to listen to what he said. I got as near him as I could, but his observations seemed to me to be absurd, so I withdrew again in some disgust. As I did so I struck against an elderly deformed man, who had been behind me, and I knocked down several books which he was carrying. I remember that as I picked them up, I observed the title of one of them, *The Origin of Tree Worship*,[16] and it struck me that the fellow must be some poor bibliophile who, either as a trade or as a hobby, was a collector of obscure volumes. I endeavoured to apologize for the accident, but it was evident that these books which I had so unfortunately maltreated were very precious objects in the eyes of their owner. With a snarl of contempt he turned upon his heel, and I saw his curved back and white side-whiskers disappear among the throng.

My observations of No. 427, Park Lane, did little to clear up the problem in which I was interested. The house was separated from the street by a low wall and railing, the whole not more than five feet high. It was perfectly easy, therefore, for anyone to get into the garden, but the window was entirely inaccessible, since there was no water-pipe or anything which could help the most active man to climb it. More puzzled than ever, I retraced my steps to Kensington. I had not been in my study five minutes when the maid entered to say that a person desired to see me. To my astonishment it was none other than my strange old book collector, his sharp, wizened face peering

I knocked down several books which he was carrying.
Charles Raymond Macaulay, *Return of Sherlock Holmes*
(McClure Phillips), 1905

With a snarl he turned upon his heel.
Frederick Dorr Steele, *Collier's*, 1903

out from a frame of white hair, and his precious volumes, a dozen of them at least, wedged under his right arm.

"You're surprised to see me, sir," said he, in a strange, croaking voice.

I acknowledged that I was.

"Well, I've a conscience, sir, and when I chanced to see you go into this house, as I came hobbling after you, I thought to myself, I'll just step in and see that kind gentleman, and tell him that if I was a bit gruff in my manner there was not any harm meant, and that I am much obliged to him for picking up my books."

"You make too much of a trifle," said I. "May I ask how you knew who I was?"

"Well, sir, if it isn't too great a liberty, I am a neighbour of yours, for you'll find my little bookshop at the corner of Church Street, and very happy to see you, I am sure. Maybe you collect yourself, sir—here's *British Birds*, and Catullus,[17] and *The Holy War*—a bargain, every one of them. With five volumes you could just fill that gap on that second shelf. It looks untidy, does it not, sir?"

I moved my head to look at the cabinet behind me. When I turned again, Sherlock Holmes was standing smiling at me across my study table. I rose to my feet, stared at him for some seconds in utter amazement, and then it appears that I must have fainted for the first and the last time in my life.[18] Certainly a grey mist swirled before my eyes, and when it cleared I found my collar-ends undone and the tingling after-taste of brandy upon my lips. Holmes was bending over my chair, his flask in his hand.[19]

"My dear Watson," said the well-remembered voice, "I owe you a thousand apologies. I had no idea that you would be so affected."

I gripped him by the arm.

Sherlock Holmes stood smiling at me over my study table.
Frederic Dorr Steele, *Collier's*, 1903

17 Bliss Austin, in "Two Bibliographical Footnotes," suggests that the Catullus and the earlier mentioned *Origin of Tree Worship* might perhaps be a single book, Grant Allen's *The Attis of . . . Catullus . . . with Dissertations on . . . the Origin of Tree Worship, and on the Galliambic Metre* (1892). Book collectors argue unendingly over the exact "five volumes" carried by Holmes.

18 Even despite the drama of the situation, Watson, an ex-soldier who has seen battle, displays a surprisingly weak constitution here, leading S. C. Roberts (in *Doctor Watson*) to conclude that other emotional factors—such as the illness and death of his wife, Mary Morstan—must have also contributed to the doctor's sudden loss of consciousness. Yet Walter P. Armstrong, Jr., thinks that Watson did not faint at all, but in fact invented his dramatic reaction in a burst of poetic licence. "A Watson who in real life had never fainted," he reasons, "might easily in composing an imaginative account of an emotional scene which never happened depict Watson as fainting."

19 It does seem a bit strange that Holmes, posing as a doddering book collector, conveniently happens to be carrying a flask of brandy. "Where did this brandy come from?" asks Walter P. Armstrong, Jr. "Did Sherlock Holmes, as one of the properties in his character of an aged bibliophile, carry a hip flask? It does not seem likely. Nor can he, after a three years' absence, have known where the brandy in Watson's home was kept." In fact, Holmes would not have been familiar with the layout of Watson's current residence, which, being in Kensington, is therefore not the Paddington residence of "The Engineer's Thumb" nor the apartment that backs on Mortimer Street in "The Final Problem."

Of course, Armstrong could be underestimating Holmes, who shrewdly could have had a flask at the ready for just the purpose of reviving his friend. In *Baker Street Chronology: Commentaries on the Sacred Writings of Dr. John H. Watson*, Ernest Bloomfield Zeisler argues Holmes surely "foresaw the possibility, if not the likelihood, that his faithful old friend might be so startled [by his reappearance] as to require resuscitation; he prepared himself for this by pocketing his brandy flask."

When I turned again Sherlock Holmes was standing
smiling at me across my study table.
Sidney Paget, *Strand Magazine*, 1903

"Holmes!" I cried. "Is it really you? Can it indeed be that you are alive? Is it possible that you succeeded in climbing out of that awful abyss?"

"Wait a moment," said he. "Are you sure that you are really fit to discuss things? I have given you a serious shock by my unnecessarily dramatic reappearance."

"I am all right, but indeed, Holmes, I can hardly believe my eyes. Good heavens! to think that you—you of all men—should be standing in my study!" Again I gripped him by the sleeve, and felt the thin, sinewy arm beneath it. "Well, you're not a spirit, anyhow," said I. "My dear chap, I am overjoyed to see you. Sit down, and tell me how you came alive out of that dreadful chasm."

He sat opposite to me and lit a cigarette in his old, nonchalant manner. He was dressed in the seedy frock-coat of the book merchant, but the rest of that individual lay in a pile of white hair and old books upon the table. Holmes looked even thinner and keener than of old, but there was a dead-white tinge in his aquiline face which told me that his life recently had not been a healthy one.

"I am glad to stretch myself, Watson," said he. "It is no joke when a tall man has to take a foot off his stature for several hours on end. Now, my dear fellow, in the matter of these explanations, we have, if I may ask for your co-operation, a hard and dangerous night's work in front of us. Perhaps it would be better if I gave you an account of the whole situation when that work is finished."

"I am full of curiosity. I should much prefer to hear now."

"You'll come with me to-night?"

"When you like and where you like."

"This is, indeed, like the old days. We shall have time for a mouthful of dinner before we need go. Well, then, about that chasm. I had no serious difficulty in getting out of it, for the very simple reason that I never was in it."

"You never were in it?"

"No, Watson, I never was in it. My note to you was absolutely genuine. I had little doubt that I had come to the end of my career when I perceived the somewhat sinister figure of the late Professor Moriarty standing upon the narrow pathway which led to safety. I read an inexorable purpose in his grey eyes.[20] I exchanged some remarks with him, therefore, and obtained his courteous permission to write the short note which you afterwards received. I left it with my cigarette-box and my stick, and I walked along the pathway, Moriarty still at my heels. When I reached the end I stood at bay. He drew no weapon, but he rushed at me and threw his long arms around me. He knew that his own game was up, and was only anxious to revenge himself upon me. We tottered together upon the brink of the fall. I have some knowledge, however, of baritsu,[21] or the Japanese system of wrestling, which has more than once been very useful to me. I slipped through his grip, and he with a horrible scream kicked madly for a few seconds, and clawed the air with both his hands. But for all his efforts he could not get his balance, and over he went. With my face over the brink,

20 Here we learn that Moriarty's eyes, like Holmes's (*The Hound of the Baskervilles*), were grey.

21 See "Baritsu," page 822.

22 American editions add the word "soon."

23 Holmes's ostensible reasons for faking his own death don't quite hold up upon closer examination. He speaks of lulling Moriarty's conspirators into complacency and then having his vengeance upon them; but as T. S. Blakeney points out, Holmes had not long before been informed by the London police that the whole of Moriarty's gang—save the professor himself—had been captured. Not until after he makes the decision to fabricate his demise does Holmes learn that the police wire was not entirely accurate and that Colonel Moran was still at large. Perhaps, Blakeney suggests, Holmes's memory of the experience has (understandably) gotten somewhat jumbled, and "his statement of his thoughts, as given by Watson, must have been coloured by wisdom after the event."

24 What does this mean? By its context, "some months later," although ambiguous, seems to refer to a short period of time *after the incident at the falls*. Holmes and Moriarty clashed in the spring of 1891, and "The Final Problem" was not published in the *Strand Magazine* until December 1893. Is it reasonable to take "some months later" to mean the almost three-year period from April 1891 to February or March of 1894, when Holmes could have read the published account? Or was it the case instead that—even though Watson supposedly kept his grief private for two years until finally penning "The Final Problem"—he wrote *another* "account" of the matter, perhaps for the benefit of brother Mycroft, which the latter forwarded?

I saw him fall for a long way. Then he struck a rock, bounded off, and splashed into the water."

I listened with amazement to this explanation, which Holmes delivered between the puffs of his cigarette.

"But the tracks!" I cried. "I saw, with my own eyes, that two went down the path and none returned."

"It came about in this way. The instant that the Professor had disappeared, it struck me what a really extraordinarily lucky chance Fate had placed in my way. I knew that Moriarty was not the only man who had sworn my death. There were at least three others whose desire for vengeance upon me would only be increased by the death of their leader. They were all most dangerous men. One or other would certainly get me. On the other hand, if all the world was convinced that I was dead they would take liberties, these men; they would[22] lay themselves open, and sooner or later I could destroy them. Then it would be time for me to announce that I was still in the land of the living. So rapidly does the brain act that I believe I had thought this all out before Professor Moriarty had reached the bottom of the Reichenbach Fall.[23]

"I stood up and examined the rocky wall behind me. In your picturesque account of the matter, which I read with great interest some months later,[24] you assert that the wall was sheer. This was not literally true. A few small footholds presented themselves, and there was some indication of a ledge. The cliff is so high that to climb it all was an obvious impossibility, and it was equally impossible to make my way along the wet path without leaving some tracks. I might, it is true, have reversed my boots, as I have done on similar occasions, but the sight of three sets of tracks in one direction would certainly have suggested a deception. On the whole, then, it was best that I should risk the climb. It was not a pleasant business, Watson. The fall roared beneath me. I am not a fanciful person, but I give you my word that I seemed to hear Moriarty's voice screaming at me out of the abyss. A mistake would have been fatal. More than once, as tufts of grass came out in my hand or my foot slipped in the wet notches of the rock, I thought that I was gone. But I struggled upwards, and at last I reached a ledge several feet deep and covered with soft green moss, where I could lie unseen, in the most perfect comfort. There I was stretched, when you, my dear Watson, and all your following were investigating in the most sympathetic and inefficient manner the circumstances of my death.

"At last, when you had all formed your inevitable and totally erroneous conclusions, you departed for the hotel, and I was left alone. I had imagined that I had reached the end of my adventures, but a very unexpected occurrence showed me that there were surprises still in store for me. A huge rock, falling from above, boomed past me, struck the path, and bounded over into the chasm. For an instant I thought that it was an accident; but a moment later, looking up, I saw a man's head against the darkening sky,[25] and another stone struck the very ledge upon which I was stretched, within a foot of my head. Of course, the meaning of this was obvious. Moriarty had not been alone. A confederate—and even that one glance had told me how dangerous a man that confederate was—had kept guard while the Professor had attacked me.[26] From a distance, unseen by me, he had been a witness of his friend's death and of my escape. He had waited, and then, making his way round to the top of the cliff, he had endeavoured to succeed where his comrade had failed.

"I did not take long to think about it, Watson. Again I saw that grim face look over the cliff, and I knew that it was the precursor of another stone. I scrambled down on to the path. I don't think I could have done it in cold blood. It was a hundred times more difficult than getting up. But I had no time to think of the danger, for another stone sang past me as I hung by my hands from the edge of the ledge. Half-way down I slipped, but by the blessing of God I landed, torn and bleeding, upon the path. I took to my heels, did ten miles over the mountains in the darkness, and a week later I found myself in Florence, with the certainty that no one in the world knew what had become of me.[27]

"I had only one confidant—my brother Mycroft. I owe you many apologies, my dear Watson, but it was all-important that it should be thought I was dead, and it is quite certain that you would not have written so convincing an account of my unhappy end had you not yourself thought that it was true. Several times during the last three years I have taken up my pen to write to you, but always I feared lest your affectionate regard for me should tempt you to some indiscretion which would betray my secret.[28] For that reason I turned away from

25 Watson's (and Holmes's) time references in "The Final Problem" and "The Empty House" are severely criticised by numerous scholars, especially Holmes's reference to "the darkening sky." See the appendix on page 823.

26 While Moriarty may have brought the confederate (Colonel Moran) along as a "bodyguard," argues Noah André Trudeau, in "The Second Most Dangerous Man in London— Dangerous to Whom?," this particular henchman had a different purpose in mind. In Trudeau's scenario, Colonel Moran could see that Moriarty was about to "take a fall" through Holmes's efforts and wanted to be sure that Holmes in fact *eliminated* Moriarty, so that Moran could take over the organisation. He shot Moriarty just as he was on the verge of the falls (hence Moriarty's "horrible scream"). Holmes did not hear the shot fired by the silent air-gun. This also explains why Moran was situated atop the cliff, not at Moriarty's side. Trudeau also answers the question raised by critics of why Colonel Moran did not prepare himself with a gun to use against Holmes and was inexpediently slinging rocks. If, after killing Moriarty with the gun Moran *did* bring, Moran's gun jammed, the stone slinging is explained. Finally, Trudeau's theory explains the absence of Moriarty's body, for Moran would have retrieved it to prevent the discovery of the bullet wound.

27 Holmes's logic here is baffling. Given that Moran had witnessed his "escape" and never actually saw whether either stone he threw hit his mark, wouldn't the colonel have assumed that Holmes was still alive—and thus wouldn't Holmes have feared his cover blown? Yet Holmes instead seems strangely complacent in the certainty that no one knows his true fate. "In other words," Stanley McComas sums up in "Lhove at Lhassa," "Moran *saw him alive,* so Moran *will believe he is dead.* Every underworld character in London must have known Holmes was alive. Watson's acceptance of this incongruous tale can only be put down to his shock at seeing Holmes again."

28 June Thomson, writing in *Holmes and Watson*, is one scholar who believes Holmes's reasoning "sounds suspiciously like an attempt to excuse the inexcusable." While Holmes excels at scrutinising objective, external situations, he is far less adept at analysing his own actions and motivations, and thus has chosen to shift the burden of fault onto Watson's hapless shoulders. "[Holmes] was not given to deep or critical self-examination," Thomson explains, "and his first instinct when faced with the need to explain his own unacceptable behaviour was to look for something or someone else to blame, in this case, Watson's inability to dissemble. By doing this he could justify his conduct not only to Watson but also to himself." Thomson is unsympathetic toward Watson, labelling him "not given himself to subtle psychological inquiry and prone anyway to believe Holmes was usually right"—which, in fact, he does here.

29 Again, Holmes's explanation of his behaviour rests on thin logic. While it may be true that Holmes wanted to avoid drawing attention to himself in public, history shows that he was in little danger of Watson even giving him a second glance and therefore had no need to turn away. On nearly every occasion reported in the Canon in which Holmes disguised himself, Watson failed to see through the disguise at first glance, whether it be that of a drunken-looking groom ("A Scandal in Bohemia"—Watson said it took three looks to be sure that it was Holmes), a tall thin old man ("The Man with the Twisted Lip"), an Italian priest ("The Final Problem"), or an unshaven French workman ("The Disappearance of Lady Frances Carfax"). "Will this explanation hold water?" Walter P. Armstrong, Jr., marvels, "It is incredible that [Holmes's]

you this evening when you upset my books, for I was in danger at the time, and any show of surprise and emotion upon your part might have drawn attention to my identity and led to the most deplorable and irreparable results.[29] As to Mycroft, I had to confide in him in order to obtain the money which I needed. The course of events in London did not run so well as I had hoped, for the trial of the Moriarty gang left two of its most dangerous members, my own most vindictive enemies, at liberty. I travelled for two years in Tibet,[30] therefore, and amused myself by visiting Lhassa, and spending some days with the head Lama.[31] You may have read of the remarkable explorations of a Norwegian named Sigerson, but I am sure that it never occurred to you that you were receiving news of your friend.[32] I then passed through Persia, looked in at Mecca,[33] and paid a short but interesting visit to the Khalifa[34] at Khartoum,[35] the results of which I have communicated to the Foreign Office. Returning to France, I spent some months in a research into the coal-tar derivatives,[36] which I conducted in a laboratory at Montpellier,[37] in the South of France. Having concluded this to my satisfaction and learning that only one of my enemies was now left in London,[38] I was about to return when my movements were hastened by the news of this very remarkable Park Lane Mystery, which not only appealed to me by its own merits, but which seemed to offer some most peculiar personal opportunities. I came over at once to London, called in my own person at Baker Street, threw Mrs. Hudson into violent hysterics, and found that Mycroft had preserved my rooms and my papers exactly as they had always been.[39] So it was, my dear Watson, that at two o'clock to-day I found myself in my old arm-chair in my own old room, and only wishing that I could have seen my old friend Watson in the other chair which he has so often adorned."

Such was the remarkable narrative to which I listened on that April evening—a narrative which would have been utterly incredible to me had it not been confirmed by the actual sight of the tall, spare figure and the keen, eager face, which I had never thought to see again. In some manner he had learned of my own sad bereavement,[40] and his sympathy was shown in his manner rather than in his words. "Work is the best antidote to sorrow, my dear Watson," said he, "and I have a piece of work for us both to-night which, if we can bring it to a suc-

confidence in his art of make-up had grown so weak that he was afraid Watson would recognize in the aged bookseller a man whom he thought long dead."

30 At this time, the mountainous, secluded region of Tibet was nominally a Chinese protectorate, the ruling Qing (or Manchu) Dynasty having sent troops in 1720 to drive out the occupying Mongols. Because the Chinese had brought with them Tibet's seventh Dalai Lama (the spiritual leader had been sequestered in China for his "protection"), Tibetans welcomed the liberators and accepted a Chinese presence at the capital city of Lhasa. At least initially, these representatives, or *ambans*, wielded only symbolic power, and throughout the nineteenth century Tibet strove to ignore them and go about administering its own affairs.

In visiting Tibet, Holmes was in fact violating a century-old ban against foreigners, instituted in 1792 after a Gurkha invasion. Tibetans deeply mistrusted a British government not only connected to the Gurkhas but also plainly covetous of a trade route to China through Tibet; in this latter respect, Britain was anxious that Russia, with its own expansionist plans, might succeed where it had failed. Yet Tibet, its borders closed, continued to reject its ardent British suitor. Finally, in 1903, the thirteenth Dalai Lama's alarming reliance on his Russian adviser led Britain to send a military force, commanded by Francis Younghusband, to Lhasa to force negotiation of a trade agreement. The Tibetans, naturally, refused to cooperate, and in March 1904 Lord Curzon gave Younghusband the order to attack. Within minutes, 628 Tibetans were dead, 222 injured. (The British lost six men.) The Dalai Lama fled to Mongolia with his adviser, and in his absence Britain signed the Lhasa Convention, establishing relations with Tibet and granting the region its autonomy. Without Chinese approval, however, the Lhasa Convention held up only until 1906, when the British did an about-face and negotiated another treaty with China—a treaty that was in turn nullified when the Qing dynasty's collapse in 1912 granted Tibet a brief period of independence.

While there is much debate over whether Holmes *could* have penetrated Tibet, other foreigners had been there before him, notably, George Bogle, the first Englishman to visit (1774), Thomas Manning, who visited Lhasa in 1811, and French Lazarist priests Huc and Gabet, whose 1846 visit to Lhasa is detailed in their 1850 *Souvenirs d'un Voyage . . .*

31 Which "head Lama"? Upon Holmes's arrival in Tibet in 1891, the thirteenth Dalai Lama, Thubten Gyatso (1876–1933), would have been around fifteen years old; the ninth Panchen Lama (or Tashi Lama, the second most powerful figure in Tibet), Panchen Choekyi Nyima (1883–1937), even younger at nine or so. It is possible, but not probable, that Holmes would have spent several days consulting with a minor, regardless of his titular status.

In any event, neither the Dalai Lama nor the Panchen Lama is ever referred to as "head lama"; in fact, events to come would illustrate just how thorny and complex the sharing of spiritual leadership could be. At the close of the nineteenth century, Tibetan leadership had been marked by a string of Dalai Lamas who had either been weak leaders or who had died prematurely (some say under suspicious circumstances), whereas the Panchen Lamas had come to embody Tibetan resistance to Chinese rule. During the ensuing trade entanglements among Britain, China, and Tibet, the thirteenth Dalai Lama and the ninth Panchen Lama were pitted against each other by the Chinese government, creating a rift between the two positions that has never really been repaired. One leader, the Dalai Lama, would eventually return from exile to rule Tibet for two decades as "the Great Thirteenth," restoring faith in the institution of the Dalai Lama; the other would be forced to flee to China to spend the rest of his own life in exile. When the Panchen Lama wrote to the Dalai Lama complaining about the way he had been treated, the Dalai Lama's response was unsympathetic, to say the least: "You seem to have forgotten the sacred history of your predecessors and wandered away to a desert. . . . It is difficult to believe that a person who thinks of himself only . . . should be regarded as a lama of Buddha."

In light of the young ages of the two lamas during Holmes's visit as well as Holmes's unconventional use of the title, A. Carson Simpson identifies the "head lama" as the Regent, abbot of the Ten-gye-ling Monastery; he was referred to as the "Head Lama" in Sir Charles Bell's *Tibet, Past and Present* (1924). Bell befriended the thirteenth Dalai Lama during his exile and also wrote a biography of the Great Thirteenth.

Oddly, the word is "Llama" in the *Strand Magazine*, many other magazine publications, and early American texts. One doubts that Holmes would have spent his time in collaboration with a pack animal (one that in any case was indigenous to the Andes, not the Himalayas).

32 It is possible, notes June Thomson, that Holmes chose his assumed Scandinavian nationality out of admiration for (or competition with) the Swedish explorer Sven Hedin (1865–1952). By the early 1890s, Hedin had already published a number of books about his travels throughout Persia, Mesopotamia, and other areas of Central Asia, and his accounts were eagerly received by newspaper readers. Holmes was probably still in Tibet when Hedin embarked on a four-year exploration of Russia, China, and northern Tibet in 1893, nearly perishing in his first crossing of the great Taklamakan Desert. Hedin returned

to Asia to explore Tibet more thoroughly in an 1899–1902 expedition, publishing the first detailed maps of Tibet in 1905–1908. Unlike Holmes, Hedin was not able to visit Lhasa, his poor disguise as a Buddhist pilgrim failing to gain him entry (although he was able to meet the Panchen Lama).

33 Thomson dismisses the oft-repeated complaint that Holmes could not have entered Mecca as an Englishman or even as a Norwegian. After all, if Richard Burton could enter Mecca in disguise (in 1853), why couldn't Holmes, who had expertise in masking his appearance (although lacking Burton's fluency in languages and sincere adoption of the Muslim faith)? In fact, Holmes's visit may have been inspired by Burton's *Personal Narrative of a Pilgrimage to El- Medinah and Meccah*, published in three volumes from 1855 to 1856. "[I]t is quite possible," hypothesises Thomson, "that for this part of his journey [Holmes] adopted not only a new name and a new nationality, as he had done in Tibet, but also a new religion and appearance, passing himself off as either an Algerian or Moroccan Muslim. . . ." As proof that he might have pulled it off, Thomson draws attention to Holmes's "dark eyes and hair as well as his lean features and hawk-like nose . . . [which] already gave him a cast of features not unlike an Arab's, a similarity which would have been enhanced by the deep tan he had acquired through exposure to the sun and wind during his travels in Tibet." As for Holmes's presumed inability to speak Arabic, posing as an Algerian or Moroccan Muslim would have helped to conceal that defect, for the primary language of those countries was French at that time, "and Holmes spoke French like a native."

34 This would be Khalifa Abdallahi, or 'Abd Allah (1846–1899), who assumed leadership of the religious and political Mahdist movement following the death of Muhammad Ahmad (al-Mahdi) in 1885. (For more on al-Mahdi, see "The Cardboard Box," note 9). Abdallahi may have lacked the Mahdi's religious fervor, but he worked to establish his authority among the different Mahdist factions and to continue the Mahdi's campaign against Egypt. By the time Holmes visited him, Abdallahi had weathered famine and various unsuccessful military campaigns and was enjoying a four-year period of administrative stability. But in 1896—perhaps acting on information provided by Holmes—British and Egyptian troops again attempted to take Sudan, and the last of the Mahdists (along with Abdallahi himself) fell on November 24, 1899.

35 Immediately after the Mahdists' capture of Khartoum, the capital of Sudan, in 1885 (see "The Cardboard Box," note 9, for a discussion of the rôle of General Charles Gordon, Watson's hero), al-Mahdi and his followers abandoned the devastated city and established a new cultural and administrative centre at nearby Omdurman. This village of mud houses was higher and better-drained than Khartoum; and by moving there al-Mahdi sought to disassociate himself completely from a city that had been founded by Egyptians. (Khartoum was retaken by the British in 1898 and rebuilt under the command of Governor-General Lord Kitchener.) Given that Khalifa Abdallahi was not living in Khartoum when Holmes had his audience, Holmes presumably refers to "Khartoum" in the expansive sense of the seat of government; in the modern era the "Three Towns of Khartoum" encompass Khartoum, Khartoum North, and Omdurman.

36 Which "derivatives" (dyes? oils? carbolic acids?) and why they interested Holmes is the subject of endless speculation. One scholar points out that 80 percent of all chemical research in the last century was devoted to studies of one form or another of the "coal-tar derivatives."

37 The name is misspelled "Montpelier" in the *Strand Magazine* and various book editions. Holmes would likely have conducted his experiments at, or with the backing of, the University of Montpellier, founded in 1220 and focussed on medicine and the law, boasting a fine anatomical museum and a rich library. Suppressed by the French Revolution of 1789, the school was divided into separate faculties (of medicine, pharmacy, science, and letters) for nearly a hundred years, regaining recognition as an official university in 1896. Montepellier is also known for its many vineyards, which might have further attracted an oenophile such as Holmes.

38 This was clearly Moran; but what happened to the other, unnamed enemy?

39 The reader may recall that in "The Final Problem," Holmes reports that Moriarty's men had "set fire to our rooms" but that "no great harm was done." The image of Mycroft busily arranging Holmes's rooms to his liking might give one pause, or at least it does Walter P. Armstrong, Jr. Considering that Mycroft had previously made only a single visit to Holmes's rooms (in "The Greek Interpreter"), it seems implausible that he would have known how to restore them "exactly as they had always been," regardless of his vaunted powers of observation. Casting about for others who may have had a hand in the renovations, Armstrong also dismisses Mrs. Hudson, "for she seldom crossed the threshold," and Holmes's eccentric contraptions would most likely have baffled her. "In fact," Armstrong concludes, "only one man could have done it, and that man was Watson. Naturally he did not want his name to appear, because he is supposed to have thought that Holmes was dead."

40 Does this mean the death of Mary Morstan? Once again, some theorists, seeing that Watson rarely discusses his wife in the Canon, take the view that his marriage was an unsuccessful one and that his "bereavement" does *not* refer to grief over his wife's death. Wingate Bett, in "Watson's Second Marriage," advances the hypothesis that "bereavement" here means deprivation, either by estrangement (which he dismisses as unthinkable) or by mental derangement. Bett suggests that "the prolonged strain to which Miss Morstan's sensitive nature had been subjected during the events of *The Sign of Four* and for some years previously might well have led to a mental breakdown." C. Alan Bradley and William A. S. Sarjeant note that Watson does not even identify the name of the deceased person; "it could have been Watson's mother, his father or his brother, for all that the chronicle tells us."

Most scholars, however, accept the conventional view that Watson's "sad bereavement" was caused by the death of Mary Morstan. Watson, presumably unwilling (unable) to dwell on the details in such a public forum, never does reveal the circumstances of her death. She was still only thirty years old in 1891, which leads some to propose that she died in childbirth, as did so many other women in the Victorian era. Another theory, that Mary Morstan succumbed to tuberculosis—which could explain why Watson was so quick to leave Holmes's side to take care of the consumptive (and fictitious) Englishwoman in "The Final Problem" (see note 40)—is readily discounted by June Thomson, who observes that tuberculosis was fatal and, at that time, untreatable; patients were prescribed only rest and fresh air as they grew progressively weaker. Yet when Holmes arrived at Watson's apartment to solicit his aid in capturing Moriarty, Watson revealed that his wife was "away upon a visit," behaviour hardly appropriate for a woman suffering from

cessful conclusion, will in itself justify a man's life on this planet." In vain I begged him to tell me more. "You will hear and see enough before morning," he answered. "We have three years of the past to discuss. Let that suffice until half-past nine, when we start upon the notable adventure of the empty house."

It was indeed like old times when, at that hour, I found myself seated beside him in a hansom, my revolver in my pocket, and the thrill of adventure in my heart. Holmes was cold and stern and silent. As the gleam of the street-lamps flashed upon his austere features, I saw that his brows were drawn down in thought and his thin lips compressed. I knew not what wild beast we were about to hunt down in the dark jungle of criminal London, but I was well assured, from the bearing of this master huntsman, that the adventure was a most grave one, while the sardonic smile which occasionally broke through his ascetic gloom boded little good for the object of our quest.

I had imagined that we were bound for Baker Street, but Holmes stopped the cab at the corner of Cavendish Square. I observed that as he stepped out he gave a most searching glance to right and left, and at every subsequent street corner he took the utmost pains to assure that he was not followed. Our route was certainly a singular one. Holmes's knowledge of the by-ways of London was extraordinary, and on this occasion he passed rapidly, and with an assured step, through a network of mews and stables, the very existence of which I had never known. We emerged at last into a small road, lined with old, gloomy houses, which led us into Manchester Street, and so to Blandford Street. Here he turned swiftly down a narrow passage, passed through a wooden gate into a deserted yard, and then opened with a key[41] the back door of a house. We entered together, and he closed it behind us.

The place was pitch-dark, but it was evident to me that it was an empty house. Our feet creaked and crackled over the bare planking, and my outstretched hand touched a wall from which the paper was hanging in ribbons. Holmes's cold, thin fingers closed round my wrist and led me forwards down a long hall, until I dimly saw the murky fanlight over the door. Here Holmes turned suddenly to the right, and we found ourselves in a large, square, empty room, heavily shadowed in the corners, but faintly lit in the centre from the lights of the street beyond. There was no lamp near and the window was thick with dust, so that we could only just discern each other's figures within. My companion put his hand upon my shoulder and his lips close to my ear.

"Do you know where we are?" he whispered.

"Surely that is Baker Street," I answered, staring through the dim window.

"Exactly. We are in Camden House, which stands opposite to our own old quarters."[42]

"But why are we here?"

"Because it commands so excellent a view of that picturesque pile. Might I trouble you, my dear Watson, to draw a little nearer to the window, taking every precaution not to show yourself, and then to look up at our old rooms—the starting-point of so many of your little fairy-tales?[43] We will see if my three years of absence have entirely taken away my power to surprise you."

I crept forward and looked across at the familiar window. As my eyes fell upon it, I gave a gasp and a cry of amazement. The blind was down, and a strong light was burning in the room. The shadow of a man who was seated in a chair within was thrown in hard, black outline upon the luminous screen of the window. There was no mistaking the poise of the head, the squareness of the shoulders, the sharpness of the features. The face was turned half-round, and the effect was that of one of those black silhouettes which our grandparents loved to frame. It was a perfect reproduction of Holmes. So amazed was I that I threw out my hand to make sure that the man himself was standing beside me. He was quivering with silent laughter.

"Well?" said he.

"Good heavens!" I cried. "It is marvellous."

"I trust that age doth not wither nor custom stale my infinite variety,"[44] said he, and I recognised in his voice the joy and pride which the artist takes in his own creation. "It really is rather like me, is it not?"

"I should be prepared to swear that it was you."

"The credit of the execution is due to Monsieur Oscar Meunier, of Grenoble, who spent some days in doing the moulding. It is a bust in wax.[45] The rest I arranged myself during my visit to Baker Street this afternoon."

a debilitating disease. "Watson would not have allowed it," Thomson writes, "nor would he have been as eager to accompany Holmes abroad had he known his wife was already suffering from consumption which, as a doctor, he would almost certainly have diagnosed."

41 Holmes's possession of the key is yet another mystery. The house is empty, implying that it is available for rent or sale; June Thomson suggests that Holmes, posing as a prospective buyer, paid a fruitful visit to the real estate agent whose name must have appeared on a sign outside. Thomas L. Stix, on the other hand, expresses doubt: "Where did Holmes get the key? We do not know, but our experience is that estate agents do not casually give out keys to properties that they control."

42 Although Watson's directions are explicit, in the words of David L. Hammer in *The Game Is Afoot*, "There are as many candidates for the Empty House as for 221B, and the most which can be said is that it remains a shadowy location." The principal reason for the dilemma is that in 1881, when Holmes moved to 221 Baker Street, Baker Street had not yet merged with York Place (1921) or Upper Baker Street (1930) *and there was no 221*. In fact Baker Street was barely a quarter-mile long and consisted of eighty buildings, with the highest number No. 85. Scholars assume that Watson disguised only the number, however, and not the street. Based on their examinations of the route described in "The Empty House," the descriptive elements described in this and other stories—the mews ("The Empty House"), the back yard ("Problem of Thor Bridge"), the windows (*A Study in Scarlet*, "The Beryl Coronet"), the absence of a street-lamp ("The Empty House")—they propose other candidates on Baker Street. The most popular is No. 31, selected by Bernard Davies ("The Back Yards of Baker Street"), William S. Baring-Gould (" 'I Have My Eye on a Suite in Baker Street' "), and David L. Hammer. No. 111 also has its supporters, including the eminent Chandler Briggs and Vincent Starrett (*The Private Life of Sherlock Holmes*) and Christopher Morley ("Report from Baker Street"), although, as noted, No. 111 was not incorporated into Baker Street proper until long after Holmes had departed. For a detailed listing of candidates, see this editor's "The Location of 'A Most Desirable Residence,' " in *The Return of Sherlock Holmes* (Indianapolis: Gasogene Books, 2003).

43 In the English edition, the phrase "your little fairy-tales" has been replaced by "our little adventures."

44 Apparently a paraphrase of dialogue from Shakespeare's *Antony and Cleopatra*, in which Antony's friend Enobarbus explains to Caesar's friend Agrippa the appeal of Cleopatra to the two men: "Age cannot wither her, nor custom stale / Her infinite variety; other women cloy / The appetites they feed, but she makes hungry / Where most she satisfies . . ." (Act II, Scene 2). Modern writers make of this a paean to mature women.

45 It is tempting to wonder whether Monsieur Meunier was employed by Madame Tussaud's Exhibition, the wax museum founded by Marie Gresholtz Tussaud (1760–1850) and located on nearby Marylebone Road. Tussaud, born in France, learned how to make wax models from an uncle who owned wax museums in Paris. Among her early subjects were both Voltaire and Rousseau; but she was imprisoned during the French Revolution and forced during the Reign of Terror to make death masks from the heads of prisoners (her friends among them) who had just been executed by the guillotine. Tussaud came to London with her two sons in 1802, and they toured their collection of wax models throughout England, Scot-

"I crept forward and looked across at the familiar window."
Sidney Paget, *Strand Magazine*, 1903

"But why?"

"Because, my dear Watson, I had the strongest possible reason for wishing certain people to think that I was there when I was really elsewhere."

"And you thought the rooms were watched?"

"I *knew* that they were watched."

"By whom?"

"By my old enemies, Watson. By the charming society whose leader lies in the Reichenbach Fall. You must remember that they knew, and only they knew, that I was still alive. Sooner or later they believed that I should come back to my rooms. They watched them continuously,[46] and this morning they saw me arrive."

"How do you know?"

"Because I recognised their sentinel when I glanced out of my window. He is a harmless enough fellow, Parker by name, a garroter[47] by trade, and a remarkable performer upon the jew's-harp.[48] I cared nothing for him. But I cared a great deal for the much more formidable person who was behind him, the bosom friend of Moriarty, the man who dropped the rocks over the cliff, the most cunning and dangerous criminal in London. That is the man who is after me to-night, Watson, and that is the man who is quite unaware that we are after *him*."

My friend's plans were gradually revealing themselves. From this convenient retreat, the watchers were being watched and the trackers tracked. That angular shadow up yonder was the bait, and we were the hunters. In silence we stood together in the darkness and watched the hurrying figures who passed and repassed in front of us. Holmes was silent and motionless; but I could tell that he was keenly alert, and that his eyes were fixed intently upon the stream of passers-by. It was a bleak and boisterous night, and the wind whistled shrilly down the long street. Many people were moving to and fro, most of them muffled in their coats and cravats. Once or twice it seemed to me that I had seen the same figure before, and I especially noticed two men who appeared to be sheltering themselves from the wind in the doorway of a house some distance up the street. I tried to draw my companion's attention to them, but he gave a little ejaculation of impatience, and continued to stare into the street. More than once he fidgeted with his feet and tapped rapidly with his fingers upon the wall. It was evident to me that he was becoming uneasy, and that his plans were not working out altogether as he had hoped. At last, as midnight approached and the street gradually cleared, he paced up and down the room in uncontrollable agitation. I was about to make some remark to him, when I raised my eyes to the lighted window, and again experienced almost as great a surprise as before. I clutched Holmes's arm, and pointed upwards.

"The shadow has moved!" I cried.

It was, indeed, no longer the profile, but the back, which was turned towards us.

Three years had certainly not smoothed the asperities of his temper or his impatience with a less active intelligence than his own.

land, and Ireland for thirty-three years, finally establishing a permanent exhibition in 1835 on Baker Street and Portman Square. The museum was an immense success, featuring lifelike figures and death masks of figures such as Napoleon, Shakespeare, Admiral Horatio Nelson, Sir Walter Scott, and Benjamin Franklin—with the most popular attraction being the "Chamber of Horrors" (originally the "Separate Room," which young ladies were advised not to visit and described in 1888 in *Dickens's Dictionary of London* as "overstrong meat for babes"), in which famous murderers and other violent criminals were represented alongside their victims. Tussaud's sons moved the museum to Marylebone Road in 1888, almost immediately adjacent to the Baker Street Underground station and a statue of Sherlock Holmes erected in 1999.

46 Ronald A. Knox, the father of Sherlockian scholarship, whose thesis it is that Mycroft was a double agent aiding both his brother and Professor Moriarty (see "The Final Problem"), writes, "*Credat Judæus Apella*; you do not really watch a house on the chance of its being revisited, for three years on end. No, Colonel Moran's information will have come, as usual, from Mycroft. . . ." As before, Knox believes that Mycroft was not an entirely devious person, and that he aimed ultimately to double-cross Sherlock's enemy rather than betray his brother. While Mycroft probably did inform Moran's people that Sherlock had returned, he also must have known about the installation of the wax model and therefore was assisting his brother in setting a trap for them. Sherlock must have been concerned that Watson might not share his faith in Mycroft or understand his complex character and so hid from Watson the real story of Mycroft's conflicting loyalties.

47 Garrot, or garrote, was a method of Spanish execution in which the condemned was

strangled by a cord, wire, or iron collar. According to E. Cobham Brewer's *Dictionary of Phrase and Fable*, originally the executioner would induce asphyxiation by twisting the cord with a stick; such a method lends meaning to the term itself, garrote being Spanish for "stick." "In 1851," Brewer continues, "General Lopez was garrotted by the Spanish authorities for attempting to gain possession of Cuba; since which time the thieves of London, etc., have adopted the method of strangling their victim by throwing their arms round his throat, while an accomplice rifles his pockets."

In "Parker the Garrotter: Why Was He Harmless?," Lionel Needleman speculates that Parker had been a notorious garroter in the 1860s who was captured during the outbreak of garroting that took place in the autumn and winter of 1862–1863 in London. After a term of imprisonment, he turned to the streets, a broken man, begging and performing on the jew's-harp, where he came to Holmes's attention.

48 This small musical instrument, known for centuries all over Europe and Asia, consists of a flexible metal (or wooden) "tongue" affixed to a two-pronged metal frame. The player places the frame in his or her teeth and plucks at the metal tongue with a finger; different notes may be achieved by modifying the shape of the mouth, altering the quality of the sound. Additionally, some eighteenth- and nineteenth-century jew's harps increased their ranges by incorporating two to as many as sixteen tongues. The etymology of the name is murky, but no connection has ever been made between the instrument and Jews. (It is also sometimes referred to as a "jaw's harp.")

"Of course it has moved," said he. "Am I such a farcical bungler, Watson, that I should erect an obvious dummy, and expect that some of the sharpest men in Europe would be deceived by it? We have been in this room two hours, and Mrs. Hudson has made some change in that figure eight times, or once in every quarter of an hour. She works it from the front so that her shadow may never be seen. Ah!" He drew in his breath with a shrill, excited intake. In the dim light I saw his head thrown forward, his whole attitude rigid with attention. Outside, the street was absolutely deserted.[49] Those two men might still be crouching in the doorway, but I could no longer see them. All was still and dark, save only that brilliant yellow screen in front of us with the black figure outlined upon its centre. Again in the utter silence I heard that thin, sibilant note which spoke of intense suppressed excitement. An instant later he pulled me back into the blackest corner of the room, and I felt his warning hand upon my lips. The fingers which clutched me were quivering. Never had I known my friend more moved, and yet the dark street still stretched lonely and motionless before us.

But suddenly I was aware of that which his keener senses had already distinguished. A low, stealthy sound came to my ears, not from the direction of Baker Street, but from the back of the very house in which we lay concealed. A door opened and shut. An instant later steps crept down the passage—steps which were meant to be silent, but which reverberated harshly through the empty house. Holmes crouched back against the wall, and I did the same, my hand closing upon the handle of my revolver. Peering through the gloom, I saw the vague outline of a man, a shade blacker than the blackness of the open door. He stood for an instant, and then he crept forward, crouching, menacing, into the room. He was within three yards of us, this sinister figure, and I had braced myself to meet his spring, before I realized that he had no idea of our presence. He passed close beside us, stole over to the window, and very softly and noiselessly raised it for half a foot. As he sank to the level of this opening the light of the street, no longer dimmed by the dusty glass, fell full upon his face. The man seemed to be beside himself with excitement. His two eyes shone like stars, and his features were working convulsively. He was an elderly man, with a thin, projecting nose, a high, bald forehead, and a huge grizzled moustache. An opera-hat was pushed to

49 This sentence is omitted in the English edition.

50 Given as "whirring" in some editions.

51 A metal cover that closes the breech of a gun once the cartridges have been loaded.

"The light of the street fell full upon his face."
Sidney Paget, *Strand Magazine*, 1903

the back of his head, and an evening dress shirt-front gleamed out through his open overcoat. His face was gaunt and swarthy, scored with deep, savage lines. In his hand he carried what appeared to be a stick, but as he laid it down upon the floor it gave a metallic clang. Then from the pocket of his overcoat he drew a bulky object, and he busied himself in some task which ended with a loud, sharp click, as if a spring or bolt had fallen into its place. Still kneeling upon the floor he bent forward and threw all his weight and strength upon some lever, with the result that there came a long, whirling,[50] grinding noise, ending once more in a powerful click. He straightened himself then, and I saw that what he held in his hand was a sort of gun, with a curiously misshapen butt. He opened it at the breech, put something in, and snapped the breech-block.[51] Then, crouching down, he rested the end of the barrel upon the ledge of the open window, and I saw his long moustache droop over the stock and his eye gleam as it peered along the sights. I heard a little sigh of satisfaction as he cuddled the butt into his shoulder, and saw that amazing target, the black man on the yellow ground, standing clear at the end of his fore sight. For an instant he was rigid and motionless. Then his finger tightened on the trigger. There was a strange, loud whiz and a long, silvery tinkle of broken glass. At that instant Holmes sprang like a tiger on to the marksman's back and hurled him flat upon his face. He was up again in a moment, and with convulsive strength he seized Holmes by the throat; but I struck him on the head with the butt of my revolver and he dropped again

Then, crouching down, he rested the end of the barrel
upon the ledge of the open window.
G. A. Dowling, *Portland Oregonian*, July 9, 1911

"He seized Holmes by the throat."
Sidney Paget, *Strand Magazine*, 1903

upon the floor. I fell upon him, and as I held him my comrade blew a shrill call upon a whistle. There was the clatter of running feet upon the pavement, and two policemen in uniform, with one plain-clothes detective, rushed through the front entrance and into the room.

"That you, Lestrade?" said Holmes.

"Yes, Mr. Holmes. I took the job myself. It's good to see you back in London, sir."

"I think you want a little unofficial help. Three undetected murders in one year won't do, Lestrade. But you handled the Molesey Mystery with less than your usual—that's to say, you handled it fairly well."

We had all risen to our feet, our prisoner breathing hard, with a stalwart constable on each side of him. Already a few loiterers had begun to collect in the street. Holmes stepped up to the window, closed it, and dropped the blinds. Lestrade had produced two candles, and the policemen had uncovered their lanterns. I was able at last to have a good look at our prisoner.

It was a tremendously virile and yet sinister face which was turned towards us. With the brow of a philosopher above[52] and the jaw of a sensualist below, the man must have started with great capacities for good or for evil. But one could not look upon his cruel blue eyes, with their drooping, cynical lids, or upon the fierce, aggressive nose and the threatening, deep-lined brow, without reading Nature's plainest danger-signals. He took no heed of any of us, but his eyes were fixed upon Holmes's face with an expression in which hatred and amazement were equally blended. "You fiend!" he kept on muttering—"you clever, clever fiend!"

"Ah, Colonel!" said Holmes, arranging his rumpled collar, "'journeys end in lovers' meetings,' as the old play says.[53] I don't think I have had the pleasure of seeing you since you favoured me with those attentions as I lay on the ledge above the Reichenbach Fall."

The Colonel still stared at my friend like a man in a trance. "You cunning, cunning fiend!" was all that he could say.

"I have not introduced you yet," said Holmes. "This, gentlemen, is Colonel Sebastian[54] Moran, once of Her Majesty's Indian Army, and the best heavy game shot that our Eastern Empire has ever produced. I believe I am correct, Colonel, in saying that your bag of tigers still remains unrivalled?"

The fierce old man said nothing, but still glared at my companion; with his savage eyes and bristling moustache he was wonderfully like a tiger himself.

"I wonder that my very simple stratagem could deceive so old a shikari,"[55] said Holmes. "It must be very familiar to you. Have you not tethered a young kid under a tree, lain above it with your rifle, and waited for the bait to bring up your tiger? This empty house is my tree, and you are my tiger. You have possibly had other guns in reserve in case there should be several tigers, or in the unlikely supposition of your own aim failing you. These," he pointed around, "are my other guns. The parallel is exact."

Colonel Moran sprang forward, with a snarl of rage, but the constables dragged him back. The fury upon his face was terrible to look at.

52 See "The Final Problem," note 14, for a discussion of Victorian interest in phrenology, the study of the shape of the head.

53 Holmes apparently paraphrases Shakespeare's *Twelfth Night*, Act II, Scene 3: "Journeys end in lovers meeting." Scholars note that Holmes has a special fondness for *Twelfth Night*, as it is the only one of Shakespeare's works he quotes twice (see also "The Red Circle"). From this, some have built a case that Holmes's birthday was "twelfth night," or January 6.

54 "Aloysius" in the manuscript.

55 An Anglo-Indian term, meaning a hunter, a sportsman.

"Colonel Moran sprang forward, with a snarl of rage."
Sidney Paget, *Strand Magazine*, 1903

"I confess that you had one small surprise for me," said Holmes. "I did not anticipate that you would yourself make use of this empty house and this convenient front window. I had imagined you as operating from the street, where my friend Lestrade and his merry men were awaiting you. With that exception, all has gone as I expected."

Colonel Moran turned to the official detective.

"You may or may not have just cause for arresting me," said he, "but at least there can be no reason why I should submit to the gibes of this person. If I am in the hands of the law, let things be done in a legal way."

"Well, that's reasonable enough," said Lestrade. "Nothing further you have to say, Mr. Holmes, before we go?"

Holmes had picked up the powerful air-gun from the floor, and was examining its mechanism.

"An admirable and unique weapon," said he, "noiseless and of tremendous power. I knew Von Herder, the blind German mechanic, who constructed it to the order of the late Professor Moriarty. For years I have been aware of its existence, though I have never before had an opportunity of handling it. I commend it very specially to your attention, Lestrade, and also the bullets which fit it."

"You can trust us to look after that, Mr. Holmes," said Lestrade, as the whole party moved towards the door. "Anything further to say?"

"Only to ask what charge you intend to prefer?"

"What charge, sir? Why, of course, the attempted murder of Mr. Sherlock Holmes."

"Not so, Lestrade. I do not propose to appear in the matter at all.[56] To you, and to you only, belongs the credit of the remarkable arrest which you have effected. Yes, Lestrade, I congratulate you! With your usual happy mixture of cunning and audacity, you have got him."

"Got him! Got whom, Mr. Holmes?"

"The man that the whole force has been seeking in vain—Colonel Sebastian Moran, who shot the Honourable Ronald Adair with an expanding bullet from an air-gun through the

56 The police have no choice but to bow to Holmes's wishes, since none of them were witness to any of the events that just took place. And while Moran has been caught in possession of an air-gun (the same air-gun that Holmes professed to fear at the outset of "The Final Problem"), nothing links this weapon to the bullet fired. June Thomson wonders at Holmes's refusal to cooperate with the police. In other cases, Holmes had kept his name out of any official reports in order to induce the police to continue to refer matters to him. Here, Holmes not only declines to take any credit for the capture but indicates that he will not even press charges against Moran. "In the absence of any explanation on Holmes's part one can only assume that during the three years spent abroad he had learned to appreciate the advantages of living incognito and now preferred to avoid publicity . . ."

Colonel Moran sprang forward with a snarl of rage.
Frederick Dorr Steele, *Collier's Magazine*, 1903

57 Park Lane fronts on Hyde Park for its entire length. From where, then, did the colonel fire? Percival Wilde, in "The Bust in the Window," suggests a location inside the park near the Marble Arch entrance, though he would have faced the difficult task of escaping attention from the scores of people who frequented the park "between the hours of ten and eleven-twenty" at night. Edgar W. Smith also nominates a position within the park, but in considering the difficulties of firing accurately while aiming upward toward a target two flights above ground level, he posits that Moran must have climbed "a strategically placed tree" to reach the appropriate level. Nicholas Utechin, disregarding the height issue as well as that of any bystanders, argues that the Colonel shot Adair while standing on the pavement on the Hyde Park side of Park Lane.

58 The reference is to "Mrs. Turner" in the manuscript, corrected. Because there are earlier references to "Mrs. Hudson" in this adventure, this strongly supports the conclusion that Mrs. Turner worked for Mrs. Hudson. See "A Scandal in Bohemia" for a detailed discussion of the Hudson-Turner connection.

59 "Preserved" in the *Strand Magazine*.

60 For a discussion of the path of the colonel's bullet, see the appendix on page 825.

open window of the second-floor front[57] of No. 427, Park Lane, upon the 30th of last month. That's the charge, Lestrade. And now, Watson, if you can endure the draught from a broken window, I think that half an hour in my study over a cigar may afford you some profitable amusement."

Our old chambers had been left unchanged through the supervision of Mycroft Holmes and the immediate care of Mrs. Hudson.[58] As I entered I saw, it is true, an unwonted tidiness, but the old landmarks were all in their places. There were the chemical corner and the acid-stained, deal-topped table. There upon a shelf was the row of formidable scrap-books and books of reference which many of our fellow-citizens would have been so glad to burn. The diagrams, the violin-case, and the pipe-rack—even the Persian slipper which contained the tobacco—all met my eye as I glanced round me.

There were two occupants of the room—one Mrs. Hudson, who beamed upon us both as we entered, the other the strange dummy which had played so important a part in the evening's adventures. It was a wax-coloured model of my friend, so admirably done that it was a perfect facsimile. It stood on a small pedestal table with an old dressing-gown of Holmes's so draped round it that the illusion from the street was absolutely perfect.

"I hope you observed[59] all precautions, Mrs. Hudson?" said Holmes.

"I went to it on my knees, sir, just as you told me."

"Excellent. You carried the thing out very well. Did you observe where the bullet went?"

"Yes, sir. I'm afraid it has spoilt your beautiful bust, for it passed right through the head and flattened itself on the wall. I picked it up from the carpet. Here it is!"[60]

Holmes held it out to me. "A soft revolver bullet, as you perceive, Watson. There's genius in that—for who would expect to find such a thing fired from an air-gun? All right, Mrs. Hudson. I am much obliged for your assistance. And now, Watson, let me see you in your old seat once more, for there are several points which I should like to discuss with you."

He had thrown off the seedy frock-coat, and now he was the Holmes of old in the mouse-coloured dressing-gown which he took from his effigy.

"The old shikari's nerves have not lost their steadiness, nor his eyes their keenness," said he, with a laugh, as he inspected the shattered forehead of his bust.

"Plumb in the middle of the back of the head and smack through the brain. He was the best shot in India, and I expect that there are few better in London. Have you heard the name?"

"No, I have not."[61]

"Well, well, such is fame! But, then, if I remember aright, you had not heard the name of Professor James[62] Moriarty, who had one of the great brains of the century. Just give me down my index of biographies from the shelf."

He turned over the pages lazily, leaning back in his chair and blowing great clouds of smoke[63] from his cigar.

"My collection of M's is a fine one," said he. "Moriarty himself is enough to make any letter illustrious, and here is Morgan the poisoner, and Merridew of abominable memory, and Mathews, who knocked out my left canine in the waiting-room at Charing Cross, and, finally, here is our friend of to-night."

" 'My collection of M's is a fine one,' said he."
Sidney Paget, *Strand Magazine*, 1903

61 This professed ignorance, comments D. Martin Dakin, appears to be a literary device used by Watson—the same device that he used to explain who Professor Moriarty was in "The Final Problem." Watson did apparently know who Colonel Moran was, having noted his employment by Moriarty in *The Valley of Fear* (whose events predate those of "The Empty House").

62 Remember that Moriarty's Christian name is not disclosed in "The Final Problem," and that the Professor's brother, whose slanderous accounts of Holmes's role in Moriarty's death trouble Watson so, is named "Colonel *James* Moriarty." Ian McQueen argues that the Professor never had a brother at all, and that Colonel Moran, attempting to reconvene the Professor's gang upon his return to London, adopted Moriarty's name professionally so as to assume a greater air of authority. Moran may have seen himself as a "brother-outlaw" to Moriarty, says McQueen, and used the term in his letters to the press in the sense not of a blood relationship but rather one of kinship with a close friend and colleague.

63 The phrase "of smoke" has been added in the English edition.

64 Bangalore is the capital (since 1830) of Karnataka, in southern India, and served as the military and administrative headquarters of British India from 1831 to 1881. Notwithstanding Watson's efforts to disguise the regiment, the American editions refer to the Pioneers as the *Bangalore* Pioneers.

65 C.B. stands for "Companion of the Bath," an order of British knighthood bestowed by the monarch as reward for outstanding military or civil service. The recipient of a C.B. would not actually become a knight or be referred to as "sir" or "dame"; such titles are reserved for the two highest classes of knighthood, Knight or Dame Grand Gross (G.C.B.) and Knight or Dame Commander (K.C.B. or D.C.B.). Those knights and dames, together with the sovereign, the "great master of the order," and members of the C.B. class, make up the Most Honourable Order of the Bath.

66 The same educational career has been ascribed to another Holmes villain, John Clay in "The Red-Headed League"—meaning that both "the second most dangerous man in London" and "the fourth smartest man in London" were products of Eton and Oxford. Christopher Morley, placing Holmes as a graduate of that other well-known British university, sees the detective's fixation on both as no mere coincidence, noting, "It must be borne in mind that Holmes was a Cambridge man and might perhaps be prejudiced." Other, more favourably viewed graduates of Eton and Oxford, as culled by Morley, include Foreign Minister Anthony Eden and Monsignor Ronald A. Knox, chaplain of Trinity College at Oxford, who translated the Bible into English and "started the whole trend of modern Sherlock Holmes criticism" with the satirical essay "Studies in the Literature of Sherlock Holmes." (Knox was himself a detective novelist whose best-known such work was *Still Dead*, published in 1934.)

"My collection of M's is a fine one."
Frederick Dorr Steele, *Collier's*, 1903

He handed over the book, and I read:

Moran, Sebastian, Colonel. Unemployed. Formerly 1st Bengalore[64] Pioneers. Born London, 1840. Son of Sir Augustus Moran, C.B.,[65] once British Minister to Persia. Educated Eton and Oxford.[66] Served in Jowaki Campaign,[67] Afghan Campaign, Charasiab (despatches), Sherpur, and Cabul.[68] Author of "Heavy Game of the Western Himalayas" (1881); "Three Months in the Jungle" (1884). Address: Conduit Street. Clubs: The Anglo-Indian,[69] the Tankerville,[70] the Bagatelle Card Club.

On the margin was written, in Holmes's precise hand:

The second most dangerous man in London.

"This is astonishing," said I, as I handed back the volume. "The man's career is that of an honourable soldier."

"It is true," Holmes answered. "Up to a certain point he did well. He was always a man of iron nerve, and the story is still told in India how he crawled down a drain after a wounded man-eating tiger. There are some trees, Watson, which grow to a certain height, and then suddenly develop some unsightly eccentricity. You will see it often in humans. I have a theory that the individual represents in his development the whole procession of his ancestors, and that such a sudden turn to good or evil stands for some strong influence which came into the line of his pedigree. The person becomes, as it were, the epitome of the history of his own family."

"It is surely rather fanciful."

"Well, I don't insist upon it. Whatever the cause, Colonel Moran began to go wrong. Without any open scandal, he still made India too hot to hold him. He retired, came to London, and again acquired an evil name. It was at this time that he was sought out by Professor Moriarty,[71] to whom for a time he was chief of the staff. Moriarty supplied him liberally with money and used him only in one or two very high-class jobs, which no ordinary criminal could have undertaken. You may have some recollection of the death of Mrs. Stewart, of Lauder, in 1887. Not? Well, I am sure Moran was at the bottom of it; but nothing could be proved. So cleverly was the Colonel concealed that, even when the Moriarty gang was broken up, we could not incriminate him. You remember at that date, when I called upon you in your rooms, how I put up the shutters for fear of air-guns? No doubt you thought me fanciful. I knew exactly what I was doing, for I knew of the existence of this remarkable gun, and I knew also that one of the best shots in the world would be behind it. When we were in Switzerland he followed us with Moriarty, and it was undoubtedly he who gave me that evil five minutes on the Reichenbach ledge.

"You may think that I read the papers with some attention during my sojourn in France, on the look-out for any chance of laying him by the heels. So long as he was free in London, my life would really not have been worth living. Night and day the shadow would have been over me, and sooner or later his chance must have come. What could I do? I could not shoot him at sight, or I should myself be in the dock. There was no use appealing to a magistrate. They cannot interfere on the strength of what would appear to them to be a wild suspicion. So I could do nothing. But I watched the criminal news, knowing that sooner or later I should get him. Then came the death of this Ronald Adair. My chance had come at last! Knowing what I did, was it not certain that Colonel Moran had done it?

67 The "Jowaki Campaign" was a term for two separate British military expeditions, mounted in 1853 and 1877–1878, against the Jowaki Afridis, a Pashtun tribe whose territory encompassed the Khyber Pass in northern Pakistan. After annexing the Punjab, the British, recognising the strategic importance of the mountain gateway, clashed frequently with the resistant Afridis in an attempt to keep the pass open. The expeditions of the Jowaki Campaign were undertaken specifically as punitive strikes, meant to retaliate for Afridi raids into British territory in India and Pakistan.

68 Sherpur is a fortified plain outside Kabul (Cabul), the scene of a British victory in the Second Afghan War, in which Dr. Watson served as well.

69 Probably the East India United Service Club, located in St. James's Square.

70 In "The Five Orange Pips," we learn that Holmes saved Major Prendergast in the "Tankerville Club Scandal."

71 Nicholas Utechin makes the interesting suggestion that the young Sebastian Moran used Professor Moriarty as his army coach (see "The Final Problem") to gain his commission and that Moriarty followed young Moran's career and later "sought him out."

72 Holmes seems to be referring to the science of ballistics—the branch of physics that, in looking at the behaviour of projectiles, is more commonly understood to mean the study of bullets and firearms, particularly when used in policework. Yet Judge S. Tupper Bigelow, in "Was It Attempted Murder?," believes Holmes to be mistaken in thinking that the bullets could be indisputably linked to Moran's gun. "[I]t is useful to know," writes Bigelow, "that ballistics was unknown at Scotland Yard, and for that matter, in any police department in the world, in 1895; the police became aware of its possibilities no earlier than 1909." Bigelow goes on to note that it was only in 1910 that all U.S. police forces were using ballistics to investigate gun-related crimes. Perhaps Holmes expected to test-fire bullets from Moran's air-gun and compare them to the bullet found in Adair's body. If two bullets fired from the same gun looked alike, he must have reasoned, then two bullets that look alike must have been fired from the same gun. In this respect, "he was anticipating the part ballistics has played in the investigation of crime by about 15 years."

He had played cards with the lad; he had followed him home from the club; he had shot him through the open window. There was not a doubt of it. The bullets alone are enough to put his head in a noose.[72] I came over at once. I was seen by the sentinel, who would, I knew, direct the Colonel's attention to my presence. He could not fail to connect my sudden return with his crime, and to be terribly alarmed. I was sure that he would make an attempt to get me out of the way *at once*, and would bring round his murderous weapon for that purpose. I left him an excellent mark in the window, and, having warned the police that they might be needed—by the way, Watson, you spotted their presence in that doorway with unerring accuracy—I took up what seemed to me to be a judicious post for observation, never dreaming that he would choose the same spot for his attack. Now, my dear Watson, does anything remain for me to explain?"

"Yes," said I. "You have not made it clear what was Colonel Moran's motive in murdering the Honourable Ronald Adair."

"Ah! my dear Watson, there we come into those realms of conjecture, where the most logical mind may be at fault. Each may form his own hypothesis upon the present evidence, and yours is as likely to be correct as mine."

"You have formed one, then?"

"I think that it is not difficult to explain the facts. It came out in evidence that Colonel Moran and young Adair had between them won a considerable amount of money. Now, Moran undoubtedly played foul—of that I have long been aware. I believe that on the day of the murder Adair had discovered that Moran was cheating. Very likely he had spoken to him privately, and had threatened to expose him unless he voluntarily resigned his membership of the club, and promised not to play cards again. It is unlikely that a youngster like Adair would at once make a hideous scandal by exposing a well-known man so much older than himself. Probably he acted as I suggest. The exclusion from his clubs would mean ruin to Moran, who lived by his ill-gotten card gains. He therefore murdered Adair, who at the time was endeavouring to work out how much money he should himself return, since he could not profit by his partner's foul play. He locked the door lest the ladies should surprise him and insist upon knowing what he was doing with these names and coins. Will it pass?"

"I have no doubt that you have hit upon the truth."

"It will be verified or disproved at the trial. Meanwhile, come what may, Colonel Moran will trouble us no more,[73] the famous air-gun of Von Herder will embellish the Scotland Yard Museum, and once again Mr. Sherlock Holmes is free to devote his life to examining those interesting little problems which the complex life of London so plentifully presents." ■

THE GREAT HIATUS

THERE are far too many studies of the activities of Sherlock Holmes during the years 1891 to 1894 to be dealt with in any but the most cursory fashion in a work such as this. The following, then, should be viewed as a mere sampling of the more interesting conjectures. Pastiches that attempt to tell the "story" of the Great Hiatus, complete with descriptions of action and dialogue, although in many instances suggesting activities not that different from those outlined in "scholarship," are not discussed below:

Fundamentalism

A substantial group of scholars accept Holmes's tale of travels to Tibet, Persia, Mecca, Egypt, and France as essentially true, although perhaps lacking in explanation. The most detailed study is that of A. Carson Simpson, *Sherlock Holmes's Wanderjahre*. This consists of four volumes, *Fanget An!*; *Post Huc nec ergo Propter Huc Gabetque*; *In fernem Land, unnahbar euren Schritten*; and *Auf der Erde Rücken rührt' ich mich viel*. Simpson considers Holmes's homeward trip in detail, setting forth voluminous background material on then-current situations in Switzerland, Tibet, Lhasa, Khartoum, and other locales mentioned and exploring the precise routes by which Holmes likely travelled. Lord Donegall, in "April 1891–April 1894," clearly expresses the faith of the fundamentalist and confirms that the journey could have happened as outlined by Holmes.

Some add background or additional detail to the basic journey. For example, C. Arnold Johnson, in "An East Wind," suggests that Moriarty survived Reichenbach and pursued Holmes to Tibet, where, to gain control of the wealth and

73 Long before Moran's trial, Holmes seems terribly confident that the villain would be sentenced "with extreme prejudice." Later stories indicate that Holmes may have been premature in closing the book on London's second-most dangerous man. In "The Illustrious Client," which took place in 1902 (see *Chronological Table*), Holmes refers to "the living Sebastian Moran"; and in "His Last Bow" (definitely set in 1914), Holmes implies that Moran is still alive, saying: "The old sweet song. It was a favourite ditty of the late lamented Professor Moriarty. Colonel Sebastian Moran has also been known to warble it." How does Moran escape the predicted gallows? In the end, all the evidence against him is circumstantial, as Judge Bigelow points out. The murder of Adair, for example, was witnessed by no one. The list of numbers and club friends found in his room could have been written up by Adair solely to figure out how much money he had won and lost, and to whom; and finally, the fact that Moran shot at a wax dummy of Holmes is not grounds for attempted murder (proof of "similar acts" being inadmissible under British law). "So the overwhelmingly strong case against Moran," Bigelow concludes, "boils down to this: Adair was killed; the expanding revolver bullet that killed him was similar to one that was shot from Moran's air-gun; therefore Moran killed Adair." Bigelow reports that as a result, Moran was in fact found not guilty of Adair's murder.

resources of the Orient, he disguised himself as a Prince of the Manchus. In his madness, fiction became reality and eventually he emerged as Dr. Fu Manchu.

Others consider possible messages sent by Holmes. Jerold M. Bensky's " 'Sigerson'—What Is in a Name?" investigates Holmes's use of the name "Sigerson" as a code or cipher to inform Mycroft of the location where he was hiding or seeking seclusion. In addition, reports from "Sigerson" possibly carried vital information to Mycroft about the political situation of each country. Similarly, Patricia Dodd, in "Communicating in Code," suggests that during the Great Hiatus, Holmes continued to keep in touch with both Mycroft and Watson through an intricate network of coded messages. Watson's messages from Mycroft to Sherlock, who was disguised as a fledgling member of Moran's gang, were cleverly inserted in the cases known as the *Adventures* and the *Memoirs*.

Tibet and Holmes's sojourn there are the subjects of special study. T. S. Blakeney's "Disjecta Membra" considers the likely path of Holmes's entry into Tibet. In " 'A High-at-us,' " Ron Carlson proposes that Holmes used his visit to negotiate with the head Lama to grow a certain " 'highly' relaxing product" that was to have been marketed by Moriarty. Similarly, Patrick E. Drazen maintains, in his article "The Greater Vehicle: Holmes in Tibet," that Holmes spent two years in Tibet pursuing Tibetan Buddhism to rid himself of the cocaine habit.

In another flight of fancy, Robert S. Chambers, in "The Journey to a Lost Horizon," suggests that Holmes discovered "Shangri-La," first described in a fictionalized narrative by James Hilton. A similar suggestion is made by Dana Martin Batory, in "Hiatus in Paradise." Batory's essay theorises that Holmes and the Norwegian explorer Sigerson journeyed to Tibet to investigate the disappearance of strange cargo caravans in the Himalayas. Both found themselves "guests" at the lamasery of Shangri-La. Sigerson was never allowed to leave. Holmes was sent back into the world to finish his work.

In a fascinating piece entitled "A Norwegian Named Sigerson," Hans-Uno Bengtsson recounts how, when the thirteenth Dalai Lama came of age in 1895, Demo Rinpoche, the retired regent, plotted an assassination, using as his instrument a pair of cursed slippers. The plot was discovered through some remarkable detective work by the Dalai Lama. Bengtsson proposes that Holmes must have had an audience with the Dalai Lama, in which Holmes gave instruction in the art of detection.

Other aspects of the trip as reported by Holmes are examined. Ed Moorman, in "A Short But Interesting Visit," explains why Holmes would have visited Khartoum on behalf of the Foreign Office to see the Khalifa and how his visit affected England's involvement in world affairs well into the twentieth century.

The study of coal-tar derivatives mentioned by Holmes draws special attention. Carol Whitlam, in "Researching the Coal-Tar Derivatives," speculates on the compounds Holmes may have researched in Montpellier in 1894. In "Double 'L'— Why in the Empty House?," Donald A. Redmond considers why Holmes conducted his coal-tar research in Montpellier (France), not Montpelier (Vermont), as spelled by Watson. However, Raymond L. Holly ("A Laboratory at Montpelier") suggests that Holmes may have conducted his research in coal-tar derivatives at Montpelier in England. Brad Keefauver, in "So You Think Coal-Tar Derivatives Are Boring? Not So!," speculates that Holmes, who had considerable knowledge of perfumes, may have been researching synthetic perfumes derived from coal tar. Richard M. Caplan comes to a different conclusion in "Why Coal-Tar Derivatives at Montpellier?," where he suggests that Holmes's research focused on the prospect of identifying and tracing for forensic purposes the origins of aniline dyes and inks.

No Deposit, No Return

There is a distinct school of thought that the Great Hiatus never happened. The leading proponent is Walter P. Armstrong, Jr., in "The Truth About Sherlock Holmes." Succinctly, Armstrong argues, "Holmes did not return. He did not return because he had never been away. . . . Not only was Holmes in London, but he was living in the same house with Watson all the time. Watson has deceived us. But we cannot blame him, for the deception was necessary in order to trap the wily members of the Moriarty gang who remained."

Richard Lancelyn Green follows along the lines of Armstrong in "On Tour with Sigerson," arguing that the only logical place where Holmes could have gone into hiding and, at the same time, maintain contact with the criminal world was in London. He returned to live at 221B, venturing forth in disguise, and only Mrs. Hudson, Mycroft, and Lestrade were in his confidence.

Anthony Boucher, in "Was the Later Holmes an Imposter?," also concludes that because of numerous inconsistencies in Holmes and Watson's accounts of the events at the falls (see, for example, "The Darkening Sky," an appendix to "The Empty House"), Holmes must not have taken the reported journey and did, in fact, fall over the cliff at the Reichenbach. The man who in 1894 returned to London was, according to Boucher, in reality Holmes's cousin Sherrinford. This hypothesis is rejected by Jay Finley Christ, in "The Later Holmes An Imposter: A Sequel," who demonstrates in detail that Holmes's and Watson's accounts of the events at the Reichenbach are logically consistent. Boucher offers a reply in verse in "Ballade of the Later Holmes," which concludes:

> Christ and you others gathered here
> *Both* Holmes sprang from Vernet's seed.
> What matters which? The truth is clear:
> *A* master did return indeed.

A different imposter is suggested by Stefan Ernstson, in "The Counterfeit Sherlock Holmes Unmasked," who concludes that the Master's sister replaced Holmes.

An even more spectacular suggestion is that of Harry Halén, set forth in "Sherlock Holmes Venäjällä" ["Sherlock Holmes in Russia"]:

The author's main thesis is that the vanishing trick of the century was performed by Holmes in 1891–1893 and after. In Tibet he underwent a "tantric materialization ritual" that resulted in Sherlock Holmes II, a live copy of the detective— a phantom body with almost all the intellectual and physical faculties of the original. In the company of his newly-born identical brother, the real Holmes, in the guise of a tobacco merchant named Anaxagoras Gurr, arrived in Russia at the invitation of Anton Chekhov. The two Holmeses parted in Riga: the phantom Holmes returned to London and the real Holmes began working in Russia, first in the Baltic provinces. Halén cites several Estonian-language titles of books telling about Holmes's exploits. These books belong to the apocryphal literature on Holmes.[74]

Similarly, Robert Keller, in "Sherlock Holmes: A Spectra?," proposes that Holmes did indeed die in the fall at Reichenbach and then returned in a spiritual, resurrected form. His later adventures were actually those of "the world's first consulting ghost."

A Different Journey

A third school of writers constructs entirely different itineraries for the Great Hiatus. Anders Fage-Pedersen, in *A Case of Identity*, demonstrates that Holmes and Dr. Nikola, a mystical doctor who travelled in Tibet during the Hiatus, are the same person.

A love affair is a common theme. Benjamin Grosbayne, in "Sherlock Holmes's Honeymoon," concludes that he married Irene Adler, became a distinguished operatic conductor and toured the musical centres of the world with his wife. Martin J. King ("Holmes in Hoboken?") sees Holmes slipping off to Hoboken, New Jersey, and identifies the Meyers Hotel there as the location of Holmes's tryst with Irene Adler, resulting in the birth of their son, Nero Wolfe. Stanley McComas, in "Lhove at Lhassa," presents evidence that Holmes and Irene Adler (divorced from Godfrey Norton) were married in Florence and then spent the next three years travelling about Asia.

More farfetched is the work of Alastair Martin, in "Finding the Better Half," which identifies Moriarty as the widow of Count Dracula whom Holmes encountered at the Reichenbach, wed, and spent three years with during the Great Hiatus. An even greater leap is taken by James Nelson, in "Sherlock and the Sherpas," who proposes that in Tibet Holmes met and mated with the Abominable Snow-woman. According to Ronald B. DeWaal's *The Universal Sherlock Holmes*, "This takes the prize for the most fanciful of all Sherlockian conjectures!"

74 Summarized by Ronald B. DeWaal in *The Universal Sherlock Holmes*.

Several writers conclude that Holmes was involved with the Lizzie Borden case, which occurred in 1892. Edgar W. Smith's "Sherlock Holmes and the Great Hiatus" seems to have been the first. Allen Robertson's "Baker Street, Beecher and Borden" expands on the connection, while in Jon Borden Sisson's "Dr. Handy's Wild-Eyed Man," a document purportedly written in 1892 by Dr. Benjamin Handy of Fall River, Massachusetts, describes Holmes's acquaintance with Lizzie Borden and his investigation of the murders of her father and stepmother. Handy concludes that Holmes may have committed the murders himself, and the article further suggests that Holmes had an affair with Lizzie.

The Russians are a common theme in the "Sherlock Holmes, Secret Agent" line of theories. T. Frederick Foss, in "The Missing Years," argues that Holmes did not spend two years in Tibet posing as a Norwegian explorer named Sigerson, but, instead, assisted his country by ferreting out information on Russian intrigues in India. He expands this argument in "But That Is Another Story," contending that the Indian Government reluctantly agreed to his presence there, but arranged for Kipling's policeman, Strickland, to keep an eye on him.

The eminent writer Poul Anderson, in "Sherlock Holmes, Explorer," suggests that Holmes's travels during the Hiatus were a working out of a lifelong wish to be an explorer, although his activities in Tibet also involved counteracting the machinations of the Russian agent Dorijev. See also Manly Wade Wellman's "Scoundrels in Bohemia," suggesting far-flung espionage activities.

There was spying to be done in Persia as well, contends William P. Collins, in "It Is Time That I Should Turn to Other Memories: Sherlock Holmes and Persia, 1893." Collins's evidence strongly suggests that Holmes indeed spent at least two months in Persia, where he observed the activities of the Russians; assessed the effects of the activities of Siyyid Jamálu'd-Dín "al-Afqhání" and Mírzá Malkam Khán on British interests; and made a number of recommendations on British policy to Her Majesty's representatives.

Similarly, John P. and Susan M. Thornton, in "The Adventure of the Elusive Boundary Line: An Account of the Master's Encounter with Destiny in Central Asia," argue that "Holmes was not the casual wanderer that he made himself out to be, but the Foreign Office's master agent who masterminded much of the Empire's success in Central Asia at the turn of the century. In character with his adventures as described in the Canon, he provided the stepping-stones for many others to rise to fame while he remained in the shadows."

Another "secret agent" suggestion is that of Raymond L. Holly, in "Europeans in Lhasa in 1891." He points out that H. Rider Haggard attributes his tales *She* and *Ayesha* to one Ludwig Horace Holly, who claims to have been in Tibet with his adopted son in 1891. They were saved from execution by a friendly Chinese official, who, Raymond Holly suggests, in reality was Holmes in disguise, working as a secret operative for Her Majesty's government.

Other activities are proposed as well. Alan Olding, head of the Sherlock Holmes Society of Australia, suggests (in "Holmes in Terra Australis Incognita—Incognito") that Holmes gained his knowledge of the Australian criminal class by spending part of his Hiatus in Australia. Bob Reyom, in "The Great Hiatus, or Locked in the Music Room Without My Cello," hypothesises that the hiatus was spent studying the motets of Orlando di Lasso, while Dana Martin Batory ("Tut, Tut, Sherlock!") examines the possibility that the mysterious Egyptian "detective" Abu Tabah (of Sax Rohmer's *Tales of Secret Egypt* (1918)) was in actuality Sherlock Holmes, who spent part of his Great Hiatus in Egypt disrupting the hashish trade on behalf of the British government.

On a musical note, Gordon R. Speck's article, " '. . . And a Week Later I Was in Florence,' " considers that Holmes may have spent the first weeks and the final weeks of the Great Hiatus in Cremona collecting samples from the Stradivari workshop and in Montpellier analysing them.

According to Tomas Gejrot ("Was Sherlock Holmes a Patient of Sigmund Freud's?"), Holmes spent his Hiatus in Vienna being treated for his addiction to cocaine. Of course, this view was taken to the extreme in Nicholas Meyer's novel *The Seven-Per-Cent Solution*, who recorded not only that Freud cured Holmes of his addiction (by elucidating that the villainous Moriarty was but a projection of Holmes's mind, based on Holmes's childhood discovery that his mother had committed adultery with his tutor Professor Moriarty) but that Freud and Holmes together solved a mystery and rescued a beautiful woman.

"Infinite possibilities" here!

BARITSU

BARTITSU, as it was properly spelled, was a Japanese style of self-defence introduced by E. W. Barton-Wright (1860–1951) in an article published in the March and April 1899 issues of *Pearson's* magazine. Barton-Wright had lived in Japan for three years; during that time, he studied with a sensei to learn the art of jujitsu (or jujutsu), a weaponless method of self-defence, developed by samurais, that was once meant to complement swordsmanship. Known as "the gentle art," jujitsu emphasises temporarily yielding to the moves of one's attacker and then, in turn, controlling them—crippling or even killing the opponent—by the use of various holds, blows, and throws.

Upon his return to England, Barton-Wright opened his own martial arts school and published "The New Art of Self-Defence," which couched his methods in utterly practical terms: headings included "How to Put a Troublesome Man Out of the Room" and "One of Many Ways of Defending Yourself, When a Man Strikes at Your Face with His Right Fist." What he called "Bartitsu"—a combination of "Barton" and "jujitsu"—was essentially jujitsu with some elements of boxing and wrestling thrown in. Barton-Wright's boasts of invincibility were met with both enthusiasm and scepticism. Nonetheless, his new method created a small sensation, and he is usually credited with having brought jujitsu (which later spawned judo, karate, and aikido) to England, even bringing experts over from Japan to aid him in his teaching and exhibition endeavours.

While "The Empty House" was published four years after the *Pearson's* article appeared, Holmes's use of "baritsu" in grappling with Moriarty at Reichenbach Falls predated the Barton-Wright system by eight years. How to explain the incongruity? In "The Mystery of Baritsu: A Sidelight Upon Sherlock Holmes's Accomplishments," Ralph Judson puts forth the theory that Holmes had actually studied jujitsu and that Watson, having read the *Pearson's* article by the time he heard Holmes's account, confused the two terms (confused them so much, in fact, that he dropped the "t" in "bartitsu" to make the word sound more like "jujitsu"). Since Judson calculates that it takes seven years or so to master a defensive art completely, he puts the beginning of Holmes's jujitsu training at around 1883 or 1884. In slipping through Moriarty's grasp, Judson imagines, Holmes must have dropped to one knee, "gripped with one hand Moriarty's heel, which was closer to the abyss, and lifting the heel and with it the foot, diagonally, away from himself, he [must have] pushed hard, at the same time, with his other hand, into the groin of the captured leg, applying terrific leverage. This caused Moriarty to lose completely his balance and gave him no time to clutch at his opponent."

In their fascinating work *Some Knowledge of Baritsu: An Investigation of the Japanese System of Wrestling Used by Mr. Sherlock Holmes*, Hirayama Yuichi and John Hall take a contrary view, concluding that the Master was not proficient in jujitsu at all. In previous cases, when confronted with the prospect of physical combat, Holmes displayed little to no skill. "This is indicated," they write, "by his inability to cope with the two assailants in the middle of his career in 'The Reigate Puzzle' (1887), and by his defeat at the hands of Gruner's hired villains towards the end of Holmes's career in 'The Illustrious Client.' . . . [E]ither Holmes learned his skills from a less than masterly teacher, or . . . Holmes did study with a master, but for too short a time to learn the technique properly."

THE DARKENING SKY

ANTHONY BOUCHER, the esteemed mystery critic and author, proposes, in his essay "Was the Later Holmes an Imposter?," that there are serious problems in reconciling the time intervals described by Holmes and Watson regarding the trips to the Reichenbach Falls with Watson's statements in "The Final Problem" and Holmes's explanation in "The Empty House." Based on Watson's statements, Boucher constructs the following timetable:

Time	Event
2 P.M. ("afternoon")	Holmes and Watson depart from Meiringen
4 P.M. ("two hours" on Watson's second trip; assume the same on the first, which may have been more leisurely)	Holmes and Watson arrive at falls
4:15 P.M. (estimated)	Conversation with messenger, Watson departs for Meiringen
5:15 P.M. ("over an hour to come down")	Watson arrives back at Meiringen, discovers fraud
7:15 P.M. ("two more had passed")	Watson hurries back to Falls

At this point, Boucher asserts that Watson returned to Meiringen to fetch the "experts" and travelled back to the falls. He allows another three hours for this return. By the time the experts left, then, it would be well after 10:30 P.M. It is very puzzling, he concludes, that Holmes should describe the sky at such an hour as "darkening." Sunset must have occurred more than two hours earlier, and Holmes couldn't possibly have seen Moran's head.

But Karl Baedeker's *Switzerland and the Adjacent Portions of Italy, Savoy, and the Tyrol: Handbook for Travellers* states that it is only a quarter hour to the lower falls from the Hotel Reichenbach in Meiringen and three-quarters of an hour to the upper falls. A. Carson Simpson, in *Sherlock Holmes's Wanderjahre (Fanget An!)*, excuses Watson's error as a result of his stress: "[L]earning of Moriarty's deception when he reached Meiringen, his apprehensions were aroused and his anxiety made minutes seem like hours. . . . A simple arithmetical calculation will demonstrate that the various trips to and fro could easily be made, with ample margins between trips, before sunset at 7:10 P.M."

Ernest Bloomfield Zeisler also concludes that the timing suggested by Watson's statements is misleading. "There is not the slightest indication that Watson made the upward journey [to the Fall] *three* times. . . . Watson told Steiler that he suspected foul play, and Steiler surely fetched the police and sent them up after Watson without delay, so that they probably arrived at the Fall shortly after Watson." Under this assumption, the "experts" could have completed their investigation as early as 6:30 P.M., well before sunset. Even if another hour or so is added to the timetable, twilight would have accounted for Holmes's vision of Moran. The same conclusion is reached by Jay Finley Christ in his essay "The Later Holmes An Imposter: A Sequel": "Nowhere in *The Final Problem* or in *The Empty House* is there the slightest suggestion or basis for an assumption that Watson made *three* trips to the fall, nor that he brought experts 'later.'[75] On the contrary, there is in *The Empty House* a clear statement to the effect that Watson was accompanied by several persons when he returned to the fall after having been lured away." Actually, in "The Empty House," Holmes describes "you . . . and all your following" investigating the circumstances of his "death," and it does seem odd that if Watson made *two* return trips to the falls, Holmes did not mention them.

THE PATH OF THE COLONEL'S BULLET

PERCIVAL WILDE, in his novel *Design for Murder*, expresses, through several characters, the criticisms that a bullet fired from the ground floor of a house on one side of the street into the second storey of a house across a street the width of Baker Street cannot penetrate both the shadow and the bust of Sherlock Holmes that is casting it, because the bust must be at some distance from its shadow; or, if it strikes both shadow and bust, it should strike the lamp that is in a straight line with them; and, in either event, because of the required elevation of the gun's muzzle, it must strike the ceiling and not the far wall of the room.

Robert S. Schultz, however, writing in "The Ballistics of the Empty House," attempts to refute each of these points:

- The bust was very close to the window, rather than far away. Watson describes seeing a "hard, black outline upon the luminous screen of the window." Had the bust been any great distance removed from the window, Schultz

75 Jay Finley Christ points out that Baedeker's guide to Switzerland lists fourteen guides who were available in Meiringen, presumably the "experts" referred to by Dr. Watson.

argues, it would have cast a large, fuzzy shadow; and if it were closer to the lamp than to the window, the outline would have been even larger and more indistinct. Schultz estimates, then, that the model was approximately one foot from the window.

- The gun, shadow, bust, and lamp need not have been in a straight line. "Needless to say, all this talk about straight lines is misleading; one would think it was well known that the path of a bullet is a parabola, not a straight line." (This refutation is not well developed, however, and the parabolic distortion cannot have been significant over these short distances.)
- After an elaborate analysis of the heights and distances involved, Schultz concludes that only if the sitting room were of "palatial" dimensions could the bullet have failed to strike the wall.

To the first of these points, Wilde replies in "The Bust in the Window" that only a large light would create an indistinct shadow, with both an umbra (the main, darkest part of the silhouette) and a penumbra (the lighter, outer shadow). Since Holmes's lamp was a small one, there would have been no penumbra, leaving only a sharp outline, no matter where the bust was placed. To the third point, he argues that Schultz miscalculates the height of the room and that "[t]he height of the shadow above the muzzle of the gun was far more than [Mr. Schultz] admits, and . . . I decline to find that the angle was so small that it was inconsequential."

This editor's experiments with light sources confirm Schultz's point that, even with a brilliant lamp, the bust must have been close to the shade to produce a shadow the approximate size of the bust (and note that there is no suggestion that the bust was considerably smaller than life-sized, which would be required to produce a life-sized shadow if it were *not* close to the shade). However, personal experiments will confirm that while the distance from the lamp to the bust may affect the degree of "sharpness" of the shadow, it will *not* affect the size; only the distance of the bust from the *shade* affects that. Thus, in a darkened room, a very bright lamp some distance from the bust could produce a shadow with a "hard, black outline," and no lamp-smashing would occur with only the slightest eleva-tion of the gun muzzle.

Furthermore, both commentators fail to recognise that the critical distance in the equation is not the height of the room but the distance across Baker Street, which Schultz states to be approximately 66 feet, a distance Wilde does not challenge. While present-day scholars may question the certainty expressed by Wilde and Schultz respecting the identification of particular buildings as Camden House and 221 Baker Street, the distance at other locations on Baker Street cannot have been significantly less.

A diagram indicates this editor's understanding and the absurdity of Wilde's position. One does not even need to resort to trigonometry to do the relevant computations, only to use the basic rule that triangles with angles that are equal have sides that are proportional in length. If we accept that the dis-tance from Moran's gun to a bust placed about 1 foot from the window is 67 feet and that the height of the bust above Moran's shoulder is 10.5 feet (allowing a 5.5-foot high shoulder, 4.5 foot distance from the floor of 221B to the top of the bust, and an 11.5 foot distance from ground to the floor of 221B, roughly Schultz's assumptions), we have a triangular ratio of 10.5/67 (see diagram). Two additional triangles must be con-sidered: the length of the suite in Baker Street and the striking place of the bullet on the wall, and the distance of the lamp from the bust and the path of the bullet (and, concomitantly, whether the lamp is in the bullet's path).

If the wall of the suite were 14 feet from the bust (not an unusual length for a room), the height of the bullet's striking place must be $x/14 = 10.5/67$, or about 2.2. That is, the bullet must have struck the wall about 2' 3" higher than the top of the bust—an acceptable result. If the room is elongated to 20 feet, the height of the striking place is $x/19 = 10.5/67$, or about 3 feet above the top of the bust. Surely the ceiling was higher than 7.5 feet! Even assuming that the height of the bust above Moran's shoulder were much greater—say, 15 feet—similar results are achieved. For a 15-foot suite, the formula is $x/14 = 15/67$, or 3.14 feet, again producing a 7.5-foot ceiling. It is obvi-ous that the great distance across Baker Street produces these results.

As to the lamp-smashing, if one assumes that the lamp were no more than one foot from the bust, then the formula $x/1 = 10.5/67$ produces the information the bullet would rise 0.15 feet, or about 2" in that one-foot trip, enough to miss a carefully-positioned lamp if the bullet struck the top of the bust. The farther back from the bust the lamp is placed, the more clearance there is between the path of the bullet and the lamp. Therefore, so long as the lamp did not extend above the top of the bust, no smashing need be imagined.

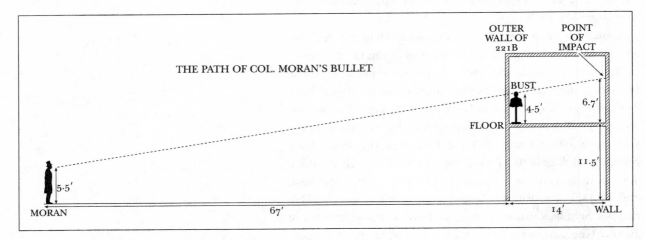

The path of the colonel's bullet.

THE ADVENTURE OF THE NORWOOD BUILDER[1]

With publication of "The Empty House" and Holmes in retirement (although the latter was unknown to the public), Watson was free at last to draw on his entire casebook of Holmes's career to select his tales. His first post-Return effort was "The Norwood Builder." The case is the first in the Canon to feature fingerprints as the key clue, and Holmes was clearly ahead of his law enforcement colleagues and the courts in recognising their significance. Scholars also raise questions about the strange will produced by Holmes's client and suggest his incompetence as a lawyer.

FROM THE POINT of view of the criminal expert," said Mr. Sherlock Holmes, "London has become a singularly uninteresting city since the death of the late lamented[2] Professor Moriarty."[3]

"I can hardly think that you would find many decent citizens to agree with you," I answered.

"Well, well, I must not be selfish," said he, with a smile, as he pushed back his chair from the breakfast-table. "The community is certainly the gainer, and no one the loser, save the poor out-of-work specialist, whose occupation has gone. With that man in the field, one's morning paper presented infinite possibilities. Often it was only the smallest trace, Watson, the faintest indication, and yet it was enough to tell me that the great malignant brain was there, as the gentlest tremors of the edges of the web remind one of the foul spider which lurks in the centre. Petty thefts, wanton assaults, purposeless outrage—to the man who held the clue all could be worked into

1 "The Norwood Builder" was published in the *Strand Magazine* in November 1903 and in *Collier's Weekly* on October 31, 1903. The manuscript is in the Berg Collection of the New York Public Library.

2 The manuscript reveals that the phrase "late lamented" has been inserted in Watson's original draft, in the same hand as the manuscript.

3 Contrast this with Watson's remark in "The Solitary Cyclist": "From the years 1894 to 1901 inclusive, Mr. Sherlock Holmes was a very busy man."

4 The phrase "as a Junior and insignificant member of the firm" is added in the manuscript.

5 Curiously, in the manuscript Watson originally refers to "Crocker."

6 The reader will recall that in "The Greek Interpreter" Holmes describes his grandmother as the sister of "Vernet, the French artist."

7 Most scholars accept this as a reference to "Wisteria Lodge," in which "ex-President Murillo" of the fictitious country of "San Pedro" figures, although the reference to "papers" is puzzling, for "papers" are not directly involved in the case.

Frederick Dorr Steele, *Collier's*, 1903

one connected whole. To the scientific student of the higher criminal world, no capital in Europe offered the advantages which London then possessed. But now—" He shrugged his shoulders in humorous deprecation of the state of things which he had himself done so much to produce.

At the time of which I speak, Holmes had been back for some months, and I, at his request, had sold my practice and returned to share the old quarters in Baker Street.[4] A young doctor, named Verner,[5] had purchased my small Kensington practice, and given with astonishingly little demur the highest price that I ventured to ask—an incident which only explained itself some years later, when I found that Verner was a distant relation of Holmes's, and that it was my friend who had really found the money.[6]

Our months of partnership had not been so uneventful as he had stated, for I find, on looking over my notes, that this period includes the case of the papers of ex-President Murillo,[7] and also the shocking affair of the Dutch steamship *Friesland*, which so nearly cost us both our lives.[8] His cold and proud nature was always averse, however, to anything in the shape of public applause, and he bound me in the most stringent terms to say no further word of himself, his methods, or his successes—a prohibition which, as I have explained, has only now been removed.

Mr. Sherlock Holmes was leaning back in his chair after his whimsical protest, and was unfolding his morning paper in a leisurely fashion, when our attention was arrested by a tremendous ring at the bell, followed immediately by a hollow drumming sound, as if someone were beating on the outer door with his fist. As it opened there came a tumultuous rush into the hall, rapid feet clattered up the stair, and an instant later a wild-eyed and frantic young man, pale, dishevelled, and palpitating, burst into the room. He looked from one to the other of us, and under our gaze of inquiry he became conscious that some apology was needed for this unceremonious entry.

8 Although Friesland is located in the Netherlands, the S.S. *Friesland* was actually of Belgian registry. The transatlantic passenger liner was owned and operated by the Red Star line, carrying scores of emigrants from Antwerp to New York throughout the 1890s. In 1903, supplanted by faster, larger steamships, she was transferred to charter service between Liverpool and Philadelphia and was finally scrapped in 1912. Christopher Morley, who sailed on the *Friesland* from Philadelphia to Liverpool in September 1910, described her as "a beauty, a smart little Red Star liner." Several scholars point out that in Arthur Conan Doyle's *The Lost World*, it was the S.S. *Friesland*, a Dutch-American liner, that sighted Professor George Edward Challenger's pterodactyl when it escaped from the Queen's Hall.

"A wild-eyed and frantic young man burst into the room."
Sidney Paget, *Strand Magazine*, 1903

"I'm sorry, Mr. Holmes," he cried. "You mustn't blame me. I am nearly mad. Mr. Holmes, I am the unhappy John Hector McFarlane."

He made the announcement as if the name alone would explain both his visit and its manner, but I could see by my companion's unresponsive face that it meant no more to him than to me.

"Have a cigarette, Mr. McFarlane," said he, pushing his case across. "I am sure that, with your symptoms, my friend Dr. Watson here would prescribe a sedative. The weather has been so very warm these last few days. Now, if you feel a little more composed, I should be glad if you would sit down in that chair and tell us very slowly and quietly who you are and what it is that you want. You mentioned your name, as if I should recognise it, but I assure you that, beyond the obvious facts that you are a bachelor, a solicitor, a Freemason, and an asthmatic, I know nothing whatever about you."

Familiar as I was with my friend's methods, it was not difficult for me to follow his deductions, and to observe the untidiness of attire, the sheaf of legal papers, the watch-charm, and the breathing which had prompted them. Our client, however, stared in amazement.

"Yes, I am all that, Mr. Holmes, and, in addition, I am the most unfortunate man at this moment in London. For heaven's sake, don't abandon me, Mr. Holmes! If they come to arrest me before I have finished my story, make them give me time, so that I may tell you the whole truth. I could go to gaol happy if I knew that you were working for me outside."

"Arrest you!" said Holmes. "This is really most grati—most interesting. On what charge do you expect to be arrested?"

"Upon the charge of murdering Mr. Jonas Oldacre, of Lower Norwood."

My companion's expressive face showed a sympathy which was not, I am afraid, entirely unmixed with satisfaction.

"Dear me," said he, "it was only this moment at breakfast that I was saying to my friend, Dr. Watson, that sensational cases had disappeared out of our papers."

Our visitor stretched forward a quivering hand and picked up the *Daily Telegraph*, which still lay upon Holmes's knee.

"If you had looked at it, sir, you would have seen at a glance what the errand is on which I have come to you this morning.

I feel as if my name and my misfortune must be in every man's mouth." He turned it over to expose the central page. "Here it is, and with your permission I will read it to you. Listen to this, Mr. Holmes. The headlines are: 'Mysterious Affair at Lower Norwood. Disappearance of a Well-Known Builder. Suspicion of Murder and Arson. A Clue to the Criminal.' That is the clue which they are already following, Mr. Holmes, and I know that it leads infallibly to me. I have been followed from London Bridge Station, and I am sure that they are only waiting for the warrant to arrest me. It will break my mother's heart—it will break her heart!" He wrung his hands in an agony of apprehension, and swayed backward and forward in his chair.

I looked with interest upon this man, who was accused of being the perpetrator of a crime of violence. He was flaxen-haired and handsome, in a washed-out negative fashion, with frightened blue eyes, and a clean-shaven face, with a weak, sensitive mouth. His age may have been about twenty-seven, his dress and bearing that of a gentleman. From the pocket of his light summer overcoat protruded the bundle of indorsed papers which proclaimed his profession.

"We must use what time we have," said Holmes. "Watson, would you have the kindness to take the paper and to read the paragraph in question?"

Underneath the vigorous headlines which our client had quoted, I read the following suggestive narrative:

Late last night, or early this morning,[9] an incident occurred at Lower Norwood which points, it is feared, to a serious crime. Mr. Jonas Oldacre is a well-known resident of that suburb, where he has carried on his business as a builder for many years. Mr. Oldacre is a bachelor, fifty-two years of age, and lives in Deep Dene House, at the Sydenham end of the road of that name. He has had the reputation of being a man of eccentric habits, secretive and retiring. For some years he has practically withdrawn from the business, in which he is said to have amassed considerable wealth. A small timber-yard still exists, however, at the back of the house, and last night, about twelve o'clock, an alarm was given that one of the stacks was on fire. The engines were soon upon the spot, but the dry wood burned with great fury, and it was impossible to arrest the conflagration until the stack had been

[9] "Now this really was swift work in the *Telegraph* office," John Hyslop writes. "The murder took place, said the newspaper, last night or in the early morning. Yet here was the *Telegraph* with a full story . . ."

10 These were a large office block in the City, located off Throgmorton Street and apparently named after Sir Thomas Gresham (1518/19–1579), English merchant, financier, and founder of the Royal Exchange. "Gresham's law"—the principle that "bad money drives out good"—was not formulated by him but named after him.

entirely consumed. Up to this point the incident bore the appearance of an ordinary accident, but fresh indications seem to point to serious crime. Surprise was expressed at the absence of the master of the establishment from the scene of the fire, and an inquiry followed, which showed that he had disappeared from the house. An examination of his room revealed that the bed had not been slept in, that a safe which stood in it was open, that a number of important papers were scattered about the room, and, finally, that there were signs of a murderous struggle, slight traces of blood being found within the room, and an oaken walking-stick, which also showed stains of blood upon the handle. It is known that Mr. Jonas Oldacre had received a late visitor in his bedroom upon that night, and the stick found has been identified as the property of this person, who is a young London solicitor named John Hector McFarlane, junior partner of Graham & McFarlane, of 426 Gresham Buildings,[10] E. C. The police believe that they have evidence in their possession which supplies a very convincing motive for the crime, and altogether it cannot be doubted that sensational developments will follow.

Later.—It is rumoured as we go to press that Mr. John Hector McFarlane has actually been arrested on the charge of the murder of Mr. Jonas Oldacre. It is at least certain that a warrant has been issued. There have been further and sinister developments in the investigation at Norwood. Besides the signs of a struggle in the room of the unfortunate builder it is now known that the French windows of his bedroom (which is on the ground floor) were found to be open, that there were marks as if some bulky object had been dragged across to the wood-pile, and, finally, it is asserted that charred remains have been found among the charcoal ashes of the fire. The police theory is that a most sensational crime has been committed, that the victim was clubbed to death in his own bedroom, his papers rifled, and his dead body dragged across to the wood-stack, which was then ignited so as to hide all traces of the crime. The conduct of the criminal investigation has been left in the experienced hands of Inspector Lestrade, of Scotland Yard, who is following up the clues with his accustomed energy and sagacity.

Sherlock Holmes listened with closed eyes and finger-tips together to this remarkable account.

"The case has certainly some points of interest," said he, in his languid fashion. "May I ask, in the first place, Mr. McFarlane, how it is that you are still at liberty, since there appears to be enough evidence to justify your arrest?"

"I live at Torrington Lodge, Blackheath, with my parents, Mr. Holmes, but last night having to do business very late with Mr. Jonas Oldacre, I stayed at an hotel in Norwood, and came to my business from there. I knew nothing of this affair until I was in the train, when I read what you have just heard. I at once saw the horrible danger of my position, and I hurried to put the case into your hands. I have no doubt that I should have been arrested either at my City office or at my home. A man followed me from London Bridge Station, and I have no doubt—Great heaven, what is that?"

It was a clang of the bell, followed instantly by heavy steps upon the stair. A moment later, our old friend Lestrade appeared in the doorway. Over his shoulder I caught a glimpse of one or two uniformed policemen outside.

"Mr. John Hector McFarlane?" said Lestrade.

Our unfortunate client rose with a ghastly face.

"I arrest you for the wilful murder of Mr. Jonas Oldacre, of Lower Norwood."

McFarlane turned to us with a gesture of despair, and sank into his chair once more like one who is crushed.

"One moment, Lestrade," said Holmes. "Half an hour more or less can make no difference to you, and the gentleman was about to give us an account of this very interesting affair, which might aid us in clearing it up."

"I think there will be no difficulty in clearing it up," said Lestrade, grimly.

"None the less, with your permission, I should be much interested to hear his account."

"Well, Mr. Holmes, it is difficult for me to refuse you anything, for you have been of use to the Force once or twice in the past, and we owe you a good turn at Scotland Yard," said Lestrade. "At the same time I must remain with my prisoner, and I am bound to warn him that anything he may say will appear in evidence against him."

"I arrest you for the wilful murder of Mr. Jonas Oldacre."
Frederick Dorr Steele, *Collier's*, 1903

"I wish nothing better," said our client. "All I ask is that you should hear and recognize the absolute truth."

Lestrade looked at his watch. "I'll give you half an hour," said he.

"I must explain first," said McFarlane, "that I knew nothing of Mr. Jonas Oldacre. His name was familiar to me, for many years ago my parents were acquainted with him, but they drifted apart. I was very much surprised, therefore, when yesterday, about three o'clock in the afternoon, he walked into my office in the city. But I was still more astonished when he told me the object of his visit. He had in his hand several sheets of a note-book, covered with scribbled writing—here they are—and he laid them on my table.

" 'Here is my will,' said he. 'I want you, Mr. McFarlane, to cast it into proper legal shape. I will sit here while you do so.'

"I set myself to copy it, and you can imagine my astonishment when I found that, with some reservations, he had left all his property to me. He was a strange little ferret-like man, with white eyelashes, and when I looked up at him I found his keen gray eyes fixed upon me with an amused expression.[11] I could hardly believe my own senses as I read the terms of the will; but he explained that he was a bachelor with hardly any living relation, that he had known my parents in his youth, and that he had always heard of me as a very deserving young man, and was assured that his money would be in worthy hands. Of course, I could only stammer out my thanks. The will was duly finished, signed, and witnessed by my clerk. This is it on the blue paper, and these slips, as I have explained, are the rough draft.[12] Mr. Jonas Oldacre then informed me that there were a number of documents—building leases, title-deeds, mortgages, scrip, and so forth—which it was necessary that I should see and understand. He said that his mind would not be easy until the whole thing was settled, and he begged me to come out to his house at Norwood that night, bringing the will with me, and to arrange matters. 'Remember, my boy, not one word to your parents about the affair until everything is settled. We will keep it as a little surprise for them.' He was very insistent upon this point, and made me promise it faithfully.

"You can imagine, Mr. Holmes, that I was not in a humour to refuse him anything that he might ask. He was my benefactor, and all my desire was to carry out his wishes in every particular. I sent a telegram home, therefore, to say that I had important business on hand, and that it was impossible for me to say how late I might be. Mr. Oldacre had told me that he would like me to have supper with him at nine, as he might not be home before that hour. I had some difficulty in finding his house, however, and it was nearly half-past before I reached it. I found him—"

"One moment!" said Holmes. "Who opened the door?"

"A middle-aged woman, who was, I suppose, his housekeeper."[13]

"And it was she, I presume, who mentioned your name?"

"Exactly," said McFarlane.

"Pray proceed."

Mr. McFarlane wiped his damp brow, and then continued his narrative:

"I was shown by this woman into a sitting-room, where a frugal supper was laid out. Afterwards, Mr. Jonas Oldacre led me into his bedroom, in which there stood a heavy safe. This he opened and took out a mass of documents, which we went over

11 In the manuscript, the phrase is "a most curious expression which certainly seemed to be more threatening than benevolent."

12 British law requires two witnesses to be present at the signing of a will; thus, with only the clerk to serve as witness, Oldacre's will would have been invalid. Perhaps McFarlane supposed himself to be the second witness, which, as S. T. L. Harbottle points out, would also have rendered much of the will null and void (under the Wills Act, 1837), since McFarlane was a primary beneficiary of the will he was purportedly witnessing. Conjecturing that McFarlane could either have made a mistake or have intended to deceive Oldacre, Harbottle comes down on the side of the latter, conjecturing that McFarlane conspired with a relative who would benefit from an intestacy. "I fear McFarlane deliberately planned that the will should be ineffective," writes Harbottle. "The fact that it was written on blue paper (at that time universally used for drafts and not for final copies or engrossments) then assumes a sinister significance." The will of Elias Openshaw in "The Five Orange Pips" must also must have suffered from "witness" problems. Apparently "Fordham, the Horsham lawyer" and McFarlane had similar gaps in their training.

Conversely, D. Martin Dakin proposes that there was no error, but that there might have been another witness present ("a clerk from a neighbouring office, or the caretaker") whom McFarlane simply did not mention. Michael Waxenberg also argues that under the Forfeiture Act of 1870, one could still inherit money or property after being arrested or convicted of a felony. Only in 1911 did English courts rule that a murderer could not benefit from killing his benefactor. "So, in 1895, it would have been possible, in theory, for McFarlane to murder Oldacre and still inherit from him. Thereafter, if McFarlane were hanged for the murder, his property would pass to his heirs. If

McFarlane were acquitted, he would be free to enjoy the harvest of his inheritance."

In the United States, modern laws do not automatically invalidate a will witnessed by an interested party. First, there may be other, disinterested witnesses present. And the fact that a will is witnessed by a beneficiary (such as McFarlane) merely creates the presumption that he or she acted fraudulently or exerted undue influence. If the suspected party can prove that there was no conflict of interest, then the presumption may be overcome.

13 Watson's notes are confused at this point, for he has deleted from the manuscript the following, which appeared after the word "housekeeper": " 'A bad shot that, Mr. McFarlane,' said Lestrade, with a cynical smile. 'Jonas Oldacre is well known as a woman hater, he has no servant except an old Charwoman who comes in for two hours every morning, and he gets all his meals at the Station restaurant. I warn you again that you are only making a bad case worse and this will all come up against you.' Our unfortunate Client had turned a ghastly colour, and he looked from one to the other of us like a hunted creature. Twice he tried to speak but his dry lips would utter no sound. At last with an effort he was able to continue his statement. 'I am speaking to you, Mr. Holmes. You will find out how far I am speaking the truth. I was shown into a sitting room . . .' "

14 Lower Norwood and Blackheath, Christopher Morley estimates, are only four miles from each other. "It has always bothered me," he comments in "Clinical Notes by a Resident Patient," "why could not the unhappy John Hector McFarlane get back from Lower Norwood to Blackheath that night?" McFarlane mentions later in his narrative that he and Jonas Oldacre completed their business "between eleven and twelve." It is possible

A mass of documents, which we went over together.
Frederick Dorr Steele, *Collier's*, 1903

together. It was between eleven and twelve when we finished. He remarked that we must not disturb the housekeeper. He showed me out through his own French window, which had been open all this time."

"Was the blind down?" asked Holmes.

"I will not be sure, but I believe that it was only half down. Yes, I remember how he pulled it up in order to swing open the window. I could not find my stick, and he said, 'Never mind, my boy, I shall see a good deal of you now, I hope, and I will keep your stick until you come back to claim it.' I left him there, the safe open, and the papers made up in packets upon the table. It was so late that I could not get back to Blackheath, so I spent the night at the Anerley Arms,[14] and I knew nothing more until I read of this horrible affair in the morning."

"Anything more that you would like to ask, Mr. Holmes?" said Lestrade, whose eyebrows had gone up once or twice during this remarkable explanation.

"Not until I have been to Blackheath."

"You mean to Norwood," said Lestrade.

"Oh, yes, no doubt that is what I must have meant," said Holmes, with his enigmatical smile. Lestrade had learned by more experiences than he would care to acknowledge that that razor-like brain could cut through that which was impenetrable to him. I saw him look curiously at my companion.

"I think I should like to have a word with you presently, Mr. Sherlock Holmes," said he. "Now, Mr. McFarlane, two of my constables are at the door, and there is a four-wheeler waiting." The wretched young man arose, and with a last beseeching glance at us walked from the room. The officers conducted him to the cab, but Lestrade remained. Holmes had picked up the pages which formed the rough draft of the will, and was looking at them with the keenest interest upon his face.

"There are some points about that document Lestrade, are there not?" said he, pushing them over.

The official looked at them with a puzzled expression.

"I can read the first few lines, and these in the middle of the second page, and one or two at the end. Those are as clear as print," said he, "but the writing in between is very bad, and there are three places where I cannot read it at all."

"What do you make of that?" said Holmes.

"Well, what do *you* make of it?"

"That it was written in a train; the good writing represents

that McFarlane may have thought this "very late," but considering the short distance to his parents' house, spending the night in a hotel seems like an unnecessary exercise and expense.

"The wretched young man arose."
Sidney Paget, *Strand Magazine*, 1903

stations, the bad writing movement, and the very bad writing passing over points. A scientific expert would pronounce at once that this was drawn up on a suburban line, since nowhere save in the immediate vicinity of a great city could there be so quick a succession of points. Granting that his whole journey was occupied in drawing up the will, then the train was an express, only stopping once between Norwood and London Bridge."

Lestrade began to laugh.

"You are too many for me when you begin to get on your theories, Mr. Holmes," said he. "How does this bear on the case?"

"Well, it corroborates the young man's story to the extent that the will was drawn up by Jonas Oldacre in his journey yesterday. It is curious—is it not?—that a man should draw up so important a document in so haphazard a fashion. It suggests that he did not think it was going to be of much practical importance. If a man drew up a will which he did not intend ever to be effective, he might do it so."

"Well, he drew up his own death-warrant at the same time," said Lestrade.

"Oh, you think so?"

"Don't you?"

"Well, it is quite possible, but the case is not clear to me yet."

"Not clear? Well, if that isn't clear, what *could* be clear? Here is a young man who learns suddenly that, if a certain older man dies, he will succeed to a fortune. What does he do? He says nothing to anyone, but he arranges that he shall go out on some pretext to see his client that night; he waits until the only other person in the house is in bed, and then in the solitude of a man's room he murders him, burns his body in the wood-pile, and departs to a neighbouring hotel. The blood-stains in the room and also on the stick are very slight. It is probable that he imagined his crime to be a bloodless one, and hoped that if the body were consumed it would hide all traces of the method of his death—traces which, for some reason, must have pointed to him. Is not all this obvious?"

"It strikes me, my good Lestrade, as being just a trifle too obvious," said Holmes. "You do not add imagination to your other great qualities, but if you could for one moment put yourself in the place of this young man, would you choose the very night after the will had been made to commit your crime? Would it not seem dangerous to you to make so very close a relation between the two incidents? Again, would you choose an occasion when you are known to be in the house, when a servant has let you in? And, finally, would you take the great pains to conceal the body, and yet leave your own stick as a sign that you were the criminal? Confess, Lestrade, that all this is very unlikely."

"As to the stick, Mr. Holmes, you know as well as I do that a criminal is often flurried, and does such things, which a cool man would avoid. He was very likely afraid to go back to the room. Give me another theory that would fit the facts."

"I could very easily give you half a dozen," said Holmes. "Here, for example, is a very possible and even probable one. I make you a free present of it. The older man is showing documents which are of evident value. A passing tramp sees them through the window, the blind of which is only half down. Exit the solicitor. Enter the tramp! He seizes a stick, which he observes there, kills Oldacre, and departs after burning the body."

"Why should the tramp burn the body?"

"For the matter of that, why should McFarlane?"

"To hide some evidence."

"Possibly the tramp wanted to hide that any murder at all had been committed."

"And why did the tramp take nothing?"

"Because they were papers that he could not negotiate."

Lestrade shook his head, though it seemed to me that his manner was less absolutely assured than before.

"Well, Mr. Sherlock Holmes, you may look for your tramp, and while you are finding him we will hold on to our man. The future will show which is right. Just notice this point, Mr. Holmes—that so far as we know, none of the papers were removed, and that the prisoner is the one man in the world who had no reason for removing them, since he was heir-at-law, and would come into them in any case."

My friend seemed struck by this remark.

"I don't mean to deny that the evidence is in some ways very strongly in favour of your theory," said he. "I only wish to point out that there are other theories possible. As you say, the future will decide. Good-morning! I dare say that in the course of the day I shall drop in at Norwood and see how you are getting on."

When the detective departed, my friend rose and made his preparations for the day's work with the alert air of a man who has a congenial task before him.

"My first movement, Watson," said he, as he bustled into his frock-coat, "must, as I said, be in the direction of Blackheath."

"And why not Norwood?"

"Because we have in this case one singular incident coming close to the heels of another singular incident. The police are making the mistake of concentrating their attention upon the second, because it happens to be the one which is actually criminal. But it is evident to me that the logical way to

" 'My first movement, Watson,' said he, 'must be in the
direction of Blackheath.' "
Sidney Paget, *Strand Magazine*, 1903

approach the case is to begin by trying to throw some light upon the first incident—the curious will, so suddenly made, and to so unexpected an heir. It may do something to simplify what followed. No, my dear fellow, I don't think you can help me. There is no prospect of danger, or I should not dream of stirring out without you. I trust that when I see you in the evening, I will be able to report that I have been able to do something for this unfortunate youngster who has thrown himself upon my protection."

It was late when my friend returned, and I could see, by a glance at his haggard and anxious face, that the high hopes with which he had started had not been fulfilled. For an hour he droned away upon his violin, endeavouring to soothe his own ruffled spirits. At last he flung down the instrument, and plunged into a detailed account of his misadventures.

"It's all going wrong, Watson—all as wrong as it can go. I kept a bold face before Lestrade, but, upon my soul, I believe that for once the fellow is on the right track and we are on the wrong. All my instincts are one way, and all the facts are the other, and I much fear that British juries have not yet attained that pitch of intelligence when they will give the preference to my theories over Lestrade's facts."

"Did you go to Blackheath?"

"Yes, Watson, I went there, and I found very quickly that the late lamented Oldacre was a pretty considerable blackguard. The father was away in search of his son. The mother was at home—a little, fluffy, blue-eyed person, in a tremor of fear and indignation. Of course, she would not admit even the possibility of his guilt. But she would not express either surprise or regret over the fate of Oldacre. On the contrary, she spoke of him with such bitterness that she was unconsciously considerably strengthening the case of the police; for, of course, if her son had heard her speak of the man in this fashion, it would predispose him towards hatred and violence. 'He was more like a malignant and cunning ape than a human being,' said she, 'and he always was, ever since he was a young man.'

" 'You knew him at that time?' said I.

" 'Yes, I knew him well; in fact, he was an old suitor of mine. Thank heaven that I had the sense to turn away from him and to marry a better, if a poorer, man. I was engaged to him, Mr. Holmes, when I heard a shocking story of how he had turned a cat loose in an aviary, and I was so horrified at his brutal cruelty that I would have nothing more to do with him.' She rummaged in a bureau, and presently she produced a photograph of a woman, shamefully defaced and mutilated with a knife. 'That is my own photograph,' she said. 'He sent it to me in that state, with his curse, upon my wedding morning.'

" 'Well,' said I, 'at least he has forgiven you now, since he has left all his property to your son.'

" 'Neither my son nor I want anything from Jonas Oldacre, dead or alive!' she cried, with a proper spirit. 'There is a God in heaven, Mr. Holmes, and that same God who has punished

"He sent it to me in that state, with his curse,
upon my wedding morning."
Sidney Paget, *Strand Magazine*, 1903

that wicked man will show, in His own good time, that my son's hands are guiltless of his blood.'

"Well, I tried one or two leads, but could get at nothing which would help our hypothesis, and several points which would make against it. I gave it up at last, and off I went to Norwood.

"This place, Deep Dene House, is a big modern villa of staring brick, standing back in its own grounds, with a laurel-clumped lawn in front of it. To the right and some distance back from the road was the timber-yard which had been the scene of the fire. Here's a rough plan on a leaf of my notebook. This window on the left is the one which opens into Oldacre's room. You can look into it from the road, you see. That is about the only bit of consolation I have had to-day. Lestrade was not there, but his head constable did the honours. They had just found a great treasure-trove. They had spent the morning raking among the ashes of the burned wood-pile, and besides the charred organic remains they had secured several discoloured metal discs. I examined them with care, and there was no doubt that they were trouser buttons. I even distinguished that one of them was marked with the name of 'Hyams,' who was Oldacre's tailor.[15] I then worked the lawn very carefully for signs and traces, but this drought has made everything as hard as iron. Nothing was to be seen save that some body or bundle had been dragged through a low privet hedge which is in a line with the wood-pile. All that, of course, fits in with the official theory. I crawled about the lawn with an August sun on my back, but I got up at the end of an hour no wiser than before.

"Well, after this fiasco I went into the bedroom and examined that also. The blood-stains were very slight, mere smears and discolourations, but undoubtedly fresh. The stick had been removed, but there also the marks were slight. There is no doubt about the stick belonging to our client. He admits it. Footmarks of both men could be made out on the carpet, but none of any third person, which again is a trick for the other side. They were piling up their score all the time, and we were at a standstill.

"Only one little gleam of hope did I get—and yet it amounted to nothing. I examined the contents of the safe, most of which had been taken out and left on the table. The papers had been made up into sealed envelopes, one or two of

15 According to Donald A. Redmond, "This was the imprint of Hyam & Co. Ltd, tailors, etc., of 134-140 Oxford Street, and of Birmingham, Wolverhampton and Leeds—one of what the duke of Plaza-Toro referred to as 'those pressing prevailers, the ready-made tailors.' A *gentleman* would patronize Bond Street and Savile Row, not Oxford Street; which tells something about the character of Oldacre."

16 Did Holmes, in 1894, plan that he would require the public to be "patient" until 1903, when "The Norwood Builder" was published?

which had been opened by the police. They were not, so far as I could judge, of any great value, nor did the bank book show that Mr. Oldacre was in such very affluent circumstances. But it seemed to me that all the papers were not there. There were allusions to some deeds—possibly the more valuable—which I could not find. This, of course, if we could definitely prove it, would turn Lestrade's argument against himself, for who would steal a thing if he knew that he would shortly inherit it?

"Finally, having drawn every other cover and picked up no scent, I tried my luck with the housekeeper. Mrs. Lexington is her name, a little, dark, silent person, with suspicious and side-long eyes. She could tell us something if she would—I am convinced of it. But she was as close as wax. Yes, she had let Mr. McFarlane in at half-past nine. She wished her hand had withered before she had done so. She had gone to bed at half-past ten. Her room was at the other end of the house, and she could hear nothing of what passed. Mr. McFarlane had left his hat, and to the best of her belief his stick, in the hall. She had been awakened by the alarm of fire. Her poor, dear master had certainly been murdered. Had he any enemies? Well, every man had enemies, but Mr. Oldacre kept himself very much to himself, and only met people in the way of business. She had seen the buttons, and was sure that they belonged to the clothes which he had worn last night. The wood-pile was very dry, for it had not rained for a month. It burned like tinder, and by the time she reached the spot, nothing could be seen but flames. She and all the firemen smelled the burned flesh from inside it. She knew nothing of the papers, nor of Mr. Oldacre's private affairs.

"So, my dear Watson, there's my report of a failure. And yet—and yet"—he clenched his thin hands in a paroxysm of conviction—"I *know* it's all wrong. I feel it in my bones. There is something that has not come out, and that housekeeper knows it. There was a sort of sulky defiance in her eyes which only goes with guilty knowledge. However, there's no good talking any more about it, Watson; but unless some lucky chance comes our way I fear that the Norwood Disappearance Case will not figure in that chronicle of our successes which I foresee that a patient public will sooner or later have to endure."[16]

There was a sort of sulky defiance in her eyes.
Frederick Dorr Steele, *Collier's*, 1903

"Surely," said I, "the man's appearance would go far with any jury?"

"That is a dangerous argument, my dear Watson. You remember that terrible murderer, Bert Stevens, who wanted us to get him off in '87? Was there ever a more mild-mannered, Sunday-school young man?"

"It is true."

"Unless we succeed in establishing an alternative theory, this man is lost. You can hardly find a flaw in the case which can now be presented against him, and all further investigation has served to strengthen it. By the way, there is one curious little point about those papers which may serve us as the starting-point for an inquiry. On looking over the bank book I found that the low state of the balance was principally due to large cheques which have been made out during the last year to Mr. Cornelius. I confess that I should be interested to know who this Mr. Cornelius may be with whom a retired builder has had such very large transactions. Is it possible that he has had a hand in the affair? Cornelius might be a broker, but we have found no scrip to correspond with these large payments. Failing any other indication, my researches must now take the direction of an inquiry at the bank for the gentleman who has cashed these cheques. But I fear, my dear fellow, that our case will end ingloriously by Lestrade hanging our client, which will certainly be a triumph for Scotland Yard."

I do not know how far Sherlock Holmes took any sleep that night, but when I came down to breakfast I found him pale and harassed, his bright eyes the brighter for the dark shadows round them. The carpet round his chair was littered with cigarette ends, and with the early editions of the morning papers. An open telegram lay upon the table.

"What do you think of this, Watson?" he asked, tossing it across. It was from Norwood, and ran as follows:

Important fresh evidence to hand. McFarlane's guilt definitely established. Advise you to abandon case.

Lestrade.

"This sounds serious," said I.

"It is Lestrade's little cock-a-doodle of victory," Holmes answered with a bitter smile. "And yet it may be premature to abandon the case. After all, important fresh evidence is a two-edged thing, and may possibly cut in a very different direction to that which Lestrade imagines. Take your breakfast, Watson, and we will go out together and see what we can do. I feel as if I shall need your company and your moral support to-day."

My friend had no breakfast himself, for it was one of his peculiarities that in his more intense moments he would permit himself no food, and I have known him to presume upon his iron strength until he has fainted from pure inanition. "At present I cannot spare energy and nerve force for digestion," he would say, in answer to my medical remonstrances. I was not surprised, therefore, when this morning he left his untouched meal behind him and started with me for Norwood. A crowd of morbid sightseers were still gathered round Deep Dene House, which was just such a suburban villa as I had pictured. Within the gates Lestrade met us, his face flushed with victory, his manner grossly triumphant.

"Well, Mr. Holmes, have you proved us to be wrong yet? Have you found your tramp?" he cried.

"I have formed no conclusion whatever," my companion answered.

"But we formed ours yesterday, and now it proves to be correct; so you must acknowledge that we have been a little in front of you this time, Mr. Holmes."

"You certainly have the air of something unusual having occurred," said Holmes.

Lestrade laughed loudly.

"You don't like being beaten any more than the rest of us do," said he. "A man can't expect always to have it his own way—can he, Dr. Watson? Step this way, if you please, gentlemen, and I think I can convince you once for all that it was John McFarlane who did this crime."

He led us through the passage and out into a dark hall beyond.

"This is where young McFarlane must have come out to get his hat after the crime was done," said he. "Now look at this." With dramatic suddenness he struck a match, and by its light exposed a stain of blood upon the whitewashed wall. As he held the match nearer I saw that it was more than a stain. It was the well-marked print of a thumb.

"Look at that with your magnifying glass, Mr. Holmes."

"Yes, I am doing so."

"You are aware that no two thumb-marks are alike?"

"I have heard something of the kind."[17]

"Well, then, will you please compare that print with this wax impression of young McFarlane's right thumb, taken by my orders this morning?"

As he held the waxen print close to the blood-stain, it did not take a magnifying glass to see that the two were undoubtedly from the same thumb. It was evident to me that our unfortunate client was lost.

"That is final," said Lestrade.

17 See "Sherlock Holmes and Fingerprinting," page 860.

It was more than a stain.
It was a well-marked print of a thumb.
Frederick Dorr Steele, *Collier's*, 1903

"Yes, that is final," I involuntarily echoed.

"It is final," said Holmes.

Something in his tone caught my ear, and I turned to look at him. An extraordinary change had come over his face. It was writhing with inward merriment. His two eyes were shining like stars. It seemed to me that he was making desperate efforts to restrain a convulsive attack of laughter.

"Dear me! Dear me!" he said at last. "Well, now, who would have thought it? And how deceptive appearances may be, to be sure! Such a nice young man to look at! It is a lesson to us not to trust our own judgment—is it not, Lestrade?"

"Yes, some of us are a little too much inclined to be cocksure, Mr. Holmes," said Lestrade. The man's insolence was maddening, but we could not resent it.

"What a providential thing that this young man should press his right thumb against the wall in taking his hat from the peg! Such a very natural action, too, if you come to think if it."

Holmes was outwardly calm, but his whole body gave a wriggle of suppressed excitement as he spoke.

"By the way, Lestrade, who made this remarkable discovery?"

"It was the housekeeper, Mrs. Lexington, who drew the night constable's attention to it."

"Where was the night constable?"

"He remained on guard in the bedroom where the crime was committed, so as to see that nothing was touched."

"But why didn't the police see this mark yesterday?"

"Well, we had no particular reason to make a careful exami-

"Look at that with your magnifying glass, Mr. Holmes."
Sidney Paget, *Strand Magazine*, 1903

nation of the hall. Besides, it's not in a very prominent place, as you see."

"No, no, of course not. I suppose there is no doubt that the mark was there yesterday?"

Lestrade looked at Holmes as if he thought he was going out of his mind. I confess that I was myself surprised both at his hilarious manner and at his rather wild observation.

"I don't know whether you think that McFarlane came out of gaol in the dead of the night in order to strengthen the evidence against himself," said Lestrade. "I leave it to any expert in the world whether that is not the mark of his thumb."

"It is unquestionably the mark of his thumb."

"There, that's enough," said Lestrade. "I am a practical man, Mr. Holmes, and when I have got my evidence I come to my conclusions. If you have anything to say you will find me writing my report in the sitting-room."

Holmes had recovered his equanimity, though I still seemed to detect gleams of amusement in his expression.

"Dear me, this is a very sad development, Watson, is it not?" said he. "And yet there are singular points about it which hold out some hopes for our client."

"I am delighted to hear it," said I, heartily. "I was afraid it was all up with him."

"I would hardly go so far as to say that, my dear Watson. The fact is that there is one really serious flaw in this evidence to which our friend attaches so much importance."

"Indeed, Holmes! What is it?"

"Only this—that I *know* that that mark was not there when I examined the hall yesterday. And now, Watson, let us have a little stroll round in the sunshine." With a confused brain, but with a heart into which some warmth of hope was returning, I accompanied my friend in a walk round the garden. Holmes took each face of the house in turn and examined it with great interest. He then led the way inside, and went over the whole building from basement to attics. Most of the rooms were unfurnished, but none the less Holmes inspected them all minutely. Finally, on the top corridor, which ran outside three untenanted bedrooms, he again was seized with a spasm of merriment.

"There are really some very unique features about this case,

Watson," said he. "I think it is time now that we took our friend Lestrade into our confidence. He has had his little smile at our expense, and perhaps we may do as much by him if my reading of this problem proves to be correct. Yes, yes; I think I see how we should approach it."

The Scotland Yard inspector was still writing in the parlour when Holmes interrupted him.

"I understood that you were writing a report of this case," said he.

"So I am."

"Don't you think it may be a little premature? I can't help thinking that your evidence is not complete."

Lestrade knew my friend too well to disregard his words. He laid down his pen and looked curiously at him.

"What do you mean, Mr. Holmes?"

"Only that there is an important witness whom you have not seen."

"Can you produce him?"

"I think I can."

"Then do so."

"I will do my best. How many constables have you?"

"There are three within call."

"Excellent!" said Holmes. "May I ask if they are all large, able-bodied men with powerful voices?"

"I have no doubt they are, though I fail to see what their voices have to do with it."

"Perhaps I can help you to see that, and one or two other things as well," said Holmes. "Kindly summon your men, and I will try."

Five minutes later three policemen had assembled in the hall.

"In the outhouse you will find a considerable quantity of straw," said Holmes. "I will ask you to carry in two bundles of it. I think it will be of the greatest assistance in producing the witness whom I require. Thank you very much. I believe you have some matches in your pocket, Watson. Now, Mr. Lestrade, I will ask you all to accompany me to the top landing."

As I have said, there was a broad corridor there, which ran outside three empty bedrooms. At one end of the corridor we were all marshalled by Sherlock Holmes, the constables grinning and Lestrade staring at my friend with amazement, expectation, and derision chasing each other across his features. Holmes stood before us with the air of a conjurer who is performing a trick.

"Would you kindly send one of your constables for two buckets of water? Put the straw on the floor here, free from the wall on either side. Now I think that we are all ready."

Lestrade's face had begun to grow red and angry.

"I don't know whether you are playing a game with us, Mr. Sherlock Holmes," said he. "If you know anything you can surely say it without all this tomfoolery."

"I assure you, my good Lestrade, that I have an excellent reason for everything that I do. You may possibly remember that you chaffed me a little some hours ago, when the sun seemed on your side of the hedge, so you must not grudge me a little pomp and ceremony now. Might I ask you, Watson, to open that window, and then to put a match to the edge of the straw?" I did so, and driven by the draught, a coil of grey smoke swirled down the corridor, while the dry straw crackled and flamed.

"Now we must see if we can find this witness for you, Lestrade. Might I ask you all to join in the cry of 'Fire'? Now, then; one, two, three—"

"Fire!" we all yelled.

"Thank you. I will trouble you once again."

"Fire!"

"Just once more, gentlemen, and all together."

"Fire!" The shout must have rung over Norwood.

It had hardly died away when an amazing thing happened. A door suddenly flew open out of what appeared to be solid wall at the end of the corridor, and a little wizened man darted out of it, like a rabbit out of its burrow.

"Capital!" said Holmes calmly. "Watson, a bucket of water over the straw. That will do! Lestrade, allow me to present you with your principal missing witness, Mr. Jonas Oldacre."

The detective stared at the new-comer with blank amazement. The latter was blinking in the bright light of the corridor, and peering at us and at the smouldering fire. It was an odious face—crafty, vicious, malignant, with shifty, light-gray eyes and white eyelashes.

"What's this, then?" said Lestrade at last. "What have you been doing all this time, eh?"

"A little, wizened man darted out."
Sidney Paget, *Strand Magazine*, 1903

Oldacre gave an uneasy laugh, shrinking back from the furious red face of the angry detective.

"I have done no harm."

"No harm? You have done your best to get an innocent man hanged. If it wasn't for this gentleman here, I am not sure that you would not have succeeded." The wretched creature began to whimper.

"I am sure, sir, it was only my practical joke."

"Oh! a joke, was it? You won't find the laugh on your side, I promise you. Take him down and keep him in the sitting-room until I come. Mr. Holmes," he continued, when they had gone, "I could not speak before the constables, but I don't mind saying, in the presence of Dr. Watson, that this is the brightest thing that you have done yet, though it is a mystery to me how

Mr. Jonas Oldacre.
Charles Raymond Macaulay, *Return of Sherlock Holmes*
(McClure Phillips), 1905

you did it. You have saved an innocent man's life, and you have prevented a very grave scandal, which would have ruined my reputation in the Force."

Holmes smiled and clapped Lestrade upon the shoulder.

"Instead of being ruined, my good sir, you will find that your reputation has been enormously enhanced. Just make a few alterations in that report which you were writing, and they will understand how hard it is to throw dust in the eyes of Inspector Lestrade."

"And you don't want your name to appear?"

"Not at all. The work is its own reward. Perhaps I shall get the credit also at some distant day when I permit my zealous historian to lay out his foolscap once more—eh, Watson? Well, now, let us see where this rat has been lurking."

A lath-and-plaster partition had been run across the passage six feet from the end, with a door cunningly concealed in it. It was lit within by slits under the eaves. A few articles of furniture and a supply of food and water were within, together with a number of books and papers.

"There's the advantage of being a builder," said Holmes as we came out. "He was able to fix up his own little hiding-place without any confederate—save, of course, that precious house-keeper of his, whom I should lose no time in adding to your bag, Lestrade."

"Holmes smiled and clapped Lestrade upon the shoulder."
Sidney Paget, *Strand Magazine*, 1903

"I'll take your advice. But how did you know of this place, Mr. Holmes?"

"I made up my mind that the fellow was in hiding in the house. When I paced one corridor and found it six feet shorter than the corresponding one below, it was pretty clear where he was. I thought he had not the nerve to lie quiet before an alarm of fire. We could, of course, have gone in and taken him, but it amused me to make him reveal himself; besides, I owed you a little mystification, Lestrade, for your chaff in the morning."

"Well, sir, you certainly got equal with me on that. But how in the world did you know that he was in the house at all?"

"The thumb-mark, Lestrade. You said it was final; and so it was, in a very different sense. I knew it had not been there the day before. I pay a good deal of attention to matters of detail, as you may have observed, and I had examined the hall, and was sure that the wall was clear. Therefore, it had been put on during the night."

"But how?"

"Very simply. When those packets were sealed up, Jonas Oldacre got McFarlane to secure one of the seals by putting his thumb upon the soft wax. It would be done so quickly and so naturally that I daresay the young man himself has no recollection of it. Very likely it just so happened, and Oldacre had himself no notion of the use he would put it to. Brooding over the case in that den of his, it suddenly struck him what absolutely damning evidence he could make against McFarlane by using that thumb-mark. It was the simplest thing in the world for him to take a wax impression from the seal, to moisten it in as much blood as he could get from a pin-prick, and to put the mark upon the wall during the night, either with his own hand or with that of his housekeeper. If you examine among these documents which he took with him into his retreat, I will lay you a wager that you find the seal with the thumb-mark upon it."

"Wonderful!" said Lestrade. "Wonderful! It's all as clear as crystal, as you put it. But what is the object of this deep deception, Mr. Holmes?"

It was amusing to me to see how the detective's overbearing manner had changed suddenly to that of a child asking questions of its teacher.

"Well, I don't think that is very hard to explain. A very deep, malicious, vindictive person is the gentleman who is now awaiting us downstairs. You know that he was once refused by McFarlane's mother? You don't! I told you that you should go to Blackheath first and Norwood afterwards. Well, this injury, as he would consider it, has rankled in his wicked, scheming brain, and all his life he has longed for vengeance, but never seen his chance. During the last year or two things have gone against him—secret speculation, I think—and he finds himself in a bad way. He determines to swindle his creditors, and for this purpose he pays large cheques to a certain Mr. Cornelius, who is, I imagine, himself under another name. I have not traced these cheques yet, but I have no doubt that they were banked under that name at some provincial town where Oldacre from time to time led a double existence. He intended to change his name altogether, draw this money, and vanish, starting life again elsewhere."

"Well, that's likely enough."

"It would strike him that in disappearing he might throw all pursuit off his track, and at the same time have an ample and crushing revenge upon his old sweetheart, if he could give the impression that he had been murdered by her only child. It was a masterpiece of villainy, and he carried it out like a master. The idea of the will, which would give an obvious motive for the crime, the secret visit unknown to his own parents, the retention of the stick, the blood, and the animal remains and buttons in the wood-pile, all were admirable. It was a net from which it seemed to me, a few hours ago, that there was no possible escape. But he had not that supreme gift of the artist, the knowledge of when to stop. He wished to improve that which was already perfect—to draw the rope tighter yet round the neck of his unfortunate victim—and so he ruined all. Let us descend, Lestrade. There are just one or two questions that I would ask him."

The malignant creature was seated in his own parlour with a policeman upon each side of him.

"It was a joke, my good sir, a practical joke, nothing more," he whined incessantly. "I assure you, sir, that I simply concealed myself in order to see the effect of my disappearance, and I am sure that you would not be so unjust as to imagine that I would have allowed any harm to befall poor young Mr. McFarlane."

18 Several scholars complain that it should have been a simple matter for investigators to distinguish rabbit bones from human bones (if, indeed, a rabbit was the animal cast upon the fire). The report only mentioned "remains" lying in the ashes, but a wood-pile certainly could not have generated a fire that burned long enough or hot enough to melt bones, human or otherwise.

"That's for the jury to decide," said Lestrade. "Anyhow, we shall have you on a charge of conspiracy, if not for attempted murder."

"And you'll probably find that your creditors will impound the banking account of Mr. Cornelius," said Holmes.

The little man started and turned his malignant eyes upon my friend.

"I have to thank you for a good deal," said he. "Perhaps I'll pay my debt some day."

Holmes smiled indulgently.

"I fancy that for some few years you will find your time very fully occupied," said he. "By the way, what was it you put into the wood-pile besides your old trousers? A dead dog, or rabbits, or what? You won't tell? Dear me, how very unkind of you! Well, well, I daresay that a couple of rabbits would account both for the blood and for the charred ashes.[18] If ever you write an account, Watson, you can make rabbits serve your turn." ∎

SHERLOCK HOLMES AND FINGERPRINTING

ONE OF the first significant developments in forensic science was the ability to identify people by their fingerprints. As early as 1858, Sir William Herschel, a magistrate in Jungipoor, India, began requiring locals to impress their handprints (and later, their fingerprints) on the backs of contracts when signing them. Because the native Indians believed that physical contact with a document was more binding than a mere signature, Herschel's procedure was meant more to enforce the contract's legitimacy than to provide any sort of personal identification. Still, through this experience he came to realise that each individual's fingerprints were unique. He began collecting the prints of family members and friends, studying how they remained unchanged over time.

Meanwhile, Dr. Henry Faulds, while working as a surgeon in Japan, discovered ancient fingerprint markings in prehistoric clay pottery and began taking people's fingerprints so as to examine the properties and distinctions of "skin-furrows." He even managed to use his collection to discover who had stolen a bottle of alcohol from his medical clinic, matching the greasy fingerprints found on a cocktail glass to those of one of his medical students, whose prints he had on file. (This is the first reported example of a crime being solved through fingerprinting.) From his research, Faulds published a letter in the October 28, 1880, edition of *Nature*, stating, "When blood finger-marks or impressions on clay, glass, *etc.*, exist, they may lead to the scientific identification of criminals. . . . There can be no doubt as to the advantage of having, besides their photographs, a nature-copy of the for-ever unchangeable finger-furrows of important criminals." Herschel published a letter in the following month's edition of *Nature*, detailing his own use of fingerprints as identifying "sign-manuals."

Despite Faulds's attempts to persuade Scotland Yard to create some sort of fingerprint identification system, it was Francis Galton, an anthropologist and cousin of Sir Charles Darwin, who would get most of the credit for fathering the science of fingerprinting. Faulds had sent a summary of his research to Darwin, who, being advanced in age, had promised to forward it to his cousin. Using Faulds's as well as Herschel's research, Galton began conducting his own experiments and collaborating with Herschel, a man whose family credentials and social status were more elevated than Faulds's.

Although Galton had to concede failure in his attempts to establish a link between fingerprints and race, intelligence, or genetic history, his work progressed, and in 1892—acknowledging the research of Herschel, but not Faulds—he published the book *Finger Prints*, which not only determined that no two people's fingerprints were alike but also introduced a classification system that broke down the patterns of each print's loops, arches, and whorls. This system was developed further by Edward R. Henry, future commissioner of the London metropolitan police. Following the 1893 endorsement of the Troup Committee, fingerprinting was successfully introduced in India in 1897, and in 1901 Scotland Yard established its own fingerprint bureau using the so-called Galton-Henry system (or Galton's Details), which remains the preferred classification system today. Galton was knighted in 1909. Faulds, on the other hand, received no recognition for his work until the mid-1900s.

Scholars have long pondered how much Holmes might have known about this fledgling science. As "The Adventure of the

Norwood Builder" is thought to have taken place in 1894, Holmes could certainly have read Herschel and Faulds's letters in *Nature*, read Galton's book, or attended Galton's lecture on "Personal Identification and Description," given on Friday evening, May 25, 1888, at the Royal Institution. (Alternatively, Holmes may have seen the reprint of that lecture in the June 28, 1888, issue of *Nature*, which discussed Herschel's work and the use of fingerprints in China to identify criminals.) Additional work by Galton was published in *Nature* on December 4, 1890, and referenced by Henry E. Varigny in an article entitled "Anthropology—The Finger Prints According to M. F. Galton," in *Revue Scientifique* (May 1891). During this time, fingerprinting was also being utilised in Argentina, where police official Juan Vucetich solved a murder case in 1892—of a mother who killed her two sons—by extracting a bloody fingerprint left on a doorpost. In 1904 Vucetich developed his own, Galton-based classification system, which is now used in most Spanish-speaking countries.

Holmes's stated admiration in "The Naval Treaty" for Alphonse Bertillon, founder of a sophisticated system of measurement to identify criminals, leads some scholars to wonder why he did not similarly reference Galton when speaking to Lestrade about fingerprinting. Vernon Rendall, noting specifically that Holmes made no mention of Galton's *Finger-prints and the Detection of Crime in India*, a paper he presented to the British Association in 1899, concludes that egotism in this situation prevented Holmes from giving others proper credit: "All one can suggest is that Holmes was not eager to take up other people's methods. With his vanity, he found it difficult to use another expert to help him."

William S. Baring-Gould makes nonsense of Rendall's claim, exposing his error in thinking Holmes would have read a paper that would not be presented for another four or five years. (Baring-Gould puts "The Adventure of the Norwood Builder" as occurring in 1895, not 1894, as most other chronologists have determined.). "On the contrary," Baring-Gould declares, "the obviously sarcastic tone of Holmes' 'I have heard something of the kind' clearly indicates that he had studied fingerprints and was aware of their importance in the detection of crime. It is more difficult to explain how Lestrade, in 1895, was aware that 'no two thumb-prints are alike,' since the system was not adopted by Scotland Yard until 1901." Of course, Lestrade, while lacking Holmes's prodigious intelligence, may also have read any of the various publications about this intriguing new science.

Holmes clearly understood the importance of fingerprints; indeed, his knowledge is demonstrated by his observations in five other reported cases, three occurring prior to "The Norwood Builder": *The Sign of Four* (thumb-mark on letter sent by Thaddeus Sholto to Mary Morstan); "The Man with the Twisted Lip" (letter to Mrs. St. Clair posted by "a man with a dirty thumb"); "The Cardboard Box" (box had "nothing distinctive save two thumb-marks"); "The Three Students" (there are no finger impressions on the examination papers); and "The Red Circle" (paper torn away to eliminate thumbprint). In "The Three Gables," even the police are aware of finger-marks, as evidenced by the anonymous inspector's remark to Holmes as he passes Holmes a sheet of foolscap.

Therefore, it is safe to assume that by 1894 or 1895, Holmes would indeed have been familiar with the technique of fingerprinting and the uniqueness of fingerprints. Clearly Watson was ("It was evident to me that our unfortunate client was lost"); and Lestrade was apparently aware of the notion as well, regardless of whether the Yard had officially adopted a system of fingerprinting. Until a bank of fingerprint data was available, however, the technique alone would have limited value.

THE ADVENTURE OF THE DANCING MEN[1]

When Hilton Cubitt hires Sherlock Holmes to discover his wife's secret past, Holmes must decipher the message of "The Dancing Men." Some would rank this case as one of Holmes's few failures, for he is unable to prevent tragedy; yet he does bring the criminal to justice. Although Americans figure in numerous cases, only twice before had Watson written of an American criminal (in A Study in Scarlet *and "The Five Orange Pips"). The case, with its mention of Holmes's friend Wilson Hargreave of the New York Police Bureau, hints that Holmes may have been to America himself. Conan Doyle had travelled there for lecture tours, and the play "Angels of Darkness" suggests that Watson, too, spent some time in America. Here we also learn a bit more about Watson: his friend Thurston, his fondness for billiards, and his apparent spendthrift nature. The cipher itself has been the subject of extensive study, by professional and amateur cryptanalysts as well as Sherlockians, and its ingenuity and originality make Dr. Watson's tale a perennial favourite.*

1 "The Dancing Men" was published in the *Strand Magazine* in December 1903 and in *Collier's Weekly* on December 5, 1903.

2 The 1886 discovery of a phenomenally rich, forty-mile vein of gold in the Transvaal's Witwatersrand (or the Rand, the area of land between the Vaal and Olifants Rivers) brought to South Africa a rapidly expanding economy and hundreds of thousands of foreign white settlers, known as *Uitlanders* (outlanders). By 1898, according to A. N. Wilson, a staggering £15 million worth of gold was being taken from the mines every year. In the previous few decades, Britain had annexed much of South Africa, including the Transvaal in 1877, though in 1881 the province's independence had been restored. Still, British *Uit-*

HOLMES HAD BEEN seated for some hours in silence with his long, thin back curved over a chemical vessel in which he was brewing a particularly malodorous product. His head was sunk upon his breast, and he looked from my point of view like a strange, lank bird, with dull gray plumage and a black top-knot.

"So, Watson," said he suddenly, "you do not propose to invest in South African securities?"[2]

I gave a start of astonishment. Accustomed as I was to Holmes's curious faculties, this sudden intrusion into my most intimate thoughts was utterly inexplicable.

"How on earth do you know that?" I asked.

He wheeled round upon his stool, with a steaming test-tube in his hand and a gleam of amusement in his deep-set eyes.

"Now, Watson, confess yourself utterly taken aback," said he.

"I am."

"I ought to make you sign a paper to that effect."

"Why?"

"Because in five minutes you will say that it is all so absurdly simple."

"I am sure that I shall say nothing of the kind."

"You see, my dear Watson"—he propped his test-tube in the rack, and began to lecture with the air of a professor addressing his class—"it is not really difficult to construct a series of inferences, each dependent upon its predecessor and each simple in itself. If, after doing so, one simply knocks out all the central inferences and presents one's audience with the starting-point and the conclusion, one may produce a startling, though possibly a meretricious, effect. Now, it was not really difficult, by an inspection of the groove between your left forefinger and thumb, to feel sure that you did not propose to invest your small capital in the gold fields."

"I see no connection."

"Very likely not; but I can quickly show you a close connection. Here are the missing links of the very simple chain: 1. You had chalk between your left finger and thumb[3] when you returned from the club[4] last night. 2. You put chalk there when you play billiards to steady the cue. 3. You never play billiards except with Thurston.[5] 4. You told me four weeks ago that Thurston had an option on some South African property which would expire in a month, and which he desired you to share with him. 5. Your cheque book is locked in my drawer,[6] and you have not asked for the key. 6. You do not propose to invest your money in this manner."

"How absurdly simple!" I cried.

"Quite so!" said he, a little nettled. "Every problem becomes very childish when once it is explained to you. Here is an unexplained one. See what you can make of that, friend Watson." He tossed a sheet of paper upon the table, and turned once more to his chemical analysis.

I looked with amazement at the absurd hieroglyphics upon the paper.

"Why, Holmes, it is a child's drawing," I cried.

"Oh, that's your idea!"

"What else should it be?"

"That is what Mr. Hilton Cubitt,[7] of Ridling Thorpe Manor,[8] Norfolk, is very anxious to know. This little conun-

landers made up a large portion of the Rand's population, earning higher wages and garnering greater power than did the unskilled African migrant workers. British speculators, eager to cash in on the boom, traded enthusiastically in South African securities; the British government, meanwhile, was keen to claim the Transvaal for its own. Continued tension between Great Britain and the resistant Transvaal government—which, despite collecting enormous amounts of taxes from the *Uitlanders*, began depriving them of the vote, public education, and other political rights—led to the onset of the Boer War in 1899, one year after this conversation between Watson and Holmes is thought to have occurred. Britain would claim victory in the Boer War in 1902. See "The Blanched Soldier" for further discussion of the conflict.

3 The placement of the chalk mark is consistent with Watson's right-handedness (see "The Yellow Face"). However, it is remarkable that a man who holds his left arm in a "stiff, unnatural manner" (*A Study in Scarlet*) has sufficient flexibility to manipulate a billiard cue.

4 It is tempting to consider this to be *Watson's* club, for Watson was an eminently "clubbable" man, and to identify it as the United Service Club, founded in May 1831 as the general military club for naval and military officers. Ralph Nevill, in his *London Clubs: Their History and Treasures*, observes that the club had the nickname of "Cripplegate"—"from the prevailing advanced years and infirmity of its members . . . The United Service contains many interesting pictures, [including a portrait of] Major-General Charles G. Gordon, by Dickinson, from a photograph. . . . In the upper billiard-room is a picture of the Battle of Trafalgar, the frame of which is wood from the timbers of the *Victory*." The United Service Club faces Pall Mall, and Watson

The United Service Club.
Queen's London (1897)

must have joined it *after* the events of "The Greek Interpreter," for he would surely otherwise have mentioned the proximity of "his" club to that of Mycroft. Was Thurston also a military man? Or was the "club" Thurston's?

5 Ralph Hodgson, in a long letter to Christopher Morley, reprinted in the *Baker Street Journal*, reports that John Thurston of 78 Margaret Street, Cavendish Square, started making "superior" billiard tables sometime prior to 1814. A few years later he moved to 14 Catherine Street, The Strand. In 1869, Messrs. Thurston & Coy, still on Catherine Street, were one of the chief table-makers in England.

6 That Watson was, apparently, not to be trusted with his own money may have been rooted in his family's profligate tendencies, according to S. C. Roberts's *Doctor Watson*. Watson himself tells Holmes in "Shoscombe Old Place" that he spends half of his army pension betting on racing. In addition, writes Roberts, "Watson père had gambled on his luck as an Australian prospector—and won;

his elder son gambled on life—and lost. . . . It is evident, however, that Holmes kept the watchful eye of an elder brother upon Watson's gambling propensities." Roberts's familial observations can hardly be accepted as fact, however, for all that is definitely known of the brother is that he died of drink, and all that is known of the father is that he left a gold watch as a legacy (*The Sign of Four*). Indeed, rejecting the image of Watson as a man reckless with his funds, D. Martin Dakin suggests instead that the doctor may have temporarily broken the lock or mislaid his own desk key, or that his desk simply wasn't the kind that locked.

7 In searching out the geographical locations mentioned in the case, numerous writers identify various residences belonging to various members of the Cubitt family in Norfolk, where the last name is prevalent. Philip Weller, however, points out in "The Norfolk Dance Hall and Other Locations: The Geography of 'The Dancing Men,'" that it is illogical to accept (as almost all scholars do) that

drum came by the first post, and he was to follow by the next train. There's a ring at the bell, Watson. I should not be very much surprised if this were he."

A heavy step was heard upon the stairs, and an instant later there entered a tall, ruddy, clean-shaven gentleman, whose clear eyes and florid cheeks told of a life led far from the fogs of Baker Street. He seemed to bring a whiff of his strong, fresh, bracing, east-coast air with him as he entered. Having shaken hands with each of us, he was about to sit down, when his eye rested upon the paper with the curious markings, which I had just examined and left upon the table.

"Well, Mr. Holmes, what do you make of these?" he cried. "They told me that you were fond of queer mysteries, and I

while Watson routinely changed the names of Holmes's clients, Watson did not do so here. "It is more logical to accept that Watson, or his agent, used the name of Cubitt as a means of disguise precisely because it was, and still is, so common in Norfolk."

8 Riding Thorpe in the first mention in the *Strand Magazine*; in other texts, Ridling Thorp or plain Ridling. It appears from the English book edition that the text given is the correct one.

"What do you make of these?"
Frederick Dorr Steele, *Collier's*, 1903

"Holmes held up the paper."
Sidney Paget, *Strand Magazine*, 1903

don't think you can find a queerer one than that. I sent the paper on ahead so that you might have time to study it before I came."

"It is certainly rather a curious production," said Holmes. "At first sight it would appear to be some childish prank. It consists of a number of absurd little figures dancing across the paper upon which they are drawn. Why should you attribute any importance to so grotesque an object?"

"I never should, Mr. Holmes. But my wife does. It is frightening her to death. She says nothing, but I can see terror in her eyes. That's why I want to sift the matter to the bottom."

Holmes held up the paper so that the sunlight shone full upon it. It was a page torn from a notebook. The markings were done in pencil, and ran in this way:

Holmes examined it for some time, and then, folding it carefully up, he placed it in his pocketbook.

"This promises to be a most interesting and unusual case," said he. "You gave me a few particulars in your letter, Mr. Hilton Cubitt, but I should be very much obliged if you would kindly go over it all again for the benefit of my friend, Dr. Watson."

"I'm not much of a story-teller," said our visitor, nervously clasping and unclasping his great, strong hands. "You'll just ask me anything that I don't make clear. I'll begin at the time of my marriage last year; but I want to say first of all that, though I'm not a rich man, my people have been at Ridling Thorpe for a matter of five centuries, and there is no better known family in the County of Norfolk. Last year I came up to London for the Jubilee,[9] and I stopped at a boarding-house in Russell Square, because Parker, the vicar of our parish, was staying in it. There was an American young lady there—Patrick was the name—Elsie Patrick. In some way we became friends, until

9 Victoria asssumed the throne in 1837, celebrating her Golden Jubilee in 1887 and her Diamond Jubilee in 1897. Most chronologists accept Cubitt's reference as being to the latter event (see *Chronological Table*). Not just a commemoration of Victoria's reign, the Diamond Jubilee was a final, grand tribute to the dominance of the British Empire, which at that time spanned over a fifth of the globe and seemed nearly invincible. Of the festivities themselves, Simon Schama writes that 50,000 troops—Gurkhas, Canadians, Jamaicans— paraded through London in tribute to the queen: "The tabloid imperialist press (above all, the *Daily Mail*) had been ecstatic; the crowds drunk with top-nation elation. Up and down the country, on 22 June schoolchildren were given the day off, herded into parks and, courtesy of the queen, given two buns and an orange. . . . The queen, now very lame, conceded just enough to the delirium to decorate her black satin with Cape ostrich feathers."

The Queen's carriage leaving the Quadrangle, Buckingham Palace, as the Jubilee procession commences (1897).
Queen's London (1897)

10 The name "Hilton" is replaced with "John" in *Collier's Weekly*. Shades of the "James/John" slip of "The Man with the Twisted Lip"!

Russell Square.
Queen's London (1897)

before my month was up I was as much in love as a man could be. We were quietly married at a registry office, and we returned to Norfolk a wedded couple. You'll think it very mad, Mr. Holmes, that a man of a good old family should marry a wife in this fashion, knowing nothing of her past or of her people; but if you saw her and knew her, it would help you to understand.

"She was very straight about it, was Elsie. I can't say that she did not give me every chance of getting out of it if I wished to do so. 'I have had some very disagreeable associations in my life,' said she; 'I wish to forget all about them. I would rather never allude to the past, for it is very painful to me. If you take me, Hilton,[10] you will take a woman who has nothing that she need be personally ashamed of; but you will have to be content with my word for it, and to allow me to be silent as to all that passed up to the time when I became yours. If these conditions are too hard, then go back to Norfolk and leave me to the lonely life in which you found me.' It was only the day before our wedding that she said those very words to me. I told her that I was content to take her on her own terms, and I have been as good as my word.

"Well, we have been married now for a year, and very happy we have been. But about a month ago, at the end of June, I saw for the first time signs of trouble. One day my wife received a letter from America. I saw the American stamp. She turned deadly white, read the letter, and threw it into the fire. She made no allusion to it afterwards, and I made none, for a promise is a promise; but she has never known an easy hour from that moment. There is always a look of fear upon her face—a look as if she were waiting and expecting. She would do better to trust me. She would find that I was her best friend. But until she speaks I can say nothing. Mind you, she is a truthful woman, Mr. Holmes, and whatever trouble there may have been in her past life it has been no fault of hers. I am only a simple Norfolk squire, but there is not a man in England who ranks his family honour more highly than I do. She knows it well, and she knew it well before she married me. She would never bring any stain upon it—of that I am sure.

"Well, now I come to the queer part of my story. About a week ago—it was the Tuesday of last week—I found on one of the window-sills a number of absurd little dancing figures, like these upon the paper. They were scrawled with chalk. I thought that it was the stable-boy who had drawn them, but the lad swore he knew nothing about it. Anyhow, they had come there during the night. I had them washed out, and I only mentioned the matter to my wife afterwards. To my surprise she took it very seriously, and begged me if any more came to let her see them. None did come for a week, and then yesterday morning I found this paper lying on the sun-dial in the garden. I showed it to Elsie, and down she dropped in a dead faint. Since then she has looked like a woman in a dream, half dazed, and with terror always lurking in her eyes. It was then that I wrote and sent the paper to you, Mr. Holmes. It was not a thing that I could take to the police, for they would have laughed at me, but you will tell me what to do. I am not a rich man; but if there is any danger threatening my little woman, I would spend my last copper to shield her."

He was a fine creature, this man of the old English soil—simple, straight, and gentle, with his great, earnest blue eyes and broad, comely face. His love for his wife and his trust in her shone in his features. Holmes had listened to his story with the utmost attention, and now he sat for some time in silent thought.

"Don't you think, Mr. Cubitt," said he, at last, "that your best plan would be to make a direct appeal to your wife, and to ask her to share her secret with you?"

Hilton Cubitt shook his massive head.

"A promise is a promise, Mr. Holmes. If Elsie wished to tell me, she would. If not, it is not for me to force her confidence. But I am justified in taking my own line—and I will."

"Then I will help you with all my heart. In the first place, have you heard of any strangers being seen in your neighbourhood?"

"No."

"I presume that it is a very quiet place. Any fresh face would cause comment?"

"In the immediate neighbourhood, yes. But we have several small watering-places not very far away. And the farmers take in lodgers."

"These hieroglyphics have evidently a meaning. If it is a purely arbitrary one, it may be impossible for us to solve it. If, on the other hand, it is systematic, I have no doubt that we shall get to the bottom of it. But this particular sample is so short that I can do nothing, and the facts which you have brought me are so indefinite that we have no basis for an investigation. I would suggest that you return to Norfolk, that you keep a keen lookout, and that you take an exact copy of any fresh dancing men which may appear. It is a thousand pities that we have not a reproduction of those which were done in chalk upon the window-sill. Make a discreet inquiry, also, as to any strangers in the neighbourhood. When you have collected some fresh evidence, come to me again. That is the best advice which I can give you, Mr. Hilton Cubitt. If there are any pressing fresh developments, I shall be always ready to run down and see you in your Norfolk home."

The interview left Sherlock Holmes very thoughtful, and several times in the next few days I saw him take his slip of paper from his notebook and look long and earnestly at the curious figures inscribed upon it. He made no allusion to the affair, however, until one afternoon a fortnight or so later. I was going out, when he called me back.

"You had better stay here, Watson."

"Why?"

"Because I had a wire from Hilton Cubitt this morning—you

remember Hilton Cubitt, of the dancing men? He was to reach Liverpool Street at one-twenty. He may be here at any moment. I gather from his wire that there have been some new incidents of importance."

We had not long to wait, for our Norfolk squire came straight from the station as fast as a hansom could bring him. He was looking worried and depressed, with tired eyes and a lined forehead.

"It's getting on my nerves, this business, Mr. Holmes," said he, as he sank, like a wearied man, into an arm-chair. "It's bad enough to feel that you are surrounded by unseen, unknown folk, who have some kind of design upon you, but when, in addition to that, you know that it is just killing your wife by inches, then it becomes as much as flesh and blood can endure. She's wearing away under it—just wearing away before my eyes."

"Has she said anything yet?"

"No, Mr. Holmes, she has not. And yet there have been times when the poor girl has wanted to speak, and yet could not quite bring herself to take the plunge. I have tried to help her; but I daresay I did it clumsily, and scared her from it. She has spoken about my old family, and our reputation in the county, and our pride in our unsullied honour, and I always felt it was leading to the point; but somehow it turned off before we got there."

"But you have found out something for yourself?"

"A good deal, Mr. Holmes. I have several fresh dancing men pictures for you to examine, and, what is more important, I have seen the fellow."

"What—the man who draws them?"

"Yes, I saw him at his work. But I will tell you everything in order. When I got back after my visit to you, the very first thing I saw next morning was a fresh crop of dancing men. They had been drawn in chalk upon the black wooden door of the tool-house, which stands beside the lawn in full view of the front windows. I took an exact copy, and here it is." He unfolded a paper and laid it upon the table. Here is a copy of the hieroglyphics:

"Excellent!" said Holmes. "Excellent! Pray continue."

"When I had taken the copy I rubbed out the marks, but two mornings later a fresh inscription had appeared. I have a copy of it here":

Holmes rubbed his hands and chuckled with delight.

"Our material is rapidly accumulating," said he.

"Three days later a message was left scrawled upon paper, and placed under a pebble upon the sundial. Here it is. The characters are, as you see, exactly the same as the last one. After that I determined to lie in wait; so I got out my revolver and I sat up in my study, which overlooks the lawn and garden. About two in the morning I was seated by the window, all being dark save for the moonlight outside, when I heard steps behind me, and there was my wife in her dressing-gown. She implored me to come to bed. I told her frankly that I wished to see who it was who played such absurd tricks upon us. She answered that it was some senseless practical joke, and that I should not take any notice of it.

" 'If it really annoys you, Hilton, we might go and travel, you and I, and so avoid this nuisance.'

" 'What, be driven out of our own house by a practical joker?' said I. 'Why, we should have the whole county laughing at us!'

" 'Well, come to bed,' said she, 'and we can discuss it in the morning.'

"Suddenly, as she spoke, I saw her white face grow whiter yet in the moonlight, and her hand tightened upon my shoulder. Something was moving in the shadow of the tool-house. I saw a dark, creeping figure which crawled round the corner and squatted in front of the door. Seizing my pistol I was rushing out, when my wife threw her arms round me and held me with convulsive strength. I tried to throw her off, but she clung to me most desperately. At last I got clear, but by the time I had opened the door and reached the house the creature was gone. He had left a trace of his presence, however, for there on the

"Three days later a message was left under
a pebble upon the sun-dial."
Charles Raymond Macaulay, *Return of
Sherlock Holmes* (McClure Phillips), 1905

door was the very same arrangement of dancing men which
had already twice appeared, and which I have copied on that
paper. There was no other sign of the fellow anywhere, though
I ran all over the grounds. And yet the amazing thing is that he
must have been there all the time, for when I examined the
door again in the morning he had scrawled some more of his
pictures under the line which I had already seen."

"Have you that fresh drawing?"

"Yes; it is very short, but I made a copy of it, and here it is."

Again he produced a paper. The new dance was in this form:

"My wife threw her arms round me."
Sidney Paget, *Strand Magazine*, 1903

"Tell me," said Holmes—and I could see by his eyes that he was much excited—"was this a mere addition to the first, or did it appear to be entirely separate?"

"It was on a different panel of the door."

"Excellent! This is by far the most important of all for our purpose. It fills me with hopes. Now, Mr. Hilton Cubitt, please continue your most interesting statement."

"I have nothing more to say, Mr. Holmes, except that I was angry with my wife that night for having held me back when I might have caught the skulking rascal. She said that she feared that I might come to harm. For an instant it had crossed my mind that perhaps what she really feared was that *he* might come to harm, for I could not doubt that she knew who this man was and what he meant by these strange signals. But there is a tone in my wife's voice, Mr. Holmes, and a look in her eyes which forbid doubt, and I am sure that it was indeed my own safety that was in her mind. There's the whole case, and now I want your advice as to what I ought to do. My own inclination is to put half a dozen of my farm lads in the shrubbery, and when this fellow comes again to give him such a hiding that he will leave us in peace for the future."

"I fear it is too deep a case for such simple remedies," said Holmes. "How long can you stop in London?"

"I must go back to-day. I would not leave my wife alone at night for anything. She is very nervous and begged me to come back."

"I daresay you are right. But if you could have stopped I might possibly have been able to return with you in a day or two. Meanwhile, you will leave me these papers, and I think that it is very likely that I shall be able to pay you a visit shortly and to throw some light upon your case."

Sherlock Holmes preserved his calm professional manner until our visitor had left us, although it was easy for me, who knew him so well, to see that he was profoundly excited. The moment that Hilton Cubitt's broad back had disappeared through the door my comrade rushed to the table, laid out all the slips of paper containing dancing men in front of him, and threw himself into an intricate and elaborate calculation. For two hours I watched him as he covered sheet after sheet of paper with figures and letters, so completely absorbed in his task that he had evidently forgotten my presence. Sometimes he was making progress, and whistled and sang at his work; sometimes he was puzzled, and would sit for long spells with a furrowed brow and a vacant eye. Finally he sprang from his chair with a cry of satisfaction, and walked up and down the room rubbing his hands together. Then he wrote a long telegram upon a cable form. "If my answer to this is as I hope, you will have a very pretty case to add to your collection, Watson," said he. "I expect that we shall be able to go down to Norfolk to-morrow, and to take our friend some very definite news as to the secret of his annoyance."

I confess that I was filled with curiosity, but I was aware that Holmes liked to make his disclosures at his own time and in his own way; so I waited until it should suit him to take me into his confidence. But there was a delay in that answering telegram, and two days of impatience followed, during which

11 "Holmes and Watson do not seem to have appreciated the urgency involved," chides Philip Weller in *The Company Canon: The Adventure of the Dancing Men*. Weller suggests that a mail train could have taken them to Norwich, depositing them there at 2:00 in the morning, after which they might have ridden a carriage to the manor.

Holmes pricked up his ears at every ring of the bell. On the evening of the second there came a letter from Hilton Cubitt. All was quiet with him, save that a long inscription had appeared that morning upon the pedestal of the sundial. He inclosed a copy of it, which is here reproduced:

𐊣𐊡𐊢𐊤𐊣𐊢𐊤𐊡𐊣𐊣𐊢𐊤 𐊣𐊢𐊣𐊣𐊣𐊡 𐊣𐊢𐊣𐊡 𐊣𐊢𐊣

Holmes bent over this grotesque frieze for some minutes, and then suddenly sprang to his feet with an exclamation of surprise and dismay. His face was haggard with anxiety.

"We have let this affair go far enough," said he. "Is there a train to North Walsham to-night?"

I turned up the time-table. The last had just gone.

"Then we shall breakfast early and take the very first in the morning," said Holmes.[11] "Our presence is most urgently needed. Ah! here is our expected cablegram. One moment, Mrs. Hudson, there may be an answer. No, that is quite as I expected. This message makes it even more essential that we should not lose an hour in letting Hilton Cubitt know how matters stand, for it is a singular and a dangerous web in which our simple Norfolk squire is entangled."

So, indeed, it proved, and as I come to the dark conclusion of a story which had seemed to me to be only childish and bizarre, I experience once again the dismay and horror with which I was filled. Would that I had some brighter ending to communicate to my readers; but these are the chronicles of fact, and I must follow to their dark crisis the strange chain of events which for some days made Ridling Thorpe Manor a household word through the length and breadth of England.

We had hardly alighted at North Walsham, and mentioned the name of our destination, when the station-master hurried towards us. "I suppose that you are the detectives from London?" said he.

A look of annoyance passed over Holmes's face.

"What makes you think such a thing?"

"Because Inspector Martin from Norwich has just passed through. But maybe you are the surgeons. She's not dead—or wasn't by last accounts. You may be in time to save her yet—though it be for the gallows."

"'I suppose that you are the detectives
from London?' said he."
Sidney Paget, *Strand Magazine*, 1903

12 Despite Holmes's evident dismay at having been too late to save his client, scholars such as Ian McQueen say that Holmes has no one but himself to blame. McQueen calls Holmes's demeanour the previous evening "lackadaisacal," especially considering that the detective claimed to have "expected" the alarming contents of Cubitt's message (and later, upon arrival at the manor, admits to having "anticipated" the unfortunate turn of events). "If Holmes had been honest with himself . . . ," McQueen sternly declares, "he might have confessed with some justification that he had suffered the greatest blow to have befallen him in his career. It was unquestionably a blow for which, owing to his gross negligence, he was personally responsible." "The Five Orange Pips" is a similar case in which Holmes failed to warn his client adequately, to the client's fatal detriment.

13 Although the word is "blank" in all other published texts, the word "black" seems more likely to be correct.

Holmes's brow was dark with anxiety.

"We are going to Ridling Thorpe Manor," said he, "but we have heard nothing of what has passed there."

"It's a terrible business," said the station-master. "They are shot, both Mr. Hilton Cubitt and his wife. She shot him and then herself—so the servants say. He's dead, and her life is despaired of. Dear, dear, one of the oldest families in the county of Norfolk, and one of the most honoured."

Without a word Holmes hurried to a carriage, and during the long seven-miles drive he never opened his mouth.[12] Seldom have I seen him so utterly despondent. He had been uneasy during all our journey from town, and I had observed that he had turned over the morning papers with anxious attention; but now this sudden realization of his worst fears left him in a blank[13] melancholy. He leaned back in his seat, lost in gloomy speculation. Yet there was much around to interest us, for we

14 This historical region, encompassing the counties of Norfolk, Suffolk, and parts of Essex, has deep Anglo-Saxon roots; it was settled in the late fifth century by immigrants from northern Germany and Scandinavia. The wealth and power of the East Anglian kings was demonstrated with the 1939 discovery at Sutton Hoo (in Suffolk) of a seventh-century burial ship, intended to carry its "owner" to the afterlife. Laden with treasures including forty-one pieces of solid gold, the ship is thought to have been meant for the East Anglian king Raedwald, who died in 624.

15 The German Ocean, before the First World War, was an alternative name for the North Sea, and on maps of this period "The North Sea or German Ocean" was generally given.

16 A portico is an archway supported by columns.

17 That is, a lawn devoted to the play of lawn tennis, so-called to distinguish it from "real tennis," a twelfth-century, racquetball-type game of French origin that was played indoors. Lawn tennis, a product of the Victorian age, gained rapidly in popularity among the fashionable set after Major Walter Winfield created an outdoor version of real tennis in 1874, utilising a new rubber ball that could bounce on grass. He introduced his new game at a lawn party in Wales and dubbed it "sphairistike" (from spaira, the Greek word for ball), but, as no one could remember—let alone pronounce!—such a name, the alternative of "lawn tennis" was suggested, and it stuck. The All England Croquet Club at Wimbledon held its first lawn tennis championship, restricted to men only, in 1877. (Women got their first Wimbledon tournament in 1884). Its inaugural champion was Spencer Gore, a surveyor, cricket aficionado, and skilled athlete, who, despite his newly

were passing through as singular a countryside as any in England, where a few scattered cottages represented the population of to-day, while on every hand enormous square-towered churches bristled up from the flat, green landscape and told of the glory and prosperity of old East Anglia.[14] At last the violet rim of the German Ocean appeared over the green edge of the Norfolk coast,[15] and the driver pointed with his whip to two old brick-and-timber gables which projected from a grove of trees. "That's Ridling Thorpe Manor," said he.

As we drove up to the porticoed[16] front door, I observed in front of it, beside the tennis lawn,[17] the black tool-house and the pedestalled sundial with which we had such strange associations. A dapper little man, with a quick, alert manner and a waxed moustache, had just descended from a high dog-cart. He introduced himself as Inspector Martin, of the Norfolk Constabulary, and he was considerably astonished when he heard the name of my companion.

"Why, Mr. Holmes, the crime was only committed at three this morning! How could you hear of it in London and get to the spot as soon as I?"

"I anticipated it. I came in the hope of preventing it."

"Then you must have important evidence of which we are ignorant, for they were said to be a most united couple."

"I have only the evidence of the dancing men," said Holmes. "I will explain the matter to you later. Meanwhile, since it is too late to prevent this tragedy, I am very anxious that I should use the knowledge which I possess in order to insure that justice be done. Will you associate me in your investigation, or will you prefer that I should act independently?"

"I should be proud to feel that we were acting together, Mr. Holmes," said the Inspector, earnestly.

"In that case I should be glad to hear the evidence and to examine the premises without an instant of unnecessary delay."

Inspector Martin had the good sense to allow my friend to do things in his own fashion, and contented himself with carefully noting the results. The local surgeon, an old, white-haired man, had just come down from Mrs. Hilton Cubitt's room, and he reported that her injuries were serious, but not necessarily fatal. The bullet had passed through the front of her brain, and it would probably be some time before she could regain consciousness. On the question of whether she had been shot or had shot herself he would not venture to express any decided opinion. Certainly the bullet had been discharged at very close quarters. There was only the one pistol found in the room, two barrels of which had been emptied. Mr. Hilton Cubitt had been shot through the heart. It was equally conceivable that he had shot her and then himself, or that she had been the criminal, for the revolver lay upon the floor midway between them.

"Has he been moved?" asked Holmes.

"We have moved nothing except the lady. We could not leave her lying wounded upon the floor."

"How long have you been here, Doctor?"

"Since four o'clock."

"Anyone else?"

"Yes, the constable here."

"And you have touched nothing?"

"Nothing."

"You have acted with great discretion. Who sent for you?"

"The housemaid, Saunders."

"Was it she who gave the alarm?"

"She and Mrs. King, the cook."

"Where are they now?"

"In the kitchen, I believe."

"Then I think we had better hear their story at once."

The old hall, oak-panelled and high-windowed, had been turned into a court of investigation. Holmes sat in a great, old-fashioned chair, his inexorable eyes gleaming out of his haggard face. I could read in them a set purpose to devote his life to this quest until the client whom he had failed to save should at last be avenged. The trim inspector Martin, the old, grey-headed country doctor, myself, and a stolid village policeman made up the rest of that strange company.

The two women told their story clearly enough. They had been aroused from their sleep by the sound of an explosion, which had been followed a minute later by a second one. They slept in adjoining rooms, and Mrs. King had rushed in to Saunders. Together they had descended the stairs. The door of the study was open and a candle was burning upon the table. Their master lay upon his face in the centre of the room. He was quite dead. Near the window his wife was crouching, her head

won laurels, described tennis as "a monotonous game compared with others." The Lawn Tennis Association was founded in 1888.

leaning against the wall. She was horribly wounded, and the side of the face was red with blood. She breathed heavily, but was incapable of saying anything. The passage, as well as the room, was full of smoke and the smell of powder. The window was certainly shut and fastened upon the inside. Both women were positive upon the point. They had at once sent for the doctor and for the constable. Then, with the aid of the groom and the stable-boy, they had conveyed their injured mistress to her room. Both she and her husband had occupied the bed. She was clad in her dress—he in his dressing-gown, over his night-clothes. Nothing had been moved in the study. So far as they knew, there had never been any quarrel between husband and wife. They had always looked upon them as a very united couple.

These were the main points of the servants' evidence. In answer to Inspector Martin they were clear that every door was fastened upon the inside and that no one could have escaped from the house. In answer to Holmes, they both remembered

"They both remembered that they were conscious of the smell of powder."
Sidney Paget, *Strand Magazine*, 1903

Our first attention was given to the body
of the unfortunate squire.
Frederick Dorr Steele, *Collier's*, 1903

that they were conscious of the smell of powder from the moment that they ran out of their rooms upon the top floor. "I commend that fact very carefully to your attention," said Holmes to his professional colleague. "And now I think that we are in a position to undertake a thorough examination of the room."

The study proved to be a small chamber, lined on three sides with books, and with a writing-table facing an ordinary window, which looked out upon the garden. Our first attention was given to the body of the unfortunate squire, whose huge frame lay stretched across the room. His disordered dress showed that he had been hastily aroused from sleep. The bullet had been fired at him from the front, and had remained in his body after penetrating the heart. His death had certainly been instantaneous and painless. There was no powder-marking either upon his dressing-gown or on his hands. According to the country surgeon, the lady had stains upon her face, but none upon her hand.

"The absence of the latter means nothing, though its presence may mean everything," said Holmes. "Unless the powder from a badly fitting cartridge happens to spurt backwards, one may fire many shots without leaving a sign. I would suggest that Mr. Cubitt's body may now be removed. I suppose, Doctor, you have not recovered the bullet which wounded the lady?"

"A serious operation will be necessary before that can be done. But there are still four cartridges in the revolver. Two have been fired and two wounds inflicted, so that each bullet can be accounted for."

"So it would seem," said Holmes. "Perhaps you can account also for the bullet which has so obviously struck the edge of the window?"

He had turned suddenly, and his long, thin finger was pointing to a hole which had been drilled right through the lower window-sash about an inch above the bottom.

"By George!" cried the Inspector.

"How ever did you see that?"

"Because I looked for it."

"Wonderful!" said the country doctor. "You are certainly right, sir. Then a third shot has been fired, and therefore a third person must have been present. But who could that have been, and how could he have got away?"

"That is the problem which we are now about to solve," said Sherlock Holmes. "You remember, Inspector Martin, when the servants said that on leaving their room they were at once conscious of a smell of powder, I remarked that the point was an extremely important one?"

"Yes, sir; but I confess I did not quite follow you."

"It suggested that at the time of the firing the window as well as the door of the room had been open. Otherwise the fumes of powder could not have been blown so rapidly through the house. A draught in the room was necessary for that. Both door and window were only open for a very short time, however."

"How do you prove that?"

"Because the candle has not guttered."

"Capital!" cried the Inspector. "Capital!"

"Feeling sure that the window had been open at the time of the tragedy, I conceived that there might have been a third person in the affair, who stood outside this opening and fired through it. Any shot directed at this person might hit the sash. I looked, and there, sure enough, was the bullet mark!"

"But how came the window to be shut and fastened?"

"The woman's first instinct would be to shut and fasten the window. But, halloa! what is this?"

It was a lady's hand-bag which stood upon the study table—a trim little hand-bag of crocodile-skin and silver. Holmes opened it and turned the contents out. There were twenty fifty-pound notes of the Bank of England, held together by an india-rubber band—nothing else.

"This must be preserved, for it will figure in the trial," said Holmes, as he handed the bag with its contents to the Inspector. "It is now necessary that we should try to throw some light upon this third bullet, which has clearly, from the splintering of the wood, been fired from inside the room. I should like to see Mrs. King, the cook, again. . . . You said, Mrs. King, that you were awakened by a *loud* explosion. When you said that, did you mean that it seemed to you to be louder than the second one?"

"Well, sir, it wakened me from my sleep, and so it is hard to judge. But it did seem very loud."

"You don't think that it might have been two shots fired almost at the same instant?"

"I am sure I couldn't say, sir."

"I believe that it was undoubtedly so. I rather think, Inspector Martin, that we have now exhausted all that this room can teach us. If you will kindly step round with me we shall see what fresh evidence the garden has to offer."

A flower-bed extended up to the study window, and we all broke into an exclamation as we approached it. The flowers were trampled down, and the soft soil was imprinted all over with footmarks. Large, masculine feet they were, with peculiarly long, sharp toes. Holmes hunted about among the grass and leaves like a retriever after a wounded bird. Then, with a cry of satisfaction, he bent forward and picked up a little brazen cylinder.

"I thought so," said he; "the revolver had an ejector, and here is the third cartridge. I really think, Inspector Martin, that our case is almost complete."

The country inspector's face had shown his intense amazement at the rapid and masterful progress of Holmes's investi-

"He bent forward and picked up a little brazen cylinder."
Sidney Paget, *Strand Magazine*, 1903

gations. At first he had shown some disposition to assert his own position, but now he was overcome with admiration, and ready to follow without question wherever Holmes led.

"Whom do you suspect?" he asked.

"I'll go into that later. There are several points in this problem which I have not been able to explain to you yet. Now that I have got so far I had best proceed on my own lines, and then clear the whole matter up once and for all."

"Just as you wish, Mr. Holmes, so long as we get our man."

"I have no desire to make mysteries, but it is impossible at the moment of action to enter into long and complex explanations. I have the threads of this affair all in my hand. Even if this lady should never recover consciousness we can still reconstruct the events of last night and insure that justice be done. First of all, I wish to know whether there is any inn in this neighbourhood known as 'Elrige's'?"

The servants were cross-questioned, but none of them had heard of such a place. The stable-boy threw a light upon the matter by remembering that a farmer of that name lived some miles off, in the direction of East Ruston.

"Is it a lonely farm?"

"Very lonely, sir."

"Perhaps they have not heard yet of all that happened here during the night?"

"Maybe not, sir."

Holmes thought for a little, and then a curious smile played over his face.

"Saddle a horse, my lad," said he. "I shall wish you to take a note to Elrige's Farm."

He took from his pocket the various slips of the dancing men. With these in front of him he worked for some time at the study table. Finally he handed a note to the boy, with directions to put it into the hands of the person to whom it was addressed, and especially to answer no questions of any sort which might be put to him. I saw the outside of the note, addressed in straggling, irregular characters, very unlike Holmes's usual precise hand. It was consigned to Mr. Abe Slaney, Elrige's Farm, East Ruston, Norfolk.

"I think, Inspector," Holmes remarked, "that you would do well to telegraph for an escort, as, if my calculations prove to be correct, you may have a particularly dangerous prisoner to convey to the county gaol. The boy who takes this note could no doubt forward your telegram. If there is an afternoon train to town, Watson, I think we should do well to take it, as I have a chemical analysis of some interest to finish, and this investigation draws rapidly to a close."

When the youth had been despatched with the note, Sherlock Holmes gave his instructions to the servants. If any visitor were to call asking for Mrs. Hilton Cubitt no information should be given as to her condition, but he was to be shown at once into the drawing-room. He impressed these points upon them with the utmost earnestness. Finally he led the way into the drawing-room, with the remark that the business was now out of our hands, and that we must while away the time as best we might until we could see what was in store for us. The doctor had departed to his patients, and only the Inspector and myself remained.

"I think that I can help you to pass an hour in an interesting and profitable manner," said Holmes, drawing his chair up to the table and spreading out in front of him the various papers upon which were recorded the antics of the dancing men. "As to you, friend Watson, I owe you every atonement for having allowed your natural curiosity to remain so long unsatisfied. To you, Inspector, the whole incident may appeal as a remarkable professional study. I must tell you first of all the interesting circumstances connected with the previous consultations which Mr. Hilton Cubitt has had with me in Baker Street." He then shortly recapitulated the facts which have already been recorded.

"I have here in front of me these singular productions, at which one might smile, had they not proved themselves to be the forerunners of so terrible a tragedy. I am fairly familiar with all forms of secret writings, and am myself the author of a trifling monograph upon the subject, in which I analyze one hundred and sixty separate ciphers; but I confess that this is entirely new to me. The object of those who invented the system has apparently been to conceal that these characters convey a message, and to give the idea that they are the mere random sketches of children.

"Having once recognised, however, that the symbols stood for letters, and having applied the rules which guide us in all forms of secret writings, the solution was easy enough. The first message submitted to me was so short that it was impossible for me to do more than to say with some confidence that the symbol 𝓍 stood for E. As you are aware, E is the most common letter in the English alphabet and it predominates to so marked an extent that even in a short sentence one would expect to find it most often. Out of fifteen symbols in the first message four were the same, so it was reasonable to set this down as E. It is true that in some cases the figure was bearing a flag, and in some cases not, but it was probable from the way in which the flags were distributed that they were used to break the sentence up into words. I accepted this as a hypothesis, and noted that E was represented by 𝓍

"But now came the real difficulty of the inquiry. The order of the English letters after E is by no means well-marked, and any preponderance which may be shown in an average of a printed sheet may be reversed in a single short sentence. Speaking roughly, T, A, O, I, N, S, H, R, D, and L are the numerical order in which letters occur; but T, A, O, and I are very nearly abreast of each other, and it would be an endless task to try each combination until a meaning was arrived at.[18] I, therefore, waited for fresh material. In my second interview with Mr. Hilton Cubitt he was able to give me two other short sentences and one message, which appeared—since there was no flag—to be a single word. Here are the symbols. Now, in the single word I have already got the two E's coming second and fourth in a word of five letters. It might be 'sever,' or 'lever,' or 'never.'[19] There can be no question that the latter as a reply to an appeal is far the most probable, and the circumstances pointed to its being a reply written by the lady. Accepting it as correct, we are now able to say that the symbols 夫ㄔ人 stand respectively for N, V, and R.

"Even now I was in considerable difficulty, but a happy thought put me in possession of several other letters. It occurred to me that if these appeals came, as I expected, from someone who had been intimate with the lady in her early life, a combination which contained two E's with three letters between might very well stand for the name 'ELSIE.' On examination I found that such a combination formed the termination of the message which was three times repeated. It was certainly some appeal to 'Elsie.' In this way I had got my L, S, and I. But what appeal could it be? There were only four letters in the word which preceded 'Elsie,' and it ended in E. Surely the word must be 'COME.' I tried all other four letters ending in E, but could find none to fit the case. So now I was in possession of C, O, and M, and I was in a position to attack the first message once more, dividing it into words and putting dots for each symbol which was still unknown. So treated it worked out in this fashion:

.M .ERE . .E SL.NE.

"Now, the first letter can only be A, which is a most useful discovery, since it occurs no fewer than three times in this short sentence, and the H is also apparent in the second word. Now it becomes:

AM HERE A.E SLANE.

Or, filling in the obvious vacancies in the name:

18 *Encyclopædia Britannica* (9th Ed.) provides additional assistance to budding cryptographers: "All the single letters must be *a, I,* or *O.* Letters occurring together are *ee, oo, ff, ll, ss,* &c [which stands for "etc."]. The commonest words of two letters are (roughly arranged in the order of their frequency) *of, to, in, it, is, be, he, by, or, as, at, an, so,* &c. The commonest words of three letters are *the* and *and* (in great excess), *for, are, but, all, not,* &c." For a further tutorial, *Britannica* points readers to Edgar Allan Poe's 1843 story "The Gold-Bug," in which William Legrand, after deconstructing a complicated cipher, is able to unearth a fortune in buried treasure.

19 "This dictum implies that the five-letter word must be one of these alternatives," Colin Prestige writes in "Agents of Evil." "Never! A simple mental exercise reveals more than 30 alternatives, some possible and some improbable." For example, such disparate words as "seven," "repel," "renew," "jewel," "sewer," and "deter" all fit the requirements.

20 Richard Warshauer identifies "Hargreave" as Thomas Byrnes, superintendent of the New York Police Department in 1892, who, from 1882 to 1892, was the renowned (and first) chief of the brand-new Detective Bureau of the NYPD. In 1898, Byrnes retired from the police department amidst charges of corruption (though none against Byrnes himself) and went to work for an insurance company. "There can be little doubt that in 1898 he was still as knowledgeable about the world of crime as he was in 1886 when he wrote [the classic *Professional Criminals of America*]. What could be more natural than for Holmes to have consulted a man so well acquainted with 'the annals of crime'?" During the height of the Whitechapel murders that terrorized London in 1888, Byrnes was quoted in the British paper, *The Star*, on the "commonsense way" in which he would pursue Jack the Ripper, criticising the work of Scotland Yard. He concluded with the brag that if he had conducted the investigation, "[t]he murderer would have been caught long ago."

21 Correctly, the New York Police *Department* or the New York Police Detective Bureau.

AM HERE ABE SLANEY.

I had so many letters now that I could proceed with considerable confidence to the second message, which worked out in this fashion:

A. ELRI.ES.

Here I could only make sense by putting T and G for the missing letters, and supposing that the name was that of some house or inn at which the writer was staying."

Inspector Martin and I had listened with the utmost interest to the full and clear account of how my friend had produced results which had led to so complete a command over our difficulties.

"What did you do then, sir?" asked the Inspector.

"I had every reason to suppose that this Abe Slaney was an American, since Abe is an American contraction, and since a letter from America had been the starting-point of all the trouble. I had also every cause to think that there was some criminal secret in the matter. The lady's allusions to her past and her refusal to take her husband into her confidence, both pointed in that direction. I therefore cabled to my friend, Wilson Hargreave,[20] of the New York Police Bureau,[21] who has more than once made use of my knowledge of London crime. I asked him whether the name of Abe Slaney was known to him. Here is his reply: 'The most dangerous crook in Chicago.' On the very evening upon which I had his answer Hilton Cubitt sent me the last message from Slaney. Working with known letters, it took this form:

ELSIE .RE.ARE TO MEET THY GO.

"The addition of a P and a D completed a message which showed me that the rascal was proceeding from persuasion to threats, and my knowledge of the crooks of Chicago prepared me to find that he might very rapidly put his words into action. I at once came to Norfolk with my friend and colleague, Dr. Watson, but, unhappily, only in time to find that the worst had already occurred."

"It is a privilege to be associated with you in the handling of a case," said the Inspector, warmly. "You will excuse me, however, if I speak frankly to you. You are only answerable to yourself, but I have to answer to my superiors. If this Abe Slaney, living at Elrige's, is indeed the murderer, and if he has made his escape while I am seated here, I should certainly get into serious trouble."

"You need not be uneasy. He will not try to escape."

"How do you know?"

"To fly would be a confession of guilt."

"Then let us go to arrest him."

"I expect him here every instant."

"But why should he come?"

"Because I have written and asked him."

"But this is incredible, Mr. Holmes! Why should he come because you have asked him? Would not such a request rather rouse his suspicions and cause him to fly?"

"I think I have known how to frame the letter," said Sherlock Holmes. "In fact, if I am not very much mistaken, here is the gentleman himself coming up the drive."

A man was striding up the path which led to the door. He was a tall, handsome, swarthy fellow, clad in a suit of gray flannel, with a Panama hat, a bristling black beard, and a great, aggressive hooked nose, and flourishing a cane as he walked. He swaggered up the path as if the place belonged to him, and we heard his loud, confident peal at the bell.

"I think, gentlemen," said Holmes, quietly, "that we had best take up our position behind the door. Every precaution is necessary when dealing with such a fellow. You will need your handcuffs, Inspector. You can leave the talking to me."

We waited in silence for a minute—one of those minutes which one can never forget. Then the door opened, and the man stepped in. In an instant Holmes clapped a pistol to his head, and Martin slipped the handcuffs over his wrists. It was all done so swiftly and deftly that the fellow was helpless before he knew that he was attacked. He glared from one to the other of us with a pair of blazing black eyes. Then he burst into a bitter laugh.

"Well, gentlemen, you have the drop on me this time. I seem to have knocked up against something hard. But I came here in answer to a letter from Mrs. Hilton Cubitt. Don't tell me that she is in this? Don't tell me that she helped to set a trap for me?"

"Mrs. Hilton Cubitt was seriously injured, and is at death's door."

"Holmes clapped a pistol to his head and Martin
slipped the handcuffs over his wrists."
Sidney Paget, *Strand Magazine*, 1903

The man gave a hoarse cry of grief which rang through the
house.

"You're crazy!" he cried, fiercely. "It was he that was hurt,
not she. Who would have hurt little Elsie? I may have threatened her, God forgive me, but I would not have touched a hair
of her pretty head. Take it back—you! Say that she is not hurt!"

"She was found badly wounded by the side of her dead husband."

He sank with a deep groan on to the settee, and buried his
face in his manacled hands. For five minutes he was silent.
Then he raised his face once more, and spoke with the cold
composure of despair.

"I have nothing to hide from you, gentlemen," said he. "If I shot the man he had his shot at me, and there's no murder in that. But if you think I could have hurt that woman, then you don't know either me or her. I tell you there was never a man in this world loved a woman more than I loved her. I had a right to her. She was pledged to me years ago. Who was this Englishman that he should come between us? I tell you that I had the first right to her, and that I was only claiming my own."

"She broke away from your influence when she found the man that you are," said Holmes, sternly. "She fled from America to avoid you, and she married an honourable gentleman in England. You dogged her and followed her, and made her life a misery to her, in order to induce her to abandon the husband whom she loved and respected in order to fly with you, whom

"Well, gentlemen, you have the drop on me this time."
Frederick Dorr Steele, *Collier's*, 1903

"He buried his face in his manacled hands."
Sidney Paget, *Strand Magazine*, 1903

she feared and hated. You have ended by bringing about the death of a noble man and driving his wife to suicide. That is your record in this business, Mr. Abe Slaney, and you will answer for it to the law."

"If Elsie dies I care nothing what becomes of me," said the American. He opened one of his hands and looked at a note crumpled up in his palm. "See here, mister," he cried, with a gleam of suspicion in his eyes, "you're not trying to scare me over this, are you? If the lady is hurt as bad as you say, who was it that wrote this note?" He tossed it forward on to the table.

"I wrote it to bring you here."

"You wrote it? There was no one on earth outside the Joint who knew the secret of the dancing men. How came you to write it?"

"What one man can invent another can discover," said Holmes. "There is a cab coming to convey you to Norwich, Mr. Slaney. But, meanwhile, you have time to make some small reparation for the injury you have wrought. Are you aware that Mrs. Hilton Cubitt has herself lain under grave suspicion of the murder of her husband, and that it was only my presence here and the knowledge which I happened to possess, which has saved her from the accusation? The least that you owe her is to make it clear to the whole world that she was in no way directly or indirectly responsible for his tragic end."

"I ask nothing better," said the American. "I guess the very best case I can make for myself is the absolute naked truth."

"It is my duty to warn you that it will be used against you," cried the Inspector, with the magnificent fair-play of the British criminal law.[22]

Slaney shrugged his shoulders.

22 The *Police Code* (12th Ed., 1904) makes it clear that the arresting officer must not induce a confession: "A confession must be entirely voluntary. This will not be the case if it appears to the Judge to have been caused by any inducement, threat, or promise, proceeding from a person in authority . . ."

The composure of despair.
Sidney Paget, *Strand Magazine*, 1903

THE RETURN OF SHERLOCK HOLMES

23 Two decades before Al Capone arrived in Chicago and became king of the city's organised crime scene, Chicago was already a rough, industrial town overcrowded with newly arrived working-class European immigrants and their children. In many ways proud of its reputation for rowdiness and even corruption, Chicago was ripe for the kind of gang warfare that employed Abe Slaney and Elsie's father and that paved the way for the rise of Capone. Rudyard Kipling was appalled by the city's grime, writing in his *American Notes* (1891), "Having seen it [Chicago], I urgently desire never to see it again. It is inhabited by savages. . . . I looked down interminable vistas flanked with nine, ten, and fifteen-storied houses, and crowded with men and women, and the show impressed me with a great horror. Except in London—and I have forgotten what London was like—I had never seen so many white people together, and never such a collection of miserables."

24 Several theories exist as to what Elsie's father used as the basis for his unique alphabet (presuming that the system was not entirely his own original creation). William Smith concludes that the cipher was likely derived from one used by the Army Signal Corps, published by Major Albert J. Myer in his *A Manual of Signals* (1864), which involved men using flags. Renowned cryptographer David Shulman puts forward a remarkably similar cipher published in the *United Service Magazine*, a British publication, in 1832, also using flags. Irving Kamil points out the similarities of the cipher to the Easter Island and Indus Valley scripts discussed by Charles Berlitz in his *Mysteries from Forgotten Worlds* (1972). And an article in *The Bookman* by Lyndon Orr (April 1910) suggests that the cipher was based on that detailed in "The Language of the Restless Imps" using stick-figures, which appeared in *St. Nicholas Magazine* in June 1874.

"I'll chance that," said he. "First of all, I want you gentlemen to understand that I have known this lady since she was a child. There were seven of us in a gang in Chicago, and Elsie's father was the boss of the Joint.[23] He was a clever man, was old Patrick. It was he who invented that writing,[24] which would pass as a child's scrawl unless you just happened to have the key to it. Well, Elsie learned some of our ways; but she couldn't stand the business, and she had a bit of honest money of her own, so she gave us all the slip and got away to London. She had been engaged to me, and she would have married me, I believe, if I had taken over another profession; but she would have nothing to do with anything on the cross. It was only after her marriage to this Englishman that I was able to find out where she was. I wrote to her, but got no answer. After that I came over, and, as letters were no use, I put my messages where she could read them.

"Well, I have been here a month now. I lived in that farm, where I had a room down below, and could get in and out every night, and no one the wiser. I tried all I could to coax Elsie away. I knew that she read the messages, for once she wrote an answer under one of them. Then my temper got the better of me, and I began to threaten her. She sent me a letter then, imploring me to go away, and saying that it would break her heart if any scandal should come upon her husband. She said that she would come down when her husband was asleep at three in the morning, and speak with me through the end window, if I would go away afterwards and leave her in peace. She came down and brought money with her, trying to bribe me to go.[25] This made me mad, and I caught her arm and tried to pull her through the window. At that moment in rushed the husband with his revolver in his hand. Elsie had sunk down upon the floor, and we were face to face. I was heeled[26] also, and I held up my gun to scare him off and let me get away. He fired and missed me. I pulled off almost at the same instant, and down he dropped. I made away across the garden, and as I went I heard the window shut behind me.[27] That's God's truth, gentlemen, every word of it, and I heard no more about it until that lad came riding up with a note which made me walk in here, like a jay,[28] and give myself into your hands."

A cab had driven up whilst the American had been talking.

25 Recall that in Elsie's purse were found "twenty fifty-pound notes of the Bank of England, held together by an india-rubber band." Where did Elsie get this enormous sum of money? Was it part of the "bit of honest money" with which, Slaney tells us, she left Chicago? Or savings from household expenses? Or did she steal it from her husband? John B. Koelle finds the entire notion improbable, surmising instead that Elsie and Slaney together killed Cubitt, stole his money, and then quarrelled over a division of the spoils. Alternatively, Slaney may have been blackmailing the Cubitts, and they brought the money to a meeting with him, where they intended to kill him.

John Hall, in *Sidelights on Holmes*, also finds Slaney's account dubious. Surely Slaney would have realised that his efforts to woo Elsie were doomed, in light of the strength of character she had already shown in refusing to marry a criminal. "[T]hen why should he imagine for one moment," marvels Hall, "that, having settled down to a happy enough life in the English countryside, she would agree to commit adultery? It makes no sense at all." Naturally, Slaney must have been half-mad with jealousy and rejection, which leads to the inevitable conclusion that he came to Ridling Thorpe Manor with revenge, not reconciliation, on his mind. "The only explanation that does make any sort of sense," continues Hall, "is surely that Slaney had intended all along to kill Mr. Cubitt, and very probably Elsie as well, as revenge for what he saw as her desertion of him."

26 Armed. The term is also used in *The Valley of Fear*.

27 That Elsie would take the time to close the window before shooting herself seems like an unnecessary bit of business. Clifton R. Andrew suggests that Elsie, still in love with Abe Slaney, closed the window in order to protect him, so that a third party's involvement in the shooting would not be discovered.

28 According to E. Cobham Brewer's *Dictionary of Phrase and Fable*, "A plunger; one who spends his money recklessly; a simpleton. This is simply the letter J, the initial letter of Juggins, who, in 1887, made a fool of himself by losses on the turf."

29 The six messages (in translation) are:

1 AM HERE ABE SLANEY
2 AT ELRIGES
3 COME ELSIE
4 NEVER
5 ELSIE PREPARE TO MEET THY GOD
6 COME HERE AT ONCE

William S. Baring-Gould notes that the symbol used for "V" in message #4 is the same as that used for "P" in message #5 in virtually every published text. In addition, in some texts, the symbol used for "C" in message #6 is the same as that used for "M" throughout, and different from that used for "C" in message #3. Whether these mistakes resulted from Watson's careless copying or the printer's errors cannot be determined at this time.

30 The nature of those "mitigating circumstances" that led to the commutation of Slaney's sentence is unclear. Harry Ober argues righteously that "Threatening a woman with death, coming to her house armed, probably flourishing a gun, and mortally wounding her husband who was defending his wife properly, all constitute to me a chain of criminal acts, which add up to murder in the first degree." However, a British court may have concluded that there was little evidence that Slaney intended to kill anyone (only the ambiguous advice "PREPARE TO MEET THY GOD") and that he was merely acting in self-defence when he fired the shot that killed Cubitt.

Two uniformed policemen sat inside. Inspector Martin rose and touched his prisoner on the shoulder.

"It is time for us to go."

"Can I see her first?"

"No, she is not conscious. Mr. Sherlock Holmes, I only hope that if ever again I have an important case I shall have the good fortune to have you by my side."

We stood at the window and watched the cab drive away. As I turned back my eye caught the pellet of paper which the prisoner had tossed upon the table. It was the note with which Holmes had decoyed him. "See if you can read it, Watson," said he, with a smile.

It contained no word, but this little line of dancing men:

"If you use the code which I have explained," said Holmes, "you will find that it simply means 'Come here at once.'[29] I was convinced that it was an invitation which he would not refuse, since he could never imagine that it could come from anyone but the lady. And so, my dear Watson, we have ended by turning the dancing men to good when they have so often been the agents of evil, and I think that I have fulfilled my promise of giving you something unusual for your notebook. Three-forty is our train, and I fancy we should be back in Baker Street for dinner."

Only one word of epilogue. The American, Abe Slaney, was condemned to death at the winter assizes at Norwich; but his penalty was changed to penal servitude in consideration of mitigating circumstances,[30] and the certainty that Hilton Cubitt had fired the first shot. Of Mrs. Hilton Cubitt I only know that I have heard she recovered entirely, and that she still remains a widow, devoting her whole life to the care of the poor and to the administration of her husband's estate. ∎

THE DANCING MEN ALPHABET

"THE FACT that a code of such transparent simplicity baffled the Master for such a time has long been a matter of wonder," Ed. S. Woodhead notes in "In Defense of Dr. Watson." Woodhead's explanation? That the "dancing men" cipher was in fact far more complex than the one presented by Watson, and that Watson, in writing up the story, vastly simplified the code, substituting it with one that was just difficult enough to stump the reader but not too difficult to explain.

Fletcher Pratt agrees with this view, calling the dancing men cipher "far too simple for practical use, with its single unvarying character for each letter, [and] it is also far too complex for a simple substitution cipher." In fact, in the figures of the dancing men themselves—and the ways in which they might be positioned—he sees myriad cryptic opportunities that are never utilised or discussed. Looking more closely at the code shown in Slaney's various messages, Pratt considers the "various leg possibilities" and the "various arm possibilities" and comes up with 784 versions of dancing men that might have been used as components of the cipher. In addition, he observes, "D, G and T show the little figures standing on their heads, and T is simply an E in reverse. Obviously the meaning of any one of the 784 characters can be changed by turning it upside down, which doubles the total, giving 1,568 characters."

By stunning coincidence, writes Pratt, the seventeenth-century cryptographers Antoine and Bonaventure Rossignol created for Louis XIV a "Great Cipher" which, after the Rossignols' deaths, remained unsolved until Étienne Bazeries cracked it in the 1890s. (Pratt suggests that Holmes may have given Bazeries assistance on one of his trips to France.) The "Great Cipher," was a "homophonic substitution cipher," in which substitutions of strings of numbers were made for *syllables*, not letters. When all the permutations of the Great Cipher's characters were added up, according to Pratt, the total was precisely 1,568.

Certainly the two codes must have been related in some way, if not in every way. "We have good reason to believe," writes Pratt, "that it [the similarity of combinations] was not accidental; that with the connivance of Holmes, Watson deliberately eliminated from the record the cipher used by Abe Slaney . . . and inserted in its place this other."

The completion of the alphabet of the "dancing men" has been attempted by numerous cryptologists and enthusiasts. The definitive work, however, is likely that of Michael J. Sare, who brilliantly devised a simple method for constructing and memorising a "dancing men" grid to encode and decode messages. Sare argues that if the code was to be used by a rough bunch of criminals, it needed to be easily constructed on principles readily memorised, requiring no codebooks or "cribs." Sare's "grid" follows:

THE ADVENTURE OF THE
SOLITARY CYCLIST[1]

In "The Solitary Cyclist," we glimpse one of the British "frontiers," the mines of South Africa, which are the source of unexpected danger to yet another Violet (there are four damsels in distress with that name in the Canon). Bicycles, the great fad of the late Victorian era, play a central rôle in the case, which is set in 1895. Although Watson records in A Study in Scarlet *that Holmes is an expert boxer, we have only two instances of his pugilistic skills, "The Naval Treaty" and here. While the case has very little mystery about it, scholars raise interesting questions about the marriage laws of England and the irrational behaviour of the villains.*

FROM THE YEARS 1894 to 1901 inclusive, Mr. Sherlock Holmes was a very busy man.[2] It is safe to say that there was no public case of any difficulty in which he was not consulted during those eight years, and there were hundreds of private cases, some of them of the most intricate and extraordinary character, in which he played a prominent part. Many startling successes and a few unavoidable failures were the outcome of this long period of continuous work. As I have preserved very full notes of all these cases, and was myself personally engaged in many of them, it may be imagined that it is no easy task to know which I should select to lay before the public. I shall, however, preserve my former rule, and give the preference to those cases which derive their interest not so much from the brutality of the crime as from the ingenuity and dramatic quality of the solution. For this reason I will now lay before the reader the facts connected with Miss Violet Smith, the solitary cyclist[3] of Charlington, and the curious sequel of our investi-

1 "The Solitary Cyclist" was published in *Collier's Weekly* on December 26, 1903, and in the *Strand Magazine* in January 1904.

2 Contrast this with Holmes's remark in "The Norwood Builder" about how "uninteresting" London has become since the death of Moriarty.

3 That the "solitary cyclist" does not refer to Miss Smith is evident from the manuscript, the greater part of which is owned by Maurice F. Neville of Santa Barbara, California. The manuscript bears the title "The Adventure of the Solitary Man," and the phrase here reads "the facts connected with the solitary man of Charlington Common."

4 "Admit" in the *Strand Magazine* and American editions.

5 Watson kept a series of year-books concerning Holmes's cases ("The Veiled Lodger"), and mentions specifically his records for 1887 ("The Five Orange Pips"), for 1890 ("The Final Problem"), for 1894 ("The Golden Pince-Nez"), and for 1895 ("The Solitary Cyclist").

6 April 23, 1895, was a Tuesday. As may be expected, the chronologists are in some disagreement regarding the correct date of "The Solitary Cyclist." See *Chronological Table*.

Frederick Dorr Steele, *Collier's*, 1903

gation, which culminated in unexpected tragedy. It is true that the circumstance did not permit[4] any striking illustration of those powers for which my friend was famous, but there were some points about the case which made it stand out in those long records of crime from which I gather the material for these little narratives.

On referring to my notebook for the year 1895,[5] I find that it was upon Saturday, April 23,[6] that we first heard of Miss Violet Smith. Her visit was, I remember, extremely unwelcome to Holmes, for he was immersed at the moment in a very abstruse and complicated problem concerning the peculiar persecution to which John Vincent Harden, the well-known tobacco millionaire, had been subjected. My friend, who loved above all things precision and concentration of thought, resented anything which distracted his attention from the matter in hand. And yet without a harshness which was foreign to his nature it was impossible to refuse to listen to the story of the young and beautiful woman, tall, graceful, and queenly, who presented herself at Baker Street late in the evening and implored his assistance and advice. It was vain to urge that his time was already fully occupied, for the young lady had come with the determination to tell her story, and it was evident that nothing short of force could get her out of the room until she had done so. With a resigned air and a somewhat weary smile, Holmes begged the beautiful intruder to take a seat and to inform us what it was that was troubling her.

"At least it cannot be your health," said he, as his keen eyes darted over her; "so ardent a bicyclist must be full of energy."[7]

She glanced down in surprise at her own feet, and I observed

Miss Violet Smith, teacher of music.
Frederick Dorr Steele, *Collier's*, 1903

7 See "Bicycling in the Time of Sherlock Holmes," page 928.

8 The word is "she" in various American editions, but the manuscript version of the story clearly states "he."

the slight roughening of the side of the sole caused by the friction of the edge of the pedal.

"Yes, I bicycle a good deal, Mr. Holmes, and that has something to do with my visit to you to-day."

My friend took the lady's ungloved hand and examined it with as close an attention and as little sentiment as a scientist would show to a specimen.

"You will excuse me, I am sure. It is my business," said he, as he dropped it. "I nearly fell into the error of supposing that you were typewriting. Of course, it is obvious that it is music. You observe the spatulate finger-end, Watson, which is common to both professions? There is a spirituality about the face, however"—he[8] gently turned it towards the light—"which the typewriter does not generate. This lady is a musician."

"Yes, Mr. Holmes, I teach music."

"In the country, I presume, from your complexion."

"Yes, sir; near Farnham, on the borders of Surrey."

"My friend took the lady's ungloved hand and examined it."
Sidney Paget, *Strand Magazine*, 1903

"A beautiful neighbourhood, and full of the most interesting associations. You remember, Watson, that it was near there that we took Archie Stamford, the forger.[9] Now, Miss Violet, what has happened to you near Farnham, on the borders of Surrey?"

The young lady, with great clearness and composure, made the following curious statement:

"My father is dead, Mr. Holmes. He was James Smith, who conducted the orchestra at the old Imperial Theatre.[10] My mother and I were left without a relation in the world except one uncle, Ralph Smith, who went to Africa twenty-five years ago, and we have never had a word from him since. When father died we were left very poor, but one day we were told that there was an advertisement in the *Times* inquiring for our whereabouts. You can imagine how excited we were, for we thought that someone had left us a fortune. We went at once to the lawyer whose name was given in the paper. There we met two gentlemen, Mr. Carruthers and Mr. Woodley, who were home on a visit from South Africa. They said that my uncle was a friend of theirs, that he had died some months before in poverty[11] in Johannesburg,[12] and that he had asked them with his last breath to hunt up his relations and see that they were in no want. It seemed strange to us that Uncle Ralph, who took no notice of us when he was alive, should be so careful to look after us when he was dead; but Mr. Carruthers explained that the reason was that my uncle had just heard of the death of his brother, and so felt responsible for our fate."

"Excuse me," said Holmes; "when was this interview?"

"Last December—four months ago."

"Pray proceed."

"Mr. Woodley seemed to me to be a most odious person. He was for ever making eyes at me—a coarse, puffy-faced, red-moustached young man, with his hair plastered down on each side of his forehead. I thought that he was perfectly hateful—and I was sure that Cyril would not wish me to know such a person."

"Oh! Cyril is his name!" said Holmes, smiling.

The young lady blushed and laughed.

"Yes, Mr. Holmes, Cyril Morton, an electrical engineer, and we hope to be married at the end of the summer. Dear me, how *did* I get talking about him? What I wished to say was that Mr. Woodley was perfectly odious, but that Mr. Carruthers, who

9 In "The Sad Case of Young Stamford," Jerry Neal Williamson speculates that he was the "Archie" of "The Red-Headed League" and also the young Stamford who introduced Holmes to Watson. The manuscript of "The Solitary Cyclist" continues here: "Hughes, the poisoner, also came from there." Apparently Watson was not then ready to reveal the facts of the Hughes case.

10 The Imperial Theatre, part of the Royal Aquarium in Westminster, presented music hall-type entertainment or, as *Baedeker* reported in 1896, "[c]omedies, burlesques, and farces." After it closed in 1899, the Imperial fell under the care of three popular actors: Lillie Langtry ("the Jersey Lily"), who had appeared there in 1882 and who reopened the theatre on April 22, 1901; Ellen Terry, who served as the Imperial's manager in 1903, producing and starring in Ibsen's *The Vikings* under the direction of her son, Edward Gordon Craig; and Lewis Waller, who from 1903 to 1906 presented a series of romantic plays there, one of the most successful of which was *Brigadier Gerard* in 1906, from the pen of Arthur Conan Doyle. The last play performed at the Imperial was Dix and Sutherland's *Boy O'Carrol*, in 1906. The theatre was dismantled the following year; thus, in 1895, the Imperial had not yet closed. Miss Smith must have been thinking of the theatre's incarnation prior to 1901 as the "old" Imperial Theatre, or else perhaps Watson himself made that distinction, inserting the word "old" here to clarify the difference for his readers.

11 It is "great poverty" in the *Strand Magazine* and American editions.

12 Johannesburg was founded in 1886 as the administrative centre for the goldmines that flourished in the Witwatersrand (see "The Adventure of the Dancing Men," note 2). A true boomtown, the city swelled as prospec-

tors arrived from all over the world to seek their fortunes; by the turn of the century, Johannesburg had 100,000 residents, with the mines worked mostly by black Africans under short-term contract. Almost inevitably, the sudden influx of humanity combined with the stimulus of greed led to an environment in which debauchery flourished; prostitution, heavy drinking, and crime-world activities linked to New York and London were a part of Johannesburg's daily life. A journalist named Pratt, writing in 1913 to warn incoming English and Australian workers, summed up the young city's atmosphere: "Ancient Nineveh and Babylon have been revived. . . . Johannesburg is their twentieth century prototype. It is a city of unbridled squalor and unfathomable squander."

13 A "grange" is a farmhouse with outbuildings.

14 Scholars seize upon Miss Smith's description here for clues as to the real locations of Chiltern Grange, Crooksbury Hill, Charlington Heath, and Charlington Hall. Michael Harrison, in *In the Footsteps of Sherlock Holmes*, declares that one district fits all of the proper distance and direction qualifications and also has a "hill" located between it and Farnham. He names the Surrey district of Charleshill and ventures, " 'Crooksbury Hill' may be either Crooksbury Heath, which could be called a hill, or it may be that part of Crooksbury Common known as Monk's Hill. I feel that the latter is more likely." Bernard Davies, in "Three Distressed Gentlewomen," goes on to identify Chiltern Grange as Lascombe, a house built in 1894 and situated about six miles from Farnham station and 6 1/2 miles from Godalming.

was a much older man, was more agreeable. He was a dark, sallow, clean-shaven, silent person; but he had polite manners and a pleasant smile. He inquired how we were left, and on finding that we were very poor he suggested that I should come and teach music to his only daughter, aged ten. I said that I did not like to leave my mother, on which he suggested that I should go home to her every week-end, and he offered me a hundred a year, which was certainly splendid pay. So it ended by my accepting, and I went down to Chiltern Grange,[13] about six miles from Farnham. Mr. Carruthers was a widower, but he had engaged a lady-housekeeper, a very respectable, elderly person, called Mrs. Dixon, to look after his establishment. The child was a dear, and everything promised well. Mr. Carruthers was very kind and very musical, and we had most pleasant evenings together. Every week-end I went home to my mother in town.

"The first flaw in my happiness was the arrival of the red-moustached Mr. Woodley. He came for a visit of a week, and oh, it seemed three months to me. He was a dreadful person, a bully to everyone else, but to me something infinitely worse. He made odious love to me, boasted of his wealth, said that if I married him I could have the finest diamonds in London, and finally, when I would have nothing to do with him, he seized me in his arms one day after dinner—he was hideously strong—and he swore that he would not let me go until I had kissed him. Mr. Carruthers came in, and tore him from me, on which he turned upon his own host, knocking him down and cutting his face open. That was the end of his visit, as you can imagine. Mr. Carruthers apologized to me next day, and assured me that I should never be exposed to such an insult again. I have not seen Mr. Woodley since.

"And now, Mr. Holmes, I come at last to the special thing which has caused me to ask your advice to-day. You must know that every Saturday forenoon I ride on my bicycle to Farnham Station in order to get the 12:22 to town. The road from Chiltern Grange is a lonely one, and at one spot it is particularly so, for it lies for over a mile between Charlington Heath upon one side and the woods which lie round Charlington Hall upon the other. You could not find a more lonely tract of road anywhere, and it is quite rare to meet so much as a cart, or a peasant, until you reach the high-road near Crooksbury Hill.[14]

Two weeks ago I was passing this place, when I chanced to look back over my shoulder, and about two hundred yards behind me I saw a man, also on a bicycle. He seemed to be a middle-aged man, with a short, dark beard. I looked back before I reached Farnham, but the man was gone, so I thought no more about it. But you can imagine how surprised I was, Mr. Holmes, when on my return on the Monday I saw the same man on the same stretch of road. My astonishment was increased when the incident occurred again, exactly as before, on the following Saturday and Monday. He always kept his distance, and did not molest me in any way, but still it certainly was very odd. I mentioned it to Mr. Carruthers, who seemed interested in what I said, and told me that he had ordered a horse and trap, so that in future I should not pass over these lonely roads without some companion.

"The horse and trap were to have come this week, but for

"He always kept so far from me that
I could not clearly see his face."
Anonymous, *Portland Oregonian*, July 23, 1911

15 Geoffrey Stavert, in "In the Wheelmarks of Violet Smith," identifies Charlington Hall as Hampton Lodge, on the Hampton Estate.

16 "Electrical" in the *Strand Magazine* and American editions. There is a company named "Midland Electrical Factors, Ltd.," in Coventry, which may be a "descendant" of the firm.

some reason they were not delivered, and again I had to cycle to the station. That was this morning. You can think that I looked out when I came to Charlington Heath, and there, sure enough, was the man, exactly as he had been the two weeks before. He always kept so far from me that I could not clearly see his face, but it was certainly someone whom I did not know. He was dressed in a dark suit with a cloth cap. The only thing about his face that I could clearly see was his dark beard. To-day I was not alarmed, but I was filled with curiosity, and I determined to find out who he was and what he wanted. I slowed down my machine, but he slowed down his. Then I stopped altogether, but he stopped also. Then I laid a trap for him. There is a sharp turning of the road, and I pedalled very quickly round this, and then I stopped and waited. I expected him to shoot round and pass me before he could stop. But he never appeared. Then I went back and looked round the corner. I could see a mile of road, but he was not on it. To make it the more extraordinary there was no side road at this point down which he could have gone."

Holmes chuckled and rubbed his hands.

"This case certainly presents some features of its own," said he. "How much time elapsed between your turning the corner and your discovery that the road was clear?"

"Two or three minutes."

"Then he could not have retreated down the road, and you say that there are no side roads?"

"None."

"Then he certainly took a footpath on one side or the other."

"It could not have been on the side of the heath or I should have seen him."

"So, by the process of exclusion we arrive at the fact that he made his way toward Charlington Hall, which, as I understand, is situated in its own grounds on one side of the road.[15] Anything else?"

"Nothing, Mr. Holmes, save that I was so perplexed that I felt I should not be happy until I had seen you and had your advice."

Holmes sat in silence for some little time.

"Where is the gentleman to whom you are engaged?" he asked at last.

"He is in the Midland Electric[16] Company, at Coventry."

"I slowed down my machine."
Sidney Paget, *Strand Magazine*, 1904

"He would not pay you a surprise visit?"

"Oh, Mr. Holmes! As if I should not know him!"

"Have you had any other admirers?"

"Several before I knew Cyril."

"And since?"

"There was this dreadful man, Woodley, if you can call him an admirer."

"No one else?"

Our fair client seemed a little confused.

"Who was he?" asked Holmes.

"Oh, it may be a mere fancy of mine; but it has seemed to me sometimes that my employer, Mr. Carruthers, takes a great deal of interest in me. We are thrown rather together. I play his accompaniments in the evening. He has never said anything. He is a perfect gentleman. But a girl always knows."

"Ha!" Holmes looked grave. "What does he do for a living?"

17 A reminder of the economics of 1895—the "going rate" for a governess was £50 per year (the modern equivalent of £3,200, or about U.S.$5,200), plus room and board. See also "The Copper Beeches," note 8, regarding the position of governesses; Violet Hunter, the reader will recall, had been paid £4 per month in her position previous to the Rucastle household.

"He is a rich man."

"No carriages or horses?"

"Well, at least he is fairly well-to-do. But he goes into the city two or three times a week. He is deeply interested in South African gold shares."

"You will let me know any fresh development, Miss Smith. I am very busy just now, but I will find time to make some inquiries into your case. In the meantime, take no step without letting me know. Good-bye, and I trust that we shall have nothing but good news from you."

"It is part of the settled order of Nature that such a girl should have followers," said Holmes, as he pulled at his meditative pipe, "but for choice not on bicycles in lonely country roads. Some secretive lover, beyond all doubt. But there are curious and suggestive details about the case, Watson."

"That he should appear only at that point?"

"Exactly. Our first effort must be to find who are the tenants of Charlington Hall. Then, again, how about the connection between Carruthers and Woodley, since they appear to be men of such different types? How came they *both* to be so keen upon looking up Ralph Smith's relations? One more point. What sort of a *ménage* is it which pays double the market price for a governess,[17] but does not keep a horse, although six miles from the station? Odd, Watson—very odd!"

"You will go down?"

"No, my dear fellow, you will go down. This may be some trifling intrigue, and I cannot break my other important research for the sake of it. On Monday you will arrive early at Farnham; you will conceal yourself near Charlington Heath; you will observe these facts for yourself, and act as your own judgment advises. Then, having inquired as to the occupants of the Hall, you will come back to me and report. And now, Watson, not another word of the matter until we have a few solid stepping-stones on which we may hope to get across to our solution."

We had ascertained from the lady that she went down upon the Monday by the train which leaves Waterloo at 9.50, so I started early and caught the 9.13. At Farnham Station I had no difficulty in being directed to Charlington Heath. It was impossible to mistake the scene of the young lady's adventure, for the road runs between the open heath on one side, and an old yew hedge upon the other, surrounding a park which is studded with magnificent trees. There was a main gateway of lichen-studded stone, each side-pillar surmounted by mouldering heraldic emblems, but besides this central carriage drive I observed several points where there were gaps in the hedge and paths leading through them. The house was invisible from the road, but the surroundings all spoke of gloom and decay.

The heath was covered with golden patches of flowering gorse, gleaming magnificently in the light of the bright spring sunshine. Behind one of these clumps I took up my position, so as to command both the gateway of the Hall and a long stretch of the road upon either side. It had been deserted when I left it, but now I saw a cyclist riding down it from the opposite direction to that in which I had come. He was clad in a dark suit, and I saw that he had a black beard. On reaching the end of the Charlington grounds he sprang from his machine and led it through a gap in the hedge, disappearing from my view.

A quarter of an hour passed and then a second cyclist appeared. This time it was the young lady coming from the station. I saw her look about her as she came to the Charlington hedge. An instant later the man emerged from his hiding-place, sprang upon his cycle, and followed her. In all the broad landscape those were the only moving figures, the graceful girl sitting very straight upon her machine,[18] and the man behind her bending low over his handle-bar, with a curiously furtive suggestion in every movement. She looked back at him and slowed her pace. He slowed also. She stopped. He at once stopped, too, keeping two hundred yards behind her. Her next movement was as unexpected as it was spirited. She suddenly whisked her wheels round and dashed straight at him! He was as quick as she, however, and darted off in desperate flight. Presently she came back up the road again, her head haughtily in the air, not deigning to take further notice of her silent attendant. He had turned also, and still kept his distance until the curve of the road hid them from my sight.

I remained in my hiding-place, and it was well that I did so, for presently the man reappeared cycling slowly back. He turned in at the Hall gates, and dismounted from his machine. For some few minutes I could see him standing among the trees. His hands were raised, and he seemed to be settling his

18 Proper Victorian women were expected to ride bicycles while wearing ankle-length skirts, petticoats, a jacket, and a hat. This created a pretty picture but did not provide much in the way of comfort. "There were some so-called liberated women," writes Richard Warner, "who chose to dress for comfort instead of propriety and wore those instruments of the Devil, the bifurcated attire. These could be bloomers, knickerbockers, or even, Heaven forbid, the convertible dress." The skirt of this last outfit could be unbuttoned in the front and then refastened around the legs, forming a rudimentary pair of pants. The upright manner in which Violent Smith rides her bike suggests that she is, indeed, a proper woman. Warner also points out that she must have been conventionally dressed, since Watson makes no particular mention of her attire: "If she had been wearing bifurcated costume, he as a ladies' man would have made some comment. After all, her limbs would have been revealed."

necktie. Then he mounted his bicycle, and rode away from me down the drive towards the Hall. I ran across the heath and peered through the trees. Far away I could catch glimpses of the old grey building with its bristling Tudor chimneys, but the drive ran through a dense shrubbery, and I saw no more of my man.

However, it seemed to me that I had done a fairly good morning's work, and I walked back in high spirits to Farnham. The local house agent could tell me nothing about Charlington Hall, and referred me to a well-known firm in Pall Mall. There I halted on my way home, and met with courtesy from the representative. No, I could not have Charlington Hall for the summer. I was just too late. It had been let about a month ago. Mr. Williamson was the name of the tenant. He was a respectable elderly gentleman. The polite agent was afraid he could say no more, as the affairs of his clients were not matters which he could discuss.

Mr. Sherlock Holmes listened with attention to the long report which I was able to present to him that evening, but it did not elicit that word of curt praise which I had hoped for and should have valued. On the contrary, his austere face was even more severe than usual as he commented upon the things that I had done and the things that I had not.

"Your hiding-place, my dear Watson, was very faulty. You should have been behind the hedge; then you would have had a close view of this interesting person. As it is, you were some hundreds of yards away, and can tell me even less than Miss Smith. She thinks she does not know the man; I am convinced she does. Why, otherwise, should he be so desperately anxious that she should not get so near him as to see his features? You describe him as bending over the handle-bar. Concealment again, you see. You really have done remarkably badly. He returns to the house, and you want to find out who he is. You come to a London house agent!"

"What should I have done?" I cried, with some heat.

"Gone to the nearest public-house. That is the centre of country gossip. They would have told you every name, from the master to the scullery-maid. Williamson! It conveys nothing to my mind. If he is an elderly man he is not this active cyclist who sprints away from that athletic young lady's pursuit. What have we gained by your expedition? The knowledge that

the girl's story is true. I never doubted it. That there is a connection between the cyclist and the Hall. I never doubted that
either. That the Hall is tenanted by Williamson. Who's the better for that? Well, well, my dear sir, don't look so depressed, we
can do little more until next Saturday, and in the meantime I
may make one or two inquiries myself."

Next morning we had a note from Miss Smith, recounting
shortly and accurately the very incidents which I had seen, but
the pith of the letter lay in the postscript:

> I am sure that you will respect my confidence, Mr. Holmes,
> when I tell you that my place here has become difficult owing
> to the fact that my employer has proposed marriage to me. I
> am convinced that his feelings are most deep and most hon-
> ourable. At the same time my promise is of course given. He
> took my refusal very seriously, but also very gently. You can
> understand, however, that the situation is a little strained.

"Our young friend seems to be getting into deep waters,"
said Holmes thoughtfully, as he finished the letter. "The case
certainly presents more features of interest and more possibility of development than I had originally thought. I should be
none the worse for a quiet, peaceful day in the country, and I
am inclined to run down this afternoon and test one or two theories which I have formed."

Holmes's quiet day in the country had a singular termination, for he arrived at Baker Street late in the evening with a
cut lip and a discoloured lump upon his forehead, besides a
general air of dissipation which would have made his own person the fitting object of a Scotland Yard investigation. He was
immensely tickled by his own adventures, and laughed
heartily as he recounted them.

"I get so little active exercise that it is always a treat," said
he. "You are aware that I have some proficiency in the good old
British sport of boxing.[19] Occasionally it is of service. To-day,
for example, I should have come to very ignominious grief
without it."

I begged him to tell me what had occurred.

"I found that country pub which I had already recommended to your notice, and there I made my discreet inquiries.
I was in the bar, and a garrulous landlord was giving me all that

19 Holmes's collegiate boxing is mentioned
in "The 'Gloria Scott.'" In "The Yellow
Face," "The Five Orange Pips," and *A Study
in Scarlet*, Watson comments on his prowess,
and Holmes himself recounts using his skill in
encounters with a street tough ("The Final
Problem") and Joseph Harrison ("The Naval
Treaty"). In *The Sign of Four*, McMurdo, a professional boxer, compliments Holmes on his
boxing talents, and Holmes reminds him that
they fought against each other in a benefit
match. See also "The Yellow Face," note 4.

20 In the sense of enthusiastic or exuberant.

"A straight left against a slogging ruffian."
Sidney Paget, *Strand Magazine*, 1904

I wanted. Williamson is a white-bearded man, and he lives alone with a small staff of servants at the Hall. There is some rumour that he is or has been a clergyman; but one or two incidents of his short residence at the Hall struck me as peculiarly unecclesiastical. I have already made some inquiries at a clerical agency, and they tell me that there was a man of that name in orders whose career has been a singularly dark one. The landlord further informed me that there are usually week-end visitors—'a warm[20] lot, sir'—at the Hall, and especially one gentleman with a red moustache, Mr. Woodley by name, who was always there. We had got as far as this when who should walk in but the gentleman himself, who had been drinking his beer in the tap-room, and had heard the whole conversation.

Who was I? What did I want? What did I mean by asking questions? He had a fine flow of language, and his adjectives were very vigorous. He ended a string of abuse by a vicious backhander, which I failed to entirely avoid. The next few minutes were delicious. It was a straight left against a slogging ruffian. I emerged as you see me. Mr. Woodley went home in a cart. So ended my country trip, and it must be confessed that, however enjoyable, my day on the Surrey border has not been much more profitable than your own."

The Thursday brought us another letter from our client.

You will not be surprised, Mr. Holmes to hear that I am leaving Mr. Carruthers's employment. Even the high pay cannot reconcile me to the discomforts of my situation. On Saturday I come up to town, and I do not intend to return. Mr. Carruthers has got a trap, and so the dangers of the lonely road, if there ever were any dangers, are now over.

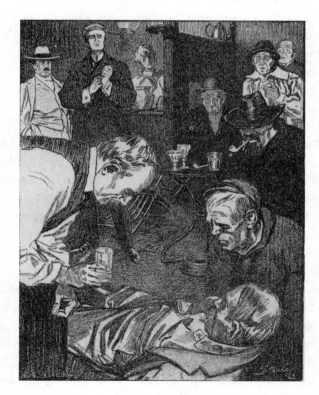

"It was a straight left against a slogging ruffian."
Frederick Dorr Steele, *Collier's*, 1903

21 This is pure Victorian sexism (or Holmesian misogyny), for Watson has earlier described Miss Smith as "tall, graceful and queenly."

As to the special cause of my leaving, it is not merely the strained situation with Mr. Carruthers, but it is the reappearance of that odious man, Mr. Woodley. He was always hideous, but he looks more awful than ever now, for he appears to have had an accident and he is much disfigured. I saw him out of the window, but I am glad to say I did not meet him. He had a long talk with Mr. Carruthers, who seemed much excited afterwards. Woodley must be staying in the neighbourhood, for he did not sleep here, and yet I caught a glimpse of him again this morning slinking about in the shrubbery. I would sooner have a savage wild animal loose about the place. I loathe and fear him more than I can say. How *can* Mr. Carruthers endure such a creature for a moment? However, all my troubles will be over on Saturday.

"So I trust, Watson, so I trust," said Holmes gravely. "There is some deep intrigue going on round that little woman,[21] and it is our duty to see that no one molests her upon that last journey. I think, Watson, that we must spare time to run down together on Saturday morning and make sure that this curious and inclusive investigation has no untoward ending."

I confess that I had not up to now taken a very serious view of the case, which had seemed to me rather grotesque and bizarre than dangerous. That a man should lie in wait for and follow a very handsome woman is no unheard-of thing, and if he has so little audacity that he not only dared not address her, but even fled from her approach, he was not a very formidable assailant. The ruffian Woodley was a very different person, but, except on one occasion, he had not molested our client, and now he visited the house of Carruthers without intruding upon her presence. The man on the bicycle was doubtless a member of those week-end parties at the Hall of which the publican had spoken, but who he was, or what he wanted, was as obscure as ever. It was the severity of Holmes's manner and the fact that he slipped a revolver into his pocket before leaving our rooms which impressed me with the feeling that tragedy might prove to lurk behind this curious train of events.

A rainy night had been followed by a glorious morning, and the heath-covered country-side, with the glowing dumps of flowering gorse, seemed all the more beautiful to eyes which were weary of the duns and drabs and slate-greys of London.

Holmes and I walked along the broad, sandy road inhaling the fresh morning air, and rejoicing in the music of the birds and the fresh breath of the spring. From a rise of the road on the shoulder of Crooksbury Hill we could see the grim Hall bristling out from amidst the ancient oaks, which, old as they were, were still younger than the building which they surrounded. Holmes pointed down the long tract of road which wound, a reddish yellow band, between the brown of the heath and the budding green of the woods. Far away, a black dot, we could see a vehicle moving in our direction. Holmes gave an exclamation of impatience.

"I had given a margin of half an hour," said he. "If that is her trap she must be making for the earlier train. I fear, Watson, that she will be past Charlington before we can possibly meet her."

From the instant that we passed the rise we could no longer see the vehicle, but we hastened onward at such a pace that my sedentary life began to tell upon me, and I was compelled to fall behind.[22] Holmes, however, was always in training, for he had inexhaustible stores of nervous energy upon which to draw. His springy step never slowed, until suddenly, when he was a hundred yards in front of me, he halted, and I saw him throw up his hand with a gesture of grief and despair. At the same instant an empty dog-cart, the horse cantering, the reins trailing, appeared round the curve of the road and rattled swiftly towards us.

"Too late, Watson; too late!" cried Holmes, as I ran panting to his side. "Fool that I was not to allow for the earlier train! It's abduction, Watson—abduction! Murder! Heaven knows what! Block the road! Stop the horse! That's right. Now jump in, and let us see if I can repair the consequences of my own blunder."

We had sprung into the dog-cart, and Holmes, after turning the horse, gave it a sharp cut with the whip, and we flew back along the road. As we turned the curve the whole stretch of road between the Hall and the heath was opened up. I grasped Holmes's arm.

"That's the man!" I gasped.

A solitary cyclist was coming towards us. His head was down and his shoulders rounded as he put every ounce of energy that he possessed on to the pedals. He was flying like a racer.[23] Suddenly he raised his bearded face, saw us close to him, and

22 Also as a result of his wounded leg? Compare Watson's statement in *The Hound of the Baskervilles*: "[Sir Henry and I] were both swift runners and in fairly good training . . ."

23 Cycling as sport was becoming increasingly popular in Europe in the 1890s, with city-to-city races that lasted up to a full day and beyond. France, which had hosted the first official road race on May 31, 1868 (a 12,000-meter affair near Paris), and the first city-to-city race on November 7, 1869 (from Paris to Rouen), was the leader in this field, establishing the one-day Paris-Roubaix race in 1896 and the twenty-one-day Tour de France in 1903. Road races in Belgium, Italy, Spain, and the Netherlands were also being founded around this time. In England, however, the poor condition of the roads meant that most bicycle racing was limited to specially constructed tracks, such as the ones located at the Crystal Palace, Sydenham, or the Alexandra Palace, Muswell Hill, in greater London. Watson's remark here suggests that he may well have attended the London races, which were held regularly on Saturday afternoons during the summer.

" 'Too late, Watson; too late!' cried Holmes."
Sidney Paget, *Strand Magazine*, 1904

pulled up, springing from his machine. That coal-black beard was in singular contrast to the pallor of his face, and his eyes were as bright as if he had a fever. He stared at us and at the dog-cart. Then a look of amazement came over his face.

"Halloa! Stop there!" he shouted, holding his bicycle to block our road. "Where did you get that dog-cart? Pull up, man!" he yelled, drawing a pistol from his side pocket. "Pull up, I say, or, by George, I'll put a bullet into your horse."

Holmes threw the reins into my lap and sprang down from the cart.

"You're the man we want to see. Where is Miss Violet Smith?" he said in his quick, clear way.

"That's what I'm asking you. You're in her dog-cart. You ought to know where she is."

"We met the dog-cart on the road. There was no one in it. We drove back to help the young lady."

"Good Lord! Good Lord! What shall I do?" cried the

stranger, in an ecstasy of despair. "They've got her, that hell-hound Woodley and the blackguard parson. Come, man, come, if you really are her friend. Stand by me and we'll save her, if I have to leave my carcass in Charlington Wood."

He ran distractedly, his pistol in his hand, towards a gap in the hedge. Holmes followed him, and I, leaving the horse grazing beside the road, followed Holmes.

"This is where they came through," said he, pointing to the marks of several feet upon the muddy path. "Halloa! Stop a minute! Who's this in the bush?"

It was a young fellow about seventeen, dressed like an ostler, with leather cords[24] and gaiters. He lay upon his back, his knees drawn up, a terrible cut upon his head. He was insen-

24 Leather corduroy breeches.

A solitary cyclist was coming toward us.
Charles Raymond Macaulay, *Return of Sherlock Holmes*
(McClure Phillips), 1905

25 A long lawn or turf upon which lawn bowling, also known as lawn bowls, was played. Possibly played in ancient Egypt and popularised throughout Europe in the Middle Ages, lawn bowling was banned for commoners by Henry VIII in the sixteenth century because it distracted them from the practice of archery. Yet noblemen continued to play the game, and the Scots introduced a formal code of rules in 1849. The English Bowling Association was established in 1903.

sible, but alive. A glance at his wound told me that it had not penetrated the bone.

"That's Peter, the groom," cried the stranger. "He drove her. The beasts have pulled him off and clubbed him. Let him lie; we can't do him any good, but we may save her from the worst fate that can befall a woman."

We ran frantically down the path, which wound among the trees. We had reached the shrubbery which surrounded the house when Holmes pulled up.

"They didn't go to the house. Here are their marks on the left—here, beside the laurel bushes! Ah, I said so."

As he spoke a woman's shrill scream—a scream which vibrated with a frenzy of horror—burst from the thick green clump of bushes in front of us. It ended suddenly on its highest note with a choke and a gurgle.

"This way! This way! They are in the bowling alley,"[25] cried the stranger, darting through the bushes. "Ah, the cowardly dogs! Follow me, gentlemen! Too late! too late! by the living Jingo!"

We had broken suddenly into a lovely glade of greensward surrounded by ancient trees. On the farther side of it, under the shadow of a mighty oak, there stood a singular group of three people. One was a woman, our client, drooping and faint, a handkerchief round her mouth. Opposite her stood a brutal, heavy-faced, red-moustached young man, his gaitered legs parted wide, one arm akimbo, the other waving a riding crop, his whole attitude suggestive of triumphant bravado. Between them an elderly, grey-bearded man, wearing a short surplice over a light tweed suit, had evidently just completed the wedding service, for he pocketed his Prayer Book as we appeared and slapped the sinister bridegroom upon the back in jovial congratulation.

"They're married?" I gasped.

"Come on!" cried our guide; "come on!" He rushed across the glade, Holmes and I at his heels. As we approached, the lady staggered against the trunk of the tree for support. Williamson, the ex-clergyman, bowed to us with mock politeness, and the bully Woodley advanced with a shout of brutal and exultant laughter.

"You can take your beard off, Bob," said he. "I know you

"As we approached, the lady staggered against
the trunk of the tree."
Sidney Paget, *Strand Magazine*, 1904

right enough. Well, you and your pals have just come in time
for me to be able to introduce you to Mrs. Woodley."

Our guide's answer was a singular one. He snatched off the
dark beard which had disguised him and threw it on the
ground, disclosing a long, sallow, clean-shaven face below it.
Then he raised his revolver and covered the young ruffian,
who was advancing upon him with his dangerous riding crop
swinging in his hand.

"Yes," said our ally, "I *am* Bob Carruthers, and I'll see this
woman righted if I have to swing for it. I told you what I'd do
if you molested her, and, by the Lord! I'll be as good as my
word."

"You're too late. She's my wife!"

"No, she's your widow."

His revolver cracked, and I saw the blood spurt from the

"No, she's your widow."
Anonymous, *Portland Oregonian*, July 23, 1911

front of Woodley's waistcoat. He spun round with a scream and fell upon his back, his hideous red face turning suddenly to a dreadful mottled pallor. The old man, still clad in his surplice, burst into such a string of foul oaths as I have never heard, and pulled out a revolver of his own, but, before he could raise it, he was looking down the barrel of Holmes's weapon.

"Enough of this," said my friend, coldly. "Drop that pistol! Watson, pick it up! Hold it to his head! Thank you. You, Carruthers, give me that revolver. We'll have no more violence. Come, hand it over!"

"Who are you, then?"

"My name is Sherlock Holmes."

"Good Lord!"

"You have heard of me, I see. I will represent the official

police until their arrival. Here, you!" he shouted to the frightened groom,[26] who had appeared at the edge of the glade. "Come here. Take this note as hard as you can ride to Farnham." He scribbled a few words upon a leaf from his notebook. "Give it to the superintendent at the police-station. Until he comes, I must detain you all under my personal custody."

The strong, masterful personality of Holmes dominated the tragic scene, and all were equally puppets in his hands. Williamson and Carruthers found themselves carrying the wounded Woodley into the house, and I gave my arm to the frightened girl. The injured man was laid on his bed, and at Holmes's request I examined him. I carried my report to where he sat in the old tapestry-hung dining-room with his two prisoners before him.

26 The *Strand Magazine* and American editions strangely refer to "a" frightened groom, as if there were more than one.

"He spun round with a scream and fell upon his back."
Sidney Paget, *Strand Magazine*, 1904

27 Holmes offers two reasons that the marriage might be invalid: the illegitimacy of Williamson's status as a clergyman, and Violet Smith's lack of consent to being married. Rev. Otis Rice contends that Holmes is right in one instance, but not the other. "The sacraments and sacramentals administered by a priest are valid whether he is inhibited, deposed, or not," Rice explains. "In this respect Williamson's flippant remark, 'Once a clergyman, always a clergyman' was in a sense true." Williamson might have faced disciplinary action—from the church or the state—for conducting a ceremony after being deposed, but nonetheless the marriage itself would have stood up under scrutiny.

Where Holmes is correct is in pointing out that Violet Smith had never intended nor wanted to marry—being gagged is a sure sign of proof—and this condition therefore renders the marriage itself invalid. Rice clarifies further: The Church of England stipulates that in a wedding, the bride and groom are actually the ministers of the ceremony, not the priest. The priest is merely a sort of witness who is present to bless and affirm the union in the eyes of the church. If either the bride or groom is unwilling to perform the marriage rites, then naturally the ceremony itself cannot be properly administered. "One wonders why Williamson did not know this," muses Rice. "Possibly his theological education had been as fragmentary as had been his liturgical training. What informed Anglican clergyman would have believed he was 'solemnizing a marriage' while wearing 'a short surplice over a light tweed suit?'"

It is doubtful that performance of a forced marriage is a "very serious felony"; however, Williamson's complicity in the matter made him equally guilty of the "abduction" and "assault" committed by Woodley, and Holmes's remark here should be taken to refer to Williamson's overall conduct.

"He will live," said I.

"What!" cried Carruthers, springing out of his chair. "I'll go upstairs and finish him first. Do you tell me that that girl, that angel, is to be tied to Roaring Jack Woodley for life?"

"You need not concern yourself about that," said Holmes. "There are two very good reasons why she should, under no circumstances, be his wife. In the first place, we are very safe in questioning Mr. Williamson's right to solemnize a marriage."

"I have been ordained," cried the old rascal.

"And also unfrocked."

"Once a clergyman, always a clergyman."

"I think not. How about the licence?"

"We had a licence for the marriage. I have it here in my pocket."

"Then you got it by a trick. But, in any case a forced marriage is no marriage, but it is a very serious felony,[27] as you will discover before you have finished. You'll have time to think the point out during the next ten years or so, unless I am mistaken. As to you, Carruthers, you would have done better to keep your pistol in your pocket."

"I begin to think so, Mr. Holmes; but when I thought of all the precaution I had taken to shield this girl—for I loved her, Mr. Holmes, and it is the only time that ever I knew what love was—it fairly drove me mad to think that she was in the power of the greatest brute and bully in South Africa, a man whose name is a holy terror from Kimberley[28] to Johannesburg. Why, Mr. Holmes, you'll hardly believe it, but ever since that girl has been in my employment I never once let her go past this house, where I knew these rascals were lurking, without following her on my bicycle just to see that she came to no harm. I kept my distance from her, and I wore a beard, so that she should not recognise me, for she is a good and high-spirited girl, and she wouldn't have stayed in my employment long if she had thought that I was following her about the country roads."

"Why didn't you tell her of her danger?"

"Because then, again, she would have left me, and I couldn't bear to face that. Even if she couldn't love me it was a great deal to me just to see her dainty form about the house, and to hear the sound of her voice."

"Well," said I, "you call that love, Mr. Carruthers, but I should call it selfishness."

"Maybe the two things go together. Anyhow, I couldn't let her go. Besides, with this crowd about, it was well that she should have someone near to look after her. Then when the cable came I knew they were bound to make a move."

"What cable?"

Carruthers took a telegram from his pocket.

"That's it," said he.

It was short and concise:

THE OLD MAN IS DEAD.

"Hum!" said Holmes. "I think I see how things worked, and I can understand how this message would, as you say, bring them to a head. But while you wait you might tell me what you can."

The old reprobate with the surplice burst into a volley of bad language.

"By heaven!" said he, "if you squeal on us, Bob Carruthers, I'll serve you as you served Jack Woodley. You can bleat about the girl to your heart's content, for that's your own affair, but if you round on your pals to this plain-clothes copper it will be the worst day's work that ever you did."

"Your reverence need not be excited," said Holmes, lighting a cigarette. "The case is clear enough against you, and all I ask is a few details for my private curiosity. However, if there's any difficulty in your telling me I'll do the talking, and then you will see how far you have a chance of holding back your secrets. In the first place, three of you came from South Africa on this game—you, Williamson, you, Carruthers, and Woodley."

"Lie number one," said the old man; "I never saw either of them until two months ago, and I have never been in Africa in my life, so you can put that in your pipe and smoke it, Mr. Busybody Holmes!"

"What he says is true," said Carruthers.

"Well, well, two of you came over. His reverence is our own home-made article. You had known Ralph Smith in South Africa. You had reason to believe he would not live long. You found out that his niece would inherit his fortune. How's that—eh?"

Carruthers nodded, and Williamson swore.

"She was next of kin, no doubt, and you were aware that the old fellow would make no will."

28 Kimberley was founded in 1871 after an intensely rich diamond mine was found at that site in 1870. South Africa, previously an agricultural nation, was transformed by the discovery of diamonds (and later, in the Witwatersrand, of gold). When individual digging gave way to organised mining, not only was the South African economy rerouted toward one of industrialisation, but the workforce also began to skew along racial lines, with black African migrant workers performing most of the manual labour and whites assuming supervisory and skilled-labour positions. In 1888, Kimberley's diamond fields were taken over by De Beers Consolidated Mines, under the control of Cecil Rhodes. As prime minister of Cape Colony (of which Kimberley was a part) and an *Uitlander* sympathiser, Rhodes would lead an unsuccessful attempt to overthrow Paul Kruger's Transvaal government in 1895. (See "The Adventure of the Dancing Men," note 2. For a detailed discussion of the upheavals in South Africa, see "The Blanched Soldier.") Rhodes's legacy upon his death in 1902 made possible the Rhodes Scholarships to Oxford.

29 Some editions have "outcast padre."

"Couldn't read or write," said Carruthers.

"So you came over, the two of you, and hunted up the girl. The idea was that one of you was to marry her, and the other have a share of the plunder. For some reason Woodley was chosen as the husband. Why was that?"

"We played cards for her on the voyage. He won."

"I see. You got the young lady into your service, and there Woodley was to do the courting. She recognised the drunken brute that he was, and would have nothing to do with him. Meanwhile your arrangement was rather upset by the fact that you had yourself fallen in love with the lady. You could no longer bear the idea of this ruffian owning her."

"No, by George, I couldn't!"

"There was a quarrel between you. He left you in a rage, and began to make his own plans independently of you."

"It strikes me, Williamson, there isn't very much that we can tell this gentleman," cried Carruthers, with a bitter laugh. "Yes, we quarrelled, and he knocked me down. I am level with him on that, anyhow. Then I lost sight of him. That was when he picked up with this cast padre[29] here. I found that they had set up housekeeping together at this place on the line that she had to pass for the station. I kept my eye on her after that, for I knew there was some devilry in the wind. I saw them from time to time, for I was anxious to know what they were after. Two days ago Woodley came up to my house with this cable, which showed that Ralph Smith was dead. He asked me if I would stand by the bargain. I said I would not. He asked me if I would marry the girl myself and give him a share. I said I would willingly do so, but that she would not have me. He said, 'Let us get her married first, and after a week or two she may see things a bit different.' I said I would have nothing to do with violence. So he went off cursing, like the foul-mouthed blackguard that he was, and swearing that he would have her yet. She was leaving me this week-end, and I had got a trap to take her to the station, but I was so uneasy in my mind that I followed her on my bicycle. She had got a start, however, and before I could catch her the mischief was done. The first thing I knew about it was when I saw you two gentlemen driving back in her dog-cart."

Holmes rose and tossed the end of his cigarette into the grate. "I have been very obtuse, Watson," said he. "When in

"Holmes tossed the end of his cigarette into the grate."
Sidney Paget, *Strand Magazine*, 1904

30 What is Holmes driving at here? Is he suggesting that Miss Smith planned to keep the matter a secret from Mr. Morton, but that he, Holmes, would reveal it? This seems unlikely in light of the forthcoming trials. Perhaps he is suggesting that Miss Smith would not want her fiancé to see her so dishevelled.

your report you said that you had seen the cyclist as you thought arrange his necktie in the shrubbery, that alone should have told me all. However, we may congratulate ourselves upon a curious and, in some respects, a unique case. I perceive three of the country constabulary in the drive, and I am glad to see that the little ostler is able to keep pace with them; so it is likely that neither he nor the interesting bridegroom will be permanently damaged by their morning's adventures. I think, Watson, that in your medical capacity you might wait upon Miss Smith and tell her that if she is sufficiently recovered, we shall be happy to escort her to her mother's home. If she is not quite convalescent you will find that a hint that we were about to telegraph to a young electrician in the Midlands would probably complete the cure.[30] As to you, Mr. Carruthers, I think that you have done what you could to make amends for your share in an evil plot. There is my card, sir, and if my evidence can be of help in your trial it shall be at your disposal."

In the whirl of our incessant activity it has often been difficult for me, as the reader has probably observed, to round off my narratives, and to give those final details which the curious might expect. Each case has been the prelude to another, and the crisis once over, the actors have passed for ever out of our busy lives. I find, however, a short note at the end of my manuscripts dealing with this case, in which I have put it upon record that Miss Violet Smith did indeed inherit a large fortune, and that she is now the wife of Cyril Morton, the senior partner of Morton & Kennedy, the famous Westminster electricians. Williamson and Woodley were both tried for abduction and assault, the former getting seven years and the latter ten. Of the fate of Carruthers I have no record, but I am sure that his assault was not viewed very gravely by the Court, since Woodley had the reputation of being a most dangerous ruffian, and I think that a few months were sufficient to satisfy the demands of justice. ■

BICYCLING IN THE TIME OF SHERLOCK HOLMES

IN THE century following the 1819 introduction of the first two-wheeled vehicle, a wooden contraption (invented by Baron Karl Drais von Sauerbronn) that the rider moved by pushing his feet along the ground, the bicycle went through numerous incarnations on its way to its current form. There was the first self-propelled two-wheeler, which was invented by Scottish blacksmith Kirkpatrick Macmillan in 1839 and made use of swinging foot cranks that were moved back and forth; the first popular two-wheeler, invented by the French Pierre and Ernest Michaux—father and son—in 1861 and propelled by rotating pedals attached to the front wheel; and the ordinary or "penny-farthing" model invented in 1870 by James Starley of the Coventry Sewing Machine Company. Incorporating a large front wheel and smaller back wheel (the penny and the farthing were England's largest and smallest coins) and weighing far less than previous versions of the vehicle, Star-

Cycling in London.
Queen's London (1897)

ley's bicycle remained fashionable for twenty years until the arrival of the chain-driven "safety" bicycle, which boasted two wheels of equal size and was far less likely to tip over. First manufactured in 1885 by Starley's nephew John, the safety bicycle had supplanted the ordinary bicycle by the early 1890s.

Cycling's popularity spread rapidly in the 1880s; clubs were founded, and both men and women enjoyed taking leisurely bicycle rides in the country, either separately or in tandem. But the bicycle's importance extended beyond mere novelty and sport. As a means of transportation, this new vehicle vastly expanded employment opportunities for working people who, unable to afford carriages or train fare, had previously been forced to work only as far away as they could walk. According to M. Haddon-MacRoberts's "The Mystery of the Missing Bicycles," millions of bicycles were being used between 1870 and 1890. Brand-new bicycles were expensive, naturally, but cheaper second- and third-hand models were always available for rent or sale as newer, more innovative models were continually being introduced and snapped up by enthusiasts. Victorians, once sedentary, became gloriously mobile. "It apparently was truly a sight," writes Haddon-MacRoberts, "to see the thousands of cyclists pouring out of the cities on weekends to escape the smog-congested haunts where they lived and worked, and to experience, for a few hours at least, an individual freedom never before known to so many people."

Some, by contrast, viewed the phenomenon with alarm, fearing the implications of this newfound emancipation, particularly in regard to young women. In 1897, Mrs. F. Harcourt Williamson, in "The Cycle in Society," moralised, "The beginning of cycling was the end of the chaperon in England, and now women, even young girls, ride alone or attended only by some casual man friend for miles together through deserted country roads. The danger of this is apparent; but parents and guardians will probably only become wise after the event. Given a lonely road, and a tramp desperate with hunger or naturally vicious, and it stands to reason that a girl, or indeed any woman riding alone must be in some considerable peril." There seems little doubt that Mrs. Williamson would have greeted Violet Smith's predicament with a knowing, "I told you so."

It is easy, then, to picture Miss Smith as a member of this new, bicyling society, taking advantage of a liberty—as well as the consequences of that liberty—largely unavailable to her a mere two decades before. It is even easier to picture her in light of the surprising discovery of the apparent origin of her bicycle. The Raleigh Bicycle Company was founded in 1890 by an Englishman named Frank Bowden, who, told by doctors he had six months to live, began bicycling and became not only healthy but also a cycling champion. Of the many bicycles manufactured by Bowden's company, one may have been delivered for the use of Violet Smith. The *Catalogue of an Exhibition on Sherlock Holmes Held at Abbey House Baker Street, London NW1, May-September 1951* sets forth (without comment) a letter from Mr. George H. B. Wilson, the managing director of Raleigh Industries Limited, Nottingham, which accompanied a bicycle lent to the exhibition by Raleigh. It reads:

> Dear Lord Donegall,
> Referring to your letter of the 20th April, in which you inform me of your present researches into the whereabouts of the cycle belonging to Miss Violet Smith . . . , I am pleased to be able to tell you that on looking back through our files for 1895 and 1896 we have been able to trace a Humber bicycle which we delivered to Miss Smith's father at Charlington Hall. As

you recall in your letter, Miss Smith married and having no further use for the vehicle sold it back to us. Many years later when it became apparent that our earliest products would be of historical interest, it was placed among other examples of this firm's craftsmanship. It was not, however, until your letter called attention to the fact, that Raleigh Industries Limited realised the very special value of this bicycle, in view of its association with the immortal detective, Mr. Sherlock Holmes.

The company records are obviously in error, however, for Charlington Hall was, at the time of the events recounted by Miss Smith, occupied by Williamson, who lived there alone, and Miss Smith's father was deceased. It is possible that when the delivery person discovered the distance to Chiltern Grange from the station, the bicycle was negligently presented to Williamson, who was thought to be Miss Smith's father.

THE ADVENTURE OF THE PRIORY SCHOOL[1]

"The Priory School" begins comically enough, with the preposterous figure of Thorneycroft Huxtable, M.A., Ph.D., etc., lying prostrate on the bearskin rug at 221 Baker Street. The case soon darkens, however, when Holmes learns that he must save a kidnapped boy from great danger. Even Holmes is surprised by the revelation of the kidnapper. Scholars argue over the true identity of the "Duke of Holdernesse," Watson's pseudonym for the boy's father, and Holmes's bold deductions from bicycle tracks (and his acceptance of an enormous fee) are questioned by many.

1 "The Priory School" appeared in *Collier's Weekly* on January 30, 1904, and in the *Strand Magazine* in February 1904.

WE HAVE HAD some dramatic entrances and exits upon our small stage at Baker Street, but I cannot recollect anything more sudden and startling than the first appearance of Dr. Thorneycroft Huxtable, M.A., Ph.D., *etc.* His card, which seemed too small to carry the weight of his academic distinctions, preceded him by a few seconds, and then he entered himself—so large, so pompous, and so dignified that he was the very embodiment of self-possession and solidity. And yet his first action, when the door had closed behind him, was to stagger against the table, whence he slipped down upon the floor, and there was that majestic figure prostrate and insensible upon our bearskin hearthrug.

We had sprung to our feet, and for a few moments we stared in silent amazement at this ponderous piece of wreckage, which told of some sudden and fatal storm far out on the ocean of life. Then Holmes hurried with a cushion for his head, and I with brandy for his lips. The heavy white face was seamed

Frederick Dorr Steele, *Collier's*, 1904

2 The manuscript, published in facsimile in 1985, reveals that the fictional town of "Mackleton" was substituted for "Castleton, in Derbyshire," a real village ten miles north-east of Buxton, in the north of England.

with lines of trouble, the hanging pouches under the closed eyes were leaden in colour, the loose mouth drooped dolorously at the corners, the rolling chins were unshaven. Collar and shirt bore the grime of a long journey, and the hair bristled unkempt from the well-shaped head. It was a sorely stricken man who lay before us.

"What is it, Watson?" asked Holmes.

"Absolute exhaustion—possibly mere hunger and fatigue," said I, with my finger on the thready pulse, where the stream of life trickled thin and small.

"Return ticket from Mackleton, in the North of England,"[2] said Holmes, drawing it from the watch-pocket. "It is not twelve o'clock yet. He has certainly been an early starter."

The puckered eyelids had begun to quiver, and now a pair of vacant grey eyes looked up at us. An instant later the man had scrambled on to his feet, his face crimson with shame.

"Forgive this weakness, Mr. Holmes; I have been a little

3 Watson mentions this case in "The Blanched Soldier," but strangely refers to the "Abbey School" and the "Duke of Greyminster" when he does so. Both sets of names—Priory/Holdernesse and Abbey/Greyminster—are patently false. June Thomson suggests that Watson may have originally chosen the Abbey School and the Duke of Greyminster as his pseudonyms, meaning to protect the identities of the participants involved; his publisher might have then pointed out that such names were similar to those of the Abbey Grange case and the real Duke of Westminster. Not wanting to confuse his readers, Watson would have obligingly altered the pseudonyms to "the Priory School" and the "Duke of Holdernesse" yet forgotten to register the change when writing up "The Blanched Soldier."

4 The "Foreign Secretary" in the manuscript.

"The heavy white face was seamed with lines of trouble."
Sidney Paget, *Strand Magazine*, 1904

overwrought. Thank you, if I might have a glass of milk and a biscuit I have no doubt that I should be better. I came personally, Mr. Holmes, in order to insure that you would return with me. I feared that no telegram would convince you of the absolute urgency of the case."

"When you are quite restored—"

"I am quite well again. I cannot imagine how I came to be so weak. I wish you, Mr. Holmes, to come to Mackleton with me by the next train."

My friend shook his head.

"My colleague, Dr. Watson, could tell you that we are very busy at present. I am retained in this case of the Ferrers Documents, and the Abergavenny murder is coming up for trial. Only a very important issue could call me from London at present."

"Important!" Our visitor threw up his hands. "Have you heard nothing of the abduction of the only son of the Duke of Holdernesse?"[3]

"What! the late Cabinet Minister?"[4]

"Exactly. We had tried to keep it out of the papers, but there was some rumour in the *Globe* last night. I thought it might have reached your ears."

Holmes shot out his long, thin arm and picked out Volume "H" in his encyclopaedia of reference.

" 'Holdernesse, Sixth Duke, K.G.,[5] P.C.[6]'—half the alphabet! 'Baron Beverley, Earl of Carston'—dear me, what a list! 'Lord Lieutenant[7] of Hallamshire,[8] since 1900. Married Edith, daughter of Sir Charles Appledore,[9] 1888. Heir and only child, Lord Saltire. Owns about two hundred and fifty thousand acres. Minerals in Lancashire and Wales. Address: Carlton House Terrace; Holdernesse Hall, Hallamshire; Carston Castle, Bangor, Wales. Lord of the Admiralty, 1872; Chief Secretary of State for—'[10] Well, well, this man is certainly one of the greatest subjects of the Crown!"[11]

"The greatest and perhaps the wealthiest. I am aware, Mr. Holmes, that you take a very high line in professional matters,

"I can not imagine how I came to be so weak."
Frederick Dorr Steele, *Collier's*, 1904

5 The K.G. stands for "Knight Garter." The Most Noble Order of the Garter, as it is officially known, was founded in 1348 by Edward III and is the highest and most exclusive level of knighthood. Its origins are murky, but legend has it that Edward was dancing with a lady of his court when a blue garter fell off her leg and onto the floor. Seeking to make light of a mortifying (for the lady) situation, Edward picked the garter up and placed it on his own leg, subsequently establishing the Order of the Garter to commemorate the incident. One of the many distinguished persons to become a Knight Garter was Winston Churchill, who in fact refused the honour when it was first offered him in 1945; his party having just been voted out of office, the prime minister declared, "I can hardly accept the Order of the Garter from the king after the people have given me the Order of the Boot." He later changed his mind, accepting the knighthood when he was back in office in 1953.

6 The P.C. stands for "Privy Councillor." Having advised the king on diplomatic matters in the sixteenth and seventeenth centuries, the Privy Council was stripped of most of its formal authority in the eighteenth century, when the cabinet officially assumed most advisory duties. The Privy Council became a largely symbolic body, with political officers of particularly high ranking (including the cabinet ministers, the archbishops of Canterbury and York, and the speaker of the House of Commons) earning membership as well as the title "the Right Honourable."

7 As the principal official of an English county, the lord lieutenant (who is appointed by the Crown) controls the appointment of justices of the peace and issues commissions in the local military organisations.

8 Here Watson's disguise of the location slips

a bit: The ancient lordship of Hallamshire embraced parts of Yorkshire and Derbyshire, and this historic place name is preserved in the community of West Hallam, which still remains in Derbyshire.

9 There is no apparent connection to "Appledore Towers," the home of the worst man in London ("Charles Augustus Milverton").

10 The manuscript description—perhaps closer to the truth—reads: "Holdernesse. 6th Duke. K.G., P.C., . . . Baron Beverley, Earl of Carston. . . . Lord Lieutenant of Hallamshire since 1900. Married Edith, daughter of Sir Charles *Appleby*, 1888. Heir and only child Lord Saltire. Owns about 250,000 acres. Minerals in Lancashire and Wales. Address Carlton House Terrace, Holdernesse Hall, *Lancashire*. Carson Castle, Bangor, Wales. Lord of the Admiralty 1871. Chief Secretary of State *for India. Foreign Secretary.*"

11 See "The Duke of Holdernesse," page 972, for a discussion of the identity of the duke.

12 "Ten thousand pounds" in the manuscript. These are enormous amounts, even for the era—in today's economics, £1,000 is the equivalent of almost £63,000, or over $100,000.

13 Anne Jordan argues that Holmes did not take the case out of concern for his own fame or pocket, but that the substantial reward money offered, along with the duke's seeming desire to deal with the matter quietly, gave the detective pause—in other words, Holmes surmised that the situation "was suggestive of a father who had a guilty secret; a secret which he was prepared to keep hidden even if it meant putting his own son's life at risk." Holmes, Jordan guesses, felt an imperative to investigate if he was to save the life of Holdernesse's son.

and that you are prepared to work for the work's sake. I may tell you, however, that his Grace has already intimated that a cheque for five thousand pounds[12] will be handed over to the person who can tell him where his son is and another thousand to him who can name the man, or men, who have taken him."

"It is a princely offer," said Holmes.[13] "Watson, I think that we shall accompany Dr. Huxtable back to the North of England. And now, Dr. Huxtable, when you have consumed that milk you will kindly tell me what has happened, when it happened, how it happened, and, finally, what Dr. Thorneycroft Huxtable, of the Priory School, near Mackleton, has to do with the matter, and why he comes three days after an event—the state of your chin gives the date—to ask for my humble services."

Our visitor had consumed his milk and biscuits. The light had come back to his eyes and the colour to his cheeks as he set himself with great vigour and lucidity to explain the situation.

"I must inform you, gentlemen, that the Priory is a preparatory school, of which I am the founder and principal. *Huxtable's Sidelights on Horace* may possibly recall my name to your memories. The Priory is, without exception, the best and most select preparatory school in England.[14] Lord Leverstoke, the Earl of Blackwater, Sir Cathcart Soames—they all have intrusted their sons to me. But I felt that my school had reached its zenith when, three weeks ago, the Duke of Holdernesse sent Mr. James Wilder, his secretary, with the intimation that young Lord Saltire, ten years old, his only son and heir, was about to be committed to my charge. Little did I think that this would be the prelude to the most crushing misfortune of my life.

"On May 1 the boy arrived, that being the beginning of the summer term. He was a charming youth, and he soon fell into our ways. I may tell you—I trust that I am not indiscreet; but half-confidences are absurd in such a case—that he was not entirely happy at home. It is an open secret that the Duke's married life had not been a peaceful one, and the matter had ended in a separation by mutual consent, the Duchess taking up her residence in the south of France. This had occurred very shortly before, and the boy's sympathies are known to have been strongly with his mother. He moped after her departure from Holdernesse Hall, and it was for this reason that the Duke desired to send him to my establishment. In a fortnight the boy was quite at home with us, and was apparently absolutely happy.

"He was last seen on the night of May 13th—that is, the night of last Monday. His room was on the second floor, and was approached through another larger room, in which two boys were sleeping. These boys saw and heard nothing, so that it is certain that young Saltire did not pass out that way. His window was open, and there is a stout ivy plant leading to the ground. We could trace no footmarks below, but it is sure that this is the only possible exit.

"His absence was discovered at seven o'clock on Tuesday morning. His bed had been slept in. He had dressed himself fully, before going off, in his usual school suit of black Eton jacket[15] and dark grey trousers. There were no signs that any-one had entered the room, and it is quite certain that anything in the nature of cries or a struggle would have been heard, since Caunter, the elder boy in the inner room, is a very light sleeper.

"When Lord Saltire's disappearance was discovered I at once called a roll of the whole establishment—boys, masters, and servants. It was then that we ascertained that Lord Saltire had not been alone in his flight. Heidegger, the German mas-ter, was missing. His room was on the second floor, at the far-ther end of the building, facing the same way as Lord Saltire's. His bed had also been slept in; but he had apparently gone away partly dressed, since his shirt and socks were lying on the floor. He had undoubtedly let himself down by the ivy, for we could see the marks of his feet where he had landed on the lawn. His bicycle was kept in a small shed beside this lawn, and it also was gone.

"He had been with me for two years, and came with the best references; but he was a silent, morose man, not very popular either with masters or boys. No trace could be found of the fugitives, and now, on Thursday morning, we are as ignorant as we were on Tuesday. Inquiry was, of course, made at once at Holdernesse Hall. It is only a few miles away, and we imagined that, in some sudden attack of homesickness, he had gone back to his father, but nothing had been heard of him. The Duke is greatly agitated—and, as to me, you have seen yourselves the state of nervous prostration to which the suspense and the responsibility have reduced me. Mr. Holmes, if ever you put

14 See "The Naval Treaty," note 35, for a dis-cussion of the state of preparatory education in England in Victorian times.

15 A short jacket cut above the waist, first worn by pupils of Eton College and later adopted by other schools for their uniforms.

16 Watson here tones down Holmes's original cutting remark; the manuscript reads, "Had the object been to lose the heir instead of to find him, you could have hardly acted with greater indiscretion."

forward your full powers, I implore you to do so now, for never in your life could you have a case which is more worthy of them."

Sherlock Holmes had listened with the utmost intentness to the statement of the unhappy schoolmaster. His drawn brows and the deep furrow between them showed that he needed no exhortation to concentrate all his attention upon a problem which, apart from the tremendous interests involved, must appeal so directly to his love of the complex and the unusual. He now drew out his notebook and jotted down one or two memoranda.

"You have been very remiss in not coming to me sooner," said he severely. "You start me on my investigation with a very serious handicap. It is inconceivable, for example, that this ivy and this lawn would have yielded nothing to an expert observer."

"I am not to blame, Mr. Holmes. His Grace was extremely desirous to avoid all public scandal. He was afraid of his family unhappiness being dragged before the world. He has a deep horror of anything of the kind."

"But there has been some official investigation?"

"Yes, sir, and it has proved most disappointing. An apparent clue was at once obtained, since a boy and a young man were reported to have been seen leaving a neighbouring station by an early train. Only last night we had news that the couple had been hunted down in Liverpool, and they prove to have no connection whatever with the matter in hand. Then it was that in my despair and disappointment, after a sleepless night, I came straight to you by the early train."

"I suppose the local investigation was relaxed while this false clue was being followed up?"

"It was entirely dropped."

"So that three days have been wasted. The affair has been most deplorably handled."[16]

"I feel it and admit it."

"And yet the problem should be capable of ultimate solution. I shall be very happy to look into it. Have you been able to trace any connection between the missing boy and this German master?"

"None at all."

"Was he in the master's class?"

"No; he never exchanged a word with him, so far as I know."

"That is certainly very singular. Had the boy a bicycle?"

"No."

"Was any other bicycle missing?"

"No."

"Is that certain?"

"Quite."

"Well, now, you do not mean to seriously suggest that this German rode off upon a bicycle in the dead of the night bearing the boy in his arms?"

"Certainly not."

"Then what is the theory in your mind?"

"The bicycle may have been a blind. It may have been hidden somewhere, and the pair gone off on foot."

"Quite so; but it seems rather an absurd blind, does it not? Were there other bicycles in this shed?"

"Several."

"Would he not have hidden a *couple*, had he desired to give the idea that they had gone off upon them?"

"I suppose he would."

"What is the theory in your mind?"
Sidney Paget, *Strand Magazine*, 1904

"Of course he would. The blind theory won't do. But the incident is an admirable starting-point for an investigation. After all, a bicycle is not an easy thing to conceal or to destroy. One other question. Did anyone call to see the boy on the day before he disappeared?"

"No."

"Did he get any letters?"

"Yes; one letter."

"From whom?"

"From his father."

"Do you open the boys' letters?"

"No."

"How do you know it was from the father?"

"The coat of arms was on the envelope, and it was addressed in the Duke's peculiar stiff hand. Besides, the Duke remembers having written."

"When had he a letter before that?"

"Not for several days."

"Had he ever one from France?"

"No; never."

"You see the point of my questions, of course. Either the boy was carried off by force or he went of his own free will. In the latter case, you would expect that some prompting from outside would be needed to make so young a lad do such a thing. If he has had no visitors, that prompting must have come in letters. Hence I try to find out who were his correspondents."

"I fear I cannot help you much. His only correspondent, so far as I know, was his own father."

"Who wrote to him on the very day of his disappearance. Were the relations between father and son very friendly?"

"His Grace is never very friendly with anyone. He is completely immersed in large public questions, and is rather inaccessible to all ordinary emotions. But he was always kind to the boy in his own way."

"But the sympathies of the latter were with the mother?"

"Yes."

"Did he say so?"

"No."

"The Duke, then?"

"Good heavens, no!"

"Then how could you know?"

"I have had some confidential talk with Mr. James Wilder, his Grace's secretary.[17] It was he who gave me the information about Lord Saltire's feelings."

"I see. By the way, that last letter of the Duke's—was it found in the boy's room after he was gone?"

"No; he had taken it with him. I think, Mr. Holmes, it is time that we were leaving for Euston."[18]

"I will order a four-wheeler. In a quarter of an hour we shall be at your service. If you are telegraphing home, Mr. Huxtable, it would be well to allow the people in your neighbourhood to imagine that the inquiry is still going on in Liverpool, or wherever else that red herring led your pack. In the meantime, I will do a little quiet work at your own doors, and perhaps the scent is not so cold but that two old hounds like Watson and myself[19] may get a sniff of it."

That evening found us in the cold, bracing atmosphere of the Peak country, in which Dr. Huxtable's famous school is situ-

17 Watson has suppressed Huxtable's full and revealingly sycophantic statement, set forth in the manuscript: "He is an excellent person—indeed I may tell you that it was through his good offices that the boy came to my school. He has the interest of the family very much at heart and he came to the conclusion that Holdernesse Hall was an unhealthy atmosphere for a young lad."

18 E. P. Greenwood comments that such a trip would have been "no mean feat," as the Derbyshire Peak District, where the Priory School was likely situated, was only serviced by the Midland Railway, which left from St. Pancras Station, not Euston Station.

19 Watson, anxious to emphasise his rôle, added himself; the manuscript reads, "one old hound like myself."

The Duke and his secretary.
Frederick Dorr Steele, *Collier's*, 1904

20 Watson modestly suppresses his own observations, to heighten the drama of Holmes's later detection: "I remember that it crossed my mind as I looked at him that it was impossible to imagine anyone more unlike the man of affairs whom one would expect to find as the agent of such a man as the Duke, a powerful nobleman." Perhaps he realised that his observations were the result of hindsight.

ated. It was already dark when we reached it. A card was lying on the hall table, and the butler whispered something to his master, who turned to us with agitation in every heavy feature.

"The Duke is here," said he. "The Duke and Mr. Wilder are in the study. Come, gentlemen, and I will introduce you."

I was, of course, familiar with the pictures of the famous statesman, but the man himself was very different from his representation. He was a tall and stately person, scrupulously dressed, with a drawn, thin face, and a nose which was grotesquely curved and long. His complexion was of a dead pallor, which was more startling by contrast with a long, dwindling beard of vivid red, which flowed down over his white waistcoat, with his watch-chain gleaming through its fringe. Such was the stately presence who looked stonily at us from the centre of Dr. Huxtable's hearthrug. Beside him stood a very young man, whom I understood to be Wilder, the private secretary. He was small, nervous, alert, with intelligent light-blue eyes and mobile features.[20] It was he who at once, in an incisive and positive tone, opened the conversation.

"I called this morning, Dr. Huxtable, too late to prevent you from starting for London. I learned that your object was to invite Mr. Sherlock Holmes to undertake the conduct of this case. His Grace is surprised, Dr. Huxtable, that you should have taken such a step without consulting him."

"When I learned that the police had failed—"

"His Grace is by no means convinced that the police have failed."

"But surely, Mr. Wilder—"

"You are well aware, Dr. Huxtable, that his Grace is particularly anxious to avoid all public scandal. He prefers to take as few people as possible into his confidence."

"The matter can be easily remedied," said the browbeaten doctor; "Mr. Sherlock Holmes can return to London by the morning train."

"Hardly that, Doctor, hardly that," said Holmes, in his blandest voice. "This northern air is invigorating and pleasant, so I propose to spend a few days upon your moors, and to occupy my mind as best I may. Whether I have the shelter of your roof or of the village inn is, of course, for you to decide."

I could see that the unfortunate doctor was in the last stage of indecision, from which he was rescued by the deep,

"Beside him stood a very young man."
Sidney Paget, *Strand Magazine*, 1904

sonorous voice of the red-bearded Duke, which boomed out like a dinner-gong.

"I agree with Mr. Wilder, Dr. Huxtable, that you would have done wisely to consult me. But since Mr. Holmes has already been taken into your confidence, it would indeed be absurd that we should not avail ourselves of his services. Far from going to the inn, Mr. Holmes, I should be pleased if you would come and stay with me at Holdernesse Hall."

"I thank your Grace. For the purposes of my investigation, I think that it would be wiser for me to remain at the scene of the mystery."

"Just as you like, Mr. Holmes. Any information which Mr. Wilder or I can give you is, of course, at your disposal."

"It will probably be necessary for me to see you at the Hall," said Holmes. "I would only ask you now, sir, whether you have formed any explanation in your own mind as to the mysterious disappearance of your son?"

"No, sir, I have not."

"Excuse me if I allude to that which is painful to you, but I have no alternative. Do you think that the Duchess had anything to do with the matter?"

The great minister showed perceptible hesitation.

"I do not think so," he said, at last.

"The other most obvious explanation is that the child has been kidnapped for the purpose of levying ransom. You have not had any demand of the sort?"

"No, sir."

"One more question, your Grace. I understand that you wrote to your son upon the day when this incident occurred."

"No, I wrote upon the day before."

"Exactly. But he received it on that day?"

"Yes."

"Was there anything in your letter which might have unbalanced him or induced him to take such a step?"

"No, sir, certainly not."

"Did you post that letter yourself?"

The nobleman's reply was interrupted by his secretary, who broke in with some heat.

"His Grace is not in the habit of posting letters himself," said he. "This letter was laid with others upon the study table, and I myself put them in the post-bag."

"You are sure this one was among them?"

"Yes, I observed it."

"How many letters did your Grace write that day?"

"Twenty or thirty. I have a large correspondence. But surely this—is somewhat irrelevant?"

"Not entirely," said Holmes.

"For my own part," the Duke continued, "I have advised the police to turn their attention to the South of France. I have already said that I do not believe that the Duchess would encourage so monstrous an action, but the lad had the most wrong-headed opinions, and it is possible that he may have fled to her, aided and abetted by this German. I think, Dr. Huxtable, that we will now return to the Hall."

I could see that there were other questions which Holmes would have wished to put but the nobleman's abrupt manner showed that the interview was at an end. It was evident that to his intensely aristocratic nature this discussion of his intimate family affairs with a stranger was most abhorrent, and that he feared lest every fresh question would throw a fiercer light into the discreetly shadowed corners of his ducal history.

When the nobleman and his secretary had left, my friend flung himself at once with characteristic eagerness into the investigation.

The boy's chamber was carefully examined, and yielded nothing save the absolute conviction that it was only through the window that he could have escaped. The German master's room and effects gave no further clue. In his case a trailer of ivy had given way under his weight, and we saw by the light of a lantern the mark on the lawn where his heels had come down. That one dint in the short, green grass was the only material witness left of this inexplicable nocturnal flight.

Sherlock Holmes left the house alone, and only returned after eleven. He had obtained a large ordnance map of the neighbourhood, and this he brought into my room, where he laid it out on the bed, and, having balanced the lamp in the middle of it, he began to smoke over it, and occasionally to point out objects of interest with the reeking amber of his pipe.

"This case grows upon me, Watson," said he. "There are decidedly some points of interest in connection with it. In this early stage, I want you to realize those geographical features which may have a good deal to do with our investigation.

"Look at this map. This dark square is the Priory School. I'll put a pin in it. Now, this line is the main road.[21] You see that it runs east and west past the school, and you see also that there is no side road for a mile either way. If these two folk passed away by road, it was *this* road."

"Exactly."

"By a singular and happy chance, we are able to some extent to check what passed along this road during the night in question. At this point, where my pipe is now resting, a county constable was on duty from twelve to six. It is, as you perceive, the first cross-road on the east side. This man declares that he was not absent from his post for an instant,[22] and he is positive that neither boy nor man could have gone that way unseen. I have

21 Another excision made by Watson to conceal the location: The manuscript reads, "the main road between Manchester and Buxton."

22 Surely, as D. Martin Dakin comments, this constable's job was a peculiar (if not pointless) one. "[W]hat was the idea of having a policeman on duty all night on a lonely road in the heart of the country," marvels Dakin, "where apparently no one was likely to pass? It seems an extraordinary waste of the poor man's time and energy. What was he supposed to be doing? He wasn't even patrolling the roads, just standing still in an isolated spot for six hours at night!"

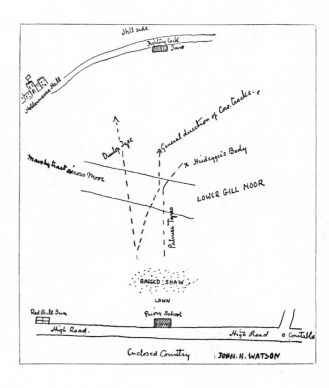

23 Watson has deleted an uncharacteristic remark of concern expressed by Holmes; the manuscript continues here: "That unfortunate Dr. Huxtable will be seriously ill, I fear. Do you hear him pacing up and down the passage?"

24 Described in the manuscript as "to the Black Gill Hills."

25 "Twelve miles" in the manuscript.

26 Omitted from the manuscript is "Here eight miles north is a simple house, Lower Gill House, now untenanted."

spoken with this policeman to-night, and he appears to me to be a perfectly reliable person. That blocks this end. We have now to deal with the other. There is an inn here, the 'Red Bull', the landlady of which was ill. She had sent to Mackleton for a doctor, but he did not arrive until morning, being absent at another case. The people at the inn were alert all night, awaiting his coming, and one or other of them seems to have continually had an eye upon the road. They declare that no one passed. If their evidence is good, then we are fortunate enough to be able to block the west, and also to be able to say that the fugitives did *not* use the road at all."

"But the bicycle?" I objected.

"Quite so. We will come to the bicycle presently.[23] To continue our reasoning: if these people did not go by the road, they must have traversed the country to the north of the house or to the south of the house. That is certain. Let us weigh the one against the other. On the south of the house is, as you perceive, a large district of arable land, cut up into small fields, with stone walls between them. There, I admit that a bicycle is impossible. We can dismiss the idea. We turn to the country on the north. Here there lies a grove of trees, marked as the 'Ragged Shaw,' and on the farther side stretches a great rolling moor, Lower Gill Moor, extending for ten miles and sloping gradually upward.[24] Here, at one side of this wilderness, is Holdernesse Hall, ten miles[25] by road, but only six across the moor. It is a peculiarly desolate plain. A few moor farmers have small holdings, where they rear sheep and cattle.[26] Except these, the plover and the curlew are the only inhabitants until you come to the Chesterfield high road. There is a church there, you see, a few cottages, and an inn. Beyond that the hills become precipitous. Surely it is here to the north that our quest must lie."

"But the bicycle?" I persisted.

"Well, well!" said Holmes impatiently. "A good cyclist does not need a high road. The moor is intersected with paths, and the moon was at the full. Halloa! what is this?"

There was an agitated knock at the door, and an instant afterwards Dr. Huxtable was in the room. In his hand he held a blue cricket-cap, with a white chevron on the peak.

"At last we have a clue!" he cried. "Thank heaven! at last we are on the dear boy's track! It is his cap."

"Where was it found?"

"In the van of the gipsies who camped on the moor. They left on Tuesday. To-day the police traced them down and examined their caravan. This was found."

"How do they account for it?"

"They shuffled and lied—said that they found it on the moor on Tuesday morning. They know where he is, the rascals! Thank goodness, they are all safe under lock and key. Either the fear of the law or the Duke's purse will certainly get out of them all that they know."

"So far, so good," said Holmes, when the doctor had at last left the room. "It at least bears out the theory that it is on the side of the Lower Gill Moor that we must hope for results. The police have really done nothing locally, save the arrest of these gipsies. Look here, Watson! There is a watercourse across the moor. You see it marked here in the map. In some parts it widens into a morass. This is particularly so in the region between Holdernesse Hall and the school. It is vain to look elsewhere for tracks in this dry weather; but at *that* point there is certainly a chance of some record being left. I will call you early to-morrow morning, and you and I will try if we can throw some little light upon the mystery."

The day was just breaking when I woke to find the long, thin form of Holmes by my bedside. He was fully dressed, and had apparently already been out.

"I have done the lawn and the bicycle shed," said he. "I have also had a ramble through the Ragged Shaw. Now, Watson, there is cocoa ready in the next room. I must beg you to hurry, for we have a great day before us."

His eyes shone, and his cheek was flushed with the exhilaration of the master workman who sees his work lie ready before him.[27] A very different Holmes, this active, alert man, from the introspective and pallid dreamer of Baker Street. I felt, as I looked upon that supple figure, alive with nervous energy, that it was indeed a strenuous day that awaited us.

And yet it opened in the blackest disappointment. With high hopes we struck across the peaty, russet moor, intersected with a thousand sheep paths, until we came to the broad, light-green belt which marked the morass between us and Holdernesse. Certainly, if the lad had gone homeward, he must have passed this, and he could not pass it without leaving his traces.

27 Watson has deleted from the manuscript an artistic allusion, "the artist whose pigments are set out, and who has only to blend them into the expression of his own soul."

28 Rosemary Michaud, in an article entitled "Who Dung It? A Trifling Manure-graph," suggests that "sheep-marks" was Watson's polite way of referring to sheep dung. Holmes, the scion of country squires, Michaud argues, surely could distinguish horse droppings from cow manure. When Holmes later called himself a "blind beetle," he was referring to his overlooking the obvious lack of cow manure where there were "cattle-tracks"—and perhaps the presence of horse droppings?

29 Not surprisingly, there were dozens of tyre manufacturers producing a variety of tyres at the time of "The Priory School." Holmes obviously limited his knowledge to the most popular brands and models.

30 Although the first patent for a pneumatic (air-filled) tyre was taken out by Robert William Thomson in England in 1845, it was not until Scottish veterinarian John Boyd Dunlop sought to improve the performance of his son's tricycle—patenting the first pneumatic bicycle tyre in 1888—that air-filled tyres began to supersede solid rubber tyres in practicality and popularity. In 1889 Dunlop began manufacturing and marketing his invention, registering his company as Byrne Brothers India Rubber Company, Ltd., in 1896, and the Dunlop Rubber Company, Ltd., in 1900. He began manufacturing automobile tyres in 1906.

31 The first pneumatic tyres had no treads. As tyres become fully moulded, plain circumferential ribs were added to prevent lateral skidding. The Palmer tyre had such a tread.

Dunlop historian Eric Tompkins reports that by 1891, marketing departments had seen a prime opportunity presenting itself on the surface of the tyre, and they began adding the maker's name as a central feature of the

But no sign of him or the German could be seen. With a darkening face my friend strode along the margin, eagerly observant of every muddy stain upon the mossy surface. Sheep-marks there were in profusion, and at one place, some miles down, cows had left their tracks. Nothing more.[28]

"Check number one," said Holmes, looking gloomily over the rolling expanse of the moor, "There is another morass down yonder, and a narrow neck between. Halloa! halloa! halloa! what have we here?"

We had come on a small black ribbon of pathway. In the middle of it, clearly marked on the sodden soil was the track of a bicycle.

"Hurrah!" I cried. "We have it."

But Holmes was shaking his head, and his face was puzzled and expectant rather than joyous.

"A bicycle, certainly, but not *the* bicycle," said he. "I am familiar with forty-two different impressions left by tyres.[29] This, as you perceive, is a Dunlop,[30] with a patch upon the outer cover. Heidegger's tyres were Palmer's, leaving longitudinal stripes.[31] Aveling, the mathematical master, was sure upon the point. Therefore, it is not Heidegger's track."

"The boy's, then?"

"Possibly, if we could prove a bicycle to have been in his possession. But this we have utterly failed to do. This track, as you perceive, was made by a rider who was going from the direction of the school."

"Or towards it?"

"No, no, my dear Watson. The more deeply sunk impression is, of course, the hind wheel, upon which the weight rests. You perceive several places where it has passed across and obliterated the more shallow mark of the front one. It was undoubtedly heading away from the school.[32] It may or may not be connected with our inquiry, but we will follow it backwards before we go any farther."

We did so, and at the end of a few hundred yards lost the tracks as we emerged from the boggy portion of the moor. Following the path backwards, we picked out another spot, where a spring trickled across it. Here, once again, was the mark of the bicycle, though nearly obliterated by the hoofs of cows. After that there was no sign, but the path ran right on into

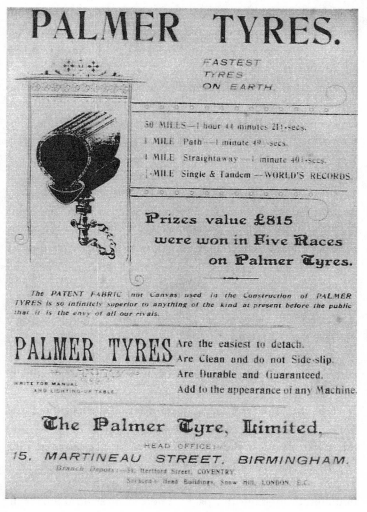

Tread of Palmer tyre.

Tread of Dunlop tyre.

tread. The logo was typically surrounded by the ribs. Therefore, "the cyclist had the joy of leaving a trail of DUNLOP DUNLOP DUN-LOP along the road, in the soft mud on wet days and in the dust on dry ones. . . . And so," Tompkins remarks, "an era of fancy tread patterns started." Could it be that Holmes differentiated the two types of tyres not by their treads, but by their logos? No wonder that he was "familiar with forty-two different impressions"!

32 For a discussion of the problem of the tyre-tracks, see "Which Way Did the Bicycle Travel?" page 973.

33 Curiously, Watson records himself smoking cigarettes only in one other adventure, namely, *The Hound of the Baskervilles*, generally dated in the twentieth century along with "The Priory School" (see *Chronological Table*). Was cigarette smoking a late-acquired and short-lived vice for Watson? Or was the doctor instead unable to embrace the rebellious image that cigarettes conveyed? (Holmes, ever the bohemian, smoked cigars, cigarettes, and various pipes.) According to Iain Gately's *Tobacco: A Cultural History of How an Exotic Plant Seduced Civilization*, those who smoked cigarettes once fared poorly when compared with those who favoured pipes and cigars; as Gately puts it, "cigarette smokers were naturally inferior specimens and best shunned." Oscar Wilde, who smoked cigarettes in order to shock people, played upon this image of perversity in *The Picture of Dorian Gray* (1891), drawling, "A cigarette is the perfect type of a perfect pleasure. It is exquisite, and it leaves me satisfied. What more can one want?" See also "The Golden Pince-Nez," note 15, for a discussion of the history of cigarette smoking in Victorian England.

Ragged Shaw, the wood which backed on to the school. From this wood the cycle must have emerged. Holmes sat down on a boulder and rested his chin in his hands. I had smoked two cigarettes before he moved.[33]

"Well, well," said he, at last. "It is, of course, possible that a cunning man might change the tyres of his bicycle in order to leave unfamiliar tracks. A criminal who was capable of such a thought is a man whom I should be proud to do business with. We will leave this question undecided and hark back to our morass again, for we have left a good deal unexplored."

We continued our systematic survey of the edge of the sodden portion of the moor, and soon our perseverance was gloriously rewarded. Right across the lower part of the bog lay a miry path. Holmes gave a cry of delight as he approached it. An impression like a fine bundle of telegraph wires ran down the centre of it. It was the Palmer tyre.

"Here is Herr Heidegger, sure enough!" cried Holmes exultantly. "My reasoning seems to have been pretty sound, Watson."

"I congratulate you."

"But we have a long way still to go. Kindly walk clear of the path. Now let us follow the trail. I fear that it will not lead very far."

We found, however, as we advanced, that this portion of the moor is intersected with soft patches, and, though we frequently lost sight of the track, we always succeeded in picking it up once more.

"Do you observe," said Holmes, "that the rider is now undoubtedly forcing the pace? There can be no doubt of it. Look at this impression, where you get both tyres clear. The one is as deep as the other. That can only mean that the rider is throwing his weight on to the handle-bar, as a man does when he is sprinting. By Jove! he has had a fall."

There was a broad, irregular smudge covering some yards of the track. Then there were a few footmarks, and the tyres reappeared once more.

"A side-slip," I suggested.

Holmes held up a crumpled branch of flowering gorse. To my horror I perceived that the yellow blossoms were all dabbled with crimson. On the path, too, and among the heather were dark stains of clotted blood.

"An impression like a fine bundle of telegraph
wires ran down the centre of it."
Sidney Paget, *Strand Magazine*, 1904

"Bad!" said Holmes. "Bad! Stand clear, Watson! Not an
unnecessary footstep! What do I read here? He fell wounded—
he stood up—he remounted—he proceeded. But there is no
other track. Cattle on this side path. He was surely not gored
by a bull? Impossible! But I see no traces of anyone else. We
must push on, Watson. Surely, with stains as well as the track
to guide us, he cannot escape us now."

Our search was not a very long one. The tracks of the tyre
began to curve fantastically upon the wet and shining path.
Suddenly, as I looked ahead, the gleam of metal caught my eye

34 Watson cuts Holmes's refreshingly naive statement that follows in the manuscript: "If it were with someone then it was probably with someone whom he knew and trusted. A lad of that age does not willingly set out alone in the dark with a stranger."

from amid the thick gorse-bushes. Out of them we dragged a bicycle, Palmer-tyred, one pedal bent, and the whole front of it horribly smeared and slobbered with blood. On the other side of the bushes, a shoe was projecting. We ran round, and there lay the unfortunate rider. He was a tall man, full-bearded, with spectacles, one glass of which had been knocked out. The cause of his death was a frightful blow upon the head, which had crushed in part of his skull. That he could have gone on after receiving such an injury said much for the vitality and courage of the man. He wore shoes, but no socks, and his open coat disclosed a nightshirt beneath it. It was undoubtedly the German master.

Holmes turned the body over reverently, and examined it with great attention. He then sat in deep thought for a time, and I could see by his ruffled brow that this grim discovery had not, in his opinion, advanced us much in our inquiry.

"It is a little difficult to know what to do, Watson," said he, at last. "My own inclinations are to push this inquiry on, for we have already lost so much time that we cannot afford to waste another hour. On the other hand, we are bound to inform the police of the discovery, and to see that this poor fellow's body is looked after."

"I could take a note back."

"But I need your company and assistance. Wait a bit! There is a fellow cutting peat up yonder. Bring him over here, and he will guide the police."

I brought the peasant across, and Holmes despatched the frightened man with a note to Dr. Huxtable.

"Now, Watson," said he, "we have picked up two clues this morning. One is the bicycle with the Palmer tyre, and we see what that has led to. The other is the bicycle with the patched Dunlop. Before we start to investigate that, let us try to realize what we *do* know, so as to make the most of it, and to separate the essential from the accidental.

"First of all, I wish to impress upon you that the boy certainly left of his own free will. He got down from his window and he went off, either alone or with someone.[34] That is sure."

I assented.

"Well, now, let us turn to this unfortunate German master. The boy was fully dressed when he fled. Therefore, he fore-

"There lay the unfortunate rider."
Sidney Paget, *Strand Magazine*, 1904

saw what he would do. But the German went without his socks. He certainly acted on very short notice."

"Undoubtedly."

"Why did he go? Because, from his bedroom window, he saw the flight of the boy. Because he wished to overtake him and bring him back. He seized his bicycle, pursued the lad, and in pursuing him met his death."

"So it would seem."

"Now I come to the critical part of my argument. The natural action of a man in pursuing a little boy would be to run after him. He would know that he could overtake him. But the German does not do so. He turns to his bicycle. I am told that he was an excellent cyclist. He would not do this if he did not see that the boy had some swift means of escape."

"The other bicycle."

"Let us continue our reconstruction. He meets his death

five miles from the school—not by a bullet, mark you, which even a lad might conceivably discharge, but by a savage blow dealt by a vigorous arm. The lad, then, *had* a companion in his flight. And the flight was a swift one, since it took five miles before an expert cyclist could overtake them. Yet we survey the ground round the scene of the tragedy. What do we find? A few cattle-tracks, nothing more. I took a wide sweep round, and there is no path within fifty yards. Another cyclist could have had nothing to do with the actual murder, nor were there any human footmarks."

"Holmes," I cried, "this is impossible."

"Admirable!" he said. "A most illuminating remark. It *is* impossible as I state it, and therefore I must in some respect have stated it wrong. Yet you saw for yourself. Can you suggest any fallacy?"

"He could not have fractured his skull in a fall?"

"In a morass, Watson?"

"I am at my wit's end."

"Tut, tut; we have solved some worse problems. At least we have plenty of material, if we can only use it. Come, then, and, having exhausted the Palmer, let us see what the Dunlop with the patched cover has to offer us."

We picked up the track and followed it onwards for some distance; but soon the moor rose into a long, heather-tufted curve, and we left the watercourse behind us. No further help from tracks could be hoped for. At the spot where we saw the last of the Dunlop tyre it might equally have led to Holdernesse Hall, the stately towers of which rose some miles to our left, or to a low, grey village which lay in front of us and marked the position of the Chesterfield high-road.

As we approached the forbidding and squalid inn, with the sign of a game-cock above the door, Holmes gave a sudden groan, and clutched me by the shoulder to save himself from falling. He had had one of those violent strains of the ankle which leave a man helpless. With difficulty he limped up to the door, where a squat, dark, elderly man was smoking a black clay pipe.

"How are you, Mr. Reuben Hayes?" said Holmes.

"Who are you, and how do you get my name so pat?" the countryman answered, with a suspicious flash of a pair of cunning eyes.

"With difficulty he limped up to the door."
Sidney Paget, *Strand Magazine*, 1904

"Well, it's printed on the board above your head. It's easy to see a man who is master of his own house. I suppose you haven't such a thing as a carriage in your stables?"

"No, I have not."

"I can hardly put my foot to the ground."

"Don't put it to the ground."

"But I can't walk."

"Well, then, hop."

Mr. Reuben Hayes's manner was far from gracious, but Holmes took it with admirable good-humour.

35 A dealer in corn, wheat, and other grains.

"Look here, my man," said he. "This is really rather an awkward fix for me. I don't mind how I get on."

"Neither do I," said the morose landlord.

"The matter is very important. I would offer you a sovereign for the use of a bicycle."

The landlord pricked up his ears.

"Where do you want to go?"

"To Holdernesse Hall."

"Pals of the Dook, I suppose?" said the landlord, surveying our mud-stained garments with ironical eyes.

Holmes laughed good-naturedly.

"He'll be glad to see us, anyhow."

"Why?"

"Because we bring him news of his lost son."

The landlord gave a very visible start.

"What, you're on his track?"

"He has been heard of in Liverpool. They expect to get him every hour."

Again a swift change passed over the heavy, unshaven face. His manner was suddenly genial.

"I've less reason to wish the Dook well than most men," said he, "for I was his head coachman once, and cruel bad he treated me. It was him that sacked me without a character on the word of a lying corn-chandler.[35] But I'm glad to hear that the young lord was heard of in Liverpool, and I'll help you to take the news to the Hall."

"Thank you," said Holmes. "We'll have some food first. Then you can bring round the bicycle."

"I haven't got a bicycle."

Holmes held up a sovereign.

"I tell you, man, that I haven't got one. I'll let you have two horses as far as the Hall."

"Well, well," said Holmes, "we'll talk about it when we've had something to eat."

When we were left alone in the stone-flagged kitchen, it was astonishing how rapidly that sprained ankle recovered. It was nearly nightfall, and we had eaten nothing since early morning, so that we spent some time over our meal. Holmes was lost in thought, and once or twice he walked over to the window and stared earnestly out. It opened on to a squalid courtyard. In the far corner was a smithy, where a grimy lad was at work. On the other side were the stables. Holmes had sat down again after one of these excursions, when he suddenly sprang out of his chair with a loud exclamation.

"By heaven, Watson, I believe that I've got it!" he cried. "Yes, yes, it must be so. Watson, do you remember seeing any cow-tracks to-day?"

"Yes, several."

"Where?"

"Well, everywhere. They were at the morass, and again on the path, and again near where poor Heidegger met his death."

"Exactly. Well, now, Watson, how many cows did you see on the moor?"

"I don't remember seeing any."

"Strange, Watson, that we should see tracks all along our line, but never a cow on the whole moor; very strange, Watson, eh?"

"Yes, it is strange."

"Now, Watson, make an effort, throw your mind back. Can you see those tracks upon the path?"

"Yes, I can."

"Can you recall that the tracks were sometimes like that, Watson"—he arranged a number of bread-crumbs in this fashion—: : : : :—"and sometimes like this"—: . : . : . : .—"and occasionally like this"—· · · · · . "Can you remember that?"

"No, I cannot."

"But I can. I could swear to it. However, we will go back at our leisure and verify it. What a blind beetle I have been not to draw my conclusion."

"And what is your conclusion?"

"Only that it is a remarkable cow which walks, canters, and gallops.[36] By George, Watson, it was no brain of a country publican that thought out such a blind as that. The coast seems to be clear, save for that lad in the smithy. Let us slip out and see what we can see."

There were two rough-haired, unkempt horses in the tumble-down stable. Holmes raised the hind-leg of one of them and laughed aloud.

"Old shoes, but newly shod—old shoes, but new nails. This case deserves to be a classic. Let us go across to the smithy."

36 In "The Hoof-Marks in 'The Priory School'" S. Tupper Bigelow contends that the walk of a horse is more correctly depicted in dots as:

· · · · · · · ·

· · · · · · · ·

the canter as

· ·   · ·

· · · · · · · ·   · · · ·

and the gallop more or less as above.

The lad continued his work without regarding us. I saw Holmes's eye darting to right and left among the litter of iron and wood which was scattered about the floor. Suddenly, however, we heard a step behind us, and there was the landlord, his heavy eyebrows drawn down over his savage eyes, his swarthy features convulsed with passion. He held a short, metal-headed stick in his hand, and he advanced in so menacing a fashion that I was right glad to feel the revolver in my pocket.

"You infernal spies!" the man cried. "What are you doing there?"

"Why, Mr. Reuben Hayes," said Holmes, coolly, "one might think that you were afraid of our finding something out."

"You infernal spies!" the man cried.
Frederick Dorr Steele, *Collier's*, 1904

The man mastered himself with a violent effort, and his grim mouth loosened into a false laugh, which was more menacing than his frown.

"You're welcome to all you can find out in my smithy," said he. "But look here, mister, I don't care for folk poking about my place without my leave, so the sooner you pay your score and get out of this the better I shall be pleased."

"All right, Mr. Hayes—no harm meant," said Holmes. "We have been having a look at your horses, but I think I'll walk, after all. It's not far, I believe."

"Not more than two miles to the Hall gates. That's the road to the left." He watched us with sullen eyes until we had left his premises.

We did not go very far along the road, for Holmes stopped the instant that the curve hid us from the landlord's view.

"We were warm, as the children say, at that inn," said he. "I seem to grow colder every step that I take away from it. No, no, I can't possibly leave it."

"I am convinced," said I, "that this Reuben Hayes knows all about it. A more self-evident villain I never saw."

"Oh! he impressed you in that way, did he? There are the horses, there is the smithy. Yes, it is an interesting place, this 'Fighting Cock'. I think we shall have another look at it in an unobtrusive way."

A long, sloping hillside, dotted with grey limestone boulders, stretched behind us. We had turned off the road, and were making our way up the hill, when, looking in the direction of Holdernesse Hall, I saw a cyclist coming swiftly along.

"Get down, Watson!" cried Holmes, with a heavy hand upon my shoulder. We had hardly sunk from view when the man flew past us on the road. Amid a rolling cloud of dust, I caught a glimpse of a pale, agitated face—a face with horror in every lineament, the mouth open, the eyes staring wildly in front. It was like some strange caricature of the dapper James Wilder whom we had seen the night before.

"The Duke's secretary!" cried Holmes. "Come, Watson, let us see what he does."

We scrambled from rock to rock, until in a few moments we had made our way to a point from which we could see the front door of the inn. Wilder's bicycle was leaning against the wall beside it. No one was moving about the house, nor could we

37 Curiously, the manuscript reads, "Two men in the dogcart, so far as I could see. Wilder and Hayes—a curious couple to run together." Is this evidence of Holmes's failing vision? He obviously corrected himself when he turned and saw Wilder behind him.

"The man flew past us on the road."
Sidney Paget, *Strand Magazine*, 1904

catch a glimpse of any faces at the windows. Slowly the twilight crept down as the sun sank behind the high towers of Holdernesse Hall. Then, in the gloom, we saw the two side-lamps of a trap light up in the stable-yard of the inn, and shortly afterwards heard the rattle of hoofs, as it wheeled out into the road and tore off at a furious pace in the direction of Chesterfield.

"What do you make of that, Watson?" Holmes whispered.

"It looks like a flight."

"A single man in a dog-cart, so far as I could see.[37] Well, it certainly was not Mr. James Wilder, for there he is at the door."

A red square of light had sprung out of the darkness. In the middle of it was the black figure of the secretary, his head advanced, peering out into the night. It was evident that he was expecting someone. Then at last there were steps in the road, a second figure was visible for an instant against the light, the door shut, and all was black once more. Five minutes later a lamp was lit in a room upon the first floor.

"It seems to be a curious class of custom that is done by the 'Fighting Cock'," said Holmes.

"The bar is on the other side."

"Quite so. These are what one may call the private guests. Now, what in the world is Mr. James Wilder doing in that den at this hour of night, and who is the companion who comes to meet him there? Come, Watson, we must really take a risk and try to investigate this a little more closely."

Together we stole down to the road and crept across to the door of the inn. The bicycle still leaned against the wall. Holmes struck a match and held it to the back wheel,[38] and I heard him chuckle as the light fell upon a patched Dunlop tyre. Up above us was the lighted window.

"I must have a peep through that, Watson. If you bend your back and support yourself upon the wall, I think that I can manage."

An instant later, his feet were on my shoulders, but he was hardly up before he was down again.

"Come, my friend," said he, "our day's work has been quite long enough. I think that we have gathered all that we can. It's a long walk to the school, and the sooner we get started the better."

He hardly opened his lips during that weary trudge across the moor, nor would he enter the school when he reached it, but went on to Mackleton Station, whence he could send some telegrams. Late at night I heard him consoling Dr. Huxtable, prostrated by the tragedy of his master's death, and later still he entered my room as alert and vigorous as he had been when he started in the morning. "All goes well, my friend," said he. "I promise that before to-morrow evening we shall have reached the solution of the mystery."

At eleven o'clock next morning my friend and I were walking up the famous yew avenue of Holdernesse Hall. We were ushered through the magnificent Elizabethan doorway and

38 Watson apparently concluded that a struck match was more dramatic, for the manuscript reads, "The lamp still gleamed from the bicycle. Holmes slipped it off, and turned it towards the machine. I heard him chuckle in the darkness as the narrow tunnel of vivid light fell upon the patch of a Dunlop tyre."

"I heard him chuckle as the light fell upon a
patched Dunlop tyre."
Sidney Paget, *Strand Magazine*, 1904

into his Grace's study. There we found Mr. James Wilder,
demure and courtly, but with some trace of that wild terror of
the night before still lurking in his furtive eyes and in his
twitching features.

"You have come to see his Grace? I am sorry; but the fact is
that the Duke is far from well. He has been very much upset
by the tragic news. We received a telegram from Dr. Huxtable
yesterday afternoon, which told us of your discovery."

"I must see the Duke, Mr. Wilder."

"But he is in his room."

"Then I must go to his room."

"I believe he is in his bed."

"I will see him there."

Holmes's cold and inexorable manner showed the secretary that it was useless to argue with him.

"Very good, Mr. Holmes, I will tell him that you are here."

After half an hour's delay, the great nobleman appeared. His face was more cadaverous than ever, his shoulders had rounded, and he seemed to me to be an altogether older man than he had been the morning before. He greeted us with a stately courtesy and seated himself at his desk, his red beard streaming down on the table.

"Well, Mr. Holmes?" said he.

An instant later, his feet were on my shoulder.
Charles Raymond Macaulay, *Return of Sherlock Holmes*
(McClure Phillips), 1905

39 Holmes meant that the duke should write the name of his banking company across the face of the cheque between two lines provided for that purpose, thereby limiting deposit to the particular bank (similar to a limiting endorsement).

40 This was also the bank of Neville St. Clair ("The Man with the Twisted Lip") and Arthur Cadogan West ("The Bruce-Partington Plans"), as well as that of Arthur Conan Doyle. In 1918 it merged into Lloyds Bank, now Lloyds TSB Bank.

But my friend's eyes were fixed upon the secretary, who stood by his master's chair.

"I think, your Grace, that I could speak more freely in Mr. Wilder's absence."

The man turned a shade paler and cast a malignant glance at Holmes.

"If your Grace wishes—"

"Yes, yes; you had better go. Now, Mr. Holmes, what have you to say?"

My friend waited until the door had closed behind the retreating secretary.

"The fact is, your Grace," said he, "that my colleague, Dr. Watson, and myself had an assurance from Dr. Huxtable that a reward had been offered in this case. I should like to have this confirmed from your own lips."

"Certainly, Mr. Holmes."

"It amounted, if I am correctly informed, to five thousand pounds to anyone who will tell you where your son is?"

"Exactly."

"And another thousand to the man who will name the person or persons who keep him in custody?"

"Exactly."

"Under the latter heading is included, no doubt, not only those who may have taken him away, but also those who conspire to keep him in his present position?"

"Yes, yes," cried the Duke, impatiently. "If you do your work well, Mr. Sherlock Holmes, you will have no reason to complain of niggardly treatment."

My friend rubbed his thin hands together with an appearance of avidity which was a surprise to me, who knew his frugal tastes.

"I fancy that I see your Grace's cheque-book upon the table," said he. "I should be glad if you would make me out a cheque for six thousand pounds. It would be as well, perhaps, for you to cross it.[39] The Capital and Counties Bank, Oxford Street branch[40] are my agents."

His Grace sat very stern and upright in his chair and looked stonily at my friend.

"Is this a joke, Mr. Holmes? It is hardly a subject for pleasantry."

"Not at all, your Grace. I was never more earnest in my life."

"What do you mean, then?"

"I mean that I have earned the reward. I know where your son is, and I know some, at least, of those who are holding him."

The Duke's beard had turned more aggressively red than ever against his ghastly white face.

"Where is he?" he gasped.

"He is, or was last night, at the Fighting Cock Inn, about two miles from your park gate."

The Duke fell back in his chair.

"And whom do you accuse?"

Sherlock Holmes's answer was an astounding one. He stepped swiftly forward and touched the Duke upon the shoulder.

"I accuse *you*," said he. "And now, your Grace, I'll trouble you for that cheque."

Never shall I forget the Duke's appearance as he sprang up and clawed with his hand, like one who is sinking into an abyss. Then, with an extraordinary effort of aristocratic self-command, he sat down and sank his face in his hands. It was some minutes before he spoke.

"How much do you know?" he asked at last, without raising his head.

"I saw you together last night."

"Does anyone else beside your friend know?"

"I have spoken to no one."

The Duke took a pen in his quivering fingers and opened his cheque-book.

"I shall be as good as my word, Mr. Holmes. I am about to write your cheque, however unwelcome the information which you have gained may be to me. When the offer was first made I little thought the turn which events might take. But you and your friend are men of discretion, Mr. Holmes?"

"I hardly understand your Grace."

"I must put it plainly, Mr. Holmes. If only you two know of the incident, there is no reason why it should go any farther. I think twelve thousand pounds[41] is the sum that I owe you, is it not?"

But Holmes smiled and shook his head.

"I fear, your Grace, that matters can hardly be arranged so easily. There is the death of this schoolmaster to be accounted for."

41 Why £12,000 and not the previously mentioned £6,000? T. S. Blakeney suggests that the duke might have felt Watson deserved a reward as well, whereas most other commentators regard this view as naive and argue that the duke intended to bribe Holmes into silence.

42 Most American statutes and, until 1957, British law proscribed "felony murder," a killing committed while a felony or "serious crime of violence" is being perpetrated. Because Wilder was clearly an accessory to the felony, he would be guilty of the murder as well.

"But James knew nothing of that. You cannot hold him responsible for that. It was the work of this brutal ruffian whom he had the misfortune to employ."

"I must take the view, your Grace, that when a man embarks upon a crime, he is morally guilty of any other crime which may spring from it."

"Morally, Mr. Holmes. No doubt you are right. But surely not in the eyes of the law. A man cannot be condemned for a murder at which he was not present,[42] and which he loathes and abhors as much as you do. The instant that he heard of it he made a complete confession to me, so filled was he with horror and remorse. He lost not an hour in breaking entirely with the murderer. Oh, Mr. Holmes, you must save him—you must save him! I tell you that you must save him!" The Duke had dropped the last attempt at self-command, and was pacing the room with a convulsed face and with his clenched hands raving in the air. At last he mastered himself and sat down once more at his desk. "I appreciate your conduct in coming here before you spoke to anyone else," said he. "At least we may take counsel how far we can minimize this hideous scandal."

"Exactly," said Holmes. "I think, your Grace, that this can only be done by absolute frankness between us. I am disposed to help your Grace to the best of my ability; but, in order to do so, I must understand to the last detail how the matter stands. I realize that your words applied to Mr. James Wilder, and that he is not the murderer."

"No; the murderer has escaped."

Sherlock Holmes smiled demurely.

"Your Grace can hardly have heard of any small reputation which I possess, or you would not imagine that it is so easy to escape me. Mr. Reuben Hayes was arrested at Chesterfield on my information at eleven o'clock last night. I had a telegram from the head of the local police before I left the school this morning."

The Duke leaned back in his chair and stared with amazement at my friend.

"You seem to have powers that are hardly human," said he. "So Reuben Hayes is taken? I am right glad to hear it, if it will not react upon the fate of James."

"Your secretary?"

"No, sir; my son."

"The murderer has escaped."
Sidney Paget, *Strand Magazine*, 1904

It was Holmes's turn to look astonished.

"I confess that this is entirely new to me, your Grace. I must beg you to be more explicit."

"I will conceal nothing from you. I agree with you that complete frankness, however painful it may be to me, is the best policy in this desperate situation to which James's folly and jealousy have reduced us. When I was a very young man, Mr. Holmes, I loved with such a love as comes only once in a lifetime. I offered the lady marriage, but she refused it on the grounds that such a match might mar my career. Had she lived, I would certainly never have married anyone else. She died, and left this one child, whom for her sake I have cherished and cared for. I could not acknowledge the paternity to the world, but I gave him the best of educations, and since he came to manhood I have kept him near my person. He surprised my secret, and has presumed ever since upon the claim which he has upon me, and upon his power of provoking a scandal which would be abhorrent to me. His presence had something to do with the unhappy issue of my marriage. Above all, he hated my young legitimate heir from the first with a persistent hatred. You may well ask me why, under these circumstances, I still kept James under my roof. I answer that it was because I could see his mother's face in his, and that for her dear sake there was no end to my long-suffering. All her pretty ways, too—there was not one of them which he could not suggest and bring back to my memory. I *could* not send him away. But I feared so much lest he should do Arthur—that is, Lord Saltire—a mischief that I despatched him for safety to Dr. Huxtable's school.

"James came into contact with this fellow Hayes because the man was a tenant of mine, and James acted as agent. The fellow was a rascal from the beginning; but, in some extraordinary way, James became intimate with him. He had always a taste for low company. When James determined to kidnap Lord Saltire, it was of this man's service that he availed himself. You remember that I wrote to Arthur upon that last day. Well, James opened the letter and inserted a note asking Arthur to meet him in a little wood called the Ragged Shaw, which is near to the school. He used the Duchess's name, and in that way got the boy to come. That evening James cycled over—I am telling you what he has himself confessed to me—and he told Arthur, whom he met in the wood, that his mother longed to see him, that she was awaiting him on the moor, and that if he would come back into the wood at midnight he would find a man with a horse, who would take him to her. Poor Arthur fell into the trap. He came to the appointment and found this fellow Hayes with a led pony. Arthur mounted, and they set off together. It appears—though this James only heard yesterday—that they were pursued, that Hayes struck the pursuer with his stick, and that the man died of his injuries. Hayes brought Arthur to his public-house, the 'Fighting Cock,' where he was confined in an upper room, under the care of Mrs.

Hayes, who is a kindly woman, but entirely under the control of her brutal husband.

"Well, Mr. Holmes, that was the state of affairs when I first saw you two days ago. I had no more idea of the truth than you. You will ask me what was James's motive in doing such a deed. I answer that there was a great deal which was unreasoning and fanatical in the hatred which he bore my heir. In his view he should himself have been heir of all my estates, and he deeply resented those social laws which made it impossible.[43] At the same time, he had a definite motive also. He was eager that I should break the entail,[44] and he was of opinion that it lay in my power to do so. He intended to make a bargain with me—to restore Arthur if I would break the entail, and so make it possible for the estate to be left to him by will. He knew well that I should never willingly invoke the aid of the police against him. I say that he would have proposed such a bargain to me; but he did not actually do so, for events moved too quickly for him, and he had not time to put his plans into practice.

"What brought all his wicked scheme to wreck was your discovery of this man Heidegger's dead body. James was seized with horror at the news. It came to us yesterday, as we sat together in this study. Dr. Huxtable had sent a telegram. James was so overwhelmed with grief and agitation that my suspicions, which had never been entirely absent, rose instantly to a certainty, and I taxed him with the deed.[45] He made a complete voluntary confession.[46] Then he implored me to keep his secret for three days longer, so as to give his wretched accomplice a chance of saving his guilty life. I yielded—as I have always yielded—to his prayers, and instantly James hurried off to the 'Fighting Cock' to warn Hayes and give him the means of flight. I could not go there by daylight without provoking comment, but as soon as night fell I hurried off to see my dear Arthur. I found him safe and well, but horrified beyond expression by the dreadful deed he had witnessed. In deference to my promise, and much against my will, I consented to leave him there for three days, under the charge of Mrs. Hayes, since it was evident that it was impossible to inform the police where he was without telling them also who was the murderer, and I could not see how that murderer could be punished without ruin to my unfortunate James. You asked for frankness, Mr.

43 Earlier, in a remark eventually cut by Watson from the manuscript, the duke remarks, "The estates are all entailed and he was aware that even if I wished I could not divert them from the direct succession."

44 A restricted course of descent or inheritance—for example, a restriction that property could only be left to the eldest child.

45 To "tax," in this sense, meaning to call to account or take to task, to accuse.

46 One may wonder how "voluntary" a confession may be said to be when one is "taxed . . . with the deed" by one's father.

47 One might argue that, no matter how persuasive the duke was, Reuben Hayes would believe it in his best interest not to keep quiet. As T. S. Blakeney observes, a man facing the gallows would be inclined to bring others down with him; in particular, the duke, whom Hayes disliked extremely, would certainly not escape unscathed. "We presume," writes Blakeney, "that the Crown so presented their case as to leave out all possible mention of the Duke, though one hardly sees how they could avoid bringing in Mr. Wilder's complicity in the abduction of Lord Saltire."

Holmes, and I have taken you at your word, for I have now told you everything without an attempt at circumlocution or concealment. Do you in your turn be as frank with me."

"I will," said Holmes. "In the first place, your Grace, I am bound to tell you that you have placed yourself in a most serious position in the eyes of the law. You have condoned a felony, and you have aided the escape of a murderer; for I cannot doubt that any money which was taken by James Wilder to aid his accomplice in his flight came from your Grace's purse."

The Duke bowed his assent.

"This is, indeed, a most serious matter. Even more culpable in my opinion, your Grace, is your attitude towards your younger son. You leave him in this den for three days."

"Under solemn promises—"

"What are promises to such people as these? You have no guarantee that he will not be spirited away again. To humour your guilty elder son you have exposed your innocent younger son to imminent and unnecessary danger. It was a most unjustifiable action."

The proud lord of Holdernesse was not accustomed to be so rated in his own ducal hall. The blood flushed into his high forehead, but his conscience held him dumb.

"I will help you, but on one condition only. It is that you ring for the footman and let me give such orders as I like."

Without a word, the Duke pressed the electric bell. A servant entered.

"You will be glad to hear," said Holmes, "that your young master is found. It is the Duke's desire that the carriage shall go at once to the Fighting Cock Inn to bring Lord Saltire home.

"Now," said Holmes, when the rejoicing lackey had disappeared, "having secured the future, we can afford to be more lenient with the past. I am not in an official position, and there is no reason, so long as the ends of justice are served, why I should disclose all that I know. As to Hayes, I say nothing. The gallows awaits him, and I would do nothing to save him from it. What he will divulge I cannot tell, but I have no doubt that your Grace could make him understand that it is to his interest to be silent.[47] From the police point of view he will have kidnapped the boy for the purpose of ransom. If they do not themselves find it out, I see no reason why I should prompt them to take a broader point of view. I would warn your Grace, however, that the continued presence of Mr. James Wilder in your household can only lead to misfortune."

"I understand that, Mr. Holmes, and it is already settled that he shall leave me forever, and go to seek his fortune in Australia."

"In that case, your Grace, since you have yourself stated that any unhappiness in your married life was caused by his presence, I would suggest that you make such amends as you can to the Duchess, and that you try to resume those relations which have been so unhappily interrupted."

"That also I have arranged, Mr. Holmes. I wrote to the Duchess this morning."

"In that case," said Holmes, rising, "I think that my friend and I can congratulate ourselves upon several most happy results from our little visit to the North. There is one other small point upon which I desire some light. This fellow Hayes had shod his horses with shoes which counterfeited the tracks of cows. Was it from Mr. Wilder that he learned so extraordinary a device?"

The Duke stood in thought for a moment, with a look of intense surprise on his face. Then he opened a door and showed us into a large room furnished as a museum. He led the way to a glass case in a corner, and pointed to the inscription.

"These shoes," it ran, "were dug up in the moat of Holdernesse Hall. They are for the use of horses, but they are shaped below with a cloven foot of iron,[48] so as to throw pursuers off the track. They are supposed to have belonged to some of the marauding Barons of Holdernesse in the Middle Ages."

Holmes opened the case, and moistening his finger he passed it along the shoe. A thin film of recent mud was left upon his skin.

"Thank you," said he, as he replaced the glass. "It is the second most interesting object that I have seen in the North."

"And the first?"

Holmes folded up his cheque, and placed it carefully in his notebook. "I am a poor man,"[49] said he, as he patted it affectionately, and thrust it into the depths of his inner pocket. ∎

48 In the "Curiosities" section of the *Strand Magazine* in May 1903, accompanying a photograph, appeared: "These false horseshoes were found in the moat at Birtsmorton Court, near Tewkesbury. It is supposed that they were used in the time of the Civil Wars, so as to deceive any person tracking the marks. The one on the left is supposed to leave the mark of a cow's hoof, the one on the right that of a child's foot."

49 D. Martin Dakin expresses the view that Holmes's statement here is made sarcastically—"in contrast with the enormous wealth of the duke"—because "The Adventure of the Priory School" occurs near the end of Holmes's career, by which time the detective had prospered financially.

THE DUKE OF HOLDERNESSE

WATSON'S attempts to conceal the Duke of Holdernesse's real identity are deemed "somewhat clumsy" by Michael Harrison, who points out in his *In the Footsteps of Sherlock Holmes* that the dukes of Norfolk similarly owned a great deal of land in the north of England (in Sheffield) and that Watson's description of the Duke of Holdernesse, with his "long, dwindling beard of vivid red," calls to mind the Duke of Norfolk who served as postmaster-general toward the end of the Victorian era.

Several other scholars seek to pierce the veil of the duke's identity, though they come to different conclusions than does Harrison. Julian Wolff, in his *Practical Handbook of Sherlockian Heraldry*, proposes that the duke could have been a member of the Neville family, whose coat of arms features a saltire (a cross honoring St. Andrew), which in turn may have given Watson the idea to name the duke's son Lord Saltire; yet several other inconsistencies lead Wolff ultimately to discard the Neville family in favor of Spencer Compton Cavendish, the 8th Duke of Devonshire, K.G., P.C. (1833–1908). Among several other points of comparison, the Duke of Devonshire's residence, Hardwick Hall, appears to match up well with Holdernesse Hall.

While T. H. B. Symons concurs that the 8th Duke of Devonshire seems a likely choice, he notes that the character description provided by Watson does not seem to match that of the estimable political figure who was "courteous and honest" and who, despite being leading the Liberal opposition, enjoyed the favour of both Disraeli—who nicknamed the duke (who also bore the title of Marquis of Hartington) "Harty-Tarty"—and Queen Victoria. The Duke of Holdernesse, by contrast, is depicted by Watson as being cold and abrupt, wary of Holmes's assistance in the disappearance of his son. "Similarly," Symons continues, "it is difficult to recognize in Watson's duke, who went to pieces on learning of the murder of Herr Heidegger by Reuben Hayes, the great Devonshire who had in 1882 to cope with the wretched murder of his brother by Fenian assassins, and who had the firmness to insist that Gladstone send an army to the relief of General Gordon." Symons also looks at the figure of Lord Saltire, who appears to throw another wrench into the equation. According to Symons, the Duke of Devonshire had a son, the 9th Duke of Devonshire, who was born in 1868 and would have been around thirty-three years old at the time of "The Priory School"—not ten years old. ("The Priory School" is thought to have occurred in 1901. Looking at it in the reverse manner, Symons points out that the 9th Duke became governor-general of Canada in 1916, at which point Lord Saltire would have been only twenty-five and hardly prepared to assume such an important post.) But Symons's grasp of the Cavendishes is a bit confused. Sir Victor Christian William Cavendish, the 9th Duke of Devonshire, was in fact the 8th Duke's *nephew*, the son of his younger brother, Lord Edward Cavendish (1838–1891). The 8th Duke himself actually had no children at all, and the title was passed down to his nephew upon the 8th Duke's death in 1908.

Richard Lancelyn Green notes that the 8th Duke of Devonshire was Lord Lieutenant of Derbyshire, a Lord of the Admiralty, and Secretary of State for India, a title given to the Duke of Holdernesse in the original manuscript version of "The Priory School." Bernard Davies points out that the only "Chief Secretary" title then extant was Chief Secretary of State for Ireland, a title also held by the 8th Duke of Devonshire. His detailed examination of the correlations between the *curriculum vitæ* of "Holdernesse" and "Devonshire" is compelling and seems to represent the consensus of opinion.

Nonetheless, there remains room for debate: Marshall S. Berdan, in "The Great Derbyshire Duke-Out," nominates the second Baron Newton, who, while lacking many of the requisite characteristics, fit Berdan's geographical conclusions. In short, it may be said that no single figure matches all of the geographical, political, and personal characteristics of "one of the greatest subjects of the Crown"—a testament to Watson's obfuscatory powers.

WHICH WAY DID THE BICYCLE TRAVEL?

CRUCIAL to Holmes's investigation of "The Priory School" is his deduction concerning the direction of travel of the fleeing bicycle, based solely on the tyre tracks. William S. Baring-Gould complains, "Much, perhaps too much, has been written about these tyre tracks." Holmes's deduction respecting the direction in which the bicycle was travelling is challenged by A. D. Galbraith in "The Real Moriarty," who, typical of the critics, says, "But it is clear that the tracks would look the same both ways, unless the tread had some lack of symmetry, or other peculiarity, and the manner of mounting it on the wheel were known."

But there are numerous defenders of the Master's conclusion. T. S. Blakeney points readers toward an article in a 1917 issue of the *Strand Magazine*, which states that the rear wheel of a bicycle would sink more deeply on an upward slope than a downward one. "In any case," writes Blakeney, covering his bases, "Holmes probably had a dozen other small indications to guide him; though he might mention only one factor, he usually had others in reserve as evidenced by the twenty-three additional points of difference in the joint letter of the Cunninghams ['The Reigate Squires']."

Even Arthur Conan Doyle, in his autobiography *Memories and Adventures*, comments on the problem: "I had so many remonstrances upon this point, varying from pity to anger, that I took out my bicycle and tried. I had imagined that the observations of the way in which the track of the hind wheel overlaid the track of the front one when the machine was not running dead straight would show the direction. I found that my correspondents were right and I was wrong, for this would be the same whichever way the cycle was moving. On the other hand the real solution was much simpler, for on an undulating moor the wheels make a much deeper impression uphill and a more shallow one downhill, so Holmes was justified of his wisdom after all."

Several writers suggest that the very nature of bicycle manufacture—with a stationary rear wheel and a mobile front wheel—necessarily produces distinct tracks. Others pursue Blakeney's notion that other indications would have guided the conclusion. For example, M. Haddon-MacRoberts conducted his own experiments, riding a bicycle through mud, on which he reports in "On Determining the Direction of Travel of a Bicycle from Its Tracks." He discovered that in order to keep upright, he had to make extensive side-to-side movements of the front wheel, leaving a track much as that described by Holmes. These tracks, he found, also allowed him to determine the direction of travel. Perhaps the most fascinating study is the discovery by Hirayama Yuichi (which he announces in "The More Deeply Sunk Impression") of a Japanese textbook written by Sanekita Masayoshi, published in 1940, entitled *Hanzai Sousa Gijuturon* (The Techniques of Crime Detection). Sanekita provides a detailed chapter on "How to Know the Direction from Wheel Impressions," with seven concrete indicators.

Peter Coleman, in "Sherlock Holmes and the Bicycle," reports on his own experiments, riding a bicycle over good ground and difficult ground. He observed that on more difficult terrain, the front wheel had to be turned more to stay erect and left distinctive tracks. If one could distinguish front tracks from rear, one could form an opinion about the direction of travel. He concludes that "when writing the adventure for publication Watson decided that a complicated explanation would interrupt the flow of his narrative and he settled for a more simplified version. This has proved unfortunate for Holmes's reputation as some sceptics have tended to dismiss his claims regarding bicycle tracks."

The most authoritative word is from the mathematical text *Which Way Did the Bicycle Go? . . . and Other Intriguing Mathematical Mysteries*, by Joseph D. E. Konhauser, Dan Velleman, and Stan Wagon. The authors provide an elegant solution involving analysis of tangent segments to the curving bicycle tracks, demonstrating that the direction can be determined purely from the shape of the curving tracks. As to Holmes's explanation: "Balderdash!" they write. "As observed by Dennis Thron (Dartmouth Medical School), it is true that the rear wheel would obliterate the track of the front wheel at the crossings, but this would be true no matter which direction the bicyclist was going. This information, by itself, does not solve the problem. We could, perhaps, give Holmes the benefit of the doubt and assume that he carried out the proper solution in his head. But we cannot believe that he would have expected Watson to grasp it from his comments alone."

THE ADVENTURE OF BLACK PETER[1]

It is hard to decide whether the criminal in "Black Peter" is worse than his victim. This tale of mistaken identity and murder begins with Holmes returning from the butcher's, where he has been busy mysteriously harpooning pigs. We follow Holmes to one of the few undisguised locations in the Canon, the Brambletye Hotel in Forest Row, which now sports a Black Peter Bar. There Holmes saves his client by clearing up a twelve-year-old mystery. Dr. Watson's account also includes tantalising references to two more unpublished cases, the "death of Cardinal Tosca" (explored by J. Regis O'Connor in The Sacred Seal, *1998), and "the notorious canary-trainer," revealed in* The Canary Trainer *by Nicholas Meyer (author of the highly successful* Seven-Per-Cent Solution, *1974) to be a story of Holmes and the Phantom of the Opera.*

1 "Black Peter" was published in *Collier's Weekly* on February 27, 1904, and in the *Strand Magazine* in March 1904.

2 A mere two years later, in "The Devil's Foot," Holmes seems a far different man than the one described here, as Ian McQueen observes in his *Sherlock Holmes Detected*. Although Holmes is not yet fifty years old, his doctor forces him in that case to vacation in Cornwall so as to rest and "avert a complete mental breakdown." One wonders whether Holmes's health takes a drastic downturn in the intervening two years, or whether Watson's observation here is misguided.

3 Watson refers to "The Priory School," published the previous month.

I HAVE NEVER known my friend to be in better form, both mental and physical, than in the year '95.[2] His increasing fame had brought with it an immense practice, and I should be guilty of an indiscretion if I were even to hint at the identity of some of the illustrious clients who crossed our humble threshold in Baker Street. Holmes, however, like all great artists, lived for his art's sake, and, save in the case of the Duke of Holdernesse,[3] I have seldom known him claim any large reward for his inestimable services. So unworldly was he—or so capricious—that he frequently refused his help to the powerful and wealthy where the problem made no appeal to his sympathies, while he would devote weeks of most intense application to the affairs of some humble client whose case presented those strange and dramatic qualities which appealed to his imagination and challenged his ingenuity.

In this memorable year '95, a curious and incongruous succession of cases had engaged his attention, ranging from his

Frederick Dorr Steele, *Collier's*, 1904

4 Cardinal "Tosca" is identified by Francis Albert Young as Cardinal Luigi Ruffo-Scilla, whose collapse and death at the age of fifty-five in Rome on May 29, 1895, came as a great surprise to many. A different churchman is suggested by Mark E. Levitt, namely, the Monsignor Isidoro Carini, who was a significant part of the effort to bring the church and the Italian government to a *rapprochement* in the 1890s and who died in 1895 in a "sudden and mysterious" way (according to the *London Times* of February 1, 1895).

5 Leo XIII was elected pope on February 20, 1878, and held the office until his death on July 20, 1903. An intellectual devoted to the philosophy of St. Thomas Aquinas, Leo XIII insisted that there was no conflict between faith and scientific advancement, and his papacy was marked by a new spirit of openness between the church and the rest of the world. In *The Hound of the Baskervilles*, Holmes obliged the same pope in connection with "that little affair of the Vatican cameos."

6 The meaning of Watson's allusion here is murky. According to E. Cobham Brewer's *Dictionary of Phrase and Fable*, a canary can be slang for a guinea or sovereign—gold coins are yellow in colour. So, too, does the dictionary list "canary-bird" as a convict: Certain "desperate" prisoners once wore yellow uniforms, and the jail was considered their cage. Donald A. Redmond adds that "The Old Canaries" was the nickname given to the Third Dragoon Guards, after their yellow facings (although there were no Third Dragoon officers named Wilson). Redmond continues that "canary" could be taken to mean any soldier sporting a yellow armband, or "an instructor at a gas school, or one of the Sanitary Corps of the R.A.M.C.; battalion Sanitary Orderlies.' "

Some dismiss the idea that the "canary" of Wilson's infamy is anything but a bird. "There is absolutely nothing whatsoever in any way,

famous investigation of the sudden death of Cardinal Tosca[4]—an inquiry which was carried out by him at the express desire of his Holiness the Pope[5]—down to his arrest of Wilson, the notorious canary-trainer,[6] which removed a plague-spot from the East End of London. Close on the heels of these two famous cases came the tragedy of Woodman's Lee,[7] and the very obscure circumstances which surrounded the death of Captain Peter Carey. No record of the doings of Mr. Sherlock Holmes would be complete which did not include some account of this very unusual affair.

During the first week of July my friend had been absent so often and so long from our lodgings that I knew he had something on hand. The fact that several rough-looking men called during that time and inquired for Captain Basil made me understand that Holmes was working somewhere under one of the numerous disguises and names with which he concealed his own formidable identity.[8] He had at least five small

shape, or form notorious about canaries," declares "Red" Smith in "The Nefarious Holmes." "However, a bird trainer can branch out, as Hirsch Jacobs has demonstrated in our day; Mr. Jacobs began with pigeons and went on to become America's leading horse-trainer in eleven of twelve consecutive years. It stands to reason that Holmes's man, Wilson, followed a similar course. . . ."

Numerous contradictory theories abound. *New York Times* music critic Harold C. Schonberg, in "Sherlock and Malocchio!," argues that the case may have been connected with threats against the life of the famous soprano Adelina Patti. David Roberts proposes that Wilson was in the business of training informants, or "stool-pigeons." Carol Paul Woods suggests that Wilson was a trainer of prize-fighters, and that he and his fighter protégé hailed from the Canary Islands.

7 "Woodman's Lee" is generally believed to be Coleman's Hatch, near Forest Row in Sussex.

8 Although there may be numerous unreported disguises, Watson records the following in addition to "Captain Basil": "a common loafer" ("The Beryl Coronet"), a rakish young plumber named Escott ("Charles Augustus Milverton"), a venerable Italian priest ("The Final Problem"), an elderly, deformed bibliophile ("The Empty House"), a French *ouvrier* ("The Disappearance of Lady Frances Carfax"), a workman looking for a job, described as "an old sporting man" ("The Mazarin Stone"), an old woman ("The Mazarin Stone"), a "drunken-looking groom" ("A Scandal in Bohemia"), an "amiable and simple-minded" Nonconformist clergyman ("A Scandal in Bohemia"), a sailor (*The Sign of Four*), an asthmatic old master mariner (*The Sign of Four*), a doddering opium smoker ("The Man with the Twisted Lip"), Mr. Harris, an accountant ("The Stock-Broker's

refuges[9] in different parts of London in which he was able to change his personality. He said nothing of his business to me, and it was not my habit to force a confidence. The first positive sign which he gave me of the direction which his investigation was taking was an extraordinary one. He had gone out before breakfast,[10] and I had sat down to mine, when he strode into the room, his hat upon his head and a huge, barbed-headed spear tucked like an umbrella under his arm.

"Good gracious, Holmes!" I cried. "You don't mean to say that you have been walking about London with that thing?"

"I drove to the butcher's and back."

"The butcher's?"

"And I return with an excellent appetite. There can be no question, my dear Watson, of the value of exercise before

" 'Good gracious, Holmes!' I cried. 'You don't mean to say that you have been walking about London with that thing?' "
Sidney Paget, *Strand Magazine*, 1904

breakfast. But I am prepared to bet that you will not guess the form that my exercise has taken."

"I will not attempt it."

He chuckled as he poured out the coffee.

"If you could have looked into Allardyce's back shop you would have seen a dead pig swung from a hook in the ceiling, and a gentleman in his shirt-sleeves furiously stabbing at it with this weapon. I was that energetic person, and I have satisfied myself that by no exertion of my strength can I transfix the pig with a single blow. Perhaps you would care to try?"

"Not for worlds. But why were you doing this?"

"Because it seemed to me to have an indirect bearing upon the mystery of Woodman's Lee. Ah, Hopkins, I got your wire last night, and I have been expecting you. Come and join us."

Our visitor was an exceedingly alert man, thirty years of age, dressed in a quiet tweed suit, but retaining the erect bearing of one who was accustomed to official uniform. I recognised him at once as Stanley Hopkins, a young police inspector, for whose future Holmes had high hopes, while he in turn professed the admiration and respect of a pupil for the scientific methods of the famous amateur. Hopkins's brow was clouded and he sat down with an air of deep dejection.

"No, thank you, sir. I breakfasted before I came round. I spent the night in town, for I came up yesterday to report."

"And what had you to report?"

"Failure, sir—absolute failure."

"You have made no progress?"

"None."

"Dear me! I must have a look at the matter."

"I wish to heavens that you would, Mr. Holmes. It's my first big chance, and I am at my wit's end. For goodness' sake, come down and lend me a hand."

"Well, well, it just happens that I have already read all the available evidence, including the report of the inquest, with some care. By the way, what do you make of that tobacco-pouch, found on the scene of the crime? Is there no clue there?"

Hopkins looked surprised.

"It was the man's own pouch, sir. His initials were inside it. And it was of sealskin—and he an old sealer."

"But he had no pipe."

Clerk"), a registration agent ("The Crooked Man"), a Norwegian explorer named "Sigerson" ("The Empty House"), and an Irish-American spy named Altamont ("His Last Bow").

9 "The reference is tantalizing and obscure," Vincent Starrett writes in *The Private Life of Sherlock Holmes*. "The rooms of Mycroft Holmes, opposite the Diogenes Club, would certainly be one of them; but it would be satisfying to know the others. . . . It may be assumed that in all of his five refuges he stored the materials of deception, as well as quantities of shag tobacco."

10 This appears to be another example of Holmes's wildly erratic morning routine, examined in depth by Ian McQueen. In "The Engineer's Thumb," for example, Watson expects to discover Holmes taking his breakfast soon after seven o'clock.

"No, sir, we could find no pipe; indeed, he smoked very little, and yet he might have kept some tobacco for his friends."

"No doubt. I only mention it because if I had been handling the case I should have been inclined to make that the starting-point of my investigation. However, my friend, Dr. Watson, knows nothing of this matter, and I should be none the worse for hearing the sequence of events once more. Just give us some short sketch of the essentials."

Stanley Hopkins drew a slip of paper from his pocket.

"I have a few dates here which will give you the career of the dead man, Captain Peter Carey. He was born in '45—fifty years of age. He was a most daring and successful seal and whale fisher. In 1883 he commanded the steam sealer *Sea Unicorn*, of Dundee. He had then had several successful voyages in succession, and in the following year, 1884, he retired. After that he travelled for some years, and finally he bought a small place called Woodman's Lee, near Forest Row, in Sussex. There he has lived for six years, and there he died just a week ago to-day.

"There were some most singular points about the man. In ordinary life he was a strict Puritan—a silent, gloomy fellow. His household consisted of his wife, his daughter, aged twenty, and two female servants. These last were continually changing, for it was never a very cheery situation, and sometimes it became past all bearing. The man was an intermittent drunkard, and when he had the fit on him he was a perfect fiend. He has been known to drive his wife and daughter out of doors in the middle of the night and flog them through the park until the whole village outside the gates was aroused by their screams.

"He was summoned once for a savage assault upon the old vicar, who had called upon him to remonstrate with him upon his conduct. In short, Mr. Holmes, you would go far before you found a more dangerous man than Peter Carey, and I have heard that he bore the same character when he commanded his ship. He was known in the trade as Black Peter, and the name was given him, not only on account of his swarthy features and the colour of his huge beard, but for the humours which were the terror of all around him. I need not say that he was loathed and avoided by every one of his neighbours, and that I have not heard one single word of sorrow about his terrible end.

"You must have read in the account of the inquest about the

man's cabin, Mr. Holmes, but perhaps your friend here has not heard of it. He had built himself a wooden outhouse—he always called it 'the cabin'—a few hundred yards from his house, and it was here that he slept every night. It was a little, single-roomed hut, sixteen feet by ten. He kept the key in his pocket, made his own bed, cleaned it himself, and allowed no other foot to cross the threshold. There are small windows on each side, which were covered by curtains, and never opened. One of these windows was turned towards the high-road, and when the light burned in it at night the folk used to point it out to each other, and wonder what Black Peter was doing in there. That's the window, Mr. Holmes, which gave us one of the few bits of positive evidence that came out at the inquest.

"You remember that a stonemason, named Slater, walking from Forest Row about one o'clock in the morning—two days before the murder—stopped as he passed the grounds and looked at the square of light still shining among the trees. He swears that the shadow of a man's head turned sideways was clearly visible on the blind, and that this shadow was certainly not that of Peter Carey, whom he knew well. It was that of a bearded man, but the beard was short and bristled forward in a way very different from that of the captain. So he says, but he had been two hours in the public-house, and it is some distance from the road to the window. Besides, this refers to the Monday, and the crime was done upon the Wednesday.

"On the Tuesday Peter Carey was in one of his blackest moods, flushed with drink and as savage as a dangerous wild beast. He roamed about the house, and the women ran for it when they heard him coming. Late in the evening he went down to his own hut. About two o'clock the following morning, his daughter, who slept with her window open, heard a most fearful yell from that direction, but it was no unusual thing for him to bawl and shout when he was in drink, so no notice was taken. On rising at seven one of the maids noticed that the door of the hut was open, but so great was the terror which the man caused that it was midday before anyone would venture down to see what had become of him. Peeping into the open door, they saw a sight which sent them flying, with white faces, into the village. Within an hour I was on the spot, and had taken over the case.

"Well, I have fairly steady nerves, as you know, Mr. Holmes,

11 Brownish or tawny with streaks of other colour.

but I give you my word that I got a shake when I put my head into that little house. It was droning like a harmonium with the flies and bluebottles, and the floor and walls were like a slaughter-house. He had called it a cabin, and a cabin it was, sure enough, for you would have thought that you were in a ship. There was a bunk at one end, a sea-chest, maps and charts, a picture of the *Sea Unicorn*, a line of log-books on a shelf, all exactly as one would expect to find it in a captain's room. And there, in the middle of it was the man himself—his face twisted like a lost soul in torment, and his great brindled[11] beard stuck upwards in his agony. Right through his broad breast a steel harpoon had been driven, and it had sunk deep

"I got a shake when I put my head into that little house"
Charles Raymond Macaulay, *Return of Sherlock Holmes*
(McClure Phillips), 1905

He was pinned like a beetle on a card.
G. A. Dowling, *Portland Oregonian*, July 30, 1911

into the wood of the wall behind him. He was pinned like a beetle on a card. Of course, he was quite dead, and had been so from the instant that he had uttered that last yell of agony.

"I know your methods, sir, and I applied them. Before I permitted anything to be moved I examined most carefully the ground outside, and also the floor of the room. There were no footmarks."

"Meaning that you saw none?"

"I assure you, sir, that there were none."

"My good Hopkins, I have investigated many crimes, but I have never yet seen one which was committed by a flying creature. As long as the criminal remains upon two legs so long must there be some indentation, some abrasion, some trifling displacement which can be detected by the scientific searcher. It is incredible that this blood-bespattered room contained no

12 A stand containing decanters that in some fashion locks the decanters in place. Reference is made to what may be one on the premises of 221B Baker Street (in "A Scandal in Bohemia") as the "spirit-case."

13 Watson also smoked "ship's," as mentioned in *A Study in Scarlet*.

trace which could have aided us. I understand, however, from the inquest that there were some objects which you failed to overlook?"

The young inspector winced at my companion's ironical comments.

"I was a fool not to call you in at the time, Mr. Holmes. However, that's past praying for now. Yes, there were several objects in the room which called for special attention. One was the harpoon with which the deed was committed. It had been snatched down from a rack on the wall. Two others remained there, and there was a vacant place for the third. On the stock was engraved 'SS. *Sea Unicorn*, Dundee.' This seemed to establish that the crime had been done in a moment of fury, and that the murderer had seized the first weapon which came in his way. The fact that the crime was committed at two in the morning, and yet Peter Carey was fully dressed, suggested that he had an appointment with the murderer, which is borne out by the fact that a bottle of rum and two dirty glasses stood upon the table."

"Yes," said Holmes; "I think that both inferences are permissible. Was there any other spirit but rum in the room?"

"Yes, there was a tantalus[12] containing brandy and whisky on the sea-chest. It is of no importance to us, however, since the decanters were full and it had therefore not been used."

"For all that, its presence has some significance," said Holmes. "However, let us hear some more about the objects which do seem to you to bear upon the case."

"There was this tobacco-pouch upon the table."

"What part of the table?"

"It lay in the middle. It was of coarse sealskin—the straight-haired skin, with a leather thong to bind it. Inside was 'P. C.' on the flap. There was half an ounce of strong ship's tobacco[13] in it."

"Excellent! What more?"

Stanley Hopkins drew from his pocket a drab-covered notebook. The outside was rough and worn, the leaves discoloured. On the first page were written the initials "J. H. N." and the date "1883." Holmes laid it on the table and examined it in his minute way, while Hopkins and I gazed over each shoulder. On the second page were the printed letters "C. P. R.," and then came several sheets of numbers. Another heading was "Argen-

"Holmes examined it in his minute way."
Sidney Paget, *Strand Magazine*, 1904

14 This appears to be a misspelling (or Anglicisation) of São Paulo, the largest city in Brazil and the capital of the province of the same name. A boom in the cultivation of coffee in the 1880s brought the region economic prosperity, as well as a wave of European immigrants.

15 Established under terms of the agreement that brought British Columbia into the confederation in 1871, the privately owned Canadian Pacific Railway was North America's first transcontinental railroad. Construction on the main line, from Montreal to Port Moody (in Vancouver), was completed in 1885.

16 "The House" here refers to the London Stock Exchange. See "The Stock-Broker's Clerk," note 22.

tine," another "Costa Rica," and another "San Paulo,"[14] each with pages of signs and figures after it.

"What do you make of these?" asked Holmes.

"They appear to be lists of Stock Exchange securities. I thought that 'J. H. N.' were the initials of a broker, and that 'C. P. R.' may have been his client."

"Try Canadian Pacific Railway,"[15] said Holmes.

Stanley Hopkins swore between his teeth, and struck his thigh with his clenched hand.

"What a fool I have been!" he cried. "Of course it is as you say. Then 'J. H. N.' are the only initials we have to solve. I have already examined the old Stock Exchange lists, and I can find no one in 1883, either in the House[16] or among the outside brokers, whose initials correspond with these. Yet I feel that the clue is the most important one that I hold. You will admit, Mr. Holmes, that there is a possibility that these initials are those of the second person who was present—in other words, of the murderer. I would also urge that the introduction into the case of a document relating to large masses of valuable securities gives us for the first time some indication of a motive for the crime."

Sherlock Holmes's face showed that he was thoroughly taken aback by this new development.

"I must admit both your points," said he. "I confess that the notebook, which did not appear at the inquest, modifies any views which I may have formed. I had come to a theory of the crime in which I can find no place for this. Have you endeavoured to trace any of the securities here mentioned?"

"Inquiries are now being made at the offices, but I fear that the complete register of the stockholders of these South American concerns is in South America, and that some weeks must elapse before we can trace the shares." Holmes had been examining the cover of the notebook with his magnifying lens.

"Surely there is some discolouration here," said he.

"Yes, sir, it is a blood-stain. I told you that I picked the book off the floor."

"Was the blood-stain above or below?"

"On the side next the boards."

"Which proves, of course, that the book was dropped after the crime was committed."

"Exactly, Mr. Holmes. I appreciated that point, and I conjectured that it was dropped by the murderer in his hurried flight. It lay near the door."

"I suppose that none of these securities have been found among the property of the dead man?"

"No, sir."

"Have you any reason to suspect robbery?"

"No, sir. Nothing seemed to have been touched."

"Dear me, it is certainly a very interesting case. Then there was a knife, was there not?"

"A sheath-knife, still in its sheath. It lay at the feet of the dead man. Mrs. Carey has identified it as being her husband's property."

Holmes was lost in thought for some time.

"Well," said he, at last. "I suppose I shall have to come out and have a look at it."

Stanley Hopkins gave a cry of joy.

"Thank you, sir. That will, indeed, be a weight off my mind."

Holmes shook his finger at the Inspector.

"It would have been an easier task a week ago," said he. "But even now my visit may not be entirely fruitless. Watson, if you can spare the time, I should be very glad of your company. If you will call a four-wheeler, Hopkins, we shall be ready to start for Forest Row in a quarter of an hour."

Alighting at the small wayside station, we drove for some miles through the remains of widespread woods, which were once part of that great forest which for so long held the Saxon invaders at bay—the impenetrable "weald,"[17] for sixty years the bulwark of Britain. Vast sections of it have been cleared, for this is the seat of the first ironworks of the country, and the trees have been felled to smelt the ore. Now the richer fields of the North have absorbed the trade, and nothing save these ravaged groves and great scars in the earth show the work of the past. Here in a clearing upon the green slope of a hill, stood a long, low, stone house, approached by a curving drive running through the fields. Nearer the road, and surrounded on three sides by bushes, was a small outhouse, one window and the door facing in our direction. It was the scene of the murder.

Stanley Hopkins led us first to the house, where he introduced us to a haggard, grey-haired woman, the widow of the murdered man, whose gaunt and deep-lined face, with the furtive look of terror in the depths of her red-rimmed eyes, told of the years of hardship and ill-usage which she had endured. With her was her daughter, a pale, fair-haired girl, whose eyes blazed defiantly at us as she told us that she was glad that her father was dead, and that she blessed the hand which had struck him down. It was a terrible household that Black Peter Carey had made for himself, and it was with a sense of relief that we found ourselves in the sunlight again and making our way along a path which had been worn across the fields by the feet of the dead man.

The outhouse was the simplest of dwellings, wooden walled, shingle-roofed, one window beside the door, and one on the farther side. Stanley Hopkins drew the key from his

17 The ancient stretch of forest known as the Weald (from the Old English *wald*, or *weald*, meaning forest) is nearly forty miles wide and rests between the chalk hills of the North and South Downs. It was once part of the much larger forest of Andredsweald ("the wood or forest without habitations"). As Watson notes, the Weald was heavily forested and once served as a centre for the iron industry, but the area remains one of England's most wooded places.

pocket, and had stooped to the lock, when he paused with a look of attention and surprise upon his face.

"Someone has been tampering with it," he said. There could be no doubt of the fact. The woodwork was cut, and the scratches showed white through the paint, as if they had been that instant done. Holmes had been examining the window.

"Someone has tried to force this also. Whoever it was has failed to make his way in. He must have been a very poor burglar."

"This is a most extraordinary thing," said the Inspector, "I could swear that these marks were not here yesterday evening."

" 'Someone has been tampering with it,' he said."
Sidney Paget, *Strand Magazine*, 1904

"Some curious person from the village, perhaps," I suggested.

"Very unlikely. Few of them would dare to set foot in the grounds, far less try to force their way into the cabin. What do you think of it, Mr. Holmes?"

"I think that fortune is very kind to us."

"You mean that the person will come again?"

"It is very probable. He came expecting to find the door open. He tried to get in with the blade of a very small penknife.[18] He could not manage it. What would he do?"

"Come again next night with a more useful tool."

"So I should say. It will be our fault if we are not there to receive him. Meanwhile, let me see the inside of the cabin."

The traces of the tragedy had been removed, but the furniture of the little room still stood as it had been on the night of the crime. For two hours, with most intense concentration, Holmes examined every object in turn, but his face showed that his quest was not a successful one. Once only he paused in his patient investigation.

"Have you taken anything off this shelf, Hopkins?"

"No, I have moved nothing."

"Something has been taken. There is less dust in this corner of the shelf than elsewhere. It may have been a book lying on its side. It may have been a box. Well, well, I can do nothing more. Let us walk in these beautiful woods, Watson, and give a few hours to the birds and the flowers.[19] We shall meet you here later, Hopkins, and see if we can come to closer quarters with the gentleman who has paid this visit in the night."

It was past eleven o'clock when we formed our little ambuscade. Hopkins was for leaving the door of the hut open, but Holmes was of the opinion that this would rouse the suspicions of the stranger. The lock was a perfectly simple one, and only a strong blade was needed to push it back. Holmes also suggested that we should wait, not inside the hut, but outside it, among the bushes which grew round the farther window. In this way we should be able to watch our man if he struck a light, and see what his object was in this stealthy nocturnal visit.

It was a long and melancholy vigil, and yet brought with it something of the thrill which the hunter feels when he lies beside the water-pool, and waits for the coming of the thirsty

18 The manuscript originally continued, "He has left half of it, which you would do well to secure, in the slit of the sash of . . ." The evidence turned out to be meaningless, perhaps explaining why Watson suppressed this false clue.

19 Contrast this action with Watson's obviously erroneous statement in "The Cardboard Box": "Appreciation of nature found no place among his many gifts, and his only change was when he turned his mind from the evil-doer of the town to track down his brother of the country."

20 Obviously Watson is thinking of Colonel Sebastian Moran, the big-game hunter captured on a similar nighttime vigil in "The Empty House" and described with similar metaphors. ("This empty house is my tree," Holmes says to him, "and you are my tiger.")

21 Curiously, in the manuscript and in the *Collier's Weekly* version, the time is given as "three o'clock."

22 A loose pleated coat with a waistband.

23 "Knickerbockers," knee-length breeches, were worn by sportsmen. The short pants got their name from George Cruikshank's illustrations in Washington Irving's *A History of New York from the Beginning of the World to the End of the Dutch Dynasty* (1809), whose fictional author was named Diedrich Knickerbocker. In the book, Dutch people were pictured wearing loose-fitting breeches that stopped at the knee. Eventually, "knickerbocker" also came to mean anyone of Dutch origin.

According to Holmes's later comments, the young nocturnal visitor did in fact play golf, hence his wearing of knickerbockers; or else he obtained the outfit to complete his disguise.

Golfers at their sport.

beast of prey. What savage creature was it which might steal upon us out of the darkness? Was it a fierce tiger of crime, which could only be taken fighting hard with flashing fang and claw,[20] or would it prove to be some skulking jackal, dangerous only to the weak and unguarded?

In absolute silence we crouched amongst the bushes, waiting for whatever might come. At first the steps of a few belated villagers, or the sound of voices from the village, lightened our vigil, but one by one these interruptions died away, and an absolute stillness fell upon us, save for the chimes of the distant church, which told us of the progress of the night, and for the rustle and whisper of a fine rain falling amid the foliage which roofed us in.

Half-past two had chimed,[21] and it was the darkest hour which precedes the dawn, when we all started as a low but sharp click came from the direction of the gate. Someone had entered the drive. Again there was a long silence, and I had begun to fear that it was a false alarm, when a stealthy step was heard upon the other side of the hut, and a moment later a metallic scraping and clinking. The man was trying to force the lock! This time his skill was greater or his tool was better, for there was a sudden snap and the creak of the hinges. Then a match was struck, and next instant the steady light from a candle filled the interior of the hut. Through the gauze curtain our eyes were all riveted upon the scene within.

The nocturnal visitor was a young man, frail and thin, with a black moustache, which intensified the deadly pallor of his face. He could not have been much above twenty years of age. I have never seen any human being who appeared to be in such a pitiable fright, for his teeth were visibly chattering, and he was shaking in every limb. He was dressed like a gentleman, in Norfolk jacket[22] and knickerbocker,[23] with a cloth cap upon his head. We watched him staring round with frightened eyes. Then he laid the candle-end upon the table and disappeared from our view into one of the corners. He returned with a large book, one of the log-books which formed a line upon the shelves. Leaning on the table, he rapidly turned over the leaves of this volume until he came to the entry which he sought. Then, with an angry gesture of his clenched hand, he closed the book, replaced it in the corner, and put out the light. He had hardly turned to leave the hut when Hopkins's hand

We watched him. . . . He returned with a large book.
Frederick Dorr Steele, *Collier's*, 1904

was on the fellow's collar, and I heard his loud gasp of terror as he understood that he was taken. The candle was relit, and there was our wretched captive, shivering and cowering in the grasp of the detective. He sank down upon the sea-chest, and looked helplessly from one of us to the other.

"Now, my fine fellow," said Stanley Hopkins, "who are you, and what do you want here?"

The man pulled himself together, and faced us with an effort at self-composure.

"You are detectives, I suppose?" said he. "You imagine I am connected with the death of Captain Peter Carey. I assure you that I am innocent."

"We'll see about that," said Hopkins. "First of all, what is your name?"

"It is John Hopley Neligan."

I saw Holmes and Hopkins exchange a quick glance.

"What are you doing here?"

"Can I speak confidentially?"

"No, certainly not."

"Why should I tell you?"

"If you have no answer, it may go badly with you at the trial."

The young man winced.

"Well, I will tell you," he said. "Why should I not? And yet I hate to think of this old scandal gaining a new lease of life. Did you ever hear of Dawson & Neligan?"

"He rapidly turned over the leaves of this volume."
Sidney Paget, *Strand Magazine*, 1904

I could see, from Hopkins's face, that he never had; but Holmes was keenly interested.

"You mean the West Country bankers," said he. "They failed for a million, ruined half the county families of Cornwall, and Neligan disappeared."

"Exactly. Neligan was my father."

At last we were getting something positive, and yet it seemed a long gap between an absconding banker and Captain Peter Carey pinned against the wall with one of his own harpoons. We all listened intently to the young man's words.

"It was my father who was really concerned. Dawson had retired. I was only ten years of age at the time, but I was old enough to feel the shame and horror of it all. It has always been said that my father stole all the securities and fled. It is not true. It was his belief that if he were given time in which to realize them, all would be well and every creditor paid in full. He started in his little yacht for Norway just before the warrant was issued for his arrest. I can remember that last night, when he bade farewell to my mother. He left us a list of the securities he was taking, and he swore that he would come back with his honour cleared, and that none who had trusted him would suffer. Well, no word was ever heard from him again. Both the yacht and he vanished utterly. We believed, my mother and I, that he and it, with the securities that he had taken with him, were at the bottom of the sea. We had a faithful friend, how-

"He sank down upon the sea-chest, and looked helplessly from one of us to the other."
Sidney Paget, *Strand Magazine*, 1904

24 Humfrey Michell, in a "Letter to Baker Street," questions why the banker's son should have been so involved in—and so distraught over—tracking down the missing securities. Under English law, normally a person would have been appointed by the courts to handle such matters in the course of the bankruptcy. "It would have been a simple matter for him [the bankruptcy 'receiver'] to obtain the record of the missing securities from the family," explains Michell, "and take the appropriate steps to obtain title to them for the benefit of the creditors. The only explanation I can think of, and I admit it is very improbable, is that young Neligan was a liar and was after something else than share certificates. If so, he was a very successful one, because he bamboozled Sherlock Holmes." Indeed, in modern commerce, someone who has had securities stolen need only post a bond and may have the securities replaced. This is not so, however, if the securities are bearer securities, that is, not issued to a named owner.

ever, who is a business man, and it was he who discovered some time ago that some of the securities which my father had with him have reappeared on the London market. You can imagine our amazement. I spent months in trying to trace them, and at last, after many doubtings and difficulties, I discovered that the original seller had been Captain Peter Carey, the owner of this hut.[24]

"Naturally I made some inquiries about the man. I found that he had been in command of a whaler which was due to return from the Arctic seas at the very time when my father was crossing to Norway. The autumn of that year was a stormy one, and there was a long succession of southerly gales. My father's yacht may well have been blown to the north, and there met by Captain Peter Carey's ship. If that were so, what had become of my father? In any case, if I could prove from Peter Carey's evidence how these securities came on the market it would be a proof that my father had not sold them, and that he had no view to personal profit when he took them.

"I came down to Sussex with the intention of seeing the captain, but it was at this moment that his terrible death occurred. I read at the inquest a description of his cabin, in which it stated that the old logbooks of his vessel were preserved in it. It struck me that if I could see what occurred in the month of August, 1883, on board the *Sea Unicorn*, I might settle the mystery of my father's fate. I tried last night to get at these logbooks, but was unable to open the door. To-night I tried again and succeeded; but I find that the pages which deal with that month have been torn from the book. It was at that moment I found myself a prisoner in your hands."

"Is that all?" asked Hopkins.

"Yes, that is all." His eyes shifted as he said it.

"You have nothing else to tell us?"

He hesitated.

"No, there is nothing."

"You have not been here before last night?"

"No."

"Then how do you account for *that?*" cried Hopkins, as he held up the damning notebook, with the initials of our prisoner on the first leaf, and the blood-stain on the cover.

The wretched man collapsed. He sank his face in his hands and trembled all over.

"Where did you get it?" he groaned. "I did not know. I thought I had lost it at the hotel."

"That is enough," said Hopkins sternly. "Whatever else you have to say, you must say in court. You will walk down with me now to the police-station. Well, Mr. Holmes, I am very much obliged to you and to your friend for coming down to help me. As it turns out your presence was unnecessary, and I would have brought the case to this successful issue without you; but none the less, I am grateful. Rooms have been reserved for you at the Brambletye Hotel,[25] so we can all walk down walk down to the village together."

"Well, Watson, what do you think of it?" asked Holmes, as we travelled back next morning.

"I can see that you are not satisfied."

"Oh, yes, my dear Watson, I am perfectly satisfied. At the same time, Stanley Hopkins's methods do not commend them-

25 David L. Hammer, in *The Game is Afoot*, writes that the Brambletye Hotel "probably takes its name from the establishment mentioned in *Black Peter* rather than the other way around." The hotel features the Black Peter Bar.

"Then how do you account for that?" cried Hopkins.
Frederick Dorr Steele, *Collier's*, 1904

26 The "Ratcliff Highway Murders" are one of a number of topics on which Holmes extemporaneously spoke to Watson in *A Study in Scarlet*. These gruesome crimes were described by Thomas De Quincey in his seminal essay *On Murder Considered as One of the Fine Arts* (1827).

Ratcliff Highway, a thoroughfare running parallel to the Thames, was a bustling hub of shops, lodging houses, and saloons catering to sailors and others involved in the shipping trade. Montagu Williams, writing in *Round London: Down East and Up West* (1894) about the street's rough-and-tumble reputation in the 1860s, disdainfully called this section of town "a terrible disgrace to London. . . . [I]t would have been madness for any respectable woman, or, for the matter of that, for any well-dressed man, to proceed thither alone. The police themselves seldom ventured there save in twos and threes, and brutal assaults upon them were of frequent occurrence." Williams did concede that conditions at Ratcliff Highway had improved by the 1890s, citing a decline in maritime prosperity, the transfer of shipping activity to new docks lower down on the Thames, and the fact that ocean liners were being helmed by "a better class of men." Yet, ultimately, Williams opined that "though

Ratcliff Highway.
Queen's London (1897)

selves to me. I am disappointed in Stanley Hopkins. I had hoped for better things from him. One should always look for a possible alternative and provide against it. It is the first rule of criminal investigation."

"What, then, is the alternative?"

"The line of investigation which I have myself been pursuing. It may give nothing. I cannot tell. But at least I shall follow it to the end." Several letters were waiting for Holmes at Baker Street. He snatched one of them up, opened it, and burst out into a triumphant chuckle of laughter.

"Excellent, Watson. The alternative develops. Have you telegraph forms? Just write a couple of messages for me: 'Sumner, Shipping Agent, Ratcliff Highway.[26] Send three men on, to arrive ten to-morrow morning.—Basil.' That's my name in those parts. The other is 'Inspector Stanley Hopkins, 46 Lord Street, Brixton. Come breakfast to-morrow at nine-thirty. Important. Wire if unable to come.—Sherlock Holmes.' There, Watson, this infernal case has haunted me for ten days. I hereby banish it completely from my presence. To-morrow, I trust that we shall hear the last of it forever."

Sharp at the hour named Inspector Stanley Hopkins appeared, and we sat down together to the excellent breakfast which Mrs. Hudson had prepared. The young detective was in high spirits at his success.

"You really think that your solution must be correct?" asked Holmes.

"I could not imagine a more complete case."

"It did not seem to me conclusive."

"You astonish me, Mr. Holmes. What more could one ask for?"

"Does your explanation cover every point?"

"Undoubtedly. I find that young Neligan arrived at the Brambletye Hotel on the very day of the crime. He came on the pretence of playing golf. His room was on the ground floor, and he could get out when he liked. That very night he went down to Woodman's Lee, saw Peter Carey at the hut, quarrelled with him, and killed him with the harpoon. Then, horrified by what he had done, he fled out of the hut, dropping the notebook which he had brought with him in order to question Peter Carey about these different securities. You may have observed that some of them were marked with ticks, and the others—the great majority—were not. Those which are ticked have been traced on the London market; but the others, presumably, were still in the possession of Carey, and young Neligan, according to his own account, was anxious to recover them in order to do the right thing by his father's creditors. After his flight he did not dare to approach the hut again for some time, but at last he forced himself to do so in order to obtain the information which he needed. Surely that is all simple and obvious?"

Holmes smiled and shook his head.

"It seems to me to have only one drawback, Hopkins, and that is that it is intrinsically impossible. Have you tried to drive a harpoon through a body? No? Tut, tut, my dear sir, you must really pay attention to these details. My friend Watson could tell you that I spent a whole morning in that exercise. It is no easy matter, and requires a strong and practised arm. But this blow was delivered with such violence that the head of the weapon sank deep into the wall. Do you imagine that this anaemic youth was capable of so frightful an assault? Is he the man who hobnobbed in rum and water with Black Peter in the dead of the night? Was it his profile that was seen on the blind two nights before? No, no, Hopkins; it is another and more formidable person for whom we must seek."

The detective's face had grown longer and longer during Holmes's speech. His hopes and his ambitions were all crumbling about him. But he would not abandon his position without a struggle.

"You can't deny that Neligan was present that night, Mr. Holmes. The book will prove that. I fancy that I have evidence enough to satisfy a jury, even if you are able to pick a hole in it. Besides, Mr. Holmes, I have laid my hand upon *my* man. As to this terrible person of yours, where is he?"

"I rather fancy that he is on the stair," said Holmes serenely. "I think, Watson, that you would do well to put that revolver where you can reach it." He rose and laid a written paper upon a side-table. "Now we are ready," said he.

There had been some talking in gruff voices outside, and now Mrs. Hudson opened the door to say that there were three men inquiring for Captain Basil.

"Show them in one by one," said Holmes.

it gives me great satisfaction to record that Ratcliff Highway is better than it was, I confess I could wish to see it better than it is."

27 A variety of winter apple with a red skin. It was highly prized as a dessert apple in Victorian England.

28 Presumably Holmes's bedroom.

The first who entered was a little ribston-pippin[27] of a man, with ruddy cheeks and fluffy white side-whiskers. Holmes had drawn a letter from his pocket.

"What name?" he asked.

"James Lancaster."

"I am sorry, Lancaster, but the berth is full. Here is half a sovereign for your trouble. Just step into this room[28] and wait there for a few minutes."

The second man was a long, dried-up creature, with lank hair and sallow cheeks. His name was Hugh Pattins. He also received his dismissal, his half-sovereign, and the order to wait.

The third applicant was a man of remarkable appearance. A fierce bull-dog face was framed in a tangle of hair and beard, and two bold, dark eyes gleamed behind the cover of thick, tufted, overhung eyebrows. He saluted and stood sailor-fashion, turning his cap round in his hands.

The third applicant was a man of remarkable appearance.
Frederick Dorr Steele, *Collier's*, 1904

"Your name?" asked Holmes.

"Patrick Cairns."

"Harpooner?"

"Yes, sir. Twenty-six voyages."

"Dundee, I suppose?"

"Yes, sir."

"And ready to start with an exploring ship?"

"Yes, sir."

"What wages?"

"Eight pounds a month."

"Could you start at once?"

"As soon as I get my kit."

"Have you your papers?"

"Yes, sir." He took a sheaf of worn and greasy forms from his pocket. Holmes glanced over them and returned them.

"You are just the man I want," said he. "Here's the agreement on the side-table. If you sign it the whole matter will be settled."

The seaman lurched across the room and took up the pen.

"Shall I sign here?" he asked, stooping over the table.

Holmes leaned over his shoulder and passed both hands over his neck.

"This will do," said he.

I heard a click of steel and a bellow like an enraged bull. The next instant Holmes and the seaman were rolling on the ground together. He was a man of such gigantic strength that, even with the handcuffs which Holmes had so deftly fastened upon his wrists, he would have very quickly overpowered my friend had Hopkins and I not rushed to his rescue. Only when I pressed the cold muzzle of the revolver to his temple did he at last understand that resistance was vain. We lashed his ankles with cord and rose breathless from the struggle.

"I must really apologize, Hopkins," said Sherlock Holmes. "I fear that the scrambled eggs are cold. However, you will enjoy the rest of your breakfast all the better, will you not, for the thought that you have brought your case to a triumphant conclusion?"

Stanley Hopkins was speechless with amazement.

"I don't know what to say, Mr. Holmes," he blurted out at last, with a very red face. "It seems to me that I have been making a fool of myself from the beginning. I understand now,

" 'Shall I sign here?' he asked."
Sidney Paget, *Strand Magazine*, 1904

what I should never have forgotten, that I am the pupil and you
are the master. Even now I see what you have done, but I don't
know how you did it or what it signifies."

"Well, well," said Holmes, good-humouredly. "We all learn
by experience, and your lesson this time is that you should
never lose sight of the alternative. You were so absorbed in
young Neligan that you could not spare a thought to Patrick
Cairns, the true murderer of Peter Carey."

The hoarse voice of the seaman broke in on our conversation.

"See here, mister," said he, "I make no complaint of being
man-handled in this fashion, but I would have you call things
by their right names. You say I murdered Peter Carey; I say I
killed Peter Carey, and there's all the difference. Maybe you
don't believe what I say. Maybe you think I am just slinging
you a yarn."

"Not at all," said Holmes. "Let us hear what you have to say."

"It's soon told, and, by the Lord, every word of it is truth. I knew Black Peter, and when he pulled out his knife I whipped a harpoon through him sharp, for I knew that it was him or me. That's how he died. You can call it murder. Anyhow, I'd as soon die with a rope round my neck as with Black Peter's knife in my heart."

"How came you there?" asked Holmes.

"I'll tell it you from the beginning. Just sit me up a little so as I can speak easy. It was in '83 that it happened—August of that year. Peter Carey was master of the *Sea Unicorn*, and I was spare harpooner. We were coming out of the ice-pack on our way home, with head winds and a week's southerly gale, when we picked up a little craft that had been blown north. There was one man on her—a landsman. The crew had thought she would founder, and had made for the Norwegian coast in the dinghy. I guess they were all drowned. Well, we took him on board, this man, and he and the skipper had some long talks in the cabin. All the baggage we took off with him was one tin box. So far as I know, the man's name was never mentioned, and on the second night he disappeared as if he had never been. It was given out that he had either thrown himself overboard or fallen overboard in the heavy weather that we were having. Only one man knew what had happened to him, and that was me, for with my own eyes I saw the skipper tip up his heels and put him over the rail in the middle watch of a dark night, two days before we sighted the Shetland Lights.

"Well, I kept my knowledge to myself, and waited to see what would come of it. When we got back to Scotland it was easily hushed up, and nobody asked any questions. A stranger died by accident, and it was nobody's business to inquire. Shortly after Peter Carey gave up the sea, and it was long years before I could find where he was. I guessed that he had done the deed for the sake of what was in that tin box, and that he could afford now to pay me well for keeping my mouth shut.

"I found out where he was through a sailor man that had met him in London, and down I went to squeeze him. The first night he was reasonable enough, and was ready to give me what would make me free of the sea for life. We were to fix it all two nights later. When I came I found him three-parts

29 Steve Clarkson, in a "Letter to Baker Street," takes issue with Cairns's story, doubting that Cairns's blow would be capable not only of stopping Carey's rapid forward motion but also of throwing the captain backward and pinning him securely against the wall. "I wonder whether even Arnold Schwarzenegger's arm would contain such power." As an alternate scenario, Clarkson envisions Carey in retreat, having backed up toward the wall when Cairns decided to harpoon him in order both to forestall Carey's taking action against him and to gain access to the tin box. The sailor's story of self-defence would earn him leniency during trial, but in Clarkson's opinion, "Cairns should have swung for it."

James A. Coffin proposes that Carey, repentant over the killing of Neligan and the theft of the securities, planned to goad Cairns into killing him, thus accomplishing a suicide and perhaps revenge on Cairns as well.

"We sat down and we drank and we yarned about old times."
Sidney Paget, *Strand Magazine*, 1904

drunk and in a vile temper. We sat down and we yarned about old times, but the more he drank the less I liked the look on his face. I spotted that harpoon upon the wall, and I thought I might need it before I was through. Then at last he broke out at me, spitting and cursing, with murder in his eyes and a great clasp-knife in his hand. He had not time to get it from the sheath before I had the harpoon through him.[29] Heavens! what a yell he gave; and his face gets between me and my sleep! I stood there, with his blood splashing round me, and I waited for a bit, but all was quiet, so I took heart once more. I looked round, and there was the tin box on a shelf. I had as much right to it as Peter Carey, anyhow, so I took it with me and left the hut. Like a fool I left my baccy-pouch upon the table.

"Now I'll tell you the queerest part of the whole story. I had hardly got outside the hut when I heard someone coming, and I hid among the bushes. A man came slinking along, went into the hut, gave a cry as if he had seen a ghost, and legged it as hard as he could run until he was out of sight.[30] Who he was or what he wanted is more than I can tell. For my part, I walked ten miles, got a train at Tunbridge Wells, and so reached London, and no one the wiser.

"Well, when I came to examine the box I found there was no money in it, and nothing but papers that I would not dare to sell. I had lost my hold on Black Peter, and was stranded in London without a shilling. There was only my trade left. I saw these advertisements about harpooners and high wages, so I went to the shipping agents, and they sent me here. That's all I know, and I say again that if I killed Black Peter, the law should give me thanks, for I saved them the price of a hempen rope."

"A very clear statement," said Holmes, rising and lighting his pipe. "I think, Hopkins, that you should lose no time in conveying your prisoner to a place of safety. This room is not well adapted for a cell, and Mr. Patrick Cairns occupies too large a portion of our carpet."[31]

"Mr. Holmes," said Hopkins, "I do not know how to express my gratitude. Even now I do not understand how you attained this result."

"Simply by having the good fortune to get the right clue from the beginning. It is very possible if I had known about this notebook it might have led away my thoughts, as it did yours. But all I heard pointed in the one direction. The amazing strength, the skill in the use of the harpoon, the rum and water, the sealskin tobacco-pouch with the coarse tobacco—all these pointed to a seaman, and one who had been a whaler. I was convinced that the initials 'P. C.' upon the pouch were a coincidence, and not those of Peter Carey, since he seldom smoked, and no pipe was found in his cabin. You remember that I asked whether whisky and brandy were in the cabin. You said they were. How many landsmen are there who would drink rum when they could get these other spirits? Yes, I was certain it was a seaman."

30 Are we really expected to believe that twelve years after the disappearance of Neligan's father, Neligan chooses to visit Peter Carey *on the very same night* that Carey is visited by the only other man who knows what happened on that fateful night in 1883? This seems to stretch the limits of coincidence and suggests that Neligan and Cairns acted in concert—perhaps Cairns had confessed to young Neligan and was then used by Neligan as the "muscle" of an effort to force information from Carey. However, when Carey and Cairns confronted each other, Cairns was goaded into an impulsive act of violence, and Neligan decided to dissociate himself from Cairns.

31 This is a far different conclusion than Holmes reaches in the case of the killer of another wife-beater, Captain Croker in "The Abbey Grange." However, most commentators assume that Cairns would quickly have gained his freedom on a plea of self-defence.

32 Apparently, it did not occur to Holmes to pick up a telephone, which would have been far quicker. Colonel E. Ennalls Berl considers Holmes's extremely limited and reluctant use of the phone throughout his career, noting that in this case Holmes uses a telegram to invite Hopkins to breakfast and requests that he wire if he is unable to attend. Whether or not Holmes was a telephone subscriber, in *The Sign of Four* it is revealed that there was a telephone across the road; surely Holmes could have phoned the Brixton Police Station and either spoken to Hopkins or left him a message. Even more inefficient, Berl chides, was Holmes's wasting three days wiring Dundee for crew lists when "it seems almost certain that a much shorter telephone struggle through the Dundee police would have given him the information." It seems odd that Holmes, always on the cutting edge of his own field, would shy away from the use of the telephone, which was spreading rapidly through England. See "The Man with the Twisted Lip," note 39. Whatever the reason, Holmes has apparently overcome his unexplained aversion by the time of "The Three Garridebs" (likely set in 1898).

33 Holmes's casual mention of a trip to Norway, where Neligan's father was headed before meeting his demise, is bafflingly oblique. D. Martin Dakin struggles to make some concrete connection to the case, coming up largely empty-handed. "He cannot have been after some of Neligan's securities, for, even if it had been any business of his, neither he nor they ever got as far as Norway. (What did Neligan senior hope to do there anyway?)" Howard Brody, in "That Trip to Norway," suggests that Holmes and Watson were off to investigate whether Neligan's dinghy had been swept into the maelstrom off the Norwegian coast that Edgar Allan Poe wrote

"And how did you find him?"

"My dear sir, the problem had become a very simple one. If it were a seaman, it could only be a seaman who had been with him on the *Sea Unicorn*. So far as I could learn, he had sailed in no other ship. I spent three days in wiring to Dundee,[32] and at the end of that time I had ascertained the names of the crew of the *Sea Unicorn* in 1883. When I found Patrick Cairns among the harpooners, my research was nearing its end. I argued that the man was probably in London, and that he would desire to leave the country for a time. I therefore spent some days in the East End, devised an Arctic expedition, put forth tempting terms for harpooners who would serve under Captain Basil—and behold the result!"

"Wonderful!" cried Hopkins. "Wonderful!"

"You must obtain the release of young Neligan as soon as possible," said Holmes. "I confess that I think you owe him some apology. The tin box must be returned to him, but, of course, the securities which Peter Carey has sold are lost forever. There's the cab, Hopkins, and you can remove your man. If you want me for the trial, my address and that of Watson will be somewhere in Norway—I'll send particulars later."[33]

about in "A Descent into the Maelstrom." In "Somewhere in Norway," Chris Redmond makes the even more tantalising suggestion that Neligan was not, in fact, murdered, but instead bribed Carey to report his death, and that Holmes went to Norway to attempt to trace his whereabouts (and the whereabouts of the missing securities).

THE ADVENTURE OF
CHARLES AUGUSTUS MILVERTON[1]

After threats and subtleties fail, Holmes and Watson turn lawbreakers in the case of Charles Augustus Milverton as they seek to foil the blackmail plot of "the worst man in London." The two men find themselves unwilling witnesses to murder, and some question the ethics of their behaviour and wonder how the murderer got away. Whether the case occurred before or after Holmes's Great Hiatus from 1891 to 1894 is unclear, but Watson withheld publication until 1904. He may have done so solely out of concern for those victims whose reputations might still be damaged by Watson's revelations, or possibly out of concern that the police might still be chasing him!

1 "Charles Augustus Milverton" was published in *Collier's Magazine* on March 26, 1904, and in the *Strand Magazine* in April 1904. Arthur Conan Doyle featured Charles Augustus Milverton in his play *The Speckled Band* in 1910; he was a blackmailer attempting to extort the Duchess of Ferrers before her marriage.

2 While there is much dispute among the chronologists on the dating of this case, most place it in 1899. The five-year gap between 1899 and publication does not seem to fit the spirit of Watson's remarks here, but there are other clues. Two specific dates are mentioned in Watson's record: a wedding on the eighteenth (not a Sunday, for no marriages could be performed on Sundays in Victorian times) and a stroll on the fourteenth. Because Wat-

I T IS YEARS since the incidents of which I speak took place,[2] and yet it is with diffidence that I allude to them. For a long time, even with the utmost discretion and reticence, it would have been impossible to make the facts public; but now the principal person concerned is beyond the reach of human law, and with due suppression the story may be told in such fashion as to injure no one. It records an absolutely unique experience in the career both of Mr. Sherlock Holmes and of myself. The reader will excuse me if I conceal the date or any other fact by which he might trace the actual occurrence.

We had been out for one of our evening rambles, Holmes and I, and had returned about six o'clock on a cold, frosty winter's evening. As Holmes turned up the lamp the light fell upon a card on the table. He glanced at it, and then, with an ejaculation of disgust, threw it on the floor. I picked it up and read:

Frederick Dorr Steele, *Collier's*, 1904

Charles Augustus Milverton,
Appledore[3] Towers,
Hampstead.[4]
Agent.

"Who is he?" I asked.

"The worst man in London," Holmes answered, as he sat down and stretched his legs before the fire. "Is anything on the back of the card?"

I turned it over.

"Will call at 6.30.—C. A. M.," I read.

"Hum! He's about due. Do you feel a creeping, shrinking sensation, Watson, when you stand before the serpents in the Zoo[5] and see the slithery, gliding, venomous creatures, with their deadly eyes and wicked, flattened faces? Well, that's how Milverton impresses me. I've had to do with fifty murderers in my career, but the worst of them never gave me the repulsion which I have for this fellow. And yet I can't get out of doing business with him—indeed, he is here at my invitation."

son remarks on looking in shop windows on the fourteenth, scholars proclaim that that day was also not a Sunday (when the windows would have been shuttered), nor was the previous day, on which Holmes and Watson dressed as theatre-goers (the theatres would have been dark). If certain months are ruled out, because of weather and lighting clues, a number of possible years are eliminated, and the chronologists choose 1899 as the most likely among the remaining.

3 The astute reader will recall that Edith, the wife of the Duke of Holdernesse ("The Priory School"), was the daughter of Sir Charles Appledore. See "The Priory School." Why Watson repeated the obvious pseudonym is unknown.

4 A residential borough (now part of Camden) popular with the artistic and literary crowd, Hampstead was the home of George Du Maurier, John Keats, and Karl Marx, among others. Hampstead's Highgate Cemetery contains the graves of several luminaries, including Marx, George Eliot, Michael Faraday, Christina Rossetti, and Herbert Spencer.

5 The London Zoo in Regent Park, with its south entrance about three-quarters of a mile

Royal Zoological Garden.
Queen's London (1897)

from the Baker Street station of the Metropolitan Railway, was founded as a scientific endeavour in 1828 by the Zoological Society. The initial 430 animals were donated by the Royal Menagerie at the Tower of London. For the zoo's first two decades, admission was granted only to members of the Zoological Society and their guests; still, the new attraction was immensely popular, and it became even more so when opened up to the general public. Victorian visitors were tickled and awed to be able to witness these exotic animals up close for the first time, and their delight was tinged also with the thrill that the zoo's powerful captives might potentially escape. Here, Holmes's fascination with the zoo's serpentine residents is shared by William Makepeace Thackeray, whose own description of the London Zoo (as quoted in Peter Ackroyd's *London: The Biography*) involves "an immense boa constrictor swallowing a live rabbit—swallowing a live rabbit, sir, and looking as if he would have swallowed one of my little children afterwards."

"Charles Augustus Milverton."
Sidney Paget, *Strand Magazine*, 1904

"But who is he?"

"I'll tell you, Watson. He is the king of all the blackmailers. Heaven help the man, and still more the woman, whose secret and reputation come into the power of Milverton. With a smiling face and a heart of marble he will squeeze and squeeze until he has drained them dry. The fellow is a genius in his way, and would have made his mark in some more savoury trade. His method is as follows: He allows it to be known that he is prepared to pay very high sums for letters which compromise people of wealth or position. He receives these wares not only from treacherous valets or maids, but frequently from genteel ruffians, who have gained the confidence and affection of trusting women. He deals with no niggard hand. I happen to know that he paid seven hundred pounds to a footman for a note two lines in length, and that the ruin of a noble family was the result. Everything which is in the market goes to Milverton, and there are hundreds in this great city who turn white at his name. No one knows where his grip may fall, for he is far too rich and far too cunning to work from hand to mouth. He will hold a card back for years in order to play it at the moment when the stake is best worth winning. I have said that he is the worst man in London, and I would ask you how could one compare the ruffian who in hot blood bludgeons his mate with this man, who methodically and at his leisure tortures the soul and wrings the nerves in order to add to his already swollen money-bags?"

I had seldom heard my friend speak with such intensity of feeling.

"But surely," said I, "the fellow must be within the grasp of the law?"

"Technically, no doubt, but practically not. What would it

Staff artists "Cargs" and E. S. Morris,
Chicago Sunday Tribune, August 20, 1911

6 A telling phrase, suggest many commentators, revealing Holmes's innate snobbery, which manifests itself most particularly in "The Illustrious Client." However, Holmes's *lack* of snobbery—and indeed, disdain for the "upper classes"—is in evidence in his treatment of the king in "A Scandal in Bohemia" and his high-handed manner with Lord Robert St. Simon in "The Noble Bachelor." Charles A. Meyer suggests that Lady Eva was involved with Albert Edward, Prince of Wales, that Albert requested Holmes's assistance (see L. W. Bailey's similar reasoning in note 27 below), and that the Crown's involvement justified in Holmes's mind his ungentlemanly treatment of Milverton's housemaid.

7 Given as "Blackwell" in American editions.

8 Samuel Pickwick, Esq., is the protagonist of Charles Dickens's farcical novel *The Pickwick Papers* (1836–1837), first published in serial form under Dickens's pseudonym, Boz. Founder of the Pickwick Club (whose members travel throughout England and report on their observations and adventures), Mr. Pickwick, a simple-minded and morally upright fellow, is bald and has eyes that twinkle from behind his spectacles. The benevolence Watson refers to is fully on display in Pickwick's opening speech to the club, wherein he informs his fellow members that "if ever the fire of self-importance broke out in his bosom, the desire to benefit the human race in preference effectually quenched it. The praise of mankind was his swing; philanthropy was his insurance office."

profit a woman, for example, to get him a few months' imprisonment if her own ruin must immediately follow? His victims dare not hit back. If ever he blackmailed an innocent person, then, indeed, we should have him; but he is as cunning as the Evil One. No, no; we must find other ways to fight him."

"And why is he here?"

"Because an illustrious client[6] has placed her piteous case in my hands. It is the Lady Eva Brackwell,[7] the most beautiful *débutante* of last season. She is to be married in a fortnight to the Earl of Dovercourt. This fiend has several imprudent letters—imprudent, Watson, nothing worse—which were written to an impecunious young squire in the country. They would suffice to break off the match. Milverton will send the letters to the Earl unless a large sum of money is paid him. I have been commissioned to meet him, and—to make the best terms I can."

At that instant there was a clatter and a rattle in the street below. Looking down I saw a stately carriage and pair, the brilliant lamps gleaming on the glossy haunches of the noble chestnuts. A footman opened the door, and a small, stout man in a shaggy astrakhan overcoat descended. A minute later he was in the room.

Charles Augustus Milverton was a man of fifty, with a large, intellectual head, a round, plump, hairless face, a perpetual frozen smile, and two keen gray eyes, which gleamed brightly from behind broad, golden-rimmed glasses. There was something of Mr. Pickwick's benevolence[8] in his appearance, marred only by the insincerity of the fixed smile and by the hard glitter of those restless and penetrating eyes. His voice was as smooth and suave as his countenance, as he advanced with a plump little hand extended, murmuring his regret for having missed us at his first visit. Holmes disregarded the outstretched hand and looked at him with a face of granite. Milverton's smile broadened; he shrugged his shoulders, removed his overcoat, folded it with great deliberation over the back of a chair, and then took a seat.

"This gentleman?" said he, with a wave in my direction. "Is it discreet? Is it right?"

"Dr. Watson is my friend and partner."

"Very good, Mr. Holmes. It is only in your client's interests that I protested. The matter is so very delicate—"

There was something of Mr. Pickwick's
benevolence in his looks.
Frederick Dorr Steele, *Collier's*, 1904

"Dr. Watson has already heard of it."

"Then we can proceed to business. You say that you are acting for Lady Eva. Has she empowered you to accept my
terms?"

"What are your terms?"

"Seven thousand pounds."

"And the alternative?"

"My dear sir, it is painful to me to discuss it, but if the
money is not paid on the 14th, there certainly will be no marriage on the 18th." His insufferable smile was more complacent than ever.

Holmes thought for a little.

9 This sentence makes little sense, unless Watson means that Holmes was "baffled" as to his next step; if Watson means that Holmes is baffled by the *meaning* of Milverton's remark, it seems more logical that the sentence should read, "I could see clearly that he did not."

"You appear to me," he said, at last, "to be taking matters too much for granted. I am, of course, familiar with the contents of these letters. My client will certainly do what I may advise. I shall counsel her to tell her future husband the whole story and to trust to his generosity."

Milverton chuckled.

"You evidently do not know the Earl," said he.

From the baffled look upon Holmes's face, I could see clearly that he did.[9]

"What harm is there in the letters?" he asked.

"They are sprightly—very sprightly," Milverton answered. "The lady was a charming correspondent. But I can assure you that the Earl of Dovercourt would fail to appreciate them. However, since you think otherwise, we will let it rest at that. It is purely a matter of business. If you think that it is in the best interests of your client that these letters should be placed in the hands of the Earl, then you would indeed be foolish to pay so large a sum of money to regain them." He rose and seized his astrakhan coat.

Holmes was gray with anger and mortification.

"Wait a little," he said. "You go too fast. We would certainly make every effort to avoid scandal in so delicate a matter."

Milverton relapsed into his chair.

"I was sure that you would see it in that light," he purred.

"At the same time," Holmes continued, "Lady Eva is not a wealthy woman. I assure you that two thousand pounds would be a drain upon her resources, and that the sum you name is utterly beyond her power. I beg, therefore, that you will moderate your demands, and that you will return the letters at the price I indicate, which is, I assure you, the highest that you can get."

Milverton's smile broadened and his eyes twinkled humorously.

"I am aware that what you say is true about the lady's resources," said he. "At the same time, you must admit that the occasion of a lady's marriage is a very suitable time for her friends and relatives to make some little effort upon her behalf. They may hesitate as to an acceptable wedding present. Let me assure them that this little bundle of letters would give more joy than all the candelabra and butter-dishes in London."

"It is impossible," said Holmes.

"Dear me, dear me, how unfortunate!" cried Milverton, taking out a bulky pocketbook. "I cannot help thinking that ladies are ill-advised in not making an effort. Look at this!" He held up a little note with a coat-of-arms upon the envelope. "That belongs to—well, perhaps it is hardly fair to tell the name until to-morrow morning. But at that time it will be in the hands of the lady's husband. And all because she will not find a beggarly sum which she could get in an hour by turning her diamonds into paste. It is such a pity. Now, you remember the sudden end of the engagement between the Honourable Miss Miles and Colonel Dorking? Only two days before the wedding there was a paragraph in the *Morning Post* to say that it was all off. And why? It is almost incredible, but the absurd sum of twelve hundred pounds would have settled the whole question. Is it not pitiful? And here I find you, a man of sense, boggling about terms when your client's future and honour are at stake. You surprise me, Mr. Holmes."

"What I say is true," Holmes answered. "The money cannot be found. Surely it is better for you to take the substantial sum which I offer than to ruin this woman's career, which can profit you in no way?"

"There you make a mistake, Mr. Holmes. An exposure would profit me indirectly to a considerable extent. I have eight or ten similar cases maturing.[10] If it was circulated among them that I had made a severe example of the Lady Eva, I should find all of them much more open to reason. You see my point?"

Holmes sprang from his chair.

"Get behind him, Watson! Don't let him out! Now, sir, let us see the contents of that notebook."

Milverton had glided as quick as a rat to the side of the room and stood with his back against the wall.

"Mr. Holmes, Mr. Holmes!" he said, turning the front of his coat and exhibiting the butt of a large revolver, which projected from the inside pocket. "I have been expecting you to do something original. This has been done so often, and what good has ever come from it? I assure you that I am armed to the teeth, and I am perfectly prepared to use my weapon, knowing that the law will support me. Besides, your supposition that I would bring the letters here in a notebook is entirely mistaken.

10 Difficult as it may be to believe that so many unfaithful spouses would risk exposure by exchanging risqué love letters—and would actually be caught doing so—the realities of the time make this scenario entirely plausible. As L. W. Bailey points out, private telephones were unavailable, and secret lovers were often forced to send word to each other via notes conveyed by their servants. Naturally, should an opportunist such as Milverton come calling with a large sum of money, many a valet or maid might be tempted to hand the evidence over. "[T]oo often," writes Bailey, "as in other fields of human activity, avarice proved stronger than loyalty." At the same time, what Milverton has in hand may not be torrid declarations of passion, but merely straightforward arrangements to meet at a certain location. For a married man or woman, such a message would be considered scandalous enough.

"Exhibiting the butt of a large revolver,
which projected from the inside pocket."
Sidney Paget, *Strand Magazine*, 1904

I would do nothing so foolish. And now, gentlemen, I have one or two little interviews this evening, and it is a long drive to Hampstead." He stepped forward, took up his coat, laid his hand on his revolver, and turned to the door. I picked up a chair, but Holmes shook his head, and I laid it down again. With a bow, a smile, and a twinkle, Milverton was out of the room, and a few moments after we heard the slam of the carriage door and the rattle of the wheels as he drove away.

Holmes sat motionless by the fire, his hands buried deep in his trouser pockets, his chin sunk upon his breast, his eyes fixed upon the glowing embers. For half an hour he was silent and still. Then, with the gesture of a man who has taken his decision, he sprang to his feet and passed into his bedroom. A little later a rakish young workman with a goatee beard and a swagger lit his clay pipe at the lamp before descending into the street. "I'll be back some time, Watson," said he, and vanished into the night. I understood that he had opened his campaign against Charles Augustus Milverton; but I little dreamed the strange shape which that campaign was destined to take.

For some days Holmes came and went at all hours in this attire, but beyond a remark that his time was spent at Hampstead, and that it was not wasted, I knew nothing of what he was doing. At last, however, on a wild, tempestuous evening, when the wind screamed and rattled against the windows, he returned from his last expedition, and, having removed his disguise, he sat before the fire and laughed heartily in his silent, inward fashion.

"You would not call me a marrying man, Watson?"

"No, indeed!"

"You'll be interested to hear that I'm engaged."

"My dear fellow! I congrat—"

"To Milverton's housemaid."

"Good heavens, Holmes!"

"I wanted information, Watson."

Sherlock Holmes in disguise.
Frederick Dorr Steele, *Collier's*, 1904

11 David Galerstein points out that it was winter and the weather was severe; it is therefore obvious that Holmes and Milverton's maid would have to meet indoors, in her bedroom. Only by sleeping with the maid, Galerstein insists, could Holmes acquire the inside information he so urgently needed. "We have seen cases where the Master risked his life to help a client," Galerstein writes admiringly. "We now see that his profession made other demands on him too, and marvel at the extent to which a private detective must sometimes go to help his client." Judy L. Buddle expresses a similar view, although she suggests that Holmes's "swagger" evidences some enthusiasm for the job. Finally, Alan Wilson spins the fanciful theory that Holmes and Agatha eventually had a son, one Sylvanus Escott.

12 "Is it not a tribute to Holmes's versatility," Richard Asher writes admiringly in "Holmes and the Fair Sex," "that he, a man accustomed to discourse upon the Chaldean roots of the ancient Cornish language and the Polyphonic Motets of Lassus, should be equally capable of love talk with a housemaid? Is it not remarkable that a man accustomed to the company of khalifas, dukes, headmasters and lamas should be such a success with a servant?"

13 D. Martin Dakin, among others, takes Holmes to task for his cavalier treatment of Milverton's hapless employee. "We may well ask if the happiness of a housemaid was not just as important as that of a society lady—even if she was the most beautiful débutante of the season." While this was decidedly not the case in Victorian society, the detective who elsewhere shows disdain for those placing too much importance on social rank might be expected to show more respect for the feelings of an innocent housemaid than he does here. Holmes's next comment, that his

"Surely you have gone too far?"

"It was a most necessary step. I am a plumber with a rising business, Escott by name. I have walked out with her each evening,[11] and I have talked with her. Good heavens, those talks![12] However, I have got all I wanted. I know Milverton's house as I know the palm of my hand."

"But the girl, Holmes?"

He shrugged his shoulders.

"You can't help it, my dear Watson. You must play your cards as best you can when such a stake is on the table.[13] However, I rejoice to say that I have a hated rival, who will certainly cut me out the instant that my back is turned. What a splendid night it is!"

"You like this weather?"

"It suits my purpose. Watson, I mean to burgle Milverton's house to-night."

I had a catching of the breath, and my skin went cold at the words, which were slowly uttered in a tone of concentrated resolution. As a flash of lightning in the night shows up in an instant every detail of a wild landscape, so at one glance I seemed to see every possible result of such an action—the detection, the capture, the honoured career ending in irreparable failure and disgrace, my friend himself lying at the mercy of the odious Milverton.

"For heaven's sake, Holmes, think what you are doing," I cried.[14]

"My dear fellow, I have given it every consideration. I am never precipitate in my actions, nor would I adopt so energetic and, indeed, so dangerous a course if any other were possible. Let us look at the matter clearly and fairly. I suppose that you will admit that the action is morally justifiable, though technically criminal. To burgle his house is no more than to forcibly take his pocket-book—an action in which you were prepared to aid me."

I turned it over in my mind.

"Yes," I said, "it is morally justifiable so long as our object is to take no articles save those which are used for an illegal purpose."

"Exactly. Since it is morally justifiable, I have only to consider the question of personal risk. Surely a gentleman should not lay much stress upon this, when a lady is in most desperate need of his help?"

"You will be in such a false position."

"Well, that is part of the risk. There is no other possible way of regaining these letters. The unfortunate lady has not the money, and there are none of her people in whom she could confide. To-morrow is the last day of grace, and unless we can get the letters to-night, this villain will be as good as his word and will bring about her ruin. I must, therefore, abandon my client to her fate, or I must play this last card. Between ourselves, Watson, it's a sporting duel between this fellow Milverton and me. He had, as you saw, the best of the first exchanges; but my self-respect and my reputation are concerned to fight it to a finish."

"Well, I don't like it, but I suppose it must be," said I. "When do we start?"

"You are not coming."

"Then you are not going," said I. "I give you my word of honour—and I never broke it in my life—that I will take a cab straight to the police-station and give you away unless you let me share this adventure with you."

"You can't help me."

"How do you know that? You can't tell what may happen. Anyway, my resolution is taken. Other people besides you have self-respect, and even reputations."

Holmes had looked annoyed, but his brow cleared, and he clapped me on the shoulder.

"Well, well, my dear fellow, be it so. We have shared the same room for some years, and it would be amusing if we ended by sharing the same cell. You know, Watson, I don't mind confessing to you that I have always had an idea that I would have made a highly efficient criminal. This is the chance of my lifetime in that direction. See here!" He took a neat little leather case out of a drawer, and opening it he exhibited a number of shining instruments. "This is a first-class, up-to-date burgling kit, with nickel-plated jemmy, diamond-tipped glass cutter, adaptable keys, and every modern improvement which the march of civilization demands. Here, too, is my dark lantern.[15] Everything is in order. Have you a pair of silent shoes?"

putative fiancée will be well taken care of by a "hated rival" the instant Holmes has departed, might seem to express some concern as to her fate. But, admonishes Dakin, "this remark, based as it was on the Victorian tradition that the *affaires du coeur* of domestic servants were something comic and not to be taken seriously, only adds insult to injury."

Brad Keefauver, in *Sherlock and the Ladies*, rises to Holmes's defence, elevating the housemaid (whose name is later revealed to be Agatha) from victim to shrewd manipulator. "I don't think the engagement was his fault," he argues. "What man, carefully trying to win a girl's heart, proposes after seeing her for only a few days, especially if he knows his intentions aren't sincere? Holmes could have gained the information he needed by simply romancing her; he needn't have asked her to marry him . . . unless, of course, it was Agatha who forced the proposal out of him."

14 This remark seems uncharacteristic of Watson—contrast his courage displayed in "The Speckled Band" and *The Hound of the Baskervilles* and his lack of hesitancy to break the law in a good cause in "A Scandal in Bohemia" and "The Bruce-Partington Plans"—and is likely to have been inserted by him later for dramatic effect.

15 See "The Red-Headed League," note 63, for a description of this device. A dark lantern would prove extremely useful to the stealth of a burglar, observes Bruce Kennedy: "With the shutter open only a crack, a faint glimmer of light can shine on the subject which would be invisible to the passer-by."

16 Why? Was Watson's wound so little trouble that he could play tennis? The plague of wearing tennis shoes as daily wear had not yet affected men's fashions.

17 Technically, plethora is a medical condition in which one's body contains too much blood; a person who is "plethoric" may be defined as moving slowly and having a ruddy complexion. Holmes is likely using the more familiar meaning of the term—"excessive"—for he has already stated that Milverton is a heavy sleeper.

"I have rubber-soled tennis shoes."[16]

"Excellent! And a mask?"

"I can make a couple out of black silk."

"I can see that you have a strong natural turn for this sort of thing. Very good; do you make the masks. We shall have some cold supper before we start. It is now nine-thirty. At eleven we shall drive as far as Church Row. It is a quarter of an hour's walk from there to Appledore Towers. We shall be at work before midnight. Milverton is a heavy sleeper, and retires punctually at ten-thirty. With any luck we should be back here by two, with the Lady Eva's letters in my pocket."

Holmes and I put on our dress-clothes, so that we might appear to be two theatre-goers homeward bound. In Oxford Street we picked up a hansom and drove to an address in Hampstead. Here we paid off our cab, and with our great coats buttoned up—for it was bitterly cold, and the wind seemed to blow through us—we walked along the edge of the heath.

"It's a business that needs delicate treatment," said Holmes. "These documents are contained in a safe in the fellow's study, and the study is the ante-room of his bed chamber. On the other hand, like all these stout, little men who do themselves well, he is a plethoric[17] sleeper. Agatha—that's my fiancée—says it is a joke in the servants' hall that it's impossible to wake the master. He has a secretary who is devoted to his interests,

Hampstead Road, joining Euston Road (1904).
Victorian and Edwardian London

and never budges from the study all day. That's why we are going at night. Then he has a beast of a dog which roams the garden. I met Agatha late the last two evenings, and she locks the brute up so as to give me a clear run. This is the house, this big one in its own grounds.[18] Through the gate—now to the right among the laurels. We might put on our masks here, I think. You see, there is not a glimmer of light in any of the windows, and everything is working splendidly."

With our black silk face-coverings, which turned us into two of the most truculent figures in London, we stole up to the silent, gloomy house. A sort of tiled veranda extended along one side of it, lined by several windows and two doors.

"That's his bedroom," Holmes whispered. "This door opens straight into the study. It would suit us best, but it is bolted as well as locked, and we should make too much noise getting in. Come round here. There's a greenhouse which opens into the drawing-room."

The place was locked, but Holmes removed a circle of glass and turned the key from the inside. An instant afterwards he had closed the door behind us, and we had become felons in the eyes of the law. The thick warm air of the conservatory and the rich choking fragrance of exotic plants took us by the throat. He seized my hand in the darkness and led me swiftly past banks of shrubs which brushed against our faces. Holmes had remarkable powers, carefully cultivated, of seeing in the dark. Still holding my hand in one of his, he opened a door, and I was vaguely conscious that we had entered a large room in which a cigar had been smoked not long before. He felt his way among the furniture, opened another door, and closed it behind us. Putting out my hand I felt several coats hanging from the wall, and I understood that I was in a passage. We passed along it, and Holmes very gently opened a door upon the right-hand side. Something rushed out at us, and my heart sprang into my mouth, but I could have laughed when I realized that it was the cat. A fire was burning in this new room, and again the air was heavy with tobacco smoke. Holmes entered on tiptoe, waited for me to follow, and then very gently closed the door. We were in Milverton's study, and a *portière*[19] at the farther side showed the entrance to his bedroom.

It was a good fire, and the room was illuminated by it. Near the door I saw the gleam of an electric switch, but it was unnec-

18 Humphrey Morton identifies Appledore Towers as the house now known as The Logs, located at the corner of East Heath Road and Well Walk and built in 1868. The first existing record of the house's occupant is Edward Gotto, who lived there from 1873 to 1896—after which The Logs, curiously, is said to have stood empty for two years. "Cannot we assume," proposes Morton, ". . . that Milverton moved to The Logs in 1896, changed its name to Appledore Towers and was in residence until his timely and unlamented death a year or two later?" Morton's identification seems generally correct, in light of the fugitives' later run across the Heath. Yet this location leaves unexplained Holmes and Watson's drive to Church Row, farther west than the location in question. They were then required to walk back toward Appledore Towers, when they could just as well have alighted at Hampstead Heath Station and walked a short way west.

19 A heavy curtain hung over the doorway of a room.

"He stood with slanting head listening intently."
Sidney Paget, *Strand Magazine*, 1904

essary, even if it had been safe, to turn it on. At one side of the fireplace was a heavy curtain, which covered the bay window we had seen from outside. On the other side was the door which communicated with the veranda. A desk stood in the centre, with a turning chair of shining red leather. Opposite was a large bookcase, with a marble bust of Athene on the top. In the corner between the bookcase and the wall there stood a tall, green safe, the firelight flashing back from the polished brass knobs upon its face. Holmes stole across and looked at it. Then he crept to the door of the bedroom, and stood with slanting head listening intently. No sound came from within. Meanwhile it had struck me that it would be wise to secure our retreat through the outer door, so I examined it. To my amazement it was neither locked nor bolted. I touched Holmes on the arm, and he turned his masked face in that direction. I saw him start, and he was evidently as surprised as I.

"I don't like it," he whispered, putting his lips to my very ear. "I can't quite make it out. Anyhow, we have no time to lose."

"Can I do anything?"

"Yes; stand by the door. If you hear anyone come, bolt it on the inside, and we can get away as we came. If they come the other way, we can get through the door if our job is done, or hide behind these window curtains if it is not. Do you understand?"

I nodded and stood by the door. My first feeling of fear had passed away, and I thrilled now with a keener zest than I had ever enjoyed when we were the defenders of the law instead of its defiers. The high object of our mission, the consciousness that it was unselfish and chivalrous, the villainous character of our opponent, all added to the sporting interest of the adventure. Far from feeling guilty, I rejoiced and exulted in our dangers. With a glow of admiration I watched Holmes unrolling his case of instruments and choosing his tool with the calm, scientific accuracy of a surgeon who performs a delicate operation. I knew that the opening of safes was a particular hobby with him, and I understood the joy which it gave him to be confronted with this green and gold monster, the dragon which held in its maw the reputations of many fair ladies. Turning up the cuffs of his dress coat—he had placed his overcoat on a chair—Holmes laid out two drills, a jemmy, and several skeleton keys. I stood at the centre door with my eyes glancing at each of the others, ready for any emergency; though, indeed, my plans were somewhat vague as to what I should do if we were interrupted. For half an hour Holmes worked with concentrated energy, laying down one tool, picking up another, handling each with the strength and delicacy of the trained mechanic. Finally I heard a click, the broad green door swung open, and inside I had a glimpse of a number of paper packets, each tied, sealed, and inscribed. Holmes picked one out, but it was hard to read by the flickering fire, and he drew out his little dark lantern, for it was too dangerous, with Milverton in the next room, to switch on the electric light. Suddenly I saw him halt, listen intently, and then in an instant he

20 The light switch, which does make a sort of sharp, clicking noise when flipped on or off ("snick!"), was not in public use when the events of "The Adventure of Charles August Milverton" are thought to have taken place, writes William E. Plimental in a letter to the *Baker Street Journal.* Rather, prior to the light switch, one would turn off a light by using "the little square attached to a table lamp, and the push-button in the wall for a chandelier, neither of which gave what might be called a 'snick.' " Plimental uses that information to date "Charles August Milverton" later than most chronologists do, placing its occurrence in 1900 or 1901.

had swung the door of the safe to, picked up his coat, stuffed his tools into the pockets, and darted behind the window curtain, motioning me to do the same.

It was only when I had joined him there that I heard what had alarmed his quicker senses. There was a noise somewhere within the house. A door slammed in the distance. Then a confused, dull murmur broke itself into the measured thud of heavy footsteps rapidly approaching. They were in the passage outside the room. They paused at the door. The door opened. There was a sharp snick[20] as the electric light was turned on. The door closed once more, and the pungent reek of a strong cigar was borne to our nostrils. Then the footsteps continued backward and forwards, backward and forwards, within a few yards of us. Finally there was a creak from a chair, and the footsteps ceased. Then a key clicked in a lock, and I heard the rustle of papers.

So far I had not dared to look out, but now I gently parted the division of the curtains in front of me and peeped through. From the pressure of Holmes's shoulder against mine I knew that he was sharing my observations. Right in front of us, and almost within our reach, was the broad, rounded back of Milverton. It was evident that we had entirely miscalculated his movements, that he had never been to his bedroom, but that he had been sitting up in some smoking- or billiard-room in the farther wing of the house, the windows of which we had not seen. His broad, grizzled head, with its shining patch of baldness, was in the immediate foreground of our vision. He was leaning far back in the red leather chair, his legs outstretched, a long black cigar projecting at an angle from his mouth. He wore a semi-military smoking jacket, claret-coloured, with a black velvet collar. In his hand he held a long legal document which he was reading in an indolent fashion, blowing rings of tobacco smoke from his lips as he did so. There was no promise of a speedy departure in his composed bearing and his comfortable attitude.

I felt Holmes's hand steal into mine and give me a reassuring shake, as if to say that the situation was within his powers, and that he was easy in his mind. I was not sure whether he had seen what was only too obvious from my position, that the door of the safe was imperfectly closed, and that Milverton might at any moment observe it. In my own mind I had determined that if I were sure, from the rigidity of his gaze, that it had caught his eye, I would at once spring out, throw my great coat over his head, pinion him, and leave the rest to Holmes. But Milverton never looked up. He was languidly interested by the papers in his hand, and page after page was turned as he followed the argument of the lawyer. At least, I thought, when he has finished the document and the cigar he will go to his room but before he had reached the end of either, there came a remarkable development, which turned our thoughts into quite another channel.

Several times I had observed that Milverton looked at his watch, and once he had risen and sat down again with a gesture of impatience. The idea, however, that he might have an appointment at so strange an hour never occurred to me until a faint sound reached my ears from the veranda outside. Milverton dropped his papers and sat rigid in his chair. The sound was repeated, and then there came a gentle tap at the door. Milverton rose and opened it.

"Well," said he curtly, "you are nearly half an hour late."

So this was the explanation of the unlocked door and of the nocturnal vigil of Milverton. There was the gentle rustle of a woman's dress. I had closed the slit between the curtains as Milverton's face turned in our direction, but now I ventured very carefully to open it once more. He had resumed his seat, the cigar still projecting at an insolent angle from the corner of his mouth. In front of him, in the full glare of the electric light, there stood a tall, slim, dark woman, a veil over her face, a mantle drawn round her chin. Her breath came quick and fast, and every inch of the lithe figure was quivering with strong emotion.

"Well," said Milverton, "you made me lose a good night's rest, my dear. I hope you'll prove worth it. You couldn't come any other time—eh?"

The woman shook her head.

"Well, if you couldn't you couldn't. If the Countess is a hard mistress, you have your chance to get level with her now. Bless the girl, what are you shivering about? That's right! Pull yourself together! Now, let us get down to business." He took a notebook from the drawer of his desk. "You say that you have five letters which compromise the Countess d'Albert. You want to sell them. I want to buy them. So far so good. It only

"You couldn't come any other time—eh?"
Frederick Dorr Steele, *Collier's*, 1904

remains to fix a price. I should want to inspect the letters, of course. If they are really good specimens—Great heavens, is it you?"

The woman without a word had raised her veil and dropped the mantle from her chin. It was a dark, handsome, clear-cut face which confronted Milverton, a face with a curved nose, strong, dark eyebrows, shading hard, glittering eyes, and a straight, thin-lipped mouth set in a dangerous smile.

"It is I," she said, "the woman whose life you have ruined."

Milverton laughed, but fear vibrated in his voice. "You were so very obstinate," said he. "Why did you drive me to such extremities? I assure you I wouldn't hurt a fly of my own accord, but every man has his business, and what was I to do? I put the price well within your means. You would not pay."

"So you sent the letters to my husband, and he—the noblest gentleman that ever lived, a man whose boots I was never worthy to lace—he broke his gallant heart and died. You remember that last night, when I came through that door, I begged and prayed you for mercy, and you laughed in my face as you are trying to laugh now, only your coward heart cannot keep your lips from twitching? Yes; you never thought to see me here again, but it was that night which taught me how I could meet you face to face, and alone. Well, Charles Milverton, what have you to say?"

"Don't imagine that you can bully me," said he, rising to his feet. "I have only to raise my voice, and I could call my servants and have you arrested. But I will make allowance for your natural anger. Leave the room at once as you came, and I will say no more."

The woman stood with her hand buried in her bosom, and the same deadly smile on her thin lips.

"You will ruin no more lives as you ruined mine. You will wring no more hearts as you wrung mine. I will free the world of a poisonous thing. Take that, you hound, and that!—and that!—and that!—and that!"

She had drawn a little gleaming revolver, and emptied barrel after barrel into Milverton's body, the muzzle within two feet of his shirt front. He shrank away and then fell forward upon the table, coughing furiously and clawing among the papers. Then he staggered to his feet, received another shot,

"You couldn't come any other time—eh?"
Sidney Paget, *Strand Magazine*, 1904

21 "Where did she go?" D. Martin Dakin astutely asks. Holmes and Watson's escape will require scaling a six-foot wall, but "Victorian costume, including in this case mantle and veil, did not encourage that form of exercise. . . ." Instead, Dakin believes that the woman, having infiltrated Milverton's household as a servant, returned to some other portion of the house to resume her duties, providing her with the perfect cover.

He fell forward upon the table, coughing
furiously and clawing among the papers.
Charles Raymond Macaulay, *Return of Sherlock Holmes*
(McClure Phillips), 1905

and rolled upon the floor. "You've done me," he cried, and lay still. The woman looked at him intently and ground her heel into his upturned face. She looked again, but there was no sound or movement. I heard a sharp rustle, the night air blew into the heated room, and the avenger was gone.[21]

No interference upon our part could have saved the man from his fate; but, as the woman poured bullet after bullet into Milverton's shrinking body I was about to spring out, when I felt Holmes's cold, strong grasp upon my wrist. I understood the whole argument of that firm, restraining grip—that it was no affair of ours; that justice had overtaken a villain; that we had our own duties and our own objects which were not to be lost sight of. But hardly had the woman rushed from the room when Holmes, with swift, silent steps, was over at the other door. He turned the key in the lock. At the same instant we heard voices in the house and the sound of hurrying feet. The revolver shots had roused the household. With perfect coolness Holmes slipped across to the safe, filled his two arms with bundles of letters, and poured them all into the fire. Again and again he did it, until the safe was empty. Someone turned the handle and beat upon the outside of the door. Holmes looked swiftly round. The letter which had been the messenger of death for Milverton lay, all mottled with his blood, upon the table. Holmes tossed it in among the blazing papers. Then he drew the key from the outer door, passed through after me, and

"Then he staggered to his feet and received another shot."
Sidney Paget, *Strand Magazine*, 1904

22 The shout given by a fox-hunter when he sees a fox break cover.

23 Gavin Brend (and others) doubts that the two-mile run ever took place. "By the time a runner has travelled one mile (let alone two) he will have a fairly accurate idea of the pursuit behind him," observes Brend, in a private letter to William S. Baring-Gould. "He will know how many men are following him, whether they are gaining or losing ground and how he manages finally to shake them off." Since Watson makes no mention of such a chase, Brend disabuses the notion that he and Holmes felt compelled to run for two miles—although he does allow that they may have travelled two miles across Hampstead Heath, running part of the way. Even those commentators who accept the two-mile run observe that the wound in Watson's leg had obviously healed considerably by the time of this tale.

locked it on the outside. "This way, Watson," said he, "we can scale the garden wall in this direction."

I could not have believed that an alarm could have spread so swiftly. Looking back, the huge house was one blaze of light. The front door was open, and figures were rushing down the drive. The whole garden was alive with people, and one fellow raised a view-halloa[22] as we emerged from the veranda and followed hard at our heels. Holmes seemed to know the grounds perfectly, and he threaded his way swiftly among a plantation of small trees, I close at his heels, and our foremost pursuer panting behind us. It was a six-foot wall which barred our path, but he sprang to the top and over. As I did the same I felt the hand of the man behind me grab at my ankle; but I kicked myself free and scrambled over a glass-strewn coping. I fell upon my face among some bushes; but Holmes had me on my feet in an instant, and together we dashed away across the huge expanse of Hampstead Heath. We had run two miles, I suppose, before Holmes at last halted and listened intently.[23] All was absolute silence behind us. We had shaken off our pursuers and were safe.

We had breakfasted and were smoking our morning pipe on the day after the remarkable experience which I have

Hampstead Heath.
Queen's London (1897)

recorded, when Mr. Lestrade, of Scotland Yard, very solemn and impressive, was ushered into our modest sitting-room.

"Good-morning, Mr. Holmes," said he; "good-morning. May I ask if you are very busy just now?"

"Not too busy to listen to you."

"I thought that, perhaps, if you had nothing particular on hand, you might care to assist us in a most remarkable case, which occurred only last night at Hampstead."

"Dear me!" said Holmes. "What was that?"

"A murder—a most dramatic and remarkable murder. I know how keen you are upon these things, and I would take it as a great favour if you would step down to Appledore Towers and give us the benefit of your advice. It is no ordinary crime. We have had our eyes upon this Mr. Milverton for some time, and, between ourselves, he was a bit of a villain. He is known to have held papers which he used for blackmailing purposes. These papers have all been burned by the murderers. No article of value was taken, as it is probable that the criminals were men of good position, whose sole object was to prevent social exposure."

"Criminals!" said Holmes. "Plural!"

"Yes, there were two of them. They were, as nearly as possible, captured red-handed. We have their footmarks, we have their description, it's ten to one that we trace them. The first fellow was a bit too active, but the second was caught by the under-gardener, and only got away after a struggle. He was a middle-sized, strongly built man—square jaw, thick neck, moustache, a mask over his eyes."

"That's rather vague," said Sherlock Holmes. "Why, it might be a description of Watson!"

"It's true," said the Inspector, with amusement. "It might be a description of Watson."

"Well, I'm afraid I can't help you, Lestrade," said Holmes. "The fact is that I knew this fellow Milverton, that I considered him one of the most dangerous men in London, and that I think there are certain crimes which the law cannot touch, and which therefore, to some extent, justify private revenge.[24] No, it's no use arguing. I have made up my mind. My sympathies are with the criminals rather than with the victim, and I will not handle this case."

24 Although it seems possible that it was Holmes, not the mystery lady, who actually killed Milverton, Bruce Harris's seemingly ludicrous contention that Holmes and Milverton had a homosexual affair—and that Holmes eliminated him to suppress the evidence—has stirred up its share of controversy. John Linsenmeyer, who was editor of the *Baker Street Journal* when Harris made his theory public, voices his "strong conviction" that while Holmes might have killed Milverton for "good and sufficient reason . . . , [Harris's] suggestion . . . is unacceptable."

25 The manuscript originally continued, "Yes, yes. It is she."

Holmes had not said one word to me about the tragedy which we had witnessed, but I observed all the morning that he was in his most thoughtful mood, and he gave me the impression, from his vacant eyes and his abstracted manner, of a man who is striving to recall something to his memory. We were in the middle of our lunch, when he suddenly sprang to his feet. "By Jove, Watson, I've got it!"[25] he cried. "Take your hat! Come with me!" He hurried at his top speed down Baker Street and along Oxford Street, until we had almost reached Regent Circus. Here on the left hand there stands a shop window filled with photographs of the celebrities and beauties of the day.

"Following his gaze I saw the picture of a regal and stately lady in Court dress."
Sidney Paget, *Strand Magazine*, 1904

Holmes's eyes fixed themselves upon one of them, and following his gaze I saw the picture of a regal and stately lady in Court dress, with a high diamond tiara upon her noble head. I looked at that delicately curved nose, at the marked eyebrows, at the straight mouth, and the strong little chin beneath it. Then I caught my breath as I read the time-honoured title of the great nobleman and statesman whose wife she had been.[26] My eyes met those of Holmes, and he put his finger to his lips as we turned away from the window.[27]

26 The identity of the lady is never revealed, but based on Watson's description of her, both earlier (when he notes her "dark, handsome, clear-cut face . . . a face with a curved nose, strong, dark eyebrows, shading hard, glittering eyes, and a straight, thin-lipped mouth") and here, L. W. Bailey concludes that she must have been a member of a titled Jewish family.

According to Bailey, Jews were allowed entrance into the titled aristocracy only after the rise of the Rothschilds, headed by patriarch Mayer Amschel Rothschild. And even for that esteemed family, an official place in British high society was slow in coming. The Rothschild brothers—Amschel Mayer, Salomon, Nathan Mayer, Karl, and James—were made barons by the emperor of Austria in 1822; Nathan, who had established the flourishing London branch of the family's banking operations, accepted the title but stated that he still wished to be referred to as "plain Mr. Rothschild." Yet Lionel de Rothschild, the son of Nathan Mayer, was denied a peerage in his father's adopted country when Queen Victoria said in 1869, "To make a Jew a peer is a step the Queen could not assent to." This despite the fact that his father had aided the British government against Napoleon and had essentially saved the London stock market from collapse after the allied victory at Waterloo; and despite the fact that Lionel had become the first Jew elected to Parliament in 1847. (Refusing to take an oath containing the words "in the true faith of a Christian," Lionel left his seat empty for eleven years until the oath was revised.)

A decade after the queen's snub, the social landscape had altered significantly, with the Jewish-born Benjamin Disraeli serving two terms as prime minister in 1868 and 1874–1880 and enjoying the queen's particular favour. In 1876, Queen Victoria bestowed a peerage upon Disraeli, making him the Earl of Beaconsfield, and in 1885 she granted one to Lionel de Rothschild's son, Nathaniel Rothschild. Meanwhile, the queen's eldest son, the Prince of Wales (Albert Edward, later Edward VII), had become great friends with the Rothschilds, blithely ignoring the disapproval of the British elite.

Considering how long Jewish people had been excluded from the nobility, it seems likely that the mystery murderess acquired her aristocratic status via a gentile husband. "If the lady was of Jewish extraction," Bailey concludes, "it is quite clear that her husband was not, since he had a 'time-honoured title.' One may surmise therefore that he had married into one of the Jewish families he had met through the Prince of Wales."

27 Watson has obviously taken great pains to disguise the murdereress's identity from the public; remember that he begins this narrative by stating his longstanding refusal to expose the details of Milverton's death "even with the utmost discretion and reticence . . . but now the principal person concerned is beyond the reach of human law." Most readers (and scholars) assume that this means the woman in question had recently passed away, but L. W. Bailey has a different theory. Calculating backward from the story's April 1904 publication date, Bailey assumes that Watson began writing up the events early in 1903. "On the 26th of June, 1902, Edward VII had been crowned King of England," Bailey muses,

"and had thus become technically above the law and so 'beyond its reach.' Is it not possible that by his choice of words Watson was hinting at a truth he dare not reveal, and into which even now it would be indelicate to probe any further?"

D. Martin Dakin adopts the more mundane view that Watson's words must refer to the demise of the lady who shot Milverton, but he raises some telling questions about Watson's publication of the tale. Why would Watson risk confessing his and Holmes's illegal activities (not to mention their suppression of evidence regarding a murder) at all? Surely he must have realised that legal repercussions were inevitable. No, Dakin concludes, something must have occurred to assure Watson that there would be no risk to himself from publication of the tale. In 1902, Holmes was involved in a case—"The Illustrious Client" —that also involved burglary supposedly committed for a good cause. Holmes's service to that client, reasons Dakin, would have put him in such good graces with royalty that Watson deemed it safe to reveal his and Holmes's own previous turn at playing Robin Hood. "But it cannot have been very agreeable to Inspector Lestrade," Dakin considers, ". . . to know how he had been led up the garden path. It is probable, however, that by then he had also retired, and might therefore have been more inclined to look indulgently on Holmes's past treatment of him."

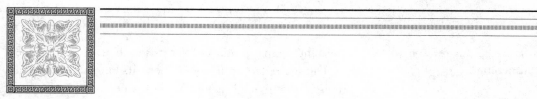

THE ADVENTURE OF THE
SIX NAPOLEONS[1]

A favourite of readers, "The Six Napoleons" finds Holmes on the track of a jewel thief, just as in "The Blue Carbuncle." However, where Holmes sees the traces of a relentless burglar, Inspector Lestrade sees only a madman on the loose. Set in the closing years of Holmes's career, the case reveals that notwithstanding Holmes's constant criticism of Scotland Yard, he is revered there. In perhaps the first recorded instance of deliberate manipulation of the news, Holmes declares, "The Press, Watson, is a most valuable institution, if you only know how to use it."

IT WAS NO very unusual thing for Mr. Lestrade, of Scotland Yard, to look in upon us of an evening, and his visits were welcome to Sherlock Holmes, for they enabled him to keep in touch with all that was going on at the police headquarters. In return for the news which Lestrade would bring, Holmes was always ready to listen with attention to the details of any case upon which the detective was engaged, and was able occasionally, without any active interference, to give some hint or suggestion drawn from his own vast knowledge and experience.

On this particular evening Lestrade had spoken of the weather and the newspapers. Then he had fallen silent, puffing thoughtfully at his cigar. Holmes looked keenly at him.

"Anything remarkable on hand?" he asked.

"Oh, no, Mr. Holmes, nothing very particular."

"Then tell me about it."

Lestrade laughed.

"Well, Mr. Holmes, there is no use denying that there *is*

1 "The Six Napoleons" was published in the *Strand Magazine* in May 1904 and in *Collier's Weekly* on April 30, 1904.

2 The words "which are not his own" have been added in the manuscript.

3 Manly Wade Wellman, in "The Great Man's Great Son: An Inquiry into the Most Private Life of Mr. Sherlock Holmes," identifies Morse Hudson both as the Hudson who blackmailed Squire Trevor ("The 'Gloria Scott'") and as the estranged husband of Holmes's landlady, Mrs. Hudson.

4 The location may explain Lestrade's supposition that he is dealing with a lunatic wrong-doer, for according to Augustus J. C. Hare, in his *Walks in London* (1878), "At the junction of Kennington Road and Lambeth Road is the new Bethlem Hospital, best known as Bedlam. It was called Bedlam even by Sir Thomas More, in whose time it was already a lunatic asylum." England's first institution devoted to the care of the mentally ill, the Bethlem Royal Hospital was founded in 1247 in Bishopsgate as the Priory of St. Mary of Bethlehem, and given over to the City of London as an insane asylum by Henry VIII in 1547. The institution—from whose name the word "bedlam" is derived—was more prison than hospital: "treatment" consisted largely of shackling the patients, and violence and anarchy were the rule rather than the exception. For a time, visitors could pay a penny to gawk at the chaotic spectacle, giving Bethlem more of the air of a madhouse than ever before.

Hare's 1878 reference to the hospital's being "new" is somewhat disingenuous; by then, Bethlem had been at its Lambeth Road location (in Southwark, which already hosted several prisons) for sixty-three years, having moved there in 1815 from Moorfields. Of course, given that Moorfields was Bethlem's home for 140 years as well as the scene of its greatest notoriety, it is understandable that Bethlem and Moorfields would be married in the popular imagination. Conditions eventually improved at the Southwark location in the

something on my mind. And yet it is such an absurd business that I hesitated to bother you about it. On the other hand, although it is trivial, it is undoubtedly queer, and I know that you have a taste for all that is out of the common. But, in my opinion, it comes more in Dr. Watson's line than ours."

"Disease?" said I.

"Madness, anyhow. And a queer madness too! You wouldn't think there was anyone living at this time of day who had such a hatred of Napoleon the First that he would break any image of him that he could see."

Holmes sank back in his chair.

"That's no business of mine," said he.

"Exactly. That's what I said. But then, when the man commits burglary in order to break images which are not his own,[2] that brings it away from the doctor and on to the policeman."

Holmes sat up again.

"Burglary! This is more interesting. Let me hear the details."

Lestrade took out his official notebook and refreshed his memory from its pages.

"The first case reported was four days ago," said he. "It was at the shop of Morse Hudson,[3] who has a place for the sale of pictures and statues in the Kennington Road.[4] The assistant had left the front shop for an instant, when he heard a crash, and hurrying in he found a plaster bust of Napoleon, which stood with several other works of art upon the counter, lying shivered into fragments. He rushed out into the road, but, although several passers-by declared that they had noticed a man run out of the shop, he could neither see anyone nor could he find any means of identifying the rascal. It seemed to be one of those senseless acts of Hooliganism[5] which occur from time to time, and it was reported to the constable on the beat as such. The plaster cast was not worth more than a few shillings, and the whole affair appeared to be too childish for any particular investigation.

"The second case, however, was more serious, and also more singular. It occurred only last night.

"In Kennington Road, and within a few hundred yards of Morse Hudson's shop, there lives a well-known medical practitioner, named Dr. Barnicot, who has one of the largest practices upon the south side of the Thames. His residence and

mid-1800s, with occupational and drug therapy being offered to patients in lieu of restraints. In 1930 the hospital relocated to Beckenham; today, the Southwark building houses the Imperial War Museum.

5 The Oxford English Dictionary defines the word as meaning "wanton acts of vandalism" and notes the earliest recorded use in 1898. Kelvin Jones, in his *Sherlock Holmes Dictionary*, gives the origin as "said to be the name of a leader of a gang, possibly *Hooley's gang*, a family resident in the mid-1890's in Islington (W. Ware). The alternative theory is that the word derives from the Houlihans, an Irish family resident in the Borough (London)."

6 "Devine" may be Paul de Vigne (1843–1901), a Belgian sculptor who lived in Paris until 1882, or possibly British sculptor James S. Deville (1776–1846).

"Lestrade took out his official notebook."
Sidney Paget, *Strand Magazine*, 1904

principal consulting-room is at Kennington Road, but he has a branch surgery and dispensary at Lower Brixton Road, two miles away. This Dr. Barnicot is an enthusiastic admirer of Napoleon, and his house is full of books, pictures, and relics of the French Emperor. Some little time ago he purchased from Morse Hudson two duplicate plaster casts of the famous head of Napoleon by the French sculptor, Devine.[6] One of these he placed in his hall in the house at Kennington Road, and the other on the mantelpiece of the surgery at Lower Brixton. Well, when Dr. Barnicot came down this morning he was astonished to find that his house had been burgled during the night, but that nothing had been taken save the plaster head from the hall. It had been carried out and had been dashed savagely

7 The original iconoclasts were destroyers of art (from Medieval Greek, *Eikonoklasts*, meaning "image breaker"). In the Byzantine empire of the eighth and ninth centuries, Christian sculptures and paintings were either destroyed or banned by those who considered them idolatrous, citing the Ten Commandments' condemnation of images. Another wave of iconoclasm struck during the Protestant Reformation, and it was not until the nineteenth century that the word took on the more secular meaning of one who works to overthrow ideas or institutions. In this instance, Holmes would be familiar with the modern usage, but calls upon his vast historical knowledge to invoke the more literal definition.

8 French: A fixed idea; a monomania, also called "partial moral mania."

against the garden wall, under which its splintered fragments were discovered."

Holmes rubbed his hands.

"This is certainly very novel," said he.

"I thought it would please you. But I have not got to the end yet. Dr. Barnicot was due at his surgery at twelve o'clock, and you can imagine his amazement when, on arriving there, he found that the window had been opened in the night and that the broken pieces of his second bust were strewn all over the room. It had been smashed to atoms where it stood. In neither case were there any signs which could give us a clue as to the criminal or lunatic who had done the mischief. Now, Mr. Holmes, you have got the facts."

"They are singular, not to say grotesque," said Holmes. "May I ask whether the two busts smashed in Dr. Barnicot's rooms were the exact duplicates of the one which was destroyed in Morse Hudson's shop?"

"They were taken from the same mould."

"Such a fact must tell against the theory that the man who breaks them is influenced by any general hatred of Napoleon. Considering how many hundreds of statues of the great Emperor must exist in London, it is too much to suppose such a coincidence as that a promiscuous iconoclast[7] should chance to begin upon three specimens of the same bust."

"Well, I thought as you do," said Lestrade. "On the other hand, this Morse Hudson is the purveyor of busts in that part of London, and these three were the only ones which had been in his shop for years. So, although, as you say, there are many hundreds of statues in London, it is very probable that these three were the only ones in that district. Therefore, a local fanatic would begin with them. What do you think, Dr. Watson?"

"There are no limits to the possibilities of monomania," I answered. "There is the condition which the modern French psychologists have called the '*idée fixe*,'[8] which may be trifling in character, and accompanied by complete sanity in every other way. A man who had read deeply about Napoleon, or who had possibly received some hereditary family injury through the great war, might conceivably form such an '*idée fixe*' and under its influence be capable of any fantastic outrage."

"That won't do, my dear Watson," said Holmes, shaking his

head; "for no amount of '*ideé fixe*' would enable your interesting monomaniac to find out where these busts were situated."

"Well, how do you explain it?"

"I don't attempt to do so. I would only observe that there is a certain method in the gentleman's eccentric proceedings. For example, in Dr. Barnicot's hall, where a sound might arouse the family, the bust was taken outside before being broken, whereas in the surgery, where there was less danger of an alarm, it was smashed where it stood. The affair seems absurdly trifling, and yet I dare call nothing trivial when I reflect that some of my most classic cases have had the least promising commencement. You will remember, Watson, how the dreadful business of the Abernetty family was first brought to my notice by the depth which the parsley had sunk into the butter upon a hot day.[9] I can't afford, therefore, to smile at your three broken busts, Lestrade, and I shall be very much obliged to you if you will let me hear of any fresh developments of so singular a chain of events."

The development for which my friend had asked came in a quicker and an infinitely more tragic form than he could have imagined. I was still dressing in my bedroom next morning, when there was a tap at the door and Holmes entered, a telegram in his hand. He read it aloud:

Come instantly, 131 Pitt Street, Kensington.

—LESTRADE.

"What is it, then?" I asked.

"Don't know—may be anything. But I suspect it is the sequel of the story of the statues. In that case our friend the image-breaker has begun operations in another quarter of London. There's coffee on the table, Watson, and I have a cab at the door."

In half an hour we had reached Pitt Street, a quiet little backwater just beside one of the briskest currents of London life. No. 131 was one of a row, all flat-chested, respectable, and most unromantic dwellings. As we drove up we found the railings in front of the house lined by a curious crowd. Holmes whistled.

"By George! it's attempted murder at the least. Nothing less will hold the London message boy. There's a deed of violence

9 Numerous pastiches and analyses of the "Abernetty business" have been written and are surveyed in detail in William Hyder's "Parsley and Butter: The Abernetty Business." Hyder concludes, without foundation, that no less than murder was involved. Is it not equally likely that a business—perhaps an inn or tavern—run by the Abernetty family was "dreadful" (that is, kept in poor sanitation), and that that condition was first brought to Holmes's notice by the butter having been left out on a hot day? The connection between this observation and the ensuing investigation remains undetermined. A number of scholars consider whether and how fast parsley will sink into butter. Not surprisingly, they do not agree.

10 The observation of "round shoulders" has been added in the manuscript.

11 While "Central Press Syndicate" is a fabricated name, the Central News Agency was an English association for the collection and distribution of news to newspapers subscribing to its services. There were at least ten press and telegraphic associations in London in 1888. "It was to the Central News Agency," observes William S. Baring-Gould, "that Jack the Ripper mailed two horribly jocund notes in late September and early October, 1888."

indicated in that fellow's round shoulders[10] and outstretched neck. What's this, Watson? The top steps swilled down and the other ones dry. Footsteps enough, anyhow! Well, well, there's Lestrade at the front window, and we shall soon know all about it."

The official received us with a very grave face and showed us into a sitting-room, where an exceedingly unkempt and agitated elderly man, clad in a flannel dressing-gown, was pacing up and down. He was introduced to us as the owner of the house—Mr. Horace Harker, of the Central Press Syndicate.[11]

"It's the Napoleon bust business again," said Lestrade. "You seemed interested last night, Mr. Holmes, so I thought perhaps you would be glad to be present now that the affair has taken a very much graver turn."

"What has it turned to, then?"

"He was introduced to us as the owner of the house—
Mr. Horace Harker."
Sidney Paget, *Strand Magazine*, 1904

"To murder. Mr. Harker, will you tell these gentlemen exactly what has occurred?"

The man in the dressing-gown turned upon us with a most melancholy face.

"It's an extraordinary thing," said he, "that all my life I have been collecting other people's news, and now that a real piece of news has come my own way I am so confused and bothered that I can't put two words together. If I had come in here as a journalist I should have interviewed myself and had two columns in every evening paper. As it is, I am giving away valuable copy by telling my story over and over to a string of different people, and I can make no use of it myself. However, I've heard your name, Mr. Sherlock Holmes, and if you'll only explain this queer business I shall be paid for my trouble in telling you the story."

Holmes sat down and listened.

"It all seems to centre round that bust of Napoleon which I bought for this very room about four months ago. I picked it up cheap from Harding Brothers,[12] two doors from the High Street Station. A great deal of my journalistic work is done at night, and I often write until the early morning. So it was to-day. I was sitting in my den, which is at the back of the top of the house, about three o'clock, when I was convinced that I heard some sounds downstairs. I listened, but they were not repeated, and I concluded that they came from outside. Then suddenly, about five minutes later, there came a most horrible yell—the most dreadful sound, Mr. Holmes, that ever I heard. It will ring in my ears as long as I live. I sat frozen with horror for a minute or two. Then I seized the poker and went downstairs. When I entered this room I found the window wide open, and I at once observed that the bust was gone from the mantelpiece. Why any burglar should take such a thing passes my understanding, for it was only a plaster cast and of no real value whatever.

"You can see for yourself that anyone going out through that open window could reach the front doorstep by taking a long stride. This was clearly what the burglar had done, so I went round and opened the door. Stepping out into the dark, I nearly fell over a dead man who was lying there. I ran back for a light, and there was the poor fellow,[13] a great gash in his throat and the whole place swimming in blood. He lay on his

12 Richard Lancelyn Green identifies this as Ponting Brothers, a shop that was located at 123-127 Kensington High Street and adjacent to the Metropolitan and District Railway Station. He further suggests that Watson's fictional name for it was lifted from *Harding's Art Manuals*, a popular series of books on art techniques.

13 The word is "devil" in the manuscript but has been softened to "fellow" in the *Strand Magazine* and book texts, a change (one among several in "The Six Napoleons") that this editor discovered by using a computer to compare a typescript of the manuscript, prepared by William Hyder and published in *"The Napoleon Bust Business Again,"* to a typescript of the published text. The results, while not startling here, raise the tantalising question of who made the changes noted— Dr. Watson, the *Strand Magazine* editor, or perhaps Conan Doyle?

14 The original description, deleted in the manuscript, was "his great black beard bristling upwards." Whether Mr. Harker imagined the beard or whether Watson suppressed the beard in order to conceal the victim's true identity is unknown.

15 In the manuscript, this is originally "Camden Road," amended to "Camden House Road." However, "Campden House Road" appears in the *Strand Magazine* and all book editions. The *Camden* Road is a large street in Kentishtown, while *Campden House* Road is in Kensington. There is no "Camden House Road" in London. Someone apparently noted Watson's error and corrected it before the manuscript was published. Newt and Lillian Williams note, in the *Annotated "Annotated,"* that this is a natural mistake, inasmuch as the "empty house" across from 221B Baker Street was *Camden House* (see "The Empty House"). H. W. Bell, in "Three Identifications," states that there was no Campden House Road, but this is plainly contradicted by several Victorian atlases, which show the road as parallel to Campden *Hill* Road and adjacent to Campden House in Kensington.

16 Since 1703, the racecourse at Doncaster has been the venue for numerous horse races, including the celebrated St. Leger Stakes event, first held in 1776.

back, his knees drawn up, and his mouth horribly open.[14] I shall see him in my dreams. I had just time to blow on my police whistle, and then I must have fainted, for I knew nothing more until I found the policeman standing over me in the hall."

"Well, who was the murdered man?" asked Holmes.

"There's nothing to show who he was," said Lestrade. "You shall see the body at the mortuary, but we have made nothing of it up to now. He is a tall man, sunburned, very powerful, not more than thirty. He is poorly dressed, and yet does not appear to be a labourer. A horn-handled clasp-knife was lying in a pool of blood beside him. Whether it was the weapon which did the deed, or whether it belonged to the dead man, I do not know. There was no name on his clothing, and nothing in his pockets save an apple, some string, a shilling map of London, and a photograph. Here it is."

It was evidently taken by a snap-shot from a small camera. It represented an alert, sharp-featured simian man with thick eyebrows and a very peculiar projection of the lower part of the face, like the muzzle of a baboon.

"And what became of the bust?" asked Holmes, after a careful study of this picture.

"We had news of it just before you came. It has been found in the front garden of an empty house in Campden House Road.[15] It was broken into fragments. I am going round now to see it. Will you come?"

"Certainly. I must just take one look round." He examined the carpet and the window. "The fellow had either very long legs or was a most active man," said he. "With an area beneath, it was no mean feat to reach that window-ledge and open that window. Getting back was comparatively simple. Are you coming with us to see the remains of your bust, Mr. Harker?"

The disconsolate journalist had seated himself at a writing-table.

"I must try and make something of it," said he, "though I have no doubt that the first editions of the evening papers are out already with full details. It's like my luck! You remember when the stand fell at Doncaster?[16] Well, I was the only journalist in the stand, and my journal the only one that had no account of it, for I was too shaken to write it. And now I'll be too late with a murder done on my own doorstep."

As we left the room, we heard his pen travelling shrilly over the foolscap.

The spot where the fragments of the bust had been found was only a few hundred yards away. For the first time our eyes rested upon this presentment of the great Emperor, which seemed to raise such frantic and destructive hatred in the mind of the unknown. It lay scattered, in splintered shards upon the grass. Holmes picked up several of them and examined them carefully. I was convinced, from his intent face and his purposeful manner, that at last he was upon a clue.

"Well?" asked Lestrade.

Holmes shrugged his shoulders.

"We have a long way to go yet," said he. "And yet—and yet—well, we have some suggestive facts to act upon. The possession of this trifling bust was worth more, in the eyes of this strange criminal, than a human life. That is one point. Then there is the singular fact that he did not break it in the house, or immediately outside the house, if to break it was his sole object."

"He was rattled and bustled[17] by meeting this other fellow. He hardly knew what he was doing."

"Well, that's likely enough. But I wish to call your attention very particularly to the position of this house in the garden of which the bust was destroyed."

Lestrade looked about him.

"It was an empty house, and so he knew that he would not be disturbed in the garden."

"Yes, but there is another empty house farther up the street which he must have passed before he came to this one. Why did he not break it there, since it is evident that every yard that he carried it increased the risk of someone meeting him?"

"I give it up," said Lestrade.

Holmes pointed to the street lamp above our heads.

"He could see what he was doing here, and he could not there. That was his reason."

"By Jove! that's true," said the detective. "Now that I come to think of it, Dr. Barnicot's bust was broken not far from his red lamp.[18] Well, Mr. Holmes, what are we to do with that fact?"

"To remember it—to docket it. We may come on something later which will bear upon it. What steps do you propose to take now, Lestrade?"

17 The word appears to be "hustled" in the manuscript, which makes sense, but apparently the editor had "busts" on his mind, and no one corrected this minor slip in either the *Strand Magazine* or the book texts.

18 " 'You ask about the Red Lamp,' says the postscript to the preface of the American edition of Arthur Conan Doyle's *Round the Red Lamp* (1894): 'It is the usual sign of the general practitioner in England.' " The manuscript originally stated that the bust was broken "right under" the red lamp.

"Holmes pointed to the street lamp above our heads."
Sidney Paget, *Strand Magazine*, 1904

"The most practical way of getting at it, in my opinion, is to identify the dead man. There should be no difficulty about that. When we have found who he is and who his associates are, we should have a good start in learning what he was doing in Pitt Street last night, and who it was who met him and killed him on the doorstep of Mr. Horace Harker. Don't you think so?"

"No doubt; and yet it is not quite the way in which I should approach the case."

"What would you do then?"

"Oh, you must not let me influence you in any way. I suggest that you go on your line and I on mine. We can compare notes afterwards, and each will supplement the other."

"Very good," said Lestrade.

"If you are going back to Pitt Street, you might see Mr. Horace Harker. Tell him for me that I have quite made up my mind, and that it is certain that a dangerous homicidal lunatic with Napoleonic delusions was in his house last night.[19] It will be useful for his article."

Lestrade stared.

"You don't seriously believe that?"

Holmes smiled.

"Don't I? Well, perhaps I don't. But I am sure that it will interest Mr. Horace Harker and the subscribers of the Central Press Syndicate. Now, Watson, I think that we shall find that we have a long and rather complex day's work before us. I should be glad, Lestrade, if you could make it convenient to meet us at Baker Street at six o'clock this evening. Until then I should like to keep this photograph found in the dead man's pocket.[20] It is possible that I may have to ask your company and assistance upon a small expedition which will have to be undertaken to-night, if my chain of reasoning should prove to be correct. Until then good-bye and good luck."

Sherlock Holmes and I walked together to the High Street, where we stopped at the shop of Harding Brothers, whence the bust had been purchased. A young assistant informed us that Mr. Harding would be absent until afternoon, and that he was himself a new-comer, who could give us no information. Holmes's face showed his disappointment and annoyance.

"Well, well, we can't expect to have it all our own way, Watson," he said at last. "We must come back in the afternoon, if Mr. Harding will not be here until then. I am, as you have no doubt surmised, endeavouring to trace these busts to their source, in order to find if there is not something peculiar which may account for their remarkable fate. Let us make for Mr. Morse Hudson, of the Kennington Road, and see if he can throw any light upon the problem."

A drive of an hour brought us to the picture-dealer's establishment. He was a small, stout man with a red face and a peppery manner.

"Yes, sir. On my very counter, sir," said he. "What we pay rates and taxes for I don't know, when any ruffian can come in and break one's goods. Yes, sir, it was I who sold Dr. Barnicot his two statues. Disgraceful, sir! A Nihilist plot, that's what I

19 Taking Holmes's remark to Lestrade literally, Charles Fisher argues that Horace Harker was himself Jack the Ripper. Or, could Mr. Harker have been related to Jonathan Harker, solicitor and counsellor to Count Dracula, a portion of whose correspondence was first published in 1897?

20 This sentence has been added in the manuscript.

21 Radical leaders of the French Revolution were known as Red Republicans, after the red "liberty caps" (or the Bonnet Rouge) they wore to signify their support for republicanism. There was also a London socialist newspaper called the *Red Republican*. Founded by George Julian Harney, it published the first English translation of *The Communist Manifesto* in 1850. From Hudson's context, it is difficult to determine which political movement he was referring to, although both may be seen as having violent connotations.

22 Originally described in the manuscript as an "odd job man."

23 James Edward Holroyd, in *Baker Street By-Ways*, questions this narrative. "How, in driving from Kennington to Stepney, would you pass successively through 'fashionable London, hotel London, theatrical London and literary London?' " he asks, pointing out that those neighbourhoods lie north of the Thames, but that the quickest route to Stepney would involve staying on the south side of the river and crossing over at London Bridge or Tower Bridge. Perhaps, suggests Holroyd, either Watson or Conan Doyle wrote up this passage while mistakenly envisioning the journey from Kensington (from which the directions are correct), rather than Kennington. "This might have been excusable in Conan Doyle," he writes, "but not surely in Watson who had been in practice in Kensington for some years."

But D. Martin Dakin rises to Watson's defence, imagining that Holmes had to make a stop at Scotland Yard that, being inconsequential, was not dwelt upon by Watson. Such a trip would involve crossing the Thames near Westminster, which could have constituted "the fringe of fashionable London" (if leaving from Kensington, Dakin notes, they would have passed through the middle of Westminster, not "the fringe"). From there, Dakin

make it. No one but an Anarchist would go about breaking statues. Red republicans[21]—that's what I call 'em. Who did I get the statues from? I don't see what that has to do with it. Well, if you really want to know, I got them from Gelder & Co., in Church Street, Stepney. They are a well-known house in the trade, and have been this twenty years. How many had I? Three—two and one are three—two of Dr. Barnicot's, and one smashed in broad daylight on my own counter. Do I know that photograph? No, I don't. Yes, I do, though. Why, it's Beppo! He was a kind of Italian piece-work man,[22] who made himself useful in the shop. He could carve a bit, and gild and frame, and do odd jobs. The fellow left me last week, and I've heard nothing of him since. No, I don't know where he came from nor where he went to. I had nothing against him while he was here. He was gone two days before the bust was smashed."

"Well, that's all we could reasonably expect to get from Morse Hudson," said Holmes, as we emerged from the shop. "We have this Beppo as a common factor, both in Kennington and in Kensington, so that is worth a ten-mile drive. Now, Watson, let us make for Gelder & Co., of Stepney, the source and origin of the busts. I shall be surprised if we don't get some help down there."

In rapid succession we passed through the fringe of fashionable London, hotel London, theatrical London, literary London, commercial London, and, finally, maritime London,[23] till we came to a river-side city of a hundred thousand souls, where the tenement houses swelter and reek with the outcasts of Europe. Here, in a broad thoroughfare, once the abode of wealthy City merchants, we found the sculpture works for which we searched. Outside was a considerable yard full of monumental masonry. Inside was a large room in which fifty workers were carving or moulding. The manager, a big blond German, received us civilly, and gave a clear answer to all Holmes's questions. A reference to his books showed that hundreds of casts had been taken from a marble copy of Devine's head of Napoleon, but that the three which had been sent to Morse Hudson a year or so before had been half of a batch of six, the other three being sent to Harding Brothers, of Kensington. There was no reason why those six should be different to any of the other casts. He could suggest no possible cause why anyone should wish to destroy them—in fact, he laughed at the idea. Their wholesale price was six shillings, but the retailer would get twelve or more. The cast was taken in two moulds from each side of the face, and then these two profiles of plaster of Paris were joined together to make the complete bust. The work was usually done by Italians in the room we were in. When finished, the busts were put on a table in the passage to dry, and afterwards stored. That was all he could tell us.

But the production of the photograph had a remarkable effect upon the manager. His face flushed with anger, and his brows knotted over his blue Teutonic eyes.

"Ah, the rascal!" he cried. "Yes, indeed, I know him very well. This has always been a respectable establishment, and the only time that we have ever had the police in it was over this very fellow. It was more than a year ago now. He knifed

traces their journey through "the Embankment and Northumberland Avenue for hotel London (plenty of big hotels there), and the Strand for theatrical London; and from there on it is plain sailing."

"'Ah, the rascal!' he cried."
Sidney Paget, *Strand Magazine*, 1904

24 The manager did not know Beppo's last name, yet he had no trouble finding his name in the ledger, observes James Edward Holroyd. "I should like to have seen the index to that pay-list. How do you enter the name of a man who has no surname? As Beppo 'X'? Or was the index conducted on the simple Holmesian principle of first names first as in Victor Lynch, the forger?" (Holroyd here refers to the entry under "V" in Holmes's "good old index," mentioned in "The Sussex Vampire.")

another Italian in the street, and then he came to the works with the police on his heels, and he was taken here. Beppo was his name—his second name I never knew. Serve me right for engaging a man with such a face. But he was a good workman—one of the best."

"What did he get?"

"The man lived, and he got off with a year. I have no doubt he is out now; but he has not dared to show his nose here. We have a cousin of his here, and I daresay he could tell you where he is."

"No, no," cried Holmes, "not a word to the cousin—not a word, I beg of you. The matter is very important and the farther I go with it the more important it seems to grow. When you referred in your ledger to the sale of those casts I observed that the date was June 3 of last year. Could you give me the date when Beppo was arrested?"

"I could tell you roughly by the pay-list," the manager answered. "Yes," he continued, after some turning over of pages,[24] "he was paid last on May 20."

"Thank you," said Holmes. "I don't think that I need intrude upon your time and patience any more." With a last word of caution that he should say nothing as to our researches, we turned our faces westward once more.

The afternoon was far advanced before we were able to snatch a hasty luncheon at a restaurant. A news-bill at the entrance announced "Kensington Outrage. Murder by a Madman," and the contents of the paper showed that Mr. Horace Harker had got his account into print after all. Two columns were occupied with a highly sensational and flowery rendering of the whole incident. Holmes propped it against the cruet-stand and read it while he ate. Once or twice he chuckled.

"This is all right, Watson," said he. "Listen to this: 'It is satisfactory to know that there can be no difference of opinion upon this case, since Mr. Lestrade, one of the most experienced members of the official force, and Mr. Sherlock Holmes, the well-known consulting expert, have each come to the conclusion that the grotesque series of incidents, which have ended in so tragic a fashion, arise from lunacy rather than from deliberate crime. No explanation save mental aberration can cover the facts.' The Press, Watson, is a most valuable institution, if you only know how to use it. And now, if you have quite finished, we will hark back to Kensington and see what the manager of Harding Brothers has to say to the matter."[25]

The founder of that great emporium proved to be a brisk, crisp little person, very dapper and quick, with a clear head and a ready tongue.

"Yes, sir, I have already read the account in the evening papers. Mr. Horace Harker is a customer of ours. We supplied him with the busts[26] some months ago. We ordered three busts of that sort from Gelder & Co., of Stepney. They are all sold now. To whom? Oh, I daresay by consulting our sales book we could very easily tell you. Yes, we have the entries here. One to Mr. Harker, you see, and one to Mr. Josiah Brown, of Laburnum Lodge, Laburnum Vale, Chiswick, and one to Mr. Sandeford, of Lower Grove Road,[27] Reading. No, I have never seen this face which you show me in the photograph. You would hardly forget it, would you, sir—for I've seldom seen an uglier. Have we any Italians on the staff? Yes, sir, we have several among our workpeople and cleaners. I daresay they might get a peep at that sales book if they wanted to. There is no particular reason for keeping a watch upon that book. Well, well, it's a very strange business, and I hope that you will let me know if anything comes of your inquiries."

Holmes had taken several notes during Mr. Harding's evidence, and I could see that he was thoroughly satisfied by the turn which affairs were taking. He made no remark, however, save that, unless we hurried, we should be late for our appointment with Lestrade. Sure enough, when we reached Baker Street the detective was already there, and we found him pacing up and down in a fever of impatience. His look of importance showed that his day's work had not been in vain.

"Well?" he asked. "What luck, Mr. Holmes?"

"We have had a very busy day, and not entirely a wasted one," my friend explained. "We have seen both the retailers and also the wholesale manufacturers. I can trace each of the busts now from the beginning."

"The busts!" cried Lestrade. "Well, well, you have your own methods, Mr. Sherlock Holmes, and it is not for me to say a word against them, but I think I have done a better day's work than you. I have identified the dead man."

"You don't say so?"

"And found a cause for the crime."

25 Deleted in the manuscript is the incomplete phrase "I may tell you that it is his evidence which is I depend upon to."

26 In English editions of the Canon, the word is curiously "busts." The original *Strand Magazine* text reads "bust," as does the Doubleday edition of the Canon.

27 The street identification has been added in the manuscript.

28 The Italian consul, Signor Silvestrelli, published a report at Rome in February 1895 that there were two great Italian centres in London, the oldest being in Holborn (and known as "Saffron Hill") and composed of "organ-men, ice-vendors, ambulant merchants, *plaster-bust sellers*, models for artists, &c [italics added]." The other, newer centre was in Soho, where Italians with a slightly higher class of occupation resided: artists, cooks, hoteliers, restauranteurs, tailors, teachers, and watchmakers. In all, Signor Silvestrelli reported, there were about 12,000 Italians living in London at the time, with Holborn representing "the black point, as it is mostly composed of Southern Italians, whose reputation is not good."

In *Street Life in London* (1877), Adolphe Smith came to something of a similar conclusion, describing Saffron Hill as a uniquely self-enclosed society that was noisy with the bustle of the ubiquitous "ice-men" who sold Italian ices throughout the rest of London. Matter-of-factly labelling some of these men "the worst characters that Italy produces," Smith charged that those who claimed to be Neapolitan had likely never even seen Naples, and were merely covering up for a more unsavoury background. "As a matter of fact, a very large number of the street ice-

"Little Italy," Holborn.
Victorian and Edwardian London

"Splendid!"

"We have an inspector who makes a specialty of Saffron Hill[28] and the Italian Quarter. Well, this dead man had some Catholic emblem round his neck, and that, along with his colour, made me think he was from the South. Inspector Hill knew him the moment he caught sight of him. His name is Pietro Venucci, from Naples,[29] and he is one of the greatest cut-throats in London. He is connected with the Mafia, which, as you know, is a secret political society, enforcing its decrees by murder.[30] Now you see how the affair begins to clear up. The other fellow is probably an Italian also, and a member of the Mafia. He has broken the rules in some fashion. Pietro is set upon his track. Probably the photograph we found in his pocket is the man himself, so that he may not knife the wrong person. He dogs the fellow, he sees him enter a house, he waits outside for him, and in the scuffle he receives his own death-wound. How is that, Mr. Sherlock Holmes?"

Holmes clapped his hands approvingly.

"Excellent, Lestrade, excellent!" he cried. "But I didn't quite follow your explanation of the destruction of the busts."

"The busts! You never can get those busts out of your head. After all, that is nothing; petty larceny, six months at the most. It is the murder that we are really investigating, and I tell you that I am gathering all the threads into my hands."

"And the next stage?"

"Is a very simple one. I shall go down with Hill to the Italian Quarter, find the man whose photograph we have got and arrest him on the charge of murder. Will you come with us?"

"I think not. I fancy we can attain our end in a simpler way. I can't say for certain, because it all depends—well, it all depends upon a factor which is completely outside our control. But I have great hopes—in fact, the betting is exactly two to one[31]—that if you will come with us to-night, I shall be able to help you to lay him by the heels."

"In the Italian Quarter?"

"No; I fancy Chiswick is an address which is more likely to find him. If you will come with me to Chiswick to-night, Lestrade, I'll promise to go to the Italian Quarter with you to-morrow, and no harm will be done by the delay. And now I think that a few hours' sleep would do us all good, for I do not propose to leave before eleven o'clock,[32] and it is unlikely that

Italian ice-man.
John Thomson, *Street Life
in London* (1877)

sellers are Calabrians, and are, therefore, semi-barbarous mountaineers."

Despite their purportedly mean and ignorant ways, Smith admired the ice-men for pursuing an honest living in their new country ("They can make more selling ices in our thoroughfares than in cutting throats round and about Naples"), but this sympathy was not necessarily shared by those Italians, such as Beppo, who created statuettes. These men, "better educated and skilful Italian artisans," were elevated in social rank above the Calabrians, and tended to "express the profoundest contempt for their fellow-countrymen who sell ices in the streets."

29 The manuscript replaces "Florence" with "Naples." This may be Watson's deliberate concealment—see note 30, below.

30 The secret criminal society known as the Mafia began as a number of private Sicilian armies, created in the late Middle Ages to repel foreign conquerers and then hired by landowners to protect their property from roving bandits. In the eighteenth and nineteenth centuries, Sicilians distrustful of ineffectual (and frequently oppressive) local governments grew to rely instead upon the Mafia's private form of justice, based as it was on *omerta*, a strict code of silence that forbade one from turning to the legal authorities for help. Victims and their family members were permitted to undertake *vendettas* (direct retribution) against those who had wronged them, and punishment for breaking the code of silence was severe. By 1900, the various Mafia families, loosely organised, had taken control of the economy in many parts of Sicily.

It is curious that Venucci, ostensibly from Naples, would be connected to the Mafia, which at that time was still centered in Sicily. Naples had its own criminal society, the Camorra. In the latter half of the eighteeenth century, the Camorra, an association that specialised in blackmail, bribery, and smuggling, was encouraged by the corrupt Bourbon regime to police the city and eliminate the opposition. A crackdown was instituted in the 1880s after the unification of Italy, and the Camorra began to decline in power; its grip was fatally loosened in 1911, after several of its members were convicted in a high-profile murder trial. While it is possible that Venucci could have been linked to the Mafia through Sicilian connections, it is equally likely that Lestrade (or the Saffron Hill inspector) was mistaken, and that Venucci was a member of the Camorra instead. In "The Red Circle," Watson deliberately conceals Gorgiano's membership in the "Black Hand" with a fictitious name for the secret society—perhaps here he is also taking steps to avoid displeasing the true organisation.

31 Watson originally miscounted the busts and made the odds "three to one" in the manuscript.

32 Originally "midnight" in the manuscript.

33 A special messenger who would convey a letter at a pre-paid or partly pre-paid rate. The Express Delivery Service was established by the post office in 1891. It was not until the queen's Diamond Jubilee in 1897 that the post office established free postal service for all households in England.

34 A storage room, usually at the top of a house. "Why on earth did Holmes not simply rely on the newspapers' own files, or the public libraries?" wonders John Hall in *Sidelights on Holmes*. "In fact as late as 1887 at the time of *The Sign of Four*, that is precisely what he did do, for after being out a couple of hours he returns to tell Watson that he was 'consulting the back files of the *Times*.' "

35 We see it in use as a weapon, however, only in "The Red-Headed League" and "A Case of Identity."

we shall be back before morning. You'll dine with us, Lestrade, and then you are welcome to the sofa until it is time for us to start. In the meantime, Watson, I should be glad if you would ring for an express messenger,[33] for I have a letter to send, and it is important that it should go at once."

Holmes spent the evening in rummaging among the files of the old daily papers with which one of our lumber-rooms[34] was packed. When at last he descended it was with triumph in his eyes, but he said nothing to either of us as to the result of his researches. For my own part, I had followed step by step the methods by which he had traced the various windings of this complex case, and, though I could not yet perceive the goal which we would reach, I understood clearly that Holmes expected this grotesque criminal to make an attempt upon the two remaining busts, one of which, I remember, was at Chiswick. No doubt the object of our journey was to catch him in the very act, and I could not but admire the cunning with which my friend had inserted a wrong clue in the evening paper so as to give the fellow the idea that he could continue his scheme with impunity. I was not surprised when Holmes suggested that I should take my revolver with me. He had himself picked up the loaded hunting-crop which was his favourite weapon.[35]

A four-wheeler was at the door at eleven, and in it we drove to a spot at the other side of Hammersmith Bridge. Here the cabman was directed to wait. A short walk brought us to a secluded road fringed with pleasant houses, each standing in its own grounds. In the light of a street lamp we read "Laburnum Villa" upon the gate-post of one of them. The occupants had evidently retired to rest, for all was dark save for a fanlight over the hall door, which shed a single blurred circle on to the garden path. The wooden fence which separated the grounds from the road threw a dense black shadow upon the inner side, and here it was that we crouched.

"I fear that you'll have a long wait," Holmes whispered. "We may thank our stars that it is not raining. I don't think we can even venture to smoke to pass the time. However, it's a two to one chance that we get something to pay us for our trouble."

It proved, however, that our vigil was not to be so long as Holmes had led us to fear, and it ended in a very sudden and singular fashion. In an instant, without the least sound to warn

Hammersmith Bridge.
Queen's London (1897)

36 In the manuscript, the phrase is "utter silence" but has been altered in the *Strand Magazine* and book texts.

us of his coming, the garden gate swung open, and a lithe, dark figure, as swift and active as an ape, rushed up the garden path. We saw it whisk past the light thrown from over the door and disappear against the black shadow of the house. There was a long pause, during which we held our breath, and then a very gentle creaking sound came to our ears. The window was being opened. The noise ceased, and again there was a long silence. The fellow was making his way into the house. We saw the sudden flash of a dark lantern inside the room. What he sought was evidently not there, for again we saw the flash through another blind, and then through another.

"Let us get to the open window. We will nab him as he climbs out," Lestrade whispered.

But before we could move the man had emerged again. As he came out into the glimmering patch of light we saw that he carried something white under his arm. He looked stealthily all round him. The silence[36] of the deserted street reassured him. Turning his back upon us, he laid down his burden, and the next instant there was the sound of a sharp tap, followed by a clatter and rattle. The man was so intent upon what he was doing that he never heard our steps as we stole across the grass plot. With the bound of a tiger Holmes was on his back, and an

But before we could move, the man had emerged again.
Anonymous, *Portland Oregonian*, August 27, 1911

instant later Lestrade and I had him by either wrist, and the handcuffs had been fastened. As we turned him over I saw a hideous, sallow face, with writhing, furious features glaring up at us, and I knew that it was indeed the man of the photograph whom we had secured.

But it was not our prisoner to whom Holmes was giving his attention. Squatted on the doorstep, he was engaged in most carefully examining that which the man had brought from the house. It was a bust of Napoleon like the one which we had seen that morning, and it had been broken into similar fragments. Carefully Holmes held each separate shard to the light, but in no way did it differ from any other shattered piece of plaster. He had just completed his examination when the hall lights flew up, the door opened, and the owner of the house, a jovial, rotund figure in shirt and trousers, presented himself.

"Mr. Josiah Brown, I suppose?" said Holmes.

"Yes, sir; and you no doubt are Mr. Sherlock Holmes? I had the note which you sent by the express messenger, and I did exactly what you told me. We locked every door on the inside and awaited developments. Well, I'm very glad to see that you have got the rascal.[37] I hope, gentlemen, that you will come in and have some refreshment."

However, Lestrade was anxious to get his man into safe quarters, so within a few minutes our cab had been summoned and we were all four upon our way to London. Not a word would our captive say; but he glared at us from the shadow of his matted hair, and once, when my hand seemed within his reach, he snapped at it like a hungry wolf. We stayed long enough at the police-station to learn that a search of his cloth-

37 Deleted in the manuscript is the phrase "and the Burglary Insurance people will have to pay me for my bust, so I have nothing to complain of."

We saw that he carried something white under his arm.
Charles Raymond Macaulay, *Return of Sherlock Holmes*
(McClure Phillips), 1905

38 Lestrade is making a rare joke here. Clearly—unless appearances are monstrously deceiving—the villain is not a landowner whose family bears a coat of arms.

"With the bound of a tiger Holmes was on his back."
Sidney Paget, *Strand Magazine*, 1904

ing revealed nothing save a few shillings and a long sheath knife, the handle of which bore copious traces of recent blood.

"That's all right," said Lestrade, as we parted. "Hill knows all these gentry,[38] and he will give a name to him. You'll find that my theory of the Mafia will work out all right. But I'm sure I am exceedingly obliged to you, Mr. Holmes, for the workmanlike way in which you laid hands upon him. I don't quite understand it all yet."

"I fear it is rather too late an hour for explanations," said Holmes. "Besides, there are one or two details which are not finished off, and it is one of those cases which are worth working out to the very end. If you will come round once more to my rooms at six o'clock to-morrow, I think I shall be able to show you that even now you have not grasped the entire meaning of this business, which presents some features which make it absolutely original in the history of crime. If ever I permit you to chronicle any more of my little problems,[39] Watson, I foresee that you will enliven your pages by an account of the singular adventure of the Napoleonic busts."

When we met again next evening, Lestrade was furnished with much information concerning our prisoner. His name, it appeared, was Beppo, second name unknown. He was a well-known ne'er-do-well among the Italian colony. He had once been a skilful sculptor and had earned an honest living, but he had taken to evil courses, and had twice already been in gaol— once for a petty theft, and once, as we had already heard, for stabbing a fellow-countryman. He could talk English perfectly well. His reasons for destroying the busts were still unknown, and he refused to answer any questions upon the subject; but the police had discovered that these same busts might very well have been made by his own hands, since he was engaged in this class of work at the establishment of Gelder & Co. To all this information, much of which we already knew, Holmes listened with polite attention, but I, who knew him so well,

39 For reasons that may be connected with his disappearance from 1891 to 1894, Holmes apparently forbade Watson from publishing any post-Reichenbach tales until 1903, when publication of the stories later collected in the *Return* commenced in the *Strand Magazine*. (*The Hound of the Baskervilles*, which Watson published in serial form commencing in 1901, was likely a pre-Reichenbach case.)

Holmes had just completed his examination
when the door opened.
Frederick Dorr Steele, *Collier's*, 1904

"The door opened, and the owner of the
house presented himself."
Sidney Paget, *Strand Magazine*, 1904

could clearly see that his thoughts were elsewhere, and I
detected a mixture of mingled uneasiness and expectation
beneath that mask which he was wont to assume. At last he
started in his chair and his eyes brightened. There had been a
ring at the bell. A minute later we heard steps upon the stairs,
and an elderly, red-faced man with grizzled side-whiskers was
ushered in. In his right hand he carried an old-fashioned
carpet-bag, which he placed upon the table.

"Is Mr. Sherlock Holmes here?"

My friend bowed and smiled. "Mr. Sandeford, of Reading, I
suppose?" said he.

"Yes, sir. I fear that I am a little late; but the trains were awkward. You wrote to me about a bust that is in my possession."

"Exactly."

"I have your letter here. You said, 'I desire to possess a copy of Devine's Napoleon, and am prepared to pay you ten pounds for the one which is in your possession.' Is that right?"

"Certainly."

"I was very much surprised at your letter, for I could not imagine how you knew that I owned such a thing."

"Of course you must have been surprised, but the explanation is very simple. Mr. Harding, of Harding Brothers, said that they had sold you their last copy, and he gave me your address."

"Oh, that was it, was it? Did he tell you what I paid for it?"

He carried an old-fashioned carpet-bag.
Frederick Dorr Steele, *Collier's*, 1904

"No, he did not."

"Well, I am an honest man, though not a very rich one. I only gave fifteen shillings for the bust, and I think you ought to know that before I take ten pounds from you."

"I am sure the scruple does you honour, Mr. Sandeford. But I have named that price, so I intend to stick to it."

"Well, it is very handsome of you, Mr. Holmes. I brought the bust up with me, as you asked me to do. Here it is!"

He opened his bag, and at last we saw placed upon our table a complete specimen of that bust which we had already seen more than once in fragments.

Holmes took a paper from his pocket and laid a ten-pound note upon the table.

"You will kindly sign that paper, Mr. Sandeford, in the presence of these witnesses. It is simply to say that you transfer every possible right that you ever had in the bust to me. I am a methodical man, you see, and you never know what turn

"I brought the bust up with me, as you asked me to do."
Sidney Paget, *Strand Magazine*, 1904

He picked up his hunting-crop and struck Napoleon.
Frederick Dorr Steele, *Collier's*, 1904

events might take afterwards. Thank you, Mr. Sandeford; here is your money, and I wish you a very good evening."

When our visitor had disappeared Sherlock Holmes's movements were such as to rivet our attention. He began by taking a clean white cloth from a drawer and laying it over the table. Then he placed his newly acquired bust in the centre of the cloth. Finally he picked up his hunting-crop and struck Napoleon a sharp blow on the top of the head. The figure broke into fragments, and Holmes bent eagerly over the shattered remains. Next instant, with a loud shout of triumph, he held up one splinter, in which a round, dark object was fixed like a plum in a pudding.

"Gentlemen," he cried, "let me introduce you to the famous black pearl of the Borgias!"[40]

Lestrade and I sat silent for a moment, and then, with a spontaneous impulse, we both broke out clapping as at the well-wrought crisis of a play. A flush of colour sprang to Holmes's pale cheeks, and he bowed to us like the master

40 The Borgia family, originally from Spain, came to wield considerable religious and political power in Italy, gaining a reputation for political ruthlessness in the process. Alfonso de Borja (1378–1458), the cardinal-archbishop of Valencia, moved to Rome when selected to serve as Pope Callixtus III in 1455; his nephew, Rodrigo (1431–1503), followed in his uncle's footsteps and was named Pope Alexander VI in 1492. He fathered several illegitimate children, among them Cesare (1476–1507) and Lucrezia (1480–1523).

At first, Cesare also took the religious path, becoming the archbishop of Valencia and a cardinal. But after the death of his older brother (in whose murder Cesare may have had a hand), Cesare turned to politics, marrying the Frenchwoman Charlotte d'Albret to bolster a Borgia alliance with Louis XII. Named duke of Romagna by his father, Cesare strengthened his rule by conquering several territories, eliminating his enemies by luring them to a castle and strangling them. So brutal and absolute were Cesare's methods that Machiavelli used him as a model in *The Prince*. His power declining following the death of Alexander, the succession of adversary Julius II, and a bout with debilitating illness, Cesare lost his land (even Louis XII turned on him, demanding the return of territories he'd seized) and his titles, fleeing to Spain, where he was arrested and thrown in prison. After escaping, Cesare died fighting rebel forces for his brother-in-law, the king of Navarre.

Lucrezia Borgia played less of an active role in her family's many crimes, instead functioning mainly as a sort of pawn in forging alliances. In all, she married three times, each marriage serving a handy political purpose for her father and her brother. Her first marriage, to Giovanni Sforza in 1492, was annulled when the pope switched allegiances from Milan to Naples; Sforza left Rome fearing for his life. Alexander then played up the Naples angle, marrying Lucrezia off to Alfonso, the illegitimate son to Alfonso II of the powerful Aragón family. Yet the advantages of this marriage, too, crumbled, when Cesare established his own alliance with Louis XII and began amassing power in Romagna, thereby threatening Naples. Alfonso, now expendable, narrowly escaped death on the steps of St. Peter's and later, recovering from his wounds, was strangled by a servant of Cesare's. (A year after Alfonso's death, Lucrezia was seen with a three-year-old boy, whom many allege was her son with either Cesare or Alexander.) Lucrezia's third union, to Alfonso d'Este, duke of Ferrera, was intended to aid Cesare's Romagna campaign but also proved the balm to Lucrezia's tumultuous life. As duchess of Ferrera, Lucrezia opened her court to artists and poets, and in the history of the Italian Renaissance she is renowned as a brilliant and generous patron of the arts.

41 According to Donald Redmond, two princes of Colonna were living in 1900: Don Fabrizio of Avella, a soldier and civic official who was named senator in 1888, and Don Prospero of Sonnino, a cavalry officer who became senator in 1900.

Finally, he picked up his hunting crop and struck Napoleon a sharp blow on the top of the head.
Anonymous, *Portland Oregonian*, August 27, 1911

dramatist who receives the homage of his audience. It was at such moments that for an instant he ceased to be a reasoning machine, and betrayed his human love for admiration and applause. The same singularly proud and reserved nature which turned away with disdain from popular notoriety was capable of being moved to its depths by spontaneous wonder and praise from a friend.

"Yes, gentlemen," said he, "it is the most famous pearl now existing in the world, and it has been my good fortune, by a connected chain of inductive reasoning, to trace it from the Prince of Colonna's[41] bedroom at the Dacre Hotel, where it was lost, to the interior of this, the last of the six busts of Napoleon which were manufactured by Gelder & Co., of Stepney. You will remember, Lestrade, the sensation caused by the disappearance of this valuable jewel, and the vain efforts of the London police to recover it. I was myself consulted upon the case; but I was unable to throw any light upon it. Suspicion fell upon the maid of the Princess, who was an Italian; and it was proved that she had a brother in London, but we failed to trace any connection between them. The maid's name was Lucretia Venucci, and there is no doubt in my mind that this Pietro who was murdered two nights ago was the brother. I have been looking up the dates in the old files of the paper, and I find that the disappearance of the pearl was exactly two days before the arrest of Beppo, for some crime of violence—an event which took place in the factory of Gelder & Co., at the very moment when these busts were being made. Now you clearly see the sequence of events, though you see them, of course, in the inverse order to the way in which they presented themselves to me. Beppo had the pearl in his possession. He may have stolen it from Pietro, he may have been Pietro's confederate, he may have been the go-between of Pietro and his sister. It is of no consequence to us which is the correct solution.

"The main fact is that he *had* the pearl, and at that moment, when it was on his person, he was pursued by the police. He made for the factory in which he worked, and he knew that he had only a few minutes in which to conceal this enormously valuable prize, which would otherwise be found on him when he was searched. Six plaster casts of Napoleon were drying in the passage. One of them was still soft. In an instant Beppo, a skilful workman, made a small hole in the wet plaster, dropped in the pearl, and with a few touches covered over the aperture once more. It was an admirable hiding-place. No one could possibly find it. But Beppo was condemned to a year's imprisonment, and in the meanwhile his six busts were scattered over London. He could not tell which contained his treasure. Only by breaking them could he see. Even shaking would tell him nothing for as the plaster was wet it was probable that the pearl would adhere to it—as, in fact, it has done. Beppo did not despair, and he conducted his search with considerable ingenuity and perseverance. Through a cousin who works with Gelder he found out the retail firms who had bought the busts. He managed to find employment with Morse Hudson,[42] and in that way tracked down three of them. The pearl was not

42 In the manuscript, the employer is not identified, and the phrase "one of them" appears in place of "Morse Hudson." Evidently, someone determined later that the reader needed to be reminded that Holmes had already determined that Beppo was employed by Morse Hudson, for the *Strand Magazine* and book texts all read as above.

One of the plaster casts.
Frederick Dorr Steele, *Collier's*, 1904

there. Then with the help of some Italian employeé he succeeded in finding out where the other three busts had gone.
The first was at Harker's. There he was dogged by his confederate, who held Beppo responsible for the loss of the pearl, and
he stabbed him in the scuffle which followed."

"If he was his confederate, why should he carry his photograph?" I asked.

"As a means of tracing him if he wished to inquire about him
from any third person. That was the obvious reason. Well, after
the murder I calculated that Beppo would probably hurry
rather than delay his movements. He would fear that the police
would read his secret, and so he hastened on before they
should get ahead of him. Of course, I could not say that he had
not found the pearl in Harker's bust. I had not even concluded
for certain that it was the pearl; but it was evident to me that
he was looking for something, since he carried the bust past

the other houses in order to break it in the garden which had a lamp overlooking it. Since Harker's bust was one in three, the chances were exactly as I told you—two to one against the pearl being inside it. There remained two busts, and it was obvious that he would go for the London one first. I warned the inmates of the house, so as to avoid a second tragedy, and we went down, with the happiest results. By that time, of course, I knew for certain that it was the Borgia pearl that we were after. The name of the murdered man linked the one event with the other. There only remained a single bust—the Reading one—and the pearl must be there. I bought it in your presence from the owner—and there it lies."

We sat in silence for a moment.

"Well," said Lestrade, "I've seen you handle a good many cases, Mr. Holmes, but I don't know that I ever knew a more workmanlike one than that. We're not jealous of you at Scotland Yard. No, sir, we are very[43] proud of you, and if you come down to-morrow there's not a man, from the oldest inspector to the youngest constable, who wouldn't be glad to shake you by the hand."

"Thank you!" said Holmes. "Thank you!" and as he turned away it seemed to me that he was more nearly moved by the softer human emotions than I had ever seen him. A moment later he was the cold and practical thinker once more. "Put the pearl in the safe, Watson,"[44] said he, "and get out the papers of the Conk-Singleton forgery case. Good-bye, Lestrade. If any little problem comes your way I shall be happy, if I can, to give you a hint or two as to its solution."

[43] The word "damned" has been replaced with "very" in the manuscript.

[44] Holmes handled this and other cases ("The Reigate Squires," "Black Peter," "The Golden Pince-Nez," "The Abbey Grange," "The Cardboard Box," "The Dying Detective," *A Study in Scarlet*, *The Valley of Fear*) solely for the experience, that is, without a paying client. Some scholars speculate that Holmes may have been quietly compensated by the police inspectors, to enhance their careers. While there is no evidence that Lestrade paid Holmes (in this case, anyway), Holmes appears to turn his experience to tangible profit. He displays no qualms about keeping the fruits of his investigation, figuring, perhaps, that "to the victor go the spoils." The pearl's rightful owner—the Prince of Colonna—on the other hand, still has no idea his treasure has been recovered. "Holmes had no title to the pearl at all," S. T. L. Harbottle charges. "He was in fact a receiver of stolen goods." And yet Holmes acts as if he is merely the next person in the line of succession to the pearl. "There was no suggestion of returning the pearl to the Prince—far from it," continues Harbottle. " 'Put the pearl in the safe, Watson,' said Holmes quite unblushingly. . . ."

Not only was the pearl "enormously valuable," but it likely would have been heavily insured. Ian McQueen believes that Holmes ultimately did not keep the pearl but instead turned it in for a reward. Surely, McQueen observes, Holmes had a dual purpose in "looking up the dates in the old files of the paper," as he simultaneously would have searched for any advertisement that the loss adjuster would have run. Note that when he received the bust from Sandeford, he had a document of transfer already prepared, with Watson and Lestrade conveniently serving as his two witnesses.

THE ADVENTURE OF THE
THREE STUDENTS[1]

"The Three Students" provides a trove of background information for scholars regarding Holmes's university years. The crime presented here—regarding a student who cheats on an exam—pales in comparison to those of other stories, but the wealth of details regarding college life makes for a rewarding tale. What also makes the case memorable is that one of the first published pieces of Sherlockian scholarship, written by editor and critic Andrew Lang, examined its events at length. So implausible are the facts of "The Three Students" that some suggest the entire case was a diversion, a joke created by Watson and an old friend of Holmes to mystify the detective.

1 "The Three Students" appeared in the *Strand Magazine* in June 1904 and in *Collier's Weekly* on September 24, 1904.

2 As will be seen, Watson's cautionary words are completely ignored by the commentators, who endeavour to discern whether the university was Cambridge or Oxford. Holmes's evident familiarity with the town, the customs, and some of its inhabitants leads many scholars to conclude that whatever university is depicted in "The Three Students" *must* be the university Holmes himself attended. However, the clues are ambiguous, at best, and the controversy remains unsettled.

IT WAS IN THE YEAR '95 that a combination of events, into which I need not enter, caused Mr. Sherlock Holmes and myself to spend some weeks in one of our great University towns, and it was during this time that the small but instructive adventure which I am about to relate befell us. It will be obvious that any details which would help the reader to exactly identify the college or the criminal would be injudicious and offensive.[2] So painful a scandal may well be allowed to die out. With due discretion the incident itself may, however, be described, since it serves to illustrate some of those qualities for which my friend was remarkable. I will endeavour in my statement to avoid such terms as would serve to limit the events to any particular place, or give a clue as to the people concerned.

We were residing at the time in furnished lodgings close to a library where Sherlock Holmes was pursuing some labourious researches in early English charters—researches which led

"The Adventure of the Three Students"

Frederick Dorr Steele, *Collier's*, 1904

3 See the appendix on page 1089 for a discussion of the Oxford vs. Cambridge aspects of the study of early English charters.

4 In this case, "tutor" is meant to describe a fellow who instructs the undergraduates at one of Oxford or Cambridge's many colleges. Being a tutor is quite prestigious—the position carries both a stipend and permanent membership on the college's governing board. It is awarded on the basis of superior performance on one's undergraduate exams. The *Encyclopædia Britannica* (11th Ed.) distinguishes the responsibilities of the tutor at Oxford and the tutor at Cambridge, noting that the former lectures and supervises undergraduates, whereas the latter is not required to teach. Is this a point for Oxford?

5 Although scholars analyse "The Three Students" in detail considering whether it displays evidence of *Holmes's* familiarity with the University town, this phrase implies that Watson knew Soames well before "the year '95." How Watson and Soames came into contact with each other remains a mystery, for Watson never mentions any university career (in *A Study in Scarlet*) other than his years at the University of London, where he eventually obtained his M.D. Perhaps Soames was earlier employed as an instructor at the public school attended by Percy Phelps and Watson ("The Naval Treaty")?

to results so striking that they may be the subject of one of my future narratives.[3] Here it was that one evening we received a visit from an acquaintance, Mr. Hilton Soames, tutor[4] and lecturer at the College of St. Luke's. Mr. Soames was a tall, spare man, of a nervous and excitable temperament. I had always known him[5] to be restless in his manner, but on this particular occasion he was in such a state of uncontrollable agitation that it was clear something very unusual had occurred.

"I trust, Mr. Holmes, that you can spare me a few hours of your valuable time. We have had a very painful incident at St. Luke's, and really, but for the happy chance of your being in the town, I should have been at a loss what to do."

"I am very busy just now, and I desire no distractions," my friend answered. "I should much prefer that you called in the aid of the police."

6 Christopher Redmond, in *A Sherlock Holmes Handbook*, finds it "improbable" that avoiding scandal was Soames's main goal, noting that a university (or tutor) truly interested in keeping things quiet would try to settle the matter internally rather than call in a famous detective to investigate the matter.

7 "The true Holmes is never discourteous to a client," contends Ronald A. Knox, who, in "Studies in the Literature of Sherlock Holmes," rejects all of the stories of *Return of Sherlock Holmes* as "lucubrations of [Watson's] unaided inventions."

8 The manuscript, owned by the Houghton Library of Harvard University, originally read "day after tomorrow."

9 One of ancient Greece's greatest historians, the Athenian Thucydides (ca. 460–400 B.C.) served as a general in the Peloponnesian War and was exiled after failing to prevent the city of Amphipolis from falling to the Spartans. During the twenty years he was banished from Athens, Thucydides wrote his only work, *History of the Peloponnesian War*, a military history of relations between Athens and Sparta that incorporated a chronological narrative as well as imagined speeches that were inserted into the narration. (The most famous of these is Pericles's funeral oration.) It differed significantly from previous historical accounts in that it was a work meant to be read, not recited. Rather than just recording events, Thucydides analysed their significance and strived for factual accuracy, clearly attempting to create a definitive history that would be studied by future generations.

Soames's choice of a passage from Thucydides for students to translate strikes some as a bit of poor judgement. Lord Donegall, in *Baker Street and Beyond*, presumes that any student hoping to qualify for such a prestigious scholarship would surely have studied

"I trust, Mr. Holmes, that you can spare me a few hours."
Frederick Dorr Steele, *Collier's*, 1904

"No, no, my dear sir; such a course is utterly impossible. When once the law is evoked it cannot be stayed again, and this is just one of those cases where, for the credit of the college, it is most essential to avoid scandal.[6] Your discretion is as well known as your powers, and you are the one man in the world who can help me. I beg you, Mr. Holmes, to do what you can."

My friend's temper had not improved since he had been deprived of the congenial surroundings of Baker Street. Without his scrap-books, his chemicals, and his homely untidiness, he was an uncomfortable man. He shrugged his shoulders in ungracious acquiescence,[7] while our visitor in hurried words and with much excitable gesticulation poured forth his story.

"I must explain to you, Mr. Holmes, that to-morrow[8] is the first day of the examination for the Fortescue Scholarship. I am one of the examiners. My subject is Greek, and the first of the papers consists of a large passage of Greek translation which the candidate has not seen. This passage is printed on the examination paper, and it would naturally be an immense advantage if the candidate could prepare it in advance. For this reason great care is taken to keep the paper secret.

"To-day about three o'clock the proofs of this paper arrived from the printers. The exercise consists of half a chapter of Thucydides.[9] I had to read it over carefully, as the text must be absolutely[10] correct. At four-thirty my task was not yet completed.[11] I had, however, promised to take tea in a friend's rooms, so I left the proof upon my desk. I was absent rather more than an hour.

"You are aware, Mr. Holmes, that our college doors are double—a green baize[12] one within and a heavy oak one without. As I approached my outer door I was amazed to see a key in it. For an instant I imagined that I had left my own there, but on feeling in my pocket I found that it was all right. The only duplicate which existed, so far as I knew, was that which belonged to my servant, Bannister, a man who has looked after my room for ten years, and whose honesty is absolutely above suspicion. I found that the key was indeed his, that he had entered my room to know if I wanted tea, and that he had very carelessly left the key in the door when he came out. His visit to my room must have been within a very few minutes of my leaving it. His forgetfulness about the key would have mattered little upon any other occasion, but on this one day it has produced the most deplorable consequences.

"The moment I looked at my table I was aware that some one had rummaged among my papers. The proof was in three long slips.[13] I had left them all together. Now, I found that one of them was lying on the floor, one was on the side-table near the window, and the third was where I had left it."

Holmes stirred for the first time.

"The first page on the floor, the second in the window, and the third where you left it," said he.

"Exactly, Mr. Holmes. You amaze me. How could you possibly know that?"

"Pray continue your very interesting statement."

"For an instant I imagined that Bannister had taken the unpardonable liberty of examining my papers. He denied it, however, with the utmost earnestness, and I am convinced that he was speaking the truth. The alternative was that someone passing had observed the key in the door, had known that I was out, and had entered to look at the papers. A large sum of money is at stake, for the scholarship is a very valuable one, and an unscrupulous man might very well run a risk in order to gain an advantage over his fellows.

"Bannister was very much upset by the incident. He had nearly fainted when we found that the papers had undoubtedly been tampered with. I gave him a little brandy and left

Thucydides rigourously and would therefore know his work "as well as an Honours Student in English Literature knows his *Hamlet*." Any excerpt Soames used would then not qualify as "a large passage of Greek translation which the candidate has not seen." However, Tony Bird suggests that Soames could have used portions of the less-studied speeches, not the narratives, because the speeches generally contain few contextual clues (personal names, places) and thus are harder to recognise. Bird also points out that the scholarship was likely to be an award given to a student early on in his career, before an undergraduate would have completed his reading of Thucydides, required only in the *second* part of Oxford's Classics course.

10 The manuscript originally read "grammatically," which is nonsense in the context of a Greek passage.

11 Ronald A. Knox is the first to comment on this extraordinary statement: "Is it likely . . . that [only] half a chapter should take the examiner an hour and a half to correct for the press?"

12 A coarse woollen cloth used for curtains, door covers, and table covers.

13 Numerous commentators, beginning with Andrew Lang, point out that not even a whole chapter of Thucydides is as long as three long slips of printers' proofs.

14 Copying the entire thing may have been unnecessary, observes Andrew Lang, who guesses that a more expedient culprit could have gotten all the information he would need merely by jotting down one sentence from the beginning, one from the end, and a note on the subject matter. This should have been enough to allow the student to look the passage up at his leisure, in his own rooms.

"How could you possibly know that?"
Sidney Paget, *Strand Magazine*, 1904

him collapsed in a chair while I made a most careful examination of the room. I soon saw that the intruder had left other traces of his presence besides the rumpled papers. On the table in the window were several shreds from a pencil which had been sharpened. A broken tip of lead was lying there also. Evidently the rascal had copied the paper[14] in a great hurry, had broken his pencil, and had been compelled to put a fresh point to it."

"Excellent!" said Holmes, who was recovering his good humour as his attention became more engrossed by the case. "Fortune has been your friend."

"This was not all. I have a new writing-table with a fine surface of red leather. I am prepared to swear, and so is Bannister, that it was smooth and unstained. Now I found a clean cut in it about three inches long—not a mere scratch, but a positive cut. Not only this, but on the table I found a small ball of black dough, or clay, with specks of something which looks like sawdust in it, I am convinced that these marks were left by the man who rifled the papers. There were no foot marks and no other evidence as to his identity. I was at my wit's end, when suddenly the happy thought occurred to me that you were in the town, and I came straight round to put the matter into your hands. Do help me, Mr. Holmes! You see my dilemma. Either I must find the man, or else the examination must be postponed until fresh papers are prepared, and since this cannot be done without explanation, there will ensue a hideous scandal, which will throw a cloud not only on the college but on the University. Above all things, I desire to settle the matter quietly and discreetly."

"I shall be happy to look into it and to give you such advice as I can," said Holmes, rising and putting on his overcoat. "The case is not entirely devoid of interest. Had anyone visited you in your room after the papers came to you?"

"Yes; young Daulat Ras, an Indian student, who lives on the same stair, came in to ask me some particular about the examination."

"For which he was entered?"

"Yes."

"And the papers were on your table?"

"To the best of my belief they were rolled up."

"But might be recognized as proofs?"

"Possibly."

"No one else in your room?"

"No."

"Did anyone know that these proofs would be there?"

"No one save the printer."

"Did this man Bannister know?"

"No, certainly not. No one knew."

"Where is Bannister now?"

"He was very ill, poor fellow! I left him collapsed in the chair. I was in such a hurry to come to you."

"You left your door open?"

"I locked up the papers first."

"Then it amounts to this, Mr. Soames, that, unless the Indian student recognised the roll as being proofs, the man who tampered with them came upon them accidentally without knowing that they were there."

15 The first of several insulting remarks Holmes aims at Watson in the course of "The Three Students," evidence, as Watson says, that "his temper had not improved" by leaving Baker Street.

Daulat Ras.
Frederick Dorr Steele, *Collier's*, 1904

"So it seems to me."

Holmes gave an enigmatic smile.

"Well," said he, "let us go round. Not one of your cases, Watson—mental, not physical.[15] All right; come if you want to. Now, Mr. Soames—at your disposal!"

The sitting-room of our client opened by a long, low, latticed window on to the ancient lichen-tinted court of the old college. A Gothic arched door led to a worn stone staircase. On the ground floor was the tutor's room. Above were three students, one on each story. It was already twilight when we reached the scene of our problem. Holmes halted and looked earnestly at the window. Then he approached it, and, standing on tiptoe with his neck craned, he looked into the room.

"He must have entered through the door. There is no opening except the one pane," said our learned guide.

"Dear me!" said Holmes, and he smiled in a singular way as he glanced at our companion. "Well, if there is nothing to be learned here, we had best go inside."

The lecturer unlocked the outer door and ushered us into his room. We stood at the entrance while Holmes made an examination of the carpet.

"I am afraid there are no signs here," said he. "One could hardly hope for any upon so dry a day. Your servant seems to have quite recovered. You left him in a chair, you say; which chair?"

"By the window there."

"I see. Near this little table. You can come in now. I have finished with the carpet. Let us take the little table first. Of course, what has happened is very clear. The man entered and took the papers, sheet by sheet, from the central table. He carried them over to the window table, because from there he

"With his neck craned, he looked into the room."
Sidney Paget, *Strand Magazine*, 1904

16 Johann Lothar von Faber (1817–1896) and John Eberhard Faber (1822–1879), were German brothers who took the family pencil business of their great-grandfather, Kaspar Faber, and turned it into a worldwide enterprise. After assuming control of Kaspar's operations near Nuremberg, Lothar expanded into the rest of Europe and the United States, in 1856 contracting exclusive rights to all the graphite being mined in eastern Siberia. Meanwhile, his brother had gone to New York, establishing America's first significant pencil factory in 1861. Eventually, the German portion of the Faber brothers' business was sold (in 1903), but the U.S.-based Eberhard Faber Pencil Company remained under the family's control and was incorporated in 1898. Most likely, the chip that Holmes is examining originated in Germany, where the company was known as "Johann Faber."

The earliest "pencils" were nothing more than lumps of chalk or lead styluses, the latter used by ancient Egyptians and medieval monks. It was the 1564 discovery of graphite in Borrowdale, England, that led to the invention of the pencil as we know it today. (The word "graphite" comes from the Greek *graphein*, "to write.") Because graphite was more pliable than lead, it required a "holder," or encasing, to stabilise it. String wrapped around the graphite sticks first served this purpose, and later the graphite came to be inserted into hollowed-out wooden tubes. Nuremberg became the new centre for pencil manufacturing, but its pencils—which utilised a composite of graphite and sulfur— were inferior to those made with high-quality graphite in England, until French chemist Jacques Conté developed an advanced new technique in 1795. The process, which involved mixing powdered graphite and clay (the amount of clay used varied depending upon the hardness desired) and firing them in a furnace, was gradually adopted by the German factories, and presumably capitalised

could see if you came across the courtyard, and so could effect an escape."

"As a matter of fact, he could not," said Soames, "for I entered by the side-door."

"Ah, that's good! Well, anyhow, that was in his mind. Let me see the three strips. No finger impressions—no! Well, he carried over this one first, and he copied it. How long would it take him to do that, using every possible contraction? A quarter of an hour, not less. Then he tossed it down and seized the next. He was in the midst of that when your return caused him to make a very hurried retreat—*very* hurried, since he had not time to replace the papers which would tell you that he had been there. You were not aware of any hurrying feet on the stair as you entered the outer door?"

"No, I can't say I was."

"Well, he wrote so furiously that he broke his pencil, and had, as you observe, to sharpen it again. This is of interest, Watson. The pencil was not an ordinary one. It was above the usual size, with a soft lead; the outer colour was dark blue, the maker's name was printed in silver lettering, and the piece remaining is only about an inch and a half long. Look for such a pencil, Mr. Soames, and you have got your man. When I add that he possesses a large and very blunt knife, you have an additional aid."

Mr. Soames was somewhat overwhelmed by this flood of information. "I can follow the other points," said he, "but really, in this matter of the length—"

Holmes held out a small chip with the letters *NN* and a space of clear wood after them.

"You see?"

"No, I fear that even now—"

"Watson, I have always done you an injustice. There are others. What could this *NN* be? It is at the end of a word. You are aware that Johann Faber[16] is the most common maker's name. Is it not clear that there is just as much of the pencil left as usually follows the *Johann*?"[17] He held the small table sideways to the electric light. "I was hoping that if the paper on which he wrote was thin some trace of it might come through upon this polished surface. No, I see nothing. I don't think there is anything more to be learned here. Now for the central table. This small pellet is, I presume, the black doughy mass you spoke of.

Roughly pyramidal in shape and hollowed out, I perceive. As you say, there appear to be grains of sawdust in it. Dear me, this is very interesting. And the cut—a positive tear, I see. It began with a thin scratch and ended in a jagged hole. I am much indebted to you for directing my attention to this case, Mr. Soames. Where does that door lead to?"

"To my bedroom."

"Have you been in it since your adventure?"

"No; I came straight away for you."

"I should like to have a glance round. What a charming, old-fashioned room! Perhaps you will kindly wait a minute until I have examined the floor. No, I see nothing. What about this curtain? You hang your clothes behind it. If anyone were forced to conceal himself in this room he must do it there, since the bed is too low and the wardrobe too shallow. No one there, I suppose?"

As Holmes drew the curtain I was aware, from some little rigidity and alertness of his attitude, that he was prepared for an emergency. As a matter of fact, the drawn curtain disclosed nothing but three or four suits of clothes hanging from a line of pegs. Holmes turned away, and stooped suddenly to the floor.

"Halloa! What's this?" said he.

It was a small pyramid of black, putty-like stuff, exactly like the one upon the table of the study. Holmes held it out on his open palm in the glare of the electric light.

"Your visitor seems to have left traces in your bedroom as well as in your sitting-room, Mr. Soames."

"What could he have wanted there?"

"I think it is clear enough. You came back by an unexpected way, and so he had no warning until you were at the very door. What could he do? He caught up everything which would betray him, and he rushed into your bedroom to conceal himself."

"Good gracious, Mr. Holmes, do you mean to tell me that all the time I was talking to Bannister in this room we had the man prisoner if we had only known it?"

"So I read it."

"Surely there is another alternative, Mr. Holmes? I don't know whether you observed my bedroom window?"

"Lattice-paned, lead framework, three separate windows, one swinging on hinge, and large enough to admit a man."

upon by the Faber brothers. The Conté technique remains the basis of pencil manufacture today.

17 Ronald A. Knox astutely observes that a pencil marked with the words JOHANN FABER would not leave the letters "NN" near the stump, but rather "ER." But Bruce Holmes (no relation) suggests in a letter to the *Baker Street Journal* that the initials were not on the stump but instead on a small chip evidently cut off the pencil when sharpened.

18 For an athlete (at either Oxford or Cambridge) to "get his Blue" is the equivalent of earning a "letter" in American high school or college sports. It derives from the colour of the team caps, dark blue for Oxford and light blue for Cambridge.

According to W. S. Bristowe, Oxford's long-jump team was led by C. B. Fry from 1892 to 1895, meaning that Gilchrist was either Fry's "second string" at Oxford or his rival at Cambridge. Harold Abrahams, the famed long-jumper and runner (immortalised in the film *Chariots of Fire*), wrote Bristowe a letter providing further detail in which he said, "We are told that Gilchrist was a Blue for the long jump and hurdles. There was no Blue at Cambridge for those two events in 1895, but it is not without interest to note that C. B. Fry's second string, W. J. Oakley, was a Blue for both these events in 1895 and in fact got his Blue for them in 1894."

"Exactly. And it looks out on an angle of the courtyard so as to be partly invisible. The man might have effected his entrance there, left traces as he passed through the bedroom, and, finally, finding the door open, have escaped that way."

Holmes shook his head impatiently.

"Let us be practical," said he. "I understand you to say that there are three students who use this stair and are in the habit of passing your door?"

"Yes, there are."

"And they are all in for this examination?"

"Yes."

"Have you any reason to suspect any one of them more than the others?"

Soames hesitated.

"It is a very delicate question," said he. "One hardly likes to throw suspicion where there are no proofs."

"Let us hear the suspicions. I will look after the proofs."

"I will tell you, then, in a few words the character of the three men who inhabit these rooms. The lower of the three is Gilchrist, a fine scholar and athlete, plays in the Rugby team and the cricket team for the college, and got his Blue for the hurdles and the long jump.[18] He is a fine, manly fellow. His father was the notorious Sir Jabez Gilchrist, who ruined himself on the turf. My scholar has been left very poor, but he is hard-working and industrious. He will do well.

"The second floor is inhabited by Daulat Ras, the Indian. He is a quiet, inscrutable fellow, as most of those Indians are. He is well up in his work, though his Greek is his weak subject. He is steady and methodical.

"The top floor belongs to Miles McLaren. He is a brilliant fellow when he chooses to work—one of the brightest intellects of the University; but he is wayward, dissipated, and unprincipled. He was nearly expelled over a card scandal in his first year. He has been idling all this term, and he must look forward with dread to the examination."

"Then it is he whom you suspect?"

"I dare not go so far as that. But, of the three, he is perhaps the least unlikely."

"Exactly. Now, Mr. Soames, let us have a look at your servant, Bannister."

He was a little, white-faced, clean-shaven, grizzly-haired fel-

Gilchrist.
Frederick Dorr Steele, *Collier's*, 1904

low of fifty. He was still suffering from this sudden disturbance of the quiet routine of his life. His plump face was twitching with his nervousness, and his fingers could not keep still.

"We are investigating this unhappy business, Bannister," said his master.

"Yes, sir."

"I understand," said Holmes, "that you left your key in the door?"

"Yes, sir."

"Was it not very extraordinary that you should do this on the very day when there were these papers inside?"

"It was most unfortunate, sir. But I have occasionally done the same thing at other times."

"When did you enter the room?"

"It was about half-past four. That is Mr. Soames's tea-time."

"How long did you stay?"

"When I saw that he was absent I withdrew at once."

"Did you look at these papers on the table?"

"No, sir; certainly not."

19 The word "many" is "fifteen" in the original manuscript.

Miles McLaren.
Frederick Dorr Steele, *Collier's*, 1904

"How came you to leave the key in the door?"

"I had the tea-tray in my hand. I thought I would come back for the key. Then I forgot."

"Has the outer door a spring lock?"

"No, sir."

"Then it was open all the time?"

"Yes, sir."

"Any one in the room could get out?"

"Yes, sir."

"When Mr. Soames returned and called for you, you were very much disturbed?"

"Yes, sir. Such a thing has never happened during the many[19] years that I have been here. I nearly fainted, sir."

"So I understand. Where were you when you began to feel bad?"

"Where was I, sir? Why, here, near the door."

"That is singular, because you sat down in that chair over yonder near the corner. Why did you pass these other chairs?"

"I don't know, sir, it didn't matter to me where I sat."

"I really don't think he knew much about it, Mr. Holmes. He was looking very bad—quite ghastly."

"You stayed here when your master left?"

"Only for a minute or so. Then I locked the door and went to my room."

"Whom do you suspect?"

"Oh, I would not venture to say, sir. I don't believe there is any gentleman in this University who is capable of profiting by such an action. No, sir, I'll not believe it."

"Thank you; that will do," said Holmes. "Oh, one more word. You have not mentioned to any of the three gentlemen whom you attend that anything is amiss?"

"No, sir; not a word."

"You haven't seen any of them?"

"No, sir."

"Very good. Now, Mr. Soames, we will take a walk in the quadrangle, if you please."

"How came you to leave the key in the door?"
Sidney Paget, *Strand Magazine*, 1904

Three yellow squares of light shone above us in the gathering gloom.

"Your three birds are all in their nests," said Holmes, looking up. "Halloa! What's that? One of them seems restless enough."

It was the Indian, whose dark silhouette appeared suddenly upon the blind. He was pacing swiftly up and down his room.

"I should like to have a peep at each of them," said Holmes. "Is it possible?"

"No difficulty in the world," Soames answered. "This set of rooms is quite the oldest in the college, and it is not unusual for visitors to go over them. Come along, and I will personally conduct you."

"No names, please!" said Holmes, as we knocked at Gilchrist's door. A tall, flaxen-haired, slim young fellow opened it, and made us welcome when he understood our errand.

Three yellow squares of light shone above us
in the gathering gloom.
Charles Raymond Macaulay, *Return of Sherlock Holmes*
(McClure Phillips), 1905

"He insisted on drawing it in his note-book."
Sidney Paget, *Strand Magazine*, 1904

There were some really curious pieces of mediæval domestic architecture within. Holmes was so charmed with one of them that he insisted on drawing it on his note-book, broke his pencil, had to borrow one from our host, and finally borrowed a knife to sharpen his own. The same curious accident happened to him in the rooms of the Indian—a silent, little, hook-nosed fellow, who eyed us askance and was obviously glad when Holmes's architectural studies had come to an end. I could not see that in either case Holmes had come upon the clue for which he was searching. Only at the third did our visit prove abortive. The outer door would not open to our knock, and nothing more substantial than a torrent of bad language came from behind it. "I don't care who you are. You can go to blazes!" roared the angry voice. "To-morrow's the exam., and I won't be drawn by anyone."

"A rude fellow," said our guide, flushing with anger as we withdrew down the stair. "Of course, he did not realize that it was I who was knocking, but none the less his conduct was very uncourteous, and, indeed, under the circumstances, rather suspicious."

Holmes's response was a curious one.

"Can you tell me his exact height?" he asked.

"Really, Mr. Holmes, I cannot undertake to say. He is taller than the Indian, not so tall as Gilchrist. I suppose five foot six would be about it."

"That is very important," said Holmes. "And now, Mr. Soames, I wish you good-night."

Our guide cried aloud in his astonishment and dismay. "Good gracious, Mr. Holmes, you are surely not going to leave me in this abrupt fashion! You don't seem to realize the position. To-morrow is the examination. I must take some definite action to-night. I cannot allow the examination to be held if one of the papers has been tampered with. The situation must be faced."

"You must leave it as it is. I shall drop round early to-morrow morning and chat the matter over. It is possible that I may be in a position then to indicate some course of action. Meanwhile you change nothing—nothing at all."

"Very good, Mr. Holmes."

"You can be perfectly easy in your mind. We shall certainly find some way out of your difficulties. I will take the black clay with me, also the pencil cuttings. Good-bye."

When we were out in the darkness of the quadrangle we again looked up at the windows. The Indian still paced his room. The others were invisible.

"Well, Watson, what do you think of it?" Holmes asked as we came out into the main street. "Quite a little parlour game—sort of three-card trick, is it not? There are your three men. It must be one of them. You take your choice. Which is yours?"

"The foul-mouthed fellow at the top. He is the one with the worst record. And yet that Indian was a sly fellow also. Why should he be pacing his room all the time?"

"There is nothing in that. Many men do it when they are trying to learn anything by heart."

"He looked at us in a queer way."

"So would you if a flock of strangers came in on you when you were preparing for an examination next day, and every moment was of value. No, I see nothing in that. Pencils, too, and knives—all was satisfactory. But that fellow *does* puzzle me."

"Who?"

"Why, Bannister, the servant. What's his game in the matter?"

"He impressed me as being a perfectly honest man."

"So he did me. That's the puzzling part. Why should a perfectly honest man—well, well, here's a large stationer's. We shall begin our researches here."

There were only four stationers of any consequences in the town, and at each Holmes produced his pencil chips and bid high for a duplicate. All were agreed that one could be ordered, but that it was not a usual size of pencil, and that it was seldom kept in stock. My friend did not appear to be depressed by his failure, but shrugged his shoulders in half-humorous resignation.

"No good, my dear Watson. This, the best and only final clue, has run to nothing. But, indeed, I have little doubt that we can build up a sufficient case without it. By Jove! my dear fellow, it is nearly nine, and the landlady babbled of green peas[20] at seven-thirty. What with your eternal tobacco, Watson, and your irregularity at meals,[21] I expect that you will get notice to quit, and that I shall share your downfall—not, however, before we have solved the problem of the nervous tutor, the careless servant, and the three enterprising students."

Holmes made no further allusion to the matter that day, though he sat lost in thought for a long time after our belated dinner. At eight in the morning he came into my room just as I finished my toilet.

"Well, Watson," said he, "it is time we went down to St. Luke's. Can you do without breakfast?"

"Certainly."

"Soames will be in a dreadful fidget until we are able to tell him something positive."

"Have you anything positive to tell him?"

"I think so."

"You have formed a conclusion?"

20 Holmes here misquotes Shakespeare frivolously—see *Henry V*, Act 2, Scene 3, where hostess Mistress Quickly speaks of Falstaff "babbl[ing] of green fields" on his deathbed.

21 The pot calling the kettle black!

"Yes, my dear Watson; I have solved the mystery."

"But what fresh evidence could you have got?"

"Aha! It is not for nothing that I have turned myself out of bed at the untimely hour of six. I have put in two hours' hard work and covered at least five miles, with something to show for it. Look at that!"

He held out his hand. On the palm were three little pyramids of black, doughy clay.

"Why, Holmes, you had only two yesterday."

"And one more this morning. It is a fair argument that wherever No. 3 came from is also the source of Nos. 1 and 2. Eh, Watson? Well, come along and put friend Soames out of his pain."

The unfortunate tutor was certainly in a state of pitiable agitation when we found him in his chambers. In a few hours the examinations would commence, and he was still in the dilemma between making the facts public and allowing the culprit to compete for the valuable scholarship. He could hardly stand still, so great was his mental agitation, and he ran towards Holmes with two eager hands outstretched.

"Thank heaven that you have come! I feared that you had given it up in despair. What am I to do? Shall the examination proceed?"

"Yes; let it proceed, by all means."

"But this rascal—?"

"He shall not compete."

"You know him?"

"I think so. If this matter is not to become public we must give ourselves certain powers, and resolve ourselves into a small private court-martial.[22] You there, if you please, Soames! Watson, you here! I'll take the arm chair in the middle. I think that we are now sufficiently imposing to strike terror into a guilty breast. Kindly ring the bell!"

Bannister entered, and shrank back in evident surprise and fear at our judicial appearance.

"You will kindly close the door," said Holmes. "Now, Bannister, will you please tell us the truth about yesterday's incident?"

The man turned white to the roots of his hair.

"I have told you everything, sir."

"Nothing to add?"

"Nothing at all, sir."

"Well, then, I must make some suggestions to you. When you sat down on that chair yesterday, did you do so in order to conceal some object which would have shown who had been in the room?"

Bannister's face was ghastly.

"No, sir, certainly not."

"It is only a suggestion," said Holmes, suavely. "I frankly admit that I am unable to prove it. But it seems probable enough, since the moment that Mr. Soames's back was turned you released the man who was hiding in that bedroom."

Bannister explains.
Frederick Dorr Steele, *Collier's*, 1904

Bannister licked his dry lips.

"There was no man, sir."

"Ah, that's a pity, Bannister. Up to now you may have spoken the truth, but now I know that you have lied."

The man's face set in sullen defiance.

"There was no man, sir."

"Come, come, Bannister!"

"No, sir, there was no one."

"In that case you can give us no further information. Would you please remain in the room? Stand over there near the bedroom door. Now, Soames, I am going to ask you to have the great kindness to go up to the room of young Gilchrist, and to ask him to step down into yours."

An instant later the tutor returned, bringing with him the student. He was a fine figure of a man, tall, lithe, and agile, with a springy step and a pleasant, open face. His troubled blue eyes glanced at each of us, and finally rested with an expression of blank dismay upon Bannister in the farther comer.

"Just close the door," said Holmes. "Now, Mr. Gilchrist, we are all quite alone here, and no one need ever know one word of what passes between us. We can be perfectly frank with each other. We want to know, Mr. Gilchrist, how you, an honourable man, ever came to commit such an action as that of yesterday?"

The unfortunate young man staggered back, and cast a look full of horror and reproach at Bannister.

"No, no, Mr. Gilchrist, sir; I never said a word—never one word!" cried the servant.

"No, but you have now," said Holmes. "Now, sir, you must see that after Bannister's words your position is hopeless, and that your only chance lies in a frank confession."

For a moment Gilchrist, with upraised hand, tried to control his writhing features. The next he had thrown himself on his knees beside the table, and, burying his face in his hands, he had burst into a storm of passionate sobbing.

"Come, come," said Holmes kindly; "it is human to err, and at least no one can accuse you of being a callous criminal. Perhaps it would be easier for you if I were to tell Mr. Soames what occurred, and you can check me where I am wrong. Shall I do so? Well, well, don't trouble to answer. Listen, and see that I do you no injustice.

"An instant later the tutor returned,
bringing with him the student."
Sidney Paget, *Strand Magazine*, 1904

"From the moment, Mr. Soames, that you said to me that no
one, not even Bannister, could have told that the papers were
in your room, the case began to take a definite shape in my
mind. The printer one could, of course, dismiss. He could
examine the papers in his own office. The Indian I also
thought nothing of. If the proofs were in roll, he could not possibly know what they were. On the other hand, it seemed an
unthinkable coincidence that a man should dare to enter the
room, and that by chance on that very day the papers were on
the table. I dismissed that. The man who entered knew that
the papers were there. How did he know?

"When I approached your room I examined the window. You
amused me by supposing that I was contemplating the possibility of someone having in broad daylight, under the eyes of
all these opposite rooms, forced himself through it. Such an
idea was absurd. I was measuring how tall a man would need

" 'Come, come,' said Holmes, kindly, 'it is human to err.' "
Sidney Paget, *Strand Magazine*, 1904

to be in order to see, as he passed, what papers were on the central table. I am six feet high, and I could do it with an effort. No one less than that would have a chance. Already you see I had reason to think that, if one of your three students was a man of unusual height, he was the most worth watching of the three.

"I entered, and I took you into my confidence as to the suggestions of the side-table. Of the centre table I could make nothing, until in your description of Gilchrist you mentioned that he was a long-distance jumper. Then the whole thing came to me in an instant, and I only needed certain corroborative proofs, which I speedily obtained.

"What happened was this: This young fellow had employed his afternoon at the athletic grounds, where he had been practising the jump. He returned carrying his jumping-shoes, which are provided, as you are aware, with several sharp spikes.

As he passed your window he saw, by means of his great height, these proofs upon your table, and conjectured what they were. No harm would have been done had it not been that, as he passed your door, he perceived the key which had been left by the carelessness of your servant. A sudden impulse came over him to enter and see if they were indeed the proofs. It was not a dangerous exploit, for he could always pretend that he had simply looked in to ask a question.

"Well, when he saw that they were indeed the proofs, it was then that he yielded to temptation. He put his shoes on the table. What was it you put on that chair near the window?"

"Gloves," said the young man.

Holmes looked triumphantly at Bannister. "He put his gloves on the chair, and he took the proofs, sheet by sheet, to copy them. He thought the tutor must return by the main gate, and that he would see him. As we know, he came back by the side-gate. Suddenly he heard him at the very door. There was no possible escape. He forgot his gloves, but he caught up his shoes and darted into the bedroom. You observe that the scratch on that table is slight at one side, but deepens in the direction of the bedroom door, That in itself is enough to show us that the shoes had been drawn in that direction, and that the culprit had taken refuge there. The earth round the spike had been left on the table, and a second sample was loosened and fell in the bedroom. I may add that I walked out to the athletic grounds this morning, saw that tenacious black clay is used in the jumping-pit,[23] and carried away a specimen of it, together with some of the fine tan[24] or sawdust which is strewn over it to prevent the athlete from slipping. Have I told the truth, Mr. Gilchrist?"

The student had drawn himself erect.

"Yes, sir, it is true," said he.

"Good heavens! have you nothing to add?" cried Soames.

"Yes, sir, I have, but the shock of this disgraceful exposure has bewildered me. I have a letter here, Mr. Soames, which I wrote to you early this morning in the middle of a restless night. It was before I knew that my sin had found me out. Here it is, sir. You will see that I have said, 'I have determined not to go in for the examination. I have been offered a commission in the Rhodesian Police,[25] and I am going out to South Africa at once.' "

23 W. S. Bristowe finds the presence of this black clay conclusive evidence that the locale of "The Three Students" is Cambridge. The same C. B. Fry who led the Oxford long-jump team wrote a 1902 *Strand* article in which he recalled that a groundsman at Fenners (a cricket lawn at Cambridge) had invented a type of clay that was duplicated by the Queen's Club in London (the site of numerous Oxford vs. Cambridge athletic events, although, confusingly enough, not affiliated with either Queen's College (Oxford) or Queens' College (Cambridge)). The club began using the clay in its long-jump pit in 1902, thereby introducing the substance to the world outside Cambridge. After writing a letter to Fry, Bristowe received a reply on December 21, 1955, in which the long-jumping captain confirmed that Oxford jumpers landed in sand, not clay. "I saw no damped semi-clay soil in the Long Jump pit till at Queens in 1903," wrote Fry. "Here, I submit," writes Bristowe triumphantly, "we have positive proof from this distinguished contemporary of Gilchrist that the mud which led to his detection was invented by the Cambridge groundsman and was unique to Cambridge in 1895 [the date commonly accepted for 'The Three Students'—see *Chronological Table*]."

This remarkable piece of evidence is independently corroborated in the diary of James Agate, quoting a letter from his friend George Lyttelton dated October 29, 1946. Lyttelton, a member of the Cambridge Union Athletic Club in 1895, verifies that the special clay was found only at Cambridge and not at Oxford.

24 Oak bark or other material used for tanning.

25 The state of Rhodesia, now Zimbabwe, was founded via the impetus of Cecil Rhodes, future prime minister of South Africa's Cape Colony (see "The Solitary Cyclist," note 28).

In 1889, Rhodes was granted a charter for his new British South Africa Company, which he had formed with the purpose of exploring commercial, colonial, transportation, and mining interests in the area northeast of South Africa. His company sent settlers deep into the region in 1890, establishing Fort Salisbury at the site of the future Rhodesian capital and quickly encountering resistance from the native Ndebele. Rhodes's troops, controlled by him in his capacity as the Parliament-appointed high commissioner, engaged in months of fighting but emerged victorious. The British South Africa Company took over administration of the territory, officially naming it Rhodesia in 1895. The military force Gilchrist intended to join (technically, the British South African Police) had more action ahead, however, as the Nbedele and the Shona tribes rose in resistance in 1896 and 1897. The police remained Rhodesia's internal security force until 1980, when the country became an independent member of the Commonwealth.

26 And what was that purpose? Soames describes Gilchrist as "a fine scholar . . . hard-working and industrious. He will do well." John Hall, in *Sidelights on Holmes*, suggests, "[P]erhaps Gilchrist had been devoting so much of his time to rugby, cricket, hurdles and the long jump that he had rather neglected his more academic interests?"

"I am indeed pleased to hear that you did not intend to profit by your unfair advantage," said Soames. "But why did you change your purpose?[26]

Gilchrist pointed to Bannister.

"There is the man who set me in the right path," said he.

"Come now, Bannister," said Holmes. "It will be clear to you, from what I have said, that only you could have let this young man out, since you were left in the room and must have locked the door when you went out. As to his escaping by that window, it was incredible. Can you not clear up the last point in this mystery, and tell us the reason for your action?"

"It was simple enough, sir, if you only had known; but, with all your cleverness, it was impossible that you could know. Time was, sir, when I was butler to old Sir Jabez Gilchrist, this young gentleman's father. When he was ruined I came to the college as servant, but I never forgot my old employer because he was down in the world. I watched his son all I could for the sake of the old days. Well, sir, when I came into this room yes-

"Here it is, sir."
Sidney Paget, *Strand Magazine*, 1904

terday, when the alarm was given, the very first thing I saw was Mr. Gilchrist's tan gloves a-lying in that chair. I knew those gloves well, and I understood their message. If Mr. Soames saw them, the game was up. I flopped down into that chair, and nothing would budge me until Mr. Soames went for you. Then out came my poor young master, whom I had dandled on my knee, and confessed it all to me. Wasn't it natural, sir, that I should save him, and wasn't it natural also that I should try to speak to him as his dead father would have done, and make him understand that he could not profit by such a deed? Could you blame me, sir?"

"No, indeed!" said Holmes, heartily, springing to his feet. "Well, Soames, I think we have cleared your little problem up, and our breakfast awaits us at home. Come, Watson! As to you, sir, I trust that a bright future awaits you in Rhodesia. For once you have fallen low. Let us see in the future how high you can rise."[27] ■

THE STUDY OF EARLY ENGLISH CHARTERS

WATSON'S casual remark that Holmes was conducting research into early English charters may be a significant clue in the controversy over whether Holmes attended Oxford or Cambridge—or at least several scholars seize upon it as such. The first to lean heavily on this point is T. S. Blakeney, who declares in "The Location of 'The Three Students' " that Holmes's research must have been conducted at Oxford. As proof, he lauds Oxford's history department, claiming that its status was unparalleled in England at this time. In part, the department owed its lofty reputation to the eminent William Stubbs, regius professor of history (as well as bishop respectively of Chester and Oxford), whose published works include the three-volume *The Constitutional History of England in Its Origin and Development (1873–78), Select Charters and Other Illustrations of English Constitutional History from the Earliest Times to the Reign of Edward the First* (1870) and nineteen volumes of medieval English chronicles that he edited for the government's ambitious Rolls series. In addition, Blakeney notes, William H. Turner's *Calendar of Charters and Rolls* was pub-

27 In July 1904, a mere month following publication of "The Three Students," famed editor and critic Andrew Lang analysed the case in his monthly column "At the Sign of the Ship" in *Longman's Magazine*. Lang contends that Holmes and Watson were, in this case, made the victims of an elaborate hoax—prepared and brilliantly acted by Hilton Soames, with the aid and connivance of Gilchrist, if not of Bannister. Playing on Holmes's complete ignorance of Greek literature, "Soames of St. Luke's came to [Holmes] with a cock-and-bull story, which would not have taken in a Fifth Form boy."

In *The London Nights of Belsize*, published in 1917, Vernon Rendall suggests that Watson, Gilchrist, Soames, and Bannister were in league together, their purpose being to give Holmes something to do. "Watson feared his relapse into the drug-habit . . . , and Watson got up this pretty little case for him." T. S. Blakeney disagrees with this scenario, arguing that Watson was never a good enough actor to pull off such a stunt. "We have no special reason to think Watson was a good deceiver," Blakeney explains, recalling various examples from the Canon in which Watson demonstrates a chronic facility for giving himself away: in "The Cardboard Box," Holmes easily guesses Watson's thoughts on General Gordon and Henry Ward Beecher merely by the expression on Watson's face; in *The Hound of the Baskervilles*, Watson's cigarette betrays him to Holmes; in "The Crooked Man," it is the doctor's habit of carrying his handkerchief in his sleeve that identifies him as a former soldier; and in "The Disappearance of Lady Frances Carfax," Watson's method of tying his bootlaces catches him out. Blakeney concedes that "Watson was not averse to 'taking a rise' out of Holmes if he had the chance [*The Valley of Fear*], [but] his straightforward character and complete honesty do not fit him for any high degree of deception." In any case, Blakeney concludes that Holmes was in no need of diversion, given the "striking" results he had evidently obtained in his study of English charters.

lished by Oxford in 1878 and housed in Oxford's Bodleian Library. Turner's work was "just the sort of volume that an amateur historian, as Holmes was, would find invaluable. Against this solidly enthroned tradition of the Oxford Medieval History School, what had Cambridge to offer?"

Christopher Morley agrees with Blakeney and surmises that Holmes may have been at Oxford to consult with Stubbs on the eighth edition of *Select Charters*, which by this time had become a widely used textbook. Morley directs readers to the tenth section of *Dialogus de Scaccario* (Dialogue on the Exchequer), an essay, drawn up circa 1200, that comments upon the biannual meeting of the treasurer of England, as well as other matters of taxation and revenue. The tenth section is concerned with murder. In medieval times, apparently, murder was defined it as "the secret death of somebody, whose slayer is not known," on the basis of the fact that the Old English word "murdrum" meant "hidden" or "occult." (Stubbs explains that Anglo-Saxons seeking vengeance frequently laid ambushes for their Norman enemies, killing them in remote places.) Given Holmes's general interest in things medieval (miracle plays and medieval pottery are mentioned in *The Sign of Four*, and in "The Bruce-Partington Plans" he has made a hobby of the music of the Middle Ages) and in British criminal law (Watson assesses him as having a "good practical knowledge" of it in *A Study in Scarlet*), Morley suggests that Holmes would find this particular work especially interesting.

Cambridge has its supporters, as well. While granting that Blakeney is "entirely fair" in making such an "erudite review" of charters at Oxford and Cambridge, W. S. Bristowe writes (in "Oxford or Cambridge?") that Blakeney's assessment passes over the many old, valuable documents at Cambridge that were being somewhat belatedly recognised as important. Bristowe seizes upon M. R. James's "Catalogues of Manuscripts" series, published at Cambridge from 1895 to 1914, and observes that Holmes could have caught up with James just as he was at the cusp of his research. "This surely would be the very moment when a man interested in research in the same field would be eager to meet Dr. James and to examine documents freshly coming to light."

A. Carson Simpson is another Cambridge supporter, writing in a letter to the *Baker Street Journal* that he changed his early backing of Oxford after reading F. E. Harmer's *Anglo-Saxon Writs* (1952) and finding that most of the documents mentioned were located in Cambridge libraries. Acknowledging that these documents were writs and not charters, Simpson ventures that the distinction between charters, which are legal contracts, and writs, which are official declarations, has been established only fairly recently. Sorting out the differences could very well have been connected to Holmes's "striking results."

The foregoing arguments are made without any apparent regard to Watson's explicit statement, in the first sentence of the case, that "a combination of events, into which I need not enter, caused Mr. Sherlock Holmes and myself to spend some weeks in one of our great university towns." That is, Holmes did not come to the university town solely to study charters. This point is clearly understood by Trevor H. Hall, in "Sherlock Holmes's University and College," where he states that "the opportunity to consult Early English charters was only *one* ingredient in Holmes's motive in visiting Cambridge or Oxford [italics added]." Hall suggests that the reason for Holmes's interest in the charters was probably an investigation of a forged historical document. If a "combination of events" brought Holmes to the university town, Hall concludes, the richness of the collection of one or the other had no bearing on the matter.

THE ADVENTURE OF THE
GOLDEN PINCE-NEZ[1]

The period following Holmes's return in the year 1894 was apparently a busy one for Holmes and Watson, because in "The Golden Pince-Nez," Watson notes no fewer than five unpublished cases, and at least three other published cases occur in that year. We learn that Holmes earned the French Order of the Legion of Honour for his capture of "the Boulevard assassin," leading to speculation about Holmes's French connections. The case is also noteworthy for its Russian background: Although Russia and its recent violent history was much on the public's mind in 1904 (the Russo-Japanese War broke out in February 1904, and in 1903, a general strike in Russia was widely reported), this is the only Canonical reference to nihilism and the terrors of the czarist police state.

W HEN I LOOK at the three massive manuscript volumes which contain our work for the year 1894, I confess that it is very difficult for me, out of such a wealth of material, to select the cases which are most interesting in themselves and at the same time most conducive to a display of those peculiar powers for which my friend was famous. As I turn over the pages, I see my notes upon the repulsive story of the red leech[2] and the terrible death of Crosby the banker. Here also I find an account of the Addleton tragedy and the singular contents of the ancient British barrow. The famous Smith-Mortimer[3] succession case comes also within this period, and so does the tracking and arrest of Huret, the Boulevard assassin[4]—an exploit which won for Holmes an autograph letter of thanks from the French President and the Order of the Legion of Honour. Each of these would furnish a narrative, but on the whole I am of opinion that none of them unites so many singular points of interest as the episode of Yoxley Old Place,

1 "The Golden Pince-Nez" was published in the *Strand Magazine* in July 1904 and in *Collier's Weekly* on October 29, 1904.

2 It is the rare leech that is red in colour. Most such parasites, as Lord Gore-Booth comments in "The Journeys of Sherlock Holmes: A Topographical Monograph," are olive-green or brown. A. Carson Simpson gathers that Watson might have been using the word's more archaic meaning and making a derogatory reference to a physician, perhaps one who had red hair (taking a name such as "Eric the Red"), wore predominantly red clothing (Count Amedeo VII of Savoy was known as "il Conte Rosso"), favoured blood-letting as a treatment, or had Communist sympathies.

THE ADVENTURE *of the* GOLDEN PINCE-NEZ

Frederick Dorr Steele, *Collier's*, 1904

which includes not only the lamentable death of young Willoughby Smith, but also those subsequent developments which threw so curious a light upon the causes of the crime.

It was a wild, tempestuous night, towards the close of November. Holmes and I sat together in silence all the evening, he engaged with a powerful lens deciphering the remains of the original inscription upon a palimpsest,[5] I deep in a recent treatise upon surgery.[6] Outside the wind howled down Baker Street, while the rain beat fiercely against the windows. It was strange there, in the very depths of the town, with ten miles of man's handiwork on every side of us, to feel the iron grip of Nature, and to be conscious that to the huge elemental forces all London was no more than the molehills that dot the fields. I walked to the window and looked out on the deserted street. The occasional lamps gleamed on the expanse of muddy road and shining pavement. A single cab was splashing its way from the Oxford Street end.

3 Presumably there is no connection to Willoughby Smith or Mortimer, the secretary and gardener who feature prominently in this case.

4 "The Golden Pince-Nez" is generally thought to have occurred in the late autumn of 1894 (see *Chronological Table*). M. Jean-Paul-Pierre Casimir-Périer (1847–1907) was the President of France from June 24, 1894 to January 15, 1895, succeeding Marie-François Sadi-Carnot, who was assassinated by the Italian anarchist Sante or Santos Caserio.

William E. Fleischauer considers which president of France would have been the target of the "Boulevard assassin" and which wrote the letter of thanks. He concludes that Sadi-Carnot was the target but rejects the identification of Huret with Caserio, for although the assassination took place in a *boulevard* (old fortification) in Paris, there was no "tracking" involved—Caserio was arrested on the spot. Sadi-Carnot, Fleischauer suggests, was the intended victim of another, earlier assassin, supplied by the Moriarty organisation. Holmes was able to stop that assassin (and thus won the gratitude of Sadi-Carnot) but failed to prevent the subsequent successful attempt. Watson, anxious to mention Holmes's medal but embarrassed to lay out the facts in light of the eventual assassination of Sadi-Carnot, obfuscated.

Michael Harrison, in *The World of Sherlock Holmes*, reaches a contrary conclusion. He asserts that Holmes tracked Huret, and that in December, using then-President Casimir-Périer as the "bait," Holmes lured the would-be assassin to Montpellier. Montpellier was of course well known to Holmes, for he had just finished his researches into coal-tar derivatives there before returning to London in April 1894 ("The Final Problem"). Huret hid himself in the old fortifications in Montpellier, but Holmes quickly flushed and captured him, leading Casimir-Périer to express his gratitude.

1093

5 A term applied to any material from which writing has been removed to make room for another text, and which has thus been prepared or scraped a second time. It is most commonly applied to ancient manuscripts that have undergone this treatment. Figuratively, a palimpsest can also be a metaphor for a text or situation with several layers of meaning—as in the title of Gore Vidal's 1995 memoir, *Palimpsest*, or the line from M. E. W. Sherwood's *Epistle to Posterity* (1897): "They linger, each of these dinners, in our palimpsest memories, each recorded clearly, so that it does not blot out the others."

6 Watson's medical reading in "The Golden Pince-Nez" is not an isolated example, as evidently he is conscientious about keeping up with the latest trends. In *The Sign of Four*, he peruses the latest textbook on pathology; in "The Stock-Broker's Clerk" he reads the *British Medical Journal*; in "The Resident Patient" he professes familiarity with Percy Trevelyan's monograph *Obscure Nervous Lesions*.

"Well, Watson, it's as well we have not to turn out to-night," said Holmes, laying aside his lens and rolling up the palimpsest. "I've done enough for one sitting. It is trying work for the eyes. So far as I can make out, it is nothing more exciting than an Abbey's accounts dating from the second half of the fifteenth century. Halloa! halloa! halloa! What's this?"

Amid the droning of the wind there had come the stamping of a horse's hoofs and the long grind of a wheel as it rasped against the kerb. The cab which I had seen had pulled up at our door.

"What can he want?" I ejaculated, as a man stepped out of it.

"Want! He wants us. And we, my poor Watson, want overcoats and cravats and goloshes, and every aid that man ever invented to fight the weather. Wait a bit, though! There's the cab off again! There's hope yet. He'd have kept it if he had wanted us to come. Run down, my dear fellow, and open the door, for all virtuous folk have been long in bed."

When the light of the hall lamp fell upon our midnight visitor, I had no difficulty in recognizing him. It was young Stanley Hopkins, a promising detective, in whose career Holmes had several times shown a very practical interest.

"Is he in?" he asked, eagerly.

"Come up, my dear sir," said Holmes's voice from above. "I hope you have no designs upon us such a night as this."

The detective mounted the stairs, and our lamp gleamed upon his shining waterproof. I helped him out of it, while Holmes knocked a blaze out of the logs in the grate.

"Now, my dear Hopkins, draw up and warm your toes," said he. "Here's a cigar, and the doctor has a prescription containing hot water and a lemon which is good medicine on a night like this. It must be something important which has brought you out in such a gale."

"It is indeed, Mr. Holmes. I've had a bustling afternoon, I promise you. Did you see anything of the Yoxley case in the latest editions?"

"I've seen nothing later than the fifteenth century to-day."

"Well, it was only a paragraph, and all wrong at that, so you have not missed anything. I haven't let the grass grow under my feet. It's down in Kent, seven miles from Chatham and three from the railway line. I was wired for at three-fifteen, reached Yoxley Old Place at five, conducted my investigation,

"It was young Stanley Hopkins, a promising detective."
Sidney Paget, *Strand Magazine*, 1904

was back at Charing Cross by the last train, and straight to you by cab."

"Which means, I suppose, that you are not quite clear about your case?"

"It means that I can make neither head nor tail of it. So far as I can see, it is just as tangled a business as ever I handled, and yet at first it seemed so simple that one couldn't go wrong. There's no motive, Mr. Holmes. That's what bothers me—I can't put my hand on a motive. Here's a man dead—there's no denying that—but, so far as I can see, no reason on earth why anyone should wish him harm."

Holmes lit his cigar and leaned back in his chair.

"Let us hear about it," said he.

7 Invented by James Heath of Bath circa 1750, the Bath chair was used to transport Victorian ladies and invalids, frequently at seaside resorts. It had three wheels: two underneath the seat and one small, pivoting wheel that supported the footrest and could be steered (via a connecting rod) by the occupant.

"Now, my dear Hopkins, draw up and warm your toes."
Frederick Dorr Steele, *Collier's*, 1904

"I've got my facts pretty clear," said Stanley Hopkins. "All I want now is to know what they all mean. The story, so far as I can make it out, is like this. Some years ago this country house, Yoxley Old Place, was taken by an elderly man, who gave the name of Professor Coram. He was an invalid, keeping his bed half the time, and the other half hobbling round the house with a stick or being pushed about the grounds by the gardener in a Bath chair.[7] He was well liked by the few neighbours who called upon him, and he has the reputation down there of being a very learned man. His household used to consist of an elderly housekeeper, Mrs. Marker, and of a maid, Susan Tarlton. These have both been with him since his arrival, and they seem to be women of excellent character. The professor is writing a learned book, and he found it necessary about a year ago to engage a secretary. The first two that he tried were not successes, but the third, Mr. Willoughby Smith, a very young man straight from the university, seems to have been just what his employer wanted. His work consisted in writing all the morning to the professor's dictation, and he usually spent the evening in hunting up references and passages which bore upon the next day's work. This Willoughby Smith has nothing against him, either as a boy at Uppingham[8] or as a young man at Cambridge. I have seen his testimonials, and from the first he was a decent, quiet, hard-working fellow, with no weak spot in him at all. And yet this is the lad who has met his death this morning in the professor's study under circumstances which can point only to murder."

The wind howled and screamed at the windows. Holmes and I drew closer to the fire, while the young inspector slowly and point by point developed his singular narrative.

"If you were to search all England," said he, "I don't suppose you could find a household more self-contained or freer from outside influences. Whole weeks would pass, and not one of them go past the garden gate. The professor was buried in his work and existed for nothing else. Young Smith knew nobody in the neighbourhood, and lived very much as his employer did. The two women had nothing to take them from the house. Mortimer, the gardener, who wheels the Bath-chair, is an Army pensioner—an old Crimean man of excellent character. He does not live in the house, but in a three-roomed cottage at the other end of the garden. Those are the only people that you would find within the grounds of Yoxley Old Place. At the same time, the gate of the garden is a hundred yards from the main London to Chatham road. It opens with a latch, and there is nothing to prevent anyone from walking in.

"Now I will give you the evidence of Susan Tarlton, who is the only person who can say anything positive about the matter. It was in the forenoon, between eleven and twelve. She was engaged at the moment in hanging some curtains in the upstairs front bedroom. Professor Coram was still in bed, for when the weather is bad he seldom rises before midday. The housekeeper was busied with some work in the back of the house. Willoughby Smith had been in his bedroom, which he uses as a sitting-room; but the maid heard him at that moment pass along the passage and descend to the study immediately below her. She did not see him, but she says that she could not be mistaken in his quick, firm tread. She did not hear the study door close, but a minute or so later there was a dreadful cry in the room below. It was a wild, hoarse scream, so strange and unnatural that it might have come either from a man or a woman. At the same instant there was a heavy thud, which

8 Smith may have been a classmate of E. W. Hornung, who was the brother-in-law of Arthur Conan Doyle and attended the prestigious Uppingham School from 1880 to 1883. Hornung was the author of the popular "Raffles" series, tales of witty gentleman thief A. J. Raffles and his sidekick, "Bunny" Manders—"a kind of inverse Holmes and Watson," according to Conan Doyle's biographer, Daniel Stashower.

9 The word is "old" in the *Strand Magazine* and American texts.

shook the whole[9] house, and then all was silence. The maid stood petrified for a moment, and then, recovering her courage, she ran downstairs. The study door was shut, and she opened it. Inside, young Mr. Willoughby Smith was stretched upon the floor. At first she could see no injury, but as she tried to raise him she saw that blood was pouring from the under side of his neck. It was pierced by a very small but very deep wound, which had divided the carotid artery. The instrument with which the injury had been inflicted lay upon the carpet beside him. It was one of those small sealing-wax knives to be found on old-fashioned writing-tables, with an ivory handle and a stiff blade. It was part of the fittings of the professor's own desk.

"At first the maid thought that young Smith was already dead, but on pouring some water from the carafe over his forehead, he opened his eyes for an instant. 'The professor,' he murmured—'it was she.' The maid is prepared to swear that those were the exact words. He tried desperately to say something else, and he held his right hand up in the air. Then he fell back dead.

"In the meantime the housekeeper had also arrived upon the scene, but she was just too late to catch the young man's dying words. Leaving Susan with the body, she hurried to the professor's room. He was sitting up in bed, horribly agitated, for he had heard enough to convince him that something terrible had occurred. Mrs. Marker is prepared to swear that the professor was still in his night-clothes, and, indeed, it was impossible for him to dress without the help of Mortimer, whose orders were to come at twelve o'clock. The professor declares that he heard the distant cry, but that he knows nothing more. He can give no explanation of the young man's last words, 'The professor—it was she,' but imagines that they were the outcome of delirium. He believes that Willoughby Smith had not an enemy in the world, and can give no reason for the crime. His first action was to send Mortimer, the gardener, for the local police. A little later the chief constable sent for me. Nothing was moved before I got there, and strict orders were given that no one should walk upon the paths leading to the house. It was a splendid chance of putting your theories into practice, Mr. Sherlock Holmes. There was really nothing wanting."

"Except Mr. Sherlock Holmes!" said my companion, with a

somewhat bitter smile. "Well, let us hear about it. What sort of a job did you make of it?"

"I must ask you first, Mr. Holmes, to glance at this rough plan, which will give you a general idea of the position of the professor's study and the various points of the case. It will help you in following my investigation."

He unfolded the rough chart, which I here reproduce, and he laid it across Holmes's knee. I rose and, standing behind Holmes, studied it over his shoulder.

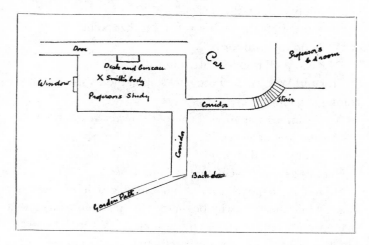

"It is very rough, of course, and it only deals with the points which seem to me to be essential. All the rest you will see later for yourself. Now, first of all, presuming that the assassin entered the house, how did he or she come in? Undoubtedly by the garden path and the back door, from which there is direct access to the study. Any other way would have been exceedingly complicated. The escape must have also been made along that line, for of the two other exits from the room one was blocked by Susan as she ran downstairs and the other leads straight to the professor's bedroom. I therefore directed my attention at once to the garden path, which was saturated with recent rain, and would certainly show any footmarks.

"My examination showed me that I was dealing with a cautious and expert criminal. No footmarks were to be found on the path. There could be no question, however, that someone had passed along the grass border which lines the path, and that he had done so in order to avoid leaving a track. I could not find anything in the nature of a distinct impression, but the grass was trodden down, and someone had undoubtedly passed. It could only have been the murderer, since neither the gardener nor anyone else had been there that morning, and the rain had only begun during the night."

"One moment," said Holmes. "Where does this path lead to?"

"To the road."

"How long is it?"

"A hundred yards or so."

"At the point where the path passes through the gate, you could surely pick up the tracks?"

"Unfortunately the path was tiled at that point."

"Well, on the road itself?"

"No; it was all trodden into mire."

"Tut-tut! Well, then, these tracks upon the grass—were they coming or going?"

"It was impossible to say. There was never any outline."

"A large foot or a small?"

"You could not distinguish."

Holmes gave an ejaculation of impatience.

"It has been pouring rain and blowing a hurricane ever since," said he. "It will be harder to read now than that palimpsest. Well, well, it can't be helped. What did you do, Hopkins, after you had made certain that you had made certain of nothing?"

"I think I made certain of a good deal, Mr. Holmes. I knew that someone had entered the house cautiously from without. I next examined the corridor. It is lined with cocoanut matting and had taken no impression of any kind. This brought me into the study itself. It is a scantily furnished room. The main article is a large writing-table with a fixed bureau. This bureau consists of a double column of drawers, with a central small cupboard between them. The drawers were open, the cupboard locked. The drawers, it seems, were always open, and nothing of value was kept in them. There were some papers of importance in the cupboard, but there were no signs that this had been tampered with, and the professor assures me that nothing was missing. It is certain that no robbery has been committed.

"I come now to the body of the young man. It was found near the bureau, and just to the left of it, as marked upon that chart. The stab was on the right side of the neck and from behind forwards, so that it is almost impossible that it could have been self-inflicted."

"Unless he fell upon the knife," said Holmes.

"Exactly. The idea crossed my mind. But we found the knife some feet away from the body, so that seems impossible. Then, of course, there are the man's own dying words. And, finally, there was this very important piece of evidence which was found clasped in the dead man's right hand."

From his pocket Stanley Hopkins drew a small paper packet. He unfolded it and disclosed a golden pince-nez, with two broken ends of black silk cord dangling from the end of it.

"The body was found near the bureau, and just to the left of it, as marked upon that chart."
Sidney Paget, *Strand Magazine*, 1904

"Willoughby Smith had excellent sight," he added. "There can be no question that this was snatched from the face or the person of the assassin."

Sherlock Holmes took the glasses into his hand, and examined them with the utmost attention and interest. He held them on his nose, endeavoured to read through them, went to the window and stared up the street with them, looked at them most minutely in the full light of the lamp, and finally, with a chuckle, seated himself at the table and wrote a few lines upon a sheet of paper, which he tossed across to Stanley Hopkins.

"That's the best I can do for you," said he. "It may prove to be of some use."

The astonished detective read the note aloud. It ran as follows:

Wanted, a woman of good address, attired like a lady. She has a remarkably thick nose, with eyes which are set close upon

"He endeavoured to read through them."
Sidney Paget, *Strand Magazine*, 1904

either side of it. She has a puckered forehead, a peering expression, and probably rounded shoulders. There are indications that she has had recourse to an optician at least twice during the last few months. As her glasses are of remarkable strength, and as opticians are not very numerous, there should be no difficulty in tracing her.

Holmes smiled at the astonishment of Hopkins, which must have been reflected upon my features.

"Surely my deductions are simplicity itself," said he. "It would be difficult to name any articles which afford a finer field for inference than a pair of glasses, especially so remarkable a pair as these. That they belong to a woman I infer from their delicacy, and also, of course, from the last words of the dying man. As to her being a person of refinement and well dressed, they are, as you perceive, handsomely mounted in solid gold, and it is inconceivable that anyone who wore such glasses could be slatternly in other respects.[10] You will find that the clips are too wide for your nose, showing that the lady's nose was very broad at the base. This sort of nose is usually a short and coarse one, but there is a sufficient number of exceptions to prevent me from being dogmatic or from insisting upon this point in my description. My own face is a narrow one, and yet I find that I cannot get my eyes into the centre, or near the centre, of these glasses. Therefore, the lady's eyes are set very near to the sides of the nose. You will perceive, Watson, that the glasses are concave[11] and of unusual strength. A lady whose vision has been so extremely contracted all her life is sure to have the physical characteristics of such vision, which are seen in the forehead, the eyelids, and the shoulders."

"Yes," I said, "I can follow each of your arguments. I confess, however, that I am unable to understand how you arrive at the double visit to the optician."

Holmes took the glasses into his hand.

"You will perceive," he said, "that the clips are lined with tiny bands of cork to soften the pressure upon the nose. One of these is discoloured and worn to some slight extent, but the other is new. Evidently one has fallen off and been replaced. I should judge that the older of them has not been there more than a few months. They exactly correspond, so I gather that the lady went back to the same establishment for the second."

10 "The conclusion that a woman who wears gold pince-nez must be well-dressed is unconvincing," Vernon Rendall complains. A good salesperson, after all, can persuade a customer that she needs an expensive, fashionable pair of spectacles—trimmed with gold, even—before price is ever discussed. Eyeglasses, while dating back to ancient China, were once not as ubiquitous as they are today, and thus it stands to reason that a woman might be willing to spend extra money on an accessory that must be worn so prominently and so often. Perhaps the glasses were bought during a temporary prosperity (compare Henry Baker's hat in "The Blue Carbuncle") and kept as a no longer affordable luxury.

11 "Convex" in the manuscript and *Collier's Weekly*, noted in a letter to *The Bookman* in July 1905.

12 That is, the police-boat pursuit of the blowgun-wielding pygmy Tonga, the companion of Jonathan Small, down the Thames —events recorded in *The Sign of Four* and especially memorable to Watson for the connection to his wooing of Mary Morstan.

"By George, it's marvellous!" cried Hopkins, in an ecstasy of admiration. "To think that I had all that evidence in my hand and never knew it! I had intended, however, to go the round of the London opticians."

"Of course you would. Meanwhile, have you anything more to tell us about the case?"

"Nothing, Mr. Holmes. I think that you know as much as I do now—probably more. We have had inquiries made as to any stranger seen on the country roads or at the railway station. We have heard of none. What beats me is the utter want of all object in the crime. Not a ghost of a motive can anyone suggest."

"Ah! there I am not in a position to help you. But I suppose you want us to come out to-morrow?"

"If it is not asking too much, Mr. Holmes. There's a train from Charing Cross to Chatham at six in the morning, and we should be at Yoxley Old Place between eight and nine."

"Then we shall take it. Your case has certainly some features of great interest, and I shall be delighted to look into it. Well, it's nearly one, and we had best get a few hours' sleep. I daresay you can manage all right on the sofa in front of the fire. I'll light my spirit-lamp, and give you a cup of coffee before we start."

The gale had blown itself out next day, but it was a bitter morning when we started upon our journey. We saw the cold winter sun rise over the dreary marshes of the Thames and the long, sullen reaches of the river, which I shall ever associate with our pursuit of the Andaman Islander[12] in the earlier days of our career. After a long and weary journey we alighted at a small station some miles from Chatham. While a horse was being put into a trap at the local inn, we snatched a hurried breakfast, and so we were all ready for business when we at last arrived at Yoxley Old Place. A constable met us at the garden gate.

"Well, Wilson, any news?"

"No, sir, nothing."

"No reports of any stranger seen?"

"No, sir. Down at the station they are certain that no stranger either came or went yesterday."

"Have you had inquiries made at inns and lodgings?"

"Yes, sir: there is no one that we cannot account for."

"Well, it's only a reasonable walk to Chatham. Anyone might stay there or take a train without being observed. This is the garden path of which I spoke, Mr. Holmes. I'll pledge my word there was no mark on it yesterday."

"On which side were the marks on the grass?"

"This side, sir. This narrow margin of grass between the path and the flower-bed. I can't see the traces now, but they were clear to me then."

"Yes, yes: someone has passed along," said Holmes, stooping over the grass border. "Our lady must have picked her steps carefully, must she not, since on the one side she would leave a track on the path, and on the other an even clearer one on the soft bed?"

"Yes, sir, she must have been a cool hand."

I saw an intent look pass over Holmes's face.

"You say that she must have come back this way?"

"Yes, sir; there is no other."

"On this strip of grass?"

"Certainly, Mr. Holmes."

"Hum! It was a very remarkable performance—very remarkable. Well, I think we have exhausted the path. Let us go farther. This garden door is usually kept open, I suppose? Then this visitor had nothing to do but to walk in. The idea of murder was not in her mind, or she would have provided herself with some sort of weapon, instead of having to pick this knife off the writing-table. She advanced along this corridor, leaving no traces upon the cocoanut matting. Then she found herself in this study. How long was she there? We have no means of judging."

"Not more than a few minutes, sir. I forgot to tell you that Mrs. Marker, the housekeeper, had been in there tidying not very long before—about a quarter of an hour, she says."

"Well, that gives us a limit. Our lady enters this room, and what does she do? She goes over to the writing-table. What for? Not for anything in the drawers. If there had been anything worth her taking, it would surely[13] have been locked up. No, it was for something in that wooden bureau. Halloa! what is that scratch upon the face of it? Just hold a match, Watson. Why did you not tell me of this, Hopkins?"

The mark which he was examining began upon the brass-work on the right-hand side of the keyhole, and extended for about four inches, where it had scratched the varnish from the surface.

[13] Curiously, the English edition has the word "scarcely," which is plainly wrong.

14 A patent lock with tumblers, named from its inventor, and believed at the time to be pick-proof.

"I noticed it, Mr. Holmes. But you'll always find scratches round a keyhole."

"This is recent—quite recent. See how the brass shines where it is cut. An old scratch would be the same colour as the surface. Look at it through my lens. There's the varnish, too, like earth on each side of a furrow. Is Mrs. Marker there?"

A sad-faced, elderly woman came into the room.

"Did you dust this bureau yesterday morning?"

"Yes, sir."

"Did you notice this scratch?"

"No, sir, I did not."

"I am sure you did not, for a duster would have swept away these shreds of varnish. Who has the key of this bureau?"

"The professor keeps it on his watch-chain."

"Is it a simple key?"

"No, sir; it is a Chubb's key."[14]

"Very good. Mrs. Marker, you can go. Now we are making a little progress. Our lady enters the room, advances to the bureau, and either opens it or tries to do so. While she is thus engaged, young Willoughby Smith enters the room. In her hurry to withdraw the key, she makes this scratch upon the door. He seizes her, and she, snatching up the nearest object, which happens to be this knife, strikes at him in order to make him let go his hold. The blow is a fatal one. He falls and she escapes, either with or without the object for which she has come. Is Susan, the maid, there? Could anyone have got away through that door after the time that you heard the cry, Susan?"

"No, sir; it is impossible. Before I got down the stair, I'd have seen anyone in the passage. Besides, the door never opened, or I would have heard it."

"That settles this exit. Then no doubt the lady went out the way she came. I understand that this other passage leads only to the professor's room. There is no exit that way?"

"No, sir."

"We shall go down it and make the acquaintance of the professor. Halloa, Hopkins! this is very important, very important indeed. The professor's corridor is also lined with cocoanut matting."

"Well, sir, what of that?"

"Don't you see any bearing upon the case? Well, well. I don't

"Did you dust this bureau yesterday morning?"
Sidney Paget, *Strand Magazine*, 1904

insist upon it. No doubt I am wrong. And yet it seems to me to be suggestive. Come with me and introduce me."

We passed down the passage, which was of the same length as that which led to the garden. At the end was a short flight of steps ending in a door. Our guide knocked, and then ushered us into the professor's bedroom.

It was a very large chamber, lined with innumerable volumes, which had overflowed from the shelves and lay in piles in the corners, or were stacked all round at the base of the cases. The bed was in the centre of the room, and in it, propped up with pillows, was the owner of the house. I have seldom seen a more remarkable-looking person. It was a gaunt, aquiline face which was turned towards us, with piercing dark eyes, which

15 The cigarette manufacturer Ionides & Co. was located at 3 Swallow Street, off Regent Street, in London. The "Alexandria" reference may be to the blend of tobacco, which might have been sweetened with molasses, as it is smoked in Egyptian hookahs. (Or perhaps the professor did have a source in Alexandria, and the Ionides name is merely a coincidence.) Cigarettes, as opposed to pipes, cigars, or snuff, were a relatively new phenomenon in the West, having been introduced in England only within the previous thirty years. In his book *The Victorians*, historian A. N. Wilson traces England's cigarette craze to the Crimean War, during which Scotsman Robert Peacock Gloag—whose exact involvement in the war is unknown—witnessed Turks and Russians smoking cigarettes. He brought the curiosity back to London with him, selling rolled, strawberry-coloured paper filled with Latakia tobacco. Others caught on, and by the early 1860s there were a number of shops in London hawking "Turkish cigarettes." Meanwhile, Gloag was experiencing considerable entrepreneurial success, having expanded operations to six houses and founded a factory in Walworth.

Although the health effects of tobacco were not as well known in the nineteenth century as they are today, many physicians did recognise that there were risks associated with smoking. Cigarettes, lacking the drawing-room sophistication of pipes and cigars, came in for particular scorn, and the habit tended to be condemned as unsavoury and low. Surgeon Arthur E. J. Longhurst blamed cigarettes for having brought down the Ottoman Empire, saying, "We may also take warning from the history of another nation, who some few centuries ago . . . were the terror of Christendom, but who since then having become more addicted to tobacco-smoking than any of the European nations, are now the lazy and lethargic Turks, held in contempt by all civilized communities."

lurked in deep hollows under overhung and tufted brows. His hair and beard were white, save that the latter was curiously stained with yellow around his mouth. A cigarette glowed amid the tangle of white hair, and the air of the room was fetid with stale tobacco smoke. As he held out his hand to Holmes, I perceived that it was also stained with yellow nicotine.

"A smoker, Mr. Holmes?" said he, speaking in well-chosen English, with a curious little mincing accent. "Pray take a cigarette. And you, sir? I can recommend them, for I have them especially prepared by Ionides of Alexandria.[15] He sends me a thousand at a time, and I grieve to say that I have to arrange for a fresh supply every fortnight. Bad, sir, very bad, but an old

It was a gaunt, aquiline face which was turned towards us.
Charles Raymond Macaulay, *Return of Sherlock Holmes*
(McClure Phillips), 1905

man has few pleasures. Tobacco and my work—that is all that is left to me."

Holmes had lit a cigarette and was shooting little darting glances all over the room.

"Tobacco and my work, but now only tobacco," the old man exclaimed. "Alas! what a fatal interruption! Who could have foreseen such a terrible catastrophe? So estimable a young man! I assure you that, after a few months' training, he was an admirable assistant. What do you think of the matter, Mr. Holmes?"

"I have not yet made up my mind."

"I shall indeed be indebted to you if you can throw a light where all is so dark to us. To a poor bookworm and invalid like myself such a blow is paralysing. I seem to have lost the faculty of thought. But you are a man of action—you are a man of affairs. It is part of the everyday routine of your life. You can preserve your balance in every emergency. We are fortunate, indeed, in having you at our side."

Holmes was pacing up and down one side of the room whilst the old professor was talking. I observed that he was smoking with extraordinary rapidity. It was evident that he shared our host's liking for the fresh Alexandrian cigarettes.

"Yes, sir, it is a crushing blow," said the old man. "That is my *magnum opus*—the pile of papers on the side-table yonder. It is my analysis of the documents found in the Coptic[16] monasteries of Syria and Egypt, a work which will cut deep at the very foundations of revealed religion. With my enfeebled health I do not know whether I shall ever be able to complete it, now that my assistant has been taken from me. Dear me! Mr. Holmes; why, you are even a quicker smoker than I am myself."

Holmes smiled.

"I am a connoisseur," said he, taking another cigarette from the box—his fourth—and lighting it from the stub of that which he had finished. "I will not trouble you with any lengthy cross-examination, Professor Coram, since I gather that you were in bed at the time of the crime, and could know nothing about it. I would only ask this: What do you imagine that this poor fellow meant by his last words: 'The professor—it was she'?"

The professor shook his head.

But once Gloag had gotten the wheels rolling, there was no stopping the momentum: England was hooked on this inexpensive new addiction. The cigarette's biggest breakthrough came in 1883, when tobacconists W. D. and H. O. Wills bought their first Bonsack machine, an American invention that could manufacture two hundred cigarettes per minute. "Between 1860 and 1900," Wilson writes, "Britain became a smoking nation." Smoking, once banned from clubs and railway cars, became ubiquitous. Cigarettes were far more affordable than pipes or cigars, particularly after the introduction of "penny cigarettes" in the 1880s; and thus the vice of the Russians and Turks became the vice of the British working class. (See "The Priory School," note 33, for more on the social perception of cigarettes.)

Holmes himself was of course an inveterate smoker of tobacco in all forms. Although Holmes is most often associated with pipes in his public image and his storage of his cigars in the coal scuttle is well-known ("The Musgrave Ritual"), there are ample records of the variety of his smoking habit. Jay Finley Christ, in "Keeping Score on Sherlock Holmes," from his *Flashes by Fanlight*, notes twenty-nine tales in which Holmes smokes only pipes, five only cigarettes, and three only cigars; three tales mention pipe and cigars, two pipe and cigarettes, and two others cigars and cigarettes. In *The Hound of the Baskervilles* he indulges in all three! Only in twelve tales does he refrain from smoking.

16 Copts are Egyptian Christians whose cultural roots predate the seventh-century Arab conquest of Egypt. While much of the rest of Egypt was converting to Islam, the Copts remained devoted to the "Egyptian Church" (now the Coptic Orthodox Church), which was founded in the fifth century and adhered to the doctrine Monophysitism—that is, the notion that Christ's nature was singularly

divine, but not human. The Coptic language, an early form of Egyptian, died out in the twelfth century, and in most ways Copts seem no different from most Egyptian Muslims. Yet through the centuries they have remained a tight-knit community, and the Coptic Orthodox Church continues to play a vital administrative role in educational and theological matters. The Copts' isolationist tendencies may have once led some to look askance at this peculiar minority. The *Encyclopædia Britannica* (9th Ed.) disparaged the Copts as "exceedingly bigoted, prone to be converted to Islamism, sullen, as Ammianus Marcellinus describes the Egyptians, false, faithless, and deceitful, but extremely useful as secretaries and accountants and skilful workmen." Holmes was engaged in the "case of the two Coptic Patriarchs" at the beginning of "The Retired Colourman," but that case is generally placed in 1898, and Holmes had no reason to study the Copts beforehand.

17 A gage is an item offered as a token or a pledge. More specifically, it used to refer to the glove offered (or thrown down) as challenge to a duel. Here, the word is used in its secondary sense, a "love-gage" being a sign of the affection one lover pledges to another.

"Yes, sir, it is a crushing blow," said the old man.
Frederick Dorr Steele, *Collier's*, 1904

"Susan is a country girl," said he, "and you know the incredible stupidity of that class. I fancy that the poor fellow murmured some incoherent, delirious words, and that she twisted them into this meaningless message."

"I see. You have no explanation yourself of the tragedy?"

"Possibly an accident, possibly—I only breathe it among ourselves—a suicide. Young men have their hidden troubles—some affair of the heart, perhaps, which we have never known. It is a more probable supposition than murder."

"But the eyeglasses?"

"Ah! I am only a student—a man of dreams. I cannot explain the practical things of life. But still, we are aware, my friend, that love-gages[17] may take strange shapes. By all means take another cigarette. It is a pleasure to see anyone appreciate them so. A fan, a glove, glasses—who knows what article may be carried as a token or treasured when a man puts an end to his life? This gentleman speaks of footsteps on the grass, but, after all, it is easy to be mistaken on such a point. As to the knife, it might well be thrown far from the unfortunate man as he fell. It is possible that I speak as a child, but to me it seems that Willoughby Smith has met his fate by his own hand."

Holmes seemed struck by the theory thus put forward, and he continued to walk up and down for some time, lost in thought and consuming cigarette after cigarette.

"Tell me, Professor Coram," he said, at last, "what is in that cupboard in the bureau?"

"Nothing that would help a thief. Family papers, letters from my poor wife, diplomas of universities which have done me honour. Here is the key. You can look for yourself."

Holmes picked up the key and looked at it for an instant, then he handed it back.

"No; I hardly think that it would help me," said he. "I should prefer to go quietly down to your garden, and turn the whole matter over in my head. There is something to be said for the theory of suicide which you have put forward. We must apologize for having intruded upon you, Professor Coram, and I promise that we won't disturb you until after lunch. At two o'clock we will come again and report to you anything which may have happened in the interval."

Holmes was curiously distrait, and we walked up and down the garden path for some time in silence.

"Have you a clue?" I asked, at last.

"It depends upon those cigarettes that I smoked," said he. "It is possible that I am utterly mistaken. The cigarettes will show me."

"My dear Holmes," I exclaimed, "how on earth—"

"Well, well, you may see for yourself. If not, there's no harm done. Of course, we always have the optician clue to fall back upon, but I take a short cut when I can get it. Ah, here is the good Mrs. Marker! Let us enjoy five minutes of instructive conversation with her."

I may have remarked before that Holmes had, when he liked, a peculiarly ingratiating way with women, and that he very readily established terms of confidence with them. In half the time which he had named, he had captured the housekeeper's goodwill and was chatting with her as if he had known her for years.

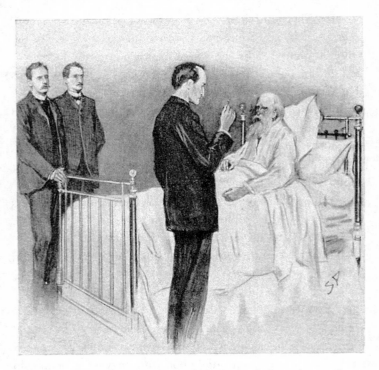

"Holmes picked up the key and looked at it for an instant."
Sidney Paget, *Strand Magazine*, 1904

"Yes, Mr. Holmes, it is as you say, sir. He does smoke something terrible. All day and sometimes all night, sir. I've seen that room of a morning—well, sir, you'd have thought it was a London fog. Poor young Mr. Smith, he was a smoker also, but not as bad as the professor. His health—well, I don't know that it's better nor worse for the smoking."

"Ah!" said Holmes, "but it kills the appetite."

"Well, I don't know about that, sir."

"I suppose the professor eats hardly anything?"

"Well, he is variable. I'll say that for him."

"I'll wager he took no breakfast this morning, and won't face his lunch after all the cigarettes I saw him consume."

"Well, you're out there, sir, as it happens, for he ate a remarkable big breakfast this morning. I don't know when I've known him make a better one, and he's ordered a good dish of cutlets for his lunch. I'm surprised myself, for since I came into that room yesterday and saw young Mr. Smith lying there on the floor, I couldn't bear to look at food. Well, it takes all sorts to make a world, and the professor hasn't let it take his appetite away."

We loitered the morning away in the garden. Stanley Hopkins had gone down to the village to look into some rumours of a strange woman who had been seen by some children on the Chatham Road the previous morning. As to my friend, all his usual energy seemed to have deserted him. I had never known him handle a case in such a half-hearted fashion. Even the news brought back by Hopkins that he had found the children and that they had undoubtedly seen a woman exactly corresponding with Holmes's description, and wearing either spectacles or eyeglasses, failed to rouse any sign of keen interest. He was more attentive when Susan, who waited upon us at lunch, volunteered the information that she believed Mr. Smith had been out for a walk yesterday morning, and that he had only returned half an hour before the tragedy occurred. I could not myself see the bearing of this incident, but I clearly perceived that Holmes was weaving it into the general scheme which he had formed in his brain. Suddenly he sprang from his chair and glanced at his watch. "Two o'clock, gentlemen," said he. "We must go up and have it out with our friend, the professor."

The old man had just finished his lunch, and certainly his empty dish bore evidence to the good appetite with which his housekeeper had credited him. He was, indeed, a weird figure as he turned his white mane and his glowing eyes towards us. The eternal cigarette smouldered in his mouth. He had been dressed and was seated in an arm-chair by the fire.

"Well, Mr. Holmes, have you solved this mystery yet?" He shoved the large tin of cigarettes which stood on a table beside him towards my companion. Holmes stretched out his hand at the same moment, and between them they tipped the box over the edge. For a minute or two we were all on our knees retrieving stray cigarettes from impossible places. When we rose again I observed Holmes's eyes were shining and his cheeks tinged with colour. Only at a crisis have I seen those battle-signals flying.

"Yes," said he, "I have solved it."

Stanley Hopkins and I stared in amazement. Something like a sneer quivered over the gaunt features of the old professor.

"Indeed! In the garden?"

"No, here."

The Professor was seated by the fire.
Frederick Dorr Steele, *Collier's*, 1904

"Here! When?"

"This instant."

"You are surely joking, Mr. Sherlock Holmes. You compel me to tell you that this is too serious a matter to be treated in such a fashion."

"I have forged and tested every link of my chain, Professor Coram, and I am sure that it is sound. What your motives are, or what exact part you play in this strange business, I am not yet able to say. In a few minutes I shall probably hear it from your own lips. Meanwhile I will reconstruct what is past for your benefit, so that you may know the information which I still require.

"A lady yesterday entered your study. She came with the intention of possessing herself of certain documents which were in your bureau. She had a key of her own. I have had an opportunity of examining yours, and I do not find that slight discolouration which the scratch made upon the varnish would have produced. You were not an accessory, therefore, and she came, so far as I can read the evidence, without your knowledge to rob you."

The professor blew a cloud from his lips. "This is most interesting and instructive," said he. "Have you no more to add? Surely, having traced this lady so far, you can also say what has become of her."

"I will endeavour to do so. In the first place, she was seized by your secretary, and stabbed him in order to escape. This catastrophe I am inclined to regard as an unhappy accident, for I am convinced that the lady had no intention of inflicting so grievous an injury. An assassin does not come unarmed. Horrified by what she had done, she rushed wildly away from the scene of the tragedy. Unfortunately for her she had lost her glasses in the scuffle, and as she was extremely short-sighted she was really helpless without them. She ran down a corridor, which she imagined to be that by which she had come—both were lined with cocoanut matting—and it was only when it was too late that she understood that she had taken the wrong passage, and that her retreat was cut off behind her. What was she to do? She could not go back. She could not remain where she was. She must go on. She went on. She mounted a stair, pushed open a door, and found herself in your room."

The old man sat with his mouth open, staring wildly at Holmes. Amazement and fear were stamped upon his expressive features. Now, with an effort, he shrugged his shoulders and burst into insincere laughter.

"All very fine, Mr. Holmes," said he. "But there is one little flaw in your splendid theory. I was myself in my room, and I never left it during the day."

"I am aware of that, Professor Coram."

"And you mean to say that I could lie upon that bed and not be aware that a woman had entered my room?"

"I never said so. You *were* aware of it. You spoke with her. You recognized her. You aided her to escape."

Again the professor burst into high-keyed laughter. He had risen to his feet, and his eyes glowed like embers.

"You are mad!" he cried. "You are talking insanely. I helped her to escape? Where is she now?"

"She is there," said Holmes, and he pointed to a high bookcase in the corner of the room.

I saw the old man throw up his arms, a terrible convulsion passed over his grim face, and he fell back in his chair. At the same instant the bookcase at which Holmes pointed swung round upon a hinge, and a woman rushed out into the room. "You are right!" she cried, in a strange foreign voice. "You are right, I am here."

She was brown with the dust and draped with the cobwebs which had come from the walls of her hiding-place. Her face, too, was streaked with grime, and at the best she could never have been handsome, for she had the exact physical characteristics which Holmes had divined, with, in addition, a long and obstinate chin. What with her natural blindness, and what with the change from dark to light, she stood as one dazed, blinking about her to see where and who we were. And yet, in spite of

"A woman rushed out into the room."
Sidney Paget, *Strand Magazine*, 1904

all these disadvantages, there was a certain nobility in the woman's bearing—a gallantry in the defiant chin and in the upraised head, which compelled something of respect and admiration.

Stanley Hopkins had laid his hand upon her arm and claimed her as his prisoner, but she waved him aside gently, and yet with an overmastering dignity which compelled obedience. The old man lay back in his chair, with a twitching face, and stared at her with brooding eyes.

"Yes, sir, I am your prisoner," she said. "From where I stood I could hear everything, and I know that you have learned the truth. I confess it all. It was I who killed the young man. But you are right, you who say it was an accident. I did not even know that it was a knife which I held in my hand, for in my despair I snatched anything from the table and struck at him to make him let me go. It is the truth that I tell."

"Madam," said Holmes, "I am sure that it is the truth. I fear that you are far from well."

She had turned a dreadful colour, the more ghastly under the dark dust-streaks upon her face. She seated herself on the side of the bed; then she resumed.

"I have only a little time here," she said, "but I would have you to know the whole truth. I am this man's wife. He is not an Englishman. He is a Russian. His name I will not tell."

For the first time the old man stirred. "God bless you, Anna!" he cried. "God bless you!"

She cast a look of the deepest disdain in his direction. "Why should you cling so hard to that wretched life of yours, Sergius?" said she.[18] "It has done harm to many and good to none—not even to yourself. However, it is not for me to cause the frail thread to be snapped before God's time. I have enough already upon my soul since I crossed the threshold of this cursed house. But I must speak or I shall be too late.

"I have said, gentlemen, that I am this man's wife. He was fifty and I a foolish girl of twenty when we married. It was in a city of Russia, a University—I will not name the place."

"God bless you, Anna!" murmured the old man again.

"We were reformers—revolutionists—Nihilists,[19] you understand. He and I and many more. Then there came a time of trouble, a police officer was killed, many were arrested, evidence was wanted, and in order to save his own life and to earn

18 Oops—so much for not revealing his name! Anna evidently thought that the matter would become public (was she a reader of Watson's works?) but believed that using only Coram's real first name would leave him untraceable.

19 Although the term "nihilism" had been floating around since the Middle Ages—encompassing definitions ranging from scepticism to a rejection of morality (the word comes from the Latin nihil, or "nothing")—it was Ivan Turgenev's 1862 novel *Fathers and Sons* that brought the concept into the popular imagination. In the novel, Turgenev's protagonist, Bazarov, embodies the radicalism of a new generation by scorning the traditional aristocracy. Nihilists were dedicated to the rejection of aestheticism and the destruction of the existing social order; they loathed ignorance and trusted only the pursuit of scientific knowledge. Even the bonds of family were considered suspect and undesirable. And while violence was not an officially sanctioned aspect of nihilism, it was not discouraged either, leaving more extremist individuals and terrorist organisations to embark upon campaigns that imprinted the movement with the permanent stamp of violence. The assassination of Czar Alexander II in 1881 was one such act, with hundreds of nihilists being exiled or hanged in its aftermath. One wonders whether this period was the "time of trouble" Anna mentions.

a great reward, my husband betrayed his own wife and his companions. Yes; we were all arrested upon his confession. Some of us found our way to the gallows, and some to Siberia. I was among these last, but my term was not for life. My husband came to England with his ill-gotten gains and has lived in quiet ever since, knowing well that if the Brotherhood knew where he was not a week would pass before justice would be done."

The old man reached out a trembling hand and helped himself to a cigarette. "I am in your hands, Anna," said he. "You were always good to me."

"I have not yet told you the height of his villainy," said she. "Among our comrades of the Order, there was one who was the friend of my heart. He was noble, unselfish, loving—all that my husband was not. He hated violence. We were all guilty—if that is guilt—but he was not. He wrote for ever dissuading us from such a course. These letters would have saved him. So would my diary, in which, from day to day, I had entered both my feelings towards him and the view which each of us had taken. My husband found and kept both diary and letters. He hid them, and he tried hard to swear away the young man's life.

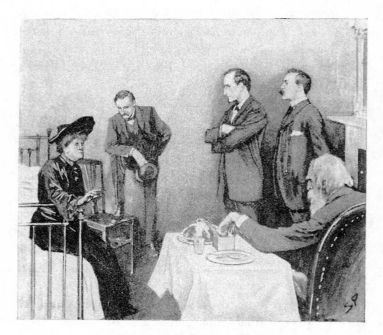

"'I am in your hands, Anna,' said he."
Sidney Paget, *Strand Magazine*, 1904

In this he failed, but Alexis was sent a convict to Siberia, where now, at this moment, he works in a salt mine. Think of that, you villain, you villain!—now, now, at this very moment, Alexis, a man whose name you are not worthy to speak, works and lives like a slave, and yet I have your life in my hands, and I let you go."

"You were always a noble woman, Anna," said the old man, puffing at his cigarette.

She had risen, but she fell back again with a little cry of pain.

"I must finish," she said. "When my term was over I set myself to get the diary and letters which, if sent to the Russian Government, would procure my friend's release. I knew that my husband had come to England. After months of searching I discovered where he was. I knew that he still had the diary, for when I was in Siberia I had a letter from him once, reproaching me and quoting some passages from its pages. Yet I was sure that with his revengeful nature he would never give it to me of his own free will. I must get it for myself. With this object I engaged an agent from a private detective firm, who entered my husband's house as secretary—it was your second secretary, Sergius, the one who left you so hurriedly. He found that papers were kept in the cupboard, and he got an impression of the key. He would not go farther. He furnished me with a plan of the house, and he told me that in the forenoon the study was always empty, as the secretary was employed up here. So at last I took my courage in both hands, and I came down to get the papers for myself. I succeeded, but at what a cost!

"I had just taken the papers and was locking the cupboard, when the young man seized me. I had seen him already that morning. He had met me on the road and I had asked him to tell me where Professor Coram lived, not knowing that he was in his employ."

"Exactly! Exactly!" said Holmes. "The secretary came back and told his employer of the woman he had met. Then, in his last breath, he tried to send a message that it was she—the she whom he had just discussed with him."

"You must let me speak," said the woman, in an imperative voice, and her face contracted as if in pain. "When he had fallen I rushed from the room, chose the wrong door, and found myself in my husband's room. He spoke of giving me up, I

20 Would Holmes have let Anna go free if she survived? After all, the slaying of the secretary was accidental. Brad Keefauver, in *Sherlock and the Ladies*, is not convinced that Anna actually killed herself. He finds it "a little too convenient" that Anna is the only witness to her self-poisoning and, in a melodramatic scene, collapses "only after she's had time to tell her story in its entirety," complete with amateurish exclamations of "My head swims. I am going!" It is possible, Keefauver surmises, that a sympathetic Holmes—who had only just that year come back from the dead himself—knowingly allowed Anna to fake her own demise and escape with her life. "If Anna Coram did put on a death scene that could fool both an experienced policeman and a doctor, I think we can rest assured that Sherlock Holmes was not taken it by it."

showed him that if he did so, his life was in my hands. If he gave me to the law, I could give him to the Brotherhood. It was not that I wished to live for my own sake, but it was that I desired to accomplish my purpose. He knew that I would do what I said—that his own fate was involved in mine. For that reason, and for no other, he shielded me. He thrust me into that dark hiding-place—a relic of old days, known only to himself. He took his meals in his own room, and so was able to give me part of his food. It was agreed that when the police left the house I should slip away by night and come back no more. But in some way you have read our plans." She tore from the bosom of her dress a small packet. "These are my last words," said she; "here is the packet which will save Alexis. I confide it to your honour and to your love of justice. Take it! You will deliver it at the Russian Embassy. Now, I have done my duty, and—"

"Stop her!" cried Holmes. He had bounded across the room and had wrenched a small phial from her hand.

"Too late!" she said, sinking back on the bed. "Too late! I took the poison before I left my hiding-place. My head swims! I am going! I charge you, sir, to remember the packet."[20]

"A simple case, and yet, in some ways, an instructive one," Holmes remarked, as we travelled back to town. "It hinged from the outset upon the pince-nez. But for the fortunate chance of the dying man having seized these, I am not sure that we could ever have reached our solution. It was clear to me from the strength of the glasses that the wearer must have been very blind and helpless when deprived of them. When you asked me to believe that she walked along a narrow strip of grass without once making a false step, I remarked, as you may remember, that it was a noteworthy performance. In my mind, I set it down as an impossible performance, save in the unlikely case that she had a second pair of glasses. I was forced, therefore, to consider seriously the hypothesis that she had remained within the house. On perceiving the similarity of the two corridors, it became clear that she might very easily have made such a mistake, and, in that case, it was evident that she must have entered the professor's room. I was keenly on the alert, therefore, for whatever would bear out this supposition, and I examined the room narrowly for anything in the shape of a hiding-place. The carpet seemed continuous and firmly nailed, so I dismissed the idea of a trap-door. There might well be a recess behind the books. As you are aware, such devices are common in old libraries. I observed that books were piled on the floor at all other points, but that one bookcase was left clear. This, then, might be the door. I could see no marks to guide me, but the carpet was of a dun colour, which lends itself very well to examination. I therefore smoked a great number of those excellent cigarettes, and I dropped the ash all over the space in front of the suspected bookcase. It was a simple trick, but exceedingly effective. I then went downstairs, and I ascertained, in your presence, Watson, without your perceiving the drift of my remarks, that Professor Coram's consumption of

"Holmes had bounded across the room and had
wrenched a small phial from her hand."
Sidney Paget, *Strand Magazine*, 1904

21 Holmes's ingenious method of detection had its precedents. Stephen F. Crocker points out that a similar approach is used in the story of Bel and the Dragon, one of the Old Testament apocrypha deleted from the book of Daniel and not considered part of the established biblical canon. In the story, a king demands to know why Daniel does not worship the idol Bel, and Daniel responds that Bel is not a living god but merely a false idol made of clay and brass. When the king points out that the great quantities of food brought before Bel every day are always consumed before the morning, Daniel is forced to defend himself or suffer death. By sprinkling ashes on the floor, Daniel is able to detect the footprints of the priests and their families who have been entering the temple and eating the food—and who, upon their discovery, are immediately executed. Crocker suggests that Holmes's methodology was "inspired" by the biblical tale.

Dorothy L. Sayers, in her introduction to *Omnibus of Crime*, notes a parallel to Daniel's detective methods in the story of Tristan and Iseult, where the king's spy spreads flour between their beds to show their movements; Tristan defeats the plan by leaping from one bed to another. Sayers, a thoughtful Sherlockian scholar, makes no connection to "The Golden Pince-Nez." However, Professor Clarke Olney credits Holmes with familiarity with the operatic tale and proposes that he adapted it to his use.

food had increased—as one would expect when he is supplying a second person. We then ascended to the room again, when, by upsetting the cigarette-box, I obtained a very excellent view of the floor, and was able to see quite clearly, from the traces upon the cigarette ash, that the prisoner had in our absence come out from her retreat.[21] Well, Hopkins, here we are at Charing Cross, and I congratulate you on having brought your case to a successful conclusion. You are going to headquarters, no doubt. I think, Watson, you and I will drive together to the Russian Embassy."

THE ADVENTURE OF THE
MISSING THREE-QUARTER[1]

"The Missing Three-Quarter" is the only case in the Canon to involve amateur sports directly. Conan Doyle and Watson both were active team sportsmen, the former an avid cricket player, the latter a rugby player (as we learn in "The Sussex Vampire"). Holmes himself excelled at individual sports, such as fencing, singlestick, and boxing. Here, he is called in to find a star rugby player in time for a crucial match. Two other players in the drama draw our attention: Lord Mount-James, perhaps the richest man in England (and the stingiest), and one Dr. Leslie Armstrong, who bids to be a most interesting villain only to turn out to be a friend. The Cambridge setting of the case provides scholars with more clues to Holmes's own university years, adding to the hints in "The Three Students," published two months earlier. Here Holmes's efforts to use a dog as a tracker prove successful, reversing his failure with the mongrel Toby in The Sign of Four.

W**E WERE FAIRLY** accustomed to receive weird telegrams at Baker Street, but I have a particular recollection of one which reached us on a gloomy February morning some seven or eight years ago, and gave Mr. Sherlock Holmes a puzzled quarter of an hour. It was addressed to him, and ran thus:

Please await me. Terrible misfortune. Right wing[2] three-quarter missing; indispensable to-morrow.
> Overton.

"Strand postmark, and despatched ten thirty-six," said Holmes, reading it over and over. "Mr. Overton was evidently considerably excited when he sent it, and somewhat incoherent in consequence. Well, well, he will be here, I daresay, by the time I have looked through *The Times*,[3] and then we shall know all about it. Even the most insignificant problem would be welcome in these stagnant days."

1 "The Missing Three-Quarter" was published in the *Strand Magazine* in August 1904 and in *Collier's Weekly* on November 26, 1904. The manuscript is at the British Library.

2 In rugby, the position of the forwards on either side of the centre. For an explanation of the game of rugby and its associated terms, see "The Rules of Rugby," page 1153.

3 The manuscript has "by the time that the table is cleared."

4 Watson's concern about Holmes's cocaine habit appears touching. Yet, considering that Holmes is actually seen using cocaine in the accounts of only two cases—*The Sign of Four* and "A Scandal in Bohemia"—it is hard to describe the addiction as having jeopardised Holmes's career. Troubling as the habit was, Watson may be indulging in a bit of vanity here, identifying himself as Holmes's saviour and the one person able to stop him from imminent relapse. Jack Tracey and Jim Berkey, in *Subcutaneously, My Dear Watson*, trace the course of Holmes's drug dependence from 1887 to 1902, with only short intermittent drug-free periods; and even they label Watson's statement here an "insupportable boast."

Frederick Dorr Steele, *Collier's*, 1904

Things had indeed been very slow with us, and I had learned to dread such periods of inaction, for I knew by experience that my companion's brain was so abnormally active that it was dangerous to leave it without material upon which to work. For years I had gradually weaned him from that drug mania which had threatened once to check his remarkable career.[4] Now I knew that under ordinary conditions he no longer craved for this artificial stimulus; but I was well aware that the fiend was not dead, but sleeping; and I have known that the sleep was a light one and the waking near when in periods of idleness I have seen the drawn look upon Holmes's ascetic face, and the brooding of his deep-set and inscrutable eyes. Therefore I blessed this Mr. Overton, whoever he might be, since he had come with his enigmatic message to break that dangerous calm which brought more peril to my friend than all the storms of his tempestuous life.

As we had expected, the telegram was soon followed by its sender, and the card of Mr. Cyril Overton, of Trinity College, Cambridge, announced the arrival of an enormous young man, sixteen stone of solid bone and muscle, who spanned the door-way with his broad shoulders, and looked from one of us to the other with a comely face which was haggard with anxiety.

"Mr. Sherlock Holmes?"

My companion bowed.

"I've been down to Scotland Yard, Mr. Holmes. I saw Inspector Stanley Hopkins. He advised me to come to you. He said the case, so far as he could see, was more in your line than in that of the regular police."

"Pray sit down, and tell me what is the matter."

"It's awful, Mr. Holmes, simply awful! I wonder my hair isn't grey. Godfrey Staunton—you've heard of him, of course? He's simply the hinge that the whole team turns on. I'd rather spare two from the pack and have Godfrey for my three-quarter line. Whether it's passing, or tackling, or dribbling, there's no one to touch him; and then, he's got the head and can hold us all together. What am I to do? That's what I ask you, Mr. Holmes.

Frederick Dorr Steele, *Collier's*, 1904

5 The Reverend Arthur Henry Stanton, according to Donald Redmond's *Sherlock Holmes: A Study in Sources*, was wrongly accused of authorship of a book of Catholic prayers.

6 Michael Harrison, in *In the Footsteps of Sherlock Holmes*, points out the omission of Louis A. Staunton, who with others of his family was convicted of murdering his wife in 1877 and surely would have been in Holmes's index.

7 C. Alan Bradley and William A. S. Sarjeant regard Holmes's ignorance as unfathomable, and an indication that Holmes must not have attended an English public school, where students could not help but learn at least the basics of rugby. "Indeed," Bradley and Sarjeant exclaim, "could any man who had grown up in England—even if privately tutored, and however little interested in sport he might be—remain so ignorant?" This evidence leads them to decide that Holmes was not, in fact, a man, but a woman in disguise; a less bizarre conclusion might be that Holmes's early education took place wholly outside England.

8 " 'Varsity" was originally a colloquial abbreviation of "University."

9 "Two years" in the manuscript.

10 The first rugby game in Cambridge took place in 1839, but the Cambridge University Rugby Union Football Club was not officially founded until 1872. The university's rival, Oxford, can claim superiority at least in this instance, having established its own rugby club three years earlier.

11 The Blackheath Football Club was founded in 1858 as the world's first "open" rugby club. Blackheath was one of the founding members of the fledgling, eleven-club Football Association, formed in 1863. But

There's Moorhouse, first reserve, but he is trained as a half, and he always edges right in on to the scrum instead of keeping out on the touch-line. He's a fine place-kick, it's true, but, then, he has no judgment and he can't sprint for nuts. Why, Morton or Johnson, the Oxford fliers, could romp round him. Stevenson is fast enough, but he couldn't drop from the twenty-five line, and a three-quarter who can't either punt or drop isn't worth a place for pace alone. No, Mr. Holmes, we are done unless you can help me to find Godfrey Staunton."

My friend had listened with amused surprise to this long speech, which was poured forth with extraordinary vigour and earnestness, every point being driven home by the slapping of a brawny hand upon the speaker's knee. When our visitor was silent Holmes stretched out his hand and took down letter "S" of his commonplace book. For once he dug in vain into that mine of varied information.

"There is Arthur H. Staunton, the rising young forger,"[5] said he, "and there was Henry Staunton, whom I helped to hang,[6] but Godfrey Staunton is a new name to me."

It was our visitor's turn to look surprised.

"Why, Mr. Holmes, I thought you knew things," said he. "I suppose, then, if you have never heard of Godfrey Staunton, you don't know Cyril Overton either?"

Holmes shook his head good-humouredly.[7]

"Great Scott!" cried the athlete. "Why, I was first reserve for England against Wales, and I've skippered the 'Varsity[8] all this year.[9] But that's nothing! I didn't think there was a soul in England who didn't know Godfrey Staunton, the crack three-quarter, Cambridge,[10] Blackheath,[11] and five Internationals.[12] Good Lord! Mr. Holmes, where have you lived?"[13]

Holmes laughed at the young giant's naïve astonishment.

"You live in a different world to me, Mr. Overton, a sweeter and healthier one. My ramifications stretch out into many sections of society, but never, I am happy to say, into amateur sport, which is the best and soundest thing in England.[14] However, your unexpected visit this morning shows me that even in that world of fresh air and fair play, there may be work for me to do; so now, my good sir, I beg you to sit down and to tell me, slowly and quietly, exactly what it is that has occurred, and how you desire that I should help you."

Young Overton's face assumed the bothered look of the man

when the association proposed to adopt Cambridge rules, in which "hacking" (kicking in the shins) and running with the ball were disallowed, Blackheath withdrew from the association and in 1871 formed the Rugby Football Union, comprising twenty clubs and following a set of rules that the club had written up in 1862. It was this split that helped to clarify the distinction between football (or American soccer) and rugby. See "The Rules of Rugby," page 1153, for more on the Rugby Football Union.

12 On March 27, 1871, the first international match was played, organised by Blackheath and pitting England against Scotland in Edinburgh. In the following decade and a half, the countries of the United Kingdom (England, Scotland, Ireland, and Wales) began playing one another annually, and have done so continuously with only a few exceptions occurring over national disputes. The "Internationals" are now known as the "Six Nations" and include Italy and France.

13 According to J. P. W. Mallalieu, Holmes is not the only person whose lack of rugby knowledge is being exposed by this exchange. In "The Sussex Vampire," Watson passes himself off as a former rugby player for Blackheath, but Mallalieu, a rugby fan and a former M.P., uses Overton's speech here to demonstrate that Watson probably never played the game. After all, the doctor has clearly never heard of Staunton nor of Over-

ton. And Mallalieu looks skeptically upon some of the statements that Watson attributes to Overton, claiming that no skilled rugby player would speak in such a manner. For example, in considering candidates to replace Staunton, Overton bemoans that one player, Stevenson, despite his speed, "couldn't drop from the twenty-five line, and a three-quarter who can't either punt or drop isn't worth a place for pace alone." To this, Mallalieu cries, "Twaddle!" explaining that any other player might "drop from the twenty-five line" in Stevenson's place, and that a three-quarter rarely has the opportunity to score (hence there is little need for him to kick the ball). For Mallalieu, Overton's incongruous references indicate plainly that Watson's familiarity with the sport is not much greater than Holmes's, that he misstated Overton's comments about the game, and that he did not play at Blackheath so much as accidentally wander onto the field from the stands.

14 Of course, neither Holmes nor Watson, both in their forties ("The Missing Three-Quarter" is usually placed in 1896 by the chronologists—see *Chronological Table*), would have participated in amateur team sports for some years. "[Football]," remarks the *Encyclopædia Britannica* (9th Ed.), "is a game more adapted to youths than to middle-aged persons, and should not be indulged in after the frame is full-grown and set, when the tumbles and scrimmages incidental to the Rugby code are apt to be baneful."

15 "Rugger" is simply another word for rugby.

16 The very first Cambridge-Oxford match was played at Oxford in 1872, the year Cambridge's club was founded. (Oxford emerged the victor, a fact that remains notably unreported on Cambridge's website.) Two years later, the match was moved to a neutral site, Kennington Oval, and various other venues, including Blackheath's Rectory Field, were subsequently tried out until the game moved to Queen's Club in 1887. With the exception of the years during World War I, when all rugby matches were suspended, Queen's Club continued to host the so-called Varsity Match—which came to be held every second Tuesday in December—until it was determined that the location had become too small for the throngs of fans that turned out to witness the intense rivalry. In 1921 the game was moved to Twickenham Stadium, where it has been played ever since.

"'Why, Mr. Holmes, I thought you knew things,' said he."
Sidney Paget, *Strand Magazine*, 1904

who is more accustomed to using his muscles than his wits; but by degrees, with many repetitions and obscurities which I may omit from his narrative, he laid his strange story before us.

"It's this way, Mr. Holmes. As I have said, I am the skipper of the Rugger[15] team of Cambridge 'Varsity, and Godfrey Staunton is my best man. To-morrow we play Oxford.[16] Yesterday we all came up, and we settled at Bentley's private hotel. At ten o'clock I went round and saw that all the fellows had gone to roost, for I believe in strict training and plenty of sleep to keep a team fit. I had a word or two with Godfrey before he turned in. He seemed to me to be pale and bothered. I asked him what was the matter. He said he was all right—just a touch of headache. I bade him good-night and left him. Half an hour later the porter tells me that a rough-looking man with a beard called with a note for Godfrey. He had not gone to bed, and the note was taken to his room. Godfrey read it and fell back in a chair as if he had been pole-axed. The porter was so scared that he was going to fetch me, but Godfrey stopped him, had a drink of water, and pulled himself together. Then he went downstairs, said a few words to the man who was waiting in the hall, and the two of them went off together. The last that the porter saw of them, they were almost running down the street in the direction of the Strand.[17] This morning Godfrey's room was empty, his bed had never been slept in, and his things were all just as I had seen them the night before. He had gone off at a moment's notice with this stranger, and no word has come from him since. I don't believe he will ever come back. He was a sportsman, was Godfrey, down to his marrow, and he wouldn't have stopped his training and let in[18] his skipper if it were not for some cause that was too strong for him. No; I feel as if he were gone for good, and we should never see him again."

Sherlock Holmes listened with the deepest attention to this singular narrative.

"What did you do?" he asked.

17 The manuscript reads "down Northumberland Avenue in the direction of the Thames Embankment."

18 To cheat or victimise.

The Strand.
Queen's London (1897)

19 Gout is a disorder that strikes men, usually over the age of thirty, and is characterised by chronic inflammation of the joints. A buildup of urate deposits in the tissue surrounding the joints can cause deformity and extreme stiffness, particular in the feet and hands. In a remarkable case of coincidence, this editor discovered that Sir Thomas Watson (1792–1882), in his *Lectures on the Principles and Practice of Physic*, wrote: "A namesake of mine, Mr. Henry Watson, describes in the first volume of *Medical Communications*, the case of a Mr. Middleton, who was accustomed, when playing at cards, to chalk or score the game upon the table with his gouty knuckles." Did Overton use this phrase by chance in describing Lord Mount-James? Was he perhaps repeating a remark by the physician of Lord Mount-James—who may have even been Sir Thomas Watson? Or did John H. Watson, who may well have attended a lecture by his namesake or read his great work, interpolate the remark himself in reporting the incident?

"I wired to Cambridge to learn if anything had been heard of him there. I have had an answer. No one has seen him."

"Could he have got back to Cambridge?"

"Yes, there is a late train—quarter-past eleven."

"But, so far as you can ascertain, he did not take it?"

"No, he has not been seen."

"What did you do next?"

"I wired to Lord Mount-James."

"Why to Lord Mount-James?"

"Godfrey is an orphan, and Lord Mount-James is his nearest relative—his uncle, I believe."

"Indeed. This throws new light upon the matter. Lord Mount-James is one of the richest men in England."

"So I've heard Godfrey say."

"And your friend was closely related?"

"Yes, he was his heir, and the old boy is nearly eighty—cram full of gout, too. They say he could chalk his billiard-cue with his knuckles.[19] He never allowed Godfrey a shilling in his life, for he is an absolute miser, but it will all come to him right enough."

"Have you heard from Lord Mount-James?"

"No."

"What motive could your friend have in going to Lord Mount-James?"

"Well, something was worrying him the night before, and if it was to do with money it is possible that he would make for his nearest relative, who had so much of it, though from all I have heard he would not have much chance of getting it. Godfrey was not fond of the old man. He would not go if he could help it."

"Well, we can soon determine that. If your friend was going to his relative Lord Mount-James, you have then to explain the visit of this rough-looking fellow at so late an hour, and the agitation that was caused by his coming."

Cyril Overton pressed his hands to his head. "I can make nothing of it," said he.

"Well, well, I have a clear day, and I shall be happy to look into the matter," said Holmes. "I should strongly recommend you to make your preparations for your match without reference to this young gentleman. It must, as you say, have been an overpowering necessity which tore him away in such a fashion, and the same necessity is likely to hold him away. Let us step round together to this hotel, and see if the porter can throw any fresh light upon the matter."

Sherlock Holmes was a past master in the art of putting a humble witness at his ease, and very soon, in the privacy of Godfrey Staunton's abandoned room, he had extracted all that the porter had to tell. The visitor of the night before was not a gentleman, neither was he a workingman. He was simply what the porter described as a "medium-looking chap;" a man of fifty, beard grizzled, pale face, quietly dressed. He seemed himself to be agitated. The porter had observed his hand trembling when he had held out the note. Godfrey Staunton had crammed the note into his pocket. Staunton had not shaken hands with the man in the hall. They had exchanged a few sentences, of which the porter had only distinguished the one word "time." Then they had hurried off in the manner described. It was just half-past ten by the hall clock.

"Let me see," said Holmes, seating himself on Staunton's bed. "You are the day porter, are you not?"

"Yes, sir, I go off duty at eleven."

"The night porter saw nothing, I suppose?"

"No, sir; one theatre party came in late. No one else."

"Were you on duty all day yesterday?"

"Yes, sir."

"Did you take any message to Mr. Staunton?"

"Yes, sir; one telegram."

"Ah! that is interesting. What o'clock was this?"

"About six."

"Where was Mr. Staunton when he received it?"

"Here in his room."

"Were you present when he opened it?"

"Yes, sir; I waited to see if there was an answer."

"Well, was there?"

"Yes, sir, he wrote an answer."

"Did you take it?"

"No, he took it himself."

"But he wrote it in your presence?"

"Yes, sir. I was standing by the door, and he with his back turned to that table. When he had written it, he said, 'All right, porter, I will take this myself.'"

"What did he write it with?"

"Did you take any messages to Mr. Staunton?"
Sidney Paget, *Strand Magazine*, 1904

"A pen, sir."

"Was the telegraphic form one of these on the table?"

"Yes, sir; it was the top one."

Holmes rose. Taking the forms, he carried them over to the window and carefully examined that which was uppermost.

"It is a pity he did not write in pencil," said he, throwing them down again with a shrug of disappointment. "As you have no doubt frequently observed, Watson, the impression usually goes through—a fact which has dissolved many a happy marriage. However, I can find no trace here. I rejoice, however, to perceive that he wrote with a broad-pointed quill pen, and I can hardly doubt that we will find some impression upon this blotting-pad. Ah, yes, surely this is the very thing!"

He tore off a strip of the blotting-paper and turned towards us the following hieroglyphic:

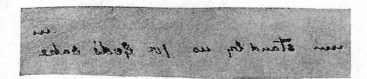

Cyril Overton was much excited. "Hold it to the glass!" he cried.

"That is unnecessary," said Holmes. "The paper is thin, and the reverse will give the message. Here it is." He turned it over, and we read:

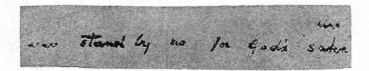

"So that is the tail end of the telegram which Godfrey Staunton despatched within a few hours of his disappearance. There are at least six words of the message which have escaped us; but what remain—'Stand by us for God's sake!'—proves that this young man saw a formidable danger which approached him, and from which someone else could protect him. 'Us,' mark you! Another person was involved. Who should it be but the pale-faced, bearded man, who seemed himself in so nervous a state? What, then, is the connection between Godfrey Staunton and the bearded man? And what is the third source from which each of them sought for help against pressing danger? Our inquiry has already narrowed down to that."

"We have only to find to whom that telegram is addressed," I suggested.

"Exactly, my dear Watson. Your reflection, though profound, had already crossed my mind. But I daresay it may have come to your notice that if you walk into a post-office and demand to see the counterfoil of another man's message, there may be some disinclination on the part of the officials to oblige you. There is so much red tape in these matters! However, I have

20 In football, a cut or gash in the skin caused by a kick. In some editions the word is "back."

21 A mute was an undertaker's attendant, assigned to walk in the funeral procession alongside the coffin. An example is provided in Charles Dickens's *Oliver Twist* (1838), in which the orphan Oliver is apprenticed out by Mr. Bumble to Mr. Sowerberry, the undertaker, who eventually sets him to work as a mute for children's funerals. It is the solemnity of the orphan's face that strikes the undertaker as useful: " 'There's an expression of melancholy in his face, my dear,' resumed Mr. Sowerberry, 'which is very interesting. He would make a delightful mute, my love.' "

22 The "Bayswater" omnibus ran every five minutes from Burdett Road to Shepherd's Bush Green.

no doubt that with a little delicacy and finesse the end may be attained. Meanwhile, I should like in your presence, Mr. Overton, to go through these papers which have been left upon the table."

There were a number of letters, bills, and notebooks, which Holmes turned over and examined with quick, nervous fingers and darting, penetrating eyes. "Nothing here," he said, at last. "By the way, I suppose your friend was a healthy young fellow—nothing amiss with him?"

"Sound as a bell."

"Have you ever known him ill?"

"Not a day. He has been laid up with a hack,[20] and once he slipped his knee-cap, but that was nothing."

"Perhaps he was not so strong as you suppose. I should think he may have had some secret trouble. With your assent, I will put one or two of these papers in my pocket, in case they should bear upon our future inquiry."

"One moment—one moment!" cried a querulous voice, and we looked up to find a queer little old man, jerking and twitching in the doorway. He was dressed in rusty black, with a very broad-brimmed top-hat and a loose white necktie—the whole effect being that of a very rustic parson or of an undertaker's mute.[21] Yet, in spite of his shabby and even absurd appearance, his voice had a sharp crackle, and his manner a quick intensity which commanded attention.

"Who are you, sir, and by what right do you touch this gentleman's papers?" he asked.

"I am a private detective, and I am endeavouring to explain his disappearance."

"Oh, you are, are you? And who instructed you, eh?"

"This gentleman, Mr. Staunton's friend, was referred to me by Scotland Yard."

"Who are you, sir?"

"I am Cyril Overton."

"Then it is you who sent me a telegram. My name is Lord Mount-James. I came round as quickly as the Bayswater bus[22] would bring me. So you have instructed a detective?"

"Yes, sir."

"And are you prepared to meet the cost?"

"I have no doubt, sir, that my friend Godfrey, when we find him, will be prepared to do that."

We looked up to find a queer little old man, jerking and
twitching in the doorway.
Frederick Dorr Steele, *Collier's*, 1904

23 This no doubt explains why "one of the richest men in England" travelled by bus, which charged a fare of 1*d*. to 6*d*., depending on the destination.

"But if he is never found, eh? Answer me that!"

"In that case, no doubt his family—"

"Nothing of the sort, sir!" screamed the little man. "Don't look to me for a penny—not a penny! You understand that, Mr. Detective! I am all the family that this young man has got, and I tell you that I am not responsible. If he has any expectations it is due to the fact that I have never wasted money,[23] and I do not propose to begin to do so now. As to those papers with which you are making so free, I may tell you that in case there should be anything of any value among them, you will be held strictly to account for what you do with them."

"Very good, sir," said Sherlock Holmes. "May I ask in the meanwhile whether you have yourself any theory to account for this young man's disappearance?"

"No, sir, I have not. He is big enough and old enough to look

" 'One moment, one moment!' cried a querulous voice."
Sidney Paget, *Strand Magazine*, 1904

after himself, and if he is so foolish as to lose himself I entirely refuse to accept the responsibility of hunting for him."

"I quite understand your position," said Holmes, with a mischievous twinkle in his eyes. "Perhaps you don't quite understand mine. Godfrey Staunton appears to have been a poor man. If he has been kidnapped it could not have been for anything which he himself possesses. The fame of your wealth has gone abroad, Lord Mount-James, and it is entirely possible that a gang of thieves have secured your nephew in order to gain from him some information as to your house, your habits, and your treasure."

The face of our unpleasant little visitor turned as white as his neckcloth.

"Heavens, sir, what an idea! I never thought of such villainy! What inhuman rogues there are in the world! But Godfrey is a fine lad—a staunch lad. Nothing would induce him to give his old uncle away. I'll have the plate moved over to the bank this evening. In the meantime spare no pains, Mr. Detective, I beg you to leave no stone unturned to bring him safely back. As to money, well, so far as a fiver, or even a tenner, goes, you can always look to me."

Even in his chastened frame of mind the noble miser could give us no information which could help us, for he knew little of the private life of his nephew. Our only clue lay in the truncated telegram, and with a copy of this in his hand Holmes set forth to find a second link for his chain. We had shaken off Lord Mount-James, and Overton had gone to consult with the other members of his team over the misfortune which had befallen them.

There was a telegraph office[24] at a short distance from the hotel. We halted outside it.

"It's worth trying, Watson," said Holmes. "Of course, with a warrant we could demand to see the counterfoils, but we have not reached that stage yet. I don't suppose they remember faces in so busy a place. Let us venture it."

"I am sorry to trouble you," said he in his blandest manner to the young woman behind the grating; "there is some small mistake about a telegram I sent yesterday. I have had no answer, and I very much fear that I must have omitted to put my name at the end. Could you tell me if this was so?"

The young woman turned over a sheaf of counterfoils.

"What o'clock was it?" she asked.

"A little after six."

"Whom was it to?"

Holmes put his finger to his lips and glanced at me. "The last words in it were 'for God's sake,' " he whispered confidentially; "I am very anxious at getting no answer."

The young woman separated one of the forms.

"This is it. There is no name," said she, smoothing it out upon the counter.

"Then that, of course, accounts for my getting no answer," said Holmes. "Dear me, how very stupid of me, to be sure! Good-morning, miss, and many thanks for having relieved my

24 In the manuscript, "two telegraph offices at equal distances from the hotel." Watson is evidently engaging in some geographical obfuscation here and elsewhere in the manuscript.

25 "Fenchurch Street Station" in the manuscript.

26 In the manuscript, originally "we rattled down the Strand."

27 This comment seems to contradict Holmes's earlier remark that "amateur sport . . . is the best and soundest thing in England."

mind." He chuckled and rubbed his hands when we found ourselves in the street once more.

"Well?" I asked.

"We progress, my dear Watson, we progress. I had seven different schemes for getting a glimpse of that telegram, but I could hardly hope to succeed the very first time."

"And what have you gained?"

"A starting-point for our investigation." He hailed a cab. "King's Cross Station,"25 said he.

"We have a journey, then?"

"Yes, I think we must run down to Cambridge together. All the indications seem to me to point in that direction."

"Tell me," I asked as we rattled up Gray's Inn Road,26 "have you any suspicion yet as to the cause of the disappearance? I don't think that among all our cases I have known one where the motives were more obscure. Surely you don't really imagine that he may be kidnapped in order to give information against his wealthy uncle?"

"I confess, my dear Watson, that that does not appeal to me as a very probable explanation. It struck me, however, as being the one which was most likely to interest that exceedingly unpleasant old person."

"It certainly did that. But what are your alternatives?"

"I could mention several. You must admit that it is curious and suggestive that this incident should occur on the eve of this important match, and should involve the only man whose presence seems essential to the success of the side. It may, of course, be coincidence, but it is interesting. Amateur sport is free from betting, but a good deal of outside betting goes on among the public,27 and it is possible that it might be worth someone's while to get at a player as the ruffians of the Turf get at a race-horse. There is one explanation. A second very obvious one is that this young man really is the heir of a great property, however modest his means may at present be, and it is not impossible that a plot to hold him for ransom might be concocted."

"These theories take no account of the telegram."

"Quite true, Watson. The telegram still remains the only solid thing with which we have to deal, and we must not permit our attention to wander away from it. It is to gain light upon the purpose of this telegram that we are now upon our way to Cambridge. The path of our investigation is at present obscure, but I shall be very much surprised if before evening we have not cleared it up, or made a considerable advance along it."

It was already dark when we reached the old University city. Holmes took a cab at the station and ordered the man to drive to the house of Dr. Leslie Armstrong. A few minutes later, we had stopped at a large mansion on the busiest thoroughfare. We were shown in, and after a long wait were at last admitted into the consulting-room, where we found the doctor seated behind his table.

It argues the degree in which I had lost touch with my profession that the name of Leslie Armstrong was unknown to me.[28] Now I am aware that he is not only one of the heads of the medical school of the University, but a thinker of European reputation in more than one branch of science. Yet even without knowing his brilliant record one could not fail to be impressed by a mere glance at the man—the square, massive face, the brooding eyes under the thatched brows, and the

28 While Watson had sold his practice in 1894 (see "The Norwood Builder") this statement seemingly contradicts Watson's continued diligent reading of medical texts, reported in "The Golden Pince-Nez" only a few years earlier.

Dr. Leslie Armstrong.
Frederick Dorr Steele, *Collier's*, 1904

granite moulding of the inflexible jaw. A man of deep character, a man with an alert mind, grim, ascetic, self-contained, formidable—so I read Dr. Leslie Armstrong. He held my friend's
card in his hand, and he looked up with no very pleased
expression upon his dour features.

"I have heard your name, Mr. Sherlock Holmes, and I am
aware of your profession—one of which I by no means
approve."

"In that, Doctor, you will find yourself in agreement with
every criminal in the country," said my friend quietly.

"So far as your efforts are directed towards the suppression
of crime, sir, they must have the support of every reasonable
member of the community, though I cannot doubt that the
official machinery is amply sufficient for the purpose. Where
your calling is more open to criticism is when you pry into the

"He looked up with no very pleased expression
on his dour features."
Sidney Paget, *Strand Magazine*, 1904

secrets of private individuals, when you rake up family matters which are better hidden, and when you incidentally waste the time of men who are more busy than yourself. At the present moment, for example, I should be writing a treatise instead of conversing with you."

"No doubt, Doctor; and yet the conversation may prove more important than the treatise. Incidentally I may tell you that we are doing the reverse of what you very justly blame, and that we are endeavouring to prevent anything like public exposure of private matters which must necessarily follow when once the case is fairly in the hands of the official police. You may look upon me simply as an irregular pioneer, who goes in front of the regular forces of the country. I have come to ask you about Mr. Godfrey Staunton."

"What about him?"

"You know him, do you not?"

"He is an intimate friend of mine."

"You are aware that he has disappeared?"

"Ah, indeed!" There was no change of expression in the rugged features of the doctor.

"He left his hotel last night. He has not been heard of."

"No doubt he will return."

"To-morrow is the 'Varsity football match."

"I have no sympathy with these childish games. The young man's fate interests me deeply, since I know him and like him. The football match does not come within my horizon at all."

"I claim your sympathy, then, in my investigation of Mr. Staunton's fate. Do you know where he is?"

"Certainly not."

"You have not seen him since yesterday?"

"No, I have not."

"Was Mr. Staunton a healthy man?"

"Absolutely."

"Did you ever know him ill?"

"Never."

Holmes popped a sheet of paper before the doctor's eyes. "Then perhaps you will explain this receipted bill for thirteen guineas, paid by Mr. Godfrey Staunton last month to Dr. Leslie Armstrong, of Cambridge. I picked it out from among the papers upon his desk."

The doctor flushed with anger.

29 This remark contrasts with "The Creeping Man," in which Holmes refers to the unnamed university locale of that tale as "this charming town." Scholars of course seize upon the point to insist that the university locale of "The Missing Three-Quarter"—most assuredly Cambridge—was not Holmes's alma mater.

"I do not feel that there is any reason why I should render an explanation to you, Mr. Holmes."

Holmes replaced the bill in his notebook. "If you prefer a public explanation, it must come sooner or later," said he. "I have already told you that I can hush up that which others will be bound to publish, and you would really be wiser to take me into your complete confidence."

"I know nothing about it."

"Did you hear from Mr. Staunton in London?"

"Certainly not."

"Dear me, dear me! the post-office again!" Holmes sighed, wearily. "A most urgent telegram was despatched to you from London by Godfrey Staunton at six-fifteen yesterday evening—a telegram which is undoubtedly associated with his disappearance—and yet you have not had it. It is most culpable. I shall certainly go down to the office here and register a complaint."

Dr. Leslie Armstrong sprang up from behind his desk, and his dark face was crimson with fury.

"I'll trouble you to walk out of my house, sir," said he. "You can tell your employer, Lord Mount-James, that I do not wish to have anything to do either with him or with his agents. No, sir, not another word!" He rang the bell furiously. "John, show these gentlemen out." A pompous butler ushered us severely to the door, and we found ourselves in the street. Holmes burst out laughing.

"Dr. Leslie Armstrong is certainly a man of energy and character," said he. "I have not seen a man who, if he turns his talents that way, was more calculated to fill the gap left by the illustrious Moriarty. And now, my poor Watson, here we are, stranded and friendless, in this inhospitable town,[29] which we cannot leave without abandoning our case. This little inn just opposite Armstrong's house is singularly adapted to our needs. If you would engage a front room and purchase the necessaries for the night, I may have time to make a few inquiries."

These few inquiries proved, however, to be a more lengthy proceeding than Holmes had imagined, for he did not return to the inn until nearly nine o'clock. He was pale and dejected, stained with dust, and exhausted with hunger and fatigue. A cold supper was ready upon the table, and when his needs were satisfied and his pipe alight he was ready to take that half-comic and wholly philosophic view which was natural to him when his affairs were going awry. The sound of carriage wheels caused him to rise and glance out of the window. A brougham and pair of greys, under the glare of a gas-lamp, stood before the doctor's door.

"It's been out three hours," said Holmes; "started at half-past six, and here it is back again. That gives a radius of ten or twelve miles, and he does it once, or sometimes twice, a day."

"No unusual thing for a doctor in practice."

"But Armstrong is not really a doctor in practice. He is a lecturer and a consultant, but he does not care for general practice, which distracts him from his literary work. Why, then, does he make these long journeys, which must be exceedingly irksome to him, and who is it that he visits?"

"His coachman—"

"My dear Watson, can you doubt that it was to him that I first applied? I do not know whether it came from his own innate depravity or from the promptings of his master, but he was rude enough to set a dog at me. Neither dog nor man liked the look of my stick, however, and the matter fell through. Relations were strained after that, and further inquiries out of the question. All that I have learned I got from a friendly native in the yard of our own inn. It was he who told me of the doctor's habits and of his daily journey. At that instant, to give point to his words, the carriage came round to the door."

"Could you not follow it?"

"Excellent, Watson! You are scintillating this evening. The idea did cross my mind. There is, as you may have observed, a bicycle shop next to our inn. Into this I rushed, engaged a bicycle, and was able to get started before the carriage was quite out of sight. I rapidly overtook it, and then, keeping at a discreet distance of a hundred yards or so, I followed its lights until we were clear of the town. He had got well out on the country road when a somewhat mortifying incident occurred. The carriage stopped, the doctor alighted, walked swiftly back to where I had also halted, and told me in an excellent sardonic fashion that he feared the road was narrow, and that he hoped his carriage did not impede the passage of my bicycle. Nothing could have been more admirable than his way of putting it. I at

30 A whist reference—see "The Norwood Builder."

once rode past the carriage, and, keeping to the main road, I went on for a few miles, and then halted in a convenient place to see if the carriage passed. There was no sign of it, however, and so it became evident that it had turned down one of several side-roads which I had observed. I rode back, but again saw nothing of the carriage, and now, as you perceive, it has returned after me. Of course, I had at the outset no particular reason to connect these journeys with the disappearance of Godfrey Staunton, and was only inclined to investigate them on the general grounds that everything which concerns Dr. Armstrong is at present of interest to us, but, now that I find he keeps so keen a lookout upon anyone who may follow him on these excursions, the affair appears more important, and I shall not be satisfied until I have made the matter clear."

"We can follow him to-morrow."

"Can we? It is not so easy as you seem to think. You are not familiar with Cambridgeshire scenery, are you? It does not lend itself to concealment. All this country that I passed over to-night is as flat and clean as the palm of your hand, and the man we are following is no fool, as he very clearly showed to-night. I have wired to Overton to let us know any fresh London developments at this address, and in the meantime we can only concentrate our attention upon Dr. Armstrong, whose name the obliging young lady at the office allowed me to read upon the counterfoil of Staunton's urgent message. He knows where that young man is—to that I'll swear, and if he knows, then it must be our own fault if we cannot manage to know also. At present it must be admitted that the odd trick is in his possession, and, as you are aware, Watson, it is not my habit to leave the game in that condition."[30]

And yet the next day brought us no nearer to the solution of the mystery. A note was handed in after breakfast, which Holmes passed across to me with a smile.

Sir:

I can assure you that you are wasting your time in dogging my movements. I have, as you discovered last night, a window at the back of my brougham, and if you desire a twenty-mile ride which will lead you to the spot from which you started, you have only to follow me. Meanwhile, I can inform you that no spying upon me can in any way help Mr. Godfrey Staunton, and I am convinced that the best service you can do to that gentleman is to return at once to London and to report to your employer that you are unable to trace him. Your time in Cambridge will certainly be wasted.

Yours faithfully,

Leslie Armstrong

"An outspoken, honest antagonist is the doctor," said Holmes. "Well, well, he excites my curiosity, and I must really know before I leave him."

"His carriage is at his door now," said I. "There he is stepping into it. I saw him glance up at our window as he did so. Suppose I try my luck upon the bicycle?"

"No, no, my dear Watson! With all respect for your natural acumen, I do not think that you are quite a match for the worthy doctor. I think that possibly I can attain our end by some independent explorations of my own. I am afraid that I must leave you to your own devices, as the appearance of *two* inquiring strangers upon a sleepy country-side might excite more gossip than I care for. No doubt you will find some sights to amuse you in this venerable city, and I hope to bring back a more favourable report to you before evening."

Once more, however, my friend was destined to be disappointed. He came back at night weary and unsuccessful.

"I have had a blank day, Watson. Having got the doctor's general direction, I spent the day in visiting all the villages upon that side of Cambridge, and comparing notes with publicans and other local news agencies. I have covered some ground. Chesterton, Histon, Waterbeach, and Oakington have each been explored, and have each proved disappointing. The daily appearance of a brougham and pair could hardly have been overlooked in such Sleepy Hollows. The doctor has scored once more. Is there a telegram for me?"

"Yes; I opened it. Here it is: 'Ask for Pompey from Jeremy Dixon, Trinity College.'[31] I don't understand it."

"Oh, it is clear enough. It is from our friend Overton, and is in answer to a question from me. I'll just send round a note to Mr. Jeremy Dixon, and then I have no doubt that our luck will turn. By the way, is there any news of the match?"

"Yes, the local evening paper has an excellent account in its

31 "St. John's College" in the manuscript.

32 See "The Rules of Rugby," page 1153, for an explanation of the scoring of the match. Richard Lancelyn Green, in trying to determine the exact year that "The Missing Three-Quarter" might have taken place, notes that since matches between Oxford and Cambridge were played every second Tuesday of December at the Queen's Club, "if the dates in the story are taken literally, then the match would have been played either in 1894, 1895, or 1896. The last would be the most likely as it was the only one of the three won by Oxford." A different theory is put forth by D. Martin Dakin (among others), who observes that Oxford won by two tries in 1897. Neither the 1896 nor the 1897 game fits the score exactly. Jay Finley Christ reports that *Whitaker's Almanac* says of the 1897 game that "the Cambridge three-quarter line did not come off," which seems to refer to "The Missing Three-Quarter."

33 The English text omits the word "instrument" here, found in both the *Strand Magazine* and American texts.

34 That portion of a stable where horses are kept untied.

last edition. Oxford won by a goal and two tries.[32] The last sentences of the description say:

> The defeat of the Light Blues may be entirely attributed to the unfortunate absence of the crack International, Godfrey Staunton, whose want was felt at every instant of the game. The lack of combination in the three-quarter line and their weakness both in attack and defence more than neutralized the efforts of a heavy and hard-working pack.

"Then our friend Overton's forebodings have been justified," said Holmes. "Personally I am in agreement with Dr. Armstrong, and football does not come within my horizon. Early to bed to-night, Watson, for I foresee that to-morrow may be an eventful day."

I was horrified by my first glimpse of Holmes next morning, for he sat by the fire holding his tiny hypodermic syringe. I associated that[33] with the single weakness of his nature, and I feared the worst when I saw it glittering in his hand. He laughed at my expression of dismay and laid it upon the table.

"No, no, my dear fellow, there is no cause for alarm. It is not upon this occasion the instrument of evil, but it will rather prove to be the key which will unlock our mystery. On this syringe I base all my hopes. I have just returned from a small scouting expedition, and everything is favourable. Eat a good breakfast, Watson, for I propose to get upon Dr. Armstrong's trail to-day, and once on it I will not stop for rest or food until I run him to his burrow."

"In that case," said I, "we had best carry our breakfast with us, for he is making an early start. His carriage is at the door."

"Never mind. Let him go. He will be clever if he can drive where I cannot follow him. When you have finished, come downstairs with me, and I will introduce you to a detective who is a very eminent specialist in the work that lies before us."

When we descended I followed Holmes into the stable yard, where he opened the door of a loose-box[34] and led out a squat, lop-eared, white-and-tan dog, something between a beagle and a foxhound.

"Let me introduce you to Pompey," said he. "Pompey is the pride of the local draghounds[35]—no very great flier, as his build will show, but a staunch hound on a scent. Well, Pompey, you may not be fast, but I expect you will be too fast for a couple of middle-aged London gentlemen, so I will take the liberty of fastening this leather leash to your collar. Now, boy, come along, and show what you can do." He led him across to the doctor's door. The dog sniffed round for an instant, and then with a shrill whine of excitement started off down the street, tugging at his leash in his efforts to go faster. In half an hour, we were clear of the town and hastening down a country road.

"What have you done, Holmes?" I asked.

35 Hounds trained to race by following a scent left by a "drag" over a predetermined course. Originally, the dogs followed the scent of a fox let loose on the course, but later, to bring control to the event, an artificial scent, usually aniseed, was applied to an object dragged over the ground.

"We were clear of the town and hastening down a country road."
Sidney Paget, *Strand Magazine*, 1904

36 The village of John o' Groats was founded during the reign of James IV (1488–1513) when Dutchman Jan de Groot and his two brothers settled near Dunnet Head in Scotland, at the northernmost tip of the British mainland. In order to appease his descendants, who argued over their precedence in the family, de Groot built an octagonal house with eight doors and eight windows. (He also built an octagonal table—in some stories, a round table—so that no one person was ever seated at the head.) A mound and a flagpole now mark the site of the original house. The expression "from Land's End to John o' Groats" means from one end of Great Britain to the other.

37 The river upon which Cambridge stands.

38 And what "excellent qualities" are those that would draw the renowned head of the medical school and European "thinker" to an athlete with no obvious intellectual tendencies? Marshall S. Berdan suggests only one: money. The heir to Lord Mount-James's fortune surely must have provided an enticing mark for a doctor on a university salary. "With the parsimonious old nobleman racked with gout," Berdan deduces, "Armstrong saw an easy way to finance his future research and altogether dispense with his bothersome practice."

"A threadbare and venerable device, but useful upon occasion. I walked into the doctor's yard this morning, and shot my syringe full of aniseed over the hind wheel. A draghound will follow aniseed from here to John o' Groat's,[36] and our friend Armstrong would have to drive through the Cam[37] before he would shake Pompey off his trail. Oh, the cunning rascal! This is how he gave me the slip the other night."

The dog had suddenly turned out of the main road into a grass-grown lane. Half a mile farther this opened into another broad road, and the trail turned hard to the right in the direction of the town, which we had just quitted. The road took a sweep to the south of the town and continued in the opposite direction to that in which we started.

"This detour has been entirely for our benefit, then?" said Holmes. "No wonder that my inquiries among those villagers led to nothing. The doctor has certainly played the game for all it is worth, and one would like to know the reason for such elaborate deception.[38] This should be the village of Trumpington to the right of us. And, by Jove! here is the brougham coming round the corner. Quick, Watson, quick, or we are done!"

He sprang through a gate into a field, dragging the reluctant Pompey after him. We had hardly got under the shelter of the hedge when the carriage rattled past. I caught a glimpse of Dr. Armstrong within, his shoulders bowed, his head sunk on his hands, the very image of distress. I could tell by my companion's graver face that he also had seen.

"I fear there is some dark ending to our quest," said he. "It cannot be long before we know it. Come, Pompey! Ah, it is the cottage in the field!"

There could be no doubt that we had reached the end of our journey. Pompey ran about and whined eagerly outside the gate, where the marks of the brougham's wheels were still to be seen. A footpath led across to the lonely cottage. Holmes tied the dog to the hedge, and we hastened onwards. My friend knocked at the little rustic door, and knocked again without response. And yet the cottage was not deserted, for a low sound came to our ears—a kind of drone of misery and despair, which was indescribably melancholy. Holmes paused irresolute, and then he glanced back at the road which he had just traversed.

"The carriage rattled past."
Sidney Paget, *Strand Magazine*, 1904

A brougham was coming down it, and there could be no mistaking those grey horses.

"By Jove, the doctor is coming back!" cried Holmes. "That settles it. We are bound to see what it means before he comes."

He opened the door, and we stepped into the hall. The droning sound swelled louder upon our ears until it became one long, deep wail of distress. It came from upstairs. Holmes darted up, and I followed him. He pushed open a half-closed door, and we both stood appalled at the sight before us.

A woman, young and beautiful, was lying dead upon the bed. Her calm, pale face, with dim, wide-opened blue eyes,

I caught a glimpse of Dr. Armstrong within.
Charles Raymond Macaulay, *Return of Sherlock Holmes*
(McClure Phillips), 1905

looked upwards from amid a great tangle of golden hair. At the
foot of the bed, half sitting, half kneeling, his face buried in the
clothes, was a young man, whose frame was racked by his sobs.
So absorbed was he by his bitter grief that he never looked up
until Holmes's hand was on his shoulder.

"Are you Mr. Godfrey Staunton?"

"Yes, yes; I am—but you are too late. She is dead."

The man was so dazed that he could not be made to understand that we were anything but doctors who had been sent to
his assistance. Holmes was endeavouring to utter a few words
of consolation and to explain the alarm which had been caused
to his friends by his sudden disappearance when there was a

step upon the stairs, and there was the heavy, stern, questioning face of Dr. Armstrong at the door.

"So, gentlemen," said he, "you have attained your end and have certainly chosen a particularly delicate moment for your intrusion. I would not brawl in the presence of death, but I can assure you that if I were a younger man your monstrous conduct would not pass with impunity."

"Excuse me, Dr. Armstrong, I think we are a little at cross purposes," said my friend, with dignity. "If you could step downstairs with us, we may each be able to give some light to the other upon this miserable affair."

A minute later the grim doctor and ourselves were in the sitting-room below.

"Well, sir?" said he.

"I wish you to understand, in the first place, that I am not employed by Lord Mount-James, and that my sympathies in this matter are entirely against that nobleman. When a man is

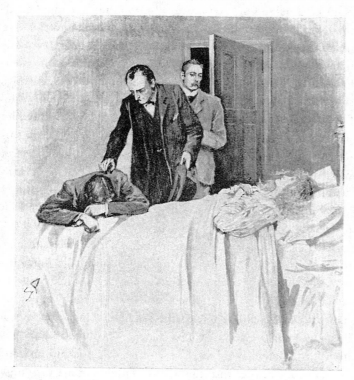

"He never looked up until Holmes's hand was
on his shoulder."
Sidney Paget, *Strand Magazine*, 1904

39 See "The Final Problem," note 40, for a discussion of the prevalence and impact of consumption in Victorian England.

lost it is my duty to ascertain his fate, but having done so the matter ends so far as I am concerned; and so long as there is nothing criminal, I am much more anxious to hush up private scandals than to give them publicity. If, as I imagine, there is no breach of the law in this matter, you can absolutely depend upon my discretion and my co-operation in keeping the facts out of the papers!"

Dr. Armstrong took a quick step forward and wrung Holmes by the hand.

"You are a good fellow," said he. "I had misjudged you. I thank heaven that my compunction at leaving poor Staunton all alone in this plight caused me to turn my carriage back; and so to make your acquaintance. Knowing as much as you do, the situation is very easily explained. A year ago Godfrey Staunton lodged in London for a time and became passionately attached to his landlady's daughter, whom he married. She was as good as she was beautiful and as intelligent as she was good. No man need be ashamed of such a wife. But Godfrey was the heir to this crabbed old nobleman, and it was quite certain that the news of his marriage would have been the end of his inheritance. I knew the lad well, and I loved him for his many excellent qualities. I did all I could to help him to keep things straight. We did our very best to keep the thing from everyone, for, when once such a whisper gets about, it is not long before everyone has heard it. Thanks to this lonely cottage and his own discretion, Godfrey has up to now succeeded. Their secret was known to no one save to me and to one excellent servant who has at present gone for assistance to Trumpington. But at last there came a terrible blow in the shape of dangerous illness to his wife. It was consumption[39] of the most virulent kind. The poor boy was half crazed with grief, and yet he had to go to London to play this match, for he could not get out of it without explanations which would expose the secret. I tried to cheer him up by a wire, and he sent me one in reply, imploring me to do all I could. This was the telegram which you appear in some inexplicable way to have seen. I did not tell him how urgent the danger was, for I knew that he could do no good here, but I sent the truth to the girl's father, and he very injudiciously communicated it to Godfrey. The result was that he came straight away in a state bordering on frenzy, and has remained in the same state, kneeling at the end of her bed, until this morning death put an end to her sufferings. That is all, Mr. Holmes, and I am sure that I can rely upon your discretion and that of your friend."

Holmes grasped the doctor's hand.

"Come, Watson," said he, and we passed from that house of grief into the pale sunlight of the winter day.[40] ∎

THE RULES OF RUGBY

And then follows rush upon rush, and scrummage upon scrummage, the ball now driven through into the School-house quarters, and now into the School goal. . . . You say you don't see much in it all—nothing but a struggling mass of boys, and a leather ball which seems to excite them all to great fury, as a red rag does a bull. My dear sir, a battle would look much the same to you, except that the boys would be men, and the balls iron; but a battle would be worth your looking at for all that, and so is a football match. You can't be expected to appreciate the delicate strokes of play, the turns by which a game is lost and won—it takes an old player to do that; but the broad philosophy of football you can understand if you will. Come along with me a little nearer, and let us consider it.

—THOMAS HUGHES,
Tom Brown's School Days (1857)

LEGEND has it that the game of rugby was "invented" in 1823 during a game of football (American soccer) when William Webb Ellis, a student at Rugby School in Warwickshire picked up the ball and began running downfield with it. The story, probably apocryphal, has elicited its share of controversy, and certainly there were other sporting events at which a ball was carried rather than kicked. Nonetheless, a plaque at Rugby School—where *Tom Brown's School Days* is set—proudly commemorates the antics of the sixteen-year-old "who with a fine disregard for the rules of football as played in his time, first took the ball in his arms and ran with it." Other schools and universities played variations of the game in the mid-nineteenth century, but a clear delineation between football

40 Sportswriter Red Smith scandalously suggests, in "Dear Me, Mr. Holmes," that Holmes made bets on the match and that his actions in the case were designed to assure his winnings. While Holmes immediately grasped the importance of Dr. Armstrong, he allowed himself "to be put off with windy bluff. . . ." Attempting to trail Armstrong, Holmes carelessly loses him on a stretch of land "as flat and clean as the palm of your hand" and then forbids Watson to give chase to Armstrong. Why, ponders Smith? "Well, the match hadn't been played yet," Smith notes. Holmes had induced Overton to admit that Cambridge was likely to lose the match without Staunton. Spotting an opportunity to make a quick profit, Smith proposes, Holmes busily spent his time in Cambridge corresponding by telegram with bookies. Only after Oxford's victory, notes Smith, did Holmes finally manage to find Armstrong and Staunton.

Marshall S. Berdan attempts to refute Smith's character assassination, arguing that Holmes's delay in solving the case may be explained on the basis that he perceived no urgency and was experiencing a temporary lack of work. Further, Berdan suggests, he may have wanted, as an alumnus of Oxford, to see Oxford win. While this latter point suggests an interest in amateur sports that Holmes flatly denies, Berdan goes on to propose that *Watson*, the incorrigible gambler (see "Shoscombe Old Place"), who—despite having played rugby himself ("The Sussex Vampire"), feigned ignorance of both Overton and Rugby—arranged to bet on the game with clubmen friends. "All of the discrepancies in the adventure can thus be accounted for without having to resort to the unacceptable depravity of the Master alleged by Mr. Smith. Smith, it seems, had the right charge but the wrong suspect."

and "rugby football" was not established until several rugby teams, rebuffed by the prohibitive rules of the newly formed Football Association, formed the Rugby Football Union in 1871 (see note 11, above).

Before too long, tensions within the new league arose, this time not over rules of play but over rules of payment. In order to ensure that they could field full teams, working-class clubs from the north began compensating players for "broken time," or time that they lost at their mining or factory jobs while playing rugby. Clubs from the south—the domain, for the most part, of "gentlemen" players with less pressing financial considerations—failed to understand the need for such compensation, and they indignantly protested what they considered a violation of the purity of amateur sport. The Rugby Football Union agreed, insisting that all payments to players cease. After years in which the opposing factions could not reach a compromise, twenty-two clubs split off in 1895 to form the Northern Rugby Union, which later became known as Rugby League. This league became the home for professional rugby teams, and Rugby Football Union league, or "Rugby Union," became that of amateur play. (In 1995, finally acknowledging the complications inherent in trying to maintain strict amateur standards, Rugby Union dropped its restrictions and permitted its players to be paid.) Even in the current era, the clubs in Rugby League—now co-owned by Australian tycoon Rupert Murdoch—are concentrated in the north of Britain and championed by the working class, whereas Rugby Union clubs retain a distinctly middle- and upper-class fan base.

As amateur clubs, Cambridge and Oxford would have been playing according to Rugby Union rules, which remain the most widely adopted in Britain. The game incorporates some elements of American football and soccer, being played with an oval ball on a rectangular field, or "pitch," measuring 70 meters (229.7 feet) wide by 146 meters (160 yards) long. There are two opposing scoring zones and upright goalposts, rather like in American football, although the goalposts in rugby take more of a letter "H" shape, with the goalposts 5.6 metres (18.3 feet) apart and the crossbar 3 metres (10 feet) above the ground. Teams of fifteen players each (thirteen in Rugby League) play two halves, each forty minutes in length, with a ten-minute halftime in between. The team usually consists of eight forwards, who form the scrummage (discussed below); two halfbacks, who are posted outside the scrummage; four three-quarter backs, who are arranged in a line across the field behind the scrummage; and the last line of defence, the fullback or "back."

Play is continuous, resembling that of American soccer. A player moves the ball downfield by carrying the ball, kicking it, or passing it behind him or to the side; no forward passing is allowed. Neither is blocking allowed—the ball carrrier's teammates must stay behind him as play progresses down the field—but the abrupt tackling with which defensive players may stop ball carriers, not to mention the fact that rugby players may wear (voluntarily) only "scrumcap" headgear and a limited amount of shoulder protection, is largely what lends the sport its historically rough reputation. Some seventy deaths were reported in English rugby games from 1890 to 1893 alone, although numerous regulations enacted since then, including the prohibition of tripping and "hacking," have greatly lessened the risk of serious injury.

Once a player is tackled and the ball touches the ground, he must immediately relinquish it, either passing the ball backward to a teammate or surrendering it to a member of the opposing team. More common is the loose maul, a sort of multiplayer semi-tackle in which the ball carrier's progress is temporarily halted and offensive and defensive players swarm around him, fighting for possession. (When the ball touches the ground, the situation becomes known as a ruck.) In this position, the ball may change hands from the carrier to a teammate, and as long as the players remain on their feet and locked in a cohesive unit, they may drive the ball down the pitch in what is known as a rolling maul.

Should the ball carrier drop or pass the ball in any sort of forward motion, or should a team be called offside, then play is stopped, resulting in a scrum, or scrummage. Here, the forwards on each team lock arms and face off against each other, pushing forward to form a roiling mass into which the attacking team's "scrum-half" rolls the ball. Both teams attempt to kick the ball backward out of the scrum, and play continues at the same chaotic pace as before. Members of the scrum must remain bound together and on their feet until the ball has been ejected.

A ball that strays out of bounds, or goes "into touch," leads to another striking formation of Rugby Union (but not Rugby League): the visually spectacular lineout. The team that was not last to touch the ball is awarded the throw-in, and the forwards of each team arrange themselves in two straight lines, facing the sideline ("touchline"). At a coded signal, the player known as the hooker throws the ball toward a selected player (the "jumper"), who is hoisted straight upward by his teammates—his feet at the level of their shoulders—to receive the inbound pass. Players may not make use of the jumper's clothing in lifting him up, but must physically lay hands on his person (thus cutting down on past injuries in which the unfortunate jumper was choked by his own jersey). Simultaneously, the other team elevates its own player, who attempts to intercept the inbound pass by whatever means necessary; and the two players duel for the ball, occupying their own midair playing field, in what can appear for all the world like some strange form of human puppetry.

Of course, the aim of this entire endeavour is to score as many points as possible, and there are two primary methods of doing so, although the weight given to each has varied through the years. A goal consists of a player's kicking the ball through the opponent's goalposts, above the crossbar. A try is achieved by bringing the ball across the opponent's goal line and touching it down ("bringing it to ground") in the opponent's goal area. (For readers weaned on American football, a goal is roughly similar to a field goal, a try to a touchdown.) In the earliest days of rugby, a try scored no points but allowed a team the opportunity to place-kick a "free" goal. But the concept of the try gradually gained in significance, particularly with Rugby Union's adoption, in the 1886–1887 season, of Cheltenham College's system, in which three tries were the equivalent of one goal. Presumably, the Oxford-Cambridge match of "The Missing Three-Quarter," which chronologists date anywhere between 1894 and 1897, used some version of this system of scoring. Rugby Union rules were changed again in 1905 such that a try equalled three points, a follow-up conversion goal two points, a dropped goal (a ball drop-kicked through the goalposts from the field during play) four points, and a penalty goal three points. Later rules changes finally brought Rugby Union's scoring system to its current levels, in which a try is worth five points, a conversion two points, and a dropped goal or a penalty goal three points.

THE ADVENTURE OF THE ABBEY GRANGE[1]

In this, one of the four cases in which Holmes protégé Inspector Stanley Hopkins appears (the others being "The Missing Three-Quarter," "Black Peter," and "The Golden Pince-Nez," all recorded in The Return*), we witness Holmes's knowledge of wine, contrasted with a disdain for the upper class first viewed in "The Noble Bachelor." Most emblematic of the detective's complicated views is the wealthy Sir Eustace Brackenstall, the murder victim, who is unfavourably contrasted with the plucky heroine and her seaman friend. The self-reliant Lady Mary Brackenstall awakens Holmes's usual sympathy for Australians (as seen by his treatment of them in "The 'Gloria Scott'" and "The Boscombe Valley Mystery"), and as in those cases, Holmes takes the law into his own hands. Here, however, his sympathies may have overridden his judgement: Many scholars believe that Holmes lets himself be fooled by a villainess cleverer than he credited.*

1 "The Abbey Grange" was published in the *Strand Magazine* in September 1904 and in *Collier's Weekly* on December 31, 1904.

2 The manuscript of "The Abbey Grange" is owned by the Bibliotheca Bodmeriana, Cologny/Geneva. Both the manuscript and the *Collier's Weekly* appearance have the opening line as: "It was a bitterly cold and frosty morning towards the end of '97," which would place the story in December 1897, as compared to "the end of the winter of '97," which most chronologists take to mean January 1897.

3 Holmes, drawing on his knowledge of Shakespeare (learnt, some suggest, in the course of a brief acting career), paraphrases *The First Part of Henry the Fourth*, Act I, Scene

I̅t was on a bitterly cold night and frosty morning, towards the end of the winter of '97[2] that I was wakened by a tugging at my shoulder. It was Holmes. The candle in his hand shone upon his eager, stooping face, and told me at a glance that something was amiss.

"Come, Watson, come!" he cried. "The game is afoot.[3] Not a word! Into your clothes and come!"

Ten minutes later we were both in a cab and rattling through the silent streets on our way to Charing Cross Station. The first faint winter's dawn was beginning to appear, and we could dimly see the occasional figure of an early workman as he passed us, blurred and indistinct in the opalescent London reek. Holmes nestled in silence into his heavy coat, and I was glad to do the same, for the air was most bitter, and neither of us had broken our fast.

It was not until we had consumed some hot tea at the station and taken our places in the Kentish[4] train that we were suffi-

THE ADVENTURE
of the
ABBEY GRANGE

Frederick Dorr Steele, *Collier's*, 1904

3: "Before the game's a-foot . . ." and *The Life of Henry the Fifth*, Act III, Scene 1: "The game's afoot!" Despite the public identification of the phrase with Holmes, he is not recorded as uttering it in any other context; Watson himself uses the phrase once, in "Wisteria Lodge." It is therefore one degree more respectable than the popular "Elementary, my dear Watson," which appears nowhere in the Canon.

4 "Chislehurst" in the manuscript.

5 Abbey *Wood* is a hamlet near Chislehurst, eleven miles from London. "Marsham" is the name of a village in Norfolk.

6 Holmes also worked with Hopkins in "The Golden Pince-Nez," "Black Peter," and "The Missing Three-Quarter," none of which had yet seen print in 1897. What were the other three or four cases?

ciently thawed, he to speak and I to listen. Holmes drew a note from his pocket and read aloud:

ABBEY GRANGE,[5] MARSHAM, KENT, 3:30 A.M.
MY DEAR MR. HOLMES—I should be very glad of your immediate assistance in what promises to be a most remarkable case. It is something quite in your line. Except for releasing the lady I will see that everything is kept exactly as I have found it, but I beg you not to lose an instant, as it is difficult to leave Sir Eustace there.—

> Yours faithfully,
> STANLEY HOPKINS.

"Hopkins has called me in seven times,[6] and on each occasion his summons has been entirely justified," said Holmes. "I fancy that every one of his cases has found its way into your collection, and I must admit, Watson, that you have some

7 "The Blanched Soldier" and "The Lion's Mane," both written by Holmes, were first published in 1926. In both, Holmes acknowledges that his "plain way" of writing will not have the reader-appeal of Watson's work.

" 'Come, Watson, come!' he cried. 'The game is afoot.' "
Sidney Paget, *Strand Magazine*, 1904

power of selection, which atones for much which I deplore in your narratives. Your fatal habit of looking at everything from the point of view of a story instead of as a scientific exercise has ruined what might have been an instructive and even classical series of demonstrations. You slur over work of the utmost finesse and delicacy, in order to dwell upon sensational details which may excite, but cannot possibly instruct, the reader."

"Why do you not write them yourself?" I said, with some bitterness.

"I will, my dear Watson, I will.[7] At present I am, as you know, fairly busy, but I propose to devote my declining years to the composition of a textbook which shall focus the whole art of detection into one volume. Our present research appears to be a case of murder."

"You think this Sir Eustace is dead, then?"

"I should say so. Hopkins's writing shows considerable agitation, and he is not an emotional man. Yes, I gather there has been violence, and that the body is left for our inspection. A mere suicide would not have caused him to send for me. As to the release of the lady, it would appear that she has been locked in her room during the tragedy. We are moving in high life, Watson, crackling paper, 'E. B.' monogram, coat-of-arms, picturesque address. I think that friend Hopkins will live up to his reputation, and that we shall have an interesting morning. The crime was committed before twelve last night."

"How can you possibly tell?"

"By an inspection of the trains and by reckoning the time. The local police had to be called in, they had to communicate with Scotland Yard, Hopkins had to go out, and he in turn had to send for me. All that makes a fair night's work. Well, here we are at Chislehurst Station, and we shall soon set our doubts at rest."

A drive of a couple of miles through narrow country lanes brought us to a park gate, which was opened for us by an old lodge-keeper, whose haggard face bore the reflection of some great disaster. The avenue ran through a noble park, between lines of ancient elms, and ended in a low, widespread house,[8] pillared in front after the fashion of Palladio.[9] The central part was evidently of a great age and shrouded in ivy, but the large windows showed that modern changes had been carried out, and one wing of the house appeared to be entirely new. The youthful figure and alert, eager face of Inspector Stanley Hopkins confronted us in the open doorway.

"I'm very glad you have come, Mr. Holmes. And you, too, Dr. Watson. But, indeed, if I had my time over again, I should not have troubled you, for since the lady has come to herself, she has given so clear an account of the affair that there is not much left for us to do. You remember that Lewisham gang of burglars?"

"What, the three Randalls?"

"Exactly; the father and two sons. It's their work. I have not a doubt of it. They did a job at Sydenham a fortnight ago and were seen and described. Rather cool to do another so soon and so near; but it is they, beyond all doubt. It's a hanging matter this time."

"Sir Eustace is dead, then?"

"Yes; his head was knocked in with his own poker."

"Sir Eustace Brackenstall,[10] the driver tells me."

"Exactly—one of the richest men in Kent. Lady Brackenstall is in the morning-room. Poor lady, she has had a most

8 Michael Harrison suggests that "Marsham, Kent" may reasonably be identified with the town of St. Mary Cray. In *In the Footsteps of Sherlock Holmes*, he writes: "Most of the old houses in this once most select of all London's suburbs remain: turned . . . into golf-clubs, or hospitals or schools or lunatic asylums . . . if 'Abbey Grange' . . . still survives, it will no longer be in private occupation."

9 Andrea Palladio (1508–1580) was an Italian Renaissance architect celebrated for his palaces and villas, most notably the Villa Rotonda near Vicenza. Combining a classic Roman style with principles of simplicity and order, Palladio favored temple-like arches and columns; strict symmetry (a central hall surrounded by smaller rooms, for example) governed the interiors of his structures. In the eighteenth century Palladio's style was widely imitated in England, Italy, and the United States. His influence may be seen in the façade of Thomas Jefferson's Monticello, completed in 1809. Palladio's most famous published work is *I quattro libri dell'architectura* (1570, translated as *The Four Books of Architecture* in 1716), a landmark study of classical architecture.

10 "Heppenstall" in the manuscript.

dreadful experience. She seemed half dead when I saw her first. I think you had best see her and hear her account of the facts. Then we will examine the dining-room together."

Lady Brackenstall was no ordinary person. Seldom have I seen so graceful a figure, so womanly a presence, and so beautiful a face. She was a blonde, golden-haired, blue-eyed, and would no doubt have had the perfect complexion which goes with such colouring had not her recent experience left her drawn and haggard. Her sufferings were physical as well as mental, for over one eye rose a hideous, plum-coloured swelling, which her maid, a tall, austere woman, was bathing assiduously with vinegar and water. The lady lay back exhausted upon a couch, but her quick, observant gaze as we entered the room and the alert expression of her beautiful features, showed that neither her wits nor her courage had been shaken by her terrible experience. She was enveloped in a loose dressing-gown of blue and silver, but a black sequin-covered dinner-dress was hung upon the couch beside her.

"I have told you all that happened, Mr. Hopkins," she said

The lady lay back exhausted upon a couch enveloped in a loose dressing-gown of blue and silver.
Frederick Dorr Steele, *Collier's*, 1904

wearily; "could you not repeat it for me? Well, if you think it necessary, I will tell these gentlemen what occurred. Have they been in the dining-room yet?"

"I thought they had better hear your ladyship's story first."

"I shall be glad when you can arrange matters. It is horrible to me to think of him still lying there." She shuddered and buried her face for a moment in her hands. As she did so the loose gown fell back from her forearms. Holmes uttered an exclamation.

"You have other injuries, madam! What is this?" Two vivid red spots stood out on one of the white, round limbs. She hastily covered it.

"It is nothing. It has no connection with this hideous business of last night.[11] If you and your friend will sit down, I will tell you all I can.

"I am the wife of Sir Eustace Brackenstall. I have been married about a year. I suppose that it is no use my attempting to conceal that our marriage has not been a happy one. I fear that all our neighbours would tell you that, even if I were to attempt to deny it. Perhaps the fault may be partly mine. I was brought up in the freer, less conventional atmosphere of South Australia, and this English life, with its proprieties and its primness, is not congenial to me. But the main reason lies in the one fact, which is notorious to everyone, and that is that Sir Eustace was a confirmed drunkard. To be with such a man for an hour is unpleasant. Can you imagine what it means for a sensitive and high-spirited woman to be tied to him for day and night? It is a sacrilege, a crime, a villainy to hold that such a marriage is binding. I say that these monstrous laws of yours[12] will bring a curse upon the land—Heaven[13] will not let such wickedness endure." For an instant she sat up, her cheeks flushed, and her eyes blazing from under the terrible mark upon her brow. Then the strong, soothing hand of the austere maid drew her head down on to the cushion, and the wild anger died away into passionate sobbing. At last she continued:

"I will tell you about last night. You are aware, perhaps, that in this house all servants sleep in the modern wing. This central block is made up of the dwelling-rooms, with the kitchen behind and our bedroom above. My maid Theresa sleeps above my room. There is no one else, and no sound could alarm those who are in the farther wing. This must have been

11 Curiously, "to-night" in the American editions.

12 What Lady Brackenstall likely refers to here is the 1857 Divorce and Matrimonial Causes Act, which laid out provisions by which men and women could divorce and created a civil court to handle such matters. (Prior to passage of the bill, anyone seeking a divorce had to do so through the Church of England, in a process that essentially entailed men suing their wives for adultery.) While the new law purported to afford more rights to women, historian Simon Schama reveals that "it was not what it seemed. Enacted specifically to pre-empt a measure that would have given married women property rights, this piece of legislation perpetuated, rather than corrected, the inequities between the sexes." A man was now allowed to file for divorce on grounds of adultery, whereas a woman could do so only if her husband's adultery also involved rape, sodomy, incest, bestiality, physical cruelty, or two years' desertion. In addition, the cost of getting a divorce was well beyond the means of most Victorian women. Sir Eustace's being a drunken, abusive lout would never have earned his wife a hearing in court; certainly, today's complaints of irreconcilable differences or emotional cruelty were a long way off. As Schama writes, "The notion that a divorce action might be brought . . . for mere incompatibility remained the most fantastic prospect." See "A Case of Identity" for more on the property rights (or lack thereof) of married women in the Victorian age.

13 The editor of the American edition makes a number of changes in phraseology in the story, coarsening the dialogue, perhaps in an effort to appeal to what the editor perceived to be a less-refined readership. Here the word "God" is substituted for "Heaven;" elsewhere, "devil" replaces "fiend," and "curse" replaces "damn."

"I am the wife of Sir Eustace Brackenstall."
Sidney Paget, *Strand Magazine*, 1904

well known to the robbers, or they would not have acted as they did.

"Sir Eustace retired about half-past ten. The servants had already gone to their quarters. Only my maid was up, and she had remained in her room at the top of the house until I needed her services. I sat until after eleven in this room, absorbed in a book. Then I walked round to see that all was right before I went upstairs. It was my custom to do this myself, for, as I have explained, Sir Eustace was not always to be trusted. I went into the kitchen, the butler's pantry, the gun-room, the billiard-room, the drawing-room, and finally the dining-room. As I approached the window, which is covered with thick curtains, I suddenly felt the wind blow upon my face and realized that it was open. I flung the curtain aside and found myself face to face with a broad-shouldered elderly man, who had just stepped into the room. The window is a long French one, which really forms a door leading to the lawn. I held my bedroom candle lit in my hand, and, by its light, behind the first man I saw two others, who were in the act of entering. I stepped back, but the fellow was on me in an instant. He caught me first by the wrist and then by the throat. I opened my mouth to scream, but he struck me a savage blow with his fist over the eye, and felled me to the ground. I must have been unconscious for a few minutes, for when I came to myself, I found that they had torn down the bell-rope, and had secured me tightly to the oaken chair which stands at the head of the dining-table. I was so firmly bound that I could not move, and a handkerchief round my mouth prevented me from uttering any sound. It was at this instant that my unfortunate husband entered the room. He had evidently heard some suspicious sounds, and he came prepared for such a scene as he found. He was dressed in his shirt[14] and trousers, with his favourite blackthorn cudgel in his hand.[15] He rushed at one of[16] the burglars, but another—it was an elderly man[17]—stooped, picked the poker out of the grate and struck him a horrible blow as he passed. He fell without[18] a groan and never moved again. I fainted once more, but again it could only have been a very few minutes during which I was insensible. When I opened my eyes I found that they had collected the silver from the sideboard, and they had drawn a bottle of wine which stood there. Each of them had a glass in his hand. I have already told you, have I not, that one was elderly, with a beard, and the others young, hairless lads. They might have been a father with his two sons. They talked together in whispers. Then they came over and made sure that I was still securely bound. Finally they withdrew, closing the window after them. It was quite a quarter of an hour before I got my mouth free. When I did so, my screams brought the maid to my assistance. The other servants were soon alarmed, and we sent for the local police, who instantly communicated with London. That is really all that I can tell you, gentlemen, and I trust that it will not be necessary for me to go over so painful a story again."

"Any questions, Mr. Holmes?" asked Hopkins.

"I will not impose any further tax upon Lady Brackenstall's patience and time," said Holmes. "Before I go into the dining-room, I should like to hear your experience." He looked at the maid.

"I saw the men before ever they came into the house," said she. "As I sat by my bedroom window I saw three men in the

14 "Nightshirt" in the American edition. There is specific reference later to Brackenstall's nightshirt, and the American editor apparently did not want the readers confused by the use of this British colloquialism.

15 A "cudgel" is a weapon of punishment—why, one may ask, did Sir Eustace have a "favourite" (implying more than one)? Perhaps Lady Brackenstall meant that when he felt threatened, he favoured a cudgel rather than a poker or other object with which to defend himself.

16 "One of" is omitted in American editions.

17 "One of the younger ones" in the manuscript. Note that, a few sentences before, Lady Brackenstall refers to "a broad-shouldered elderly man." Why would she here say "an" elderly man, not "the" elderly man? In other words, the manuscript record is more likely to be accurate. Did Watson go back and deliberately introduce inconsistencies in her account after the truth was known, as hints?

18 Curiously changed to "with" in American editions.

moonlight down by the lodge gate yonder, but I thought nothing of it at the time. It was more than an hour after that I heard my mistress scream, and down I ran, to find her, poor lamb, just as she says, and him on the floor, with his blood and brains over the room. It was enough to drive a woman out of her wits, tied there, and her very dress spotted with him; but she never wanted courage, did Miss Mary Fraser of Adelaide, and Lady Brackenstall of Abbey Grange hasn't learned new ways. You've questioned her long enough, you gentlemen, and now she is coming to her own room, just with her old Theresa, to get the rest that she badly needs."

With a motherly tenderness the gaunt woman put her arm round her mistress and led her from the room.

"She has been with her all her life," said Hopkins. "Nursed her as a baby, and came with her to England when they first left Australia, eighteen months ago. Theresa Wright is her name, and the kind of maid you don't pick up nowadays. This way, Mr. Holmes, if you please!"

The keen interest had passed out of Holmes's expressive face, and I knew that with the mystery all the charm of the case had departed. There still remained an arrest to be effected, but what were these commonplace rogues that he should soil his hands with them? An abstruse and learned specialist who finds that he has been called in for a case of measles would experience something of the annoyance which I read in my friend's eyes. Yet the scene in the dining-room of the Abbey Grange was sufficiently strange to arrest his attention and to recall his waning interest.

It was a very large and high chamber, with carved oak ceiling, oaken panelling, and a fine array of deer's heads and ancient weapons around the walls. At the further end from the door was the high French window of which we had heard. Three smaller windows on the right-hand side filled the apartment with cold winter sunshine. On the left was a large, deep fireplace, with a massive, overhanging oak mantelpiece. Beside the fireplace was a heavy oaken chair with arms and crossbars at the bottom. In and out through the open woodwork was woven a crimson cord, which was secured at each side to the crosspiece below. In releasing the lady, the cord had been slipped off her, but the knots with which it had been secured still remained. These details only struck our attention afterwards, for our thoughts were entirely absorbed by the terrible object which lay upon the tiger-skin hearthrug in front of the fire.

It was the body of a tall, well-made man, about forty years of age. He lay upon his back, his face upturned, with his white teeth grinning through his short, black beard. His two clenched hands were raised above his head, and a heavy blackthorn stick lay across them. His dark, handsome, aquiline features were convulsed into a spasm of vindictive hatred, which had set his dead face in a terribly fiendish expression. He had evidently been in his bed when the alarm had broken out, for he wore a foppish, embroidered nightshirt, and his bare feet projected from his trousers. His head was horribly injured, and the whole room bore witness to the savage ferocity of the blow

"It was the body of a tall, well-made man,
about forty years of age."
Sidney Paget, *Strand Magazine*, 1904

which had struck him down. Beside him lay the heavy poker, bent into a curve by the concussion. Holmes examined both it and the indescribable wreck which it had wrought.

"He must be a powerful man, this elder Randall," he remarked.

"Yes," said Hopkins. "I have some record of the fellow, and he is a rough customer."

"You should have no difficulty in getting him."

"Not the slightest. We have been on the look-out for him, and there was some idea that he had got away to America. Now that we know that the gang are here, I don't see how they can escape. We have the news at every seaport already, and a reward will be offered before evening. What beats me is how they could have done so mad a thing, knowing that the lady could describe them and that we could not fail to recognise the description."

"Exactly. One would have expected that they would have silenced Lady Brackenstall as well."

"They may not have realized," I suggested, "that she had recovered from her faint."

"That is likely enough. If she seemed to be senseless, they would not take her life. What about this poor fellow, Hopkins? I seem to have heard some queer stories about him."

"He was a good-hearted man when he was sober, but a perfect fiend when he was drunk, or rather when he was half drunk, for he seldom really went the whole way. The devil seemed to be in him at such times, and he was capable of anything. From what I hear, in spite of all his wealth and his title, he very nearly came our way once or twice. There was a scandal about his drenching a dog with petroleum and setting it on fire—her ladyship's dog, to make the matter worse—and that was only hushed up with difficulty. Then he threw a decanter at that maid, Theresa Wright; there was trouble about that. On the whole, and between ourselves, it will be a brighter house without him. What are you looking at now?"

Holmes was down on his knees, examining with great attention the knots upon the red cord with which the lady had been secured. Then he carefully scrutinized the broken and frayed end where it had snapped off when the burglar had dragged it down.

"When this was pulled down, the bell in the kitchen must have rung loudly," he remarked.

"No one could hear it. The kitchen stands right at the back of the house."

"How did the burglar know no one would hear it? How dared he pull at a bell-rope in that reckless fashion?"

"Exactly, Mr. Holmes, exactly. You put the very question which I have asked myself again and again. There can be no doubt that this fellow must have known the house and its habits. He must have perfectly understood that the servants would all be in bed at that comparatively early hour, and that no one could possibly hear a bell ring in the kitchen. Therefore, he must have been in close league with one of the servants. Surely that is evident. But there are eight servants, and all of good character."

"Other things being equal," said Holmes, "one would suspect the one at whose head the master threw a decanter. And yet that would involve treachery towards the mistress to whom this woman seems devoted. Well, well, the point is a minor one, and when you have Randall you will probably find no difficulty in securing his accomplice. The lady's story certainly seems to be corroborated, if it needed corroboration, by every detail which we see before us." He walked to the French window and threw it open. "There are no signs here, but the ground is iron hard, and one would not expect them. I see that these candles in the mantelpiece have been lighted."

"Yes, it was by their light and that of the lady's bedroom candle that the burglars saw their way about."

"And what did they take?"

"Well, they did not take much—only half a dozen articles of plate[19] off the sideboard. Lady Brackenstall thinks that they were themselves so disturbed by the death of Sir Eustace that they did not ransack the house as they would otherwise have done."

"No doubt that is true. And yet they drank some wine, I understand."

"To steady their nerves."

"Exactly. These three glasses upon the sideboard have been untouched, I suppose?"

"Yes; and the bottle stands as they left it."

19 Dishes, cups, or other household articles covered in precious metals such as silver or gold.

20 Beeswing is a translucent, flaky film found in older wines, particularly those, such as port, that are bottle-aged for many years. The *Dictionary of Phrase and Fable* provides that "A port drinker is very particular not to 'break the beeswing' by shaking the bottle, or turning it the wrong way up."

21 What was the wine? The most important clue is the presence of the beeswing, which generally manifests itself in crusted port, a rare and costly wine. But there are other telling signs: (a) The wine had been left on the sideboard after dinner, suggesting that it was not drunk with dinner but perhaps was intended for later drinking. This confirms that the wine was an "after-dinner" wine such as port. (b) Sir Eustace was "one of the richest men in Kent," according to Hopkins. His life style was more *nouveau riche* than that of the landed gentry, and he made a show of his wealth, using monogrammed paper, displaying a coat-of-arms, and sporting a "foppish" nightshirt. Thus, despite the fact that he was a "confirmed drunkard" and probably no longer particular about his own source of intoxication, for the sake of appearances he would have stocked his wine cellar with the showiest, most expensive wines available. This suggests a bottle from the 1834 vintage, "one of the most renowned of the mid-19th century," according to Michael Broadbent's *The New Great Vintage Wine Book*. The "giant of the vintage" was Kopke's Quinta do Roriz. Although this type of port is no longer in existence, Nicholas Utechin verifies, in "Some Remarkable Wines," that it was sold by Harrod's in 1895 for £60 a dozen. Of course, there can be no certainty with such scant evidence, but the 1834 Kopke's Quinta do Roriz does seem a likely candidate for the sideboard.

"These three glasses upon the sideboard have been untouched, I suppose."
Charles Raymond Macaulay, *Return of Sherlock Holmes* (McClure Phillips), 1905

"Let us look at it. Halloa, halloa! What is this?"

The three glasses were grouped together, all of them tinged with wine, and one of them containing some dregs of beeswing.[20] The bottle stood near them, two-thirds full, and beside it lay a long, deeply stained cork. Its appearance and the dust upon the bottle showed that it was no common vintage which the murderers had enjoyed.[21]

A change had come over Holmes's manner. He had lost his listless expression, and again I saw an alert light of interest in his keen, deep-set eyes. He raised the cork and examined it minutely.

"How did they draw it?" he asked.

Hopkins pointed to a half-opened drawer. In it lay some table linen and a large corkscrew.

"Did Lady Brackenstall say that screw was used?"

"No; you remember that she was senseless at the moment when the bottle was opened."

"Quite so. As a matter of fact, that screw was *not* used. This bottle was opened by a pocket-screw, probably contained in a knife, and not more than an inch and a half long. If you will examine the top of the cork, you will observe that the screw was driven in three times before the cork was extracted. It has never been transfixed. This long screw would have transfixed it and drawn it up with a single pull. When you catch this fellow, you will find that he has one of these multiplex knives[22] in his possession."

"Excellent!" said Hopkins.

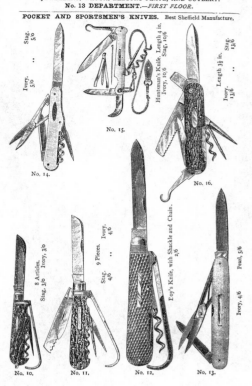

Pocket knives including corkscrews.

"Halloa, halloa, what is this?"
Sidney Paget, *Strand Magazine*, 1904

22 In the late 1880s, the Swiss army decided that its soldiers would be best served if several of their necessary implements were combined into one pocket knife. Such a knife would require a screwdriver (with which the soldier's rifle could be disassembled), a can opener, a utensil with which holes could be bored, and, of course, a blade. This design evolved into pocket knives for the general public with a wide variety of tools incorporated. Harrod's 1895 catalogue, for example, illustrates six different types of pocket knives that include a corkscrew.

"But these glasses do puzzle me, I confess. Lady Brackenstall actually *saw* the three men drinking, did she not?"

"Yes; she was clear about that."

"Then there is an end of it. What more is to be said? And yet, you must admit that the three glasses are very remarkable, Hopkins. What? You see nothing remarkable? Well, well, let it pass. Perhaps, when a man has special knowledge and special powers like my own, it rather encourages him to seek a complex explanation when a simpler one is at hand. Of course, it must be a mere chance about the glasses. Well, good-morning, Hopkins. I don't see that I can be of any use to you, and you appear to have your case very clear. You will let me know when Randall is arrested, and any further developments which may occur. I trust that I shall soon have to congratulate you upon a

Sherlock Holmes examines the glasses.
Frederick Dorr Steele, *Collier's*, 1904

"I could see by Holmes's face that he was much puzzled."
Sidney Paget, *Strand Magazine*, 1904

successful conclusion. Come, Watson, I fancy that we may employ ourselves more profitably at home."

During our return journey I could see by Holmes's face that he was much puzzled by something which he had observed. Every now and then, by an effort, he would throw off the impression, and talk as if the matter were clear, but then his doubts would settle down upon him again, and his knitted brows and abstracted eyes would show that his thoughts had gone back once more to the great dining-room of the Abbey Grange, in which this midnight tragedy had been enacted. At last by a sudden impulse, just as our train was crawling out of a suburban station, he sprang on to the platform and pulled me out after him.

"Excuse me, my dear fellow," said he, as we watched the

23 Latin: anew, afresh. A trial *de novo* is one at which none of the evidence or rulings from any previous trial is automatically placed before the judge.

24 Note that the level of the contents of the bottle changes without any explanation by Dr. Watson. When previously observed, the Doctor records that the bottle is "two-thirds full." Perhaps Holmes poured some wine off to conduct an actual experiment, instead of simply imagining the result. William R. Cochran, in "The Magic Wine Bottle," suggests that Holmes and Watson drank the missing beverage.

rear carriages of our train disappearing round a curve; "I am sorry to make you the victim of what may seem a mere whim, but on my life, Watson, I simply *can't* leave that case in this condition. Every instinct that I possess cries out against it. It's wrong—it's all wrong—I'll swear that it's wrong. And yet the lady's story was complete, the maid's corroboration was sufficient, the detail was fairly exact. What have I to put up against that? Three wine-glasses, that is all. But if I had not taken things for granted, if I had examined everything with care which I should have shown had we approached the case *de novo*[23] and had no cut-and-dried story to warp my mind, should I not then have found something more definite to go upon? Of course I should. Sit down on this bench, Watson, until a train for Chislehurst arrives, and allow me to lay the evidence before you, imploring you in the first instance to dismiss from your mind the idea that anything which the maid or her mistress may have said must necessarily be true. The lady's charming personality must not be permitted to warp our judgment.

"Surely there are details in her story which, if we looked at in cold blood, would excite our suspicion. These burglars made a considerable haul at Sydenham a fortnight ago. Some account of them and of their appearance was in the papers, and would naturally occur to anyone who wished to invent a story in which imaginary robbers should play a part. As a matter of fact, burglars who have done a good stroke of business are, as a rule, only too glad to enjoy the proceeds in peace and quiet without embarking on another perilous undertaking. Again, it is unusual for burglars to operate at so early an hour; it is unusual for burglars to strike a lady to prevent her screaming, since one would imagine that was the sure way to make her scream; it is unusual for them to commit murder when their numbers are sufficient to overpower one man; it is unusual for them to be content with a limited plunder when there was much more within their reach; and finally, I should say that it was very unusual for such men to leave a bottle half empty.[24] How do all these unusuals strike you, Watson?"

"Their cumulative effect is certainly considerable, and yet each of them is quite possible in itself. The most unusual thing of all, as it seems to me, is that the lady should be tied to the chair."

"Well, I am not so clear about that, Watson, for it is evident that they must either kill her or else secure her in such a way that she could not give immediate notice of their escape. But at any rate I have shown, have I not, that there is a certain element of improbability about the lady's story? And now on the top of this comes the incident of the wineglasses."

"What about the wineglasses?"

"Can you see them in your mind's eye?"

"I see them clearly."

"We are told that three men drank from them. Does that strike you as likely?"

"Why not? There was wine in each glass."

"Exactly; but there was beeswing only in one glass. You must have noticed that fact. What does that suggest to your mind?"

"The last glass filled would be most likely to contain beeswing."

"Not at all. The bottle was full of it, and it is inconceivable that the two glasses were clear and the third heavily charged with it. There are two possible explanations, and only two. One is that after the second glass was filled the bottle was violently agitated, and so the third glass received the beeswing. That does not appear probable. No, no, I am sure that I am right."

"What, then, do you suppose?"

"That only two glasses were used, and that the dregs of both were poured into a third glass, so as to give the false impression that three people had been here. In that way all the beeswing would be in the last glass, would it not? Yes, I am convinced that this is so. But if I have hit upon the true explanation of this one small phenomenon, then in an instant the case rises from the commonplace to the exceedingly remarkable, for it can only mean that Lady Brackenstall and her maid have deliberately lied to us, that not one word of their story is to be believed, that they have some very strong reason for covering the real criminal, and that we must construct our case for ourselves without any help from them. That is the mission which now lies before us, and here, Watson, is the Chislehurst[25] train."

The household of the Abbey Grange were much surprised at our return, but Sherlock Holmes, finding that Stanley Hopkins had gone off to report to headquarters, took possession of the dining-room, locked the door upon the inside, and devoted

25 American editions inexplicably have "Sydenham."

26 Ranking below barons, baronets are given precedence over most knights, various companions, and various descendants of the younger sons of peers. As a baronet, Brackenstall would be formally addressed as "Sir Eustace Brackenstall, Bt." (or the fuller abbreviation "Bart," now considered old-fashioned). His wife would be known as "Your Ladyship" and addressed, as Holmes and Watson have done properly, as "Lady Brackenstall," her Christian name being dropped. Only the daughter of a duke, marquis, or earl would retain her Christian name in the formal address. See, for example, Lady Hilda Trelawney Hope, the youngest daughter of the Duke of Belminster ("The Second Stain").

Note that a mere knight would also be referred to as "Sir Eustace . . ." and his wife as "Lady Brackenstall." However, a baronetage was hereditary, while a knighthood was not. Even if Watson did not actually know that Brackenstall was a baronet, his evident lack of merits strongly implies that his title was an hereditary honour, rather than earned. Of course, it is unthinkable that Watson would refer to someone as a baronet who was not.

himself for two hours to one of those minute and laborious investigations which form the solid basis on which his brilliant edifices of deduction were reared. Seated in a corner like an interested student who observes the demonstration of his professor, I followed every step of that remarkable research. The window, the curtains, the carpet, the chair, the rope—each in turn was minutely examined and duly pondered. The body of the unfortunate baronet[26] had been removed, and all else remained as we had seen it in the morning. Then, to my astonishment, Holmes climbed up on to the massive mantelpiece. Far above his head hung the few inches of red cord which were still attached to the wire. For a long time he gazed upwards at it, and then in an attempt to get nearer to it he rested his knee upon a wooden bracket on the wall. This brought his hand within a few inches of the broken end of the rope; but it was not this so much as the bracket itself which seemed to engage his attention. Finally he sprang down with an ejaculation of satisfaction.

"It's all right, Watson," said he. "We have got our case—one of the most remarkable in our collection. But, dear me, how slow-witted I have been, and how nearly I have committed the blunder of my lifetime! Now, I think that with a few missing links my chain is almost complete."

"You have got your men?"

"Man, Watson, man. Only one, but a very formidable person. Strong as a lion—witness the blow which bent that poker! Six foot three in height, active as a squirrel, dexterous with his fingers; finally, remarkably quick-witted, for this whole ingenious story is of his concoction. Yes, Watson, we have come upon the handiwork of a very remarkable individual. And yet in that bell-rope he has given us a clue which should not have left us a doubt."

"Where was the clue?"

"Well, if you were to pull down a bell-rope, Watson, where would you expect it to break? Surely at the spot where it is attached to the wire. Why should it break three inches from the top, as this one has done?"

"Because it is frayed there?"

"Exactly. This end, which we can examine, is frayed. He was cunning enough to do that with his knife. But the other end is not frayed. You could not observe that from here, but if

"Look at that mark on the seat of the oaken chair."
Sidney Paget, *Strand Magazine*, 1904

you were on the mantelpiece you would see that it is cut clean off without any mark of fraying whatever. You can reconstruct what occurred. The man needed the rope. He would not tear it down for fear of giving the alarm by ringing the bell. What did he do? He sprang up on the mantelpiece, could not quite reach it, put his knee on the bracket—you will see the impression in the dust—and so got his knife to bear upon the cord. I could not reach the place by at least three inches, from which I infer that he is at least three inches a bigger man than I. Look at that mark upon the seat of the oaken chair! What is it?"

"Blood."

"Undoubtedly it is blood. This alone puts the lady's story out of court. If she were seated on the chair when the crime was done, how comes that mark? No, no, she was placed in the

27 The Battle of Marengo—a major engagement in the French Revolutionary Wars—was fought on June 14, 1800, between the French, commanded by Napoleon Bonaparte, and the Austrians, led by General Michael Friedrich von Melas. Having miscalculated where Melas was, Napoleon came upon the village of Marengo in Piedmont, northern Italy, with his forces scattered and unprepared for combat. Melas's surprise attack drove the French four miles backward, spelling certain victory for the Austrians. But here the overconfident Melas made an error, handing over command to a subordinate officer and departing for Alessandria. In a matter of hours, a French division headed by General Louis Desaix returned to launch a vicious counterattack, turning the tide and sending the Austrians into retreat. Napoleon later came to regard the Battle of Marengo as the most brilliant victory of his career, despite the fact that he was only very narrowly saved from defeat.

"Chicken Marengo," a traditional Provençal dish, is popularly supposed to have been invented for Napoleon after the battle. Reportedly, foragers were only able to find chicken, tomatoes, eggs, crayfish, garlic, olive oil, and cognac, as well as the soldiers' bread, and the dish was cobbled together with the ingredients on hand. Napoleon is said to have so liked the dish (or was so superstitious) that he ordered that it be prepared after every succeeding battle.

28 To apply hot, moist cloths to the body; to treat with a poultice or warm medicinal compress.

chair after the death of her husband. I'll wager that the black dress shows a corresponding mark to this. We have not yet met our Waterloo, Watson, but this is our Marengo, for it begins in defeat and ends in victory.27 I should like now to have a few words with the nurse Theresa. We must be wary for a while, if we are to get the information which we want."

She was an interesting person, this stern Australian nurse. Taciturn, suspicious, ungracious, it took some time before Holmes's pleasant manner and frank acceptance of all that she said thawed her into a corresponding amiability. She did not attempt to conceal her hatred for her late employer.

"Yes, sir, it is true that he threw the decanter at me. I heard him call my mistress a name, and I told him that he would not dare to speak so if her brother had been there. Then it was that he threw it at me. He might have thrown a dozen if he had but left my bonny bird alone. He was forever ill-treating her, and she was too proud to complain. She will not even tell me all that he has done to her. She never told me of those marks on her arm that you saw this morning, but I know very well that they come from a stab with a hat-pin. The sly fiend—Heaven forgive me that I should speak of him so, now that he is dead, but a fiend he was, if ever one walked the earth. He was all honey when first we met him, only eighteen months ago, and we both feel as if it were eighteen years. She had only just arrived in London. Yes, it was her first voyage—she had never been from home before. He won her with his title and his money and his false London ways. If she made a mistake she has paid for it, if ever a woman did. What month did we meet him? Well, I tell you it was just after we arrived. We arrived in June, and it was July. They were married in January of last year. Yes, she is down in the morning-room again, and I have no doubt she will see you, but you must not ask too much of her, for she has gone through all that flesh and blood will stand."

Lady Brackenstall was reclining on the same couch, but looked brighter than before. The maid had entered with us, and began once more to foment28 the bruise upon her mistress's brow.

"I hope," said the lady, "that you have not come to cross-examine me again?"

"No," Holmes answered, in his gentlest voice, "I will not cause you any unnecessary trouble, Lady Brackenstall, and my whole desire is to make things easy for you, for I am convinced that you are a much-tried woman. If you will treat me as a friend and trust me, you may find that I will justify your trust."

"What do you want me to do?"

"To tell me the truth."

"Mr. Holmes!"

"No, no, Lady Brackenstall, it is no use. You may have heard of any little reputation which I possess. I will stake it all on the fact that your story is an absolute fabrication."

Mistress and maid were both staring at Holmes with pale faces and frightened eyes.

"You are an impudent fellow!" cried Theresa. "Do you mean to say that my mistress has told a lie?"

Holmes rose from his chair.

"Have you nothing to tell me?"

"I have told you everything."

"Think once more, Lady Brackenstall. Would it not be better to be frank?"

For an instant there was hesitation in her beautiful face. Then some new strong thought caused it to set like a mask.

"I have told you all I know."

Holmes took his hat and shrugged his shoulders. "I am sorry," he said, and without another word we left the room and the house. There was a pond in the park, and to this my friend led the way. It was frozen over, but a single hole was left for the convenience of a solitary swan. Holmes gazed at it, and then passed on to the lodge gate. There he scribbled a short note for Stanley Hopkins, and left it with the lodge-keeper.

"It may be a hit, or it may be a miss, but we are bound to do something for friend Hopkins, just to justify this second visit," said he. "I will not quite take him into my confidence yet. I think our next scene of operations must be the shipping office of the Adelaide-Southampton line, which stands at the end of Pall Mall, if I remember right. There is a second line of steamers which connect South Australia with England, but we will draw the larger cover[29] first."

Holmes's card sent in to the manager ensured instant attention, and he was not long in acquiring all the information which he needed. In June of '95, only one of their line had reached a home port. It was the *Rock of Gibraltar*, their largest and best boat. A reference to the passenger list showed that Miss Fraser

29 A shooting metaphor, meaning to draw the fox from its covert or temporary lair. When the animal "breaks cover," the hunt begins.

30 "Crocker" in the American editions.

"Holmes gazed at it and then passed on."
Sidney Paget, *Strand Magazine*, 1904

of Adelaide, with her maid, had made the voyage in her. The boat was now on her way to Australia, somewhere to the south of the Suez Canal. Her officers were the same as in '95, with one exception. The first officer, Mr. Jack Croker,[30] had been made a captain and was to take charge of their new ship, the *Bass Rock*, sailing in two days' time from Southampton. He lived at Sydenham, but he was likely to be in that morning for instructions, if we cared to wait for him.

No; Mr. Holmes had no desire to see him, but would be glad to know more about his record and character.

His record was magnificent. There was not an officer in the fleet to touch him. As to his character, he was reliable on duty, but a wild, desperate fellow off the deck of his ship, hotheaded, excitable, but loyal, honest, and kind-hearted. That was the pith of the information with which Holmes left the office of the Adelaide-Southampton Company. Thence he drove to Scotland Yard, but, instead of entering, he sat in his cab with his brows drawn down, lost in profound thought. Finally he drove round to the Charing Cross telegraph office, sent off a message, and then, at last, we made for Baker Street once more.

"No, I couldn't do it, Watson," said he, as we reentered our room. "Once that warrant was made out, nothing on earth would save him. Once or twice in my career I feel that I have done more real harm by my discovery of the criminal than ever he had done by his crime. I have learned caution now, and I had rather play tricks with the law of England than with my own conscience. Let us know a little more before we act."

Before evening, we had a visit from Inspector Stanley Hopkins. Things were not going very well with him.

"I believe that you are a wizard, Mr. Holmes. I really do sometimes think that you have powers that are not human. Now, how on earth could you know that the stolen silver was at the bottom of that pond?"

"I didn't know it."

"But you told me to examine it."

"You got it, then?"

"Yes I got it."

"I am very glad if I have helped you."

"But you haven't helped me. You have made the affair far more difficult. What sort of burglars are they who steal silver and then throw it into the nearest pond?"

"It was certainly rather eccentric behaviour. I was merely going on the idea that if the silver had been taken by persons who did not want it, who merely took it for a blind, as it were, then they would naturally be anxious to get rid of it."

"But why should such an idea cross your mind?"

"Well, I thought it was possible. When they came out through the French window, there was the pond, with one tempting little hole in the ice, right in front of their noses. Could there be a better hiding-place?"

"Ah, a hiding-place—that is better!" cried Stanley Hopkins. "Yes, yes, I see it all now! It was early, there were folk upon the roads, they were afraid of being seen with the silver, so they sank it in the pond, intending to return for it when the coast was clear. Excellent, Mr. Holmes—that is better than your idea of a blind."

"Quite so; you have got an admirable theory. I have no doubt that my own ideas were quite wild, but you must admit that they have ended in discovering the silver."

"Yes, sir; yes. It was all your doing. But I have had a bad set-back."

"A set-back?"

"Yes, Mr. Holmes. The Randall gang were arrested in New York this morning."

"Dear me, Hopkins. That is certainly rather against your theory that they committed a murder in Kent last night."

"It is fatal, Mr. Holmes, absolutely fatal. Still, there are other gangs of three besides the Randalls, or it may be some new gang of which the police have never heard."

"Quite so, it is perfectly possible. What, are you off?"

"Yes, Mr. Holmes; there is no rest for me until I have got to the bottom of the business. I suppose you have no hint to give me?"

"I have given you one."

"Which?"

"Well, I suggested a blind."

"But why, Mr. Holmes, why?"

"Ah, that's the question, of course. But I commend the idea to your mind. You might possibly find that there was something in it. You won't stop for dinner? Well, good-bye, and let us know how you get on."

Dinner was over, and the table cleared before Holmes alluded to the matter again. He had lit his pipe and held his slippered feet to the cheerful blaze of the fire. Suddenly he looked at his watch.

"I expect developments, Watson."

"When?"

"Now—within a few minutes. I dare say you thought I acted rather badly to Stanley Hopkins just now?"

"I trust your judgment."

"A very sensible reply, Watson. You must look at it this way: what I know is unofficial; what he knows is official. I have the right to private judgment, but he has none. He must disclose all, or he is a traitor to his service. In a doubtful case I would not put him in so painful a position, and so I reserve my information until my own mind is clear upon the matter."

"But when will that be?"

"The time has come. You will now be present at the last scene of a remarkable little drama."

There was a sound upon the stairs, and our door was opened to admit as fine a specimen of manhood as ever passed through it. He was a very tall young man, golden-moustached, blue-eyed, with a skin which had been burned by tropical suns, and a springy step which showed that the huge frame was as active as it was strong. He closed the door behind him, and then he stood with clenched hands and heaving breast, choking down some overmastering emotion.

"Sit down, Captain Croker. You got my telegram?"

Our visitor sank into an arm-chair and looked from one to the other of us with questioning eyes.

"I got your telegram, and I came at the hour you said. I heard that you had been down to the office. There was no getting away from you. Let's hear the worst. What are you going to do

"The door was opened to admit as fine a specimen of
manhood as ever passed through it."
Sidney Paget, *Strand Magazine*, 1904

31 Subtly racist, drawn from U.S. slang, the phrase meant "honest." The *Oxford English Dictionary* records its first usage in English writing in 1883.

He stood with clenched hands and heaving breast.
Frederick Dorr Steele, *Collier's*, 1904

with me? Arrest me? Speak out, man! You can't sit there and play with me like a cat with a mouse."

"Give him a cigar," said Holmes. "Bite on that, Captain Croker, and don't let your nerves run away with you. I should not sit here smoking with you if I thought that you were a common criminal, you may be sure of that. Be frank with me, and we may do some good. Play tricks with me, and I'll crush you."

"What do you wish me to do?"

"To give me a true account of all that happened at the Abbey Grange last night—a *true* account, mind you, with nothing added and nothing taken off. I know so much already that if you go one inch off the straight, I'll blow this police whistle from my window and the affair goes out of my hands forever."

The sailor thought for a little. Then he struck his leg with his great sunburned hand.

"I'll chance it," he cried. "I believe you are a man of your word, and a white man,[31] and I'll tell you the whole story. But one thing I will say first. So far as I am concerned, I regret nothing and I fear nothing, and I would do it all again and be proud of the job. Curse the beast, if he had as many lives as a cat, he would owe them all to me! But it's the lady, Mary—Mary Fraser—for never will I call her by that accursed name. When I think of getting her into trouble, I who would give my life just to bring one smile to her dear face, it's that that turns my soul into water. And yet—and yet—what less could I do? I'll tell you my story, gentlemen, and then I'll ask you, as man to man, what less could I do?

"I must go back a bit. You seem to know everything, so I expect that you know that I met her when she was a passenger and I was first officer of the *Rock of Gibraltar*. From the first day I met her, she was the only woman to me. Every day of that voyage I loved her more, and many a time since have I kneeled down in the darkness of the night watch and kissed the deck of that ship because I knew her dear feet had trod it. She was never engaged to me. She treated me as fairly as ever a woman treated a man. I have no complaint to make. It was all love on my side, and all good comradeship and friendship on hers. When we parted she was a free woman, but I could never again be a free man.

"Next time I came back from sea, I heard of her marriage. Well, why shouldn't she marry whom she liked? Title and money—who could carry them better than she? She was born for all that is beautiful and dainty. I didn't grieve over her marriage. I was not such a selfish hound as that. I just rejoiced that good luck had come her way, and that she had not thrown herself away on a penniless sailor.[32] That's how I loved Mary Fraser.

"Well, I never thought to see her again, but last voyage I was promoted, and the new boat was not yet launched, so I had to wait for a couple of months with my people at Sydenham. One day out in a country lane I met Theresa Wright, her old maid. She told me all about her, about him, about everything. I tell you, gentlemen, it nearly drove me mad. This drunken hound, that he should dare to raise his hand to her whose boots he was not worthy to lick! I met Theresa again. Then I met Mary herself—and met her again. Then she would meet me no more. But the other day I had a notice that I was to start on my voyage within a week, and I determined that I would see her once

32 Despite Croker's adoring portrait of her, some commentators suggest tartly that Mary Fraser of Adelaide, in throwing aside a man who truly loved her, got only what she deserved in marrying Sir Eustace. John Hall, for instance, in *Sidelights on Holmes*, sees her as little more than a social climber, commenting that "Miss Fraser evidently agreed with [Croker's] view, and the title and money outweighed Sir Eustace's manifest defects." Conversely, drawing only upon her character as evidence (and in flat contrast to Theresa Wright's statement that Sir Eustace's "title and his money" attracted Mary), David Brown comes to the unique conclusion that Mary herself was a wealthy woman and that Sir Eustace married her for her money. Others propose that Holmes was in fact taken in by Mary Fraser, who married Sir Eustace Brackenstall for his money and plotted to use Captain Croker to kill her new husband.

33 John Hall makes the case that that name was "bitch," and grants that even a person of delicate sensibilities "could not really blame Sir Eustace for the stray naughty word, considering that he had come down from his lonely bedroom to find his wife entertaining a jolly sailor in his ancestral dining-room."

34 Holmes earlier reached the conclusion that, because two glasses of wine were clear of beeswing and one was full of it, "only two glasses were used, and that the dregs of both were poured into a third glass, so as to give the false impression that three people had been here." With Captain Croker's explanation, it becomes evident that Holmes's conclusion was indeed correct, although one of the glasses likely still had a trace of beeswing. Yet his *reasoning* was actually incorrect. A little further thought would have shown Holmes that the beeswing would be heaviest not in the third glass, but in the first glass poured— that is, the one offered to Lady Brackenstall— and that only one glass would be clear of the sediment altogether.

Captain Croker never says that a third glass was poured as part of the plan. In fact, Theresa Wright, who was as "cool as ice," could well have used a glass herself! At any rate, Holmes appears to be accurate in assuming that the plotters decided to fill a third glass for appearances. The ensuing situation is where Holmes's thinking goes slightly awry. Instead of the third glass, filled partly from each of the other two, having the most sediment, it would contain the least, being poured from the top portion of the wine in each glass. Lady Brackenstall's glass would likely be the fullest, with only "a little [poured] between [her] lips," while Captain Croker's would have been vigorously drunk. The third glass would have been filled, then, by pouring off wine from Lady Brackenstall's glass into an empty third glass. Because her glass would

before I left. Theresa was always my friend, for she loved Mary and hated this villain almost as much as I did. From her I learned the ways of the house. Mary used to sit up reading in her own little room downstairs. I crept round there last night and scratched at the window. At first she would not open to me, but in her heart I know that now she loves me, and she could not leave me in the frosty night. She whispered to me to come round to the big front window, and I found it open before me, so as to let me into the dining-room. Again I heard from her own lips things that made my blood boil, and again I cursed this brute who mishandled the woman I loved. Well, gentlemen, I was standing with her just inside the window, in all innocence, as Heaven is my judge, when he rushed like a madman into the room, called her the vilest name that a man could use to a woman,33 and welted her across the face with the stick he had in his hand. I had sprung for the poker, and it was a fair fight between us. See here on my arm where his first blow fell. Then it was my turn, and I went through him as if he had been a rotten pumpkin. Do you think I was sorry? Not I! It was his life or mine; but far more than that, it was his life or hers, for how could I leave her in the power of this madman? That was how I killed him. Was I wrong? Well, then, what would either of you gentlemen have done if you had been in my position?

"She had screamed when he struck her, and that brought old Theresa down from the room above. There was a bottle of wine on the sideboard, and I opened it and poured a little between Mary's lips, for she was half dead with shock. Then I took a drop myself.34 Theresa was as cool as ice, and it was her plot as much as mine. We must make it appear that burglars had done the thing. Theresa kept on repeating our story to her mistress, while I swarmed up and cut the rope of the bell. Then I lashed her in her chair, and frayed out the end of the rope to make it look natural, else they would wonder how in the world a burglar could have got up there to cut it. Then I gathered up a few plates and pots of silver, to carry out the idea of the robbery, and there I left them, with orders to give the alarm when I had a quarter of an hour's start. I dropped the silver into the pond and made off for Sydenham, feeling that for once in my life I had done a real good night's work. And that's the truth and the whole truth, Mr. Holmes, if it costs me my neck."

Holmes smoked for some time in silence. Then he crossed the room and shook our visitor by the hand.

"That's what I think," said he. "I know that every word is true, for you have hardly said a word which I did not know. No one but an acrobat or a sailor could have got up to that bell-rope from the bracket, and no one but a sailor could have made the knots with which the cord was fastened to the chair. Only once had this lady been brought into contact with sailors, and that was on her voyage, and it was someone of her own class of life, since she was trying hard to shield him, and so showing that she loved him. You see how easy it was for me to lay my hands upon you when once I had started upon the right trail."

"I thought the police never could have seen through our dodge."

"And the police haven't; nor will they, to the best of my belief. Now, look here, Captain Croker, this is a very serious matter, though I am willing to admit that you acted under the most extreme provocation to which any man could be subjected. I am not sure that in defence of your own life your action will not be pronounced legitimate. However, that is for a British jury to decide. Meanwhile I have so much sympathy for you that if you choose to disappear in the next twenty-four hours I will promise you that no one will hinder you."

"And then it will all come out?"

"Certainly it will come out."

The sailor flushed with anger.

"What sort of proposal is that to make a man? I know enough of law to understand that Mary would be had as accomplice. Do you think I would leave her alone to face the music while I slunk away? No, sir; let them do their worst upon me, but for Heaven's sake, Mr. Holmes, find some way of keeping my poor Mary out of the courts."

Holmes for the second time held out his hand to the sailor.

"I was only testing you, and you ring true every time. Well, it is a great responsibility that I take upon myself, but I have given Hopkins an excellent hint, and if he can't avail himself of it I can do no more. See here, Captain Croker, we'll do this in due form of law. You are the prisoner. Watson, you are a British jury, and I never met a man who was more eminently fitted to represent one. I am the judge. Now, gentleman of the

have sat the longest, the sediment would have settled to the greatest extent in her glass.

A simple experiment conducted by this editor demonstrates the result: one glass nearly clear of sediment, one glass with a moderate amount (Captain Croker's glass), and one glass heavily charged with sediment (the remains of Lady Brackenstall's original glass). So, while Holmes reached the right conclusion—namely, that there was something wrong with the amount of beeswing in each glass—he certainly explained his reasoning incorrectly. Perhaps this was simply an insight produced by his "special knowledge and special powers."

35 "The voice of the people is the voice of God," a proverb attributed to William of Malmesbury in the twelfth century. Legal scholars credit the growth of the jury as an institution in the Middle Ages to its rôle in ameliorating the "divine" justice dispensed by the royal court.

36 "The Abbey Grange" was first published in 1904, and the events of the case were said by Watson to have occurred "towards the end of the winter of '97." D. Martin Dakin asks, "[H]ow could Watson have been authorised to let the cat out of the bag less than seven years later? Would it not make Croker liable to instant arrest, not to mention Lady Brackenstall and the maid? Possibly even Holmes himself as an accessory after?" The only solution, as far as Dakin sees it, is that Croker and the former Lady Brackenstall (now, presumably, Mrs. Croker) had died in the intervening seven years, thus releasing Watson to write his tale. Still, publication of "The Abbey Grange" would surely have upset Hopkins once he realised how Holmes had kept him in the dark—unless, Dakin suggests hopefully, Hopkins realised that Holmes's motives were pure, and that he had wished to spare Hopkins the unpleasantness of arresting and trying a man as decent as Croker.

Notwithstanding that the case was not published by Watson until 1904, the facts were apparently made known by him to his literary agent, Dr. Arthur Conan Doyle, who, in March 1899, published in the *Strand Magazine* a remarkably similar tale entitled "B.24" (later republished in Conan Doyle's *Round the Fire Stories)*, involving a beautiful woman who murders her sadistic husband and arranges for a burglar to be hanged for it.

jury, you have heard the evidence. Do you find the prisoner guilty or not guilty?"

"Not guilty, my lord," said I.

"*Vox populi, vox Dei*.[35] You are acquitted, Captain Croker. So long as the law does not find some other victim you are safe from me. Come back to this lady in a year, and may her future and yours justify us in the judgment which we have pronounced this night!"[36]

THE ADVENTURE OF THE SECOND STAIN[1]

In "The Naval Treaty," Dr. Watson mentions "The Adventure of the Second Stain" as a case involving "interests of such importance and implicat[ing] so many of the first families in the kingdom that for many years it will be impossible to make it public." That case is definitely not this case. (For one thing, the former was published in 1892, over a decade before the definite setting of 1904 given by Dr. Watson here.) Yet this "Second Stain" is also a case of great international importance and one of the few reported matters to involve Holmes with political crimes, the others being "The Naval Treaty" and "The Bruce-Partington Plans." The events that take place are reminiscent of those in Edgar Allan Poe's "Purloined Letter," and it becomes clear that Holmes—who, in A Study in Scarlet, *decries C. Auguste Dupin, the detective of the "Purloined Letter," as "a very inferior fellow"—is not above copying the tactics of the era's other famous detective. "The Second Stain" is also noteworthy as the last case handled by Holmes before his retirement. The news of Holmes's retirement closed the series of stories known as* The Return of Sherlock Holmes, *and the public had to wait until 1908 for any further tales of the detective.*

I HAD INTENDED the "Adventure of the Abbey Grange" to be the last of those exploits of my friend, Mr. Sherlock Holmes, which I should ever communicate to the public.[2] This resolution of mine was not due to any lack of material, since I have notes of many hundreds of cases to which I have never alluded, nor was it caused by any waning interest on the part of my readers in the singular personality and unique methods of this remarkable man. The real reason lay in the reluctance which Mr. Holmes has shown to the continued publication of his experiences. So long as he was in actual professional practice the records of his successes were of some practical value to him;[3] but since he has definitely retired from London and betaken himself to study and bee-farming on the Sussex Downs,[4] notoriety has become hateful to him, and he has peremptorily requested that his wishes in this matter should be strictly observed.[5] It was only upon my representing to him that I had given a promise that the "Adventure of the Second

1 "The Second Stain" was published in the *Strand Magazine* in December 1904 and in the January 28, 1905, issue of *Collier's Weekly.* The manuscript is in the possession of Haverford College.

2 "The Abbey Grange" was published in the *Strand Magazine* in September 1904, three months before publication of "The Second Stain."

3 Roger T. Clapp underlines the practical value of Watson's writing, observing in "The Curious Problem of the Railway Timetables" that, as a businessman, Holmes made shrewd use of Watson's abilities to generate new clients. Word of mouth from satisfied clients and referrals from Scotland Yard could only

create so much business, and outright advertising by professionals was considered unseemly. Holmes must have realised that publication of Watson's records of his cases would advertise the detective's services to the wider public. "That this was his underlying plan," Clapp goes on, "is quite clearly evidenced by his repeated—although subtle—suggestions that Watson select for his published stories those cases which best illustrated Holmes's deductive powers and resources . . . and his frequent complaints that Watson was sacrificing technical detail which would reflect Holmes's brilliance for the purely dramatic aspects of his cases." Holmes's constant apathy and even belittling of Watson's efforts (sprinkled with offhand suggestions of cases Watson might want to write up) was a psychological tactic, Clapp argues, designed to let Watson think the entire project was his own idea, not some manipulative marketing ploy.

4 Watson writes in the preface to *His Last Bow* (1917) that the farm was "five miles from Eastbourne," and in "The Lion's Mane," the villa is said to be "situated upon the southern slope of the Downs, commanding a great view of the Channel."

5 Edgar W. Smith adamantly disputes this image of Holmes as publicity-shy recluse. "The facts flatly contradict this assertion," Edgar W. Smith declares in "Dr. Watson and the Great Censorship." Although the public had been told that Holmes had died in 1891—in the story "The Final Problem," published in 1893—no sooner did Holmes retire than "The Empty House" was published in the *Strand*, revealing that Holmes, still very much alive, had returned to London in 1894 to solve Ronald Adair's murder. It may be that what Watson meant here was that Holmes did not want any publicity about the details of his *retirement*, and as will be seen in "The Lion's

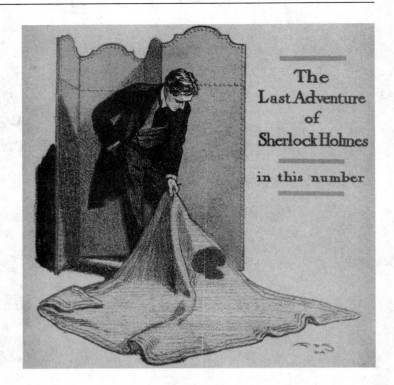

Frederick Dorr Steele, *Collier's*, 1905

Stain" should be published when the times were ripe, and pointed out to him that it is only appropriate that this long series of episodes should culminate in the most important international case which he has ever been called upon to handle,[6] that I at last succeeded in obtaining his consent that a carefully guarded account of the incident should at last be laid before the public. If in telling the story I seem to be somewhat vague in certain details, the public will readily understand that there is an excellent reason for my reticence.

It was, then, in a year, and even in a decade, that shall be nameless, that upon one Tuesday morning in autumn we found two visitors of European fame within the walls of our humble room in Baker Street. The one, austere, high-nosed, eagle-eyed, and dominant, was none other than the illustrious Lord Bellinger,[7] twice Premier of Britain. The other, dark, clear-cut, and elegant, hardly yet of middle age, and endowed with every beauty of body and of mind, was the Right Honourable Trelawney Hope, Secretary for European Affairs, and the most rising statesman in the country. They sat side by side upon our paper-littered settee, and it was easy to see from their worn and anxious faces that it was business of the most pressing importance which had brought them. The Premier's thin, blue-veined hands were clasped tightly over the ivory head of his umbrella, and his gaunt, ascetic face looked gloomily from Holmes to me. The European Secretary pulled nervously at his moustache[8] and fidgeted with the seals of his watch-chain.

"When I discovered my loss, Mr. Holmes, which was at eight o'clock this morning, I at once informed the Prime Minister. It was at his suggestion that we have both come to you."

"Have you informed the police?"

"No, sir," said the Prime Minister, with the quick, decisive manner for which he was famous.

"We have not done so, nor is it possible that we should do so. To inform the police must, in the long run, mean to inform the public. This is what we particularly desire to avoid."

"And why, sir?"

Mane," and "His Last Bow," both post-retirement tales, Holmes's place of refuge is obscure.

6 The manuscript originally read "one supreme example of the international influences he has exercised."

7 See the appendix on page 1222 for a discussion of the identities of "Lord Bellinger" and the "Right Honourable Trelawney Hope."

8 In the manuscript, Watson originally wrote that he "puffed a cigarette."

"They sat side by side."
Sidney Paget, *Strand Magazine*, 1904

9 The manuscript omits the phrase "until I missed the paper this morning."

"Because the document in question is of such immense importance that its publication might very easily—I might almost say probably—lead to European complications of the utmost moment. It is not too much to say that peace or war may hang upon the issue. Unless its recovery can be attended with the utmost secrecy, then it may as well not be recovered at all, for all that is aimed at by those who have taken it is that its contents should be generally known."

"I understand. Now, Mr. Trelawney Hope, I should be much obliged if you would tell me exactly the circumstances under which this document disappeared."

"That can be done in a very few words, Mr. Holmes. The letter—for it was a letter from a foreign potentate—was received six days ago. It was of such importance that I have never left it in my safe, but I have taken it across each evening to my house in Whitehall Terrace, and kept it in my bedroom in a locked despatch-box. It was there last night. Of that I am certain. I actually opened the box while I was dressing for dinner and saw the document inside. This morning it was gone. The despatch-box had stood beside the glass upon my dressing-table all night. I am a light sleeper, and so is my wife. We are both prepared to swear that no one could have entered the room during the night. And yet I repeat that the paper is gone."

"What time did you dine?"

"Half-past seven."

"How long was it before you went to bed?"

"My wife had gone to the theatre. I waited up for her. It was half-past eleven before we went to our room."

"Then for four hours the despatch-box had lain unguarded?"

"No one is ever permitted to enter that room save the housemaid in the morning, and my valet, or my wife's maid, during the rest of the day. They are both trusty servants who have been with us for some time. Besides, neither of them could possibly have known that there was anything more valuable than the ordinary departmental papers in my despatch-box."

"Who did know of the existence of that letter?"

"No one in the house."

"Surely your wife knew?"

"No, sir; I had said nothing to my wife until I missed the paper this morning."9

The Premier nodded approvingly.

"I have long known, sir, how high is your sense of public duty," said he. "I am convinced that in the case of a secret of this importance it would rise superior to the most intimate domestic ties."

The European Secretary bowed.

"You do me no more than justice, sir. Until this morning I have never breathed one word to my wife upon this matter."

"Could she have guessed?"

"No, Mr. Holmes, she could not have guessed—nor could anyone have guessed."

"Have you lost any documents before?"

"No, sir."

"Who is there in England who did know of the existence of this letter?"

"Each member of the Cabinet was informed of it yesterday; but the pledge of secrecy which attends every Cabinet meeting was increased by the solemn warning which was given by the Prime Minister. Good heavens, to think that within a few hours I should myself have lost it!" His handsome face was distorted with a spasm of despair, and his hands tore at his hair. For a moment we caught a glimpse of the natural man—impulsive, ardent, keenly sensitive. The next the aristocratic mask was replaced, and the gentle voice had returned. "Besides the members of the Cabinet there are two, or possibly three, departmental officials who know of the letter. No one else in England, Mr. Holmes, I assure you."

"But abroad?"

"I believe that no one abroad has seen it save the man who wrote it. I am well convinced that his Ministers—that the usual official channels have not been employed."

Holmes considered for some little time.

"Now, sir, I must ask you more particularly what this document is, and why its disappearance should have such momentous consequences?"

The two statesmen exchanged a quick glance, and the Premier's shaggy eyebrows gathered in a frown.

"Mr. Holmes, the envelope is a long, thin one of pale blue colour. There is a seal of red wax stamped with a crouching lion. It is addressed in large, bold handwriting to—"

"I fear, sir," said Holmes, "that, interesting and indeed

essential as these details are, my inquiries must go more to the root of things. What *was* the letter?"

"That is a State secret of the utmost importance, and I fear that I cannot tell you, nor do I see that it is necessary. If by the aid of the powers which you are said to possess you can find such an envelope as I describe with its enclosure, you will have deserved well of your country, and earned any reward which it lies in our power to bestow."

Sherlock Holmes rose with a smile.

"You are two of the most busy men in the country," said he, "and in my own small way I have also a good many calls upon me. I regret exceedingly that I cannot help you in this matter, and any continuation of this interview would be a waste of time."

The Premier sprang to his feet with that quick, fierce gleam of his deep-set eyes before which a Cabinet had cowered. "I am not accustomed—" he began, but mastered his anger and

"The Premier sprang to his feet."
Sidney Paget, *Strand Magazine*, 1904

resumed his seat. For a minute or more we all sat in silence. Then the old statesman shrugged his shoulders.

"We must accept your terms, Mr. Holmes. No doubt you are right, and it is unreasonable for us to expect you to act unless we give you our entire confidence."

"I agree with you, sir," said the younger statesman.

"Then I will tell you, relying entirely upon your honour and that of your colleague, Dr. Watson. I may appeal to your patriotism also, for I could not imagine a greater misfortune for the country than that this affair should come out."

"You may safely trust us."

"The letter, then, is from a certain foreign potentate who has been ruffled by some recent Colonial developments of this country. It has been written hurriedly and upon his own responsibility entirely. Inquiries have shown that his Ministers know nothing of the matter. At the same time it is couched in so unfortunate a manner, and certain phrases in it are of so provocative a character, that its publication would undoubtedly lead to a most dangerous state of feeling in this country. There would be such a ferment, sir, that I do not hesitate to say that within a week of the publication of that letter this country would be involved in a great war."

Holmes wrote a name upon a slip of paper and handed it to the Premier.

"Exactly. It was he.[10] And it is this letter—this letter which may well mean the expenditure of a thousand millions and the lives of a hundred thousand men—which has become lost in this unaccountable fashion."

"Have you informed the sender?"

"Yes, sir, a cipher telegram has been despatched."

"Perhaps he desires the publication of the letter."

"No, sir, we have strong reason to believe that he already understands that he has acted in an indiscreet and hot-headed manner. It would be a greater blow to him and to his country than to us if this letter were to come out."

"If this is so, whose interest is it that the letter should come out? Why should anyone desire to steal it or to publish it?"[11]

"There, Mr. Holmes, you take me into regions of high international politics. But if you consider the European situation you will have no difficulty in perceiving the motive. The whole of Europe is an armed camp. There is a double league[12]

10 Commentators suggest that the "foreign potentate" who sent the ill-advised letter must have been Kaiser Wilhelm II (1859–1941), also known as William II. The emperor of Germany and king of Prussia from 1888 to 1918, William had already earned himself a rocky reputation in Britain, despite the traditional friendship between the two nations. In 1895, he famously sent a telegram to South African president Paul Kruger congratulating him on his defeat of the British-supported Jameson Raid. The strengthening of Germany's navy and the expansion of its colonial interests further incited British suspicions, and the two countries began to feel the strain of competition. Germany's creation of the Triple Alliance with Italy and Austria-Hungary in 1881 (see "The Naval Treaty," note 19) divided the two nations still more, and in 1907 Britain countered by joining with Russia and longtime rival France to form the Triple Entente. The rising tensions between Germany and Britain, combined with William's lack of political tact, seem to lend themselves to a letter containing "provocative" phrases and of such import that it could involve Britain in a "great war." In fact, Germany and Britain would face off against each other in the Great War only eight years after publication of "The Second Stain."

11 This seems a stunningly naive statement by Holmes, who has just been informed of the highly delicate nature of the letter's contents. Aubrey C. Roberts expresses his disappointment in what he sees as only one of Holmes's "lapses" in "The Second Stain," chiding, "With questions like these right up front, it is a great wonder that the illustrious Premier did not take his business elsewhere, post haste."

12 This could allude either to the Triple Alliance or, more likely, to the then-Dual Alliance between France and Russia (preliminarily formed in 1891, and confirmed in 1894), which Britain had yet to join. See note 10, above. Scholars reach little concurrence on the dating of "The Second Stain," ranging from 1886 to 1894, although those proposing the later date do so on the existence of the Dual Alliance.

which makes a fair balance of military power. Great Britain holds the scales. If Britain were driven into war with one confederacy, it would assure the supremacy of the other confederacy, whether they joined in the war or not. Do you follow?"

"Very clearly. It is then the interest of the enemies of this potentate to secure and publish this letter, so as to make a breach between his country and ours?"

"Yes, sir."

"And to whom would this document be sent if it fell into the hands of an enemy?"

"To any of the great Chancelleries of Europe. It is probably speeding on its way thither at the present instant as fast as steam can take it."

Mr. Trelawney Hope dropped his head on his chest and groaned aloud. The Premier placed his hand kindly upon his shoulder.

"It is your misfortune, my dear fellow. No one can blame you. There is no precaution which you have neglected. Now, Mr. Holmes, you are in full possession of the facts. What course do you recommend?"

Holmes shook his head mournfully.

"You think, sir, that unless this document is recovered there will be war?"

"I think it is very probable."

"Then, sir, prepare for war."

"That is a hard saying, Mr. Holmes."

"Consider the facts, sir. It is inconceivable that it was taken after eleven-thirty at night, since I understand that Mr. Hope and his wife were both in the room from that hour until the loss was found out. It was taken, then, yesterday evening between seven-thirty and eleven-thirty, probably near the earlier hour, since whoever took it evidently knew that it was there and would naturally secure it as early as possible. Now, sir, if a document of this importance were taken at that hour, where can it be now? No one has any reason to retain it. It has been passed rapidly on to those who need it. What chance have we now to overtake or even to trace it? It is beyond our reach."

The Prime Minister rose from the settee.

"What you say is perfectly logical, Mr. Holmes. I feel that the matter is indeed out of our hands."

"Let us presume, for argument's sake, that the document was taken by the maid or by the valet—"

"They are both old and tried servants."

"I understand you to say that your room is on the second floor, that there is no entrance from without, and that from within no one could go up unobserved. It must, then, be somebody in the house who has taken it. To whom would the thief take it? To one of several international spies and secret agents, whose names are tolerably familiar to me. There are three[13] who may be said to be the heads of their profession. I will begin my research by going round and finding if each of them is at his post. If one is missing—especially if he has disappeared since last night—we will have some indication as to where the document has gone."

"Why should he be missing?" asked the European Secretary. "He would take the letter to an Embassy in London, as likely as not."

"I fancy not. These agents work independently, and their relations with the Embassies are often strained."

The Prime Minister nodded his acquiescence.

"I believe you are right, Mr. Holmes. He would take so valuable a prize to headquarters with his own hands. I think that your course of action is an excellent one. Meanwhile, Hope, we cannot neglect our other duties on account of this one misfortune. Should there be any fresh developments during the day we shall communicate with you, and you will no doubt let us know the results of your own inquiries."

The two statesmen bowed and walked gravely from the room.

When our illustrious visitors had departed, Holmes lit his pipe in silence and sat for some time lost in the deepest thought. I had opened the morning paper and was immersed in a sensational crime which had occurred in London the night before, when my friend gave an exclamation, sprang to his feet, and laid his pipe down upon the mantelpiece.

"Yes," said he, "there is no better way of approaching it. The situation is desperate, but not hopeless. Even now, if we could be sure which of them has taken it, it is just possible that it has not yet passed out of his hands. After all, it is a question of money with these fellows, and I have the British Treasury

13 "Half-a-dozen," according to the manuscript.

14 This would have been a pretty penny indeed! In *A Sherlock Holmes Handbook*, Christopher Redmond explains that income tax in the 1890s stood at 2.5 percent. Remembering that a pound consists of twenty shillings, each shilling twelve pennies, the tax was 2.5% x 240 pennies/pound, or 6 pennies per pound. Holmes's "another penny on the income tax" would be a one-sixth increase in the tax and would, according to Redmond's calculations, "add more than £2 million to the annual collections of only £13 million, out of a total public revenue of £100 million."

15 The first two reappear, with Oberstein as a principal character, in "The Bruce-Partington Plans."

The Treasury.
Queen's London (1897)

behind me. If it's on the market I'll buy it—if it means another penny on the income tax.[14] It is conceivable that the fellow might hold it back to see what bids come from this side before he tries his luck on the other. There are only those three capable of playing so bold a game; there are Oberstein, La Rothière, and Eduardo Lucas.[15] I will see each of them."

I glanced at my morning paper.

"Is that Eduardo Lucas of Godolphin Street?"

"Yes."

"You will not see him."

"Why not?"

"He was murdered in his house last night."

My friend has so often astonished me in the course of our adventures that it was with a sense of exultation that I realized how completely I had astonished him. He stared in amazement, and then snatched the paper from my hands. This was the paragraph which I had been engaged in reading when he rose from his chair:

MURDER IN WESTMINSTER

A crime of a mysterious character was committed last night at 16 Godolphin Street, one of the old-fashioned and secluded rows of eighteenth-century houses which lie between the river and the Abbey, almost in the shadow of the great Tower of the Houses of Parliament. This small but select mansion has been inhabited for some years by Mr. Eduardo Lucas, well known in society circles both on account of his charming personality and because he has the well-deserved reputation of being one of the best amateur tenors in the country. Mr. Lucas is an unmarried man, thirty-four years of age, and his establishment consists of Mrs. Pringle, an elderly housekeeper, and of Mitton, his valet. The former retires early and sleeps at the top of the house. The valet was out for the evening, visiting a friend at Hammersmith. From ten o'clock onwards Mr. Lucas had the house to himself. What occurred during that time has not yet transpired, but at a quarter to twelve Police-constable Barrett, passing along Godolphin Street, observed that the door of No. 16 was ajar. He knocked, but received no answer. Perceiving a light in the front room, he advanced into the passage and again knocked, but without reply. He then pushed open the door and entered. The room was in a state of wild disorder, the furniture being all swept to one side, and one chair lying on its back in the centre. Beside this chair, and still grasping one of its legs, lay the unfortunate tenant of the house. He had been stabbed to the heart and must have died instantly. The knife with which the crime had been committed was a curved Indian dagger, plucked down from a trophy of Oriental arms which adorned one of the walls. Robbery does not appear to have been the motive of the crime, for there had been no attempt to remove the valuable contents of the room. Mr. Eduardo Lucas was so well known and popular that his violent and mysterious fate will arouse painful interest and intense sympathy in a wide-spread circle of friends.

"Well, Watson, what do you make of this?" asked Holmes, after a long pause.

"It is an amazing coincidence."

"A coincidence! Here is one of the three men whom we had named as possible actors in this drama, and he meets a violent death during the very hours when we know that that drama was being enacted. The odds are enormous against its being coincidence. No figures could express them. No, my dear Watson, the two events are connected—*must* be connected. It is for us to find the connection."

16 Kensington and Notting Hill are the addresses of Oberstein and La Rothiere given in "The Bruce-Partington Plans."

17 A tray upon which food or drinks are served. From the French *salve*, to save; the Spanish *salva*, to taste food to detect poison; and the Latin *salvare*, to save.

"My dear Watson, the two events are connected—
must be connected."
Sidney Paget, *Strand Magazine*, 1904

"But now the official police must know all."

"Not at all. They know all they see at Godolphin Street. They know—and shall know—nothing of Whitehall Terrace. Only *we* know of both events, and can trace the relation between them. There is one obvious point which would, in any case, have turned my suspicions against Lucas. Godolphin Street, Westminster, is only a few minutes' walk from White-hall Terrace. The other secret agents whom I have named live in the extreme West End.[16] It was easier, therefore, for Lucas than for the others to establish a connection or receive a message from the European Secretary's household—a small thing, and yet where events are compressed into a few hours it may prove essential. Halloa! what have we here?"

Mrs. Hudson had appeared with a lady's card upon her salver.[17] Holmes glanced at it, raised his eyebrows, and handed it over to me.

"Ask Lady Hilda Trelawney Hope if she will be kind enough to step up," said he.

A moment later our modest apartment, already so distinguished that morning, was further honoured by the entrance of the most lovely woman in London. I had often heard of the beauty of the youngest daughter of the Duke of Belminster, but no description of it, and no contemplation of colourless photographs, had prepared me for the subtle, delicate charm and the beautiful colouring of that exquisite head. And yet as we saw it that autumn morning, it was not its beauty which would be the first thing to impress the observer. The cheek was lovely but it was paled with emotion; the eyes were bright, but it was the brightness of fever; the sensitive mouth was tight and drawn in an effort after self-command. Terror—not beauty—was what sprang first to the eye as our fair visitor stood framed for an instant in the open door.

"Has my husband been here, Mr. Holmes?"

"Yes, madam, he has been here."

"Mr. Holmes, I implore you not to tell him that I came here." Holmes bowed coldly and motioned the lady to a chair.

"Your ladyship places me in a very delicate position. I beg that you will sit down and tell me what you desire; but I fear that I cannot make any unconditional promise."

She swept across the room and seated herself with her back to the window. It was a queenly presence—tall, graceful, and intensely womanly.

"Mr. Holmes," she said—and her white-gloved hands clasped and unclasped as she spoke—"I will speak frankly to you in the hope that it may induce you to speak frankly in return. There is complete confidence between my husband and me on all matters save one. That one is politics. On this his lips are sealed. He tells me nothing. Now, I am aware that there was a most deplorable occurrence in our house last night. I know that a paper has disappeared. But because the matter is political my husband refuses to take me into his complete confidence. Now it is essential—essential, I say—that I should thoroughly understand it. You are the only other person, save only these politicians, who knows the true facts. I beg you, then, Mr. Holmes, to tell me exactly what has happened and what it will lead to. Tell me all, Mr. Holmes. Let no regard for your client's interests keep you silent, for I assure you that his

She seated herself with her back to the window.
Frederick Dorr Steele, *Collier's*, 1905

interests, if he would only see it, would be best served by taking me into his complete confidence. What was this paper that
was stolen?"

"Madam, what you ask me is really impossible."

She groaned and sank her face in her hands.

"You must see that this is so, madam. If your husband thinks
fit to keep you in the dark over this matter, is it for me, who
have only learned the true facts under the pledge of professional secrecy, to tell what he has withheld? It is not fair to ask
it. It is him whom you must ask."

"I have asked him. I come to you as a last resource. But without your telling me anything definite, Mr. Holmes, you may do
a great service if you would enlighten me on one point."

"What is it, madam?"

"Is my husband's political career likely to suffer through this
incident?"

"Well, madam, unless it is set right it may certainly have a very unfortunate effect."

"Ah!" She drew in her breath sharply as one whose doubts are resolved.

"One more question, Mr. Holmes. From an expression which my husband dropped in the first shock of this disaster I understood that terrible public consequences might arise from the loss of this document."[18]

"If he said so, I certainly cannot deny it."

"Of what nature are they?"

"Nay, madam, there again you ask me more than I can possibly answer."

"Then I will take up no more of your time. I cannot blame you, Mr. Holmes, for having refused to speak more freely, and you on your side will not, I am sure, think the worse of me because I desire, even against his will, to share my husband's anxieties. Once more I beg that you will say nothing of my visit." She looked back at us from the door, and I had a last impression of that beautiful haunted face, the startled eyes, and the drawn mouth. Then she was gone.

"Now, Watson, the fair sex is your department,"[19] said Holmes, with a smile, when the dwindling *frou-frou* of skirts had ended in the slam of the door. "What was the fair lady's game? What did she really want?"

"Surely her own statement is clear and her anxiety very natural."

"Hum! Think of her appearance, Watson, her manner, her suppressed excitement, her restlessness, her tenacity in asking questions. Remember that she comes of a caste who do not lightly show emotion."

"She was certainly much moved."

"Remember also the curious earnestness with which she assured us that it was best for her husband that she should know all. What did she mean by that? And you must have observed, Watson, how she manœuvred to have the light at her back. She did not wish us to read her expression."

"Yes; she chose the one chair in the room."[20]

"And yet the motives of women are so inscrutable. You remember the woman at Margate whom I suspected for the same reason. No powder on her nose—that proved to be the correct solution. How can you build on such a quicksand?

18 Lady Hilda's demeanour here departs markedly from that of today's political wives, who tend to be somewhat savvier about their husbands' affairs. Her naivete about what the theft of the letter might imply is surely a product of the age, D. Martin Dakin comments, observing that "Nowadays any politician fortunate enough to be married to a society beauty would be sure to have her active assistance in his election campaign and writing part of his address to his constituents."

19 The manuscript originally read, " 'Now, Watson, what's the meaning of this?' asked Holmes."

20 Watson means the one chair in the room that would have put the light at her back, not that there are no other chairs present. Holmes and Watson's armchairs are mentioned in "The Three Gables," "The Five Orange Pips," and "The 'Gloria Scott'." The basket chair, generally used by clients, is noted in "The Noble Bachelor" and "The Blue Carbuncle." Holmes and Watson would (as gentlemen) clearly have been standing when she entered the room, and Lady Hilda thus had a choice of at least three chairs.

"She looked back at us from the door."
Sidney Paget, *Strand Magazine*, 1904

Their most trivial action may mean volumes, or their most extraordinary conduct may depend upon a hairpin or a curling-tongs. Good-morning, Watson."

"You are off?"

"Yes, I will while away the morning at Godolphin Street with our friends of the regular establishment. With Eduardo Lucas lies the solution of our problem, though I must admit that I have not an inkling as to what form it may take. It is a capital mistake to theorize in advance of the facts. Do you stay on guard, my good Watson, and receive any fresh visitors. I'll join you at lunch if I am able."

All that day and the next and the next Holmes was in a mood which his friends would call taciturn, and others morose. He ran out and ran in, smoked incessantly, played snatches on his violin, sank into reveries, devoured sandwiches at irregular hours, and hardly answered the casual questions which I put to him. It was evident to me that things were not going well with him or his quest. He would say nothing of the case, and it was from the papers that I learned the particulars of the inquest, and the arrest with the subsequent release of John Mitton, the valet of the deceased. The coroner's jury brought in the obvious "Wilful Murder," but the parties remained as unknown as ever. No motive was suggested. The room was full of articles of value, but none had been taken. The dead man's papers had not been tampered with. They were carefully examined, and showed that he was a keen student of international politics, an indefatigable gossip, a remarkable linguist, and an untiring letter-writer. He had been on intimate terms with the leading politicians of several countries. But nothing sensational was discovered among the documents which filled his drawers. As to his relations with women, they appeared to have been promiscuous but superficial. He had many acquaintances among them, but few friends, and no one whom he loved. His habits were regular, his conduct inoffensive. His death was an absolute mystery and likely to remain so.

As to the arrest of John Mitton, the valet, it was a council of despair as an alternative to absolute inaction. But no case could be sustained against him. He had visited friends in Hammersmith that night. The *alibi* was complete. It is true that he started home at an hour which should have brought him to Westminster before the time when the crime was discovered, but his own explanation that he had walked part of the way seemed probable enough in view of the fineness of the night. He had actually arrived at twelve o'clock, and appeared to be overwhelmed by the unexpected tragedy. He had always been on good terms with his master. Several of the dead man's possessions—notably a small case of razors—had been found in the valet's boxes, but he explained that they had been presents from the deceased, and the housekeeper was able to corroborate the story. Mitton had been in Lucas's employment for three years. It was noticeable that Lucas did not take Mitton on the Continent with him. Sometimes he visited Paris for three months on end, but Mitton was left in charge of the Godolphin Street house. As to the housekeeper, she had heard nothing on the night of the crime. If her master had a visitor, he had himself admitted him.

So for three mornings the mystery remained, so far as I could follow it in the papers. If Holmes knew more, he kept his own counsel, but, as he told me that Inspector Lestrade had taken him into his confidence in the case, I knew that he was in close touch with every development. Upon the fourth day there appeared a long telegram from Paris which seemed to solve the whole question.

A discovery has just been made by the Parisian police [said the *Daily Telegraph*] which raises the veil which hung round the tragic fate of Mr. Eduardo Lucas, who met his death by violence last Monday night at Godolphin Street, Westminster. Our readers will remember that the deceased gentleman was found stabbed in his room, and that some suspicion attached to his valet, but that the case broke down on an *alibi*. Yesterday a lady, who has been known as Mme. Henri Fournaye, occupying a small villa in the Rue Austerlitz, was reported to the authorities by her servants as being insane. An examination showed she had indeed developed mania of a dangerous and permanent form. On inquiry the police have discovered that Mme. Henri Fournaye only returned from a journey to London on Tuesday last, and there is evidence to connect her with the crime at Westminster. A comparison of photographs has proved conclusively that M. Henri Fournaye and Eduardo Lucas were really one and the same person, and that the deceased had for some reason lived a double life in London and Paris. Mme. Fournaye, who is of Creole origin, is of an extremely excitable nature, and has suffered in the past from attacks of jealousy which have amounted to frenzy. It is conjectured that it was in one of these that she committed the terrible crime which has caused such a sensation in London. Her movements upon the Monday night have not yet been traced, but it is undoubted that a woman answering to her description attracted much attention at Charing Cross Station on Tuesday morning by the wildness of her appearance and the violence of her gestures. It is probable, therefore, that the crime was either committed when insane, or that its immediate effect was to drive the unhappy woman out of her mind. At present she is unable to give any coherent account of the past, and the doctors hold out no hopes of the re-establishment of her reason. There is evidence that a woman, who might have been Mme. Fournaye, was seen for some hours upon Monday night watching the house in Godolphin Street.[21]

"What do you think of that, Holmes?" I had read the account aloud to him, while he finished his breakfast.

"My dear Watson," said he, as he rose from the table and paced up and down the room, "you are most long-suffering, but if I have told you nothing in the last three days, it is because there is nothing to tell. Even now this report from Paris does not help us much."

"Surely it is final as regards the man's death."

"The man's death is a mere incident—a trivial episode—in comparison with our real task, which is to trace this document and save a European catastrophe. Only one important thing has happened in the last three days, and that is that nothing has happened.[22] I get reports almost hourly from the Government, and it is certain that nowhere in Europe is there any sign of trouble. Now, if this letter were loose—no, it *can't* be loose—but if it isn't loose, where can it be? Who has it? Why is it held back? That's the question that beats in my brain like a hammer. Was it, indeed, a coincidence that Lucas should meet his death on the night when the letter disappeared? Did the letter ever reach him? If so, why is it not among his papers? Did this mad wife of his carry it off with her? If so, is it in her house in Paris? How could I search for it without the French police having their suspicions aroused? It is a case, my dear Watson, where the law is as dangerous to us as the criminals are. Every man's hand is against us, and yet the interests at stake are colossal. Should I bring it to a successful conclusion, it will certainly represent the crowning glory of my career. Ah, here is my latest from the front!" He glanced hurriedly at the note which had been handed in. "Halloa! Lestrade seems to have observed something of interest. Put on your hat, Watson, and we will stroll down together to Westminster."

21 Who would have possibly noticed Mme. Fournaye—until now, a person of seemingly no importance—at both Godolphin Street on Monday and Charing Cross Station on Tuesday? Certainly she appears undeserving of attention. It is also unlikely, argues George J. McCormack, that responsible doctors would have so quickly concluded that she was permanently insane. Based on such dubious reporting, McCormack proposes that the entire newspaper article was a fabrication, planted by Holmes. McCormack goes on to conclude that Lady Hilda herself murdered Lucas and that Watson invented the story of the French wife at Holmes's insistence, to shield her and to conceal his role as a criminal accessory.

22 Felix Morley points out that Holmes might have remembered the value of his own observation, in "Silver Blaze," that a dog that "did nothing in the night-time" could prove a vital piece of "negative evidence." In this situation, Morley writes, "Holmes failed to make an equally brilliant—and obvious—deduction."

23 A rug made of coarse wool or wool and cotton.

It was my first visit to the scene of the crime—a high, dingy, narrow-chested house, prim, formal, and solid, like the century which gave it birth. Lestrade's bulldog features gazed out at us from the front window, and he greeted us warmly when a big constable had opened the door and let us in. The room into which we were shown was that in which the crime had been committed, but no trace of it now remained, save an ugly, irregular stain upon the carpet. This carpet was a small square drugget²³ in the centre of the room, surrounded by a broad expanse of beautiful, old-fashioned, wood-flooring in square blocks, highly polished. Over the fireplace was a magnificent trophy of weapons, one of which had been used on that tragic night. In the window was a sumptuous writing-desk, and every detail of the apartment, the pictures, the rugs, and the hangings, all pointed to a taste which was luxurious to the verge of effeminacy.

"Seen the Paris news?" asked Lestrade.

Holmes nodded.

"Our French friends seem to have touched the spot this time. No doubt it's just as they say. She knocked at the door—surprise visit, I guess, for he kept his life in water-tight compartments—he let her in, couldn't keep her in the street. She told him how she had traced him, reproached him. One thing led to another, and then with that dagger so handy the end soon came. It wasn't all done in an instant, though, for these chairs were all swept over yonder, and he had one in his hand as if he had tried to hold her off with it. We've got it all clear as if we had seen it."

Holmes raised his eyebrows.

"And yet you have sent for me?"

"Ah, yes, that's another matter—a mere trifle, but the sort of thing you take an interest in—queer, you know, and what you might call freakish. It has nothing to do with the main fact—can't have, on the face of it."

"What is it, then?"

"Well, you know, after a crime of this sort we are very careful to keep things in their position. Nothing has been moved. Officer in charge here day and night. This morning, as the man was buried and the investigation over—so far as this room is concerned—we thought we could tidy up a bit. This carpet.

You see, it is not fastened down; only just laid there. We had occasion to raise it. We found—"

"Yes? You found—"

Holmes's face grew tense with anxiety.

"Well, I'm sure you would never guess in a hundred years what we did find. You see that stain on the carpet? Well, a great deal must have soaked through, must it not?"

"Undoubtedly it must."

"Well, you will be surprised to hear that there is no stain on the white woodwork to correspond."

"No stain! But there must—"

"Yes; so you would say. But the fact remains that there isn't."

He took the corner of the carpet in his hand and, turning it over, he showed that it was indeed as he said.

"He took the corner of the carpet in his hand."
Sidney Paget, *Strand Magazine*, 1904

"There is a second stain."
Frederick Dorr Steele, *Collier's*, 1905

"But the under side is as stained as the upper. It must have left a mark."

Lestrade chuckled with delight at having puzzled the famous expert.

"Now I'll show you the explanation. There *is* a second stain, but it does not correspond with the other. See for yourself." As he spoke he turned over another portion of the carpet, and there, sure enough, was a great crimson spill upon the square white facing of the old-fashioned floor. "What do you make of that, Mr. Holmes?"

"Why, it is simple enough. The two stains did correspond, but the carpet has been turned round. As it was square and unfastened, it was easily done."

"The official police don't need you, Mr. Holmes, to tell them that the carpet must have been turned round. That's clear enough, for the stains lie above each other—if you lay it over this way. But what I want to know is, who shifted the carpet, and why?"

I could see from Holmes's rigid face that he was vibrating with inward excitement.

"Look here, Lestrade!" said he, "has that constable in the passage been in charge of the place all the time?"

"Yes, he has."

"Well, take my advice. Examine him carefully. Don't do it before us. We'll wait here. You take him into the back room. You'll be more likely to get a confession out of him alone. Ask him how he dared to admit people and leave them alone in this room. Don't ask him if he has done it. Take it for granted. Tell him you *know* someone has been here. Press him. Tell him that a full confession is his only chance of forgiveness. Do exactly what I tell you!"

"By George, if he knows I'll have it out of him!" cried Lestrade. He darted into the hall, and a few moments later his bullying voice sounded from the back room.

"Now, Watson, now!" cried Holmes, with frenzied eagerness. All the demoniacal force of the man masked behind that listless manner burst out in a paroxysm of energy. He tore the drugget from the floor, and in an instant was down on his hands and knees clawing at each of the squares of wood beneath it. One turned sideways as he dug his nails into the edge of it. It hinged back like the lid of a box. A small black cavity opened beneath it. Holmes plunged his eager hand into it and drew it out with a bitter snarl of anger and disappointment. It was empty.

"Quick, Watson, quick! Get it back again!" The wooden lid was replaced, and the drugget had only just been drawn straight when Lestrade's voice was heard in the passage. He found Holmes leaning languidly against the mantelpiece, resigned and patient, endeavouring to conceal his irrepressible yawns.

"Sorry to keep you waiting, Mr. Holmes. I can see that you are bored to death with the whole affair. Well, he has confessed all right. Come in here, MacPherson. Let these gentlemen hear of your most inexcusable conduct."

The big constable, very hot and penitent, sidled into the room.

"I meant no harm, sir, I'm sure. The young woman came to the door last evening—mistook the house, she did. And then we got talking. It's lonesome, when you're on duty here all day."

"Well, what happened then?"

"She wanted to see where the crime was done—had read about it in the papers, she said. She was a very respectable,

"It hinged back like the lid of a box."
Sidney Paget, *Strand Magazine*, 1904

well-spoken young woman, sir, and I saw no harm in letting her have a peep. When she saw that mark on the carpet, down she dropped on the floor, and lay as if she were dead. I ran to the back and got some water, but I could not bring her to. Then I went round the corner to the Ivy Plant for some brandy, and by the time I had brought it back the young woman had recovered and was off—ashamed of herself, I daresay, and dared not face me!"

"How about moving that drugget?"

"Well, sir, it was a bit rumpled, certainly, when I came back. You see, she fell on it and it lies on a polished floor with nothing to keep it in place. I straightened it out afterwards."

"It's a lesson to you that you can't deceive me, Constable MacPherson," said Lestrade, with dignity. "No doubt you thought that your breach of duty could never be discovered, and yet a mere glance at that drugget was enough to convince me that someone had been admitted to the room. It's lucky for you, my man, that nothing is missing, or you would find yourself in Queer Street.[24] I'm sorry to have called you down over such a petty business, Mr. Holmes, but I thought the point of the second stain not corresponding with the first would interest you."

"Certainly it was most interesting. Has this woman only been here once, Constable?"

"Yes, sir, only once."

"Who was she?"

"Don't know the name, sir. Was answering an advertisement

24 E. Cobham Brewer's *Dictionary of Phrase and Fable* supplies that "to live in Queer Street" meant "To be of doubtful solvency. To be one marked in a tradesman's ledger with a *quære* (inquire), meaning, make inquiries about this customer." Similarly, in Robert Louis Stevenson's *Strange Case of Dr. Jekyll and Mr. Hyde*, one character remarks, "No, sir, I make it a rule of mine: the more it looks like Queer Street, the less I ask." Although historian Graham Robb ventures that the word "queer" had come to imply homosexuality as early as 1894 (see "The Greek Interpreter," note 8), the implication was far from universal, and generally the word was still used to refer to irregularity or to counterfeit goods.

He found Holmes leaning languidly against the mantelpiece.
Charles Raymond Macaulay, *Return of Sherlock Holmes*
(McClure Phillips), 1905

25 In English editions, the word "incident" is "accident."

about typewriting and came to the wrong number—very pleasant, genteel young woman, sir."

"Tall? Handsome?"

"Yes, sir; she was a well-grown young woman. I suppose you might say she was handsome. Perhaps some would say she was very handsome. 'Oh, officer, do let me have a peep!' says she. She had pretty, coaxing ways, as you might say, and I thought there was no harm in letting her just put her head through the door."

"How was she dressed?"

"Quiet, sir—a long mantle down to her feet."

"What time was it?"

"It was just growing dusk at the time. They were lighting the lamps as I came back with the brandy."

"Very good," said Holmes. "Come, Watson, I think that we have more important work elsewhere."

As we left the house Lestrade remained in the front room, while the repentant constable opened the door to let us out. Holmes turned on the step and held up something in his hand. The constable stared intently.

"Good Lord, sir!" he cried, with amazement on his face. Holmes put his finger on his lips, replaced his hand in his breast-pocket, and burst out laughing as we turned down the street. "Excellent!" said he. "Come, friend Watson, the curtain rings up for the last act. You will be relieved to hear that there will be no war, that the Right Honourable Trelawney Hope will suffer no setback in his brilliant career, that the indiscreet Sovereign will receive no punishment for his indiscretion, that the Prime Minister will have no European complication to deal with, and that with a little tact and management upon our part nobody will be a penny the worse for what might have been a very ugly incident."[25]

My mind filled with admiration for this extraordinary man.

"You have solved it!" I cried.

"Hardly that, Watson. There are some points which are as dark as ever. But we have so much that it will be our own fault if we cannot get the rest. We will go straight to Whitehall Terrace and bring the matter to a head."

When we arrived at the residence of the European Secretary it was for Lady Hilda Trelawney Hope that Sherlock Holmes inquired. We were shown into the morning-room.

"Mr. Holmes!" said the lady, and her face was pink with her indignation. "This is surely most unfair and ungenerous upon your part. I desired, as I have explained, to keep my visit to you a secret, lest my husband should think that I was intruding into his affairs. And yet you compromise me by coming here and so showing that there are business relations between us."

"Unfortunately, madam, I had no possible alternative. I have been commissioned to recover this immensely important paper. I must therefore ask you, madam, to be kind enough to place it in my hands."

The lady sprang to her feet, with the colour all dashed in an instant from her beautiful face. Her eyes glazed—she tottered—I thought that she would faint. Then with a grand effort she rallied from the shock, and a supreme astonishment and indignation chased every other expression from her features.

"You—you insult me, Mr. Holmes."

"Come, come, madam, it is useless. Give up the letter."

She darted to the bell.

"The butler shall show you out."

"Madam, I have been commissioned to recover this
immensely important paper."
Frederick Dorr Steele, *Collier's*, 1905

"You insult me, Mr. Holmes."
Sidney Paget, *Strand Magazine*, 1904

"Do not ring, Lady Hilda. If you do, then all my earnest efforts to avoid a scandal will be frustrated. Give up the letter, and all will be set right. If you will work with me I can arrange everything. If you work against me, I must expose you."

She stood grandly defiant, a queenly figure, her eyes fixed upon his as if she would read his very soul. Her hand was on the bell, but she had forborne to ring it.

"You are trying to frighten me. It is not a very manly thing, Mr. Holmes, to come here and browbeat a woman. You say that you know something. What is it that you know?"

"Pray sit down, madam. You will hurt yourself there if you fall. I will not speak until you sit down. Thank you."

"I give you five minutes, Mr. Holmes."

"One is enough, Lady Hilda. I know of your visit to Eduardo Lucas, and of your giving him this document, of your ingenious return to the room last night, and of the manner in which you took the letter from the hiding-place under the carpet."

She stared at him with an ashen face and gulped twice before she could speak.

"You are mad, Mr. Holmes—you are mad!" she cried, at last.

He drew a small piece of cardboard from his pocket. It was the face of a woman cut out of a portrait.

"I have carried this because I thought it might be useful," said he.[26] "The policeman has recognised it."

She gave a gasp, and her head dropped back in the chair.

"Come, Lady Hilda. You have the letter. The matter may still be adjusted. I have no desire to bring trouble to you. My duty ends when I have returned the lost letter to your husband. Take my advice and be frank with me; it is your only chance."

Her courage was admirable. Even now she would not own defeat.[27]

"I tell you again, Mr. Holmes, that you are under some absurd illusion."

Holmes rose from his chair.

"I am sorry for you, Lady Hilda. I have done my best for you; I can see that it is all in vain."

He rang the bell. The butler entered.

"Is Mr. Trelawney Hope at home?"

"He will be home, sir, at a quarter to one."

Holmes glanced at his watch.

"Still a quarter of an hour," said he. "Very good, I shall wait."

The butler had hardly closed the door behind him when Lady Hilda was down on her knees at Holmes's feet, her hands outstretched, her beautiful face upturned and wet with her tears.

"Oh, spare me, Mr. Holmes! Spare me!" she pleaded, in a frenzy of supplication. "For heaven's sake, don't tell him! I love him so! I would not bring one shadow on his life, and this I know would break his noble heart."

Holmes raised the lady. "I am thankful, madam, that you have come to your senses even at this last moment! There is not an instant to lose. Where is the letter?"

She darted across to a writing-desk, unlocked it, and drew out a long blue envelope.

"Here it is, Mr. Holmes. Would to heaven I had never seen it!"

26 This is prescient of Holmes, for there is surely no prior hint that any third party might be called upon to identify any of the principals of the case. Did he also have a photograph of Trelawney Hope?

27 At this point in the manuscript, a substantial portion appears in a handwriting that is not that of Conan Doyle, the scrivener of virtually all of the other manuscripts. Several suggestions were considered, including that the writing was that of Alfred Wood, Conan Doyle's secretary; that of Sir Arthur but his so-called resting hand; or even that of Dr. Watson! The editors of *Baker Street Miscellanea*, however, wisely asked Dame Jean Conan Doyle, the daughter of Arthur Conan Doyle, who promptly identified it as that of her mother, then Jean Leckie, later Sir Arthur's second wife.

28 The phrase "written before my marriage" was added to the manuscript.

29 B. George Isen asserts that the letter was written to Eduardo Lucas himself, a "man whose relations with women . . . appeared to have been promiscuous but superficial." Isen concludes that Lady Hilda killed Lucas mere moments before the "French wife" burst into the room but that Holmes, out of concern for both Lady Hilda and England, concealed the facts (rather as he did for the mysterious lady culprit in "Charles Augustus Milverton").

30 This sentence has been added to the original manuscript, and nothing further is said about Lucas's spy. Who was the spy? Surprisingly, observes B. George Isen, no one—not even Holmes—seems significantly worried about "this dangerous creature in the presumably secure government office who not only had known that Mr. Trelawney Hope always carried the missive with him but knew, too, that Hope deposited it in his dispatch box at home." Surely Holmes must have sought to discover the identity of the spy and expose him or her to the government.

John Hall, in *Sidelights on Holmes*, suggests that while Holmes would not have dropped the matter, exposure may have been unnecessary. "Perhaps Holmes thought that, with Lucas dead and thus any hold he had over the spy gone, the furore [over Lucas's death] would ensure that the spy behaved himself in the future. It might even be that Holmes had a discreet word with the offender, and satisfied himself that there would be no further lapses."

31 This sentence was added to the manuscript in the handwriting of Conan Doyle.

"How can we return it?" Holmes muttered. "Quick, quick, we must think of some way! Where is the despatch-box?"

"Still in his bedroom."

"What a stroke of luck! Quick, madam, bring it here!"

A moment later she had appeared with a red flat box in her hand. "How did you open it before? You have a duplicate key? Yes, of course you have. Open it!"

From out of her bosom Lady Hilda had drawn a small key. The box flew open. It was stuffed with papers. Holmes thrust the blue envelope deep down into the heart of them, between the leaves of some other document. The box was shut, locked, and returned to his bedroom.

"Now we are ready for him," said Holmes; "we have still ten minutes. I am going far to screen you, Lady Hilda. In return you will spend the time in telling me frankly the real meaning of this extraordinary affair."

"Mr. Holmes, I will tell you everything," cried the lady. "Oh, Mr. Holmes, I would cut off my right hand before I gave him a moment of sorrow! There is no woman in all London who loves her husband as I do, and yet if he knew how I have acted—how I have been compelled to act—he would never forgive me. For his own honour stands so high that he could not forget or pardon a lapse in another. Help me, Mr. Holmes! My happiness, his happiness, our very lives are at stake!"

"Quick, madam, the time grows short!"

"It was a letter of mine, Mr. Holmes, an indiscreet letter written before my marriage[28]—a foolish letter, a letter of an impulsive, loving girl.[29] I meant no harm, and yet he would have thought it criminal. Had he read that letter his confidence would have been forever destroyed. It is years since I wrote it. I had thought that the whole matter was forgotten. Then at last I heard from this man, Lucas, that it had passed into his hands, and that he would lay it before my husband. I implored his mercy. He said that he would return my letter if I would bring him a certain document which he described in my husband's despatch-box. He had some spy in the office who had told him of its existence.[30] He assured me that no harm could come to my husband. Put yourself in my position, Mr. Holmes! What was I to do?"

"Take your husband into your confidence."[31]

"I could not, Mr. Holmes, I could not! On the one side

seemed certain ruin; on the other, terrible as it seemed to take my husband's papers, still in a matter of politics I could not understand the consequences, while in a matter of love and trust they were only too clear to me. I did it, Mr. Holmes! I took an impression of his key; this man, Lucas, furnished a duplicate. I opened his despatch-box, took the paper, and conveyed it to Godolphin Street."

"What happened there, madam?"

"I tapped at the door as agreed. Lucas opened it. I followed him into his room, leaving the hall door ajar behind me, for I feared to be alone with the man. I remembered that there was a woman outside as I entered.[32] Our business was soon done. He had my letter on his desk; I handed him the document. He gave me the letter. At this instant there was a sound at the door. There were steps in the passage. Lucas quickly turned back the drugget, thrust the document into some hiding-place there, and covered it over.

"What happened after that is like some fearful dream. I have a vision of a dark, frantic face, of a woman's voice, which screamed in French, 'My waiting is not in vain.[33] At last, at last I have found you with her!' There was a savage struggle. I saw him with a chair in his hand, a knife gleamed in hers. I rushed from the horrible scene, ran from the house, and only next morning in the paper did I learn the dreadful result.[34] That night I was happy, for I had my letter, and I had not seen yet what the future would bring.

"It was the next morning that I realized that I had only exchanged one trouble for another. My husband's anguish at the loss of his paper went to my heart. I could hardly prevent myself from there and then kneeling down at his feet and telling him what I had done. But that again would mean a confession of the past. I came to you that morning in order to understand the full enormity of my offence. From the instant that I grasped it my whole mind was turned to the one thought of getting back my husband's paper. It must still be where Lucas had placed it, for it was concealed before this dreadful woman entered the room. If it had not been for her coming, I should not have known where his hiding-place was. How was I to get into the room? For two days I watched the place, but the door was never left open. Last night I made a last attempt. What I did and how I succeeded, you have already learned. I

32 This sentence does not appear in the original manuscript.

33 This sentence also was added to the original manuscript.

34 And so it emerges that Watson, in judging Lucas's murder "an amazing coincidence," was right after all, whereas an uncharacteristically rash Holmes, who insisted, "No, my dear Watson, the two events are connected—must be connected," was in the wrong. In considering Lucas's death, Nathan L. Bengis writes in "Sherlock Stays After School," the practical Watson took a less cerebral approach and came to the correct conclusion "but allowed himself to be shouted down" by Holmes, who normally lectures against leaping to conclusions but did the opposite here. Of course, even upon learning the true sequence of events, Holmes declines to give his friend proper credit. Bengis complains, "One would expect Holmes to have been big enough to admit his error to Watson in some words as these: 'You were perfectly right. It was an amazing coincidence. I was too rash in jumping to conclusions.' Watson, of course, was too fine to recriminate his friend with 'I told you so,' but he had been made so often to eat humble pie that for once he should have insisted that his friend eat some!"

35 The phrase "and thought of destroying it" is not in the manuscript.

36 Scornfully, D. Martin Dakin deems Lady Hilda "one of the most dim-witted of lovelies" for seeing no way out of her dilemma. "As she had a duplicate key and the dispatch-box was still in the bedroom, there was no reason why she should not have put it back on the quiet at any time, without waiting for Holmes to do it for her."

37 "His" in some American editions.

brought the paper back with me, and thought of destroying it,[35] since I could see no way of returning it without confessing my guilt to my husband.[36] Heavens, I hear his step upon the stair!"

The European Secretary burst excitedly into the room.

"Any news, Mr. Holmes, any news?" he cried.

"I have some hopes."

"Ah, thank heaven!" His face became radiant. "The Prime Minister is lunching with me. May he share your hopes? He has nerves of steel, and yet I know that he has hardly slept since this terrible event. Jacobs, will you ask the Prime Minister to come up? As to you, dear, I fear that this is a matter of politics. We will join you in a few minutes in the dining-room."

The Prime Minister's manner was subdued, but I could see by the gleam of his eyes and the twitchings of his bony hands that he shared the excitement of his young colleague.

"I understand that you have something to report, Mr. Holmes?"

"Purely negative as yet," my friend answered. "I have inquired at every point where it might be, and I am sure that there is no danger to be apprehended."

"But that is not enough, Mr. Holmes. We cannot live forever on such a volcano. We must have something definite."

"I am in hopes of getting it. That is why I am here. The more I think of the matter the more convinced I am that the letter has never left this house."

"Mr. Holmes!"

"If it had it would certainly have been public by now."

"But why should anyone take it in order to keep it in this[37] house?"

"I am not convinced that anyone did take it."

"Then how could it leave the despatch-box?"

"I am not convinced that it ever did leave the despatch-box."

"Mr. Holmes, this joking is very ill-timed. You have my assurance that it left the box."

"Have you examined the box since Tuesday morning?"

"No; it was not necessary."

"You may conceivably have overlooked it."

"Impossible, I say."

"But I am not convinced of it; I have known such things to happen. I presume there are other papers there. Well, it may have got mixed with them."

"It was on the top."

"Someone may have shaken the box and displaced it."

"No, no; I had everything out."

"Surely it is easily decided, Hope," said the Premier. "Let us have the despatch-box brought in."

The Secretary rang the bell.

"Jacobs, bring down my despatch-box. This is a farcical waste of time, but still, if nothing else will satisfy you, it shall be done. Thank you, Jacobs; put it here. I have always had the key on my watch-chain. Here are the papers, you see. Letter from Lord Merrow, report from Sir Charles Hardy, memorandum from Belgrade, note on the Russo-German grain taxes, letter from Madrid, note from Lord Flowers—Good heavens! what is this? Lord Bellinger! Lord Bellinger!"

The Premier snatched the blue envelope from his hand.

"The Premier snatched the blue envelope from his hand."
Sidney Paget, *Strand Magazine*, 1904

38 "Let us face it," concludes Aubrey Roberts. "[Holmes's] number one ally in this case was 'Lady Luck.'" His risky gamble in challenging the premier with pointed questions paid off; the ensuing murder of Lucas was, in the end, a fluke that opened the door to important new evidence. So, too, was Lestrade's sudden summoning of Holmes to consult with him about the second stain a happy stroke of luck. In the end, the clues dropped into Holmes's lap fortuitously, assembling themselves into a pattern quite beyond his initial line of thought. "However," Roberts sighs, "would this arrogant egocentric be expected to say, 'Sir, it was an uncommon bit of luck; a chance shot in the dark'? No, of course not. Still he must have been smiling at that possibility as he turned away to hide such thoughts from the 'keen scrutiny' of the Premier. . . ."

George McCormack decides that Holmes's "diplomatic secret" was the guilt of Lady Hilda, and further surmises that Holmes did not in fact replace the state papers in the despatch-box, since doing so would have exposed Lady Hilda as the sole suspect (assuming that Trelawney Hope did not fall for such a cheap parlour trick). Instead, McCormack theorises, Watson created out of whole cloth the touching scene at the Hope residence; in reality, Holmes extracted the paper from Lady Hilda and then handed it over outright to Hope and Lord Bellinger at the Baker Street office, without telling them from which channels he had procured it. "It was to encourage such speculation," McCormack writes, "that Holmes, in declining to explain how he had recovered the paper, said to Lord Bellinger, 'We also have our diplomatic secrets.' In this way, Lady Hilda was in no way implicated."

Yet Lord Bellinger had no such illusions, concludes Ian McQueen, which "Holmes clearly perceived as he 'turned away smiling from the keen scrutiny of those wonderful

"Yes, it is it—and the letter intact. Hope, I congratulate you!"

"Thank you! Thank you! What a weight from my heart. But this is inconceivable—impossible! Mr. Holmes, you are a wizard, a sorcerer! How did you know it was there?"

"Because I knew it was nowhere else."

"I cannot believe my eyes!" He ran wildly to the door. "Where is my wife? I must tell her that all is well. Hilda! Hilda!" we heard his voice on the stairs.

The Premier looked at Holmes with twinkling eyes.

"Come, sir," said he. "There is more in this than meets the eye. How came the letter back in the box?"

Holmes turned away smiling from the keen scrutiny of those wonderful eyes.

"We also have our diplomatic secrets,"[38] said he and, picking up his hat, he turned to the door. ■

"LORD BELLINGER" AND THE "RIGHT HONOURABLE TRELAWNEY HOPE"

"The one, austere, high-nosed, eagle-eyed, and dominant, was none other than the illustrious Lord Bellinger, twice Premier of Britain. The other, dark, clear-cut, and elegant, hardly yet of middle age, and endowed with every beauty of body and of mind, was the Right Honourable Trelawney Hope, Secretary for European Affairs, and the most rising statesman in the country."

IS IT POSSIBLE to identify the faces behind the masks created by Dr. Watson in "The Second Stain"?

The first to be considered is "the illustrious Lord Bellinger," who Watson reveals was "twice Premier of Britain." Since Watson deliberately hides the year and even the decade of "The Second Stain" from readers, relying upon chronological clues is an uncertain task. Only three prime ministers held office more than once during the lifetimes of Holmes and Watson: Benjamin Disraeli (1868, 1874–1880), William Gladstone (1868–1874, 1880–1885, 1886, 1892–1894), and Robert Salisbury (1885–1886, 1886–1892, 1895–1902). Only Salisbury and Gladstone did so for a second time during the Partnership.

Gavin Brend makes a case for Lord Salisbury, placing "The Second Stain" during Salisbury's second term. Acknowledging that Holmes's description of Lord Bellinger as "austere, high-nosed, eagle-eyed, and dominant" resembles Gladstone more than it does Salisbury, he insists that this is another point in Salisbury's favour, because Watson was so careful in disguising his characters that he would never give Gladstone such an accurate portrait. June Thomson contrarily argues that Salisbury *would* be described as "dominant" and "eagle-eyed" and therefore agrees with Brend's identification. She also finds the letter in "The Second Stain" consistent with the kaiser's dispatch of the Kruger telegram (see note 10, above) and therefore likely to have occurred between December 1895 and January 1896, during Salisbury's second term of office.

Others disagree with Brend's assessment, taking Watson's description at its face value, so to speak. O. F. Grazebrook, in Volume 2 of *Studies in Sherlock Holmes*, identifies Lord Bellinger as Mr. Gladstone on that basis, suggesting also that Gladstone's involvement explains Lord Holdhurst's remark to Holmes in "The Naval Treaty": "Your name is very familiar to me, Mr. Holmes." Presumably, Grazebrook deduces, Gladstone had told his successor, Lord Salisbury—Grazebrook identifies Salisbury with Lord Holdhurst—about Holmes's involvement with the affair of the missing document. Otherwise, it would have been nearly impossible for Holdhurst/Salisbury to have heard of Holmes, given that by 1889, the date generally assigned to "The Naval Treaty," only *A Study in Scarlet* (1887) had been published and had not achieved much attention.

Jon L. Lellenberg, in "Revised Treatise," claims to have confirmed conclusively the identification of Lord Bellinger as Gladstone, using documentation, not description, as his triumphal proof. Turning to the British government's official history of World War II, *SOE in France: An Account of the Work of the British Special Operations Executive 1940–1944*, written by M. R. D. Foot and published by the government in 1966, Lellenberg opens to the third chapter, which discusses recruiting and training. This chapter, according to Lellenberg, addresses

the necessity of avoiding public disclosure and recognition of even successful exploits; and a footnote on page 44 comments: "Sherlock Holmes's interview with a thinly disguised

eyes.' The next Cabinet reshuffle probably saw Trelawney Hope stripped of office and sent to occupy a back bench in the Lords. In time he may even have guessed that his wife was branded as a security risk. Bellinger's twinkle of mystification was not to be satisfied by Holmes's disarming remark about diplomatic secrets. And Holmes knew it; or why the hurried exit?"

Mr. Gladstone during his adventure of 'The Second Stain' is the *locus classicus*." No doubt this passing reference by Professor Foot, a distinguished historian with access to the classified archives, escaped the notice of the Foreign Office censor during the security review.

Several alternate identifications for Lord Bellinger have been made. Marcella Holmes, in "Sherlock Holmes and the Prime Minister," reviews the cases for Disraeli (who held the title of Lord Beaconsfield), Gladstone, Salisbury, and Archibald Rosebery (1894–1895). She concludes that Watson had no part in the affair, which took place in 1878 or 1879, and that Lord Beaconsfield was Lord Bellinger. Her case rests on Disraeli's two terms in office, the similar initial of "Beaconsfield" and "Bellinger," and the similarity of physical appearance to Watson's description. Based solely on chronology, T. S. Blakeney identifies Lord Bellinger as Lord Rosebery and congratulates Watson on his skill in hiding Rosebery's personality by claiming that he served as prime minister twice. The most surprising identification of Lord Bellinger must be D. A. Redmond's, in "Lord Bellinger—Who Else?," demonstrating that Lord Bellinger was John Albert Bellinger, first Baron Bellinger, and not the prime minister at all.

Turning to the "Right Honourable Trelawney Hope," Watson has said that he was "hardly of middle age"; but no foreign secretary (Watson's "Secretary for European Affairs") throughout the relevant period was that young a man. Still, Gavin Brend calculates that if the events of "The Second Stain" had to have taken place, as Watson describes, "one Tuesday morning in autumn" when the prime minister and foreign secretary were two different people, then only 1886, the first year of Lord Salisbury's second term, would fit the bill. Sir Stafford Northcote (the Earl of Iddesleigh) was Salisbury's foreign minister that year, with Salisbury taking over the responsibilities of the office the following year, after Northcote's death in January 1887.

Felix Morley, who also casts his vote with Salisbury and Northcote, elaborates upon the political situation in "The Significance of the Second Stain." Northcote's death came close upon the heels of relative turmoil in Salisbury's cabinet. On Christmas Eve, Lord Randolph Churchill, Salisbury's chancellor of the exchequer (or finance minister), resigned after submitting his first budget; soon after, W. H. Smith, the secretary of state for war—with whom Churchill had clashed—resigned as well. Northcote had just come to an agreement with Salisbury for his own resignation when he died suddenly, in the anteroom of the prime minister's official residence. "How tragic the circumstances were the reader of *The Adventure of the Second Stain* can fully realize," Morley explains. He theorises that after Holmes's recovery of the document, word of Northcote's "reckless carelessness with state papers" would surely have spread to other members of the cabinet. Morley blames Lady Hilda's feminine naivete for the leak, writing, "I am on delicate ground, but it may be stated as a general rule that a lady who has twice been terribly indiscreet is not unlikely to err a third time." Assuming that Lady Hilda may have foolishly spoken to the butler about Holmes's restoration of her husband's mysterious document, Morley continues, "At any rate a new light is thrown on the unexplained resignation from Lord Salisbury's Cabinet and the sudden, 'almost tragic' death of his Foreign Secretary."

Taking a contrary view, C. Arnold Johnson, in "Lord Iddesleigh?," suggests that Trelawney Hope was not Northcote but rather Lord Randolph Churchill, with his true cabinet position disguised by Watson. Similarly, June Thomson proposes Joseph Chamberlain for the rôle, during his term of service as "Secretary of State for the Colonies" for Salisbury during his second term. Chamberlain fits the description as well, as an "elegant" man.

Adherents of the "Gladstone" identification of Lord Bellinger generally point to Lord Rosebery, who served as Gladstone's foreign secretary in 1886 (for five months) and from 1892 to 1894, as the original of Trelawney Hope. Rosebery, who served as prime minister in late 1894–early 1895, certainly qualified as a "rising statesman in the country." Lady Hannah Rosebery was the only daughter of Baron Meyer Amschel de Rothschild of Mentmore and thus might well have been disguised as Lady Hilda.

Watson's "carefully guarded" account succeeds in leaving little definitive evidence of the faces behind the masks!

HIS LAST BOW [1]

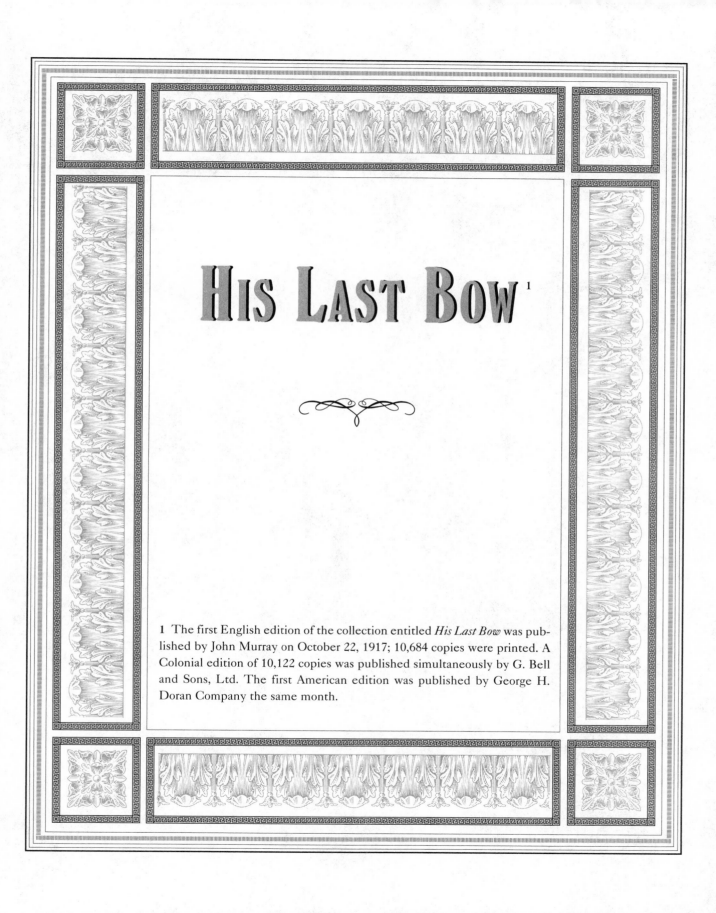

1 The first English edition of the collection entitled *His Last Bow* was published by John Murray on October 22, 1917; 10,684 copies were printed. A Colonial edition of 10,122 copies was published simultaneously by G. Bell and Sons, Ltd. The first American edition was published by George H. Doran Company the same month.

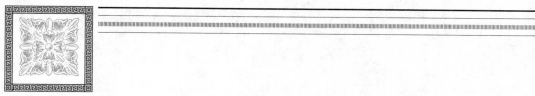

PREFACE

T HE FRIENDS OF Mr. Sherlock Holmes will be glad to learn that he is still alive and well, though somewhat crippled by occasional attacks of rheumatism.[1] He has, for many years, lived in a small farm upon the Downs[2] five miles from Eastbourne, where his time is divided between philosophy and agriculture. During this period of rest he has refused the most princely offers to take up various cases, having determined that his retirement was a permanent one. The approach of the German war caused him, however, to lay his remarkable combination of intellectual and practical activity at the disposal of the Government, with historical results which are recounted in "His Last Bow." Several previous experiences which have lain long in my portfolio, have been added to *His Last Bow* so as to complete the volume.[3]

JOHN H. WATSON, M.D.

1 Holmes's rheumatism is studied in detail in Rosemary Michaud's insightful "All in Your Hands, Mr. Holmes." Michaud concludes from the Canonical evidence that Holmes's arthritis was in his hands and that it became severe after the Great Hiatus. This explains why Holmes virtually gave up the violin and perhaps explains Holmes's inability to prevent the attack on Watson in "The Three Garridebs." The incident, argues Michaud, revealed to Holmes once and for all that he could no longer continue certain aspects of his detective work without endangering Watson and himself and led him to retire soon thereafter. John Hall, however, in *Sidelights on Holmes*, suggests that Watson is deliberately deceiving the reader here, to provide a "cover" for Holmes's post-"Last Bow" espionage activities.

2 Ensuing details reveal that Watson is referring here to the South Downs or Sussex Downs, the range of chalk hills that divides the county of Sussex into the coastal district and the Wealden district of forested land.

3 "The Cardboard Box," which originally appeared in book form following "Wisteria Lodge," has been restored to its rightful place in *The Memoirs of Sherlock Holmes*. See "The Cardboard Box."

THE ADVENTURE OF
WISTERIA LODGE[1]

As Watson reported in the preface to His Last Bow, *a collection of eight stories published in 1917, Holmes may have been retired, but the accounts of plenty of his cases remained to delight his fans. The seven new stories that Watson added to "His Last Bow" as part of the collection (also included was "The Cardboard Box," properly part of* The Memoirs) *had appeared in the* Strand *sporadically from 1908 through 1917. "Wisteria Lodge," the first, is misdated by Watson (probably by accident), who places it in 1892, when Holmes was missing and thought dead. Here, as in "The Golden Pince-Nez," Holmes deals with a political fugitive, this time from South America. Although voodoo is a staple of twentieth-century thrillers, the earliest book in the British Library on the subject was published in 1893, and this story may be the earliest literary reference to voodoo. Unusually, Holmes is assisted in the case by that rarity in Dr. Watson's accounts, a competent local policeman.*

I.
THE SINGULAR EXPERIENCE OF
MR. JOHN SCOTT ECCLES

I FIND IT RECORDED in my notebook that it was a bleak and windy day towards the end of March in the year 1892.[2] Holmes had received a telegram whilst we sat at our lunch, and he had scribbled a reply. He made no remark, but the matter remained in his thoughts, for he stood in front of the fire afterwards with a thoughtful face, smoking his pipe, and casting an occasional glance at the message. Suddenly he turned upon me with a mischievous twinkle in his eyes.

"I suppose, Watson, we must look upon you as a man of letters,"[3] said he. "How do you define the word 'grotesque'?"

"Strange—remarkable," I suggested.

He shook his head at my definition.

"There is surely something more than that," said he; "some underlying suggestion of the tragic and the terrible. If you cast your mind back to some of those narratives with which you

1 "The Adventure of Wisteria Lodge" appeared as a title for this story only when book and omnibus editions were published. In *Collier's Magazine* (August 15, 1908), the whole story was entitled "The Singular Experience of Mr. J. Scott Eccles," and in England the *Strand Magazine* titled it "A Reminiscence of Mr. Sherlock Holmes," calling the first installment (September 1908) "The Singular Experience of Mr. John Scott Eccles" and the second installment (October 1908) "The Tiger of San Pedro." Indeed, until collected in book form, the entire series of stories, appearing from September 1908 to December 1913 (not including "The Cardboard Box" or

"His Last Bow"), was entitled the "Reminiscences of Sherlock Holmes."

2 This date is of course incorrect, for between April 1891 and April 1894 Holmes was absent from London (and public view) on the Great Hiatus. See "The Empty House."

3 The first of numerous snide remarks to Watson during the course of this tale, which Watson, to his everlasting credit, faithfully records.

4 The day-and-night post office in Charing Cross was one of the oldest of the London post offices. In Holmes and Watson's day, it was tucked away on the ground floor of Morley's Hotel, but had its entrance on the south side of the Strand. The central post office—a "magnificent pile," in the words of one Victorian writer—was located in St. Martins-le-Grand, and there were only four branch offices, at Lombard Street; Charing Cross; Cavendish Street, Oxford Street; and 266 Borough High Street.

5 Although the question may seem strange to an American reader, the "Scott" was obviously part of a typical English compound name (for example, Conan Doyle) and not the writer's first name. There would have been no reason for the writer to have wasted money on including his or her first name in the telegram.

6 This is not Bob Carruthers of "The Solitary Cyclist," who had no apparent military connections. Carruthers is another in the long line of colonels of questionable integrity—see, for example, Colonel Lysander Stark, no doubt an alias ("The Engineer's Thumb"); Colonel Dorking, whose conduct may have been cause for blackmail ("Charles Augustus Milverton"); Colonel James Barclay, "David" to his wife's "Bathsheba" ("The Crooked Man"); Colonel Warburton, the madman

have afflicted a long-suffering public, you will recognise how often the grotesque has deepened into the criminal. Think of that little affair of the red-headed men. That was grotesque enough in the outset, and yet it ended in a desperate attempt at robbery. Or, again, there was that most grotesque affair of the five orange pips, which led straight to a murderous conspiracy. The word puts me on the alert."

"Have you it there?" I asked.

He read the telegram aloud.

Have just had most incredible and grotesque experience. May I consult you?

SCOTT ECCLES,
Post Office, Charing Cross.[4]

"Man or woman?" I asked.[5]

"Oh, man, of course. No woman would ever send a reply-paid telegram. She would have come."

"Will you see him?"

"My dear Watson, you know how bored I have been since we locked up Colonel Carruthers.[6] My mind is like a racing engine, tearing itself to pieces because it is not connected up with the work for which it was built.[7] Life is commonplace, the papers are sterile; audacity and romance seem to have passed for ever from the criminal world. Can you ask me, then, whether I am ready to look into any new problem, however trivial it may prove? But here, unless I am mistaken, is our client."

A measured step was heard upon the stairs, and a moment later a stout, tall, grey-whiskered and solemnly respectable person was ushered into the room. His life history was written in his heavy features and pompous manner. From his spats to his gold-rimmed spectacles he was a Conservative, a Churchman, a good citizen, orthodox and conventional to the last degree. But some amazing experience had disturbed his native composure and left its traces in his bristling hair, his flushed, angry cheeks, and his flurried, excited manner. He plunged instantly into his business.

"I have had a most singular and unpleasant experience, Mr. Holmes," said he. "Never in my life have I been placed in such a situation. It is most improper—most outrageous. I must insist upon some explanation." He swelled and puffed in his anger.

"Pray sit down, Mr. Scott Eccles," said Holmes, in a soothing voice. "May I ask, in the first place, why you came to me at all?"

"Well, sir, it did not appear to be a matter which concerned the police, and yet, when you have heard the facts, you must admit that I could not leave it where it was. Private detectives are a class with whom I have absolutely no sympathy, but none the less, having heard your name—"

"Quite so. But, in the second place, why did you not come at once?"

"What do you mean?"

Holmes glanced at his watch.

"It is a quarter past two," he said. "Your telegram was dispatched about one. But no one can glance at your toilet and attire without seeing that your disturbance dates from the moment of your waking."

Our client smoothed down his unbrushed hair and felt his unshaven chin.

"You are right, Mr. Holmes. I never gave a thought to my toilet. I was only too glad to get out of such a house. But I have been running round making inquiries before I came to you. I went to the house agents, you know, and they said that Mr. Garcia's rent was paid up all right and that everything was in order at Wisteria Lodge."

"Come, come, sir," said Holmes, laughing. "You are like my friend Dr. Watson, who has a bad habit of telling his stories wrong end foremost. Please arrange your thoughts and let me know, in their due sequence, exactly what those events are which have sent you out unbrushed and unkempt, with dress boots and waistcoat buttoned awry, in search of advice and assistance."

Our client looked down with a rueful face at his own unconventional appearance.

"I'm sure it must look very bad, Mr. Holmes, and I am not aware that in my whole life such a thing has ever happened before. But I will tell you the whole queer business, and when I have done so you will admit, I am sure, that there has been enough to excuse me."

But his narrative was nipped in the bud. There was a bustle outside, and Mrs. Hudson opened the door to usher in two robust and official-looking individuals, one of whom was well

("The Engineer's Thumb"); Colonel Openshaw of the Confederate Army ("The Five Orange Pips"); Colonel Upwood, guilty of scandalous conduct (*The Hound of the Baskervilles*); Colonel Emsworth, guilty of overreaction ("The Blanched Soldier"); Colonel Valentine Walker, guilty of treason ("The Bruce-Partington Plans"); Colonel James Moriarty, guilty of brotherhood ("The Empty House"); and Colonel Sebastian Moran, guilty of almost everything ("The Empty House"). Only Colonel Ross of "Silver Blaze," Colonel Spence Munro of "The Copper Beeches," Colonel Hayter of "The Reigate Squires," and Colonel Sir James Damery of "The Illustrious Client" seem free of taint.

7 Holmes uses a similar analogy in "The Devil's Foot" when he says, "To let the brain work without sufficient material is like racing an engine. It racks itself to pieces."

8 Gregson appears only here and in *A Study in Scarlet* and "The Greek Interpreter."

9 How, exactly, Eccles was traced is not discussed, but Colonel E. Ennalls Berl speculates that Gregson and Baynes must have possessed some undisclosed information as to Eccles's movements, since he visited several other locations before heading to Charing Cross Post Office and therefore, theoretically, could have wired the telegram from anywhere.

"I have been running round making inquiries
before I came to you."
Arthur Twidle, *Strand Magazine*, 1908

known to us as Inspector Gregson[8] of Scotland Yard, an energetic, gallant, and, within his limitations, a capable officer. He shook hands with Holmes, and introduced his comrade as Inspector Baynes of the Surrey Constabulary.

"We are hunting together, Mr. Holmes, and our trail lay in this direction." He turned his bulldog eyes upon our visitor. "Are you Mr. John Scott Eccles, of Popham House, Lee?"

"I am."

"We have been following you about all the morning."

"You traced him through the telegram, no doubt," said Holmes.[9]

"Exactly, Mr. Holmes. We picked up the scent at Charing Cross Post Office and came on here."

"But why do you follow me? What do you want?"

"We wish a statement, Mr. Scott Eccles, as to the events which led up to the death last night of Mr. Aloysius Garcia, of Wisteria Lodge, near Esher."

Our client had sat up with staring eyes and every tinge of colour struck from his astonished face.

"Dead? Did you say he was dead?"

"Yes, sir, he is dead."

"But how? An accident?"

"Murder, if ever there was one upon earth."

"Good God! This is awful! You don't mean—you don't mean that I am suspected?"

"A letter of yours was found in the dead man's pocket, and we know by it that you had planned to pass last night at his house."

"So I did."

"Oh, you did, did you?"

Our client sat up with staring eyes.
Frederick Dorr Steele, *Collier's*, 1908

"This is awful! You don't mean—
you don't mean that I am suspected?"
Arthur Twidle, *Strand Magazine*, 1908

Out came the official notebook.

"Wait a bit, Gregson," said Sherlock Holmes. "All you desire is a plain statement, is it not?"

"And it is my duty to warn Mr. Scott Eccles that it may be used against him."

"Mr. Eccles was going to tell us about it when you entered the room. I think, Watson, a brandy and soda would do him no harm. Now, sir, I suggest that you take no notice of this addition to your audience, and that you proceed with your narrative exactly as you would have done had you never been interrupted."

Our visitor had gulped off the brandy and the colour had

returned to his face. With a dubious glance at the inspector's notebook, he plunged at once into his extraordinary statement.

"I am a bachelor," said he, "and, being of a sociable turn, I cultivate a large number of friends. Among these are the family of a retired brewer called Melville, living at Albemarle Mansion, Kensington. It was at his table that I met some weeks ago a young fellow named Garcia. He was, I understood, of Spanish descent and connected in some way with the Embassy. He spoke perfect English, was pleasing in his manners, and as good-looking a man as ever I saw in my life.

"In some way we struck up quite a friendship, this young fellow and I. He seemed to take a fancy to me from the first, and within two days of our meeting he came to see me at Lee. One thing led to another, and it ended in his inviting me out to spend a few days at his house, Wisteria Lodge, between Esher and Oxshott. Yesterday evening I went to Esher to fulfil this engagement.[10]

"He had described his household to me before I went there. He lived with a faithful servant, a countryman of his own, who looked after all his needs. This fellow could speak English and did his housekeeping for him. Then there was a wonderful cook, he said, a half-breed whom he had picked up in his travels, who could serve an excellent dinner. I remember that he remarked what a queer household it was to find in the heart of Surrey, and that I agreed with him, though it has proved a good deal queerer than I thought.

"I drove to the place—about two miles on the south side of Esher. The house was a fair-sized one, standing back from the road, with a curving drive which was banked with high evergreen shrubs. It was an old, tumble-down building in a crazy state of disrepair. When the trap pulled up on the grass-grown drive in front of the blotched and weather-stained door, I had doubts as to my wisdom in visiting a man whom I knew so slightly. He opened the door himself, however, and greeted me with a great show of cordiality. I was handed over to the manservant, a melancholy, swarthy individual, who led the way, my bag in his hand, to my bedroom. The whole place was depressing. Our dinner was *tête-à-tête*, and though my host did his best to be entertaining, his thoughts seemed to continually wander, and he talked so vaguely and wildly that I could hardly understand him. He continually drummed his fingers on the

10 Commentators contend that Eccles and Garcia's "friendship" was a homosexual relationship, albeit unconsummated. While male-male friendships were very different in Victorian times, and certainly many were free from homoerotic content (for example, as this editor firmly believes, that between Holmes and Watson), there are unexplained incidents in this tale, the implications of which seem to slide right by Watson, which suggest the initiation of an erotic relationship here. Holmes, perhaps to avoid shocking Watson, invents quite other reasons for the friendship.

table, gnawed his nails, and gave other signs of nervous impatience. The dinner itself was neither well served nor well cooked, and the gloomy presence of the taciturn servant did not help to enliven us. I can assure you that many times in the course of the evening I wished that I could invent some excuse which would take me back to Lee.

"One thing comes back to my memory which may have a bearing upon the business that you two gentlemen are investigating. I thought nothing of it at the time. Near the end of dinner a note was handed in by the servant. I noticed that after my host had read it he seemed even more distrait and strange than before. He gave up all pretence at conversation and sat, smoking endless cigarettes, lost in his own thoughts, but he made no remark as to the contents. About eleven I was glad to go to bed. Some time later Garcia looked in at my door—the room was dark at the time—and asked me if I had rung. I said that I had not. He apologised for having disturbed me so late, saying that it was nearly one o'clock. I dropped off after this and slept soundly all night.

"And now I come to the amazing part of my tale. When I woke it was broad daylight. I glanced at my watch, and the time was nearly nine. I had particularly asked to be called at eight, so I was very much astonished at this forgetfulness. I sprang up and rang for the servant. There was no response. I rang again and again, with the same result. Then I came to the conclusion that the bell was out of order. I huddled on my clothes and hurried downstairs in an exceedingly bad temper to order some hot water. You can imagine my surprise when I found that there was no one there. I shouted in the hall. There was no answer. Then I ran from room to room. All were deserted. My host had shown me which was his bedroom the night before, so I knocked at the door. No reply. I turned the handle and walked in. The room was empty, and the bed had never been slept in. He had gone with the rest. The foreign host, the foreign footman, the foreign cook, all had vanished in the night! That was the end of my visit to Wisteria Lodge."

Sherlock Holmes was rubbing his hands and chuckling as he added this bizarre incident to his collection of strange episodes.

"Your experience is, so far as I know, perfectly unique," said he. "May I ask, sir, what you did then?"

"I was furious. My first idea was that I had been the victim of some absurd practical joke. I packed my things, banged the hall door behind me, and set off for Esher, with my bag in my hand. I called at Allan Brothers', the chief land agents in the village, and found that it was from this firm that the villa had been rented. It struck me that the whole proceeding could hardly be for the purpose of making a fool of me, and that the main object must be to get out of the rent. It is late in March, so quarter-day is at hand.[11] But this theory would not work. The agent was obliged to me for my warning, but told me that the rent had been paid in advance. Then I made my way to town and called at the Spanish Embassy. The man was unknown there. After this I went to see Melville, at whose house I had first met Garcia, but I found that he really knew rather less about him than I did. Finally, when I got your reply to my wire I came out to you, since I understand that you are a person who gives advice in difficult cases. But now, Mr. Inspector, I gather, from what you said when you entered the room, that you can carry the story on, and that some tragedy has occurred. I can assure you that every word I have said is the truth, and that, outside of what I have told you, I know absolutely nothing about the fate of this man. My only desire is to help the law in every possible way."

"I am sure of it, Mr. Scott Eccles—I am sure of it," said Inspector Gregson, in a very amiable tone. "I am bound to say that everything which you have said agrees very closely with the facts as they have come to our notice. For example, there was that note which arrived during dinner. Did you chance to observe what became of it?"

"Yes, I did. Garcia rolled it up and threw it into the fire."

"What do you say to that, Mr. Baynes?"

The country detective was a stout, puffy, red man, whose face was only redeemed from grossness by two extraordinarily bright eyes, almost hidden behind the heavy creases of cheek and brow. With a slow smile he drew a folded and discoloured scrap of paper from his pocket.

"It was a dog-grate,[12] Mr. Holmes, and he overpitched it. I picked this out unburned from the back of it."

Holmes smiled his appreciation.

"You must have examined the house very carefully, to find a single pellet of paper."

11 This would have been Lady Day, March 25. The four "quarter-days," upon which quarterly payments (such as rents) are due, derive from the medieval church calendar and indicate the start of a new fiscal season. In England, Wales, and Northern Ireland they are Lady Day (also referenced in "The Resident Patient"), Midsummer (June 24), Michaelmas (September 29), and Christmas (December 25). In 1991 the dates were synchronised to February 28, May 28, August 28, and November 28.

12 A detached fire-grate standing in a fireplace on supports called dogs.

"It was a dog-grate, Mr. Holmes, and he overpitched it.
I picked this out unburned from the back of it."
Arthur Twidle, *Strand Magazine*, 1908

"I did, Mr. Holmes. It's my way. Shall I read it, Mr. Gregson?"

The Londoner nodded.

"The note is written upon ordinary cream-laid paper without watermark. It is a quarter-sheet. The paper is cut off in two snips with a short-bladed scissors. It has been folded over three times and sealed with purple wax, put on hurriedly and pressed down with some flat, oval object. It is addressed to Mr. Garcia, Wisteria Lodge. It says:

Our own colours, green and white. Green open, white shut.
Main stair, first corridor, seventh right, green baize. God speed.

D.

It is a woman's writing, done with a sharp-pointed pen, but the address is either done with another pen or by someone else. It is thicker and bolder, as you see."

"A very remarkable note," said Holmes, glancing it over. "I must compliment you, Mr. Baynes, upon your attention to detail in your examination of it. A few trifling points might perhaps be added. The oval seal is undoubtedly a plain sleeve-link[13]—what else is of such a shape? The scissors were bent nail-scissors. Short as the two snips are, you can distinctly see the same slight curve in each."

The country detective chuckled.

"I thought I had squeezed all the juice out of it, but I see there was a little over," he said. "I'm bound to say that I make nothing of the note except that there was something on hand, and that a woman, as usual, was at the bottom of it."

Mr. Scott Eccles had fidgeted in his seat during this conversation.

"I am glad you found the note, since it corroborates my story," said he. "But I beg to point out that I have not yet heard what has happened to Mr. Garcia, nor what has become of his household."

"As to Garcia," said Gregson, "that is easily answered. He was found dead this morning upon Oxshott Common, nearly a mile from his home. His head had been smashed to pulp by heavy blows of a sand-bag or some such instrument, which had crushed rather than wounded. It is a lonely corner, and there is no house within a quarter of a mile of the spot. He had apparently been struck down first from behind, but his assailant had gone on beating him long after he was dead. It was a most furious assault. There are no footsteps nor any clue to the criminals."

"Robbed?"

"No, there was no attempt at robbery."

"This is very painful—very painful and terrible," said Mr. Scott Eccles, in a querulous voice; "but it is really uncommonly hard upon me. I had nothing to do with my host going off upon a nocturnal excursion and meeting so sad an end. How do I come to be mixed up with the case?"

"Very simply, sir," Inspector Baynes answered. "The only document found in the pocket of the deceased was a letter from you saying that you would be with him on the night of his death. It was the envelope of this letter which gave us the dead man's name and address. It was after nine this morning when we reached his house and found neither you nor anyone else inside it. I wired to Mr. Gregson to run you down in London

13 A cuff-link.

while I examined Wisteria Lodge. Then I came into town, joined Mr. Gregson, and here we are."

"I think now," said Gregson, rising, "we had best put this matter into an official shape. You will come round with us to the station, Mr. Scott Eccles, and let us have your statement in writing."

"Certainly, I will come at once. But I retain your services, Mr. Holmes. I desire you to spare no expense and no pains to get at the truth."

My friend turned to the country inspector.

"I suppose that you have no objection to my collaborating with you, Mr. Baynes?"

"Highly honoured, sir, I am sure."

"You appear to have been very prompt and businesslike in all that you have done. Was there any clue, may I ask, as to the exact hour that the man met his death?"

"He had been there since one o'clock. There was rain about that time, and his death had certainly been before the rain."

"But that is perfectly impossible, Mr. Baynes," cried our client. "His voice is unmistakable. I could swear to it that it was he who addressed me in my bedroom at that very hour."

"Remarkable, but by no means impossible," said Holmes, smiling.

"You have a clue?" asked Gregson.

"On the face of it the case is not a very complex one, though it certainly presents some novel and interesting features. A further knowledge of facts is necessary before I would venture to give a final and definite opinion. By the way, Mr. Baynes, did you find anything remarkable besides this note in your examination of the house?"

The detective looked at my friend in a singular way.

"There were," said he, "one or two *very* remarkable things. Perhaps when I have finished at the police-station you would care to come out and give me your opinion of them."

"I am entirely at your service," said Sherlock Holmes, ringing the bell. "You will show these gentlemen out, Mrs. Hudson, and kindly send the boy with this telegram. He is to pay a five-shilling reply."

We sat for some time in silence after our visitors had left. Holmes smoked hard, with his brows drawn down over his keen eyes, and his head thrust forward in the eager way characteristic of the man.

"Well, Watson," he asked, turning suddenly upon me, "what do you make of it?"

"I can make nothing of this mystification of Scott Eccles."

"But the crime?"

"Well, taken with the disappearance of the man's companions, I should say that they were in some way concerned in the murder and had fled from justice."

"That is certainly a possible point of view. On the face of it you must admit, however, that it is very strange that his two servants should have been in a conspiracy against him and should have attacked him on the one night when he had a guest. They had him alone at their mercy every other night in the week."

"Then why did they fly?"

"Quite so. Why did they fly? There is a big fact. Another big fact is the remarkable experience of our client, Scott Eccles. Now, my dear Watson, is it beyond the limits of human ingenuity to furnish an explanation which would cover both these big facts? If it were one which would also admit of the mysterious note with its very curious phraseology, why, then it would be worth accepting as a temporary hypothesis. If the fresh facts which come to our knowledge all fit themselves into the scheme, then our hypothesis may gradually become a solution."

"But what is our hypothesis?"

Holmes leaned back in his chair with half-closed eyes.

"You must admit, my dear Watson, that the idea of a joke is impossible. There were grave events afoot, as the sequel showed, and the coaxing of Scott Eccles to Wisteria Lodge had some connection with them."

"But what possible connection?"

"Let us take it link by link. There is, on the face of it, something unnatural about this strange and sudden friendship between the young Spaniard and Scott Eccles. It was the former who forced the pace. He called upon Eccles at the other end of London on the very day after he first met him, and he kept in close touch with him until he got him down to Esher. Now, what did he want with Eccles? What could Eccles supply? I see no charm in the man. He is not particularly intelli-

14 Such a comment seems "rather unfair," remarks Cathy Fraser, "about someone who had the presence of mind to search the house, visit the house-agents, the Spanish Embassy and Melville, in his attempt to unravel the mystery, before resorting to Holmes." Perhaps Holmes has not yet forgiven Eccles for his earlier declaration that "Private detectives are a class with whom I have absolutely no sympathy."

15 Garcia's plan hinged on Eccles's believing that it was 1:00 A.M. when he disturbed his houseguest's sleep; but Eccles had his own watch, having glanced at it when he awoke in the morning. "[I]t is rather unreasonable," writes Edward F. Clark, Jr., in "Wisteria Lodge Revisited (A Model Cop, a Model Laundry Item, and a Not-So-Model Culinary Artist)," "to expect that a sly schemer, a plotter, like Garcia, would stake his alibi—everything—on the chance that Scott Eccles might not strike a light and check the hour." Clark theorises that Garcia's cook added some sort of sleeping potion to Eccles's soup, rendering him so drowsy that he would not think to look at the time during the night.

D. Martin Dakin, on the other hand, takes issue with Garcia's strategy regarding the actual timing of his alibi. If Garcia did leave the house at midnight, presumably he was to carry out his mission by 12:30 A.M. and return by 1:00 A.M.—meaning that he would need an alibi for 12:30, not 1:00.

16 This would mean the colours worn by racehorses and their jockeys, as in the program descriptions listed in "Silver Blaze." That Holmes makes such an association for Watson's benefit should not be surprising, given Watson's admitted knowledge of the Turf (see "Shoscombe Old Place").

gent[14]—not a man likely to be congenial to a quick-witted Latin. Why, then, was he picked out from all the other people whom Garcia met as particularly suited to his purpose? Has he any one outstanding quality? I say that he has. He is the very type of conventional British respectability, and the very man as a witness to impress another Briton. You saw yourself how neither of the inspectors dreamed of questioning his statement, extraordinary as it was."

"But what was he to witness?"

"Nothing, as things turned out, but everything had they gone another way. That is how I read the matter."

"I see, he might have proved an alibi."

"Exactly, my dear Watson; he might have proved an alibi. We will suppose, for argument's sake, that the household of Wisteria Lodge are confederates in some design. The attempt, whatever it may be, is to come off, we will say, before one o'clock. By some juggling of the clocks it is quite possible that they may have got Scott Eccles to bed earlier than he thought, but in any case it is likely that when Garcia went out of his way to tell him that it was one it was really not more than twelve. If Garcia could do whatever he had to do and be back by the hour mentioned he had evidently a powerful reply to any accusation.[15] Here was this irreproachable Englishman ready to swear in any court of law that the accused was in his house all the time. It was an insurance against the worst."

"Yes, yes, I see that. But how about the disappearance of the others?"

"I have not all my facts yet, but I do not think there are any insuperable difficulties. Still, it is an error to argue in front of your data. You will find yourself insensibly twisting them round to fit your theories."

"And the message?"

"How did it run? 'Our own colours, green and white.' Sounds like racing.[16] 'Green open, white shut.' That is clearly a signal. 'Main stair, first corridor, seventh right, green baize.' This is an assignation. We may find a jealous husband at the bottom of it all. It was clearly a dangerous quest. She would not have said 'God speed' had it not been so. 'D.'—that should be a guide."

"The man was a Spaniard. I suggest that 'D' stands for Dolores, a common female name in Spain."

"Good, Watson, very good—but quite inadmissible. A

Spaniard would write to a Spaniard in Spanish. The writer of this note is certainly English. Well, we can only possess our souls in patience, until this excellent inspector comes back for us. Meanwhile we can thank our lucky fate which has rescued us for a few short hours from the insufferable fatigues of idleness."

An answer had arrived to Holmes's telegram before our Surrey officer had returned. Holmes read it, and was about to place it in his notebook when he caught a glimpse of my expectant face. He tossed it across with a laugh.

"We are moving in exalted circles," said he.

The telegram was a list of names and addresses:

Lord Harringby, The Dingle; Sir George Ffolliott, Oxshott Towers; Mr. Hynes Hynes, J.P., Purdey Place; Mr. James Baker Williams, Forton Old Hall; Mr. Henderson, High Gable; Rev. Joshua Stone, Nether Walsling.

"He tossed it across with a laugh."
Arthur Twidle, *Strand Magazine*, 1908

"This is a very obvious way of limiting our field of operations," said Holmes. "No doubt Baynes, with his methodical mind, has already adopted some similar plan."

"I don't quite understand."

"Well, my dear fellow, we have already arrived at the conclusion that the message received by Garcia at dinner was an appointment or an assignation. Now, if the obvious reading of it is correct, and in order to keep this tryst one has to ascend a main stair and seek the seventh door in a corridor, it is perfectly clear that the house is a very large one. It is equally certain that this house cannot be more than a mile or two from Oxshott, since Garcia was walking in that direction, and hoped, according to my reading of the facts, to be back in Wisteria Lodge in time to avail himself of an alibi, which would only be valid up to one o'clock. As the number of large houses close to Oxshott must be limited, I adopted the obvious method of sending to the agents mentioned by Scott Eccles and obtaining a list of them. Here they are in this telegram, and the other end of our tangled skein must lie among them."

It was nearly six o'clock before we found ourselves in the pretty Surrey village of Esher, with Inspector Baynes as our companion.

Holmes and I had taken things for the night, and found comfortable quarters at the Bull. Finally we set out in the company of the detective on our visit to Wisteria Lodge. It was a cold, dark March evening, with a sharp wind and a fine rain beating upon our faces, a fit setting for the wild common over which our road passed and the tragic goal to which it led us.

II. THE TIGER OF SAN PEDRO

A COLD AND MELANCHOLY walk of a couple of miles brought us to a high wooden gate, which opened into a gloomy avenue of chestnuts. The curved and shadowed drive led us to a low, dark house, pitch-black against a slate-coloured sky. From the front window upon the left of the door there peeped a glimmer of a feeble light.

"There's a constable in possession," said Baynes. "I'll knock at the window." He stepped across the grass plot and tapped with his hand on the pane. Through the fogged glass I dimly saw a man spring up from a chair beside the fire, and heard a sharp cry from within the room. An instant later a white-faced, hard-breathing policeman had opened the door, the candle wavering in his trembling hand.

"What's the matter, Walters?" asked Baynes, sharply.

The man mopped his forehead with his handkerchief and gave a long sigh of relief.

"I am glad you have come, sir. It has been a long evening, and I don't think my nerve is as good as it was."

"Your nerve, Walters? I should not have thought you had a nerve in your body."

"Well, sir, it's this lonely, silent house and the queer thing in the kitchen. Then when you tapped at the window I thought it had come again."

The queer thing in the kitchen.
Frederick Dorr Steele, *Collier's*, 1908

It was at the window.
Lee Conrey, *Seattle Post-Intelligencer*, November 24, 1912

"That what had come again?"

"The devil, sir, for all I know. It was at the window."

"What was at the window, and when?"

"It was just about two hours ago. The light was just fading. I was sitting reading in the chair. I don't know what made me look up, but there was a face looking in at me through the lower pane. Lord, sir, what a face it was! I'll see it in my dreams."

"Tut, tut, Walters! This is not talk for a police-constable."

"I know, sir, I know; but it shook me, sir, and there's no use to deny it. It wasn't black, sir, nor was it white, nor any colour that I know, but a kind of queer shade like clay with a splash of milk in it. Then there was the size of it—it was twice yours, sir. And the look of it—the great staring goggle eyes, and the line of white teeth like a hungry beast. I tell you, sir, I couldn't move a finger, nor get my breath, till it whisked away and was gone. Out I ran and through the shrubbery, but thank God there was no one there."

"If I didn't know you were a good man, Walters, I should put a black mark against you for this. If it were the devil himself a constable on duty should never thank God that he could not lay his hands upon him. I suppose the whole thing is not a vision and a touch of nerves?"

"That, at least, is very easily settled," said Holmes, lighting his little pocket lantern. "Yes," he reported, after a short examination of the grass bed, "a number twelve shoe, I should say. If he was all on the same scale as his foot he must certainly have been a giant."

"What became of him?"

"He seems to have broken through the shrubbery and made for the road."

"Well," said the inspector, with a grave and thoughtful face, "whoever he may have been, and whatever he may have wanted, he's gone for the present, and we have more immediate things to attend to. Now, Mr. Holmes, with your permission, I will show you round the house."

The various bedrooms and sitting-rooms had yielded nothing to a careful search. Apparently the tenants had brought little or nothing with them, and all the furniture down to the smallest details had been taken over with the house. A good

"There was a face looking in at me through the lower pane."
Arthur Twidle, *Strand Magazine*, 1908

deal of clothing with the stamp of Marx and Co., High Holborn, had been left behind. Telegraphic inquiries had been already made which showed that Marx knew nothing of his customer save that he was a good payer. Odds and ends, some pipes, a few novels, two of them in Spanish, an old-fashioned pinfire revolver, and a guitar were amongst the personal property.

"Nothing in all this," said Baynes, stalking, candle in hand, from room to room. "But now, Mr. Holmes, I invite your attention to the kitchen."

It was a gloomy, high-ceilinged room at the back of the house, with a straw litter in one corner, which served apparently as a bed for the cook. The table was piled with half-eaten dishes and dirty plates, the debris of last night's dinner.

"Look at this," said Baynes. "What do you make of it?"

He held up his candle before an extraordinary object which stood at the back of the dresser. It was so wrinkled and shrunken and withered that it was difficult to say what it might have been. One could but say that it was black and leathery and that it bore some resemblance to a dwarfish, human figure. At first, as I examined it, I thought that it was a mummified negro baby, and then it seemed a very twisted and ancient

He held up the candle before an extraordinary object
which stood at the back of the dresser.
Lee Conrey, *Seattle Post-Intelligencer*, December 1, 1912

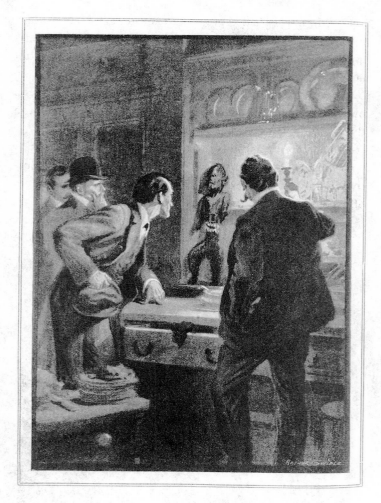

" 'Very interesting, indeed,' said Holmes."
Arthur Twidle, *Strand Magazine*, 1908

monkey. Finally I was left in doubt as to whether it was animal or human. A double band of white shells was strung round the centre of it.

"Very interesting—very interesting, indeed!" said Holmes peering at this sinister relic. "Anything more?"

In silence Baynes led the way to the sink and held forward his candle. The limbs and body of some large, white bird, torn savagely to pieces with the feathers still on, were littered all over it. Holmes pointed to the wattles on the severed head.

"A white cock," said he; "most interesting! It is really a very curious case."

But Mr. Baynes had kept his most sinister exhibit to the last. From under the sink he drew a zinc pail which contained a quantity of blood. Then from the table he took a platter heaped with small pieces of charred bone.

"Something has been killed and something has been burned. We raked all these out of the fire. We had a doctor in this morning. He says that they are not human."

Holmes smiled and rubbed his hands.

"I must congratulate you, inspector, on handling so distinctive and instructive a case. Your powers, if I may say so without offence, seem superior to your opportunities."

Inspector Baynes's small eyes twinkled with pleasure.

"You're right, Mr. Holmes. We stagnate in the provinces. A

"From under the sink he drew a zinc pail."
Arthur Twidle, *Strand Magazine*, 1908

case of this sort gives a man a chance, and I hope that I shall take it. What do you make of these bones?"

"A lamb, I should say, or a kid."

"And the white cock?"

"Curious, Mr. Baynes, very curious. I should say almost unique."

"Yes, sir, there must have been some very strange people with some very strange ways in this house. One of them is dead. Did his companions follow him and kill him? If they did we should have them, for every port is watched. But my own views are different. Yes, sir, my own views are very different."

"You have a theory then?"

"And I'll work it myself, Mr. Holmes. It's only due to my own credit to do so. Your name is made, but I have still to make mine. I should be glad to be able to say afterwards that I had solved it without your help."

Holmes laughed good-humouredly.

"Well, well, inspector," said he. "Do you follow your path and I will follow mine. My results are always very much at your service if you care to apply to me for them. I think that I have seen all that I wish in this house, and that my time may be more profitably employed elsewhere. *Au revoir* and good luck!"

I could tell by numerous subtle signs, which might have been lost upon anyone but myself, that Holmes was on a hot scent. As impassive as ever to the casual observer, there were none the less a subdued eagerness and suggestion of tension in his brightened eyes and brisker manner which assured me that the game was afoot. After his habit he said nothing, and after mine I asked no questions. Sufficient for me to share the sport and lend my humble help to the capture without distracting that intent brain with needless interruption. All would come round to me in due time.

I waited, therefore—but, to my ever-deepening disappointment I waited in vain. Day succeeded day, and my friend took no step forward. One morning he spent in town, and I learned from a casual reference that he had visited the British Museum. Save for this one excursion, he spent his days in long, and often solitary walks, or in chatting with a number of village gossips whose acquaintance he had cultivated.

"I'm sure, Watson, a week in the country will be invaluable

17 A small spade used for digging out weeds. "Spud" as slang for potato is said to have derived from this word, since a spud or any other number of digging implements could be used to dig up potatoes.

18 Few would regard Holmes as a nature-lover; in fact, Humfrey Michell reminds readers that Holmes's admiration of the moss-rose, in "The Naval Treaty," is the only occasion on which he is recorded even noticing flowers. "Can we really believe that he would deceive a child when he prowled about with a spud, a tin box and an elementary book on botany during his singularly inept investigation . . . ? Assuredly that strange story should be classed among the Apocrypha."

to you," he remarked. "It is very pleasant to see the first green shoots upon the hedges and the catkins on the hazels once again. With a spud,[17] a tin box, and an elementary book on botany, there are instructive days to be spent." He prowled about with this equipment himself,[18] but it was a poor show of plants which he would bring back of an evening.

Occasionally in our rambles we came across Inspector Baynes. His fat, red face wreathed itself in smiles and his small eyes glittered as he greeted my companion. He said little about the case, but from that little we gathered that he also was not dissatisfied at the course of events. I must admit, however, that I was somewhat surprised when, some five days after the crime, I opened my morning paper to find in large letters:

THE OXSHOTT MYSTERY
A SOLUTION
ARREST OF SUPPOSED ASSASSIN

Holmes sprang in his chair as if he had been stung when I read the head-lines.

"By Jove!" he cried. "You don't mean that Baynes has got him?"

"Apparently," said I, as I read the following report:

Great excitement was caused in Esher and the neighbouring district when it was learned late last night that an arrest had been effected in connection with the Oxshott murder. It will be remembered that Mr. Garcia, of Wisteria Lodge, was found dead on Oxshott Common, his body showing signs of extreme violence, and that on the same night his servant and his cook fled, which appeared to show their participation in the crime. It was suggested, but never proved, that the deceased gentleman may have had valuables in the house, and that their abstraction was the motive of the crime. Every effort was made by Inspector Baynes, who has the case in hand, to ascertain the hiding place of the fugitives, and he had good reason to believe that they had not gone far, but were lurking in some retreat which had already been prepared. It was certain from the first, however, that they would eventually be detected, as the cook, from the evidence of one or two tradespeople who have caught a glimpse of him through the window, was a man of most remarkable appearance—being a huge and hideous mulatto,[19] with yellowish features of a pronounced negroid type. This man has been seen since the crime, for he was detected and pursued by Constable Walters on the same evening, when he had the audacity to revisit Wisteria Lodge. Inspector Baynes, considering that such a visit must have some purpose in view, and was likely, therefore, to be repeated, abandoned the house, but left an ambuscade in the shrubbery. The man walked into the trap, and was captured last night after a struggle, in which Constable Downing was badly bitten by the savage. We understand that when the prisoner is brought before the magistrates a remand[20] will be applied for by the police, and that great developments are hoped from his capture.

"Really we must see Baynes at once," cried Holmes, picking up his hat. "We will just catch him before he starts." We hurried down the village street and found, as we had expected, that the inspector was just leaving his lodgings.

"You've seen the paper, Mr. Holmes?" he asked, holding one out to us.

"Yes, Baynes, I've seen it. Pray don't think it a liberty if I give you a word of friendly warning."

"Of warning, Mr. Holmes?"

"I have looked into this case with some care, and I am not convinced that you are on the right lines. I don't want you to commit yourself too far, unless you are sure."

"You're very kind, Mr. Holmes."

"I assure you I speak for your good."

It seemed to me that something like a wink quivered for an instant over one of Mr. Baynes's tiny eyes.

"We agreed to work on our own lines, Mr. Holmes. That's what I am doing."

"Oh, very good," said Holmes. "Don't blame me."

"No, sir; I believe you mean well by me. But we all have our own systems, Mr. Holmes. You have yours, and maybe I have mine."

"Let us say no more about it."

"You're welcome always to my news. This fellow is a perfect savage, as strong as a cart-horse and as fierce as the devil. He chewed Downing's thumb nearly off before they could master

19 In the strictest terms, a mulatto was said to be the child of one black parent and one white parent. Reflecting the racial climate of the day, there were further terms that specified one's mixed-race lineage to an even greater degree: a "quadroon" (one-quarter black) was the child of a mulatto and a white, while an "octoroon" (one-eighth black) was the child of a quadroon and a white. The child of an octoroon and a white was finally considered to be white, according to Brewer's *Dictionary of Phrase and Fable*, whose listing of "Negro Offspring" tellingly only presents situations in which a white man would mate with a "negro" or mixed-race woman. The word "mulatto" was derived from the Portuguese diminutive of *mulo*, or mule, the crossbred offspring of a male donkey and female horse.

20 In this context, a judicial order for committal of an alleged offender to custody pending trial.

him. He hardly speaks a word of English, and we can get nothing out of him but grunts."

"And you think you have evidence that he murdered his late master?"

"I didn't say so, Mr. Holmes; I didn't say so. We all have our little ways. You try yours and I will try mine. That's the agreement."

Holmes shrugged his shoulders as we walked away together. "I can't make the man out. He seems to be riding for a fall. Well, as he says, we must each try our own way and see what comes of it. But there's something in Inspector Baynes which I can't quite understand."

"Just sit down in that chair, Watson," said Sherlock Holmes, when we had returned to our apartment at the Bull. "I want to put you in touch with the situation, as I may need your help tonight. Let me show you the evolution of this case, so far as I have been able to follow it. Simple as it has been in its leading features, it has none the less presented surprising difficulties in the way of an arrest. There are gaps in that direction which we have still to fill.

"We will go back to the note which was handed in to Garcia upon the evening of his death. We may put aside this idea of Baynes's that Garcia's servants were concerned in the matter. The proof of this lies in the fact that it was *he* who had arranged for the presence of Scott Eccles, which could only have been done for the purpose of an alibi. It was Garcia, then, who had an enterprise, and apparently a criminal enterprise, in hand that night, in the course of which he met his death. I say criminal because only a man with a criminal enterprise desires to establish an alibi. Who, then, is most likely to have taken his life? Surely the person against whom the criminal enterprise was directed. So far it seems to me that we are on safe ground.

"We can now see a reason for the disappearance of Garcia's household. They were *all* confederates in the same unknown crime. If it came off then Garcia returned, any possible suspicion would be warded off by the Englishman's evidence, and all would be well. But the attempt was a dangerous one, and if Garcia did *not* return by a certain hour it was probable that his own life had been sacrificed. It had been arranged, therefore, that in such a case his two subordinates were to make for some pre-arranged spot, where they could escape investigation and be in a position afterwards to renew their attempt. That would fully explain the facts, would it not?"

The whole inexplicable tangle seemed to straighten out before me. I wondered, as I always did, how it had not been obvious to me before.

"But why should one servant return?"

"We can imagine that, in the confusion of flight, something precious, something which he could not bear to part with, had been left behind. That would explain his persistence, would it not?"

"Well, what is the next step?"

"The next step is the note received by Garcia at the dinner. It indicates a confederate at the other end. Now, where was the other end? I have already shown you that it could only lie in some large house, and that the number of large houses is limited. My first days in this village were devoted to a series of walks, in which in the intervals of my botanical researches I made a reconnaissance of all the large houses and an examination of the family history of the occupants. One house, and only one, riveted my attention. It is the famous old Jacobean[21] grange of High Gable, one mile on the farther side of Oxshott, and less than half a mile from the scene of the tragedy. The other mansions belonged to prosaic and respectable people who live far aloof from romance. But Mr. Henderson, of High Gable, was by all accounts a curious man, to whom curious adventures might befall. I concentrated my attention, therefore, upon him and his household.

"A singular set of people, Watson—the man himself the most singular of them all. I managed to see him on a plausible pretext, but I seemed to read in his dark, deep-set, brooding eyes that he was perfectly aware of my true business. He is a man of fifty, strong, active, with iron-grey hair, great bunched black eyebrows, the step of a deer, and the air of an emperor— a fierce, masterful man, with a red-hot spirit behind his parchment face. He is either a foreigner or has lived long in the Tropics, for he is yellow and sapless, but tough as whipcord. His friend and secretary, Mr. Lucas, is undoubtedly a foreigner, chocolate brown, wily, suave and cat-like with a poisonous gentleness of speech. You see, Watson, we have come already upon

21 Jacobean architecture, which originated during the reign of James I (1603–1625), bridged Elizabethan with English Renaissance style, combining the old ornamental decorations and grand manor flourishes with more formal design elements such as columns, arches, and flat roofs featuring low, protective parapets.

two sets of foreigners—one at Wisteria Lodge and one at High Gable—so our gaps are beginning to close.

"These two men, close and confidential friends, are the centre of the household; but there is one other person, who for our immediate purpose may be even more important. Henderson has two children—girls of eleven and thirteen. Their governess is a Miss Burnet, an Englishwoman of forty or thereabouts. There is also one confidential manservant. This little group forms the real family, for they travel about together and Henderson is a great traveller, always on the move. It is only within the last few weeks that he has returned, after a year's absence, to High Gable. I may add that he is enormously rich, and whatever his whims may be he can very easily satisfy them. For the rest, his house is full of butlers, footmen, maidservants, and the usual overfed, underworked staff of a large English country-house.

"So much I learned partly from village gossip and partly from my own observation. There are no better instruments than discharged servants with a grievance, and I was lucky enough to find one. I call it luck, but it would not have come my way had I not been looking out for it. As Baynes remarks, we all have our systems. It was my system which enabled me to find John Warner, late gardener of High Gable, sacked in a moment of temper by his imperious employer. He in turn had friends among the indoor servants, who unite in their fear and dislike of their master. So I had my key to the secrets of the establishment.

"Curious people, Watson! I don't pretend to understand it all yet, but very curious people anyway. It's a double-winged house, and the servants live on one side, the family on the other. There's no link between the two save for Henderson's own servant, who serves the family's meals. Everything is carried to a certain door, which forms the one connection. Governess and children hardly go out at all, except into the garden. Henderson never by any chance walks alone. His dark secretary is like his shadow. The gossip among the servants is that their master is terribly afraid of something. 'Sold his soul to the devil in exchange for money,' says Warner, 'and expects his creditor to come up and claim his own.' Where they came from, or who they are, nobody has an idea. They are very violent. Twice Henderson has lashed at folk with his dog-whip, and only his long purse and heavy compensation have kept him out of the courts.

"Well, now, Watson, let us judge the situation by this new information. We may take it that the letter came out of this strange household, and was an invitation to Garcia to carry out some attempt which had already been planned. Who wrote the note? It was someone within the citadel, and it was a woman. Who then, but Miss Burnet, the governess? All our reasoning seems to point that way. At any rate, we may take it as a hypothesis, and see what consequences it would entail. I may add that Miss Burnet's age and character make it certain that my first idea that there might be a love interest in our story is out of the question.

"If she wrote the note she was presumably the friend and confederate of Garcia. What, then, might she be expected to do if she heard of his death? If he met it in some nefarious enterprise her lips might be sealed. Still, in her heart she must retain bitterness and hatred against those who had killed him, and would presumably help so far as she could to have revenge upon them. Could we see her, then, and try to use her? That was my first thought. But now we come to a sinister fact. Miss Burnet has not been seen by any human eye since the night of the murder. From that evening she has utterly vanished. Is she alive? Has she perhaps met her end on the same night as the friend whom she had summoned? Or is she merely a prisoner? There is the point which we still have to decide.

"You will appreciate the difficulty of the situation, Watson. There is nothing upon which we can apply for a warrant. Our whole scheme might seem fantastic if laid before a magistrate. The woman's disappearance counts for nothing, since in that extraordinary household any member of it might be invisible for a week. And yet she may at the present moment be in danger of her life. All I can do is to watch the house and leave my agent, Warner, on guard at the gates. We can't let such a situation continue. If the law can do nothing we must take the risk ourselves."

"What do you suggest?"

"I know which is her room. It is accessible from the top of an outhouse. My suggestion is that you and I go to-night and see if we can strike at the very heart of the mystery."

It was not, I must confess, a very alluring prospect. The old house with its atmosphere of murder, the singular and formidable inhabitants, the unknown dangers of the approach, and the fact that we were putting ourselves legally in a false position, all combined to damp my ardour. But there was something in the ice-cold reasoning of Holmes which made it impossible to shrink from any adventure which he might recommend. One knew that thus, and only thus, could a solution be found. I clasped his hand in silence, and the die was cast.

But it was not destined that our investigation should have so adventurous an ending. It was about five o'clock, and the shadows of the March evening were beginning to fall, when an excited rustic rushed into our room.

"They've gone, Mr. Holmes. They went by the last train. The lady broke away, and I've got her in a cab downstairs."

"Excellent, Warner!" cried Holmes, springing to his feet. "Watson, the gaps are closing rapidly."

In the cab was a woman, half-collapsed from nervous exhaustion. She bore upon her aquiline and emaciated face the traces of some recent tragedy. Her head hung listlessly upon her breast, but as she raised it and turned her dull eyes upon us, I saw that her pupils were dark dots in the centre of the broad grey iris. She was drugged with opium.

"I watched at the gate, same as you advised, Mr. Holmes," said our emissary, the discharged gardener. "When the carriage came out I followed it to the station. She was like one walking in her sleep; but when they tried to get her into the train she came to life and struggled. They pushed her into the carriage. She fought her way out again. I took her part, got her into a cab, and here we are. I shan't forget the face at the carriage window as I led her away. I'd have a short life if he had his way—the black-eyed, scowling, yellow devil."

We carried her upstairs, laid her on the sofa, and a couple of cups of the strongest coffee soon cleared her brain from the mists of the drug. Baynes had been summoned by Holmes, and the situation rapidly explained to him.

"Why, sir, you've got me the very evidence I want," said the inspector, warmly, shaking my friend by the hand. "I was on the same scent as you from the first."

"What! You were after Henderson?"

"Why, Mr. Holmes, when you were crawling in the shrubbery at High Gable I was up one of the trees in the plantation

"She fought her way out again."
Arthur Twidle, *Strand Magazine*, 1908

and saw you down below. It was just who would get his evidence first."

"Then why did you arrest the mulatto?"

Baynes chuckled.

"I was sure Henderson, as he calls himself, felt that he was suspected, and that he would lie low and make no move so long as he thought he was in any danger. I arrested the wrong man to make him believe that our eyes were off him. I knew he would be likely to clear off then and give us a chance of getting at Miss Burnet."

Holmes laid his hand upon the inspector's shoulder.

"You will rise high in your profession. You have instinct and intuition," said he.

Baynes flushed with pleasure.

22 A Spanish title applied in courtesy to all of the "better" classes. It precedes the bearer's Christian name (as in "Don Juan"). Thus the inspector's reference to "Don Murillo" is improper.

The light from the window streamed across the shrubbery.
Frederick Dorr Steele, *Collier's*, 1908

"I've had a plain-clothes man waiting at the station all the week. Wherever the High Gable folk go he will keep them in sight. But he must have been hard put to it when Miss Burnet broke away. However, your man picked her up, and it all ends well. We can't arrest without her evidence, that is clear, so the sooner we get a statement the better."

"Every minute she gets stronger," said Holmes, glancing at the governess. "But tell me, Baynes, who is this man Henderson?"

"Henderson," the inspector answered, "is Don[22] Murillo, once called the Tiger of San Pedro."

The Tiger of San Pedro! The whole history of the man came back to me in a flash. He had made his name as the most lewd and bloodthirsty tyrant that had ever governed any country with a pretence to civilization. Strong, fearless, and energetic, he had sufficient virtue to enable him to impose his odious vices upon a cowering people for ten or twelve years. His name was a terror through all Central America.[23] At the end of that time there was a universal rising against him. But he was as cunning as he was cruel, and at the first whisper of coming trouble he had secretly conveyed his treasures aboard a ship which was manned by devoted adherents. It was an empty palace which was stormed by the insurgents next day. The Dictator, his two children, his secretary, and his wealth had all escaped them. From that moment he had vanished from the world, and his identity had been a frequent subject for comment in the European Press.[24]

"Yes, sir; Don Murillo, the Tiger of San Pedro," said Baynes. "If you look it up you will find that the San Pedro colours are green and white, same as in the note, Mr. Holmes. Henderson he called himself, but I traced him back, Paris and Rome and Madrid to Barcelona, where his ship came in in '86. They've been looking for him all the time for their revenge, but it is only now that they have begun to find him out."

"They discovered him a year ago," said Miss Burnet, who had sat up and was now intently following the conversation. "Once already his life has been attempted; but some evil spirit shielded him. Now, again, it is the noble, chivalrous Garcia who has fallen, while the monster goes safe. But another will come, and yet another, until some day justice will be done; that is as certain as the rise of to-morrow's sun." Her thin hands clenched, and her worn face blanched with the passion of her hatred.

"But how come you into this matter, Miss Burnet?" asked Holmes. "How can an English lady join in such a murderous affair?"

"I join in it because there is no other way in the world by which justice can be gained. What does the law of England care for the rivers of blood shed years ago in San Pedro, or for the ship-load of treasure which this man has stolen? To you they are like crimes committed in some other planet. But *we* know. We have learned the truth in sorrow and in suffering. To us there is no fiend in hell like Juan Murillo, and no peace in life while his victims still cry for vengeance."

"No doubt," said Holmes, "he was as you say. I have heard that he was atrocious. But how are you affected?"

23 Any attempt to guess the true location of "San Pedro" by looking for clues in the fateful note ("Our own colours, green and white") is fruitless, for green and white, as Julian Wolff points out in *Practical Handbook of Sherlockian Heraldry*, are not the colours of any Central American flag. Wolff does notice that green and *yellow* are the colours of Brazil's flag, a close enough match to support a possible correlation there. Cindy Stevens makes an excellent case for Hispaniola as "San Pedro." Other suggestions include Nicaragua, El Salvador, and Guatemala. (See note 24 for further details.)

24 Operating on the assumption that the green and white colours of Garcia's note were actually meant to be the green and yellow colours of the Brazilian flag, Julian Wolff identifies the "Tiger" as Dom Pedro de Alcântara, or Pedro II, the last emperor of Brazil. Pedro II reigned from 1831 until 1889, when a military coup forced him into exile in Europe. Far from being a "lewd and bloodthirsty tyrant," Pedro II was widely popular; under his reign the slaves were emancipated, export revenues increased, and the railway system expanded. It was the monarchy's ties to a traditionally elite feudal system, more than dissatisfaction with Pedro II himself, that caused pro-capitalist groups—among them the urban middle class, coffee farmers, and the military—to push for a new system of government. Wolff explains the contradiction between Pedro II's actual nature and the violent description accorded him here by pointing out that Holmes and Watson were getting information from the point of view of the opposition. Although Watson seems to recall reading about Dom Pedro in the press, his recollection of those press reports may well have been coloured by the passions of Garcia and his confederates. As Wolff puts it, "Anyone who has read the opposition's opinion of our best and wisest men will easily understand."

Evan Wilson concludes instead that the country in question is El Salvador, the dictator Rafael Zaldívar, who ruled from 1876 to 1885 and oversaw numerous Indian uprisings. Charles Higham, in *Adventures of Conan Doyle*, suggests José Santos Zelaya (1893–1909), president of Nicaragua. Zelaya, a true dictator who annexed the Mosquito Coast, incited revolutions in neighboring countries, and attempted to assume control of the Central American Federation, made plenty of enemies—including the U.S. government, which, frustrated by his refusal to allow a canal to be built through Nicaragua, encouraged his Conservative opposition to revolt. Zelaya was forced to resign and go into exile, but not until one year after "Wisteria Lodge" was first published. In a detailed examination of the problem, Henry Dietz also fingers Zelaya as the Tiger, arguing that Watson "anticipated the end of the adventure before it took place in the hopes of hurrying Zelaya's downfall."

Klas Lithner is persuasive in arguing for Justo Rufino Barrios, a dictator of Guatemala from 1873 to 1885. Most fancifully, Rick Lai proposes that Murillo was the man named Mayes, known as the "Tiger of Haiti," whose evil deeds were recorded by Arthur Morrison in *The Red Triangle* (1903), a record of the adventures of Holmes's rival Martin Hewitt.

25 Watson undoubtedly means "Señora"; "Signora" is an Italian title.

"I will tell you it all. This villain's policy was to murder, on one pretext or another, every man who showed such promise that he might in time come to be a dangerous rival. My husband—yes, my real name is Signora[25] Victor Durando—was the San Pedro Minister in London. He met me and married me there. A nobler man never lived upon earth. Unhappily, Murillo heard of his excellence, recalled him on some pretext, and had him shot. With a premonition of his fate he had refused to take me with him. His estates were confiscated, and I was left with a pittance and a broken heart.

"Then came the downfall of the tyrant. He escaped as you have just described. But the many whose lives he had ruined, whose nearest and dearest had suffered torture and death at his hands, would not let the matter rest. They banded themselves into a society which should never be dissolved until the work was done. It was my part after we had discovered in the transformed Henderson the fallen despot, to attach myself to his household and keep the others in touch with his movements. This I was able to do by securing the position of governess in his family. He little knew that the woman who faced him at every meal was the woman whose husband he had hurried at an hour's notice into eternity. I smiled on him, did my duty to his children, and bided my time. An attempt was made in Paris, and failed. We zigzagged swiftly here and there over Europe, to throw off the pursuers, and finally returned to this house, which he had taken upon his first arrival in England.

"But here also the ministers of justice were waiting. Knowing that he would return there, Garcia, who is the son of the former highest dignitary in San Pedro, was waiting with two trusty companions of humble station, all three fired with the same reasons for revenge. He could do little during the day, for Murillo took every precaution, and never went out save with his satellite Lucas, or Lopez as he was known in the days of his greatness. At night, however, he slept alone, and the avenger might find him. On a certain evening, which had been prearranged, I sent my friend final instructions, for the man was for ever on the alert, and continually changed his room. I was to see that the doors were open and the signal of a green or white light in a window which faced the drive was to give notice if all was safe, or if the attempt had better be postponed.

"But everything went wrong with us. In some way I had

excited the suspicion of Lopez, the secretary. He crept up behind me, and sprang upon me just as I had finished the note. He and his master dragged me to my room, and held judgment upon me as a convicted traitress. Then and there they would have plunged their knives into me, could they have seen how to escape the consequence of the deed. Finally, after much debate, they concluded that my murder was too dangerous. But they determined to get rid for ever of Garcia.[26] They had gagged me, and Murillo twisted my arm round until I gave him the address. I swear that he might have twisted it off had I understood what it would mean to Garcia. Lopez addressed the note which I had written, sealed it with his sleeve-link, and sent it by the hand of the servant, Jose.[27] How they murdered him I do not know, save that it was Murillo's hand who struck him down, for Lopez had remained to guard me. I believe he must have waited among the gorse bushes through which the

"He crept up behind me just as I had finished the note."
Lee Conrey, *Seattle Post-Intelligencer*, December 8, 1912

26 The logic of killing Garcia but not Señora Durando seems convoluted, argues D. Martin Dakin, seeing as how "his body was bound to be discovered, whereas she could have disappeared without anyone being the wiser." Chris Wills-Wood answers that Murillo and his confederates were seeking to avoid drawing attention to High Gable itself. Señora Durando's death would have caused the police to make troublesome inquiries of her employers, whereas Garcia's murder could have—had not the wily Holmes and Baynes been involved—presumably eluded any connection with the house down the road.

27 "But why didn't the fool Lopez wait to pounce until she'd addressed the envelope herself?" D. Martin Dakin asks. "It would have saved them the trouble of torturing her, as well as giving the letter a more authentic appearance. It is strange enough as it is that the address in a different handwriting didn't arouse Garcia's suspicions." That Garcia did notice is the contention of Chris Wills-Wood, who remembers that, after receiving the letter, Garcia seemed (according to Eccles's account) "even more distrait and strange than before" and later became "lost in his own thoughts."

"He and his master dragged me to my room."
Arthur Twidle, *Strand Magazine*, 1908

path winds and struck him down as he passed. At first they were of a mind to let him enter the house and to kill him as a detected burglar; but they argued that if they were mixed up in an inquiry their own identity would at once be publicly disclosed and they would be open to further attacks. With the death of Garcia the pursuit might cease, since such a death might frighten others from the task.

"All would now have been well for them had it not been for my knowledge of what they had done. I have no doubt that there were times when my life hung in the balance. I was confined to my room, terrorised by the most horrible threats, cruelly ill-used to break my spirit—see this stab on my shoulder and the bruises from end to end of my arms—and a gag was thrust into my mouth on the one occasion when I tried to call from the window. For five days this cruel imprisonment continued, with hardly enough food to hold body and soul together. This afternoon a good lunch was brought me, but the moment after I took it I knew that I had been drugged. In a sort of dream I remember being half-led, half-carried to the carriage; in the same state I was conveyed to the train. Only then, when the wheels were almost moving did I suddenly realise that my liberty lay in my own hands. I sprang out, they tried to drag me back, and had it not been for the help of this good man, who led me to the cab, I should never have broken away. Now, thank God, I am beyond their power for ever."

"They had gagged me, and Murillo twisted my arm round."
Frederick Dorr Steele, *Collier's*, 1908

28 As the county seat of Surrey, Guildford would have hosted the semiannual legal hearings for the entire county.

29 In England, a rank of the peerage below that of a duke and above that of an earl. In other countries, the title has been debased.

30 Clearly "Signor" should be "Señor," and "Rulli" is an unlikely Spanish name.

31 See "The Golden Pince-Nez," note 19.

We had all listened intently to this remarkable statement. It was Holmes who broke the silence.

"Our difficulties are not over," he remarked, shaking his head. "Our police work ends, but our legal work begins."

"Exactly," said I. "A plausible lawyer could make it out as an act of self-defence. There may be a hundred crimes in the background, but it is only on this one that they can be tried."

"Come, come," said Baynes, cheerily; "I think better of the law than that. Self-defence is one thing. To entice a man in cold blood with the object of murdering him is another, whatever danger you may fear from him. No, no; we shall all be justified when we see the tenants of High Gable at the next Guildford Assizes."[28]

It is a matter of history, however, that a little time was still to elapse before the Tiger of San Pedro should meet with his deserts. Wily and bold, he and his companion threw their pursuer off their track by entering a lodging-house in Edmonton Street and leaving by the back-gate into Curzon Square. From that day they were seen no more in England. Some six months afterwards the Marquess[29] of Montalva and Signor Rulli,[30] his secretary, were both murdered in their rooms at the Hotel Escurial at Madrid. The crime was ascribed to Nihilism,[31] and the murderers were never arrested. Inspector Baynes visited us at Baker Street with a printed description of the dark face of the secretary, and of the masterful features, the magnetic black

The crime was ascribed to Nihilism, and the
murderers were never arrested.
Frederick Dorr Steele, *Collier's*, 1908

"The man walked into the trap and was captured."
Arthur Twidle, *Strand Magazine*, 1908

eyes, and the tufted brows of his master. We could not doubt that justice, if belated, had come at last.

"A chaotic case, my dear Watson," said Holmes, over an evening pipe. "It will not be possible for you to present it in that compact form which is dear to your heart. It covers two continents, concerns two groups of mysterious persons, and is further complicated by the highly respectable presence of our friend Scott Eccles, whose inclusion shows me that the deceased Garcia had a scheming mind and a well-developed instinct of self-preservation. It is remarkable only for the fact that amid a perfect jungle of possibilities we, with our worthy

32 The magical power attributed to a fetish (which may be either the remnant of a living thing, such as a bone, a shell, or a claw; or an artificially constructed object, such as a wooden carving) is said to come from a god that inhabits the item and imbues it with his desires. In some cases, the fetish is thought to have a will of its own. Had the cook placed a "taboo" on his fetish, it would have taken on even greater power, and no one but the cook would have been able to touch it.

collaborator the inspector, have kept our close hold on the essentials and so been guided along the crooked and winding path. Is there any point which is not quite clear to you?"

"The object of the mulatto cook's return?"

"I think that the strange creature in the kitchen may account for it. The man was a primitive savage from the backwoods of San Pedro, and this was his fetish.[32] When his companion and he had fled to some prearranged retreat—already occupied, no doubt, by a confederate—the companion had persuaded him to leave so compromising an article of furniture. But the mulatto's heart was with it, and he was driven back to it next day, when, on reconnoitring through the window, he found policeman Walters in possession. He waited three days longer, and then his piety or his superstition drove him to try once more. Inspector Baynes, who, with his usual astuteness, had minimised the incident before me, had really recognised its importance, and had left a trap into which the creature walked. Any other point, Watson?"

"The torn bird, the pail of blood, the charred bones, all the mystery of that weird kitchen?"

Holmes smiled as he turned up an entry in his notebook.

"I spent a morning in the British Museum reading up that and other points. Here is a quotation from Eckermann's *Voodooism and the Negroid Religions*:

Sacrifices to propitiate his unclean gods.
Frederick Dorr Steele, *Collier's*, 1908

The true Voodoo-worshipper attempts nothing of importance without certain sacrifices which are intended to propitiate his unclean gods. In extreme cases these rites take the form of human sacrifices followed by cannibalism. The more usual victims are a white cock, which is plucked in pieces alive, or a black goat, whose throat is cut and body burned.[33]

"So you see our savage friend was very orthodox in his ritual. It is grotesque, Watson," Holmes added, as he slowly fastened his notebook; "but, as I have had occasion to remark, there is but one step from the grotesque to the horrible."

33 The references to "unclean gods" and cannibalism reflect a Victorian revulsion for voodoo that largely persists today. Yet the staying power of Haiti's primary religion has forced even the Catholic church to come to uneasy terms with its practices. In fact, some of voodoo's rituals are derived from Catholicism itself. Brought to Haiti by West African slaves (particularly those from Benin), voodoo holds that the world is governed by spiritual forces, or *loas*, who must be appeased through ritual animal sacrifice, food offerings, and ceremonial song and dance. *Loas*, which may be identified with deceased ancestors, African gods, or Catholic saints, are sometimes said to inhabit the bodies of voodoo devotees who have entered into a trance state.

It is from voodoo that the leering, lurching zombies of horror films originate. A zombie is the soul of a deceased person summoned by an evil sorcerer to enact magic, or a corpse raised from the grave to perform manual labor. Voodoo priests may also appear to create zombies by administering a poison that renders one paralysed for several hours.

Despite some of voodoo's more idiosyncratic aspects, cannibalism's role in the belief system is no more than an urban legend, as is the sticking of pins into so-called voodoo dolls. Varieties of voodoo are practised not only in Haiti but also in the Guyanas, Cuba, Jamaica, Brazil, and the United States. In light of Don Murillo's flight from one capital of Europe to another, it is not surprising to find a servant without references in the Don's retinue, and the cook, whom the Don "picked up in his travels," is of indeterminate geographic origin.

THE ADVENTURE OF THE
RED CIRCLE[1]

Long before Mario Puzo and Francis Ford Coppola romanticised the Mafia for the American public, "The Red Circle" involved Holmes with an Italian secret society so powerful that Watson was compelled to disguise its name. The "Italian colony" in London, although a distinct feature of the landscape, by and large kept itself apart from the rest of the population, and only one other case, "The Six Napoleons," involves Italians. Here, Holmes accidentally joins forces with the Pinkertons, America's premier private detective agency of the nineteenth century, to capture a cross-Atlantic killer. The Pinkertons appear again in The Valley of Fear, *but this is the only record of Holmes working with them. Scholars consider that Holmes may well have been duped by the beautiful heroine into letting the real murderer go.*

[1] The original title in the manuscript is "The Adventure of the Bloomsbury Lodger." The manuscript is owned by the Lilly Library at Indiana University and is described by Spencer C. Kennedy in "The Adventure of the Red Circle: An Examination of the Original Manuscript." "The Red Circle" was published in the *Strand Magazine* in March and April 1911.

PART I

WELL, MRS. WARREN, I cannot see that you have any particular cause for uneasiness, nor do I understand why I, whose time is of some value, should interfere in the matter. I really have other things to engage me." So spoke Sherlock Holmes, and turned back to the great scrapbook in which he was arranging and indexing some of his recent material.

But the landlady had the pertinacity, and also the cunning, of her sex. She held her ground firmly.

"You arranged an affair for a lodger of mine last year," she said—"Mr. Fairdale Hobbs."

"Ah, yes—a simple matter."

"But he would never cease talking of it—your kindness, sir, and the way in which you brought light into the darkness. I remembered his words when I was in doubt and darkness myself. I know you could if you only would."

Holmes was accessible upon the side of flattery, and also, to do him justice, upon the side of kindliness. The two forces

A Reverie.
H. M. Brock, R. I., and Joseph Simpson, R. B. A.,
Strand Magazine, 1911

2 Mrs. Warrren's maid-servant, that is.

3 *Baedeker* lists several boarding houses in Mrs. Warren's vicinity, near the British Museum (those belonging to Misses Wright, for example, on Upper Woburn Place, or to Mrs. Snell, on Bedford Place) that had rates of 7-8s. per day, although less expensive locations might run as little as 30s. to 40s. per week. Of course, Holmes and Watson are themselves lodgers, although Mrs. Hudson may appear to be the ideal landlady and no other tenants are ever mentioned. The "B" in 221B implies that there was a 221A which also formed a part of the premises at Baker Street, and there may well have been shared facilities (such as the water closets). In *A Study in Scarlet*, Watson reveals that upon his return to London from India, when he is receiving a wound pension of 11s. per day, he has been living in a hotel. The expense has been too much for him, however, and he eagerly agrees to share a "suite" with Holmes, who has been looking for someone to go in with him on the Baker Street apartment. Private apartments, such as those in which Holmes and Watson lodge at Baker Street, tended to run 15 to 21s. per week in the less-expensive neighbourhoods, but included only breakfast. We may deduce, therefore, that Watson's share of the cost of lodgings must have been closer to the 7-8s. per day that a boarding house would have cost, although eventually Holmes paid Mrs. Hudson a "princely sum" for the suite ("The Dying Detective").

4 People who tended to "take lodgings" were generally bachelors, spinsters, widows, out-of-towners, or working people who had missed their trains out of London. All sought economical accommodations and were willing to sacrifice some degree of privacy. Unless one was willing to pay top dollar, the quality of the rooms and service was certainly not up the level of a hotel, and landladies could be both

made him lay down his gum-brush with a sigh of resignation and push back his chair.

"Well, well, Mrs. Warren, let us hear about it, then. You don't object to tobacco, I take it? Thank you, Watson—the matches! You are uneasy, as I understand, because your new lodger remains in his rooms and you cannot see him. Why, bless you, Mrs. Warren, if I were your lodger you often would not see me for weeks on end."

"No doubt, sir; but this is different. It frightens me, Mr. Holmes. I can't sleep for fright. To hear his quick step moving here and moving there from early morning to late at night, and yet never to catch so much as a glimpse of him—it's more than I can stand. My husband is as nervous over it as I am, but he is out at his work all day, while I get no rest from it. What is he hiding for? What has be done? Except for the girl,[2] I am all alone in the house with him, and it's more than my nerves can stand."

Holmes leaned forward and laid his long, thin fingers upon the woman's shoulder. He had an almost hypnotic power of soothing when he wished. The scared look faded from her eyes, and her agitated features smoothed into their usual commonplace. She sat down in the chair which he had indicated. "If I take it up I must understand every detail," said he. "Take time to consider. The smallest point may be the most essential. You say that the man came ten days ago, and paid you for a fortnight's board and lodging?"

"He asked my terms, sir. I said fifty shillings a week.[3] There is a small sitting-room and bedroom, and all complete, at the top of the house.[4]

"Well?"

"He said, 'I'll pay you five pounds a week if I can have it on my own terms.' I'm a poor woman, sir, and Mr. Warren earns little, and the money meant much to me. He took out a ten-pound note, and he held it out to me then and there. 'You can have the same every fortnight for a long time to come if you keep the terms,' he said. 'If not, I'll have no more to do with you.' "

"What were the terms?"

"Well, sir, they were that he was to have a key of the house. That was all right. Lodgers often have them. Also that he was to be left entirely to himself and never, upon any excuse, to be disturbed."

"Nothing wonderful in that, surely?"

"Not in reason, sir. But this is out of all reason. He has been there for ten days, and neither Mr. Warren, nor I, nor the girl has once set eyes upon him. We can hear that quick step of his pacing up and down, up and down, night, morning, and noon; but except on that first night he has never once gone out of the house."

"Oh, he went out the first night, did he?"

"Yes, sir, and returned very late—after we were all in bed. He told me after he had taken the rooms that he would do so, and asked me not to bar the door. I heard him come up the stair after midnight."

"But his meals?"

"It was his particular direction that we should always, when he rang, leave his meal upon a chair, outside his door. Then he rings again when he has finished and we take it down from the same chair. If he wants anything else he prints it on a slip of paper and leaves it."

"Prints it?"

"Yes, sir; prints it in pencil. Just the word, nothing more. Here's one I brought to show you—SOAP. Here's another—MATCH. This is one he left the first morning—DAILY GAZETTE.[5] I leave that paper with his breakfast every morning."

"Dear me, Watson," said Holmes, staring with great curiosity at the slips of foolscap which the landlady had handed to him, "this is certainly a little unusual. Seclusion I can understand; but why print? Printing is a clumsy process. Why not write? What would it suggest, Watson?"

"That he desired to conceal his handwriting."

"But why? What can it matter to him that his landlady should have a word of his writing? Still, it may be as you say. Then, again, why such laconic messages?"

"I cannot imagine."

"It opens a pleasing field for intelligent speculation. The words are written with a broad-pointed, violet-tinted pencil of a not unusual pattern. You will observe that the paper is torn away at the side here after the printing was done, so that the 'S' of 'SOAP' is partly gone. Suggestive, Watson, is it not?"

"Of caution?"

"Exactly. There was evidently some mark, some thumb-print, something which might give a clue to the person's iden-

solicitous and baldly opportunistic, charging extra for any variety of amenities. "Lodging houses," declared *Punch* magazine cheekily in its January–June 1842 issue, "[a]re distinguished by square inscriptions wafered to squares of glass, which usually intimate a desire on the part of the exhibitors (generally blooming widows) to share their domiciles with a 'single gentleman.' When introduced to the lady, she declares that everything is 'clean and comfortable' especially the window-curtains, whose colour cannot be seen for the dust; and the bed-room which was fumigated by the last lodger with tobacco smoke."

Still, Mrs. Warren's sole lodger may count himself fortunate (or sufficiently well funded) to have avoided the typical London boarding house, where the residents were more numerous and the scene slightly more disorderly. *London Characters and the Humorous Side of London Life* (1870), by Henry Mayhew et al., described such an environment as "neither public nor private," a living situation in which "individual freedom is lost, and, instead of living an independent life as at an hotel, the members of a 'circle' find themselves surrounded by such amenities as may be supposed to belong a rather large and singularly disunited family."

5 A fictitious newspaper.

"Holmes stared with great curiosity at the slips of foolscap."
H. M. Brock, R. I., and Joseph Simpson, R. B. A.,
Strand Magazine, 1911

tity. Now, Mrs. Warren, you say that the man was of middle size, dark, and bearded. What age would he be?"

"Youngish, sir—not over thirty."

"Well, can you give me no further indications?"

"He spoke good English, sir, and yet I thought he was a foreigner by his accent."

"And he was well dressed?"

"Very smartly dressed, sir—quite the gentleman. Dark clothes—nothing you would note."

"He gave no name?"

"No, sir."

"And has had no letters or callers?"

"None."

"But surely you or the girl enter his room of a morning?"

"No, sir; he looks after himself entirely."

"Dear me! That is certainly remarkable. What about his luggage?"

"He had one big brown bag with him—nothing else."

"Well, we don't seem to have much material to help us. Do you say nothing has come out of that room—absolutely nothing?"

The landlady drew an envelope from her bag; from it she shook out two burnt matches and a cigarette-end upon the table.

"They were on his tray this morning. I brought them because I had heard that you can read great things out of small ones."

Holmes shrugged his shoulders.

"There is nothing here," said he. "The matches have, of course, been used to light cigarettes. That is obvious from the shortness of the burnt end. Half the match is consumed in lighting a pipe or cigar. But, dear me! This cigarette stub is certainly remarkable. The gentleman was bearded and moustached, you say?"

"Yes, sir."

"I don't understand that. I should say that only a clean-shaven man could have smoked this. Why, Watson, even your modest moustache would have been singed."

"A holder?" I suggested.

"No, no; the end is matted. I suppose there could not be two people in your rooms, Mrs. Warren?"

"No, sir. He eats so little that I often wonder it can keep life in one."

"Well, I think we must wait for a little more material. After all, you have nothing to complain of. You have received your rent, and he is not a troublesome lodger, though he is certainly an unusual one. He pays you well, and if he chooses to lie concealed it is no direct business of yours. We have no excuse for an intrusion upon his privacy until we have some reason to think that there is a guilty reason for it. I've taken up the matter, and I won't lose sight of it. Report to me if anything fresh occurs, and rely upon my assistance if it should be needed.

"There are certainly some points of interest in this case, Watson," he remarked, when the landlady had left us. "It may, of course, be trivial—individual eccentricity; or it may be very much deeper than appears on the surface. The first thing that

6 "But surely a letter (which could have been addressed simply to Mrs. Warren's lodger, without a name) would have been more secret than a newspaper entry that could be read by anyone!" remarks D. Martin Dakin. He proposes that the lodger garnered a sort of thrill out of acting clandestinely and courting risk—a tendency that Holmes, for that matter, often displayed himself.

7 This reference to the *Daily Gazette* was to the *Daily Telegraph* in the original manuscript, the agony columns of which Holmes referred to in "The Six Napoleons." Watson apparently determined, for reasons unknown, to change the name of the actual newspaper; he slipped up and used the real name in the manuscript, only to correct his slip-up later.

strikes one is the obvious possibility that the person now in the rooms may be entirely different from the one who engaged them."

"Why should you think so?"

"Well, apart from this cigarette-end, was it not suggestive that the only time the lodger went out was immediately after his taking the rooms? He came back—or someone came back—when all witnesses were out of the way. We have no proof that the person who came back was the person who went out. Then, again, the man who took the rooms spoke English well. This other, however, prints 'match' when it should have been 'matches.' I can imagine that the word was taken out of a dictionary, which would give the noun but not the plural. The laconic style may be to conceal the absence of knowledge of English. Yes, Watson, there are good reasons to suspect that there has been a substitution of lodgers."

"But for what possible end?"

"Ah! there lies our problem. There is one rather obvious line of investigation." He took down the great book in which, day by day, he filed the agony columns of the various London journals. "Dear me!" said he, turning over the pages, "what a chorus of groans, cries, and bleatings! What a rag-bag of singular happenings! But surely the most valuable hunting-ground that ever was given to a student of the unusual! This person is alone and cannot be approached by letter without a breach of that absolute secrecy which is desired. How is any news or any message to reach him from without? Obviously by advertisement through a newspaper.[6] There seems no other way, and fortunately we need concern ourselves with the one paper only. Here are the *Daily Gazette* extracts of the last fortnight.[7] 'Lady with a black boa at Prince's Skating Club'—that we may pass. 'Surely Jimmy will not break his mother's heart'—that appears to be irrelevant. 'If the lady who fainted in the Brixton bus'—she does not interest me. 'Every day my heart longs—' Bleat, Watson—unmitigated bleat! Ah, this is a little more possible. Listen to this: 'Be patient. Will find some sure means of communication. Meanwhile, this column.—G.' That is two days after Mrs. Warren's lodger arrived. It sounds plausible, does it not? The mysterious one could understand English, even if he could not print it. Let us see if we can pick up the trace again. Yes, here we are—three days later. 'Am making successful arrangements. Patience and prudence. The clouds will pass.—G.' Nothing for a week after that. Then comes something much more definite: 'The path is clearing. If I find chance signal message remember code agreed—one A, two B, and so on. You will hear soon.—G.' That was in yesterday's paper, and there is nothing in to-day's. It's all very appropriate to Mrs. Warren's lodger. If we wait a little, Watson, I don't doubt that the affair will grow more intelligible."

So it proved; for in the morning I found my friend standing on the hearthrug with his back to the fire, and a smile of complete satisfaction upon his face.

"How's this, Watson?" he cried, picking up the paper from the table. " 'High red house with white stone facings. Third floor. Second window left. After dusk.—G.' That is definite enough. I think after breakfast we must make a little reconnaissance of Mrs. Warren's neighbourhood. Ah, Mrs. Warren! what news do you bring us this morning?"

Our client had suddenly burst into the room with an explosive energy which told of some new and momentous development.

"It's a police matter, Mr. Holmes!" she cried. "I'll have no more of it! He shall pack out of that[8] with his baggage. I would have gone straight up and told him so, only I thought it was but fair to you to take your opinion first. But I'm at the end of my patience, and when it comes to knocking my old man about—"

"Knocking Mr. Warren about?"

"Using him roughly, anyway."

"But who used him roughly?"

"Ah! that's what we want to know! It was this morning, sir. Mr. Warren is a timekeeper at Morton and Waylight's, in Tottenham Court Road. He has to be out of the house before seven. Well, this morning he had not got ten paces down the road when two men came up behind him, threw a coat over his head, and bundled him into a cab that was beside the kerb. They drove him an hour, and then opened the door and shot him out. He lay in the roadway so shaken in his wits that he never saw what became of the cab. When he picked himself up he found he was on Hampstead Heath; so he took a bus home, and there he lies now on the sofa, while I came straight round to tell you what had happened."

"Most interesting," said Holmes. "Did he observe the appearance of these men—did he hear them talk?"

8 The word "that" appears in the *Strand Magazine* and American texts; it has been amended to "there" in the English first edition of *His Last Bow*.

9 For some reason, the word "lawyer" appears here in the manuscript in place of "lodger." Watson may have had legal problems on his mind at the time of writing up his notes, presumably in late 1910 or early 1911. By that time, Watson's writings had been widely published and pirated (in America especially), and Watson must have had frequent need to consult his solicitors.

"They bundled him into a cab that was beside the kerb."
H. M. Brock, R. I., and Joseph Simpson, R. B. A.,
Strand Magazine, 1911

"No; he is clean dazed. He just knows that he was lifted up as if by magic and dropped as if by magic. Two at least were in it, and maybe three."

"And you connect this attack with your lodger?"

"Well, we've lived there fifteen years and no such happenings ever came before. I've had enough of him. Money's not everything. I'll have him out of my house before the day is done."

"Wait a bit, Mrs. Warren. Do nothing rash. I begin to think that this affair may be very much more important than appeared at first sight. It is clear now that some danger is threatening your lodger. It is equally clear that his enemies, lying in wait for him near your door, mistook your husband for him in the foggy morning light. On discovering their mistake they released him. What they would have done had it not been a mistake, we can only conjecture."

"Well, what am I to do, Mr. Holmes?"

"I have a great fancy to see this lodger[9] of yours, Mrs. Warren."

"I don't see how that is to be managed, unless you break in the door. I always hear him unlock it as I go down the stair after I leave the tray."

"He has to take the tray in. Surely we could conceal ourselves and see him do it."

The landlady thought for a moment.

"Well, sir, there's the box-room opposite. I could arrange a looking-glass, maybe, and if you were behind the door—"

"Excellent!" said Holmes. "When does he lunch?"

"About one, sir."

"Then Dr. Watson and I will come round in time. For the present, Mrs. Warren, good-bye."

At half-past twelve we found ourselves upon the steps of Mrs. Warren's house—a high, thin, yellow-brick edifice in Great Orme Street, a narrow thoroughfare at the northeast side of the British Museum. Standing as it does near the corner of

Great Orme Street, properly Great Ormond Street.
Old London

10 This sentence and the previous sentence have been added to the manuscript.

the street, it commands a view down Howe Street, with its more pretentious houses. Holmes pointed with a chuckle to one of these, a row of residential flats, which projected so that they could not fail to catch the eye.

"See, Watson!" said he. " 'High red house with stone facings.' There is the signal station all right. We know the place, and we know the code; so surely our task should be simple. There's a 'To Let' card in that window. It is evidently an empty flat to which the confederate has access.[10] Well, Mrs. Warren, what now?"

"I have it all ready for you. If you will both come up and leave your boots below on the landing, I'll put you there now."

It was an excellent hiding-place which she had arranged.

"I caught a glimpse of a dark, beautiful, horrified face glaring at the narrow opening of the box-room."
H. M. Brock, R. I., and Joseph Simpson, R. B. A.,
Strand Magazine, 1911

The mirror was so placed that, seated in the dark, we could very plainly see the door opposite. We had hardly settled down in it, and Mrs. Warren left us, when a distant tinkle announced that our mysterious neighbour had rung. Presently the landlady appeared with the tray, laid it down upon a chair beside the closed door, and then, treading heavily, departed. Crouching together in the angle of the door, we kept our eyes fixed upon the mirror. Suddenly, as the landlady's footsteps died away, there was the creak of a turning key, the handle revolved, and two thin hands darted out and lifted the tray from the chair. An instant later it was hurriedly replaced, and I caught a glimpse of a dark, beautiful, horrified face glaring at the narrow opening of the box-room. Then the door crashed to, the key turned once more, and all was silence. Holmes twitched my sleeve, and together we stole down the stair.

"I will call again in the evening," said he to the expectant landlady. "I think, Watson, we can discuss this business better in our own quarters."

"My surmise, as you saw, proved to be correct," said he, speaking from the depths of his easy-chair. "There has been a substitution of lodgers. What I did not foresee is that we should find a woman, and no ordinary woman,[11] Watson."

"She saw us."

"Well, she saw something to alarm her. That is certain. The general sequence of events is pretty clear, is it not? A couple seek refuge in London from a very terrible and instant danger. The measure of that danger is the rigour of their precautions. The man, who has some work which he must do, desires to leave the woman in absolute safety while he does it. It is not an easy problem, but he solved it in an original fashion, and so effectively that her presence was not even known to the landlady who supplies her with food. The printed messages, as is now evident, were to prevent her sex being discovered by her writing. The man cannot come near the woman, or he will guide their enemies to her.[12] Since he cannot communicate with her direct, he has recourse to the agony column of a paper. So far all is clear."

"But what is at the root of it?"

"Ah, yes, Watson—severely practical, as usual! What is at the root of it all? Mrs. Warren's whimsical problem enlarges somewhat and assumes a more sinister aspect as we proceed.

11 The phrase is "a beautiful woman" in the manuscript.

12 He has apparently already done so, unless the attack on Mr. Warren was mere hooliganism.

13 The manuscript reads nineteen, which under no circumstances (see the discussion of the letter "K" in "The Secret Message," page 1297) could be correct. Watson apparently checked the results against his notes later.

This much we can say: that it is no ordinary love escapade. You saw the woman's face at the sign of danger. We have heard, too, of the attack upon the landlord, which was undoubtedly meant for the lodger. These alarms, and the desperate need for secrecy, argue that the matter is one of life or death. The attack upon Mr. Warren further shows that the enemy, whoever they are, are themselves not aware of the substitution of the female lodger for the male. It is very curious and complex, Watson."

"Why should you go further in it? What have you to gain from it?"

"What, indeed? It is Art for Art's sake, Watson. I suppose when you doctored you found yourself studying cases without thought of a fee?"

"For my education, Holmes."

"Education never ends, Watson. It is a series of lessons with the greatest for the last. This is an instructive case. There is neither money nor credit in it, and yet one would wish to tidy it up. When dusk comes we should find ourselves one stage advanced in our investigation."

When we returned to Mrs. Warren's rooms, the gloom of a London winter evening had thickened into one grey curtain, a dead monotone of colour, broken only by the sharp yellow squares of the windows and the blurred haloes of the gaslamps. As we peered from the darkened sitting-room of the lodging-house, one more dim light glimmered high up through the obscurity.

"Someone is moving in that room," said Holmes in a whisper, his gaunt and eager face thrust forward to the window-pane. "Yes, I can see his shadow. There he is again! He has a candle in his hand. Now he is peering across. He wants to be sure that she is on the look-out. Now he begins to flash. Take the message also, Watson, that we may check each other. A single flash—that is 'A,' surely. Now, then. How many did you make it? Twenty.[13] So did I. That should mean 'T.' A T—that's intelligible enough! Another 'T.' Surely this is the beginning of a second word. Now, then—TENTA. Dead stop. That can't be all, Watson? ATTENTA gives no sense. Nor is it any better as three words AT, TEN, TA, unless 'T.A.' are a person's initials. There it goes again! What's that? ATTE—why, it is the same message over again. Curious, Watson, very curious! Now he is off once more! AT—why, he is repeating it for the third time. 'ATTENTA' three times! How often will he repeat it? No, that seems to be the finish. He has withdrawn from the window. What do you make of it, Watson?"

"A cipher message, Holmes."

My companion gave a sudden chuckle of comprehension. "And not a very obscure cipher, Watson," said he. "Why, of course, it is Italian! The 'A' means that it is addressed to a woman. 'Beware! Beware! Beware!' How's that Watson?"[14]

"I believe you have hit it."

"Not a doubt of it. It is a very urgent message, thrice repeated to make it more so. But beware of what? Wait a bit; he is coming to the window once more."

Again we saw the dim silhouette of a crouching man and the whisk of the small flame across the window as the signals were renewed. They came more rapidly than before—so rapid that it was hard to follow them.

" 'PERICOLO'—'pericolo'—eh, what's that, Watson? 'Danger,' isn't it? Yes, by Jove, it's a danger signal. There he goes again! 'PERI.' Halloa, what on earth—"

The light had suddenly gone out, the glimmering square of window had disappeared, and the third floor formed a dark band round the lofty building, with its tiers of shining casements. That last warning cry had been suddenly cut short. How, and by whom? The same thought occurred on the instant to us both. Holmes sprang up from where he crouched by the window.

"This is serious, Watson," he cried. "There is some devilry going forward! Why should such a message stop in such a way?[15] I should put Scotland Yard in touch with this business—and yet, it is too pressing for us to leave."

"Shall I go for the police?"

"We must define the situation a little more clearly. It may bear some more innocent interpretation. Come, Watson, let us go across ourselves and see what we can make of it."

PART II

As we walked rapidly down Howe Street I glanced back at the building which we had left. There, dimly outlined at the top window, I could see the shadow of a head, a woman's head,

14 See "The Secret Message," page 1299, for a discussion of the cipher.

15 In the manuscript, this question was followed by the line, "Scribbling a note, he rang for Mrs. Warren and directed her to drive with it instantly to Scotland Yard." Apparently Watson subsequently recollected the true events and corrected the manuscript. Spencer Kennedy notes that if in fact Mrs. Warren had delivered the note, Holmes and Watson would not have met the Pinkerton agent, and it is probable that Watson's realisation of this spurred his memory.

16 See also "The Empty House," in which Holmes misquotes in a slightly different manner Shakespeare's *Twelfth Night*, Act II, Scene 3.

17 The Pinkerton National Detective Agency was founded by Allan Pinkerton (1819–1884), a Scotsman who emigrated to Illinois in 1842. He settled in West Dundee, near Chicago, and opened up a cooper's shop there. An ardent abolitionist, Pinkerton allowed his shop to serve as one of the many stations on the Underground Railroad.

While chopping wood one day on an uninhabited island in Fox River, Pinkerton stumbled upon evidence that led to the arrest and capture of a gang of counterfeiters. His pivotal role in bringing down the gang resulted in his being named deputy sheriff of Kane County in 1846, then the first city detective of Chicago's police force. But Pinkerton quickly saw that he would never make his fortune as a cop. In 1850, he left the Chicago force to start his own private detective agency, the first of its kind in Chicago and one of only a handful in the country.

Pinkerton National Detective Agency specialised in train robberies and achieved many spectacular successes, including no less than the thwarting of an 1861 assassination attempt on President-elect Lincoln in Baltimore. During the Civil War, Pinkerton worked for the Union side, heading an organisation that gathered intelligence on Confederate activity. After the war, detectives from the Pinkerton Agency infiltrated and broke up the Molly Maguires, an Irish-American secret society that controlled Pennyslvania's coal-mining industry (events central to *The Valley of Fear*). The sign above the door of the agency featured the motto "We Never Sleep" accompanying an illustration of an eye, an indelible image that gave rise to the term "public eye." Among the sixteen books attributed to Pinkerton (as part of "Allan Pinkerton's Detective Stories") are *The Molly Maguires and*

gazing tensely, rigidly, out into the night, waiting with breathless suspense for the renewal of that interrupted message. At the doorway of the Howe Street flats a man, muffled in a cravat and greatcoat, was leaning against the railing. He started as the hall-light fell upon our faces.

"Holmes!" he cried.

"Why, Gregson!" said my companion as he shook hands with the Scotland Yard detective. "Journeys end with lovers' meetings.[16] What brings you here?"

"The same reasons that bring you, I expect," said Gregson. "How you got on to it I can't imagine."

"Different threads, but leading up to the same tangle. I've been taking the signals."

"Signals?"

"Yes, from that window. They broke off in the middle. We came over to see the reason. But since it is safe in your hands I see no object in continuing the business."

"Wait a bit!" cried Gregson, eagerly. "I'll do you this justice, Mr. Holmes, that I was never in a case yet that I didn't feel stronger for having you on my side. There's only the one exit to these flats, so we have him safe."

"Who is he?"

"Well, well, we score over you for once, Mr. Holmes. You must give us best this time." He struck his stick sharply upon the ground, on which a cabman, his whip in his hand, sauntered over from a four-wheeler which stood on the far side of the street. "May I introduce you to Mr. Sherlock Holmes?" he said to the cabman. "This is Mr. Leverton, of Pinkerton's American Agency."[17]

"The hero of the Long Island Cave Mystery?"[18] said Holmes. "Sir, I am pleased to meet you."

The American, a quiet, businesslike young man, with a clean-shaven, hatchet face, flushed up at the words of commendation. "I am on the trail of my life now, Mr. Holmes," said he. "If I can get Gorgiano—"

"What! Gorgiano of the Red Circle?"[19]

"Oh, he has a European fame, has he? Well, we've learned all about him in America. We *know* he is at the bottom of fifty murders, and yet we have nothing positive we can take him on. I tracked him over from New York, and I've been close to him for a week in London, waiting some excuse to get my hand on

the Detectives (1877), viewed by many historians now as a highly biased work on the labour dispute, and *Criminal Reminiscences and Detective Sketches* (1879).

It is unlikely that Pinkerton himself and Holmes ever met, although some scholars posit a trip to America by Holmes prior to the 1881 events of *A Study in Scarlet*. While Holmes may have been intrigued by the idea of establishing an "agency" (a term he himself uses in "The Sussex Vampire"), he would likely have been appalled at Pinkerton's lack of education in the "science of detection," which Holmes essentially invented.

Many chronologists place the events of "The Red Circle" in 1902, at which point Pinkerton's sons, Robert and William, would have been in charge, having taken over the agency upon Pinkerton's death in 1882. Clearly, the Pinkerton National Detective Agency was eminently qualified to investigate the events at hand. But who, exactly, is the Pinkerton client in this case?

18 "The mystery, on true Sherlockian principles, is that there are no caves on Long Island," writes Christopher Morley, the quintessential New Yorker, in "Was Sherlock Holmes an American?" W. E. Edwards suggests that the word was "cove," noting that Glen Cove is a landmark for the golfer and the starch-manufacturer. David H. Galerstein, in "A Solution to the Long Island Cave Mystery," proposes a *man-made* cave on the north shore of Long Island.

Other scholars challenge the assumption that Long Island, NY, was meant: Long Island, Tennessee, and Long Island, Alabama, are suggested. D. Martin Dakin proposes that Cave (spelled with a capital) was the name of the criminal or victim involved. William Ulrich makes the interesting suggestion that the "Cave" referred to was a term used to describe a cell of the Bohemian Brethren, a secret society, located on Long Island.

19 In the manuscript, Holmes responds, "What, the Black Hand Captain?" Evidently Watson (perhaps fearing reprisal) determined at this point to conceal the identity of the organisation of which Gorgiano was a member and changed the title of the manuscript.

his collar. Mr. Gregson and I ran him to ground in that big tenement house, and there's only the one door, so he can't slip us. There's three folk come out since he went in, but I'll swear he wasn't one of them."

"Mr. Holmes talks of signals," said Gregson. "I expect, as usual, he knows a good deal that we don't."

In a few clear words Holmes explained the situation as it had appeared to us. The American struck his hands together with vexation.

"He's on to us!" he cried.

"Why do you think so?"

"Well, it figures out that way, does it not? Here he is, sending out messages to an accomplice—there are several of his gang in London. Then suddenly, just as by your own account he was telling them that there was danger, he broke short off. What could it mean except that from the window he had suddenly either caught sight of us in the street, or in some way come to understand how close the danger was, and that he must act right away if he was to avoid it? What do you suggest, Mr. Holmes?"

"That we go up at once and see for ourselves."

"But we have no warrant for his arrest."

"He is in unoccupied premises under suspicious circumstances," said Gregson. "That is good enough for the moment. When we have him by the heels we can see if New York can't help us to keep him. I'll take the responsibility of arresting him now."

Our official detectives may blunder in the matter of intelligence, but never in that of courage. Gregson climbed the stair to arrest this desperate murderer with the same absolutely quiet and businesslike bearing with which he would have ascended the official staircase of Scotland Yard. The Pinkerton man had tried to push past him, but Gregson had firmly elbowed him back. London dangers were the privilege of the London force.

The door of the left-hand flat upon the third landing was standing ajar. Gregson pushed it open. Within all was absolute silence and darkness. I struck a match, and lit the detective's lantern. As I did so, and as the flicker steadied into a flame, we all gave a gasp of surprise. On the deal boards of the carpetless floor there was outlined a fresh track of blood. The red steps pointed towards us and led away from an inner room, the door of which was closed. Gregson flung it open and held his light full blaze in front of him, whilst we all peered eagerly over his shoulders.

In the middle of the floor of the empty room was huddled the figure of an enormous man, his clean-shaven, swarthy face grotesquely horrible in its contortion, and his head encircled by a ghastly crimson halo of blood, lying in a broad wet circle upon the white woodwork. His knees were drawn up, his hands thrown out in agony, and from the centre of his broad, brown, upturned throat there projected the white haft of a knife driven blade-deep into his body. Giant as he was, the man must have gone down like a pole-axed ox before that terrific blow. Beside his right hand a most formidable horn-handled, two-edged dagger lay upon the floor, and near it a black kid glove.

"By George! it's Black Gorgiano himself!" cried the American detective. "Someone has got ahead of us this time."

" 'By George! It's Black Gorgiano himself!'
cried the American detective."
H. M. Brock, R. I., *Strand Magazine*, 1911

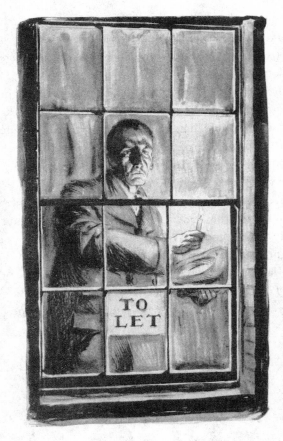

"Holmes was passing the candle backwards and forwards
across the window-panes."
H. M. Brock, R. I., *Strand Magazine*, 1911

"Here is the candle in the window, Mr. Holmes," said Gregson. "Why, whatever are you doing?"

Holmes had stepped across, had lit the candle, and was passing it backwards and forwards across the window-panes. Then he peered into the darkness, blew the candle out, and threw it on the floor.

"I rather think that will be helpful," said he. He came over and stood in deep thought while the two professionals were examining the body. "You say that three people came out from the flat while you were waiting downstairs," said he, at last. "Did you observe them closely?"

"Yes, I did."

"Was there a fellow about thirty, black-bearded, dark, of middle size?"

"Yes; he was the last to pass me."

"That is your man, I fancy. I can give you his description, and we have a very excellent outline of his footmark. That should be enough for you."

"Not much, Mr. Holmes, among the millions of London."

"Perhaps not. That is why I thought it best to summon this lady to your aid."

We all turned round at the words. There, framed in the doorway, was a tall and beautiful woman—the mysterious lodger of Bloomsbury. Slowly she advanced, her face pale and drawn

"Slowly she advanced, her face pale and drawn
with a frightful apprehension."
H. M. Brock, R. I., *Strand Magazine*, 1911

20 "There has never been anything in the world absolutely like Notting Hill," wrote G. K. Chesterton in *The Napoleon of Notting Hill* (1904). "There will never be anything quite like it to the crack of doom." Formerly open countryside that was built up with houses, villas, and shops, Notting Hill was an area "at once urban and suburban," in the words of historian Peter Ackroyd, cyclically cursed with periods of rejuvenation and decline. Ackroyd quotes an 1860s issue of *Building News* in describing the beleaguered neighbourhood as "a graveyard of buried hopes . . . naked carcasses, crumbling decorations, fractured walls, slimy cement. All who touch them lose heart and money by the venture." In a further display of its feast-or-famine history, the neighbourhood, the setting for the fluffy eponymous romantic comedy film *Notting Hill* (1999), now epitomises what one long-time resident, British filmmaker Stephen Frears, in a recent *Los Angeles Times* interview, calls "trendy-spendy" London, with shops selling $300 eyeglasses and cafes serving spaghettini with caramelized squid.

21 The concept that a British citizen should not be compelled to incriminate him- or herself had existed since the mid-seventeenth century, when it was written into British common law. At that time, both interrogation and the trial process were handled by the courts; with the introduction of the Metropolitan Police Force in 1829, the task of interrogation was transferred from the magistrates to the police. Yet official policy on the rules of police interrogation remained somewhat muddled until 1912, when passage of the Judges' Rules established the administrative guideline (but not concrete law) that, prior to questioning a suspect, a police officer had to inform him or her of the right to remain silent.

Even though informing a suspect of these rights may not have become standard procedure until 1912, the London police did

with a frightful apprehension, her eyes fixed and staring, her terrified gaze rivetted upon the dark figure on the floor.

"You have killed him!" she muttered. "Oh, *Dio mio*, you have killed him!" Then I heard a sudden sharp intake of her breath, and she sprang into the air with a cry of joy. Round and round the room she danced, her hands clapping, her dark eyes gleaming with delighted wonder, and a thousand pretty Italian exclamations pouring from her lips. It was terrible and amazing to see such a woman so convulsed with joy at such a sight. Suddenly she stopped and gazed at us all with a questioning stare.

"But you! You are police, are you not? You have killed Giuseppe Gorgiano. Is it not so?"

"We are police, madam."

She looked round into the shadows of the room.

"But where, then, is Gennaro?" she asked. "He is my husband, Gennaro Lucca. I am Emilia Lucca, and we are both from New York. Where is Gennaro? He called me this moment from this window, and I ran with all my speed."

"It was I who called," said Holmes.

"You! How could you call?"

"Your cipher was not difficult, madam. Your presence here was desirable. I knew that I had only to flash '*Vieni*' and you would surely come."

The beautiful Italian looked with awe at my companion.

"I do not understand how you know these things," she said. "Giuseppe Gorgiano—how did he—" She paused, and then suddenly her face lit up with pride and delight. "Now I see it! My Gennaro! My splendid, beautiful Gennaro, who has guarded me safe from all harm, he did it, with his own strong hand he killed the monster. Oh, Gennaro, how wonderful you are! What woman could ever be worthy of such a man?"

"Well, Mrs. Lucca," said the prosaic Gregson, laying his hand upon the lady's sleeve with as little sentiment as if she were a Notting Hill hooligan,[20] "I am not very clear yet who you are or what you are; but you've said enough to make it very clear that we shall want you at the Yard."

"One moment, Gregson," said Holmes. "I rather fancy that this lady may be as anxious to give us information as we can be to get it. You understand, madam, that your husband will be arrested and tried for the death of the man who lies before us? What you say may be used in evidence.[21] But if you think that he has acted from motives which are not criminal, and which he would wish to have known, then you cannot serve him better than by telling us the whole story."

"Now that Gorgiano is dead we fear nothing," said the lady. "He was a devil and a monster, and there can be no judge in the world who would punish my husband for having killed him."

"In that case," said Holmes, "my suggestion is that we lock this door, leave things as we found them, go with this lady to her room, and form our opinion after we have heard what it is that she has to say to us."

Half an hour later we were seated, all four, in the small sitting-room of Signora Lucca, listening to her remarkable narrative of those sinister events, the ending of which we had chanced to witness. She spoke in rapid and fluent but very unconventional English, which, for the sake of clearness, I will make grammatical.

"I was born in Posilippo, near Naples," she said "and was the daughter of Augusto Barelli, who was the chief lawyer and once the deputy of that part. Gennaro was in my father's employment, and I came to love him, as any woman must. He had neither money nor position—nothing but his beauty and strength and energy—so my father forbade the match. We fled together, were married at Bari, and sold my jewels to gain the money which would take us to America. This was four years ago, and we have been in New York ever since.

"Fortune was very good to us at first. Gennaro was able to do a service to an Italian gentleman—he saved him from some ruffians in the place called the Bowery, and so made a powerful friend. His name was Tito Castalotte, and he was the senior partner of the great firm of Castalotte and Zamba, who are the chief fruit importers of New York. Signor Zamba is an invalid, and our new friend Castalotte has all power within the firm, which employs more than three hundred men. He took my husband into his employment, made him head of a department, and showed his goodwill towards him in every way. Signor Castalotte was a bachelor, and I believe that he felt as if Gennaro was his son, and both my husband and I loved him as if he were our father. We had taken and furnished a little house in Brooklyn, and our whole future seemed assured, when that black cloud appeared which was soon to overspread our sky.

attempt to adhere to an unofficial protocol in the years before. Eight years prior to the passage of the Judges' Rules, Lord Brampton, in an "Address to the Police on their Duties," reproduced in the *Police Code of 1904*, carefully delineated between the process of investigation and that of interrogation. He explained that when one was attempting to discover the perpetrator of a crime, asking questions of any person who might have had relevant information was acceptable. The rules changed, however, at the moment arrest was imminent. Lord Brampton wrote that when "a Constable has a warrant to arrest, or is about to arrest a person on his own authority, or has a person in custody for a crime, it is wrong to question such person touching the crime of which he is accused. . . . On arresting a man a Constable ought simply to read his warrant, or tell the accused the nature of the charge upon which he is arrested, leaving it to the person so arrested to say anything or nothing as he pleases. . . . [H]e ought not, by anything he says or does, to invite or encourage an accused person to make any statement, without first cautioning him that he is not bound to say anything tending to criminate himself, and that anything he says may be used against him."

Although Signora Lucca apparently was not herself a suspect (but see note 23, below), Holmes here was apparently thinking of the general rule of British law that a spouse might not be compelled to testify against his or her spouse.

22 The Carbonari (Italian for "Charcoal Burners") were members of a secret political society that was active in early nineteenth-century southern Italy and may have originated with the Freemasonry. These dissidents first began agitating for political freedom during the reign of Gioacchino Murat, Napoleon's brother-in-law and the king of Naples (1808–1815). In general, while the Carbonari tended to advocate Italian unification and some form of constitutional and representative government, a more precise agenda was never defined.

As with the Freemasonry and other secret societies, the Carbonari had their own ritual language, gestures, initiation ceremony, and hierarchy (in this case, made up of "apprentices" and "masters"). Their revolutionary fervour spread from Naples to like-minded areas such as Piedmont, the Papal States, Bologna, Parma, and Modena; and to other countries, including Spain and France. In 1831, the nationalist *Risorgimento* movement was formed and eventually subsumed most of the Carbonari.

Violent uprisings and assassination attempts characterised the Carbonari movement, but still, the political aims of the group seem at odds with the "dreadful" terrorist society Signora Lucca describes here. This incongruence may be explained by the fact that in the manuscript, Gennaro is linked to "the famous Camorra" rather than to the Carbonari. The Camorra remained in existence through the end of the nineteenth century and had an agenda that was more criminal than political (see "The Six Napoleons," note 30, for a fuller description), and therefore it is likely that Genarro was in fact ensnared by the Camorra rather than the Carbonari. Watson, fearing repercussions for his portrayal of Genarro's terrifying countryman, must have thought better of his initial candour and altered the reference to a Neapolitan society far less likely to seek retribution.

"One night, when Gennaro returned from his work, he brought a fellow-country-man back with him. His name was Gorgiano, and he had come also from Posilippo. He was a huge man, as you can testify, for you have looked upon his corpse. Not only was his body that of a giant, but everything about him was grotesque, gigantic, and terrifying. His voice was like thunder in our little house. There was scarce room for the whirl of his great arms as he talked. His thoughts, his emotions, his passions, all were exaggerated and monstrous. He talked, or rather roared, with such energy that others could but sit and listen, cowed with the mighty stream of words. His eyes blazed at you and held you at his mercy. He was a terrible and wonderful man. I thank God that he is dead!

"He came again and again. Yet I was aware that Gennaro was no more happy than I was in his presence. My poor husband would sit pale and listless, listening to the endless raving upon politics and upon social questions which made up our visitor's conversation. Gennaro said nothing, but I who knew him so well could read in his face some emotion which I had never seen there before. At first I thought that it was dislike. And then, gradually, I understood that it was more than dislike. It was fear—a deep, secret, shrinking fear. That night—the night that I read his terror—I put my arms round him and I implored him by his love for me and by all that he held dear to hold nothing from me, and to tell me why this huge man overshadowed him so.

"He told me, and my own heart grew cold as ice as I listened. My poor Gennaro, in his wild and fiery days, when all the world seemed against him and his mind was driven half mad by the injustices of life, had joined a Neapolitan society, the Red Circle, which was allied to the old Carbonari.[22] The oaths and secrets of this brotherhood were frightful; but once within its rule no escape was possible. When we had fled to America Gennaro thought that he had cast it all off forever. What was his horror one evening to meet in the streets the very man who had initiated him in Naples, the giant Gorgiano, a man who had earned the name of 'Death' in the South of Italy, for he was red to the elbow in murder! He had come to New York to avoid the Italian police, and he had already planted a branch of this dreadful society in his new home. All this Gennaro told me, and showed me a summons which he had received that very day, a Red Circle drawn upon the head of it telling him that a lodge would be held upon a certain date, and that his presence at it was required and ordered.

"That was bad enough, but worse was to come. I had noticed for some time that when Gorgiano came to us, as he constantly did, in the evening, he spoke much to me; and even when his words were to my husband those terrible, glaring, wild-beast eyes of his were always turned upon me. One night his secret came out. I had awakened what he called 'love' within him—the love of a brute—a savage. Gennaro had not yet returned when he came. He pushed his way in, seized me in his mighty arms, hugged me in his bear's embrace, covered me with kisses, and implored me to come away with him. I was struggling and screaming when Gennaro entered and attacked him. He struck Gennaro senseless and fled from the house which he was never more to enter. It was a deadly enemy that we made that night.

"A few days later came the meeting. Gennaro returned from it with a face which told me that something dreadful had occurred. It was worse than we could have imagined possible. The funds of the society were raised by blackmailing rich Italians and threatening them with violence should they refuse the money. It seems that Castalotte, our dear friend and benefactor, had been approached. He had refused to yield to threats, and he had handed the notices to the police. It was resolved now that such an example should be made of him as would prevent any other victim from rebelling. At the meeting it was arranged that he and his house should be blown up with dynamite. There was a drawing of lots as to who should carry out the deed. Gennaro saw our enemy's cruel face smiling at him as he dipped his hand in the bag. No doubt it had been pre-arranged in some fashion, for it was the fatal disc with the Red Circle upon it, the mandate for murder which lay upon his palm. He was to kill his best friend, or he was to expose himself and me to the vengeance of his comrades. It was part of their fiendish system to punish those whom they feared or hated by injuring not only their own person, but those whom they loved, and it was the knowledge of this which hung as a terror over my poor Gennaro's head and drove him nearly crazy with apprehension.

"All that night we sat together, our arms round each other,

23 Daniel Griffin concludes that Emilia lied about who was pursuing whom, that she had run off with Gorgiano and that Gennaro Lucca pursued them. John Hall, in *Sidelights on Holmes*, poses much the same theory, except that in his version, Lucca killed his wife, disguised himself as a woman, killed Gorgiano, and then emerged as "Signora" Lucca, to test the waters as to his own safety.

each strengthening each for the troubles that lay before us. The very next evening had been fixed for the attempt. By mid-day my husband and I were on our way to London, but not before he had given our benefactor full warning of his danger, and had also left such information for the police as would safeguard his life for the future.

"The rest, gentlemen, you know for yourselves. We were sure that our enemies would be behind us like our own shadows. Gorgiano had his private reasons for vengeance, but in any case we knew how ruthless, cunning, and untiring he could be. Both Italy and America are full of stories of his dreadful powers. If ever they were exerted it would be now. My darling made use of the few clear days which our start had given us in arranging for a refuge for me in such a fashion that no possible danger could reach me. For his own part, he wished to be free that he might communicate both with the American and with the Italian police. I do not myself know where he lived, or how. All that I learned was through the columns of a newspaper. But once, as I looked through my window, I saw two Italians watching the house, and I understood that in some way Gorgiano had found out our retreat. Finally Gennaro told me, through the paper, that he would signal to me from a certain window, but when the signals came they were nothing but warnings, which were suddenly interrupted. It is very clear to me now that he knew Gorgiano to be close upon him, and that, thank God! he was ready for him when he came. And now, gentlemen, I would ask you whether we have anything to fear from the Law, or whether any judge upon earth would condemn my Gennaro for what he has done?"

"Well, Mr. Gregson," said the American, looking across at the official, "I don't know what your British point of view may be, but I guess that in New York this lady's husband will receive a pretty general vote of thanks."[23]

"She will have to come with me and see the Chief," Gregson answered. "If what she says is corroborated, I do not think she or her husband has much to fear. But what I can't make head or tail of, Mr. Holmes, is how on earth *you* got yourself mixed up in the matter."

"Education, Gregson, education. Still seeking knowledge at the old university. Well, Watson, you have one more specimen of the tragic and grotesque to add to your collection. By the way, it is not eight o'clock, and a Wagner night at Covent Garden! If we hurry, we might be in time for the second act." ∎

THE SECRET MESSAGE

THERE are apparent problems with the secret message as decoded by Sherlock Holmes. Professor Louis E. Lord of the Classics Department at Oberlin College points out that the Italian alphabet contains no K (and, he might have added, no W, X, or Y, and only occasionally J). More complicated still, Holmes was initially unaware that the message was being transmitted in Italian, and thus would have seen no need to consider any but the twenty-six-letter English alphabet. Professor Lord argues, as reported by Vincent Starrett in his "Explanation" (Introduction) to *221B: Studies in Sherlock Holmes*, that in Italian, twenty flashes is not a "T" (as immediately interpreted by Holmes) but—by virtue of the missing "K"—actually a "U." He continues, "The full message as read by Holmes is 'Attenta, pericolo!' Yet the omission of K must have misplaced every letter below it, and Holmes should have read, not 'Attenta pericolo!' but 'Assemsa, oeqicnkn!' Or, if Signor Lucca, sending his warning, had—for the convenience of Holmes and Watson—used the English alphabet, his wife, who knew little English and was expecting the message in Italian, would have read 'Auueoua, qesicpmp!' Well, it is a sufficiently startling message, either way; and it is no slight testimony to the ability of Sherlock Holmes that he brought off the case with honours."

Careful study of Lord's argument reveals a basic contradiction in his own work. S. F. Blake writes that "it is unfortunately necessary for me to point out [an error] which Prof. Lord himself committed. He says that Holmes should have read the message 'Assemsa, oeqicnkn.' Since Holmes counted the first three series of flashes as 1, 20, 20, and then translated them A, T, T, we have to infer that he counted the other flashes in this word as 5, 14, 20, 1 in order to translate it as 'attenta.' But 1, 20, 20, 5, 14, 20, 1 flashes do not spell out 'assemsa' in any language known to me, certainly not in English or Italian, the only two in question here. They spell 'attenta' in the English alphabet and 'auueoua' in the Italian. In the English alphabet, 'assemsa' would call for 1, 19, 19, 5, 13, 19, 1 flashes, and in Italian, 1, 18, 18, 5, 12, 18, 1. A similar situation holds, obviously, with regard to the word 'pericolo' (or oeqicnkn). It is clearly *lèse majesté*, or something approaching it, to accuse the keen-eyed Holmes of being unable to count up to 20."

Donald A. Yates expresses the view that the code agreed upon must have been to spell Italian in the English alphabet ("A Final Illumination of the Lucca Code"). He argues that Gennaro selected English so as to make the code unreadable by Gorgiano. Further, Yates points to Signora Lucca's "smooth flow of perfect, well-phrased English sentences." However, Blake contends that Gorgiano undoubtedly learned English in New York and observes that the sentences of Signora Lucca to which Yates refers were expressly made grammatical by Dr. Watson. Blake argues instead that Gennaro selected the English language alphabet because he needed the letter K to transmit specific words (for example, "Black Joe"). Josh Pachter argues that Gennaro Lucca gave his wife the "key" to the cipher, consisting of using the Italian alphabet *but inserting the letter K*.

D. Martin Dakin comments, "I wonder if an unnecessary fuss has not been made over this. Although Italian does not use K (or W, X or Y), I doubt if Italians are taught an alphabet without them, and surely it is not unreasonable to suggest that a common alphabet of twenty-six traditional letters is generally accepted all over western Europe." This seems borne out by the *Encyclopædia Britannica* (9th Ed.), which lists the Russian and Cyrillic alphabets as the only European alphabet variants of note.

Blake performed the interesting experiment of attempting to flash a lighted candle as rapidly as possible across a window to convey the recorded message. He concludes that about 477 candle waves are required, consuming almost five minutes, for the brief message recorded. This experiment was redone by Allen Mackler and Sheldon Wesson, who report in "Light Upon the Candle" that while Blake is in error and the message requires only 384 passes, 7 minutes 7 seconds seems to be a more likely time.

Dakin responds: "A greater mystery is why Gennaro should have chosen such a protracted and cumbersome way of sending Emilia a (three times repeated, with Gorgiano at his heels at any moment!) rather pointless message about a danger of which she was already aware and couldn't do anything about anyway. He could have said it just as well in his newspaper advertisements."

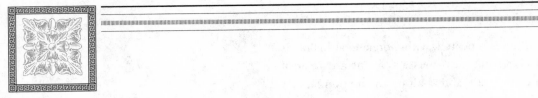

THE ADVENTURE OF THE
BRUCE-PARTINGTON PLANS[1]

Regarded as one of the finest mystery stories in the annals of detection, both for its innovative clues and for its unexpected villain, "The Bruce-Partington Plans" is only the second case in which Sherlock's brother Mycroft plays an active rôle (the other is "The Greek Interpreter"). Here, Sherlock reveals to Watson that his brother is not just an auditor working for the British government, as he told him in "The Greek Interpreter"; occasionally his brother is the British government. At the core of the story is an important government secret: the plans for the "Bruce-Partington" submarine, which Mycroft predicts will make naval warfare impossible. Submarines fascinated Conan Doyle, who wrote a story entitled "Danger!" in 1914, warning of the perils of submarine warfare before they were widely appreciated. Scholars ponder why the British failed to develop the "Bruce-Partington," which could have played a significant rôle in the Great War. There is also much argument about Watson's description of the railways of London and puzzlement over the strange security procedures of the Admiralty.

1 "The Bruce-Partington Plans" was published in the *Strand Magazine* in December 1908 and in *Collier's Weekly* on December 12, 1908.

I

N THE THIRD week of November, in the year 1895, a dense yellow fog settled down upon London. From the Monday to the Thursday I doubt whether it was ever possible from our windows in Baker Street to see the loom of the opposite houses. The first day Holmes had spent in cross-indexing his huge book of references. The second and third had been patiently occupied upon a subject which he had recently made his hobby—the music of the Middle Ages. But when, for the fourth time, after pushing back our chairs from breakfast we saw the greasy, heavy brown swirl still drifting past us and condensing in oily drops upon the window-panes, my comrade's impatient and active nature could endure this drab existence no longer. He paced restlessly about our sitting-room in a fever of suppressed energy, biting his nails, tapping the furniture, and chafing against inaction.

"Nothing of interest in the paper, Watson?" he said.

I was aware that by anything of interest, Holmes meant anything of criminal interest. There was the news of a revolution, of a possible war, and of an impending change of Government;[2] but these did not come within the horizon of my companion. I could see nothing recorded in the shape of crime which was not commonplace and futile. Holmes groaned and resumed his restless meanderings.

"The London criminal is certainly a dull fellow," said he, in the querulous voice of the sportsman whose game has failed him. "Look out of this window, Watson. See how the figures loom up, are dimly seen, and then blend once more into the cloud-bank. The thief or the murderer could roam London on such a day as the tiger does the jungle, unseen until he pounces, and then evident only to his victim."

"There have," said I, "been numerous petty thefts."

Holmes snorted his contempt.

"This great and sombre stage is set for something more worthy than that," said he. "It is fortunate for this community that I am not a criminal."

"It is, indeed!" said I, heartily.

"Suppose that I were Brooks or Woodhouse, or any of the fifty men who have good reason for taking my life, how long could I survive against my own pursuit? A summons, a bogus appointment, and all would be over. It is well they don't have days of fog in the Latin countries—the countries of assassination. By Jove! Here comes something at last to break our dead monotony."

It was the maid with a telegram. Holmes tore it open and burst out laughing.

"Well, well! What next?" said he. "Brother Mycroft is coming round."

"Why not?" I asked.

"Why not? It is as if you met a tram-car[3] coming down a country lane. Mycroft has his rails and he runs on them. His Pall Mall lodgings, the Diogenes Club, Whitehall[4]—that is his cycle. Once, and only once, he has been here.[5] What upheaval can possibly have derailed him?"

"Does he not explain?"

Holmes handed me his brother's telegram.

Must see you over Cadogan West. Coming at once.
                                        MYCROFT.

2 See "An Impending Change of Government," page 1334.

3 A passenger vehicle, drawn by a horse along rails.

4 See "The Greek Interpreter" for discussions of Whitehall and the possible identity of the Diogenes Club.

5 Presumably Holmes is referring to Mycroft's Baker Street visit in "The Greek Interpreter," generally dated from 1884 to 1890. Yet in "The Empty House," Mycroft is said to have "preserved [Holmes's] rooms and papers exactly as they had always been"; W. E. Edwards marvels, "it appears that, eminently characteristically, he had accomplished this feat without going near them. . . ."

6 In a bimetallic system, both gold and silver are minted and made available as legal tender. For most of the nineteenth century, all countries practised bimetallism except England, which had established a gold standard in 1798 and 1816.

"Cadogan West? I have heard the name."

"It recalls nothing to my mind. But that Mycroft should break out in this erratic fashion! A planet might as well leave its orbit. By the way, do you know what Mycroft is?"

I had some vague recollection of an explanation at the time of the Adventure of the Greek Interpreter.

"You told me that he had some small office under the British Government."

Holmes chuckled.

"I did not know you quite so well in those days. One has to be discreet when one talks of high matters of state. You are right in thinking that he is under the British Government. You would also be right in a sense if you said that occasionally he *is* the British Government."

"My dear Holmes!"

"I thought I might surprise you. Mycroft draws four hundred and fifty pounds a year, remains a subordinate, has no ambitions of any kind, will receive neither honour nor title, but remains the most indispensable man in the country."

"But how?"

"Well, his position is unique. He has made it for himself. There has never been anything like it before, nor will be again. He has the tidiest and most orderly brain, with the greatest capacity for storing facts, of any man living. The same great powers which I have turned to the detection of crime he has used for this particular business. The conclusions of every department are passed to him, and he is the central exchange, the clearing-house, which makes out the balance. All other men are specialists, but his specialism is omniscience. We well suppose that a Minister needs information as to a point which involves the Navy, India, Canada and the bimetallic question;[6] he could get his separate advices from various departments upon each, but only Mycroft can focus them all, and say offhand how each factor would affect the other. They began by using him as a short-cut, a convenience; now he has made himself an essential. In that great brain of his everything is pigeon-holed, and can be handed out in an instant. Again and again his word has decided the national policy. He lives in it. He thinks of nothing else save when, as an intellectual exercise, he unbends if I call upon him and ask him to advise me on one of my little problems. But Jupiter is descending to-day. What on earth can it mean? Who is Cadogan West, and what is he to Mycroft?"

"I have it," I cried, and plunged among the litter of papers upon the sofa. "Yes, yes, here he is, sure enough! Cadogan West was the young man who was found dead on the Underground on Tuesday morning."

Holmes sat up at attention, his pipe half-way to his lips.

"This must be serious, Watson. A death which has caused my brother to alter his habits can be no ordinary one. What in the world can he have to do with it? The case was featureless as I remember it. The young man had apparently fallen out of the train and killed himself. He had not been robbed, and there was no particular reason to suspect violence. Is that not so?"

"There has been an inquest," said I, "and a good many fresh facts have come out. Looked at more closely, I should certainly say that it was a curious case."

"Judging by its effect upon my brother, I should think it must be a most extraordinary one." He snuggled down in his armchair. "Now, Watson, let us have the facts."

"The man's name was Arthur Cadogan West. He was twenty-seven years of age, unmarried, and a clerk at Woolwich Arsenal."[7]

7 The Royal Arsenal of military institutions, located in the town of Woolwich, was established in 1805 and included the Royal Military Academy and the Royal Artillery. *Baedeker* described the arsenal as "one of the most imposing establishments in existence for the manufacture of materials of war.... The chief departments are the Gun Factory, established in 1716 by a German named Schalch (the new Woolwich guns are not cast, but formed of forged steel and wire); the Laboratory for making cartridges and projectiles; and the Gun-carriage and Waggon Department. The arsenal covers an area of 598 acres, and affords employment to over 14,000 men."

Woolwich Arsenal.
Queen's London (1897)

8 A workman on the track or roadbed.

9 Several train routes convened at Willesden Junction, where the suburban lines of the London & North Western, North London, and Great Western railways connected with London & North Western's main line.

10 A passenger would generally have had to show his ticket to railway officials twice: once after purchasing the ticket, in order to ascertain the correct platform; and once upon completing the trip. *Baedeker* explained that "the tickets themselves are marked with a large red O or I (for 'outer' and 'inner' line of rails), corresponding with notices in the stations. . . . Passengers leave the platform by the 'Way Out,' where their tickets are given up. Those who are travelling with through-tickets to a station situated on one of the branch-lines show their tickets at the junction where carriages are changed, and where the officials will indicate the proper train."

"Government employ. Behold the link with Brother Mycroft!"

"He left Woolwich suddenly on Monday night. Was last seen by his *fiancée*, Miss Violet Westbury, whom he left abruptly in the fog about 7:30 that evening. There was no quarrel between them and she can give no motive for his action. The next thing heard of him was when his dead body was discovered by a plate-layer[8] named Mason, just outside Aldgate Station on the Underground system in London."

"When?"

"The body was found at six on the Tuesday morning. It was lying wide of the metals upon the left hand of the track as one goes eastward, at a point close to the station, where the line emerges from the tunnel in which it runs. The head was badly crushed—an injury which might well have been caused by a fall from the train, the body could only have come on the line in that way. Had it been carried down from any neighbouring street, it must have passed the station barriers, where a collector is always standing. This point seems absolutely certain."

"Very good. The case is definite enough. The man, dead or alive, either fell or was precipitated from a train. So much is clear to me. Continue."

"The trains which traverse the lines of rail beside which the body was found are those which run from west to east, some being purely Metropolitan, and some from Willesden[9] and outlying junctions. It can be stated for certain that this young man, when he met his death, was travelling in this direction at some late hour of the night, but at what point he entered the train it is impossible to state."

"His ticket, of course, would show that."

"There was no ticket in his pockets."

"No ticket! Dear me, Watson, this is really very singular. According to my experience it is not possible to reach the platform of a Metropolitan train without exhibiting one's ticket.[10] Presumably, then, the young man had one. Was it taken from him in order to conceal the station from which he came? It is possible. Or did he drop it in the carriage? That also is possible. But the point is of curious interest. I understand that there was no sign of robbery?"

"Apparently not. There is a list here of his possessions. His purse contained two pounds fifteen. He had also a check-book on the Woolwich branch of the Capital and Counties Bank. Through this his identity was established. There were also two dress-circle[11] tickets for the Woolwich Theatre, dated for that very evening. Also a small packet of technical papers."

Holmes gave an exclamation of satisfaction.

"There we have it at last, Watson! British Government— Woolwich. Arsenal—Technical papers—Brother Mycroft, the chain is complete. But here he comes, if I am not mistaken, to speak for himself."

A moment later the tall and portly form of Mycroft Holmes was ushered into the room. Heavily built and massive, there was a suggestion of uncouth physical inertia in the figure, but above this unwieldy frame there was perched a head so masterful in its brow, so alert in its steel-grey, deep-set eyes, so firm in its lips, and so subtle in its play of expression, that after the first glance one forgot the gross body and remembered only the dominant mind.

At his heels came our old friend Lestrade, of Scotland

11 The lowest balcony of the theatre, for which the wearing of evening dress was then obligatory.

"The tall and portly form of Mycroft Holmes
was ushered into the room."
Arthur Twidle, *Strand Magazine*, 1908

12 Siam (Thailand), long the only country in Southeast Asia to avoid European colonisation, was at the time of "The Bruce-Partington Plans" being subjected to a turf war between England and France. Fighting to retain Siam's independence, the Thai monarch Chulalongkorn, or Rama V (son of Mongkut, the king immortalised in the films *Anna and the King of Siam* and *The King and I*), was forced to make several concessions toward the two expansionist Western powers in the form not only of trade treaties and diplomatic emissaries but also of land. In 1893, after France sent warships up the Chao Phraya River to Bangkok, Siam agreed to give up its claims to the Laotian territory east of the Mekong River. Meanwhile, the British, having acquired nearby Burma in 1886, had interests of their own, and were competing with the French for the territory north of Siam, from Chiang Saen up to China. France and England would settle their differences with an 1896 agreement stating that neither country would go to war over Siam or its disputed territories, acknowledging (but not guaranteeing) Siam's sovereignty. Siam itself had no part in the treaty. It would lose Laos and Cambodia to France in 1907, and four Malay states to Britain in 1909.

13 The prime minister in 1895 was Lord Salisbury.

14 The first underwater vehicle was built in 1620 (by a Dutch inventor who tested his craft fifteen feet below the surface of the Thames), and inventors such as Robert Fulton attempted to refine the craft; but efforts to develop a working submarine intensified in the late nineteenth century. During the Civil War, the Confederacy constructed several vessels designed to affix explosives to the hulls of enemy ships. Of the three submarines, which were powered by hand-cranked propellers,

Yard—thin and austere. The gravity of both their faces foretold some weighty quest. The detective shook hands without a word. Mycroft Holmes struggled out of his overcoat and subsided into an armchair.

"A most annoying business, Sherlock," said he. "I extremely dislike altering my habits, but the powers that be would take no denial. In the present state of Siam[12] it is most awkward that I should be away from the office. But it is a real crisis. I have never seen the Prime Minister so upset.[13] As to the Admiralty—it is buzzing like an overturned bee-hive. Have you read up the case?"

"We have just done so. What were the technical papers?"

"Ah, there's the point! Fortunately, it has not come out. The Press would be furious if it did. The papers which this wretched youth had in his pocket were the plans of the Bruce-Partington submarine."[14]

Mycroft Holmes spoke with a solemnity which showed his sense of the importance of the subject. His brother and I sat expectant.

"Surely you have heard of it? I thought everyone had heard of it."

"Only as a name."

The Admiralty.
Queen's London (1897)

only one, the *H. L. Hunley*, had any success in attacking a Union warship.

The greatest strides in submarine technology began taking place sometime around 1880, when English clergyman George W. Garrett built an underwater vehicle powered by a coal-fired boiler. The steam generated prior to launch could power the submarine for several miles. In 1886, fellow Englishmen Andrew Campbell and James Ash had slightly better success with the *Nautilus*, which used an electric motor and could travel a maximum of eighty miles before the battery had to be recharged. The French equivalent was Gustave Zédé's *Gymnote*, built in 1888 but prone to control problems. France's designs improved (with Zédé's collaboration) over the next decade, and the *Narval*, built by naval engineer Maxime Laubeuf and launched in 1899, made several satisfactory dives. It was powered by steam on the surface of the water and electricity when submerged. At the dawn of the new century, in 1905, the French navy would be the first to lay claim to a diesel-powered submarine, the *Aigrette*.

Competition in the U.S. between two rival inventors precipitated tremendous advances. For an 1895 naval contract, Irish immigrant John P. Holland designed the *Plunger*, which would have used steam on the surface and electricity below the surface. The craft was never completed, and Holland poured his own financial resources into his next design, that of the *Holland VI* (gasoline on the surface, electricity below). Launched in 1897, *Holland VI* carried a crew of nine and could fire torpedoes and guns. It was adopted by the U. S. Navy in 1900. Simultaneously, another U.S. inventor, British-born Simon Lake, was developing submarines intended for research rather than warfare. The gasoline- and electricity-powered *Argonaut I*—one of several submarines built by Lake—was com-

pleted in 1894, and four years later it sailed from Norfolk, Virginia, to New York City, becoming the first underwater vessel to navigate extensively in the open sea.

France and the United States had become innovators in the field of submarine development, and technology was progressing even further still. By 1911, the *Encyclopædia Britannica* (11th Ed.) acknowledged, "By far the greater number of submarine boats in existence in 1910 were developments through a process of continuous experiment and improvement of the *Gymnote* and of the early Holland boats, although the process of evolution had been so rapid and extensive that the parentage of these modern boats is barely recognizable. . . ." The British navy, however, declined to participate in the race for invention, choosing to commission five Holland-design submarines in 1901. The first was completed in 1903. Germany did not build its first submarine, the U-1, until 1905.

Ronald S. Bonn suggests that, in contrast to outward appearances, the Germans already had the Bruce-Partington submarines—which were superior to the Holland boats—and thus refrained from purchasing any of the latter. Germany, Bonn proposes, obtained the plans from Doctor Watson, "the greatest nongovernmental criminal who ever lived." Michael H. Kean, in *Who Was Bruce-Partington*, concludes that "Bruce-Partington" was not an individual, for no single Englishman solved all the major challenges of the submarine, but rather that the plans were the joint product of Simon Lake and the Reverend Garrett, who, between them, solved all of the problems of constructing efficacious submarines. Sadly, it appears that the plans were (in the words of one scholar, "like many more modern British defence projects") abandoned as too sophisticated for the times.

15 "How to reconcile this remark with Mycroft's previous 'I thought everyone had heard of it' is something we will not attempt," comments William S. Baring-Gould wryly.

16 Mycroft seems to echo the preventative sentiments of inventor John P. Holland (see note 14), who wrote, in "The Submarine Boat and Its Future" (published in the *North American Review* for December 1900), that with the invention of the submarine, "Nations with sea ports will have to refrain from making war." See "Naval Warfare," page 1335, for a consideration of Mycroft's inaccurate prediction.

17 The annual requests to Parliament for money allotments during the forthcoming year.

18 Presumably the director of naval construction, in the department of the controller of the Admiralty Board, is meant.

19 Secrecy aside, there may be even more to the "international problem" than Mycroft lets on. June Thomson makes note of the fact that William II, the emperor of Germany (see "The Second Stain," note 10), began expanding his navy after dismissing his chancellor, Otto von Bismarck, in 1890. "The theft of the Bruce-Partington submarine plans," Thomson writes, "was almost certainly connected with the young Kaiser's naval ambitions, which so alarmed France and Russia that in 1894 they signed the Dual Alliance."

20 The "honours list" was the announcement of peerages, knighthoods, medals, etc., awarded by the sovereign. In "The Three Garridebs," we learn that Holmes declined a knighthood.

"Its importance can hardly be exaggerated. It has been the most jealously guarded of all Government secrets.[15] You may take it from me that naval warfare becomes impossible[16] within the radius of a Bruce-Partington's operation. Two years ago a very large sum was smuggled through the Estimates[17] and was expended in acquiring a monopoly of the invention. Every effort has been made to keep the secret. The plans, which are exceedingly intricate, comprising some thirty separate patents, each essential to the working of the whole, are kept in an elaborate safe in a confidential office adjoining the Arsenal, with burglar-proof doors and windows. Under no conceivable circumstances were the plans to be taken from the office. If the Chief Constructor of the Navy[18] desired to consult them, even he was forced to go to the Woolwich office for the purpose. And yet here we find them in the pockets of a dead junior clerk in the heart of London. From an official point of view it's simply awful."

"But you have recovered them?"

"No, Sherlock, no! That's the pinch. We have not. Ten papers were taken from Woolwich. There were seven in the pockets of Cadogan West. The three most essential are gone—stolen, vanished. You must drop everything, Sherlock. Never mind your usual petty puzzles of the police-court. It's a vital international problem that you have to solve.[19] Why did Cadogan West take the papers, where are the missing ones, how did he die, how came his body where it was found, how can the evil be set right? Find an answer to all these questions, and you will have done good service for your country."

"Why do you not solve it yourself, Mycroft? You can see as far as I."

"Possibly, Sherlock. But it is a question of getting details. Give me your details, and from an armchair I will return you an excellent expert opinion. But to run here and run there, to cross-question railway guards, and lie on my face with a lens to my eye—it is not my *métier*. No, you are the one man who can clear the matter up. If you have a fancy to see your name in the next honours list—"[20]

My friend smiled and shook his head.

"I play the game for the game's own sake," said he. "But the problem certainly presents some points of interest, and I shall be very pleased to look into it. Some more facts, please."

"I have jotted down the more essential ones upon this sheet of paper, together with a few addresses which you will find of service. The actual official guardian of the papers is the famous Government expert, Sir James Walter, whose decorations and sub-titles fill two lines of a book of reference. He has grown grey in the Service, is a gentleman, a favoured guest in the most exalted houses, and above all, a man whose patriotism is beyond suspicion. He is one of two who have a key of the safe. I may add that the papers were undoubtedly in the office during working hours on Monday, and that Sir James left for London about three o'clock taking his key with him. He was at the house of Admiral Sinclair at Barclay Square[21] during the whole of the evening when this incident occurred."

"Has the fact been verified?"

"Yes; his brother, Colonel Valentine Walter, has testified to his departure from Woolwich, and Admiral Sinclair to his arrival in London; so Sir James is no longer a direct factor in the problem."

"Who was the other man with a key?"

"The senior clerk and draughtsman, Mr. Sidney Johnson. He is a man of forty, married, with five children. He is a silent, morose man, but he has, on the whole, an excellent record in the public service. He is unpopular with his colleagues, but a hard worker. According to his own account, corroborated only by the word of his wife, he was at home the whole of Monday evening after office hours, and his key has never left the watch-chain upon which it hangs."

"Tell us about Cadogan West."

"He has been ten years in the Service and has done good work. He has the reputation of being hot-headed and impetuous, but a straight, honest man. We have nothing against him. He was next Sidney Johnson in the office. His duties brought him into daily, personal contact with the plans. No one else had the handling of them."

"Who locked the plans up that night?"

"Mr. Sidney Johnson, the senior clerk."

"Well, it is surely perfectly clear who took them away. They are actually found upon the person of this junior clerk, Cadogan West. That seems final, does it not?"

"It does, Sherlock, and yet it leaves so much unexplained. In the first place, why did he take them?"

"I presume they were of value?"

21 There is no *Barclay* Square in London, and this likely refers to *Berkeley* Square, a short distance from Baker Street.

22 Two thousand pounds in 1895 is over £128,000 in modern equivalency, or almost $210,000.

"He could have got several thousands for them very easily."[22]

"Can you suggest any possible motive for taking the papers to London except to sell them?"

"No, I cannot."

"Then we must take that as our working hypothesis. Young West took the papers. Now this could only be done by having a false key."

"Several false keys. He had to open the building and the room."

"He had, then, several false keys. He took the papers to London to sell the secret intending, no doubt to have the plans themselves back in the safe next morning before they were missed. While in London on this treasonable mission he met his end."

"How?"

"We will suppose that he was travelling back to Woolwich when he was killed and thrown out of the compartment."

"Aldgate, where the body was found, is considerably past the station for London Bridge, which would be his route to Woolwich."

"Many circumstances could be imagined under which he would pass London Bridge. There was someone in the carriage, for example, with whom he was having an absorbing interview. This interview led to a violent scene in which he lost his life. Possibly he tried to leave the carriage, fell out on the line, and so met his end. The other closed the door. There was a thick fog, and nothing could be seen."

"No better explanation can be given with our present knowledge; and yet consider, Sherlock, how much you leave untouched. We will suppose, for argument's sake, that young Cadogan West *had* determined to convey these papers to London. He would naturally have made an appointment with the foreign agent and kept his evening clear. Instead of that he took two tickets for the theatre, escorted his fiancée half-way there, and then suddenly disappeared."

"A blind," said Lestrade, who had sat listening with some impatience to the conversation.

"A very singular one. That is objection No. 1. Objection No. 2: We will suppose that he reaches London and sees the foreign agent. He must bring back the papers before morning or the loss will be discovered. He took away ten. Only seven were in his pocket. What had become of the other three? He certainly would not leave them of his own free will. Then, again, where is the price of his treason? One would have expected to find a large sum of money in his pocket."

"It seems to me perfectly clear," said Lestrade. "I have no doubt at all as to what occurred. He took the papers to sell them. He saw the agent. They could not agree as to price. He started home again, but the agent went with him. In the train the agent murdered him, took the more essential papers, and threw his body from the carriage. That would account for everything, would it not?"

"Why had he no ticket?"

"The ticket would have shown which station was nearest the agent's house. Therefore he took it from the murdered man's pocket."

"Good, Lestrade, very good," said Holmes. "Your theory holds together. But if this is true, then the case is at an end. On the one hand the traitor is dead. On the other the plans of the Bruce-Partington submarine are presumably already on the Continent. What is there for us to do?"

"To act, Sherlock—to act!" cried Mycroft, springing to his feet. "All my instincts are against this explanation. Use your powers! Go to the scene of the crime! See the people concerned! Leave no stone unturned! In all your career you have never had so great a chance of serving your country."

"Well, well!" said Holmes, shrugging his shoulders. "Come, Watson! And you, Lestrade, could you favour us with your company for an hour or two? We will begin our investigation by a visit to Aldgate Station. Good-bye, Mycroft. I shall let you have a report before evening, but I warn you in advance that you have little to expect."

An hour later Holmes, Lestrade and I stood upon the Underground railroad at the point where it emerges from the tunnel immediately before Aldgate Station. A courteous red-faced old gentleman represented the railway company.

"This is where the young man's body lay," said he, indicating a spot about three feet from the metals. "It could not have fallen from above, for these, as you see, are all blank walls.

23 These were the railway switches, movable rails permitting a train to change lines.

Therefore, it could only have come from a train, and that train, so far as we can trace it, must have passed about midnight on Monday."

"Have the carriages been examined for any sign of violence?"

"There are no such signs, and no ticket has been found."

"No record of a door being found open?"

"None."

"We have had some fresh evidence this morning," said Lestrade. "A passenger who passed Aldgate in an ordinary Metropolitan train about 11:40 on Monday night declares that he heard a heavy thud, as of a body striking the line, just before the train reached the station. There was dense fog, however, and nothing could be seen. He made no report of it at the time. Why, whatever is the matter with Mr. Holmes?"

My friend was standing with an expression of strained intensity upon his face, staring at the railway metals where they curved out of the tunnel. Aldgate is a junction, and there was a network of points.[23] On these his eager, questioning eyes were fixed, and I saw on his keen, alert face that tightening of the lips, that quiver of the nostrils, and concentration of the heavy tufted brows which I knew so well.

"Points," he muttered; "the points."

"What of it? What do you mean?"

"I suppose there are no great number of points on a system such as this?"

"No; there are very few."

"And a curve, too. Points, and a curve. By Jove! if it were only so."

"What is it, Mr. Holmes? Have you a clue?"

"An idea—an indication, no more. But the case certainly grows in interest. Unique, perfectly unique, and yet why not? I do not see any indications of bleeding on the line."

"There were hardly any."

"But I understand that there was a considerable wound."

"The bone was crushed, but there was no great external injury."

"And yet one would have expected some bleeding. Would it be possible for me to inspect the train which contained the passenger who heard the thud of a fall in the fog?"

"My friend was standing with an expression of
strained intensity upon his face."
Arthur Twidle, *Strand Magazine*, 1908

"I fear not, Mr. Holmes. The train has been broken up
before now, and the carriages redistributed."

"I can assure you, Mr. Holmes," said Lestrade, "that every
carriage has been carefully examined. I saw to it myself."

It was one of my friend's most obvious weaknesses that he
was impatient with less alert intelligences than his own.

"Very likely," said he, turning away. "As it happens, it was
not the carriages which I desired to examine. Watson, we have
done all we can here. We need not trouble you any further, Mr.
Lestrade. I think our investigations must now carry us to Woolwich."

At London Bridge, Holmes wrote a telegram to his brother,
which he handed to me before dispatching it. It ran thus:

See some light in the darkness, but it may possibly flicker out. Meanwhile, please send by messenger, to await return at Baker Street, a complete list of all foreign spies or international agents known to be in England, with full address.

SHERLOCK.

"That should be helpful, Watson," he remarked as we took our seats in the Woolwich train. "We certainly owe Brother Mycroft a debt for having introduced us to what promises to be a really very remarkable case."

His eager face still wore that expression of intense and high-strung energy, which showed me that some novel and suggestive circumstance had opened up a stimulating line of thought. See the foxhound with hanging ears and drooping tail as it lolls about the kennels, and compare it with the same hound as, with gleaming eyes and straining muscles, it runs upon a breast-high scent—such was the change in Holmes since the morning. He was a different man from the limp and lounging figure in the mouse-coloured dressing-gown who had prowled so restlessly only a few hours before round the fog-girt room.

"There is material here. There is scope." said he. "I am dull indeed not to have understood its possibilities."

"Even now they are dark to me."

"The end is dark to me also, but I have hold of one idea which may lead us far. The man met his death elsewhere, and his body was on the *roof* of a carriage."

"On the roof?"

"Remarkable, is it not? But consider the facts. Is it a coincidence that it is found at the very point where the train pitches and sways as it comes round on the points? Is not that the place where an object upon the roof might be expected to fall off? The points would affect no object inside the train. Either the body fell from the roof, or a very curious coincidence has occurred. But now consider the question of the blood. Of course, there was no bleeding on the line if the body had bled elsewhere. Each fact is suggestive in itself. Together they have a cumulative force."

"And the ticket, too!" I cried.

"Exactly. We could not explain the absence of a ticket. This would explain it. Everything fits together."

"But suppose it were so, we are still as far as ever from unravelling the mystery of his death. Indeed, it becomes not simpler but stranger."

"Perhaps," said Holmes, thoughtfully; "perhaps." He relapsed into a silent reverie, which lasted until the slow train drew up at last in Woolwich Station. There he called a cab and drew Mycroft's paper from his pocket.

"We have quite a little round of afternoon calls to make," said he. "I think that Sir James Walter claims our first attention."

The house of the famous official was a fine villa with green lawns stretching down to the Thames. As we reached it the fog was lifting, and a thin, watery sunshine was breaking through. A butler answered our ring.

"Sir James, sir!" said he, with solemn face. "Sir James died this morning."

"Good heavens!" cried Holmes, in amazement. "How did he die?"

"Perhaps you would care to step in, sir, and see his brother, Colonel Valentine?"

"Yes, we had best do so."

We were ushered into a dim-lit drawing-room, where an instant later we were joined by a very tall, handsome, light-bearded man of fifty, the younger brother of the dead scientist. His wild eyes, stained cheeks, and unkempt hair all spoke of the sudden blow which had fallen upon the household. He was hardly articulate as he spoke of it.

"It was this horrible scandal," said he. "My brother, Sir James, was a man of very sensitive honour, and he could not survive such an affair. It broke his heart. He was always so proud of the efficiency of his department, and this was a crushing blow."

"We had hoped that he might have given us some indications which would have helped us to clear the matter up."

"I assure you that it was all a mystery to him as it is to you and to all of us. He had already put all his knowledge at the disposal of the police. Naturally he had no doubt that Cadogan West was guilty. But all the rest was inconceivable."

"You cannot throw any new light upon the affair?"

"I know nothing myself save what I have read or heard. I

24 The third of the quartet of Canonical "Violets," which include Violet Hunter ("The Copper Beeches"), Violet Smith ("The Solitary Cyclist"), and Violet De Merville ("The Illustrious Client").

have no desire to be discourteous, but you can understand, Mr. Holmes, that we are much disturbed at present, and I must ask you to hasten this interview to an end."

"This is indeed an unexpected development," said my friend when we had regained the cab. "I wonder if the death was natural, or whether the poor old fellow killed himself! If the latter, may it be taken as some sign of self-reproach for duty neglected? We must leave that question to the future. Now we shall turn to the Cadogan Wests."

A small but well-kept house in the outskirts of the town sheltered the bereaved mother. The old lady was too dazed with grief to be of any use to us, but at her side was a white-faced young lady, who introduced herself as Miss Violet Westbury,[24] the *fiancée* of the dead man, and the last to see him upon that fatal night.

"I cannot explain it, Mr. Holmes," she said. "I have not shut an eye since the tragedy, thinking, thinking, thinking, night and day, what the true meaning of it can be. Arthur was the most single-minded, chivalrous, patriotic man upon earth. He would have cut his right hand off before he would sell a State secret confided to his keeping. It is absurd, impossible, preposterous to anyone who knew him."

"But the facts, Miss Westbury?"

"Yes, yes; I admit I cannot explain them."

"Was he in any want of money?"

"No; his needs were very simple and his salary ample. He had saved a few hundreds, and we were to marry at the New Year."

"No signs of any mental excitement? Come, Miss Westbury, be absolutely frank with us."

The quick eye of my companion had noted some change in her manner. She coloured and hesitated.

"Yes," she said at last, "I had a feeling that there was something on his mind."

"For long?"

"Only for the last week or so. He was thoughtful and worried. Once I pressed him about it. He admitted that there was something, and that it was concerned with his official life. 'It is too serious for me to speak about, even to you,' said he. I could get nothing more."

Holmes looked grave.

"Go on, Miss Westbury. Even if it seems to tell against him, go on. We cannot say what it may lead to."

"Indeed, I have nothing more to tell. Once or twice it seemed to me that he was on the point of telling me something. He spoke one evening of the importance of the secret and I have some recollection that he said that no doubt foreign spies would pay a great deal to have it."

My friend's face grew graver still.

"Anything else?"

"He said that we were slack about such matters—that it would be easy for a traitor to get the plans."

"Was it only recently that he made such remarks?"

"Yes, quite recently."

"Now tell us of that last evening."

"We were to go to the theatre. The fog was so thick that a cab was useless. We walked, and our way took us close to the office. Suddenly he darted away into the fog."

"Without a word?"

"He gave an exclamation; that was all. I waited but he never returned. Then I walked home. Next morning, after the office opened, they came to inquire. About twelve o'clock we heard the terrible news. Oh, Mr. Holmes, if you could only, only save his honour! It was so much to him."

Holmes shook his head sadly.

"Come, Watson," said he, "our ways lie elsewhere. Our next station must be the office from which the papers were taken.

"It was black enough before against this young man, but our inquiries make it blacker," he remarked as the cab lumbered off. "His coming marriage gives a motive for the crime. He naturally wanted money. The idea was in his head, since he spoke about it. He nearly made the girl an accomplice in the treason by telling her his plans. It is all very bad."

"But surely, Holmes, character goes for something? Then, again, why should he leave the girl in the street and dart away to commit a felony?"

"Exactly! There are certainly objections. But it is a formidable case which they have to meet."

Mr. Sidney Johnson, the senior clerk, met us at the office and received us with that respect which my companion's card always commanded. He was a thin, gruff, bespectacled man of

25 It is frankly impossible for "the last man out" every evening not to possess keys with which to lock the doors. "Why did he conceal the fact that he had such a set?" ponders R. Kelf-Cohen, in a symposium entitled "The Bruce-Partington Keys" edited by Lord Gore-Booth. "You will agree that it is normal Civil Service practice for Sidney Johnson, the Senior Clerk, to be responsible for closing the office and making everything secure."

Paul Gore-Booth (Lord Gore-Booth) retorts that a civil servant would never lie; thus Sidney Johnson must telling the truth in saying he does not possess keys to the doors. Perhaps, Lord Gore-Booth proposes, the doors were locked with spring locks (a theory he admits is unlikely, given that if Johnson were ever to step outside momentarily, he would essentially be locking himself out and would be, ludicrously, forced to call upon Sir James for assistance). Alternatively, perhaps the office had keys that did not leave the grounds but were turned in at some central location after use. Such a practice was in use at other civil service offices. "The Head of the Department," Lord Gore-Booth muses, "probably would have his private keys of the doors but there was no good reason to make a lot of spares, if there was some way of getting at the Departmental set. Perhaps they were left with the 'old soldier and . . . most trustworthy man.' "

middle age, his cheeks haggard, and his hands twitching from the nervous strain to which he had been subjected.

"It is bad, Mr. Holmes, very bad! Have you heard of the death of the chief?"

"We have just come from his house."

"The place is disorganized. The chief dead, Cadogan West dead, our papers stolen. And yet, when we closed our door on Monday evening we were as efficient an office as any in the Government service. Good God, it's dreadful to think of! That West, of all men, should have done such a thing!"

"You are sure of his guilt, then?"

"I can see no other way out of it. And yet I would have trusted him as I trust myself."

"At what hour was the office closed on Monday?"

"At five."

"Did you close it?"

"I am always the last man out."

"Where were the plans?"

"In that safe. I put them there myself."

"Is there no watchman to the building?"

"There is, but he has other departments to look after as well. He is an old soldier and a most trustworthy man. He saw nothing that evening. Of course, the fog was very thick."

"Suppose that Cadogan West wished to make his way into the building after hours; he would need three keys, would he not, before he could reach the papers?"

"Yes, he would. The key of the outer door, the key of the office, and the key of the safe."

"Only Sir James Walter and you had those keys?"

"I had no keys of the doors—only of the safe."[25]

"Was Sir James a man who was orderly in his habits?"

"Yes, I think he was. I know that so far as those three keys are concerned he kept them on the same ring. I have often seen them there."

"And that ring went with him to London?"

"He said so."

"And your key never left your possession?"

"Never."

"Then West, if he is the culprit, must have had a duplicate. And yet none was found upon his body. One other point: if a clerk in this office desired to sell the plans, would it not be simpler to copy the plans for himself than to take the originals, as was actually done?"

"It would take considerable technical knowledge to copy the plans in an effective way."

"But I suppose either Sir James, or you, or West had that technical knowledge?"

"No doubt we had, but I beg you won't try to drag me into the matter, Mr. Holmes. What is the use of our speculating in this way when the original plans were actually found on West?"

"Well, it is certainly singular that he should run the risk of taking originals if he could safely have taken copies, which would have equally served his turn."

"Singular, no doubt—and yet he did so."

"Every inquiry in this case reveals something inexplicable. Now there are three papers still missing. They are, as I understand, the vital ones."

"Yes, that is so."

"Do you mean to say that anyone holding these three papers, and without the seven others, could construct a Bruce-Partington submarine?"

"I reported to that effect to the Admiralty. But to-day, I have

"Do you mean to say that anyone holding these three papers, and without the seven others, could construct a Bruce-Partington submarine?"
Arthur Twidle, *Strand Magazine*, 1908

26 Rex Stout, famed biographer of Nero Wolfe, complains that Holmes—after having meticulously observed and examined every clue up until this point—finds out that West took the 8:15 train yet fails to inquire about the train's other passengers, thus missing an opportunity to see if anything may be learned about West's murderer. "This is indeed," Stout writes indignantly, "unacceptable."

been over the drawings again, and I am not so sure of it. The double valves with the automatic self-adjusting slots are drawn in one of the papers which have been returned. Until the foreigners had invented that for themselves they could not make the boat. Of course, they might soon get over the difficulty."

"But the three missing drawings are the most important?"

"Undoubtedly."

"I think, with your permission, I will now take a stroll round the premises. I do not recall any other question which I desired to ask." He examined the lock of the safe, the door of the room, and finally the iron shutters of the window. It was only when we were on the lawn outside that his interest was strongly excited. There was a laurel bush outside the window, and several of the branches bore signs of having been twisted or snapped. He examined them carefully with his lens, and then some dim and vague marks upon the earth beneath. Finally he asked the chief clerk to close the iron shutters, and he pointed out to me that they hardly met in the centre, and that it would be possible for anyone outside to see what was going on within the room.

"The indications are ruined by the three days' delay. They may mean something or nothing. Well, Watson, I do not think that Woolwich can help us further. It is a small crop which we have gathered. Let us see if we can do better in London."

Yet we added one more sheaf to our harvest before we left Woolwich Station. The clerk in the ticket office was able to say with confidence that he saw Cadogan West—whom he knew well by sight—upon the Monday night, and that he went to London by the 8.15 to London Bridge. He was alone, and took a single third-class ticket. The clerk was struck at the time by his excited and nervous manner. So shaky was he that he could hardly pick up his change, and the clerk had helped him with it. A reference to the timetable showed that the 8.15 was the first train which it was possible for West to take after he had left the lady about 7.30.[26]

"Let us reconstruct, Watson," said Holmes, after half an hour of silence. "I am not aware that in all our joint researches we have ever had a case which was more difficult to get at. Every fresh advance which we make only reveals a fresh ridge beyond. And yet we have surely made some appreciable progress.

"The effect of our inquiries at Woolwich has in the main

been against young Cadogan West; but the indications at the window would lend themselves to a more favourable hypothesis. Let us suppose, for example, that he had been approached by some foreign agent. It might have been done under such pledges as would have prevented him from speaking of it, and yet would have affected his thoughts in the direction indicated by his remarks to his *fiancée*. Very good. We will now suppose that as he went to the theatre with the young lady he suddenly, in the fog, caught a glimpse of this same agent going in the direction of the office. He was an impetuous man, quick in his decisions. Everything gave way to his duty. He followed the man, reached the window, saw the abstraction of the documents, and pursued the thief. In this way we get over the objection that no one would take originals when he could make copies. This outsider had to take originals. So far it holds together."

"What is the next step?"

"Then we come into difficulties. One would imagine that under such circumstances the first act of young Cadogan West would be to seize the villain and raise the alarm. Why did he not do so? Could it have been an official superior who took the papers? That would explain West's conduct. Or could the thief[27] have given West the slip in the fog, and West started at once to London to head him off from his own rooms, presuming that he knew where the rooms were? The call must have been very pressing, since he left his girl standing in the fog, and made no effort to communicate with her. Our scent runs cold here, and there is a vast gap between either hypothesis and the laying of West's body, with seven papers in his pocket, on the roof of a Metropolitan train. My instinct now is to work from the other end. If Mycroft has given us the list of addresses we may be able to pick our man and follow two tracks instead of one."

Surely enough, a note awaited us at Baker Street. A Government messenger had brought it post-haste. Holmes glanced at it and threw it over to me.

There are numerous small fry, but few who would handle so big an affair. The only men worth considering are Adolph

27 In the *Strand Magazine* and numerous editions of *His Last Bow*, there is a typographical error, with the word given as "chief."

28 Oberstein and La Rothière are also mentioned in "The Second Stain," as two of the "only . . . three capable of playing so bold a game" as to purchase and resell the valuable diplomatic letter.

Meyer, of 13, Great George Street, Westminster; Louis La Rothière, of Campden Mansions, Notting Hill; and Hugo Oberstein,[28] 13 Caulfield Gardens, Kensington. The latter was known to be in town on Monday, and is now reported as having left. Glad to hear you have seen some light. The cabinet awaits your final report with the utmost anxiety. Urgent representations have arrived from the very highest quarter. The whole force of the State is at your back if you should need it.

—MYCROFT.

"I'm afraid," said Holmes, smiling, "that all the Queen's horses and all the Queen's men cannot avail in this matter." He had spread out his big map of London, and leaned eagerly over it. "Well, well," said he presently with an exclamation of satisfaction, "things are turning a little in our direction at last. Why, Watson, I do honestly believe that we are going to pull it off after all." He slapped me on the shoulder with a sudden burst of hilarity. "I am going out now. It is only a reconnaissance. I will do nothing serious without my trusted comrade and biographer at my elbow. Do you stay here, and the odds are that you will see me again in an hour or two. If time hangs heavy get foolscap and a pen, and begin your narrative of how we saved the State."

I felt some reflection of his elation in my own mind, for I knew well that he would not depart so far from his usual austerity of demeanour unless there was good cause for exultation. All the long November evening I waited, filled with impatience for his return. At last, shortly after nine o'clock there arrived a messenger with a note:

Am dining at Goldini's Restaurant, Gloucester Road, Kensington. Please come at once and join me there. Bring with you a jemmy, a dark lantern, a chisel, and a revolver.

—S. H.

It was a nice equipment for a respectable citizen to carry through the dim, fog-draped streets. I stowed them all discreetly away in my overcoat, and drove straight to the address given. There sat my friend at a little round table near the door of the garish Italian restaurant.

"Have you had something to eat? Then join me in a coffee and curaçao.[29] Try one of the proprietor's cigars. They are less poisonous than one would expect. Have you the tools?"

"They are here, in my overcoat."

"Excellent. Let me give you a short sketch of what I have done, with some indication of what we are about to do. Now it must be evident to you, Watson, that this young man's body was *placed* on the roof of the train. That was clear from the instant that I determined the fact that it was from the roof, and not from a carriage, that he had fallen."

"Could it not have been dropped from a bridge?"

"I should say it was impossible. If you examine the roofs you will find that they are slightly rounded, and there is no railing round them. Therefore, we can say for certain that young Cadogan West was placed on it."

"How could he be placed there?"

"That was the question which we had to answer. There is only one possible way. You are aware that the Underground runs clear of tunnels at some points in the West-End. I had a vague memory that as I have travelled by it I have occasionally seen windows just above my head. Now, suppose that a train halted under such a window, would there be any difficulty in laying a body upon the roof?"

"It seems most improbable."

"We must fall back upon the old axiom that when all other contingencies fail, whatever remains, however improbable, must be the truth. Here all other contingencies *have* failed. When I found that the leading international agent, who had just left London, lived in a row of houses which abutted upon the Underground, I was so pleased that you were a little astonished at my sudden frivolity."

"Oh, that was it, was it?"

"Yes, that was it. Mr. Hugo Oberstein, of 13 Caulfield Gardens, had become my objective. I began my operations at Gloucester Road Station, where a very helpful official walked with me along the track, and allowed me to satisfy myself, not only that the back-stair windows of Caulfield Gardens open on the line but the even more essential fact that, owing to the intersection of one of the larger railways, the Underground trains are frequently held motionless for some minutes at that very spot."

29 A liqueur flavoured with bitter orange peel, distilled on the eponymous island in the Caribbean, which is part of the Dutch Antilles.

30 The definition of a "suspicious character" may be found in the *Police Code of 1904*, which stated, "Every one is liable to penal servitude . . . [w]ho is found, by night, having in his possession, without lawful excuse (proof of which excuse lies upon him), any picklock or false key, jemmy, centre-bit, chisel, bradawl, gimlet, or other instrument adapted for housebreaking and forcing windows, doors, or locks. . . ." It's little wonder Holmes was concerned about Watson's culpability.

"Splendid, Holmes! You have got it!"

"So far—so far, Watson. We advance, but the goal is afar. Well, having seen the back of Caulfield Gardens, I visited the front and satisfied myself that the bird was indeed flown. It is a considerable house, unfurnished, so far as I could judge, in the upper rooms. Oberstein lived there with a single valet, who was probably a confederate entirely in his confidence. We must bear in mind that Oberstein has gone to the Continent to dispose of his booty, but not with any idea of flight; for he had no reason to fear a warrant, and the idea of an amateur domiciliary visit would certainly never occur to him, Yet that is precisely what we are about to make."

"Could we not get a warrant and legalise it?"

"Hardly on the evidence."

"What can we hope to do?"

"We cannot tell what correspondence may be there."

"I don't like it, Holmes."

"My dear fellow, you shall keep watch in the street. I'll do the criminal part. It's not a time to stick at trifles. Think of Mycroft's note, of the Admiralty, the Cabinet, the exalted person who waits for news. We are bound to go."

My answer was to rise from the table.

"You are right, Holmes. We are bound to go."

He sprang up and shook me by the hand.

"I knew you would not shrink at the last," said he, and for a moment I saw something in his eyes which was nearer to tenderness than I had ever seen. The next instant he was his masterful, practical self once more.

"It is nearly half a mile, but there is no hurry. Let us walk," said he. "Don't drop the instruments, I beg. Your arrest as a suspicious character would be a most unfortunate complication."[30]

Caulfield Gardens was one of those lines of flat-faced pillared, and porticoed houses which are so prominent a product of the middle Victorian epoch in the West-End of London. Next door there appeared to be a children's party, for the merry buzz of young voices and the clatter of a piano resounded through the night. The fog still hung about and screened us with its friendly shade. Holmes had lit his lantern and flashed it upon the massive door.

"This is a serious proposition," said he. "It is certainly

bolted as well as locked. We would do better in the area.[31] There is an excellent archway down yonder in case a too zealous policeman should intrude. Give me a hand, Watson, and I'll do the same for you."

A minute later we were both in the area. Hardly had we reached the dark shadows before the step of the policeman was heard in the fog above. As its soft rhythm died away, Holmes set to work upon the lower door. I saw him stoop and strain until with a sharp crash it flew open. We sprang through into the dark passage, closing the area door behind us. Holmes led the way up the curving, uncarpeted stair. His little fan of yellow light shone upon a low window.

"Here we are, Watson—this must be the one." He threw it open, and as he did so there was a low, harsh murmur, growing steadily into a loud roar as a train dashed past us in the darkness. Holmes swept his light along the window-sill. It was thickly coated with soot from the passing engines, but the black surface was blurred and rubbed in places.

"You can see where they rested the body. Halloa, Watson!

31 The open space below the pavement level, giving light to the basement windows and entrance to service quarters.

"Halloa, Watson! What is this?"
Arthur Twidle, *Strand Magazine*, 1908

32 That is, the American "second floor."

What is this? There can be no doubt that it is a blood mark." He was pointing to faint discolourations along the woodwork of the window. "Here it is on the stone of the stair also. The demonstration is complete. Let us stay here until a train stops."

We had not long to wait, the very next train roared from the tunnel as before, but slowed in the open, and then, with a creaking of brakes, pulled up immediately beneath us. It was not four feet from the window-ledge to the roof of the carriages. Holmes softly closed the window.

"So far we are justified," said he. "What do you think of it, Watson?"

"A masterpiece. You have never risen to a greater height."

"I cannot agree with you there. From the moment that I conceived the idea of the body being upon the roof, which surely was not a very abstruse one, all the rest was inevitable. If it were not for the grave interests involved the affair up to this point would be insignificant. Our difficulties are still before us. But perhaps we may find something here which may help us."

We had ascended the kitchen stair and entered the suite of rooms upon the first floor.[32] One was a dining-room, severely furnished and containing nothing of interest. A second was a bedroom, which also drew blank. The remaining room appeared more promising, and my companion settled down to a systematic examination. It was littered with books and papers, and was evidently used as a study. Swiftly and methodically Holmes turned over the contents of drawer after drawer and cupboard after cupboard, but no gleam of success came to brighten his austere face. At the end of an hour he was no further than when he started.

"The cunning dog has covered his tracks," said he. "He has left nothing to incriminate him. His dangerous correspondence has been destroyed or removed. This is our last chance."

It was a small tin cash-box which stood upon the writing-desk. Holmes prised it open with his chisel. Several rolls of paper were within, covered with figures and calculations, without any note to show to what they referred. The recurring words, "Water pressure" and "Pressure to the square inch" suggested some possible relation to a submarine. Holmes tossed them all impatiently aside. There only remained an envelope with some small newspaper slips inside it. He shook them out on the table, and at once I saw by his eager face that his hopes had been raised.

"What's this, Watson? Eh? What's this? Record of a series of messages in the advertisements of a paper. *Daily Telegraph* agony column by the print and paper.[33] Right-hand top corner of a page. No dates—but messages arrange themselves. This must be the first:

Hoped to hear sooner. Terms agreed to. Write fully to address given on card.

—PIERROT.

"Next comes:

Too complex for description. Must have full report. Stuff awaits you when goods delivered.

—PIERROT.

"Then comes:

Matter presses. Must withdraw offer unless contract completed. Make appointment by letter. Will confirm by advertisement.

—PIERROT.

"Finally:

Monday night after nine. Two taps. Only ourselves. Do not be so suspicious. Payment in hard cash when goods delivered.

—PIERROT.

"A fairly complete record, Watson![34] If we could only get at the man at the other end!" He sat lost in thought, tapping his fingers on the table. Finally he sprang to his feet.

"Well, perhaps it won't be so difficult after all. There is nothing more to be done here, Watson. I think we might drive round to the offices of the *Daily Telegraph*, and so bring a good day's work to a conclusion."

Mycroft Holmes and Lestrade had come round by appointment after breakfast next day and Sherlock Holmes had

33 Holmes's knowledge of newspaper print is featured in *The Hound of the Baskervilles*, where Holmes tells Dr. Watson: "The detection of types is one of the most elementary branches of knowledge to the special expert in crime, though I confess that once when I was very young I confused the *Leeds Mercury* with the *Western Morning News.*"

34 "What possessed [Oberstein]," wonders D. Martin Dakin, "after clearing his house of all other suspicious papers, to leave . . . his newspaper advertisements to his confederate? Why should he keep them at all, once they had served their purpose? Just to make it easier for Holmes?"

35 A traditional toast in the Royal Navy and oft-cited phrase in literature. Its earliest published appearance seems to have been in the song "The Death of Nelson," from the opera *The Americans* by John Braham (with words by S. J. Arnold), first staged in 1811: "But dearly was that conquest bought / Too well the gallant Hero fought, / For England, home and beauty. / He cried as 'midst the fire he ran, / 'England shall find that ev'ry man / This day will do his duty!' "

36 One must wonder, here, how Holmes knew the *place* of the meeting. There was no evidence at Oberstein's flat that he had met his confidant there—was this just a lucky shot, or did Holmes know something which Watson failed to record?

37 Orlando di Lasso (1532–1594), also called Roland de Lassus, was a prolific Flemish composer whose more than two thousand compositions included a collection of 516 Latin motets (religious choral works), published posthumously as *Magnus Opus Musicum* in 1604. He was equally comfortable composing masses, Italian madrigals, French chansons, and German lieder, and setting love songs to the words of Petrarch. Emperor Maximilian II raised him to the nobility in 1570, and he received the knighthood of the Golden Spur from Pope Gregory XIII in 1574, after dedicating a collection of masses to him. Lasso's best-known work is *Penitential Psalms of David* (published in 1584). See "The Polyphonic Motets of Lassus," page 1338, for further consideration of Holmes's monograph and his musical abilities.

recounted to them our proceedings of the day before. The professional shook his head over our confessed burglary.

"We can't do these things in the force, Mr. Holmes," said he. "No wonder you get results that are beyond us. But some of these days you'll go too far, and you'll find yourself and your friend in trouble."

"For England, home and beauty[35]—eh, Watson? Martyrs on the altar of our country. But what do you think of it, Mycroft?"

"Excellent, Sherlock! Admirable! But what use will you make of it?"

Holmes picked up the *Daily Telegraph* which lay upon the table.

"Have you seen Pierrot's advertisement to-day?"

"What! Another one?"

"Yes, here it is:

To-night. Same hour. Same place.[36] Two taps. Most vitally important. Your own safety at stake.

—PIERROT.

"By George!" cried Lestrade. "If he answers that we've got him!"

"That was my idea when I put it in. I think if you could both make it convenient to come with us about eight o'clock to Caulfield Gardens we might possibly get a little nearer to a solution."

One of the most remarkable characteristics of Sherlock Holmes was his power of throwing his brain out of action and switching all his thoughts on to lighter things whenever he had convinced himself that he could no longer work to advantage. I remember that during the whole of that memorable day he lost himself in a monograph which he had undertaken upon the Polyphonic Motets of Lassus.[37] For my own part I had none of this power of detachment, and the day, in consequence, appeared to be interminable. The great national importance of the issue, the suspense in high quarters, the direct nature of the experiment which we were trying—all combined to work upon my nerve. It was a relief to me, when at last, after a light dinner, we set out upon our expedition. Lestrade and Mycroft met us by appointment at the outside of Gloucester Road Station. The area door of Oberstein's house had been left open the night before, and it was necessary for me, as Mycroft Holmes absolutely and indignantly declined to climb the railings, to pass in and open the hall door. By nine o'clock we were all seated in the study, waiting patiently for our man.

An hour passed and yet another. When eleven struck, the measured beat of the great church clock seemed to sound the dirge of our hopes. Lestrade and Mycroft were fidgeting in their seats and looking twice a minute at their watches. Holmes sat silent and composed, his eyelids half shut, but every sense on the alert. He raised his head with a sudden jerk.

"He is coming," said he.

There had been a furtive step past the door. Now it returned. We heard a shuffling sound outside, and then two sharp taps with the knocker. Holmes rose, motioning to us to remain seated. The gas in the hall was a mere point of light. He opened the outer door, and then as a dark figure slipped past him he closed and fastened it. "This way!" we heard him say, and a moment later our man stood before us. Holmes had followed him closely, and as the man turned with a cry of surprise and alarm he caught him by the collar and threw him back into the room. Before our prisoner had recovered his balance the door was shut and Holmes standing with his back against it. The man glared round him, staggered, and fell senseless upon the floor. With the shock, his broad-brimmed hat flew from his head, his cravat slipped down from his lips, and there were the long light beard and the soft, handsome delicate features of Colonel Valentine Walter.

Holmes gave a whistle of surprise.

"You can write me down an ass this time, Watson," said he. "This was not the bird that I was looking for."[38]

"Who is he?" asked Mycroft eagerly.

"The younger brother of the late Sir James Walter, the head of the Submarine Department. Yes, yes; I see the fall of the cards. He is coming to. I think that you had best leave his examination to me."

We had carried the prostrate body to the sofa. Now our prisoner sat up, looked round him with a horror-stricken face, and passed his hand over his forehead, like one who cannot believe his own senses.

"What is this?" he asked. "I came here to visit Mr. Oberstein."

38 "Now the puzzle is this," writes Nathan L. Bengis, in a letter to the *Sherlock Holmes Journal*: "Who, if not Walter, was the 'bird' Holmes was expecting? There can be little doubt that the man Holmes had in mind was Sidney Johnson, the senior clerk." Johnson does seem a likely (perhaps too likely?) suspect, considering his easy access to the papers and the fact that he was the last to leave the building on the night in question. Thus it is not difficult to see why Holmes may have guessed wrong. Bengis credits him for a quick recovery, but otherwise cuts the Master little slack, writing, "In view . . . of his failure to identify the culprit in advance, Holmes must no longer be assigned full marks in this adventure."

39 Holmes's innate snobbery is revealed here. It would be expected, he implies, that a man of the middle classes, such as Mr. Sidney Johnson, might commit treason, but a gentleman—never!

"Before our prisoner had recovered his balance the door was shut and Holmes was standing with his back against it."
Arthur Twidle, *Strand Magazine*, 1908

"Everything is known, Colonel Walter," said Holmes. "How an English gentleman[39] could behave in such a manner is beyond my comprehension. But your whole correspondence and relations with Oberstein are within our knowledge. So also are the circumstances connected with the death of young Cadogan West. Let me advise you to gain at least the small credit for repentance and confession, since there are still some details which we can only learn from your lips."

The man groaned and sank his face in his hands. We waited, but he was silent.

"I can assure you," said Holmes, "that every essential is already known. We know that you were pressed for money; that you took an impress of the keys which your brother held;

and that you entered into a correspondence with Oberstein, who answered your letters through the advertisement columns of the *Daily Telegraph*. We are aware that you went down to the office in the fog on Monday night, but that you were seen and followed by young Cadogan West, who had probably some previous reason to suspect you. He saw your theft, but could not give the alarm, as it was just possible that you were taking the papers to your brother in London. Leaving all his private concerns, like the good citizen that he was, he followed you closely in the fog, and kept at your heels until you reached this very house. There he intervened, and then it was, Colonel Walter, that to treason you added the more terrible crime of murder."

"I did not! I did not! Before God I swear that I did not!" cried our wretched prisoner.

"Tell us, then, how Cadogan West met his end before you laid him upon the roof of a railway carriage."

"I will. I swear to you that I will. I did the rest. I confess it. It was just as you say. A Stock Exchange debt had to be paid. I needed the money badly. Oberstein offered me five thousand. It was to save myself from ruin. But as to murder, I am as innocent as you."

"What happened then?"

"He had his suspicions before,[40] and he followed me as you describe. I never knew it until I was at the very door. It was thick fog, and one could not see three yards. I had given two taps and Oberstein had come to the door. The young man rushed up and demanded to know what we were about to do with the papers. Oberstein had a short life-preserver.[41] He always carried it with him. As West forced his way after us into the house Oberstein struck him on the head. The blow was a fatal one. He was dead within five minutes. There he lay in the hall, and we were at our wit's end what to do. Then Oberstein had this idea about the trains which halted under his back window. But first he examined the papers which I had brought. He said that three of them were essential, and that he must keep them. 'You cannot keep them,' said I. 'There will be a dreadful row at Woolwich if they are not returned.' 'I must keep them,' said he, 'for they are so technical that it is impossible in the time to make copies.' 'Then they must all go back together to-night,' said I. He thought for a little, and then he cried out that he had it. 'Three I will keep,' said he. 'The others we will

40 If Cadogan West was suspicious of Colonel Walter—and the origin of those suspicions is never revealed—it seems logical that he would have informed Sir James; yet he did not. Also unrevealed is the manner in which Colonel Walter first realised West suspected him. Naturally, West's recognition of the delicate hierarchy and etiquette involved may have dictated his actions. "If West knew of Colonel Walter's financial embarrassment," D. Martin Dakin reasons, "and heard him asking fishy questions about the plans, it might be enough to arouse his suspicions, but it would be acutely awkward for him, a junior official, to express them about his boss's own brother. It would be easier for him to drop a few tactful hints to the colonel himself."

41 E. Cobham Brewer's *Dictionary of Phrase and Fable* provides: "[A] loaded staff or knuckle-duster for self-defence."

42 The exact path of the train is worked out in enormous detail by various scholars, who—shockingly—fail to agree. Norman Crump painstakingly reconstructs Holmes's investigation on the ground, both at Aldgate and in Kensington. The essential issue he considers is whether the body travelled from Gloucester Road to Aldgate via the north side (that is, via Baker Street) of the Inner Circle (the name of the oval train route including Gloucester Road and Aldgate) or via the south (via Victoria). On the "outer" rail of the Inner Circle, the trains orbited in a clockwise direction, while on the "inner" rail they ran counter-clockwise. Crump neither finds a window overlooking the inner rail nor locates Herr Oberstein's house but, despite six "extreme improbabilities" of his own reasoning, concludes that the outer rail was the path in question.

In "The Bruce-Partington Railway Geography," Wayne B. Swift gives great attention to signalling and attempts to bolster Crump's arguments by postulating how and where trains might have been held by signals in 1895. Bernard Davies cuts the Gordian knot by concluding that the train was not on the Inner Circle at all, demonstrating at length that each and every problem of the text can be explained. The most telling piece of evidence brought forth by Davies is that "*Inner Circle trains were never normally broken up*; the standard sets of 5 Metropolitan eight-wheelers or 9 District four-wheelers being always kept coupled unless a particular vehicle needed repairs." Although historical detective work such as Davies's can never be wholly certain, his analysis certainly seems definitively to place the train on the Outer Circle.

"That was the end of the matter."
Arthur Twidle, *Strand Magazine*, 1908

stuff into the pocket of this young man. When he is found the whole business will assuredly be put to his account.' I could see no other way out of it, so we did as he suggested. We waited half an hour at the window before a train stopped. It was so thick that nothing could be seen, and we had no difficulty in lowering West's body on to the train. That was the end of the matter so far as I was concerned."[42]

"And your brother?"

"He said nothing, but he had caught me once with his keys, and I think that he suspected. I read in his eyes that he suspected. As you know, he never held up his head again."

There was silence in the room. It was broken by Mycroft Holmes.

"Can you not make reparation? It would ease your conscience, and possibly your punishment."

"What reparation can I make?"

"Where is Oberstein with the papers?"

"I do not know."

"Did he give you no address?"

"He said that letters to the Hôtel du Louvre, Paris, would eventually reach him."

"Then reparation is still within your power," said Sherlock Holmes.

"I will do anything I can. I owe this fellow no particular good-will. He has been my ruin and my downfall."

"Here are paper and pen. Sit at this desk and write to my dictation. Direct the envelope to the address given. That is right. Now the letter:

DEAR SIR,—

With regard to our transaction, you will no doubt have observed by now that one essential detail is missing. I have a tracing which will make it complete. This has involved me in extra trouble, however, and I must ask you for a further advance of five hundred pounds. I will not trust it to the post, nor will I take anything but gold or notes. I would come to you abroad, but it would excite remark if I left the country at present. Therefore I shall expect to meet you in the smoking-room of the Charing Cross Hotel at noon on Saturday. Remember that only English notes, or gold, will be taken.

"That will do very well. I shall be very much surprised if it does not fetch our man."

And it did! It is a matter of history—that secret history of a nation which is often so much more intimate and interesting than its public chronicles—that Oberstein, eager to complete the coup of his lifetime, came to the lure and was safely engulfed for fifteen years in a British prison.[43] In his trunk were found the invaluable Bruce-Partington plans, which he had put up for auction in all the naval centres of Europe.

Colonel Walter died in prison towards the end of the second year of his sentence. As to Holmes, he returned refreshed to

43 "[W]hat were the extenuating circumstances whereby Oberstein got only 15 years for as cold-blooded and indefensible a murder as can be found?" Felix Morley asks. W. E. Edwards posits that Oberstein may have been in a position to blackmail major British figures into using their influence to have his death sentence commuted.

his monograph upon the Polyphonic Motets of Lassus, which has since been printed for private circulation, and is said by experts to be the last word upon the subject. Some weeks afterwards I learned incidentally that my friend spent a day at Windsor, whence he returned with a remarkably fine emerald tie-pin. When I asked him if he had bought it, he answered that it was a present from a certain gracious lady in whose interests he had once been fortunate enough to carry out a small commission. He said no more; but I fancy that I could guess at that lady's august name, and I have little doubt that the emerald pin will forever recall to my friend's memory the adventure of the Bruce-Partington plans. ■

AN IMPENDING CHANGE OF GOVERNMENT

"I was aware that by anything of interest, Holmes meant anything of criminal interest. There was the news of a revolution, of a possible war, and of an impending change of Government; but these did not come within the horizon of my companion."

THE EVENTS of November 1895 to which Dr. Watson refers have proved tantalisingly difficult to identify. In "1896–1964, 'The Wheel Has Come Full Circle,'" Jennifer Chorley proposes that the "revolution" was that of Turkey; that the threat of "possible war" impelled troops to be sent to Ashanti, in Ghana; and that the "impending change of Government" involved Bechuanaland's becoming part of Cape Colony. A different sort of "change of Government" is named by Owen F. Grazebrook, in Volume 3 of *Studies in Sherlock Holmes*. He posits that the naming of Lord Farnet Joseph Wolseley as the new commander in chief of the army would have been a suitably delicate situation, since Queen Victoria had favoured the previous commander in chief, the Duke of Cambridge. "It may well be that in Dr. Watson's somewhat slipshod mind," Grazebrook reasons, "and being an old army veteran, the office of Commander-in-chief was connected with the governance of the country, and that the substitution of the Duke of Cambridge by Wolseley meant, to him at any rate, 'an impending change of Government.' If this is so, November 1895 may stand as being correct; for in November of that year the Queen graciously received Lord Wolseley and, to continue a military metaphor, 'buried the hatchet.' "

Still other political affairs are noted by Christopher Morley in *Sherlock Holmes and Dr. Watson: A Textbook of Friendship.* Without specifically identifying the events alluded to by Watson, Morley fingers South Africa, where brewing conflicts between the Boers and British settlers would lead to Sir Leander Jameson's ill-fated Transvaal Raid on December 29, 1895. Further political tension arose from a dispute with Venezuela over the border of British Guiana. And awkward relations with Germany were somewhat complicated by the completion, in the summer of 1895, of the Kiel Canal, giving the large German Baltic fleet direct access to the North Sea and the adjacent English Channel.

W. E. Edwards states definitively that the revolution involved the Japanese assassination of Korea's Queen Min in October 1895 and the subsequent imprisonment of King Kojong. The massacres of Armenians in Turkey, he continues, suggest the "possible war" that was only avoided after France expressed reluctance to commit to military action; and the "change of government" was then occurring in France, where the socialist Léon Bourgeois assumed the premiership on November 1, 1895.

Then as now, the state of international affairs at any given time leaves the possibilities of revolution, impending war, and regime change infinitely open to debate. *Plus ça change . . .*

NAVAL WARFARE

MYCROFT HOLMES grandly claims that the "Bruce-Partington" submarine would make naval warfare impossible within the radius of the submarine. But recall that the Royal Navy never ended up building any submarines of its own, and rather ordered several based on John Holland's design, six years after the Bruce-Partingon plans were lost and recovered. (See note 14.) What caused Mycroft's prediction to fail?

Fletcher Pratt, in "Holmes and the Royal Navy," writes, "[There is not] very much doubt that [Mycroft's] hopes were completely disappointed. The date was 1895; and not for a

Could this be a "Bruce-Partington" submersible?
The Victorians: A World Built to Last

decade and a half thereafter was any submarine produced which made the operations of surface ships even dangerous, to say nothing of impossible. . . ." In attempting to build the submarine, Pratt concludes, the Admiralty quickly discovered serious design flaws. Knowing the plans had depreciated in value, the Sea Lords then *allowed* them to be stolen, hoping to flush out a rumoured traitor and simultaneously to set back their enemies' submarine programs. The Admiralty could hardly have been pleased, Pratt surmises, with Holmes's recovery of the plans, but fortunately copies had apparently been made by the thief before the Royal Navy's "disintelligence" efforts could be spoiled. Pratt sees support for this theory in the construction of the French submarine *Morse*, which was built in 1896 and did not last beyond a few disappointing sea voyages. He suggests that the *Morse* was designed on the basis of the flawed Bruce-Partington plans.

J. S. Callaway, U.S.N., in "An Enquiry into the Identity of the Bruce-Partington Submarine," rejects this identification. Pratt, he notes, ignores that a working model of the Bruce-Partington submarine would have already existed in 1895, a date that eliminates identification with the *Morse*, which was not built until 1896. Instead, Callaway observes that in 1893 the French navy had completed work on the submarine *Gustave Zede* (named after the designer of the *Gymnote*) and theorises that the British must have acquired the plans for that boat from a third party in order to prevent either the United States or Germany from obtaining them. Callaway suggests that army funds were used to purchase the plans, thus explaining why the plans were kept at Woolwich, an army arsenal, rather than a navy depot. In "What Were the Technical Papers, Mycroft?," Daniel Morrow proposes a British-built version of the Holland submarine, a theory that involves redating "The Bruce-Partington Plans" to 1901. See *Chronological Table*.

Arguing on the basis of Sir William Laird Clowes's *The Royal Navy: History*, published in 1903, Jack Crelling (in "The Mystery of the Bruce-Partington Plans") suggests that the plans were not for a submarine at all. Sir William wrote, "Until the Autumn of 1900 British Admiralty appeared to pay but little attention to the assiduity with which certain foreign powers had been experimenting with submarines during the previous twelve or fifteen years," and Crelling proposes that the plans were instead for a steam turbine PT boat, along the lines of the *Turbinia*, demonstrated at the Diamond Jubilee Review of 1887.

Peter H. Wood, in "An Automatic Self-Adjusting Solution: Bruce-Partington Dives Again," points out that the word "submersible" is a noun meaning a submarine boat. If the term "submarine" is meant to serve as an adjective, it must have modified the missing word "torpedo." Wood goes on to lay out an ingenious case involving fraudulent plans for an improvement to the accuracy problems of the Mark III torpedo (already in use by the Royal Navy), covered up by the theft of the plans.

Joseph A. Coppola, in an impressive article entitled "Submarine Technology and the Bruce-Partington Adventures," contends that inventor John Holland himself obtained the Bruce-Partington plans and incorporated them into his successful design for the *Holland VI*, which was launched in 1897. Michael Kean, in a letter headed "The Politics of Defense," notes that if Holland did indeed use these plans as the basis for the modern submarine, "then he might also be accused of 'adding insult to injury' with respect to the Royal Navy; for John Holland actually sold his plans back to the British!"

THE POLYPHONIC MOTETS OF LASSUS

HOLMES'S special interest in Roland de Lassus's motets, as opposed to the thousands of other pieces the master musician composed, has long intrigued Sherlockians of a musical bent. Benjamin Grosbayne takes the placid view that after retiring to his bee farm, Holmes took a more detailed look at de Lassus's *oeuvre*, turning out monographs on the composer's other works. "As for being 'the last word upon the subject,' " Grosbayne writes sceptically, "the enthusiasms of friendship must be taken into consideration. Tovey, Koechlin, Jeppesen, Matthieu, Bäumker, Sandberger, E. Van der Straeten and other authorities make no mention of Holmes's monograph."

Edward R. Staubach, in "The Polyphonic Motets of Lassus," addresses the possible appeal of the motets to a thinking man such as Holmes:

> The unexpected has been described as typical in Lassus's motets with frequent changes from fast to slow, sudden breaks, unexpected beginnings and endings, and from regular accents to strong offbeat accents (syncopation). The personality reflected in these motets would certainly gain the interest of a man whose violin playing Watson described in *A Study in Scarlet* as sometimes "sonorous and melancholy," then "fantastic and cheerful," maybe the result of "a whim or fancy."

In writing his monograph, Staubach surmises that Holmes would have focused on de Lassus's "highly individualized style and approach . . . the emotions and character of the works, and their compositional techniques."

Whether the monograph actually exists, however, is not free from controversy. Guy Warrack, writing in *Sherlock Holmes and Music*, expresses grave reservations about the entire enterprise, particularly since the music of de Lassus was not widely performed in London. "It seems very doubtful whether Holmes had ever heard any of de Lassus's Motets," Warrack writes, considering not only the detective's lack of opportunity to hear the music but also the demands of his career in 1895, a year in which chronologists generally place "Wisteria Lodge," "The Three Students" (with Holmes travelling in connection with his researches into early English charters), "The Solitary Cyclist," and "Black Peter" as well as "The Bruce-Partington Plans." Holmes's familiarity with de Lassus's motets would likely have been from the printed music, rather than from the experience of listening to the music being sung. Even then, it has never been firmly established as to whether or not Holmes could read music, or whether he played by ear. Warrack observes that the vocally polyphonic complexities of de Lassus's motets would be difficult to grasp by one who was not a skilled reader of music, or by one who played violin rather than sang. Morever, he argues, to speak of "polyphonic motets" is redundant, exposing Holmes's lack of knowledge on the subject of sixteenth-century music. Of course, as Warrack admits, this may be easily explained by attributing the error to Watson. Holmes might have mentioned that motets were polyphonic pieces of music, and in writing up his notes, Watson could have looked at "motets (polyphonic)" and transcribed it as "polyphonic motets." Ultimately, given these many doubts and the fact that no scholars have ever been able to track down the monograph (supposedly printed only for private circulation), Warrack deduces that Holmes's claim to have written such an authoritative work was nothing more than a boast: "When we come to balance probabilities, we may be driven to the melancholy conclusion that the monograph was at best only projected, at the worst a complete myth."

But Staubach disagrees, even going so far as to write an article entitled "Taking Issue with Mr. Warrack." He points out that Warrack's contention that Holmes was not an expert reader of music is unsubstantiated. He also claims that lack of exposure to the performance of de Lassus's music is but a mere technicality in this case, arguing, "There have been and are a few outstanding artists, conductors, and composers, who can look at a page of a symphonic score and hear the music by sight; some even with the timbre of the instruments for which the piece is scored. . . . Could not such a case be made for the analytical genius of Sherlock Holmes to extend into a not so distant field?" As to the demands on Holmes's time, Staubach argues that "a definitive article on the works could have been published by studying a representative sampling of each classification." "The monograph did indeed exist," he asserts. "Each decade seems to bring forth a 'lost' cello concerto of Haydn or preludes of Bach. We can hope."

THE ADVENTURE OF THE DYING DETECTIVE[1]

The only one of the seven new cases reported in His Last Bow *to occur before Holmes's disappearance in 1894, "The Dying Detective" (which scholars generally place between 1887 and 1890) has stirred up controversy over Holmes's cruel treatment of his closest friend, Dr. Watson. Here Holmes feigns illness (the practice known in Victorian times as "malingering") to deceive a murderer. In doing so, he not only allows Watson to believe that he is dying, he pretends to denigrate Watson's talents as a doctor. While Holmes's capture of the criminal is undeniably dramatic, it is the strain on the relationship between Holmes and Watson that holds our attention. Holmes's deception of Watson foreshadows his far greater (and crueller) deception in "The Final Problem" in 1891, when he allowed Watson to believe for three years that he, Holmes, was dead. The late publication of this tale may indicate Watson's reluctance to reveal this cold side of his beloved friend's character.*

M RS. HUDSON, THE landlady of Sherlock Holmes, was a long-suffering woman. Not only was her first-floor flat invaded at all hours by throngs of singular and often undesirable characters, but her remarkable lodger showed an eccentricity and irregularity in his life which must have sorely tried her patience. His incredible untidiness, his addiction to music at strange hours, his occasional revolver practice within doors, his weird and often malodorous scientific experiments, and the atmosphere of violence and danger which hung around him made him the very worst tenant in London. On the other hand, his payments were princely.[2] I have no doubt that the house might have been purchased at the price which Holmes paid for his rooms during the years that I was with him.

The landlady stood in the deepest awe of him and never dared to interfere with him, however outrageous his proceedings might seem. She was fond of him, too, for he had a remarkable gentleness and courtesy in his dealings with

1 A facsimile of Sir Arthur Conan Doyle's manuscript of "The Dying Detective" was published in 1991. There are minor textual differences between the manuscript dated July 27, 1913, and the version eventually published in the *Strand Magazine* in December 1913; significant differences are noted below.

2 What a change from Holmes's situation in *A Study in Scarlet*! The cost of the rooms at Baker Street was, in 1878, "too much for [Holmes's] purse," and so he arranged to split the cost with Watson. Watson's income of eleven shillings and sixpence a day led him to the same conclusion; therefore, it may be assumed that Holmes's income had at that time approximated Watson's. The amount of Watson's current writing income is impossible

to determine; Arthur Conan Doyle became wealthy from his involvement with Dr. Watson, but nothing is known about their financial arrangements.

3 Gustave Doré and Blanchard Jerrold, in their magnificent *London: A Pilgrimage* (1872), describe Rotherhithe, the neighborhood of the Thames dockyards, as "shabby, slatternly places" with "low and poor houses, amid shiftless riverside loungers," and note "the intensity of the squalid recklessness" of the area. The residents of Rotherhithe had little use for "swells" or "West-enders," and few Londoners ventured there unescorted at night.

4 What room is this? William S. Baring-Gould identifies it as Holmes's bedroom, as does Watson, who explicitly refers to it as such by alluding to the "opening and closing of the bedroom door." Julian Wolff, however, argues in "I Have My Eye on a Suite in Baker Street" that the room is the sitting-room *made over* into a sick-room.

5 A "hectic" fever is one that is fluctuating but persistently recurrent.

women. He disliked and distrusted the sex, but he was always a chivalrous opponent. Knowing how genuine was her regard for him, I listened earnestly to her story when she came to my rooms in the second year of my married life and told me of the sad condition to which my poor friend was reduced. "He's dying, Dr. Watson," said she. "For three days he has been sinking, and I doubt if he will last the day. He would not let me get a doctor. This morning when I saw his bones sticking out of his face and his great bright eyes looking at me I could stand no more of it. 'With your leave or without it, Mr. Holmes, I am going for a doctor this very hour,' said I. 'Let it be Watson, then,' said he. I wouldn't waste an hour in coming to him, sir, or you may not see him alive."

I was horrified, for I had heard nothing of his illness. I need not say that I rushed for my coat and my hat. As we drove back I asked for the details.

"There is little I can tell you, sir. He has been working at a case down at Rotherhithe,[3] in an alley near the river, and he has brought this illness back with him. He took to his bed on Wednesday afternoon and has never moved since. For these three days neither food nor drink has passed his lips."

"Good God! Why did you not call in a doctor?"

"He wouldn't have it, sir. You know how masterful he is. I didn't dare to disobey him. But he's not long for this world, as you'll see for yourself the moment that you set eyes on him."

He was indeed a deplorable spectacle. In the dim light of a foggy November day the sick-room[4] was a gloomy spot, but it was that gaunt, wasted face staring at me from the bed which sent a chill to my heart. His eyes had the brightness of fever, there was a hectic[5] flush upon either cheek, and dark crusts clung to his lips; the thin hands upon the coverlet twitched incessantly, his voice was croaking and spasmodic. He lay listlessly as I entered the room, but the sight of me brought a gleam of recognition to his eyes.

"Well, Watson, we seem to have fallen upon evil days," said he, in a feeble voice, but with something of his old carelessness of manner.

"My dear fellow!" I cried, approaching him.

"Stand back! Stand right back!" said he, with the sharp imperiousness which I had associated only with moments of crisis. "If you approach me, Watson, I shall order you out of the house."

"But why?"

"Because it is my desire. Is that not enough?"

Yes, Mrs. Hudson was right. He was more masterful than ever. It was pitiful, however, to see his exhaustion.

"I only wished to help," I explained.

"Exactly! You will help best by doing what you are told."

"Certainly, Holmes."

He relaxed the austerity of his manner.

"You are not angry?" he asked, gasping for breath.

Poor devil, how could I be angry when I saw him lying in such a plight before me?

"It's for your own sake, Watson," he croaked.

"For *my* sake?"

"I know what is the matter with me. It is a coolie[6] disease from Sumatra[7]—a thing that the Dutch know more about than we, though they have made little of it up to date. One thing only is certain. It is infallibly deadly, and it is horribly contagious."

He spoke now with a feverish energy, the long hands twitching and jerking as he motioned me away.

"Contagious by touch, Watson—that's it, by touch. Keep your distance and all is well."

"Good heavens, Holmes! Do you suppose that such a consideration weighs with me for an instant? It would not affect me in the case of a stranger. Do you imagine it would prevent me from doing my duty to so old a friend?"

Again I advanced, but he repulsed me with a look of furious anger.

"If you will stand there I will talk. If you do not you must leave the room."

I have so deep a respect for the extraordinary qualities of Holmes that I have always deferred to his wishes, even when I least understood them. But now all my professional instincts were aroused. Let him be my master elsewhere, I at least was his in a sick-room.

"Holmes," said I, "you are not yourself. A sick man is but a child, and so I will treat you. Whether you like it or not, I will examine your symptoms and treat you for them."

6 An unskilled labourer from Asia, generally from India or China (from the Hindi word *Kuli*, an aboriginal tribe; or Tamil *kuli*, meaning "wages"). In the 1840s, the abolition of slavery drove employers in the British colonies to rely increasingly upon the cheap labour provided by coolies. These workers functioned as indentured servants, signing contracts to work for a period of five years (although the amount of time varied) in exchange for minimal wages and the cost of passage. Conditions of passage for Chinese coolies in particular were horrendous: Thousands died in the crowded, miserable conditions on board the ships. Occasionally, coolies were kidnapped and forced into labour. British India largely prohibited the emigration of its unskilled workers in 1922; other countries, such as the United States, Canada, and Australia, resented the influx of cheap labour and, toward the end of the nineteenth century and the beginning of the twentieth, began passing laws specifically designed to prevent Chinese immigrants from entering the country.

7 The second-largest island in Indonesia, Sumatra was coveted, and battled over, by the British and the Dutch throughout the nineteenth century. The Dutch, having first arrived in 1596, had the greater claim, and by the early twentieth century had established administrative and economic authority over the island.

8 "Obstinate old Watson!" in the manuscript. The manuscript version of the remark seems inappropriate for the early date of this adventure, occurring at best eight or nine years after 1881 (see *Chronological Table*). However, when it is recalled that Dr. Watson wrote the narrative of this adventure over twenty-five years after it occurred, the remark may be viewed as a fond interpolation.

9 Many scholars have discounted these two diseases as fabrications, but William S. Baring-Gould, among others, declares that both are actually scrub typhus, also known as tsutsuga-mushi fever. Transmitted by mites carrying the parasite *rickettsia* (named after American pathologist Harold Taylor Ricketts, who identified the microorganism before dying of typhus in 1910), scrub typhus carries many of the symptoms purportedly exhibited by Holmes. A person suffering from scrub typhus will develop a black, encrusted lesion at the point of the bite, followed by headache, fever, chills, general aches and pains, and swollen lymph glands. After a week, a pinkish rash spreads across the torso and occasionally to the arms and legs. In the most extreme cases, delirium, apathy, heart and lung abnormalities, and circulatory failure may develop during the second symptomatic week.

Baring-Gould's argument is advanced by Hugh L'Etang, who, in "Some Observations on the Black Formosa Corruption and Tapanuli Fever," notes that the disease is found in the South Pacific, notably Formosa, Sumatra, Japan, New Guinea, northern Australia, and the Philippines. Whereas Formosa (Taiwan) is well known, "the name Tapanuli," L'Etang admits, "sounds decidedly spurious." Yet he points out that Tapanuli is in fact a mountainous region of 15,084 square miles located on Sumatra's northwest coast.

Note that Holmes does not say that he has *contracted* either of these diseases, only that he knows of them and Watson does not.

He looked at me with venomous eyes.

"If I am to have a doctor whether I will or not, let me at least have someone in whom I have confidence," said he.

"Then you have none in me?"

"In your friendship, certainly. But facts are facts, Watson, and after all you are only a general practitioner with very limited experience and mediocre qualifications. It is painful to have to say these things, but you leave me no choice."

I was bitterly hurt.

"Such a remark is unworthy of you, Holmes. It shows me very clearly the state of your own nerves. But if you have no confidence in me I would not intrude my services. Let me bring Sir Jasper Meek or Penrose Fisher, or any of the best men in London. But someone you *must* have, and that is final. If you think that I am going to stand here and see you die without either helping you myself or bringing anyone else to help you, then you have mistaken your man."

"You mean well, Watson,"[8] said the sick man, with something between a sob and a groan. "Shall I demonstrate your own ignorance? What do you know, pray, of Tapanuli fever? What do you know of the black Formosa corruption?"[9]

"I have never heard of either."[10]

"There are many problems of disease, many strange pathological possibilities, in the East, Watson." He paused after each sentence to collect his failing strength. "I have learned so much during some recent researches which have a medico-criminal aspect. It was in the course of them that I contracted this complaint.[11] You can do nothing."

"Possibly not. But I happen to know that Dr. Ainstree, the greatest living authority upon tropical disease, is now in London. All remonstrance is useless, Holmes. I am going this instant to fetch him." I turned resolutely to the door.

Never have I had such a shock! In an instant, with a tiger-spring, the dying man had intercepted me. I heard the sharp snap of a twisted key. The next moment he had staggered back to his bed, exhausted and panting after his one tremendous outflame of energy.

"You won't take the key from me by force, Watson. I've got you, my friend. Here you are, and here you will stay until I will otherwise. But I'll humour you." (All this in little gasps, with terrible struggles for breath between.) "You've only my own

"I heard the sharp snap of a twisted key."
Walter Paget, *Strand Magazine*, 1913

10 The fact that Watson is unfamiliar with these diseases should not, according to Roger Butters, be added to the litany of Sherlockian criticism that Watson's medical abilities are somewhat wanting. Butters dismisses these sorts of assessments as unfair, reasoning that, at least in this case, "there would presumably have been little call for treating [Tapanuli fever and black Formosa corruption] in Kensington. Anyway, Holmes very likely invented them."

11 The manuscript adds the tantalisingly deleted phrase "which threatens to remove the last restraint [from/upon] one or two gentlemen whom I could mention."

good at heart. Of course I know that very well. You shall have your way, but, give me time to get my strength. Not now, Watson, not now. It's four o'clock. At six you can go."

"This is insanity, Holmes."

"Only two hours, Watson. I promise you will go at six. Are you content to wait?"

"I seem to have no choice."

"None in the world, Watson. Thank you, I need no help in arranging the clothes. You will please keep your distance. Now, Watson, there is one other condition that I would make. You will seek help, not from the man you mention, but from the one that I choose."

"By all means."

12 Despite Holmes's prodigious smoking habit, this is the only instance in which Holmes is indicated to have used a *traditional* receptacle for his tobacco, in lieu of the oft-mentioned Persian slipper ("The Empty House," "The Illustrious Client," "The Musgrave Ritual," "The Naval Treaty") or coal-scuttle ("The Mazarin Stone").

13 Presumably these were used to inject cocaine. In *The Sign of Four*, it is clear that Holmes takes cocaine subcutaneously.

"The first three sensible words that you have uttered since you entered this room, Watson. You will find some books over there. I am somewhat exhausted; I wonder how a battery feels when it pours electricity into a non-conductor? At six, Watson, we resume our conversation."

But it was destined to be resumed long before that hour, and in circumstances which gave me a shock hardly second to that caused by his spring to the door. I had stood for some minutes looking at the silent figure in the bed. His face was almost covered by the clothes and he appeared to be asleep. Then, unable to settle down to reading, I walked slowly round the room, examining the pictures of celebrated criminals with which every wall was adorned. Finally, in my aimless perambulation, I came to the mantelpiece. A litter of pipes, tobacco-pouches,[12] syringes,[13] penknives, revolver cartridges, and other *débris* was scattered over it. In the midst of these was a small black and white ivory box with a sliding lid. It was a neat little thing, and I had stretched out my hand to examine it more closely, when—

It was a dreadful cry that he gave—a yell which might have been heard down the street. My skin went cold and my hair bristled at that horrible scream. As I turned I caught a glimpse of a convulsed face and frantic eyes. I stood paralyzed, with the little box in my hand.

"Put it down! Down, this instant, Watson—this instant, I say!" His head sank back upon the pillow and he gave a deep sigh of relief as I replaced the box upon the mantelpiece. "I hate to have my things touched, Watson. You know that I hate it. You fidget me beyond endurance. You, a doctor—you are enough to drive a patient into an asylum. Sit down, man, and let me have my rest!"

The incident left a most unpleasant impression upon my mind. The violent and causeless excitement, followed by this brutality of speech, so far removed from his usual suavity, showed me how deep was the disorganization of his mind. Of all ruins, that of a noble mind is the most deplorable. I sat in silent dejection until the stipulated time had passed. He seemed to have been watching the clock as well as I, for it was hardly six before he began to talk with the same feverish animation as before.

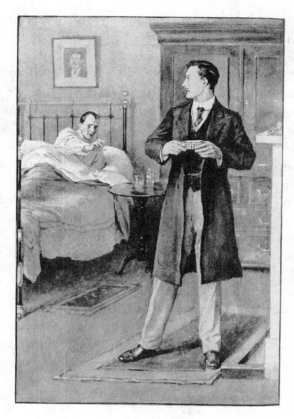

"Put it down! Down, this instant, Watson—
this instant, I say!"
Walter Paget, *Strand Magazine*, 1913

"Now, Watson," said he. "Have you any change in your pocket?"

"Yes."

"Any silver?"

"A good deal."

"How many half-crowns?"

"I have five."

"Ah, too few! Too few! How very unfortunate, Watson! However, such as they are you can put them in your watch-pocket. And all the rest of your money in your left trouserpocket. Thank you. It will balance you so much better like that."

This was raving insanity. He shuddered, and again made a sound between a cough and a sob.

14 Stephen Hayes suggests that the "giant rat of Sumatra"—the mystifying case that Holmes mentions in passing in "The Sussex Vampire"—may have been an experimental animal used by Culverton Smith in his study of bacteria. It was, Hayes continues, Holmes's investigation of the plague-stricken ship *Matilda Briggs* (also mentioned in "The Sussex Vampire") that carried the rat from Sumatra to London and led Holmes to uncover Smith's misdeeds. Mary Ann Kluge identifies Smith himself as the giant rat of Sumatra.

"You will now light the gas, Watson, but you will be very careful that not for one instant shall it be more than half on. I implore you to be careful, Watson. Thank you, that is excellent. No, you need not draw the blind. Now you will have the kindness to place some letters and papers upon this table within my reach. Thank you. Now some of that litter from the mantelpiece. Excellent, Watson! There is a sugar-tongs there. Kindly raise that small ivory box with its assistance. Place it here among the papers. Good! You can now go and fetch Mr. Culverton Smith, of 13, Lower Burke Street."

To tell the truth, my desire to fetch a doctor had somewhat weakened, for poor Holmes was so obviously delirious that it seemed dangerous to leave him. However, he was as eager now to consult the person named as he had been obstinate in refusing.

"I never heard the name," said I.

"Possibly not, my good Watson. It may surprise you to know that the man upon earth who is best versed in this disease is not a medical man, but a planter. Mr. Culverton Smith is a well-known resident of Sumatra,[14] now visiting London. An outbreak

Lee Conrey, *Portland Oregonian*, January 25, 1914

of the disease upon his plantation, which was distant from medical aid, caused him to study it himself, with some rather far-reaching consequences.[15] He is a very methodical person, and I did not desire you to start before six because I was well aware that you would not find him in his study. If you could persuade him to come here and give us the benefit of his unique experience of this disease, the investigation of which has been his dearest hobby, I cannot doubt that he could help me."

I give Holmes's remarks as a consecutive whole, and will not attempt to indicate how they were interrupted by gaspings for breath and those clutchings of his hands which indicated the pain from which he was suffering. His appearance had changed for the worse during the few hours that I had been with him. Those hectic spots were more pronounced, the eyes shone more brightly out of darker hollows, and a cold sweat glimmered upon his brow. He still retained, however, the jaunty gallantry of his speech. To the last gasp he would always be the master.

"You will tell him exactly how you have left me," said he. "You will convey the very impression which is in your own mind—a dying man—a dying and delirious man. Indeed, I cannot think why the whole bed of the ocean is not one solid mass of oysters, so prolific the creatures seem. Ah, I am wandering! Strange how the brain controls the brain! What was I saying, Watson?"

"My directions for Mr. Culverton Smith."

"Ah, yes, I remember. My life depends upon it. Plead with him, Watson. There is no good feeling between us. His nephew, Watson—I had suspicions of foul play and I allowed him to see it. The boy died horribly. He has a grudge against me. You will soften him, Watson. Beg him, pray him, get him here by any means. He can save me—only he!"

"I will bring him in a cab, if I have to carry him down to it."

"You will do nothing of the sort. You will persuade him to come. And then you will return in front of him. Make any excuse so as not to come with him. Don't forget, Watson. You won't fail me. You never did fail me. No doubt there are natural enemies which limit the increase of the creatures. You and I, Watson, we have done our part. Shall the world, then, be overrun by oysters? No, no; horrible! You'll convey all that is in your mind."

15 This sentence is substituted (whether by Watson or another is unknown) for the following bizarre sentence in the manuscript: "You will find the gentleman, whose habits I have studied, seated at this present moment in a bamboo chair, his feet extended, a tumbler by his side, and a long manilla cigar between his curiously animal teeth." If Watson accurately recorded Holmes's statement in the manuscript, he may himself have changed the text to avoid embarrassing Holmes, for when Watson meets Smith, he is seated in a "reclining" chair (certainly *not* bamboo); there is no sign of a beverage or tobacco (save a "smoking-cap") and no mention of noteworthy dentition.

16 This is the only mention by name of Holmes's "old acquaintance." He cannot be identified with Morton, the Oxford rugby player ("The Missing Three-Quarter"), Cyril Morton, the betrothed of Violet Smith ("The Solitary Cyclist"), or the Morton of Morton & Waylight, the firm for whom Mr. Warren was a timekeeper ("The Red Circle"), because all three of these cases unquestionably occurred long after the latest date assigned to "The Dying Detective" (see *Chronological Table*). Could he be one of the many unidentified constables or other policemen, now promoted? Or the partner of Inspector Brown in *The Sign of Four*? That he was an acquaintance of Holmes and not of Watson is implied by the "sir" at the end of his enquiry into Holmes's health.

I left him full of the image of this magnificent intellect babbling like a foolish child. He had handed me the key, and with a happy thought I took it with me lest he should lock himself in. Mrs. Hudson was waiting, trembling and weeping, in the passage. Behind me as I passed from the flat I heard Holmes's high, thin voice in some delirious chant. Below, as I stood whistling for a cab, a man came on me through the fog.

"How is Mr. Holmes, sir?" he asked.

It was an old acquaintance, Inspector Morton,[16] of Scotland Yard, dressed in unofficial tweeds.

"He is very ill," I answered.

He looked at me in a most singular fashion. Had it not been too fiendish, I could have imagined that the gleam of the fan-light showed exultation in his face.

"I heard some rumour of it," said he.

The cab had driven up, and I left him.

Lower Burke Street proved to be a line of fine houses lying in the vague borderland between Notting Hill and Kensington. The particular one at which my cabman pulled up had an air of smug and demure respectability in its old-fashioned iron railings, its massive folding-door, and its shining brasswork. All was in keeping with a solemn butler who appeared framed in the pink radiance of a tinted electric light behind him.

"Yes, Mr. Culverton Smith is in. Dr. Watson! Very good, sir, I will take up your card."

My humble name and title did not appear to impress Mr. Culverton Smith. Through the half-open door I heard a high, petulant penetrating voice.

"Who is this person? What does he want? Dear me, Staples, how often have I said that I am not to be disturbed in my hours of study?"

There came a gentle flow of soothing explanation from the butler.

"Well, I won't see him, Staples. I can't have my work interrupted like this. I am not at home. Say so. Tell him to come in the morning if he really must see me."

Again the gentle murmur.

"Well, well, give him that message. He can come in the morning, or he can stay away. My work must not be hindered."

I thought of Holmes tossing upon his bed of sickness, and counting the minutes, perhaps, until I could bring help to him.

It was not a time to stand upon ceremony. His life depended upon my promptness. Before the apologetic butler had delivered his message I had pushed past him and was in the room.

With a shrill cry of anger a man rose from a reclining chair beside the fire. I saw a great yellow face, coarse-grained and greasy, with heavy, double-chin, and two sullen, menacing grey eyes which glared at me from under tufted and sandy brows. A high bald head had a small velvet smoking-cap poised coquettishly upon one side of its pink curve. The skull was of enormous capacity, and yet, as I looked down I saw to my amazement that the figure of the man was small and frail, twisted in the shoulders and back like one who has suffered from rickets in his childhood.

"What's this?" he cried, in a high, screaming voice. "What is

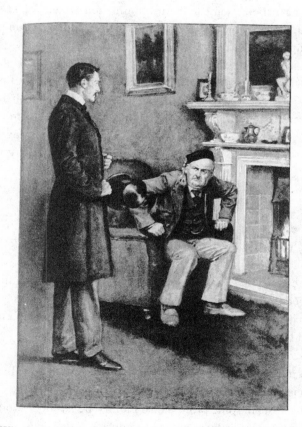

" 'What's this?' he cried, in a high, screaming voice. 'What is the meaning of this intrusion?' "
Walter Paget, *Strand Magazine*, 1913

the meaning of this intrusion? Didn't I send you word that I would see you to-morrow morning?"

"I am sorry," said I, "but the matter cannot be delayed. Mr. Sherlock Holmes—".

The mention of my friend's name had an extraordinary effect upon the little man. The look of anger passed in an instant from his face. His features became tense and alert.

"Have you come from Holmes?" he asked.

"I have just left him."

"What about Holmes? How is he?"

"He is desperately ill. That is why I have come."

The man motioned me to a chair, and turned to resume his own. As he did so I caught a glimpse of his face in the mirror over the mantelpiece. I could have sworn that it was set in a malicious and abominable smile. Yet I persuaded myself that it must have been some nervous contraction which I had surprised, for he turned to me an instant later with genuine concern upon his features.

"I am sorry to hear this," said he. "I only know Mr. Holmes through some business dealings which we have had, but I have every respect for his talents and his character. He is an amateur of crime, as I am of disease. For him the villain, for me the microbe. There are my prisons," he continued, pointing to a row of bottles and jars which stood upon a side table. "Among those gelatine cultivations some of the very worst offenders in the world are now doing time."

"It was on account of your special knowledge that Mr. Holmes desired to see you. He has a high opinion of you, and thought that you were the one man in London who could help him."

The little man started, and the jaunty smoking-cap slid to the floor.

"Why?" he asked. "Why should Mr. Holmes think that I could help him in his trouble?"

"Because of your knowledge of Eastern diseases."

"But why should he think that this disease which he has contracted is Eastern?"

"Because, in some professional inquiry, he has been working among Chinese sailors down in the docks."

Mr. Culverton Smith smiled pleasantly and picked up his smoking-cap.

"Oh, that's it—is it?" said he. "I trust the matter is not so grave as you suppose. How long has he been ill?"

"About three days."

"Is he delirious?"

"Occasionally."

"Tut, tut! This sounds serious. It would be inhuman not to answer his call. I very much resent any interruption to my work, Dr. Watson, but this case is certainly exceptional. I will come with you at once."

I remembered Holmes's injunction.

"I have another appointment," said I.

"Very good. I will go alone.[17] I have a note of Mr. Holmes's address. You can rely upon my being there within half an hour at most."[18]

It was with a sinking heart that I re-entered Holmes's bedroom. For all that I knew the worst might have happened in my absence. To my enormous relief, he had improved greatly in the interval. His appearance was as ghastly as ever, but all trace of delirium had left him and he spoke in a feeble voice, it is true, but with even more than his usual crispness and lucidity.

"Well, did you see him, Watson?"

"Yes; he is coming."

"Admirable, Watson! Admirable! You are the best of messengers."

"He wished to return with me."

"That would never do, Watson. That would be obviously impossible. Did he ask what ailed me?"

"I told him about the Chinese in the East End."

"Exactly! Well, Watson, you have done all that a good friend could. You can now disappear from the scene."

"I must wait and hear his opinion, Holmes."

"Of course you must. But I have reasons to suppose that this opinion would be very much more frank and valuable if he imagines that we are alone. There is just room behind the head of my bed, Watson."

"My dear Holmes!"

"I fear there is no alternative, Watson. The room does not lend itself to concealment, which is as well, as it is the less likely to arouse suspicion. But just there, Watson, I fancy that it could be done." Suddenly he sat up with a rigid intentness

17 The manuscript indicates that the phrase replaces the phrase "I will follow after you."

18 This is substituted for "almost as soon as yourself" in the manuscript and, together with the previous alteration, make much more sense than the deleted phrases, because Watson has just indicated that he will *not* return to Baker Street but has "another appointment."

19 Smith positions himself here as a virtuous but vengeful man following Saint Paul's advice to the Romans, to "overcome evil with good": "If thine enemy hunger, feed him; if he thirst, give him drink; for in so doing thou shalt heap coals of fire on his head." (Romans 12:21)

upon his haggard face. "There are the wheels, Watson. Quick, man, if you love me! And don't budge, whatever happens—whatever happens, do you hear? Don't speak! Don't move! Just listen with all your ears." Then in an instant his sudden access of strength departed, and his masterful, purposeful talk droned away into the low, vague murmurings of a semi-delirious man.

From the hiding-place into which I had been so swiftly hustled I heard the footfalls upon the stair, with the opening and the closing of the bedroom door. Then, to my surprise, there came a long silence, broken only by the heavy breathings and gaspings of the sick man. I could imagine that our visitor was standing by the bedside and looking down at the sufferer. At last that strange hush was broken.

"Holmes!" he cried. "Holmes!" in the insistent tone of one who awakens a sleeper. "Can't you hear me, Holmes?" There was a rustling, as if he had shaken the sick man roughly by the shoulder.

"Is that you, Mr. Smith?" Holmes whispered. "I hardly dared hope that you would come."

The other laughed.

"I should imagine not," he said. "And yet, you see, I am here. Coals of fire, Holmes—coals of fire!"[19]

"It is very good of you—very noble of you. I appreciate your special knowledge."

Our visitor sniggered.

"You do. You are, fortunately, the only man in London who does. Do you know what is the matter with you?"

"The same," said Holmes.

"Ah! You recognize the symptoms?"

"Only too well."

"Well, I shouldn't be surprised, Holmes. I shouldn't be surprised if it *were* the same. A bad look-out for you if it is. Poor Victor was a dead man on the fourth day—a strong, hearty young fellow. It was certainly, as you said, very surprising that he should have contracted an out-of-the-way Asiatic disease in the heart of London—a disease, too, of which I had made such a very special study. Singular coincidence, Holmes. Very smart of you to notice it, but rather uncharitable to suggest that it was cause and effect."

"I knew that you did it."

"Oh, you did, did you? Well, you couldn't prove it, anyhow. But what do you think of yourself spreading reports about me like that, and then crawling to me for help the moment you are in trouble? What sort of a game is that—eh?"

I heard the rasping, laboured breathing of the sick man. "Give me the water!" he gasped.

"You're precious near your end, my friend, but I don't want you to go till I have had a word with you. That's why I give you water. There, don't slop it about! That's right. Can you understand what I say?"

Holmes groaned.

"Do what you can for me. Let bygones be bygones," he whispered. "I'll put the words out of my head—I swear I will. Only cure me, and I'll forget it."

"Forget what?"

"Well, about Victor Savage's death. You as good as admitted just now that you had done it. I'll forget it."

"You can forget it or remember it, just as you like. I don't see you in the witness-box. Quite another shaped box, my good Holmes, I assure you. It matters nothing to me that you should know how my nephew died. It's not him we are talking about. It's you."

"Yes, yes."

"The fellow who came for me—I've forgotten his name—said that you contracted it down in the East End among the sailors."

"I could only account for it so."

"You are proud of your brains, Holmes, are you not? Think yourself smart, don't you? You came across someone who was smarter this time. Now cast your mind back, Holmes. Can you think of no other way you could have got this thing?"

"I can't think. My mind is gone. For heaven's sake help me!"

"Yes, I will help you. I'll help you to understand just where you are and how you got there. I'd like you to know before you die."[20]

"Give me something to ease my pain."

"Painful, is it? Yes, the coolies used to do some squealing towards the end. Takes you as cramp, I fancy."

"Yes, yes; it is cramp."

"Well, you can hear what I say, anyhow. Listen now! Can you

20 The device of inducing the villain to confess in front of a hidden witness is used again by Holmes in "The Mazarin Stone." The latter story was evidently developed as a stage play before it became a short story, and the "staginess" of the similar scene there leads numerous critics to dispute the veracity of the tale. However, no scholar disputes the truthfulness of Watson's report of "The Dying Detective."

21 What was the mystery weapon that Culverton Smith used? George B. Koelle, in "Poisons of the Canon," suggests that it was the plague bacillus, or the rod-shaped bacteria (named *Pasterella pestis* or *Yersinia pestis*, after Alexandre Yersin, the scientist who isolated it in 1894 and developed an antiserum) that is responsible for bubonic, pneumonic, and septicemic plague. Of these, bubonic is the mildest form and represents three-quarters of all plague cases; pneumonic plague affects the lungs, and septicemic plague rapidly infects the bloodstream and may cause death within twenty-four hours. Left untreated, these two latter two types are almost always fatal.

Twenty-five million Europeans, or anywhere between one-fourth and one-third the total population of Europe, lost their lives to the so-called Black Death (comprising both pneumonic and bubonic plague) between 1347 and 1351; 70,000 people died in the 1664–1665 Great Plague of London; and 80,000 to 100,000 people died in an 1894 outbreak in Canton and Hong Kong. All three forms of the disease are transmitted by rat fleas, coincident with the theories connecting Smith to the giant rat of Sumatra (see note 14 above). Koelle does not name which type of plague might have struck Victor Savage, but N. Joel Ehrenkranz, in "A. Conan Doyle, Sherlock Holmes, and Murder by Tropical Infection," names septicemic plague as the murder weapon. Relatively little was known about the plague at the time of "The Dying Detective," and Koelle recognises that the first published account of the bacillus did not appear until 1894. Thus Smith's unpublished studies would surely have been groundbreaking had they reached a wider audience.

Snake venom is the nominee of Hugh L'Etang, who cites the poison's convenience and guesses that the "sharp spring" could have been fashioned like a snake's fang, hollowed out or grooved to inject poison into a finger. "It seems likely that Victor Savage was

remember any unusual incident in your life just about the time your symptoms began?"

"No, no; nothing."

"Think again."

"I'm too ill to think."

"Well, then, I'll help you. Did anything come by post?"

"By post?"

"A box by chance?"

"I'm fainting—I'm gone!"

"Listen, Holmes!" There was a sound as if he was shaking the dying man, and it was all that I could do to hold myself quiet in my hiding-place. "You must hear me. You *shall* hear me. Do you remember a box—an ivory box? It came on Wednesday. You opened it—do you remember?"

"Yes, yes, I opened it. There was a sharp spring inside it. Some joke—"

"It was no joke, as you will find to your cost. You fool, you would have it and you have got it. Who asked you to cross my path? If you had left me alone I would not have hurt you."

"I remember," Holmes gasped. "The spring! It drew blood. This box—this on the table."

"The very one, by George! And it may as well leave the room in my pocket. There goes your last shred of evidence. But you have the truth now, Holmes, and you can die with the knowledge that I killed you. You knew too much of the fate of Victor Savage, so I have sent you to share it.[21] You are very near your end, Holmes. I will sit here and I will watch you die."

Holmes's voice had sunk to an almost inaudible whisper.

"What is that?" said Smith. "Turn up the gas? Ah, the shadows begin to fall, do they? Yes, I will turn it up, that I may see you the better." He crossed the room and the light suddenly brightened. "Is there any other little service that I can do you, my friend?"

"A match and a cigarette."

I nearly called out in my joy and my amazement. He was speaking in his natural voice—a little weak, perhaps, but the very voice I knew. There was a long pause, and I felt that Culverton Smith was standing in silent amazement looking down at his companion.

"What's the meaning of this?" I heard him say at last in a dry, rasping tone.

Lee Conrey, *Seattle Post-Intelligencer*, January 4, 1914

"The best way of successfully acting a part is to be it," said Holmes. "I give you my word that for three days I have tasted neither food nor drink until you were good enough to pour me out that glass of water. But it is the tobacco which I find most irksome. Ah, here *are* some cigarettes." I heard the striking of a match. "That is very much better. Halloa! halloa! Do I hear the step of a friend?"

There were footfalls outside, the door opened, and Inspector Morton appeared.

"All is in order and this is your man," said Holmes.

The officer gave the usual cautions.

"I arrest you on the charge of the murder of one Victor Savage," he concluded.

killed by a neuro-toxic or nerve poison," L'Etang writes. "This could certainly be produced by the King Cobra of Malaya and the East Indies." W. E. Edwards disagrees, arguing that venom from a king cobra would kill its victim in a very short period of time. Recall that in "The Speckled Band," the unfortunate Julia Stoner lost consciousness within minutes of being bitten by a snake; by contrast, Culverton Smith mentions that Victor Savage "was a dead man on the fourth day," and Holmes's putative illness likewise lasted several days.

Edwards throws his lot instead with an injection of the germ of some form of tropical disease—such as Tapanuli fever or the black Formosa corruption, the two ailments mentioned by Holmes, "or something worse." Dr. Robert S. Katz (" 'It is Horribly Contagious' ") proposes that the germ in question is *pseudomonas pseudomallei*, which causes acute septicemic melioidosis (ASM)—a bacterial infection transmitted when a skin abrasion comes into contact with contaminated water and soil.

Most of these theories are rejected by S. E. Dahlinger, who, in "Of Mites and Men," decides that Holmes's symptoms do not correspond with either the plague, typhus, or acute septicemic melioidosis. She proposes some combination of infectious bacteria that was concocted by Culverton Smith, and writes, "It would have been easy enough for Smith to incubate the bacilli in a culture medium maintained in a Petri jar ('those jars upon the side table') in which, as he remarked, 'Some of the very worst offenders in the world are now doing time.' . . . The exotic bacteria could only have travelled to England via a culture medium or an infected host. No flea or mite bite would be necessary if the bacilli and a bit of gelatine for it to feed on were transferred to the point of a sharp spring—an extremely nasty box lunch."

"And you might add of the attempted murder of one Sherlock Holmes," remarked my friend with a chuckle. "To save an invalid trouble, Inspector, Mr. Culverton Smith was good enough to give our signal by turning up the gas. By the way, the prisoner has a small box in the right-hand pocket of his coat which it would be as well to remove. Thank you. I would handle it gingerly if I were you. Put it down here. It may play its part in the trial."

There was a sudden rush and a scuffle, followed by the clash of iron and a cry of pain.

"You'll only get yourself hurt," said the inspector. "Stand still, will you?" There was the click of the closing handcuffs.

"A nice trap!" cried the high, snarling voice. "It will bring *you* into the dock, Holmes, not me. He asked me to come here to cure him. I was sorry for him and I came. Now he will pre-

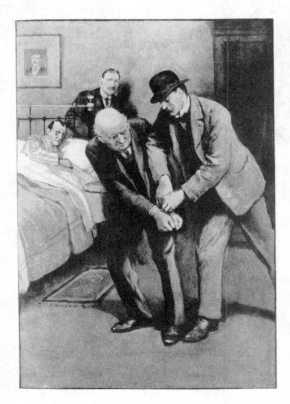

"You'll only get yourself hurt,' said the Inspector.
'Stand still, will you?'"
Walter Paget, *Strand Magazine*, 1913

tend, no doubt, that I have said anything which he may invent which will corroborate his insane suspicions. You can lie as you like, Holmes. My word is always as good as yours."

"Good heavens!" cried Holmes. "I had totally forgotten him. My dear Watson, I owe you a thousand apologies. To think that I should have overlooked you! I need not introduce you to Mr. Culverton Smith, since I understand that you met somewhat earlier in the evening. Have you the cab below? I will follow you when I am dressed, for I may be of some use at the station."

"I never needed it more," said Holmes as he refreshed himself with a glass of claret and some biscuits in the intervals of his toilet. "However, as you know, my habits are irregular, and such a feat means less to me than to most men. It was very essential that I should impress Mrs. Hudson with the reality of my condition, since she was to convey it to you, and you in turn to him. You won't be offended, Watson? You will realise that among your many talents dissimulation finds no place, and that if you had shared my secret you would never have been able to impress Smith with the urgent necessity of his presence, which was the vital point of the whole scheme.[22] Knowing his vindictive nature, I was perfectly certain that he would come to look upon his handiwork."

"But your appearance, Holmes—your ghastly face?"

"Three days of absolute fast does not improve one's beauty, Watson. For the rest, there is nothing which a sponge may not cure. With vaseline upon one's forehead, belladonna[23] in one's eyes, rouge over the cheek-bones, and crusts of beeswax[24] round one's lips, a very satisfying effect can be produced. Malingering is a subject upon which I have sometimes thought of writing a monograph.[25] A little occasional talk about half-crowns, oysters, or any other extraneous subject produces a pleasing effect of delirium."

"But why would you not let me near you, since there was in truth no infection?"

"Can you ask, my dear Watson? Do you imagine that I have no respect for your medical talents? Could I fancy that your astute judgment would pass a dying man who, however weak, had no rise of pulse or temperature? At four yards, I could deceive you. If I failed to do so, who would bring my Smith within my grasp? No, Watson, I would not touch that box. You

22 June Thomson agrees that it was not in Watson's nature to lie with any kind of conviction. "But this is hardly an acceptable excuse," she chides Holmes—no matter how heartfelt the detective's apology and his reassurances as to Watson's medical abilities. (Recall, too, that Watson dropped everything to rush to Holmes's side.) And what of Mrs. Hudson, who was equally anguished over her tenant's health? "Holmes is far more concerned with the success of his deception," Thomson concludes, "than with its effects on his old friend and his landlady." This certainly fits with Holmes's cold character, assessed as early as *A Study in Scarlet* by his friend Stamford: " 'Holmes is a little too scientific for my tastes—it approaches to cold-bloodedness. I could imagine his giving a friend a little pinch of the latest vegetable alkaloid, not out of malevolence, you understand, but simply out of a spirit of inquiry in order to have an accurate idea of the effects.' "

23 The poisonous belladonna, also known as deadly nightshade, is a dark, purple-red plant with bell-shaped leaves and shiny black berries that emit a sweet, inky juice. Indigenous to central and southern Europe, the plant derives its toxicity mainly from the alkaloid atropine, which has its highest concentration in the root of the plant. In ancient times, belladonna was sometimes used as a poison and a hallucinogen by cults that practised witchcraft. When applied medicinally, belladonna extract serves as a narcotic and a sedative; it has been used to treat everything from intestinal cramps, motion sickness, asthma, and nasal congestion to scarlet fever, typhoid fever, heart palpitations, pneumonia, and the effects of opium. The name—Italian for "beautiful lady"—is said to derive either from a belief that the plant would transform itself into an enchantress of tempting beauty, or, more likely, from the fact that sixteenth-century Italian women would use small amounts of extract to dilate their pupils, thereby making their eyes seem brighter. (Eye doctors still use atropine in examining their patients.) In Holmes's case, dilating his pupils achieves the same results desired by those Italian women but the opposite effect, causing him to appear glassy-eyed rather than more attractive.

24 Beeswax was widely used in Victorian times for the stiffening of moustaches, and as a polish.

25 William S. Baring-Gould expresses doubt that Holmes ever wrote such a monograph, but grants that he might have intended it as a chapter in his planned textbook on the art of detection (referred to in "The Abbey Grange"). Even if published, Holmes's monograph was not, Baring-Gould observes, mentioned in Sir John Collie's expert *Malingering and Feigned Sickness*, published in 1913. Yet there is room for possibility. In his book, Collie alludes to an 1836 essay on "Feigned and Factitious Diseases, chiefly of Soldiers and Sailors," and (as quoted by Baring-Gould) states that "[s]ince then only one small similar treatise has appeared." Could the "small similar treatise" have been Holmes's?

26 There is no indication that Holmes determined the nature of the threat posed to him by the needle from a bacteriological examination of the box, and indeed such a determination would have been beyond the scope of Holmes's skills as we know them. Therefore Holmes's depiction of various symptoms depended on his observations of Victor Savage and replicating Savage's symptoms, not merely acting out a textbook description of a certain disease.

27 In this instance, "reversion" refers to the undisposed-of part of an estate, which will presumably fall into possession of the original

can just see if you look at it sideways where the sharp spring like a viper's tooth emerges as you open it.[26] I dare say it was by some such device that poor Savage, who stood between this monster and a reversion,[27] was done to death. My correspondence, however, is, as you know, a varied one, and I am somewhat upon my guard against any packages which reach me.[28] It was clear to me, however, that by pretending that he had really succeeded in his design I might surprise a confession. That pretence I have carried out with the thoroughness of the true artist. Thank you, Watson, you must help me on with my coat. When we have finished at the police-station I think that something nutritious at Simpson's[29] would not be out of place."

grantor or his representative. Note that in "Shoscombe Old Place," the eponymous residence reverts to the brother of the late Sir James Falder upon the death of Sir James's widow, Lady Beatrice.

28 S. E. Dahlinger remarks on the mental attitude of Holmes displayed in "The Dying Detective": "Does he simply open a package arriving in the post? Noooo! Instead, he thinks, 'A surprise package for *me*? Who wants to kill me now?' Who wants to kill me now? *There's* a well-adjusted question, but reasonable, one feels, given his line of work."

29 In 1828, Samuel Reiss opened the Grand Cigar Divan, a club located on the Strand that quickly became a companionable coffeehouse. As friendly competition with other coffeehouses grew more serious, Reiss's club established a reputation as the centre of chess in England. Caterer John Simpson partnered with Reiss in 1848, and the two men undertook an ambitious expansion, renaming the club Simpson's Grand Cigar Tavern and serving food and wine to such luminaries as Benjamin Disraeli, William Gladstone, and Charles Dickens. In 1898, Simpson's was acquired by the Savoy Group, a hotel-and-restaurant developer; in 1904 (after a year of renovation while the Strand was being widened), the club acquired its current, rather unwieldy name: Simpson's-in-the-Strand, Grand Divan Tavern.

THE DISAPPEARANCE OF
LADY FRANCES CARFAX[1]

Watson plays an unusually active rôle in "The Disappearance of Lady Frances Carfax"
when Holmes asks him to travel to the Continent to hunt down "a stray chicken in a world
of foxes." The case is revealing of social attitudes in the late nineteenth century (and Holmes's
"male chauvinism"), for the "chicken" is a wealthy middle-aged single woman, whom
Holmes describes as "one of the most dangerous classes in the world . . . an inciter of crimes
in others." Watson energetically pursues the matter, but Holmes is, as usual, highly critical
of Watson's work. Scholars are equally critical of Holmes's performance in the case.

1 "The Disappearance of Lady Frances Carfax" was published in the *Strand Magazine* in December 1911 and in the *American Magazine* (New York) the same month (entitled there "The Disappearance of Lady Carfax"). The manuscript of "The Disappearance of Lady Frances Carfax" is in the hands of a private collector. Peter Blau reports, in " 'It Is an Old Manuscript,' " that in the original text, Lady Frances is Lady Maria.

2 Holmes's own rheumatism is discussed in the Preface. There is little agreement among the chronologists about the date of "Lady Frances Carfax," but those who agree place it after 1900, when Watson would have been just fifty (see *Chronological Table*). According to *Whitaker's Almanack* for 1900, at age fifty,

UT WHY TURKISH?" asked Mr. Sherlock Holmes, gazing fixedly at my boots. I was reclining in a cane-backed chair at the moment, and my protruded feet had attracted his ever-active attention.

"English," I answered, in some surprise. "I got them at Latimer's, in Oxford Street."

Holmes smiled with an expression of weary patience.

"The bath!" he said; "the bath! Why the relaxing and expensive Turkish rather than the invigorating home-made article?"

"Because for the last few days I have been feeling rheumatic[2] and old. A Turkish bath is what we call an alterative in medicine[3]—a fresh starting-point, a cleanser of the system.

"By the way, Holmes," I added. "I have no doubt the connection between my boots and a Turkish bath is a perfectly self-evident one to a logical mind, and yet I should be obliged to you if you would indicate it."

"The train of reasoning is not very obscure, Watson," said Holmes, with a mischievous twinkle. "It belongs to the same elementary class of deduction which I should illustrate if I were to ask you who shared your cab in your drive this morning."

"I don't admit that a fresh illustration is an explanation," said I, with some asperity.

"Bravo, Watson! A very dignified and logical remonstrance. Let me see, what were the points? Take the last one first—the cab. You observe that you have some splashes on the left sleeve and shoulder of your coat. Had you sat in the centre of a hansom you would probably have had no splashes, and if you had they would certainly have been symmetrical. Therefore it is clear that you sat at the side. Therefore it is equally clear that you had a companion."

"That is very evident."

"Absurdly commonplace, is it not?"

"But the boots and the bath?"

"Equally childish. You are in the habit of doing up your boots in a certain way. I see them on this occasion fastened with an elaborate double bow, which is not your usual method of tying them. You have, therefore, had them off. Who has tied them? A bootmaker—or the boy at the bath. It is unlikely that it is the bootmaker, since your boots are nearly new. Well, what remains? The bath. Absurd, is it not?[4] But, for all that, the Turkish bath has served a purpose."

"What is that?"

"You say that you have had it because you need a change. Let me suggest that you take one. How would Lausanne do, my dear Watson—first-class tickets and all expenses paid on a princely scale?"

"Splendid! But why?"

Holmes leaned back in his armchair and took his notebook from his pocket.

"One of the most dangerous classes in the world," said he, "is the drifting and friendless woman. She is the most harmless, and often the most useful of mortals, but she is the inevitable inciter of crime in others.[5] She is helpless. She is migratory. She has sufficient means to take her from country to country and from hotel to hotel. She is lost, as often as not, in a maze of obscure *pensions* and boarding-houses. She is a stray

Watson's life expectancy was about another twenty years (today, his life expectancy would be about another thirty-three years). Therefore, his feeling old was not wholly imaginary.

3 Often misspelled as "alternative," an alterative is any drug used to alter the course of an ailment and restore the sufferer to full health.

4 Philip Weller remarks, "It is absurd, since there are other possibilities, such as that Watson was buying a new pair of shoes or a second pair of boots." But Derham Groves, in "The Reason Behind the Reasoning," explains that Holmes reasoned from a recent change in the weather that, in order to ease the ache of his old wound, Watson would seek out the Turkish baths.

5 "Holmes's experience of women was, of course, limited," notes T. S. Blakeney wryly.

6 Famed science-fiction writer Philip José Farmer concludes that Lady Frances was the descendant of the Lord Rufton mentioned in "How the Brigadier Triumphed in England," first published in the *Strand Magazine* in 1903 and later published as a chapter of the memoirs edited by Sir Arthur Conan Doyle under the title *Adventures of Gerard*. Of course, the name "Rufton" is fictitious in both accounts, but, Farmer proposes, Doyle, knowing of the relationship, suggested that Dr. Watson use the same pseudonym that he had used.

7 Mark Hunter Purvis reaches the conclusion that Miss Dobney was engaged in blackmailing Lady Frances.

8 The Hôtel National, notes Michael Kaser, is not listed in *Baedeker's* Switzerland guide until 1902. Scholars propose from 1895 to 1902 for the dates of "Lady Frances Carfax," and this fact tends to support the possibility of a later dating. However, Kaser sticks to 1901, the date selected by most writers, and surmises that the hotel, while sufficiently luxurious for a woman of Lady Frances's standing, might have taken a while to achieve the international reputation required for inclusion in a guide as venerable as Baedeker.

9 A hunting metaphor, one of many used by Holmes, perhaps reflecting his country upbringing.

10 Spelled (incorrectly) "Montpelier" in all British texts. Holmes spent "some months" in a laboratory in Montpellier between 1891 and 1894, pursuing research into the coal-tar derivatives ("The Empty House").

chicken in a world of foxes. When she is gobbled up she is hardly missed. I much fear that some evil has come to the Lady Frances Carfax."

I was relieved at this sudden descent from the general to the particular. Holmes consulted his notes.

"Lady Frances," he continued, "is the sole survivor of the direct family of the late Earl of Rufton.[6] The estates went, as you may remember, in the male line. She was left with limited means, but with some very remarkable old Spanish jewellery of silver and curiously cut diamonds to which she was fondly attached—too attached, for she refused to leave them with her banker and always carried them about with her. A rather pathetic figure, the Lady Frances, a beautiful woman, still in fresh middle age, and yet, by a strange chance, the last derelict of what only twenty years ago was a goodly fleet."

"What has happened to her, then?"

"Ah, what has happened to the Lady Frances? Is she alive or dead? There is our problem. She is a lady of precise habits, and for four years it has been her invariable custom to write every second week to Miss Dobney, her old governess, who has long retired, and lives in Camberwell.[7] It is this Miss Dobney who has consulted me. Nearly five weeks have passed without a word. The last letter was from the Hôtel National at Lausanne.[8] Lady Frances seems to have left there and given no address. The family are anxious, and, as they are exceedingly wealthy, no sum will be spared if we can clear the matter up."

"Is Miss Dobney the only source of information? Surely she had other correspondents?"

"There is one correspondent who is a sure draw,[9] Watson. That is the bank. Single ladies must live, and their passbooks are compressed diaries. She banks at Silvester's. I have glanced over her account. The last cheque but one paid her bill at Lausanne, but it was a large one and probably left her with cash in hand. Only one cheque has been drawn since."

"To whom, and where?"

"To Miss Marie Devine. There is nothing to show where the cheque was drawn. It was cashed at the Crédit Lyonnais at Montpellier[10] less than three weeks ago. The sum was fifty pounds."

"And who is Miss Marie Devine?"

"That also I have been able to discover. Miss Marie Devine

"What has happened to the Lady Frances? Is she alive
or dead? There is our problem."
Frederick Dorr Steele, *American Magazine*, 1911

was the maid of Lady Frances Carfax. Why she should have paid
her this cheque we have not yet determined. I have no doubt,
however, that your researches will soon clear the matter up."

"*My* researches!"

"Hence the health-giving expedition to Lausanne. You
know that I cannot possibly leave London while old Abrahams
is in such mortal terror of his life. Besides, on general principles
it is best that I should not leave the country. Scotland Yard
feels lonely without me, and it causes an unhealthy excitement
among the criminal classes. Go, then, my dear Watson, and if
my humble counsel can ever be valued at so extravagant a rate
as two pence a word, it waits your disposal night and day at the
end of the Continental wire."

Two days later found me at the National Hôtel at Lausanne,
where I received every courtesy at the hands of M. Moser, the

11 "A wild man, truly a wild man!"

12 Is this the former Baden, Germany (now known as Baden-Baden), with its famous thermal baths? Or Baden, Switzerland, also known for its mineral springs? The principal scholars are divided on the issue.

well-known manager. Lady Frances, as he informed me, had stayed there for several weeks. She had been much liked by all who met her. Her age was not more than forty. She was still handsome, and bore every sign of having in her youth been a very lovely woman. M. Moser knew nothing of any valuable jewellery, but it had been remarked by the servants that the heavy trunk in the lady's bedroom was always scrupulously locked. Marie Devine, the maid, was as popular as her mistress. She was actually engaged to one of the head waiters in the hotel, and there was no difficulty in getting her address. It was 11, Rue de Trajan, Montpellier. All this I jotted down, and felt that Holmes himself could not have been more adroit in collecting his facts.

Only one corner still remained in the shadow. No light which I possessed could clear up the cause for the lady's sudden departure. She was very happy at Lausanne. There was every reason to believe that she intended to remain for the season in her luxurious rooms overlooking the lake. And yet she had left at a single day's notice, which involved her in the useless payment of a week's rent. Only Jules Vibart, the lover of the maid, had any suggestion to offer. He connected the sudden departure with the visit to the hotel a day or two before of a tall, dark, bearded man. *"Un sauvage—un véritable sauvage!"*[11] cried Jules Vibart. The man had rooms somewhere in the town. He had been seen talking earnestly to Madame on the promenade by the lake. Then he had called. She had refused to see him. He was English, but of his name there was no record. Madame had left the place immediately afterwards. Jules Vibart, and, what was of more importance, Jules Vibart's sweetheart, thought that this call and this departure were cause and effect. Only one thing Jules would not discuss. That was the reason why Marie had left her mistress. Of that he could or would say nothing. If I wished to know, I must go to Montpellier and ask her.

So ended the first chapter of my inquiry. The second was devoted to the place which Lady Frances Carfax had sought when she left Lausanne. Concerning this there had been some secrecy, which confirmed the idea that she had gone with the intention of throwing someone off her track. Otherwise why should not her luggage have been openly labelled for Baden?[12] Both she and it reached the Rhenish spa by some circuitous route. This much I gathered from the manager of Cook's local office.[13] So to Baden I went, after dispatching to Holmes an account of all my proceedings, and receiving in reply a telegram of half-humorous commendation.

At Baden the track was not difficult to follow. Lady Frances had stayed at the Englischer Hof[14] for a fortnight. Whilst there she had made the acquaintance of a Dr. Shlessinger and his wife, a missionary from South America. Like most lonely ladies, Lady Frances found her comfort and occupation in religion. Dr. Shlessinger's remarkable personality, his whole-hearted devotion, and the fact that he was recovering from a disease contracted in the exercise of his apostolic duties, affected her deeply. She had helped Mrs. Shlessinger in the nursing of the convalescent saint. He spent his day, as the manager described it to me, upon a lounge-chair on the verandah, with an attendant lady upon either side of him. He was preparing a map of the Holy Land, with special reference to the kingdom of the Midianites,[15] upon which he was writing a monograph. Finally, having improved much in health, he and his wife had returned to London, and Lady Frances had started thither in their company. This was just three weeks before, and the manager had heard nothing since. As to the maid, Marie, she had gone off some days beforehand in floods

"He spent his day upon a lounge-chair on the veranda, with an attendant lady upon either side of him."
Alec Ball, *Strand Magazine*, 1911

13 The Thomas Cook travel agency was conceived at a June 9, 1841, temperance meeting in Leicester. Interested in attending a July 5 meeting at Loughborough, cabinet-maker and former Baptist preacher Thomas Cook (1808–1892) suggested that his fellow temperance workers make the journey together. Cook persuaded the Midland Railway Company to arrange a train to carry five hundred passengers the twelves miles to Loughborough and back again at the cost of one shilling per person. The success of the trip encouraged Cook to continue arranging excursions for temperance societies and Sunday schools, printing up posters and handbills to advertise his services. Eventually, Cook—today widely considered the founder of modern tourism—began taking an even more active rôle in the travel plans, researching the routes to be taken, writing up accompanying handbooks (precursors to the modern travel guide), and publishing a newspaper promoting his tours. In 1855, Cook was able to expand his business beyond Britain by taking tourists on a Grand Tour of Europe, from Leicester to the international exhibition in Paris on a circuitous route that included Brussels, Heidelberg, Baden-Baden, and Strasbourg. By the 1870s, he was conducting tours around the world. So dominant in the travel field was the firm that in 1884, the British government asked it to organise the relief expedition sent to attempt a rescue of General George Gordon at Khartoum (see "The Cardboard Box," note 9).

According to Michael Kaser, the Thomas Cook office in Lausanne was opened on April, 1891, at No. 1 Rue Pépinet. At that point, the business would have been known officially as Thos. Cook and Son, as the business affairs were being managed by Cook's son, John Mason Cook.

14 Furthering the argument for Baden, Germany, Kaser notes that an Englischer Hof for that town is listed in *Baedeker's* 1893 and 1902

southern Germany editions. In addition, there is no Englischer Hof listed for Baden in the 1887 edition of *Baedeker's* Switzerland.

15 The Midianites, also referred to as Ishmaelites in the Old Testament, were a group of nomadic tribes related to the Israelites. Residing mostly in the northwestern Arabian Desert, they are described in Genesis as having been descended from Midian, the son of Abraham by his second wife, Keturah. In Exodus, Moses marries Zipporah, a daughter of the Midianite priest Jethro. There was no "kingdom of the Midianites."

of tears, after informing the other maids that she was leaving service forever. Dr. Shlessinger had paid the bill of the whole party before his departure.

"By the way," said the landlord, in conclusion, "you are not the only friend of Lady Frances Carfax who is inquiring after her just now. Only a week or so ago we had a man here upon the same errand."

"Did he give a name?" I asked.

"None; but he was an Englishman, though of an unusual type."

"A savage?" said I, linking my facts after the fashion of my illustrious friend.

"Exactly. That describes him very well. He is a bulky, bearded, sunburned fellow, who looks as if he would be more at home in a farmers' inn than in a fashionable hotel. A hard, fierce man, I should think, and one whom I should be sorry to offend."

Already the mystery began to define itself, as figures grow clearer with the lifting of a fog. Here was this good and pious lady pursued from place to place by a sinister and unrelenting figure. She feared him, or she would not have fled from Lausanne. He had still followed. Sooner or later he would overtake her. Had he already overtaken her? Was *that* the secret of her continued silence? Could the good people who were her companions not screen her from his violence or his blackmail? What horrible purpose, what deep design, lay behind this long pursuit? There was the problem which I had to solve.

To Holmes I wrote showing how rapidly and surely I had got down to the roots of the matter. In reply I had a telegram asking for a description of Dr. Shlessinger's left ear. Holmes's ideas of humour are strange and occasionally offensive, so I took no notice of his ill-timed jest—indeed, I had already reached Montpellier in my pursuit of the maid, Marie, before his message came.

I had no difficulty in finding the ex-servant and in learning all that she could tell me. She was a devoted creature, who had only left her mistress because she was sure that she was in good hands, and because her own approaching marriage made a separation inevitable in any case. Her mistress had, as she confessed with distress, shown some irritability of temper towards her during their stay in Baden, and had even questioned her once as if she had suspicions of her honesty, and this had made the parting easier than it would otherwise have been. Lady Frances had given her fifty pounds as a wedding-present. Like me, Marie viewed with deep distrust the stranger who had driven her mistress from Lausanne. With her own eyes she had seen him seize the lady's wrist with great violence on the public promenade by the lake. He was a fierce and terrible man. She believed that it was out of dread of him that Lady Frances had accepted the escort of the Shlessingers to London. She had never spoken to Marie about it, but many little signs had convinced the maid that her mistress lived in a state of continual nervous apprehension. So far she had got in her narrative, when suddenly she sprang from her chair and her face was convulsed with surprise and fear. "See!" she cried. "The miscreant follows still! There is the very man of whom I speak."

Through the open sitting-room window I saw a huge, swarthy man with a bristling black beard walking slowly down the centre of the street and staring eagerly at the numbers of the houses. It was clear that, like myself, he was on the track

"See!" she cried. "The miscreant follows still!
There is the very man of whom I speak!"
Frederick Dorr Steele, *American Magazine*, 1911

of the maid. Acting upon the impulse of the moment, I rushed out and accosted him.

"You are an Englishman," I said.

"What if I am?" he asked, with a most villainous scowl.

"May I ask what your name is?"

"No, you may not," said he with decision.

The situation was awkward, but the most direct way is often the best.

"Where is the Lady Frances Carfax?" I asked.

He stared at me in amazement.

"What have you done with her? Why have you pursued her? I insist upon an answer!" said I.

The fellow gave a bellow of anger and sprang upon me like a tiger. I have held my own in many a struggle, but the man had a grip of iron and the fury of a fiend. His hand was on my throat and my senses were nearly gone before an unshaven

"The fellow gave a bellow of anger and sprang upon me like a tiger."
Alec Ball, *Strand Magazine*, 1911

French *ouvrier*[16] in a blue blouse, darted out from a *cabaret* opposite, with a cudgel in his hand, and struck my assailant a sharp crack over the forearm, which made him leave go his hold. He stood for an instant fuming with rage and uncertain whether he should not renew his attack. Then, with a snarl of anger, he left me and entered the cottage from which I had just come. I turned to thank my preserver, who stood beside me in the roadway.

"Well, Watson," said he, "a very pretty hash you have made of it! I rather think you had better come back with me to London by the night express."

An hour afterwards, Sherlock Holmes, in his usual garb and style, was seated in my private room at the hotel. His explanation of his sudden and opportune appearance was simplicity itself, for, finding that he could get away from London, he determined to head me off at the next obvious point of my travels. In the disguise of a working-man he had sat in the *cabaret* waiting for my appearance.[17]

"And a singularly consistent investigation you have made, my dear Watson," said he. "I cannot at the moment recall any possible blunder which you have omitted. The total effect of your proceedings has been to give the alarm everywhere and yet to discover nothing."

"Perhaps you would have done no better," I answered, bitterly.

"There is no 'perhaps' about it. I *have* done better. Here is the Hon. Philip Green, who is a fellow-lodger with you in this hotel, and we may find in him the starting-point for a more successful investigation."

A card had come up on a salver, and it was followed by the same bearded ruffian who had attacked me in the street. He started when he saw me.

"What is this, Mr. Holmes?" he asked. "I had your note and I have come. But what has this man to do with the matter?"

"This is my old friend and associate, Dr. Watson, who is helping us in this affair."

The stranger held out a huge, sunburned hand, with a few words of apology.

"I hope I didn't harm you. When you accused me of hurting her I lost my grip of myself. Indeed, I'm not responsible in these days. My nerves are like live wires. But this situation is

16 French: workman.

17 Benjamin Clark sees Holmes's behaviour, both here and further on, as "illogical and bizarre." If Watson had wired Holmes that Lady Frances was on her way to London, Holmes had no reason to disguise himself in Montpellier. And yet, Clark puzzles, "the detective chose this moment to indulge his craving for fancy dress by disguising himself as a French workman. Was his only purpose in doing so to have the pleasure of startling Watson?" Indeed, Watson had done excellent work, picking up Lady Frances's trail, identifying the persons with whom she left Baden, and, notwithstanding Holmes's accusation, doing nothing to alarm the criminals.

18 A high, frilly, cotton cap with a crown, worn indoors by women in the eighteenth and early nineteenth centuries. The usage possibly originates from the obscure Dutch *mop-muts*, *mop* meaning "to cover up" and *muts* meaning "cap."

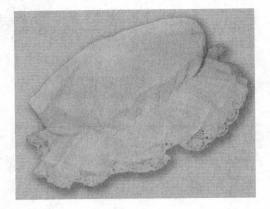

A mobcap.

19 Located in the De Kaap Valley of South Africa's Makonjwa mountain range, Barberton became a gold rush town after the rich deposits of Barber's Reef were discovered there in June 1884.

20 A large hotel in Portland Place. It was here that Arthur Conan Doyle first met with the commissioning editor of *Lippincott's*, Joseph Marshall Stoddart, and arranged for publication of *The Sign of Four*. Captain Morstan (*The Sign of Four*) stayed here, as did the King of Bohemia ("A Scandal in Bohemia").

beyond me. What I want to know, in the first place, Mr. Holmes, is, how in the world you came to hear of my existence at all."

"I am in touch with Miss Dobney, Lady Frances's governess."

"Old Susan Dobney with the mob cap![18] I remember her well."

"And she remembers you. It was in the days before—before you found it better to go to South Africa."

"Ah, I see you know my whole story. I need hide nothing from you. I swear to you, Mr. Holmes, that there never was in this world a man who loved a woman with a more whole-hearted love than I had for Frances. I was a wild youngster, I know—not worse than others of my class. But her mind was pure as snow. She could not bear a shadow of coarseness. So, when she came to hear of things that I had done, she would have no more to say to me. And yet she loved me—that is the wonder of it!—loved me well enough to remain single all her sainted days just for my sake alone. When the years had passed and I had made my money at Barberton[19] I thought perhaps I could seek her out and soften her. I had heard that she was still unmarried. I found her at Lausanne, and tried all I knew. She weakened, I think, but her will was strong, and when next I called she had left the town. I traced her to Baden, and then after a time heard that her maid was here. I'm a rough fellow, fresh from a rough life, and when Dr. Watson spoke to me as he did I lost hold of myself for a moment. But for God's sake tell me what has become of the Lady Frances."

"That is for us to find out," said Sherlock Holmes, with peculiar gravity. "What is your London address, Mr. Green?"

"The Langham Hotel[20] will find me."

"Then may I recommend that you return there and be on hand in case I should want you? I have no desire to encourage false hopes, but you may rest assured that all that can be done will be done for the safety of Lady Frances. I can say no more for the instant. I will leave you this card so that you may be able to keep in touch with us. Now, Watson, if you will pack your bag I will cable to Mrs. Hudson to make one of her best efforts for two hungry travellers at seven-thirty to-morrow."

A telegram was awaiting us when we reached our Baker Street rooms, which Holmes read with an exclamation of interest and threw across to me. "Jagged or torn," was the message, and the place of origin, Baden.

"What is this?" I asked.

"It is everything," Holmes answered. "You may remember my seemingly irrelevant question as to this clerical gentleman's left ear. You did not answer it."

"I had left Baden, and could not inquire."

"Exactly. For this reason I sent a duplicate to the manager of the Englischer Hof, whose answer lies here."

"What does it show?"

"It shows, my dear Watson, that we are dealing with an exceptionally astute and dangerous man. The Rev. Dr. Shlessinger, missionary from South America, is none other than Holy Peters, one of the most unscrupulous rascals that Australia has ever evolved—and for a young country it has turned out some very finished types. His particular speciality is the beguiling of lonely ladies by playing upon their religious feelings, and his so-called wife, an Englishwoman named Fraser, is a worthy helpmate. The nature of his tactics suggested his identity to me, and this physical peculiarity—he was badly bitten in a saloon-fight at Adelaide[21] in '89—confirmed my suspicion. This poor lady is in the hands of a most infernal couple, who will stick at nothing, Watson. That she is already dead is a very likely supposition. If not, she is undoubtedly in some sort of confinement, and unable to write to Miss Dobney or her other friends. It is always possible that she never reached London, or that she has passed through it, but the former is improbable, as, with their system of registration, it is not easy for foreigners to play tricks with the Continental police;[22] and the latter is also unlikely, as these rogues could not hope to find any other place where it would be as easy to keep a person under restraint. All my instincts tell me that she is in London, but, as we have at present no possible means of telling where, we can only take the obvious steps, eat our dinner, and possess our souls in patience. Later in the evening I will stroll down and have a word with friend Lestrade at Scotland Yard."

But neither the official police nor Holmes's own small, but

21 The capital of South Australia. Mary Fraser, Lady Brackenstall, of "The Abbey Grange," was also from Adelaide. In the manuscript, "Adelaide" is Omaha, Nebraska, a world away.

22 Philip Weller remarks: "This is a typical piece of arrogant nonsense from Holmes, since the Continental registration system (which was not as efficient as Holmes suggests anyway) could not have shown that Lady Frances might not have reached London."

23 One must assume that this refers to the Baker Street Irregulars, mentioned by name only in *A Study in Scarlet*, *The Sign of Four*, and "The Crooked Man." Or is this the "Agency" referred to in "The Sussex Vampire"?

24 "Bovington's" in American texts, a thinly disguised version of Bravington's, the fashionable Victorian jewellers.

25 Holmes most likely means Westminster Bridge Road, which runs from Westminster Bridge to St. George's Square.

very efficient, organization[23] sufficed to clear away the mystery. Amid the crowded millions of London the three persons we sought were as completely obliterated as if they had never lived. Advertisements were tried, and failed. Clues were followed, and led to nothing. Every criminal resort which Shlessinger might frequent was drawn in vain. His old associates were watched, but they kept clear of him. And then suddenly, after a week of helpless suspense, there came a flash of light. A silver-and-brilliant pendant of old Spanish design had been pawned at Bevington's,[24] in Westminster Road.[25] The pawner was a large, clean-shaven man of clerical appearance. His name and address were demonstrably false. The ear had escaped notice, but the description was surely that of Shlessinger.

Three times had our bearded friend from the Langham called for news—the third time within an hour of this fresh development. His clothes were getting looser on his great body. He seemed to be wilting away in his anxiety. "If you will only give me something to do!" was his constant wail. At last Holmes could oblige him.

"He has begun to pawn the jewels. We should get him now."

"But does this mean that any harm has befallen the Lady Frances?"

Holmes shook his head very gravely.

"Supposing that they have held her prisoner up to now, it is clear that they cannot let her loose without their own destruction. We must prepare for the worst."

"What can I do?"

"These people do not know you by sight?"

"No."

"It is possible that he will go to some other pawnbroker in the future. In that case, we must begin again. On the other hand, he has had a fair price and no questions asked, so if he is in need of ready-money he will probably come back to Bevington's. I will give you a note to them, and they will let you wait in the shop. If the fellow comes you will follow him home. But no indiscretion, and above all, no violence. I put you on your honour that you will take no step without my knowledge and consent."

For two days the Hon. Philip Green (he was, I may mention, the son of the famous admiral of that name who commanded the Sea of Azof[26] fleet in the Crimean War[27]) brought us no news. On the evening of the third he rushed into our sitting-room, pale, trembling, with every muscle of his powerful frame quivering with excitement.

"We have him! We have him!" he cried.

He was incoherent in his agitation. Holmes soothed him with a few words, and thrust him into an armchair.

"Come, now, give us the order of events," said he.

"She came only an hour ago. It was the wife, this time, but the pendant she brought was the fellow of the other. She is a tall, pale woman, with ferret eyes."

"That is the lady," said Holmes.

"She left the office and I followed her. She walked up the Kennington Road, and I kept behind her. Presently she went into a shop. Mr. Holmes, it was an undertaker's."

My companion started. "Well?" he asked, in that vibrant voice which told of the fiery soul behind the cold, grey face.

26 Also known as the Azov or Azoff Sea, this inland body of water is a northern extension of the Black Sea and is connected to it by the Kerch Strait. The Azof is the world's shallowest sea, measuring only forty-six feet deep at its deepest point.

27 See "The 'Gloria Scott'," note 30.

"'We have him! We have him!' he cried."
Alec Ball, *Strand Magazine*, 1911

28 Watson misspeaks here, for the "client" is declared by Holmes to be the family of Lady Frances, not her lover.

29 See note 23. Holmes here does not refer to his gang of "street urchins" but only means that he and Watson will act in a manner different from the "regular forces." Irregular troops, for example, were used in the British Army as harassing forces or for infiltration behind enemy lines.

"She was talking to the woman behind the counter. I entered as well. 'It is late,' I heard her say, or words to that effect. The woman was excusing herself. 'It should be there before now,' she answered. 'It took longer, being out of the ordinary.' They both stopped and looked at me, so I asked some question and then left the shop."

"You did excellently well. What happened next?"

"The woman came out, but I had hid myself in a doorway. Her suspicions had been aroused, I think, for she looked round her. Then she called a cab and got in. I was lucky enough to get another and so to follow her. She got down at last at No. 36, Poultney Square, Brixton. I drove past, left my cab at the corner of the square, and watched the house."

"Did you see anyone?"

"The windows were all in darkness save one on the lower floor. The blind was down, and I could not see in. I was standing there, wondering what I should do next, when a covered van drove up with two men in it. They descended, took something out of the van, and carried it up the steps to the hall door. Mr. Holmes, it was a coffin."

"Ah!"

"For an instant I was on the point of rushing in. The door had been opened to admit the men and their burden. It was the woman who had opened it. But as I stood there she caught a glimpse of me, and I think that she recognized me. I saw her start, and she hastily closed the door. I remembered my promise to you, and here I am."

"You have done excellent work," said Holmes scribbling a few words upon a half-sheet of paper. "We can do nothing legal without a warrant, and you can serve the cause best by taking this note down to the authorities and getting one. There may be some difficulty, but I should think that the sale of the jewellery should be sufficient. Lestrade will see to all details."

"But they may murder her in the meanwhile. What could the coffin mean, and for whom could it be but for her?"

"We will do all that can be done, Mr. Green. Not a moment will be lost. Leave it in our hands. Now, Watson," he added as our client[28] hurried away, "he will set the regular forces on the move. We are, as usual, the irregulars,[29] and we must take our own line of action. The situation strikes me as so desperate

The door had opened to admit the men and their burden.
Frederick Dorr Steele, *American Magazine*, 1911

that the most extreme measures are justified. Not a moment is to be lost in getting to Poultney Square.

"Let us try to reconstruct the situation," said he as we drove swiftly past the Houses of Parliament and over Westminster Bridge. "These villains have coaxed this unhappy lady to London, after first alienating her from her faithful maid. If she has written any letters they have been intercepted. Through some confederate they have engaged a furnished house. Once inside it they have made her a prisoner, and they have become possessed of the valuable jewellery which has been their object from the first. Already they have begun to sell part of it, which seems safe enough to them, since they have no reason to think

30 "No reason to think anyone is interested in the lady's fate!" Benjamin Clark complains. "Why, for a week, Holmes, with what he describes as his own small but very efficient organization, together with Scotland Yard, has been investigating, advertising, combing Shlessinger's haunt, watching his old associates, and heaven knows what else. . . . No! If Peters failed to be alarmed under the above-described conditions, he certainly does not deserve the title of astute." Clark further observes that making two separate trips to pawn the pendants was a monumental error, one that led directly to Peters's downfall.

Westminster Bridge.
Queen's London (1897)

that anyone is interested in the lady's fate.[30] When she is released she will, of course, denounce them. Therefore, she must not be released. But they cannot keep her under lock and key forever. So murder is their only solution."

"That seems very clear."

"Now we will take another line of reasoning. When you follow two separate chains of thought, Watson, you will find some point of intersection which should approximate to the truth. We will start now, not from the lady, but from the coffin and argue backward. That incident proves, I fear, beyond all doubt that the lady is dead. It points also to an orthodox burial with proper accompaniment of medical certificate and official sanction. Had the lady been obviously murdered, they would have buried her in a hole in the back garden. But here all is open and regular. What does that mean? Surely that they have done her to death in some way which has deceived the doctor and simulated a natural end—poisoning, perhaps. And yet how strange that they should ever let a doctor approach her unless he were a confederate, which is hardly a credible proposition."

"Could they have forged a medical certificate?"

"Dangerous, Watson, very dangerous. No, I hardly see them doing that. Pull up, cabby! This is evidently the undertaker's, for we have just passed the pawnbroker's. Would you go in,

Watson? Your appearance inspires confidence. Ask what hour the Poultney Square funeral takes place to-morrow."

The woman in the shop answered me without hesitation that it was to be at eight o'clock in the morning. "You see, Watson, no mystery; everything above-board! In some way the legal forms have undoubtedly been complied with, and they think that they have little to fear. Well, there's nothing for it now but a direct frontal attack. Are you armed?"

"My stick!"

"Well, well, we shall be strong enough. 'Thrice is he armed who hath his quarrel just.'[31] We simply can't afford to wait for the police, or to keep within the four corners of the law. You can drive off, cabby. Now, Watson, we'll just take our luck together, as we have occasionally done in the past."

He had rung loudly at the door of a great dark house in the centre of Poultney Square. It was opened immediately, and the figure of a tall woman was outlined against the dim-lit hall.

"Well, what do you want?" she asked, sharply, peering at us through the darkness.

"I want to speak to Dr. Shlessinger," said Holmes.

"There is no such person here," she answered, and tried to close the door, but Holmes had jammed it with his foot.

"Well, I want to see the man who lives here, whatever he may call himself," said Holmes, firmly.

She hesitated. Then she threw open the door. "Well, come in!" said she. "My husband is not afraid to face any man in the world." She closed the door behind us, and showed us into a sitting-room on the right side of the hall, turning up the gas as she left us. "Mr. Peters will be with you in an instant," she said.

Her words were literally true, for we had hardly time to look around the dusty and moth-eaten apartment in which we found ourselves before the door opened and a big, clean-shaven bald-headed man stepped lightly into the room. He had a large red face, with pendulous cheeks, and a general air of superficial benevolence which was marred by a cruel, vicious mouth.

"There is surely some mistake here, gentlemen," he said in an unctuous, make-everything-easy voice. "I fancy that you have been misdirected. Possibly if you tried farther down the street—"

"That will do; we have no time to waste," said my compan-

31 Holmes quotes King Henry, caught between the quarreling Dukes of Suffolk and Warwick, just after the murder of the Duke of Gloucester, from Shakespeare's *The Second Part of King Henry the Sixth*, Act III, Scene 2.

32 Holmes was not committing burglary or the daytime crime of housebreaking here because he had no felonious intent, that is, he had no intention to remove anything belonging to Peters or to attack Peters. Trespass is not a criminal offence; at worst, Holmes may have been guilty of conduct tending to provoke a breach of the peace. Of course, Peters was not making a formal accusation of Holmes, only speaking in the vernacular.

ion firmly. "You are Henry Peters, of Adelaide, late the Rev. Dr. Shlessinger, of Baden and South America. I am as sure of that as that my own name is Sherlock Holmes."

Peters, as I will now call him, started and stared hard at his formidable pursuer. "I guess your name does not frighten me, Mr. Holmes," said he coolly. "When a man's conscience is easy you can't rattle him. What is your business in my house?"

"I want to know what you have done with the Lady Frances Carfax, whom you brought away with you from Baden."

"I'd be very glad if you could tell me where that lady may be," Peters answered, coolly. "I've a bill against her for nearly a hundred pounds, and nothing to show for it but a couple of trumpery pendants that the dealer would hardly look at. She attached herself to Mrs. Peters and me at Baden (it is a fact that I was using another name at the time), and she stuck on to us until we came to London. I paid her bill and her ticket. Once in London, she gave us the slip, and, as I say, left these out-of-date jewels to pay her bills. You find her, Mr. Holmes, and I'm your debtor."

"I *mean* to find her," said Sherlock Holmes. "I'm going through this house till I do find her."

"Where is your warrant?"

Holmes half drew a revolver from his pocket. "This will have to serve till a better one comes."

"Why, you are a common burglar."[32]

"So you might describe me," said Holmes, cheerfully. "My companion is also a dangerous ruffian. And together we are going through your house."

Our opponent opened the door.

"Fetch a policeman, Annie!" said he. There was a whisk of feminine skirts down the passage, and the hall door was opened and shut.

"Our time is limited, Watson," said Holmes. "If you try to stop us, Peters, you will most certainly get hurt. Where is that coffin which was brought into your house?"

"What do you want with the coffin? It is in use. There is a body in it."

"I must see that body."

"Never with my consent."

"Then without it." With a quick movement Holmes pushed the fellow to one side and passed into the hall. A door half

"Holmes half drew a revolver from his pocket."
Alec Ball, *Strand Magazine*, 1911

opened stood immediately before us. We entered. It was the dining-room. On the table, under a half-lit chandelier, the coffin was lying. Holmes turned up the gas and raised the lid. Deep down in the recesses of the coffin lay an emaciated figure. The glare from the lights above beat down upon an aged and withered face. By no possible process of cruelty, starvation, or disease could this worn-out wreck be the still beautiful Lady Frances. Holmes's face showed his amazement, and also his relief.

"Thank God!" he muttered. "It's someone else."

"Ah, you've blundered badly for once, Mr. Sherlock Holmes," said Peters, who had followed us into the room.

"Who is this dead woman?"

"Well, if you really must know, she is an old nurse of my wife's, Rose Spender her name, whom we found in the Brixton Workhouse Infirmary.[33] We brought her round here, called in Dr. Horsom, of 13, Firbank Villas—mind you take the address,

33 The first "workhouses" were built in response to the Poor Law of 1601, which handed responsibility for the indigent to individual parishes. While workhouses were meant to provide the poor with gainful employment, the work available was minimal, and they began to resemble prisons more than viable social institutions. The situation grew even more taxed with passage of the Poor Law Amendment Act of 1834, which limited aid for the poor exclusively to the workhouses, prohibiting any "outdoor" or "home" relief. Many of those in need of assistance were desperately ill, and vice versa. Workhouses were forced to add infirmaries, complete with isolation wards, to treat the overwhelming number of applicants afflicted with cholera, smallpox, scarlet fever, and whooping cough.

This centralised system was orchestrated by Edwin Chadwick, whose draconian rules made him, as historian Roy Porter puts it, "the most hated man in England." His idea was to solve the poverty problem by making conditions at workhouses so bleak and demeaning—even punitive—that the indigent would seek to lift themselves out of poverty. To Chadwick, as Porter explains, the workhouses were "a self-operating mechanism for eliminating pauperism: the workhouse being intended as nastier than work." Married couples were routinely separated, as were parents and children. The "work" usually consisted of breaking stones or picking okum. By law, after 1833, unclaimed workhouse bodies were used for dissection by anatomists (see "The Cardboard Box," note 17). (When poverty levels failed to diminish, Chadwick blamed sickness itself, and he became obsessed not with improving the workhouses but with cleaning up the city's sewage system.)

The reference to the Brixton Workhouse Infirmary is fictitious, but Philip Weller suggests that the name may be a euphemism for

Brixton Prison, "where there was a female prisoner section and an infirmary, although this seems harsh for a woman of 90."

"Our time is limited, Watson," said Holmes. "If you try to stop us, Peters, you will most certainly get hurt. Where is that coffin which was brought into your house?"
Frederick Dorr Steele, *American Magazine*, 1911

Mr. Holmes—and had her carefully tended, as Christian folk should. On the third day she died—certificate says senile decay—but that's only the doctor's opinion, and, of course, you know better. We ordered her funeral to be carried out by Stimson and Co., of the Kennington Road, who will bury her at eight o'clock to-morrow morning. Can you pick any hole in that, Mr. Holmes? You've made a silly blunder, and you may as well own up to it. I'd give something for a photograph of your gaping, staring face when you pulled aside that lid expecting to see the Lady Frances Carfax, and only found a poor old woman of ninety."

Holmes's expression was as impassive as ever under the jeers of his antagonist, but his clenched hands betrayed his acute annoyance.

"I am going through your house," said he.

"Are you, though!" cried Peters, as a woman's voice and heavy steps sounded in the passage. "We'll soon see about that. This way, officers, if you please. These men have forced their way into my house, and I cannot get rid of them. Help me to put them out."

A sergeant and a constable stood in the doorway. Holmes drew his card from his case.

"This is my name and address. This is my friend, Dr. Watson."

"Bless you, sir, we know you very well," said the sergeant, "but you can't stay here without a warrant."

"Of course not. I quite understand that."

"Arrest him!" cried Peters.

"We know where to lay our hands on this gentleman if he is wanted," said the sergeant, majestically, "but you'll have to go, Mr. Holmes."

"Yes, Watson, we shall have to go."

A minute later we were in the street once more. Holmes was as cool as ever, but I was hot with anger and humiliation. The sergeant had followed us.

"Sorry, Mr. Holmes, but that's the law."

"Exactly, Sergeant, you could not do otherwise."

"I expect there was good reason for your presence there. If there is anything I can do—"

"It's a missing lady, Sergeant, and we think she is in that house. I expect a warrant presently."

"Then I'll keep my eye on the parties, Mr. Holmes. If anything comes along, I will surely let you know."

It was only nine o'clock, and we were off full cry upon the trail at once. First we drove to Brixton Workhouse Infirmary, where we found that it was indeed the truth that a charitable couple had called some days before, that they had claimed an imbecile old woman as a former servant and that they had obtained permission to take her away with them. No surprise was expressed at the news that she had since died.

The doctor was our next goal. He had been called in, had found the woman dying of pure senility, had actually seen her pass away, and had signed the certificate in due form. "I assure you that everything was perfectly normal and there was no room for foul play in the matter," said he. Nothing in the house had struck him as suspicious, save that for people of their class it was remarkable that they should have no servant. So far and no farther went the doctor.

Finally we found our way to Scotland Yard. There had been difficulties of procedure in regard to the warrant. Some delay was inevitable. The magistrate's signature might not be obtained until next morning. If Holmes would call about nine he could go down with Lestrade and see it acted upon. So ended the day, save that near midnight our friend, the sergeant, called to say that he had seen flickering lights here and there in the windows of the great dark house, but that no one had left it and none had entered. We could but pray for patience, and wait for the morrow.

Sherlock Holmes was too irritable for conversation and too restless for sleep. I left him smoking hard, with his heavy, dark brows knotted together, and his long nervous fingers tapping upon the arms of his chair, as he turned over in his mind every possible solution of the mystery. Several times in the course of the night I heard him prowling about the house. Finally, just after I had been called in the morning, he rushed into my

"Quick, man, quick! It's life or death!"
Frederick Dorr Steele, *American Magazine*, 1911

A funeral procession outside London.
A Hundred Years Ago

room. He was in his dressing-gown, but his pale, hollow-eyed face told me that his night had been a sleepless one.

"What time was the funeral? Eight, was it not?" he asked, eagerly. "Well, it is seven-twenty now. Good heavens, Watson, what has become of any brains that God has given me? Quick, man, quick! It's life or death—a hundred chances on death to one on life. I'll never forgive myself, never, if we are too late!"

Five minutes had not passed before we were flying in a hansom down Baker Street. But even so it was twenty-five to eight as we passed Big Ben, and eight struck as we tore down the Brixton Road. But others were late as well as we. Ten minutes after the hour the hearse was still standing at the door of the house, and even as our foaming horse came to a halt the coffin, supported by three men, appeared on the threshold. Holmes darted forward and barred their way.

"Take it back!" he cried, laying his hand on the breast of the foremost. "Take it back this instant!"

"What the devil do you mean? Once again I ask you, where is your warrant?" shouted the furious Peters, his big red face glaring over the farther end of the coffin.

"The warrant is on its way. This coffin shall remain in the house until it comes."

The authority in Holmes's voice had its effect upon the

34 Dr. Alvin Rodin and Jack D. Key observe that whatever Peters's cleverness elsewhere, his use of chloroform is not particularly ingenious. Chloroform had been used as a medical anaesthetic since Sir James Simpson first administered it in 1847; and the technique gained popular acceptance after Queen Victoria authorised her physician, John Snow, to administer chloroform during the delivery of Prince Leopold, her eighth child, in 1853. Apparently, criminals such as Peters had already discovered alternate uses for chloroform. Rodin and Key find that the substance was used to subdue potential victims during a rash of robberies in 1850. They quote Thomson's 1936 *Story of Scotland Yard*, which reports that "two notorious women used it to render a Mr. Jewett, a solicitor . . . unconscious. He woke to find himself stripped of his clothing and valuables, lying on a filthy bed in a wretched lodging."

"Holmes darted forward and barred their way."
Alec Ball, *Strand Magazine*, 1911

bearers. Peters had suddenly vanished into the house, and they obeyed these new orders. "Quick, Watson, quick! Here is a screw-driver!" he shouted, as the coffin was replaced upon the table. "Here's one for you, my man! A sovereign if the lid comes off in a minute! Ask no questions—work away! That's good! Another! And another! Now pull all together! It's giving! It's giving! Ah, that does it at last!"

With a united effort we tore off the coffin-lid. As we did so there came from the inside a stupefying and overpowering smell of chloroform.[34] A body lay within, its head all wreathed in cotton-wool, which had been soaked in the narcotic. Holmes plucked it off and disclosed the statuesque face of a handsome and spiritual woman of middle age. In an instant he had passed his arm round the figure and raised her to a sitting position.

"Is she gone, Watson? Is there a spark left? Surely we are not too late!"

For half an hour it seemed that we were. What with actual suffocation, and what with the poisonous fumes of the chloroform, the Lady Frances seemed to have passed the last point of recall. And then, at last, with artificial respiration, with injected ether,[35] with every device that science could suggest, some flutter of life, some quiver of the eyelids, some dimming of a mirror, spoke of the slowly returning life. A cab had driven up, and Holmes, parting the blind, looked out at it. "Here is Lestrade with his warrant," said he. "He will find that his birds have flown. And here," he added, as a heavy step hurried along the passage, "is someone who has a better right to nurse this lady than we have. Good morning, Mr. Green; I think that the sooner we can move the Lady Frances the better. Meanwhile, the funeral may proceed, and the poor old woman who still lies in that coffin may go to her last resting-place alone."

"Should you care to add the case to your annals, my dear Watson," said Holmes that evening, "it can only be as an example of that temporary eclipse to which even the best-balanced mind may be exposed. Such slips are common to all mortals, and the greatest is he who can recognize and repair them. To this modified credit I may, perhaps, make some claim. My night was haunted by the thought that somewhere a clue, a strange sentence, a curious observation, had come under my notice and had been too easily dismissed. Then, suddenly, in the grey of the morning, the words came back to me. It was the remark of the undertaker's wife, as reported by Philip Green. She had said, 'It should be there before now. It took longer, being out of the ordinary.' It was the coffin of which she spoke. It had been out of the ordinary. That could only mean that it had been made to some special measurement. But why? Why? Then in an instant I remembered the deep sides, and the little wasted figure at the bottom. Why so large a coffin for so small a body? To leave room for another body. Both would be buried under the one certificate. It had all been so clear, if only my own sight had not been dimmed. At eight the Lady Frances would be buried. Our one chance was to stop the coffin before it left the house.[36]

"It was a desperate chance that we might find her alive, but it *was* a chance, as the result showed. These people had never,

35 While ether in gaseous form was then used as an anaesthetic, it was also recommended in injected form as a stimulant. The *Encyclopædia Britannica* (11th Ed.) calls it "perhaps the most rapid and powerful cardiac stimulant known." The source of the ether that Watson injects here, however, remains a puzzle to D. Martin Dakin, who writes that carrying it around would have required "a black bag of colossal proportions." Presumably, Watson could not have dashed into a local shop to purchase ether, and nor could he have approached a local hospital, which would have demanded he admit the patient rather than treat her himself. "Perhaps," Dakin muses, "although this is not mentioned, the truth is that Holmes, anticipating the need for ether, had asked Watson to bring some; just as he must have pocketed the two screwdrivers he so opportunely produced to open the coffin, and since Peters was not likely to have left such things lying about for their convenience."

36 Philip Weller questions the conduct of the undertakers, who, even if not in league with Lady Frances's kidnappers, "might be considered to be morally guilty by omission, in not passing on the suspicions which must have been aroused during the various stages of their involvement with the burial of Rose Spender."

37 " 'Unusual' might have been a better adjective," Benjamin Clark concludes. "Surely it was a device with truly extraordinary risks. In the first place, the extraction from the workhouse had to be done in an innocent and plausible manner. Then it was important that the Shlessingers pick an inmate who had to be, one might say, 'just right'—not yet dead, but *awful close*: and yet not so close but what she could be moved. A very 'nice' calculation, all things considered."

to my knowledge, done a murder. They might shrink from actual violence at the last. They could bury her with no sign of how she met her end, and even if she were exhumed there was a chance for them. I hoped that such considerations might prevail with them. You can reconstruct the scene well enough. You saw the horrible den upstairs, where the poor lady had been kept so long. They rushed in and overpowered her with their chloroform, carried her down, poured more into the coffin to insure against her waking, and then screwed down the lid. A clever device, Watson.37 It is new to me in the annals of crime. If our ex-missionary friends escape the clutches of Lestrade, I shall expect to hear of some brilliant incidents in their future career." ■

"THEY COULD BURY HER . . ."

THE premature burial that Lady Frances narrowly escaped represented a very real fear in the nineteenth century, albeit one long concentrated in Germany and France. Horrifying stories of presumed corpses having destroyed coffin lids, torn their garments, and even eaten their own fingers in panic and terror (many of these stories, but not all of them, apocryphal) had been circulating for centuries, proliferating in the wake of plague and cholera epidemics and reaching particular intensity during the eighteenth century. Some became the basis for legends of vampires, others fuelled justifiable fears of physicians and the "science" of medicine.

Pivotal to the movement was physician Jean-Jacques Bruhier d'Ablaincourt's translation of a 1740 thesis written, in Latin, by Danish-born anatomist Jacques-Bénigne Winslow. Fervent in his convictions, Winslow claimed to have twice been mistaken for dead himself, only to have been revived each time at the last minute. He stated that traditional methods of determining death were frequently inadequate (which, in fact, they were) and, maintaining that only signs of putrefaction constituted definitive proof, insisted that numerous attempts be made to resuscitate a corpse—including sticking a sharp object up the nose, cutting the feet with razors, and pouring vinegar or urine into the mouth—before preparing it for burial.

Bruhier not only translated Winslow's thesis into French but also added his own treatise, listing further stories and proposing that corpses should rest in mortuaries, supervised by physicians, for a period of seventy-two hours before being buried. Bruhier's book became a publishing sensation and eventually turned into the two-volume *Dissertation sur l'incertitude des signes de la mort*, published as a complete work (and dropping mention of Winslow as coauthor) in 1749. Translated into several languages, Bruhier's books swept through Europe, making their greatest impact in Germany. There, a number of "waiting mortuaries" (known as *Leichenhäuser*) were constructed in the 1790s. Corpses from wealthy families had the privilege of being watched by an attendant or having their lifeless fingers attached by string to a bell. Germany was also the pioneer in inventing security coffins, which were similarly rigged with bells meant to ring at the sign of any movement. The fixation spread to France, where, in the first half of the nineteenth century, doctors published pamphlets suggesting new methods of testing for signs of death. These ranged from holding a corpse's finger above a flame to see if a blister would form, to systemically pulling a corpse's tongue for three hours to aid in artificial respiration.

Britain managed to remain apart from the fray for quite some time. Indeed, as late as 1852, Dr. John Simon, in the *City of London Medical Reports*, decried the custom of delayed burials among the poor, writing, "Fears of premature interment, which had much to do with it, are now seldom spoken of but with a smile." Jan Bondeson, author of the absorbing *Buried Alive: The Terrifying History of Our Most Primal Fear*, writes that when French interest began to pick up in the 1830s, "the [English] medical establishment was wholly complacent, viewing the Continental preoccupation with premature burial with a mixture of amusement and disgust." Some of the French pamphlets made their way to Britain and led to various alarmist articles and books being published throughout the early 1800s, although none particularly caught fire with the general public.

Yet just as French and German fascination with premature burial was waning, the British experienced a late surge, stimulated in large part by the 1896 appearance of *Premature Burial and How It May Be Prevented*, which was written by political activist William Tebb and coauthored by the American Edward

Perry Vollum, M.D. Tebb was an abolitionist and an antivacci-nationist, an aficionado of medical science but not a physician himself. His book attracted its share of exasperated critics, notably among the clergy and the medical establishment—who pointed out the extreme unreliability of newspaper and verbal accounts—but it was generally well received and sold so well that a second edition appeared in 1905. While more extensive than Bruhier's book, *Premature Burial* contained many of the same stories Bruhier had cited, with slight varia-tions. Naturally, Tebb and Vollum dismissed any similarities between accounts, chalking them up to coincidence rather than to any sort of pattern that might have called their veracity into question.

The same year that his book was published, Tebb, ever the savvy promoter, helped form the London Society for the Pre-vention of Premature Burial, primarily to help publicise *Pre-mature Burial*. The society would become the leading agitator in the anti–premature-burial movement, holding regular meet-ings, organising the occasional lecture, and launching a journal, the *Burial Reformer*, in 1905. In addition to reporting on the society's meetings, the journal published articles on premature burial and stories from the world's newspapers. One example is "The Accrington Sensation" (1905), in which Mrs. Elizabeth Holden escaped burial only when an undertaker saw her eye-lid twitch. According to the *Burial Reformer*, her trauma did not preclude her from talking to the press: "pale, wan, extremely weak, she feebly lisped out to a representative of the *Manches-ter Courier* her recollections of her terrible experience." The journal also published poetry, exposing the public to such gems as Mark Melford's "Living with the Dead," printed in 1913 and containing the immortal lines: "Alive! Within the jaws of death, / No fate was ever worse! / No enemy invoked on me / So terrible a curse! / Conveyed still living to my grave! / Within a funeral hearse." It was clear that by this time, the journal, now named *Perils of Premature Burial*, had taken on an increasingly sensationalist tone, running stories—such as that of a baby found within its coffin, sucking placidly from a bot-tle—that were frankly preposterous. Its audience dwindling, the journal ceased publication in 1914, although the society itself continued to exist until the 1930s.

Edgar Allan Poe and Wilkie Collins were among those literary figures sufficiently spooked by the prospect of being buried alive, or at least intrigued by it, to pen fiction in which premature burial played a central role. Poe, of course, qualifies as "[t]he writer with the most premature burials per page," according to Bondeson. "[His] unwholesome fascination with this subject is apparent to every devotee of his horror stories." Chief among these is "The Premature Burial" (1844), in which the protagonist so fears being buried alive that he takes elaborate precautions to avoid the scenario—preparations that come to naught when he suffers a cataleptic fit while travelling (see "The Resident Patient," note 8). Poe's creepy tale was made into a macabre 1962 film by Roger Corman, starring the fine actor Ray Milland as the death-obsessed protagonist (Milland also appeared in the 1984 Sherlock Holmes film *The Masks of Death*, starring Peter Cushing as Holmes). Wilkie Collins and Mark Twain both wrote works of fiction set in waiting mortuaries, and other authors wrote stories featuring characters, presumed dead, who saved themselves from a horrible fate by belatedly awakening and extracting themselves from their coffins. But in terms of sheer enthusiasm, none of these writers matched Friederike Kempner, who made a name for herself by writing, in German, a popular 1853 pamphlet on the subject. She also wrote poetry, including "The Prematurely Buried Child," which describes a "coffin'd child" crying out, "Mummy, where are you!?" and continues in similarly dramatic fashion: "His bloody hands they knock / Unyielding coffin walls / Half dead with fright and shock / 'Hear, I am not dead!' / But no one heeds his call."

Regardless of whether Lady Frances suffered from "taphophobia," as the fear of premature burial has been termed, Holmes surely saved her from becoming what John Snart, author of the near-hysterical *Thesaurus of Horror, or, The Charnel-House Explored* (1817), deemed "a fermentable mass of *murdered, senseless, decomposing matter*!!!"

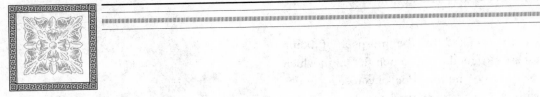

THE ADVENTURE OF THE DEVIL'S FOOT[1]

The exploration of Africa captured the public imagination in the mid-nineteenth century, but the continent was no longer considered terra incognita *by 1897, when the events of "The Devil's Foot" occurred (or 1910, when it was published). Hence the "great lion hunter and explorer" Dr. Leon Sterndale, the central figure of the case, is already something of an anomaly—even a bit of a caricature—when Holmes and Watson encounter him while on holiday in Cornwall. The case has been scrutinised in detail by scholars, who argue over the Cornwall locations and the nature of the "devilish drug" (reminiscent of LSD and PCP), but its real value lies in the revelation of the depth of the friendship between Holmes and Watson. Here, too, is the unforgettable repartée between Holmes and a suspect: "I followed you." "I saw no one." "That is what you may expect to see when I follow you."*

1 "The Devil's Foot" was published in the *Strand Magazine* in December 1910. The manuscript is in the Berg Collection of the New York Public Library.

IN RECORDING FROM time to time some of the curious experiences and interesting recollections which I associate with my long and intimate friendship with Mr. Sherlock Holmes, I have continually been faced by difficulties caused by his own aversion to publicity. To his sombre and cynical spirit all popular applause was always abhorrent, and nothing amused him more at the end of a successful case than to hand over the actual exposure to some orthodox official, and to listen with a mocking smile to the general chorus of misplaced congratulation. It was indeed this attitude upon the part of my friend, and certainly not any lack of interesting material which has caused me of late years to lay very few of my records before the public. My participation in some of his adventures was always a privilege which entailed discretion and reticence upon me.

It was, then, with considerable surprise that I received a telegram from Holmes last Tuesday—he has never been known to write where a telegram would serve—in the following terms:

> Why not tell them of the Cornish horror—strangest case I have handled.

I have no idea what backward sweep of memory had brought the matter fresh to his mind, or what freak had caused him to desire that I should recount it; but I hasten, before another cancelling telegram may arrive, to hunt out the notes which give me the exact details of the case, and to lay the narrative before my readers.

It was, then, in the spring of the year 1897 that Holmes's iron constitution showed some symptoms of giving way in the face of constant hard work of a most exacting kind,[2] aggravated, perhaps, by occasional indiscretions of his own.[3] In March of that year Dr. Moore Agar,[4] of Harley Street,[5] whose dramatic introduction to Holmes I may some day recount,[6] gave positive injunctions that the famous private agent would[7] lay aside all his cases and surrender himself to complete rest if he wished to avert an absolute break-down. The state of his health was not a matter in which he himself took the faintest interest, for his mental detachment was absolute, but he was induced at last, on the threat of being permanently disqualified from work, to give himself a complete change of scene and air. Thus it was that in the early spring of that year we found ourselves together in a small cottage near Poldhu Bay,[8] at the further extremity of the Cornish peninsula.[9]

It was a singular spot, and one peculiarly well suited to the grim humour of my patient. From the windows of our little white-washed house, which stood high upon a grassy headland, we looked down upon the whole sinister semicircle of Mounts Bay,[10] that old death trap of sailing vessels, with its fringe of black cliffs and surge-swept reefs on which innumerable seamen have met their end. With a northerly breeze it lies placid and sheltered, inviting the storm-tossed craft to tack into it for rest and protection.

Then comes the sudden swirl round of the wind, the blustering gale from the south-west, the dragging anchor, the lee shore,[11] and the last battle in the creaming breakers. The wise mariner stands far out from that evil place.

---

2 A recurrence, June Thomson suggests, of the toll of Holmes's "workaholism" recorded in "The Reigate Squires."

3 Watson must refer here to Holmes's drug habit, from which Watson reported weaning him in "The Missing Three-Quarter." He there stated, however, that "I was well aware that the [drug] fiend was not dead but sleeping," and that Holmes's cure was not permanent—the sleep was "a light one and the waking near when in periods of idleness I have seen the drawn look upon Holmes's ascetic face." Earle F. Walbridge interprets the phrase differently, suggesting that Holmes's "indiscretions" consisted of over-indulgence in oysters, which Walbridge terms "one of Holmes's little weaknesses" (mentioning his indulgence of Athelney Jones in *The Sign of Four* and his babbling of oysters in "The Dying Detective").

4 Charles Thomas, writing as "Percy Trevelyan," in *Mr. Holmes in Cornwall* identifies Agar as the cousin of the Agar-Robartes family, chief landowners of the parish of Mullion. He suggests that Dr. Agar specifically directed Holmes to travel to Poldhu, thinking that his cousins might be of assistance and that the ozone-laden air of Cornwall would have "therapeutic values."

5 This street in London's Cavendish Square was associated almost exclusively with medical practices; in "The Resident Patient," Dr. Percy Trevelyan mentions having set up shop in the area (see "The Resident Patient," note 9).

6 Watson never published this case.

7 The word is "should" in the *Strand Magazine* text, perhaps a significant difference in light of subsequent events.

8 On December 12, 1901, the world's first

transatlantic radio transmission (consisting of three Morse code dots, or the letter "S") was sent from Poldhu, Cornwall, to St. John's, Newfoundland, where it was received by the Italian physicist Guglielmo Marconi (1874–1937). See "His Last Bow," note 22. There is no actual Poldhu Bay, but there is a Poldhu Cove in Mounts Bay.

9 Watson means the *southern* extremity, according to Philip Weller, although, as Weller points out, Poldhu Cove in fact lies four miles off Lizard Point, the true southernmost point of the peninsula (as well as the southernmost point in England).

10 Located at the point where the English Channel meets the Atlantic Ocean, the area of sheltered Mounts Bay provided the setting for W. S. Gilbert and Arthur Sullivan's 1879 operetta *The Pirates of Penzance*. The town of Penzance, overlooking Mounts Bay, was subjected to occasional Mediterranean pirate raids up until the eighteenth century.

11 The part of the shore that is sheltered from the wind.

12 Cornish was a member of the Brythonic, or British, subfamily of the Celtic language, spoken by the Britons during the time of Julius Caesar. The other British languages include Breton and Welsh, both of which are still in use. The earliest recorded examples of Cornish date back to the tenth century A.D., and while the language was spoken by residents of Cornwall, it died out completely in the eighteenth century.

13 The Semitic language of Chaldean, better known as Aramaic, resembles Hebrew, Syriac, and Phoenician. After Aramaeans brought the language with them to Syria in the seventh century B.C., it became the common language of the Fertile Crescent and for a time served

On the land side our surroundings were as sombre as on the sea. It was a country of rolling moors, lonely and dun-coloured, with an occasional church tower to mark the site of some old-world village. In every direction upon these moors there were traces of some vanished race which had passed utterly away, and left as its sole record strange monuments of stone, irregular mounds which contained the burned ashes of the dead, and curious earthworks which hinted at prehistoric strife. The glamour and mystery of the place, with its sinister atmosphere of forgotten nations, appealed to the imagination of my friend, and he spent much of his time in long walks and solitary meditations upon the moor. The ancient Cornish language[12] had also arrested his attention, and he had, I remember, conceived the idea that it was akin to the Chaldean,[13] and had been largely derived from the Phoenician[14] traders in tin. He had

"Holmes spent much of his time in long walks and solitary meditations."
Gilbert Holiday, *Strand Magazine*, 1910

received a consignment of books upon philology and was settling down to develop this thesis, when suddenly, to my sorrow
and to his unfeigned delight, we found ourselves, even in that
land of dreams, plunged into a problem at our very doors which
was more intense, more engrossing, and infinitely more mysterious than any of those which had driven us from London. Our
simple life and peaceful, healthy routine were violently interrupted, and we were precipitated into the midst of a series of
events which caused the utmost excitement not only in Cornwall, but throughout the whole West of England. Many of my
readers may retain some recollection of what was called at the
time "The Cornish Horror," though a most imperfect account
of the matter reached the London Press. Now, after thirteen
years I will give the true details of this inconceivable affair to
the public.

I have said that scattered towers marked the villages which
dotted this part of Cornwall. The nearest of these was the hamlet of Tredannick Wollas, where the cottages of a couple of
hundred inhabitants clustered round an ancient, moss-grown
church. The vicar of the parish, Mr. Roundhay,[15] was something of an archæologist, and as such Holmes had made his
acquaintance. He was a middle-aged man, portly and affable,
with a considerable fund of local lore. At his invitation we had
taken tea at the vicarage, and had come to know, also, Mr. Mortimer Tregennis, an independent gentleman, who increased
the clergyman's scanty resources by taking rooms in his large,
straggling house. The vicar, being a bachelor, was glad to come
to such an arrangement, though he had little in common with
his lodger, who was a thin, dark, spectacled man, with a stoop
which gave the impression of actual, physical deformity. I
remember that during our short visit we found the vicar garrulous, but his lodger strangely reticent, a sad-faced, introspective man, sitting with averted eyes, brooding apparently upon
his own affairs.

These were the two men who entered abruptly into our little sitting-room on Tuesday, March the 16th, shortly after our
breakfast hour, as we were smoking together, preparatory to
our daily excursion upon the moors.

"Mr. Holmes," said the vicar, in an agitated voice, "the most
extraordinary and tragic affair has occurred during the night. It
is the most unheard-of business. We can only regard it as a spe-

as the official language of the Persian empire.
In the sixth century B.C., Aramaic supplanted
Hebrew as the spoken language of the Jews,
although Hebrew remained in use for religious and government functions. Jesus Christ
and his apostles were said to have spoken Aramaic—portions of the Old Testament and the
Jewish prayer for the dead, known as the *kad-
dish* and still used in contemporary Jewish
liturgy, are written in the language—and it
was widely spoken in Palestine and Syria until
the sixth century A.D., when Arabic became
the dominant language.

14 The Phoenicians were the ancient Semitic
inhabitants of what is now Lebanon, and were
known for their extensive trading and colonisation ventures. Their travels took them as far
away as England, probably during the first
millennium B.C., although the trading may
have ceased when Phoenicia became a mere
province of the Persian Empire after 539 B.C.
According to Bernard Davies, writing in "The
Ancient Cornish Language," if Holmes
indeed asserted the linguistic theory that Watson attributes to him, he must also have
known that that theory was not original. "The
briefest study of the subject would have
shown," remarks Davies, "that it had been
around for a very long while—certainly since
Renaissance times." However, linguistic studies in the early nineteenth century by scholars
such as Rasmus Rask, Franz Bopp, and fairy-
tale collector Jakob Grimm subsequently
showed that the sources of the Cornish language were many members of the Indo-
European family of languages, including
ancient Celtic, Latin, Greek, Russian, and
ancient Sanskrit. While Holmes may well
have been interested in the history of the language, then, Watson must have misunderstood Holmes to have asserted the idea of a
single Chaldean source.

15 Charles Thomas identifies Mr. Roundhay

as the Reverend James Henry Scholefield of
Corpus Christi College, Cambridge, the Vicar
of Mullion in 1897.

"'The most extraordinary and tragic affair has occurred
during the night,' said the vicar."
Gilbert Holiday, *Strand Magazine*, 1910

cial Providence that you should chance to be here at the time,
for in all England you are the one man we need."

I glared at the intrusive vicar with no very friendly eyes; but
Holmes took his pipe from his lips and sat up in his chair like
an old hound who hears the view-halloa. He waved his hand to
the sofa, and our palpitating visitor with his agitated companion sat side by side upon it. Mr. Mortimer Tregennis was more
self-contained than the clergyman, but the twitching of his
thin hands and the brightness of his dark eyes showed that
they shared a common emotion.

"Shall I speak or you?" he asked of the vicar.

"Well, as you seem to have made the discovery, whatever it may be, and the vicar to have had it second-hand, perhaps you had better do the speaking," said Holmes.

I glanced at the hastily-clad clergyman, with the formally-dressed lodger seated beside him, and was amused at the surprise which Holmes's simple deduction had brought to their faces.

"Perhaps I had best say a few words first," said the vicar, "and then you can judge if you will listen to the details from Mr. Tregennis, or whether we should not hasten at once to the scene of this mysterious affair. I may explain, then, that our friend here spent last evening in the company of his two brothers, Owen and George, and of his sister Brenda, at their house of Tredannick Wartha, which is near the old stone cross[16] upon the moor. He left them shortly after ten o'clock, playing cards round the dining-room table, in excellent health and spirits. This morning, being an early riser, he walked in that direction before breakfast, and was overtaken by the carriage of Dr. Richards, who explained that he had just been sent for on a most urgent call to Tredannick Wartha. Mr. Mortimer Tregennis naturally went with him. When he arrived at Tredannick Wartha he found an extraordinary state of things. His two brothers and his sister were seated round the table exactly as he had left them, the cards still spread in front of them and the candles burned down to their sockets. The sister lay back stone-dead in her chair, while the two brothers sat on each side of her laughing, shouting, and singing, the senses stricken clean out of them. All three of them, the dead woman and the two demented men, retained upon their faces an expression of the utmost horror—a convulsion of terror which was dreadful to look upon. There was no sign of the presence of anyone in the house, except Mrs. Porter, the old cook and housekeeper, who declared that she had slept deeply and heard no sound during the night. Nothing had been stolen or disarranged, and there is absolutely no explanation of what the horror can be which has frightened a woman to death and two strong men out of their senses. There is the situation, Mr. Holmes, in a nutshell, and if you can help us to clear it up you will have done a great work."

I had hoped that in some way I could coax my companion back into the quiet which had been the object of our journey;

16 There is indeed a prominent stone cross on the moor, just north of Predannack Wartha.

17 This is simply wrong, according to Pamela Bruxner; there is no stone cross on the moor a mile away in any direction from the coastline of the Bay. "Mr. Roundhay was of course in an agitated state of mind at the time, and Watson's notes, as we know, were not always models of accuracy."

but one glance at his intense face and contracted eyebrows told me how vain was now the expectation. He sat for some little time in silence, absorbed in the strange drama which had broken in upon our peace.

"I will look into this matter," he said at last. "On the face of it, it would appear to be a case of a very exceptional nature. Have you been there yourself, Mr. Roundhay?"

"No, Mr. Holmes. Mr. Tregennis brought back the account to the vicarage, and I at once hurried over with him to consult you."

"How far is it to the house where this singular tragedy occurred?"

"About a mile inland."[17]

"Then we shall walk over together. But, before we start, I must ask you a few questions, Mr. Mortimer Tregennis."

The other had been silent all this time, but I had observed that his more controlled excitement was even greater than the obtrusive emotion of the clergyman. He sat with a pale, drawn face, his anxious gaze fixed upon Holmes, and his thin hands clasped convulsively together. His pale lips quivered as he listened to the dreadful experience which had befallen his family, and his dark eyes seemed to reflect something of the horror of the scene.

"Ask what you like, Mr. Holmes," said he eagerly. "It is a bad thing to speak of, but I will answer you the truth."

"Tell me about last night."

"Well, Mr. Holmes, I supped there, as the vicar has said, and my elder brother George proposed a game of whist afterwards. We sat down about nine o'clock. It was a quarter-past ten when I moved to go. I left them all round the table, as merry as could be."

"Who let you out?"

"Mrs. Porter had gone to bed, so I let myself out. I shut the hall door behind me. The window of the room in which they sat was closed, but the blind was not drawn down. There was no change in door or window this morning, nor any reason to think that any stranger had been to the house. Yet there they sat, driven clean mad with terror, and Brenda lying dead of fright, with her head hanging over the arm of the chair. I'll never get the sight of that room out of my mind so long as I live."

"The facts, as you state them, are certainly most remarkable," said Holmes. "I take it that you have no theory yourself which can in any way account for them?"

"It's devilish, Mr. Holmes; devilish!" cried Mortimer Tregennis. "It is not of this world. Something has come into that room which has dashed the light of reason from their minds. What human contrivance could do that?"

"I fear," said Holmes, "that if the matter is beyond humanity it is certainly beyond me. Yet we must exhaust all natural explanations before we fall back upon such a theory as this. As to yourself, Mr. Tregennis, I take it you were divided in some way from your family, since they lived together and you had rooms apart?"

"That is so, Mr. Holmes, though the matter is past and done with. We were a family of tin-miners at Redruth, but we sold out our venture to a company, and so retired with enough to keep us. I won't deny that there was some feeling about the division of the money and it stood between us for a time, but it was all forgiven and forgotten, and we were the best of friends together."

"Looking back at the evening which you spent together, does anything stand out in your memory as throwing any possible light upon the tragedy? Think carefully, Mr. Tregennis, for any clue which can help me."

"There is nothing at all, sir."

"Your people were in their usual spirits?"

"Never better."

"Were they nervous people? Did they ever show any apprehension of coming danger?"

"Nothing of the kind."

"You have nothing to add then, which could assist me?"

Mortimer Tregennis considered earnestly for a moment.

"There is one thing occurs to me," said he at last. "As we sat at the table my back was to the window, and my brother George, he being my partner at cards,[18] was facing it. I saw him once look hard over my shoulder, so I turned round and looked also. The blind was up and the window shut, but I could just make out the bushes on the lawn, and it seemed to me for a moment that I saw something moving among them. I couldn't even say if it were man or animal, but I just thought there was something there. When I asked him what he was looking at, he told me that he had the same feeling. That is all that I can say."

18 Bob Jones, in "A Missed Clue in The Devil's Foot," points out that this is a lie, which Holmes should have recognised immediately. Whist is a game played by two teams of two, seated *opposite* each other. If George had been Mortimer's partner, then Brenda and Owen would have been seated opposite each other, not next to each other, as is described.

"Did you not investigate?"

"No; the matter passed as unimportant."

"You left them, then, without any premonition of evil?"

"None at all."

"I am not clear how you came to hear the news so early this morning."

"I am an early riser, and generally take a walk before breakfast. This morning I had hardly started when the doctor in his carriage overtook me. He told me that old Mrs. Porter had sent a boy down with an urgent message. I sprang in beside him and we drove on. When we got there we looked into that dreadful room. The candles and the fire must have burned out hours before, and they had been sitting there in the dark until dawn had broken. The doctor said Brenda must have been dead at least six hours. There were no signs of violence. She just lay across the arm of the chair with that look on her face. George and Owen were singing snatches of songs and gibbering like two great apes. Oh, it was awful to see! I couldn't stand it, and the doctor was as white as a sheet. Indeed, he fell into a chair in a sort of faint, and we nearly had him on our hands as well."

"Remarkable—most remarkable!" said Holmes, rising and taking his hat. "I think, perhaps, we had better go down to Tredannick Wartha without further delay. I confess that I have seldom known a case which at first sight presented a more singular problem."

Our proceedings of that first morning did little to advance the investigation. It was marked, however, at the outset by an incident which left the most sinister impression upon my mind. The approach to the spot at which the tragedy occurred is down a narrow, winding, country lane. While we made our way along it we heard the rattle of a carriage coming towards us, and stood aside to let it pass. As it drove by us I caught a glimpse through the closed window of a horribly contorted, grinning face glaring out at us. Those staring eyes and gnashing teeth flashed past us like a dreadful vision.

"My brothers!" cried Mortimer Tregennis, white to his lips. "They are taking them to Helston."

We looked with horror after the black carriage, lumbering

19 "Flower-pots" in the English first edition.

"Those staring eyes and gnashing teeth flashed past us
like a dreadful vision."
Gilbert Holiday, *Strand Magazine*, 1910

upon its way. Then we turned our steps towards this ill-omened house in which they had met their strange fate.

It was a large and bright dwelling, rather a villa than a cottage, with a considerable garden which was already, in that Cornish air, well filled with spring flowers. Towards this garden the window of the sitting-room fronted, and from it, according to Mortimer Tregennis, must have come that thing of evil which had by sheer horror in a single instant blasted their minds. Holmes walked slowly and thoughtfully among the flower-plots[19] and along the path before we entered the porch. So absorbed was he in his thoughts, I remember, that he stumbled over the watering-pot, upset its contents, and deluged both our feet and the garden path. Inside the house we were met by the elderly Cornish housekeeper, Mrs. Porter, who, with the aid of a young girl, looked after the wants of the family. She readily answered all Holmes's questions. She had heard nothing in the night. Her employers had all been in excellent spirits lately, and she had never known them more cheerful and prosperous. She had fainted with horror upon entering the room in the morning and seeing that dreadful company round the table. She had, when she recovered, thrown open the window to let the morning air in, and had run down to the lane, whence she sent a farm-lad for the doctor. The lady was on her bed upstairs, if we cared to see her. It took four strong men to get the brothers into the asylum carriage. She would not herself stay in the house another day, and was starting that very afternoon to rejoin her family at St. Ives.

We ascended the stairs and viewed the body. Miss Brenda Tregennis had been a very beautiful girl, though now verging upon middle age. Her dark, clear-cut face was handsome, even in death, but there still lingered upon it something of that convulsion of horror which had been her last human emotion. From her bedroom we descended to the sitting-room where this strange tragedy had actually occurred. The charred ashes of the overnight fire lay in the grate. On the table were the four guttered and burned-out candles, with the cards scattered over its surface. The chairs had been moved back against the walls, but all else was as it had been the night before. Holmes paced with light, swift steps about the room; he sat in the various chairs, drawing them up and reconstructing their positions. He tested how much of the garden was visible; he examined the floor, the ceiling, and the fireplace; but never once did I see that sudden brightening of his eyes and tightening of his lips which would have told me that he saw some gleam of light in this utter darkness.

"Why a fire?" he asked once. "Had they always a fire in this small room on a spring evening?"

Mortimer Tregennis explained that the night was cold and damp. For that reason, after his arrival, the fire was lit. "What are you going to do now, Mr. Holmes?" he asked.

My friend smiled and laid his hand upon my arm. "I think, Watson, that I shall resume that course of tobacco-poisoning which you have so often and so justly condemned," said he.

"We ascended the stairs and viewed the body."
Gilbert Holiday, *Strand Magazine*, 1910

"With your permission, gentlemen, we will now return to our cottage, for I am not aware that any new factor is likely to come to our notice here. I will turn the facts over in my mind, Mr. Tregennis, and should anything occur to me I will certainly communicate with you and the vicar. In the meantime I wish you both good morning."

It was not until long after we were back in Poldhu Cottage that Holmes broke his complete and absorbed silence. He sat coiled in his armchair, his haggard and ascetic face hardly visible amid the blue swirl of his tobacco smoke, his black brows drawn down, his forehead contracted, his eyes vacant and far away. Finally, he laid down his pipe and sprang to his feet.

"It won't do, Watson!" said he, with a laugh. "Let us walk along the cliffs together and search for flint arrows. We are more likely to find them than clues to this problem. To let the brain work without sufficient material is like racing an engine. It racks itself to pieces. The sea air, sunshine, and patience, Watson—all else will come.

"Now, let us calmly define our position, Watson," he continued, as we skirted the cliffs together. "Let us get a firm grip of the very little which we do know, so that when fresh facts arise we may be ready to fit them into their places. I take it, in the first place, that neither of us is prepared to admit diabolical intrusions into the affairs of men. Let us begin by ruling that entirely out of our minds. Very good. There remain three persons who have been grievously stricken by some conscious or unconscious human agency. That is firm ground. Now, when did this occur? Evidently, assuming his narrative to be true, it was immediately after Mr. Mortimer Tregennis had left the room. That is a very important point. The presumption is that it was within a few minutes afterwards. The cards still lay upon the table. It was already past their usual hour for bed. Yet they had not changed their position or pushed back their chairs. I repeat, then, that the occurrence was immediately after his departure, and not later than eleven o'clock last night.

"Our next obvious step is to check, so far as we can, the movements of Mortimer Tregennis after he left the room. In this there is no difficulty, and they seem to be above suspicion. Knowing my methods as you do, you were, of course, conscious of the somewhat clumsy water-pot expedient by which I obtained a clearer impress of his foot than might otherwise have been possible. The wet, sandy path took it admirably. Last night was also wet, you will remember, and it was not difficult—having obtained a sample print—to pick out his track among others and to follow his movements. He appears to have walked away swiftly in the direction of the vicarage.

"If, then, Mortimer Tregennis disappeared from the scene, and yet some outside person affected the card-players, how can we reconstruct that person, and how was such an impression of horror conveyed? Mrs. Porter may be eliminated. She is evidently harmless. Is there any evidence that someone crept up to the garden window and in some manner produced so terrific an effect that he drove those who saw it out of their senses? The only suggestion in this direction comes from Mortimer Tregennis himself, who says that his brother spoke about some movement in the garden. That is certainly remarkable, as the night was rainy, cloudy, and dark. Anyone who had the design to alarm these people would be compelled to place his very face against the glass before he could be seen. There is a three-foot flower-border outside this window, but no indication of a footmark. It is difficult to imagine, then, how an outsider could have made so terrible an impression upon the company, nor have we found any possible motive for so strange and elaborate an attempt. You perceive our difficulties, Watson?"

"They are only too clear," I answered, with conviction.

"And yet, with a little more material, we may prove that they are not insurmountable," said Holmes. "I fancy that among your extensive archives, Watson, you may find some which were nearly as obscure. Meanwhile, we shall put the case aside until more accurate data are available, and devote the rest of our morning to the pursuit of neolithic man."

I may have commented upon my friend's power of mental detachment, but never have I wondered at it more than upon that spring morning in Cornwall when for two hours he discoursed upon celts,[20] arrowheads, and shards, as lightly as if no sinister mystery was waiting for his solution. It was not until we had returned in the afternoon to our cottage that we found a visitor awaiting us, who soon brought our minds back to the matter in hand. Neither of us needed to be told who that visitor was. The huge body, the craggy and deeply-seamed face with the fierce eyes and hawk-like nose, the grizzled hair which nearly brushed our cottage ceiling, the beard—golden at the fringes and white near the lips, save for the nicotine stain from his perpetual cigar—all these were as well known in London as in Africa, and could only be associated with the tremendous personality of Dr. Leon Sterndale,[21] the great lion-hunter and explorer.[22]

We had heard of his presence in the district, and had once or twice caught sight of his tall figure upon the moorland paths. He made no advances to us, however, nor would we have dreamed of doing so to him, as it was well known that it was his love of seclusion which caused him to spend the greater part of the intervals between his journeys in a small bungalow buried in the lonely wood of Beauchamp Arriance.[23] Here, amid his books and his maps, he lived an absolutely lonely life, attending to his own simple wants, and paying little apparent heed to the affairs of his neighbours. It was a surprise to me, therefore, to hear him asking Holmes in an eager voice, whether he had made any advance in his reconstruction of this mysterious episode. "The county police are utterly at fault," said he; "but perhaps your wider experience has suggested some conceivable explanation. My only claim to being taken into your confidence is that during my many residences here I have come to know this family of Tregennis very well—indeed, upon my Cornish mother's side I could call them cousins—and their strange fate has naturally been a great shock to me. I may tell

20 In the English book text (but not the *Strand Magazine* or American book text), the word is "Celts." Although Celts are persons of Celtic ancestry, based on the context Holmes is more likely referring to celts, which are prehistoric stone tools ground into wedge- or chisel-like shapes.

21 Charles Thomas suggests that Sterndale is the nephew of Richard Lemon Lander (1804–1834) of Truro, Cornwall, a pioneering explorer of West Africa. On an 1830–1831 expedition, he discovered the source of the Niger River in the Bight of Benin. He was killed by tribesmen on an 1832–1834 trading expedition up the Niger.

22 Several other great explorers of Africa may have inspired Sterndale to choose that continent as his travelling grounds. The famed David Livingstone (1813–1873), for example, was a Scottish missionary whose thirty-year African odyssey started in South Africa as a member of the London Missionary Society in 1841. His part in the discovery of Lake Ngami in 1849 earned him a gold medal from the British National Geographic Society. In 1853, saying, "I shall open up a path into the interior, or perish," Livingstone set off with a small party of Africans, reaching Luanda after a gruelling six-month expedition. Making his way homeward along the Zambezi River, Livingstone discovered Victoria Falls in 1855 and became a hero in Britain, having inspired public curiosity about the uncharted wilds of Africa. Named British consul at Quelimane, he returned to Africa in 1857 to explore the Zambezi region in 1857–1863; but his determination to uncover the source of the Nile brought Livingstone his greatest celebrity. Arriving in Africa in 1866, Livingstone discovered Lake Mweru and Lake Bangweulu before reaching Nyangwe, farther west in Africa than any European had ever travelled. Illness forced Livingstone to return to Ujiji on

Lake Tanganyika, and it was there that Henry Stanley—a *New York Herald* reporter sent to find the missing explorer and bring him food and medicine—came upon him on November 10, 1871, and uttered the immortal words, "Dr. Livingstone, I presume?" Stanley joined him on a journey to Unyanyembe but was unable to persuade Livingstone to leave the continent. Livingstone pressed onward, still seeking the source of the Nile. He died in 1873 in the village of Chitambo, in what is now Zambia, and was buried with great ceremony in Westminster Abbey—although his heart remained behind in Africa, having been removed by his African servants and buried in the soil there.

Far more successful in locating the source of the Nile was John Speke (1827–1864), who with Sir Richard Burton discovered Lake Tanganyika in February 1858. Journeying on alone, Speke reached the lake believed to be the legendary source of the Nile on July 30. He named it Lake Victoria and was honoured by the National Geographic Society for his efforts. Burton disputed Speke's claim, but Speke, on a return journey to Lake Victoria in 1862, was able to identify the Nile's exit from the lake at the spot he named Ripon Falls. Speke was killed by his own gun on a hunting expedition in 1864.

The African hunter-adventurer was a popular subject of books as well, such as the works of H. Rider Haggard, recording the tales of Allan Quatermain, the hero of fourteen books including *King Solomon's Mines* (1885)—the latter one of the best-selling books of the nineteenth century. Quatermain, the quintessential "Great White Adventurer," became the subject of numerous films, and, most recently, has been revealed by writer Alan Moore to have been a member of the League of Extraordinary Gentlemen, an alliance of secret agents probably formed by Mycroft Holmes.

23 Venton or Venten or Fenten (variant spellings) Arriance is noted on period maps as a residence one mile southwest of Poldhu Cove.

you that I had got as far as Plymouth upon my way to Africa, but the news reached me this morning, and I came straight back again to help in the inquiry."

Holmes raised his eyebrows.

"Did you lose your boat through it?"

"I will take the next."

"Dear me! that is friendship indeed."

"I tell you they were relatives."

"Quite so—cousins of your mother. Was your baggage aboard the ship?"

"Some of it, but the main part at the hotel."

"I see. But surely this event could not have found its way into the Plymouth morning papers?"

"No, sir; I had a telegram."

"Might I ask from whom?"

A shadow passed over the gaunt face of the explorer.

"You are very inquisitive, Mr. Holmes."

"It is my business."

With an effort, Dr. Sterndale recovered his ruffled composure.

"I have no objection to telling you," he said. "It was Mr. Roundhay, the vicar, who sent me the telegram which recalled me."

"Thank you," said Holmes. "I may say in answer to your original question, that I have not cleared my mind entirely on the subject of this case, but that I have every hope of reaching some conclusion. It would be premature to say more."

"Perhaps you would not mind telling me if your suspicions point in any particular direction?"

"No, I can hardly answer that."

"Then I have wasted my time, and need not prolong my visit." The famous doctor strode out of our cottage in considerable ill-humour, and within five minutes Holmes had followed him. I saw him no more until the evening, when he returned with a slow step and haggard face which assured me that he had made no great progress with his investigation. He glanced at a telegram which awaited him, and threw it in the grate.

"From the Plymouth hotel, Watson," he said. "I learned the name of it from the vicar, and I wired to make certain that Dr. Leon Sterndale's account was true. It appears that he did indeed spend last night there, and that he has actually allowed some of his baggage to go on to Africa, while he returned to be present at this investigation. What do you make of that, Watson?"

"He is deeply interested."

"Deeply interested—yes. There is a thread here which we have not yet grasped, and which might lead us through the tangle. Cheer up, Watson, for I am very sure that our material has not yet all come to hand. When it does, we may soon leave our difficulties behind us."

Little did I think how soon the words of Holmes would be realised, or how strange and sinister would be that new development which opened up an entirely fresh line of investigation. I was shaving at my window in the morning when I heard the rattle of hoofs, and, looking up, saw a dogcart coming at a gallop down the road. It pulled up at our door, and our friend the vicar sprang from it and rushed up our garden path. Holmes was already dressed, and we hastened down to meet him.

Our visitor was so excited that he could hardly articulate, but at last in gasps and bursts his tragic story came out of him.

"We are devil-ridden, Mr. Holmes! My poor parish is devil-ridden!" he cried. "Satan himself is loose in it! We are given over into his hands!" He danced about in his agitation, a ludicrous object if it were not for his ashy face and startled eyes. Finally he shot out his terrible news.

"Mr. Mortimer Tregennis died during the night, and with exactly the same symptoms as the rest of his family."

Holmes sprang to his feet, all energy in an instant.

"Can you fit us both into your dogcart?"

"Yes, I can."

"Then, Watson, we will postpone our breakfast. Mr. Roundhay, we are entirely at your disposal. Hurry—hurry, before things get disarranged."

The lodger occupied two rooms at the vicarage, which were in an angle by themselves, the one above the other. Below was a large sitting-room; above, his bedroom. They looked out upon a croquet lawn which came up to the windows. We had arrived before the doctor or the police, so that everything was absolutely undisturbed. Let me describe exactly the scene as we saw it upon that misty March morning. It has left an impression which can never be effaced from my mind.

The atmosphere of the room was of a horrible and depressing stuffiness. The servant who had first entered had thrown up the window, or it would have been even more intolerable. This might partly be due to the fact that a lamp stood flaring and smoking on the centre table. Beside it sat the dead man, leaning back in his chair, his thin beard projecting, his spectacles pushed up on to his forehead, and his lean, dark face turned towards the window and twisted into the same distortion of terror which had marked the features of his dead sister. His limbs were convulsed and his fingers contorted as though he had died in a very paroxysm of fear. He was fully clothed, though there were signs that his dressing had been done in a

"Beside it sat the dead man, leaning back in his chair."
Gilbert Holiday, *Strand Magazine*, 1910

24 A hand-lamp with a tall *standard*, or stem.

hurry. We had already learned that his bed had been slept in, and that the tragic end had come to him in the early morning.

One realised the red-hot energy which underlay Holmes's phlegmatic exterior when one saw the sudden change which came over him from the moment that he entered the fatal apartment. In an instant he was tense and alert, his eyes shining, his face set, his limbs quivering with eager activity. He was out on the lawn, in through the window, round the room, and up into the bedroom, for all the world like a dashing foxhound drawing a cover. In the bedroom he made a rapid cast around, and ended by throwing open the window, which appeared to give him some fresh cause for excitement, for he leaned out of it with loud ejaculations of interest and delight. Then he rushed down the stair, out through the open window, threw himself upon his face on the lawn, sprang up and into the room once more, all with the energy of the hunter who is at the very heels of his quarry. The lamp, which was an ordinary standard,[24] he examined with minute care, making certain measurements upon its bowl. He carefully scrutinised with his lens the talc shield which covered the top of the chimney, and scraped off some ashes which adhered to its upper surface, putting some of them into an envelope, which he placed in his pocket-book. Finally, just as the doctor and the official police put in an appearance, he beckoned to the vicar and we all three went out upon the lawn.

"I am glad to say that my investigation has not been entirely barren," he remarked. "I cannot remain to discuss the matter with the police, but I should be exceedingly obliged, Mr. Roundhay, if you would give the inspector my compliments and direct his attention to the bedroom window and to the sitting-room lamp. Each is suggestive, and together they are almost conclusive. If the police would desire further information I shall be happy to see any of them at the cottage. And now, Watson, I think that, perhaps, we shall be better employed elsewhere."

It may be that the police resented the intrusion of an amateur, or that they imagined themselves to be upon some hopeful line of investigation; but it is certain that we heard nothing from them for the next two days. During this time Holmes spent some of his time smoking and dreaming in the cottage; but a greater portion in country walks which he undertook alone, returning after many hours without remark as to where he had been. One experiment served to show me the line of his investigation. He had bought a lamp which was the duplicate of the one which had burned in the room of Mortimer Tregennis on the morning of the tragedy. This he filled with the same oil as that used at the vicarage, and he carefully timed the period which it would take to be exhausted. Another experiment which he made was of a more unpleasant nature, and one which I am not likely ever to forget.

"You will remember, Watson," he remarked one afternoon, "that there is a single common point of resemblance in the varying reports which have reached us. This concerns the effect of the atmosphere of the room in each case upon those who had first entered it. You will recollect that Mortimer Tregennis, in describing the episode of his last visit to his brother's house, remarked that the doctor on entering the room fell into a chair? You had forgotten? Well, I can answer for it that it was so. Now, you will remember also that Mrs. Porter, the housekeeper, told us that she herself fainted upon entering the room and had afterwards opened the window. In the second case—that of Mortimer Tregennis himself—you cannot have forgotten the horrible stuffiness of the room when we arrived, though the servant had thrown open the window. That servant, I found upon inquiry, was so ill that she had gone to her bed. You will admit, Watson, that these facts are very suggestive. In each case there is evidence of a poisonous atmosphere. In each case, also, there is combustion going on in the room—in the one case a fire, in the other a lamp. The fire was needed, but the lamp was lit—as a comparison of the oil consumed will show—long after it was broad daylight. Why? Surely because there is some connection between three things—the burning, the stuffy atmosphere, and, finally, the madness or death of those unfortunate people. That is clear, is it not?"

"It would appear so."

"At least we may accept it as a working hypothesis. We will suppose, then, that something was burned in each case which produced an atmosphere causing strange toxic effects. Very good. In the first instance—that of the Tregennis family—this substance was placed in the fire. Now the window was shut, but the fire would naturally carry fumes to some extent up the chimney. Hence one would expect the effects of the poison to

25 In a letter headed "Tregennis and Poe," Stephen Saxe suggests that the murderer in "The Devil's Foot" must have derived his idea for the murder from reading Edgar Allan Poe's story, "The Imp of the Perverse" (1845), in which the murderer committed his crime with a poisoned candle, just as the murderer in that story got the idea from reading some French memoirs.

be less than in the second case, where there was less escape for the vapour. The result seems to indicate that it was so, since in the first case only the woman, who had presumably the more sensitive organism, was killed, the others exhibiting that temporary or permanent lunacy which is evidently the first effect of the drug. In the second case the result was complete. The facts, therefore, seem to bear out the theory of a poison which worked by combustion.[25]

"With this train of reasoning in my head I naturally looked about in Mortimer Tregennis's room to find some remains of this substance. The obvious place to look was the talc shield or smoke-guard of the lamp. There, sure enough, I perceived a number of flaky ashes, and round the edges a fringe of brownish powder, which had not yet been consumed. Half of this I took, as you saw, and I placed it in an envelope."

"Why half, Holmes?"

"It is not for me, my dear Watson, to stand in the way of the official police force. I leave them all the evidence which I found. The poison still remained upon the talc, had they the wit to find it. Now, Watson, we will light our lamp; we will, however, take the precaution to open our window to avoid the premature decease of two deserving members of society, and you will seat yourself near that open window in an armchair, unless, like a sensible man, you determine to have nothing to do with the affair. Oh, you will see it out, will you? I thought I knew my Watson. This chair I will place opposite yours, so that we may be the same distance from the poison, and face to face. The door we will leave ajar. Each is now in a position to watch the other and to bring the experiment to an end should the symptoms seem alarming. Is that all clear? Well, then, I take our powder—or what remains of it—from the envelope, and I lay it above the burning lamp. So! Now, Watson, let us sit down and await developments."

They were not long in coming. I had hardly settled in my chair before I was conscious of a thick, musky odour, subtle and nauseous. At the very first whiff of it my brain and my imagination were beyond all control. A thick, black cloud swirled before my eyes, and my mind told me that in this cloud, unseen as yet, but about to spring out upon my appalled senses, lurked all that was vaguely horrible, all that was monstrous and inconceivably wicked in the universe. Vague shapes swirled and swam amid the dark cloud-bank, each a menace and a warning of something coming, the advent of some unspeakable dweller upon the threshold, whose very shadow would blast my soul. A freezing horror took possession of me. I felt that my hair was rising, that my eyes were protruding, that my mouth was opened, and my tongue like leather. The turmoil within my brain was such that something must surely snap. I tried to scream, and was vaguely aware of some hoarse croak which was my own voice, but distant and detached from myself. At the same moment, in some effort of escape, I broke through that cloud of despair, and had a glimpse of Holmes's face, white, rigid, and drawn with horror—the very look which I had seen upon the features of the dead. It was that vision

"We lurched through the door, and an instant afterwards had thrown ourselves down upon the grass plot."
Gilbert Holiday, *Strand Magazine,* 1910

26 Watson apparently forgets this episode over the course of the following decade, considering that in "The Three Garridebs" (published in 1920) he writes, "For the one and only time I caught a glimpse of a great heart as well as of a great brain."

27 Watson had, after all, been warned of this trait of Holmes's. Stamford, as recorded in the first chapter of *A Study in Scarlet*, told Watson, "I could imagine his giving a friend a little pinch of the latest vegetable alkaloid, not out of malevolence, you understand, but simply out of a spirit of inquiry in order to have an accurate idea of the effects. To do him justice, I think that he would take it himself with the same readiness."

which gave me an instant of sanity and of strength. I dashed from my chair, threw my arms round Holmes, and together we lurched through the door, and an instant afterwards had thrown ourselves down upon the grass plot and were lying side by side, conscious only of the glorious sunshine which was bursting its way through the hellish cloud of terror which had girt us in. Slowly it rose from our souls like the mists from a landscape, until peace and reason had returned, and we were sitting upon the grass, wiping our clammy foreheads, and looking with apprehension at each other to mark the last traces of that terrific experience which we had undergone.

"Upon my word, Watson!" said Holmes at last, with an unsteady voice, "I owe you both my thanks and an apology. It was an unjustifiable experiment even for oneself, and doubly so for a friend. I am really very sorry."

"You know," I answered, with some emotion, for I had never seen so much of Holmes's heart before,[26] "that it is my greatest joy and privilege to help you."[27]

He relapsed at once into the half-humorous, half-cynical vein which was his habitual attitude to those about him. "It would be superfluous to drive us mad, my dear Watson," said he. "A candid observer would certainly declare that we were so already before we embarked upon so wild an experiment. I confess that I never imagined that the effect could be so sudden and so severe." He dashed into the cottage, and reappearing with the burning lamp held at full arm's length, he threw it among a bank of brambles. "We must give the room a little time to clear. I take it, Watson, that you have no longer a shadow of a doubt as to how these tragedies were produced?"

"None whatever."

"But the cause remains as obscure as before. Come into the arbour here, and let us discuss it together. That villainous stuff seems still to linger round my throat. I think we must admit that all the evidence points to this man, Mortimer Tregennis, having been the criminal in the first tragedy, though he was the victim in the second one. We must remember, in the first place, that there is some story of a family quarrel, followed by a reconciliation. How bitter that quarrel may have been, or how hollow the reconciliation we cannot tell. When I think of Mortimer Tregennis, with the foxy face and the small shrewd, beady eyes, behind the spectacles, he is not a man whom I should judge to be of a particularly forgiving disposition. Well, in the next place, you will remember that this idea of someone moving in the garden, which took our attention for a moment from the real cause of the tragedy, emanated from him. He had a motive in misleading us. Finally, if he did not throw this substance into the fire at the moment of leaving the room, who did do so? The affair happened immediately after his departure. Had anyone else come in, the family would certainly have risen from the table.[28] Besides, in peaceful Cornwall, visitors do not arrive after ten o'clock at night. We may take it, then, that all the evidence points to Mortimer Tregennis as the culprit."

"Then his own death was suicide!"

"Well, Watson, it is on the face of it a not impossible supposition. The man who had the guilt upon his soul of having brought such a fate upon his own family might well be driven by remorse to inflict it upon himself. There are, however, some cogent reasons against it. Fortunately, there is one man in England who knows all about it, and I have made arrangements by which we shall hear the facts this afternoon from his own lips. Ah! he is a little before his time. Perhaps you would kindly step this way, Dr. Leon Sterndale. We have been conducting a chemical experiment indoors which has left our little room hardly fit for the reception of so distinguished a visitor."

I had heard the click of the garden gate, and now the majestic figure of the great African explorer appeared upon the path. He turned in some surprise towards the rustic arbour in which we sat.

"You sent for me, Mr. Holmes. I had your note about an hour ago, and I have come, though I really do not know why I should obey your summons."

"Perhaps we can clear the point up before we separate," said Holmes. "Meanwhile, I am much obliged to you for your courteous acquiescence. You will excuse this informal reception in the open air, but my friend Watson and I have nearly furnished an additional chapter to what the papers call the Cornish Horror, and we prefer a clear atmosphere for the present. Perhaps, since the matters which we have to discuss will affect you personally in a very intimate fashion, it is as well that we should talk where there can be no eavesdropping."

The explorer took his cigar from his lips and gazed sternly at my companion.

28 Bob Jones, who has earlier pointed out that the seated positions of the Tregennises do not match with the purported details of the whist game—that is, that if George and Mortimer had been partners, then Brenda and Owen should have been seated across from one another—surmises that Mortimer may have seen the difficulty of claiming that *Brenda*, his actual partner, had faced the window and seen a possible intruder. Using a dead woman to divert suspicion from himself may have seemed like questionable strategy, and therefore Mortimer turned George into his false witness instead. "Mortimer would know that, although George was alive, in his demented condition he couldn't testify at the inquest," Jones decides. Watson's own testimony as to the speed of working of the devil's foot root is evidence, Jones argues, that the three would not have had time to reseat themselves. But Holmes himself notes that the dispersion of the smoke up the chimney would have slowed the effect of the drug. Who is to say that the Tregennises did not re-seat themselves to play a *three*-handed card game?

"I am at a loss to know, sir," he said, "what you can have to speak about which affects me personally in a very intimate fashion."

"The killing of Mortimer Tregennis," said Holmes.

For a moment I wished that I were armed. Sterndale's fierce face turned to a dusky red, his eyes glared, and the knotted, passionate veins started out in his forehead, while he sprang forward with clenched hands towards my companion. Then he stopped, and with a violent effort he resumed a cold, rigid calmness which was, perhaps, more suggestive of danger than his hot-headed out-burst.

"I have lived so long among savages and beyond the law," said he, "that I have got into the way of being a law to myself.

"He sprang forward with clenched
hands towards my companion."
Gilbert Holiday, *Strand Magazine*, 1910

You would do well, Mr. Holmes, not to forget it, for I have no desire to do you an injury."

"Nor have I any desire to do you an injury, Dr. Sterndale. Surely the clearest proof of it is that, knowing what I know, I have sent for you and not for the police."

Sterndale sat down with a gasp, overawed for, perhaps, the first time in his adventurous life. There was a calm assurance of power in Holmes's manner which could not be withstood. Our visitor stammered for a moment, his great hands opening and shutting in his agitation.

"What do you mean?" he asked, at last. "If this is bluff upon your part, Mr. Holmes, you have chosen a bad man for your experiment. Let us have no more beating about the bush. What *do* you mean?"

"I will tell you," said Holmes, "and the reason why I tell you is that I hope frankness may beget frankness. What my next step may be will depend entirely upon the nature of your own defence."

"My defence?"

"Yes, sir."

"My defence against what?"

"Against the charge of killing Mortimer Tregennis."

Sterndale mopped his forehead with his handkerchief. "Upon my word, you are getting on," said he. "Do all your successes depend upon this prodigious power of bluff?"

"The bluff," said Holmes, sternly, "is upon your side, Dr. Leon Sterndale, and not upon mine. As a proof I will tell you some of the facts upon which my conclusions are based. Of your return from Plymouth, allowing much of your property to go on to Africa, I will say nothing save that it first informed me that you were one of the factors which had to be taken into account in reconstructing this drama—"

"I came back—"

"I have heard your reasons and regard them as unconvincing and inadequate. We will pass that. You came down here to ask me whom I suspected. I refused to answer you. You then went to the vicarage, waited outside it for some time, and finally returned to your cottage."

"How do you know that?"

"I followed you."

"I saw no one."

"That is what you may expect to see when I follow you. You spent a restless night at your cottage, and you formed certain plans, which in the early morning you proceeded to put into execution. Leaving your door just as day was breaking, you filled your pocket with some reddish gravel that was lying heaped beside your gate."

Sterndale gave a violent start and looked at Holmes in amazement.

"You then walked swiftly for the mile which separated you from the vicarage. You were wearing, I may remark, the same pair of ribbed tennis shoes which are at the present moment upon your feet. At the vicarage you passed through the orchard and the side hedge, coming out under the window of the lodger Tregennis. It was now daylight, but the household was not yet stirring. You drew some of the gravel from your pocket, and you threw it up at the window above you."

Sterndale sprang to his feet.

"I believe that you are the devil himself!" he cried.

Holmes smiled at the compliment. "It took two, or possibly three, handfuls before the lodger came to the window. You beckoned him to come down. He dressed hurriedly and descended to his sitting-room. You entered by the window. There was an interview—a short one—during which you walked up and down the room. Then you passed out and closed the window, standing on the lawn outside smoking a cigar and watching what occurred. Finally, after the death of Tregennis, you withdrew as you had come. Now, Dr. Sterndale, how do you justify such conduct, and what were the motives for your actions? If you prevaricate or trifle with me, I give you my assurance that the matter will pass out of my hands for ever."

Our visitor's face had turned ashen grey as he listened to the words of his accuser. Now he sat for some time in thought with his face sunk in his hands. Then with a sudden impulsive gesture he plucked a photograph from his breast-pocket and threw it on the rustic table before us.

"That is why I have done it," said he.

It showed the bust and face of a very beautiful woman. Holmes stooped over it.

"Brenda Tregennis," said he.

"Yes, Brenda Tregennis," repeated our visitor. "For years I

have loved her. For years she has loved me. There is the secret of that Cornish seclusion which people have marvelled at. It has brought me close to the one thing on earth that was dear to me. I could not marry her, for I have a wife who has left me for years and yet whom, by the deplorable laws of England, I could not divorce.[29] For years Brenda waited. For years I waited. And this is what we have waited for."[30] A terrible sob shook his great frame, and he clutched his throat under his brindled beard. Then with an effort he mastered himself and spoke on.

"The vicar knew. He was in our confidence. He would tell you that she was an angel upon earth. That was why he telegraphed to me and I returned.[31] What was my baggage or Africa to me when I learned that such a fate had come upon my darling? There you have the missing clue to my action, Mr. Holmes."

"Proceed," said my friend.

Dr. Sterndale drew from his pocket a paper packet and laid it upon the table. On the outside was written *Radix pedis diaboli*, with a red poison label beneath it. He pushed it towards me. "I understand that you are a doctor, sir. Have you ever heard of this preparation?"

"Devil's-foot root! No, I have never heard of it."

"It is no reflection upon your professional knowledge," said he, "for I believe that, save for one sample in a laboratory at Buda,[32] there is no other specimen in Europe. It has not yet found its way either into the pharmacopœia or into the literature of toxicology.[33] The root is shaped like a foot, half human, half goat-like; hence the fanciful name given by a botanical missionary. It is used as an ordeal poison[34] by the medicine-men in certain districts of West Africa, and is kept as a secret among them. This particular specimen I obtained under very extraordinary circumstances in the Ubanghi country."[35] He opened the paper as he spoke, and disclosed a heap of reddish-brown, snuff-like powder.

"Well, sir?" asked Holmes sternly.

"I am about to tell you, Mr. Holmes, all that actually occurred, for you already know so much that it is clearly to my interest that you should know all. I have already explained the relationship in which I stood to the Tregennis family. For the sake of the sister I was friendly with the brothers. There was a

29 See "The Abbey Grange," note 12, for a discussion of contemporary divorce laws.

30 By the time of publication of "The Devil's Foot," the waiting of Arthur Conan Doyle for his love Jean Leckie had ended, albeit more happily (see the Foreword to this edition). Conan Doyle's first wife died in 1906, and he and Jean, whom he had met and loved passionately but platonically since 1897, were married in 1907. "The Devil's Foot" was published only a few weeks after the birth of their son Adrian.

31 "This excitable clergyman fails to strike me as a likely recipient of Brenda Tregennis and Dr. Sterndale's confidences," writes Pamela Bruxner; "one can't help wondering whether they ever regretted it. One is also curious as to the wording of the telegram sent by the vicar to recall Sterndale from his journey; if it was couched in the same sort of terms as his remarks to Holmes, what on earth did the local post office make of it?"

32 The capital of Hungary since 1361, the hilly town of Buda was home to many of the palaces and villas of the landed gentry. In 1873, Buda joined with the city of Pest to form Budapest. Although the nineteenth century saw Pest flourish as a commercial and industrial center, Buda still housed several government and university buildings, one of which may have contained the laboratory that Sterndale mentions here.

33 George B. Koelle, writing in 1959 (in his masterful "Poisons in the Canon"), shortly after the discovery of lysergic acid diethylamide, or LSD-25, expresses the hope that a compound similar to the synthetic drug might be found in some unidentified root and thus the mystery of the "devil's foot root" be finally solved. However, scholars seem no closer today than in 1959 to a definitive iden-

tification. F. A. Allen, M.P.S., in "Devilish Drugs, Part One" proposes an unknown member of the rauwolfia species, which, in at least one known variety, produces nightmares among its undesirable possible side-effects. There could be, he suggests, a "secret and nightmare-enhanced African species."

In "Radix Pedis Diabolis: A Speculative Identification," Verner Andersen nominates the Calabar bean, the dried seed of the Central African *Physostigma venenosum*, as the culprit. As early as 1855, after self-experimentation, Robert Christison published a paper on the seeds and their toxic effects, and the Calabar bean was known to be used in connection with the "poison-water ordeal" (see note 34, below). This nomination is seconded by James G. Ravin, M.D., in "The Devil's-Foot Root Identified: Eserine," who describes the drug called eserine, now known to be derived from the Calabar bean.

Peter Cooper, F.P.S. ("The Devil's Foot: An Excursion into Holmesian Toxicology") makes a case for *muavi* or *moavi*, a Kiswahili name (*Erythrophleum guineense*), a "well-documented ordeal drug of the Congo region." In a letter to the *Pharmaceutical Journal*, Dr. Varro E. Tyler, dean and professor of pharmacognosy at Purdue University, prefers *niando* (*Alchornea floribunda*), a native plant used by Congolese as an intoxicant, as causing effects closer to Watson's description. Without naming a candidate, Robert S. Ennis speculates ("Devil's Foot or Angel Dust?") that the drug may have been an early and natural form of P.C.P., a manufactured drug with many effects similar to the devil's foot root. Marina Stajic, Ph.D., a toxicologist, in "However Improbable . . . ," makes the interesting suggestion that the toxic substance in question was devil's claw root, in itself a harmless herb, which had been infected with ergot, a hallucinogen-containing fungus.

In short, although there are numerous candidates, no definitive identification has been made. Indeed, John Hall, in *Sidelights on Holmes*, suggests that Watson may have intentionally misdescribed the drug out of a sense of responsibility to suppress its use.

34 The "poison-water ordeal" was a method of criminal judgement used in some parts of Africa. The *Encyclopædia Britannica* (9th Ed.) describes it thus: "The accused, with solemn ceremony and invocation, drinks freely of [the poison]; if it nauseates him and he throws it up he is triumphantly acquitted, but if he becomes dizzy he is guilty, and the assembly fall on him, pelt him with stones, and even drag him over the rocks till he is dead. . . ." *Britannica* lists the *mbundu* root, the Calabar bean (see note 33, above), and the tangena nut (*Tanghinia veneniflua*) as the drugs used for this purpose.

35 The Ubangi or Ubanghi, also known as the Mubangi, Mobangi, or Oubangui, is a river in central Africa, the chief northern tributary of the Congo. In 1897, the Ubangi and the Mbomu formed the frontier between Belgian Congo and French Congo.

family quarrel about money which estranged this man Mortimer, but it was supposed to be made up, and I afterwards met him as I did the others. He was a sly, subtle, scheming man, and several things arose which gave me a suspicion of him, but I had no cause for any positive quarrel.

"One day, only a couple of weeks ago, he came down to my cottage and I showed him some of my African curiosities. Among other things I exhibited this powder, and I told him of its strange properties, how it stimulates those brain centres which control the emotion of fear, and how either madness or death is the fate of the unhappy native who is subjected to the ordeal by the priest of his tribe. I told him also how powerless European science would be to detect it. How he took it I cannot say, for I never left the room, but there is no doubt that it was then, while I was opening cabinets and stooping to boxes, that he managed to abstract some of the devil's-foot root. I well remember how he plied me with questions as to the amount and the time that was needed for its effect, but I little dreamed that he could have a personal reason for asking.

"I thought no more of the matter until the vicar's telegram reached me at Plymouth. This villain had thought that I would be at sea before the news could reach me, and that I should be lost for years in Africa. But I returned at once.[36] Of course, I could not listen to the details without feeling assured that my poison had been used. I came round to see you on the chance that some other explanation had suggested itself to you. But there could be none. I was convinced that Mortimer Tregennis was the murderer; that for the sake of money, and with the idea, perhaps, that if the other members of his family were all insane he would be the sole guardian of their joint property, he had used the devil's-foot powder upon them, driven two of them out of their senses, and killed his sister Brenda, the one human being whom I have ever loved or who has ever loved me. There was his crime; what was to be his punishment?

"Should I appeal to the law? Where were my proofs? I knew that the facts were true, but could I help to make a jury of countrymen believe so fantastic a story? I might or I might not. But I could not afford to fail. My soul cried out for revenge. I have said to you once before, Mr. Holmes, that I have spent much of my life outside the law, and that I have come at last to be a law to myself. So it was now. I determined that the fate

36 Because there was no urgency to the timing of the murders, Rex Stout finds it incredible that "the murderer would not have postponed his deed until Dr. Sterndale was in the middle of the ocean—or, better still, buried in Central Africa." In light of Tregennis's evident shrewdness, then, one must conclude that either he was badly misinformed about the date of Sterndale's departure or the sailing was unexpectedly delayed.

37 Ah, the innocence of those days before Surgeon General warnings!

38 Holmes may turn a blind eye to Sterndale's form of vigilante justice, but Rex Stout, for one, does not. Recognising that Holmes cares little about being an accessory to murder, Stout asks, "[B]ut what of the moral issue? Is the lyncher to be excused if the lynchee had in fact offended?" At least Watson, Stout imagines, "lifts an eye-brow as Sterndale raises his giant figure, bows gravely, and walks from the arbor."

which he had given to others should be shared by himself. Either that or I would do justice upon him with my own hand. In all England there can be no man who sets less value upon his own life than I do at the present moment.

"Now I have told you all. You have yourself supplied the rest. I did, as you say, after a restless night, set off early from my cottage. I foresaw the difficulty of arousing him, so I gathered some gravel from the pile which you have mentioned, and I used it to throw up to his window. He came down and admitted me through the window of the sitting-room. I laid his offence before him. I told him that I had come both as judge and executioner. The wretch sank into a chair paralysed at the sight of my revolver. I lit the lamp, put the powder above it, and stood outside the window, ready to carry out my threat to shoot him should he try to leave the room. In five minutes he died. My God! how he died! But my heart was flint, for he endured nothing which my innocent darling had not felt before him. There is my story, Mr. Holmes. Perhaps, if you loved a woman, you would have done as much yourself. At any rate, I am in your hands. You can take what steps you like. As I have already said, there is no man living who can fear death less than I do."

Holmes sat for some little time in silence.

"What were your plans?" he asked, at last.

"I had intended to bury myself in Central Africa. My work there is but half finished."

"Go and do the other half," said Holmes. "I, at least, am not prepared to prevent you."

Dr. Sterndale raised his giant figure, bowed gravely, and walked from the arbour. Holmes lit his pipe and handed me his pouch.

"Some fumes which are not poisonous[37] would be a welcome change," said he. "I think you must agree, Watson, that it is not a case in which we are called upon to interfere. Our investigation has been independent, and our action shall be so also. You would not denounce the man?"

"Certainly not," I answered.

"I have never loved, Watson, but if I did and if the woman I loved had met such an end, I might act even as our lawless lion-hunter has done.[38] Who knows? Well, Watson, I will not offend your intelligence by explaining what is obvious. The gravel upon the window-sill was, of course, the starting-point of my research. It was unlike anything in the vicarage garden. Only when my attention had been drawn to Dr. Sterndale and his cottage did I find its counterpart.[39] The lamp shining in broad daylight and the remains of powder upon the shield were successive links in a fairly obvious chain. And now, my dear Watson, I think we may dismiss the matter from our mind, and go back with a clear conscience to the study of those Chaldean roots which are surely to be traced in the Cornish branch of the great Celtic speech."

39 D. Martin Dakin, amazed that Sterndale would carry gravel from his own cottage grounds, asks, "Was he *trying* to make it easy for Holmes?"

HIS LAST BOW[1]

In the tale entitled "His Last Bow," we learn of Holmes's undercover service in the Great War. Conan Doyle reported that while touring the front lines in 1916, he was asked what Holmes was doing for his country. Out of ignorance, he answered, "He is too old to serve." Happily, that was not so. Like only one other story in the Canon, "The Mazarin Stone," "His Last Bow" is written in the third person, not as a Watsonian narrative, raising questions about its authorship. Scholars generally agree that it is Watson's work—otherwise, it seems unlikely that Watson would have included it in the collection under his preface. Because Watson was not present for much of the action of the episode, he may have felt more comfortable adopting an "omniscient" point of view. Here we learn details of Holmes's retirement and his celebrated beekeeping, and there are hints of Watson's retirement as well. The tale is a sentimental favourite of many readers, and the 1940s Holmes films starring Basil Rathbone and Nigel Bruce echoed its patriotic themes. Published in 1917, before the end of World War I, Holmes's vision of a beneficial "east wind coming" (that is, a wind that would blow over England from the Continent) expressed the hopes of the millions of people around the world who wished for peace.

AN EPILOGUE OF SHERLOCK HOLMES[2]

Iᴛ ᴡᴀs ɴɪɴᴇ o'clock at night upon the second of August— the most terrible August in the history of the world.[3] One[4] might have thought already that God's curse hung heavy over a degenerate world, for there was an awesome hush and a feeling of vague expectancy in the sultry and stagnant air. The sun had long set, but one blood-red gash like an open wound lay low in the distant west. Above, the stars were shining brightly; and below, the lights of the shipping glimmered in the bay. The two famous Germans stood beside the stone parapet of the garden walk, with the long low, heavily gabled house behind them, and they looked down upon the broad sweep of the beach at the foot of the great chalk cliff on which Von Bork, like some wandering eagle, had perched himself four years

1 "His Last Bow" was published in the *Strand Magazine* in September 1917 and in *Collier's Weekly* on September 22, 1917. The manuscript is owned by a private collector. Dr. Watson may not have shared the manuscript with Arthur Conan Doyle before June 1916, for Sir Arthur reported (in *A Visit to Three Fronts*) that when he visited the Argonne French front at that time, its director, General Georges-Louis Humbert questioned him about Holmes: " 'Sherlock Holmes, est ce qu'il est un soldat dans l'armée anglaise?' The whole table waited in an awful hush. 'Mais, mon général,' I stammered, 'il est trop vieux pour service.' "

2 The subtitle in the *Strand Magazine* is "The War Service of Sherlock Holmes."

3 August of 1914 saw the culmination of long-simmering friction between the countries of the Triple Alliance, comprising Germany, Italy, and Austria-Hungary; and those of the Triple Entente, comprising Britain, Russia, and France (see "The Naval Treaty," note 19, and "The Second Stain," note 10). Following the assassination by Serbian nationalists of Archduke Francis Ferdinand, heir to the Austrian throne, and his wife on June 28, 1914, the Austrian government presented a nearly unacceptable ultimatum to Serbia, designed to punish that country and establish its own authority. Serbia, while unable to accept the terms most threatening to its sovereignty, offered to send the matter to international arbitration; but Austria-Hungary dismissed the suggestion, severing diplomatic relations and—with the encouragement of Germany—declaring war on Serbia on July 28. The declaration produced a domino effect: Russia began mobilizing forces in support of Serbia, prompting Germany to issue an ultimatum to Russia and another to France requesting that the French maintain neutrality. When both demands were ignored, Germany declared war on Russia on August 1 and on France on August 3. The incursion of German troops into Belgium, in violation of a neutrality agreement, gave Britain its rationale for entering the fray, which it did by declaring war on Germany on August 4. Further declarations of war filled the rest of August: Austria-Hungary made its official declaration against Russia on August 5, Serbia against Germany on August 6, France against Austria-Hungary on August 10, Great Britain against Austria-Hungary on August 12, Japan against Germany on August 23, Austria-Hungary against Japan on August 25, and Austria-Hungary against Belgium on August 28. Across Europe many, little realising the mass devastation that lay ahead, thought that hostilities would end within a matter of months.

4 Who wrote this story? There is widespread speculation. Edgar W. Smith, in "Adventure of the Veiled Author," argues for Mycroft, partly on the grounds that only he would know the secret Foreign Office history that lay behind Holmes's career as Altamont. H. W. Bell, in *Sherlock Holmes and Dr. Watson: The Chronology of their Adventures*, contends that "His Last Bow" and "The Mazarin Stone" were written by the same author, without identifying who that author was. S. C. Roberts suggests, in *Dr. Watson*, that a wife of Watson's (that is, his post-Mary Morstan wife, mentioned in "The Blanched Soldier") wrote both stories. Graeme Decarie argues that Holmes himself wrote "His Last Bow," a story that is "almost entirely fictitious." Leaning on Watson's remark, in his introduction to "Thor Bridge," that "in [other cases] I was either not present or played so small a part that they could only be told *as by a third person*" (italics added), D. Martin Dakin concludes that Dr. Watson wrote the tale. And Lord Donegall, going perhaps the furthest afield, suggests Billy the page!

5 William II, Friedrich Wilhelm Victor Albert (1859–1941), king of Prussia and German emperor. See "The Second Stain," note 10.

before. They stood with their heads close together, talking in low, confidential tones. From below the two glowing ends of their cigars might have been the smouldering eyes of some malignant fiend looking down in the darkness.

A remarkable man this Von Bork—a man who could hardly be matched among all the devoted agents of the Kaiser.[5] It was his talents which had first recommended him for the English mission, the most important mission of all, but since he had taken it over, those talents had become more and more manifest to the half-dozen people in the world who were really in touch with the truth. One of these was his present companion, Baron Von Herling, the chief secretary of the legation, whose huge 100-horse-power Benz car was blocking the country lane as it waited to waft its owner back to London.

"So far as I can judge the trend of events, you will probably be back in Berlin within the week," the secretary was saying. "When you get there, my dear Von Bork, I think you will be surprised at the welcome you will receive. I happen to know what is thought in the highest quarters of your work in this country." He was a huge man, the secretary, deep, broad, and tall, with a slow, heavy fashion of speech which had been his main asset in his political career.

Von Bork laughed.

"They are not very hard to deceive," he remarked. "A more docile, simple folk could not be imagined."

"I don't know about that," said the other thoughtfully. "They have strange limits and one must learn to observe them. It is that surface simplicity of theirs which makes a trap for the stranger. One's first impression is that they are entirely soft. Then one comes suddenly upon something very hard, and you know that you have reached the limit, and must adapt yourself to the fact. They have, for example, their insular conventions which simply *must* be observed."

"Meaning, 'good form' and that sort of thing?" Von Bork sighed, as one who had suffered much.

"Meaning British prejudice in all its queer manifestations. As an example I may quote one of my own worst blunders— I can afford to talk of my blunders, for you know my work well enough to be aware of my successes. It was on my first arrival. I was invited to a week-end gathering at the country house of a cabinet minister. The conversation was amazingly indiscreet."

Von Bork nodded. "I've been there," said he dryly.

"Exactly. Well, I naturally sent a resume of the information to Berlin. Unfortunately our good Chancellor is a little heavy-handed in these matters,[6] and he transmitted a remark which showed that he was aware of what had been said. This, of course, took the trail straight up to me. You've no idea the harm that it did me. There was nothing soft about our British hosts on that occasion, I can assure you. I was two years living it down. Now you, with this sporting pose of yours."

"No, no, don't call it a pose. A pose is an artificial thing. This is quite natural. I am a born sportsman. I enjoy it."

"Well, that makes it the more effective. You yacht against them, you hunt with them, you play polo, you match them in every game, your four-in-hand[7] takes the prize at Olympia.[8] I have even heard that you go the length of boxing with the young officers. What is the result? Nobody takes you seriously. You are a 'good old sport,' 'quite a decent fellow for a German,' a hard-drinking, night-club, knock-about-town, devil-may-care young fellow. And all the time this quiet country house of yours is the centre of half the mischief in England, and the sporting squire the most astute secret-service man in Europe. Genius, my dear Von Bork—genius!"

"You flatter me, Baron. But certainly I may claim that my four years in this country have not been unproductive. I've never shown you my little store. Would you mind stepping in for a moment?"

The door of the study opened straight on to the terrace. Von Bork pushed it back, and, leading the way, he clicked the switch of the electric light. He then closed the door behind the bulky form which followed him, and carefully adjusted the heavy curtain over the latticed window. Only when all these precautions had been taken and tested did he turn his sunburned aquiline face to his guest.

"Some of my papers have gone," said he, "when my wife and the household left yesterday for Flushing[9] they took the less important with them. I must, of course, claim the protection of the Embassy for the others."

"Your name has already been filed as one of the personal

6 Theobald von Bethmann-Hollweg (1856–1921), who served as chancellor from 1909 to 1917, stumbled in many of his diplomatic efforts. His enlarging of Germany's peacetime army played a substantial role in exacerbating the tensions that led to war, as did his support for Austria-Hungary's aggressiveness toward Serbia and his compliance with the aims of the war-hungry German General Staff. He did, however, attempt to secure U.S. mediation of the conflict and worked to restrict submarine warfare once it was apparent that the United States would not remain neutral. Bethmann-Hollweg was forced to resign in 1917 by conservatives angry over his proposed electoral reforms for Prussia.

7 A vehicle drawn by four horses.

8 The Olympia amphitheatre in Kensington could hold 10,000 people (according to *Baedeker*) and hosted sporting events, concerts, roller-skating, and large-scale performances, including the Barnum and Bailey circus.

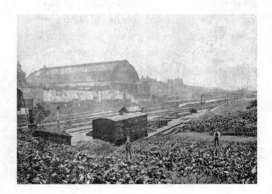

The Olympia.
Queen's London (1897)

9 Known in Dutch as Vlissingen, the city of Flushing lies on the southern coast of the island of Walcheren, in the Veeland province of the Netherlands. Because it blocks outside

access to Antwerp, the medieval seaport has traditionally been a site of great strategic importance, and several battles have been fought there. Napoleon used it as a naval base during French occupation of the Netherlands (1795–1814).

10 Even though the outbreak of World War I effectively negated Parliament's 1914 passage of Home Rule, or self-government for Ireland, the notion continued to be fiercely resisted by Unionists and Protestants in Ulster, who preferred outright independence to inclusion in the British union. Opposition was also strong among Irish Catholics, motivating Arthur Griffith—a former member of the revolutionary Fenian society—to found Sinn Féin ("We Ourselves" in Gaelic), a cultural organisation dedicated to preserving Irish traditions and language. Germany was sympathetic to the anti-British sentiment, supplying some arms to two insurgent militia forces, the Ulster Volunteers and the Dublin-based Irish Volunteers (the military arm of Sinn Féin and precursor to the Irish Republican Army). In the so-called Easter Rising of 1916, which Germany aided through the manipulation of Sir Roger Casement, violence finally erupted in a week's worth of fighting in Dublin; the overwhelmed rebellion forces were put down, but Irish support for the movement swelled after the British government executed leaders of the opposition.

11 In Greek mythology, the Furies were the vengeful daughters (three in number, according to Euripides) of Mother Earth. By "window-breaking Furies," Von Herling could be thinking of the Women's Social & Political Union, the militant organisation fighting for women's voting rights. From 1910 to 1914, many members were taking part in window-smashing raids, and some committed arson. Alternatively, Jack Tracy suggests that Von Herling might have had labour unrest in

suite. There will be no difficulties for you or your baggage. Of course, it is just possible that we may not have to go. England may leave France to her fate. We are sure that there is no binding treaty between them."

"And Belgium?"

"Yes, and Belgium, too."

Von Bork shook his head. "I don't see how that could be. There is a definite treaty there. She could never recover from such a humiliation."

"She would at least have peace for the moment."

"But her honour?"

"Tut, my dear sir, we live in a utilitarian age. Honour is a mediæval conception. Besides England is not ready. It is an inconceivable thing, but even our special war tax of fifty million, which one would think made our purpose as clear as if we had advertised it on the front page of the *Times*, has not roused these people from their slumbers. Here and there one hears a question. It is my business to find an answer. Here and there also there is an irritation. It is my business to soothe it. But I can assure you that so far as the essentials go—the storage of munitions, the preparation for submarine attack, the arrangements for making high explosives—nothing is prepared. How then can England come in, especially when we have stirred her up such a devil's brew of Irish civil war,[10] window-breaking Furies,[11] and God knows what to keep her thoughts at home?"

"She must think of her future."

"Ah, that is another matter. I fancy that in the future, we have our own very definite plans about England, and that your information will be very vital to us. It is to-day or to-morrow with Mr. John Bull. If he prefers to-day we are perfectly ready. If it is to-morrow we shall be more ready still. I should think they would be wiser to fight with allies than without them, but that is their own affair. This week is their week of destiny. But you were speaking of your papers." He sat in the armchair with the light shining upon his broad bald head, while he puffed sedately at his cigar.

The large oak-panelled, book-lined room had a curtain hung in the further corner. When this was drawn it disclosed a large brass-bound safe. Von Bork detached a small key from his watch-chain, and after some considerable manipulation of the lock he swung open the heavy door.

"Look!" said he, standing clear, with a wave of his hand.

The light shone vividly into the opened safe, and the secretary of the Embassy gazed with an absorbed interest at the rows of stuffed pigeon-holes with which it was furnished. Each pigeon-hole had its label, and his eyes as he glanced along them read a long series of such titles as "Fords," "Harbour-defences," "Aeroplanes," "Ireland," "Egypt," "Portsmouth forts,"[12] "The Channel," "Rosyth,"[13] and a score of others. Each compartment was bristling with papers and plans.

"Colossal!" said the secretary. Putting down his cigar he softly clapped his fat hands.

"And all in four years, Baron. Not such a bad show for the hard-drinking, hard-riding country squire. But the gem of my collection is coming and there is the setting all ready for it." He pointed to a space over which "Naval Signals" was printed.

"But you have a good dossier there already."

"Out of date and waste paper. The Admiralty in some way got the alarm and every code has been changed. It was a blow, Baron—the worst set-back in my whole campaign. But thanks to my cheque-book and the good Altamont all will be well to-night."

The Baron looked at his watch, and gave a guttural exclamation of disappointment.

"Well, I really can wait no longer. You can imagine that things are moving at present in Carlton Terrace[14] and that we have all to be at our posts. I had hoped to be able to bring news of your great coup. Did Altamont name no hour?"

Von Bork pushed over a telegram.

Will come without fail to-night and bring new sparking plugs.
ALTAMONT

"Sparking plugs, eh?"

"You see he poses as a motor expert and I keep a full garage. In our code everything likely to come up is named after some spare part. If he talks of a radiator it is a battleship, of an oil pump a cruiser, and so on. Sparking plugs are naval signals."

"From Portsmouth at mid-day," said the secretary, examining the superscription. "By the way, what do you give him?"

"Five hundred pounds for this particular job. Of course he has a salary as well."

mind, as violent retribution was also the goal in the several major labour strikes and related riots that crippled the country in 1912. Because the Furies were female, however, it seems most likely that Von Herling's reference is to the suffragettes.

12 Portsmouth was the chief naval station of England. For more on the forts of Portsmouth, see "The Five Orange Pips," note 23.

13 A town and important naval base in Scotland, located upon the northern shore of the Firth of Forth, a few miles to the west of Edinburgh. The naval base served as a ship-repair station in World War I.

14 The German Embassy was 9 Carlton House Terrace in London, E.C.

15 As members of the landed gentry in Prussia and eastern Germany, Junkers (German for "country squire") were politically conservative, supporting the monarchy, the military, and agricultural protectionism. Otto von Bismarck, the chancellor from 1871 to 1890, was a Junker of old Brandenburg stock.

16 A bronze statue of the Duke of York (second son of George III) perches atop the York Column, located at the head of the steps on Waterloo Place's southern side. The German Embassy is located to the west of the column.

17 This sweet white wine is produced in the area around the Hungarian town of Tokay (or Tokaj, in Hungarian), in the foothills of the Carpathian Mountains. It is made from three grapes: Furmint, Hárslevelü, and, occasionally, Muscat or Muskotály, with the Furmint contributing approximately 50 percent. The bottle's label would have read Tokaji (the possessive) followed by Aszu, Szamorodui, or Essencia, indicating the *terroir*.

18 The Essex seaport was then the base for the British destroyer and submarine fleets.

19 Count Ferdinand von Zeppelin (1838–1917) was a German military officer who, after retiring from the army in 1890, dedicated himself to developing motor-driven airships. In 1900 he invented a rigid airship, or dirigible, called the *LZ-1*. Although it launched with only limited success, the performance satisfied the German government sufficiently to fund Zeppelin's research thereafter, granting him a commission for an entire fleet after he accomplished a twenty-four-hour flight in 1906. The Zeppelin Foundation was founded at Friedrichschafen in 1908, and the German military would end up using more than one hundred Zeppelins during World War I.

"The greedy rogue. They are useful, these traitors, but I grudge them their blood money."

"I grudge Altamont nothing. He is a wonderful worker. If I pay him well, at least he delivers the goods, to use his own phrase. Besides he is not a traitor. I assure you that our most pan-Germanic Junker[15] is a sucking dove in his feelings towards England as compared with a real bitter Irish-American."

"Oh, an Irish-American?"

"If you heard him talk you would not doubt it. Sometimes I assure you I can hardly understand him. He seems to have declared war on the King's English as well as on the English King. Must you really go? He may be here any moment."

"No. I'm sorry but I have already overstayed my time. We shall expect you early to-morrow, and when you get that signal book through the little door on the Duke of York's steps[16] you can put a triumphant *Finis* to your record in England. What! Tokay!"[17] He indicated a heavily sealed dust-covered bottle which stood with two high glasses upon a salver.

"May I offer you a glass before your journey?"

"No, thanks. But it looks like revelry."

"Altamont has a nice taste in wines, and he took a fancy to my Tokay. He is a touchy fellow, and needs humouring in small things. I have to study him, I assure you." They had strolled out on to the terrace again, and along it to the further end where at a touch from the Baron's chauffeur the great car shivered and chuckled. "Those are the lights of Harwich,[18] I suppose," said the secretary, pulling on his dust coat. "How still and peaceful it all seems. There may be other lights within the week, and the English coast a less tranquil place! The heavens, too, may not be quite so peaceful if all that the good Zeppelin[19] promises us comes true. By the way, who is that?"

Only one window showed a light behind them; in it there stood a lamp, and beside it, seated at a table, was a dear old ruddy-faced woman in a country cap. She was bending over her knitting and stopping occasionally to stroke a large black cat upon a stool beside her.

"That is Martha, the only servant I have left."

The secretary chuckled.

"She might almost personify Britannia," said he, "with her

complete self absorption and general air of comfortable somnolence. Well, *au revoir*, Von Bork!"—with a final wave of his hand he sprang into the car, and a moment later the two golden cones from the headlights shot forward through the darkness. The secretary lay back in the cushions of the luxurious Limousine, with his thoughts so full of the impending European tragedy that he hardly observed that as his car swung round the village street it nearly passed over a little Ford[20] coming in the opposite direction.

Von Bork walked slowly back to the study when the last gleams of the motor lamps had faded into the distance. As he passed he observed that his old housekeeper had put out her lamp and retired. It was a new experience to him, the silence and darkness of his widespread house, for his family and household had been a large one. It was a relief to him, however, to think that they were all in safety and that, but for that one old woman who had lingered in the kitchen, he had the whole place to himself. There was a good deal of tidying up to do inside his study and he set himself to do it, until his keen, handsome face was flushed with the heat of the burning papers. A leather valise stood beside his table, and into this he began to pack very neatly and systematically the precious contents of his safe. He had hardly got started with the work, however, when his quick ears caught the sound of a distant car. Instantly he gave an exclamation of satisfaction, strapped up the valise, shut the safe, locked it, and hurried out on to the terrace. He was just in time to see the lights of a small car come to a halt at the gate. A passenger sprang out of it and advanced swiftly towards him while the chauffeur, a heavily built, elderly man, with a grey moustache, settled down, like one who resigns himself to a long vigil.

"Well?" asked Von Bork eagerly, running forward to meet his visitor.

For answer the man waved a small brown-paper parcel triumphantly above his head.

"You can give me the glad hand[21] to-night, Mister," he cried. "I'm bringing home the bacon at last."

"The signals?"

"Same as I said in my cable. Every last one of them, semaphore, lamp code, Marconi[22]—a copy, mind you, not the original. That was too dangerous. But it's the real goods, and you

20 By mid-1914 there were more than 500,000 Model Ts on the roads of the world. John L. Benton challenges the identification of the vehicle as a "Ford," stating that the word "came to be used nearly in generic fashion to describe almost any kind of small, light car." Benton concludes that, based on the description of the "spare seat," the car was a three-wheeled Morgan.

21 To welcome someone enthusiastically.

22 That is, radio telegraphy. Guglielmo Marconi was not the first to produce and transmit radio waves, but the system of wireless communication that he developed gave birth to modern radio. Having experimented with a signalling system that could transmit radio waves for over a mile, Marconi filed his first patent in 1894. Over the next several years he gave public demonstrations to show off his new technology; at La Spezia in 1897, he was able to communicate with Italian warships up to 19 kilometers (11.8 miles) away. That same year, with his brother's financial backing, Marconi established the Wireless Telegraph and Signal Company, Ltd., to further the development and marketing of his efforts. The value of his public demonstrations paid off handsomely in situations such as the 1899 America's Cup, when he enabled two American yachts to report back to New York City on their ongoing progress in the race. Excitement about Marconi's efforts spread around the globe. In 1901, at St. John's, Newfoundland, he received history's first transatlantic message, sent from Poldhu, Cornwall (see "The Devil's Foot," note 8). He was awarded the 1909 Nobel Prize in Physics en route to even more triumphs, including successful experiments with shortwave communication during World War I and a transmission from England to Australia in 1918.

can lay to that," he slapped the German upon the shoulder with a rough familiarity from which the other winced.

"Come in," he said. "I'm all alone in the house. I was only waiting for this. Of course a copy is better than the original. If an original were missing they would change the whole thing. You think it's all safe about the copy?"

The Irish-American had entered the study and stretched his long limbs from the armchair. He was a tall, gaunt man of sixty, with clear-cut features and a small goatee beard which gave him a general resemblance to the caricatures of Uncle Sam. A half-smoked, sodden cigar hung from the corner of his mouth, and as he sat down he struck a match and relit it. "Making ready for a move?" he remarked as he looked round him. "Say, Mister," he added, as his eyes fell upon the safe from which the curtain was now removed, "you don't tell me you keep your papers in that?"

"Why not?"

"Gosh, in a wide-open contraption like that! And they reckon you to be some spy. Why a Yankee crook would be into that with a can-opener. If I'd known that any letter of mine was goin' to lie loose in a thing like that I'd have been a mug to write to you at all."

"It would puzzle any crook to force that safe," Von Bork answered. "You won't cut that metal with any tool."

"But the lock?"

"No, it's a double combination lock. You know what that is?"

"Search me," said the American.

"Well, you need a word as well as a set of figures before you can get the lock to work." He rose and showed a double-radiating disc round the keyhole. "This outer one is for the letters, the inner one for the figures."

"Well, well, that's fine."

"So it's not quite as simple as you thought. It was four years ago that I had it made, and what do you think I chose for the word and figures?"

"It's beyond me."

"Well, I chose August for the word, and 1914 for the figures, and here we are."

The American's face showed his surprise and admiration.

"My, but that was smart! You had it down to a fine thing."

"Yes, a few of us even then could have guessed the date. Here it is, and I'm shutting down to-morrow morning."

"Well, I guess you'll have to fix me up also. I'm not staying in this goldarned country all on my lonesome. In a week or less from what I see, John Bull will be on his hind legs and fair ramping. I'd rather watch him from over the water."

"But you're an American citizen?"

"Well, so was Jack James an American citizen, but he's doing time in Portland[23] all the same. It cuts no ice with a British copper to tell him you're an American citizen. 'It's British law and order over here,' says he. By the way, Mister, talking of Jack James it seems to me you don't do much to cover your men."

"What do you mean?" Von Bork asked sharply.

"Well, you are their employer, ain't you? It's up to you to see that they don't fall down. But they do fall down, and when did you ever pick them up? There's James—"

"It was James's own fault. You know that yourself. He was too self-willed for the job."

"James was a bonehead—I give you that. Then there was Hollis."

"The man was mad."

"Well, he went a bit woozy towards the end. It's enough to make a man bughouse when he has to play a part from morning to night with a hundred guys all ready to set the coppers wise to him. But now there is Steiner—"

Von Bork started violently, and his ruddy face turned a shade paler.

"What about Steiner?"

"Well, they've got him, that's all. They raided his store last night, and he and his papers and all are in Portsmouth gaol. You'll go off and he, poor devil, will have to stand the racket, and lucky if he gets off with his life. That's why I want to get over the water as soon as you do."

Von Bork was a strong, self-contained man, but it was easy to see that the news had shaken him.

"How could they have got on to Steiner?" he muttered. "That's the worst blow yet."

"Well, you nearly had a worse one, for I believe they are not far off me."

23 The Isle of Portland, properly a peninsula of the coast of Devonshire, England, which then was the seat of a 1,600-inmate prison and a naval base.

"You don't mean that!"

"Sure thing. My landlady down Fratton way had some inquiries, and when I heard of it I guessed it was time for me to hustle. But what I want to know, Mister, is how the coppers know these things? Steiner is the fifth man you've lost since I signed on with you, and I know the name of the sixth if I don't get a move on. How do you explain it, and ain't you ashamed to see your men go down like this?"

Von Bork flushed crimson.

"How dare you speak in such a way!"

"If I didn't dare things, Mister, I wouldn't be in your service. But I'll tell you straight what is in my mind. I've heard that with you German politicians when an agent has done his work you are not sorry to see him put away."

Von Bork sprang to his feet.

"Do you dare to suggest that I have given away my own agents!"

"I don't stand for that, Mister, but there's a stool pigeon or a cross somewhere, and it's up to you to find out where it is. Anyhow I am taking no more chances. It's me for little Holland, and the sooner the better."

Von Bork had mastered his anger.

"We have been allies too long to quarrel now at the very hour of victory," he said. "You've done splendid work, and taken risks and I can't forget it. By all means go to Holland, and you can get a boat from Rotterdam to New York. No other line will be safe a week from now. I'll take that book and pack it with the rest."

The American held the small parcel in his hand, but made no motion to give it up.

"What about the dough?" he asked.

"The what?"

"The boodle. The reward. The £500. The gunner turned damned nasty at the last, and I had to square him with an extra hundred dollars or it would have been nitsky for you and me. 'Nothin' doin'!' says he, and he meant it too, but the last hundred did it. It's cost me two hundred pound from first to last, so it isn't likely I'd give it up without gettin' my wad."

Von Bork smiled with some bitterness. "You don't seem to have a very high opinion of my honour," said he, "you want the money before you give up the book."

"Well, Mister, it is a business proposition."

"All right. Have your way." He sat down at the table and scribbled a cheque, which he tore from the book, but he refrained from handing it to his companion. "After all, since we are to be on such terms, Mr. Altamont," said he, "I don't see why I should trust you any more than you trust me. Do you understand?" he added, looking back over his shoulder at the American. "There's the cheque upon the table. I claim the right to examine that parcel before you pick the money up."

The American passed it over without a word. Von Bork undid a winding of string and two wrappers of paper. Then he sat gazing for a moment in silent amazement at a small blue book which lay before him. Across the cover was printed in golden letters *Practical Handbook of Bee Culture*. Only for one

"He was gripped at the back of his neck by a grasp
of iron, and a chloroformed sponge was held in front of
his writhing face."
A. Gilbert, *Strand Magazine*, 1917

24 With the passing of the Victorian age into that of the Edwardian, Edgar W. Smith is amused to note, in "On the Forms of Address," that Holmes and Watson have conceded nothing to familiarity and are still addressing each other by their last names. Certainly nicknames such as "Jack" might seem inappropriate, writes Smith, but "perhaps 'John' and 'Sherlock,' in deference to the mellowing times and their own mellowing middle-age? But no—in 1914, when they had shared each others' lives for a full thirty-three years, we find them still ingrained in their old habit . . ."

25 Imperial Tokay came from one particular vineyard and is no longer made. Michael Broadbent reports tasting a bottle of 1885 Imperial Tokay but says it was not particularly distinguished. The 1889 and 1906 vintages of Tokay were exceptional (Broadbent calls the latter "the last great vintage of the Austro-Hungarian empire"), and, given the provenance of the bottle and the refined tastes of the Baron, it was likely from the former vintage.

26 Schönbrunn Palace (or Schloss Schönbrunn) in Vienna was the summer residence of the Austrian royal family. A former hunting lodge, it became the glittering centre of imperial life and politics during the reign of Maria Theresa in the mid-1700s. It is celebrated for its exquisite gardens and its zoo, believed to be the oldest in Europe and opened to the public in 1779.

Franz Joseph I (1830–1916) was the emperor of Austria and the king of Hungary, the uncle of Francis Ferdinand, whose assassination was the trigger that started World War I—although Franz Joseph took his own, proactive role in precipitating war, issuing the ultimatum to Serbia that brought events to a head.

27 Vincent Starrett, in "The Singular Adventures of Martha Hudson," advances the con-

instant did the master spy glare at this strangely irrelevant inscription. The next he was gripped at the back of his neck by a grasp of iron, and a chloroformed sponge was held in front of his writhing face.

"Another glass, Watson!"[24] said Mr. Sherlock Holmes, as he extended the bottle of Imperial Tokay.[25]

The thickset chauffeur, who had seated himself by the table, pushed forward his glass with some eagerness.

"It is a good wine, Holmes."

"A remarkable wine, Watson. Our friend upon the sofa has assured me that it is from Franz Joseph's special cellar at the Schoenbrunn Palace.[26] Might I trouble you to open the window, for chloroform vapour does not help the palate."

The safe was ajar, and Holmes standing in front of it was removing dossier after dossier, swiftly examining each, and then packing it neatly in Von Bork's valise. The German lay upon the sofa sleeping stertorously with a strap round his upper arms and another round his legs.

"We need not hurry ourselves, Watson. We are safe from interruption. Would you mind touching the bell. There is no one in the house except old Martha,[27] who has played her part to admiration. I got her the situation here when first I took the matter up. Ah, Martha, you will be glad to hear that all is well."

The pleasant old lady had appeared in the doorway. She curtseyed with a smile to Mr. Holmes, but glanced with some apprehension at the figure upon the sofa.

"It is all right, Martha. He has not been hurt at all."

"I am glad of that, Mr. Holmes. According to his lights he has been a kind master. He wanted me to go with his wife to Germany yesterday, but that would hardly have suited your plans, would it, sir?"

"No, indeed, Martha. So long as you were here I was easy in my mind. We waited some time for your signal to-night."

"It was the secretary, sir."

"I know. His car passed ours."[28]

"I thought he would never go. I knew that it would not suit your plans, sir, to find him here."

"No, indeed. Well, it only meant that we waited half an hour or so until I saw your lamp go out and knew that the coast was clear. You can report to me to-morrow in London, Martha, at Claridge's Hotel."

"Very good, sir."

"I suppose you have everything ready to leave."

"Yes, sir. He posted seven letters to-day. I have the addresses as usual."

"Very good, Martha. I will look into them to-morrow. Good night. These papers," he continued, as the old lady vanished, "are not of very great importance for, of course, the information which they represent has been sent off long ago to the German Government. These are the originals which could not safely be got out of the country."

"Then they are of no use."

"I should not go so far as to say that, Watson. They will at least show our people what is known and what is not. I may say that a good many of these papers have come through me, and I need not add are thoroughly untrustworthy. It would brighten my declining years to see a German cruiser navigating the Solent[29] according to the minefield plans which I have furnished. But you, Watson," he stopped his work and took his old friend by the shoulders, "I've hardly seen you in the light yet. How have the years[30] used you? You look the same blithe boy as ever."

"I feel twenty years younger, Holmes. I have seldom felt so happy as when I got your wire asking me to meet you at Harwich with the car. But you, Holmes—you have changed very little—save for that horrible goatee."

"These are the sacrifices one makes for one's country, Watson," said Holmes, pulling at his little tuft. "To-morrow it will be but a dreadful memory. With my hair cut and a few other superficial changes I shall no doubt reappear at Claridge's to-morrow as I was before this American stunt—I beg your pardon, Watson, my well of English seems to be permanently defiled—before this American job came my way."

"But you had retired, Holmes. We heard of you as living the life of a hermit among your bees and your books in a small farm upon the South Downs."

"Exactly, Watson. Here is the fruit of my leisured ease, the magnum opus of my latter years!" He picked up the volume from the table and read out the whole title, *Practical Handbook of Bee Culture, with some Observations upon the Segregation of the*

troversial theory that "Martha" was Mrs. Hudson, Holmes's former landlady. Although taken up by many later commentators without any analysis, the theory was finally exploded in William Hyder's "The Martha Myth," in which he demonstrates that (a) Mrs. Hudson is never referred to by her full name and (b) there is no basis in "His Last Bow" on which to identify "Martha" with Mrs. Hudson.

28 In the *Strand Magazine* version of "His Last Bow," Holmes says: "I know. His car passed ours. But for your excellent driving, Watson, we should have been the very type of Europe under the Prussian Juggernaut." Holmes jokes here that the secretary nearly ran them over. Perhaps Watson, in 1917, as the war staggered to its finish, wanted to temper Holmes's inflammatory remark.

29 An arm of the English Channel between the south coast of England and the Isle of Wight.

30 "His Last Bow" occurs in 1914. The penultimate *recorded* meeting of Holmes and Watson took place in "The Creeping Man," in September 1903.

31 Holmes quotes the proud warrior Gaius Marcius Coriolanus in Shakespeare's *Coriolanus*, Act V, Scene 6. In this final scene, Coriolanus's reluctant brokering of peace between the Romans and the Volscians has brought forth accusations of betrayal and cowardice from Tullus Aufidius, the general of the Volscian army and Coriolanus's sometime ally. In response, Coriolanus reminds Aufidius that it was he who once roused the Roman army to conquer the Volscians: "If you have writ your annals true, 'tis there / That, like an eagle in a dovecote, I / Fluttered your Volscians in Corioli. / Alone I did it." Immediately after Coriolanus utters this line, the Volscians turn upon him, killing the warrior in a wave of rage. Holmes knew his audience better, however, likely arousing only murmurs of "Marvellous! Wonderful!" from the loyal Dr. Watson.

32 Those who believe that Watson penned "His Last Bow" might take note of the doctor's questioning of Holmes here. As D. Martin Dakin reminds us, Watson was not present during the opening scene between Von Bork and Von Herling—and nor was anyone else, for that matter—thus making it difficult to recreate that conversation with any true fidelity. "[U]nless old Martha had her ear to the keyhole all the time, and was a stenographic genius," Dakin writes, "then what passed between Von Bork and Von Herling . . . could not possibly be known to any third person; and as neither of them is likely to have obliged Watson with a transcript, [the author] must have been drawing on his imagination, aided by such facts as Holmes could give him about his previous dealings with the master spy." Indeed, the inclusion of such details seems to support those who regard the entire story as fiction. See note 4, above.

33 Herbert Henry Asquith, Earl of Oxford and Asquith (1852–1928), was prime minister of England from 1908 to 1916. He was not

Queen. Alone I did it.[31] Behold the fruit of pensive nights and laborious days, when I watched the little working gangs as once I watched the criminal world of London."

"But how did you get to work again?"[32]

"Ah, I have often marvelled at it myself. The Foreign Minister alone I could have withstood, but when the Premier[33] also deigned to visit my humble roof—![34] The fact is, Watson, that this gentleman upon the sofa was a bit too good for our people. He was in a class by himself.[35] Things were going wrong, and no one could understand why they were going wrong. Agents were suspected or even caught, but there was evidence of some strong and secret central force. It was absolutely necessary to expose it. Strong pressure was brought upon me to look into the matter. It has cost me two years, Watson, but they have not been devoid of excitement. When I say that I started my pilgrimage at Chicago, graduated in an Irish secret society at Buffalo, gave serious trouble to the constabulary[36] at Skibbereen[37] and so eventually caught the eye of a subordinate agent of Von Bork,[38] who recommended me as a likely man, you will realise that the matter was complex. Since then I have been honoured by his confidence, which has not prevented most of his plans going subtly wrong and five of his best agents being in prison. I watched them, Watson, and I picked them as they ripened. Well, sir, I hope that you are none the worse!"

The last remark was addressed to Von Bork himself, who after much gasping and blinking had lain quietly listening to Holmes's statement. He broke out now into a furious stream of German invective, his face convulsed with passion. Holmes continued his swift investigation of documents while his prisoner cursed and swore.

"Though unmusical, German is the most expressive of all languages," he observed, when Von Bork had stopped from pure exhaustion. "Hullo! Hullo!" he added, as he looked hard at the corner of a tracing before putting it in the box. "This should put another bird in the cage. I had no idea that the paymaster was such a rascal, though I have long had an eye upon him. Mister Von Bork, you have a great deal to answer for."

The prisoner had raised himself with some difficulty upon the sofa and was staring with a strange mixture of amazement and hatred at his captor.

"I shall get level with you, Altamont," he said, speaking with

considered a particularly strong wartime leader, and, facing conflicts within his cabinet, heavy British losses on the Western Front, and a vicious press campaign attacking his competency, he was forced to resign before the war had ended.

34 June Thomson theorises that Mycroft must have had a hand in nominating his brother to infiltrate the German spy ring—and may have even persuaded Holmes personally to come out of retirement in service of his country. Calculating that Mycroft would have retired himself upon reaching the age of sixty-five in 1912, Thomson reasons that he would likely have maintained his connections with the government, meeting with former colleagues occasionally at the Diogenes Club.

35 Gordon R. Speck, in "Spy and Counterspy," scoffs at this characterisation, citing Von Bork's vast incompetence as a spy, at least as displayed in the events of this story. "What does Von Bork do with the fruits of his genius and enterprise?" Speck marvels. "He commits a baffling array of fundamental mistakes that would shame a neophyte. He retains originals of copied secret documents. He keeps them in a carelessly concealed safe in his home. He schedules a grossly ostentatious meeting with Baron Von Herling, whose 'large Benz car' blocks the rural road. He gratuitously divulges vital information (date of German offensive and combination to the safe) to a subordinate foreign agent. He sends his wife off 'with less important papers,' papers that could get the old girl jailed if not hanged." Von Herlin's assessment of Von Bork as "the most astute secret-service man in Europe" certainly casts doubt on the quality of the entire German organisation (a point, in 1917 when "His Last Bow" was published and the war not yet ended, which the author certainly intended).

36 The Royal Irish Constabulary, a paramilitary force, was established in 1822. It was frequently called upon to suppress violence instigated by the Fenian society.

37 In the county of Cork, Ireland. Ian Smyth suggests that Holmes had not only become a member of the Fenians but had also participated in gun-running at Skibbereen for the society's military arm (which would become the IRA). By working for the British government, Holmes would have been regarded by the Fenians as an opponent and a traitor—hence the secrecy over his place of retirement.

38 Belden Wigglesworth argues, in "The Road to Skibbereen," that Holmes would not make a direct approach to Von Bork, for such a tactic might well have been suspicious, but instead went to Russia (another sphere of German interest) from Skibbereen, to attract the attention of this subordinate.

39 Donald Hayne suggests that Holmes first migrated to the town of *Altamont*, New York, and took as his own the name of that village. Willis B. Wood suggests that "Altamont" took his alias in memory of an eponymous station on the St. Louis and San Francisco Railway between Joplin, Missouri, and Wichita, Kansas. Mrs. Crighton Sellars observes that William Makepeace Thackaray in *Pendennis* and Sir Walter Scott in *The Pirate* chose "Altamont" as the alias of their villains and suggests that Holmes did so to taunt the Germans. William S. Baring-Gould points out that the full name of Arthur Conan Doyle's father was Charles *Altamont* Doyle, but there is no suggestion that Holmes knew this.

40 Anthony Boucher notes that in infiltrating the German spy ring, Holmes has paid the ultimate compliment to Birdy Edwards, the Pinkerton agent whom he met in *The Valley of Fear*: imitation. The events of "His Last Bow" take place in the same year that *The Valley of Fear* was published, and Holmes's tactics here bear striking resemblance to Edwards's in that case. According to Boucher, Holmes not only changed his name in going deep undercover but also "seemed one of the most dangerous and active men in the organization, while slyly seeing to it that all its plans went awry, and finally upset the whole apple-cart immediately after discussing with the top man the terrible possibility that 'there's a stool-pigeon or a cross somewhere.'"

slow deliberation, "if it takes me all my life I shall get level with you!"

"The old sweet song," said Holmes. "How often have I heard it in days gone by. It was a favourite ditty of the late lamented Professor Moriarty. Colonel Sebastian Moran has also been known to warble it. And yet I live and keep bees upon the South Downs."

"Curse you, you double traitor!" cried the German, straining against his bonds and glaring murder from his furious eyes.

"No, no, it is not so bad as that," said Holmes, smiling. "As my speech surely shows you Mr. Altamont of Chicago had no existence in fact.[39] I used him and he is gone."[40]

"Then who are you?"

"It is really immaterial who I am, but since the matter seems

"'Curse you, you double traitor!' cried the German, straining against his bonds and glaring murder from his furious eyes."
A. Gilbert, *Strand Magazine*, 1917

to interest you, Mr. Von Bork, I may say that this is not my first acquaintance with the members of your family. I have done a good deal of business in Germany in the past and my name is probably familiar to you."

"I would wish to know it," said the Prussian grimly.

"It was I who brought about the separation[41] between Irene Adler and the late King of Bohemia when your cousin Heinrich was the Imperial Envoy. It was I also who saved from murder, by the Nihilist Klopman, Count Von und Zu Grafenstein, who was your mother's elder brother. It was I—"

Von Bork sat up in amazement.

"There is only one man," he cried.

"Exactly," said Holmes.

Von Bork groaned and sank back on the sofa. "And most of that information came through you," he cried. "What is it worth? What have I done? It is my ruin for ever!"

"It is certainly a little untrustworthy," said Holmes. "It will require some checking and you have little time to check it. Your admiral may find the new guns rather larger than he expects, and the cruisers perhaps a trifle faster."[42]

Von Bork clutched at his own throat in despair.

"There are a good many other points of detail which will, no doubt, come to light in good time. But you have one quality which is very rare in a German, Mr. Von Bork: you are a sportsman and you will bear me no ill-will when you realise that you, who have outwitted so many other people, have at last been outwitted yourself. After all, you have done your best for your country, and I have done my best for mine, and what could be more natural? Besides," he added, not unkindly, as he laid his hand upon the shoulder of the prostrate man, "it is better than to fall before some more ignoble foe. These papers are now ready, Watson. If you will help me with our prisoner, I think that we may get started for London at once."

It was no easy task to move Von Bork, for he was a strong and a desperate man. Finally, holding either arm, the two friends walked him very slowly down the garden walk which he had trod with such proud confidence when he received the congratulations of the famous diplomatist only a few hours before. After a short, final struggle he was hoisted, still bound hand and foot, into the spare seat of the little car. His precious valise was wedged in beside him.

41 Astute readers may recall that it was not Holmes who separated Irene Adler from the king of Bohemia but Adler herself, who fled with her new husband upon learning that Holmes was on her trail. D. Martin Dakin suggests that sometime after Watson wrote up the account, the king might have retained Holmes once again, this time successfully persuading Adler to return the implicating photograph. Thus Holmes would feel entitled to take final responsibility for settling matters between them.

42 Admiral Alfred von Tirpitz (1849–1930) was appointed secretary of state for naval affairs in 1897. He built up the German navy in the years leading up to World War I and was an advocate of using unrestricted submarine warfare to defeat the Allies. When the navy began to falter in the face of superior Allied strength, von Tirpitz (who had apparently been misled as predicted by Holmes's disinformation) resigned his post in 1916.

"Holding either arm, the two friends walked him
very slowly down the garden path."
A. Gilbert, *Strand Magazine*, 1917

"I trust that you are as comfortable as circumstances permit," said Holmes, when the final arrangements were made.
"Should I be guilty of a liberty if I lit a cigar and placed it
between your lips?"

But all amenities were wasted upon the angry German.

"I suppose you realise, Mr. Sherlock Holmes," said he, "that
if your Government bears you out in this treatment it becomes
an act of war."

"What about your Government and all this treatment?" said
Holmes, tapping the valise.

"You are a private individual. You have no warrant for my
arrest. The whole proceeding is absolutely illegal and outrageous."

"Absolutely," said Holmes.

"Kidnapping a German subject."

"And stealing his private papers."

"Well, you realise your position, you and your accomplice here. If I were to shout for help as we pass through the village—"

"My dear sir, if you did anything so foolish you would probably enlarge the too limited titles of our village inns by giving us 'The Dangling Prussian' as a sign-post. The Englishman is a patient creature, but at present his temper is a little inflamed and it would be as well not to try him too far. No, Mr. Von Bork, you will go with us in a quiet, sensible fashion to Scotland Yard, whence you can send for your friend Baron Von Herling and see if even now you may not fill that place which he has reserved for you in the ambassadorial suite.[43] As to you, Watson, you are joining us with your old service,[44] as I understand, so London won't be out of your way. Stand with me here upon the terrace, for it may be the last quiet talk that we shall ever have."

The two friends chatted in intimate converse for a few minutes, recalling once again the days of the past[45] whilst their prisoner vainly wriggled to undo the bonds that held him. As they turned to the car, Holmes pointed back to the moonlit sea, and shook a thoughtful head.

"There's an east wind coming, Watson."

"I think not, Holmes. It is very warm."

"Good old Watson! You are the one fixed point in a changing age. There's an east wind coming all the same, such a wind as never blew on England yet. It will be cold and bitter, Watson, and a good many of us may wither before its blast.[46] But it's God's own wind none the less, and a cleaner, better, stronger land will lie in the sunshine when the storm has cleared. Start her up, Watson, for it's time that we were on our way. I have a cheque for five hundred pounds which should be cashed early, for the drawer is quite capable of stopping it, if he can."

43 The German ambassador to Britain from 1912 to 1914 was Prince Karl Max Lichnowsky (1860–1928), whose opposition to the war eventually led to his dismissal and exile. Holmes is undoubtedly joking here, for Von Bork would never have been allowed to return to Germany after it was learned that the information supplied by "Altamont" was false.

44 "What further part Watson took in the war remains unknown," S. C. Roberts writes. At this point he was likely past the age of permissible duty in the field, but as a loyal veteran he may have offered his medical services at a nearby military hospital. His friend Arthur Conan Doyle also found his offer of military service rejected and instead formed a volunteer corps of local militia.

45 Edgar W. Smith speculates, "[E]ven as Watson was sitting . . . in Von Bork's parlour on that fateful August 2nd, with the war-clouds looming heavy in the east, he may have had in his breast-pocket at that very moment, ready for mailing, the manuscript of *The Valley of Fear*—for that long novel out of the past began to run in the *Strand* just a month later."

46 That neither Holmes nor Watson was killed in the Great War is evident, for as late as 1926, Holmes apparently wrote and published "The Blanched Soldier" and "The Lion's Mane," and Watson continued to write and publish until 1927, when "The Retired Colourman," "The Veiled Lodger," and "Shoscombe Old Place" were published. It is unclear whether Dr. Watson had a hand in the publication of *The Case-Book of Sherlock Holmes*, for, in contrast to *His Last Bow*, the Preface is written by Arthur Conan Doyle.

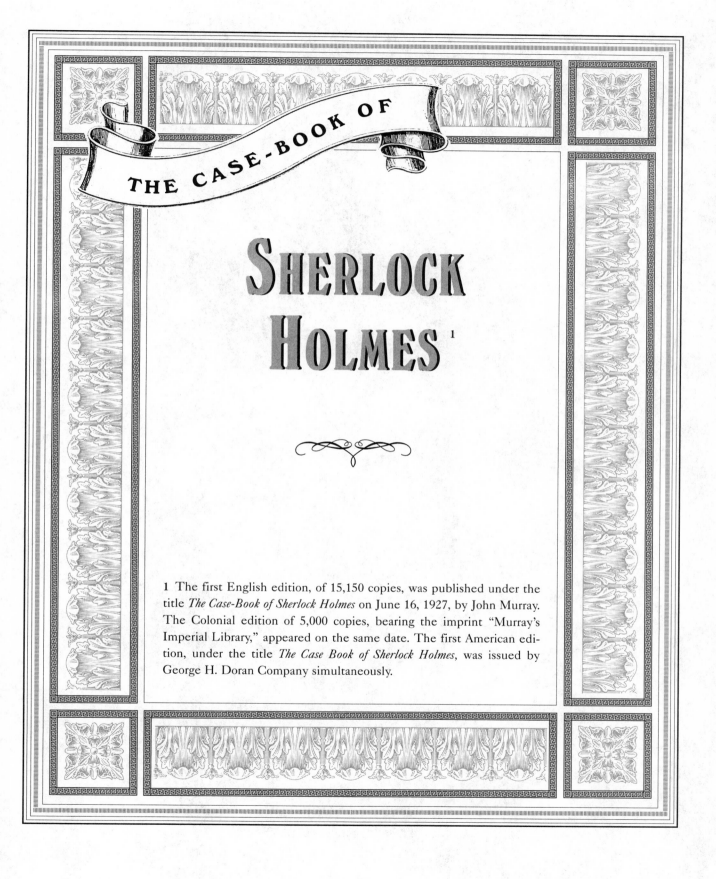

THE CASE-BOOK OF

SHERLOCK HOLMES [1]

⁂

1 The first English edition, of 15,150 copies, was published under the title *The Case-Book of Sherlock Holmes* on June 16, 1927, by John Murray. The Colonial edition of 5,000 copies, bearing the imprint "Murray's Imperial Library," appeared on the same date. The first American edition, under the title *The Case Book of Sherlock Holmes*, was issued by George H. Doran Company simultaneously.

PREFACE[1]

FEAR THAT MR. Sherlock Holmes may become like one of those popular tenors who, having outlived their time, are still tempted to make repeated farewell bows to their indulgent audiences.[2] This must cease and he must go the way of all flesh, material or imaginary. One likes to think that there is some fantastic limbo for the children of imagination, some strange, impossible place where the beaux of Fielding may still make love to the belles of Richardson, where Scott's heroes still may strut, Dickens's delightful Cockneys still raise a laugh, and Thackeray's worldlings continue to carry on their reprehensible careers. Perhaps in some humble corner of such a Valhalla, Sherlock and his Watson may for a time find a place, while some more astute sleuth with some even less astute comrade may fill the stage which they have vacated.

His career has been a long one—though it is possible to exaggerate it; decrepit gentlemen who approach me and declare that his adventures formed the reading of their boyhood do not meet the response from me which they seem to expect. One is not anxious to have one's personal dates handled so unkindly. As a matter of cold fact Holmes made his *début* in *A Study in Scarlet* and in *The Sign of Four*, two small booklets which appeared between 1887 and 1889. It was in 1891 that "A Scandal in Bohemia," the first of the long series of short stories, appeared in *The Strand Magazine*. The public seemed appreciative and desirous of more, so that from that date, thirty-six years ago, they have been produced in a broken series which now contains no fewer than fifty-six stories, republished in *The Adventures*, *The Memoirs*, *The Return*, and *His Last Bow*, and there remain these twelve published during the last few years which are here produced under the title of *The Case-Book*

---

1 The Preface first appeared in slightly altered form in the *Strand Magazine* in March 1927.

2 Conan Doyle may have thought here of William Gillette, who, in 1923, appeared in a revival of the play *Sherlock Holmes* as the Master himself, a role Gillette originated in 1899. Gillette went on to reprise the rôle in America again in 1928 and finally in a "farewell tour" that began in 1929 and ended only in 1932.

of Sherlock Holmes. He began his adventures in the very heart of the later Victorian Era, carried it through the all-too-short reign of Edward, and has managed to hold his own little niche even in these feverish days. Thus it would be true to say that those who first read of him, as young men, have lived to see their own grown-up children following the same adventures in the same magazine. It is a striking example of the patience and loyalty of the British public.

I had fully determined at the conclusion of *The Memoirs* to bring Holmes to an end, as I felt that my literary energies should not be directed too much into one channel. That pale, clear-cut face and loose-limbed figure were taking up an undue share of my imagination. I did the deed, but, fortunately, no coroner had pronounced upon the remains, and so, after a long interval, it was not difficult for me to respond to the flattering demand and to explain my rash act away. I have never regretted it, for I have not in actual practice found that these lighter sketches have prevented me from exploring and finding my limitations in such varied branches of literature as history, poetry, historical novels, psychic research, and the drama. Had Holmes never existed I could not have done more, though he may perhaps have stood a little in the way of the recognition of my more serious literary work.

And so, reader, farewell to Sherlock Holmes! I thank you for your past constancy, and can but hope that some return has been made in the shape of that distraction from the worries of life and stimulating change of thought which can only be found in the fairy kingdom of romance.

ARTHUR CONAN DOYLE

THE ADVENTURE OF THE
ILLUSTRIOUS CLIENT[1]

This final collection of short adventures, entitled The Case-Book of Sherlock Holmes, *consists of twelve stories published from 1921 through 1927 in the* Strand Magazine. *Curiously, it contains a preface by Arthur Conan Doyle, and doubt has been raised as to whether Dr. Watson wrote all of the stories credited to him in the volume. There are suggestions that some of the stories were penned by Watson's wife or cousin; some may even have been written by Sir Arthur Conan Doyle! "The Illustrious Client" is a tale of the mature Holmes, set in 1902. Holmes is physically attacked in the case, but as in "The Six Napoleons," he uses the power of the press to fool the villain. Although Holmes calls upon Watson to disguise himself as a connoisseur of Chinese pottery, scholars point out that Holmes's plan makes little sense. The case opens with another example of Holmes's "reverse snobbery" in his dealings with the foppish Sir James Damery, and the contrast is startling when we later meet "Porky" Shinwell Johnson, an "underworld" operative of Holmes's.*

"IT CAN'T HURT now," was Mr. Sherlock Holmes's comment when, for the tenth time in as many years, I asked his leave to reveal the following narrative. So it was that at last I obtained permission to put on record what was, in some ways, the supreme moment of my friend's career.

Both Holmes and I had a weakness for the Turkish Bath.[2] It was over a smoke in the pleasant lassitude of the drying-room that I have found him less reticent and more human than anywhere else. On the upper floor of the Northumberland Avenue establishment there is an isolated corner where two couches lie side by side, and it was on these that we lay upon September 3, 1902, the day when my narrative begins. I had asked him whether anything was stirring, and for answer he had shot his long, thin, nervous arm out of the sheets which enveloped him and had drawn an envelope from the inside pocket of the coat which hung beside him.

"It may be some fussy, self-important fool, it may be a matter of life or death," said he as he handed me the note." I know no more than this message tells me."

1 "The Illustrious Client" was published in two parts in the *Strand Magazine* in February and March 1925, and its first American appearance was in *Collier's Weekly Magazine* on November 8, 1924.

2 In a Victorian Turkish bath, the bather would visit a series of hot, dry rooms of increasing temperature, cooling down with the occasional cold shower or bath. Afterward would follow a washing-down, a massage, and finally a lengthy relaxation period in a room outfitted with couches. Turkish baths were introduced to Victorian society by David Urquhart, a diplomat who served in the British embassy in Turkey from 1831 to 1837; he returned home to become a member of Parliament and a passionate advocate of all things Turkish. His house was decorated in the Turkish style, luxuriously outfitted with

Iznik tiles and a working Turkish bath. In 1856, inspired by Urquhart's book *The Pillars of Hercules* (1850), which described the Turkish *hammam*, a physician named Richard Barter built—with Urquhart's help—a bath at St. Ann's Hill in Blarney, Ireland, to be used for therapeutic purposes. The following year, Urquhart assisted in building England's first public Turkish bath, on Broughton Lane in Manchester. Hundreds of similar establishments proliferated thereafter, including the fashionable Urquhart's London & Provincial Turkish Bath Company (opened in 1862) and Nevill's Turkish Baths, a chain of nine baths located throughout London. Nevill's had a pair of establishments on Northumberland Avenue, one designated for men and one for women. Watson's use of the baths was apparently a symptom of middle age; his first recorded visit was in "The Disappearance of Lady Frances Carfax" (text accompanying note 3), set by most chronologists after 1900. Holmes is not recorded as a visitor in any other story.

3 *Baedeker* reports that the Conservative Carlton Club, located at 94 Pall Mall, boasted 1,800 members in 1896. In "The Greek Interpreter," Dr. Watson places Mycroft Holmes's Diogenes Club "some little distance" from the Carlton Club (see "The Greek Interpreter," note 12).

4 According to O. F. Grazebrook, the first record of a telephone at the Carlton Club is in the directory dated October 31, 1883, issued by the United Telephone Company.

It was from the Carlton Club,[3] and dated the evening before. This is what I read:

Sir James Damery presents his compliments to Mr. Sherlock Holmes and will call upon him at 4:30 to-morrow. Sir James begs to say that the matter upon which he desires to consult Mr. Holmes is very delicate and also very important. He trusts, therefore, that Mr. Holmes will make every effort to grant this interview, and that he will confirm it over the telephone to the Carlton Club.[4]

"I need not say that I have confirmed it, Watson," said Holmes, as I returned the paper. "Do you know anything of this man Damery?"

"Only that this name is a household word in Society."

"Well, I can tell you a little more than that. He has rather a reputation for arranging delicate matters which are to be kept out of the papers. You may remember his negotiations with Sir George Lewis[5] over the Hammerford Will case. He is a man of the world with a natural turn for diplomacy. I am bound, therefore, to hope that it is not a false scent and that he has some real need for our assistance."

"Our?"

"Well, if you will be so good, Watson."

"I shall be honoured."

"Then you have the hour—four-thirty. Until then we can put the matter out of our heads."

5 Sir George Lewis (1833–1911), of the firm of Lewis and Lewis, was the most famous solicitor in England, the confidant of the Prince of Wales and countless others.

Sherlock Holmes shot his long, thin, nervous arm out of the sheets and drew an envelope from the inside pocket of the coat which hung beside him.
Howard Elcock, *Strand Magazine*, 1925

6 Queen Anne Street was located in the Cavendish Square neighbourhood of medical establishments (see "The Resident Patient" and "The Devil's Foot"), a short walk from Baker Street. Watson's relocation to quarters in this area of respected professionals indicates a step up socially from the days of his Paddington practice, where, writes Vernon Pennell, "early patients were drawn from the porters and their like of the Great Western Railway, via Kensington. . . ." D. Martin Dakin rejects some scholars' contentions that the move to Queen Anne Street was connected with a second marriage; rather, he contends, it was made out of necessity, "for financial reasons possibly connected with his unfortunate losses at gambling touched on in Shoscombe Old Place." The location is not mentioned in any other story.

7 Bliss Austin uses this piece of dialogue as evidence of Holmes's "subtle wit," expressed here with the intent of belittling the dandily attired Colonel Damery. As the exchange ensues, Austin explains, it becomes clear that Damery has not yet removed his gloves ("Colonel Damery threw up his kid-gloved hands with a laugh"), indicating either that the colonel felt Holmes's apartments were unclean, or, in a worse display of manners, that he had not yet shaken Holmes's hand. Holmes's question of "Don't you smoke?" was a pointed means of "baiting" Damery, writes Austin, who continues, "The trap was not obvious but it was there. Unless the Colonel refused altogether, he must either remove his gloves or treat Holmes to the delicious sight of a man in lavender spats smoking with kid gloves on. But refuse he did, so Holmes continued: 'Then you will excuse me if I light my pipe.' And one can be certain that he smiled as he said it."

8 Holmes also refers to Moran in "His Last Bow" (that is, in 1914) in a manner implying

I was living in my own rooms in Queen Anne Street[6] at the time, but I was round at Baker Street before the time named. Sharp to the half-hour, Colonel Sir James Damery was announced. It is hardly necessary to describe him, for many will remember that large, bluff, honest personality, that broad, clean-shaven face, above all, that pleasant, mellow voice. Frankness shone from his grey Irish eyes, and good humour played round his mobile, smiling lips. His lucent top-hat, his dark frock-coat, indeed, every detail, from the pearl pin in the black satin cravat to the lavender spats over the varnished shoes, spoke of the meticulous care in dress for which he was famous. The big, masterful aristocrat dominated the little room.

"Of course, I was prepared to find Dr. Watson," he remarked, with a courteous bow. "His collaboration may be very necessary, for we are dealing on this occasion, Mr. Holmes, with a man to whom violence is familiar and who will, literally, stick at nothing. I should say that there is no more dangerous man in Europe."

"I have had several opponents to whom that flattering term has been applied," said Holmes, with a smile. "Don't you smoke? Then you will excuse me if I light my pipe.[7] If your man is more dangerous than the late Professor Moriarty, or than the living[8] Colonel Sebastian Moran, then he is indeed worth meeting. May I ask his name?"

"Have you ever heard of Baron Gruner?"

"You mean the Austrian murderer?"

Colonel Damery threw up his kid-gloved hands with a laugh. "There is no getting past you, Mr. Holmes! Wonderful! So you have already sized him up as a murderer?"

"It is my business to follow the details of Continental crime. Who could possibly have read what happened at Prague and have any doubts as to the man's guilt! It was a purely technical legal point and the suspicious death of a witness that saved him! I am as sure that he killed his wife when the so-called 'accident' happened in the Splügen Pass[9] as if I had seen him do it.[10] I knew, also, that he had come to England and had a presentiment that sooner or later he would find me some work to do. Well, what has Baron Gruner been up to? I presume it is not this old tragedy which has come up again?"

Colonel Damery threw up his kid-gloved hands with a laugh.
"There is no getting past you, Mr. Holmes! Wonderful!"
Howard Elcock, *Strand Magazine*, 1925

that he was still alive. How Moran may have escaped the gallows for the killing of the Honourable Ronald Adair is explored in the notes to "The Empty House."

9 A pass on the boundary between Switzerland and Italy.

10 Michael Kaser questions the logic of the trial's taking place in Prague for a murder that occurred at the Swiss Splügen Pass. Even an appeal of the verdict reached by the provincial court would have been heard in Vienna. Bliss Austin explains the incongruity by suggesting, "Perhaps the Baron's reputation in Vienna was so bad that he requested, and because of his high position was granted, a change of venue."

"No, it is more serious than that. To revenge crime is important, but to prevent it is more so. It is a terrible thing, Mr. Holmes, to see a dreadful event, an atrocious situation, preparing itself before your eyes, to clearly understand whither it will lead and yet to be utterly unable to avert it. Can a human being be placed in a more trying position?"

"Perhaps not."

"Then you will sympathize with the client in whose interests I am acting."

"I did not understand that you were merely an intermediary. Who is the principal?"

"Mr. Holmes, I must beg you not to press that question. It is important that I should be able to assure him that his honoured

11 The battle of the Khyber Pass occurred in the second Afghan war (1878–1879), one of three wars in which Britain—threatened by Russia's interest in Afghanistan—attempted to seize control of the territory for itself. Under terms of the 1879 Treaty of Gandamak, Yakub Khan, the emir of Afghanistan, ceded Khyber Pass to the British; and by the end of the year, following the murder of a British envoy, British forces had occupied Kabul. Watson carried out his military service in this second Afghan campaign.

12 This would have been an early type of passenger cruise, predating the transatlantic voyages of the great ocean liners like the *Lusitania* and the *Titanic*. According to O. F. Grazebrook, the first cruise operated by the Orient Line took place aboard the *Garonne* on February 20, 1889, and carried passengers to Algiers, Genoa, Lisbon, Malaga, and Naples en route to Gibraltar and back. Thereafter, the Orient Line conducted cruises annually from 1889 to 1900.

name has been in no way dragged into the matter. His motives are, to the last degree, honourable and chivalrous, but he prefers to remain unknown. I need not say that your fees will be assured and that you will be given a perfectly free hand. Surely the actual name of your client is immaterial?"

"I am sorry," said Holmes. "I am accustomed to have mystery at one end of my cases, but to have it at both ends is too confusing. I fear, Sir James, that I must decline to act."

Our visitor was greatly disturbed. His large, sensitive face was darkened with emotion and disappointment.

"You hardly realize the effect of your own action, Mr. Holmes," said he. "You place me in a most serious dilemma, for I am perfectly certain that you would be proud to take over the case if I could give you the facts, and yet a promise forbids me from revealing them all. May I, at least, lay all that I can before you?"

"By all means, so long as it is understood that I commit myself to nothing."

"That is understood. In the first place, you have no doubt heard of General de Merville?"

"De Merville of Khyber fame?[11] Yes, I have heard of him."

"He has a daughter, Violet de Merville, young, rich, beautiful, accomplished, a wonder-woman in every way. It is this daughter, this lovely, innocent girl, whom we are endeavouring to save from the clutches of a fiend."

"Baron Gruner has some hold over her, then?"

"The strongest of all holds where a woman is concerned—the hold of love. The fellow is, as you may have heard, extraordinarily handsome, with a most fascinating manner, a gentle voice, and that air of romance and mystery which means so much to a woman. He is said to have the whole sex at his mercy and to have made ample use of the fact."

"But how came such a man to meet a lady of the standing of Miss Violet de Merville?"

"It was on a Mediterranean yachting voyage. The company, though select, paid their own passages.[12] No doubt the promoters hardly realized the Baron's true character until it was too late. The villain attached himself to the lady, and with such effect that he has completely and absolutely won her heart. To say that she loves him hardly expresses it. She dotes upon him, she is obsessed by him. Outside of him there is nothing on earth. She will not hear one word against him. Everything has been done to cure her of her madness, but in vain. To sum up, she proposes to marry him next month. As she is of age and has a will of iron, it is hard to know how to prevent her."

"Does she know about the Austrian episode?"

"The cunning devil has told her every unsavoury public scandal of his past life, but always in such a way as to make himself out to be an innocent martyr. She absolutely accepts his version and will listen to no other."

"Dear me! But surely you have inadvertently let out the name of your client? It is no doubt General de Merville."

Our visitor fidgeted in his chair.

"I could deceive you by saying so, Mr. Holmes, but it would not be true. De Merville is a broken man. The strong soldier has been utterly demoralized by this incident. He has lost the nerve which never failed him on the battlefield and has become a weak, doddering old man, utterly incapable of contending with a brilliant, forceful rascal like this Austrian. My client, however, is an old friend, one who has known the General intimately for many years and taken a paternal interest in this young girl since she wore short frocks. He cannot see this tragedy consummated without some attempt to stop it. There is nothing in which Scotland Yard can act. It was his own suggestion that you should be called in, but it was, as I have said, on the express stipulation that he should not be personally involved in the matter. I have no doubt, Mr. Holmes, with your great powers you could easily trace my client back through me, but I must ask you, as a point of honour, to refrain from doing so, and not to break in upon his incognito."

Holmes gave a whimsical smile.

"I think I may safely promise that," said he. "I may add that your problem interests me, and that I shall be prepared to look into it. How shall I keep in touch with you?"

"The Carlton Club will find me. But, in case of emergency, there is a private telephone call, 'XX.31.' "

Holmes noted it down and sat, still smiling, with the open memorandum-book upon his knee.

"The Baron's present address, please?"

"Vernon Lodge, near Kingston. It is a large house. He has been fortunate in some rather shady speculations and is a rich man, which, naturally, makes him a more dangerous antagonist."

13 The Hurlingham Club in Fulham was considered the headquarters of polo in England. Originating in Persia sometime between the sixth century B.C. and the first century A.D., the equestrian sport eventually made its way to Arabia, Tibet, China, Japan, and India, where it was picked up by British officers stationed there. Polo—from the Balti, or Tibeto-Burman, word for ball—was introduced to England in 1869, and its popularity spread rapidly throughout the country. Soon after hosting its first polo match in 1874, Hurlingham was attracting thousands of spectators and hosting competitions such as the Champion Cup (which debuted in 1876) and the annual Oxford vs. Cambridge match (starting in 1878). In 1875, the Hurlingham Polo Committee took on responsibility for drawing up a set of polo rules, which were adopted for use throughout England.

14 Irving Fenton describes Charles Peace (1832–1879) as a "burglar, murderer, liar, wifebeater, braggart, actor, inventor, [and] violin virtuoso." A native of Sheffield, Peace started his criminal career as a teenager, spending several stints in jail for burglarising people's houses. Between prison terms, he taught himself to play a violin with one string, billing himself as "the modern Paganini" at fairs and other venues. Fenton credits Peace with inventing the burglar's kit, improving the machinery at Dartmoor's prison, and fashioning a "smoke helmet" for firemen, among other innovations. His downfall was the 1876 murder of Arthur Dyson, the husband of Peace's purported mistress. Eluding capture by living as "Mr. Thompson" in London for two years, he was finally caught committing burglary in Blackheath. Peace was recognised and quickly sentenced to death—the jury was out for only ten minutes—and, writes Fenton, "on February 25, 1879, the law ended his terrestrial friendship, at least, with Sherlock Holmes." His collection of violins and banjos,

"Is he at home at present?"

"Yes."

"Apart from what you have told me, can you give me any further information about the man?"

"He has expensive tastes. He is a horse fancier. For a short time he played polo at Hurlingham,[13] but then this Prague affair got noised about and he had to leave. He collects books and pictures. He is a man with a considerable artistic side to his nature. He is, I believe, a recognized authority upon Chinese pottery, and has written a book upon the subject."

"A complex mind," said Holmes." All great criminals have that. My old friend Charlie Peace[14] was a violin virtuoso. Wainwright[15] was no mean artist. I could quote many more. Well, Sir James, you will inform your client that I am turning my mind upon Baron Gruner. I can say no more. I have some sources of information of my own, and I dare say we may find some means of opening the matter up."

When our visitor had left us Holmes sat so long in deep thought that it seemed to me that he had forgotten my presence. At last, however, he came briskly back to earth.

"Well, Watson, any views?" he asked.

"I should think you had better see the young lady herself."

"My dear Watson, if her poor old broken father cannot move her, how shall I, a stranger, prevail? And yet there is something in the suggestion if all else fails. But I think we must begin from a different angle. I rather fancy that Shinwell Johnson might be a help."

I have not had occasion to mention Shinwell Johnson in these memoirs because I have seldom drawn my cases from the latter phases of my friend's career. During the first years of the century he became a valuable assistant. Johnson, I grieve to say, made his name first as a very dangerous villain and served two terms at Parkhurst.[16] Finally, he repented and allied himself to Holmes, acting as his agent in the huge criminal underworld of London, and obtaining information which often proved to be of vital importance. Had Johnson been a "nark" of the police he would soon have been exposed, but as he dealt with cases which never came directly into the courts, his activities were never realized by his companions. With the glamour of his two convictions upon him, he had the *entrée* of every night-club, doss-house,[17] and gambling-den in the town, and

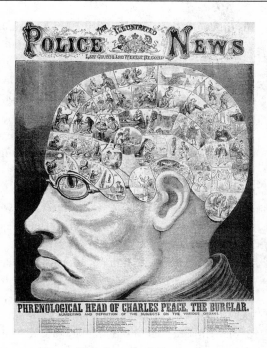

Phrenological head of Charles Peace.
The Victorians: A World Built to Last

one of the best in England, was auctioned off after his death. One wonders whether Holmes purchased one of Peace's violins as a souvenir.

Like Holmes, Peace was a master of disguise, capable of altering his appearance merely by jutting out his lower jaw or wearing a pair of goggles. For a time he posed as a one-armed man, hiding his real limb underneath his clothes. An 1894 *Strand* article entitled "Burglars and Burgling" notes that Peace used this effect to conceal the telltale fact that he was missing the forefinger of his left hand. "After he left Sheffield on 29th November,

1876," the article recounts, "his description was posted at every police station in the country. So he made himself [a false arm] which he placed in his sleeve, hanging his violin on the hook when engaged in walking about and taking stock of 'crackable' residences, and screwing in a fork in the place of the hook for use at meals. For something like two years, the irrepressible Peace walked this earth short of a hand, while the police were looking for a man short of a *finger*."

15 This might have been Thomas Griffiths Wainewright (1794–1852), a painter, art critic for *London Magazine* (writing essays under the pen names Egomet Bonmot and Janus Weathercock), and suspected murderer. Attempting to evade suspicion for the deaths of his uncle, his mother-in-law, and his sister-in-law, he lived in France for six years but, upon returning to England, was convicted on an old forgery charge and exiled to Tasmania for the remainder of his life. Or, Holmes might be referring to Henry Wainwright (?–1875), a brush manufacturer who killed his mistress and was caught attempting to dispose of her dismembered body parts. The artistic abilities of Wainwright, who maintained his innocence but confessed just before being hanged, are unknown.

16 Parkhurst, on the Isle of Wight, is a maximum-security prison, established in 1838.

17 A common lodging-house; a flop-house.

18 Some of which information Holmes may have passed on to Langdale Pike, with whom he regularly shared "knowledge" about the depths of London life (see "The Three Gables").

his quick observation and active brain made him an ideal agent for gaining information.[18] It was to him that Sherlock Holmes now proposed to turn.

It was not possible for me to follow the immediate steps taken by my friend, for I had some pressing professional business of my own, but I met him by appointment that evening at Simpson's, where, sitting at a small table in the front window, and looking down at the rushing stream of life in the Strand, he told me something of what had passed.

"Johnson is on the prowl," said he. "He may pick up some garbage in the darker recesses of the underworld, for it is down there amid the black roots of crime, that we must hunt for this man's secrets."

"But, if the lady will not accept what is already known, why should any fresh discovery of yours turn her from her purpose?"

"Who knows, Watson? Woman's heart and mind are insoluble puzzles to the male. Murder might be condoned or explained, and yet some smaller offence might rankle. Baron Gruner remarked to me—"

"He remarked to you!"

"Oh, to be sure, I had not told you of my plans! Well, Watson, I love to come to close grips with my man. I like to meet him eye to eye and read for myself the stuff that he is made of. When I had given Johnson his instructions, I took a cab out to Kingston and found the Baron in a most affable mood."

"Did he recognize you?"

"There was no difficulty about that, for I simply sent in my card. He is an excellent antagonist, cool as ice, silky voiced and soothing as one of your fashionable consultants and poisonous as a cobra. He has breed in him, a real aristocrat of crime, with a superficial suggestion of afternoon tea and all the cruelty of the grave behind it. Yes, I am glad to have had my attention called to Baron Adelbert Gruner."

"You say he was affable?"

"A purring cat who thinks he sees prospective mice. Some people's affability is more deadly than the violence of coarser souls. His greeting was characteristic. 'I rather thought I should see you sooner or later, Mr. Holmes,' said he. 'You have been engaged, no doubt, by General de Merville to endeavour to stop my marriage with his daughter, Violet. That is so, is it not?'

"I acquiesced.

" 'My dear man,' said he, 'you will only ruin your own well-deserved reputation. It is not a case in which you can possibly succeed. You will have barren work,[19] to say nothing of incurring some danger. Let me very strongly advise you to draw off at once.'

" 'It is curious,' I answered, 'but that was the very advice which I had intended to give you. I have a respect for your brains, Baron, and the little which I have seen of your personality has not lessened it. Let me put it to you as man to man. No one wants to rake up your past and make you unduly uncomfortable. It is over, and you are now in smooth waters, but if you persist in this marriage you will raise up a swarm of powerful enemies who will never leave you alone until they have made England too hot to hold you. Is the game worth it? Surely you would be wiser if you left the lady alone. It would not be pleasant for you if these facts of your past were brought to her notice.'

"The Baron has little waxed tips of hair under his nose, like the short antennae of an insect. These quivered with amusement as he listened, and he finally broke into a gentle chuckle.

" 'Excuse my amusement, Mr. Holmes,' said he, 'but it is really funny to see you trying to play a hand with no cards in it. I don't think anyone could do it better, but it is rather pathetic, all the same. Not a colour card[20] there, Mr. Holmes, nothing but the smallest of the small.'

" 'So you think.'

" 'So I know. Let me make the thing clear to you, for my own hand is so strong that I can afford to show it. I have been fortunate enough to win the entire affection of this lady. This was given to me in spite of the fact that I told her very clearly of all the unhappy incidents in my past life. I also told her that certain wicked and designing persons—I hope you recognize yourself—would come to her and tell her these things, and I warned her how to treat them. You have heard of post-hypnotic suggestion, Mr. Holmes? Well, you will see how it works, for a man of personality can use hypnotism without any vulgar passes or tomfoolery.[21] So she is ready for you and, I have no doubt, would give you an appointment, for she is quite amenable to her father's will—save only in the one little matter.'

"Well, Watson, there seemed to be no more to say, so I took

19 At least the *Baron* Gruner has a punning sense of humour.

20 A king, queen, or jack in a deck of playing cards, and presumably, since the most popular card game in England in 1902 was whist, in which aces outranked kings, an ace as well.

21 Hypnosis was well known in the late nineteenth century. It was first used for scientific purposes by Friedrich (or Franz) Anton Mesmer (1734–1815), a Viennese physician who treated his patients with what he thought of as "animal magnetism": an occult force that flowed from the hypnotist to the hypnotised, stimulating an invisible fluid in the body. The treatment became known as mesmerism, and although Mesmer was eventually discredited by the medical community—he was driven out of both Vienna and Paris—his methods did pave the way for the future exploration of the trance state in therapy. The "passes" scoffed at by Gruner refer to the early technique used by Mesmer of passing the hypnotist's hands slowly and regularly over the subject's face, with or without contact.

The term "hypnotism" was coined by British surgeon James Braid (1795–1860) in his book *Neurypnology* (1843). Braid debunked Mesmer's theories of the occult and proposed instead that hypnotism was a form of sleep, brought on by the fatigue that intense concentration on a fixed object could induce. With this technique he claimed to have "cured" patients of rheumatism and paralysis. As the end of the nineteenth century drew near, more physicians, among them Sigmund Freud, began utilising hypnosis to treat psychological disorders such as hysteria.

Notwithstanding popular myths of "glamour" and "hypnotic personalities," a post-hypnotic suggestion requires knowledge of the techniques of hypnotism. Where or when Gruner learned hypnotism remains unknown.

22 Gruner here refers to French criminals and not American Indians.

23 Formerly a town, Montmartre (French for "hill of the martyrs") was annexed by Paris in 1860. The famed church of Sacré Coeur rests atop the hill—the highest point in Paris—and the area has long been favoured by the city's bohemians. They gathered at nightclubs such as the Moulin Rouge, which opened in 1889 and was immortalised by the artist Henri de Toulouse-Lautrec.

my leave with as much cold dignity as I could summon, but, as I had my hand on the door-handle, he stopped me.

" 'By the way, Mr. Holmes,' said he, 'did you know Le Brun, the French agent?'

" 'Yes,' said I.

" 'Do you know what befell him?'

" 'I heard that he was beaten by some Apaches[22] in the Montmartre district[23] and crippled for life.'

" 'Quite true, Mr. Holmes. By a curious coincidence he had been inquiring into my affairs only a week before. Don't do it, Mr. Holmes; it's not a lucky thing to do. Several have found

As I had my hand on the door-handle, he stopped me.
"My last word to you is, go your own way and
let me go mine. Good-bye!"
Howard Elcock, *Strand Magazine*, 1925

that out. My last word to you is, go your own way and let me go mine. Good-bye!'

"So there you are, Watson. You are up to date now."

"The fellow seems dangerous."

"Mighty dangerous. I disregard the blusterer, but this is the sort of man who says rather less than he means."

"Must you interfere? Does it really matter if he marries the girl?"

"Considering that he undoubtedly murdered his last wife, I should say it mattered very much. Besides, the client! Well, well, we need not discuss that. When you have finished your coffee you had best come home with me, for the blithe Shinwell will be there with his report."

We found him sure enough, a huge, coarse, red-faced, scorbutic[24] man, with a pair of vivid black eyes which were the only external sign of the very cunning mind within. It seems that he had dived down into what was peculiarly his kingdom, and beside him on the settee was a brand[25] which he had brought up in the shape of a slim, flame-like young woman with a pale, intense face, youthful, and yet so worn with sin and sorrow that one read the terrible years which had left their leprous[26] mark upon her.

"This is Miss Kitty Winter,"[27] said Shinwell Johnson, waving his fat hand as an introduction." What she don't know—well, there, she'll speak for herself. Put my hand right on her, Mr. Holmes, within an hour of your message."

"I'm easy to find," said the young woman. "Hell, London, gets me every time. Same address for Porky Shinwell.[28] We're old mates, Porky, you and I. But, by Cripes! There is another who ought to be down in a lower hell than we if there was any justice in the world! That is the man you are after, Mr. Holmes."

Holmes smiled. "I gather we have your good wishes, Miss Winter."

"If I can help to put him where he belongs, I'm yours to the rattle,"[29] said our visitor with fierce energy. There was an intensity of hatred in her white, set face and her blazing eyes such as woman seldom and man never can attain. "You needn't go into my past, Mr. Holmes. That's neither here nor there. But what I am Adelbert Gruner made me. If I could pull him down!" She clutched frantically with her hands into the air.

24 That is, affected by scurvy, a disease caused by a lack of fresh vegetables and, consequently, of vitamin C. Scurvy primarily used to affect sailors, who did not have access to perishable foods. In 1747, Scottish naval surgeon James Lind treated afflicted sailors with oranges and lemons, achieving dramatic results, and in 1795 the British navy began distributing lime juice on long sea voyages. Characterised by a weakening of the capillaries, scurvy induces bleeding gums, loosened teeth, and haemorrhaging. Here, Watson likely uses "scorbutic" as another means of describing Johnson as "red-faced," since there is no other indication that he might actually be suffering from the disease.

25 A torch—in this case, a metaphor for a passionate woman (continuing with the description of Kitty Winter as "flame-like" and, later, "fiery").

26 Leprosy—caused by the bacterium *Mycobacterium leprae*, identified by Norwegian physician G. Armauer Hansen in 1874—inflicts affected persons with skin lesions. In the benign form of the disease, tuberculoid leprosy, these lesions are reddish or purplish; in the more severe lepromatous leprosy, they are yellow and brown in colour, protruding from the ears, nose, and throat. See "The Blanched Soldier," note 24, for a discussion of the spread of the disease and social attitudes towards leprosy and lepers. Here, however, Watson is likely speaking metaphorically (as with "scorbutic—see note 24) and uses the term in the sense of moral decay.

27 Whether she was related to James Winter, a k a "Killer" Evans of "The Three Garridebs," is unknown.

28 There is a confusion of names here. If the fellow's real name is "Shinwell Johnson," and "Porky" is his nickname, then why not

"Porky Johnson"? Or is this used in the sense of "Fat Albert" or "Fast Eddie"? The "Porky" epithet undoubtedly refers to his physical grossness (a "huge . . . man").

29 That is, until the death-rattle, or until death.

"Oh, if I could only pull him into the pit where he has pushed so many!"

"You know how the matter stands?"

"Porky Shinwell has been telling me. He's after some other poor fool and wants to marry her this time. You want to stop it. Well, you surely know enough about this devil to prevent any decent girl in her senses wanting to be in the same parish with him."

"She is not in her senses. She is madly in love. She has been told all about him. She cares nothing."

"Told about the murder?"

"Yes."

"My Lord, she must have a nerve!"

"She puts them all down as slanders."

"Couldn't you lay proofs before her silly eyes?"

"Well, can you help us do so?"

"Ain't I a proof myself? If I stood before her and told her how he used me."

"Would you do this?"

"Would I? Would I not!"

"Well, it might be worth trying. But he has told her most of his sins and had pardon from her, and I understand she will not reopen the question."

"I'll lay he didn't tell her all," said Miss Winter. "I caught a glimpse of one or two murders besides the one that made such a fuss. He would speak of someone in his velvet way and then look at me with a steady eye and say: 'He died within a month.' It wasn't hot air, either. But I took little notice—you see, I loved him myself at that time. Whatever he did went with me, same as with this poor fool! There was just one thing that shook me. Yes, by Cripes, if it had not been for his poisonous, lying tongue that explains and soothes, I'd have left him that very night. It's a book he has—a brown leather book with a lock, and his arms in gold on the outside. I think he was a bit drunk that night, or he would not have shown it to me."

"What was it, then?"

"I tell you, Mr. Holmes, this man collects women, and takes a pride in his collection, as some men collect moths or butterflies. He had it all in that book. Snapshot photographs, names, details, everything about them. It was a beastly book—a book no man, even if he had come from the gutter, could have put together. But it was Adelbert Gruner's book all the same. 'Souls I have ruined.' He could have put that on the outside if he had been so minded. However, that's neither here nor there, for the book would not serve you, and, if it would, you can't get it."

"Where is it?"

"How can I tell you where it is now? It's more than a year since I left him. I know where he kept it then. He's a precise, tidy cat of a man in many of his ways, so maybe it is still in the pigeon-hole of the old bureau in the inner study. Do you know his house?"

"I've been in the study," said Holmes.

"Have you, though? You haven't been slow on the job if you only started this morning. Maybe dear Adelbert has met his match this time. The outer study is the one with the Chinese crockery in it—big glass cupboard between the windows. Then behind his desk is the door that leads to the inner study—a small room where he keeps papers and things."

"Is he not afraid of burglars?"

"Adelbert is no coward. His worst enemy couldn't say that of him. He can look after himself. There's a burglar alarm at night. Besides, what is there for a burglar—unless they got away with all this fancy crockery?"

"No good," said Shinwell Johnson, with the decided voice of the expert. "No fence wants stuff of that sort that you can neither melt nor sell."

"Quite so," said Holmes. "Well, now, Miss Winter, if you would call here to-morrow evening at five, I would consider in the meanwhile whether your suggestion of seeing this lady personally may not be arranged. I am exceedingly obliged to you for your co-operation. I need not say that my clients will consider liberally—"

"None of that, Mr. Holmes," cried the young woman. "I am not out for money. Let me see this man in the mud, and I've got all I've worked for—in the mud with my foot on his cursed face. That's my price. I'm with you to-morrow or any other day so long as you are on his track. Porky here can tell you always where to find me."

I did not see Holmes again until the following evening, when we dined once more at our Strand restaurant. He shrugged his shoulders when I asked him what luck he had in his interview. Then he told the story, which I would repeat in this way. His hard, dry statement needs some little editing to soften it into the terms of real life.

"There was no difficulty at all about the appointment," said Holmes, "for the girl glories in showing abject filial obedience in all secondary things in an attempt to atone for her flagrant breach of it in her engagement. The General 'phoned that all was ready and the fiery Miss W. turned up according to schedule, so that at half-past five a cab deposited us outside 104 Berkeley Square, where the old soldier resides—one of those awful grey London castles which would make a church seem frivolous. A footman showed us into a great yellow-curtained drawing-room, and there was the lady awaiting us, demure, pale, self-contained, as inflexible and remote as a snow image on a mountain.

"I don't quite know how to make her clear to you, Watson. Perhaps you may meet her before we are through, and you can use your own gift of words. She is beautiful, but with the ethereal other-world beauty of some fanatic whose thoughts are set on high. I have seen such faces in the pictures of the old masters of the Middle Ages. How a beast-man could have laid his vile paws upon such a being of the beyond I cannot imagine. You may have noticed how extremes call to each other, the spiritual to the animal, the cave-man to the angel. You never saw a worse case than this.

"She knew what we had come for, of course—that villain had lost no time in poisoning her mind against us. Miss Winter's advent rather amazed her, I think, but she waved us into our respective chairs like a reverend abbess receiving two rather leprous mendicants. If your head is inclined to swell, my dear Watson, take a course of Miss Violet de Merville.

" 'Well, sir,' said she, in a voice like the wind from an iceberg, 'your name is familiar to me. You have called, as I understand, to malign my fiancé, Baron Gruner. It is only by my father's request that I see you at all, and I warn you in advance that anything you can say could not possibly have the slightest effect upon my mind.'

"I was sorry for her, Watson. I thought of her for the moment as I would have thought of a daughter of my own. I am not often eloquent. I use my head, not my heart. But I really did plead with her with all the warmth of words that I could find in my nature. I pictured to her the awful position of the woman who only wakes to a man's character after she is his wife—a woman who has to submit to be caressed by bloody hands and lecherous lips. I spared her nothing—the shame, the fear, the agony, the hopelessness of it all. All my hot words could not bring one tinge of colour to those ivory cheeks or one gleam of emotion to those abstracted eyes. I thought of what the rascal had said about a post-hypnotic influence. One could really believe that she was living above the earth in some ecstatic dream. Yet there was nothing indefinite in her replies.

" 'I have listened to you with patience, Mr. Holmes,' said she. 'The effect upon my mind is exactly as predicted. I am aware that Adelbert, that my fiancé, has had a stormy life in which he has incurred bitter hatreds and most unjust aspersions. You are only the last of a series who have brought their slanders before me. Possibly you mean well, though I learn that you are a paid agent who would have been equally willing to act for the Baron as against him. But in any case I wish you to understand once for all that I love him and that he loves me, and that the opinion of all the world is no more to me than the twitter of those birds outside the window. If his noble nature has ever for an instant fallen, it may be that I have been specially sent to raise it to its true and lofty level. I am not clear'—here she turned eyes upon my companion—'who this young lady may be.'

"I was about to answer when the girl broke in like a whirlwind. If ever you saw flame and ice face to face, it was those two women.

" 'I'll tell you who I am,' she cried, springing out of her chair, her mouth all twisted with passion—'I am his last mistress. I am one of a hundred that he has tempted and used and ruined and thrown into the refuse heap, as he will you also. *Your* refuse heap is more likely to be a grave, and maybe that's the best. I tell you, you foolish woman, if you marry this man he'll be the death of you. It may be a broken heart or it may be a broken neck, but he'll have you one way or the other. It's not out of love for you I'm speaking. I don't care a tinker's curse whether you live or die. It's out of hate for him and to spite him and to get back on him for what he did to me. But it's all the same, and you needn't look at me like that, my fine lady, for you may be lower than I am before you are through with it.'

" 'Mr. Holmes, I beg that you will bring this interview to an end,' said the icy voice.
With an oath Miss Winter darted forward, and if I had not caught her wrist she would have
caught this maddening woman by the hair."

Howard Elcock, *Strand Magazine*, 1925

" 'I should prefer not to discuss such matters,' said Miss de Merville coldly. 'Let me say once for all that I am aware of three passages in my fiancé's life in which he became entangled with designing women, and that I am assured of his hearty repentance for any evil that he may have done.'

" 'Three passages!' screamed my companion. 'You fool! You unutterable fool!'

" 'Mr. Holmes, I beg that you will bring this interview to an end,' said the icy voice. 'I have obeyed my father's wish in seeing you, but I am not compelled to listen to the ravings of this person.'

"With an oath Miss Winter darted forward, and if I had not caught her wrist she would have clutched this maddening woman by the hair. I dragged her towards the door and was lucky to get her back into the cab without a public scene, for she was beside herself with rage. In a cold way I felt pretty furious myself, Watson, for there was something indescribably annoying in the calm aloofness and supreme self-complaisance of the woman whom we were trying to save. So now once again you know exactly how we stand, and it is clear that I must plan some fresh opening move, for this gambit won't work. I'll keep in touch with you, Watson, for it is more than likely that you will have your part to play, though it is just possible that the next move may lie with them rather than with us."

And it did. Their blow fell—or his blow rather, for never could I believe that the lady was privy to it. I think I could show you the very paving-stone upon which I stood when my eyes fell upon the placard, and a pang of horror passed through my very soul. It was between the Grand Hotel and Charing Cross Station, where a one legged news-vender displayed his evening papers. The date was just two days after the last conversation. There, black upon yellow, was the terrible news-sheet:

MURDEROUS ATTACK
UPON SHERLOCK HOLMES

I think I stood stunned for some moments.[30] Then I have a confused recollection of snatching at a paper, of the remonstrance of the man, whom I had not paid, and, finally, of standing in the doorway of a chemist's shop while I turned up the fateful paragraph. This was how it ran:

We learn with regret that Mr. Sherlock Holmes, the well-known private detective, was the victim this morning of a murderous assault which has left him in a precarious position. There are no exact details to hand, but the event seems to have occurred about twelve o'clock in Regent Street, outside the Café Royal. The attack was made by two men armed with sticks, and Mr. Holmes was beaten about the head and body,

30 This sentence is the beginning of Part II of "The Illustrious Client," published in the March 1925 issue of the *Strand Magazine*. The part begins with the following synopsis:

The Illustrious Client on whose behalf Sherlock Holmes is consulted is anxious to prevent the marriage of the young, rich, and beautiful Miss Violet de Merville to Baron Gruner, an unscrupulous adventurer. Gruner has told her every scandal of his past life, but in such a way as to make himself out to be an innocent martyr. She absolutely accepts his version, and will listen to no other.

Sherlock Holmes interviews the Baron, who warns him of the risk he is running in interfering in his affairs. He then visits Miss de Merville in company with a Miss Winter, one of the Baron's many victims, in the hope that her story may induce the infatuated girl to change her mind. But all to no purpose.

"So now you know exactly how we stand," said Sherlock Holmes, finally, "and it is clear that I must plan some fresh opening move, for this gambit won't work. I'll keep in touch with you, Watson . . . though it is just possible that the next move may lie with them rather than with us."

And it did. For two days later Watson's eyes fell upon a newspaper placard, and a pang of horror passed through him as he read the words: "Murderous Attack upon Sherlock Holmes."

receiving injuries which the doctors describe as most serious. He was carried to Charing Cross Hospital, and afterwards insisted upon being taken to his rooms in Baker Street. The miscreants who attacked him appear to have been respectably dressed men, who escaped from the bystanders by passing through the Café Royal and out into Glasshouse Street behind it. No doubt they belonged to that criminal fraternity which has so often had occasion to bewail the activity and ingenuity of the injured man.

I need not say that my eyes had hardly glanced over the paragraph before I had sprung into a hansom and was on my way to Baker Street. I found Sir Leslie Oakshott, the famous surgeon, in the hall and his brougham waiting at the kerb.

"No immediate danger," was his report. "Two lacerated scalp wounds and some considerable bruises. Several stitches have been necessary. Morphine has been injected and quiet is essential, but an interview of a few minutes would not be absolutely forbidden."

With this permission I stole into the darkened room. The sufferer was wide awake, and I heard my name in a hoarse whisper. The blind was three-quarters down, but one ray of sunlight slanted through and struck the bandaged head of the

Charing Cross Hotel and Station.
Sherlock Holmes's London

Howard Elcock, *Strand Magazine*, 1925

31 Dr. Samuel R. Meaker criticises the vaunted Dr. Oakshott for his shoddy suturing job, which has soaked Holmes's dressing through with blood even before the doctor has left the house. Eight days later, Holmes's head is described as "girt with bloody bandages" even after his stitches are removed. Holmes's forthcoming statement about his plan to "exaggerate" his injuries to the doctor, adds Murray A. Cantor, demonstrates even more of a disconnect between Oakshott's reputation and his actual abilities.

injured man. A crimson patch had soaked through the white linen compress.[31] I sat beside him and bent my head.

"All right, Watson. Don't look so scared," he muttered in a very weak voice. "It's not as bad as it seems."

"Thank God for that!"

"I'm a bit of a single-stick expert, as you know. I took most of them on my guard. It was the second man that was too much for me."

"What can I do, Holmes? Of course, it was that damned fellow who set them on. I'll go and thrash the hide off him if you give the word."

"Good old Watson! No, we can do nothing there unless the police lay their hands on the men. But their get-away had been well prepared. We may be sure of that. Wait a little. I have my plans. The first thing is to exaggerate my injuries. They'll

32 Holmes's malingering abilities should have been well known to Watson after "The Dying Detective."

The attack was made by two men armed with sticks.
Howard Elcock, *Strand Magazine*, 1925

come to you for news. Put it on thick, Watson. Lucky if I live the week out—concussion—delirium—what you like! You can't overdo it."

"But Sir Leslie Oakshott?"

"Oh, he's all right. He shall see the worst side of me. I'll look after that."[32]

"Anything else?"

"Yes. Tell Shinwell Johnson to get that girl out of the way. Those beauties will be after her now. They know, of course, that she was with me in the case. If they dared to do me in it is not likely they will neglect her. That is urgent. Do it to-night."

"I'll go now. Anything more?"

"Put my pipe on the table—and the tobacco-slipper. Right! Come in each morning and we will plan our campaign."

I arranged with Johnson that evening to take Miss Winter to a quiet suburb and see that she lay low until the danger was past.

For six days the public were under the impression that Holmes was at the door of death. The bulletins were very grave and there were sinister paragraphs in the papers. My continual visits assured me that it was not so bad as that. His wiry constitution and his determined will were working wonders. He was recovering fast, and I had suspicions at times that he was really finding himself faster than he pretended, even to me. There was a curious secretive streak in the man which led to many dramatic effects, but left even his closest friend guessing as to what his exact plans might be. He pushed to an extreme the axiom that the only safe plotter was he who plotted alone. I was nearer him than anyone else, and yet I was always conscious of the gap between.

On the seventh day the stitches were taken out, in spite of which there was a report of erysipelas[33] in the evening papers. The same evening papers had an announcement which I was bound, sick or well, to carry to my friend. It was simply that among the passengers on the Cunard boat *Ruritania*, starting from Liverpool on Friday, was the Baron Adelbert Gruner,[34] who had some important financial business to settle in the States before his impending wedding to Miss Violet de Merville, only daughter of, *etc., etc.* Holmes listened to the news with a cold, concentrated look upon his pale face, which told me that it hit him hard.

"Friday!" he cried. "Only three clear days. I believe the rascal wants to put himself out of danger's way. But he won't, Wat-

Café Royal.
Victorian and Edwardian London

33 Arthur Conan Doyle witnessed outbreaks of this highly contagious skin infection in July 1900 at Bloemfontein, South Africa, during his investigation of the Boer War. Erysipelas is "an acute febrile infectious disease of the skin from which several orderlies [then] died," according to Alvin E. Rodin and Jack D. Key's *Medical Casebook of Doctor Arthur Conan Doyle*. "Only at the time of World War II, when penicillin became available, was it no longer a frequently fatal disease."

34 Baron Gruner was to leave Liverpool in the *Ruritania* on a Friday, despite the fact that Cunard liners then sailed for New York only on Tuesdays, Thursdays, and Saturdays, according to Jack Tracy's *Encyclopedia Sherlockiana*.

35 "Harry" is slang for the Devil. Some believe it derives from "hairy," but E. Cobham Brewer, in his *Dictionary of Phrase and Fable*, writes, "There is an ancient pamphlet entitled *The Harrowing of Hell*. I do not think it is a corruption of 'Old Hairy,' although the Hebrew *Seirim* (hairy ones) is translated devils in Lev. xvii. 7, and no doubt alludes to the he-goat, an object of worship with the Egyptians." Brewer also notes that the Scandinavian *hari* is equivalent to Baal, the Canaanite deity whose name was distorted to Baal-zebub.

36 Located at 14 St. James's Square, the London Library was a large subscription library founded in 1841 by a group that included Thomas Carlyle and John Stuart Mill. Their goal was to allow the library's members—who qualified by presenting a recommendation by another member and then paying an annual subscription fee—access to "good books in all departments of knowledge."

37 The ancient Chinese calendar consisted of six sixty-day cycles, divided up into ten-day periods. Three of those periods (what we might consider weeks) made up a month. The years, too, were grouped into major cycles of sixty, with minor cycles consisting of five years each.

38 Hung-wu (1328–1398) was the founder of the Ming dynasty, which lasted from 1368 to 1644. Born Chu Yüan-chang to a poor peasant family and orphaned at the age of sixteen, he joined a monastery and later became a leader of rebel forces that stole from the rich and gave to the poor. Educated by learned men he encountered on his travels, Chu became a formidable opponent of the Mongolian Yüan dynasty, capturing Nanking in 1356 and systematically overpowering or eliminating his rivals. In 1368, he established himself as emperor of the new Ming dynasty and gave himself the title Hung-wu, or Vastly Martial.

son! By the Lord Harry,[35] he won't! Now, Watson, I want you to do something for me."

"I am here to be used, Holmes."

"Well, then, spend the next twenty-four hours in an intensive study of Chinese pottery."

He gave no explanations and I asked for none. By long experience I had learned the wisdom of obedience. But when I had left his room I walked down Baker Street, revolving in my head how on earth I was to carry out so strange an order. Finally I drove to the London Library[36] in St. James's Square, put the matter to my friend Lomax, the sub-librarian, and departed to my rooms with a goodly volume under my arm.

It is said that the barrister who crams up a case with such care that he can examine an expert witness upon the Monday has forgotten all his forced knowledge before the Saturday. Certainly I should not like now to pose as an authority upon ceramics. And yet all that evening, and all that night with a short interval for rest, and all next morning I was sucking in knowledge and committing names to memory. There I learned of the hall-marks of the great artist-decorators, of the mystery of cyclical dates,[37] the marks of the Hung-wu[38] and the beauties of the Yung-lo,[39] the writings of Tang-ying,[40] and the glories of the primitive period of the Sung[41] and the Yuan.[42] I was charged with all this information when I called upon Holmes next evening. He was out of bed now, though you would not have guessed it from the published reports, and he sat with his much-bandaged head resting upon his hand in the depth of his favourite arm-chair.

"Why, Holmes," I said, "if one believed the paper, you are dying."

"That," said he, "is the very impression which I intended to convey. And now, Watson, have you learned your lessons?"

"At least I have tried to."

"Good. You could keep up an intelligent conversation on the subject?"

"I believe I could."

"Then hand me that little box from the mantelpiece."

He opened the lid and took out a small object most carefully wrapped in some fine Eastern silk. This he unfolded, and disclosed a delicate little saucer of the most beautiful deep-blue colour.

History regards him as a despot who restored stability and Chinese culture to the government after the reign of the Mongol invaders.

Ceramics created during the Ming period are highly prized, characterised primarily by delicate white porcelain pieces hand-painted with blue artwork. The style was widely copied in seventeenth-century Europe.

39 Yung-lo (1360–1424), born Chu Ti, was the third Ming emperor, a younger son of Hung-wu. A favourite of Hung-wu but not his official heir, Chu Ti was assigned by his father to pursue and conquer the remaining Mongols. Upon Hung-wu's death, Chu Ti's nephew (Chu Yün-wen, the young son of the deceased crown prince) became the new emperor; but Chu Ti, convinced of his own supremacy, usurped the throne in 1403 after a lengthy civil war.

40 Tang-ying (1470–1523), or Tang Yin (also T'ang Yin), was a painter and poet of the Ming dynasty. Briefly imprisoned for cheating on his governmental exams, he was forced to give up on a life of scholarly comfort and instead sold his paintings to make a living. He is best known for his landscapes. Tang-ying was also the name of the director of the imperial Chinese porcelain kilns in the eighteenth century.

41 The Sung dynasty spanned the years from 960 to 1259, achieving substantial educational, economic, and artistic progress (at least by modern American standards)—paper currency was introduced, civil service examinations were expanded, and a welfare policy was implemented—before falling to the Mongols. There were, in fact, two Sung dynasties: the Northern Sung was followed by the Southern Sung, established in 1127. Pottery in the Northern Sung dynasty was glazed brown and black, whereas the Southern Sung produced pieces in white, pale green (or celadon), and black. Both types of pottery are esteemed for their simple shapes and purity of colour.

42 The Yüan, or Mongol, dynasty (1271–1368) was established when Kublai Khan (1215–1294), the grandson of Genghis Khan, came down from northern China to overthrow the Sung dynasty in the south. Maintaining their distance from the Chinese population, the Mongols staffed the government with Central Asians and encouraged the input of Europeans, such as the European traveller Marco Polo. Art was not particularly encouraged by the state, leading artists to seek their own inspiration and to hone and enhance the styles of the T'ang and Northern Sung dynasties. Somewhat ironically, this led to a grand flourishing of the arts. Ceramics during this period began to display the blue-and-white colours that became prominent during the Ming dynasty.

43 "Eggshell" porcelains, called by the Chinese "bodyless" because of their extreme thinness, were made as early as the reign of Yung-lo.

"It needs careful handling, Watson. This is the real eggshell pottery[43] of the Ming dynasty. No finer piece ever passed through Christie's. A complete set of this would be worth a king's ransom—in fact, it is doubtful if there is a complete set outside the imperial palace of Peking. The sight of this would drive a real connoisseur wild."

"What am I to do with it?"

Holmes handed me a card upon which was printed: "Dr. Hill Barton, 369 Half Moon Street."

"That is your name for the evening, Watson. You will call upon Baron Gruner. I know something of his habits, and at half-past eight he would probably be disengaged. A note will tell him in advance that you are about to call, and you will say that you are bringing him a specimen of an absolutely unique set of Ming china. You may as well be a medical man, since that is a part which you can play without duplicity. You are a collector, this set has come your way, you have heard of the Baron's interest in the subject, and you are not averse to selling at a price."

"What price?"

"Well asked, Watson. You would certainly fall down badly if you did not know the value of your own wares. This saucer was got for me by Sir James, and comes, I understand, from the collection of his client. You will not exaggerate if you say that it could hardly be matched in the world."

"I could perhaps suggest that the set should be valued by an expert."

"Excellent, Watson! You scintillate to-day. Suggest Christie or Sotheby. Your delicacy prevents your putting a price for yourself."

"But if he won't see me?"

"Oh, yes, he will see you. He has the collection mania in its most acute form—and especially on this subject, on which he is an acknowledged authority. Sit down, Watson, and I will dictate the letter. No answer needed. You will merely say that you are coming, and why."

It was an admirable document, short, courteous, and stimulating to the curiosity of the connoisseur. A district messenger was duly dispatched with it. On the same evening, with the precious saucer in my hand and the card of Dr. Hill Barton in my pocket, I set off on my own adventure.

The beautiful house and grounds indicated that Baron

Gruner was, as Sir James had said, a man of considerable wealth. A long winding drive, with banks of rare shrubs on either side, opened out into a great gravelled square adorned with statues. The place had been built by a South African gold king in the days of the great boom, and the long, low house with the turrets at the corners, though an architectural nightmare, was imposing in its size and solidity. A butler who would have adorned a bench of bishops[44] showed me in and handed me over to a plush-clad footman, who ushered me into the Baron's presence.

He was standing at the open front of a great case which stood between the windows, and which contained part of his Chinese collection. He turned as I entered with a small brown vase in his hand.

"Pray sit down, Doctor," said he. "I was looking over my own treasures and wondering whether I could really afford to add to them. This little Tang[45] specimen, which dates from the seventeenth century, would probably interest you. I am sure you never saw finer workmanship or a richer glaze. Have you the Ming saucer with you of which you spoke?"

I carefully unpacked it and handed it to him. He seated himself at his desk, pulled over the lamp, for it was growing dark, and set himself to examine it. As he did so the yellow light beat upon his own features, and I was able to study them at my ease.

He was certainly a remarkably handsome man. His European reputation for beauty was fully deserved. In figure he was not more than of middle size, but was built upon graceful and active lines. His face was swarthy, almost Oriental, with large, dark, languorous eyes which might easily hold an irresistible fascination for women. His hair and moustache were raven black: the latter short, pointed, and carefully waxed. His features were regular and pleasing, save only his straight, thin-lipped mouth. If ever I saw a murderer's mouth it was there—a cruel, hard gash in the face, compressed, inexorable, and terrible. He was ill-advised to train his moustache away from it, for it was Nature's danger-signal, set as a warning to his victims.[46] His voice was engaging and his manners perfect. In age I should have put him at little over thirty, though his record afterwards showed that he was forty-two.

"Very fine—very fine indeed!" he said at last. "And you say you have a set of six to correspond. What puzzles me is that I

44 Bishops are automatically appointed to represent the Church of England in the House of Lords, where seating is on open benches.

45 The Tang, or T'ang, dynasty spanned the years 618 to 907. It was a glorious period for arts and culture, with poetry especially celebrated and western and other types of foreign music performed with great fanfare at imperial ceremonies. Ceramics were mostly white porcelain, tri-coloured pottery, and stoneware glazed a deep black.

46 Nature similarly bestows Colonel Sebastian Moran's facial features with signs of warning, in "The Empty House": "But one could not look upon his cruel blue eyes, with their drooping, cynical lids, or upon the fierce, aggressive nose and the threatening, deep-lined brow, without reading Nature's plainest danger-signals." Various Canonical individuals assert a connection between physical appearance and character—see, for example, Moriarty's comments on Holmes's appearance in "The Final Problem" and the discussion there of the "science" of phrenology.

should not have heard of such magnificent specimens. I only know of one in England to match this, and it is certainly not likely to be in the market. Would it be indiscreet if I were to ask you, Dr. Hill Barton, how you obtained this?"

"Does it really matter?" I asked with as careless an air as I could muster. "You can see that the piece is genuine, and, as to the value, I am content to take an expert's valuation."

"Very mysterious," said he with a quick, suspicious flash of his dark eyes. "In dealing with objects of such value, one naturally wishes to know all about the transaction. That the piece is genuine is certain. I have no doubts at all about that. But suppose—I am bound to take every possibility into account— that it should prove afterwards that you had no right to sell?"

"I would guarantee you against any claim of the sort."

"That, of course, would open up the question as to what your guarantee was worth."

"Very fine—very fine indeed! Would be indiscreet if I
were to ask you how you obtained this?"
Howard Elcock, *Strand Magazine*, 1925

"My bankers would answer that."

"Quite so. And yet the whole transaction strikes me as rather unusual."

"You can do business or not," said I, with indifference. "I have given you the first offer, as I understood that you were a connoisseur, but I shall have no difficulty in other quarters."

"Who told you I was a connoisseur?"

"I was aware that you had written a book upon the subject."

"Have you read the book?"

"No."

"Dear me, this becomes more and more difficult for me to understand! You are a connoisseur and collector with a very valuable piece in your collection, and yet you have never troubled to consult the one book which would have told you of the real meaning and value of what you held. How do you explain that?"

"I am a very busy man. I am a doctor in practice."

"That is no answer. If a man has a hobby he follows it up, whatever his other pursuits may be. You said in your note that you were a connoisseur."

"So I am."

"Might I ask you a few questions to test you? I am obliged to tell you, Doctor—if you are indeed a doctor—that the incident becomes more and more suspicious. I would ask you what do you know of the Emperor Shomu[47] and how do you associate him with the Shoso-in near Nara?[48] Dear me, does that puzzle you? Tell me a little about the Northern Wei[49] dynasty and its place in the history of ceramics."

I sprang from my chair in simulated anger.

"This is intolerable, sir," said I. "I came here to do you a favour, and not to be examined as if I were a schoolboy. My knowledge on these subjects may be second only to your own, but I certainly shall not answer questions which have been put in so offensive a way."

He looked at me steadily. The languor had gone from his eyes. They suddenly glared. There was a gleam of teeth from between those cruel lips.

"What is the game? You are here as a spy. You are an emissary of Holmes. This is a trick that you are playing upon me. The fellow is dying, I hear, so he sends his tools to keep watch upon me. You've made your way in here without leave, and, by God! you may find it harder to get out than to get in."

47 The Japanese emperor Shomu (701–756) took the throne in 715. He distinguished himself by heavily fostering Buddhism and Buddhist thought, devoting considerable state resources to the creation of Buddhist temples, monasteries, and artifacts.

48 Nara was the first permanent capital of Japan. Emperor Shomu built the enormous Todai Temple (or Todai-ji) there, dedicating it with a speech in 752 in which he declared himself subject to "Three Precious Things": Buddha, the law of Buddhism, and the organisation of the church. Shoso House (Shoso-in), the one surviving structure of the Todai Temple, houses a vast collection of more than six hundred of Emperor Shomu's personal objects, and over nine thousand works of art in all.

49 The Wei dynasty was founded in 220 by Toba nomads who ruled the northern portion of China until the dynastic wars of the sixth century. The Wei gradually assimilated to upper-class Chinese culture and in particular embraced Buddhism, promoting it as the state religion. Most of the significant art produced during this period was Buddhist in theme, but whatever relation to pottery the Baron may have had in mind is unknown.

50 Watson refers here to the highly corrosive sulphuric acid (also called "oil of vitriol"), commonly used in the nineteenth century as a bleaching agent or disinfectant. A vitriol-throwing occurred in "The Blue Carbuncle."

He had sprung to his feet, and I stepped back, bracing myself for an attack, for the man was beside himself with rage. He may have suspected me from the first; certainly this cross-examination had shown him the truth; but it was clear that I could not hope to deceive him. He dived his hand into a side-drawer and rummaged furiously. Then something struck upon his ear, for he stood listening intently.

"Ah!" he cried. "Ah!" and dashed into the room behind him.

Two steps took me to the open door, and my mind will ever carry a clear picture of the scene within. The window leading out to the garden was wide open. Beside it, looking like some terrible ghost, his head girt with bloody bandages, his face drawn and white, stood Sherlock Holmes. The next instant he was through the window and I heard the crash of his body among the laurel bushes outside. With a howl of rage the master of the house rushed after him to the open window.

And then! It was done in an instant, and yet I clearly saw it. An arm—a woman's arm—shot out from among the leaves. At the same instant the Baron uttered a horrible cry—a yell which will always ring in my memory. He clapped his two hands to his face and rushed round the room, beating his head horribly against the walls. Then he fell upon the carpet, rolling and writhing, while scream after scream resounded through the house.

"Water! For God's sake, water!" was his cry.

I seized a carafe from a side-table and rushed to his aid. At the same moment the butler and several footmen ran in from the hall. I remember that one of them fainted as I knelt by the injured man and turned that awful face to the light of the lamp. The vitriol[50] was eating into it everywhere and dripping from the ears and the chin. One eye was already white and glazed. The other was red and inflamed. The features which I had admired a few minutes before were now like some beautiful painting over which the artist has passed a wet and foul sponge. They were blurred, discoloured, inhuman, terrible.

In a few words I explained exactly what had occurred, so far as the vitriol attack was concerned. Some had climbed through the window and others had rushed out on to the lawn, but it was dark and it had begun to rain. Between his screams the victim raged and raved against the avenger. "It was that hell-cat, Kitty Winter!" he cried. "Oh, the she-devil! She shall pay for

The Baron dashed into the room. Two steps took me to the open door. Beside the window,
looking like some terrible ghost, his head girt with bandages, his face
drawn and white, stood Sherlock Holmes.
Howard Elcock, *Strand Magazine*, 1925

it! She shall pay! Oh, God in heaven, this pain is more than I
can bear!"

I bathed his face in oil, put cotton wadding on the raw sur-
faces, and administered a hypodermic of morphia. All suspicion of me had passed from his mind in the presence of this
shock, and he clung to my hands as if I might have the power
even yet to clear those dead-fish eyes which gazed up at me. I
could have wept over the ruin had I not remembered very
clearly the vile life which had led up to so hideous a change. It
was loathsome to feel the pawing of his burning hands, and I
was relieved when his family surgeon, closely followed by a
specialist, came to relieve me of my charge. An inspector of
police had also arrived, and to him I handed my real card. It
would have been useless as well as foolish to do otherwise, for
I was nearly as well known by sight at the Yard as Holmes himself. Then I left that house of gloom and terror. Within an hour
I was at Baker Street.

51 "For the wages of sin is death; but the gift of God is eternal life . . ." *Romans* 6:23.

52 Hans-Uno Bengtsson points out, in " 'It Needs Careful Handling,' " that this is an unfair criticism, for it is not Watson's limited knowledge that ends the interview abruptly but rather the unlikelihood of a sale of a unique art object well known to the baron.

53 This seems a suspiciously poor excuse to Brad Keefauver, who hardly believes Holmes to be an innocent bystander in the attack. "What did he think she was hiding?" Keefauver asks in his book *Sherlock Holmes and the Ladies*. "A gun, maybe? Nothing that could do Gruner any go--od, in any case. Sherlock Holmes does not come away from the ending to 'The Adventure of the Illustrious Client' with clean hands no matter how you look at it."

Holmes was seated in his familiar chair, looking very pale and exhausted. Apart from his injuries, even his iron nerves had been shocked by the events of the evening, and he listened with horror to my account of the Baron's transformation.

"The wages of sin, Watson—the wages of sin!" said he.[51] "Sooner or later it will always come. God knows, there was sin enough," he added, taking up a brown volume from the table. "Here is the book the woman talked of. If this will not break off the marriage, nothing ever could. But it will, Watson. It must. No self-respecting woman could stand it."

"It is his love diary?"

"Or his lust diary. Call it what you will. The moment the woman told us of it I realized what a tremendous weapon was there if we could but lay our hands on it. I said nothing at the time to indicate my thoughts, for this woman might have given it away. But I brooded over it. Then this assault upon me gave me the chance of letting the Baron think that no precautions need be taken against me. That was all to the good, I would have waited a little longer, but his visit to America forced my hand. He would never have left so compromising a document behind him. Therefore we had to act at once. Burglary at night is impossible. He takes precautions. But there was a chance in the evening if I could only be sure that his attention was engaged. That was where you and your blue saucer came in. But I had to be sure of the position of the book, and I knew I had only a few minutes in which to act, for my time was limited by your knowledge of Chinese pottery.[52] Therefore I gathered the girl up at the last moment. How could I guess what the little packet was that she carried so carefully under her cloak?[53] I thought she had come altogether on my business, but it seems she had some of her own."

"He guessed I came from you."

"I feared he would. But you held him in play just long enough for me to get the book, though not long enough for an unobserved escape. Ah, Sir James, I am very glad you have come!"

Our courtly friend had appeared in answer to a previous summons. He listened with the deepest attention to Holmes's account of what had occurred.

"You have done wonders—wonders!" he cried, when he had heard the narrative. "But if these injuries are as terrible as Dr.

Watson describes, then surely our purpose of thwarting the marriage is sufficiently gained without the use of this horrible book."

Holmes shook his head.

"Women of the De Merville type do not act like that. She would love him the more as a disfigured martyr. No, no. It is his mental side, not his physical, which we have to destroy. That book will bring her back to earth—and I know nothing else that could. It is in his own writing. She cannot get past it."

Sir James carried away both it and the precious saucer. As I was myself overdue, I went down with him into the street. A brougham was waiting for him. He sprang in, gave a hurried order to the cockaded coachman, and drove swiftly away. He flung his overcoat half out of the window to cover the armorial bearings upon the panel, but I had seen them in the glare of our fanlight none the less. I gasped with surprise. Then I turned back and ascended the stair to Holmes's room.

"I have found out who our client is," I cried, bursting with my great news. "why, Holmes, it is—"

"It is a loyal friend and a chivalrous gentleman,"[54] said Holmes, holding up a restraining hand. "Let that now and forever be enough for us."

I do not know how the incriminating book was used. Sir James may have managed it. Or it is more probable that so delicate a task was entrusted to the young lady's father. The effect, at any rate, was all that could be desired. Three days later appeared a paragraph in the *Morning Post* to say that the marriage between Baron Adelbert Gruner and Miss Violet de Merville would not take place. The same paper had the first police-court hearing of the proceedings against Miss Kitty Winter on the grave charge of vitriol-throwing. Such extenuating circumstances came out in the trial that the sentence, as will be remembered, was the lowest that was possible for such an offence. Sherlock Holmes was threatened with a prosecution for burglary, but when an object is good and a client is sufficiently illustrious, even the rigid British law becomes human and elastic. My friend has not yet stood in the dock.

54 Watson conceals the identity of Holmes's illustrious client with a method D. Martin Dakin deems so "transparent" that Watson must have meant for it to be punctured. "I do not think anyone who has ever read the story," Dakin declares, "could be in any doubt that the client was HM King Edward VII— particularly as he had already appeared under that alias in *The Beryl Coronet.* . . ." Dakin exaggerates the certainty of the identification slightly here. Although scholars generally believe that "one of the highest, noblest, most exalted names in England," whom banker Alexander Holder terms his "illustrious client," is the young King Edward, then Prince of Wales (see "The Beryl Coronet," note 7), here the phrase "illustrious client" is never used except in Watson's story title. If this is Watson revealing the client's name, it is certainly a subtle method.

THE ADVENTURE OF THE BLANCHED SOLDIER[1]

"The Blanched Soldier" is one of two cases written up by Holmes, rather than Watson. The other, "The Lion's Mane," also appears in The Case-Book. *Neither can be said to be a literary triumph: the contrast with Holmes's superb storytelling in stories such as "The 'Gloria Scott'" and "The Musgrave Ritual" is pronounced. Both stories similarly show Holmes presented with a problem which he solves by knowledge known only to him—an early style of mystery fiction that Arthur Conan Doyle publicly disdained. Published in 1926, when the Boer War was but a dim memory to the British public, "The Blanched Soldier" demonstrates Holmes's knowledge of medicine rather than his detective skills. The case is also a harsh reminder of public attitudes toward mental illness and contagious diseases, even as late as 1903, when the events occur. The real doctor in the case, Sir James Saunders, made such an impression on Sherlockians that there now exists the "Sir James Saunders Society, a dermatological scion of the Baker Street Irregulars," which meets annually and administers a strict "re-certification" examination to its members.*

1 "The Blanched Soldier" was published in the *Strand Magazine* in November 1926. Its first American publication was in *Liberty* on October 16, 1926. The manuscript is in the Berg Collection of the New York Public Library.

2 Critics have found reason to doubt that Holmes really wrote "The Blanched Soldier" and "The Lion's Mane." Joseph J. Eckrich sees a basic discrepancy between Holmes's character and the accessibility of this tale, writing, "What bothers me is my belief that had Holmes taken up [Watson's] dare, he would have written a cold, unemotional narrative, and would have published it in some specialized journal . . ."

Gavin Brend, in *My Dear Holmes*, agrees

THE IDEAS OF my friend Watson, though limited, are exceedingly pertinacious. For a long time he has worried me to write an experience of my own.[2] Perhaps I have rather invited this persecution, since I have often had occasion to point out to him how superficial are his own accounts and to accuse him of pandering to popular taste instead of confining himself rigidly to facts and figures. "Try it yourself, Holmes!" he has retorted, and I am compelled to admit that having taken my pen in my hand, I do begin to realize that the matter must be presented in such a way as may interest the reader. The following case can hardly fail to do so, as it is among the strangest happenings in my collection, though it chanced that Watson had no note of it in his collection. Speaking of my old friend and biographer, I would take this opportunity to remark that if I burden myself with a companion in my various little inquiries it is not done out of sentiment or caprice, but it is that Watson has some remarkable characteristics of his own, to which in his honesty he has given small attention amid his exaggerated estimates of my own performances. A confederate who foresees your conclusions and course of action is always dangerous, but one to whom each development comes as a perpetual surprise, and to whom the future is always a closed book, is indeed an ideal helpmate.[3]

I find from my notebook that it was in January, 1903, just after the conclusion of the Boer War,[4] that I had my visit from Mr. James M. Dodd, a big, fresh, sunburned, upstanding Briton. The good Watson had at that time deserted me for a wife,[5] the only selfish action which I can recall in our association. I was alone.

It is my habit to sit with my back to the window and to place my visitors in the opposite chair, where the light falls full upon them.[6] Mr. James M. Dodd seemed somewhat at a loss how to begin the interview. I did not attempt to help him, for his silence gave me more time for observation. I have found it wise to impress clients with a sense of power, and so I gave him some of my conclusions.

"From South Africa, sir, I perceive."

"Yes, sir," he answered, with some surprise.

"Imperial Yeomanry,[7] I fancy."

"Exactly."

"Middlesex Corps, no doubt."

"That is so. Mr. Holmes, you are a wizard."

I smiled at his bewildered expression.

"When a gentleman of virile appearance enters my room with such tan upon his face as an English sun could never give, and with his handkerchief in his sleeve instead of in his pocket, it is not difficult to place him.[8] You wear a short beard, which shows that you were not a regular. You have the cut of a riding-man. As to Middlesex, your card has already shown me that you are a stockbroker from Throgmorton Street. What other regiment would you join?"[9]

"You see everything."

"I see no more than you, but I have trained myself to notice what I see. However, Mr. Dodd, it was not to discuss the science of observation that you called upon me this morning. What has been happening at Tuxbury Old Park?"

"Mr. Holmes—!"

"My dear sir, there is no mystery. Your letter came with that

with Eckrich that the writing style of "The Blanched Soldier" does not reflect what might be expected of Holmes and points out that in "The Abbey Grange," Holmes decried Watson's degrading of "what might have been an instructive and even classical series of demonstration" into mere stories. Brend, who also thinks it unlikely that Holmes would start recording his own tales at this late stage in his career, discards the possibility of a third-party author, especially an author pretending to be Holmes.

D. Martin Dakin finds Holmes's excuses for attempting to write a popular story "singularly unconvincing. Would he not rather have reserved his analytical comments on his own cases for that monumental work on *The Whole Art of Detection* which his admirers are still eagerly awaiting?" Furthermore, Dakin argues, if Holmes were to take up a narrative pen, he would have chosen more distinguished stories than "The Blanched Soldier" and "The Lion's Mane." That Holmes *could* construct a powerful story, Dakin points out, is demonstrated in "The 'Gloria Scott'" and "The Musgrave Ritual," both of which are told primarily by Holmes.

So who wrote this story? Brend concludes that Watson is the likely author of both "The Blanched Soldier" and "The Lion's Mane," as well as the "The Mazarin Stone," which is told in the third person. O. F. Grazebrook constructs an ingenious theory that the entire *Case-Book* was from the pen of Dr. Verner, Holmes's distant cousin. B. Dean Wortman points to two distinctive writing styles in "The Blanched Soldier" and concludes that part was written by Holmes and part by Arthur Conan Doyle. But Richard M. Caplan, M.D., in "The Curious Circumstance of the Missing Brother," takes the "fundamentalist" viewpoint that at least "The Blanched Soldier" was written by Holmes. Dr. Caplan argues that Holmes selected this story to "try his hand" precisely because Watson would have had to "make himself seem grossly inadequate as a diagnostician" to tell the story.

3 Certainly a backhanded compliment! Contrast this statement with Holmes's critical remarks in cases such as "The Disappearance of Lady Frances Carfax" (" 'Well, Watson . . . a very pretty hash you have made of it!' ") and "The Retired Colourman" ("in your mission you have missed everything of importance").

4 For a brief history of the Boer War, see the appendix on page 1507.

5 The identity of the woman to whom Holmes's report refers is not recorded. Watson himself makes no reference to her at all, and the reader's awareness of her existence depends entirely on Holmes's remark. Most commentators take this reference to indicate a second marriage, post-Mary Morstan, since Watson has already suffered through the "sad bereavement" of, presumably, Mary's death (mentioned in "The Empty House" as occurring between 1891 and 1894). Others have postulated more than two marriages. For example, H. W. Bell, in *Sherlock Holmes and Dr. Watson: A Chronology of Their Adventures*, reasons that in February 1896, Watson had taken up separate quarters ("The Veiled Lodger") but had not resumed medical practice. Hence a second marriage must have taken place. Thus the remark here implies a third marriage. Trevor H. Hall, in "Dr. Watson's Marriages," concludes that Watson was married five times, and that the wife referred to in "The Blanched Soldier" is the fifth. Cameron Hollyer, in "Murk IV Meets Watson the Benedict," computes—with tongue planted firmly in cheek—that Watson had over eighty wives.

Watson's silence about the details of his second marriage leads some commentators to doubt if it ever took place. Mary Morstan did not die, they propose. Instead, Watson's "sad

bereavement" referred either to the death of a child or to a serious breakdown in Mrs. Watson's health. These commentators go on to suggest that, after 1894, Mary was confined to a sanatorium, where Watson visited her regularly. This reference, then, to Watson's desertion refers to her release from the sanatorium and return to the Watson household.

June Thomson is not a follower of this school of thought. "Quite apart from the lack of evidence to support these theories and their failure to explain satisfactorily Watson's silence over the matter," she argues, "both Watson's and Holmes's choice of words alone would tend to refute them." A serious illness would not be described as a "sad bereavement." Neither does it seem likely that Holmes, who knew Mary, would describe her as "a wife."

Then who is she? Speculation abounds, with little evidence other than a chance remark of approbation by Holmes or Dr. Watson. S. C. Roberts, for example, proposes Violet de Merville (of "The Illustrious Client"), whom Holmes describes as an "ethereal other-world beauty." Watson did not meet her in the course of the tale, but Roberts imagines that the chivalrous Watson would have called on her to inquire after her recovery and, perhaps abetted by her military father, courted her. David L. Hammer favours Violet Hunter, whom Watson appears to have seen as a candidate for Holmes's affections at the time. Two different scholars propose Lady Frances Carfax (who bore the "statuesque face of a handsome and spiritual woman of middle age") as likely to appeal to the middle-aged Watson, while June Thomson offers Grace Dunbar (of "Thor Bridge"), described by Watson as "tall, with a noble figure and commanding presence," as her candidate. J. N. Williamson audaciously suggests that Watson had an affair with Irene Adler prior to his marriage to Mary Morstan, that Mary divorced him in 1901, and that Watson then married Adler.

There is no real evidence of the identity of this mysterious "wife," nor is it even certain that it is *Watson's* wife—a point made by C. Alan Bradley and William A. S. Serjeant, who contend that it is Mrs. Neville St. Clair ("The Man with the Twisted Lip"), someone else's wife. D. Martin Dakin evades the entire topic, pointing out that if "The Blanched Soldier" was not written by Holmes—that is, is fictitious—then "with it goes the whole evidence for the much discussed second marriage of Watson. . . ."

6 A technique learned from Professor Moriarty? See *The Valley of Fear*, Chapter Two, in which Moriarty sat with the lamp shining in the face of Inspector Macdonald during their interview. In any event, Holmes found himself on the receiving end of this method of observation when Lady Hilda Trelawney Hope, in "The Second Stain," seated herself in the "one chair" that put her out of the light ("She swept across the room and seated herself with her back to the window").

7 The voluntary mounted units once known as the Yeomanry Calvary were organised in 1794 to put down riots. After providing crucial service in the Boer War—some three thousand officers and men were involved—the cavalry's name was changed to the Imperial Yeomanry in 1901.

8 Holmes used similar deductive reasoning to identify Dr. Watson as a military man in *A Study in Scarlet*, where Watson's "military air" and tan gave away his visit to Afghanistan.

9 The "Middlesex Corps" was properly the Middlesex (Duke of Cambridge's Hussars) Yeomanry Cavalry, which changed its name in 1901 to Middlesex Imperial Yeomanry (Duke of Cambridge's Hussars) and in 1908 became 1st County of London Yeomanry (Middlesex, Duke of Cambridge's Hussars). Prince George, Duke of Cambridge (the commander-in-chief of the British Army from 1856 to 1895 and cousin to Queen Victoria) became its colonel-in-chief in 1898, assuring its "tony" status (to which Holmes here alludes).

10 Originally "Gerald Emsworth" in the manuscript.

heading, and as you fixed this appointment in very pressing terms it was clear that something sudden and important had occurred."

"Yes, indeed. But the letter was written in the afternoon, and a good deal has happened since then. If Colonel Emsworth had not kicked me out—"

"Kicked you out!"

"Well, that was what it amounted to. He is a hard nail, is Colonel Emsworth. The greatest martinet in the Army in his day, and it was a day of rough language, too. I couldn't have stuck the colonel if it had not been for Godfrey's sake."

I lit my pipe and leaned back in my chair.

"Perhaps you will explain what you are talking about."

My client grinned mischievously.

"I had got into the way of supposing that you knew everything without being told," said he. "But I will give you the facts, and I hope to God that you will be able to tell me what they mean. I've been awake all night puzzling my brain, and the more I think the more incredible does it become.

"When I joined up in January, 1901, just two years ago—young Godfrey Emsworth[10] had joined the same squadron. He was Colonel Emsworth's only son—Emsworth, the Crimean

I lit my pipe and leaned back in my chair. "Perhaps you will explain what you are talking about."
Howard Elcock, *Strand Magazine*, 1926

V.C.[11]—and he had the fighting blood in him, so it is no wonder he volunteered. There was not a finer lad in the regiment. We formed a friendship—the sort of friendship which can only be made when one lives the same life—and shares the same joys and sorrows. He was my mate—and that means a good deal in the Army. We took the rough and the smooth together for a year of hard fighting. Then he was hit with a bullet from an elephant gun in the action near Diamond Hill[12] outside Pretoria. I got one letter from the hospital at Cape Town and one from Southampton. Since then not a word—not one word, Mr. Holmes, for six months and more, and he my closest pal.

"Well, when the war was over, and we all got back, I wrote to his father and asked where Godfrey was. No answer. I waited a bit and then I wrote again. This time I had a reply, short and gruff. Godfrey had gone on a voyage round the world, and it was not likely that he would be back for a year. That was all.

"I wasn't satisfied, Mr. Holmes. The whole thing seemed to me so damned unnatural. He was a good lad, and he would not drop a pal like that. It was not like him. Then, again, I happened to know that he was heir to a lot of money, and also that his father and he did not always hit it off too well. The old man was sometimes a bully, and young Godfrey had too much spirit to stand it. No, I wasn't satisfied, and I determined that I would get to the root of the matter. It happened, however, that my own affairs needed a lot of straightening out, after two years' absence, and so it is only this week that I have been able to take up Godfrey's case again. But since I have taken it up I mean to drop everything in order to see it through."

Mr. James M. Dodd appeared to be the sort of person whom it would be better to have as a friend than as an enemy. His blue eyes were stern and his square jaw had set hard as he spoke.

'Well, what have you done?" I asked.

"My first move was to get down to his home, Tuxbury Old Park, near Bedford, and to see for myself how the ground lay. I wrote to the mother, therefore—I had had quite enough of the curmudgeon of a father—and I made a clean frontal attack: Godfrey was my chum, I had a great deal of interest which I might tell her of our common experiences, I should be in the neighbourhood, would there be any objection, *et cetera*? In reply I had quite an amiable answer from her and an offer to put me up for the night. That was what took me down on Monday.

11 That is, Colonel Emsworth had won the Victoria Cross, England's highest military honour for gallantry in the face of the enemy, in the Crimean War.

12 The battle of Diamond Hill occurred on June 11–12, 1900, when British forces, having just captured Pretoria, attacked the Boers entrenched along the ridges outside the city. The Boers were forced to withdraw, but few lives were lost, and both sides ended up claiming victory.

13 Objected to; took exception to.

14 An argument, a quarrel.

"Tuxbury Old Hall is inaccessible—five miles from any-where. There was no trap at the station, so I had to walk, car-rying my suit-case, and it was nearly dark before I arrived. It is a great wandering house, standing in a considerable park. I should judge it was of all sorts of ages and styles, starting on a half-timbered Elizabethan foundation and ending in a Victo-rian portico. Inside it was all panelling and tapestry and half-effaced old pictures, a house of shadows and mystery. There was a butler, old Ralph, who seemed about the same age as the house, and there was his wife, who might have been older. She had been Godfrey's nurse, and I had heard him speak of her as second only to his mother in his affections, so I was drawn to her in spite of her queer appearance. The mother I liked also—a gentle little white mouse of a woman. It was only the colonel himself whom I barred.[13]

"We had a bit of barney[14] right away, and I should have walked back to the station if I had not felt that it might be playing his game for me to do so. I was shown straight into his study, and there I found him, a huge, bow-backed man with a smoky skin and a straggling grey beard, seated behind his lit-tered desk. A red-veined nose jutted out like a vulture's beak, and two fierce grey eyes glared at me from under tufted brows. I could understand now why Godfrey seldom spoke of his father.

" 'Well, sir,' said he in a rasping voice, 'I should be interested to know the real reasons for this visit.'

"I answered that I had explained them in my letter to his wife.

" 'Yes, yes; you said that you had known Godfrey in Africa. We have, of course, only your word for that.'

" 'I have his letters to me in my pocket.'

" 'Kindly let me see them.'

"He glanced at the two which I handed him, and then he tossed them back.

" 'Well, what then?' he asked.

" 'I was fond of your son Godfrey, sir. Many ties and memo-ries united us. Is it not natural that I should wonder at his sud-den silence and should wish to know what has become of him?'

" 'I have some recollection, sir, that I had already corre-sponded with you and had told you what had become of him. He has gone upon a voyage round the world. His health was in a poor way after his African experiences, and both his mother and I were of opinion that complete rest and change were needed. Kindly pass that explanation on to any other friends who may be interested in the matter.'

" 'Certainly,' I answered. 'But perhaps you would have the goodness to let me have the name of the steamer and of the line by which he sailed, together with the date. I have no doubt that I should be able to get a letter through to him.'

"My request seemed both to puzzle and to irritate my host. His great eyebrows came down over his eyes, and he tapped his fingers impatiently on the table. He looked up at last with the expression of one who has seen his adversary make a dangerous move at chess, and has decided how to meet it.

" 'Many people, Mr. Dodd,' said he, 'would take offence at your infernal pertinacity and would think that this insistence had reached the point of damned impertinence.'

" 'You must put it down, sir, to my real love for your son.'

" 'Exactly. I have already made every allowance upon that score. I must ask you, however, to drop these inquiries. Every family has its own inner knowledge and its own motives, which cannot always be made clear to outsiders, however well-intentioned. My wife is anxious to hear something of Godfrey's past which you are in a position to tell her, but I would ask you to let the present and the future alone. Such inquiries serve no useful purpose, sir, and place us in a delicate and difficult position.'

"So I came to a dead end, Mr. Holmes. There was no getting past it. I could only pretend to accept the situation and register a vow inwardly that I would never rest until my friend's fate had been cleared up. It was a dull evening. We dined quietly, the three of us, in a gloomy, faded old room. The lady questioned me eagerly about her son, but the old man seemed morose and depressed. I was so bored by the whole proceeding that I made an excuse as soon as I decently could and retired to my bedroom. It was a large, bare room on the ground floor, as gloomy as the rest of the house, but after a year of sleeping upon the veldt, Mr. Holmes, one is not too particular about one's quarters. I opened the curtains and looked out into the garden, remarking that it was a fine night with a bright half-moon. Then I sat down by the roaring fire with the lamp on a table beside me, and endeavoured to distract my mind with a novel. I was interrupted, however, by Ralph, the old butler, who came in with a fresh supply of coals.

" 'I thought you might run short in the night-time, sir. It is bitter weather and these rooms are cold.'

"He hesitated before leaving the room, and when I looked round he was standing facing me with a wistful look upon his wrinkled face.

" 'Beg your pardon, sir, but I could not help hearing what you said of young Master Godfrey at dinner. You know, sir, that my wife nursed him, and so I may say I am his foster-father. It's natural we should take an interest. And you say he carried himself well, sir?'

" 'There was no braver man in the regiment. He pulled me out once from under the rifles of the Boers, or maybe I should not be here.'

"The old butler rubbed his skinny hands.

" 'Yes, sir, yes, that is Master Godfrey all over. He was always courageous. There's not a tree in the park, sir, that he has not climbed. Nothing would stop him. He was a fine boy—and oh, sir, he was a fine man.'

"I sprang to my feet.

" 'Look here!' I cried. 'You say he *was*. You speak as if he were dead. What is all this mystery? What has become of Godfrey Emsworth?'

"I gripped the old man by the shoulder, but he shrank away.

" 'I don't know what you mean, sir. Ask the master about Master Godfrey. He knows. It is not for me to interfere.'

"He was leaving the room, but I held his arm.

" 'Listen,' I said. 'You are going to answer one question before you leave if I have to hold you all night. Is Godfrey dead?'

"He could not face my eyes. He was like a man hypnotized. The answer was dragged from his lips. It was a terrible and unexpected one.

" 'I wish to God he was!' he cried, and, tearing himself free, he dashed from the room.

"You will think, Mr. Holmes, that I returned to my chair in no very happy state of mind. The old man's words seemed to me to bear only one interpretation. Clearly my poor friend had become involved in some criminal or, at the least disreputable

"I gripped the old man by the shoulder, but he shrank away."
Howard Elcock, *Strand Magazine*, 1926

transaction which touched the family honour. That stern old man had sent his son away and hidden him from the world lest some scandal should come to light. Godfrey was a reckless fellow. He was easily influenced by those around him. No doubt he had fallen into bad hands and been misled to his ruin. It was a piteous business, if it was indeed so, but even now it was my duty to hunt him out and see if I could aid him. I was anxiously pondering the matter when I looked up, and there was Godfrey Emsworth standing before me."

My client had paused as one in deep emotion.

"Pray continue," I said. "Your problem presents some very unusual features."

"He was outside the window, Mr. Holmes, with his face pressed against the glass. I have told you that I looked out at the night. When I did so I left the curtains partly open. His figure was framed in this gap. The window came down to the ground and I could see the whole length of it, but it was his face which held my gaze. He was deadly pale—never have I seen a man so white. I reckon ghosts may look like that; but his eyes met mine, and they were the eyes of a living man. He sprang back when he saw that I was looking at him, and he vanished into the darkness.

"There was something shocking about the man, Mr. Holmes. It wasn't merely that ghastly face glimmering as white

"He sprang back when he saw that I was looking at him
and vanished into the darkness."
Howard Elcock, *Strand Magazine*, 1926

as cheese in the darkness. It was more subtle than that—something slinking, something furtive, something guilty—something very unlike the frank, manly lad that I had known. It left a feeling of horror in my mind.

"But when a man has been soldiering for a year or two with brother Boer as a playmate, he keeps his nerve and acts quickly. Godfrey had hardly vanished before I was at the window. There was an awkward catch, and I was some little time before I could throw it up.[15] Then I nipped through and ran down the garden path in the direction that I thought he might have taken.

"It was a long path and the light was not very good, but it seemed to me something was moving ahead of me. I ran on and called his name, but it was no use. When I got to the end of the path there were several others branching in different directions to various outhouses. I stood hesitating, and as I did so I heard distinctly the sound of a closing door. It was not behind me in the house, but ahead of me, somewhere in the darkness. That was enough, Mr. Holmes, to assure me that what I had seen was not a vision. Godfrey had run away from me, and he had shut a door behind him. Of that I was certain.

"There was nothing more I could do, and I spent an uneasy night turning the matter over in my mind and trying to find some theory which would cover the facts. Next day I found the colonel rather more conciliatory, and as his wife remarked that there were some places of interest in the neighbourhood, it gave me an opening to ask whether my presence for one more night would incommode them. A somewhat grudging acquiescence from the old man gave me a clear day in which to make my observations. I was already perfectly convinced that Godfrey was in hiding somewhere near, but where and why remained to be solved.

"The house was so large and so rambling that a regiment might be hid away in it and no one the wiser. If the secret lay there, it was difficult for me to penetrate it. But the door which I had heard close was certainly not in the house. I must explore the garden and see what I could find. There was no difficulty in the way, for the old people were busy in their own fashion and left me to my own devices.

"There were several small outhouses, but at the end of the garden there was a detached building of some size—large

15 "It was some little time before I could open it" in the *Strand Magazine* text.

enough for a gardener's or a gamekeeper's residence. Could this be the place whence the sound of that shutting door had come? I approached it in a careless fashion as though I were strolling aimlessly round the grounds. As I did so, a small, brisk, bearded man in a black coat and bowler hat—not at all the gardener type—came out of the door. To my surprise, he locked it after him and put the key in his pocket. Then he looked at me with some surprise on his face.

" 'Are you a visitor here?' he asked.

"I explained that I was and that I was a friend of Godfrey's.

" 'What a pity that he should be away on his travels, for he would have so liked to see me,' I continued.

" 'Quite so. Exactly,' said he with a rather guilty air. 'No doubt you will renew your visit at some more propitious time.' He passed on, but when I turned I observed that he was standing watching me, half-concealed by the laurels at the far end of the garden.

"I had a good look at the little house as I passed it, but the windows were heavily curtained, and, so far as one could see, it was empty. I might spoil my own game and even be ordered off the premises if I were too audacious, for I was still conscious that I was being watched. Therefore, I strolled back to the house and waited for night before I went on with my inquiry. When all was dark and quiet I slipped out of my window and made my way as silently as possible to the mysterious lodge.

"I have said that it was heavily curtained, but now I found that the windows were shuttered as well. Some light, however, was breaking through one of them, so I concentrated my attention upon this. I was in luck, for the curtain had not been quite closed, and there was a crack in the shutter, so that I could see the inside of the room. It was a cheery place enough, a bright lamp and a blazing fire. Opposite to me was seated the little man whom I had seen in the morning. He was smoking a pipe and reading a paper."

"What paper?" I asked.

My client seemed annoyed at the interruption of his narrative.

"Can it matter?" he asked.

"It is most essential."

"I really took no notice."

"Possibly you observed whether it was a broad-leafed paper or of that smaller type which one associates with weeklies."

"Now that you mention it, it was not large. It might have been the *Spectator*. However, I had little thought to spare upon such details, for a second man was seated with his back to the window, and I could swear that this second man was Godfrey. I could not see his face, but I knew the familiar slope of his shoulders. He was leaning upon his elbow in an attitude of great melancholy, his body turned towards the fire. I was hesitating as to what I should do when there was a sharp tap on my shoulder, and there was Colonel Emsworth beside me.

" 'This way, sir!' said he in a low voice. He walked in silence to the house, and I followed him into my own bedroom. He had picked up a time-table in the hall.

" 'There is a train to London at eight-thirty,' said he. 'The trap will be at the door at eight.'

"He was white with rage, and, indeed, I felt myself in so difficult a position that I could only stammer out a few incoherent apologies, in which I tried to excuse myself by urging my anxiety for my friend.

" 'The matter will not hear discussion,' said he abruptly. 'You have made a most damnable intrusion into the privacy of our family. You were here as a guest and you have become a spy. I have nothing more to say, sir, save that I have no wish ever to see you again.'

"At this I lost my temper, Mr. Holmes, and I spoke with some warmth.

" 'I have seen your son, and I am convinced that for some reason of your own you are concealing him from the world. I have no idea what your motives are in cutting him off in this fashion, but I am sure that he is no longer a free agent. I warn you, Colonel Emsworth, that until I am assured as to the safety and well-being of my friend I shall never desist in my efforts to get to the bottom of the mystery, and I shall certainly not allow myself to be intimidated by anything which you may say or do.'

"The old fellow looked diabolical, and I really thought he was about to attack me. I have said that he was a gaunt, fierce old giant, and though I am no weakling I might have been hard put to it to hold my own against him. However, after a long glare of rage he turned upon his heel and walked out of the

16 Probably a concealed reference to the "Duke of Holdernesse," with whom Holmes was involved in "The Priory School."

room. For my part, I took the appointed train in the morning, with the full intention of coming straight to you and asking for your advice and assistance at the appointment for which I had already written."

Such was the problem which my visitor laid before me. It presented, as the astute reader will have already perceived, few difficulties in its solution, for a very limited choice of alternatives must get to the root of the matter. Still, elementary as it was, there were points of interest and novelty about it which may excuse my placing it upon record. I now proceeded, using my familiar method of logical analysis, to narrow down the possible solutions.

"The servants," I asked; "how many were in the house?"

"For the best of my belief there were only the old butler and his wife. They seemed to live in the simplest fashion."

"There was no servant, then, in the detached house?"

"None, unless the little man with the beard acted as such. He seemed, however, to be quite a superior person."

"That seems very suggestive. Had you any indication that food was conveyed from the one house to the other?"

"Now that you mention it, I did see old Ralph carrying a basket down the garden walk and going in the direction of this house. The idea of food did not occur to me at the moment."

"Did you make any local inquiries?"

"Yes, I did. I spoke to the station-master and also to the innkeeper in the village. I simply asked if they knew anything of my old comrade, Godfrey Emsworth. Both of them assured me that he had gone for a voyage round the world. He had come home and then had almost at once started off again. The story was evidently universally accepted."

"You said nothing of your suspicions?"

"Nothing."

"That was very wise. The matter should certainly be inquired into. I will go back with you to Tuxbury Old Park."

"Today?"

It happened that at the moment I was clearing up the case which my friend Watson has described as that of the Abbey School, in which the Duke of Greyminster was so deeply involved.[16] I had also a commission from the Sultan of Turkey which called for immediate action, as political consequences of the gravest kind might arise from its neglect.[17] Therefore it was not until the beginning of the next week, as my diary[18] records, that I was able to start forth on my mission to Bedfordshire in company with Mr. James M. Dodd. As we drove to Euston we picked up a grave and taciturn gentleman of irongrey aspect, with whom I had made the necessary arrangements.

"This is an old friend," said I to Dodd. "It is possible that his presence may be entirely unnecessary, and, on the other hand, it may be essential. It is not necessary at the present stage to go further into the matter."

The narratives of Watson have accustomed the reader, no doubt, to the fact that I do not waste words or disclose my thoughts while a case is actually under consideration. Dodd seemed surprised, but nothing more was said, and the three of us continued our journey together. In the train I asked Dodd one more question which I wished our companion to hear.

"You say that you saw your friend's face quite clearly at the window, so clearly that you are sure of his identity?"

"I have no doubt about it whatever. His nose was pressed against the glass. The lamplight shone full upon him."

"It could not have been someone resembling him?"

"No, no, it was he."

"But you say he was changed?"

17 Abdul-Hamid II (1842–1918) assumed the throne in 1876 after his brother, Murad V, suffered a mental breakdown. A cruel despot who relied upon his secret police and censorship to keep the populace in line, Abdul-Hamid dismissed Parliament and suspended the constitution, ruling in seclusion from his palace and adopting a pan-Islamic stance for Turkey. He was deposed in 1909 by the revolutionary Young Turks movement, which was agitating for a constitutional government. In 1901 and 1902, Turkish encroachments on Aden had created dangerously high tensions between England and Turkey, and perhaps Mycroft and his cronies asked Sherlock to assist the sultan in smoothing the diplomatic waters by looking into the early stirrings of the revolution.

18 Is this Holmes's "case-book," mentioned in "The Speckled Band"? There is no other mention in the Canon of Holmes's keeping a *diary*, although Holmes undoubtedly kept notes on his cases and uses the word here in the sense of a pocket journal.

Euston Station.
Queen's London (1897)

19 But Holmes *does* engage in this trick, by concealing the identity of his taciturn "old friend" until the end of the tale.

"Only in colour. His face was—how shall I describe it?—it was of a fish-belly whiteness. It was bleached."

"Was it equally pale all over?"

"I think not. It was his brow which I saw so clearly as it was pressed against the window."

"Did you call to him?"

"I was too startled and horrified for the moment. Then I pursued him, as I have told you, but without result."

My case was practically complete, and there was only one small incident needed to round it off. When, after a considerable drive, we arrived at the strange old rambling house which my client had described, it was Ralph, the elderly butler, who opened the door. I had requisitioned the carriage for the day and had asked my elderly friend to remain within it unless we should summon him. Ralph, a little wrinkled old fellow, was in the conventional costume of black coat and pepper-and-salt trouser, with only one curious variant. He wore brown leather gloves, which at sight of us he instantly shuffled off, laying them down on the hall-table as we passed in. I have, as my friend Watson may have remarked, an abnormally acute set of senses, and a faint but incisive scent was apparent. It seemed to centre on the hall-table. I turned, placed my hat there, knocked it off, stooped to pick it up, and contrived to bring my nose within a foot of the gloves. Yes, it was undoubtedly from them that the curious tarry odour was oozing. I passed on into the study with my case complete. Alas, that I should have to show my hand so when I tell my own story. It was by concealing such links in the chain that Watson was enabled to produce his meretricious finales.[19]

Colonel Emsworth was not in his room, but he came quickly enough on receipt of Ralph's message. We heard his quick, heavy step in the passage. The door was flung open and he rushed in with bristling beard and twisted features, as terrible an old man as ever I have seen. He held our cards in his hand, and he tore them up and stamped on the fragments.

"Have I not told you, you infernal busybody, that you are warned off the premises? Never dare to show your damned face here again. If you enter again without my leave I shall be within my rights if I use violence. I'll shoot you, sir! By God, I will. As to you, sir," turning upon me, "I extend the same warning to you. I am familiar with your ignoble profession, but you

The door was flung open and he rushed in with
bristling beard and twisted features, as terrible an
old man as ever I have seen.
Howard Elcock, *Strand Magazine*, 1926

must take your reputed talents to some other field. There is no
opening for them here."

"I cannot leave here," said my client firmly, "until I hear
from Godfrey's own lips that he is under no restraint."

Our involuntary host rang the bell.

"Ralph," he said, "telephone down to the county police and
ask the inspector to send up two constables. Tell him there are
burglars in the house."

"One moment," said I. "You must be aware, Mr. Dodd, that
Colonel Emsworth is within his rights and that we have no
legal status within his house. On the other hand, he should recognize that your action is prompted entirely by solicitude for

20 Note that a telephone is available even in the countryside at this point, twenty-four years after the establishment of London's first telephone exchange in 1879. In 1902, the National Telephone Company had 25,000 lines in London and the Post Office 5,500 (still a small number for a population of about 4.5 million). According to Norman Lucas, author of a fine history of Scotland Yard entitled *The CID*, discussed in Gar Donnelson's "'Please give the Yard a call, Watson,'" a telephone was not installed at New Scotland Yard until 1903, and not all of the Metropolitan Police Stations had a telephone until 1906. However, every major provincial police force had had telephones for years.

his son. I venture to hope that if I were allowed to have five minutes' conversation with Colonel Emsworth, I could certainly alter his view of the matter."

"I am not so easily altered," said the old soldier. "Ralph, do what I have told you. What the devil are you waiting for? Ring up the police!"[20]

"Nothing of the sort," I said, putting my back to the door. "Any police interference would bring about the very catastrophe which you dread." I took out my notebook and scribbled one word upon a loose sheet. "That," said I as I handed it to Colonel Emsworth, "is what has brought us here."

He stared at the writing with a face from which every expression save amazement had vanished.

"How do you know?" he gasped, sitting down heavily in his chair.

"It is my business to know things. That is my trade."

He sat in deep thought, his gaunt hand tugging at his straggling beard. Then he made a gesture of resignation.

"Well, if you wish to see Godfrey, you shall. It is no doing of mine, but you have forced my hand. Ralph, tell Mr. Godfrey and Mr. Kent that in five minutes we shall be with them."

At the end of that time we passed down the garden path and found ourselves in front of the mystery house at the end. A small bearded man stood at the door with a look of considerable astonishment upon his face.

"This is very sudden, Colonel Emsworth," said he. "This will disarrange all our plans."

"I can't help it, Mr. Kent. Our hands have been forced. Can Mr. Godfrey see us?"

"Yes, he is waiting inside." He turned and led us into a large, plainly furnished front room. A man was standing with his back to the fire, and at the sight of him my client sprang forward with outstretched hand.

"Why, Godfrey, old man, this is fine!"

But the other waved him back.

"Don't touch me, Jimmie. Keep your distance. Yes, you may well stare! I don't quite look the smart Lance-Corporal Emsworth, of B Squadron, do I?"

His appearance was certainly extraordinary. One could see

that he had indeed been a handsome man with clear-cut features sunburned by an African sun, but mottled in patches over this darker surface were curious whitish patches which had bleached his skin.

"That's why I don't court visitors," said he. "I don't mind you, Jimmie, but I could have done without your friend. I suppose there is some good reason for it, but you have me at a disadvantage."

"I wanted to be sure that all was well with you, Godfrey. I saw you that night when you looked into my window, and I could not let the matter rest till I had cleared things up."

"Old Ralph told me you were there, and I couldn't help taking a peep at you. I hoped you would not have seen me, and I had to run to my burrow when I heard the window go up."

"But what in heaven's name is the matter?"

"Well, it's not a long story to tell," said he, lighting a cigarette. "You remember that morning fight at Buffelsspruit, outside Pretoria,[21] on the Eastern railway line?[22] You heard I was hit?"

"Yes, I heard that, but I never got particulars."

"Three of us got separated from the others. It was very broken country, you may remember. There was Simpson—the fellow we called Baldy Simpson—and Anderson, and I. We were clearing brother Boer, but he lay low and got the three of us. The other two were killed. I got an elephant bullet through my shoulder. I stuck on to my horse, however, and he galloped several miles before I fainted and rolled off the saddle.

"When I came to myself it was nightfall, and I raised myself up, feeling very weak and ill. To my surprise there was a house close beside me, a fairly large house with a broad stoep[23] and many windows. It was deadly cold. You remember the kind of numb cold which used to come at evening, a deadly, sickening sort of cold, very different from a crisp healthy frost. Well, I was cold to the bone, and my only hope seemed to lie in reaching that house. I staggered to my feet and dragged myself along, hardly conscious of what I did. I have a dim memory of slowly ascending the steps, entering a wide-opened door, passing into a large room which contained several beds, and throwing myself down with a gasp of satisfaction upon one of them. It was unmade, but that troubled me not at all. I threw the clothes over my shivering body and in a moment I was in a deep sleep.

21 Pretoria, formerly the capital of the South African Transvaal, was founded in 1855 and named after the Boer leader Andries Pretorius. During the Boer War, Winston Churchill, then a correspondent for the *Morning Post*, was captured and imprisoned in Pretoria. He managed to escape, hiding himself in a coal wagon and travelling hundreds of miles on foot until he reached safety. Enthralled audiences devoured Churchill's accounts of his Pretoria experience and flocked to his lectures (which he delivered accompanied by slides), elevating him to the level of respected journalist and war hero. Riding the wave of his newfound popularity, Churchill soon embarked upon what would be a brilliant political career.

22 This would have been the Delagoa Bay and East African Railway, which was backed by the British and lasted only from 1887 to 1889.

23 In South African Dutch, a raised verandah running along the front or sides of a house.

24 Although lepers were considered unclean and were confined to colonies to lessen their contact with the outside world, leprosy itself is not a highly contagious disease: At highest risk of infection are the children of those already afflicted, not their adult neighbours. Thus, the doctor's horrified claims to the contrary, Godfrey Emsworth's merely sleeping on a "leper's bed" would not have been enough to have infected him with the disease.

In addition to skin lesions, leprosy (from the Greek word *lepros*, or "scaly") may cause nerve damage, which leads to a loss of sensation. As even minor injuries—a cut, a mild burn—often go unnoticed and untreated, the damage becomes far more severe, leading to the "twisted or swollen or disfigured" figures that greeted Master Emsworth. By the seventeenth century, rates of leprosy in northern Europe had decreased; but Africa still suffered greatly from the disease, as it continues to do today. See "The Illustrious Client," note 26, for more on leprosy.

"It was morning when I wakened, and it seemed to me that instead of coming out into a world of sanity I had emerged into some extraordinary nightmare. The African sun flooded through the big, curtainless windows, and every detail of the great, bare, whitewashed dormitory stood out hard and clear. In front of me was standing a small, dwarf-like man with a huge, bulbous head, who was jabbering excitedly in Dutch, waving two horrible hands which looked to me like brown sponges. Behind him stood a group of people who seemed to be intensely amused by the situation, but a chill came over me as I looked at them. Not one of them was a normal human being. Every one was twisted or swollen or disfigured in some strange way. The laughter of these strange monstrosities was a dreadful thing to hear.

"It seemed that none of them could speak English, but the situation wanted clearing up, for the creature with the big head was growing furiously angry, and, uttering wild-beast cries, he had laid his deformed hands upon me and was dragging me out of bed, regardless of the fresh flow of blood from my wound. The little monster was as strong as a bull, and I don't know what he might have done to me had not an elderly man who was clearly in authority been attracted to the room by the hubbub. He said a few stern words in Dutch, and my persecutor shrank away. Then he turned upon me, gazing at me in the utmost amazement.

" 'How in the world did you come here?' he asked in amazement. 'Wait a bit, I see that you are tired out and that wounded shoulder of yours wants looking after. I am a doctor, and I'll soon have you tied up. But man alive? You are in far greater danger here than ever you were on the battlefield. You are in the Leper Hospital, and you have slept in a leper's bed.'[24]

"Need I tell you more, Jimmie? It seems that in view of the approaching battle all these poor creatures had been evacuated the day before. Then, as the British advanced, they had been brought back by this, their medical superintendent, who assured me that, though he believed he was immune to the disease, he would nonetheless never have dared to do what I had done. He put me in a private room, treated me kindly, and within a week or so I was removed to the general hospital at Pretoria.

"So there you have my tragedy. I hoped against hope, but it

was not until I had reached home that the terrible signs which you see upon my face told me that I had not escaped. What was I to do? I was in this lonely house. We had two servants whom we could utterly trust. There was a house where I could live. Under pledge of secrecy, Mr. Kent who is a surgeon, was prepared to stay with me. It seemed simple enough on those lines. The alternative was a dreadful one—segregation for life among strangers with never a hope of release. But absolute secrecy was necessary, or even in this quiet countryside there would have been an outcry, and I should have been dragged to my horrible doom. Even you, Jimmie—even you had to be kept in the dark. Why my father has relented I cannot imagine."

Colonel Emsworth pointed to me.

"This is the gentleman who forced my hand." He unfolded the scrap of paper on which I had written the word "leprosy." "It seemed to me that if he knew so much as that it was safer that he should know all."

"And so it was," said I. "No one knows but good may come of it? I understand that only Mr. Kent has seen the patient. May I ask, sir, if you are an authority on such complaints, which are, I understand, tropical or semi-tropical in their nature?"

" 'I have the ordinary knowledge of the educated medical man,' he observed with some stiffness.[25]

"I have no doubt, sir, that you are fully competent, but I am sure that you will agree that in such a case a second opinion is valuable. You have avoided this, I understand, for fear that pressure should be put upon you to segregate the patient."

"That is so," said Colonel Emsworth.

"I foresaw this situation," I explained, "and I have brought with me a friend whose discretion may absolutely be trusted. I was able once to do him a professional service, and he is ready to advise as a friend rather than as a specialist. His name is Sir James Saunders."

The prospect of an interview with Lord Roberts[26] would not have excited greater wonder and pleasure in a raw subaltern[27] than was now reflected upon the face of Mr. Kent.

"I shall indeed be proud," he murmured.

"Then I will ask Sir James to step this way. He is at present in the carriage outside the door. Meanwhile, Colonel Emsworth, we may perhaps assemble in your study, where I could give the necessary explanations."

25 An "educated medical man," even a surgeon like Mr. Kent, should have noted the absence of common symptoms of leprosy, erythema (reddening of the skin), admittedly not always present, and anaesthesia (loss of feeling), which is invariably present.

26 Frederick Sleigh Roberts, 1st Earl Roberts of Kandahar (1832–1914), was a celebrated British field marshal who earned the Victoria Cross for his service in the Indian Mutiny. He rose to the level of national hero during the Second Afghan War, winning a decisive battle against Afghan forces just outside Kandahar, and served as commander-in-chief of all forces in India from 1885 to 1893. In 1899, at the age of sixty-seven, Roberts replaced Sir Redvers Buller (whom A. N. Wilson labels "a stupid man") as commander-in-chief in the Boer War after Buller's missteps led to heavy losses, including the death of Roberts's only son. Under Roberts, British forces were brought back from the verge of defeat, and Roberts stepped down in 1900 and returned to England. As her last official engagement, an ailing Queen Victoria bestowed an earldom upon Lord Roberts on January 14, 1901, granting him the privilege of passing the title down to his daughter in the absence of a remaining male heir. Roberts was named commander-in-chief of the British Army and served until 1904, when the office was abolished.

27 The most junior commissioned officer.

Colonel Emsworth pointed to Sherlock Holmes.
"This is the gentleman who forced my hand," he said.
Howard Elcock, *Strand Magazine*, 1926

And here it is that I miss my Watson. By cunning questions and ejaculations of wonder he could elevate my simple art, which is but systematized common sense, into a prodigy. When I tell my own story I have no such aid. And yet I will give my process of thought even as I gave it to my small audience, which included Godfrey's mother in the study of Colonel Emsworth.

"That process," said I, "starts upon the supposition that when you have eliminated all which is impossible, then whatever remains, however improbable, must be the truth. It may well be that several explanations remain, in which case one

tries test after test until one or other of them has a convincing amount of support. We will now apply this principle to the case in point. As it was first presented to me, there were three possible explanations of the seclusion or incarceration of this gentleman in an outhouse of his father's mansion. There was the explanation that he was in hiding for a crime, or that he was mad and that they wished to avoid an asylum, or that he had some disease which caused his segregation. I could think of no other adequate solutions. These, then, had to be sifted and balanced against each other.

"The criminal solution would not bear inspection. No unsolved crime had been reported from that district. I was sure of that. If it were some crime not yet discovered, then clearly it would be to the interest of the family to get rid of the delinquent and send him abroad rather than keep him concealed at home. I could see no explanation for such a line of conduct.

28 Watson's friend Arthur Conan Doyle spent much time in South Africa during the Boer War, when he supervised a hospital in Cape Town. Although Conan Doyle was deeply involved with the medical issues facing South Africa and made a special study of the epidemic of enteric fever at Bloemfontein, he does not mention leprosy in either his autobiography or his history of the Boer War.

29 Also known as fish-skin disease, ichthyosis is a congenital, usually hereditary skin condition characterised by dry, scaly skin. The authoritative medical diagnosis of ichthyosis offered by Sir James Saunders is widely questioned. Numerous scholars, some doctors themselves, offer alternative and, in their view, more likely diagnoses. The earliest critic is Maurice Campbell, M.D., who, in his thoughtful *Sherlock Holmes and Dr. Watson: A Medical Digression*, asserts that Emsworth suffered from scleroderma, which manifests itself in patches of hardened skin and may affect the internal organs. Herman Beerman, M.D., in a careful review of the symptoms reported by Holmes, concludes that the disease in question is vitiligo (known also as leukoderma, or piebald skin), a loss of melanin which causes the skin to turn white in oval-shaped patches. Dr. Beerman reconsiders his diagnosis, however, in an article written with E. B. Smith, M.D., and decides upon pityriasis alba, a condition causing scaly skin but which occurs most frequently in children. Carl M. Silberman, M.D., makes his case for tinea versicolor, a fungus infection. And Carl L. Heifetz mentions still another disease—xeroderma, a condition similar to ichthyosis—but is unable to come to a conclusion respecting the disease other than that it is *not* leprosy.

"Insanity was more plausible. The presence of the second person in the outhouse suggested a keeper. The fact that he locked the door when he came out strengthened the supposition and gave the idea of constraint. On the other hand, this constraint could not be severe or the young man could not have got loose and come down to have a look at his friend. You will remember, Mr. Dodd, that I felt round for points, asking you, for example, about the paper which Mr. Kent was reading. Had it been the *Lancet* or the *British Medical Journal* it would have helped me. It is not illegal, however, to keep a lunatic upon private premises so long as there is a qualified person in attendance and that the authorities have been duly notified. Why, then, all this desperate desire for secrecy? Once again I could not get the theory to fit the facts.

"There remained the third possibility, into which, rare and unlikely as it was, everything seemed to fit. Leprosy is not uncommon in South Africa.[28] By some extraordinary chance this youth might have contracted it. His people would be placed in a very dreadful position, since they would desire to save him from segregation. Great secrecy would be needed to prevent rumours from getting about and subsequent interference by the authorities. A devoted medical man, if sufficiently paid, would easily be found to take charge of the sufferer. There would be no reason why the latter should not be allowed freedom after dark. Bleaching of the skin is a common result of the disease. The case was a strong one—so strong that I determined to act as if it were actually proved. When on arriving here I noticed that Ralph, who carries out the meals, had gloves which are impregnated with disinfectants, my last doubts were removed. A single word showed you, sir, that your secret was discovered, and if I wrote rather than said it was to prove to you that my discretion was to be trusted." I was finishing this little analysis of the case when the door was opened and the austere figure of the great dermatologist was ushered in. But for once his sphinx-like features had relaxed and there was a warm humanity in his eyes. He strode up to Colonel Emsworth and shook him by the hand.

"It is often my lot to bring ill-tidings and seldom good," said he. "This occasion is the more welcome. It is not leprosy."

"What?"

"A well-marked case of pseudo-leprosy or ichthyosis,[29] a

scale-like affection of the skin, unsightly, obstinate, but possibly curable, and certainly non-infective. Yes, Mr. Holmes, the coincidence is a remarkable one. But is it coincidence? Are there not subtle forces at work of which we know little? Are we assured that the apprehension from which this young man has no doubt suffered terribly since his exposure to its contagion may not produce a physical effect which simulates that which it fears? At any rate, I pledge my professional reputation—But the lady[30] has fainted! I think that Mr. Kent had better be with her until she recovers from this joyous shock."[31] ■

THE BOER WAR

THE BOER WAR is the name by which the South African War (1899–1902) is known in Britain, *boer* being Dutch for "farmer." Following the 1886 discovery of gold in the Witswatersrand, British prospectors swarmed to the Transvaal, or South African Republic, to stake their claims, transforming the ramshackle mining camp of Johannesburg into a bustling city of 100,000 by 1900. To the Dutch farmers who had lived on the land for generations, this mass influx of foreigners, or *uit-*

30 The colonel himself faints in the manuscript. Perhaps the author felt that this made him appear to be a weakling and altered the final version.

31 "[W]hat reader has not been struck by the incredibility of the ending, whereby Godfrey Emsworth turns out not to have leprosy at all?" writes D. Martin Dakin. "Watson was never guilty of forcing such 'happy endings' to please his readers, as witness *The Dancing Men* or *The Greek Interpreter*."

Soldiers of the Leicestershire Regiment in the Boer War.
Spectacle of Empire

landers, felt like no less than an invasion. Fearful of the growing economic and political power being wielded by British settlers, the Transvaal government, headed by the anti-British President Stephanus Johannes Paulus (Paul) Kruger, began heavily taxing the Uitlanders and restricting their civil rights (see "The Dancing Men," note 2). Britain, for its part, bent on adding to the Empire, had taken control of Cape Colony, Swaziland, Rhodesia, and other South African lands, and had briefly annexed the Transvaal itself. The gold mines and the expansionist potential of the Transvaal made Johannesburg seem the precious jewel in the crown of a unified, British South Africa.

Tensions were exacerbated by the ill-fated raid led by Dr. Leander Starr Jameson (see "The Three Garridebs," note 10) in 1895, a deliberate act of aggression that was meant to inspire the Uitlanders to revolt and that received the backing of Cecil Rhodes, prime minister of Cape Colony (see "The Solitary Cyclist," note 28). As a consequence, the Transvaal sought help from the Orange Free State province, forming a military alliance to protect the independence of both regions. Sir Alfred Milner, appointed British high commissioner for South Africa in 1897, was charged with persuading Kruger to compromise on his Uitlander policy; but talks went nowhere, and the British pushed matters to the brink by sending additional troops to its South African garrison. On October 11, 1899, the Transvaal and the Orange Free State declared war on the British.

Even with some 1,600 volunteers from Germany (remember that Kaiser Wilhelm had sent an infamous letter to Kruger, congratulating him on suppressing Jameson's raid—see "The Second Stain," note 10), Ireland, the United States, Scandinavia, France, Holland, and Russia arriving to help the Boers, the conflict seemed a mismatch from the start. Yet Boer forces had the advantage of fighting in familiar terrain and using modern rifles superior to those carried by the British; and in the war's early stages, they also far outnumbered the British troops. Initially the Boers achieved striking success, invading Northern Natal and Cape Colony; besieging Ladysmith, Kimberley, and Mafeking; and, during "Black Week" in December, scoring important victories at Stromberg, Magersfontein, and Colenso. It was this string of losses that prompted London to dismiss the flailing Sir Redvers Buller and install Frederick Sleigh Roberts as the new commander-in- chief (see note 26). As Roberts took charge and substantial British reinforcements touched down on South African shores, the tide of the war began to turn.

With the experienced Baron Kitchener (Herbert Horatio Kitchener, later Viscount Broome, 1850–1916) serving as Roberts's chief of staff, the British Army began to overwhelm the Boers, relieving Kimberley, Ladysmith, and Mafeking and capturing Bloemfontein, Johannesburg, and Pretoria. The Transvaal was officially annexed by Britain in October 1900, and Roberts returned to England, leaving Kitchener to take his place as commander-in-chief at the end of November. But the war was not yet over, and would not be for another eighteen months. The Boers embarked upon a well-coordinated guerrilla campaign in which they successfully harassed British bases, railways, and communication lines, keeping large rural areas out of British hands. In response, Kitchener saw systematic cruelty as his most effective option. He set up corrugated stone-and-iron blockhouses along the railway lines as lookout posts, then cleared the land by burning farms, killing livestock, and herding women and children into "concentration camps" (a technique probably learned from the Spanish, who used the tactic of *reconcentrado* against Cuban guerrillas in 1895). By the end of 1901, more than 100,000 Boers were living in the inadequately supplied camps; some 20,000 inmates, most of them children, died of disease brought on by unsanitary conditions. Kitchener's strategy, despite the international outrage it provoked, worked. On May 31, 1902, the Treaty of Vereeniging brought an official end to the conflict. The two Boer provinces, at last broken, formally recognised British sovereignty in exchange for the promise of future self-government and a payment of £3 million to cover the costs of property destruction.

Overall, British losses totalled 5,774 men, while the Boers lost some 4,000. As historian A. N. Wilson writes, "The war was hugely popular. . . . The songs of the war had an infectious music-hall brio. And Britain may be said to have won handsome returns on her expenditure. For her £222 million [the total cost of the war] she had won control of the richest spot on Earth." Yet the manner in which the Boer War was won casts a pall on this particular episode in British history. Whereas today

Kitchener might have stood in front of an international tribunal, in 1902, after being awarded £50,000 by Parliament, he was given the Order of Merit and made a viscount. In later years, Kitchener ruled Egypt and Sudan and served as secretary of state for war at the onset of World War I.

Arthur Conan Doyle volunteered for military service in the Boer War on Christmas Eve 1899. The British Army had no interest in the forty-year-old author, however, and Conan Doyle had to seek his own opportunities to aid the war effort, joining John Langman's volunteer hospital in February 1900 in South Africa. Upon his return to England in July 1900, he wrote two important works, *The Great Boer War*, a history, and *The War in South Africa: Its Causes and Conduct*, a response to the public criticism of British treatment of the Boers. It was probably this latter work for which Conan Doyle earned his knighthood in 1902.

THE ADVENTURE OF THE
MAZARIN STONE[1]

"The Mazarin Stone" is written in the third person, like "His Last Bow." Notwithstanding that the account opens with a passage of Watson's thoughts and emotions, most scholars doubt that he wrote it. The events all take place in one room of the Baker Street lodgings, and some suggest that the story is an adaption (by Sir Arthur Conan Doyle) of his own script for THE CROWN DIAMOND, *a moderately successful play that ran contemporaneously. Holmes seems to be uncharacteristically sarcastic. Parts of the story seem to be copied from Watson's "The Empty House," and the description of the layout of the sitting room at Baker Street contradicts Watson's accounts in other stories. When Granada Television produced "The Mazarin Stone" for television, Jeremy Brett (who had appeared in the previous thirty-nine episodes) was too ill to appear as Sherlock Holmes, and so the producers rewrote the story to make brother Mycroft the detective. In view of the likelihood that "The Mazarin Stone" is a work of fiction, they may be forgiven.*

IT WAS PLEASANT to Dr. Watson[2] to find himself once more in the untidy room of the first floor in Baker Street which had been the starting-point of so many remarkable adventures. He looked round him at the scientific charts upon the wall, the acid-charred bench of chemicals, the violin-case leaning in the corner, the coal-scuttle, which contained of old the pipes and tobacco. Finally, his eyes came round to the fresh and smiling face of Billy, the young but very wise and tactful page, who had helped a little to fill up the gap of loneliness and isolation which surrounded the saturnine figure of the great detective.

"It all seems very unchanged, Billy. You don't change, either. I hope the same can be said of him?"

Billy glanced with some solicitude at the closed door of the bedroom.

"I think he's in bed and asleep," he said.

It was seven in the evening of a lovely summer's day, but Dr.

1 "The Mazarin Stone" appeared in the *Strand Magazine* in October 1921; its first American publication was in *Hearst's International Magazine* in November 1921. Only months before, on May 2, 1921, a play by Arthur Conan Doyle entitled *The Crown Diamond: or, An Evening with Sherlock Holmes* opened at the Bristol Hippodrome, after which it toured for eighteen months. The play and the events of "The Mazarin Stone" have much in common, and it is difficult to understand why Dr. Watson would have given Sir Arthur access to his notes for purposes of producing a play. The play was published in 1958 by the Baker Street Irregulars.

2 See the appendix on page 1531 for a discussion of the author of this story.

3 This was probably Arthur James Balfour (1848–1930), who succeeded his uncle, Lord Salisbury, as prime minister in 1902. His administration was marked by educational reform and establishment of the 1904 Entente Cordiale (a "friendly understanding") with France, the precursor to the Triple Entente with Russia. But Balfour was not particularly popular, and a dispute within the Conservative party over the issue of free trade forced him to resign from office in 1905. Balfour's most recognised action was the so-called Balfour Declaration, in which, as foreign secretary under David Lloyd George, he wrote a November 2, 1917, letter to Baron Rothschild pledging British support for a Jewish homeland in Palestine.

4 The British home secretary, as head of the home office, is responsible for the maintenance of the peace and administration of the police, judicial, and penal systems. Aretas Akers-Douglas, 1st Viscount Chilston, served as home secretary from 1902 to 1905, the period in which the events of "The Mazarin Stone" likely occurred.

Watson was sufficiently familiar with the irregularity of his old friend's hours to feel no surprise at the idea.

"That means a case, I suppose?"

"Yes, sir; he is very hard at it just now. I'm frightened for his health. He gets paler and thinner, and he eats nothing. 'When will you be pleased to dine, Mr. Holmes?' Mrs. Hudson asked. 'Seven-thirty, the day after to-morrow,' said he. You know his way when he is keen on a case."

"Yes, Billy, I know."

"He's following someone. Yesterday he was out as a workman looking for a job. Today he was an old woman. Fairly took me in, he did, and I ought to know his ways by now." Billy pointed with a grin to a very baggy parasol which leaned against the sofa. "That's part of the old woman's outfit," he said.

"But what is it all about, Billy?"

Billy sank his voice, as one who discusses great secrets of State. "I don't mind telling you, sir, but it should go no farther. It's this case of the Crown diamond."

"What—the hundred-thousand-pound burglary?"

"Yes, sir. They must get it back, sir. Why, we had the Prime Minister[3] and the Home Secretary[4] both sitting on that very sofa. Mr. Holmes was very nice to them. He soon put them at their ease and promised he would do all he could. Then there is Lord Cantlemere—"

"Ah!"

"Yes, sir, you know what that means. He's a stiff 'un, sir, if I may say so. I can get along with the Prime Minister, and I've nothing against the Home Secretary, who seemed a civil, obliging sort of man, but I can't stand his Lordship. Neither can Mr. Holmes, sir. You see, he don't believe in Mr. Holmes and he was against employing him. He'd *rather* he failed."

"And Mr. Holmes knows it?"

"Mr. Holmes always knows whatever there is to know."

"Well, we'll hope he won't fail and that Lord Cantlemere will be confounded. But I say, Billy, what is that curtain for across the window?"

"Mr. Holmes had it put up there three days ago. We've got something funny behind it."

Billy advanced and drew away the drapery which screened the alcove of the bow window.

Dr. Watson could not restrain a cry of amazement. There was

a facsimile of his old friend, dressing-gown and all, the face turned three-quarter towards the window and downward, as though reading an invisible book, while the body was sunk deep in an armchair. Billy detached the head and put it in the air.

"We put it at different angles, so that it may seem more life-like. I wouldn't dare touch it if the blind were not down. But when it's up you can see this from across the way."

"We used something of the sort once before."[5]

"Before my time," said Billy. He drew the window curtains apart and looked out into the street. "There are folk who watch us from over yonder. I can see a fellow now at the window. Have a look for yourself."

Watson had taken a step forward when the bedroom door opened, and the long, thin form of Holmes emerged, his face pale and drawn, but his step and hearing as active as ever. With a single spring he was at the window, and had drawn the blind once more.

"That will do, Billy," said he. "You were in danger of your life then, my boy, and I can't do without you just yet. Well, Watson, it is good to see you in your old quarters once again. You come at a critical moment."

"So I gather."

"You can go, Billy. That boy is a problem, Watson. How far am I justified in allowing him to be in danger?"

"Danger of what, Holmes?"

"Of sudden death. I'm expecting something this evening."

"Expecting what?"

"To be murdered, Watson."

"No, no; you are joking, Holmes!"

"Even my limited sense of humour could evolve a better joke than that. But we may be comfortable in the meantime, may we not? Is alcohol permitted? The gasogene[6] and cigars are in the old place. Let me see you once more in the custom-ary armchair. You have not I hope, learned to despise my pipe and my lamentable tobacco? It has to take the place of food these days."

"But why not eat?"

"Because the faculties become refined when you starve them. Why, surely, as a doctor, my dear Watson, you must admit that what your digestion gains in the way of blood sup-ply is so much lost to the brain. I am a brain, Watson. The rest

5 In "The Empty House."

6 Despite the popular association of the gaso-gene (used to produce seltzer water) with Holmes, it is mentioned only here and in "A Scandal in Bohemia" (see "A Scandal in Bohemia," note 16).

7 That this is a pose may be evidenced by Holmes's sumptuous repasts in such tales as *The Sign of Four* and "The Noble Bachelor." Holmes certainly was no *gourmand*, for he often dined on a hurried meal (for example, his "rude meal" of a slice of beef and bread in "The Beryl Coronet") and Watson stated that "his diet was usually of the sparest . . . ," but the Canon has ample examples of Holmes's appreciation of fine dining (for example, "something nutritious at Simpson's" in "The Dying Detective").

"Billy advanced and drew away the drapery which screened the window. Dr. Watson could not restrain a cry of amazement. There was a facsimile of his old friend, dressing-gown and all."
A. Gilbert, *Strand Magazine*, 1921

of me is a mere appendix.[7] Therefore, it is the brain I must consider."

"But this danger, Holmes?"

"Ah, yes, in case it should come off, it would perhaps be as well that you should burden your memory with the name and address of the murderer. You can give it to Scotland Yard, with my love and a parting blessing. Sylvius is the name—Count Negretto Sylvius. Write it down, man, write it down! 136 Moorside Gardens, N. W.—got it?"

Watson's honest face was twitching with anxiety. He knew

only too well the immense risks taken by Holmes and was well aware that what he said was more likely to be understatement than exaggeration. Watson was always the man of action, and he rose to the occasion.

"Count me in, Holmes. I have nothing to do for a day or two."

"Your morals don't improve, Watson. You have added fibbing to your other vices. You bear every sign of the busy medical man, with calls on him every hour."

"Not such important ones. But can't you have this fellow arrested?"

"Yes, Watson, I could. That's what worries him so."

"But why don't you?"

"Because I don't know where the diamond is."

"Ah! Billy told me—the missing Crown jewel!"

8 Cardinal Jules Mazarin (1602–1661) was cardinal and chief minister of France during the youth of Louis XIV. Originally from Italy (his given name was Giulio Mazarini), the young secretary to the papal legate of Milan was sent to France in 1630, during hostilities between France and Spain, to negotiate with Louis XIII's chief minister, Cardinal Richilieu. Mazarin's ensuing friendship with the great Richelieu not only brought him back to France in 1640 to serve the French court, but it also encouraged Louis XIII to recommend him for cardinal despite his never having been ordained as a priest. Upon the deaths of Richelieu and Louis XIII, Mazarin became the minister of the French regent, Anne of Austria. Before the young Louis XIV came of age, Mazarin had the regent's implicit trust and busied himself with negotiating peace between Spain and France; after Louis XIV was crowned in 1654, Mazarin advised him on political affairs and helped him to train his staff. Some biographers make the unsubstantiated claim that the handsome, charming Mazarin was engaged in a secret affair with Anne of Austria and possibly even married her. In Mazarin's will, he bequeathed to the French Crown the major part of his jewel collection, including the eighteen diamonds thereafter called the "Mazarin Diamonds."

Peter Blau, in "In Memoriam: Muzaffar Ad-Din," points out that there were no yellow diamonds among the Mazarin Diamonds. However, in the play *The Crown Diamond*, written by Arthur Conan Doyle and perhaps based on Watson's records of this case (see note 1, above), Holmes makes no mention of Mazarin but instead describes the gem as "the great yellow Crown Diamond, 77 carats." With this added information, Blau identifies the stone as one of the Persian crown jewels, which may have been stolen during the visit of the shah of Persia to England in 1902. Blau offers no theory, however, on why the stone is here misidentified as the "Mazarin stone."

"Yes, the great yellow Mazarin stone.[8] I've cast my net and I have my fish. But I have not got the stone. What is the use of taking *them*? We can make the world a better place by laying them by the heels. But that is not what I am out for. It's the stone I want."

"And is this Count Sylvius one of your fish?"

"Yes, and he's a shark. He bites. The other is Sam Merton, the boxer. Not a bad fellow, Sam, but the Count has used him. Sam's not a shark. He is a great big silly bull-headed gudgeon.[9] But he is flopping about in my net all the same."

"Where is this Count Sylvius?"

"I've been at his very elbow all the morning. You've seen me as an old lady, Watson. I was never more convincing. He actually picked up my parasol for me once. 'By your leave, madame,' said he—half-Italian, you know, and with the Southern graces of manner when in the mood, but a devil incarnate in the other mood. Life is full of whimsical happenings, Watson."

"It might have been tragedy."

"Well, perhaps it might. I followed him to old Straubenzee's workshop in the Minories. Straubenzee made the air-gun[10]—a very pretty bit of work, as I understand, and I rather fancy it is in the opposite window at the present moment. Have you seen the dummy? Of course, Billy showed it to you. Well, it may get a bullet through its beautiful head at any moment. Ah, Billy, what is it?"

The boy had reappeared in the room with a card upon a tray. Holmes glanced at it with raised eyebrows and an amused smile.

"The man himself. I had hardly expected this. Grasp the nettle, Watson![11] A man of nerve. Possibly you have heard of his reputation as a shooter of big game.[12] It would indeed be a triumphant ending to his excellent sporting record if he added me to his bag. This is a proof that he feels my toe very close behind his heel."

"Send for the police."

"I probably shall. But not just yet. Would you glance carefully out of the window, Watson, and see if anyone is hanging about in the street?"

Watson looked warily round the edge of the curtain.

"Yes, there is one rough fellow near the door."

1516

"That will be Sam Merton—the faithful but rather fatuous Sam. Where is this gentleman, Billy?"

"In the waiting-room, sir."[13]

"Show him up when I ring."

"Yes, sir."

"If I am not in the room, show him in all the same."

"Yes, sir."

Watson waited until the door was closed, and then he turned earnestly to his companion.

"Look here, Holmes, this is simply impossible. This is a desperate man, who sticks at nothing. He may have come to murder you."

"I should not be surprised."

"I insist upon staying with you."

"You would be horribly in the way."

"In *his* way?"

"No, my dear fellow—in my way."

"Well, I can't possibly leave you."

"Yes, you can, Watson. And you will, for you have never failed to play the game. I am sure you will play it to the end.[14] This man has come for his own purpose, but he may stay for mine." Holmes took out his notebook and scribbled a few lines. "Take a cab to Scotland Yard and give this to Youghal of the C. I. D.[15] Come back with the police. The fellow's arrest will follow."

"I'll do that with joy."

"Before you return I may have just time enough to find out where the stone is." He touched the bell. "I think we will go out through the bedroom. This second exit is exceedingly useful.[16] I rather want to see my shark without his seeing me, and I have, as you will remember, my own way of doing it."

It was, therefore, an empty room into which Billy, a minute later, ushered Count Sylvius. The famous game-shot, sportsman, and man-about town was a big, swarthy fellow, with a formidable dark moustache shading a cruel, thin-lipped mouth, and surmounted by a long, curved nose like the beak of an eagle. He was well dressed, but his brilliant necktie, shining pin, and glittering rings were flamboyant in their effect. As the door closed behind him he looked round him with fierce, startled eyes, like one who suspects a trap at every turn. Then he gave a violent start as he saw the impassive head and the collar

9 A gudgeon is a small freshwater fish used for bait. Brewer's *Dictionary of Phrase and Fable* explains that "to swallow a gudgeon" means "To be bamboozled with a most palpable lie, as silly fish are caught by gudgeons." To illustrate the point, Brewer quotes the second part of Samuel Butler's satirical poem "Hudibras" (1664): "Make fools believe in their foreseeing / Of things before they are in being; / To swallow gudgeons ere they're catched, / And count their chickens ere they're hatched."

10 Holmes has a fear of air-guns, and not without reason: See "The Final Problem" and "The Empty House."

11 Holmes appears to be combining lines from "Verses written on a window in Scotland," by Aaron Hill (1685–1750), theatre impresario, poet, commercial entrepreneur, and friend of novelist Samuel Richardson and poet Alexander Pope: "Tender-handed stroke a nettle, / And it stings you for your pains; / Grasp it like a man of mettle / And it soft as silk remains." However, usage of the figure of the nettle is so common that this example can hardly be seen as contradictory of Watson's assessment of Holmes's knowledge of literature as "nil" (*A Study in Scarlet*).

12 A trait the count shared with Colonel Sebastian Moran of "The Empty House." In *The Crown Diamond* (see note 1, above), the villain *is* Colonel Sebastian Moran, a falsification perhaps suggested by this common pastime.

13 This is the only mention in the Canon of a "waiting room" at 221 Baker Street.

14 What might seem, at first blush, to be another dismissive comment directed toward Watson is, in fact, a rare showing of flattery and affection on Holmes's part. As June

Thomson clarifies, "At that period, the acknowledgement that someone had 'played the game' was one of the highest compliments one Englishman could pay to another. In praising Watson in this manner, Holmes seems to be looking back over his shoulder, as it were, at Watson's role in their relationship and, while endorsing Watson's outstanding qualities as a friend, is also signalling that the time for parting has almost come."

15 The Criminal Investigation Department (CID) branch of the London Metropolitan Police was created in 1878, separating plain-clothes detectives from the uniformed constables. (The term "Scotland Yard," the name for police headquarters, is often used when only the CID itself is meant.) For no discernible reason, Holmes refers to the police's criminal investigation unit as the CID only in "The Mazarin Stone," "The Three Garridebs," and *The Valley of Fear*. In all other cases, he prefers "the Yard."

16 This is the only mention in the Canon of a "second exit" from the sitting room. Ann Byerly makes the sensible argument that Holmes had taken over Watson's bedroom at this time, that the rooms had a door joining them, and that the "second door" was the concealed exit to Holmes's bedroom, while the unconcealed exit was to Watson's room.

"His thick stick half raised, he was crouching for his
final spring and blow when a cool, sardonic voice
greeted him from the open bedroom door:
'Don't break it, Count! Don't break it!'"
A. Gilbert, *Strand Magazine*, 1921

of the dressing-gown which projected above the armchair in
the window. At first his expression was one of pure amazement. Then the light of a horrible hope steamed in his dark,
murderous eyes. He took one more glance round to see that
there were no witnesses, and then, on tiptoe, his thick stick
half raised, he approached the silent figure. He was crouching
for his final spring and blow when a cool, sardonic voice
greeted him from the open bedroom door:

"Don't break it, Count! Don't break it!"

The assassin staggered back, amazement in his convulsed
face. For an instant he half raised his loaded cane once more,
as if he would turn his violence from the effigy to the original;

17 Holmes also sat for a wax bust made by Monsieur Oscar Meunier of Grenoble ("The Empty House").

but there was something in that steady grey eye and mocking smile which caused his hand to sink to his side.

"It's a pretty little thing," said Holmes, advancing towards the image. "Tavernier, the French modeller, made it.[17] He is as good at waxworks as your friend Straubenzee is at air-guns."

"Air-guns, sir! What do you mean?"

"Put your hat and stick on the side-table. Thank you! Pray take a seat. Would you mind to put your revolver out also? Oh, very good, if you prefer to sit upon it. Your visit is really most opportune, for I wanted badly to have a few minutes' chat with you."

The Count scowled, with heavy, threatening eyebrows.

"I, too, wished to have some words with you, Holmes. That is why I am here. I won't deny that I intended to assault you just now."

Holmes swung his leg on the edge of the table.

"I rather gathered that you had some idea of the sort in your head," said he. 'But why these personal attentions?"

"Because you have gone out of your way to annoy me. Because you have put your creatures upon my track."

"My creatures! I assure you not!"

"Nonsense! I have had them followed. Two can play at that game, Holmes."

"It is a small point Count Sylvius, but perhaps you would kindly give me my prefix when you address me. You can understand that, with my routine of work, I should find myself on familiar terms with half the rogues' gallery, and you will agree that exceptions are invidious."

"Well, *Mr.* Holmes, then."

"Excellent! But I assure you you are mistaken about my alleged agents."

Count Sylvius laughed contemptuously.

"Other people can observe as well as you. Yesterday there was an old sporting man. To-day it was an elderly woman. They held me in view all day."

"Really, sir, you compliment me. Old Baron Dowson said the night before he was hanged that in my case what the law had gained the stage had lost. And now you give my little impersonations your kindly praise?"

"It was you—you yourself?"

Holmes shrugged his shoulder. "You can see in the corner

the parasol which you so politely handed to me in the Minories before you began to suspect."

"If I had known, you might never . . ."

"Have seen this humble home again. I was well aware of it. We all have neglected opportunities to deplore. As it happens, you did not know, so here we are!"

The Count's knotted brows gathered more heavily over his menacing eyes. "What you say only makes the matter worse. It was not your agents but your play-acting, busybody self! You admit that you have dogged me. Why?"

"Come now, Count. You used to shoot lions in Algeria."

"Well?"

"But why?"

"Why? The sport—the excitement—the danger!"

"And, no doubt, to free the country from a pest?"

"Exactly."

"My reasons in a nutshell!"

The Count sprang to his feet, and his hand involuntarily moved back to his hip-pocket.

"Sit down, sir, sit down! There was another, more practical, reason. I want that yellow diamond!"

Count Sylvius lay back in his chair with an evil smile.

"Upon my word!" said he.

"You knew that I was after you for that. The real reason why you are here to-night is to find out how much I know about the matter and how far my removal is absolutely essential. Well, I should say that, from your point of view, it is absolutely essential, for I know all about it, save only one thing, which you are about to tell me."

"Oh, indeed! And pray, what is this missing fact?"

"Where the Crown diamond now is."

The Count looked sharply at his companion. "Oh, you want to know that, do you? How the devil should I be able to tell you where it is?"

"You can, and you will."

"Indeed!"

"You can't bluff me, Count Sylvius." Holmes's eyes, as he gazed at him, contracted and lightened until they were like two menacing points of steel. "You are absolute plate-glass. I see to the very back of your mind."

"Then, of course, you see where the diamond is!"

18 A whist reference. In this case, a player with all the best cards of the chosen trump suit—which beats a card of any other suit—is certain to win, and the hapless opponent may as well "throw down your hand," indicating defeat. See "The Red-Headed League" for a discussion of Holmes's whist-playing.

Holmes clapped his hands with amusement, and then pointed a derisive finger. "Then you do know. You have admitted it!"

"I admit nothing."

"Now, Count, if you will be reasonable, we can do business. If not, you will get hurt."

Count Sylvius threw up his eyes to the ceiling. "And you talk about bluff!" said he.

Holmes looked at him thoughtfully, like a master chess-player who meditates his crowning move. Then he threw open the table drawer and drew out a square notebook.

"Do you know what I keep in this book?"

"No, sir, I do not!"

"You!"

"Me!"

"Yes, sir, *you*. You are all here—every action of your vile and dangerous life."

"Damn you, Holmes!" cried the Count with blazing eyes. "There are limits to my patience!"

"It's all here, Count. The real facts as to the death of old Mrs. Harold, who left you the Blymer estate, which you so rapidly gambled away."

"You are dreaming!"

"And the complete life history of Miss Minnie Warrender."

"Tut! You will make nothing of that!"

"Plenty more here, Count. Here is the robbery in the train de-luxe to the Riviera on February 13, 1892. Here is the forged cheque in the same year on the Credit Lyonnais."

"No; you're wrong there."

"Then I am right on the others! Now, Count, you are a card-player. When the other fellow has all the trumps, it saves time to throw down your hand."[18]

"What has all this talk to do with the jewel of which you spoke?"

"Gently, Count. Restrain that eager mind! Let me get to the points in my own humdrum fashion. I have all this against you; but above all, I have a clear case against both you and your fighting bully in the case of the Crown diamond."

"Indeed!"

"I have the cabman who took you to Whitehall and the cabman who brought you away. I have the Commissionaire who saw you near the case. I have Ikey Sanders, who refused to cut it up for you. Ikey has peached,[19] and the game is up."

The veins stood out on the Count's forehead. His dark, hairy hands were clenched in a convulsion of restrained emotion. He tried to speak, but the words would not shape themselves.

"That's the hand I play from," said Holmes. "I put it all upon the table. But one card is missing. It's the king of diamonds. I don't know where the stone is."

"You never shall know."

"No? Now, be reasonable, Count. Consider the situation. You are going to be locked up for twenty years. So is Sam Merton. What good are you going to get out of your diamond? None in the world. But if you hand it over—well, I'll compound a felony. We don't want you or Sam. We want the stone. Give that up, and so far as I am concerned you can go free so long as you behave yourself in the future. If you make another slip—well, it will be the last. But this time my commission is to get the stone, not you."

"But if I refuse?"

"Why, then—alas!—it must be you and not the stone."

Billy had appeared in answer to a ring.

"I think, Count, that it would be as well to have your friend Sam at this conference. After all, his interests should be represented. Billy, you will see a large and ugly gentleman outside the front door. Ask him to come up."

"If he won't come, sir?"

"No violence, Billy.[20] Don't be rough with him. If you tell him that Count Sylvius wants him he will certainly come."

"What are you going to do now?" asked the Count as Billy disappeared.

"My friend Watson was with me just now. I told him that I had a shark and a gudgeon in my net; now I am drawing the net and up they come together."

The Count had risen from his chair, and his hand was behind his back. Holmes held something half protruding from the pocket of his dressing-gown.

"You won't die in your bed, Holmes."

"I have often had the same idea. Does it matter very much? After all, Count, your own exit is more likely to be perpendicular than horizontal.[21] But these anticipations of the future

19 To inform against or betray; a derivative of "impeach."

20 A joke, for Holmes sends the "young page" to fetch Sam Merton, a "heavily-built" prize-fighter.

21 By which Holmes means that the count will be hanged.

22 Indeed, Holmes does appear to be uncharacteristically acting the part of the "wiseacre" in "The Mazarin Stone," evidence to some of the fictitious nature of the tale.

23 A barcarolle, or barcarole, is a Venetian gondolier's song (*barcarola* is Italian for "boatman"), with a rhythm suggestive of the rowing motion. The "Hoffmann Barcarolle" is the most famous operatic example of the form; it is from the opera *Les Contes d'Hoffmann* (Tales of Hoffmann), which was written by the French composer Jacques Offenbach (1819–1880) and based on three stories by the German author E. T. A. Hoffmann. *Les Contes d'Hoffmann* was first performed in February 1881 at the Opéra Comique in Paris. The song, which opens the second act, is an empassioned duet to love and the night. Benjamin Grosbayne finds the adjectives "wailing" and "haunting" very inapt for the piece and concludes that Watson was abysmally ignorant of the literature of the violin and probably music in general. Anthony Boucher points out that there was no recording extant of the "Barcarolle" in 1902, and this must have been a private recording of Holmes's own playing.

are morbid. Why not give ourselves up to the unrestrained enjoyment of the present?"

A sudden wild-beast light sprang up in the dark, menacing eyes of the master criminal. Holmes's figure seemed to grow taller as he grew tense and ready.

"It is no use your fingering your revolver, my friend," he said in a quiet voice. "You know perfectly well that you dare not use it, even if I gave you time to draw it. Nasty, noisy things, revolvers, Count. Better stick to air-guns. Ah! I think I hear the fairy footstep of your estimable partner. Good day, Mr. Merton. Rather dull in the street, is it not?"

The prize-fighter, a heavily built young man with a stupid, obstinate, slab-sided face, stood awkwardly at the door, looking about him with a puzzled expression. Holmes's debonair manner was a new experience, and though he vaguely felt that it was hostile, he did not know how to counter it. He turned to his more astute comrade for help.

"What's the game now, Count? What's this fellow want? What's up?" His voice was deep and raucous.

The Count shrugged his shoulders, and it was Holmes who answered.

"If I may put it in a nutshell, Mr. Merton, I should say it was *all* up."

The boxer still addressed his remarks to his associate.

"Is this cove trying to be funny, or what? I'm not in the funny mood myself."[22]

"No, I expect not," said Holmes. "I think I can promise you that you will feel even less humorous as the evening advances. Now, look here, Count Sylvius. I'm a busy man and I can't waste time. I'm going into that bedroom. Pray make yourselves quite at home in my absence. You can explain to your friend how the matter lies without the restraint of my presence. I shall try over the Hoffmann 'Barcarolle'[23] upon my violin. In five minutes I shall return for your final answer. You quite grasp the alternative, do you not? Shall we take you, or shall we have the stone?"

Holmes withdrew, picking up his violin from the corner as he passed. A few moments later the long-drawn, wailing notes of that most haunting of tunes came faintly through the closed door of the bedroom.

"'I'm going into that bedroom,' said Holmes. 'Pray make yourselves quite at home in my absence. In five minutes I shall return for your final answer.'"
A. Gilbert, *Strand Magazine*, 1921

24 To inform against one's companions, to tell tales. Equivalent to "peach."

25 To "do" a person in boxing (or street fighting) is to get the best of him. A "thick 'un" is a sovereign: a crown piece, or five shillings. Thus, the total expression means something like "I'll beat him up but good," as one might say today.

"What is it, then?" asked Merton anxiously as his companion turned to him. "Does he know about the stone?"

"He knows a damned sight too much about it. I'm not sure that he doesn't know all about it . . ."

"Good Lord!" The boxer's shallow face turned a shade whiter.

"Ikey Sanders has split[24] on us."

"He has, has he? I'll do him down a thick 'un[25] for that if I swing for it."

"That won't help us much. We've got to make up our minds what to do."

"Half a mo'" said the boxer, looking suspiciously at the bed-

26 See "The Empty House," note 45.

27 To send or transport to prision.

28 The cutting of diamonds has been extensively practised in the city since the sixteenth century. Many famous diamonds were cut and polished in Amsterdam. These include the Cullinan, the largest diamond ever found, and the Koh-I-Noor (the Mountain of Light), the latter cut for the British Crown Jewels in 1852. The world's smallest diamond, 0.00012 carat, with 57 facets, was cut in Amsterdam.

room door. "He's a leary cove that wants watching. I suppose he's not listening?"

"How can he be listening with that music going?"

"That's right. Maybe somebody's behind a curtain. Too many curtains in this room." As he looked round he suddenly saw for the first time the effigy in the window, and stood staring and pointing, too amazed for words.

"Tut! it's only a dummy," said the Count.

"A fake, is it? Well, strike me! Madame Tussaud[26] ain't in it. It's the living spit of him, gown and all. But them curtains, Count!"

"Oh, confound the curtains! We are wasting our time, and there is none too much. He can lag[27] us over this stone."

"The deuce he can!"

"But he'll let us slip if we only tell him where the swag is."

"What! Give it up? Give up a hundred thousand quid?"

"It's one or the other."

Merton scratched his short-cropped pate.

"He's alone in there. Let's do him in. If his light were out we should have nothing to fear."

The Count shook his head.

"He is armed and ready. If we shot him we could hardly get away in a place like this. Besides, it's likely enough that the police know whatever evidence he has got. Hallo! What was that?"

There was a vague sound which seemed to come from the window. Both men sprang round, but all was quiet. Save for the one strange figure seated in the chair, the room was certainly empty.

"Something in the street," said Merton. "Now look here, guv'nor, you've got the brains. Surely you can think a way out of it. If slugging is no use then it's up to you."

"I've fooled better men than he," the Count answered. "The stone is here in my secret pocket. I take no chances leaving it about. It can be out of England to-night and cut into four pieces in Amsterdam[28] before Sunday. He knows nothing of Van Seddar."

"I thought Van Seddar was going next week."

"He *was*. But now he must get off by the next boat. One or other of us must slip round with the stone to Lime Street and tell him."

"But the false bottom ain't ready."

"Well, he must take it as it is and chance it. There's not a moment to lose." Again, with the sense of danger which becomes an instinct with the sportsman, he paused and looked hard at the window. Yes, it was surely from the street that the faint sound had come.

"As to Holmes," he continued, "we can fool him easily enough. You see, the damned fool won't arrest us if he can get the stone. Well, we'll promise him the stone. We'll put him on the wrong track about it, and before he finds that it *is* the wrong track it well be in Holland and we out of the country."

"That sounds good to me!" cried Sam Merton with a grin.

"You go on and tell the Dutchman to get a move on him. I'll see this sucker and fill him up with a bogus confession. I'll tell him that the stone is in Liverpool. Confound that whining music; it gets on my nerves! By the time he finds it isn't in Liverpool it will be in quarters and we on the blue water. Come back here, out of a line with that keyhole. Here is the stone."

"I wonder you dare carry it."

"Where could I have it safer? If we could take it out of Whitehall someone else could surely take it out of my lodgings."

"Let's have a look at it."

Count Sylvius cast a somewhat unflattering glance at his associate and disregarded the unwashed hand which was extended towards him.

"What—d'ye think I'm going to snatch it off you? See here, mister, I'm getting a bit tired of your ways."

"Well, well, no offence, Sam. We can't afford to quarrel. Come over to the window if you want to see the beauty properly. Now hold it to the light! Here!"

"Thank you!"

With a single spring Holmes had leaped from the dummy's chair and had grasped the precious jewel. He held it now in one hand, while his other pointed a revolver at the Count's head. The two villains staggered back in utter amazement. Before they had recovered Holmes had pressed the electric bell.[29]

"No violence, gentlemen—no violence, I beg of you! Consider the furniture! It must be very clear to you that your position is an impossible one. The police are waiting below."

29 The only appearance of this bell at Baker Street.

30 To seize, take, or lay hold of anything, as in, "I copped us some great seats." Here, Merton means that his capture (by the cops, coincidentally enough) seems just. In fact, this usage of the word "cop" probably comes from the Old French *caper* and the Latin *capere*, to capture or seize.

THE GRAMOPHONE,
OR TALKING MACHINE.

This is an apparatus for reproducing the human voice or other sounds as often as desired; it is intended to be for the voice what photography is for the features. The Gramophone bears no resemblance in a scientific aspect to the Phonograph or Graphophone. Those who have seen and heard it universally pronounce it to be a wonderful Toy.

Price 2 Guineas.

PARKINS AND GOTTO,
60, OXFORD STREET, LONDON.

Contemporary gramophone.
Victorian Advertisements

31 "Let us stress here the fact that it was a gramophone," Anthony Boucher writes. "To most modern readers, *gramophone* and *phonograph* are interchangeable words, respectively British and American, like lift and elevator. . . . But in England in 1903, *gramophone* distinctly meant the Berliner-Gramophone & Typewriter disc machine, while cylinder machines were known as *phonographs* or *graphophones*."

The gramophone was invented in the U.S. by Emile Berliner (1851–1929), a German-American inventor. Thomas Edison had

The Count's bewilderment overmastered his rage and fear.

"But how the deuce—?" he gasped.

"Your surprise is very natural. You are not aware that a second door from my bedroom leads behind that curtain. I fancied that you must have heard me when I displaced the figure, but luck was on my side. It gave me a chance of listening to your racy conversation which would have been painfully constrained had you been aware of my presence."

The Count gave a gesture of resignation.

"We give you best, Holmes. I believe you are the devil himself."

"Not far from him, at any rate," Holmes answered with a polite smile.

Sam Merton's slow intellect had only gradually appreciated the situation. Now, as the sound of heavy steps came from the stairs outside, he broke silence at last.

"A fair cop!"[30] said he. "But, I say, what about that bloomin' fiddle! I hear it yet."

"Tut, tut!" Holmes answered. "You are perfectly right. Let it play! These modern gramophones are a remarkable invention."[31]

There was an inrush of police, the handcuffs clicked and the criminals were led to the waiting cab. Watson lingered with Holmes, congratulating him upon this fresh leaf added to his laurels. Once more their conversation was interrupted by the imperturbable Billy with his card-tray.

"Lord Cantlemere, sir."

"Show him up, Billy. This is the eminent peer who represents the very highest interests," said Holmes. "He is an excellent and loyal person, but rather of the old regime. Shall we make him unbend? Dare we venture upon a slight liberty? He knows, we may conjecture, nothing of what has occurred."

The door opened to admit a thin, austere figure with a hatchet face and drooping mid-Victorian whiskers of a glossy blackness which hardly corresponded with the rounded shoulders and feeble gait. Holmes advanced affably, and shook an unresponsive hand.

"How-do-you-do, Lord Cantlemere? It is chilly for the time of year, but rather warm indoors. May I take your overcoat?"

"No, I thank you; I will not take it off."

Holmes laid his hand insistently upon the sleeve.

"Pray allow me! My friend Dr. Watson would assure you that these changes of temperature are most insidious."

His Lordship shook himself free with some impatience.

"I am quite comfortable, sir. I have no need to stay. I have simply looked in to know how your self-appointed task was progressing."

"It is difficult—very difficult."

"I feared that you would find it so."

There was a distinct sneer in the old courtier's words and manner.

"Every man finds his limitations, Mr. Holmes, but at least it cures us of the weakness of self-satisfaction."

"Yes, sir, I have been much perplexed."

"No doubt."

"Especially upon one point. Possibly you could help me upon it?"

"You apply for my advice rather late in the day. I thought that you had your own all-sufficient methods. Still, I am ready to help you."

"You see, Lord Cantlemere, we can no doubt frame a case against the actual thieves."

"When you have caught them."

"Exactly. But the question is—how shall we proceed against the receiver?"

"Is this not rather premature?"

"It is as well to have our plans ready. Now, what would you regard as final evidence against the receiver?"

"The actual possession of the stone."

"You would arrest him upon that?"

"Most undoubtedly."

Holmes seldom laughed,[32] but he got as near it as his old friend Watson could remember.

"In that case, my dear sir, I shall be under the painful necessity of advising your arrest."

Lord Cantlemere was very angry. Some of the ancient fires flickered up into his sallow cheeks.

"You take a great liberty, Mr. Holmes. In fifty years of official life I cannot recall such a case. I am a busy man, sir, engaged upon important affairs, and I have no time or taste for foolish jokes. I may tell you frankly, sir, that I have never been a believer in your power, and that I have always been of the

recorded and reproduced sound on a cylinder, but in 1887 Berliner created a flat disk, which was made of hard rubber and played on a machine that had to be continually cranked. These gramophones sold for an affordable ten dollars, but sound quality was poor, and cranking the machine for such a long time proved tiresome. Berliner's invention got a boost when Eldridge Reeves Johnson, who ran a machine shop, invented a simple spring motor for him, eliminating the gramophone's most problematic feature. To advertise his invention, Berliner trademarked (on July 10, 1900) a picture of a dog staring at a gramophone, based on the 1898 painting *His Master's Voice* by British artist Francis Barraud. (Barraud was inspired by his late dog Nipper.) He opened a London office in 1898, which became The Gramophone & Typewriter Company in 1900 and His Master's Voice (HMV) in 1910.

Expanding rapidly, the Berliner Gramophone Company hired a man named Frank Seaman to market and distribute Berliner's gramophones for him. As profits rose, Seaman grew dissatisfied with the terms of his contract and started the Zon-o-phone Company to take business away from Berliner; he then used some fancy legal manoeuvring to induce Berliner's chief rival, the Columbia Graphophone Company—which was still using cylinders—to sue the Berliner Gramophone Company and put it out of business.

Following this fiasco, Berliner essentially retired in 1900, but Eldridge Reeves Johnson continued on by establishing the Consolidated Talking Machine Company, using (with Berliner's permission) the picture of the dog and the gramophone in his company logo. After hiring engineers to improve the sound quality of Berliner's disks, Johnson offered a free, higher-quality record to anyone who owned a Berliner machine. The gimmick worked so well that Johnson attracted the attention of his old foes Seaman and Columbia, who once again took him to court.

Eldridge countersued and won, his only concession being that he could no longer use the name "gramophone," which Seaman, as official distributor for the Berliner Gramophone Company, claimed for his own. Flush with his victory, Johnson began putting "Victor Records" on his disks and eventually renamed his company the Victor Talking Machine Company, incorporating it in 1901 and partnering in England with the Gramophone & Typewriter Company, which had remained intact. In 1929, Victor Records would be purchased by RCA, which would become RCA-Victor; in 1935, Gramophone & Typewriter Company (now HMV Records) would be absorbed by the RCA-created EMI. Both continued to use Berliner's original "His Master's Voice" image.

While Holmes may have been slow in other areas to adapt to new technologies (witness the absence of a telephone at Baker Street for many years), when it came to his beloved music, Holmes apparently had to have the latest recording device.

32 This is false, at least if the Canon is a fair sampling of Holmes's behaviour. A. G. Cooper, in "Holmesian Humour," claims to have counted 292 examples of the Master's laughter, while Charles E. Lauterbach and Edward S. Lauterbach, in "The Man Who Seldom Laughed," compiled the following table:

Frequency Table Showing the
Number and Kind of Responses
Sherlock Holmes Made to Humorous
Situations and Comments in His
60 Recorded Adventures

Smile	103
Laugh	65
Joke	58
Chuckle	31
Humor	10
Amusement	9
Cheer	7
Delight	7
Twinkle	7
Miscellaneous	19
Total	316

The authors' facetious explanation for Watson's characterisation of Holmes as humorless is that Watson was deaf.

opinion that the matter was far safer in the hands of the regu-lar police force. Your conduct confirms all my conclusions. I have the honour, sir, to wish you good-evening." Holmes had swiftly changed his position and was between the peer and the door.

"One moment, sir," said Holmes. "To actually go off with the Mazarin stone would be a more serious offence than to be found in temporary possession of it."

"Sir, this is intolerable! Let me pass."

"Put your hand in the right-hand pocket of your overcoat."

"What do you mean, sir?"

"Come—come, do what I ask."

An instant later the amazed peer was standing, blinking and stammering, with the great yellow stone on his shaking palm.

"What! What! How is this, Mr. Holmes?"

"Too bad, Lord Cantlemere, too bad!" cried Holmes. "My old friend here will tell you that I have an impish habit of prac-tical joking.[33] Also that I can never resist a dramatic situation. I took the liberty—the very great liberty, I admit—of putting the stone into your pocket at the beginning of our interview."

The old peer stared from the stone to the smiling face before him.

"Sir, I am bewildered. But—yes—it is indeed the Mazarin stone. We are greatly your debtors, Mr. Holmes. Your sense of humour may, as you admit, be somewhat perverted, and its exhibition remarkably untimely, but at least I withdraw any reflection I have made upon your amazing professional powers. But how—"

"The case is but half finished; the details can wait. No doubt, Lord Cantlemere, your pleasure in telling of this successful result in the exalted circle to which you return will be some small atonement for my practical joke. Billy, you will show his Lordship out, and tell Mrs. Hudson that I should be glad if she would send up dinner for two as soon as possible." ∎

THE AUTHOR OF "THE MAZARIN STONE"

WHO WROTE this story? In the entire Canon, only "The Mazarin Stone" and "His Last Bow" are recorded in the third person. Curiously, no other Canonical tales were published in

33 While the narrator's earlier statement that "Holmes seldom laughed" may be seen as evidence that "The Mazarin Stone" is ficti-tious, June Thomson suggests that Holmes was on the verge of a breakdown and that his behaviour had altered accordingly. He had become pale and thin, and Billy "feared for his health." His behaviour was eccentric, as evidenced by the rudeness he displays here. While Holmes calls slipping the gem into Lord Cantlemere's pocket an "impish" instance of his love of practical jokes, Lord Cantlemere terms it "perverted." "It is there-fore not surprising, even if it is still inexcus-able," Thomson writes, "that given the stress Holmes was under and these signs of growing eccentricity, those quirks of personality which had always been apparent, such as his outspo-kenness and his disregard for other people's feelings, should be accentuated to such a degree that his behaviour became at times socially unacceptable."

the interval between these two stories ("His Last Bow" in 1917 and "The Mazarin Stone" in 1921). An inconclusive word count study by David Chizar, et al., in "Another Perspective on The Adventure of the Mazarin Stone" points out that the writing style in "The Mazarin Stone" (shorter, less complex sentences) is more like a play than Watson's short stories, suggesting that someone—most likely, Arthur Conan Doyle—wrote "The Mazarin Stone" on the basis of *The Crown Diamond*.

Christopher Morley, in "Watson à la Mode," proposes that Mrs. Watson wrote the story ("her first and last attempt") but insists that "Mrs. Watson" was Mary Morstan Watson (and not the "second" wife of Watson's referred to in "The Blanched Soldier"). O.F. Grazebrook suggests that the author was young Dr. Verner, while Edgar Smith proposes Arthur Conan Doyle as the author. Still another contention is that of G. B. Newton, who nominates Billy the page.

Gavin Brend and others nominate Watson as the author of "The Mazarin Stone," venturing that he wrote this story and "His Last Bow" in the third person to avoid the prohibition on writing imposed by his last wife. Thinking somewhat along the same lines is June Thomson, who expresses the belief that Watson was considering not his relationship with his wife, but that with Holmes. "Although the breach [evidenced by Watson living in his own rooms and probably caused by his marriage—see "The Illustrious Client"] was to some extent healed," she reflects, "a certain coolness remained between the two men, a state of affairs in which the use of the more impersonal third person seemed more appropriate." Page Heldenbrand joins the Watson bandwagon, pointing to the doctor's remark in "Thor Bridge" respecting cases in which he was "either not present or played so small a part as they could only be told as by a third person." And John Hall, in *Sidelights on Holmes*, sees Watson's resorting to the third person as a matter of necessity, given that he was not in the room when Count Sylvius and Sam Merton were discussing their plans. "But Holmes was [in the room], pretending to be a wax bust of himself," Hall notes. "Once the case was finished, for Holmes to inform Watson of what had transpired, and then for Watson to inform us, his readers, would have been very much of an anti-climax. This was simply the first [to occur] of the two cases where Watson had, indeed, to tell the tale as by a third person."

But D. Martin Dakin rejects any theory naming Watson as the author, declaring that it "bristles with improbabilities." Singling out numerous incongruities in the details of the story, such as the extra door to the sitting room and the fact that no violin recording of Hoffmann's "Barcarolle" was available in London until 1907, he concedes that the final scene, in which Holmes slips the diamond into Lord Cantlemere's pocket, seems to evoke the Holmes—with his fondness for the dramatic revelation—that Watson's readers have come to know. Dakin guesses that Watson, who did witness the conversation between Count Sylvius and Sam Merton, might have taken incomplete notes on the case; these were then discovered by a third party, who wrote them up to the best of his or her ability. Of course, Dakin thinks little of that ability, noting with disdain, "Holmes had a delicate vein of sarcasm and was not above twitting an adversary, as witness his interview with Colonel Sebastian Moran; but the forced facetiousness of his exchanges with the Count . . . reads like a violent caricature of this tendency, and must grate on the ear of all Holmesians."

THE ADVENTURE OF THE
THREE GABLES[1]

Another case scholars doubt Dr. Watson wrote is "The Three Gables" (not to be confused with "The Three Garridebs," which also appeared in The Case-Book*). Holmes's sarcastic remarks to Steve Dixie, certainly racist by modern standards, display an attitude markedly different from his evident racial tolerance on view in "The Yellow Face." There is little detection evident in the tale, and Holmes seems slow to grasp the clue of untouched luggage in the entry hall. Yet there are certain elements of the tale that seem accurate: Holmes's connection with Langdale Pike, a Victorian "gossip columnist," conforms with our idea of Holmes's "organization." Holmes would have needed a source of information about "society" and the "upper classes," which neither the Baker Street Irregulars (the street urchins) or even "Porky" Shinwell Johnson could provide. Holmes's high-handed meeting with Isadora Klein also rings true to Holmes's character, for we have seen him repeatedly take the law into his own hands (for example, in "The Boscombe Valley Mystery," "The Blue Carbuncle," and "The Abbey Grange"). Without careful analysis of the manuscript, which is in the hands of a private collector, the authorship of "The Three Gables" must remain unsettled.*

1 "The Three Gables" was published in the *Strand Magazine* in October 1920; its first American publication was in *Liberty* on September 18, 1926.

I DON'T THINK THAT any of my adventures with Mr. Sherlock Holmes opened quite so abruptly, or so dramatically, as that which I associate with The Three Gables. I had not seen Holmes for some days, and had no idea of the new channel into which his activities had been directed. He was in a chatty mood that morning, however, and had just settled me into the well-worn low armchair on one side of the fire, while he had curled down with his pipe in his mouth upon the opposite chair, when our visitor arrived. If I had said that a mad bull had arrived, it would give a clearer impression of what occurred.

The door had flown open and a huge negro had burst into the room. He would have been a comic figure if he had not been terrific, for he was dressed in a very loud grey check suit with a flowing salmon-coloured tie. His broad face and flat-

tened nose were thrust forward, as his sullen dark eyes, with a smouldering gleam of malice in them, turned from one of us to the other.

"Which of you genlemen is Masser Holmes?" he asked.

Holmes raised his pipe with a languid smile.

"Oh! it's you, is it?" said our visitor, coming with an unpleasant, stealthy step round the angle of the table. "See here, Masser Holmes, you keep your hands out of other folks' business. Leave folks to manage their own affairs. Got that, Masser Holmes?"

"Keep on talking," said Holmes. "It's fine."

"Oh! it's fine, is it?" growled the savage. "It won't be so damn fine if I have to trim you up a bit. I've handled your kind before now, and they didn't look fine when I was through with them. Look at that, Masser Holmes!"

He swung a huge knotted lump of a fist under my friend's nose. Holmes examined it closely with an air of great interest. "Were you born so?" he asked. "Or did it come by degrees?"

2 While this might seem a throwaway insult, Holmes could literally be detecting something familiar and unpalatable in Steve Dixie's scent—or at least, that is what Walter Shepherd deduces. He postulates that Holmes, intimate with so many parts of the city, may have detected olfactory traces on Dixie of the area known as the Old Nichol or the Jago, the haunt of the worst of criminals, into which even the police travelled only in pairs. "[T]he odour of the Jago," Shepherd writes, "was exceptional even in the most squalid areas of East London." Of course, most people of the time—when hot running water was a luxury available only to those of certain means and baths were commensurately infrequent—would be considered malodorous by today's standards. "[I]n the 1890's even the ordinary respectable citizens often carried about with them traces of what we might call 'tainted atmospheres,' " explains Shepherd. "For example, in the buses, in street crowds, or in the Underground railways, the curious smell of the early mackintoshes was prominent in wet weather, and body-odour in fine."

"See here, Mr. Holmes, you keep your hands out of other folks' business. Leave folks to manage their own affairs. Got that, Mr. Holmes?"
Howard Elcock, *Strand Magazine*, 1926

It may have been the icy coolness of my friend, or it may have been the slight clatter which I made as I picked up the poker. In any case, our visitor's manner became less flamboyant.

"Well, I've given you fair warnin'," said he. "I've a friend that's interested out Harrow way—you know what I'm meaning—and he don't intend to have no buttin' in by you. Got that? You ain't the law, and I ain't the law either, and if you come in I'll be on hand also. Don't you forget it."

"I've wanted to meet you for some time," said Holmes. "I won't ask you to sit down, for I don't like the smell of you,[2] but aren't you Steve Dixie, the bruiser?"

"That's my name, Masser Holmes, and you'll get put through it for sure if you give me any lip."

"It is certainly the last thing you need," said Holmes, staring at our visitor's hideous mouth. "But it was the killing of young Perkins outside the Holborn Bar[3]—What! you're not going?"

The negro had sprung back, and his face was leaden. "I won't listen to no such talk," said he. "What have I to do with this 'ere Perkins, Masser Holmes? I was trainin' at the Bull Ring[4] in Birmingham when this boy done gone get into trouble."

"Yes, you'll tell the magistrate about it, Steve," said Holmes. "I've been watching you and Barney Stockdale—"

"So help me the Lord! Masser Holmes—"

"That's enough. Get out of it. I'll pick you up when I want you."

"Good mornin', Masser Holmes. I hope there ain't no hard feelin's about this 'ere visit?"

"There will be unless you tell me who sent you."

"Why, there ain't no secret about that, Masser Holmes. It was that same gen'l'man that you have just done gone mention."

"And who set him on to it?"

"S'elp me. I don't know, Masser Holmes. He just say, 'Steve, you go see Mr. Holmes, and tell him his life ain't safe if he go down Harrow way.' That's the whole truth." Without waiting for any further questioning, our visitor bolted out of the room almost as precipitately as he had entered. Holmes knocked out the ashes of his pipe with a quiet chuckle.

"I am glad you were not forced to break his woolly head, Watson.[5] I observed your manoeuvres with the poker. But he is really rather a harmless fellow, a great muscular, foolish, blustering baby, and easily cowed, as you have seen. He is one of the Spencer John gang and has taken part in some dirty work of late which I may clear up when I have time. His immediate principal, Barney, is a more astute person. They specialize in assaults, intimidation, and the like. What I want to know is, who is at the back of them on this particular occasion?"

"But why do they want to intimidate you?"

"It is this Harrow Weald case. It decides me to look into the matter, for if it is worth anyone's while to take so much trouble, there must be something in it."

"But what is it?"

"I was going to tell you when we had this comic interlude. Here is Mrs. Maberley's note. If you care to come with me we will wire her and go out at once."

3 Properly the "Holborn Bars," which are stones at the junction of Gray's Inn Road and Holborn marking the edge of the City of London.

Holborn Bars.
Queen's London (1897)

4 In medieval times, the large, centrally located, open space of the Bull Ring in Birmingham was the site of a thriving market for livestock and food. The space possibly also hosted bull- or bull-and-bear–baiting, hence the name. As Birmingham through the centuries grew more modernised, so did the Bull Ring, and it came to accommodate numerous shops. (Today, the concept of a market continues: The site has been developed as the Bullring shopping centre.)

5 Many criticise Holmes's apparently racist attitude toward Dixie and note the contrast with his treatment of Grant Munro's step-daughter ("The Yellow Face") and Daulat Ras ("The Three Students") as evidence of the fakery of "The Three Gables." June Thomson attempts to take a view that de-emphasises race, admitting that "the Victorians tended to regard uneducated people of non-white races as uncivilized" but adding that Steve Dixie is, in particular, "a thoroughly unpleasant character." In support, Thomson names other examples in which

Holmes exhibits blatantly disdainful behaviour toward other men who are considered violent or cruel, such as Neil Gibson ("The Thor Bridge) or Dr. Roylott ("The Speckled Band"), both of whom are white. Yet she acknowledges that Holmes's manner here, regardless of its origin or intent, seems singularly harsh. "If it is any defence, which I doubt," she writes, "it should be added that Holmes had an 'abnormally acute set of senses.' " She further speculates, as she does for "The Mazarin Stone," that Holmes during this period of time is suffering from undue stress, a culmination of years of overwork and his separation from his good friend Watson. William P. Collins makes no excuses for Holmes, concluding that he was "moulded into a Victorian conscious of the superiority of the British and aware of class and colour separation . . ."—that is, no more (or less) prejudiced than other Victorians.

6 An official attached to (that is, employed by) the British embassy. Some nations used their attachés as spies (a practice still making headlines around the world), though there is no evidence that espionage was part of Douglas Maberley's duties.

DEAR MR. SHERLOCK HOLMES,

I have had a succession of strange incidents occur to me in connection with this house, and I should much value your advice. You would find me at home any time to-morrow. The house is within a short walk of the Weald Station. I believe that my late husband, Mortimer Maberley, was one of your early clients.

Yours faithfully,
MARY MABERLEY.

The address was "The Three Gables, Harrow Weald."

"So that's that!" said Holmes. "And now, if you can spare the time, Watson, we will get upon our way."

A short railway journey, and a shorter drive, brought us to the house, a brick and timber villa, standing in its own acre of undeveloped grassland. Three small projections above the upper windows made a feeble attempt to justify its name. Behind was a grove of melancholy, half-grown pines, and the whole aspect of the place was poor and depressing. None the less, we found the house to be well furnished, and the lady who received us was a most engaging elderly person, who bore every mark of refinement and culture.

"I remember your husband well, madam," said Holmes, "though it is some years since he used my services in some trifling matter."

"Probably you would be more familiar with the name of my son Douglas."

Holmes looked at her with great interest.

"Dear me! Are you the mother of Douglas Maberley? I knew him slightly. But of course all London knew him. What a magnificent creature he was! Where is he now?"

"Dead, Mr. Holmes, dead! He was attaché[6] at Rome, and he died there of pneumonia last month."

"I am sorry. One could not connect death with such a man. I have never known anyone so vitally alive. He lived intensely—every fibre of him!"

"Too intensely, Mr. Holmes. That was the ruin of him. You remember him as he was—debonair and splendid. You did not see the moody, morose, brooding creature into which he developed. His heart was broken. In a single month I seemed to see my gallant boy turn into a worn-out cynical man."

"A love affair—a woman?"

"Or a fiend. Well, it was not to talk of my poor lad that I asked you to come, Mr. Holmes."

"Dr. Watson and I are at your service."

"There have been some very strange happenings. I have been in this house more than a year now, and as I wished to lead a retired life I have seen little of my neighbours. Three days ago I had a call from a man who said that he was a house agent. He said that this house would exactly suit a client of his, and that if I would part with it money would be no object. It seemed to me very strange as there are several empty houses on the market which appear to be equally eligible, but naturally I was interested in what he said. I therefore named a price which was five hundred pounds more than I gave. He at once closed with the offer, but added that his client desired to buy the furniture as well and would I put a price upon it. Some of this furniture is from my old home, and it is, as you see, very good, so that I named a good round sum. To this also he at once agreed. I had always wanted to travel, and the bargain was so good a one that it really seemed that I should be my own mistress for the rest of my life.

"Yesterday the man arrived with the agreement all drawn out. Luckily I showed it to Mr. Sutro, my lawyer, who lives in Harrow. He said to me, 'This is a very strange document. Are you aware that if you sign it you could not legally take *anything* out of the house—not even your own private possessions?' When the man came again in the evening I pointed this out, and I said that I meant only to sell the furniture.

" 'No, no, everything,' said he.

" 'But my clothes? My jewels?'

" 'Well, well, some concession might be made for your personal effects. But nothing shall go out of the house unchecked. My client is a very liberal man, but he has his fads and his own way of doing things. It is everything or nothing with him.'

" 'Then it must be nothing,' said I. And there the matter was left, but the whole thing seemed to me to be so unusual that I thought—"

Here we had a very extraordinary interruption.

Holmes raised his hand for silence. Then he strode across

Holmes flung open the door and dragged in a great
gaunt woman whom he had seized by the shoulder.
Howard Elcock, *Strand Magazine*, 1926

the room, flung open the door, and dragged in a great gaunt
woman whom he had seized by the shoulder. She entered with
ungainly struggle, like some huge awkward chicken, torn,
squawking, out of its coop.

"Leave me alone! What are you a-doin' of?" she screeched.

"Why, Susan, what is this?"

"Well, ma'am, I was comin' in to ask if the visitors was
stayin' for lunch when this man jumped out at me."

"I have been listening to her for the last five minutes, but
did not wish to interrupt your most interesting narrative. Just a
little wheezy, Susan, are you not? You breathe too heavily for
that kind of work."

Susan turned a sulky but amazed face upon her captor. "Who be you, anyhow, and what right have you a-pullin' me about like this?"

"It was merely that I wished to ask a question in your presence. Did you, Mrs. Maberley, mention to anyone that you were going to write to me and consult me?"

"No, Mr. Holmes, I did not."

"Who posted your letter?"

"Susan did."

"Exactly. Now, Susan, to whom was it that you wrote or sent a message to say that your mistress was asking advice from me?"

"It's a lie. I sent no message."

"Now, Susan, wheezy people may not live long, you know. It's a wicked thing to tell fibs. Whom did you tell?"

"Susan!" cried her mistress, "I believe you are a bad, treacherous woman. I remember now that I saw you speaking to someone over the hedge."

"That was my own business," said the woman sullenly.

"Suppose I tell you that it was Barney Stockdale to whom you spoke?" said Holmes.

"Well, if you know, what do you want to ask for?"

"I was not sure, but I know now. Well now, Susan, it will be worth ten pounds to you if you will tell me who is at the back of Barney."

"Someone that could lay down a thousand pounds for every ten you have in the world."

"So, a rich man? No; you smiled—a rich woman. Now we have got so far, you may as well give the name and earn the tenner."

"I'll see you in hell first."

"Oh, Susan! Language!"

"I am clearing out of here. I've had enough of you all. I'll send for my box to-morrow." She flounced for the door.

"Good-bye, Susan. Paregoric[7] is the stuff. . . . Now," he continued, turning suddenly from lively to severe when the door had closed behind the flushed and angry woman. "This gang means business. Look how close they play the game. Your letter to me had the local P.M. postmark. And yet Susan passes the word to Barney. Barney has time to go to his employer and get instructions; he or she—I incline to the latter from Susan's grin

7 An alcohol solution made up of opium and camphor, once used in cough remedies and now predominantly used to treat diarrhea. Generally, a paregoric could be understood to mean any soothing medicine (the word comes from the Greek *parēgorikos*, or consoling). Therefore, Holmes is rather derisively telling Susan to take some medicine for her "wheeze" if she wishes to listen undetected in the future.

8 In 1861, the government decided that savings from all parts of the county of London could be collected at the rudimentary money-order branch of the post office, then transmitted to a central savings bank in London. The bank, designed to encourage the lower classes to save money, grew rapidly, and by 1883, over 2.8 million depositors had accounts there. The average balance was almost £14. By 1901, one in four used the system, for a total of more than 7.6 million depositors.

9 The great Italian Renaissance artist Raphael Santi (1483–1520)—Raffaello Santi or Raffaello Sanzio, in Italian—was given the nickname *Il Divino*, or "The Divine," for the rare combination of transcendence and humanity that he brought to his paintings. The emerging Raphael borrowed certain techniques from Michelangelo, such as lighting and shading, but strove for a more serene and universal style, leading to his celebrated series of Madonna paintings, which exhibit a touching sweetness and sense of intimacy. As the architect for the Vatican, Raphael, an atheist, was commissioned by Pope Leo X to create ten large tapestries for the Sistene Chapel, depicting the Acts of the Apostles. These were hung by 1519. Raphael died on his thirty-seventh birthday and was buried at the Pantheon in Rome.

10 Published in 1623 by John Heminge and Henry Condell under the auspices of publishers Edward Blount and William Jaggard, this volume included all thirty-six of Shakespeare's plays (excluding the disputed *Pericles*) and has widely been considered the authoritative Shakespearean text. Prior to the appearance of the First Folio, piracy in publishing was rampant and standards of authenticity difficult to enforce. Heminge and Condelle, Shakespeare's fellow actors at the Globe theatre, undertook the project in an effort to correct the various inaccuracies that

when she thought I had blundered—forms a plan. Black Steve is called in, and I am warned off by eleven o'clock next morning. That's quick work, you know."

"But what do they want?"

"Yes, that's the question. Who had the house before you?"

"A retired sea captain called Ferguson."

"Anything remarkable about him?"

"Not that ever I heard of."

"I was wondering whether he could have buried something. Of course, when people bury treasure nowadays they do it in the Post-Office bank.[8] But there are always some lunatics about. It would be a dull world without them. At first I thought of some buried valuable. But why, in that case, should they want your furniture? You don't happen to have a Raphael[9] or a first folio Shakespeare[10] without knowing it?"

"No, I don't think I have anything rarer than a Crown Derby[11] tea-set."

"That would hardly justify all this mystery. Besides, why should they not openly state what they want? If they covet your tea-set, they can surely offer a price for it without buying you out, lock, stock, and barrel. No, as I read it, there is something which you do not know that you have, and which you would not give up if you did know."

"That is how I read it," said I.

"Dr. Watson agrees, so that settles it."[12]

"Well, Mr. Holmes, what can it be?"

"Let us see whether by this purely mental analysis we can get it to a finer point. You have been in this house a year."

"Nearly two."

"All the better. During this long period no one wants anything from you. Now suddenly within three or four days you have urgent demands. What would you gather from that?"

"It can only mean," she said "that the object, whatever it may be, has only just come into the house."

"Settled once again," said Holmes. "Now, Mrs. Maberley, has any object just arrived?"

"No; I have bought nothing new this year."

"Indeed! That is very remarkable. Well, I think we had best let matters develop a little further until we have clearer data. Is that lawyer of yours a capable man?"

"Mr. Sutro is most capable."

"Have you another maid, or was the fair Susan, who has just banged your front door, alone?"

"I have a young girl."

"Try and get Sutro to spend a night or two in the house. You might possibly want protection."[13]

"Against whom?"

"Who knows? The matter is certainly obscure. If I can't find what they are after, I must approach the matter from the other end, and try to get at the principal. Did this house-agent man give any address?"

"Simply his card and occupation. Haines-Johnson, Auctioneer and Valuer."

"I don't think we shall find him in the Directory.[14] Honest business men don't conceal their place of business. Well, you will let me know any fresh development. I have taken up your case, and you may rely upon it that I shall see it through."

As we passed through the hall Holmes's eyes, which missed nothing, lighted upon several trunks and cases which were piled in a corner. The labels shone out upon them.

" 'Milano.' 'Lucerne.' These are from Italy."[15]

"They are poor Douglas's things."

"You have not unpacked them? How long have you had them?"

"They arrived last week."

"But you said—why, surely this might be the missing link. How do we know that there is not something of value there?"

"There could not possibly be, Mr. Holmes. Poor Douglas had only his pay and a small annuity. What could he have of value?"

Holmes was lost in thought.

"Delay no longer, Mrs. Maberley," he said at last. "Have these things taken upstairs to your bedroom. Examine them as soon as possible and see what they contain. I will come to-morrow and hear your report."

It was quite evident that The Three Gables was under very close surveillance, for as we came round the high hedge at the end of the lane there was the negro prize-fighter standing in the shadow. We came on him quite suddenly, and a grim and menacing figure he looked in that lonely place. Holmes clapped his hand to his pocket.

existed in published versions of Shakespeare's plays, as well as to disown the plays that had been falsely attributed to him. The collection, entitled *Mr. William Shakespeares Comedies, Histories & Tragedies, Published According to the True Originall Copies*, was nine hundred pages long and was published seven years after Shakespeare's death.

11 In 1890, Queen Victoria designated a factory in Derby, which had been producing fine English China since 1750, as "Manufacturers of porcelain to Her Majesty" and allowed it to affix the word "Royal" to its name. The Royal Crown Derby Porcelain Company (or simply Royal Crown Derby) produced delicate, richly decorated ivory and eggshell china, as well as officially sanctioned reproductions of porcelains from Persia and Japan. A piece of Derby china is distinguished by one of several marks, generally depicting a crown atop a "D" in blue or red.

12 Unwonted sarcasm, it seems.

13 This is surely a novel view of the services of a lawyer.

14 One of several annual directories of the residences and commercial establishments of London, such as the directory issued by the post office or the commercial directories issued by Kelly & Co. for various trades and cities (the name "Kelly's" remains in use today for industrial directories).

15 Michael C. Kaser calls attention to the odd fact that while the label for Milan, affixed by Italian transportation authorities, gives the city name in Italian ("Milano"), the label for Lucerne—a German-speaking town—has been written in French. The Italian for Lucerne would properly be "Lucerna," the German "Luzern." Did Douglas Maberley's baggage make an unintended detour through

France on its way to Lucerne? Holmes's eagle eye may have spotted that at least one of the bags could have been tampered with, and re-labelled, en route; hence his realisation that they would need to be carefully safeguarded and checked.

16 The three rock towers of the Langdale Pikes (named Harrison Stickle, Loft Crag, and Pike o' Stickle) are located in England's Lake District, now a national park. The area of mountains and lakes was once a favourite of literary figures, including William Wordsworth, Samuel Taylor Coleridge, and Robert Southey, who became known as the Lake poets or the Lake School. "Langdale Pike," therefore, was likely a literary pseudonym.

We came on the negro prize-fighter quite suddenly, and a grim and menacing figure he looked in that lonely place.
Howard Elcock, *Strand Magazine*, 1926

"Lookin' for your gun, Masser Holmes?"

"No, for my scent-bottle, Steve."

"You are funny, Masser Holmes, ain't you?"

"It won't be funny for you, Steve, if I get after you. I gave you fair warning this morning."

"Well, Masser Holmes, I done gone think over what you said, and I don't want no more talk about that affair of Masser Perkins. S'pose I can help you, Masser Holmes, I will."

"Well, then, tell me who is behind you on this job."

"So help me the Lord! Masser Holmes, I told you the truth before. I don't know. My boss Barney gives me orders and that's all."

"Well, just bear in mind, Steve, that the lady in that house, and everything under that roof, is under my protection. Don't you forget it."

"All right, Masser Holmes. I'll remember."

"I've got him thoroughly frightened for his own skin, Watson," Holmes remarked as we walked on. "I think he would double-cross his employer if he knew who he was. It was lucky I had some knowledge of the Spencer John crowd, and that Steve was one of them. Now, Watson, this is a case for Langdale Pike,[16] and I am going to see him now. When I get back I may be clearer in the matter."

I saw no more of Holmes during the day, but I could well imagine how he spent it, for Langdale Pike was his human book of reference upon all matters of social scandal. This strange, languid creature spent his waking hours in the bow window of a St. James's Street club,[17] and was the receiving-station, as well as the transmitter, for all the gossip of the Metropolis. He made, it was said, a four-figure income by the paragraphs which he contributed every week to the garbage papers which cater for an inquisitive public. If ever, far down in the turbid depths of London life, there was some strange swirl or eddy, it was marked with automatic exactness by this human dial upon the surface. Holmes discreetly helped Langdale to knowledge, and on occasion was helped in turn.

When I met my friend in his room early next morning, I was conscious from his bearing that all was well, but none the less a most unpleasant surprise was awaiting us. It took the shape of the following telegram:

Please come out at once. Client's house burgled in the night. Police in possession.

SUTRO.

St. James's Street.
Queen's London (1897)

17 It seems an inescapable conclusion that the club was White's, at No. 37-38 St. James Street, whose famed bow window played a central role in the hierarchy of the already tony establishment. The window was built in 1811 directly over the entrance steps, replacing the old front door. Beau Brummell, the British dandy and raconteur, used to hold court in front of the window with his admirers and friends. But he was one of only a few select club members whose right to a window seat was unquestioned. As Ralph Nevill, in *London Clubs: Their History and Treasures,* relates, "an ordinary member of the club would as soon have thought of taking his seat on the throne in the House of Lords as of appropriating one of the chairs in the bow-windows." Sitting exposed to the outside world, of course, proved tiresome when one was constantly being recognised; and so, Nevill continues, "It was decided, after anxious discussion, that no greeting should pass from the bow-window or from any window in the club. As a consequence, the hats of the dandies were doffed to no passers-by." The fact that Langdale Pike, no matter how "strange," spent so much of his time lounging by the bow window of "St. James's Street" certainly speaks volumes about his status in London's social world.

18 Holmes paraphrases the Bible here in assessing the lawyer's conduct: "Thou trusteth in the staff of this broken reed." Isaiah 36:6. Could Holmes have been insulted that Mrs. Maberley did not ask *him* to provide protection?

19 This is the only instance in the Canon in which Holmes collaborates with an unnamed Inspector. This may be another point for those who contend that "The Three Gables" is a work of fiction.

Holmes whistled. "The drama has come to a crisis, and quicker than I had expected. There is a great driving-power at the back of this business, Watson, which does not surprise me after what I have heard. This Sutro, of course, is her lawyer. I made a mistake, I fear, in not asking you to spend the night on guard. This fellow has clearly proved a broken reed.[18] Well, there is nothing for it but another journey to Harrow Weald."

We found The Three Gables a very different establishment to the orderly household of the previous day. A small group of idlers had assembled at the garden gate, while a couple of constables were examining the windows and the geranium beds. Within we met a grey old gentleman, who introduced himself as the lawyer, together with a bustling, rubicund Inspector, who greeted Holmes as an old friend.[19]

"Well, Mr. Holmes, no chance for you in this case, I'm afraid. Just a common, ordinary burglary, and well within the capacity of the poor old police. No experts need apply."

"I am sure the case is in very good hands," said Holmes. "Merely a common burglary, you say?"

"Quite so. We know pretty well who the men are and where to find them. It is that gang of Barney Stockdale, with the big nigger in it—they've been seen about here."

"Excellent! What did they get?"

"Well, they don't seem to have got much. Mrs. Maberley was chloroformed and the house was—Ah! here is the lady herself."

Our friend of yesterday, looking very pale and ill, had entered the room, leaning upon a little maidservant.

"You gave me good advice, Mr. Holmes," said she, smiling ruefully. "Alas, I did not take it. I did not wish to trouble Mr. Sutro, and so I was unprotected."

"I only heard of it this morning," the lawyer explained.

"Mr. Holmes advised me to have some friend in the house. I neglected his advice, and I have paid for it."

"You look wretchedly ill," said Holmes. "Perhaps you are hardly equal to telling me what occurred."

"It is all here," said the Inspector, tapping a bulky notebook.

"Still, if the lady is not too exhausted—"

"There is really so little to tell. I have no doubt that wicked Susan had planned an entrance for them. They must have known the house to an inch. I was conscious for a moment of the chloroform rag which was thrust over my mouth, but I have no notion how long I may have been senseless. When I woke, one man was at the bedside and another was rising with a bundle in his hand from among my son's baggage, which was partially opened and littered over the floor. Before he could get away I sprang up and seized him."

"You took a big risk," said the Inspector.

"I clung to him, but he shook me off, and the other may have struck me, for I can remember no more. Mary the maid heard the noise and began screaming out of the window. That brought the police, but the rascals had got away."

"What did they take?"

'Well, I don't think there is anything of value missing. I am sure there was nothing in my son's trunks."

"Did the men leave no clue?"

"There was one sheet of paper which I may have torn from the man that I grasped. It was lying all crumpled on the floor. It is in my son's handwriting."

"Which means that it is not of much use," said the Inspector. "Now if it had been in the burglar's—"

"Exactly," said Holmes. "What rugged common sense! None the less, I should be curious to see it."

The Inspector drew a folded sheet of foolscap from his pocketbook.

"I never pass anything, however trifling," said he, with some pomposity. "That is my advice to you, Mr. Holmes. In twenty-five years' experience I have learned my lesson. There is always the chance of finger-marks or something."

Holmes inspected the sheet of paper.

"What do you make of it, Inspector?"

"Seems to be the end of some queer novel, so far as I can see."

"It may certainly prove to be the end of a queer tale," said Holmes. "You have noticed the number on the top of the page. It is two hundred and forty-five. Where are the odd two hundred and forty-four pages?"

"Well, I suppose the burglars got those. Much good may it do them."

"It seems a queer thing to break into a house in order to steal such papers as that. Does it suggest anything to you, Inspector?"

"Yes, sir, it suggests that in their hurry the rascals just grabbed at what came first to hand. I wish them joy of what they got."

"Why should they go to my son's things?" asked Mrs. Maberley.

"Well, they found nothing valuable downstairs, so they tried their luck upstairs. That is how I read it. What do you make of it, Mr. Holmes?"

"I must think it over, Inspector. Come to the window, Watson." Then, as we stood together, he read over the fragment of paper. It began in the middle of a sentence and ran like this:

. . . face bled considerably from the cuts and blows, but it was nothing to the bleeding of his heart as he saw that lovely face, the face for which he had been prepared to sacrifice his very life, looking out at his agony and humiliation. She smiled— yes, by Heaven! she smiled, like the heartless fiend she was, as he looked up at her. It was at that moment that love died and hate was born. Man must live for something. If it is not for your embrace, my lady, then it shall surely be for your undoing and my complete revenge.

"Queer grammar!" said Holmes with a smile, as he handed the paper back to the Inspector. "Did you notice how the 'he' suddenly changed to 'my'? The writer was so carried away by his own story that he imagined himself at the supreme moment to be the hero."

"It seemed mighty poor stuff," said the Inspector as he replaced it in his book. "What! are you off, Mr. Holmes?"

"I don't think there is anything more for me to do now that the case is in such capable hands. By the way, Mrs. Maberley, did you say you wished to travel?"

"It has always been my dream, Mr. Holmes."

"Where would you like to go—Cairo, Madeira, the Riviera?"

"Oh, if I had the money I would go round the world."

"Quite so. Round the world. Well, good-morning. I may drop you a line in the evening." As we passed the window I caught a glimpse of the Inspector's smile and shake of the head. "These clever fellows have always a touch of madness." That was what I read in the Inspector's smile.

"Now, Watson, we are at the last lap of our little journey," said Holmes when we were back in the roar of Central London once more. "I think we had best clear the matter up at once, and it would be well that you should come with me, for it is safer to have a witness when you are dealing with such a lady as Isadora Klein."

We had taken a cab and were speeding to some address in Grosvenor Square. Holmes had been sunk in thought, but he roused himself suddenly.

"By the way, Watson, I suppose you see it all clearly?"

"No, I can't say that I do. I only gather that we are going to see the lady who is behind all this mischief."

"Exactly! But does the name Isadora Klein convey nothing to you? She was, of course, *the* celebrated beauty. There was never a woman to touch her.[20] She is pure Spanish, the real blood of the masterful Conquistadors, and her people have been leaders in Pernambuco[21] for generations. She married the aged German sugar king, Klein, and presently found herself the richest as well as the most lovely widow upon earth. Then there was an interval of adventure when she pleased her own tastes. She had several lovers, and Douglas Maberley, one of the most striking men in London, was one of them. It was by all accounts more than an adventure with him. He was not a Society butterfly, but a strong, proud man who gave and expected all. But she is the '*belle dame sans merci*'[22] of fiction. When her caprice is satisfied the matter is ended, and if the other party in the matter can't take her word for it she knows how to bring it home to him."

"Then that was his own story—"

"Ah! you are piecing it together now. I hear that she is about to marry the young Duke of Lomond, who might almost be her son. His Grace's ma might overlook the age, but a big scandal would be a different matter, so it is imperative—Ah! here we are."

It was one of the finest corner-houses of the West End. A machine-like footman took up our cards and returned with word that the lady was not at home. "Then we shall wait until she is," said Holmes cheerfully.

The machine broke down.

"Not at home means not at home to *you*," said the footman.

"Good," Holmes answered. "That means that we shall not have to wait. Kindly give this note to your mistress."

20 As Christopher Redmond notes, she is one of the "series of ambiguous Latin, yet English beauties who appear . . . in the later period [of Holmes's career: Beryl Garcia of *The Hound of the Baskervilles*], Maria Pinto Gibson of 'Thor Bridge,' Emilia Lucca of 'The Red Circle,' Mrs. Ferguson of 'The Sussex Vampire,' . . . Senora Durando (Burnet) of 'Wisteria Lodge.'" As late as the twentieth century, the "foreigner" (that is, any person not of English birth) was still viewed by the English with distrust and suspicion.

21 Holmes uses the phrase "She is pure Spanish" figuratively, one imagines. The province of Pernambuco had been ruled by the Portuguese, not the Spanish, since 1654 (and before that, the Dutch). Throughout the nineteenth century, Pernambuco rebelled against Portuguese rule in a series of armed insurrections, and in 1891 was finally made a state of the Brazilian Republic—whose own nobility, of course, was of Portuguese heritage. Pernambuco's capital, Recife, is also known as Pernambuco, though it unclear whether Holmes is referring to the city or the state.

22 Literally, "the beautiful lady without compassion." Holmes is likely alluding to John Keats's poem "La Belle Dame sans Merci" (1819), which in turn took its title and theme from a medieval poem by early French poet Alain Chartier. Keats's ballad concerns a knight who, wandering through a meadow, falls hopelessly in love with a mysterious woman who is "Full beautiful—a faery's child, / Her hair was long, her foot was light, / Her eyes were wild." After a brief romantic encounter, the knight falls asleep and dreams of others who have fallen under the same woman's spell. "I saw pale kings, and princes too, / Pale warriors, death-pale were they all; / They cried, 'La Belle Dame sans Merci / Hath thee in thrall!'" Upon awakening, the knight finds himself alone and heartbroken.

23 "Underrated" in the *Strand Magazine* and book editions.

He scribbled three or four words upon a sheet of his note-book, folded it and handed it to the man.

"What did you say, Holmes?" I asked.

"I simply wrote: 'Shall it be the police, then?' I think that should pass us in."

It did—with amazing celerity. A minute later we were in an Arabian Nights drawing-room, vast and wonderful, in a half gloom, picked out with an occasional pink electric light. The lady had come, I felt, to that time of life when even the proudest beauty finds the half-light more welcome. She rose from a settee as we entered: tall, queenly, a perfect figure, a lovely mask-like face, with two wonderful Spanish eyes which looked murder at us both.

"What is this intrusion—and this insulting message?" she asked, holding up the slip of paper.

"I need not explain, madame. I have too much respect for your intelligence to do so—though I confess that intelligence has been surprisingly at fault of late."

"How so, sir?"

"By supposing that your hired bullies could frighten me from my work. Surely no man would take up my profession if it were not that danger attracts him. It was you, then, who forced me to examine the case of young Maberley."

"I have no idea what you are talking about. What have I to do with hired bullies?"

Holmes turned away wearily.

"Yes, I have over-rated[23] your intelligence. Well, good-afternoon!"

"Stop! Where are you going?"

"To Scotland Yard."

We had not got halfway to the door before she had overtaken us and was holding his arm. She had turned in a moment from steel to velvet.

"Come and sit down, gentlemen. Let us talk this matter over, I feel that I may be frank with you, Mr. Holmes. You have the feelings of a gentleman. How quick a woman's instinct is to find it out. I will treat you as a friend."

"I cannot promise to reciprocate, madame. I am not the law, but I represent justice so far as my feeble powers go. I am ready to listen, and then I will tell you how I will act."

"Stop! Where are you going?" "To Scotland Yard."
Howard Elcock, *Strand Magazine*, 1926

"No doubt it was foolish of me to threaten a brave man like yourself."

"What was really foolish, madame, is that you have placed yourself in the power of a band of rascals who may blackmail or give you away."

"No, no! I am not so simple. Since I have promised to be frank, I may say that no one, save Barney Stockdale and Susan his wife, have the least idea who their employer is. As to them, well, it is not the first—" She smiled and nodded with a charming coquettish intimacy.

"I see. You've tested them before."

"They are good hounds who run silent."

"Such hounds have a way sooner or later of biting the hand

24 To calcine is to heat a substance to a high temperature just below the melting point, thus oxidising it or ridding it of moisture or other unwanted matter. In light of his training, one may forgive Dr. Watson for using such a technical word that essentially means "burned."

that feeds them. They will be arrested for this burglary. The police are already after them."

"They will take what comes to them. That is what they are paid for. I shall not appear in the matter."

"Unless I bring you into it."

"No, no; you would not. You are a gentleman. It is a woman's secret."

"In the first place, you must give back this manuscript."

She broke into a ripple of laughter, and walked to the fireplace. There was a calcined[24] mass which she broke up with the poker. "Shall I give this back?" she asked. So roguish and exquisite did she look as she stood before us with a challenging smile that I felt of all Holmes's criminals this was the one whom he would find it hardest to face. However, he was immune from sentiment.

"That seals your fate," he said coldly. "You are very prompt in your actions, madame, but you have overdone it on this occasion."

She threw the poker down with a clatter.

"How hard you are!" she cried. "May I tell you the whole story?"

"I fancy I could tell it to you."

"But you must look at it with my eyes, Mr. Holmes. You must realize it from the point of view of a woman who sees all her life's ambition about to be ruined at the last moment. Is such a woman to be blamed if she protects herself?"

"The original sin was yours."

"Yes, yes! I admit it. He was a dear boy, Douglas, but it so chanced that he could not fit into my plans. He wanted marriage—marriage, Mr. Holmes—with a penniless commoner. Nothing less would serve him. Then he became pertinacious. Because I had given he seemed to think that I still must give, and to him only. It was intolerable. At last I had to make him realize it."

"By hiring ruffians to beat him under your own window."

"You do indeed seem to know everything. Well, it is true. Barney and the boys drove him away, and were, I admit, a little rough in doing so. But what did he do then? Could I have believed that a gentleman would do such an act? He wrote a book in which he described his own story. I, of course, was the wolf; he the lamb. It was all there, under different names, of course; but who in all London would have failed to recognize it?[25] What do you say to that, Mr. Holmes?"

"Well, he was within his rights."

"It was as if the air of Italy had got into his blood and brought with it the old cruel Italian spirit. He wrote to me and sent me a copy of his book that I might have the torture of anticipation. There were two copies, he said—one for me, one for his publisher."

"How did you know the publisher's had not reached him?"

"I knew who his publisher was. It is not his only novel, you know. I found out that he had not heard from Italy. Then came Douglas's sudden death. So long as that other manuscript was in the world there was no safety for me. Of course, it must be among his effects, and these would be returned to his mother. I set the gang at work. One of them got into the house as servant. I wanted to do the thing honestly. I really and truly did. I was ready to buy the house and everything in it. I offered any price she cared to ask. I only tried the other way when everything else had failed. Now, Mr. Holmes, granting that I was too hard on Douglas—and, God knows, I am sorry for it—what else could I do with my whole future at stake?"

Sherlock Holmes shrugged his shoulders.

"Well, well," said he, "I suppose I shall have to compound a felony as usual. How much does it cost to go round the world in first-class style?"

The lady stared in amazement.

"Could it be done on five thousand pounds?"

"Well, I should think so, indeed!"

"Very good. I think you will sign me a cheque for that,[26] and I will see that it comes to Mrs. Maberley. You owe her a little change of air. Meantime, lady"—he wagged a cautionary forefinger—"have a care! Have a care! You can't play with edged tools forever without cutting those dainty hands."[27]

25 As mild as the rescued excerpt of the manuscript seemed—"it was nothing to the bleeding of his heart as he saw that lovely face"—could it be that what unnerves Isadora Klein is not a sappy love story in which she plays the villain, but something more explicit? In *In Bed with Sherlock Holmes*, Christopher Redmond guesses that the rest of Maberley's manuscript "might presumably have been racier; strong pornography was extensively written and read among the late Victorians, and a Maberley whose mind had virtually come unhinged because of the way a woman had treated him might possibly have produced some of it." Indeed, he would have had plenty of source material: An 1872 appeal of the "Society for the Suppression of Vice," based in London, proudly reported that within the two previous years the society had been "the means of bringing to punishment, by imprisonment, hard labour, and fines, upwards of forty of the most notorious dealers [in pornography]." Nonetheless, the appeal continued, "these polluting productions are still circulated throughout the country, principally through the post-office, penetrating into the schools of both sexes." Perhaps the most famous example of Victorian pornography is *My Secret Life* (1890), the supposed autobiography of "Walter," a married gentleman who seeks pleasure with some 1,500 women. (It was written in language that surely would have made Holmes blush.)

Notwithstanding such titillating speculation, however, even a tame manuscript might well have caused Mrs. Klein's mortification. "It must be stressed," Redmond reminds us, " . . . that it did not take X-rated material to make the stuff of embarrassment or blackmail for a respectable Victorian."

26 Holmes's bypassing of a fee in "The Three Gables" leads David Galerstein to contend that Isadora Klein's five thousand pounds will not, in fact, end up entirely in

Mrs. Maberley's bank account. As Mrs. Maberley does not likely have the means to pay Holmes on her own, Galerstein theorizes that Holmes plans to deduct his fee from the amount first, then give the rest to his "client." Holmes's slippery sense of ethics is clearly on display here—money for freedom—and he is not shy about letting the guilty party know it. "When he asked for the money," Galerstein observes, "he told Mrs. Klein he was compounding a felony 'as usual.' He was bluntly admitting that for a sufficient fee he would overlook a crime and that he had done so many times before."

27 Taken as a whole, "The Three Gables," though ostensibly written by Watson, raises a few scholars' suspicions as to its true authorship. "The plot is fantastic and improbable," writes D. Martin Dakin, "and is it likely that any real man would have the name of Langdale Pike?" Dakin takes particular umbrage at the characterisation of Holmes in this story. He is depicted as ridiculously cruel and unfunny toward the maid Susan, unashamedly open to bribery, and worst of all, racist in his dealings with Steve Dixie. "No admirer of Holmes can read these scenes without a blush," Dakin laments. "For Holmes was a gentleman; and one thing no gentleman does is to taunt another man for his racial characteristics." Suggesting that the author of "The Mazarin Stone" (which similarly failed in its attempt to portray Holmes as witty) might also have been the author of "The Three Gables," Dakin deems this "the poorest story of all in the generally accepted Canon. . . . [I]t was neither written by [Watson] nor represents true history."

Of course, Dakin's view is in the minority, and the story remains securely in the Canon. Walter Pond cautions, "The only proper attitude for the Sherlockian scholar is to have confidence in the integrity of Dr. Watson and his literary agent and to accord proper respect to all the stories, whether or not they conform to our own notions of ethics or plausibility."

THE ADVENTURE OF THE
SUSSEX VAMPIRE[1]

That "The Sussex Vampire" is the genuine article—a Watsonian tale—is unassailable, which means that the suspicions that swirl around other stories in the Canon are blissfully nonexistent here. No scholar questions Watson's report of Holmes's great index, with references to Victor Lynch, the forger; the giant rat of Sumatra, "a story for which the world is not yet prepared"; Vanderbilt and the yeggman; Vittoria the circus belle; and Vigor, the Hammersmith wonder. References to Watson's youth, when he played rugby for Blackheath, also support the authenticity of the account. There is no record of the reaction of Watson's friend Sir Arthur Conan Doyle to such a mystical tale. Doyle, who by 1924 was known as the "St. Paul of Spiritualism" and had committed his life to sharing his belief in the reality of the supernatural, might have harboured a particular fondness for "The Sussex Vampire." In striking contrast to Doyle, Holmes declares himself to be a confirmed sceptic: When a supernatural explanation is proffered for the mystery at hand, Holmes remarks, "This Agency stands flat-footed upon the ground, and there it must remain. . . . No ghosts need apply." This is consistent with Holmes's pragmatic attitude in The Hound of the Baskervilles, *when he rejects a diabolical explanation: "In a modest way I have combatted evil, but to take on the Father of Evil himself would, perhaps, be too ambitious a task."*

HOLMES HAD READ carefully a note which the last post had brought him. Then, with the dry chuckle which was his nearest approach to a laugh,[2] he tossed it over to me.

"For a mixture of the modern and the mediæval, of the practical and of the wildly fanciful, I think this is surely the limit," said he. "What do you make of it, Watson?"

I read as follows:

46, OLD JEWRY,[3] Nov. 19th.
Re Vampires
SIR,—
Our client, Mr. Robert Ferguson, of Ferguson & Muirhead, tea brokers, of Mincing Lane, has made some inquiry from us in a communication of even date[4] concerning vampires. As our firm specializes entirely upon the assessment of machin-

1 "The Sussex Vampire" was published in the January 1924 issues of the *Strand Magazine* and *Hearst's International Magazine*.

2 Theodore C. Blegen finds this remark disconcerting. "In case after case, the doctor has reported roars and explosions and even paroxysms of laughter by Mr. Holmes. I think we must, unhappily, assume another little lapse of memory on Dr. Watson's part." See "The Mazarin Stone," note 32, for a more detailed discussion of Holmes's pattern of laughter.

3 The area of London known as Old Jewry (originally "Jews' Street") was settled by Jewish refugees, fleeing persecution in other

parts of Europe in the early part of the twelfth century. Forbidden from practising any business except the lending of money, the Jews, to whom many of London's noble families now became indebted, were subject to periodic bouts of anti-Semitism on the part of the English public and the monarchy itself. In 1189, a riot instigated at Richard I's coronation saw many Jewish families burned alive or clubbed to death in the streets of Old Jewry. The harassment continued and intensified until 1290, when the immigration of financiers from Italy prompted Edward I to take away the Jews' state-imposed livelihood by banning them from practising usury. With the decree, some 15,000 Jews were expelled from London, the houses of Old Jewry confiscated by the crown.

4 "Of even date" means that Ferguson's letter bore the same date as the lawyers'. The phrase is still common "legalese."

5 The combination of vampires, tea brokerage, and a law firm specializing in machinery produces a rather strange marriage indeed. And later in the tale, Ferguson recounts that he met his Peruvian wife during a business transaction involving the importation of nitrates—which would not seem to have anything remotely to do with tea. Gordon R. Speck expresses scepticism of the entire situation in "The Adventure of the Sussex Vampire: Hoax, Jokes, and Hubris." The combination of vampires, South America, and nitrates suggests to him that Ferguson may well have been involved with the importation of bat guano. Was Ferguson too embarrassed to admit how he made his living?

6 Who is E.J.C.? J. W. Scheideman, noting the careful, non-judgemental tone of the letter and its delicate balance between "fact and fancy," concludes that the conservative

ery the matter hardly comes within our purview and we have therefore recommended Mr. Ferguson to call upon you and lay the matter before you.[5] We have not forgotten your successful action in the case of Matilda Briggs.
We are, Sir,

Faithfully yours,
MORRISON, MORRISON, AND DODD.
per E.J.C.[6]

"Matilda Briggs was not the name of a young woman, Watson," said Holmes in a reminiscent voice. "It was a ship[7] which is associated with the giant rat of Sumatra,[8] a story for which the world is not yet prepared. But what do we know about vampires?[9] Does it come within our purview either? Anything is better than stagnation, but really we seem to have been switched on to a Grimms' fairy tale. Make a long arm, Watson, and see what V has to say."

I leaned back and took down the great index volume to which he referred. Holmes balanced it on his knee and his eyes moved slowly and lovingly over the record of old cases, mixed with the accumulated information of a lifetime.

"Voyage of the *Gloria Scott*," he read. "That was a bad business. I have some recollection that you made a record of it, Watson, though I was unable to congratulate you upon the result. Victor Lynch, the forger. Venomous lizard or gila. Remarkable case, that! Vittoria, the circus belle. Vanderbilt and the Yeggman.[10] Vipers. Vigor,[11] the Hammersmith wonder. Hullo! Hullo! Good old index. You can't beat it. Listen to this, Watson. Vampirism in Hungary.[12] And again, Vampires in Transylvania."[13] He turned over the pages with eagerness, but after a short intent perusal he threw down the great book with a snarl of disappointment.

"Rubbish, Watson, rubbish! What have we to do with walking corpses who can only be held in their grave by stakes driven through their hearts? It's pure lunacy."

"But surely," I said, "the vampire was not necessarily a dead man? A living person might have the habit. I have read, for example, of the old sucking the blood of the young in order to retain their youth."

"You are right, Watson. It mentions the legend in one of

Messieurs Morrison, Morrison, and Dodd would probably not have written such a fair-minded note themselves. "Perhaps E.J.C. was a Cockney office-boy," Scheideman ventures, "who boldly tackled Mr. Ferguson's problem with a combination of common sense . . . and official form when other members of the firm hesitated."

7 Richard W. Clarke discovers that the *Matilda Briggs* was owned by the Oriental Trading Company, based in Shanghai. Another, more intriguing angle is pursued by Edgar W. Smith, who calls attention to the ill-fated *Mary Celeste*. Found mysteriously abandoned between the Azores and Portugal in 1872, she had sailed from New York under the leadership of Captain Benjamin Spooner Briggs. The captain had been accompanied by his wife, Sarah Elizabeth Briggs, and their daughter, Sophia Matilda Briggs.

8 This was probably the species *Sundamys infraluteus*, discovered by Guy G. Musser and Cameron Newcomb and reported in 1983 in their 270-page article in *Bulletin of the American Museum of Natural History*. They describe the adult male, indigenous to the tropical forests of Sumatra, as weighing in excess of 22 pounds and measuring 24 inches long, including the tail. Having obtained six specimens

The giant rat of Sumatra?
Baker Street Journal

for study, Musser and Newcomb note that the rat "is difficult to catch and its habits are unknown." See "The Dying Detective," note 14, for speculation on the giant rat of Sumatra in relation to Culverton Smith, who had lived in Sumatra and attempted to poison Holmes, probably with a tropical disease.

9 See " 'But What Do We Know About Vampires?' " page 1576, for an examination of the vampire literature with which Holmes, Watson, and their client might have been familiar.

10 A yegg, or yeggman, is a burglar or a safe-cracker. Although the exact origins of the term are murky, William Pinkerton, of the Pinkerton National Detective Agency (see "The Red Circle," note 17), believed both "yegg" and "hobo" to be related to gypsies. Excerpts from speeches given by Pinkerton between 1900 and 1907 reveal the following logic: "When a particularly clever thief is found among a gypsy tribe, he is selected as the 'Yegg' or chief thief. This expression is now adopted by the better class of thieves among tramps and hobos of this country. As late as twenty years ago, one tramp meeting another and wishing to be sure of his identity as a professional tramp would address him as 'Ho-Beau.' This expression subsequently developed into the word 'hobo.' If a tribe or band of tramps found among their number a particularly persistent beggar or daring thief, they, using the expression of the gypsies, called him a 'Yegg.' Then came the name of 'John Yegg' and finally the word 'Yeggman.' "

11 One is tempted to connect this "wonder" with the famous ornate fin-de-siècle gilt and velvet auditorium of the Lyric Theatre Hammersmith, which opened in 1895 and was undoubtedly well known to the musical Holmes. Howard Lachtman identifies the "wonder" as a mechanical horse produced by the Vigor company. Its virtues are described in the accompanying advertisement.

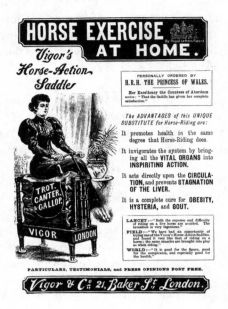

HORSE EXERCISE AT HOME.

Vigor's Horse-Action Saddle

By Royal Letters Patent

PERSONALLY ORDERED BY
H.R.H. THE PRINCESS OF WALES.

Her Excellency the Countess of Aberdeen
writes : "That the Saddle has given her complete
satisfaction."

The ADVANTAGES of this UNIQUE SUBSTITUTE for Horse-Riding are :

It promotes health in the same degree that Horse-Riding does.

It invigorates the system by bringing all the VITAL ORGANS into INSPIRITING ACTION.

It acts directly upon the CIRCULATION, and prevents STAGNATION OF THE LIVER.

It is a complete cure for OBESITY, HYSTERIA, and GOUT.

TROT. CANTER. GALLOP.

VIGOR   LONDON

LANCET :—" Both the expense and difficulty of riding on a live horse are avoided. The invention is very ingenious."

FIELD :—" We have had an opportunity of trying one of the Vigor's Horse-Action Saddles, and found it very like that of riding on a horse ; the same muscles are brought into play as when riding."

WORLD :—" It is good for the figure, good for the complexion, and especially good for the health."

PARTICULARS, TESTIMONIALS, and PRESS OPINIONS POST FREE.

Vigor & Co. 21, Baker St., London.

"Vigor the Hammersmith Wonder"?
Victorian Advertisements

12 Harold Niver suggests that Holmes may have obtained this information from the reverse side of the newspaper article he received from Hungary in the aftermath of "The Greek Interpreter" ("Months afterwards a curious newspaper cutting reached us from Buda-Pesth"). Or perhaps Holmes had some contact with Arminius Vambery, the Hungarian scholar who is said to have advised Bram Stoker in his research for *Dracula* and who may have been the model for that book's Professor Van Helsing. See "The Musgrave Ritual," note 7.

13 This region of central Romania was controlled by Hungary for much of its history, including during the Victorian era. Transylvania's popular association with vampires originates with Vlad Tepes, the "real" Dracula, who ruled over neighbouring Wallachia, just

these references. But are we to give serious attention to such things? This Agency stands flat-footed upon the ground, and there it must remain. The world is big enough for us. No ghosts need apply. I fear that we cannot take Mr. Robert Ferguson very seriously. Possibly this note may be from him and may throw some light upon what is worrying him."

He took up a second letter which had lain unnoticed upon the table whilst he had been absorbed with the first. This he began to read with a smile of amusement upon his face which gradually faded away into an expression of intense interest and concentration. When he had finished he sat for some little time lost in thought with the letter dangling from his fingers. Finally, with a start, he aroused himself from his reverie.

"Cheeseman's, Lamberley. Where is Lamberley, Watson?"

"Hullo! Hullo! Good old index. You can't beat it.
Listen to this, Watson."
Howard Elcock, *Strand Magazine*, 1924

"It is in Sussex, south of Horsham."

"Not very far, eh? And Cheeseman's?"

"I know that country, Holmes. It is full of old houses which are named after the men who built them centuries ago. You get Odley's and Harvey's and Carriton's—the folk are forgotten but their names live in their houses."

"Precisely," said Holmes coldly. It was one of the peculiarities of his proud, self-contained nature that, though he pocketed any fresh information very quietly and accurately in his brain, he seldom made any acknowledgment to the giver. "I rather fancy we shall know a good deal more about Cheeseman's, Lamberley, before we are through. This letter is, as I had hoped, from Robert Ferguson. By the way, he claims acquaintance with you."

"With me!"

"You had better read it."

He handed the letter across. It was headed with the address quoted.

DEAR MR. HOLMES,—

I have been recommended to you by my lawyers, but indeed the matter is so extraordinarily delicate that it is most difficult to discuss. It concerns a friend for whom I am acting. This gentleman married some five years ago a Peruvian lady, the daughter of a Peruvian merchant, whom he had met in connection with the importation of nitrates. The lady was very beautiful, but the fact of her foreign birth and of her alien religion always caused a separation of interests and of feelings between husband and wife, so that after a time his love may have cooled towards her and he may have come to regard their union as a mistake. He felt there were sides of her character which he could never explore or understand. This was the more painful as she was as loving a wife as a man could have—to all appearance absolutely devoted.

Now for the point which I will make more plain when we meet. Indeed, this note is merely to give you a general idea of the situation and to ascertain whether you would care to interest yourself in the matter. The lady began to show some curious traits quite alien to her ordinarily sweet and gentle disposition. The gentleman had been married twice and he had one son by the first wife. This boy was now fifteen, a very

to the south of Transylvania, in the mid-fifteenth century. A ruthless leader who is historically regarded in Romania as both a hero and a tyrant, Tepes executed his enemies and suspected traitors by impaling them upon stakes; this type of rule earned him the name Dracula, meaning "son of the dragon" (or, in some interpretations, "son of the devil"). Count Dracula, of Bram Stoker's *Dracula*, was a native of Transylvania, and the story of Dracula took place in a district just bordering Transylvania, "in the midst of the Carpathian mountains; one of the wildest and least known portions of Europe."

charming and affectionate youth, though unhappily injured through an accident in childhood.

Twice the wife was caught in the act of assaulting this poor lad in the most unprovoked way. Once she struck him with a stick and left a great weal on his arm.

This was a small matter, however, compared with her conduct to her own child, a dear boy just under one year of age. On one occasion about a month ago this child had been left by its nurse for a few minutes. A loud cry from the baby, as of pain, called the nurse back. As she ran into the room she saw her employer, the lady, leaning over the baby and apparently biting his neck. There was a small wound in the neck, from which a stream of blood had escaped. The nurse was so horrified that she wished to call the husband, but the lady implored her not to do so, and actually gave her five pounds as a price for her silence. No explanation was ever given, and for the moment the matter was passed over.

It left, however, a terrible impression upon the nurse's mind, and from that time she began to watch her mistress closely and to keep a closer guard upon the baby, whom she tenderly loved. It seemed to her that even as she watched the mother, so the mother watched her, and that every time she was compelled to leave the baby alone the mother was waiting to get at it.

Day and night the nurse covered the child, and day and night the silent, watchful mother seemed to be lying in wait as a wolf waits for a lamb. It must read most incredible to you, and yet I beg you to take it seriously, for a child's life and a man's sanity may depend upon it.

At last there came one dreadful day when the facts could no longer be concealed from the husband. The nurse's nerve had given way; she could stand the strain no longer, and she made a clean breast of it all to the man.

To him it seemed as wild a tale as it may now seem to you. He knew his wife to be a loving wife, and, save for the assaults upon her stepson, a loving mother. Why, then, should she wound her own dear little baby? He told the nurse that she was dreaming, that her suspicions were those of a lunatic, and that such libels upon her mistress were not to be tolerated. Whilst they were talking a sudden cry of pain was heard. Nurse and master rushed together to the nursery. Imagine his feelings, Mr. Holmes, as he saw his wife rise from a kneeling position beside the cot, and saw blood upon the child's exposed neck and upon the sheet. With a cry of horror, he turned his wife's face to the light and saw blood all round her lips. It was she—she beyond all question—who had drunk the poor baby's blood.

So the matter stands. She is now confined to her room. There has been no explanation. The husband is half demented. He knows, and I know, little of Vampirism beyond the name. We had thought it was some wild tale of foreign parts. And yet here in the very heart of the English Sussex— well, all this can be discussed with you in the morning. Will you see me? Will you use your great powers in aiding a dis- tracted man? If so, kindly wire to Ferguson, Cheeseman's, Lamberley, and I will be at your rooms by ten o'clock.

Yours faithfully,
Robert Ferguson.

P. S. I believe your friend Watson played Rugby for Black- heath when I was three-quarter for Richmond.[14] It is the only personal introduction which I can give.

"Of course I remember him," said I, as I laid down the let- ter. "Big Bob Ferguson, the finest three-quarter Richmond ever had. He was always a good-natured chap. It's like him to be so concerned over a friend's case."

Holmes looked at me thoughtfully and shook his head.

"I never get your limits, Watson," said he. "There are unex- plored possibilities about you. Take a wire down, like a good fellow. 'Will examine your case with pleasure.' "

"*Your* case!"

"We must not let him think that this Agency is a home for the weak-minded. Of course it is his case. Send him that wire and let the matter rest till morning."

Promptly at ten o'clock next morning Ferguson strode into our room. I had remembered him as a long, slab-sided man with loose limbs and a fine turn of speed, which had carried him round many an opposing back. There is surely nothing in life more painful than to meet the wreck of a fine athlete whom one has known in his prime. His great frame had fallen in, his

14 Blackheath, for which Watson played, was an amateur rugby club founded in 1858; Rich- mond was formed in 1861. In 1871, these clubs were among the founders of the Rugby Football Union. See "The Missing Three- Quarter," note 11.

15 In 1865, ten acres of the Old Deer Park—located near the Thames on the outskirts of Richmond, close to the Royal Botanical Gardens at Kew—were leased to the Richmond Cricket Club. In 1866, the Cricket Club let out ground to the Richmond Football Club (that is, the rugby club) for use in the winter. J.P.W. Mallelieu contends that despite Ferguson's unequivocal statement, Watson never played rugby for Blackheath and that he was thrown over the ropes at the match Ferguson recalled when, drunk, Watson wandered onto the playing field (see "The Missing Three-Quarter," note 13).

Richmond Park, the "Old Deer Park."
Queen's London (1897)

flaxen hair was scanty, and his shoulders were bowed. I fear that I roused corresponding emotions in him.

"Hullo, Watson," said he, and his voice was still deep and hearty. "You don't look quite the man you did when I threw you over the ropes into the crowd at the Old Deer Park.[15] I expect I have changed a bit also. But it's this last day or two that has aged me. I see by your telegram, Mr. Holmes, that it is no use my pretending to be anyone's deputy."

"It is simpler to deal direct," said Holmes.

"Of course it is. But you can imagine how difficult it is when you are speaking of the one woman whom you are bound to protect and help. What can I do? How am I to go to the police with such a story? And yet the kiddies have got to be protected. Is it madness, Mr. Holmes? Is it something in the blood? Have you any similar case in your experience? For God's sake, give me some advice, for I am at my wit's end."

"Very naturally, Mr. Ferguson. Now sit here and pull yourself together and give me a few clear answers. I can assure you that I am very far from being at my wit's end, and that I am confident we shall find some solution. First of all, tell me what steps you have taken. Is your wife still near the children?"

"We had a dreadful scene. She is a most loving woman, Mr. Holmes. If ever a woman loved a man with all her heart and soul, she loves me. She was cut to the heart that I should have discovered this horrible, this incredible, secret. She would not even speak. She gave no answer to my reproaches, save to gaze at me with a sort of wild, despairing look in her eyes. Then she rushed to her room and locked herself in. Since then she has refused to see me. She has a maid who was with her before her marriage, Dolores by name—a friend rather than a servant. She takes her food to her."

"Then the child is in no immediate danger?"

"Mrs. Mason, the nurse, has sworn that she will not leave it night or day. I can absolutely trust her. I am more uneasy about poor little Jack, for, as I told you in my note, he has twice been assaulted by her."

"But never wounded?"

"No, she struck him savagely. It is the more terrible as he is a poor little inoffensive cripple." Ferguson's gaunt features softened as he spoke of his boy. "You would think that the dear lad's condition would soften anyone's heart. A fall in childhood

"For God's sake, Mr. Holmes, give me some advice,
for I am at my wit's end."
Howard Elcock, *Strand Magazine*, 1924

and a twisted spine, Mr. Holmes. But the dearest, most loving heart within."

Holmes had picked up the letter of yesterday and was reading it over. "What other inmates are there in your house, Mr. Ferguson?"

"Two servants who have not been long with us. One stablehand, Michael, who sleeps in the house. My wife, myself, my boy Jack, baby, Dolores, and Mrs. Mason. That is all."

"I gather that you did not know your wife well at the time of your marriage?"

"I had only known her a few weeks."

"How long had this maid Dolores been with her?"

"Some years."

Mrs. Ferguson kneeling by the cot gave no answer to her
husband's reproaches, save to gaze at him with a wild
despairing look in her eyes.
W. T. Benda, *Hearst's International*, 1924

"Then your wife's character would really be better known
by Dolores than by you ?"

"Yes, you may say so."

Holmes made a note.

"I fancy," said he, "that I may be of more use at Lamberley
than here. It is eminently a case for personal investigation. If
the lady remains in her room, our presence could not annoy or
inconvenience her. Of course, we would stay at the inn."

Ferguson gave a gesture of relief.

"It is what I hoped, Mr. Holmes. There is an excellent train
at two from Victoria, if you could come."

"Of course we could come. There is a lull at present. I can
give you my undivided energies. Watson, of course, comes with
us. But there are one or two points upon which I wish to be
very sure before I start. This unhappy lady, as I understand it,
has appeared to assault both the children, her own baby and
your little son?"

"That is so."

"But the assaults take different forms, do they not? She has
beaten your son."

"Once with a stick and once very savagely with her hands."

"Did she give no explanation why she struck him?"

"None save that she hated him. Again and again she said so."

"Well, that is not unknown among stepmothers. A posthumous jealousy, we will say. Is the lady jealous by nature?"

"Yes, she is very jealous—jealous with all the strength of her fiery tropical love."

"But the boy—he is fifteen, I understand, and probably very developed in mind, since his body has been circumscribed in action. Did he give you no explanation of these assaults?"

"No; he declared there was no reason."

"Were they good friends at other times?"

"No; there was never any love between them."

"Yet you say he is affectionate?"

"Never in the world could there be so devoted a son. My life is his life. He is absorbed in what I say or do."

Once again Holmes made a note. For some time he sat lost in thought.

"No doubt you and the boy were great comrades before this second marriage. You were thrown very close together, were you not?"

"Very much so."

"And the boy, having so affectionate a nature, was devoted, no doubt, to the memory of his mother?"

"Most devoted."

"He would certainly seem to be a most interesting lad. There is one other point about these assaults. Were the strange attacks upon the baby and the assaults upon your son at the same period?"

"In the first case it was so. It was as if some frenzy had seized her, and she had vented her rage upon both. In the second case it was only Jack who suffered. Mrs. Mason had no complaint to make about the baby."

"That certainly complicates matters."

"I don't quite follow you, Mr. Holmes."

"Possibly not. One forms provisional theories and waits for time or fuller knowledge to explode them. A bad habit, Mr. Ferguson; but human nature is weak. I fear that your old friend here has given an exaggerated view of my scientific methods.

16 Perhaps selected by Holmes for its collegiate associations. See "The Creeping Man," set in "Camford," evidently Holmes's university, where Holmes and Watson lunch at the "Chequers," a pub recalled by Holmes with some fondness.

17 The carved, moulded, or drawn representation of a name using pictures, or some kind of hieroglyphic riddle.

However, I will only say at the present stage that your problem does not appear to me to be insoluble, and that you may expect to find us at Victoria at two o'clock."

It was evening of a dull, foggy November day when, having left our bags at the "Chequers,"[16] Lamberley, we drove through the Sussex clay of a long winding lane, and finally reached the isolated and ancient farmhouse in which Ferguson dwelt. It was a large, straggling building, very old in the centre, very new at the wings, with towering Tudor chimneys and a lichen-spotted, high-pitched roof of Horsham slabs. The doorsteps were worn into curves, and the ancient tiles which lined the porch were marked with the rebus[17] of a cheese and a man, after the original builder. Within, the ceilings were corrugated with heavy oaken beams, and the uneven floors sagged into sharp curves. An odour of age and decay pervaded the whole crumbling building.

There was one very large central room into which Ferguson led us. Here, in a huge old-fashioned fireplace with an iron screen behind it dated 1670, there blazed and spluttered a splendid log fire.

The room, as I gazed round, was a most singular mixture of dates and of places. The half-panelled walls may well have belonged to the original yeoman father of the seventeenth century. They were ornamented, however, on the lower part by a line of well-chosen modern water-colour; while above, where yellow plaster took the place of oak, there was hung a fine collection of South American utensils and weapons, which had been brought, no doubt, by the Peruvian lady upstairs. Holmes rose, with that quick curiosity which sprang from his eager mind, and examined them with some care. He returned with his eyes full of thought.

"Hullo!" he cried. "Hullo!"

A spaniel had lain in a basket in the corner. It came slowly forward towards its master, walking with difficulty. Its hind-legs moved irregularity and its tail was on the ground. It licked Ferguson's hand.

"What is it, Mr. Holmes?"

"The dog. What's the matter with it?"

"That's what puzzled the vet. A sort of paralysis. Spinal

meningitis, he thought. But it is passing. He'll be all right soon—won't you, Carlo?"

A shiver of assent passed through the drooping tail. The dog's mournful eyes passed from one of us to the other. He knew that we were discussing his case.

"Did it come on suddenly?"

"In a single night."

"How long ago?"

"It may have been four months ago."

"Very remarkable. Very suggestive."

"What do you see in it, Mr. Holmes?"

"A confirmation of what I had already thought."

"For God's sake, what *do* you think, Mr. Holmes? It may be a mere intellectual puzzle to you, but it is life and death to me! My wife a would-be murderer—my child in constant danger! Don't play with me, Mr. Holmes. It is too terribly serious."

The big Rugby three-quarter was trembling all over. Holmes put his hand soothingly upon his arm.

"I fear that there is pain for you, Mr. Ferguson, whatever the solution may be," said he. "I would spare you all I can. I cannot say more for the instant but before I leave this house I hope I may have something definite."

"Please God you may! If you will excuse me, gentlemen, I will go up to my wife's room and see if there has been any change."

He was away some minutes, during which Holmes resumed his examination of the curiosities upon the wall. When our host returned it was clear from his downcast face that he had made no progress. He brought with him a tall, slim, brown-faced girl.

"The tea is ready, Dolores," said Ferguson. "See that your mistress has everything she can wish."

"She verra ill," cried the girl, looking with indignant eyes at her master. "She no ask for food. She verra ill. She need doctor. I frightened stay alone with her without doctor."

Ferguson looked at me with a question in his eyes.

"I should be so glad if I could be of use."

"Would your mistress see Dr. Watson?"

"I take him. I no ask leave. She needs doctor."

"Then I'll come with you at once."

I followed the girl, who was quivering with strong emotion, up the staircase and down an ancient corridor. At the end was an iron-clamped and massive door. It struck me as I looked at it that if Ferguson tried to force his way to his wife he would find it no easy matter. The girl drew a key from her pocket, and the heavy oaken planks creaked upon their old hinges. I passed in and she swiftly followed, fastening the door behind her.

On the bed a woman was lying who was clearly in a high fever. She was only half conscious, but as I entered she raised a pair of frightened but beautiful eyes and glared at me in apprehension. Seeing a stranger, she appeared to be relieved and sank back with a sigh upon the pillow. I stepped up to her with a few reassuring words, and she lay still while I took her pulse and temperature. Both were high, and yet my impression was that the condition was rather that of mental and nervous excitement than of any actual seizure.

"She lie like that one day, two day. I 'fraid she die," said the girl.

The woman turned her flushed and handsome face towards me.

"Where is my husband?"

"He is below and would wish to see you."

"I will not see him. I will not see him." Then she seemed to wander off into delirium. "A fiend! A fiend! Oh, what shall I do with this devil?"

"Can I help you in any way?"

"No. No one can help. It is finished. All is destroyed. Do what I will, all is destroyed."

The woman must have some strange delusion. I could not see honest Bob Ferguson in the character of fiend or devil.

"Madame," I said, "your husband loves you dearly. He is deeply grieved at this happening."

Again she turned on me those glorious eyes.

"He loves me. Yes. But do I not love him? Do I not love him even to sacrifice myself rather than break his dear heart? That is how I love him. And yet he could think of me—he could speak of me so."

"He is full of grief but he cannot understand."

"No, he cannot understand. But he should trust."

"Will you not see him?" I suggested.

"No, no; I cannot forget those terrible words nor the look

The woman turned her flushed and handsome face toward me.
"Where is my husband?" she asked.
Howard Elcock, *Strand Magazine*, 1924

upon his face. I will not see him. Go now. You can do nothing for me. Tell him only one thing. I want my child. I have a right to my child. That is the only message I can send him." She turned her face to the wall and would say no more.

I returned to the room downstairs, where Ferguson and Holmes still sat by the fire. Ferguson listened moodily to my account of the interview.

"How can I send her the child?" he said. "How do I know what strange impulse might come upon her? How can I ever forget how she rose from beside it with its blood upon her lips?" He shuddered at the recollection. "The child is safe with Mrs. Mason, and there he must remain."

A smart maid, the only modern thing which we had seen in the house, had brought in some tea. As she was serving it the door opened and a youth entered the room. He was a remarkable lad, pale-faced and fair-haired, with excitable light blue eyes which blazed into a sudden flame of emotion and joy as they rested upon his father. He rushed forward and threw his arms round his neck with the abandon of a loving girl.

"Oh, daddy," he cried. "I did not know that you were due yet. I should have been here to meet you. Oh, I am so glad to see you!"

Ferguson gently disengaged himself from the embrace with some little show of embarrassment.

"Dear old chap," said he, patting the flaxen head with a very tender hand. "I came early because my friends, Mr. Holmes and Dr. Watson, have been persuaded to come down and spend an evening with us."

"Is that Mr. Holmes, the detective?"

"Yes."

The youth looked at us with a very penetrating and, as it seemed to me, unfriendly gaze.

"What about your other child, Mr. Ferguson?" asked Holmes. "Might we make the acquaintance of the baby?"

"Ask Mrs. Mason to bring baby down," said Ferguson. The boy went off with a curious, shambling gait which told my surgical eyes that he was suffering from a weak spine. Presently he returned, and behind him came a tall, gaunt woman bearing in her arms a very beautiful child, dark-eyed, golden-haired, a wonderful mixture of the Saxon and the Latin. Ferguson was evidently devoted to it, for he took it into his arms and fondled it most tenderly.

"Fancy anyone having the heart to hurt him," he muttered, as he glanced down at the small, angry red pucker upon the cherub throat.

It was at this moment that I chanced to glance at Holmes, and saw a most singular intentness in his expression. His face was as set as if it had been carved out of old ivory, and his eyes, which had glanced for a moment at father and child, were now fixed with eager curiosity upon something at the other side of the room. Following his gaze I could only guess that he was looking out through the window at the melancholy, dripping garden. It is true that a shutter had half closed outside and

"Fancy anyone having the heart to hurt him," Ferguson
muttered as he glanced at the angry red pucker on his
baby's throat. All this time Holmes was staring
intently at the window across the room.
W. T. Benda, *Hearst's International*, 1924

obstructed the view, but none the less it was certainly at the
window that Holmes was fixing his concentrated attention.
Then he smiled, and his eyes came back to the baby. On its
chubby neck there was this small puckered mark. Without
speaking, Holmes examined it with care. Finally he shook one
of the dimpled fists which waved in front of him.

"Good-bye, little man. You have made a strange start in life.
Nurse, I should wish to have a word with you in private."

He took her aside and spoke earnestly for a few minutes. I
only heard the last words, which were. "Your anxiety will soon,
I hope, be set at rest." The woman, who seemed to be a sour,
silent kind of creature, withdrew with the child.

"What is Mrs. Mason like?" asked Holmes.

"Not very prepossessing externally, as you can see, but a
heart of gold, and devoted to the child."

"Do you like her, Jack?" Holmes turned suddenly upon the
boy. His expressive mobile face shadowed over, and he shook
his head.

"Jacky has very strong likes and dislikes," said Ferguson,
putting his arm round the boy. "Luckily I am one of his likes."

The boy cooed and nestled his head upon his father's breast.
Ferguson gently disengaged him.

At this moment I chanced to glance at Holmes, and
saw a most singular intentness in his expression. His
eyes with fixed with eager curiosity upon something
at the other side of the room.
Howard Elcock, *Strand Magazine*, 1924

"Run away, little Jacky," said he, and he watched his son
with loving eyes until he disappeared. "Now, Mr. Holmes," he
continued when the boy was gone, "I really feel that I have
brought you on a fool's errand, for what can you possibly do
save give me your sympathy? It must be an exceedingly delicate and complex affair from your point of view."

"It is certainly delicate," said my friend with an amused
smile, "but I have not been struck up to now with its com-
plexity. It has been a case for intellectual deduction, but when
this original intellectual deduction is confined point by point
by quite a number of independent incidents, then the subjec-
tive becomes objective and we can say confidently that we
have reached our goal. I had, in fact, reached it before we left
Baker Street, and the rest has merely been observation and
confirmation."

Ferguson put his big hand to his furrowed forehead.

"For heaven's sake, Holmes," he said hoarsely, "if you can
see the truth in this matter, do not keep me in suspense. How
do I stand? What shall I do? I care nothing as to how you have
found your facts so long as you have really got them."

"Certainly I owe you an explanation, and you shall have it. But you will you permit me to handle the matter in my own way? Is the lady capable of seeing us, Watson?"

"She is ill, but she is quite rational."

"Very good. It is only in her presence that we can clear the matter up. Let us go up to her."

"She will not see me," cried Ferguson.

"Oh, yes, she will," said Holmes. He scribbled a few lines upon a sheet of paper. "You at least have the *entrée*, Watson. Will you have the goodness to give the lady this note?"

I ascended again and handed the note to Dolores, who cautiously opened the door. A minute later I heard a cry from within, a cry in which joy and surprise seemed to be blended. Dolores looked out.

"She will see them. She will leesten," said she.

At my summons Ferguson and Holmes came up. As we entered the room Ferguson took a step or two towards his wife, who had raised herself in the bed, but she held out her hand to repulse him. He sank into an arm-chair, while Holmes seated himself beside him, after bowing to the lady, who looked at him with wide-eyed amazement.

"I think we can dispense with Dolores," said Holmes. "Oh, very well, madame, if you would rather she stayed I can see no objection. Now, Mr. Ferguson, I am a busy man with many calls, and my methods have to be short and direct. The swiftest surgery is the least painful. Let me first say what will ease your mind. Your wife is a very good, a very loving, and a very ill-used woman."

Ferguson sat up with a cry of joy.

"Prove that, Mr. Holmes, and I am your debtor forever."

"I will do so, but in doing so I must wound you deeply in another direction."

"I care nothing so long as you clear my wife. Everything on earth is insignificant compared to that."

"Let me tell you, then, the train of reasoning which passed through my mind in Baker Street. The idea of a vampire was to me absurd. Such things do not happen in criminal practice in England. And yet your observation was precise. You had

18 Holmes refers to Eleanor of Castile, who accompanied her husband Edward I on a crusade to the Holy Land in 1270–1272. According to legend—possibly apocryphal—Eleanor saved Edward's life by sucking the poison from a dagger wound in his arm.

19 Curare, an extract found in tropical plants, was used in poison arrows by native South Americans for warfare and hunting. Its active ingredient is an alkaloid that causes muscle paralysis, first in the facial region and then moving on to the limbs. Finally, the poison arrests the respiratory functions, often causing death. In modern medicine, curare is used as a relaxant, an anaesthetic, and a treatment for spastic paralysis.

20 While Holmes may have seen his answer in the spaniel's injury, several scholars look at the same dog and see only controversy. Because curare acts first upon the facial muscles (which contain the most nerves), followed by those of the neck, chest, and limbs, the evidence that only Carlo's legs were paralysed seems incongruous. Stuart Palmer, noting that curare "kills within minutes or has no effect at all," speculates that the poison used was not curare at all, but possibly "an extract of the deadly nightshade, the Upas tree, or the venom of the Red Leech."

"The spaniel Carlo should have died at once," Mrs. Eleanor S. Cole confirms. Holmes himself has proclaimed that "it would mean death [for the child] if the venom were not sucked out," and therefore, the same would be true for a dog, which would have weighed less. To explain Carlo's seemingly miraculous survival, Mrs. Cole theorises that Jacky had second thoughts about his cruel action and was moved to suck some of the poison out of the wound, preventing the dog's demise but not its debilitation.

F. A. Allen, M.P.S., contemplates that Jacky

seen the lady rise from beside the child's cot with the blood upon her lips."

"I did."

"Did it not occur to you that a bleeding wound may be sucked for some other purpose than to draw the blood from it? Was there not a Queen in English history who sucked such a wound to draw poison from it?"[18]

"Poison!"

"A South American household. My instinct felt the presence of those weapons upon the wall before my eyes ever saw them. It might have been other poison, but that was what occurred to me. When I saw that little empty quiver beside the small bird-bow, it was just what I expected to see. If the child were pricked with one of those arrows dipped in curare[19] or some other devilish drug, it would mean death if the venom were not sucked out.

"And the dog! If one were to use such a poison, would one not try it first in order to see that it had not lost its power? I did not foresee the dog, but at least I understood him and he fitted into my reconstruction.[20]

"Now do you understand? Your wife feared such an attack. She saw it made and saved the child's life, and yet she shrank from telling you all the truth, for she knew how you loved the boy and feared lest it break your heart."

"Jacky!"

"I watched him as you fondled the child just now. His face was clearly reflected in the glass of the window where the shutter formed a background. I saw such jealousy, such cruel hatred, as I have seldom seen in a human face."

"My Jacky!"[21]

"You have to face it, Mr. Ferguson. It is the more painful because it is a distorted love, a maniacal exaggerated love for you, and possibly for his dead mother, which has prompted his action. His very soul is consumed with hatred for this splendid child, whose health and beauty are a contrast to his own weakness."

"Good God! It is incredible!"

"Have I spoken the truth, madame?"

The lady was sobbing, with her face buried in the pillows. Now she turned to her husband.

"How could I tell you, Bob? I felt the blow it would be to

you. It was better that I should wait and that it should come from some other lips than mine. When this gentleman, who seems to have powers of magic, wrote that he knew all, I was glad."

"I think a year at sea would be my prescription for Master Jacky," said Holmes, rising from his chair. "Only one thing is still clouded, madame. We can quite understand your attacks upon Master Jacky. There is a limit to a mother's patience. But how did you dare to leave the child these last two days?"

"I had told Mrs. Mason. She knew."

"Exactly. So I imagined."

Ferguson was standing by the bed, choking, his hands out-stretched and quivering.

"This, I fancy, is the time for our exit, Watson," said Holmes in a whisper. "If you will take one elbow of the too faithful Dolores, I will take the other. There, now," he added as he closed the door behind him, "I think we may leave them to settle the rest among themselves."

I have only one further note of this case. It is the letter which Holmes wrote in final answer to that with which the narrative begins. It ran thus:

BAKER STREET,
Nov. 21st.
Re Vampires
SIR:—
Referring to your letter of the 19th, I beg to state that I have looked into the inquiry of your client, Mr. Robert Ferguson, of Ferguson & Muirhead, tea brokers, of Mincing Lane, and that the matter has been brought to a satisfactory conclusion. With thanks for your recommendation,
     I am, Sir,
     Faithfully yours,
     SHERLOCK HOLMES.[22] ■

may have run a crude experiment on the dog, injecting a small amount of poison into Carlo's back with "a dirty half-scraped arrow-tip." The dog's continued paralysis would have been largely attributable not to the poison, which would have lacked potency, but to infection or trauma caused by gouging the dog's back with the arrow-tip. George B. Koelle agrees that Carlo was given a nonlethal dose of curare, and that the effects would have worn off in less than a day. Thus the veterinarian's diagnosis of spinal meningitis might actually have been correct, he surmises (in which case Holmes's deduction would have been little more than a fluke), or else the arrow tip might have damaged or otherwise traumatised Carlo's sciatic nerve.

21 The dynamic between father and son here could surely fill an entire psychology text-book. Jacky is a clinging, jealous, troubled little boy; but his doting father seems all too blind to his flaws. "Psychologically [Jacky] is an interesting study," D. Martin Dakin comments; "but we cannot acquit his father of some responsibility for his aberrations, by the sentimental way in which he treated him: to describe a boy of fifteen as 'poor little Jack' and 'the dear lad,' and to address him as 'dear old chap' and 'little Jacky' does not encourage a healthy relationship in the family."

22 Even D. Martin Dakin, who rejects from the Canon many of the stories in *The Case-Book of Sherlock Holmes*, accepts "The Sussex Vampire" as genuine, citing the authenticity of "trivial details about the doctor's early life" (for example, the mention of Watson's rugby days) and Holmes's immediate cynicism regarding the existence of vampires. The sarcastic Holmes is in full force here, as well, making wry comments such as, "I never get your limits, Watson. . . . There are unexplored possibilities about you." While some scholars

have noted that circumstances of the lame spaniel in "The Sussex Vampire" bear striking resemblance to those of the lame sheep of "The Silver Blaze"—in both, a would-be criminal practices upon an animal before turning to his human target—Dakin explains away the similarity by suggesting that little Jacky may have read "Silver Blaze," and thereupon was struck by inspiration.

"BUT WHAT DO WE KNOW ABOUT VAMPIRES?"

CHRONOLOGISTS place "The Sussex Vampire" in 1896, the year before publication of Bram Stoker's *Dracula*. But even if Robert Ferguson, Holmes, and Watson had not yet added Stoker's popular account to their knowledge of vampires, *Dracula* was only the culmination of a Victorian interest in accounts of vampires that had been growing since the beginning of the century.

The first significant vampire story published in English was John Polidori's "The Vampyre," appearing in the *New Monthly Magazine* for April 1819. In 1816, Polidori, a physician, had accompanied George Gordon, Lord Byron, on a trip to Italy and Switzerland. One rainy night in Geneva, Polidori was present—along with Byron's friends Percy Bysshe and Mary Shelley—at the now-famous conversation in which Byron announced, "We will each write a ghost story." Mary Shelley's effort became the novel *Frankenstein*, published two years later. Shelley wrote nothing; Byron started on a story but soon abandoned it. And Polidori's attempt was "The Vampyre," which featured the vampire Lord Ruthven, a nobleman marked by his aloof manner and the "deadly hue of his face, which never gained a warmer tint. . . ." The enigmatic yet strangely compelling Ruthven befriends a gentleman named Aubrey, eventually attacking and killing the object of Aubrey's affections and, finally, Aubrey's beloved sister. It is unsurprising that "The Vampyre" is the only literary effort for which Polidori is remembered, considering lines such as the ending, "Lord Ruthven had disappeared, and Aubrey's sister had glutted the thirst of a VAMPYRE!"

Also hugely influential was the popular *Varney the Vampyre*, written by James Malcolm Rymer and serialised in 109 weekly installments, from 1845 to 1847. Considered the first novel-length account of a vampire written in English, *Varney* is written in the style of an unabashedly sensationalist potboiler: "Her bosom heaves, and her limbs tremble, yet she cannot withdraw her eyes from that marble-looking face. . . . With a plunge he seizes her neck in his fang-like teeth—a gush of blood, and a hideous sucking noise follows. The girl has swooned, and the vampire is at his hideous repast!" Still, literary quality aside, *Varney* offers a vivid, monstrous portrait of the undead that echoes throughout later accounts of vampires. Rymer's vampire is a "tall gaunt figure" whose face, similar to Ruthven's, is "perfectly white—perfectly bloodless," with eyes like "polished tin" and "fearful-looking teeth-projecting like those of some wild animal, hideously, glaringly white, and fang-like."

The most influential record of vampires published in the 1800s, which Bram Stoker specifically acknowledged reading, is Joseph Sheridan Le Fanu's 1872 story "Carmilla." This account, which features a character that may well have resonated in Robert Ferguson's mind, records the tale of a female vampire. After a carriage accident, the charming and beautiful Carmilla is taken in by Laura, the narrator, a lonely young lady who quite literally falls under her new friend's spell. Like the vampires described before her, Carmilla exudes a powerful sexuality, and the story does not shy from depicting a charged, complicated relationship between the two women. Laura experiences terrifying dreams in which a mysterious woman visits her in bed and kisses her neck, and recalls that in the daytime the doting Carmilla occasionally "would press me more closely in her trembling embrace, and her lips in soft kisses gently glow upon my cheek. . . . In these mysterious moods I did not like her. I experienced a strange tumultuous excitement that was pleasurable, ever and anon, mingled with a vague sense of fear and disgust. . . . I was conscious of a love growing into adoration, and also of abhorrence." Carmilla, it turns out, is Millarca, Countess of Karnstein, dead for more than a century. Following the traditions of eastern European superstition, Laura and a band of men exhume Countess Millarca's body, driving a stake through her heart.

Stoker's *Dracula*, an assemblage of excerpts from the journal of Jonathan Harker, an English solicitor, the diaries of Dr. Seward and Mina Harker, and various letters, combines many of the descriptive elements of the previous accounts of vampires: the pale, intelligent aristocrat with a hypnotically sexual allure, the backdrop of eastern European folklore, the ability of the monster to pass undetected through upper-class society. Stoker's record is coy about the year in which the events of *Dracula* occurred, and Leonard Wolf, editor of the definitive *Annotated Dracula*, concludes that 1887 or any other year on a five-year cycle (that is, 1882 or 1892) would match the phases of the moon reported in the journal entries. Jonathan Harker ends by recording a visit to Transylvania "seven years" after the events, so the 1892 date can be discarded, and therefore 1887 seems most probable.

Sherlockians have their own theories about the extent of Holmes's familiarity with vampires and speculate that he may even have been involved in the Dracula case. William S. Baring-Gould expresses surprise at the lack of an entry in Holmes's index for "Vampirism in London," for surely, he believes, Holmes would have kept clippings from the *Daily-Graph*, the *Pall Mall Gazette*, and the *Westminister Gazette*, describing the attacks that Stoker's account ascribes to Count Dracula. (Those same clippings are included in *Dracula*.) Yet Baring-Gould's evidence is shaky, for he incorrectly ascribes the newspaper accounts to the year 1890, which Wolf demonstrates to be impossible.

Arthur Conan Doyle may have been familiar with these accounts as well. In 1894, he produced a novel entitled *The Parasite*, about a "psychic vampire," Miss Helen Penclosa, an older woman who preys on her victims using hypnotic powers: that is, she doesn't bite them. Professor Austin Gilroy, the narrator, falls under her spell and undertakes criminal acts, even threatening his fiancée with vitriol. In the end, Gilroy breaks free of Penclosa's influence by an exertion of will. Somewhat predictably, Conan Doyle's flight of fancy was not a popular success.

In *The Carfax Syndrome*, Kelvin Jones asserts that Holmes knew more than he let on to Watson—that he was acquainted with Bram Stoker and was moved to help investigate the mysterious affair involving Count Dracula. When the hunt for the count turned to Europe, Holmes also went abroad, joining Jonathan and Mina Harker and their companions. During the journey, he became involved in performing services for the royal family of Scandinavia and the French government. Most startlingly, Jones asserts that Miss Mary Morstan died of a vampiric attack, and that this fact alone spurred Holmes to investigate Ferguson's case and cast aside his veil of rationalism.

Harold Niver concludes, from the publicity given to the events of *Dracula*, that Holmes must have known of the existence of at least one vampire. Why would he not admit it?

Because, suggests Niver, Holmes and Dracula had reached a "peaceful co-existence" treaty? Or because Holmes had defeated Dracula himself, in the guise of Professor Van Helsing, the hero of Stoker's account?

The latter theory is taken up in some detail by William Leonard, in the article "Re: Vampires." Leonard, too, argues that Holmes must have known of the existence of Dracula. Leonard also considers the argument, first advanced by Jay Finley Christ, that Dracula and Moriarty were one and the same person, although Watson was unaware of the fact. "There were many things which Dr. Watson did not know," explained Christ, as quoted by Leonard. Christ cited Holmes's encounter with Moriarty in "The Final Problem," in which the professor accused Holmes of having pursued him since January. "Here was a clue for Dr. Watson, but he muffed it," Christ continued. "Moriarty and Dracula were two names for the same man. Mr. Holmes had been after him for over three months and began to catch up with him in January. Moriarty-Dracula knew this all the time, but Watson didn't get it."

Niver and Jones both ultimately conclude that Mrs. Ferguson was indeed a vampire and that Holmes concealed this information from her fragile husband, as well as from Watson. But their assumptions are roundly rejected in Thomas F. O'Brien's careful work "Re: Vampires, Again." Studying the physical descriptions of Van Helsing and Dracula in Stoker's text and the ambiguity of Stoker's reported dates, he concludes, unlike many Sherlockians, that Stoker's work "must be relegated to the world of fiction. . . ."

And yet the power of the figures of Holmes, Dracula, and Moriarty is such that they may, in the minds of some, be forever linked. Numerous pastiches, parodies, and comic books essay the connection. Perhaps the finest is Kim Newman's *Anno Dracula*, envisioning an England ruled by Count Dracula, recently married to Queen Victoria, an England in which vampirism has become a mark of upper-class status. Sherlockian scholar David L. Hammer concurs with this civilised view of the traditional monster, writing, "Vampirism stands a fair chance of being regarded as essentially an eccentricity in England, provided of course the vampire observes good form, adheres to what is proper, eschews excessive public displays, and doesn't harm birds or animals."

While Holmes, Watson, and Robert Ferguson could not have read Stoker's book in 1896, Watson most surely would have done so before writing "The Sussex Vampire," which was not published until 1924. Watson might also well have seen *Nosferatu* ("The Undead"), the 1922 German film that was based on *Dracula* but that, being unauthorised, used different names for the characters. In the movie, Count Dracula becomes Count Orlok, and the vampire is depicted not as a stately nobleman or romantic creature but as having, in the words of Alan Ryan, editor of *The Penguin Book of Vampire Stories*, a "hideous, ratlike appearance." Nonetheless, the magnetism of Max Shreck's performance must have reminded Watson that vampirism's hold on the public was a powerful one, a fascination not to be easily dismissed.

THE ADVENTURE OF THE
THREE GARRIDEBS[1]

No scholar has yet found anyone with the genuine name of "Garrideb," and the uniqueness of the name plays a critical rôle in this tale. "The Three Garridebs" is undoubtedly a late case, probably occurring in 1902, and it may well be that the criminal was a reader of Dr. Watson's works, for the crime strongly resembles the deceptions employed in "The Red-Headed League" and "The Stock-Broker's Clerk." The case is most noteworthy for what it reveals about the partners: As in "The Devil's Foot," another late case, Holmes expresses a moving concern for Watson's safety. Perhaps as a sign of Holmes's age (48) or his impending retirement in 1904, Holmes and Watson's relationship has grown from that of mere flatmates in 1881 to the closest of friendships.

IT MAY HAVE been a comedy, or it may have been a tragedy. It cost one man his reason, it cost me a blood-letting, and it cost yet another man the penalties of the law. Yet there was certainly an element of comedy. Well, you shall judge for yourselves.

I remember the date very well, for it was in the same month that Holmes refused a knighthood[2] for services which may perhaps some day be described. I only refer to the matter in passing, for in my position of partner and confidant I am obliged to be particularly careful to avoid any indiscretion. I repeat, however, that this enables me to fix the date, which was the latter end of June, 1902, shortly after the conclusion of the South African War. Holmes had spent several days in bed, as was his habit from time to time, but he emerged that morning with a long foolscap document in his hand and a twinkle of amusement in his austere grey eyes.

1 "The Three Garridebs" was first published in *Collier's Weekly Magazine* on October 25, 1924, and in the January 1925 issue of the *Strand Magazine*.

2 In "The Golden Pince-Nez," Watson reports that Holmes accepted a Legion of Honour from the French president for assisting in "the tracking and arrest of Huret, the Boulevard assassin." This makes Holmes's refusal of a knighthood all the more curious. Trevor H. Hall explains the discrepancy by guessing that Holmes accepted the Legion of Honour in tribute to his grandmother, the sister of the French artist Vernet. The spurned offer of a knighthood may have been part of Edward VII's coronation honours, which coin-

cidentally (or perhaps not) included the knighthood of Arthur Conan Doyle.

3 The telephone at Baker Street is mentioned only here, in "The Illustrious Client," and in "The Retired Colourman."

4 No Moorville exists in Kansas, presumably for the reason that, as Willis B. Wood writes, "In Kansas . . . [t]here are no moors."

"There is a chance for you to make some money, friend Watson," said he. "Have you ever heard the name of Garrideb?"

I admitted that I had not.

"Well, if you can lay your hand upon a Garrideb, there's money in it."

"Why?"

"Ah, that's a long story—rather a whimsical one, too. I don't think in all our explorations of human complexities we have ever come upon anything more singular. The fellow will be here presently for cross-examination, so I won't open the matter up till he comes. But, meanwhile, that's the name we want."

The telephone directory[3] lay on the table beside me, and I turned over the pages in a rather hopeless quest. But to my amazement there was this strange name in its due place. I gave a cry of triumph.

"Here you are, Holmes! Here it is!"

Holmes took the book from my hand.

" 'Garrideb, N.,' " he read. " '36 Little Ryder Street, W.' Sorry to disappoint you, my dear Watson, but this is the man himself. That is the address upon his letter. We want another to match him."

Mrs. Hudson had come in with a card upon a tray. I took it up and glanced at it.

"Why, here it is!" I cried in amazement. "This is a different initial. John Garrideb, Counsellor at Law, Moorville, Kansas,[4] U. S. A."

Holmes smiled as he looked at the card. "I am afraid you must make yet another effort, Watson," said he. "This gentleman is also in the plot already, though I certainly did not expect to see him this morning. However, he is in a position to tell us a good deal which I want to know."

A moment later he was in the room. Mr. John Garrideb, Counsellor at Law, was a short, powerful man with the round, fresh, clean-shaven face characteristic of so many American men of affairs. The general effect was chubby and rather childlike, so that one received the impression of quite a young man with a broad set smile upon his face. His eyes, however, were arresting. Seldom in any human head have I seen a pair which bespoke a more intense inward life, so bright were they, so alert, so responsive to every change of thought. His accent was American, but was not accompanied by any eccentricity of speech.

"Mr. Holmes?" he asked, glancing from one to the other. "Ah, yes! Your pictures are not unlike you, sir, if I may say so.[5] I believe you have had a letter from my namesake, Mr. Nathan Garrideb, have you not?"

"Pray sit down," said Sherlock Holmes. "We shall, I fancy, have a good deal to discuss." He took up his sheets of foolscap. "You are, of course, the Mr. John Garrideb mentioned in this document. But surely you have been in England some time?"

"Why do you say that, Mr. Holmes?" I seemed to read sudden suspicion in those expressive eyes.

"Your whole outfit is English."

Mr. Garrideb forced a laugh. "I've read of your tricks, Mr. Holmes, but I never thought I would be the subject of them. Where do you read that?"

"The shoulder cut of your coat, the toes of your boots—could anyone doubt it?"

"Well, well, I had no idea I was so obvious a Britisher. But business brought me over here some time ago, and so, as you say, my outfit is nearly all London. However, I guess your time is of value, and we did not meet to talk about the cut of my socks. What about getting down to that paper you hold in your hand?"

Holmes had in some way ruffled our visitor, whose chubby face had assumed a far less amiable expression.

"Patience! Patience, Mr. Garrideb!" said my friend in a soothing voice. "Dr. Watson would tell you that these little digressions of mine sometimes prove in the end to have some bearing on the matter. But why did Mr. Nathan Garrideb not come with you?"

"Why did he ever drag you into it at all?" asked our visitor with a sudden out-flame of anger. "What in thunder had you to do with it? Here was a bit of professional business between two gentlemen, and one of them must needs call in a detective! I saw him this morning, and he told me this fool-trick he had played me, and that's why I am here. But I feel bad about it, all the same."

"There was no reflection upon you, Mr. Garrideb. It was simply zeal upon his part to gain your end—an end which is, I understand, equally vital for both of you. He knew that I had means of getting information, and, therefore, it was very natural that he should apply to me."

5 By June 1902, there were several illustrators of Watson's stories. D. H. Friston, Charles Doyle, and George Hutchinson had done the work on *A Study in Scarlet* and *The Sign of Four*. Sidney Paget was the exclusive illustrator of the *Strand Magazine* tales, while in America, several uncredited artists, as well as the fine artist W. H. Hyde, had illustrated editions of the tales.

"Why did he ever drag you into it at all, Mr. Holmes?" asked our
visitor, with a sudden outflame of anger. "What in
thunder had you to do with it?"
Howard Elcock, *Strand Magazine*, 1925

Our visitor's angry face gradually cleared.

"Well, that puts it different," said he. "When I went to see
him this morning and he told me he had sent to a detective, I
just asked for your address and came right away. I don't want
police butting into a private matter. But if you are content just
to help us find the man, there can be no harm in that."

"Well, that is just how it stands," said Holmes. "And now, sir,
since you are here, we had best have a clear account from your
own lips. My friend here knows nothing of the details."

Mr. Garrideb surveyed me with not too friendly a gaze.

"Need he know?" he asked.

"We usually work together."

"Well, there's no reason it should be kept a secret. I'll give you the facts as short as I can make them. If you came from Kansas I would not need to explain to you who Alexander Hamilton Garrideb was. He made his money in real estate, and afterwards in the wheat pit at Chicago,[6] but he spent it in buying up as much land as would make one of your counties, lying along the Arkansas River, west of Fort Dodge.[7] It's grazing-land and lumber-land and arable-land and mineralized-land, and just every sort of land that brings dollars to the man that owns it.

"He had no kith nor kin—or, if he had, I never heard of it. But he took a kind of pride in the queerness of his name. That was what brought us together. I was in the law at Topeka, and one day I had a visit from the old man, and he was tickled to death to meet another man with his own name. It was his pet fad, and he was dead set to find out if there were any more Garridebs in the world. 'Find me another!' said he, I told him I was a busy man and could not spend my life hiking round the world in search of Garridebs. 'None the less,' said he, 'that is just what you will do if things pan out as I planned them.' I thought he was joking, but there was a powerful lot of meaning in the words, as I was soon to discover.

"For he died within a year of saying them, and he left a will behind him. It was the queerest will that has ever been filed in the State of Kansas. His property was divided into three parts, and I was to have one on condition that I found two Garridebs who would share the remainder. It's five million dollars for each if it is a cent,[8] but we can't lay a finger on it until we all three stand in a row.

"It was so big a chance that I just let my legal practice slide and I set forth looking for Garridebs. There is not one in the United States. I went through it, sir, with a fine-toothed comb and never a Garrideb could I catch. Then I tried the old country. Sure enough there was the name in the London Telephone Directory.[9] I went after him two days ago and explained the whole matter to him. But he is a lone man like myself, with some women relations, but no men. It says three adult men in the will. So you see we still have a vacancy, and if you can help to fill it we will be very ready to pay your charges."

"Well, Watson," said Holmes with a smile, "I said it was

6 The "wheat pit" was the wheat commodities exchange in Chicago, known as the Board of Trade. Frank Norris's classic 1903 novel *The Pit* chronicled the tale of the fortunes of the Jadwin family and described the workings of the Pit, where options to buy and sell wheat—"futures"—were bought and sold. In grandiloquent prose, Norris recounted how the trading at the Pit reverberated far beyond the city itself: "All through the Northwest, all through the central world of the Wheat the set and whirl of that innermost Pit made itself felt; and it spread and spread and spread till grain in the elevators of Western Iowa moved and stirred and answered to its centripetal force, and men upon the streets of New York felt the mysterious tugging of its undertow engage their feet, embrace their bodies, overwhelm them, and carry them bewildered and unresisting back and downwards to the Pit itself."

7 Fort Dodge, established in 1864, is a southwestern Kansas town on the north bank of the Arkansas River. With the laying of the Santa Fe Railway, Fort Dodge would be eclipsed by the exploits of its neighbouring cousin, Dodge City. That town was settled in 1872 a mere four miles away from Fort Dodge, and soon played host to the gunslinging adventures of Bat Masterson (1853–1921) and Wyatt Earp (1848–1929).

8 A vast sum now, this was an astronomical fortune then, the modern equivalent of over $100 million. At least one statistical source estimates that the average net worth of the top one percent of the population of Victorian England was about $265,000—roughly one-twentieth of what was being offered to each Garrideb.

9 Whether this was a directory of the National Telephone Company (which had 25,000 lines in London in 1902) or the post

office (which had 5,500 lines in London at that time) is unknown. At present there is only one N. Garrideb listed in the public directories for the United States, Canada, and the United Kingdom, that being in St. Charles, MO (actually the home telephone number of Sherlockians Michael and Kathleen Bragg), and no one has ever discovered another Garrideb.

10 Many scholars note that Holmes comes up with a fictitious name very similar to that of both Lysander Stark, the alias of the counterfeiter in "The Engineer's Thumb," and Sir Leander Starr Jameson, Bt. (1853–1917), friend and collaborator of Cecil Rhodes. After impetuously leading five hundred volunteers on a failed invasion of the South African Transvaal on December 29, 1895, "Doc Jim," as Jameson, a physician and statesman, was known, was captured and sent back to England, where he was sentenced to fifteen months in prison. Upon his release, he returned to South Africa and served as prime minister of Cape Colony from 1904 to 1908. The similarity to "Lysander Stark" may be due to Watson's penchant for disguising the names of persons figuring in his tales, while

Leander Starr Jameson, fourth from left, standing, with other officers of the Jameson Raid.
Spectacle of Empire

rather whimsical, did I not? I should have thought, sir, that your obvious way was to advertise in the agony columns of the papers."

"I have done that, Mr. Holmes. No replies."

"Dear me! Well, it is certainly a most curious little problem. I may take a glance at it in my leisure. By the way, it is curious that you should have come from Topeka. I used to have a correspondent—he is dead now—old Dr. Lysander Starr,[10] who was Mayor in 1890."

"Good old Dr. Starr!" said our visitor. "His name is still honoured. Well, Mr. Holmes, I suppose all we can do is to report to you and let you know how we progress. I reckon you will hear within a day or two." With this assurance our American bowed and departed.

Holmes had lit his pipe, and he sat for some time with a curious smile upon his face.

"Well?" I asked at last.

"I am wondering, Watson—just wondering!"

"At what?"

Holmes took his pipe from his lips.

"I was wondering, Watson, what on earth could be the object of this man in telling us such a rigmarole of lies. I nearly asked him so—for there are times when a brutal frontal attack is the best policy—but I judged it better to let him think he had fooled us. Here is a man with an English coat frayed at the elbow and trousers bagged at the knee with a year's wear, and yet by this document and by his own account he is a provincial American lately landed in London. There have been no advertisements in the agony columns. You know that I miss nothing there. They are my favourite covert for putting up a bird,[11] and I would never have overlooked such a cock pheasant as that. I never knew a Dr. Lysander Starr, of Topeka. Touch him where you would he was false. I think the fellow is really an American, but he has worn his accent smooth with years of London. What is his game, then, and what motive lies behind this preposterous search for Garridebs? It's worth our attention, for, granting that the man is a rascal, he is certainly a complex and ingenious one. We must now find out if our other correspondent is a fraud also. Just ring him up, Watson."

I did so, and heard a thin, quavering voice at the other end of the line.

"Yes, yes, I am Mr. Nathan Garrideb. Is Mr. Holmes there? I should very much like to have a word with Mr. Holmes."

My friend took the instrument and I heard the usual syncopated dialogue.

"Yes, he has been here. I understand that you don't know him. . . . How long? . . . Only two days! . . . Yes, yes, of course, it is a most captivating prospect. Will you be at home this evening? I suppose your namesake will not be there? . . . Very good, we will come then, for I would rather have a chat without him. . . . Dr. Watson will come with me. . . . I understood from your note that you did not go out often. . . . Well, we shall be round about six. You need not mention it to the American lawyer. . . . Very good. Good-bye!"

Jameson may have been on Holmes's (or Watson's) mind as the result of his recent trial and imprisonment.

11 In hunting or shooting, a covert is a blind, shelter, or bit of thick underbrush that provides cover for game. To "put up" a bird is to flush it out of the covert, alarming it so that it flies out into the open.

"Well, we shall be round about six. Dr. Watson
will come with me."
Howard Elcock, *Strand Magazine*, 1925

12 In late June?

13 The infamous tree at Tyburn was one of the sites of public executions from 1196 until 1783, when they were transferred to Newgate. The hangings at Tyburn took on a carnival-like atmosphere: A two-hour procession, heavy with drink and festivity (prisoners were often drunk by the time they reached the gallows), would lead the condemned and an accompanying crowd from Newgate prison to Tyburn on the Mondays scheduled for executions. Criminals, particularly those with any sort of élan, were treated like heroes, as was the occasional executioner. One hangman of the early 1600s, known as Derrick, was immortalised in Thomas Dekker's *Bellman of London* (1608), which wrote of a horse-thief, "And Derrick must be his host, and Tyborne the inn at which he will light." A hoisting device that could hang several criminals at once became known as a Derrick, and the name eventually came to refer to cranes aboard ships. Recent research reveals that the site of the gallows may have been at Connaught Square, not Edgware Road.

14 Named after Neander Valley in Germany, where the first remains of this early *Homo sapiens* subspecies were found in 1856, the cave-dwelling Neanderthals inhabited Europe and the Mediterranean (as well as parts of the Middle East, Central Asia, and Africa) in the late Pleistocene epoch. Their physiognomy was marked by a low, sloping brow; a chinless jaw that jutted forward; and a thick, squat build, suitable for the cold climate of the era. The large front teeth of the Neanderthals possibly derived from chewing on animal skins to soften them, as the Eskimos do. They were supplanted by Cro-Magnons some 30,000 years ago, although the exact circumstances of the Neanderthals' extinction are unknown.

It was twilight of a lovely spring evening,[12] and even Little Ryder Street, one of the smaller offshoots from the Edgware Road, within a stone-cast of old Tyburn Tree of evil memory,[13] looked golden and wonderful in the slanting rays of the setting sun. The particular house to which we were directed was a large, old-fashioned, Early Georgian edifice, with a flat brick face broken only by two deep bay windows on the ground floor. It was on this ground floor that our client lived, and, indeed, the low windows proved to be the front of the huge room in which he spent his waking hours. Holmes pointed as we passed to the small brass plate which bore the curious name.

"Up some years, Watson," he remarked, indicating its discoloured surface. "It's *his* real name, anyhow, and that is something to note."

The house had a common stair, and there were a number of names painted in the hall, some indicating offices and some private chambers. It was not a collection of residential flats, but rather the abode of Bohemian bachelors. Our client opened the door for us himself and apologized by saying that the woman in charge left at four o'clock. Mr. Nathan Garrideb proved to be a very tall, loose-jointed, round-backed person, gaunt and bald, some sixty-odd years of age. He had a cadaverous face, with the dull dead skin of a man to whom exercise was unknown. Large round spectacles and a small projecting goat's beard combined with his stooping attitude to give him an expression of peering curiosity. The general effect, however, was amiable, though eccentric.

The room was as curious as its occupant. It looked like a small museum. It was both broad and deep, with cupboards and cabinets all round, crowded with specimens, geological and anatomical. Cases of butterflies and moths flanked each side of the entrance. A large table in the centre was littered with all sorts of debris, while the tall brass tube of a powerful microscope bristled up among them. As I glanced round I was surprised at the universality of the man's interests. Here was a case of ancient coins. There was a cabinet of flint instruments. Behind his central table was a large cupboard of fossil bones. Above was a line of plaster skulls with such names as "Neanderthal,"[14] "Heidelberg,"[15] "Cro-Magnon"[16] printed beneath them. It was clear that he was a student of many subjects. As he stood in front of us now, he held a piece of chamois leather in his right hand with which he was polishing a coin.

"Syracusan—of the best period," he explained, holding it. "They degenerated greatly towards the end.[17] At their best I hold them supreme, though some prefer the Alexandrian school.[18] You will find a chair here, Mr. Holmes. Pray allow me to clear these bones. And you, sir—ah, yes, Dr. Watson—if you would have the goodness to put the Japanese vase to one side. You see round me my little interests in life. My doctor lectures me about never going out, but why should I go out when I have so much to hold me here? I can assure you that the adequate cataloguing of one of those cabinets would take me three good months."

Holmes looked round him with curiosity.

"But do you tell me that you *never* go out?" he said.

"Now and again I drive down to Sotheby's or Christie's.[19] Otherwise I very seldom leave my room. I am not too strong, and my researches are very absorbing. But you can imagine, Mr. Holmes, what a terrific shock—pleasant but terrific—it was for me when I heard of this unparalleled good fortune. It only needs one more Garrideb to complete the matter, and surely we can find one. I had a brother, but he is dead, and female relatives are disqualified. But there must surely be others in the world. I had heard that you handled strange cases, and that was why I sent to you. Of course, this American gentleman is quite right, and I should have taken his advice first, but I acted for the best."

"I think you acted very wisely indeed," said Holmes. "But are you really anxious to acquire an estate in America?"

"Certainly not, sir. Nothing would induce me to leave my collection. But this gentleman has assured me that he will buy me out as soon as we have established our claim. Five million dollars was the sum named. There are a dozen specimens in the market at the present moment which fill gaps in my collection, and which I am unable to purchase for want of a few hundred pounds. Just think what I could do with five million dollars. Why, I have the nucleus of a national collection. I shall be the Hans Sloane of my age."[20]

His eyes gleamed behind his great spectacles. It was very

15 The 400,000-year-old jawbone of Heidelberg man, thought to be an example either of *Homo erectus* (a species that lived 1.6 million to 250,000 years ago) or of an early form of *Homo sapiens*, was discovered in 1907 in a sand pit near Heidelberg, Germany. Chinless and very large, the jaw has relatively small teeth and dates to the middle Pleistocene epoch. Because the date of discovery conflicts with that of "The Three Garridebs" ("The latter end of June, 1902"), either Watson, in writing this story sometime just before its publication date in 1924, substituted the Heidelberg name for some other specimen, or Garrideb possessed a model of some hitherto unknown relic.

16 The most recent of the three types of skulls owned by Garrideb, Cro-Magnon is a modern version of *Homo sapiens*, dating from the Upper Paleolithic period of 10,000 to 35,000 years ago. Several skeletons of this type were discovered in 1868, in a cave at Cro-Magnon in the Dordogne area of southern France. More advanced than the Neanderthals that preceded them, Cro-Magnons were tall and strong, anatomically similar to modern humans but with a slightly larger brain capacity. They lived in caves and makeshift huts and created sculptures and cave paintings, the first art produced by prehistoric peoples.

17 Syracuse (a city-state in Sicily) was conquered by the Romans in 212 B.C. Coin collectors share Garrideb's high regard for Syracusan coins. According to A. Carson Simpson, in his "Numismatics in the Canon," "the period 400–336 B.C. is generally accepted as that in which the numismatic art reached the highest point of excellence it ever attained. Thereafter, although portraiture on coins became more lifelike and individual, the general level of artistic treatment declined."

18 What Garrideb means by "the Alexandrian school" is unclear. Presumably he means coins minted in the city of Alexandria—but which Alexandria? A. Carson Simpson concludes that the *Roman* city of Alexandria is probably meant, for it struck numerous coins of highly diverse design. "There were, literally, thousands of varieties issued from the time of Augustus to that of Valerius," he notes; "as a result, they offer a fertile field for study."

19 The two rival auction houses of Sotheby's and Christie's were founded in 1744 and 1766, respectively. The former got its start when bookseller Samuel Baker put the private library of the late Rt. Hon. Sir John Stanley, Bt., "containing several Hundred scarce and valuable books in all branches of Polite Literature," up for sale on March 11, 1744, earning a few hundred pounds for 457 books. In 1767 he went into business with George Leigh and began handling the sale of several more libraries, including the books that Napoleon took with him to exile on St. Helena. When Baker passed away in 1778, the business was taken over by Leigh and John Sotheby, a nephew of Baker's. Sotheby and his successors would control the fortunes of the firm for the next eighty years, until the last Sotheby's death in 1861. (Thereafter, Sotheby's was controlled by a series of partners.) Under the Sotheby family's direction, the firm focussed on rare manuscripts, prints, and coins; and it was not until after World War I that Sotheby's began branching out into paintings and other works of art, necessitating a move from 13 Wellington Street to its current quarters at 34-35 New Bond Street.

Christie's first auction was conducted by James Christie, a former navy officer, on December 5, 1766. Over the ensuing years, Christie's budding friendships with artists and aristocrats turned his auction house into a gathering place for collectors, dealers, and tastemakers of London's high society. After Christie's death, his son, also named James, assumed responsibility for the business, specialising in Greek and Italian vases and sculpture. He, in turn, was succeeded by his sons James Stirling and George Henry, who later added brothers William and Edward Manson and then Thomas J. Woods in 1859. At that point, the firm became formally known as Christie, Manson & Woods. Christie's handled many high-profile transactions in the eighteenth and nineteenth centuries, including the sale of Sir Robert Walpole's art collection to Catherine the Great, Empress of Russia, in 1778; the auction of portrait painter Sir Joshua Reynolds's studio in 1794; and the seventeen-day sale of pictures from Scotland's Hamilton Palace in 1882.

20 Sir Hans Sloane (1660–1753), naturalist, physician, collector, and benefactor of the British Museum (see "The Musgrave Ritual," note 13). Legend has it that Sloane also helped introduce chocolate to the western world, having observed locals drinking cocoa in Jamaica. Finding the drink personally unpalatable, Sloane mixed his cocoa with milk, and his recipe was manufactured as medicine in England until John Cadbury began selling the beverage at his tea-and-coffee shop in 1824.

clear that no pains would be spared by Mr. Nathan Garrideb in finding a namesake.

"I merely called to make your acquaintance, and there is no reason why I should interrupt your studies," said Holmes. "I prefer to establish personal touch with those with whom I do business. There are few questions I need ask, for I have your very clear narrative in my pocket, and I filled up the blanks when this American gentleman called. I understand that up to this week you were unaware of his existence."

"That is so. He called last Tuesday."

"Did he tell you of our interview to-day?"

"Yes, he came straight back to me. He had been very angry."

"Why should he be angry?"

"He seemed to think it was some reflection on his honour. But he was quite cheerful again when he returned."

"Did he suggest any course of action?"

"No, sir, he did not."

"Has he had, or asked for, any money from you?"

"No, sir, never!"

"You see no possible object he has in view?"

"None, except what he states."

"Did you tell him of our telephone appointment?"[21]

"Yes, sir, I did."

Holmes was lost in thought. I could see that he was puzzled.

"Have you any articles of great value in your collection?"

"No, sir. I am not a rich man. It is a good collection, but not a very valuable one."

"You have no fear of burglars?"

"Not the least."

"How long have you been in these rooms?"

"Nearly five years."

Holmes's cross-examination was interrupted by an imperative knocking at the door. No sooner had our client unlatched it than the American lawyer burst excitedly into the room.

"Here you are!" he cried, waving a paper over his head. "I thought I should be in time to get you. Mr. Nathan Garrideb, my congratulations! You are a rich man, sir. Our business is happily finished and all is well. As to you, Mr. Holmes, we can only say we are sorry if we have given you any useless trouble."

He handed over the paper to our client, who stood staring at

21 Recall that upon phoning Nathan Garrideb earlier, Holmes told him that he "need not mention [the visit] to the American lawyer"; yet here, he evinces no surprise when Garrideb confesses that he has told him of the appointment after all. "Had he already summed up the eccentric collector as a hopeless nincompoop," asks D. Martin Dakin, "who could be assumed to be incapable of carrying out instructions?"

22 A farming implement consisting of a metal or wooden frame supporting sharp teeth or circular blades. Harrows are used to break up and smooth soil, to extract weeds, and to cover newly planted seeds.

23 A four-wheeled carriage; it had a long board, running between the front and rear axles, on which a seat was placed.

"Here you are!" he cried, waving a paper over his head. "Mr. Nathan Garrideb, my congratulations. You are a rich man, sir."
Howard Elcock, *Strand Magazine*, 1925

a marked advertisement. Holmes and I leaned forward and read it over his shoulder. This is how it ran:

HOWARD GARRIDEB
Constructor of Agricultural Machinery
Binders, reapers' steam and hand plows, drills, harrows,[22]
farmers' carts, buckboards,[23] and all other appliances.
Estimates for Artesian Wells.
Apply Grosvenor Buildings, Aston.

"Glorious!" gasped our host. "That makes our third man."

"I had opened up inquiries in Birmingham," said the American, "and my agent there has sent me this advertisement from a local paper. We must hustle and put the thing through. I have written to this man and told him that you will see him in his office to-morrow afternoon at four o'clock."

"You want *me* to see him?"

"What do you say, Mr. Holmes? Don't you think it would be

wiser? Here am I, a wandering American with a wonderful tale. Why should he believe what I tell him? But you are a Britisher with solid references, and he is bound to take notice of what you say. I would go with you if you wished, but I have a very busy day to-morrow, and I could always follow you if you are in any trouble."

"Well, I have not made such a journey for years."

"It is nothing, Mr. Garrideb. I have figured out your connections. You leave at twelve and should be there soon after two. Then you can be back the same night. All you have to do is to see this man, explain the matter, and get an affidavit of his existence. By the Lord!" he added hotly, "considering I've come all the way from the centre of America, it is surely little enough if you go a hundred miles in order to put this matter through."

"Quite so," said Holmes. "I think what this gentleman says is very true."

Mr. Nathan Garrideb shrugged his shoulders with a disconsolate air. "Well, if you insist I shall go," said he. "It is certainly hard for me to refuse you anything, considering the glory of hope that you have brought into my life."

"Then that is agreed," said Holmes, "and no doubt you will let me have a report as soon as you can."

"I'll see to that," said the American. "Well," he added, looking at his watch, "I'll have to get on. I'll call to-morrow, Mr. Nathan, and see you off to Birmingham. Coming my way, Mr. Holmes? Well, then, good-bye, and we may have good news for you to-morrow night."

I noticed that my friend's face cleared when the American left the room, and the look of thoughtful perplexity had vanished.

"I wish I could look over your collection, Mr. Garrideb," said he. "In my profession all sorts of odd knowledge comes useful, and this room of yours is a storehouse of it."

Our client shone with pleasure and his eyes gleamed from behind his big glasses.

"I had always heard, sir, that you were a very intelligent man," said he. "I could take you round now if you have the time."

"Unfortunately, I have not. But these specimens are so well labelled and classified that they hardly need your personal

24 Georgian style is an umbrella term given to the various architectural trends common during the reigns of George I, II, III, and IV, from 1714 to 1830. At first inspired by the work of Renaissance architect Andrea Palladio (see "The Abbey Grange," note 9), architects of the Georgian era then turned to neoclassicism, imitating the designs of classical Greece and Rome. Toward the end of the eighteenth century and the beginning of the nineteenth, simpler lines prevailed, and the red-brick house with white woodwork became a hallmark of the Georgian style. During this period, furniture and interior design also took precedence, with wallpaper, subdued colours, and furniture pieces by Thomas Chippendale all claiming influence in London townhouses of the day. It is likely that Garrideb's house was from the later period, because Queen Anne houses also were predominately brickwork.

explanation. If I should be able to look in to-morrow, I presume that there would be no objection to my glancing over them?"

"None at all. You are most welcome. The place will, of course, be shut up, but Mrs. Saunders is in the basement up to four o'clock and would let you in with her key."

"Well, I happen to be clear to-morrow afternoon. If you would say a word to Mrs. Saunders it would be quite in order. By the way, who is your house-agent?"

Our client was amazed at the sudden question.

"Holloway and Steele, in the Edgware Road. But why?"

"I am a bit of an archaeologist myself when it comes to houses," said Holmes, laughing. "I was wondering if this was Queen Anne or Georgian."

"Georgian, beyond doubt." [24]

"Really. I should have thought a little earlier. However, it is easily ascertained. Well, good-bye, Mr. Garrideb, and may you have every success in your Birmingham journey."

The house-agent's was close by, but we found that it was closed for the day, so we made our way back to Baker Street. It was not till after dinner that Holmes reverted to the subject.

"Our little problem draws to a close," said he. "No doubt you have outlined the solution in your own mind."

"I can make neither head nor tail of it."

"The head is surely clear enough and the tail we should see to-morrow. Did you notice nothing curious about that advertisement?"

"I saw that the word 'plough' was mis-spelt."

"Oh, you did notice that, did you? Come, Watson, you improve all the time. Yes, it was bad English but good American. The printer had set it up as received. Then the buckboards. That is American also. And artesian wells are commoner with them than with us. It was a typical American advertisement, but purporting to be from an English firm. What do you make of that?"

"I can only suppose that this American lawyer put it in himself. What his object was I fail to understand."

"Well, there are alternative explanations. Anyhow, he wanted to get this good old fossil up to Birmingham. That is very clear. I might have told him that he was clearly going on a wild-goose chase, but, on second thoughts, it seemed better to clear the stage by letting him go. To-morrow, Watson—well, to-morrow will speak for itself."

Holmes was up and out early. When he returned at lunchtime I noticed that his face was very grave.

"This is a more serious matter than I had expected, Watson," said he. "It is fair to tell you so, though I know it will only be an additional reason to you for running your head into danger. I should know my Watson by now. But there *is* danger, and you should know it."

"Well, it is not the first we have shared, Holmes. I hope it may not be the last. What is the particular danger this time?"

"We are up against a very hard case. I have identified Mr. John Garrideb, Counsellor at Law. He is none other than 'Killer' Evans, of sinister and murderous reputation."

"I fear I am none the wiser."

"Ah, it is not part of your profession to carry about a portable Newgate Calendar[25] in your memory. I have been down to see friend Lestrade at the Yard. There may be an occasional want of imaginative intuition down there, but they lead the world for thoroughness and method. I had an idea that we might get on the track of our American friend in their records. Sure enough, I found his chubby face smiling up at me from the Rogues' Portrait Gallery. 'James Winter, *alias* Morecroft, *alias* Killer Evans', was the inscription below." Holmes drew an envelope from his pocket. "I scribbled down a few points from his dossier. Aged forty-four. Native of Chicago. Known to have shot three men in the States. Escaped from penitentiary through political influence. Came to London in 1893. Shot a man over cards in a night-club in the Waterloo Road in January, 1895. Man died, but he was shown to have been the aggressor in the row. Dead man was identified as Rodger Prescott,[26] famous as forger and coiner in Chicago. Killer Evans released in 1901. Has been under police supervision since, but so far as known has led an honest life. Very dangerous man, usually carries arms and is prepared to use them. That is our bird, Watson—a sporting bird, as you must admit."

"But what is his game?"

"Well, it begins to define itself. I have been to the house-agent's. Our client, as he told us, has been there five years. It

25 *The Newgate Calendar* was a series of wildly popular books containing accounts of prisoners who had been incarcerated at Newgate. In the various editions—the first of which was entitled *The Malefactor's Register or New Newgate and Tyburn Calendar*—readers could learn all about criminals such as Hannah Dagoe, from Ireland, "of that numerous class of women who ply at Covent Garden Market as basket-women." The accused broke into the

Newgate Prison, to which the "Calendar" applies.
Queen's London (1897)

house of the widow Eleanor Hussey, stealing all of her possessions, and was promptly tried and sentenced to death. According to the account, Dagoe was "a strong, masculine woman, the terror of her fellow-prisoners, and actually stabbed one of the men who had given evidence against her; but the wound happened not to prove dangerous." After being transported to Tyburn on May 4, 1763, for her execution, Dagoe wrestled free of the constraints binding her hands, struck the executioner, and began removing articles of her clothing and throwing them into the crowd. The executioner managed to get the rope around her neck, whereupon she hurled herself out of the cart, in effect killing herself before the signal was given. Or Holmes might have happened upon the story of George Allen, an epileptic who murdered his three children in 1807. "Insanity probably caused the horrid deed to be committed which we are now going to relate," the account opens sadly. Allen's wife had barely escaped her husband's attack on her when "one of the children (the girl) fell at her feet, with her head almost cut off, which he had murdered and thrown after her. The woman opened the door and screamed out that her husband was cutting off their children's heads. A neighbour soon came to her assistance, and when a light was procured the monster was found standing in the middle of the house-place with a razor in his hand. When asked what he had been doing, he replied coolly: 'Nothing yet: I have only killed three of them!' "

26 "Presbury" in the *Strand Magazine* text, here and throughout the remainder of the account.

27 This was probably a Webley Metropolitan Police Model (see appendix to "The Speckled Band"). Yet H. T. Webster considers the Webley inadequate for the task for which

was unlet for a year before then. The previous tenant was a gentleman at large named Waldron. Waldron's appearance was well remembered at the office. He had suddenly vanished and nothing more been heard of him. He was a tall, bearded man with very dark features. Now, Prescott, the man whom Killer Evans had shot, was, according to Scotland Yard, a tall, dark man with a beard. As a working hypothesis, I think we may take it that Prescott, the American criminal, used to live in the very room which our innocent friend now devotes to his museum. So at last we get a link, you see."

"And the next link?"

"Well, we must go now and look for that."

He took a revolver from the drawer and handed it to me.

"I have my old favourite[27] with me. If our Wild West friend tries to live up to his nickname, we must be ready for him. I'll give you an hour for a siesta, Watson, and then I think it will be time for our Ryder Street adventure."

It was just four o'clock when we reached the curious apartment of Nathan Garrideb. Mrs. Saunders, the caretaker, was about to leave, but she had no hesitation in admitting us, for the door shut with a spring lock, and Holmes promised to see that all was safe before we left. Shortly afterwards the outer door closed, her bonnet passed the show window, and we knew that we were alone in the lower floor of the house. Holmes made a rapid examination of the premises. There was one cupboard in a dark corner which stood out a little from the wall. It was behind this that we eventually crouched, while Holmes in a whisper outlined his intentions.

"He wanted to get our amiable friend out of his room—that is very clear, and, as the collector never went out, it took some planning to do it. The whole of this Garrideb invention was apparently for no other end. I must say, Watson, that there is a certain devilish ingenuity about it even if the queer name of the tenant did give him an opening which he could hardly have expected. He wove his plot with remarkable cunning."[28]

"But what did he want?"

"Well, that is what we are here to find out. It has nothing whatever to do with our client, so far as I can read the situation.

It is something connected with the man he murdered—the man who may have been his confederate in crime. There is some guilty secret in the room. That is how I read it. At first I thought our friend might have something in his collection more valuable than he knew—something worth the attention of a big criminal. But the fact that Rodger Prescott of evil memory inhabited these rooms points to some deeper reason. Well, Watson, we can but possess our souls in patience and see what the hour may bring."

That hour was not long in striking. We crouched closer in the shadow as we heard the outer door open and shut. Then came the sharp, metallic snap of a key,[29] and the American was in the room. He closed the door softly behind him, took a sharp glance around him to see that all was safe, threw off his overcoat, and walked up to the central table with the brisk manner of one who knows exactly what he has to do and how to do it. He pushed the table to one side, tore up the square of carpet on which it rested, rolled it completely back, and then, drawing a jemmy from his inside pocket, he knelt down and worked vigorously upon the floor. Presently we heard the sound of sliding boards, and an instant later a square had opened in the planks. Killer Evans struck a match, lit a stump of candle, and vanished from our view.

Clearly our moment had come. Holmes touched my wrist as a signal, and together we stole across to the open trap-door. Gently as we moved, however, the old floor must have creaked under our feet, for the head of our American, peering anxiously round, emerged suddenly from the open space. His face turned upon us with a glare of baffled rage, which gradually softened into a rather shamefaced grin as he realized that two pistols were pointed at his head.

"Well, well!" said he coolly, as he scrambled to the surface. "I guess you have been one too many for me, Mr. Holmes. Saw through my game, I suppose, and played me for a sucker from the first. Well, sir, I hand it to you; you have me beat and—"

In an instant he had whisked out a revolver from his breast and had fired two shots. I felt a sudden hot sear as if a red-hot iron had been pressed to my thigh. There was a crash as Holmes's pistol came down on the man's head. I had a vision of him sprawling upon the floor with blood running down his

Holmes soon uses it, which is to strike Evans over the head and render him momentarily senseless. In "Observations on Sherlock Holmes as an Athlete and Sportsman," he describes the Webley as "a very inefficient bludgeon" and guesses that Holmes was using another type of gun—perhaps a Colt Frontier Model .45 or some other type of sturdy American gun, possibly given to Holmes by a grateful client such as Sir Henry Baskerville (who lived in Canada and likely in America as well).

28 The ingenuity of the plot seems far superior to the ingenuity of the man, in the opinion of Gavin Brend. He deems the crime "a work of art" but declares Killer Evans to possess "rather a humdrum personality"—so much so that he may not have cooked up the scheme himself, but instead sought the advice of one of his more clever associates. And who might this associate have been? "There exists a theory," Brend proposes, "that most criminals repeat certain details every time they commit a crime, so that they may be said to write their signatures across it. If this be so then the signature on *The Three Garridebs* can easily be read. It is one that we have met before . . . in the matter of *The Red-Headed League*. It is the signature of the most interesting of all Holmes's opponents, our old acquaintance, John Clay, once of Eton and Oxford, the grandson of a Royal Duke." Of course, one might also recognise this case's strong similarity to "The Stock-Broker's Clerk." Perhaps Killer Evans devised the plan after a careful reading of *The Adventures of Sherlock Holmes* and *The Memoirs of Sherlock Holmes*!

29 Where, one wonders, did Evans obtain a key?

His face turned upon us with a glare of baffled rage, which
gradually softened into a rather shamefaced grin as he
realized that two pistols were pointed at his head.
Howard Elcock, *Strand Magazine*, 1925

face while Holmes rummaged him for weapons. Then my
friend's wiry arms were round me, and he was leading me to a
chair.

"You're not hurt, Watson? For God's sake, say that you are
not hurt!"

It was worth a wound—it was worth many wounds—to know
the depth of loyalty and love which lay behind that cold mask.
The clear, hard eyes were dimmed for a moment, and the firm
lips were shaking. For the one and only time I caught a
glimpse of a great heart as well as of a great brain. All my years
of humble but single-minded service culminated in that
moment of revelation.

"It's nothing, Holmes. It's a mere scratch."

He had ripped up my trousers with his pocket-knife.

"You are right," he cried with an immense sigh of relief. "It is quite superficial." His face set like flint as he glared at our prisoner, who was sitting up with a dazed face. "By the Lord, it is as well for you. If you had killed Watson, you would not have got out of this room alive. Now, sir, what have you to say for yourself?"

He had nothing to say for himself. He only lay and scowled. I leaned on Holmes's arm, and together we looked down into the small cellar which had been disclosed by the secret flap. It was still illuminated by the candle which Evans had taken down with him. Our eyes fell upon a mass of rusted machinery, great rolls of paper, a litter of bottles, and, neatly arranged upon a small table, a number of neat little bundles.

"A printing press—a counterfeiter's outfit," said Holmes.

"Yes, sir," said our prisoner, staggering slowly to his feet and then sinking into the chair. "The greatest counterfeiter London ever saw. That's Prescott's machine, and those bundles on the table are two thousand of Prescott's notes worth a hundred each and fit to pass anywhere. Help yourselves, gentlemen. Call it a deal and let me beat it."

Holmes laughed.

"We don't do things like that, Mr. Evans. There is no bolt-hole for you in this country. You shot this man Prescott, did you not?"

"Yes, sir, and got five years for it, though it was he who pulled on me. Five years—when I should have had a medal the size of a soup plate. No living man could tell a Prescott from a Bank of England, and if I hadn't put him out he would have flooded London with them. I was the only one in the world who knew where he made them. Can you wonder that I wanted to get to the place? And can you wonder that when I found this crazy boob of a bug-hunter with the queer name squatting right on the top of it, and never quitting his room, I had to do the best I could to shift him? Maybe I would have been wiser if I had put him away. It would have been easy enough, but I'm a soft-hearted guy that can't begin shooting unless the other man has a gun also. But say, Mr. Holmes, what have I done wrong, anyhow? I've not used this plant. I've not hurt this old stiff. Where do you get me?"

"Only attempted murder, so far as I can see," said Holmes.

There was a crash as Holmes's pistol came down on the man's head.
Howard Elcock, *Strand Magazine*, 1925

30 Why did Holmes not let Garrideb down easily, sparing him the shock which evidently led to his breakdown? Perhaps, asserts W. W. Robson, because Holmes was intent on capture of the criminal and (as noted above) had concluded that Garrideb could not be trusted with the truth. If so, Nathan Garrideb must join the short list of clients ill-served by having engaged Holmes's services (including John Openshaw of "The Five Orange Pips" and Hilton Cubitt of "The Dancing Men").

"But that's not our job. They take that at the next stage. What we wanted at present was just your sweet self. Please give the Yard a call, Watson. It won't be entirely unexpected."

So those were the facts about Killer Evans and his remarkable invention of the three Garridebs. We heard later that our poor old friend never got over the shock of his dissipated dreams. When his castle in the air fell down, it buried him beneath the ruins. He was last heard of at a nursing-home in Brixton.[30] It was a glad day at the Yard when the Prescott outfit was discovered, for, though they knew that it existed, they had never been able, after the death of the man, to find out where it was.[31] Evans had indeed done great service and caused several worthy C. I. D. men to sleep the sounder, for the counterfeiter stands in a class by himself as a public danger. They would willingly have subscribed to that soup-plate medal of which the criminal had spoken, but an unappreciative bench took a less favourable view, and the Killer returned to those shades from which he had just emerged.

31 It is no tribute to the "worthy C.I.D. men" that the Prescott outfit could be successfully hidden in *Prescott's own apartment* and yet not be discovered.

THE PROBLEM OF THOR BRIDGE[1]

Although Watson is surely the writer of "Thor Bridge," here he mistakenly claims service in the "Indian Army." Perhaps his memory was beginning to dim as he celebrated his seventy-first birthday in 1922, when the case was published. In this tale, Watson records another confrontation of Holmes's with money and power, in the guise of Neil Gibson, the "Gold King." Although his true identity has been the subject of much speculation, this American millionaire seems to be almost a caricature of the British idea of "Gilded Age" Americans—fabulously rich, crude, stubborn, cold, and violent. Here too are other staples of Holmes's world: the beautiful governess, the dark South American beauty. But all is not what it seems here, and Holmes must reach deep to solve the clue of the chipped stonework.

1 "Thor Bridge" was published in the *Strand Magazine* in February/March 1922 and in *Hearst's International Magazine* in February/March 1922. The title page of the manuscript, which is owned by a private collector, shows that the tale had several alternate titles: "[The Little Tin?] Box," "The Adventure of the Second Chip," and "The Problem of Rushmere Bridge"—and that the *final* title was "The Problem of Thor's [*sic*] Bridge."

2 At 48-49 The Strand is located the Charing Cross branch of Lloyds TSB Bank, and a sign above the entrance declares "Cox & Co." Sherlockians have traditionally identified this location as the home of Watson's "tin dispatch-box."

SOMEWHERE IN THE vaults of the bank of Cox & Co.,[2] at Charing Cross, there is a travel-worn and battered tin dispatch-box with my name, John H.[3] Watson, M.D., Late Indian Army,[4] painted upon the lid. It is crammed with papers, nearly all of which are records of cases to illustrate the curious problems which Mr. Sherlock Holmes had at various times to examine. Some, and not the least interesting, were complete failures, and as such will hardly bear narrating, since no final explanation is forthcoming. A problem without a solution may interest the student, but can hardly fail to annoy the casual reader. Among these unfinished tales is that of Mr. James Phillimore, who, stepping back into his own house to get his umbrella, was never more seen in this world.[5] No less remarkable is that of the cutter *Alicia*, which sailed one spring morning into a small patch of mist from where she never again emerged, nor was anything further ever heard of herself and her crew.[6] A third case worthy of note is that of Isadora Persano, the well-known journalist and duellist, who was found stark staring mad with a match box in front of him which contained a remarkable worm said to be unknown to science.[7] Apart from these unfathomed cases, there are some which involve the secrets of private families to an extent which would mean consternation in many exalted quarters if it were thought possible that they might find their way into print. I need not say that such a breach of confidence is unthinkable, and that these records will be separated and destroyed now that my friend has time to turn his energies to the matter. There remain a considerable residue of cases of greater or less interest which I might have edited before had I not feared to give the public a surfeit which might react upon the reputation of the man whom above all others I revere. In some I was myself concerned and can speak as an eye-witness, while in others I was either not present or played so small a part that they could only be told as by a third person.[8] The following narrative is drawn from my own experience.

It was a wild morning in October, and I observed as I was dressing how the last remaining leaves were being whirled from the solitary plane tree[9] which graces the yard behind our house. I descended to breakfast prepared to find my companion in depressed spirits, for, like all great artists, he was easily impressed by his surroundings, On the contrary, I found that he had nearly finished his meal, and that his mood was particularly bright and joyous, with that somewhat sinister cheerfulness which was characteristic of his lighter moments.

"You have a case, Holmes?" I remarked.

"The faculty of deduction is certainly contagious, Watson," he answered. "It has enabled you to probe my secret. Yes, I have a case. After a month of trivialities and stagnation the wheels move once more."

"Might I share it?"

"There is little to share, but we may discuss it when you have consumed the two hard-boiled eggs with which our new cook[10] favoured us. Their condition may not be unconnected with the copy of the *Family Herald*[11] which I observed yesterday upon the hall-table. Even so trivial a matter as cooking an egg demands an attention which is conscious of the passage of time, and incompatible with the love romance in that excellent periodical."

3 Watson's middle initial appears only three times: here, at the foot of the sketch plan illustrating "The Priory School" (in the *Strand Magazine* in February 1904), and on the title page of *A Study in Scarlet*. Dorothy L. Sayers, in her classic article "Dr. Watson's Christian Name," argues that the "H" stands for "Hamish," a Scotch name equivalent to "James" (see "The Man with the Twisted Lip" for an instance in which Watson's wife refers to him as "James"). Several others propose "Henry," primarily because of the high contemporary regard for cleric John Henry Newman. Still others, for varied but ultimately unconvincing reasons, propose "Hampton," "Harrington," "Hector," "Horatio," "Hubert," and "Huffham." One wag even suggests "Holmes"!

4 According to Watson's previous accounts, he served in the Berkshires and the Northumberland Fusiliers, which were regiments of the British army sent over to India. This means, as Crighton Sellars points out in her essential "Dr. Watson and the British Army," that he was never actually in the Indian Army, a separate organisation altogether.

5 Phillimore's mysterious disappearance has inspired the "James Phillimore Society," a group of Sherlockians who are devoted to magic and science fiction.

6 Philip Weller notes, "*Lloyd's Sailing Vessels* for 1891–92 includes a wooden sea bark called the 'Alicia,' which was built in 1877, and which was wrecked in 1891."

7 Speculations abound regarding the remarkable worm. Edgar W. Smith embraces the amusing suggestion of Rolfe Boswell, who thought of the worm not as a biological specimen but as an optical illusion used in the German Gestalt school of psychology. One could hypnotise oneself, or possibly go mad, by staring at a whirling spiral an inch in diameter. Boswell likened the effect to that of staring fixedly at a coiled watch spring, and noted that the *Shorter Oxford Dictionary* gave one definition of "worm" as "A spring or strip of metal of spiral shape 1724." "Presumably," Boswell wrote, "if you gaze at such a worm long enough, you'll be *Persano non grata*, if not 'stark staring mad.' "

A more serious effort is put forward by R. P. Graham, who unearths an 1819 article that was written by Sir John Ross (uncle of famed Antarctic explorer Sir James Clark Ross, both of whom sailed in search of the Northwest Passage in 1818) and entitled "A Voyage of Discovery, made under the Orders of the Admiralty, in His Majesty's Ships *Isabella* and *Alexander*, for the Purpose of Exploring Baffin's Bay and Enquiring into the Probability of a North-West Passage." Ross's work contains the intriguing text, "we sounded with the deepsea clamms, which brought up a quantity of mud, in which were *five worms of a species that had not been seen before.*" Graham asks, "Who of Ross's crew . . . preserved these Baffin Bay worms, and who put one of their

descendants into a match-box to help drive poor Isadora Persano 'stark staring mad'?"

Startlingly, in the manuscript of "Thor Bridge," Watson originally records the "worm" as a caterpillar.

8 See "The Mazarin Stone" and "His Last Bow."

9 Referred to as a sycamore or buttonwood tree in the United States.

10 Previously, Mrs. Hudson has handled the cooking; as Christopher Redmond recalls, "The incident [in 'The Three Students'] when Mrs. Hudson promises 'green peas at seven-thirty' gives no indication that they were to be prepared by anyone other than herself." Holmes's reference to a new cook must mean that Mrs. Holmes has finally hired someone else to handle the kitchen duties, or else that Holmes formerly employed a cook who has mysteriously never been mentioned.

11 A family-interest magazine established in 1842.

A quarter of an hour later the table had been cleared and we were face to face. He had drawn a letter from his pocket.

"You have heard of Neil Gibson, the Gold King?" he said.

"You mean the American Senator?"

"Well, he was once Senator for some Western state, but is better known as the greatest gold-mining magnate in the world."

"Yes, I know of him. He has surely lived in England for some time. His name is very familiar."

"Yes; he bought a considerable estate in Hampshire some five years ago. Possibly you have already heard of the tragic end of his wife?"

"Of course, I remember it now. That is why the name is familiar. But I really know nothing of the details."

Holmes waved his hand towards some papers on a chair. "I had no idea that the case was coming my way or I should have had my extracts ready," said he. "The fact is that the problem, though exceedingly sensational, appeared to present no difficulty. The interesting personality of the accused does not obscure the clearness of the evidence. That was the view taken by the coroner's jury and also in the police-court proceedings. It is now referred to the Assizes at Winchester. I fear it is a thankless business. I can discover facts, Watson, but I cannot change them. Unless some entirely new and unexpected ones come to light I do not see what my client can hope for."

"Your client?"

"Ah, I forgot I had not told you. I am getting into your involved habit, Watson, of telling a story backward. You had best read this first."

The letter which he handed to me, written in a bold, masterful hand, ran as follows:

CLARIDGE'S HOTEL,
October 3rd.
DEAR MR. SHERLOCK HOLMES:
I can't see the best woman God ever made go to her death without doing all that is possible to save her. I can't explain things—I can't even try to explain them, but I know beyond

12 At that time, a woman was considered a spinster if she had not married by her early twenties, and thus Miss Dunbar may have been no more than twenty-three. It was a different era indeed. Historian A. N. Wilson, speculating on whether Charles Dodgson (better known as Lewis Carroll, author of *Alice's Adventures in Wonderland*) might have proposed to Alice Liddell—the "real" Alice—when he was thirty-one and she was eleven, concedes that such a proposal would have been considered improper, but not necessarily criminal. "This probably seems more shocking to a twenty-first-century sensibility than it might have done to the Victorians," he writes, noting that the 1861 census reveals that 175 women in Bolton and 179 in Burnley married at the age of fifteen or younger.

Miss Dunbar is one of several women clients of Holmes's who, being unmarried, turn to governess work to support themselves (see "The Copper Beeches," note 9). The others are Violet Hunter ("The Copper Beeches") and Violet Smith ("The Solitary Cyclist").

13 In the manuscript of "Thor Bridge," the note sets the appointment for eight o'clock, and the body is found at midnight.

all doubt that Miss Dunbar is innocent. You know the facts—who doesn't? It has been the gossip of the country.

And never a voice raised for her! It's the damned injustice of it all that makes me crazy. That woman has a heart that wouldn't let her kill a fly. Well, I'll come at eleven to-morrow and see if you can get some ray of light in the dark. Maybe I have a clue and don't know it. Anyhow, all I know and all I have and all I am are for your use if only you can save her. If ever in your life you showed your powers, put them now into this case.

Yours faithfully,
J. NEIL GIBSON.

"There you have it," said Sherlock Holmes, knocking out the ashes of his after-breakfast pipe and slowly refilling it. "That is the gentleman I await. As to the story, you have hardly time to master all these papers, so I must give it to you in a nutshell if you are to take an intelligent interest in the proceedings. This man is the greatest financial power in the world, and a man, as I understand, of most violent and formidable character. He married a wife, the victim of this tragedy, of whom I know nothing save that she was past her prime,[12] which was the more unfortunate as a very attractive governess superintended the education of two young children. These are the three people concerned, and the scene is a grand old manor house, the centre of an historical English state. Then as to the tragedy. The wife was found in the grounds nearly half a mile from the house, late at night, clad in her dinner dress, with a shawl over her shoulders and a revolver bullet through her brain. No weapon was found near her and there was no local clue as to the murder. No weapon near her, Watson—mark that. The crime seems to have been committed late in the evening, and the body was found by a game-keeper about eleven o'clock,[13] when it was examined by the police and by a doctor before being carried up to the house. Is this too condensed, or can you follow it clearly?"

"It is all very clear. But why suspect the governess?"

"Well, in the first place there is some very direct evidence. A revolver with one discharged chamber and a calibre which corresponded with the bullet was found on the floor of her wardrobe." His eyes fixed and he repeated in broken words,

14 That is, the coroner's court and the police court.

"The wife was found in the grounds, late at night,
with a revolver bullet through her brain."
A. Gilbert, *Strand Magazine*, 1922

"On-the-floor-of-her-wardrobe." Then he sank into silence, and I saw that some train of thought had been set moving which I should be foolish to interrupt. Suddenly with a start he emerged into brisk life once again. "Yes, Watson, it was found. Pretty damning, eh? So the two juries[14] thought. Then the dead woman had a note upon her making an appointment at that very place and signed by the governess. How's that? Finally there is the motive. Senator Gibson is an attractive person. If his wife dies, who more likely to succeed her than the young lady who had already by all accounts received pressing attentions from her employer? Love, fortune, power, all depending upon one middle-aged life. Ugly, Watson—very ugly!"

"Yes, indeed, Holmes."

"Nor could she prove an alibi. On the contrary, she had to admit that she was down near Thor Bridge—that was the scene of the tragedy—about that hour. She couldn't deny it, for some passing villager had seen her there."

"That really seems final."

15 Billy appears only in "Thor Bridge," "The Mazarin Stone," and *The Valley of Fear*.

16 Mark Hunter-Purves makes the interesting suggestion that Bates was in love with Mrs. Gibson and stayed on at the Gibson estate only to be near her.

"And yet, Watson—and yet! This bridge—a single broad span of stone with balustraded sides—carries the drive over the narrowest part of a long, deep, reed-girt sheet of water. Thor Mere it is called. In the mouth of the bridge lay the dead woman. Such are the main facts. But here, if I mistake not, is our client, considerably before his time."

Billy[15] had opened the door, but the name which he announced was an unexpected one. Mr. Marlow Bates was a stranger to both of us. He was a thin, nervous wisp of a man with frightened eyes and a twitching, hesitating manner—a man whom my own professional eye would judge to be on the brink of an absolute nervous breakdown.

"You seem agitated, Mr. Bates," said Holmes. "Pray sit down. I fear I can only give you a short time, for I have an appointment at eleven."

"I know you have," our visitor gasped, shooting out short sentences like a man who is out of breath. "Mr. Gibson is coming. Mr. Gibson is my employer. I am manager of his estate, Mr. Holmes, he is a villain—an infernal villain."

"Strong language, Mr. Bates."

"I have to be emphatic, Mr. Holmes, for the time is so limited. I would not have him find me here for the world. He is almost due now. But I was so situated that I could not come earlier. His secretary, Mr. Ferguson, only told me this morning of his appointment with you."

"And you are his manager?"

"I have given him notice. In a couple of weeks I shall have shaken off his accursed slavery.[16] A hard man, Mr. Holmes, hard to all about him. Those public charities are a screen to cover his private iniquities. But his wife was his chief victim. He was brutal to her—yes, sir, brutal! How she came by her death I do not know, but I am sure that he had made her life a misery to her. She was a creature of the tropics, a Brazilian by birth, as no doubt you know."

"No; it had escaped me."

"Tropical by birth and tropical by nature. A child of the sun and of passion. She had loved him as such women can love, but when her own physical charms had faded—I am told that they once were great—there was nothing to hold him. We all liked her and felt for her and hated him for the way that he treated her. But he is plausible and cunning. That is all I have to say to you. Don't take him at his face value. There is more behind. Now I'll go. No, no, don't detain me! He is almost due."

With a frightened look at the clock our strange visitor literally ran to the door and disappeared.

"Well! well!" said Holmes after an interval of silence. "Mr. Gibson seems to have a nice loyal household. But the warning is a useful one, and now we can only wait till the man himself appears."

Sharp at the hour we heard a heavy step upon the stairs, and the famous millionaire was shown into the room. As I looked upon him I understood not only the fears and dislike of his manager, but also the execrations which so many business rivals have heaped upon his head. If I were a sculptor and desired to idealize the successful man of affairs, iron of nerve and leathery of conscience, I should choose Mr. Neil Gibson as my model. His tall, gaunt, craggy figure had a suggestion of hunger and rapacity. An Abraham Lincoln keyed to base uses instead of high ones would give some idea of the man. His face might have been chiselled in granite, hard-set, craggy, remorseless, with deep lines upon it, the scars of many a crisis. Cold grey eyes, looking shrewdly out from under bristling brows, surveyed us each in turn. He bowed in perfunctory fashion as Holmes mentioned my name, and then with a masterful air of possession he drew a chair up to my companion and seated himself with his bony knees almost touching him.

"Let me say right here, Mr. Holmes," he began, "that money is nothing to me in this case. You can burn it if it's any use in lighting you to the truth. This woman is innocent and this woman has to be cleared, and it's up to you to do it. Name your figure!"

"My professional charges are upon a fixed scale,"[17] said Holmes coldly. "I do not vary them, save when I remit them altogether."

"Well, if dollars make no difference to you, think of the reputation. If you pull this off every paper in England and America will be booming[18] you. You'll be the talk of two continents."

"Thank you, Mr. Gibson, I do not think that I am in need of booming. It may surprise you to know that I prefer to work anonymously, and that it is the problem itself which attracts me. But we are wasting time. Let us get down to the facts."

"I think that you will find all the main ones in the press reports. I don't know that I can add anything which will help you. But if there is anything you would wish more light upon—well, I am here to give it."

"Well, there is just one point."

"What is it?"

"What were the actual relations between you and Miss Dunbar?"

The Gold King gave a violent start and half rose from his chair. Then his massive calm came back to him.

"I suppose you are within your rights—and maybe doing your duty—in asking such a question, Mr. Holmes."

"We will agree to suppose so," said Holmes.

"Then I can assure you that our relations were entirely and always those of an employer towards a young lady whom he never conversed with, or ever saw, save when she was in the company of his children."

Holmes rose from his chair.

"I am a rather busy man, Mr. Gibson," said he, "and I have no time or taste for aimless conversations. I wish you good-morning."

Our visitor had risen also, and his great loose figure towered above Holmes. There was an angry gleam from under those bristling brows and a tinge of colour in the sallow cheeks.

"What the devil do you mean by this, Mr. Holmes? Do you dismiss my case?"

"Well, Mr. Gibson, at least I dismiss you. I should have thought my words were plain."

"Plain enough, but what's at the back of it? Raising the price on me, or afraid to tackle it, or what? I've a right to a plain answer."

"Well, perhaps you have," said Holmes. "I'll give you one. This case is quite sufficiently complicated to start with without the further difficulty of false information."

"Meaning that I lie."

"Well, I was trying to express it as delicately as I could, but if you insist upon the word I will not contradict you."

I sprang to my feet, for the expression upon the millionaire's face was fiendish in its intensity, and he had raised his great

"I sprang to my feet, for the expression upon the millionaire's
face was fiendish in its intensity, and he had raised his
great knotted fist. Holmes smiled languidly and
reached his hand out for his pipe."
A. Gilbert, *Strand Magazine*, 1922

knotted fist. Holmes smiled languidly and reached his hand
out for his pipe.

"Don't be noisy, Mr. Gibson. I find that after breakfast even
the smallest argument is unsettling. I suggest that a stroll in the
morning air and a little quiet thought will be greatly to your
advantage."

With an effort the Gold King mastered his fury. I could not
but admire him, for by a supreme self-command he had turned
in a minute from a hot flame of anger to a frigid and contemp-
tuous indifference.

"Well, it's your choice. I guess you know how to run your own business. I can't make you touch the case against your will. You've done yourself no good this morning, Mr. Holmes, for I have broken stronger men than you. No man ever crossed me and was the better for it."

"So many have said so, and yet here I am," said Holmes, "Well, good-morning, Mr. Gibson. You have a good deal yet to learn."

Our visitor made a noisy exit, but Holmes smoked in imperturbable silence with dreamy eyes fixed upon the ceiling.

"Any views, Watson?" he asked at last.

"Well, Holmes, I must confess that when I consider that this is a man who would certainly brush any obstacle from his path, and when I remember that his wife may have been an obstacle and an object of dislike, as that man Bates plainly told us, it seems to me—"

"Exactly. And to me also."

"But what were his relations with the governess, and how did you discover them?"

"Bluff, Watson, bluff! When I considered the passionate, unconventional, unbusinesslike tone of his letter and contrasted it with his self-contained manner and appearance, it was pretty clear that there was some deep emotion which centred upon the accused woman rather than upon the victim. We've got to understand the exact relations of those three people if we are to reach the truth. You saw the frontal attack which I made upon him, and how imperturbably he received it. Then I bluffed him by giving him the impression that I was absolutely certain, when in reality I was only extremely suspicious."

"Perhaps he will come back?"

"He is sure to come back. He *must* come back. He can't leave it where it is. Ha! isn't that a ring? Yes, there is his footstep. Well, Mr. Gibson, I was just saying to Dr. Watson that you were somewhat overdue."

The Gold King had re-entered the room in a more chastened mood than he had left it. His wounded pride still showed in his resentful eyes, but his common sense had shown him that he must yield if he would attain his end.

"I've been thinking it over, Mr. Holmes, and I feel that I have been hasty in taking your remarks amiss. You are justified in getting down to the facts, whatever they may be, and I think the more of you for it. I can assure you, however, that the relations between Miss Dunbar and me don't really touch this case."

"That is for me to decide, is it not?"

"Yes, I guess that is so. You're like a surgeon who wants every symptom before he can give his diagnosis."

"Exactly. That expresses it. And it is only a patient who has an object in deceiving his surgeon who would conceal the facts of his case."

"That may be so, but you will admit, Mr. Holmes, that most men would shy off a bit when they are asked point-blank what their relations with a woman may be—if there is really some serious feeling in the case. I guess most men have a little private reserve of their own in some corner of their souls where they don't welcome intruders. And you burst suddenly into it. But the object excuses you, since it was to try and save her. Well, the stakes are down and the reserve open, and you can explore where you will. What is it you want?"

"The truth."

The Gold King paused for a moment as one who marshals his thoughts. His grim, deep-lined face had become even sadder and more grave.

"I can give it to you in a very few words, Mr. Holmes," said he at last. "There are some things that are painful as well as difficult to say, so I won't go deeper than is needful. I met my wife when I was gold-hunting in Brazil.[19] Maria Pinto was the daughter of a government official at Manáos,[20] and she was very beautiful. I was young and ardent in those days, but even now, as I look back with colder blood and a more critical eye, I can see that she was rare and wonderful in her beauty. It was a deep rich nature, too, passionate, whole-hearted, tropical, ill-balanced, very different from the American women whom I had known. Well, to make a long story short, I loved her and I married her. It was only when the romance had passed—and it lingered for years—that I realized that we had nothing—absolutely nothing—in common. My love faded. If hers had faded also it might have been easier. But you know the wonderful way of women! Do what I might, nothing could turn her

19 Brazil experienced a gold rush starting in 1695, when large deposits were discovered in what is now Minas Gerais. The discovery had a tremendous impact on the settlement and economy of Brazil; prospectors quickly established mining towns, and slaves were brought in from sugar plantations and the gold mines in Africa. With so much money coming into the region, the Portuguese government moved the colonial capital from Salvador to Rio de Janeiro in 1763. The boom lasted only as long as the original deposits held out, although mining continued on a far more reduced scale. Despite the failure of many mines, however, as late as 1888, the *Encylopædia Britannica* still alluringly promised its readers that "the underground wealth of the country is as yet almost untouched." Whether Gibson made his fortune in Brazilian gold or in "some Western state," as seems more likely, is unknown.

20 The port city of Manáos (now Manaus) is the capital of the state of Amazonas, in northwestern Brazil. Overlooking the Rio Negro and located deep within the Amazonian rainforest, Manáos is sparsely populated, the only city within a six-hundred-mile radius. The majority of its wealth from 1890 to 1920—a short-lived period of glory—was generated through the production of rubber, leading to construction of a modern port in Manáos that was completed by 1900. One may surmise a lonely existence for the young, beautiful girl, and a romance with the ardent Gibson may have offered Senhorita Pinto a tantalising opportunity to leave that life behind.

from me. If I have been harsh to her, even brutal as some have said, it has been because I knew that if I could kill her love, or if it turned to hate, it would be easier for both of us. But nothing changed her. She adored me in those English woods as she had adored me twenty years ago on the banks of the Amazon. Do what I might, she was as devoted as ever.

"Then came Miss Grace Dunbar. She answered our advertisement and became governess to our two children. Perhaps you have seen her portrait in the papers. The whole world has proclaimed that she also is a very beautiful woman. Now, I make no pretence to be more moral than my neighbours, and I will admit to you that I could not live under the same roof with such a woman and in daily contact with her without feeling a passionate regard for her. Do you blame me, Mr. Holmes?"

"I do not blame you for feeling it. I should blame you if you expressed it, since this young lady was in a sense under your protection."

"Well, maybe so," said the millionaire, though for a moment the reproof had brought the old angry gleam into his eyes. "I'm not pretending to be any better than I am. I guess all my life I've been a man that reached out his hand for what he wanted, and I never wanted anything more than the love and possession of that woman. I told her so."

"Oh, you did, did you?"

Holmes could look very formidable when he was moved.

"I said to her that if I could marry her I would, but that it was out of my power. I said that money was no object and that all I could do to make her happy and comfortable would be done."

"Very generous, I am sure," said Holmes with a sneer.

"See here, Mr. Holmes. I came to you on a question of evidence, not on a question of morals. I'm not asking for your criticism."

"It is only for the young lady's sake that I touch your case at all," said Holmes sternly. "I don't know that anything she is accused of is really worse than what you have yourself admitted, that you have tried to ruin a defenceless girl who was under your roof. Some of you rich men have to be taught that all the world cannot be bribed into condoning your offences."

To my surprise the Gold King took the reproof with equanimity.

"That's how I feel myself about it now. I thank God that my

plans did not work out as I intended. She would have none of it, and she wanted to leave the house instantly."

"Why did she not?

"Well, in the first place, others were dependent upon her, and it was no light matter for her to let them all down by sacrificing her living. When I had sworn—as I did—that she should never be molested again, she consented to remain. But there was another reason. She knew the influence she had over me, and that it was stronger than any other influence in the world. She wanted to use it for good."

"How?"

"Well, she knew something of my affairs. They are large, Mr. Holmes—large beyond the belief of an ordinary man. I can make or break—and it is usually break. It wasn't individuals only. It was communities, cities, even nations. Business is a hard game, and the weak go to the wall. I played the game for all it was worth. I never squealed myself, and I never cared if the other fellow squealed. But she saw it different. I guess she was right. She believed and said that a fortune for one man that was more than he needed should not be built on ten thousand ruined men who were left without the means of life. That was how she saw it, and I guess she could see past the dollars to something that was more lasting. She found that I listened to what she said, and she believed she was serving the world by influencing my actions. So she stayed—and then this came along."

"Can you throw any light upon that?"

The Gold King paused for a minute or more, his head sunk in his hands, lost in deep thought.

"It's very black against her. I can't deny that. And women lead an inward life and may do things beyond the judgment of a man. At first I was so rattled and taken aback that I was ready to think she had been led away in some extraordinary fashion that was clean against her usual nature. One explanation came into my head. I give it to you, Mr. Holmes, for what it is worth. There is no doubt that my wife was bitterly jealous. There is a soul-jealousy that can be as frantic as any body-jealousy, and though my wife had no cause—and I think she understood this—for the latter, she was aware that this English girl exerted

21 To interview Grace Dunbar in prison.

an influence upon my mind and my acts that she herself never had. It was an influence for good, but that did not mend the matter. She was crazy with hatred, and the heat of the Amazon was always in her blood. She might have planned to murder Miss Dunbar—or we will say to threaten her with a gun and so frighten her into leaving us, then there might have been a scuffle and the gun gone off and shot the woman who held it."

"That possibility had already occurred to me," said Holmes. "Indeed, it is the only obvious alternative to deliberate murder."

"But she utterly denies it."

"Well, that is not final—is it? One can understand that a woman placed in so awful a position might hurry home still in her bewilderment holding the revolver. She might even throw it down among her clothes, hardly knowing what she was doing, and when it was found she might try to lie her way out by a total denial, since all explanation was impossible. What is against such a supposition?"

"Miss Dunbar herself."

"Well, perhaps."

Holmes looked at his watch. "I have no doubt we can get the necessary permits[21] this morning and reach Winchester by the evening train. When I have seen this young lady it is very possible that I may be of more use to you in the matter, though I cannot promise that my conclusions will necessarily be such as you desire."

There was some delay in the official pass, and instead of reaching Winchester that day we went down to Thor Place, the Hampshire estate of Mr. Neil Gibson. He did not accompany us himself, but we had the address of Sergeant Coventry, of the local police, who had first examined into the affair. He was a tall, thin, cadaverous man, with a secretive and mysterious manner which conveyed the idea that he knew or suspected a very great deal more than he dared say. He had a trick, too, of suddenly sinking his voice to a whisper as if he had come upon something of vital importance, though the information was usually commonplace enough. Behind these tricks of manner he soon showed himself to be a decent, honest fellow who was not too proud to admit that he was out of his depth and would welcome any help.

"Anyhow, I'd rather have you than Scotland Yard, Mr. Holmes," said he. "If the Yard gets called into a case, then the local loses all credit for success and may be blamed for failure. Now, you play straight, so I've heard."

"I need not appear in the matter at all," said Holmes to the evident relief of our melancholy acquaintance. "If I can clear it up I don't ask to have my name mentioned."

"Well, it's very handsome of you, I am sure. And your friend, Dr. Watson, can be trusted, I know. Now, Mr. Holmes, as we walk down to the place there is one question I should like to ask you. I'd breathe it to no soul but you." He looked round as though he hardly dare utter the words. "Don't you think there might be a case against Mr. Neil Gibson himself?"

"I have been considering that."

"You've not seen Miss Dunbar. She is a wonderfully fine woman in every way. He may well have wished his wife out of the road. And these Americans are readier with pistols than our folk are. It was his pistol, you know."

"Was that clearly made out?"

"Yes, sir. It was one of a pair that he had."

"One of a pair? Where is the other?"

"Well, the gentleman has a lot of fire-arms of one sort and another. We never quite matched that particular pistol—but the box was made for two."

"If it was one of a pair you should surely be able to match it."

"Well, we have them all laid out at the house if you would care to look them over."

"Later, perhaps. I think we will walk down together and have a look at the scene of the tragedy."

This conversation had taken place in the little front room of Sergeant Coventry's humble cottage, which served as the local police-station. A walk of half a mile or so across a wind-swept heath, all gold and bronze with the fading ferns, brought us to a side-gate opening into the grounds of the Thor Place estate. A path led us through the pheasant preserves, and then from a clearing we saw the widespread, half-timbered house, half Tudor and half Georgian, upon the crest of the hill. Beside us there was a long, reedy pool, constricted in the centre where the main carriage drive passed over a stone bridge, but swelling into small lakes on either side. Our guide paused at the mouth of this bridge, and he pointed to the ground.

"That was where Mrs. Gibson's body lay. I marked it by that stone."

"I understand that you were there before it was moved?"

"Yes; they sent for me at once."

"Who did?"

"Mr. Gibson himself. The moment the alarm was given and he had rushed down with others from the house, he insisted that nothing should be moved until the police should arrive."

"That was sensible. I gathered from the newspaper report that the shot was fired from close quarters."

"Yes, sir. Very close."

"Our guide pointed to the ground.
'That was where Mrs. Gibson's body lay.'"
A. Gilbert, *Strand Magazine*, 1922

"Near the right temple?"

"Just behind it, sir."

"How did the body lie?"

"On the back, sir. No trace of a struggle. No marks. No weapon. The short note from Miss Dunbar was clutched in her left hand."

"Clutched, you say?"

"Yes, sir, we could hardly open the fingers."

"That is of great importance. It excludes the idea that anyone could have placed the note there after death in order to furnish a false clue. Dear me! The note, as I remember, was quite short.

I will be at Thor Bridge at nine o'clock.—
                                            G. DUNBAR.

"Is that not so?"

"Yes, sir."

"Did Miss Dunbar admit writing it?"

"Yes, sir."

"What was her explanation?"

"Her defence was reserved for the Assizes. She would say nothing."

"The problem is certainly a very interesting one. The point of the letter is very obscure, is it not?"

"Well, sir," said the guide, "it seemed, if I may be so bold as to say so, the only really clear point in the whole case."

Holmes shook his head.

"Granting that the letter is genuine and was really written, it was certainly received some time before—say one hour or two. Why, then, was this lady still clasping it in her left hand? Why should she carry it so carefully? She did not need to refer to it in the interview. Does it not seem remarkable?"

"Well, sir, as you put it, perhaps it does."

"I think I should like to sit quietly for a few minutes and think it out." He seated himself upon the stone ledge of the bridge, and I could see his quick grey eyes darting their questioning glances in every direction. Suddenly he sprang up again and ran across to the opposite parapet, whipped his lens from his pocket, and began to examine the stonework.

"This is curious," said he.

"Yes, sir, we saw the chip on the ledge. I expect it's been done by some passer-by."

The stonework was grey, but at this one point it showed white for a space not larger than a sixpence. When examined closely one could see that the surface was chipped as by a sharp blow.

"It took some violence to do that," said Holmes thoughtfully. With his cane he struck the ledge several times without leaving a mark. "Yes, it was a hard knock. In a curious place, too. It was not from above but from below, for you see that it is on the *lower* edge of the parapet."

"But it is at least fifteen feet from the body."

" 'It took some violence to do that,' said Holmes, gazing at the chip on the ledge. With his cane he struck the ledge several times without leaving a mark. 'Yes, it was a hard knock.' "
A. Gilbert, *Strand Magazine*, 1922

"Yes, it is fifteen feet from the body. It may have nothing to do with the matter, but it is a point worth noting. I do not think that we have anything more to learn here. There were no foot-steps, you say?"

"The ground was iron hard, sir. There were no traces at all."

"Then we can go. We will go up to the house first and look over these weapons of which you speak. Then we shall get on to Winchester, for I should desire to see Miss Dunbar before we go farther."

Mr. Neil Gibson had not returned from town, but we saw in the house the neurotic Mr. Bates who had called upon us in the morning. He showed us with a sinister relish the formidable array of fire-arms of various shapes and sizes which his employer had accumulated in the course of an adventurous life.

"Mr. Gibson has his enemies, as anyone would expect who knew him and his methods," said he. "He sleeps with a loaded revolver in the drawer beside his bed. He is a man of violence, sir, and there are times when all of us are afraid of him. I am sure that the poor lady who has passed was often terrified."

"Did you ever witness physical violence towards her?"

"No, I cannot say that. But I have heard words which were nearly as bad—words of cold, cutting contempt, even before the servants."

"Our millionaire does not seem to shine in private life," remarked Holmes as we made our way to the station. "Well, Watson, we have come on a good many facts, some of them new ones, and yet I seem some way from my conclusion. In spite of the very evident dislike which Mr. Bates has to his employer, I gather from him that when the alarm came he was undoubtedly in his library. Dinner was over at 8:30 and all was normal up to then. It is true that the alarm was somewhat late in the evening, but the tragedy certainly occurred about the hour named in the note. There is no evidence at all that Mr. Gibson had been out of doors since his return from town at five o'clock. On the other hand, Miss Dunbar, as I understand it, admits that she had made an appointment to meet Mrs. Gib-son at the bridge. Beyond this she would say nothing, as her lawyer had advised her to reserve her defence. We have several very vital questions to ask that young lady, and my mind will not be easy until we have seen her. I must confess that the case would seem to me to be very black against her if it were not for one thing."

"And what is that, Holmes?"

"The finding of the pistol in her wardrobe."

"Dear me, Holmes!" I cried, "that seemed to me to be the most damning incident of all."

"Not so, Watson. It had struck me even at my first perfunctory reading as very strange, and now that I am in closer touch with the case it is my only firm ground for hope. We must look for consistency. Where there is a want of it we must suspect deception."

"I hardly follow you."

"Well now, Watson, suppose for a moment that we visualize you in the character of a woman who, in a cold, premeditated fashion, is about to get rid of a rival. You have planned it. A note has been written. The victim has come. You have your weapon. The crime is done. It has been workmanlike and complete. Do you tell me that after carrying out so crafty a crime you would now ruin your reputation as a criminal by forgetting to fling your weapon into those adjacent reed-beds which would forever cover it, but you must needs carry it carefully home and put it in your own wardrobe, the very first place that would be searched? Your best friends would hardly call you a schemer, Watson, and yet I could not picture you doing anything so crude as that."

"In the excitement of the moment—"

"No, no, Watson, I will not admit that it is possible. Where a crime is coolly premeditated, then the means of covering it are coolly premeditated also. I hope, therefore, that we are in the presence of a serious misconception."

"But there is so much to explain."

"Well, we shall set about explaining it. When once your point of view is changed, the very thing which was so damning becomes a clue to the truth. For example, there is this revolver. Miss Dunbar disclaims all knowledge of it. On our new theory she is speaking truth when she says so. Therefore, it was placed in her wardrobe. Who placed it there? Someone who wished to incriminate her. Was not that person the actual criminal? You see how we come at once upon a most fruitful line of enquiry."[22]

We were compelled to spend the night at Winchester, as the formalities had not yet been completed, but next morning, in the company of Mr. Joyce Cummings, the rising barrister who was entrusted with the defence,[23] we were allowed to see the young lady in her cell. I had expected from all that we had heard to see a beautiful woman, but I can never forget the effect which Miss Dunbar produced upon me. It was no wonder that even the masterful millionaire had found in her something more powerful than himself—something which could control and guide him. One felt, too, as one looked at that strong, clear-cut, and yet sensitive face, that even should she be capable of some impetuous deed, none the less there was an innate nobility of character which would make her influence always for the good. She was a brunette, tall, with a noble figure and commanding presence, but her dark eyes had in them the appealing, helpless expression of the hunted creature who feels the nets around it, but can see no way out from the toils. Now, as she realized the presence and the help of my famous friend, there came a touch of colour in her wan cheeks and a light of hope began to glimmer in the glance which she turned upon us.

"Perhaps Mr. Neil Gibson has told you something of what occurred between us?" she asked, in a low, agitated voice.

"Yes," Holmes answered; "you need not pain yourself by entering into that part of the story. After seeing you, I am prepared to accept Mr. Gibson's statement both as to the influence which you had over him and as to the innocence of your relations with him.[24] But why was the whole situation not brought out in court?"

"It seemed to me incredible that such a charge could be sustained. I thought that if we waited the whole thing must clear itself up without our being compelled to enter into painful details of the inner life of the family. But I understand that far from clearing it has become even more serious."

"My dear young lady," cried Holmes earnestly, "I beg you to have no illusions upon the point. Mr. Cummings here would

22 Here ended the first instalment in the *Strand Magazine* text. The following appeared there: "The extraordinary solution of this enthralling problem will appear next month." The second instalment of the case, published in the March 1922 issue of the *Strand Magazine*, contained a synopsis of the first part of the story, reproduced as an *Appendix*.

23 W. W. Robson is surprised that a man of Gibson's means would retain a "rising barrister" rather than a more experienced member of the Queen's Counsel. To be appointed to the Queen's Counsel (King's Counsel when the sovereign was male) was an honour of the highest distinction, and such barristers were eligible to write "Q.C." after their names as well as to wear silk gowns in court. At one point, King's and Queen's Counsel barristers served as counsel to the Crown, but that function was phased out until only the honour remained. Gibson may well have found that the Q.C.s whom he undoubtedly approached had no interest in taking on "this thankless business."

24 For someone who often cautions Watson against letting a client's appearance lead his judgement, Holmes seems to have let his guard down here to an astonishing degree. Only one look at Miss Dunbar somehow persuades Holmes that she is wholly innocent of wrongdoing. As Nathan L. Bengis marvels, "Is this the same man who boasted of never making exceptions?"

assure you that all the cards are at present against us, and that we must do everything that is possible if we are to win clear. It would be a cruel deception to pretend that you are not in very great danger. Give me all the help you can, then, to get at the truth."

"I will conceal nothing."

"Tell us, then, of your true relations with Mr. Gibson's wife."

"She hated me, Mr. Holmes. She hated me with all the fervour of her tropical nature. She was a woman who would do nothing by halves, and the measure of her love for her husband was the measure also of her hatred for me. It is probable that she misunderstood our relations. I would not wish to wrong her, but she loved so vividly in a physical sense that she could hardly understand the mental, and even spiritual, tie which held her husband to me, or imagine that it was only my desire to influence his power to good ends which kept me under his roof. I can see now that I was wrong. Nothing could justify me in remaining where I was a cause of unhappiness, and yet it is certain that the unhappiness would have remained even if I had left the house."

"Now, Miss Dunbar," said Holmes, "I beg you to tell us exactly what occurred that evening."

"I can tell you the truth so far as I know it, Mr. Holmes, but I am in a position to prove nothing, and there are points—the most vital points—which I can neither explain nor can I imagine any explanation."

"If you will find the facts, perhaps others may find the explanation."

"With regard, then, to my presence at Thor Bridge that night, I received a note from Mrs. Gibson in the morning. It lay on the table of the schoolroom, and it may have been left there by her own hand. It implored me to see her there after dinner, said she had something important to say to me, and asked me to leave an answer on the sundial in the garden, as she desired no one to be in our confidence. I saw no reason for such secrecy, but I did as she asked, accepting the appointment. She asked me to destroy her note and I burned it in the schoolroom grate. She was very much afraid of her husband, who treated her with a harshness for which I frequently reproached him, and I could only imagine that she acted in this way because she did not wish him to know of our interview."

"Yet she kept your reply very carefully?"

"Yes. I was surprised to hear that she had it in her hand when she died."

"Well, what happened then?"

"I went down as I had promised. When I reached the bridge she was waiting for me. Never did I realize till that moment how this poor creature hated me. She was like a mad woman—indeed, I think she *was* a mad woman, subtly mad with the deep power of deception which insane people may have. How else could she have met me with unconcern every day and yet had so raging a hatred of me in her heart? I will not say what she said. She poured her whole wild fury out in burning and horrible words. I did not even answer—I could not. It was dreadful to see her. I put my hands to my ears and rushed away.

"She poured her whole wild fury out in burning and horrible words—
I put my hands to my ears and rushed away."
A. Gilbert, *Strand Magazine*, 1922

When I left her she was standing still shrieking out her curses at me, in the mouth of the bridge."

"Where she was afterwards found?"

"Within a few yards from the spot."

"And yet, presuming that she met her death shortly after you left her, you heard no shot?"

"No, I heard nothing. But, indeed, Mr. Holmes, I was so agitated and horrified by this terrible outbreak that I rushed to get back to the peace of my own room, and I was incapable of noticing anything which happened."

"You say that you returned to your room. Did you leave it again before next morning?"

"Yes, when the alarm came that the poor creature had met her death I ran out with the others."

"Did you see Mr. Gibson?"

"Yes; he had just returned from the bridge when I saw him. He had sent for the doctor and the police."

"Did he seem to you much perturbed?"

"Mr. Gibson is a very strong, self-contained man. I do not think that he would ever show his emotions on the surface. But I, who knew him so well, could see that he was deeply concerned."

"Then we come to the all-important point. This pistol that was found in your room. Had you ever seen it before?"

"Never, I swear it."

"When was it found?"

"Next morning, when the police made their search."

"Among your clothes?"

"Yes; on the floor of my wardrobe under my dresses."

"You could not guess how long it had been there?"

"It had not been there the morning before."

"How do you know?"

"Because I tidied out the wardrobe."

"That is final. Then someone came into your room and placed the pistol there in order to inculpate you."

"It must have been so."

"And when?"

"It could only have been at meal-time, or else at the hours when I would be in the schoolroom with the children."

"As you were when you got the note?"

"Yes; from that time onward for the whole morning."

"Thank you, Miss Dunbar. Is there any other point which could help me in the investigation?"

"I can think of none."

"There was some sign of violence on the stonework of the bridge—a perfectly fresh chip just opposite the body. Could you suggest any possible explanation of that?"

"Surely it must be a mere coincidence."

"Curious, Miss Dunbar, very curious. Why should it appear at the very time of the tragedy, and why at the very place?"

"But what could have caused it? Only great violence could have such an effect."[25]

Holmes did not answer. His pale, eager face had suddenly assumed that tense, far-away expression which I had learned to associate with the supreme manifestations of his genius. So evident was the crisis in his mind that none of us dared to speak, and we sat, barrister, prisoner, and myself, watching him in a concentrated and absorbed silence. Suddenly he sprang from his chair, vibrating with nervous energy and the pressing need for action.

"Come, Watson, come!" he cried.

"What is it, Mr. Holmes?"

"Never mind, my dear lady. You will hear from me, Mr. Cummings. With the help of the god of justice I will give you a case which will make England ring. You will get news by to-morrow, Miss Dunbar, and meanwhile take my assurance that the clouds are lifting and that I have every hope that the light of truth is breaking through."

It was not a long journey from Winchester to Thor Place, but it was long to me in my impatience, while for Holmes it was evident that it seemed endless; for, in his nervous restlessness, he could not sit still, but paced the carriage or drummed with his long, sensitive fingers upon the cushions beside him. Suddenly, however, as we neared our destination he seated himself opposite to me—we had a first-class carriage to ourselves—and laying a hand upon each of my knees he looked into my eyes with the peculiarly mischievous gaze which was characteristic of his more imp-like moods.

"Watson," said he, "I have some recollection that you go armed upon these excursions of ours."

25 Why would Miss Dunbar exhibit such strong interest in this trivial incident? Robert Hahn explains that she did in fact murder Maria Gibson, in order to marry Neil Gibson. She planted clues and induced Gibson to call in Holmes, so that he could "save" her. When Holmes faltered, Dunbar called his attention to the vital clue—the chip.

26 In attempting to puzzle out what kind of weapon it is that Watson carries, Stanton O. Berg, a firearms consultant, calls particular attention to the mention of a safety catch. "Manual safeties on revolvers are rather rare," Berg explains, "and even more rare when one must confine it to a revolver in existence in the year 1900. *[O]nly the Webley Mark III Pocket Revolver in the .380 caliber . . . fits the time frame of this story*" [Berg's emphasis].

"Suddenly Holmes sprang from his chair. 'Come, Watson, come!' he said. 'With the help of the God of justice I will give you a case which will make England ring.' "
A. Gilbert, *Strand Magazine*, 1922

It was as well for him that I did so, for he took little care for his own safety when his mind was once absorbed by a problem, so that more than once my revolver had been a good friend in need. I reminded him of the fact.

"Yes, yes, I am a little absent-minded in such matters. But have you your revolver on you?"

I produced it from my hip-pocket, a short, handy, but very serviceable little weapon. He undid the catch,[26] shook out the cartridges, and examined it with care.

"It's heavy—remarkably heavy," said he.

"Yes, it is a solid bit of work."

He mused over it for a minute.

"Do you know, Watson," said he, "I believe your revolver is going to have a very intimate connection with the mystery which we are investigating."

"My dear Holmes, you are joking."

"No, Watson, I am very serious. There is a test before us. If the test comes off, all will be clear. And the test will depend upon the conduct of this little weapon. One cartridge out. Now we will replace the other five and put on the safety-catch. So! That increases the weight and makes it a better reproduction."

I had no glimmer of what was in his mind, nor did he enlighten me, but sat lost in thought until we pulled up in the little Hampshire station. We secured a ramshackle trap, and in a quarter of an hour were at the house of our confidential friend, the sergeant.

"A clue, Mr. Holmes? What is it?"

"It all depends upon the behaviour of Dr. Watson's revolver," said my friend. "Here it is. Now, officer, can you give me ten yards of string?"

The village shop provided a ball of stout twine.

"I think that this is all we will need," said Holmes. "Now, if you please, we will get off on what I hope is the last stage of our journey."

The sun was setting and turning the rolling Hampshire moor into a wonderful autumnal panorama. The sergeant, with many critical and incredulous glances, which showed his deep doubts of the sanity of my companion, lurched along beside us. As we approached the scene of the crime I could see that my friend under all his habitual coolness was in truth deeply agitated.

"Yes," he said in answer to my remark, "you have seen me miss my mark before, Watson. I have an instinct for such things, and yet it has sometimes played me false. It seemed a certainty when first it flashed across my mind in the cell at Winchester, but one drawback of an active mind is that one can always conceive alternative explanations which would make our scent a false one. And yet—and yet—Well, Watson, we can but try."[27]

As he walked he had firmly tied one end of the string to the handle of the revolver. We had now reached the scene of the tragedy. With great care he marked out under the guidance of the policeman the exact spot where the body had been stretched. He then hunted among the heather and the ferns

27 "The motto of the firm," according to Holmes—see "The Creeping Man," note 18.

until he found a considerable stone. This he secured to the other end of his line of string, and he hung it over the parapet of the bridge so that it swung clear above the water. He then stood on the fatal spot, some distance from the edge of the bridge, with my revolver in his hand, the string being taut between the weapon and the heavy stone on the farther side.

"Now for it!" he cried.

At the words he raised the pistol to his head, and then let go his grip. In an instant it had been whisked away by the weight of the stone, had struck with a sharp crack against the parapet, and had vanished over the side into the water. It had hardly

"Holmes was kneeling beside the stonework, and a joyous cry showed that he had found what he expected."
A. Gilbert, *Strand Magazine*, 1922

gone before Holmes was kneeling beside the stonework, and a joyous cry showed that he had found what he expected.

"Was there ever a more exact demonstration?" he cried. "See, Watson, your revolver has solved the problem!" As he spoke he pointed to a second chip of the exact size and shape of the first which had appeared on the under edge of the stone balustrade.[28]

"We'll stay at the inn to-night," he continued as he rose and faced the astonished sergeant. "You will, of course, get a grappling-hook and you will easily restore my friend's revolver. You will also find beside it the revolver, string and weight with which this vindictive woman attempted to disguise her own crime[29] and to fasten a charge of murder upon an innocent victim.[30] You can let Mr. Gibson know that I will see him in the morning, when steps can be taken for Miss Dunbar's vindication."

Late that evening, as we sat together smoking our pipes in the village inn, Holmes gave me a brief review of what had passed.

"I fear, Watson," said he, "that you will not improve any reputation which I may have acquired by adding the Case of the Thor Bridge Mystery to your annals. I have been sluggish in mind and wanting in that mixture of imagination and reality which is the basis of my art. I confess that the chip in the stonework was a sufficient clue to suggest the true solution, and that I blame myself for not having attained it sooner.

"It must be admitted that the workings of this unhappy woman's mind were deep and subtle, so that it was no very simple matter to unravel her plot. I do not think that in our adventures we have ever come across a stranger example of what perverted love can bring about. Whether Miss Dunbar was her rival in a physical or in a merely mental sense seems to have been equally unforgivable in her eyes. No doubt she blamed this innocent lady for all those harsh dealings and unkind words with which her husband tried to repel her too demonstrative affection. Her first resolution was to end her own life. Her second was to do it in such a way as to involve her victim in a fate which was worse far than any sudden death could be.

"We can follow the various steps quite clearly, and they show

28 G. Arthur Morrison disputes the result. A chip "no larger than a sixpence" would, according to his calculations, have required five times the force generated by a two-pound revolver that was flung fifteen feet by a heavy stone. "One may object that the stonework was in a cracked, crumbled condition and thus easily chipped," Morrison writes, "but if this were the case, the newly exposed surface would not be a pristine white, but a dull grey like the surrounding surface because of moisture seepage." Morrison suggests that Watson and Holmes together concocted the tale recorded by Watson (drawing on the Hans Gross book, discussed below) to conceal the real facts: that Marlo Bates and Miss Dunbar were having an affair, that Bates killed Mrs. Gibson (in a struggle initiated by her drawing her pistol), and that Bates devised a scheme to divert suspicion from Miss Dunbar by leaving too-obvious clues.

29 Suicide, or "self-murder," was a criminal offence in England—largely unpunishable, of course; but until 1870, the personal property of one who had committed suicide became forfeit to the Crown. Mrs. Gibson was far from alone in seeking to end her life of unhappiness. "London," Peter Ackroyd writes, "was the suicide capital of Europe. As early as the fourteenth century Froissart described the English as 'a very sad race,' which description applied particularly and even principally to Londoners." Half-facetiously, Ackroyd observes that others have blamed London's fog, the consumption of beef, "a contempt of death and a disgust of life," the wine sold in London taverns, and the theatre for the "London vogue for suicides." "Everything was blamed," Ackroyd concludes, "except, perhaps, for the onerous and exhausting condition of the city itself." Perhaps the melancholy of the city (combined with rabid jealousy) was especially jarring to Mrs. Gibson's "whole-hearted, tropical, ill-balanced" nature.

30 There seems little doubt that Holmes was familiar with the writings of Dr. Hans Gross, professor of criminology at the University of Graz, Austria, whose great work on criminal investigation, *Handbuch für Untersuchungsrichter*, was published in 1893. The case described by Gross is reproduced in "The Original 'Problem of Thor Bridge,'" page 1633.

31 What does the future hold for the striking governess? June Thomson concludes that Dr. Watson, rather than Neil Gibson, later married Miss Dunbar but kept her identity secret, not only because he wished to conceal that he had married a woman who had been in prison on a murder charge but also to avoid attracting the vengeance of Gibson. But John Hall thinks little of Grace Dunbar's character, charging that some of the blame for the unfortunate events should be assigned to her. She was aware that her presence in the household was straining relations between her employers, making for an awkward and ethically troubling situation. "Surely anyone with a grain of common decency would have wanted to get out of it as quickly as possible," Hall writes, "if only to avoid further embarrassment to themselves?" As to her claim that she wished only to do good with her influence, Hall mostly dismisses that line of reasoning, noting that "the cynic might well suspect that there was also a certain satisfaction to be derived from the knowledge that Mrs. Gibson was consumed with an overweening jealousy and hatred. . . . It may well be that Holmes, when he spoke of Miss Dunbar and Mr. Gibson joining forces, thought that they thoroughly deserved one another."

32 "Thor Bridge," with its superb storytelling and characterisations, is another story that escapes the authorial doubts D. Martin Dakin affixes to many tales in *The Case-Book*. "While we must decisively reject ["The Lion's Mane," "The Blanched Soldier," "The

a remarkable subtlety of mind. A note was extracted very cleverly from Miss Dunbar which would make it appear that she had chosen the scene of the crime. In her anxiety that it should be discovered she somewhat overdid it, by holding it in her hand to the last. This alone should have excited my suspicions earlier than it did.

"Then she took one of her husband's revolvers—there was, as you saw, an arsenal in the house—and kept it for her own use. A similar one she concealed that morning in Miss Dunbar's wardrobe after discharging one barrel, which she could easily do in the woods without attracting attention. She then went down to the bridge where she had contrived this exceedingly ingenious method for getting rid of her weapon. When Miss Dunbar appeared she used her last breath in pouring out her hatred, and then, when she was out of hearing, carried out her terrible purpose. Every link is now in its place and the chain is complete. The papers may ask why the mere was not dragged in the first instance, but it is easy to be wise after the event, and in any case the expanse of a reed-filled lake is no easy matter to drag unless you have a clear perception of what you are looking for and where. Well, Watson, we have helped a remarkable woman, and also a formidable man. Should they in the future join their forces, as seems not unlikely,[31] the financial world may find that Mr. Neil Gibson has learned something in that schoolroom of Sorrow where our earthly lessons are taught."[32] ∎

SYNOPSIS OF THE FIRST PART OF THE STORY

(Strand Magazine, March 1922)

"THE THREE leading figures in this Adventure are Neil Gibson, a famous gold-mining magnate, his wife, and their children's young governess, the attractive Miss Dunbar. The wife was found in the grounds of Thor Place, nearly half a mile from the house, late at night, clad in her dinner dress, with a revolver bullet through her brain. No weapon was found near her. There was no trace of a struggle, but in her left hand was clutched a note reading: 'I will be at Thor Bridge at nine o'clock.—G. Dunbar.' Later, the police discovered on the floor of the wardrobe in the governess's room a revolver with one discharged chamber and a calibre which corresponded with the bullet. Miss Dunbar, when arrested, could prove no alibi—on the contrary, she admitted she was near Thor Bridge, the scene of the tragedy, about the time of Mrs. Gibson's death. She also admitted writing the note, but would say no more.

"Gibson urges Sherlock Holmes to spare neither trouble nor expense to clear Miss Dunbar. 'It's very black against her,' he admits. 'I can't deny that. . . . And there is no doubt that my wife was bitterly jealous.'

"The revolver is found to belong to Gibson, but there is no evidence that he had been out of doors since his return from town at five o'clock. Miss Dunbar, on the other hand, admitted making the appointment with Mrs. Gibson.

"On viewing the scene of the tragedy, Sherlock Holmes's careful examination of the bridge reveals a small and apparently recently-made chip on the parapet. 'It took some violence to do that,' said Holmes, thoughtfully. 'It was a hard knock. In a curious place, too. It was not from above but from below, for you see that it is on the lower edge of the parapet.'

"As the following instalment shows, this apparently insignificant chip in the stone was really the clue to the solution of the mystery."

Mazarin Stone," and "The Three Gables"], there are others in the collection that bear just as clearly the stamp of authenticity," he writes. "*Thor Bridge* is one. The plot and style are excellent, and it shows in every line the marks of a genuine Watson reminiscence. Holmes dealing with the regrettable Mr. Neil Gibson, the Gold King, is Holmes at his best."

THE ORIGINAL "PROBLEM OF THOR BRIDGE"

DR. HANS GROSS (1847–1915) was professor of criminology at the University of Graz, Austria, and one of the founders of police science. In his monumental *Handbuch für Untersuchungsrichter* (Handbook for Criminal Investigators), Gross reports the following case:

Early one morning the authorities were informed that the corpse of a murdered man had been found. At the spot indicated, in the middle of a bridge crossing a rather deep stream, the body was found of a grain merchant, A. M., supposed to be a well-to-do man, face downward with a gunshot wound behind the ear. The bullet, after passing through the brain, had lodged in the frontal bone above the left eye. His pocket book was missing and the seam of the inside pocket in which it was usually carried was ripped up, as if the pocket-book had been rapidly and violently snatched out. His watch and chain were also missing; of the latter the ring attaching it to the waistcoat button was alone left. A policeman stated that A. M. had been seen the evening before in a spirit shop, where he drank with moderation and left about 10:30 P.M., stating he was about to return home. To reach his house he had to pass over the bridge where he was found dead. In the spirit shop there was at the same time as A. M. an unknown, wretched-looking man, who throughout the evening drank but a single glass of spirits and left shortly after A. M. The latter had several times taken out his pocket-book, which appeared well filled, though no one could say whether he had any money or how much. The supposition was therefore natural that the unknown had followed A. M., murdered him on the bridge, and robbed him; he was accordingly searched for, arrested, and brought to the spot. He denied all knowledge of the crime and said he had passed the night in a barn, which however he could not point out to the police. Just when the inquiry was concluding and the corpse was about to be removed after the postmortem, the Investigating Officer observed quite by chance that on the decayed wooden parapet of the bridge, almost opposite the spot where the corpse lay, there was a small, but perfectly fresh injury which appeared to have been caused by the violent blow on the upper edge of the parapet of a hard and angular body. He immediately suspected that this injury had some connection with the murder; examination with a magnifying glass showed nothing important, but it was impossible to avoid the impression that here the murderer had thrown something into the water and thus damaged the parapet. Accordingly the Investigating Officer determined to drag the bed of the stream below the bridge, when almost immediately there was picked up a strong cord about 14 feet long with a large stone at one end and at the other a discharged pistol, the barrel of which fitted exactly the bullet extracted from the head of A. M. The case was thus evidently one of suicide; A. M. had hung the stone over the parapet of the bridge and discharged the pistol behind his ear. The moment he fired he let go the pistol, which the weight of the stone dragged over the parapet into the water, but the pistol had struck violently against the parapet in passing over and so caused the injury observed. Experiment showed the trick to be quite easy and that the parapet was damaged every time. Subsequent inquiries disclosed that the pistol actually belonged to A. M., that his affairs were hopelessly involved, and that he had just effected an insurance on his life for the benefit of his family for a large sum. As the company did not pay in cases of suicide, A. M. had adopted this means to conceal the suicide and lead to the belief that he had been murdered.[33]

33 Translation by Patrick J. Leonard, Sr., in "Thor Bridge—A Mystery Remains."

THE ADVENTURE OF THE CREEPING MAN[1]

"The Creeping Man" is more of a science-fiction story than a mystery, but the science of the tale is well grounded in medical trends of the day. In this story, Holmes is called in to discover the reasons that the respectable Professor Presbury has taken up courting a woman his daughter's age. Watson demonstrates here that Holmes's attitude toward dogs has changed markedly from his cold (but not cruel) dog poisoning in A Study in Scarlet. *Now Holmes sees dogs as the mirror of their household, and he even plans a monograph on the topic. While the case, with its outlandish plot of a drug-based "fountain of youth," has elements that seem laughable today, the obsessions of Professor Presbury and his fellow Victorians are not dissimilar from those reflected in current medical headlines.*

1 "The Creeping Man" was published in the *Strand Magazine* and in *Hearst's International Magazine* in March 1923.

2 "Is there not something a little odd about this?" asks Catherine Cooke, in " 'The Singular Facts Connected with Professor Presbury.' " "Surely throughout most of the canon it is Watson who wants to publish and Holmes who discourages and forbids him or who pours scorn on those accounts which do see the light of day? Why then this sudden change?"

3 "We"? Is this the editorial "we"? Does Watson here refer to Arthur Conan Doyle and himself? Or is this a statement that Holmes and Watson consulted regarding publication? If the latter, then this may be taken as confir-

Mr. Sherlock Holmes was always of opinion that I should publish the singular facts connected with Professor Presbury, if only to dispel once for all the ugly rumours which some twenty years ago agitated the University and were echoed in the learned societies of London.[2] There were, however, certain obstacles in the way, and the true history of this curious case remained entombed in the tin box which contains so many records of my friend's adventures. Now we[3] have at last obtained permission to ventilate the facts which formed one of the very last cases handled by Holmes before his retirement from practice. Even now a certain reticence and discretion have to be observed in laying the matter before the public.

It was one Sunday evening early in September of the year 1903 that I received one of Holmes's laconic messages:

Come at once if convenient—if inconvenient come all the same.

S. H.

The relations between us in those latter days were peculiar. He was a man of habits, narrow and concentrated habits, and I had become one of them. As an institution I was like the violin, the shag tobacco, the old black pipe, the index books, and others perhaps less excusable. When it was a case of active work and a comrade was needed upon whose nerve he could place some reliance, my rôle was obvious. But apart from this I had uses. I was a whetstone for his mind. I stimulated him. He liked to think aloud in my presence. His remarks could hardly be said to be made to me—many of them would have been as appropriately addressed to his bedstead—but none the less, having formed the habit, it had become in some way helpful that I should register and interject. If I irritated him by a certain methodical slowness in my mentality, that irritation served only to make his own flame-like intuitions and impressions flash up the more vividly and swiftly. Such was my humble rôle in our alliance.[4]

When I arrived at Baker Street[5] I found him huddled up in his arm-chair with updrawn knees, his pipe in his mouth and his brow furrowed with thought. It was clear that he was in the throes of some vexatious problem. With a wave of his hand he indicated my old arm-chair, but otherwise for half an hour he gave no sign that he was aware of my presence. Then with a start he seemed to come from his reverie, and, with his usual whimsical smile, he greeted me back to what had once been my home.

"You will excuse a certain abstraction of mind, my dear Watson," said he. "Some curious facts have been submitted to me within the last twenty-four hours, and they in turn have given rise to some speculations of a more general character. I have serious thoughts of writing a small monograph upon the uses of dogs in the work of the detective."

"But surely, Holmes, this has been explored," said I. "Bloodhounds—sleuth-hounds—"

"No, no, Watson; that side of the matter is, of course, obvious. But there is another which is far more subtle. You may recollect that in the case which you, in your sensational way,

mation that Holmes was alive and well in 1923, twenty years after the events of this case and nine years after the events of "His Last Bow," the last recorded case of Sherlock Holmes.

4 Watson is being too modest. In "The Blanched Soldier," generally given the date of January 1903, Holmes remarks, "Speaking of my old friend and biographer . . . Watson has some remarkable characteristics of his own, to which in his honesty he has given small attention amid his exaggerated estimates of my own performances." Yet Dorothy L. Sayers sees more than meets the eye in Watson's assessment of his "humble rôle," and she wonders whether his soliloquy might be a subtle expression of bitterness at Holmes's treatment of him through the years. In "Dr. Watson, Widower," she observes that Watson seems hurt at being considered "a mere convenience, like the fiddle and the old pipe, to be picked up or cast aside as Holmes's fancy took him. His faithful heart was really wounded." For further evidence she points to "The Mazarin Stone" (thought to have occurred in 1903, the same year as "The Creeping Man"), in which Watson distances himself from his old friend, plunging himself into his practice and bearing "every sign of the busy medical man." "When the call comes," Sayers writes, "he answers it, but not quite with the old alacrity. 'Was it for so trivial a question as this that I had been summoned from my work?' he asks himself, with a touch of bitterness. . . . Never before had he resented an intrusion on his 'work.'"

5 Watson is now living, one assumes, with his wife (see "The Blanched Soldier," note 5, for a discussion of *which* wife).

6 The original title of *A Study in Scarlet*. There Holmes remarks, "There's the scarlet thread of murder running through the colourless skein of life, and our duty is to unravel it, and isolate it, and expose every inch of it."

7 Watson coyly hides the location of the tale, and scholars have debated whether "Camford" is Cambridge or Oxford. Without expressing his reasoning, T. S. Blakeney asserts flatly that this is a "transparent alias" for Cambridge. Nicholas Utechin concludes that it is Oxford, on the basis of Holmes's familiarity with the Chequers inn and the train schedules. Other observations and arguments are noted below.

coupled with the Copper Beeches, I was able, by watching the mind of the child, to form a deduction as to the criminal habits of the very smug and respectable father."

"Yes, I remember it well."

"My line of thoughts about dogs is analogous. A dog reflects the family life. Whoever saw a frisky dog in a gloomy family, or a sad dog in a happy one? Snarling people have snarling dogs, dangerous people have dangerous ones. And their passing moods may reflect the passing moods of others."

I shook my head. "Surely, Holmes, this is a little far-fetched," said I.

He had refilled his pipe and resumed his seat, taking no notice of my comment.

"The practical application of what I have said is very close to the problem which I am investigating. It is a tangled skein,[6] you understand, and I am looking for a loose end. One possible loose end lies in the question: Why does Professor Presbury's faithful wolf-hound, Roy, endeavour to bite him?"

I sank back in my chair in some disappointment. Was it for so trivial a question as this that I had been summoned from my work? Holmes glanced across at me.

"The same old Watson!" said he. "You never learn that the gravest issues may depend upon the smallest things. But is it not on the face of it strange that a staid, elderly philosopher—you've heard of Presbury, of course, the famous Camford[7] physiologist?—that such a man, whose friend has been his devoted wolf-hound, should now have been twice attacked by his own dog? What do you make of it?"

"The dog is ill."

"Well, that has to be considered. But he attacks no one else, nor does he apparently molest his master, save on very special occasions. Curious, Watson—very curious. But young Mr. Bennett is before his time, if that is his ring. I had hoped to have a longer chat with you before he came."

There was a quick step on the stairs, a sharp tap at the door, and a moment later the new client presented himself. He was a tall, handsome youth about thirty, well dressed and elegant, but with something in his bearing which suggested the shyness

There was s sharp tap at the door, and a moment later the
new client presented himself.
Howard Elcock, *Strand Magazine*, 1923

of the student rather than the self-possession of the man of the
world. He shook hands with Holmes, and then looked with
some surprise at me.

"This matter is very delicate, Mr. Holmes," he said. "Consider the relation in which I stand to Professor Presbury, both
privately and publicly. I really can hardly justify myself if I
speak before any third person."

"Have no fear, Mr. Bennett. Dr. Watson is the very soul of
discretion, and I can assure you that this is a matter in which I
am very likely to need an assistant."

"As you like, Mr. Holmes. You will, I am sure, understand
my having some reserves in the matter."

8 N. P. Metcalfe uses this statement to build a case for Camford as a stand-in for Oxford. According to his research, Cambridge had no Chair of Comparative Anatomy in 1903, the closest approximation being a Chair of Zoology and Comparative Anatomy. At Oxford, however, there was an appropriately labelled post: the Linacre Chair of Comparative Anatomy, so named in 1893, in a change from its original designation, the Linacre Chair of Human and Comparative Anatomy. In 1903 the post was held by W. F. R. Weldon, M.A., and it is he whom Metcalfe targets as the real Professor Presbury.

Jonathan McCafferty dissents, recalling that Watson frequently changes details in order to obscure the identity of Holmes's clients and would certainly have altered the name of the professorship. He selects Cambridge as the location, declaring that Professor Presbury was in fact Alexander MacAlister, professor of anatomy at Cambridge from 1893 to 1919.

"You will appreciate it, Watson, when I tell you that this gentleman, Mr. Trevor Bennett, is professional assistant to the great scientist, lives under his roof, and is engaged to his only daughter. Certainly we must agree that the Professor has every claim upon his loyalty and devotion. But it may best be shown by taking the necessary steps to clear up this strange mystery."

"I hope so, Mr. Holmes. That is my one object. Does Dr. Watson know the situation?"

"I have not had time to explain it."

"Then perhaps I had better go over the ground again before explaining some fresh developments."

"I will do so myself," said Holmes, "in order to show that I have the events in their due order. The Professor, Watson, is a man of European reputation. His life has been academic. There has never been a breath of scandal. He is a widower with one daughter, Edith. He is, I gather, a man of very virile and positive, one might almost say combative, character. So the matter stood until a very few months ago.

"Then the current of his life was broken. He is sixty-one years of age, but he became engaged to the daughter of Professor Morphy, his colleague in the chair of Comparative Anatomy.[8] It was not, as I understand, the reasoned courting of an elderly man, but rather the passionate frenzy of youth, for no one could have shown himself a more devoted lover. The lady, Alice Morphy, was a very perfect girl both in mind and body, so that there was every excuse for the Professor's infatuation. None the less, it did not meet with full approval in his own family."

"We thought it rather excessive," said our visitor.

"Exactly. Excessive and a little violent and unnatural. Professor Presbury was rich, however, and there was no objection upon the part of the father. The daughter, however, had other views, and there were already several candidates for her hand, who, if they were less eligible from a worldly point of view, were at least more of an age. The girl seemed to like the Professor in spite of his eccentricities. It was only age which stood in the way.

"About this time a little mystery suddenly clouded the normal routine of the Professor's life. He did what he had never done before. He left home and gave no indication where he was going. He was away a fortnight, and returned looking rather travel-worn. He made no allusion to where he had been, although he was usually the frankest of men. It chanced, however, that our client here, Mr. Bennett, received a letter from a fellow-student in Prague, who said that he was glad to have seen Professor Presbury there, although he had not been able to talk to him. Only in this way did his own household learn where he had been.

"Now comes the point. From that time onward a curious change came over the Professor. He became furtive and sly. Those around him had always the feeling that he was not the man that they had known, but that he was under some shadow which had darkened his higher qualities. His intellect was not affected. His lectures were as brilliant as ever. But always there was something new, something sinister and unexpected. His daughter, who was devoted to him, tried again and again to resume the old relations and to penetrate this mask which her father seemed to have put on. You, sir, as I understand, did the same—but all was in vain. And now, Mr. Bennett, tell in your own words the incident of the letters."

"You must understand, Dr. Watson, that the Professor had no secrets from me. If I were his son or his younger brother, I could not have more completely enjoyed his confidence. As his secretary I handled every paper which came to him, and I opened and subdivided his letters. Shortly after his return all this was changed. He told me that certain letters might come to him from London which would be marked by a cross under the stamp. These were to be set aside for his own eyes only. I may say that several of these did pass through my hands, that they had the E.C. mark,[9] and were in an illiterate handwriting.[10] If he answered them at all the answers did not pass through my hands nor into the letter-basket in which our correspondence was collected."

"And the box," said Holmes.

"Ah, yes, the box. The Professor brought back a little wooden box from his travels. It was the one thing which suggested a Continental tour, for it was one of those quaint carved things which one associates with Germany. This he placed in his instrument cupboard. One day, in looking for a cannula,[11] I took up the box. To my surprise he was very angry, and reproved me in words which were quite savage for my curiosity. It was the first time such a thing had happened and I was

9 That is to say, the East Central postal district of London.

10 What, asks Barbara Roisman Cooper astutely, is "illiterate handwriting"? A person who is illiterate is unable to read. "If the writer were illiterate," Cooper continues, "how could he write? What does 'illiterate handwriting' look like?" Presumably, Watson meant to write "illegible."

11 A small metal or rubber tube, used to drain fluid from the body or to administer medicine.

deeply hurt. I endeavoured to explain that it was a mere accident that I had touched the box, but all the evening I was conscious that he looked at me harshly and that the incident was rankling in his mind." Mr. Bennett drew a little diary book from his pocket. "That was on July 2nd," said he.

"You are certainly an admirable witness," said Holmes. "I may need some of these dates which you have noted."

"I learned method among other things from my great teacher. From the time that I observed abnormality in his behaviour I felt that it was my duty to study his case. Thus I have it here that it was on that very day, July 2nd, that Roy attacked the Professor, as he came from his study into the hall. Again on July 11th, there was a scene of the same sort and then I have a note of yet another upon July 20th. After that we had to banish Roy to the stables. He was a dear, affectionate animal—but I fear I weary you."

Mr. Bennett spoke in a tone of reproach, for it was very clear that Holmes was not listening. His face was rigid and his eyes gazed abstractedly at the ceiling. With an effort he recovered himself.

"Singular! Most singular!" he murmured. "These details were new to me, Mr. Bennett. I think we have now fairly gone over the old ground, have we not? But you spoke of some fresh developments."

The pleasant, open face of our visitor clouded over, shadowed by some grim remembrance. "What I speak of occurred the night before last," said he. "I was lying awake about two in the morning, when I was aware of a dull muffled sound coming from the passage. I opened my door and peeped out. I should explain that the Professor sleeps at the end of the passage—"

"The date being—?" asked Holmes.

Our visitor was clearly annoyed at so irrelevant an interruption.

"I have said, sir, that it was the night before last—that is, September 4th."

Holmes nodded and smiled.

"Pray continue," said he.

"He sleeps at the end of the passage, and would have to pass my door in order to reach the staircase. It was a really terrifying experience, Mr. Holmes. I think that I am as strong-nerved as my neighbours, but I was shaken by what I saw. The passage was dark save that one window half-way along it threw a patch of light. I could see that something was coming along the passage, something dark and crouching. Then suddenly it emerged into the light, and I saw that it was he. He was crawling, Mr. Holmes—crawling! He was not quite on his hands and knees. I should rather say on his hands and feet, with his face sunk between his hands. Yet he seemed to move with ease. I was so paralysed by the sight that it was not until he had reached my door that I was able to step forward and ask if I

"Something was moving along the passage, something dark and crouching; then suddenly it emerged into the light and I saw that it was he."
Frederick Dorr Steele, *Hearst's International*, 1923

12 Rheumatism of the lumbar muscles in the lower back, frequently caused by a muscle strain or a slipped disk.

13 A psychiatrist; from the French *aliéné*, meaning insane.

14 D. Martin Dakin, who expresses doubt about the "Canonicity" of the tale, nonetheless defends the seeming incongruity of Miss Presbury's calling Mr. Bennett "Jack" instead of his given name, Trevor. Dakin writes that this particular reference "cannot be taken as evidence against the story, in view of Watson's notorious carelessness about Christian names, including his own. . . . It could plausibly be argued that Miss Presbury had a pet name for her man, just as Effie Munro had [in 'The Yellow Face'], and as many authorities consider Mrs. Watson had ['James' in 'The Man with the Twisted Lip']."

could assist him. His answer was extraordinary. He sprang up, spat out some atrocious word at me, and hurried on past me, and down the staircase. I waited about for an hour, but he did not come back. It must have been daylight before he regained his room."

"Well, Watson, what make you of that?" asked Holmes, with the air of the pathologist who presents a rare specimen.

"Lumbago,12 possibly. I have known a severe attack make a man walk in just such a way, and nothing would be more trying to the temper."

"Good, Watson! You always keep us flat-footed on the ground. But we can hardly accept lumbago, since he was able to stand erect in a moment."

"He was never better in health," said Bennett. "In fact, he is stronger than I have known him for years. But there are the facts, Mr. Holmes. It is not a case in which we can consult the police, and yet we are utterly at our wits' end as to what to do, and we feel in some strange way that we are drifting towards disaster. Edith—Miss Presbury—feels as I do, that we cannot wait passively any longer."

"It is certainly a very curious and suggestive case. What do you think, Watson?"

"Speaking as a medical man," said I, "it appears to be a case for an alienist.13 The old gentleman's cerebral processes were disturbed by the love affair. He made a journey abroad in the hope of breaking himself of the passion. His letters and the box may be connected with some other private transaction—a loan, perhaps, or share certificates, which are in the box."

"And the wolf-hound no doubt disapproved of the financial bargain. No, no, Watson, there is more in it than this. Now, I can only suggest—"

What Sherlock Holmes was about to suggest will never be known, for at this moment the door opened and a young lady was shown into the room. As she appeared Mr. Bennett sprang up with a cry and ran forward with his hands out to meet those which she had herself outstretched.

"Edith, dear! Nothing the matter, I hope?"

"I felt I must follow you. Oh, Jack,14 I have been so dreadfully frightened! It is awful to be there alone."

The Professor spat out some atrocious word at me and hurried on down the staircase.
Howard Elcock, *Strand Magazine*, 1923

"Mr. Holmes, this is the young lady I spoke of. This is my fiancée."

"We were gradually coming to that conclusion, were we not, Watson?" Holmes answered, with a smile. "I take it, Miss Presbury, that there is some fresh development in the case, and that you thought we should know?"

Our new visitor, a bright, handsome girl of a conventional English type, smiled back at Holmes as she seated herself beside Mr. Bennett.

"When I found Mr. Bennett had left his hotel I thought I should probably find him here. Of course, he had told me that

15 The American third floor, that is.

he would consult you. But, oh, Mr. Holmes, can you do nothing for my poor father?"

"I have hopes, Miss Presbury, but the case is still obscure. Perhaps what you have to say may throw some fresh light upon it."

"It was last night, Mr. Holmes. He had been very strange all day. I am sure that there are times when he has no recollection of what he does. He lives as in a strange dream. Yesterday was such a day. It was not my father with whom I lived. His outward shell was there, but it was not really he."

"Tell me what happened."

"I was awakened in the night by the dog barking most furiously. Poor Roy, he is chained now near the stable. I may say that I always sleep with my door locked; for, as Jack—as Mr. Bennett—will tell you, we all have a feeling of impending danger. My room is on the second floor.[15] It happened that the blind was up in my window, and there was bright moonlight outside. As I lay with my eyes fixed upon the square of light, listening to the frenzied barkings of the dog, I was amazed to see my father's face looking in at me. Mr. Holmes, I nearly died of surprise and horror. There it was pressed against the window-pane, and one hand seemed to be raised as if to push up the window. If that window had opened, I think I should have gone mad. It was no delusion, Mr. Holmes. Don't deceive yourself by thinking so. I dare say it was twenty seconds or so that I lay paralysed and watched the face. Then it vanished, but I could not—I could not spring out of bed and look out after it. I lay cold and shivering till morning. At breakfast he was sharp and fierce in manner, and made no allusion to the adventure of the night. Neither did I, but I gave an excuse for coming to town—and here I am."

Holmes looked thoroughly surprised at Miss Presbury's narrative.

"My dear young lady, you say that your room is on the second floor. Is there a long ladder in the garden?"

"No, Mr. Holmes; that is the amazing part of it. There is no possible way of reaching the window—and yet he was there."

"The date being September 5th," said Holmes. "That certainly complicates matters."

It was the young lady's turn to look surprised. "This is the

"As I lay with my eyes fixed upon the square of light I was amazed to see my father's face looking in at me."
Howard Elcock, *Strand Magazine*, 1923

16 The word "lunatics," after all, comes from the Roman belief that the moon affected mysterious changes in certain people, driving them to the point of madness when it was full.

second time that you have alluded to the date, Mr. Holmes," said Bennett. "Is it possible that it has any bearing upon the case?"

"It is possible—very possible—and yet I have not my full material at present."

"Possibly you are thinking of the connection between insanity and phases of the moon?"[16]

"No, I assure you. It was quite a different line of thought. Possibly you can leave your notebook with me and I will check the dates. Now I think, Watson, that our line of action is perfectly clear. This young lady has informed us—and I have the

17 See "The Sussex Vampire," note 16. Several scholars point to Holmes's favourable recollections of the Chequers as an indication that Camford was the site of Holmes's own university.

"I dare say that it was twenty seconds or so that I lay paralyzed and watched its face. Then it vanished and I lay cold and shivering until morning."
Frederick Dorr Steele, *Hearst's International*, 1923

greatest confidence in her intuition—that her father remembers little or nothing which occurs upon certain dates. We will therefore call upon him as if he had given us an appointment upon such a date. He will put it down to his own lack of memory. Thus we will open our campaign by having a good close view of him."

"That is excellent," said Mr. Bennett. "I warn you, however, that the Professor is irascible and violent at times."

Holmes smiled. "There are reasons why we should come at once—very cogent reasons if my theories hold good. To-morrow, Mr. Bennett, will certainly see us in Camford. There is, if I remember right, an inn called the Chequers where the port used to be above mediocrity, and the linen was above reproach.[17] I think, Watson, that our lot for the next few days might lie in less pleasant places."

Monday morning found us on our way to the famous University town—an easy effort on the part of Holmes, who had no roots to pull up, but one which involved frantic planning and hurrying on my part, as my practice was by this time not inconsiderable. Holmes made no allusion to the case until after we had deposited our suit-cases at the ancient hostel of which he had spoken.

"I think, Watson, that we can catch the Professor just before lunch. He lectures at eleven, and should have an interval at home."

"What possible excuse have we for calling?"

Holmes glanced at his notebook.

"There was a period of excitement upon August 26. We will assume that he is a little hazy as to what he does at such times. If we insist that we are there by appointment I think he will hardly venture to contradict us. Have you the effrontery necessary to put it through?"

"We can but try."

"Excellent, Watson! Compound of the Busy Bee and Excelsior. We can but try—the motto of the firm.[18] A friendly native will surely guide us."

Such a one on the back of a smart hansom swept us past a row of ancient colleges,[19] and finally turning into a tree-lined drive pulled up at the door of a charming house, girt round with lawns and covered with purple wistaria. Professor Presbury was certainly surrounded with every sign not only of comfort but of luxury. Even as we pulled up a grizzled head appeared at the front window, and we were aware of a pair of keen eyes from under shaggy brows which surveyed us through large horn glasses. A moment later we were actually in his sanctum, and the mysterious scientist, whose vagaries had brought us from London, was standing before us. There was certainly no sign of eccentricity either in his manner or appearance, for he was a portly, large-featured man, grave, tall, and frock-coated, with the dignity of bearing which a lecturer needs. His eyes were his most remarkable feature, keen, observant, and clever to the verge of cunning.

He looked at our cards. "Pray sit down, gentlemen. What can I do for you?"

Mr. Holmes smiled amiably.

"It was the question which I was about to put to you, Professor."

"To me, sir!"

18 This is the second time Watson has responded to Holmes with, "We can but try," the first being in "Thor Bridge." Alan Olding suggests that Holmes is referring to two popular poems. The first, "Against Idleness and Mischief," was a popular children's rhyme by hymn writer Isaac Watts (1674–1748), published in his *Divine Songs for Children* (1715). A paean to industriousness, the poem exhorts, "How doth the little busy bee / Improve each shining hour / And gather honey all the day / From every opening flower!" Lewis Carroll later parodied the poem in *Alice's Adventures in Wonderland*, depicting a disoriented Alice, in an attempt to remember the lines, reciting instead, "How doth the little crocodile / Improve his shining tail, / And pour the waters of the Nile / On every golden scale!" As to the second part of Holmes's statement, "excelsior" is Latin for "ever upward." (It is the official motto of the state of New York.) In the poem "Excelsior" by Henry Wadsworth Longfellow (1807–1882), a young man travels through the Alps and, though warned away by those he meets, continues determinedly onward in what what turns out to be a doomed attempt to navigate the pass. " 'Oh, stay,' the maiden said, 'and rest / Thy weary head upon this breast!' / A tear stood in his bright blue eye, / But still he answered, with a sigh, / Excelsior!"

19 In another attempt to prove the true location of Camford, Gavin Brend writes that "colleges in rows, on the whole, suggest Oxford." N. P. Metcalfe is noncommittal, suggesting that the row of ancient colleges could be found either on High Street at Oxford or at King's Parade and Trinity Street in Cambridge.

"Possibly there is some mistake. I heard through a second person that Professor Presbury of Camford had need of my services."

"Oh, indeed!" It seemed to me that there was a malicious sparkle in the intense grey eyes. "You heard that, did you? May I ask the name of your informant?"

"I am sorry, Professor, but the matter was rather confidential. If I have made a mistake there is no harm done. I can only express my regret."

"Not at all. I should wish to go further into this matter. It interests me. Have you any scrap of writing, any letter or telegram, to bear out your assertion?"

"No, I have not."

"I presume that you do not go so far as to assert that I summoned you?"

"I would rather answer no questions," said Holmes.

"No, I dare say not," said the Professor, with asperity. "However, that particular one can be answered very easily without your aid."

He walked across the room to the bell. Our London friend, Mr. Bennett, answered the call.

"Come in, Mr. Bennett. These two gentlemen have come from London under the impression that they have been summoned. You handle all my correspondence. Have you a note of anything going to a person named Holmes?"

"No, sir," Bennett answered, with a flush.

"That is conclusive," said the Professor, glaring angrily at my companion. "Now, sir"—he leaned forward with his two hands upon the table—"it seems to me that your position is a very questionable one."

Holmes shrugged his shoulders.

"I can only repeat that I am sorry that we have made a needless intrusion."

"Hardly enough, Mr. Holmes!" the old man cried, in a high screaming voice, with extraordinary malignancy upon his face. He got between us and the door as he spoke, and he shook his two hands at us with furious passion. "You can hardly get out of it so easily as that." His face was convulsed and he grinned and gibbered at us in his senseless rage. I am convinced that we should have had to fight our way out of the room if Mr. Bennett had not intervened.

"My dear Professor," he cried, "consider your position! Consider the scandal at the University! Mr. Holmes is a well-known man. You cannot possibly treat him with such discourtesy."

Sulkily our host—if I may call him so—cleared the path to the door. We were glad to find ourselves outside the house, and in the quiet of the tree-lined drive. Holmes seemed greatly amused by the episode.

"Our learned friend's nerves are somewhat out of order," said he. "Perhaps our intrusion was a little crude, and yet we have gained that personal contact which I desired. But, dear me, Watson, he is surely at our heels. The villain still pursues us."

There were the sounds of running feet behind, but it was, to my relief, not the formidable Professor but his assistant

"Hardly enough, Mr. Holmes!" the old man cried
in a high screaming voice.
Frederick Dorr Steele, *Hearst's International*, 1923

The Professor's face was convulsed and he grinned and gibbered at us in his senseless rage.
I am convinced that Holmes and I would have had to fight our way out of the room if
Mr. Bennett had not intervened.
Howard Elcock, *Strand Magazine*, 1923

who appeared round the curve of the drive. He came panting up to us.

"I am so sorry, Mr. Holmes. I wished to apologize."

"My dear sir, there is no need. It is all in the way of professional experience."

"I have never seen him in a more dangerous mood. But he grows more sinister. You can understand now why his daughter and I are alarmed. And yet his mind is perfectly clear."

"Too clear!" said Holmes. "That was my miscalculation. It is evident that his memory is much more reliable than I had thought. By the way, can we, before we go, see the window of Miss Presbury's room?"

Mr. Bennett pushed his way through some shrubs and we had a view of the side of the house.

"It is there. The second on the left."

"Dear me, it seems hardly accessible. And yet you will observe that there is a creeper below and a water-pipe above which give some foothold."

"I could not climb it myself," said Mr. Bennett.

"Very likely. It would certainly be a dangerous exploit for any normal man."

"There was one other thing I wished to tell you, Mr. Holmes. I have the address of the man in London to whom the Professor writes. He seems to have written this morning and I got it from his blotting-paper. It is an ignoble position for a trusted secretary, but what else can I do?"

Holmes glanced at the paper and put it into his pocket.

"Dorak—a curious name. Slavonic, I imagine. Well, it is an important link in the chain. We return to London this afternoon, Mr. Bennett. I see no good purpose to be served by our remaining. We cannot arrest the Professor, because he has done no crime, nor can we place him under constraint, for he cannot be proved to be mad. No action is as yet possible."

"Then what on earth are we to do?"

"A little patience, Mr. Bennett. Things will soon develop. Unless I am mistaken next Tuesday may mark a crisis. Certainly we shall be in Camford on that day. Meanwhile, the general position is undeniably unpleasant, and if Miss Presbury can prolong her visit—"

"That is easy."

"Then let her stay till we can assure her that all danger is past. Meanwhile, let him have his way and do not cross him. So long as he is in a good humour all is well."

"There he is!" said Bennett, in a startled whisper. Looking between the branches we saw the tall, erect figure emerge from the hall door and look around him. He stood leaning forward, his hands swinging straight before him, his head turning from side to side. The secretary with a last wave slipped off among the trees, and we saw him presently rejoin his employer, the two entering the house together in what seemed to be animated and even excited conversation.

"I expect the old gentleman has been putting two and two together," said Holmes, as we walked hotelwards. "He struck

20 As observed by William S. Baring-Gould, Mercer is another member of that "small, but very efficient, organization" of Holmes's informants. Its members include Shinwell Johnson ("The Illustrious Client") and Langdale Pike ("The Three Gables").

me as having a particularly clear and logical brain, from the little I saw of him. Explosive, no doubt, but then from his point of view he has something to explode about if detectives are put on his track and he suspects his own household of doing it. I rather fancy that friend Bennett is in for an uncomfortable time."

Holmes stopped at a post office and sent off a telegram on our way. The answer reached us in the evening, and he tossed it across to me.

> Have visited the Commercial Road and seen Dorak. Suave person, Bohemian, elderly. Keeps large general store.—
> Mercer.

"Mercer is since your time," said Holmes.[20] "He is my general utility man who looks up routine business. It was important to know something of the man with whom our Professor was so secretly corresponding. His nationality connects up with the Prague visit."

"Thank goodness that something connects with something," said I. "At present we seem to be faced by a long series of inexplicable incidents with no bearing upon each other. For example, what possible connection can there be between an angry wolf-hound and a visit to Bohemia, or either of them with a man crawling down a passage at night? As to your dates, that is the biggest mystification of all."

Holmes smiled and rubbed his hands. We were, I may say, seated in the old sitting-room of the ancient hotel, with a bottle of the famous vintage of which Holmes had spoken on the table between us.

"Well, now, let us take the dates first," said he, his fingertips together and his manner as if he were addressing a class. "This excellent young man's diary shows that there was trouble upon July 2nd, and from then onwards it seems to have been at nine-day intervals, with, so far as I remember, only one exception. Thus the last outbreak upon Friday was on September 3rd, which also falls into the series, as did August 26th, which preceded it. The thing is beyond coincidence."

I was forced to agree.

"Let us, then, form the provisional theory that every nine

days the Professor takes some strong drug which has a passing but highly poisonous effect. His naturally violent nature is intensified by it. He learned to take this drug while he was in Prague, and is now supplied with it by a Bohemian intermediary in London. This all hangs together, Watson!"

"But the dog, the face at the window, the creeping man in the passage?"

"Well, well, we have made a beginning. I should not expect any fresh developments until next Tuesday.[21] In the meantime we can only keep in touch with friend Bennett and enjoy the amenities of this charming town."[22]

In the morning Mr. Bennett slipped round to bring us the latest report. As Holmes had imagined, times had not been easy with him. Without exactly accusing him of being responsible for our presence, the Professor had been very rough and rude in his speech, and evidently felt some strong grievance. This morning he was quite himself again, however, and had delivered his usual brilliant lecture to a crowded class. "Apart from his queer fits," said Bennett, "he has actually more energy and vitality than I can ever remember, nor was his brain ever clearer. But it's not he—it's never the man whom we have known."

"I don't think you have anything to fear now for a week at least," Holmes answered. "I am a busy man, and Dr. Watson has his patients to attend to.[23] Let us agree that we meet here at this hour next Tuesday, and I shall be surprised if before we leave you again we are not able to explain, even if we cannot perhaps put an end to, your troubles. Meanwhile, keep us posted in what occurs."

I saw nothing of my friend for the next few days, but on the following Monday evening I had a short note asking me to meet him next day at the train. From what he told me as we travelled up to Camford all was well, the peace of the Professor's house had been unruffled, and his own conduct perfectly normal. This also was the report which was given us by Mr. Bennett himself when he called upon us that evening at our old quar-

21 Holmes's "August 26th" should be the 25th, if the nine-day cycle applies. And why "next Tuesday," which does not fit the cycle at all? The relevant dates and the confusion in Watson's records are examined on page 1665.

22 In "The Missing Three-Quarter," Holmes calls the university of the adventure "this inhospitable town." Because Watson records "The Missing Three-Quarter" as occurring in Cambridge, it seems very unlikely that "The Creeping Man" could occur there.

23 Throughout this case, Holmes appears surprisingly indecisive. First, he tells Bennett that he and Watson will return to London in the afternoon after their frustrated attempt to speak with the professor, yet they do not do so. Then, while ensconced in the hotel's sitting room, Holmes announces that "I should not expect any fresh developments until next Tuesday. In the meantime we can only . . . enjoy the amenities of this charming town." By morning, he has changed his mind once again, this time declaring that he and Watson will depart for London and then come back next Tuesday. "These are clear evidences of vacillation," remark W. S. Bradley and Alan S. J. Sarjeant. "No reasonable hypothesis can give logic to such an on-again, off-again sequence." Bradley and Sarjeant, pursuing to extremes their hypothesis that Holmes was a woman, conclude that this vacillation is a symptom of (Ms.) Holmes's menopause.

ters in the "Chequers." "He heard from his London correspondent to-day. There was a letter and there was a small
packet, each with the cross under the stamp which warned me
not to touch them. There has been nothing else."

"That may prove quite enough," said Holmes grimly. "Now,
Mr. Bennett, we shall, I think, come to some conclusion to-
night. If my deductions are correct we should have an opportunity of bringing matters to a head. In order to do so it is
necessary to hold the Professor under observation. I would suggest, therefore, that you remain awake and on the look out.
Should you hear him pass your door do not interrupt him, but
follow him as discreetly as you can. Dr. Watson and I will not
be far off. By the way, where is the key of that little box of
which you spoke?"

"Upon his watch-chain."

"I fancy our researches must lie in that direction. At the
worst the lock should not be very formidable. Have you any
other able-bodied man on the premises?"

"There is the coachman, Macphail."

"Where does he sleep?"

"Over the stables."

"We might possibly want him. Well, we can do no more until
we see how things develop. Good-bye—but I expect that we
shall see you before morning."

It was nearly midnight before we took our station among
some bushes immediately opposite the hall door of the Professor. It was a fine night, but chilly, and we were glad of our warm
overcoats. There was a breeze, and clouds were scudding
across the sky, obscuring from time to time the half-moon. It
would have been a dismal vigil were it not for the expectation
and excitement which carried us along, and the assurance of
my comrade that we had probably reached the end of the
strange sequence of events which had engaged our attention.

"If the cycle of nine days holds good then we shall have the
Professor at his worst to-night," said Holmes. "The fact that
these strange symptoms began after his visit to Prague, that he
is in secret correspondence with a Bohemian dealer in London,
who presumably represents someone in Prague, and that he
received a packet from him this very day, all point in one direction. What he takes and why he takes it are still beyond our

ken, but that it emanates in some way from Prague is clear enough. He takes it under definite directions which regulate this ninth-day system, which was the first point which attracted my attention. But his symptoms are most remarkable. Did you observe his knuckles?"

I had to confess that I did not.

"Thick and horny in a way which is quite new in my experience. Always look at the hands first, Watson. Then cuffs, trouser-knees, and boots. Very curious knuckles which can only be explained by the mode of progression observed by—" Holmes paused, and suddenly clapped his hand to his forehead. "Oh, Watson, Watson, what a fool I have been! It seems incredible, and yet it must be true. All points in one direction. How could I miss seeing the connection of ideas? Those knuckles—how could I have passed those knuckles? And the dog! And the ivy! It's surely time that I disappeared into that little farm of my dreams. Look out, Watson! Here he is! We shall have the chance of seeing for ourselves."

The hall door had slowly opened, and against the lamp-lit background we saw the tall figure of Professor Presbury. He was clad in his dressing-gown. As he stood outlined in the doorway he was erect but leaning forward with dangling arms, as when we saw him last.

Now he stepped forward into the drive, and an extraordinary change came over him. He sank down into a crouching position, and moved along upon his hands and feet, skipping every now and then as if he were overflowing with energy and vitality. He moved along the face of the house and then round the corner. As he disappeared Bennett slipped through the hall door and softly followed him.

"Come, Watson, come!" cried Holmes, and we stole as softly as we could through the bushes until we had gained a spot whence we could see the other side of the house, which was bathed in the light of the half-moon. The Professor was clearly visible crouching at the foot of the ivy-covered wall. As we watched him he suddenly began with incredible agility to ascend it. From branch to branch he sprang, sure of foot and firm of grasp, climbing apparently in mere joy at his own pow-

The hall door slowly opened and against the lamp-lit background
Holmes and Watson saw the tall figure of Professor Presbury.
As he stood outlined in the doorway he was erect but
leaned forward with dangling arms.
Frederick Dorr Steele, *Hearst's International*, 1923

ers, with no definite object in view. With his dressing-gown flapping on each side of him he looked like some huge bat glued against the side of his own house, a great square dark patch upon the moonlit wall. Presently he tired of this amusement, and, dropping from branch to branch, he squatted down into the old attitude and moved towards the stables, creeping along in the same strange way as before. The wolf-hound was out now, barking furiously, and more excited than ever when it actually caught sight of its master. It was straining on its chain, and quivering with eagerness and rage. The Professor squatted down very deliberately just out of reach of the hound, and began to provoke it in every possible way. He took handfuls of pebbles from the drive and threw them in the dog's face, prodded him with a stick which he had picked up, flicked his hands about only a few inches from the gaping mouth, and endeavoured in every way to increase the animal's fury, which was already beyond all control. In all our adventures I do not know that I have ever seen a more strange sight than this impassive and still dignified figure crouching frog-like upon the ground and goading to a wilder exhibition of passion the maddened hound, which ramped and raged in front of him, by all manner of ingenious and calculated cruelty.

And then in a moment it happened! It was not the chain that broke, but it was the collar that slipped, for it had been made for a thick-necked Newfoundland. We heard the rattle of falling metal, and the next instant dog and man were rolling on the ground together, the one roaring in rage, the other scream-

With his dressing-gown flapping on each side of him he looked like some huge bat glued against . . . the moonlit wall.

Frederick Dorr Steele, *Hearst's International*, 1923

24 "This is a startling admission," observes Dr. Robert S. Katz, and it proves that Watson—himself a first-class surgeon—is uncertain about the proper course of action. To Katz, this is a telling sign of the gravity of the situation: "No highly trained surgeon would willingly make such a statement about himself in a published account unless something was very wrong indeed."

Frederick Dorr Steele, *Hearst's International*, 1923

ing in a strange shrill falsetto of terror. It was a very narrow thing for the Professor's life. The savage creature had him fairly by the throat, its fangs had bitten deep, and he was senseless before we could reach them and drag the two apart. It might have been a dangerous task for us, but Bennett's voice and presence brought the great wolf-hound instantly to reason. The uproar had brought the sleepy and astonished coachman from his room above the stables. "I'm not surprised," said he, shaking his head. "I've seen him at it before. I knew the dog would get him sooner or later."

The hound was secured, and together we carried the Professor up to his room, where Bennett, who had a medical degree, helped me to dress his torn throat. The sharp teeth had passed dangerously near the carotid artery, and the hæmorrhage was serious. In half an hour the danger was past, I had given the patient an injection of morphia, and he had sunk into deep sleep. Then, and only then, were we able to look at each other and to take stock of the situation.

"I think a first-class surgeon should see him," said I.[24]

"For God's sake, no!" cried Bennett. "At present the scandal is confined to our own household. It is safe with us. If it gets beyond these walls it will never stop. Consider his position at the University, his European reputation, the feelings of his daughter."

"Quite so," said Holmes. "I think it may be quite possible to keep the matter to ourselves, and also to prevent its recurrence now that we have a free hand. The key from the watch-chain, Mr. Bennett. Macphail will guard the patient and let us know if there is any change. Let us see what we can find in the Professor's mysterious box."

There was not much, but there was enough—an empty phial, another nearly full, a hypodermic syringe, several letters in a crabbed, foreign hand. The marks on the envelopes showed

Dog and man were rolling on the ground together,
the one roaring in rage, the other screaming in a strange
shrill falsetto of terror.
Howard Elcock, *Strand Magazine*, 1923

25 The langur is any of several species of leaf- and fruit-eating Asian monkeys with long tails and bushy eyebrows. The "black-faced Langur" would be the tree-dwelling Hanuman langur, or the sacred monkey of India, named after the Hindu monkey-god Hanuman. Monkeys of this genus have long, slender limbs; grey, black, or brown fur; tufts of hair atop their heads and around their faces; and black ears, faces, feet, and hands. They travel in packs of twenty or thirty and, regarded with reverence throughout India, roam unmolested through villages and temples, often raiding crops or stores.

Black-faced langur.

26 J. C. Prager and Albert Silverstein identify Lowenstein as Eugen Steinach (1861–1944), a Viennese physiologist who purportedly coined the word "hormone." In 1912, Steinach's research led him to implant sex glands from female guinea pigs into male guinea pigs, and vice versa. The female guinea pigs began displaying male sexual behaviour, and the males female sexual behaviour, leading some to theorise that the glands secreted substances that might account for homosexuality. Further research identified the secretions as the sex hormones testosterone and estrogen but con-

that they were those which had disturbed the routine of the secretary, and each was dated from the Commercial Road and signed "A. Dorak." They were mere invoices to say that a fresh bottle was being sent to Professor Presbury, or receipts to acknowledge money. There was one other envelope, however, in a more educated hand and bearing the Austrian stamp with the postmark of Prague. "Here we have our material!" cried Holmes, as he tore out the enclosure.

HONOURED COLLEAGUE,—

Since your esteemed visit I have thought much of your case, and though in your circumstances there are some special reasons for the treatment, I would none the less enjoin caution, as my results have shown that it is not without danger of a kind.

It is possible that the Serum of Anthropoid would have been better. I have, as I explained to you, used black-faced Langur[25] because a specimen was accessible. Langur is, of course, a crawler and climber, while Anthropoid walks erect, and is in all ways nearer.

I beg you to take every possible precaution that there be no premature revelation of the process. I have one other client in England, and Dorak is my agent for both.

Weekly reports will oblige.

Yours with high esteem,
H. LOWENSTEIN.

Lowenstein! The name brought back to me the memory of some snippet from a newspaper which spoke of an obscure scientist[26] who was striving in some unknown way for the secret of rejuvenescence and the elixir of life.[27] Lowenstein of Prague! Lowenstein with the wondrous strength-giving serum, tabooed by the profession because he refused to reveal its source. In a few words I said what I remembered. Bennett had taken a manual of Zoology from the shelves. " 'Langur,' " he read, " 'the great black-faced monkey of the Himalayan slopes, biggest and most human of climbing monkeys.' Many details are added. Well, thanks to you, Mr. Holmes, it is very clear that we have traced the evil to its source."

"The real source," said Holmes, "lies, of course, in that

untimely love affair which gave our impetuous Professor the idea that he could only gain his wish by turning himself into a younger man.[28] When one tries to rise above Nature one is liable to fall below it. The highest type of man may revert to the animal if he leaves the straight road of destiny." He sat musing for a little with the phial in his hand, looking at the clear liquid within.[29] "When I have written to this man and told him that I hold him criminally responsible for the poisons which he circulates, we will have no more trouble. But it may recur. Others may find a better way. There is danger there—a very real danger to humanity. Consider, Watson, that the material, the sensual, the worldly would all prolong their worthless lives. The spiritual would not avoid the call to something higher. It would be the survival of the least fit. What sort of cesspool may not our poor world become?" Suddenly the dreamer disappeared, and Holmes, the man of action, sprang from his chair. "I think there is nothing more to be said, Mr. Bennett. The various incidents will now fit themselves easily into the general scheme. The dog, of course, was aware of the change far more quickly than you. His smell would ensure that. It was the monkey, not the Professor, whom Roy attacked, just as it was the monkey who teased Roy.[30] Climbing was a joy to the creature, and it was a mere chance, I take it, that the pastime brought him to the young lady's window.[31] There is an early train to town, Watson, but I think we shall just have time for a cup of tea at the Chequers before we catch it."[32] ∎

cluded that hormone injections have no lasting effect on sexual orientation.

Steinach's investigations into the physical bases of sexuality were unfortunately eclipsed by his repeated attempts to develop methods for sexual rejuvenation. A tireless self-promoter, he earned the reputation of a "quack" in the contemporary press, and it may be one of these earlier accounts that Watson remembers having read. Later historians have labelled Steinach a scientific pioneer, and Prager and Silverstein argue that the brilliant researcher was duped by Presbury into believing that his "honoured colleague" would assist him with legitimate research into the effects of the serum.

27 In investigating Lowenstein's efforts, Alvin E. Rodin and Jack D. Key, in their *Medical Casebook of Dr. Arthur Conan Doyle*, comment upon the work of French physiologist Brown-Séquard (1817–1894), who somewhat damaged his distinguished reputation by attempting to invent the elixir of eternal youth. In June of 1889, already recognised for having discovered the importance of the spinal cord, Brown-Séquard announced—to much sensation in the Parisian and London journals—that he had injected himself with the testicular secretions of guinea pigs and dogs, and felt "rejuvenated" as a result. Among other findings, he reported that he was now able to engage in sexual relations with his new, younger wife, whereas previously he had found his capabilities limited. Brown-Séquard did not, however, end up prolonging his life in any meaningful way, and Rodin and Key note that injections of water alone have achieved similar results. "Even in the decade when 'The Creeping Man' was published (the 1920's)," they write, "medical fadism and quackery included transplanted monkey glands as well as extracts for rejuvenation."

Richard Brown expands upon Brown-Séquard's results, explaining that his method became known as "organotherapy" and was recommended in the United States as a treatment for epilepsy, cancer, cholera, tuberculosis, leprosy, and other infirmities. In the 1890s, testicular extract sold in New York for $2.50 per twenty-five injections, with a special syringe costing another $2.50. "These were sent by mail to any distance in the U.S.A., complete with directions," Brown reports. "Whether or not they were sent in wooden boxes is not stated, but they would need some form of protection to send glass vials and syringes by mail in the 1890s, and wood seems most likely."

28 In "The Rehabilitation of the Creeping Man," Charles A. Meyer makes the startling assertion that Holmes totally misunderstood the case and that Presbury suffered from Tourette syndrome, which has symptoms very similar to those exhibited (Meyer notes the twitching of Presbury's nose, the raising of his brows, the grimacing, the grunting, the throat clearing, the hissing, the clipping and yipping and yelping, and the obscene eruptions, as well as his unusual gait and partial amnesia). He had succeeded in masking his disease for many years, but the stress of the love affair brought pronounced occurrences. Searching for a biochemical cure, the professor began taking the drugs to suppress his symptoms.

Not content with that interesting hypothesis, Meyer presents another, in "The Real Creeps in 'The Adventure of the Creeping Man.' " He asserts that "Bennett" (in actuality a man named Jack—see note 14, above) and Edith Presbury plotted to prevent Presbury from marrying Alicia Morphy and so depriving Edith of her inheritance. They poisoned Presbury slowly with dopamine, producing the observed symptoms.

Still another "deconstruction" of the facts of Watson's narrative is presented in "The Original Holmes," by Tsukasa Kobayashi and Akane Higashiyama. The authors propose that the facts of the case are that Presbury had committed a number of murders in order to acquire male testicles, which Lowenstein made into a serum of testosterone to use on himself. He first tested the drug on Roy.

29 Might not Holmes be speaking of himself, in regard to a different sort of drug? "Past events may well have returned to Holmes," Paul Singleton writes, "as 'he sat musing for a little while with the phial in his hand, looking at the clear liquid within.' Cocaine, in its liquid form, is also clear."

30 Some scholars are wary of Holmes's fantastical deductions and prefer more realistic solutions to the puzzle. Dr. Samuel R. Meaker is one of these sceptics, flat-out proclaiming Holmes "wrong in assuming that treatment with monkey-serum could make a human being behave or smell like a monkey." Instead, Professor Presbury may have been experiencing a psychosomatic reaction to the extract, merely imagining that he was being induced into monkey-like behavior. Meaker explains that the dog did not pick up on any animalistic scent but only behaved "as any sensitive dog might do to a weird and apparently hostile change in its master's conduct." In Meaker's hypothesis, Watson was on a truer path than Holmes when he ventured, "Speaking as a medical man, it appears to be a case for an alienist."

31 "We are left to speculate about what happened later," observes science-fiction master Poul Anderson. "With the supply cut off, the professor doubtless reverted to normal. Watson implies as much when he writes about preserving reticence and discretion. Let us hope that Presbury either won his bride in

"AS TO YOUR DATES, THAT IS THE BIGGEST MYSTIFICATION OF ALL"

THE RELEVANT dates for "The Creeping Man" may be summarised as follows:

Nine-Day Cycle of Dosages	Description
Thursday, July 2, 1903	First attack noted.
Saturday, July 11, 1903	Second attack noted (nine days later).
Monday, July 20, 1903	Third attack.
Wednesday, July 29, 1903	Unnoted attack.
Friday, August 7, 1903	Unnoted attack.
Sunday, August 16, 1903	Unnoted attack.
Tuesday, August 25, 1903	"Period of excitement" noted on Wednesday, August 26, 1903.
Thursday, September 3, 1903	Attack noted. Bennett describes the attack as occurring on the 4th; since the incident occurred at 2:00 A.M. on the 4th, the dosage occurred on this date.
Saturday, September 12, 1903	Anticipated day of attack (that is, nine days after September 3, 1903).

Other relevant dates involved in the case:

Date	Description
Saturday, September 5, 1903, or early Sunday, September 6, 1903	Edith Presbury's bed chamber is visited by Professor Presbury.
Sunday, September 6, 1903	Bennett calls upon Holmes.
Monday, September 7, 1903	Holmes and Watson visit "Camford" to observe Professor Presbury; Holmes advises Bennett that "next Tuesday" (presumably Tuesday, September 15, 1903) will mark a crisis.

spite of everything and they were happy together, or he found the serene acceptance proper to old age."

32 This is yet another of the *Case-Book* adventures that D. Martin Dakin finds reason to doubt. He dismisses the obscuring of "Camford" as "the transparent device of a second-rate writer," charging that university settings have already been better depicted in "The Missing Three-Quarter" (which Dakin declares to have taken place in Cambridge) and "The Three Students" (Oxford). The aborted meeting with Professor Presbury, he continues, seems palely reminiscent of Holmes and Watson's encounter with Dr. Leslie Armstrong in "The Missing Three-Quarter," and its outcome less justified. Although swayed by Watson's typically pragmatic diagnosis of lumbago and Holmes's "delightful" telegram summoning Watson to his side, Dakin on the whole stands firmly against the authenticity of "The Creeping Man," labelling it "fantastic and more reminiscent of Dr. Jekyll or the Werewolf than a Holmes case."

As will be evident from the above, the exact nine-day cycle does not explain all of the date references. For example, the episode described as occurring on September 5, 1903, could have been the aftermath of a dosage actually taken on September 4, and Bennett was careless in describing the 2:00 A.M. attack as occurring on the 4th when it actually occurred in the early morning of the 5th. Or perhaps Presbury was not punctual about taking the drug on the date of delivery. However, even allowing some "slippage" in the intervals does not explain why Tuesday, September 15, 1903, has any relevance.

THE ADVENTURE OF THE
LION'S MANE[1]

*The principal question for the student of "The Lion's Mane" must be why Holmes wrote it.
While the case has the appearance of a crime, Holmes solves the mystery merely by recollect-
ing that he has read the true explanation in a book. In fact, there is no crime at all. The tale
is noteworthy, however, because it is the Canon's only depiction of Holmes's retirement. July
1907 sees Holmes in residence in Sussex, and the story gives many clues as to the location of
Holmes's last known home (where readers long to believe he still lives). Maud Bellamy,
whose fiancée is the victim of the alleged crime, is a singularly attractive figure, and some
suggest that Holmes had "feelings" for her. Appealing as that notion may be, we can only
speculate, for there is no mention of her in "His Last Bow."*

IT IS A most singular thing that a problem which was certainly as abstruse and unusual as any which I have faced in my
long professional career should have come to me after my
retirement, and be brought, as it were, to my very door. It
occurred after my withdrawal to my little Sussex home, when
I had given myself up entirely to that soothing life of Nature
for which I had so often yearned during the long years spent
amid the gloom of London.[2] At this period of my life the good
Watson had passed almost beyond my ken. An occasional
week-end visit was the most that I ever saw of him.[3] Thus I
must act as my own chronicler.[4] Ah! had he but been with me,
how much he might have made of so wonderful a happening
and of my eventual triumph against every difficulty! As it is,
however, I must needs tell my tale in my own plain way, showing by my words each step upon the difficult road which lay
before me as I searched for the mystery of the Lion's Mane.

My villa is situated upon the southern slope of the Downs,

1 A facsimile of the original manuscript of
"The Lion's Mane" was published by the
Westminster Libraries and the Sherlock
Holmes Society of London in 1992. There are
numerous differences between the original
text and the final published version, and significant additions to and deletions from the
initial version are discussed in context, below.

2 The very nature of the Great Detective
makes it difficult to understand why he would
ever retire in the first place. Holmes's explanation of yearning for "that soothing life of
Nature" is rejected by D. Martin Dakin, who
points to Holmes's constant need for stimula-
tion and his keen and restless mind, which
would hardly be satisfied by academic
research. Trevor H. Hall, in "The Late Mr.

Sherlock Holmes," proposes that Holmes developed amblyopia (a lazy eye) from his excessive tobacco use and faced total blindness, but this is pure speculation and seems unsupported by Holmes's own comment in "The Lion's Mane" about the "great view" from his villa. "Was there some enigmatic secret in his life to which even Watson never penetrated?" asks Dakin. "Distinction in Holmesian circles awaits the scholar who can read this perplexing riddle."

3 "These revealing sentences, surely the most melancholy in the whole saga," writes Trevor H. Hall, "refrained significantly from any mention of the detested Mrs. Watson." This would be Watson's fifth wife, Hall proposes in "The Problem of the Unpublished Cases," and he declares that she is the one to blame for keeping such intimate friends apart. Hall envisions Watson, in the manner of many widowers, having married a younger, sexually desirable woman who possessed a "selfish lack of any understanding of the bond between himself and Holmes. . . ." Perhaps, as the marriage progressed, Watson found himself driven to consult Holmes for the "occasional week-end visit" in the aftermath of bitter fights with his young wife, when the differences between them began to come to light. Nonetheless, Hall sorrowfully concludes, "It is clear that for some years her physical charms continued to be irresistible to the infatuated Watson, for only in this way can we account for his going as far as he did to meet her cruelly intolerant objections to the continuance of his association with Holmes."

June Thomson rejects Hall's theory, citing far more mundane reasons for the change in Holmes and Watson's friendship. "Their lack of contact," she contends, "is due more to a slow drifting apart, brought about by the physical distance between them, rather than through any specific alienation. Both were busy men, absorbed in their own very different lives and, as can happen in even the closest friendships, they found they had less and less in common as the years passed and there were fewer opportunities to meet."

4 The story was published, with the cooperation of Arthur Conan Doyle, in England in the *Strand Magazine* in December 1926 and in the United States in *Liberty* on November 27, 1926. The remainder of this paragraph replaces the following text in the manuscript: "It is possible that he would in any case have rejected this case from his records for in his loyalty he would always dwell upon my successes. I do not think that I can look back on the adventure of the Lion's Mane with any particular personal pride and yet in its rarity I place it very high among my collection." Perhaps on reflection, the aging Holmes decided at the last minute that if he were allowing the tale to be published, he should appear to have been proud of his part in discovering the secret. "Rarity," after all, was a very slight reason for the readers of the *Strand* to appreciate the story.

commanding a great view of the Channel. At this point the coast-line is entirely of chalk cliffs, which can only be descended by a single, long, tortuous path, which is steep and slippery. At the bottom of the path lie a hundred yards of pebbles and shingle, even when the tide is at full. Here and there, however, there are curves and hollows which make splendid swimming-pools filled afresh with each flow. This admirable beach extends for some miles in each direction, save only at one point where the little cove and village of Fulworth break the line.

My house is lonely. I, my old housekeeper,[5] and my bees have the estate all to ourselves. Half a mile off, however, is Harold Stackhurst's well-known coaching[6] establishment, The Gables, quite a large place, which contains some score of young fellows preparing for various professions, with a staff of several masters. Stackhurst himself was a well-known rowing Blue[7] in his day, and an excellent all-round scholar. He and I were always friendly from the day I came to the coast, and he was the one man who was on such terms with me that we could drop in on each other in the evenings without an invitation.

Towards the end of July, 1907, there was a severe gale, the wind blowing up-channel, heaping the seas to the base of the cliffs and leaving a lagoon at the turn of the tide. On the morning of which I speak the wind had abated, and all Nature was newly washed and fresh. It was impossible to work upon so delightful a day, and I strolled out before breakfast to enjoy the exquisite air. I walked along the cliff path which led to the steep descent to the beach. As I walked I heard a shout behind me, and there was Harold Stackhurst waving his hand in cheery greeting.

"What a morning, Mr. Holmes! I thought I should see you out."

"Going for a swim, I see."

"At your old tricks again," he laughed, patting his bulging pocket. "Yes. McPherson started early, and I expect I may find him there."

Fitzroy McPherson was the science master, a fine upstanding young fellow whose life had been crippled by heart trouble following rheumatic fever. He was a natural athlete, however, and excelled in every game which did not throw too great a

5 If she is the same housekeeper Holmes employed in 1914, we learn in "His Last Bow" that her first name was Martha. Early commentators generally assume, without foundation, that Holmes's housekeeper in retirement was Mrs. Hudson.

6 A "coach" is a private tutor, especially one employed in preparing for a particular examination. Note that Professor Moriarty was an army coach.

7 Gilchrist of "The Three Students" was a Blue in the hurdles and long jump. See "The Three Students," note 18.

strain upon him. Summer and winter he went for his swim, and, as I am a swimmer myself, I have often joined him.

At this moment we saw the man himself. His head showed above the edge of the cliff where the path ends. Then his whole figure appeared at the top, staggering like a drunken man. The next instant he threw up his hands and, with a terrible cry, fell upon his face. Stackhurst and I rushed forward—it may have been fifty yards—and turned him on his back. He was obviously dying. Those glazed sunken eyes and dreadful livid cheeks could mean nothing else. One glimmer of life came into his face for an instant, and he uttered two or three words with an eager air of warning. They were slurred and indistinct, but to my ear the last of them, which burst in a shriek from his lips, were "the Lion's Mane." It was utterly

McPherson threw up his hands and, with a terrible cry,
fell upon his face. Stackhurst and I rushed forward.
Howard Elcock, *Strand Magazine*, 1926

irrelevant and unintelligible, and yet I could twist the sound into no other sense. Then he half raised himself from the ground, threw his arms into the air and fell forward on his side. He was dead.

My companion was paralysed by the sudden horror of it, but I, as may well be imagined, had every sense on the alert. And I had need, for it was speedily evident that we were in the presence of an extraordinary case. The man was dressed only in his Burberry overcoat,[8] his trousers, and an unlaced pair of canvas shoes. As he fell over, his Burberry, which had been simply thrown round his shoulders, slipped off, exposing his trunk. We stared at it in amazement. His back was covered with dark red lines as though he had been terribly flogged by a thin wire scourge. The instrument with which this punishment had been inflicted was clearly flexible, for the long, angry weals curved round his shoulders and ribs. There was blood dripping down his chin, for he had bitten through his lower lip in the paroxysm of his agony. His drawn and distorted face told how terrible that agony had been.

I was kneeling and Stackhurst standing by the body when a shadow fell across us, and we found that Ian Murdoch was by our side. Murdoch was the mathematical coach at the establishment, a tall, dark, thin man, so taciturn and aloof that none can be said to have been his friend. He seemed to live in some high, abstract region of surds[9] and conic sections,[10] with little to connect him with ordinary life. He was looked upon as an oddity by the students, and would have been their butt, but there was some strange outlandish blood in the man, which showed itself not only in his coal-black eyes and swarthy face, but also in occasional outbreaks of temper, which could only be described as ferocious. On one occasion, being plagued by a little dog belonging to McPherson, he had caught the creature up and hurled it through the plate-glass window, an action for which Stackhurst would certainly have given him his dismissal had he not been a very valuable teacher. Such was the strange, complex man who now appeared beside us. He seemed to be honestly shocked at the sight before him, though the incident of the dog may show that there was no great sympathy between the dead man and himself.

"Poor fellow! Poor fellow! What can I do? How can I help?"

"Were you with him? Can you tell us what has happened?"

8 This would have been the modern trench coat, developed by Thomas Burberry, a former draper. Burberry became famous for inventing gabardine, an ingenious fabric made of yarn that was waterproofed before it was woven. Legend has it that his invention originated from a conversation he had with a local shepherd. When Burberry asked how it was that the shepherd's smock kept the rain at bay, the shepherd replied that oil from sheep's wool may have been a factor. Burberry patented gabardine in 1888, and eventually his name became synonymous with the unique style of overcoat manufactured by his company. Burberry opened his first shop in 1891; he would later design uniforms for the British army and outfit Roald Amundsen's South Pole expedition (in 1911) and Ernest Shackleton's Antarctic expedition (1914).

9 An irrational number (one with an infinite number of digits after the decimal point), such as the square root of three.

10 In geometry, the intersection of a right circular cone and a plane; the intersection will always be a line, a circle, an ellipse, a hyperbola, or a parabola (depending on the angle of the plane and the angle of the edge of the cone).

11 The following deleted sentences appear in the manuscript: "Dr. Mordhouse the well-known naturalist who was summering on the South Coast had joined him. Morning, noon & evening the Doctor's sunhat and butterfly net were familiar object on the Downs and along the beach. I need not explain that he is probably the most popular living writer upon the subject. What is more important at this crisis is that he was of a cheery sunny disposition a fit comrade for a man in trouble." The source of the "Mordhouse" material and possible reasons for its deletion are considered in note 46, below.

12 Clay mixed with carbonate of lime.

13 A beach or other tract covered with loose stones or pebbles.

14 The manuscript continues: "The reader will see that I take him into my confidence as I go, and have, I fear, none of the literary wiles of Watson."

"No, no, I was late this morning. I was not on the beach at all. I have come straight from The Gables. What can I do?"

"You can hurry to the police-station at Fulworth. Report the matter at once."

Without a word he made off at top speed, and I proceeded to take the matter in hand, while Stackhurst, dazed at this tragedy, remained by the body.[11] My first task naturally was to note who was on the beach. From the top of the path I could see the whole sweep of it, and it was absolutely deserted save that two or three dark figures could be seen far away moving towards the village of Fulworth. Having satisfied myself upon this point, I walked slowly down the path. There was clay or soft marl[12] mixed with the chalk, and every here and there I saw the same footstep, both ascending and descending. No one else had gone down to the beach by this track that morning. At one place I observed the print of an open hand with the fingers towards the incline. This could only mean that poor McPherson had fallen as he ascended. There were rounded depressions, too, which suggested that he had come down upon his knees more than once. At the bottom of the path was the considerable lagoon left by the retreating tide. At the side of it McPherson had undressed, for there lay his towel on a rock. It was folded and dry, so that it would seem that, after all, he had never entered the water. Once or twice as I hunted round amid the hard shingle[13] I came on little patches of sand where the print of his canvas shoe, and also of his naked foot, could be seen. The latter fact proved that he had made all ready to bathe, though the towel indicated that he had not actually done so.[14]

And here was the problem clearly defined—as strange a one as had ever confronted me. The man had not been on the beach more than a quarter of an hour at the most. Stackhurst had followed him from The Gables, so there could be no doubt about that. He had gone to bathe and had stripped, as the naked footsteps showed. Then he had suddenly huddled on his clothes again—they were all dishevelled and unfastened—and he had returned without bathing, or at any rate without drying himself. And the reason for his change of purpose had been that he had been scourged in some savage, inhuman fashion, tortured until he bit his lip through in his agony, and was left with only strength enough to crawl away and to die. Who had done this barbarous deed? There were, it is true, small grottos and caves in the base of the cliffs, but the low sun shone directly into them, and there was no place for concealment.[15] Then, again, there were those distant figures on the beach. They seemed too far away to have been connected with the crime, and the broad lagoon in which McPherson had intended to bathe lay between him and them, lapping up to the rocks. On the sea two or three fishing-boats were at no great distance. Their occupants might be examined at our leisure. There were several roads for inquiry, but none which led to any very obvious goal.

When I at last returned to the body I found that a little group of wandering folk had gathered round it. Stackhurst[16] was, of course, still there, and Ian Murdoch had just arrived with Anderson, the village constable, a big, ginger-moustached man of the slow, solid Sussex breed—a breed which covers much good sense under a heavy, silent exterior. He listened to everything, took note of all we said, and finally drew me aside.

"I'd be glad of your advice, Mr. Holmes. This is a big thing for me to handle, and I'll hear of it from Lewes[17] if I go wrong."

I advised him to send for his immediate superior, and for a doctor; also to allow nothing to be moved, and as few fresh footmarks as possible to be made, until they came. In the meantime I searched the dead man's pockets. There were his handkerchief, a large knife, and a small folding card-case. From this projected a slip of paper, which I unfolded and handed to the constable. There was written on it in a scrawling, feminine hand: "I will be there, you may be sure.—Maudie." It read like a love affair, an assignation, though when and where were a blank. The constable replaced it in the card-case and returned it with the other things to the pockets of the Burberry. Then, as nothing more suggested itself, I walked back to my house for breakfast, having first arranged that the base of the cliffs should be thoroughly searched.

Stackhurst was round in an hour or two to tell me that the body had been removed to The Gables, where the inquest would be

15 The original version reads: "No one could emerge from them now unseen and they would all be examined in turn."

16 The phrase "and Dr. Mordhurst" appears in the manuscript.

17 Lewes, as the county town of Sussex, was the location of the constabulary headquarters.

18 The first part of this sentence does not appear in the original version.

19 An enclosed, wagon-like contraption utilised by "modest" beachgoers uncomfortable with the concept of bathing attire. The vehicle could be pushed into the water, allowing bathers to enjoy the ocean without exposing themselves to the elements or—even worse—the general public.

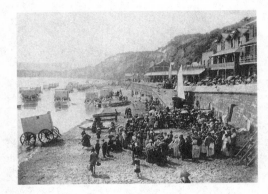

Bathing-cots.
A Hundred Years Ago

held. He brought with him some serious and definite news. As I expected, nothing had been found in the small caves below the cliff,[18] but he had examined the papers in McPherson's desk, and there were several which showed an intimate correspondence with a certain Miss Maud Bellamy, of Fulworth. We had then established the identity of the writer of the note.

"The police have the letters," he explained. "I could not bring them. But there is no doubt that it was a serious love affair. I see no reason, however, to connect it with that horrible happening save, indeed, that the lady had made an appointment with him."

"But hardly at a bathing-pool which all of you were in the habit of using," I remarked.

"It is mere chance," said he, "that several of the students were not with McPherson."

"*Was* it mere chance?"

Stackhurst knit his brows in thought.

"Ian Murdoch held them back," said he. "He would insist upon some algebraic demonstration before breakfast. Poor chap, he is dreadfully cut up about it all."

"And yet I gather that they were not friends."

"At one time they were not. But for a year or more Murdoch has been as near to McPherson as he ever could be to anyone. He is not of a very sympathetic disposition by nature."

"So I understand. I seem to remember your telling me once about a quarrel over the ill-usage of a dog."

"That blew over all right."

"But left some vindictive feeling, perhaps."

"No, no; I am sure they were real friends."

"Well, then, we must explore the matter of the girl. Do you know her?"

"Everyone knows her. She is the beauty of the neighbourhood—a real beauty, Holmes, who would draw attention everywhere. I knew that McPherson was attracted by her, but I had no notion that it had gone so far as these letters would seem to indicate."

"But who is she?"

"She is the daughter of old Tom Bellamy, who owns all the boats and bathing-cots[19] at Fulworth. He was a fisherman to start with, but is now a man of some substance. He and his son William run the business."

"Shall we walk into Fulworth and see them?"

"On what pretext?"

"Oh, we can easily find a pretext. After all, this poor man did not ill-use himself in this outrageous way. Some human hand was on the handle of that scourge, if indeed it was a scourge which inflicted the injuries. His circle of acquaintances in this lonely place was surely limited. Let us follow it up in every direction and we can hardly fail to come upon the motive, which in turn should lead us to the criminal."

It would have been a pleasant walk across the thyme-scented Downs had our minds not been poisoned by the tragedy we had witnessed. The village of Fulworth lies in a hollow curving in a semicircle round the bay. Behind the old-fashioned hamlet several modern houses have been built upon the rising ground. It was to one of these that Stackhurst guided me.

"That's The Haven, as Bellamy called it. The one with the corner tower and slate roof. Not bad for a man who started with nothing but—By Jove, look at that!"

The garden gate of The Haven had opened and a man had emerged. There was no mistaking that tall, angular, straggling figure. It was Ian Murdoch, the mathematician. A moment later we confronted him upon the road.

"Hullo!" said Stackhurst. The man nodded, gave us a[20] sideways glance from his curious dark eyes, and would have passed us, but his principal pulled him up.

"What were you doing there?" he asked.

Murdoch's face flushed with anger. "I am your subordinate, sir, under your roof. I am not aware that I owe you any account of my private actions."

Stackhurst's nerves were near the surface after all he had endured. Otherwise, perhaps, he would have waited. Now he lost his temper completely.

"In the circumstances your answer is pure impertinence, Mr. Murdoch."

"Your own question might perhaps come under the same heading."

"This is not the first time that I have had to overlook your insubordinate ways. It will certainly be the last. You will kindly make fresh arrangements for your future as speedily as you can."

[20] The original version included the phrase "rather malevolent" here.

21 This encounter, in the opinion of Julia C. Rosenblatt, hides Holmes's real reason for writing up the events of "The Lion's Mane": they mark his introduction to the lovely Maud Bellamy. Rosenblatt argues that Holmes loved Maud and married her, once her grieving over McPherson's death had passed. "Unwilling to publish his true feelings for all the world to read, he modestly conceded 'Maud Bellamy will always remain in my memory as a most complete and remarkable woman.' Never before had he confessed such regard for a woman."

"I had intended to do so. I have lost to-day the only person who made The Gables habitable."

He strode off upon his way, while Stackhurst, with angry eyes, stood glaring after him. "Is he not an impossible, intolerable man?" he cried.

The one thing that impressed itself forcibly upon my mind was that Mr. Ian Murdoch was taking the first chance to open a path of escape from the scene of the crime. Suspicion, vague and nebulous, was now beginning to take outline in my mind. Perhaps the visit to the Bellamys might throw some further light upon the matter. Stackhurst pulled himself together, and we went forward to the house.

Mr. Bellamy proved to be a middle-aged man with a flaming red beard. He seemed to be in a very angry mood, and his face was soon as florid as his hair.

"No, sir, I do not desire any particulars. My son here"—indicating a powerful young man, with a heavy, sullen face, in the corner of the sitting-room—"is of one mind with me that Mr. McPherson's attentions to Maud were insulting. Yes, sir, the word 'marriage' was never mentioned, and yet there were letters and meetings, and a great deal more of which neither of us could approve. She has no mother, and we are her only guardians. We are determined—"

But the words were taken from his mouth by the appearance of the lady herself. There was no gainsaying that she would have graced any assembly in the world. Who could have imagined that so rare a flower would grow from such a root and in such an atmosphere? Women have seldom been an attraction to me, for my brain has always governed my heart, but I could not look upon her perfect clear-cut face, with all the soft freshness of the Downlands in her delicate colouring, without realizing that no young man would cross her path unscathed.[21] Such was the girl who had pushed open the door and stood now, wide-eyed and intense, in front of Harold Stackhurst.

"I know already that Fitzroy is dead," she said. "Do not be afraid to tell me the particulars."

"This other gentleman of yours let us know the news," explained the father.

"There is no reason why my sister should be brought into the matter," growled the younger man.

The sister turned a sharp, fierce look upon him. "This is my business, William. Kindly leave me to manage it in my own way. By all accounts there has been a crime committed. If I can help to show who did it, it is the least I can do for him who is gone."

She listened to a short account from my companion, with a composed concentration which showed me that she possessed strong character as well as great beauty. Maud Bellamy will always remain in my memory as a most complete and remarkable woman. It seems that she already knew me by sight, for she turned to me at the end.

"Bring them to justice, Mr. Holmes. You have my sympathy and my help, whoever they may be." It seemed to me that she glanced defiantly at her father and brother as she spoke.

"Thank you," said I. "I value a woman's instinct in such matters. You use the word 'they.' You think that more than one was concerned?"

"I knew Mr. McPherson well enough to be aware that he was a brave and a strong man. No single person could ever have inflicted such an outrage upon him."

"Might I have one word with you alone?"

"I tell you, Maud, not to mix yourself up in the matter," cried her father angrily.

She looked at me helplessly. "What can I do?"

"The whole world will know the facts presently, so there can be no harm if I discuss them here," said I. "I should have preferred privacy, but if your father will not allow it he must share the deliberations." Then I spoke of the note which had been found in the dead man's pocket. "It is sure to be produced at the inquest. May I ask you to throw any light upon it that you can?"

"I see no reason for mystery," she answered. "We were engaged to be married, and we only kept it secret because Fitzroy's uncle, who is very old and said to be dying, might have disinherited him if he had married against his wish. There was no other reason."

"You could have told us," growled Mr. Bellamy.

"So I would, father, if you had ever shown sympathy."

"I object to my girl picking up with men outside her own station."

"It was your prejudice against him which prevented us from telling you. As to this appointment"—she fumbled in her dress and produced a crumpled note—"it was in answer to this."

DEAREST,
The old place on the beach just after sunset on Tuesday. It is the only time I can get away.

F. M.

"Tuesday was to-day, and I had meant to meet him to-night."

I turned over the paper. "This never came by post. How did you get it?"

I turned over the paper. "This never came by post. How did you get it?" "I would rather not answer that question."
Howard Elcock, *Strand Magazine*, 1926

"I would rather not answer that question. It has really nothing to do with the matter which you are investigating. But anything which bears upon that I will most freely answer."

She was as good as her word, but there was nothing which was helpful in our investigation. She had no reason to think that her *fiancé* had any hidden enemy, but she admitted that she had had several warm admirers.

"May I ask if Mr. Ian Murdoch was one of them?"

She blushed and seemed confused.

"There was a time when I thought he was. But that was all changed when he understood the relations between Fitzroy and myself."

Again the shadow round this strange man seemed to me to be taking more definite shape. His record must be examined. His rooms must be privately searched. Stackhurst was a willing collaborator, for in his mind also suspicions were forming. We returned from our visit to The Haven with the hope that one free end of this tangled skein was already in our hands.

A week passed. The inquest had thrown no light upon the matter and had been adjourned for further evidence. Stackhurst had made discreet inquiry about his subordinate, and there had been a superficial search of his room, but without result. Personally, I had gone over the whole ground again, both physically and mentally, but with no new conclusions. In all my chronicles the reader will find no case which brought me so completely to the limit of my powers. Even my imagination could conceive no solution to the mystery. And then there came the incident of the dog.

It was my old housekeeper who heard of it first by that strange wireless by which such people collect the news of the country-side.

"Sad story this, sir, about Mr. McPherson's dog," said she one evening.

I do not encourage such conversations, but the words arrested my attention.

"What of Mr. McPherson's dog?"

"Dead, sir. Died of grief for its master."

"Who told you this?"

"Why, sir, everyone is talking of it. It took on terrible, and

22 Michael Harrison, in his monograph *Cynological Mr. Holmes: Conanical Canines Considered*, remarks how far Holmes has come emotionally in his response to a dog's death, from his coldly clinical interest in the poisoning of the "experimental subject" dog in *A Study in Scarlet* to this passage.

has eaten nothing for a week. Then to-day two of the young gentlemen from The Gables found it dead—down on the beach, sir, at the very place where its master met his end."

"At the very place." The words stood out clear in my memory. Some dim perception that the matter was vital rose in my mind. That the dog should die was after the beautiful, faithful nature of dogs.[22] But "in the very place"! Why should this lonely beach be fatal to it? Was it possible that it also had been sacrificed to some revengeful feud? Was it possible—? Yes, the perception was dim, but already something was building up in my mind. In a few minutes I was on my way to The Gables, where I found Stackhurst in his study. At my request he sent for Sudbury and Blount, the two students who had found the dog.

"Yes, it lay on the very edge of the pool," said one of them. "It must have followed the trail of its dead master."

I saw the faithful little creature, an Airedale terrier, laid out upon the mat in the hall. The body was stiff and rigid, the eyes projecting, and the limbs contorted. There was agony in every line of it.

From The Gables I walked down to the bathing-pool. The sun had sunk and the shadow of the great cliff lay black across the water, which glimmered dully like a sheet of lead. The place was deserted and there was no sign of life save for two sea-birds circling and screaming overhead. In the fading light I could dimly make out the little dog's spoor upon the sand round the very rock on which his master's towel had been laid. For a long time I stood in deep meditation while the shadows grew darker around me. My mind was filled with racing thoughts. You have known what it was to be in a nightmare in which you feel that there is some all-important thing for which you search and which you know is there, though it remains forever just beyond your reach. That was how I felt that evening as I stood alone by that place of death. Then at last I turned and walked slowly homeward.

I had just reached the top of the path when it came to me. Like a flash, I remembered the thing for which I had so eagerly and vainly grasped. You will know, or Watson has written in vain, that I hold a vast store of out-of-the-way knowledge, without scientific system, but very available for the needs of my work. My mind is like a crowded box-room with packets of all sorts stowed away therein—so many that I may well have but a vague perception of what was there.[23] I had known that there was something which might bear upon this matter. It was still vague, but at least I knew how I could make it clear. It was monstrous, incredible, and yet it was always a possibility. I would test it to the full.

There is a great garret in my little house which is stuffed with books. It was into this that I plunged and rummaged for an hour. At the end of that time I emerged with a little chocolate and silver volume. Eagerly I turned up the chapter of which I had a dim remembrance. Yes, it was indeed a far-fetched and unlikely proposition, and yet I could not be at rest until I had made sure if it might, indeed, be so. It was late when I retired, with my mind eagerly awaiting the work of the morrow.

But that work met with an annoying interruption. I had hardly swallowed my early cup of tea and was starting for the beach when I had a call from Inspector Bardle of the Sussex Constabulary—a steady, solid, bovine man with thoughtful eyes, which looked at me now with a very troubled expression.

"I know your immense experience, sir," said he. "This is quite unofficial, of course, and need go no farther. But I am fairly up against it in this McPherson case. The question is, shall I make an arrest, or shall I not?"

"Meaning Mr. Ian Murdoch?"

"Yes, sir. There is really no one else when you come to think of it. That's the advantage of this solitude. We narrow it down to a very small compass. If he did not do it, then who did?"

"What have you against him?"

He had gleaned along the same furrows as I had. There was Murdoch's character and the mystery which seemed to hang round the man. His furious bursts of temper, as shown in the incident of the dog. The fact that he had quarrelled with McPherson in the past, and that there was some reason to think that he might have resented his attentions to Miss Bellamy. He had all my points, but no fresh ones, save that Murdoch seemed to be making every preparation for departure.

"What would my position be if I let him slip away with all this evidence against him?" The burly, phlegmatic man was sorely troubled in his mind.[24]

23 Holmes's observation here is in direct contradiction to what he told Watson of his mental habits in *A Study in Scarlet*. " 'I consider that a man's brain originally is like a little empty attic,' he said then, 'and you have to stock it with such furniture as you choose. A fool takes in all the lumber of every sort that he comes across, so that the knowledge which might be useful to him gets crowded out, or at best is jumbled up with a lot of other things so that he has a difficulty in laying his hands upon it. Now the skilful workman is very careful indeed as to what he takes into his brain-attic. He will have nothing but the tools which may help him in doing his work, but of these he has a large assortment, and all in the most perfect order. It is a mistake to think that that little room has elastic walls and can distend to any extent. Depend upon it there comes a time when for every addition of knowledge you forget something that you knew before. It is of the highest importance, therefore, not to have useless facts elbowing out the useful ones.' "

24 The following appears here in the original text: "It was clear to me however that a premature arrest would be fatal."

25 The following dialogue appears in the original text:

"Have you heard the Doctor about that?" asked the Inspector with a peculiar look.

"Has he anything fresh?"

"He considers that it was not a mere wire whip which could have done the mischief. He has examined the scars very carefully with a lens."

"What then?"

26 The word "doctor" is capitalised in the original text, the apparent remains of Dr. Mordhouse/Mordhurst.

27 And a new method it apparently was, for photography is not previously mentioned among the various techniques Holmes employs throughout the Canon. Holmes had certainly witnessed the phenomenon of the amateur photographer many years earlier: John Clay, the villain of "The Red-Headed League," was an avid amateur photographer, as was Jephro Rucastle of "The Copper Beeches," both of which cases likely occurred prior to 1890. Arthur Conan Doyle was also an avid amateur photographer and in the early 1880s wrote numerous articles for the *British Journal of Photography* on photographic techniques. The use of photography in connection with the solving of crimes was not new either; in the 1840s, the French Sûreté (the national police force) began storing photographs of known criminals in their records, and in 1903, the first conviction in England based on photographs of crime-scene fingerprints was obtained.

By 1907, photography had expanded well beyond the domain of journalism, thanks in no small part to the innovations of the Eastman Kodak Company, which brought out the popular Kodak camera in 1888. Targeted toward the general public under the slogan "You push the button—we do the rest," this

"Consider," I said, "all the essential gaps in your case. On the morning of the crime he can surely prove an alibi. He had been with his scholars till the last moment, and within a few minutes of McPherson's appearance he came upon us from behind. Then bear in mind the absolute impossibility that he could single-handed have inflicted this outrage upon a man quite as strong as himself. Finally, there is this question of the instrument with which these injuries were inflicted."[25]

"What could it be but a scourge or flexible whip of some sort?"

"Have you examined the marks?" I asked.

"I have seen them. So has the doctor."[26]

"But I have examined them very carefully with a lens. They have peculiarities."

"What are they, Mr. Holmes?"

I stepped to my bureau and brought out an enlarged photograph. "This is my method in such cases," I explained.[27]

"You certainly do things thoroughly, Mr. Holmes."

"I should hardly be what I am if I did not. Now let us consider this weal which extends round the right shoulder. Do you observe nothing remarkable?"

"I can't say I do."

"Surely it is evident that it is unequal in its intensity. There is a dot of extravasated[28] blood here, and another there. There are similar indications in this other weal down here. What can that mean?"

"I have no idea. Have you?"

"Perhaps I have. Perhaps I haven't. I may be able to say more soon. Anything which will define what made that mark will bring us a long way towards the criminal."[29]

"It is, of course, an absurd idea," said the policeman, "but if a red-hot net of wire had been laid across the back, then these better marked points would represent where the meshes crossed each other."

"A most ingenious comparison.[30] Or shall we say a very stiff cat-o'-nine-tails with small hard knots upon it?"

"By Jove, Mr. Holmes, I think you have hit it."

"Or there may be some very different cause, Mr. Bardle.[31]

hand camera, one of several on the market, could take up to one hundred pictures on negative film. The amateur photographer processed his or her prints by sending the entire camera to the Eastman factory in Rochester, New York. (A British factory in Harrow, Middlesex, was opened in 1891.) Soon, even children were being encouraged to take pictures, with the 1900 introduction of Kodak's Brownie camera. Named after Palmer Cox's cartoon characters, the camera cost one dollar and, according to the ads, could be "operated by any school boy or girl." In the first year of production, 150,000 units were shipped to stores. For the dedicated amateur photographer, supplies were easily at hand. Harrod's Stores' 1895 Catalogue offered a complete line of cameras, films, plates, lamps, developing chemicals, papers, and printing equipment for the hobbyist.

28 To extravasate is to force blood out from a vessel into surrounding tissue. In this case, Holmes evidently noticed several red splotches underneath the dead man's skin.

29 This paragraph replaces the following, which appears in the original text: "Neither am I bound to say have I. And yet it is of capital importance. Anything which will define the instrument used will help us towards the criminal."

30 The original text uses the word "suggestion" and goes on: "But, as you say, the idea cannot be seriously entertained. What about a wire scourge with little bands of metal upon the wires. Have I not read somewhere of such a scourge?"

31 Deleted from the original text: "Yes, yes, but how does it advance us? The one argument for an arrest is that you could search the man's possessions."

My door was flung open and Ian Murdoch staggered
into the room "Brandy! Brandy!" he gasped, and fell
groaning upon the sofa.
Howard Elcock, *Strand Magazine*, 1926

But your case is far too weak for an arrest. Besides, we have
those last words—'the Lion's Mane.' "

"I have wondered whether Ian—"

"Yes, I have considered that. If the second word had borne
any resemblance to Murdoch—but it did not. He gave it
almost in a shriek. I am sure that it was 'Mane.' "

"Have you no alternative, Mr. Holmes?"

"Perhaps I have. But I do not care to discuss it until there is
something more solid to discuss."

"And when will that be?"

"In an hour—possibly less."

The Inspector rubbed his chin and looked at me with dubious eyes.

"I wish I could see what was in your mind, Mr. Holmes. Perhaps it's those fishing-boats."

"No, no, they were too far out."

"Well, then, is it Bellamy and that big son of his? They were
not too sweet upon Mr. McPherson. Could they have done him
a mischief?"

32 The phrase "the naturalist Dr. Mordhouse" is deleted from the original text and "Stackhurst" inserted.

"No, no, you won't draw me until I am ready," said I with a smile. "Now, Inspector, we each have our own work to do. Perhaps if you were to meet me here at midday—"

So far we had got when there came the tremendous interruption which was the beginning of the end.

My outer door was flung open, there were blundering footsteps in the passage, and Ian Murdoch staggered into the room, pallid, dishevelled, his clothes in wild disorder, clawing with bony hands at the furniture to hold himself erect. "Brandy! Brandy!" he gasped, and fell groaning upon the sofa.

He was not alone. Behind him came[32] Stackhurst, hatless and panting, almost as *distrait* as his companion.

"Yes, yes, brandy!" he cried. "The man is at his last gasp. It was all I could do to bring him here. He fainted twice upon the way."

Half a tumbler of the raw spirit brought about a wondrous change. He pushed himself up on one arm and swung his coat from his shoulders. "For God's sake, oil, opium, morphia!" he cried. "Anything to ease this infernal agony!"

The Inspector and I cried out at the sight. There, crisscrossed upon the man's naked shoulder, was the same strange reticulated pattern of red, inflamed lines which had been the death-mark of Fitzroy McPherson.

The pain was evidently terrible and was more than local, for

33 The original text reads, "I turned upon the Doctor."

the sufferer's breathing would stop for a time, his face would turn black, and then with loud gasps he would clap his hand to his heart, while his brow dropped beads of sweat. At any moment he might die. More and more brandy was poured down his throat, each fresh dose bringing him back to life. Pads of cotton-wool soaked in salad-oil seemed to take the agony from the strange wounds. At last his head fell heavily upon the cushion. Exhausted Nature had taken refuge in its last storehouse of vitality. It was half a sleep and half a faint, but at least it was ease from pain.

To question him had been impossible, but the moment we were assured of his condition Stackhurst turned upon me.[33]

"My God!" he cried, "what is it, Holmes? What is it?"

"Where did you find him?"

"Down on the beach. Exactly where poor McPherson met his end. If this man's heart had been weak as McPherson's was, he would not be here now. More than once I thought he was gone as I brought him up. It was too far to The Gables, so I made for you."

"Did you see him on the beach?"

"I was walking on the cliff when I heard his cry. He was at the edge of the water, reeling about like a drunken man. I ran down, threw some clothes about him, and brought him up. For Heaven's sake, Holmes, use all the powers you have and spare no pains to lift the curse from this place, for life is becoming unendurable. Can you, with all your world-wide reputation, do nothing for us?"

"I think I can, Stackhurst. Come with me now! And you, Inspector, come along! We will see if we cannot deliver this murderer into your hands."

Leaving the unconscious man in the charge of my housekeeper, we all three went down to the deadly lagoon. On the shingle there was piled a little heap of towels and clothes left by the stricken man. Slowly I walked round the edge of the water, my comrades in Indian file behind me. Most of the pool was quite shallow, but under the cliff where the beach was hollowed out it was four or five feet deep. It was to this part that a swimmer would naturally go, for it formed a beautiful pellucid green pool as clear as crystal. A line of rocks lay above it at the base of the cliff, and along this I led the way, peering eagerly into the depths beneath me. I had reached the deepest and stillest pool when my eyes caught that for which they were searching, and I burst into a shout of triumph.

"*Cyanea*!" I[34] cried. "*Cyanea*! Behold the Lion's Mane!"

The strange object at which I pointed did indeed look like a tangled mass torn from the mane of a lion. It lay upon a rocky shelf some three feet under the water, a curious waving, vibrating, hairy creature with streaks of silver among its yellow tresses. It pulsated with a slow, heavy dilation and contraction.[35]

"It has done mischief enough. Its day is over!" I cried. "Help me, Stackhurst! Let us end the murderer forever."[36]

There was a big boulder just above the ledge, and we pushed it until it fell with a tremendous splash into the water. When the ripples had cleared we saw that it had settled upon the ledge below. One flapping edge of yellow membrane showed that our victim was beneath it. A thick oily scum oozed out from below the stone and stained the water round, rising slowly to the surface.

"Well, this gets me!" cried the inspector. "What was it, Mr. Holmes? I'm born and bred in these parts, but I never saw such a thing. It don't belong to Sussex."

"Just as well for Sussex," I remarked. "It may have been the south-west gale that brought it up. Come back to my house, both of you, and I will give you the terrible experience of one who has good reason to remember his own meeting with the same peril of the seas."

When we reached my study we found that Murdoch was so far recovered that he could sit up. He was dazed in mind, and every now and then was shaken by a paroxysm of pain. In broken words he explained that he had no notion what had occurred to him, save that terrific pangs had suddenly shot through him, and that it had taken all his fortitude to reach the bank.

"Here is a book," I said, taking up the little volume, "which first brought light into what might have been forever dark.[37] It is *Out of Doors*, by the famous observer J. G. Wood.[38] Wood himself very nearly perished from contact with this vile creature, so he wrote with a very full knowledge. *Cyanea Capillata* is the miscreant's full name, and he can be as dangerous to life as, and far more painful than, the bite of the cobra.[39] Let me briefly give this extract.

34 Tellingly, "he" in the original text.

35 *Cyanea capillata*, the Lion's Mane Jellyfish, is one of the world's largest jellyfish. Its bell can grow up to three feet across, its fine tentacles a stunning thirty feet in length.

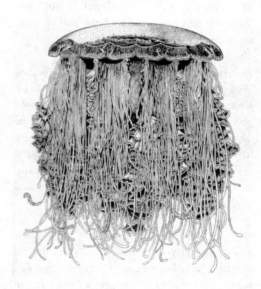

Cyanea capillata.

36 In the original text, the paragraph reads: " 'Its day is done!' cried the naturalist. 'Help me, Holmes!' "

37 This sentence is substituted in the published version for the following: "Our explanations were unnecessary for Dr. Mordhouse had arrived with a chocolate-backed book in his hand."

38 Reverend John George Wood (1827–1889) was the author of nearly sixty books and numerous popular articles—many of them geared toward children—intended to demystify the study of natural history. Neither a scientist nor a particularly skilled writer, he was nonetheless able to make natural history both interesting and comprehensible to lay people, and his work inspired countless subsequent

naturalists. Wood's *Out of Doors: A Selection of Original Articles on Practical Natural History*, was published in London by Longmans, Green in 1874 and appeared in new editions in 1882 and 1890.

39 Appearing in the original text: "I will leave the book that you may read the full account for yourself."

40 Wood's warnings are repeated in his *New Illustrated Natural History* (ca. 1895), where he writes: "Lest any of my readers should become fellow-sufferers with myself, I advise them to be very careful when bathing after a strong south-west wind has prevailed, and if ever they see a tawny mass of membranes and fibres floating along, to retreat at once, and wait until it is at least a hundred yards away."

41 "Undoubtedly the reverend gentleman was particularly sensitive to the sting of this jellyfish," Joel Hedgpeth writes, "for his account is by all odds the most harrowing in the literature of marine natural history." Fortunately, although jellyfish stings may be as alarmingly severe as Wood describes, Hedgpeth notes that, at least in North Atlantic waters, "there is no recorded fatality that can be attributed solely to jellyfish poisoning in temperate waters."

42 The word "Inspector" is substituted for "Mr. Holmes" in the original version.

43 Of course, Murdoch, living up to Holmes's initial doubts about him, might well have planted the jellyfish in the tide pool "with diabolical malice aforethought," Joel Hedgpeth theorises. His plan was to murder McPherson, then subject himself to the jellyfish's "tawny membranes" as a cover for his own crime. But Hedgpeth points out that no two jellyfish stings produce identical symptoms, and that

If the bather should see a loose roundish mass of tawny membranes and fibres, something like very large handfuls of lion's mane and silver paper, let him beware, for this is the fearful stinger, *Cyanea Capillata*.[40]

"Could our sinister acquaintance be more clearly described?

"He goes on to tell his own encounter with one when swimming off the coast of Kent. He found that the creature radiated almost invisible filaments to the distance of fifty feet, and that anyone within that circumference from the deadly centre was in danger of death. Even at a distance the effect upon Wood was almost fatal.

The multitudinous threads caused light scarlet lines upon the skin which on closer examination resolved into minute dots or pustules, each dot charged as it were with a red-hot needle making its way through the nerves.

"The local pain was, as he explains, the least part of the exquisite torment.

Pangs shot through the chest, causing me to fall as if struck by a bullet. The pulsation would cease, and then the heart would give six or seven leaps as if it would force its way through the chest.

"It nearly killed him, although he had only been exposed to it in the disturbed ocean and not in the narrow calm waters of a bathing-pool. He says that he could hardly recognize himself afterwards, so white, wrinkled and shrivelled was his face.[41] He gulped down brandy, a whole bottleful, and it seems to have saved his life. There is the book, Inspector.[42] I leave it with you, and you cannot doubt that it contains a full explanation of the tragedy of poor McPherson."

"And incidentally exonerates me," remarked Ian Murdoch with a wry smile.[43] "I do not blame you, Inspector, nor you, Mr. Holmes, for your suspicions were natural. I feel that on the very eve of my arrest I have only cleared myself by sharing the fate of my poor friend."

"No, Mr. Murdoch. I was already upon the track, and had I

been out as early as I intended I might well have saved you from this terrific experience."

"But how did you know, Mr. Holmes?"

"I am an omnivorous reader with a strangely retentive memory for trifles. That phrase 'the Lion's Mane' haunted my mind. I knew that I had seen it somewhere in an unexpected context. You have seen that it does describe the creature. I have no doubt that it was floating on the water when McPherson saw it, and that this phrase was the only one by which he could convey to us a warning as to the creature which had been his death."

"Then I, at least, am cleared," said Murdoch, rising slowly to his feet. "There are one or two words of explanation which I should give, for I know the direction in which your inquiries have run. It is true that I loved this lady, but from the day when she chose my friend McPherson my one desire was to help her to happiness. I was well content to stand aside and act as their go-between. Often I carried their messages, and it was because I was in their confidence and because she was so dear to me that I hastened to tell her of my friend's death, lest someone should forestall me in a more sudden and heartless manner. She would not tell you, sir, of our relations lest you should disapprove and I might suffer. But with your leave I must try to get back to The Gables, for my bed will be very welcome."

Stackhurst held out his hand. "Our nerves have all been at concert-pitch," said he. "Forgive what is past, Murdoch. We shall understand each other better in the future." They passed out together with their arms linked in friendly fashion. The Inspector remained, staring at me in silence with his ox-like eyes.

"Well, you've done it!" he cried at last. "I had read of you, but I never believed it. It's wonderful!"

I was forced to shake my head. To accept such praise was to lower one's own standards.

"I was slow at the outset—culpably slow.[44] Had the body been found in the water I could hardly have missed it. It was the towel which misled me. The poor fellow had never thought to dry himself, and so I in turn was led to believe that he had never been in the water. Why, then, should the attack of any water creature suggest itself to me? That was where I

the striking similarity between Murdoch's reaction and J. G. Wood's written account should have immediately raised Holmes's suspicions. "Beyond all doubt," Hedgpeth writes, "this dark, brooding, 'ferocious tempered' young man, disappointed in love and capable of throwing innocent dogs through windows, had conceived a most ingenious crime and to allay suspicion had caressed his own monstrous pet. But his own injuries were not serious enough, and so he found ways to reproduce those experienced by Dr. Wood." Hedgpeth adds that the long hair of an Airedale terrier should have protected it from the potency of the jellyfish's sting, and that therefore Murdoch must have poisoned the dog and placed it at the scene of the crime, to throw Holmes further off his scent.

44 "Fi, fi, Sherlock!" Nathan L. Bengis exclaims. "Even the 'gentlemen of the police force' should have seen through that one." He accuses Holmes of being "downright befuddled" in jumping to conclusions with the folded towel and yet not noticing that McPherson's skin, as well as his coat, shoes, and hair, would have still been wet by the time Holmes examined the body. This, not a rumpled towel, would have proved that McPherson had been in the water. "What is quite incredible and unpardonable," Bengis writes with surprising vehemence, "is your sorry attempt to exonerate yourself. Surely at least in retrospect the flimsiness of your excuse should have been apparent to you, and you should have been too ashamed of your performance to make a permanent record of it for future generations."

Edward F. Clark, Jr., defends Holmes by explaining that the ocean water would have largely dried or been blotted off and that any residue would have been commingled with sweat. He renders a verdict on Bengis's charge of "not proven."

Bengis's observation is also considered by Hirayama Yuichi and Mizuochi Masako. They argue that since Holmes could not have missed these signs, then McPherson never did enter the water. Instead, he was murdered by Tom and William Bellamy (inspired by Ian Murdoch), with the Lion's Mane used as a weapon. In *Sidelights on Holmes*, however, John Hall refutes their theory, primarily on the grounds of the size of the jellyfish and the impossibility of transportation. Instead, he suggests that McPherson, partially undressed, put his shoes back on to investigate the strange object that he saw on the beach, slipped on some rocks, and was stung.

Mary Ann Kluge makes the startling observation that all of the remarkably un-Holmesian characteristics of the detective—so overwhelmed with nature that he couldn't work, overlooking obvious clues, delighted with solving a simple mystery, following up random clues, awestruck by a beautiful woman, and trusting of a woman's intuition—fit a well-known personality: Dr. Watson! She concludes that Holmes and Watson had exchanged places to permit Holmes to carry out various secret missions.

45 "You have nearly met me at my Waterloo" and "You have nearly met me at what might have become my Waterloo" appear in the original text.

46 The perpetually dubious D. Martin Dakin concludes that "The Lion's Mane" is a pseudonymous story: a tale of "pure invention" not intended for publication, written at Holmes's request and with the use of his notes. O. F. Grazebrook uses harsher language, labelling it an "impudent forgery." But Tom Alessandri urges the reader to remember that Holmes did not write "The Lion's Mane" until 1919 or 1920, when he would have been sixty-five or sixty-six. The story therefore presents a fascinating look "as to how a genius

went astray. Well, well, Inspector,[45] I often ventured to chaff you gentlemen of the police force, but *Cyanea capillata* very nearly avenged Scotland Yard."[46]

reviews and attempts to revitalize a past career" and permits us to view "a lonely bee-keeper who seems sincerely to miss his old friend."

Examination of the changes evidenced in the manuscript of "The Lion's Mane," detailed above, suggests other possibilities. The story as originally written reflected poorly on Holmes, telling of his "Waterloo" suffered at the hands of the knowing Dr. Mordhouse/Mordhurst. It showed Holmes with little of his powers remaining. It is difficult to square this depiction with that of Holmes presented in "His Last Bow," where Holmes is as he was before retirement, in full command of his powers. Perhaps the original "Mordhouse" version of "The Lion's Mane" was fiction, written (by Holmes, Arthur Conan Doyle, or even some functionary in the war department) to establish "cover" for Holmes, designed to lull the Germans into believing that he was not a factor to be considered in their plans for England. Yet for whatever reason, the idea of publishing this cover story was abandoned. Later, Arthur Conan Doyle rewrote it for publication.

THE ADVENTURE OF THE
VEILED LODGER[1]

"The Veiled Lodger" is the shortest of Dr. Watson's stories, and there is virtually no detection on exhibit. As in "The Red Circle," a troubled landlady asks Holmes to investigate her own lodger, a woman despondent over a murder plot gone horribly wrong. Holmes, who has never hesitated to ignore society's rules himself, nonetheless moves to prevent the woman from committing the ultimate rejection of society: suicide. While some question Watson's authorship of the tale, the attitudes expressed here by Holmes about higher justice coincide with those evidenced by him in "The Blue Carbuncle" and "The Boscombe Valley Mystery." Also, none can doubt the Watsonian tone to the narrator's deliberate suppression of a "story concerning the politician, the lighthouse and the trained cormorant."

1 "The Veiled Lodger" was published in the United States in *Liberty* on January 22, 1927, and in England in the *Strand Magazine* in February 1927.

2 See "Holmes's Career," page 1705 for a consideration of the mathematics here.

WHEN ONE CONSIDERS that Mr. Sherlock Holmes was in active practice for twenty-three years, and that during seventeen of these I was allowed to co-operate with him and to keep notes of his doings,[2] it will be clear that I have a mass of material at my command. The problem has always been not to find but to choose. There is the long row of year-books which fill a shelf, and there are the dispatch-cases filled with documents, a perfect quarry for the student not only of crime but of the social and official scandals of the late Victorian era. Concerning these latter, I may say that the writers of agonized letters, who beg that the honour of their families or the reputation of famous forbears may not be touched, have nothing to fear. The discretion and high sense of professional honour which have always distinguished my friend are still at work in the choice of these memoirs, and no confidence will be abused. I deprecate, however, in the strongest way the attempts which have been made lately to get at and to destroy these papers.

The source of these outrages is known, and if they are repeated I have Mr. Holmes's authority for saying that the whole story concerning the politician, the lighthouse, and the trained cormorant will be given to the public. There is at least one reader who will understand.[3]

It is not reasonable to suppose that every one of these cases gave Holmes the opportunity of showing those curious gifts of instinct and observation which I have endeavoured to set forth in these memoirs. Sometimes he had with much effort to pick the fruit, sometimes it fell easily into his lap. But the most terrible human tragedies were often involved in those cases which brought him the fewest personal opportunities, and it is one of these which I now desire to record. In telling it, I have made a slight change of name and place, but otherwise the facts are as stated.

One forenoon—it was late in 1896—I received a hurried note from Holmes asking for my attendance.[4] When I arrived I found him seated in a smoke-laden atmosphere, with an elderly, motherly woman of the buxom landlady type in the corresponding chair in front of him.

"This is Mrs. Merrilow, of South Brixton," said my friend, with a wave of the hand. "Mrs. Merrilow does not object to tobacco, Watson, if you wish to indulge your filthy habits.[5] Mrs. Merrilow has an interesting story to tell which may well lead to further developments in which your presence may be useful."

"Anything I can do—"

"You will understand, Mrs. Merrilow, that if I come to Mrs. Ronder I should prefer to have a witness. You will make her understand that before we arrive."

"Lord bless you, Mr. Holmes," said our visitor, "she is that anxious to see you that you might bring the whole parish at your heels!"

"Then we shall come early in the afternoon. Let us see that we have our facts correct before we start. If we go over them it will help Dr. Watson to understand the situation. You say that Mrs. Ronder has been your lodger for seven years and that you have only once seen her face."

"And I wish to God I had not!" said Mrs. Merrilow.

"It was, I understand, terribly mutilated."

"Well, Mr. Holmes, you would hardly say it was a face at all. That's how it looked. Our milkman got a glimpse of her once

3 Donald A. Redmond, in "Still Sits the Cormorant," identifies the politician as Joseph Chamberlain, who was associated with a scandal in the 1890s relating to a mutual assurance society lampooned by *Punch* as the "Cormorant Friendly Society." Derek Hinrich suggests that the "politician" was "Dollmann," the pseudonym of the English traitor described in Erskine Childers's *Riddle of the Sands* (1903), whose plans for a British invasion involved a German troop ship called the *Kormoran* (cormorant).

4 Watson clearly was not living with Holmes on the precise date of this case. To explain the separation, H. W. Bell argues that Watson had married again and so was living away from Baker Street. Gavin Brend proposes that Holmes and Watson had temporarily parted because of a quarrel, which he attributes to Holmes's strictures on Watson's gambling. But neither D. Martin Dakin nor Dorothy L. Sayers puts much stock in the change of address: Dakin suggests that Watson was substituting for a colleague and living at that doctor's residence to do so, and Dorothy L. Sayers offers that Watson may have been staying with friends, such as Mr. and Mrs. Percy Phelps.

5 This is evidently a joke, for the "smoke-laden" atmosphere must have been created by Holmes himself indulging in the same habit.

6 In Victorian England, milk was not delivered in bottles. The milkman carried on his cart a large churn, from which the milk was drawn in a small can or tin.

peeping out of the upper window, and he dropped his tin[6] and the milk all over the front garden. That is the kind of face it is. When I saw her—I happened on her unawares—she covered up quick, and then she said, 'Now, Mrs. Merrilow, you know at last why it is that I never raise my veil.' "

"Do you know anything about her history?"

"Nothing at all."

"Did she give references when she came?"

"No, sir, but she gave hard cash, and plenty of it. A quarter's rent right down on the table in advance and no arguing about terms. In these times a poor woman like me can't afford to turn down a chance like that."

"Did she give any reason for choosing your house?"

"Mine stands well back from the road and is more private than most. Then, again, I only take the one, and I have no family of my own. I reckon she had tried others and found that mine suited her best. It's privacy she is after, and she is ready to pay for it."

"You say that she never showed her face from first to last save on the one accidental occasion. Well, it is a very remarkable story, most remarkable, and I don't wonder that you want it examined."

"I don't, Mr. Holmes. I am quite satisfied so long as I get my rent. You could not have a quieter lodger, or one who gives less trouble."

"Then what has brought matters to a head?"

"Her health, Mr. Holmes. She seems to be wasting away. And there's something terrible on her mind. 'Murder!' she cries. 'Murder!' And once I heard her, 'You cruel beast! You monster!' she cried. It was in the night, and it fair rang through the house and sent the shivers through me. So I went to her in the morning. 'Mrs. Ronder,' I says, 'if you have anything that is troubling your soul, there's the clergy,' I says, 'and there's the police. Between them you should get some help.' 'For God's sake, not the police!' says she, 'and the clergy can't change what is past. And yet,' she says, 'it would ease my mind if someone knew the truth before I died.' 'Well,' says I, 'if you won't have the regulars, there is this detective man what we read about'—beggin' your pardon, Mr. Holmes. And she, she fair jumped at it. 'That's the man,' says she. 'I wonder I never thought of it before. Bring him here, Mrs. Merrilow, and if he won't come, tell him I am the wife of Ronder's wild beast show. Say that, and give him the name Abbas Parva.' Here it is as she wrote it, Abbas Parva. 'That will bring him if he's the man I think he is.' "

"And it will, too," remarked Holmes. "Very good, Mrs. Merrilow. I should like to have a little chat with Dr. Watson. That will carry us till lunch-time. About three o'clock you may expect to see us at your house in Brixton."

Our visitor had no sooner waddled out of the room—no other verb can describe Mrs. Merrilow's method of progression—than Sherlock Holmes threw himself with fierce energy upon the pile of commonplace books in the corner. For a few minutes there was a constant swish of the leaves, and then with a grunt of satisfaction he came upon what he sought. So excited was he that he did not rise, but sat upon the floor like some strange Buddha, with crossed legs, the huge books all round him, and one open upon his knees.

"The case worried me at the time, Watson. Here are my marginal notes to prove it. I confess that I could make nothing of it. And yet I was convinced that the coroner was wrong. Have you no recollection of the Abbas Parva tragedy?"

"None, Holmes."

Holmes sat upon the floor like some strange Buddha,
with crossed legs, the books all round him, and
one open upon his knee.
Frank Wiles, *Strand Magazine*, 1927

7 George Wombwell (1778–1850) was the proprietor of England's largest travelling menagerie. It is said that Wombwell started his enterprise with two snakes, purchased from a sailor on the docks at the Port of London. A skilled marketer, Wombwell generated a considerable amount of publicity in 1825 by staging a controversial match between six bull mastiffs and Wombwell's two trained lions, Nero and Wallace. The public subsequently flocked to see the famed lions, and Wombwell built up an impressive collection of animals that included tigers, zebras, polar bears, and two rhinoceroses (billed as the "Largest Quadruped in the World, the Elephant Excepted"). Upon his death, *The Times* eulogised Wombwell by writing, "No one probably has done so much to forward practically the study of natural history amongst the masses."

Bostock and Wombwell's Menagerie
at the Crystal Palace, *c.* 1895.
Victorian and Edwardian London

8 In 1853, George Sanger (1827–1911) and his brother John Sanger (1816–1889) formed a small travelling circus. By 1871, it had become so popular that they were able to buy Astley's Amphitheatre and stage grand productions both there and at Agricultural Hall, all the while continuing to tour England. The brothers, who called themselves Lord George and Lord John, attracted curiosity and attention at

"And yet you were with me then. But certainly my own impression was very superficial, for there was nothing to go by, and none of the parties had engaged my services. Perhaps you would care to read the papers?"

"Could you not give me the points?"

"That is very easily done. It will probably come back to your memory as I talk. Ronder, of course, was a household word. He was the rival of Wombwell,[7] and of Sanger,[8] one of the greatest showmen of his day. There is evidence, however, that he took to drink, and that both he and his show were on the down grade at the time of the great tragedy. The caravan had halted for the night at Abbas Parva, which is a small village in Berkshire, when this horror occurred. They were on their way to Wimbledon, travelling by road, and they were simply camping and not exhibiting, as the place is so small a one that it would not have paid them to open.

"They had among their exhibits a very fine North African lion. Sahara King was its name, and it was the habit, both of Ronder and his wife, to give exhibitions inside its cage. Here, you see, is a photograph of the performance by which you will perceive that Ronder was a huge porcine person and that his wife was a very magnificent woman. It was deposed at the inquest that there had been some signs that the lion was dangerous, but, as usual, familiarity begat contempt, and no notice was taken of the fact.

"It was usual for either Ronder or his wife to feed the lion at night. Sometimes one went, sometimes both, but they never allowed anyone else to do it, for they believed that so long as they were the food-carriers he would regard them as benefactors and would never molest them. On this particular night, seven years ago, they both went, and a very terrible happening followed, the details of which have never been made clear.

"It seems that the whole camp was roused near midnight by the roars of the animal and the screams of the woman. The different grooms and *employés* rushed from their tents, carrying lanterns, and by their light an awful sight was revealed. Ronder lay, with the back of his head crushed in and deep claw-marks across his scalp, some ten yards from the cage, which was open. Close to the door of the cage lay Mrs. Ronder upon her back, with the creature squatting and snarling above her. It had torn her face in such a fashion that it was never thought that she could live. Several of the circus men, headed by Leonardo, the strong man, and Griggs, the clown, drove the creature off with poles, upon which it sprang back into the cage, and was at once locked in. How it had got loose was a mystery. It was conjectured that the pair intended to enter the cage, but that when the door was loosed the creature bounded out upon them. There was no other point of interest in the evidence save that the woman in a delirium of agony kept screaming, 'Coward! Coward!' as she was carried back to the van in which they lived. It was six months before she was fit to give evidence, but the inquest was duly held, with the obvious verdict of death from misadventure."

"What alternative could be conceived?" said I.

"You may well say so. And yet there were one or two points which worried young Edmunds, of the Berkshire Constabulary. A smart lad that! He was sent later to Allahabad.[9] That was how I came into the matter, for he dropped in and smoked a pipe or two over it."

"A thin, yellow-haired man?"

"Exactly. I was sure you would pick up the trail presently."

"But what worried him?"

"Well, we were both worried. It was so deucedly difficult to reconstruct the affair. Look at it from the lion's point of view. He is liberated. What does he do? He takes half a dozen bounds forward, which brings him to Ronder. Ronder turns to fly,—the claw-marks were on the back of his head—but the lion strikes him down. Then, instead of bounding on and escaping, he returns to the woman, who was close to the cage, and he knocks her over and chews her face up. Then, again, those cries of hers would seem to imply that her husband had in some way failed her. What could the poor devil have done to help her? You see the difficulty?"

"Quite."

"And then there was another thing. It comes back to me now as I think it over. There was some evidence that just at the time the lion roared and the woman screamed, a man began shouting in terror."

every town they visited, parading their gilded wagons and eccentric performers through the streets to the circus field. "Lord" George's wife, who danced with snakes in the lion's cage (and had once performed with Wombwell's menagerie), would often ride in the lead wagon, dressed as Britannia with a lion at her feet. The brothers dissolved their partnership and went their separate ways in the late 1870s, each forming his own travelling show.

9 Ceded to the British in 1801, the city of Allahabad, which means "City of God," was the site of heavy fighting during the Indian Mutiny. A. N. Wilson reports that British Colonel James Neill (see appendix to "The Crooked Man") "killed as many Indians in Allahabad alone as were killed on his own side in the entire two years of fighting."

10 An excellent white Burgundy, further evidence of Holmes's gourmet tastes (see "The Noble Bachelor," note 37).

"This man Ronder, no doubt."

"Well, if his skull was smashed in you would hardly expect to hear from him again. There were at least two witnesses who spoke of the cries of a man being mingled with those of a woman."

"I should think the whole camp was crying out by then. As to the other points, I think I could suggest a solution."

"I should be glad to consider it."

"The two were together, ten yards from the cage, when the lion got loose. The man turned and was struck down. The woman conceived the idea of getting into the cage and shutting the door. It was her only refuge. She made for it, and just as she reached it the beast bounded after her and knocked her over. She was angry with her husband for having encouraged the beast's rage by turning. If they had faced it they might have cowed it. Hence her cries of 'Coward!' "

"Brilliant, Watson! Only one flaw in your diamond."

"What is the flaw, Holmes?"

"If they were both ten paces from the cage, how came the beast to get loose?"

"Is it possible that they had some enemy who loosed it?"

"And why should it attack them savagely when it was in the habit of playing with them, and doing tricks with them inside the cage?"

"Possibly the same enemy had done something to enrage it."

Holmes looked thoughtful and remained in silence for some moments.

"Well, Watson, there is this to be said for your theory. Ronder was a man of many enemies. Edmunds told me that in his cups he was horrible. A huge bully of a man, he cursed and slashed at everyone who came in his way. I expect those cries about a monster, of which our visitor has spoken, were nocturnal reminiscences of the dear departed. However, our speculations are futile until we have all the facts. There is a cold partridge on the sideboard, Watson, and a bottle of Montrachet.[10] Let us renew our energies before we make a fresh call upon them."

When our hansom deposited us at the house of Mrs. Merrilow, we found that plump lady blocking up the open door of her humble but retired abode. It was very clear that her chief pre-occupation was lest she should lose a valuable lodger, and she implored us, before showing us up, to say and do nothing which could lead to so undesirable an end. Then, having reassured her, we followed her up the straight, badly carpeted staircase and were shown into the room of the mysterious lodger.

It was a close, musty, ill-ventilated place, as might be expected, since its inmate seldom left it. From keeping beasts in a cage, the woman seemed, by some retribution of fate, to have become herself a beast in a cage. She sat now in a broken armchair in the shadowy corner of the room. Long years of inaction had coarsened the lines of her figure, but at some period it must have been beautiful, and was still full and voluptuous. A thick dark veil covered her face, but it was cut off close at her upper lip and disclosed a perfectly shaped mouth and a delicately rounded chin. I could well conceive that she had indeed been a very remarkable woman. Her voice, too, was well modulated and pleasing.

"My name is not unfamiliar to you, Mr. Holmes," said she. "I thought that it would bring you."

"That is so, madam, though I do not know how you are aware that I was interested in your case."

"I learned it when I had recovered my health and was examined by Mr. Edmunds, the county detective. I fear I lied to him. Perhaps it would have been wiser had I told the truth."

"It is usually wiser to tell the truth. But why did you lie to him?"

"Because the fate of someone else depended upon it. I knew that he was a very worthless being, and yet I would not have his destruction upon my conscience. We had been so close—so close!"

"But has this impediment been removed?"

"Yes, sir. The person that I allude to is dead."

"Then why should you not now tell the police anything you know?"

"Because there is another person to be considered. That other person is myself. I could not stand the scandal and publicity which would come from a police examination. I have not long to live, but I wish to die undisturbed. And yet I wanted to find one man of judgment to whom I could tell my terrible story, so that when I am gone all might be understood."

"You compliment me, madam. At the same time, I am a responsible person. I do not promise you that when you have spoken I may not myself think it my duty to refer the case to the police."

"I think not, Mr. Holmes. I know your character and methods too well, for I have followed your work for some years. Reading is the only pleasure which fate has left me, and I miss little which passes in the world. But in any case, I will take my chance of the use which you may make of my tragedy. It will ease my mind to tell it."

"My friend and I would be glad to hear it."

The woman rose and took from a drawer the photograph of a man. He was clearly a professional acrobat, a man of magnificent physique, taken with his huge arms folded across his swollen chest and a smile breaking from under his heavy moustache—the self-satisfied smile of the man of many conquests.

"That is Leonardo," she said.

"Leonardo, the strong man, who gave evidence?"

"The same. And this—this is my husband."

It was a dreadful face—a human pig, or rather a human wild boar, for it was formidable in its bestiality. One could imagine that vile mouth champing and foaming in its rage, and one could conceive those small, vicious eyes darting pure malignancy as they looked forth upon the world. Ruffian, bully, beast—it was all written on that heavy-jowled face.

"Those two pictures will help you, gentlemen, to understand the story. I was a poor circus girl brought up on the sawdust, and doing springs through the hoop before I was ten. When I became a woman this man loved me, if such lust as his can be called love, and in an evil moment I became his wife. From that day I was in hell, and he the devil who tormented me. There was no one in the show who did not know of his treatment. He deserted me for others. He tied me down and lashed me with his riding-whip when I complained. They all pitied me and they all loathed him, but what could they do? They feared him, one and all. For he was terrible at all times, and murderous when he was drunk. Again and again he was had up for assault, and for cruelty to the beasts, but he had plenty of money and the fines were nothing to him. The best men all left us, and the show began to go downhill. It was only Leonardo and I who kept it up—with little Jimmy Griggs, the clown. Poor devil, he had not much to be funny about, but he did what he could to hold things together.

"Then Leonardo came more and more into my life. You see what he was like. I know now the poor spirit that was hidden in that splendid body, but compared to my husband he seemed like the angel Gabriel. He pitied me and helped me, till at last our intimacy turned to love—deep, deep, passionate love, such love as I had dreamed of but never hoped to feel. My husband suspected it, but I think that he was a coward as well as a bully, and that Leonardo was the one man that he was afraid of. He took revenge in his own way by torturing me more than ever. One night my cries brought Leonardo to the door of our van. We were near tragedy that night, and soon my lover and I understood that it could not be avoided. My husband was not fit to live. We planned that he should die.

"Leonardo had a clever, scheming brain. It was he who planned it. I do not say that to blame him, for I was ready to go with him every inch of the way. But I should never have had the wit to think of such a plan. We made a club—Leonardo made it—and in the leaden head he fastened five long steel nails, the points outwards, with just such a spread as the lion's paw. This was to give my husband his death-blow, and yet to leave the evidence that it was the lion which we would loose who had done the deed.

"It was a pitch-dark night when my husband and I went down, as was our custom, to feed the beast. We carried with us the raw meat in a zinc pail. Leonardo was waiting at the corner of the big van which we should have to pass before we reached the cage. He was too slow, and we walked past him before he could strike, but he followed us on tiptoe and I heard the crash as the club smashed my husband's skull. My heart leaped with joy at the sound. I sprang forward, and I undid the catch which held the door of the great lion's cage.

"And then the terrible thing happened. You may have heard how quick these creatures are to scent human blood, and how it excites them. Some strange instinct had told the creature in one instant that a human being had been slain. As I slipped the

"As I slipped the bars the lion bounded out,
and was on me in an instant."
Frank Wiles, *Strand Magazine*, 1927

bars it bounded out and was on me in an instant. Leonardo could have saved me. If he had rushed forward and struck the beast with his club he might have cowed it. But the man lost his nerve. I heard him shout in his terror, and then I saw him turn and fly. At the same instant the teeth of the lion met in my face. Its hot, filthy breath had already poisoned me and I was hardly conscious of pain. With the palms of my hands I tried to push the great steaming, blood-stained jaws away from me, and I screamed for help. I was conscious that the camp was stirring, and then dimly I remembered a group of men, Leonardo, Griggs and others, dragging me from under the creature's paws. That was my last memory, Mr. Holmes, for many a weary month. When I came to myself and saw myself in the mirror, I cursed that lion—oh, how I cursed him!—not because he had torn away my beauty but because he had not torn away my life. I had but one desire, Mr. Holmes, and I had enough money to gratify it. It was that I should cover myself so that my poor face should be seen by none, and that I should dwell where none whom I had ever known should find me. That was all that was left to me to do—and that is what I have done. A poor wounded beast that has crawled into its hole to die—that is the end of Eugenia Ronder.[11]

We sat in silence for some time after the unhappy woman had told her story. Then Holmes stretched out his long arm and patted her hand with such a show of sympathy as I had seldom known him to exhibit.

"Poor girl!" he said. "Poor girl! The ways of fate are indeed hard to understand. If there is not some compensation here-after, then the world is a cruel jest. But what of this man Leonardo?"

"I never saw him or heard from him again. Perhaps I have been wrong to feel so bitterly against him. He might as soon have loved one of the freaks whom we carried round the coun-try as the thing which the lion had left. But a woman's love is not so easily set aside. He had left me under the beast's claws, he had deserted me in my need, and yet I could not bring myself to give him to the gallows. For myself, I cared nothing what became of me. What could be more dreadful than my actual life? But I stood between Leonardo and his fate."

"And he is dead?"

"He was drowned last month when bathing near Margate. I saw his death in the paper."[12]

"And what did he do with this five-clawed club, which is the most singular and ingenious part of all your story?"

"I cannot tell, Mr. Holmes. There is a chalk-pit by the camp, with a deep green pool at the base of it. Perhaps in the depths of that pool—"

"Well, well, it is of little consequence now. The case is closed."

"Yes," said the woman, "the case is closed."

We had risen to go, but there was something in the woman's

11 Eugenia Ronder was fortunate (or unfortu-nate, according to her point of view) to escape the fate of Ellen Bright, the Lion Tamer at Wombwell's menagerie. Attacked by a tiger in 1880, she died at the age of seventeen.

12 Bill Mason makes the interesting sugges-tion that Leonardo was *not* dead. "After all," he writes, "Leonardo had 'a clever scheming brain,' and the likelihood of someone so phys-ically fit drowning at a seaside resort would appear to be as slim as it would be ironic. No, Leonardo would be more likely to end seven years of looking over his shoulder by faking his own death."

There was something in the woman's voice which arrested
Holmes's attention. He turned swiftly upon her. "Your life is not
your own," he said. "Keep your hands off it."

Frank Wiles, *Strand Magazine*, 1927

voice which arrested Holmes's attention. He turned swiftly
upon her.

"Your life is not your own," he said. "Keep your hands off
it."

"What use is it to anyone?"

"How can you tell? The example of patient suffering is in
itself the most precious of all lessons to an impatient world."

The woman's answer was a terrible one. She raised her veil
and stepped forward into the light.

"I wonder if you would bear it," she said.

It was horrible. No words can describe the framework of a

face when the face itself is gone. Two living and beautiful brown eyes looking sadly out from that grisly ruin did but make the view more awful. Holmes held up his hand in a gesture of pity and protest, and together we left the room.

Two days later, when I called upon my friend, he pointed with some pride to a small blue bottle upon his mantelpiece. I picked it up. There was a red poison label. A pleasant almondy odour rose when I opened it.

"Prussic acid?"[13] said I.

"Exactly. It came by post. 'I send you my temptation. I will follow your advice.' That was the message. I think, Watson, we can guess the name of the brave woman who sent it." ∎

HOLMES'S CAREER

THE mathematics of Watson's statement "Mr. Sherlock Holmes was in active practice for twenty-three years, and . . . during seventeen of these I was allowed to co-operate with him and to keep notes of his doings" constitute quite a puzzle. D. Martin Dakin explains the "twenty-three years" by counting back from Holmes's retirement in 1903 and adding on three years for the Great Hiatus to arrive at 1877, the year that Holmes would have started his business. (There is no direct evidence for this starting year, but "The Musgrave Ritual," which can reasonably be said to be Holmes's first real case, occurred four years after college; if Holmes was born in 1854, went up to university at the early age of seventeen, and attended for two years, as discussed elsewhere, this would place "The Musgrave Ritual" around 1877. Most chronologists assign the case to 1879.)

But the seventeen years that Watson says he was involved with Holmes's investigations—meaning that he remained uninvolved for six years—is harder to figure. It is known that Watson first joined Holmes in 1881; that accounts for four years, but leaves two unexplained. Dakin dismisses the notion that Watson is excluding the years of his marriage to Mary Morstan, as several stories indicate that Watson was continuing to assist Holmes during his marriage. Dakin may mean the year

13 Prussic acid is another name for hydrogen cyanide, an almost-colourless, volatile, and highly poisonous liquid compound that, in vaporous form, smells faintly of bitter almonds. (In water, it is called hydrocyanic acid.) It is used to produce rubbers, fibres, and plastics, and was discovered in 1782 when extracted from the pigment Prussian blue. Thirty minutes of exposure to two to five hundred parts of hydrogen cyanide per one million parts of air is usually sufficient to cause death; in one form of capital punishment, the condemned prisoner, seated in an airtight chamber, is exposed to a lethal amount of hydrogen cyanide gas, created by dropping cyanide into sulphuric acid.

from 1902 to 1903, when Watson had left Holmes "for a wife" ("The Blanched Soldier"). Yet that still leaves one year at large. Rather than try to account for the missing year, Dakin puts the discrepancy down to an error by the compositor, who might have misread Watson's "dreadful" handwriting and interpreted his figure "19" as seventeen.

William S. Baring-Gould, in his "A New Chronology of Sherlock Holmes and Dr. Watson," has a different tally. While he agrees with Dakin on the twenty-three-year period, he arrives at seventeen years by starting with 1882 to 1903 and then subtracting the three-year Great Hiatus and a "missing year" of 1895 to 1896, when, according to Baring-Gould's assignment of cases, Holmes was involved in investigations of a particularly delicate matter and could not consult even with Watson. This depends, however, on Baring-Gould's unique dating of *A Study in Scarlet* in 1882, and as is evident from the *Chronological Table*, few other scholars leave 1895 or 1896 empty of cases.

Henry T. Folsom, who adopts the more widely accepted date of 1881 for *A Study in Scarlet*, proposes the years 1881 to 1883 as the two missing years (noting, as does Dakin, nineteen years from 1881 to 1903 after subtracting the Great Hiatus). Folsom suggests that Watson served a second tour in the army from 1881 to 1883, during which he received his second wound.

A more radical approach is that of Shulamit Saltzman, in "The Other Watson," who argues that the first Watson substituted (with Holmes's permission) his nephew J. H. Watson after marrying Mary Morstan in 1889, and thus Watson II truthfully stated that he had been with Holmes for seventeen years.

THE ADVENTURE OF
SHOSCOMBE OLD PLACE[1]

There is nothing about Watson's narrative of "Shoscombe Old Place" to suggest that Watson planned it to be the last tale he would write of Sherlock Holmes. Yet it was, appearing in 1927, when Watson was seventy-six years old. Perhaps Watson suffered some sudden illness or debility preventing him from further writing. Perhaps his wife urged him to lay down his pen, or perhaps she died. There is something fitting about a case of concealed death and investigations of crypts as a finale. In any event, as this tale opens, Holmes is still on the "cutting edge" of detective work, pioneering the use of the microscope as an investigative tool. Watson reveals that he was (at least in 1902, when the case likely took place) an habitué of the race track. As in "The Creeping Man," Holmes uses his newly found skills as an observer of dogs to uncover the mystery. Once again, he demonstrates his disdain for the "upper classes," as he confronts the amoral Sir Robert Norberton: "As to the morality or decency of your own conduct, it is not for me to express an opinion," he demurs coldly.

SHERLOCK HOLMES HAD been bending for a long time over a low-power microscope. Now he straightened himself up and looked round at me in triumph.

"It is glue, Watson," said he. "Unquestionably it is glue. Have a look at these scattered objects in the field!"

I stooped to the eyepiece and focussed for my vision.

"Those hairs are threads from a tweed coat. The irregular grey masses are dust. There are epithelial scales[2] on the left. Those brown blobs in the centre are undoubtedly glue."

"Well," I said, laughing, "I am prepared to take your word for it. Does anything depend upon it?"

"It is a very fine demonstration," he answered. "In the St. Pancras case you may remember that a cap was found beside the dead policeman.[3] The accused man denies that it is his. But he is a picture-frame maker who habitually handles glue."

"Is it one of your cases?"

"No; my friend, Merivale[4] of the Yard, asked me to look into

1 At the end of "The Retired Colourman," published in the January 1927 issue of the *Strand Magazine*, a forthcoming Holmes story was announced with the title "The Adventure of the Black Spaniel." It eventually took the title "The Adventure of Shoscombe Old Place" and became the last Holmes case to be published individually, appearing first in the United States in *Liberty* in March 1927 and then in the *Strand* in April 1927. When included in the first published edition of *The Case-Book of Sherlock Holmes*, it was moved to its present position as the penultimate tale. It turns out that the story could claim not two titles, but three: Arthur Conan Doyle, who wrote a preface to the John Murray edition of *Sherlock Holmes: The Complete Short Stories* in 1928, referred to the story as "The Adventure

of Shoscombe Abbey" (although he misdated it as appearing in 1925), and the manuscript (published in facsimile in 2002 by the Bibliothèque cantonale et universitaire Lausanne) plainly bears that title.

Watson wrote no preface to *The Case-Book of Sherlock Holmes*, turning the task over to Arthur Conan Doyle. Thus for reasons forever unexplained, these were the last words that readers would hear from Holmes's devoted friend. "After this," in the words of June Thomson in *Holmes and Watson*, "the rest, as Hamlet says, is silence."

2 That is, skin.

3 The former borough of St. Pancras is home to St. Pancras Old Church, built in the fourteenth century and thought to be the first Christian church in England. That a policeman was murdered in the area evinces little surprise, for as Peter Ackroyd notes, the area around the church "has always been an isolated and somewhat mysterious place—'Walk not there too late,' counselled one Elizabethan topographer."

4 Donald A. Redmond calls him "the only policeman Holmes ever called friend and (barring reference to Charlie Peace) perhaps the only person other than Watson whom he named 'friend.' "

5 The manufacture of forged coins. See "The Engineer's Thumb" for another case involving coiners.

6 About £2 per week. Nino Cirone calculates that Watson was making 8 to 20 bets a week, certainly an active habit!

7 The racing expertise that Holmes displayed throughout "Silver Blaze" now appears to have vanished, whereas Watson, who in that case showed little interest in the

"It is glue, Watson," said Holmes.
"Unquestionably it is glue."
Frank Wiles, *Strand Magazine*, 1927

the case. Since I ran down that coiner[5] by the zinc and copper filings in the seam of his cuff they have begun to realize the importance of the microscope." He looked impatiently at his watch. "I had a new client calling, but he is overdue. By the way, Watson, you know something of racing?"

"I ought to. I pay for it with about half my wound pension."[6]

"Then I'll make you my 'Handy Guide to the Turf.'[7] What about Sir Robert Norberton? Does the name recall anything?"

"Well, I should say so. He lives at Shoscombe Old Place, and I know it well, for my summer quarters were down there once.[8] Norberton nearly came within your province once."

"How was that?"

"It was when he horsewhipped Sam Brewer, the well-known Curzon Street moneylender, on Newmarket Heath. He nearly killed the man."

"Ah, he sounds interesting! Does he often indulge in that way?"

"Well, he has the name of being a dangerous man. He is

about the most daredevil rider in England—second in the Grand National[9] a few years back. He is one of those men who have overshot their true generation. He should have been a buck in the days of the Regency—a boxer, an athlete, a plunger[10] on the turf, a lover of fair ladies, and, by all account, so far down Queer Street[11] that he may never find his way back again."

"Capital, Watson! A thumb-nail sketch. I seem to know the man. Now, can you give me some idea of Shoscombe Old Place?"

"Only that it is in the centre of Shoscombe Park, and that the famous Shoscombe stud and training quarters are to be found there."

"And the head trainer," said Holmes, "is John Mason. You need not look surprised at my knowledge, Watson, for this is a letter from him which I am unfolding. But let us have some more about Shoscombe. I seem to have struck a rich vein."

"There are the Shoscombe spaniels," said I. "You hear of them at every dog show. The most exclusive breed in England. They are the special pride of the lady of Shoscombe Old Place."

"Sir Robert Norberton's wife, I presume!"

"Sir Robert has never married. Just as well, I think, considering his prospects. He lives with his widowed sister, Lady Beatrice Falder."

"You mean that she lives with him?"

"No, no. The place belonged to her late husband, Sir James. Norberton has no claim on it at all.[12] It is only a life interest[13] and reverts to her husband's brother. Meantime, she draws the rents every year."

"And brother Robert, I suppose, spends the said rents?"

"That is about the size of it. He is a devil of a fellow and must lead her a most uneasy life. Yet I have heard that she is devoted to him. But what is amiss at Shoscombe?"

"Ah, that is just what I want to know. And here, I expect, is the man who can tell us."

The door had opened and the page had shown in a tall, clean-shaven man with the firm, austere expression which is only seen upon those who have to control horses or boys. Mr. John

sport, has now become, as William S. Baring-Gould puts it, "a slave to the turf." On the other hand, R. M. McLaren expresses considerable doubt that Watson in fact pays for racing with half of his wound pension. He believes that Watson spends the money instead on the stock market, since the doctor writes (in such stories as "The Stock-Broker's Clerk," "A Case of Identity," and "Black Peter") about the stock exchange and financial matters with "a much surer and more certain hand." However, because the stock market was not the traditional losing ground for a gentleman (as was the turf), to save face, Watson engaged in a deception about his gambling habit.

8 Although this seems to imply Watson's military period, W. W. Robson observes that in *A Study in Scarlet*, Watson is described as having spent most of his army summers in India. Perhaps, Robson speculates, Watson may have summered at Shoscombe (a rural village in Avon) when he was a medical student. Michael Duke suggests a stay there in 1892, when there was a hiatus in the partnership, occurring when Watson was as yet unmarried (note the "my summer quarters"). Bernard Davies proposes "a practical exercise, involving a few days under canvas in the Berkshire Downs country attached to some regular Army or militia manoeuvres" as the likeliest explanation but rejects the "summer" aspect as inconsistent with the evident dates of Watson's training. John Weber argues for 1892 and a summer convalescence for Mary Morstan Watson and her husband.

9 The Grand National is an annual steeplechase held at Aintree Racecourse in Liverpool. The first official Grand National race was run in 1839, and while the winner of that inaugural race was the five-to-one favourite Lottery, the race is better remembered for Captain Martin Becher, who tumbled off his

horse, Conrad, into what is now known as Becher's Brook. It is unknown whether Grand National's records reveal a second-place rider named Robert Norberton, and Watson does not mention the year in which Sir Robert achieved such a finish. Nonetheless, the list of those who may have bested Norberton's horse include Wild Man from Borneo, who won the Grand National in 1895 and whose head adorns the wall in the room where winning teams are interviewed; Manifesto, who ran the Grand National eight times and won it in 1897 and 1899; or even Cloister, who finished forty lengths ahead of his closer competitor in 1893—in which case the accomplishment of second place loses a bit of its lustre.

10 A reckless bettor; a dashing or venturesome gambler or speculator (as in, to *plunge* headlong into a risky bet).

11 See "The Second Stain," note 24.

12 Deleted in the manuscript is the sentence "In fact by all accounts it passes clean out of the family if she dies."

13 An interest in an estate that terminates with the death of the holder.

Mason had many of both under his sway, and he looked equal to the task. He bowed with cold self-possession and seated himself upon the chair to which Holmes had waved him.

"You had my note, Mr. Holmes?"[14]

"Yes, but it explained nothing."

"It was too delicate a thing for me to put the details on paper. And too complicated. It was only face to face I could do it."

"Well, we are at your disposal."

"First of all, Mr. Holmes, I think that my employer, Sir Robert, has gone mad."

Holmes raised his eyebrows. "This is Baker Street, not Harley Street,"[15] said he. "But why do you say so?"

"Well, sir, when a man does one queer thing, or two queer things, there may be a meaning to it, but when everything he does is queer, then you begin to wonder. I believe Shoscombe Prince and the Derby[16] have turned his brain."

"That is a colt you are running?"

"The best in England, Mr. Holmes. I should know, if anyone does. Now, I'll be plain with you, for I know you are gentlemen of honour and that it won't go beyond the room. Sir Robert has got to win this Derby. He's up to the neck, and it's his last chance. Everything he could raise or borrow is on the horse—and at fine odds, too! You can get forties[17] now, but it was nearer the hundred when he began to back him."

"But how is that if the horse is so good?"

"The public don't know how good he is. Sir Robert has been too clever for the touts.[18] He has the Prince's half-brother out for spins. You can't tell 'em apart. But there are two lengths in a furlong[19] between them when it comes to a gallop.[20] He thinks of nothing but the horse and the race. His whole life is on it. He's holding off the Jews till then.[21] If the Prince fails him he is done."

"It seems a rather desperate gamble, but where does the madness come in?"

"Well, first of all, you have only to look at him. I don't believe he sleeps at night. He is down at the stables at all hours. His eyes are wild. It has all been too much for his nerves. Then there is his conduct to Lady Beatrice!"

"Ah! What is that?"

"They have always been the best of friends. They had the

14 Deleted in the manuscript is the sentence "I sorely need your advice for it is not a matter I can take either to the police or to doctors."

15 By this Holmes means that one of the many physicians on Harley Street, in Cavendish Square, might be more appropriate for a case requiring psychiatric care. (See "The Resident Patient," note 9, and "The Devil's Foot," note 5.)

16 The Derby (now, changing with the times, known as the Vodafone Derby), established in 1780, is run annually at Epsom Downs, in Surrey. In 1900, the Derby stake was £6,000, £5,000 to the winner, £500 to the nominator (that is, the person in whose name the horse is entered) of the winner, £300 to the second, and £200 to the third. The winners in the years possible for "Shoscombe Old Place" were:

Year	Horse	Owner	Jockey
1882	Shotover	Duke of Westminster	T. Cannon
1883	St. Blaise	Sir F. Johnstone	T. Cannon
1887	Merry Hampton	"Mr. Abington," a k a Charles Baird	J. Watts
1888	Ayrshire	Duke of Portland	F. Barrett
1894	Ladas II	Lord Rosebery	J. Watts
1896	Persimmon	H.R.H. Prince of Wales	J. Watts
1897	Galtee More	Mr. J. Gubbins	C. Wood
1898	Jeddah	Mr. J. W. Larnach	O. Madden
1899	Flying Fox	Duke of Westminster	M. Cannon
1900	Diamond Jubilee	H.R.H. Prince of Wales	H. Jones
1901	Volodyovski	Mr. W. C. Whitney	L. Reiff
1902	Ard Patrick	Mr. J. Gubbin	J. H. Martin

Information courtesy of the Vodafone Derby website.

Francine and Wayne Swift conclusively identify the horse Shoscombe Prince as "Merry Hampton"; the owner as Charles Baird; and the year as 1887.

17 That is, odds of forty to one.

18 Agents seeking inside information on horses, for the purposes of advantageous betting. Fitzroy Simpson of "Silver Blaze," it may be recalled, was decried by a stable boy as "one of those damned touts" (see "Silver Blaze," note 9).

19 The phrase "fifty yards in the mile," which would never be used in racing parlance, has been deleted in the manuscript, and the more likely reference to furlongs inserted. A furlong is an eighth of a mile. "Two lengths in a furlong" means two lengths of a horse for every furlong run. Therefore, the Derby being one and a half miles (twelve furlongs) in length, the Prince would be expected to outrun its half-brother by twenty-four lengths. A "length" is a very imprecise distance, as the size of horses vary considerably (War Admiral, for example, was a legendarily large race horse, while Seabiscuit was very small).

20 Deleted in the manuscript is the sentence "When we have the Prince out it's where no one can ever see him. Sir Robert nearly killed one tout and was had in the police court for it."

21 That is, fighting off his creditors. While Jews no longer dominated the money-lending profession as they had during the Middle Ages before their expulsion (see "The Sussex Vampire," note 3), the image of the Jew as usurer persisted, and some did still engage in the trade. London's Jewish population had recently gotten larger, with thousands of immigrants streaming in from Russia and Poland in the 1880s. Crowded into the East End, these new arrivals worked primarily as tailors in sweatshops, although many took other factory work or peddled goods such as old clothes, fruit, jewellery, and knives out of street carts.

Anti-Semitism was a fact of life, and—despite the premiership of Benjamin Disraeli and the rise of the Rothschilds (see "Charles Augustus Milverton," note 26)—Jews tended to be viewed as either squalid or stingy (or both) and, even more perilous, likely to rise out of the ghetto and take work away from Christians. Beatrice Potter, wondering at the success of Polish and Russian Jews who immigrated "with no ready-made skill of a marketable character," wrote, in Charles Booth's survey *Life and Labour of the People in London* (1889–1903), "They are set down in an already over-stocked and demoralized labour market; they are surrounded by the drunkenness, immorality, and gambling of the East End streets; they are, in fact, placed in the midst of the very refuse of our civilization, and yet . . . whether they become bootmakers, tailors, cabinet-makers, glaziers, or dealers, the Jewish inhabitants of East London rise in the social scale. . . . [They] slowly but surely invade the higher provinces of production, bringing in their train a system of employment and a method of dealing with masters, men, and fellow-workers which arouses the antagonism of English workmen. . . . The Polish Jew regards manual work as the first rung of the social ladder, to be superseded or supplanted on the first opportunity by the estimates of the profit-maker, the transactions of the dealer, or the calculations of the money-lender; and he is only tempted from a life of continual acquisition by that vice of the intellect, gambling."

same tastes, the two of them, and she loved the horses as much as he did. Every day at the same hour she would drive down to see them—and, above all, she loved the Prince. He would prick up his ears when he heard the wheels on the gravel, and he would trot out each morning to the carriage to get his lump of sugar. But that's all over now."

"Why?"

"Well, she seems to have lost all interest[22] in the horses. For a week now she has driven past the stables with never so much as 'Good-morning'!"

"You think there has been a quarrel?"

"And a bitter, savage, spiteful quarrel at that. Why else would he give away her pet spaniel that she loved as if it were her child? He gave it a few days[23] ago to old Barnes, what keeps the 'Green Dragon,' three miles[24] off, at Crendall."

"That certainly did seem strange."

"Of course, with her weak heart and dropsy[25] one couldn't expect that she could get about with him, but he spent two hours every evening in her room. He might well do what he could, for she has been a rare good friend to him. But that's all over, too. He never goes near her. And she takes it to heart. She is brooding and sulky and drinking, Mr. Holmes—drinking like a fish."

"Did she drink before this estrangement?"

"Well, she took her glass, but now it is often a whole bottle of an evening. So Stephens, the butler, told me. It's all changed, Mr. Holmes, and there is something damned rotten about it. But then, again, what is master doing down at the old church crypt at night? And who is the man that meets him there?"

Holmes rubbed his hands.

"Go on, Mr. Mason. You get more and more interesting."

"It was the butler who saw him go. Twelve o'clock at night and raining hard. So next night I was up at the house and, sure enough, master was off again. Stephens and I went after him, but it was jumpy work, for it would have been a bad job if he had seen us. He's a terrible man with his fists if he gets started, and no respecter of persons. So we were shy of getting too near, but we marked him down all right. It was the haunted crypt that he was making for, and there was a man waiting for him there."

22 The phrase "in her brother" has been deleted from the manuscript.

23 A "week" in the original manuscript.

24 The Green Dragon is "seven" miles off in the original manuscript.

25 A build-up of fluids in body tissue, creating swelling, often in the ankles and lower legs. Now referred to as edema, the condition may be indicative of heart failure, severe malnutrition, obesity, or kidney disease, among other concerns. In Lady Beatrice's case, no doubt her weak heart, causing blood to accumulate in her veins and capillaries, was a major factor in inducing the dropsy.

26 The manuscript deletes the phrase "folk come all the way from France to see. He's got the oldest coffin in England in it."

"What is this haunted crypt?"

"Well, sir, there is an old ruined chapel in the park. It is so old that nobody could fix its date. And under it there's a crypt which[26] has a bad name among us. It's a dark, damp, lonely place by day, but there are few in that county that would have the nerve to go near it at night. But master's not afraid. He never feared anything in his life. But what is he doing there in the night-time?"

"Wait a bit!" said Holmes. "You say there is another man there. It must be one of your own stablemen, or someone from

"I guess he had not heard us coming. He let out a yell, and away he went as hard as he could lick."
Frank Wiles, *Strand Magazine*, 1927

the house! Surely you have only to spot who it is and question him?"

"It's no one I know."

"How can you say that?"

"Because I have seen[27] him, Mr. Holmes. It was on that second night. Sir Robert turned and passed us—me and Stephens, quaking in the bushes like two bunny-rabbits, for there was a bit of moon that night. But we could hear the other moving about behind. We were not afraid of him. So we up when Sir Robert was gone and pretended we were just having a walk like in the moonlight, and so we came right on him as casual and innocent as you please. 'Hullo, mate! who may you be?' says I. I guess he had not heard us coming, so he looked over his shoulder with a face as if he had seen the devil coming out of hell. He let out a yell,[28] and away he went as hard as he could lick it in the darkness. He could run!—I'll give him that. In a minute he was out of sight and hearing, and who he was, or what he was, we never found."

"But you saw him clearly in the moonlight?"

"Yes, I would swear to his yellow face—a mean dog, I should say. What could he have in common with Sir Robert?"

Holmes sat for some time lost in thought.

"Who keeps Lady Beatrice Falder company?" he asked at last.

"There is her maid, Carrie Evans. She has been with her this five years."

"And is, no doubt, devoted?"

Mr. Mason shuffled uncomfortably.

"She's devoted enough," he answered at last. "But I won't say to whom."

"Ah!" said Holmes.

"I can't tell tales out of school."

"I quite understand, Mr. Mason. Of course, the situation is clear enough. From Dr. Watson's description of Sir Robert I can realize that no woman is safe from him. Don't you think the quarrel between brother and sister may lie there?"

"Well, the scandal has been pretty clear for a long time."

"But she may not have seen it before. Let us suppose that she has suddenly found it out. She wants to get rid of the woman. Her brother will not permit it. The invalid, with her weak heart and inability to get about, has no means of enforc-

27 The manuscript reads "spoken with."

28 The manuscript deletes the phrase "dropped a sort of iron stick which was in his hand."

29 The manuscript deletes the sentence "I said no one would go near the crypt at night but there are some of us afraid of it by day too, and I told you we have to show some of them [illegible] over it."

30 The manuscript deletes "he's holding the Jews off, I expect, till after the Derby."

31 Deleted from the manuscript is the following exchange:

"How long is it since you observed the change between Sir Robert and his sister."

"About a week."

---

ing her will. The hated maid is still tied to her. The lady refuses to speak, sulks, takes to drink. Sir Robert in his anger takes her pet spaniel away from her. Does not all this hang together?"

"Well, it might do—so far as it goes."

"Exactly! As far as it goes. How would all that bear upon the visits by night to the old crypt? We can't fit that into our plot."

"No, sir, and there is something more that I can't fit in. Why should Sir Robert want to dig up a dead body?"

Holmes sat up abruptly.

"We only found it out yesterday—after I had written to you.[29] Yesterday Sir Robert had gone to London,[30] so Stephens and I went down to the crypt. It was all in order, sir, except that in one corner was a bit of a human body."

"You informed the police, I suppose?"

Our visitor smiled grimly.

"Well, sir, I think it would hardly interest them. It was just the head and a few bones of a mummy. It may have been a thousand years old. But it wasn't there before. That I'll swear, and so will Stephens. It had been stowed away in a corner and covered over with a board, but that corner had always been empty before."

"What did you do with it?"

"Well, we just left it there."

"That was wise. You say Sir Robert was away yesterday. Has he returned?"

"We expect him back to-day."[31]

"When did Sir Robert give away his sister's dog?"

"It was just a week ago to-day. The creature was howling outside the old well-house, and Sir Robert was in one of his tantrums that morning. He caught it up, and I thought he would have killed it. Then he gave it to Sandy Bain, the jockey, and told him to take the dog to old Barnes at the 'Green Dragon,' for he never wished to see it again."

Holmes sat for some time in silent thought. He had lit the oldest and foulest of his pipes.

"I am not clear yet what you want me to do in this matter, Mr. Mason," he said at last. "Can't you make it more definite?"

"Perhaps this will make it more definite, Mr. Holmes," said our visitor.[32]

He took a paper from his pocket, and, unwrapping it carefully, he exposed a charred fragment of bone.

Holmes examined it with interest.

"Where did you get it?"

"There is a central heating furnace in the cellar under Lady Beatrice's room. It's been off for some time, but Sir Robert complained of cold and had it on again. Harvey runs it—he's one of my lads. This very morning he came to me with this which he found raking out the cinders. He didn't like the look of it."

"Nor do I," said Holmes. "What do you make of it, Watson?"

It was burned to a black cinder, but there could be no question as to its anatomical significance.

"It's the upper condyle of a human femur," said I.[33]

"Exactly!" Holmes had become very serious.[34] "When does this lad tend to the furnace?"

"He makes it up every evening and then leaves it."

"Then anyone could visit it during the night?"

"Yes, sir."

"Can you enter it from outside?"

"There is one door from outside. There is another which leads up by a stair to the passage in which Lady Beatrice's room is situated."

"These are deep waters, Mr. Mason; deep and rather dirty. You say that Sir Robert was not at home last night?"

"No, sir."

"Then, whoever was burning bones, it was not he."

"That's true, sir."

"What is the name of that inn you spoke of?"

"The 'Green Dragon.' "

"Is there good fishing in that part of Berkshire?" The honest trainer showed very clearly upon his face that he was convinced that yet another lunatic had come into his harassed life.

"Well, sir, I've heard there are trout in the mill-stream and pike in the Hall lake."

"That's good enough. Watson and I are famous fishermen—are we not, Watson? You may address us in future at the 'Green Dragon.' We should reach it to-night. I need not say that we

32 An entire paragraph is deleted here in the manuscript:

"I want you to keep me from becoming as mad as my employer, Mr. Holmes. Look at my position. I have a Derby winner to attend to. Any moment it might be seized for Sir Robert's debts. There is Sir Robert himself, quarreling with the one person that could save him and has saved him in the past. There is all this coming and going at night, with Sir Robert meeting a stranger and digging up a dead body. It's more than a man's nerves can stand. And on top of it all, Mr. Holmes, what do you make of this."

33 In anatomy, the condyle is a protuberance on the end of a bone, usually meant to align with another bone. Jack Tracy comments that the condyle for the femur (or thighbone) is located on the *lower* end of the bone, at the knee joint; there is no upper condyle. Therefore, he concludes, Watson must have been using the word "condyle" in a very loose sense, referring simply to the end of a bone.

34 The manuscript deletes the sentence "I think we must get the police on this advice, Mr. Mason. You say it was only this morning so no time has been lost."

don't want to see you, Mr. Mason, but a note will reach us, and no doubt I could find you if I want you. When we have gone a little farther into the matter I will let you have a considered opinion."

Thus it was that on a bright May evening Holmes and I found ourselves alone in a first-class carriage and bound for the little "halt-on-demand" station of Shoscombe. The rack above us was covered with a formidable litter of rods, reels and baskets. On reaching our destination a short drive took us to an old-fashioned tavern, where a sporting host, Josiah Barnes, entered eagerly into our plans for the extirpation of the fish of the neighbourhood.

"What about the Hall lake and the chance of a pike?" said Holmes.

The face of the innkeeper clouded.

"That wouldn't do, sir. You might chance to find yourself in the lake before you were through."

"How's that, then?"

"It's Sir Robert, sir. He's terrible jealous of touts. If you two strangers were as near his training quarters as that he'd be after you as sure as fate. He ain't taking no chances, Sir Robert ain't."

"I've heard he has a horse entered for the Derby."

"Yes, and a good colt, too. He carries all our money for the race, and all Sir Robert's into the bargain. By the way"—he looked at us with thoughtful eyes—"I suppose you ain't on the Turf yourselves?"

"No, indeed. Just two weary Londoners who badly need some good Berkshire air."

"Well, you are in the right place for that. There is a deal of it lying about. But mind what I have told you about Sir Robert. He's the sort that strikes first and speaks afterwards. Keep clear of the park."

"Surely, Mr. Barnes! We certainly shall. By the way, that was a most beautiful spaniel that was whining in the hall."

"I should say it was. That was the real Shoscombe breed. There ain't a better in England."

"I am a dog-fancier myself," said Holmes. "Now, if it is a fair question, what would a prize dog like that cost?"

"More than I could pay, sir. It was Sir Robert himself who gave me this one. That's why I have to keep it on a lead. It would be off to the Hall in a jiffy if I gave it its head."

"We are getting some cards in our hand, Watson," said Holmes, when the landlord had left us. "It's not an easy one to play, but we may see our way in a day or two. By the way, Sir Robert is still in London, I hear. We might, perhaps, enter the sacred domain to-night without fear of bodily assault. There are one or two points on which I should like reassurance."

"Have you any theory, Holmes?"

"Only this, Watson, that something happened a week or so ago which has cut deep into the life of the Shoscombe house-hold. What is that something? We can only guess at it from its effects. They seem to be of a curiously mixed character. But that should surely help us. It is only the colourless, uneventful case which is hopeless."

"Let us consider our data. The brother no longer visits the beloved invalid sister. He gives away her favourite dog. Her dog, Watson! Does that suggest nothing to you?"

"Nothing but the brother's spite."

"Well, it might be so. Or—well, there is an alternative. Now to continue our review of the situation from the time that the quarrel, if there is a quarrel, began. The lady keeps her room, alters her habits, is not seen save when she drives out with her maid, refuses to stop at the stables to greet her favourite horse, and apparently takes to drink. That covers the case, does it not?"

"Save for the business in the crypt."

"That is another line of thought. There are two, and I beg you will not tangle them. Line A, which concerns Lady Beatrice, has a vaguely sinister flavour, has it not?"

"I can make nothing of it."

"Well, now, let us take up line B, which concerns Sir Robert. He is mad keen upon winning the Derby. He is in the hands of the Jews, and may at any moment be sold up and his racing stables seized by his creditors. He is a daring and desperate man. He derives his income from his sister. His sister's maid is his willing tool. So far we seem to be on fairly safe ground, do we not?"

35 D. Martin Dakin remarks on the extraordinary social snobbery displayed here by Watson, who should have remembered that upper-class gentlemen such as Sir George Burnwell ("The Beryl Coronet"), old Baron Dowson ("The Mazarin Stone"), and John Clay ("The Red-Headed League") were, despite their appearances, capable of immoral deeds. "Moreover," Dakin adds, "since Watson himself told Holmes that Sir Robert had been nearly guilty of murder already . . . , why should he think it incredible that a man capable of such primitive savagery towards one who had offended him should commit an even more serious crime?"

36 A dace is a small freshwater fish, a member of the minnow family. One wonders whether Holmes's comment here is meant as a subtle slight of the innkeeper; as Donald Girard Jewell writes, "While the trout and the pike were viewed worthy of the gentleman angler's attention, the dace and the eel were left to the lower strata of society. The two are lumped into a category of fish referred to by the British as 'coarse.' "

37 An artificial lure, formed from a shiny, spoon-shaped metal disk with a hook attached.

38 Any of several game fishes of the family *Carangidae*, found in tropical or temperate waters. The fish known as the greater amberjack can grow to six feet in length, but it is more likely that Holmes and Watson were seeking a more manageable catch such as the crevalle jack or the golden-coloured yellow jack, both native to warmer areas of the Atlantic.

"But the crypt?"

"Ah, yes, the crypt! Let us suppose, Watson—it is merely a scandalous supposition, a hypothesis put forward for argument's sake—that Sir Robert has done away with his sister."

"My dear Holmes, it is out of the question."[35]

"Very possibly, Watson. Sir Robert is a man of an honourable stock. But you do occasionally find a carrion crow among the eagles. Let us for a moment argue upon this supposition. He could not fly the country until he had realized his fortune, and that fortune could only be realized by bringing off this coup with Shoscombe Prince. Therefore, he has still to stand his ground. To do this he would have to dispose of the body of his victim, and he would also have to find a substitute who would impersonate her. With the maid as his confidante that would not be impossible. The woman's body might be conveyed to the crypt, which is a place so seldom visited, and it might be secretly destroyed at night in the furnace, leaving behind it such evidence as we have already seen. What say you to that, Watson?"

"Well, it is all possible if you grant the original monstrous supposition."

"I think that there is a small experiment which we may try to-morrow, Watson, in order to throw some light on the matter. Meanwhile, if we mean to keep up our characters, I suggest that we have our host in for a glass of his own wine and hold some high converse upon eels and dace,[36] which seems to be the straight road to his affections. We may chance to come upon some useful local gossip in the process."

In the morning Holmes discovered that we had come without our spoon-bait[37] for jack,[38] which absolved us from fishing for the day. About eleven o'clock we started for a walk, and he obtained leave to take the black spaniel with us.

"This is the place," said he as we came to two high park gates with heraldic griffins towering above them. "About midday, Mr. Barnes informs me, the old lady takes a drive, and the carriage must slow down while the gates are opened. When it comes through, and before it gathers speed, I want you, Watson, to stop the coachman with some question. Never mind me. I shall stand behind this holly-bush and see what I can see."

It was not a long vigil. Within a quarter of an hour we saw the big open yellow barouche[39] coming down the long avenue, with two splendid, high-stepping grey carriage horses in the shafts. Holmes crouched behind his bush with the dog. I stood unconcernedly swinging a cane in the roadway. A keeper ran out and the gates swung open.

The carriage had slowed to a walk, and I was able to get a good look at the occupants. A highly-coloured young woman with flaxen hair and impudent eyes sat on the left. At her right was an elderly person with rounded back and a huddle of shawls about her face and shoulders which proclaimed the invalid. When the horses reached the highroad I held up my

39 A four-wheeled carriage with a box in front for the driver and two double seats for the passengers, each seat facing the other. The carriage is fitted with a collapsible top, which may be raised to cover the passengers.

Holmes released the spaniel, and with a joyous cry it dashed forward to the carriage and sprang upon the step.
Frank Wiles, *Strand Magazine*, 1927

hand with an authoritative gesture, and as the coachman pulled up I inquired if Sir Robert was at Shoscombe Old Place.

At the same moment Holmes stepped out and released the spaniel. With a joyous cry it dashed forward to the carriage and sprang upon the step. Then in a moment its eager greeting changed to furious rage, and it snapped at the black skirt above it.

"Drive on! Drive on!" shrieked a harsh voice. The coachman lashed the horses, and we were left standing in the roadway.

"Well, Watson, that's done it," said Holmes, as he fastened the lead to the neck of the excited spaniel. "He thought it was his mistress, and he found it was a stranger. Dogs don't make mistakes."

"But it was the voice of a man!" I cried.

"Exactly! We have added one card to our hand, Watson, but it needs careful playing, all the same."

My companion seemed to have no further plans for the day, and we did actually use our fishing tackle in the mill-stream, with the result that we had a dish of trout for our supper. It was only after that meal that Holmes showed signs of renewed activity. Once more we found ourselves upon the same road as in the morning, which led us to the park gates. A tall, dark figure was awaiting us there, who proved to be our London acquaintance, Mr. John Mason, the trainer.

"Good-evening, gentlemen," said he. "I got your note, Mr. Holmes. Sir Robert has not returned yet, but I hear that he is expected to-night."

"How far is this crypt from the house?" asked Holmes.

"A good quarter of a mile."

"Then I think we can disregard him altogether."

"I can't afford to do that, Mr. Holmes. The moment he arrives he will want to see me to get the last news of Shoscombe Prince."

"I see! In that case we must work without you, Mr. Mason. You can show us the crypt and then leave us."

It was pitch-dark and without a moon, but Mason led us over the grass-lands until a dark mass loomed up in front of us which proved to be the ancient chapel. We entered the broken gap which was once the porch and our guide, stumbling among heaps of loose masonry, picked his way to the corner of the building, where a steep stair led down into the crypt. Striking a match, he illuminated the melancholy place—dismal and evil-smelling, with ancient crumbling walls of rough-hewn stone, and piles of coffins, some of lead and some of stone, extending upon one side right up to the arched and groined[40] roof which lost itself in the shadows above our heads. Holmes

40 A groin vault, or cross vault, is formed at the intersection of two semicircular vaults (burial chambers). The "groin" itself is the curved line along which the vaults meet.

Holmes had lit his lantern, which shot a tiny tunnel of
vivid yellow light upon the mournful scene.
Frank Wiles, *Strand Magazine*, 1927

41 Jack Tracy comments that this is an unusual body type for a jockey.

had lit his lantern, which shot a tiny tunnel of vivid yellow light upon the mournful scene. Its rays were reflected back from the coffin-plates, many of them adorned with the griffin and coronet of this old family which carried its honours even to the gate of Death.

"You spoke of some bones, Mr. Mason. Could you show them before you go?"

"They are here in this corner." The trainer strode across and then stood in silent surprise as our light was turned upon the place. "They are gone," said he.

"So I expected," said Holmes, chuckling. "I fancy the ashes of them might even now be found in that oven which had already consumed a part."

"But why in the world would anyone want to burn the bones of a man who has been dead a thousand years?" asked John Mason.

"That is what we are here to find out," said Holmes. "It may mean a long search, and we need not detain you. I fancy that we shall get our solution before morning."

When John Mason had left us, Holmes set to work making a very careful examination of the graves, ranging from a very ancient one, which appeared to be Saxon, in the centre, through a long line of Norman Hugos and Odos, until we reached the Sir William and Sir Denis Falder of the eighteenth century. It was an hour or more before Holmes came to a leaden coffin standing on end before the entrance to the vault. I heard his little cry of satisfaction, and was aware from his hurried but purposeful movements that he had reached a goal. With his lens he was eagerly examining the edges of the heavy lid. Then he drew from his pocket a short jemmy, a box-opener, which he thrust into a chink, levering back the whole front, which seemed to be secured by only a couple of clamps. There was a rending, tearing sound as it gave way, but it had hardly hinged back and partly revealed the contents before we had an unforeseen interruption.

Someone was walking in the chapel above. It was the firm, rapid step of one who came with a definite purpose and knew well the ground upon which he walked. A light streamed down the stairs, and an instant later the man who bore it was framed in the Gothic archway. He was a terrible figure, huge in stature[41] and fierce in manner. A large stable-lantern which he held in front of him shone upwards upon a strong, heavily moustached face and angry eyes, which glared round him into every recess of the vault, finally fixing themselves with a deadly stare upon my companion and myself.

"Who the devil are you?" he thundered. "And what are you doing upon my property?" Then, as Holmes returned no answer, he took a couple of steps forward and raised a heavy stick which he carried. "Do you hear me?" he cried. "Who are you? What are you doing here?" His cudgel quivered in the air.

But instead of shrinking Holmes advanced to meet him.

"I also have a question to ask you, Sir Robert," he said in his sternest tone. "Who is this? And what is it doing here?"

He turned and tore open the coffin-lid behind him. In the

"I also have a question to ask you, Sir Robert," said Holmes in his
sternest tone. "Who is this? And what is it doing here?"
Frank Wiles, *Strand Magazine*, 1927

glare of the lantern I saw a body swathed in a sheet from head to foot, with dreadful, witch-like features, all nose and chin, projecting at one end, the dim, glazed eyes staring from a discoloured and crumbling face.

The Baronet had staggered back with a cry and supported himself against a stone sarcophagus.

"How came you to know of this?" he cried. And then, with some return of his truculent manner: "What business is it of yours?"

"My name is Sherlock Holmes," said my companion. "Possibly it is familiar to you. In any case, my business is that of every other good citizen—to uphold the law. It seems to me that you have much to answer for."

Sir Robert glared for a moment, but Holmes's quiet voice and cool, assured manner had their effect.

" 'Fore God, Mr. Holmes, it's all right," said he. "Appearances are against me, I'll admit, but I could act no otherwise."

"I should be happy to think so, but I fear your explanations must be before the police."

Sir Robert shrugged his broad shoulders.

"Well, if it must be, it must. Come up to the house and you can judge for yourself how the matter stands."

A quarter of an hour later we found ourselves in what I judge, from the lines of polished barrels behind glass covers, to be the gun-room of the old house. It was comfortably furnished, and here Sir Robert left us for a few moments. When he returned he had two companions with him; the one, the florid young woman whom we had seen in the carriage; the other, a small rat-faced man with a disagreeably furtive manner. These two wore an appearance of utter bewilderment, which showed that the Baronet had not yet had time to explain to them the turn events had taken.

"There," said Sir Robert with a wave of his hand, "are Mr. and Mrs. Norlett. Mrs. Norlett, under her maiden name of Evans, has for some years been my sister's confidential maid. I have brought them here because I feel that my best course is to explain the true position to you, and they are the two people upon earth who can substantiate what I say."

"Is this necessary, Sir Robert? Have you thought what you are doing?" cried the woman.

"As to me, I entirely disclaim all responsibility," said her husband.

Sir Robert gave him a glance of contempt. "I will take all responsibility," said he. "Now, Mr. Holmes, listen to a plain statement of the facts.

"You have clearly gone pretty deeply into my affairs or I should not have found you where I did. Therefore, you know already, in all probability, that I am running a dark horse[42] for the Derby and that everything depends upon my success. If I win, all is easy. If I lose—well, I dare not think of that!"

"I understand the position," said Holmes.

"I am dependent upon my sister, Lady Beatrice, for everything. But it is well known that her interest in the estate is for her own life only. For myself, I am deeply in the hands of the Jews. I have always known that if my sister were to die my creditors would be on to my estate like a flock of vultures. Everything would be seized—my stables, my horses—everything. Well, Mr. Holmes, my sister *did* die just a week ago."

"And you told no one!"

"What could I do? Absolute ruin faced me. If I could stave things off for three weeks all would be well. Her maid's husband—this man here—is an actor. It came into our heads—it came into my head—that he could for that short period personate my sister. It was but a case of appearing daily in the carriage, for no one need enter her room save the maid. It was not difficult to arrange. My sister died of the dropsy which had long afflicted her."[43]

"That will be for a coroner to decide."

"Her doctor would certify that for months her symptoms have threatened such an end."

"Well, what did you do?"

"The body could not remain there. On the first night Norlett and I carried it out to the old well-house, which is now never used. We were followed, however, by her pet spaniel, which yapped continually at the door, so I felt some safer place was needed. I got rid of the spaniel, and we carried the body to the crypt of the church. There was no indignity or irreverence, Mr. Holmes. I do not feel that I have wronged the dead."

42 Before the term took on political implications, a "dark horse" was a promising racehorse whose potential for success was kept hidden from oddsmakers and bettors. But the dark horse had entered the political realm by 1886, when a newspaper, quoted in E. Cobham Brewer's *Dictionary of Phrase and Fable*, commented, "At last a Liberal candidate has entered the field at Croydon. The Conservatives have kept their candidate back, as a dark horse."

43 Unless Sir Robert's sister suffered from hydrocephalus—an accumulation of fluids in the skull that leads to mental retardation, paralysis, and sometimes death—then it is unlikely she died from dropsy itself; more probably, her death was brought about by the weak heart causing the dropsy. At the time, however, that particular medical distinction may not have been clear.

44 Holmes here is being somewhat disingenuous, for Holmes often demonstrated a willingness to leave the facts obscured when he felt that he had no official duty to accuse a criminal (for example, in "The Boscombe Valley Mystery" and "The Blue Carbuncle"). Some scholars darkly hint that in "The Priory School," Holmes was financially motivated by the Duke of Holdernesse to allow the fact of the rôle of James Wilder to remain hidden. Sir Robert would seem to be even more likely than the duke to be interested in giving Holmes a monetary incentive to keep silent, and although there is no suggestion that Holmes was in fact bribed, critics suggest that he may well have wagered on the Prince.

45 The figure appears to be "£40,000" in the original manuscript. In current economic equivalence, £80,000 in 1902 (the date given by most chronologists for the tale) represents over £5.1 million, or $8.2 million.

"Your conduct seems to me inexcusable, Sir Robert."

The Baronet shook his head impatiently. "It is easy to preach," said he. "Perhaps you would have felt differently if you had been in my position. One cannot see all one's hopes and all one's plans shattered at the last moment and make no effort to save them. It seemed to me that it would be no unworthy resting-place if we put her for the time in one of the coffins of her husband's ancestors lying in what is still consecrated ground. We opened such a coffin, removed the contents, and placed her as you have seen her. As to the old relics which we took out, we could not leave them on the floor of the crypt. Norlett and I removed them, and he descended at night and burned them in the central furnace. There is my story, Mr. Holmes, though how you forced my hand so that I have to tell it is more than I can say."

Holmes sat for some time lost in thought.

"There is one flaw in your narrative, Sir Robert," he said at last. "Your bets on the race, and therefore your hopes for the future, would hold good even if your creditors seized your estate."

"The horse would be part of the estate. What do they care for my bets? As likely as not they would not run him at all. My chief creditor is, unhappily, my most bitter enemy—a rascally fellow, Sam Brewer, whom I was once compelled to horsewhip on Newmarket Heath. Do you suppose that he would try to save me?"

"Well, Sir Robert," said Holmes, rising, "this matter must, of course, be referred to the police. It was my duty to bring the facts to light, and there I must leave it.[44] As to the morality or decency of your own conduct, it is not for me to express an opinion. It is nearly midnight, Watson, and I think we may make our way back to our humble abode."

It is generally known now that this singular episode ended upon a happier note than Sir Robert's actions deserved. Shoscombe Prince did win the Derby, the sporting owner did net eighty thousand pounds[45] in bets, and the creditors did hold their hand until the race was over, when they were paid in full, and enough was left to re-establish Sir Robert in a fair position in life. Both police and coroner took a lenient view of the transaction, and beyond a mild censure for the delay in registering the lady's decease, the lucky owner got away scatheless from this strange incident in a career[46] which has now outlived its shadows and promises to end in an honoured old age.

46 Deleted in the manuscript is the phrase "terminated lately in so remarkable and sensational a fashion," which was replaced by the balance of the sentence in the text.

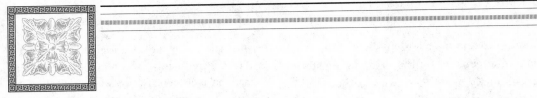

THE ADVENTURE OF THE RETIRED COLOURMAN[1]

"The Retired Colourman" is the last story of the last volume of Holmes tales. Written in late 1926, when Watson had celebrated his seventy-fifth birthday, it probably occurred several years before Holmes's retirement in 1904. Watson seems pleased to recollect his active partnership with Holmes, who, at age 72, may well have vanished from his life. Holmes first concludes that the case is merely "the old story": a fickle wife and a treacherous friend. He hands the investigation over to Watson, and (Holmes says) Watson characteristically misses everything of importance. However, when Holmes's "hated rival on the Surrey shore" (of whom we have heard nothing before) turns up in the case, Holmes realises that a cold-blooded murder has occurred. There are a few untidy details in the tale, but no account of Watson's is free of flaws, and no true Sherlockian could accept one scholar's thesis that this—the story on which we must close the book on Sherlock Holmes and Dr. Watson—is a fabricated account. As to why it appears last in the book, we can only speculate, keeping in mind that Arthur Conan Doyle (as is evident from his Preface to the Case-Book*) and not John Watson put together this last volume.*

---

1 "The Retired Colourman" was published in *Liberty* on December 18, 1926, and in the *Strand Magazine* in January 1927.

SHERLOCK HOLMES WAS in a melancholy and philosophic mood that morning. His alert practical nature was subject to such reactions.

"Did you see him?" he asked.

"You mean the old fellow who has just gone out?"

"Precisely."

"Yes, I met him at the door."

"What did you think of him?"

"A pathetic, futile, broken creature."

"Exactly, Watson. Pathetic and futile. But is not all life pathetic and futile? Is not his story a microcosm of the whole? We reach. We grasp. And what is left in our hands at the end? A shadow. Or worse than a shadow—misery."

"Is he one of your clients?"

"Well, I suppose I may call him so. He has been sent on by the Yard. Just as medical men occasionally send their incur-

2 Sufficient means, whether in the form of income or property, with which to live comfortably.

3 Professor Coram of "The Golden Pince-Nez" was engaged in a study of documents found in Coptic monasteries (see "The Golden Pince-Nez," note 16). Strangely, only in the year 1899 were there two Coptic patriarchs in office, Cyril Maqar, head of the Catholic Patriarchate (which was founded in 1895 but named no patriarch until 1899), and Cyril V, known as Hanna al-Nasikh, who served as patriarch of the Coptic Orthodox Church from 1874 to 1927 (with a short respite in 1912). Wladimir V. Bogomoletz suggests that Dr. Watson may have confused the date of "The Retired Colourman" when he stated that it occurred in the "summer of 1898." Of course, the "two Coptic patriarchs" for whom Holmes acted may not both have actually been holding that office—Holmes may have acted for both men in 1898, and Watson, writing up the story many years later, simply *called* them both patriarchs, as honorifics due them.

ables to a quack. They argue that they can do nothing more, and that whatever happens the patient can be no worse than he is."

"What is the matter?"

Holmes took a rather soiled card from the table. "Josiah Amberley. He says he was junior partner of Brickfall & Amberley, who are manufacturers of artistic materials. You will see their names upon paint-boxes. He made his little pile, retired from business at the age of sixty-one, bought a house at Lewisham, and settled down to rest after a life of ceaseless grind. One would think his future was tolerably assured."

"Yes, indeed."

Holmes glanced over some notes which he had scribbled upon the back of an envelope.

"Retired in 1896, Watson. Early in 1897 he married a woman twenty years younger than himself—a good-looking woman, too, if the photograph does not flatter. A competence,[2] a wife, leisure—it seemed a straight road which lay before him. And yet within two years he is, as you have seen, as broken and miserable a creature as crawls beneath the sun."

"But what has happened?"

"The old story, Watson. A treacherous friend and a fickle wife. It would appear that Amberley has one hobby in life, and it is chess. Not far from him at Lewisham there lives a young doctor who is also a chess-player. I have noted his name as Dr. Ray Ernest. Ernest was frequently in the house, and an intimacy between him and Mrs. Amberley was a natural sequence, for you must admit that our unfortunate client has few outward graces, whatever his inner virtues may be. The couple went off together last week—destination untraced. What is more, the faithless spouse carried off the old man's deed-box as her personal luggage with a good part of his life's savings within. Can we find the lady? Can we save the money? A commonplace problem so far as it has developed, and yet a vital one for Josiah Amberley."

"What will you do about it?"

"Well, the immediate question, my dear Watson, happens to be, What will *you* do?—if you will be good enough to understudy me. You know that I am preoccupied with this case of the two Coptic Patriarchs,[3] which should come to a head to-day. I really have not time to go out to Lewisham, and yet evidence taken on the spot has a special value. The old fellow was quite insistent that I should go, but I explained my difficulty. He is prepared to meet a representative."

"By all means," I answered. "I confess I don't see that I can be of much service, but I am willing to do my best." And so it was that on a summer afternoon I set forth to Lewisham, little dreaming that within a week the affair in which I was engaging would be the eager debate of all England.

It was late that evening before I returned to Baker Street and gave an account of my mission. Holmes lay with his gaunt figure stretched in his deep chair, his pipe curling forth slow wreaths of acrid tobacco, while his eyelids drooped over his eyes so lazily that he might almost have been asleep were it not that at any halt or questionable passage of my narrative they half lifted, and two grey eyes, as bright and keen as rapiers, transfixed me with their searching glance.

"The Haven is the name of Mr. Josiah Amberley's house," I explained. "I think it would interest you, Holmes. It is like some penurious patrician who has sunk into the company of his inferiors. You know that particular quarter, the monotonous brick streets, the weary suburban highways. Right in the mid-

Holmes's eyelids drooped so lazily that he might almost have been asleep.
Frederick Dorr Steele, *Liberty*, 1926

"Cut out the poetry, Watson," said Holmes, severely.
Frank Wiles, *Strand Magazine*, 1927

dle of them, a little island of ancient culture and comfort, lies this old home, surrounded by a high sun-baked wall mottled with lichens and topped with moss, the sort of wall—"

"Cut out the poetry, Watson," said Holmes severely. "I note that it was a high brick wall."

"Exactly. I should not have known which was The Haven had I not asked a lounger who was smoking in the street. I have a reason for mentioning him. He was a tall, dark, heavily-moustached, rather military-looking man. He nodded in answer to my inquiry and gave me a curiously questioning glance, which came back to my memory a little later.

"I had hardly entered the gateway before I saw Mr. Amberley coming down the drive. I only had a glimpse of him this morning, and he certainly gave me the impression of a strange creature, but when I saw him in full light his appearance was even more abnormal."

"I have, of course, studied it, and yet I should be interested to have your impression," said Holmes.

"He seemed to me like a man who was literally bowed down by care. His back was curved as though he carried a heavy burden. Yet he was not the weakling that I had at first imagined, for his shoulders and chest have the framework of a giant, though his figure tapers away into a pair of spindled legs."

"Left shoe wrinkled, right one smooth."

"I did not observe that."

"No, you wouldn't. I spotted his artificial limb. But proceed."

"I was struck by the snaky locks of grizzled hair which curled from under his old straw hat, and his face with its fierce, eager expression and the deeply lined features."

"Very good, Watson. What did he say?"

"He began pouring out the story of his grievances. We walked down the drive together, and of course I took a good look round. I have never seen a worse-kept place. The garden was all running to seed, giving me an impression of wild neglect in which the plants had been allowed to find the way of Nature rather than of art. How any decent woman could have tolerated such a state of things, I don't know. The house, too, was slatternly to the last degree, but the poor man seemed himself to be aware of it and to be trying to remedy it, for a great pot of green paint stood in the centre of the hall, and he was carrying a thick brush in his left hand. He had been working on the woodwork.

"He took me into his dingy sanctum, and we had a long chat. Of course, he was disappointed that you had not come yourself. 'I hardly expected,' he said, 'that so humble an individual as myself, especially after my heavy financial loss, could obtain the complete attention of so famous a man as Mr. Sherlock Holmes.'

"I assured him that the financial question did not arise. 'No, of course, it is art for art's sake with him,' said he, 'but even on the artistic side of crime he might have found something here to study. And human nature, Dr. Watson—the black ingratitude of it all! When did I ever refuse one of her requests? Was ever a woman so pampered? And that young man—he might have been my own son. He had the run of my house. And yet see how they have treated me! Oh, Dr. Watson, it is a dreadful, dreadful world!'

"That was the burden of his song for an hour or more. He had, it seems, no suspicion of an intrigue. They lived alone save for a woman who comes in by the day and leaves every evening at six. On that particular evening old Amberley, wishing to give his wife a treat, had taken two upper circle seats at the Haymarket Theatre.[4] At the last moment she had complained of a headache and had refused to go. He had gone

4 The Little Theatre in the Hay was built by carpenter John Potter in 1720 and later gave way, in 1821, to the larger Theatre Royal Haymarket, constructed next door. The original house's first success was *Hurlothrumbo*, a comic opera by Lord Flame, pseudonym for the jester and actor Samuel "Maggoty" Johnson (sometimes referred to as "Little Samuel Johnson" to distinguish him from *the* Samuel Johnson). That production ran for thirty nights in 1729. The theatre was occasionally the site of surprising violence: Twenty people died in 1794 when an eager crowd surged forward for a glimpse of George III, who was attending a performance there; and a small riot occurred in 1879, when the pit was done away with to make room for orchestra stalls, depriving theatregoers of cheap seats near the stage. Violence aside, the theatrical productions were many and varied. Tom Taylor's *Our American Cousin* (the play that Abraham Lincoln would be watching at Ford's Theater on a fateful night in 1865) ran at the Haymarket for four hundred nights beginning in 1861; and Oscar Wilde debuted *A Woman of No Importance* there in 1893 and *An Ideal Husband* in 1895. The ghost of John Baldwin Buckstone, a friend of Charles Dickens and manager of the Haymarket from 1853 to 1879, is said to haunt the theatre's auditorium and dressing rooms.

5 W. W. Robson explains that "in boarding schools each pupil is given a number, for purposes of identification, which he keeps throughout his school career."

6 In the Haymarket's current upper circle—the second balcony above the orchestra stalls, situated above the royal circle but below the gallery—the rows run from A through G, and the seat numbers run upward from right to left. This would make Amberley's seats two rows up, to the far left side of the balcony. Neither the 1896 nor the 1905 *Baedeker* mentions an upper circle, but both indicate prices for the Haymarket as "[s]talls 10*s.* 6*d.*, balcony stalls 7*s.*, balcony 5*s.*, pit-circle 2*s.* 6*d.*, upper boxes 2*s.*, gallery 1*s.*"

Theatre Royal Haymarket.
Sherlock Holmes's London

alone. There seemed to be no doubt about the fact, for he produced the unused ticket which he had taken for his wife."

"That is remarkable—most remarkable," said Holmes, whose interest in the case seemed to be rising. "Pray continue, Watson. I find your narrative most arresting. Did you personally examine this ticket? You did not, perchance, take the number?"

"It so happens that I did," I answered with some pride. "It chanced to be my old school number,[5] thirty-one, and so it stuck in my head."

"Excellent, Watson! His seat, then, was either thirty or thirty-two."

"Quite so," I answered, with some mystification. "And on B row."[6]

"That is most satisfactory. What else did he tell you?"

"He showed me his strong-room, as he called it. It really is a strong-room—like a bank—with iron door and shutter—burglar-proof, as he claimed. However, the woman seems to have had a duplicate key, and between them they had carried off some seven thousand pounds' worth of cash and securities."

"Securities! How could they dispose of those?"

"He said that he had given the police a list and that he hoped they would be unsaleable. He had got back from the theatre about midnight and found the place plundered, the door and window open, and the fugitives gone. There was no letter or message, nor has he heard a word since. He at once gave the alarm to the police."

Holmes brooded for some minutes.

"You say he was painting. What was he painting?"

"Well, he was painting the passage. But he had already painted the door and woodwork of this room I spoke of."

"Does it not strike you as a strange occupation in the circumstances?"

" 'One must do something to ease an aching heart.' That was his own explanation. It was eccentric, no doubt, but he is clearly an eccentric man. He tore up one of his wife's photographs in my presence—tore it up furiously in a tempest of passion. 'I never wish to see her damned face again,' he shrieked."

"Anything more, Watson?"

"Yes, one thing which struck me more than anything else. I had driven to the Blackheath Station and had caught my train there when, just as it was starting, I saw a man dart into the carriage next to my own. You know that I have a quick eye for faces, Holmes. It was undoubtedly the tall, dark man whom I

He tore up one of his wife's photographs in my presence. "I never wish to see her damned face again!" he shrieked.
Frederick Dorr Steele, *Liberty*, 1926

He tore up one of his wife's photographs
in a tempest of passion.
Frank Wiles, *Strand Magazine*, 1927

had addressed in the street. I saw him once more at London
Bridge, and then I lost him in the crowd. But I am convinced
that he was following me."

"No doubt! No doubt!" said Holmes. "A tall, dark, heavily-
moustached man, you say, with grey-tinted sun-glasses?"

"Holmes, you are a wizard. I did not say so, but he *had* grey-
tinted sun-glasses."

"And a Masonic tie-pin?"

"Holmes!"

"Quite simple, my dear Watson. But let us get down to what
is practical. I must admit to you that the case, which seemed to
me to be so absurdly simple as to be hardly worth my notice, is
rapidly assuming a very different aspect. It is true that though

in your mission you have missed everything of importance, yet even those things which have obtruded themselves upon your notice give rise to serious thought."

"What have I missed?"

"Don't be hurt, my dear fellow. You know that I am quite impersonal. No one else would have done better. Some possibly not so well. But clearly you have missed some vital points. What is the opinion of the neighbours about this man Amberley and his wife? That surely is of importance. What of Dr. Ernest? Was he the gay Lothario[7] one would expect? With your natural advantages, Watson, every lady is your helper and accomplice. What about the girl at the post-office, or the wife of the greengrocer? I can picture you whispering soft nothings with the young lady at the Blue Anchor,[8] and receiving hard somethings in exchange. All this you have left undone."

"It can still be done."

"It has been done. Thanks to the telephone[9] and the help of the Yard, I can usually get my essentials without leaving this room. As a matter of fact, my information confirms the man's story. He has the local repute of being a miser as well as a harsh and exacting husband. That he had a large sum of money in that strong-room of his is certain. So also is it that young Dr. Ernest, an unmarried man, played chess with Amberley, and probably played the fool with his wife. All this seems plain sailing, and one would think that there was no more to be said—and yet!—and yet!"

"Where lies the difficulty?"

"In my imagination, perhaps. Well, leave it there, Watson. Let us escape from this weary workaday world by the side door of music. Carina[10] sings to-night at the Albert Hall,[11] and we still have time to dress, dine and enjoy."

In the morning I was up betimes, but some toast crumbs and two empty egg-shells told me that my companion was earlier still. I found a scribbled note upon the table.

DEAR WATSON,—

There are one or two points of contact which I should wish to establish with Mr. Josiah Amberley. When I have done so we can dismiss the case—or not. I would only ask you to be on

7 A rake, a seducer, a lady's man, a cad; derived from the character of Lothario in Nicholas Rowe's enormously popular play *The Fair Penitent* (1703). In addition to adding a word to the dictionary, the "haughty, gallant, gay Lothario"—who seduces and then abandons the heroine Calista, driving her to suicide—would serve as the prototype for Robert Lovelace, the predatory gentleman suitor of Samuel Richardson's seminal novel *Clarissa Harlowe* (1747–1748).

8 Although Holmes may have been simply tossing out an exemplary name, Jonathan Oates takes the remark seriously and suggests that Holmes had in mind the Anchor, a pub at 66 Algernon Road, Lewisham.

9 Gar Donnelson labels this the earliest date at which a telephone appears at Baker Street ("The Illustrious Client" and "The Three Garridebs," which also make mention of a telephone, both clearly occurred in 1902). But he doubts that Holmes would have depended on the device as heavily as he claims, and writes, "Given the state of telephony in London at the time, one does have to doubt Holmes's statement to Watson. . . . [T]elephone messages could be sent to the post offices for transmission as telegrams, and telegrams received at the post offices could be transmitted by telephone. So, whether or not the Yard yet had a telephone is perhaps beside the point."

10 The identity of "Carina" is discussed on page 1751.

11 Royal Albert Hall was inaugurated on March 29, 1871, in honor of the late Prince Albert, whose dream it had been to create a vast artistic, scientific, and cultural centre near the site of the Great Exhibition. With seven thousand seats, Albert Hall is the largest concert hall in England, and it has

played host to countless balls, fairs, concerts, sporting events, and plays, including several events of state. While esteemed for the quality of its performances, the hall was notoriously cursed with bad acoustics—namely echoes and reverberations—until renovations were made in the 1960s. The finale of Alfred Hitchcock's classic film *The Man Who Knew Too Much* is set at a concert held there, and of course, the Beatles' "A Day in the Life" reported the news that it was now known "how many holes it takes to fill the Albert Hall."

12 *Crockford's Clerical Directory* was published by Oxford University Press commencing in 1869 and continues in print today.

13 "Living of Mossmoor cum Little Purlington" means that Elman's parish (his "living") was Mossmoor *combined with* Little Purlington.

hand about three o'clock, as I conceive it possible that I may want you.

S. H.

I saw nothing of Holmes all day, but at the hour named he returned, grave, preoccupied, and aloof. At such times it was wiser to leave him to himself.

"Has Amberley been here yet?"

"No."

"Ah! I am expecting him."

He was not disappointed, for presently the old fellow arrived with a very worried and puzzled expression upon his austere face.

"I've had a telegram, Mr. Holmes. I can make nothing of it." He handed it over, and Holmes read it aloud.

Come at once without fail. Can give you information as to your recent loss.

Elman.
The Vicarage.

"Dispatched at 2:10 from Little Purlington," said Holmes. "Little Purlington is in Essex, I believe, not far from Frinton. Well, of course you will start at once. This is evidently from a responsible person, the vicar of the place. Where is my Crockford?[12] Yes, here we have him: 'J. C. Elman, M.A., Living of Mossmoor cum Little Purlington.'[13] Look up the trains, Watson."

"There is one at 5:20 from Liverpool Street."

"Excellent. You had best go with him, Watson. He may need help or advice. Clearly we have come to a crisis in this affair."

But our client seemed by no means eager to start.

"It's perfectly absurd, Mr. Holmes," he said. "What can this man possibly know of what has occurred? It is waste of time and money."

"He would not have telegraphed to you if he did not know something. Wire at once that you are coming."

"I don't think I shall go."

Holmes assumed his sternest aspect.

"It would make the worst possible impression both on the police and upon myself, Mr. Amberley, if when so obvious a clue arose you should refuse to follow it up. We should feel that you were not really in earnest in this investigation."

Our client seemed horrified at the suggestion.

"Why, of course I shall go if you look at it in that way," said he. "On the face of it, it seems absurd to suppose that this parson knows anything, but if you think—"

"I *do* think," said Holmes, with emphasis, and so we were launched upon our journey. Holmes took me aside before we left the room and gave me one word of counsel, which showed that he considered the matter to be of importance. "Whatever you do, see that he really *does* go," said he. "Should he break away or return, get to the nearest telephone exchange and send the single word 'Bolted.' I will arrange here that it shall reach me wherever I am."

Little Purlington is not an easy place to reach, for it is on a branch line. My remembrance of the journey is not a pleasant one, for the weather was hot, the train slow, and my companion sullen and silent, hardly talking at all save to make an occasional sardonic remark as to the futility of our proceedings. When we at last reached the little station it was a two-mile drive before we came to the Vicarage, where a big, solemn, rather pompous clergyman received us in his study. Our telegram lay before him.

"Well, gentlemen," he asked, "what can I do for you?"

"We came," I explained, "in answer to your wire."

"My wire! I sent no wire."

"I mean the wire which you sent to Mr. Josiah Amberley about his wife and his money."

"If this is a joke, sir, it is a very questionable one," said the vicar angrily. "I have never heard of the gentleman you name, and I have not sent a wire to anyone."

Our client and I looked at each other in amazement.

"Perhaps there is some mistake," said I; "are there perhaps two vicarages? Here is the wire itself, signed Elman and dated from the Vicarage."

"There is only one vicarage, sir, and only one vicar, and this wire is a scandalous forgery, the origin of which shall certainly be investigated by the police. Meanwhile, I can see no possible object in prolonging this interview."

So Mr. Amberley and I found ourselves on the roadside in what seemed to me to be the most primitive village in Eng-

"If this is a joke, sir, it is a very questionable one,"
said the vicar, angrily.
Frank Wiles, *Strand Magazine*, 1927

land. We made for the telegraph office, but it was already closed. There was a telephone, however, at the little Railway Arms, and by it I got into touch with Holmes, who shared in our amazement at the result of our journey.

"Most singular!" said the distant voice. "Most remarkable! I much fear, my dear Watson, that there is no return train to-night. I have unwittingly condemned you to the horrors of a country inn. However, there is always Nature, Watson—Nature and Josiah Amberley—you can be in close commune with both." I heard his dry chuckle as he turned away.

It was soon apparent to me that my companion's reputation as a miser was not undeserved. He had grumbled at the expense of the journey, had insisted upon travelling third-class, and was now clamorous in his objections to the hotel bill. Next morning, when we did at last arrive in London, it was hard to say which of us was in the worse humour.

"You had best take Baker Street as we pass," said I. "Mr. Holmes may have some fresh instructions."

"If they are not worth more than the last ones they are not of much use," said Amberley, with a malevolent scowl. None the less, he kept me company. I had already warned Holmes by telegram of the hour of our arrival, but we found a message waiting that he was at Lewisham and would expect us there. That was a surprise, but an even greater one was to find that he was not alone in the sitting-room of our client. A stern-looking, impassive man sat beside him, a dark man with grey-tinted glasses and a large Masonic pin projecting from his tie.[14]

"This is my friend Mr. Barker," said Holmes. "He has been interesting himself also in your business, Mr. Josiah Amberley, though we have been working independently. But we both have the same question to ask you!"

Mr. Amberley sat down heavily. He sensed impending danger. I read it in his straining eyes and his twitching features.

"What is the question, Mr. Holmes?"

"Only this: What did you do with the bodies?"

The man sprang to his feet with a hoarse scream. He clawed into the air with his bony hands. His mouth was open, and for the instant he looked like some horrible bird of prey. In a flash we got a glimpse of the real Josiah Amberley, a misshapen demon with a soul as distorted as his body. As he fell back into his chair he clapped his hand to his lips as if to stifle a cough. Holmes sprang at his throat like a tiger and twisted his face towards the ground. A white pellet fell from between his gasping lips.[15]

"No short cuts, Josiah Amberley. Things must be done decently and in order.[16] What about it, Barker?"

"I have a cab at the door," said our taciturn companion.

"It is only a few hundred yards to the station. We will go together. You can stay here, Watson. I shall be back within half an hour."

The old colourman had the strength of a lion in that great trunk of his, but he was helpless in the hands of the two expe-

14 Is this, like Jabez Wilson, another Mason who improperly flaunts his membership in that secret society? In "The Red-Headed League," Holmes chastises Wilson for wearing a similar breastpin "against the strict rules of your order."

15 The highly lethal potassium cyanide seems a likely culprit for Amberley's attempted suicide, surmises Dr. J. W. Sovine. "Only an extremely rapid deadly poison effective in small dose would suffice for Josiah's purpose," he writes. "Cyanide of potassium qualifies." And Amberley's career in the manufacture of artistic materials would provide him with access to either potassium cyanide—which is used in photographic processing—or potassium ferrocyanide, the latter of which may be used to prepare the former.

16 "Let all things be done decently and in order" (I Corinthians.) Holmes, who frequently has taken justice into his own hands (see, for example, "The Abbey Grange"), here insists that Amberley stand trial, perhaps to provide an example for other criminals who might think themselves smarter than the Great Detective.

17 This statement seems inconsistent with Holmes's later statement that Barker "had done nothing save what I told him," which itself contradicts Holmes's statement that they had "been working independently." D. Martin Dakin suggests that this is further evidence of the spurious nature of the tale but also conjectures that Barker "may have been the detective noticed by Watson in *The Empty House . . .* , who was showing off in Park Lane—perhaps doing his best to make hay while the sun shone on him during Holmes's absence." S. E. Dahlinger comes to the same conclusion about the man, who is then described as wearing "coloured glasses" (see "The Empty House," note 15). Several scholars equate Barker as the "well-known criminal investigator" who wrote the letter to the press reproduced in "The Man with the Watches," published in the *Strand Magazine* in July 1898 through the agency of Arthur Conan Doyle and later collected in Conan Doyle's *Tales of Mystery* (1908). Darlene Cypser identifies him with *Cecil* Barker of *The Valley of Fear* (although that Barker is definitely an American), while David R. McCallister concludes that Barker was the "hated rival" for the hand of maid Agatha in "Charles Augustus Milverton." Gordon McCauley adds to the ferment by suggesting that Barker was a former Irregular.

The man sprang to his feet with a hoarse scream.
He clawed into the air with his bony hands, and looked
like some horrible bird of prey.
Frank Wiles, *Strand Magazine*, 1927

rienced man-handlers. Wriggling and twisting he was dragged to the waiting cab, and I was left to my solitary vigil in the ill-omened house. In less time than he had named, however, Holmes was back, in company with a smart young police inspector.

"I've left Barker to look after the formalities," said Holmes. "You had not met Barker, Watson. He is my hated rival upon the Surrey shore. When you said a tall dark man it was not difficult for me to complete the picture. He has several good cases to his credit, has he not, Inspector?"[17]

"He has certainly interfered several times," the Inspector answered with reserve.

"His methods are irregular, no doubt, like my own. The irregulars are useful sometimes, you know. You, for example, with your compulsory warning about whatever he said being used against him, could never have bluffed this rascal into what is virtually a confession."[18]

"Perhaps not. But we get there all the same, Mr. Holmes. Don't imagine that we had not formed our own views of this case, and that we would not have laid our hands on our man. You will excuse us for feeling sore when you jump in with methods which we cannot use, and so rob us of the credit."

"There shall be no such robbery, MacKinnon. I assure you that I efface myself from now onward, and as to Barker, he has done nothing save what I told him."

The Inspector seemed considerably relieved.

"That is very handsome of you, Mr. Holmes. Praise or blame can matter little to you, but it is very different to us when the newspapers begin to ask questions."

18 The London police, like their American counterparts, were governed by rules barring them from coercing confessions (see "The Dancing Men," note 22).

Holmes sprang at him like a tiger, and twisted
his face toward the floor.
Frederick Dorr Steele, *Liberty*, 1926

19 Broadmoor Prison for criminal lunatics (now a psychiatric hospital) was located in Crowthorne, Berkshire. It opened in 1863 with ninety-five female inmates; men were admitted the following year.

20 There is no direct evidence as to whether Holmes played chess. Svend Peterson cites numerous references in Holmes's remarks throughout his career to games, gambits, moves, checks, and other chess terminology, leading Peterson to the inescapable conclusion that Holmes was an avid player of the game.

21 John Hall, in *Sidelights on Holmes*, suggests that Amberley had perhaps seen his wife and Dr. Ernest look around inside the strong-room, driving him to kill them out of greed rather than jealousy. "The possibility that Ernest may indeed have intended to run off with both Mrs. Amberley and the cash and securities is somewhat played down [by Watson], perhaps in order to retain the reader's sympathy for the murdered couple."

"Quite so. But they are pretty sure to ask questions anyhow, so it would be as well to have answers. What will you say, for example, when the intelligent and enterprising reporter asks you what the exact points were which aroused your suspicion, and finally gave you a certain conviction as to the real facts?"

The Inspector looked puzzled.

"We don't seem to have got any real facts yet, Mr. Holmes. You say that the prisoner, in the presence of three witnesses, practically confessed, by trying to commit suicide, that he had murdered his wife and her lover. What other facts have you?"

"Have you arranged for a search?"

"There are three constables on their way."

"Then you will soon get the clearest fact of all. The bodies cannot be far away. Try the cellars and the garden. It should not take long to dig up the likely places. This house is older than the water-pipes. There must be a disused well somewhere. Try your luck there."

"But how did you know of it, and how was it done?"

"I'll show you first how it was done, and then I will give the explanation which is due to you, and even more to my long-suffering friend here, who has been invaluable throughout. But, first, I would give you an insight into this man's mentality. It is a very unusual one—so much so that I think his destination is more likely to be Broadmoor[19] than the scaffold. He has, to a high degree, the sort of mind which one associates with the mediaeval Italian nature rather than with the modern Briton. He was a miserable miser who made his wife so wretched by his niggardly ways that she was a ready prey for any adventurer. Such a one came upon the scene in the person of this chess-playing doctor. Amberley excelled at chess—one mark, Watson, of a scheming mind.[20] Like all misers, he was a jealous man, and his jealousy became a frantic mania.[21] Rightly or wrongly, he suspected an intrigue. He determined to have his revenge, and he planned it with diabolical cleverness. Come here!"

Holmes led us along the passage with as much certainty as if he had lived in the house and halted at the open door of the strong-room.

"Pooh! What an awful smell of paint!" cried the Inspector.

"That was our first clue," said Holmes. "You can thank Dr.

Watson's observation for that, though he failed to draw the inference. It set my foot upon the trail. Why should this man at such a time be filling his house with strong odours? Obviously, to cover some other smell which he wished to conceal— some guilty smell which would suggest suspicions. Then came the idea of a room such as you see here with iron door and shutter—a hermetically sealed room. Put those two facts together, and whither do they lead? I could only determine that by examining the house myself. I was already certain that the case was serious, for I had examined the box-office chart at the Haymarket Theatre—another of Dr. Watson's bull's-eyes—and ascertained that neither B thirty nor thirty-two of the upper circle had been occupied that night. Therefore, Amberley had not been to the theatre, and his alibi fell to the ground. He made a bad slip when he allowed my astute friend to notice the number of the seat taken for his wife. The question now arose how I might be able to examine the house. I sent an agent to the most impossible village I could think of, and summoned my man to it at such an hour that he could not possibly get back. To prevent any miscarriage, Dr. Watson accompanied him. The good vicar's name I took, of course, out of my Crockford. Do I make it all clear to you?"

"It is masterly," said the Inspector in an awed voice.

"There being no fear of interruption I proceeded to burgle the house.[22] Burglary has always been an alternative profession had I cared to adopt it, and I have little doubt that I should have come to the front. Observe what I found. You see the gas-pipe along the skirting here. Very good. It rises in the angle of the wall, and there is a tap here in the corner. The pipe runs out into the strong-room, as you can see, and ends in that plaster rose in the centre of the ceiling, where it is concealed by the ornamentation. That end is wide open. At any moment by turning the outside tap the room could be flooded with gas. With door and shutter closed and the tap full on I would not give two minutes of conscious sensation to anyone shut up in that little chamber. By what devilish device he decoyed them there I do not know, but once inside the door they were at his mercy."[23]

The Inspector examined the pipe with interest. "One of our officers mentioned the smell of gas," said he, "but of course the window and door were open then, and the paint—or some

22 S. Tupper Bigelow shows, in "Sherlock Holmes Was No Burglar," that technically, under British law, Holmes was innocent of burglary as well as unlawful entry—both crimes require a specific intent to commit a felony in the structure entered.

23 Charles A. Meyer makes the interesting suggestion that Amberley modelled his room after those in the well-publicised "murder castle" of mass-murderer H. H. Holmes. (Holmes was a pseudonym for his given name, Herman Mudgett, and thus there is no chance that he and Sherlock Holmes were related.) In the late 1800s, Holmes, a physician, constructed a three-storey hotel at the corner of Sixty-Third and Wallace in Chicago. Hidden behind the hotel's façade was a bizarrely outfitted interior of secret passages, sealed chambers, trapdoors, surgeon's tools, kilns, and a stretching machine. Once the hotel was completed, Holmes began gassing young women—some of whom he was linked to romantically—and dissecting them, selling their skeletons to medical schools. He struck pay dirt in 1893, when Chicago hosted the World's Columbian Exposition, a celebration of the four hundredth anniversary of Columbus's voyage to the New World. At least fifty tourists checked into Holmes's hotel and were never heard from again. Holmes's next project was an insurance scam in which his associate, Ben Pitezel, was to fake his own death. Travelling from city to city with Pitezel's young children in tow, Holmes caught the interest of the Pinkerton Detective Agency and was finally captured on November 17, 1894. In all, Holmes claimed to have killed 133 people, among them Pitezel and Pitezel's children. He was hanged in 1896. Holmes's story is brilliantly told in *The Devil in the White City: Murder, Magic, and Madness at the Fair That Changed America*, by Erik Larson (New York, 2003). Holmes is also the subject of a new documentary film titled *H. H. Holmes: America's First*

Serial Killer. Probably not coincidentally, celebrated writer/critic William Anthony Parker White (an avid Sherlockian), more commonly known as "Anthony Boucher," wrote several mysteries under the second pseudonym of "H. H. Holmes."

Motivated by Holmes's exploits, Amberley may well have murdered other individuals in the room to test its capabilities. But this leaves unanswered the basic question: Why did he build it? Was it built expressly to murder his wife?

of it—was already about. He had begun the work of painting the day before, according to his story. But what next, Mr. Holmes?"

"Well, then came an incident which was rather unexpected to myself. I was slipping through the pantry window in the early dawn when I felt a hand inside my collar, and a voice said: 'Now, you rascal, what are you doing in there?' When I could twist my head round I looked into the tinted spectacles of my friend and rival, Mr. Barker. It was a curious forgathering and set us both smiling. It seems that he had been engaged by Dr. Ray Ernest's family to make some investigations and had come to the same conclusion as to foul play. He had watched the house for some days and had spotted Dr. Watson as one of the obviously suspicious characters who had called there. He could hardly arrest Watson, but when he saw a man actually climbing

"I felt a hand inside my collar, and a voice said: 'Now, you rascal, what are you doing in there?'"
Frank Wiles, *Strand Magazine*, 1927

I was slipping through the pantry window in the early dawn
when I felt a hand inside my collar.
Frederick Dorr Steele, *Liberty*, 1926

out of the pantry window there came a limit to his restraint. Of
course, I told him how matters stood and we continued the
case together."

"Why him? Why not us?"

"Because it was in my mind to put that little test which
answered so admirably. I fear you would not have gone so far."

The Inspector smiled.

"Well, maybe not. I understand that I have your word, Mr.
Holmes, that you step right out of the case now and that you
turn all your results over to us."

"Certainly, that is always my custom."

24 T. V. Ramamurthy quite astutely points out that a dying man who managed only four letters before expiring would hardly have had the strength (or presence of mind) to put the pencil back into his pocket. And who would have placed the pencil with Dr. Ernest's body? Certainly not Amberley. In possible recognition of this anomaly, the words "on the body" do not appear in the *Liberty* publication of "The Retired Colourman." But William G. Miller ingeniously explains: "[This] is, in fact, an incomplete sentence. Had not the eager inspector cut off Holmes in mid-sentence, the full statement would have been 'If you find an indelible pencil on the body I will be very much surprised. . . . Instead, you will find the pencil in Josiah Amberley's *own* pocket.'" He goes on to suggest that the pencil was inside the room before the murders and was probably used by Amberley to keep his records.

"Well, in the name of the Force I thank you. It seems a clear case, as you put it, and there can't be much difficulty over the bodies."

"I'll show you a grim little bit of evidence," said Holmes, "and I am sure Amberley himself never observed it. You'll get results, Inspector, by always putting yourself in the other fellow's place, and thinking what you would do yourself. It takes some imagination, but it pays. Now, we will suppose that you were shut up in this little room, had not two minutes to live, but wanted to get even with the fiend who was probably mocking at you from the other side of the door. What would you do?"

"Write a message."

"Exactly. You would like to tell people how you died. No use writing on paper. That would be seen. If you wrote on the wall some eye might rest upon it. Now, look here! Just above the skirting is scribbled with a purple indelible pencil: 'We we—' That's all."

"What do you make of that?"

"Well, it's only a foot above the ground. The poor devil was on the floor dying when he wrote it. He lost his senses before he could finish."

"He was writing, 'We were murdered.'"

"That's how I read it. If you find an indelible pencil on the body—"[24]

"We'll look out for it, you may be sure. But those securities? Clearly there was no robbery at all. And yet he *did* possess those bonds. We verified that."

"You may be sure he has them hidden in a safe place. When the whole elopement had passed into history, he would suddenly discover them and announce that the guilty couple had relented and sent back the plunder or had dropped it on the way."

"You certainly seem to have met every difficulty," said the Inspector. "Of course, he was bound to call us in, but why he should have gone to you I can't understand."

"Pure swank!" Holmes answered. "He felt so clever and so sure of himself that he imagined no one could touch him. He could say to any suspicious neighbour, 'Look at the steps I have taken. I have consulted not only the police, but even Sherlock Holmes.'"

The Inspector laughed.

"We must forgive you your 'even,' Mr. Holmes," said he, "it's as workmanlike a job as I can remember."

A couple of days later my friend tossed across to me a copy of the bi-weekly *North Surrey Observer*. Under a series of flaming headlines, which began with "The Haven Horror," and ended with "Brilliant Police Investigation," there was a packed column of print which gave the first consecutive account of the affair. The concluding paragraph is typical of the whole. It ran thus:

> The remarkable acumen by which Inspector MacKinnon deduced from the smell of paint that some other smell, that of gas, for example, might be concealed; the bold deduction that the strong-room might also be the death-chamber, and the subsequent inquiry which led to the discovery of the bodies in a disused well, cleverly concealed by a dog-kennel, should live in the history of crime as a standing example of the intelligence of our professional detectives.

"Well, well, MacKinnon is a good fellow," said Holmes with a tolerant smile. "You can file it in our archives, Watson. Some day the true story may be told."[25] ■

THE IDENTITY OF "CARINA"

WHO WAS the mysterious "Carina," whose concert Holmes and Watson attended at Albert Hall? Guy Warrack, in *Sherlock Holmes and Music*, identifies her with Annie Louise Cary (1841–1921), a preeminent American contralto with a three-octave range. She toured extensively throughout Europe yet retired in May 1882, making her ultimately an unlikely candidate for Carina. In "Carina: An Identification," Allen Mackler selects the Croatian soprano Milka Ternina (1863-1941), who, after enjoying a decade's worth of success in Munich, debuted at Covent Garden as Isolde in June 1898. Donald A. Redmond mentions an untitled paper prepared by Patrick Drazen that argues for the Venezuelan pianist, composer, and singer Maria Teresa Carreño (1853–1917), of whom there is no record of a London appearance; but Redmond also points out that *Carina*

25 D. Martin Dakin wonders how this story could be told without embarrassing Inspector MacKinnon, even if he had long since retired. Might "MacKinnon" be an alias created by Dr. Watson? But then, he considers, could Lestrade, Gregson, Hopkins, and Athelney Jones all be aliases? Why, even the names of Watson and Holmes might be false identities! "[H]orror of horrors!" Dakin exclaims; "I recoil in guilty dismay from the hideous spectre I have raised, and hasten to disclaim the whole idea before I am indicted for heresy by the united membership of all the Sherlock Holmes societies."

was the title of a comic opera written by Edward Litt Laman Blanchard and C. Bridgeman, with music by Sophia Julia Woolf and performed prior to 1888. And in a daring but convincing article, Richard Lancelyn Green rejects the musical identification altogether, noting that Karina (the only name by which she was known) was the *première danseuse* at the Royal Opera House. Founder of "Madame Karina's Royal School of Dancing," under "the patronage of Her Majesty Queen Alexandra [of Denmark]," she was a stalwart of the opera ballet from 1913 through the 1920s. Despite Green's conclusion that it was "surely" she whom Dr. Watson had in mind, however, there is no evidence that she was on stage in London in 1898 or 1899, the only years considered by chronologists for "The Retired Colourman."

More romantically, Anthony Boucher argues in "The Records of Baker Street" that because every other musician in the Canon (besides Carina) is an eminent historical personage, then "Carina" must not be the singer's actual name. Instead, he believes that Holmes was using the Italian term of endearment *carina*, meaning "darling." "Then imagine the typography of the passage altered," Boucher explains, "to read, 'Let us escape from this weary workaday world by the side door of music; carina sings to-night at the Albert Hall . . .' " To Boucher, this constitutes a "momentary indiscretion on the part of Holmes, an obtuseness on the part of Watson," and a tantalising reference to Holmes's love life that will never be explained. William S. Baring-Gould does Boucher one better, suggesting that "Carina" was a reference to Irene Adler (who was not, in his view, deceased at that time), whereas Samuel Feinberg argues that it disguised Holmes's relationship with noted American soprano Lillian Nordica (1857–1914), best known for her Wagner roles. These various conclusions, while satisfying to those who yearn to find the "softer emotions" present in Holmes, can hardly be supported by the single remark.

In the end, none of the candidates mentioned above, with the exception of the unsatisfying "Ternina," fits the dates in question, and neither is there any real evidence for the more pleasant suggestions of the romantics. The intriguing mystery of Carina, then, to this day remains unsolved.

SELECTED SOURCES

GENERAL

Ackroyd, Peter. LONDON: THE BIOGRAPHY. London: Chatto & Windus, 2000.

Baedeker, Karl. GREAT BRITAIN: HANDBOOK FOR TRAVELLERS. Leipzic: Karl Baedeker, 1894.

Baedeker, Karl. LONDON AND ITS ENVIRONS. Leipsic: Karl Baedeker, 1896.

Baedeker, Karl. SWITZERLAND AND THE ADJACENT PORTIONS OF ITALY, SAVOY, AND THE TYROL: HANDBOOK FOR TRAVELLERS. Leipsic: Karl Baedeker, 1887.

Baring-Gould, William S. ANNOTATED SHERLOCK HOLMES. New York: Clarkson N. Potter, 1967. 2 vols.

Baring-Gould, William. S. CHRONOLOGICAL HOLMES. New York: Privately printed, 1955.

Baring-Gould, William S. SHERLOCK HOLMES OF BAKER STREET. New York: Clarkson N. Potter, 1962.

Baring-Gould, William S. "New Chronology of Sherlock Holmes and Dr. Watson," *Baker Street Journal* [O. S.] 3, No. 2 (1948): 107–125, and No. 3 (1948): 238–251.

Beach, C. B., ed. THE STUDENT'S CYCLOPEDIA. St. Louis, Mo.: H. M. Dixon & Co., 1901. 2 vols.

Beckson, Karl. LONDON IN THE 1890S: A CULTURAL HISTORY. New York and London: W. W. Norton, 1992.

Beeton, S. O. BEETON'S BRITISH GAZETTEER: A TOPOGRAPHICAL AND HISTORICAL GUIDE TO THE UNITED KINGDOM. London: Ward, Lock and Co., 1870.

Bell, H. W. SHERLOCK HOLMES AND DR. WATSON: THE CHRONOLOGY OF THEIR ADVENTURES. London: Constable & Co., 1932.

Betjeman, John. VICTORIAN AND EDWARDIAN LONDON FROM OLD PHOTOGRAPHS. London: B. T. Batsford Ltd., 1969.

Bigelow, S. Tupper. AN IRREGULAR ANGLO-AMERICAN GLOSSARY OF MORE OR LESS UNFAMILIAR WORDS, TERMS AND PHRASES IN THE SHERLOCK HOLMES SAGA. Toronto: Castalotte & Zamba, 1959.

Blackbeard, Bill. SHERLOCK HOLMES IN AMERICA. New York: Harry N. Abrams, 1981.

Blakeney, T. S. SHERLOCK HOLMES: FACT OR FICTION? London: John Murray, 1932.

Bondeson, Jan. BURIED ALIVE: THE TERRIFYING HISTORY OF OUR MOST PRIMAL FEAR. New York: W. W. Norton, 2001.

Booth, Charles. LIFE AND LABOUR OF THE PEOPLE IN LONDON. 17 vols. London and New York: MacMillan and Co., 1889–1903.

Bradley, C. Alan, and William A. S. Sargeant. MS. HOLMES OF BAKER STREET: THE TRUTH ABOUT SHERLOCK. Dubuque, Iowa: Gasogene Press, Ltd., 1989.

BRADSHAW'S GENERAL RAILWAY AND STEAM NAVIGATION GUIDE FOR GREAT BRITAIN AND IRELAND: AUGUST 1887. Newton Abbot: David & Charles Reprints, 1968.

Brend, Gavin. MY DEAR HOLMES. London: George Allen & Unwin, Ltd., 1951.

Brewer, E. Cobham. DICTIONARY OF PHRASE AND FABLE. Philadelphia: Henry Altemus, 1898.

Bush, Gerald. OLD LONDON. London: Academy Editions, 1975.

Butters, Roger. FIRST PERSON SINGULAR: A REVIEW OF THE LIFE AND WORK OF MR. SHERLOCK HOLMES, THE WORLD'S FIRST CONSULTING DETECTIVE, AND HIS FRIEND AND COLLEAGUE, DR. JOHN H. WATSON. New York: Vantage Press, 1984.

Campbell, Maurice. SHERLOCK HOLMES AND DR. WATSON: A MEDICAL DIGRESSION. London: Ash & Co., Ltd., 1935.

Carr, John Dickson. LIFE OF SIR ARTHUR CONAN DOYLE. London: John Murray, 1949.

Christ, Jay Finley. AN IRREGULAR CHRONOLOGY OF SHERLOCK HOLMES OF BAKER STREET. Ann Arbor, Mich.: The Fanlight House, 1947.

Clunn, Harold P. THE FACE OF LONDON. New edition, revised by E. R. Wethersett. London: Spring Books, n.d.

Cummings, Carey. THE BIORHYTHMIC HOLMES: A CHRONOLOGICAL PERSPECTIVE, Vol. 1, SIGN—STUD and the Adventures. Privately printed, 1980.

Dakin, D. Martin. A SHERLOCK HOLMES COMMENTARY. Newton Abbot: David & Charles, 1972.

DeVries, Leonard, and James Laver. VICTORIAN ADVERTISEMENTS. Philadelphia: J. B. Lippincott Co., 1968.

DeWaal, Ronald B. THE UNIVERSAL SHERLOCK HOLMES. Toronto: Metropolitan Toronto Reference Library, 1994. 4 vols. and Index.

Dickens, Charles, Jr. DICKENS'S DICTIONARY OF LONDON, 1890–1891. London: Charles Dickens & Evans, 1891.

Donegall, Lord. BAKER STREET AND BEYOND. Westminster, England: Westminster Libraries and Sherlock Holmes Society of London, 1993.

Doyle, Arthur Conan. MEMORIES AND ADVENTURES. Boston: Little, Brown and Company, 1924.

ENCYCLOPÆDIA BRITANNICA, 9th Edition. The R. S. Peale Reprint. Chicago: The Werner Company, 1893.

ENCYCLOPÆDIA BRITANNICA. 11th Edition. New York: The Encyclopædia Britannica Company, 1910.

Folsom, Henry T. THROUGH THE YEARS AT BAKER STREET: A CHRONOLOGY OF SHERLOCK HOLMES, REVISED EDITION. Washington, N.J.: Privately printed, 1964.

Ford, Colin, and Brian Harrison. A HUNDRED YEARS AGO: BRITAIN IN THE 1880s IN WORDS AND PICTURES. Cambridge: Harvard University Press, 1983.

Gascoigne, Bamber. ENCYLOPEDIA OF BRITAIN. London: Macmillan, 1994.

Gately, Iain. TOBACCO: A CULTURAL HISTORY OF HOW AN EXOTIC PLANT SEDUCED CIVILIZATION. New York: Grove Press, 2002.

Grazebrook, O. F. STUDIES IN SHERLOCK HOLMES. 4 vols. London: Privately printed, ca. 1949.

Green, Richard Lancelyn, and John Michael Gibson. A BIBLIOGRAPHY OF A. CONAN DOYLE. Boston, London, New York: Hudson House, 2000.

Guy, Patricia. BACCHUS AT BAKER STREET: OBSERVATIONS ON THE BIBULOUS PREFERENCES OF MR. SHERLOCK HOLMES AND HIS CONTEMPORARIES. Essex, England: Ian Henry Publications, 1995.

Hall, John. THE ABOMINABLE WIFE AND OTHER UNRECORDED CASES OF MR. SHERLOCK HOLMES. Ashcroft, British Columbia: Calabash Press, 1998.

————. "I REMEMBER THE DATE VERY WELL": A CHRONOLOGY OF THE SHERLOCK HOLMES STORIES OF ARTHUR CONAN DOYLE. Essex, England: Ian Henry Publications, 1993.

————. SIDELIGHTS ON HOLMES. Ashcroft, British Columbia: Calabash Press, 1998.

————. UNEXPLORED POSSIBILITIES. Leeds, England: Tai Xu Press, 1995.

Hammer, David L. THE BEFORE-BREAKFAST PIPE OF MR. SHERLOCK HOLMES. Dubuque, Iowa: Gasogene Press, Ltd., 1995.

————. A DANGEROUS GAME. Indianapolis, Ind.: Gasogene Press, Ltd., 1997.

————. FOR THE SAKE OF THE GAME. Dubuque, Iowa: Gasogene Press, Ltd., 1986.

————. THE GAME IS AFOOT: A TRAVEL GUIDE TO THE ENGLAND OF SHERLOCK HOLMES. Bloomington, Ind.: Gaslight Publications, 1983.

————. THE WORTH OF THE GAME. Dubuque, Iowa: Gasogene Press, Ltd., 1993.

Hardwick, Michael. COMPLETE GUIDE TO SHERLOCK HOLMES. New York: St. Martin's Press, 1986.

Hare, Augustus J. C. WALKS IN LONDON. New York: George Routledge and Sons, 1884.

Harrison, Michael. CYNOLOGICAL MR. HOLMES. New York: Magico Magazine, 1985.

————. IN THE FOOTSTEPS OF SHERLOCK HOLMES. Newton Abbot: David & Charles, 1971.

————. THE LONDON OF SHERLOCK HOLMES. New York: Drake Publishers, 1972.

————. THE WORLD OF SHERLOCK HOLMES. London: Frederick Muller, Ltd., 1973.

Herbert, Rosemary, ed. OXFORD COMPANION TO CRIME & MYSTERY WRITING. New York and Oxford: Oxford University Press, 1999.

Higham, Charles. ADVENTURES OF CONAN DOYLE: THE LIFE OF THE CREATOR OF SHERLOCK HOLMES. London: Hamish Hamilton, 1976.

Holroyd, James Edward. BAKER STREET BY-WAYS. London: George Allen and Unwin Ltd., 1959.

Hotten, John Camden. THE SLANG DICTIONARY; OR, THE VULGAR WORDS, STREET PHRASES, AND "FAST" EXPRESSIONS OF HIGH AND LOW SOCIETY. London: John Camden Hotten, Piccadilly, 1865.

Hughes, Thomas. TOM BROWN'S SCHOOL DAYS. New York: Oxford University Press, 1989 (reprint edition).

Inwood, Stephen. A HISTORY OF LONDON. New York: Carroll & Graf Publishers, 1998.

Jones, Kelvin I. A SHERLOCK HOLMES DICTIONARY: AN ETYMOLOGICAL GUIDE TO THE LESS FAMILIAR WORDS AND PHRASES IN THE SHERLOCK HOLMES STORIES. New York: Magico Magazine, 1988.

Keefauver, Brad. SHERLOCK AND THE LADIES. New York: Magico Magazine, 1988.

Kobayashi, Tsukasa, Akane Higashiyama, and Masaharu Uemura. SHERLOCK HOLMES'S LONDON. San Francisco, Chronicle books, 1986.

La Cour, Tage. EX BIBLIOTHECA HOLMESIANA: THE FIRST EDITIONS OF THE WRITINGS OF SHERLOCK HOLMES. Copenhagen: Danish Baker Street Irregulars, 1952.

McQueen, Ian. SHERLOCK HOLMES DETECTED: THE PROBLEMS OF THE LONG STORIES. Newton Abbot, London and Vancouver: David & Charles, 1974.

Miles, Alfred H., ed. THE HOUSEHOLD ORACLE: A POPULAR REFEREE ON SUBJECTS OF HOUSEHOLD ENQUIRY. London: Hutchinson & Co., 1898.

Morley, Christopher. SHERLOCK HOLMES AND DR. WATSON: A TEXTBOOK OF FRIENDSHIP. New York: Harcourt, Brace and Company, 1944.

Morris, Jan. SPECTACLE OF EMPIRE. Garden City, NY: Doubleday & Co., 1982.

Peck, Andrew Jay. THE DATE BEING . . . ? New York: Privately printed, 1970.

Peck, Andrew Jay, and Leslie S. Klinger. THE DATE BEING—?: A COMPENDIUM OF CHRONOLOGICAL DATA. New York: Magico Magazine, 1996.

Perry, George, and Nicholas Mason, eds. VICTORIANS: A WORLD BUILT TO LAST. New York: Viking Press, 1974.

Porter, Roy. LONDON: A SOCIAL HISTORY. London: Hamish Hamilton Co., 1994.

QUEEN'S LONDON. London: Cassell & Co., 1897.

Redmond, Christopher. IN BED WITH SHERLOCK HOLMES. Toronto: Simon & Pierre, 1984.

————. A SHERLOCK HOLMES HANDBOOK. Toronto: Simon & Pierre, 1993.

Redmond, Donald A. SHERLOCK HOLMES: A STUDY IN SOURCES. Kingston and Montreal: McGill-Queen's University Press, 1982.

Roberts, S. C. DOCTOR WATSON. London: Faber & Faber, 1931 (Criterion Miscellany No. 28).

———. HOLMES & WATSON: A MISCELLANY. London, New York, and Toronto: Oxford University Press, 1953.

Rodin, Alvin E., and Jack D. Key. MEDICAL CASEBOOK OF DOCTOR ARTHUR CONAN DOYLE. Malabar, Fla.: Robert E. Krieger Publishing Company, Inc., 1984.

Schama, Simon. A HISTORY OF BRITAIN: THE FATE OF EMPIRE 1776–2000. New York: Hyperion, 2002.

Shepherd, Walter. ON THE SCENT WITH SHERLOCK HOLMES. London: Arthur Barker Limited, 1978.

SHERLOCK HOLMES: CATALOGUE OF AN EXHIBITION HELD AT ABBEY HOUSE, BAKER STREET, LONDON, MAY–SEPTEMBER 1951. London: Wightman & Co., 1951.

Spence, Jonathan D. THE SEARCH FOR MODERN CHINA. New York: W. W. Norton, 1990.

Starrett, Vincent. THE PRIVATE LIFE OF SHERLOCK HOLMES. New York: The Macmillan Company, 1933.

Stashower, Daniel. TELLER OF TALES: THE LIFE OF ARTHUR CONAN DOYLE. New York: Henry Holt and Company, 1999.

Steinbrunner, Chris, and Otto Penzler, eds. ENCYCLOPEDIA OF MYSTERY & DETECTION. New York, St. Louis, San Francisco: McGraw-Hill, 1976.

Stern, Madeleine B. THE GAME'S A HEAD: A PHRENOLOGICAL STUDY OF SHERLOCK HOLMES AND ARTHUR CONAN DOYLE. London: Privately printed, 1983.

———. SHERLOCK HOLMES: RARE-BOOK COLLECTOR. Rockville Centre, N.Y.: Paulette Greene, 1981.

Strachey, Lytton. EMINENT VICTORIANS. New York: G. P. Putnam, 1918.

Thomson, John, and Adolphe Smith. VICTORIAN STREET LIFE IN HISTORIC PHOTOGRAPHS (originally, STREET LIFE IN LONDON). Reprint. New York: Dover, 1994.

THREE VICTORIAN TELEPHONE DIRECTORIES, 1884–5. Newton Abbot: David & Charles, 1970.

Tracy, Jack, ed. THE ENCYCLOPEDIA SHERLOCKIANA, OR A UNIVERSAL DICTIONARY OF SHERLOCK HOLMES AND HIS BIOGRAPHER JOHN H. WATSON, M.D. Rev. ed. New York: Avon Books, 1979.

Van Liere, Edward J. A DOCTOR ENJOYS SHERLOCK HOLMES. New York, Washington, and Hollywood: Vantage Press, 1959.

VICTORIAN SHOPPING: HARROD'S CATALOGUE 1895. Newton Abbot: David & Charles, 1972.

Vincent, Col. Sir Howard. THE POLICE CODE AND GENERAL MANUAL OF THE

CRIMINAL LAW. London: Francis Edwards and Limpkin, Marshall, Hamilton, Kent & Co., Ltd., 1904.

Warner, William R. WARNER'S POCKET MEDICAL DICTIONARY. Philadelphia: William R. Warner & Co., 1897.

Weller, Philip. LIFE AND TIMES OF SHERLOCK HOLMES. London: Studio Editions, 1992.

Whitaker, Joseph. ALMANACK 1900. Facsimile ed. London: The Stationery Office, 2000.

Williams, Montagu. ROUND LONDON: DOWN EAST AND UP WEST. London: Macmillan and Co., 1892.

Williams, Newt and Lillian. Unpublished handwritten clarifications, comments, and footnotes to Baring-Gould's THE ANNOTATED SHERLOCK HOLMES (*supra*), known as the ANNOTATED "ANNOTATED," now in the library of the Occupants of the Empty House, DuQuoin, Ill., made available to the editor.

Wilson, A. N. THE VICTORIANS. London: Hutchinson, 2002.

Wolff, Julian. PRACTICAL HANDBOOK OF SHERLOCKIAN HERALDRY. New York: Privately printed, 1955.

————. THE SHERLOCKIAN ATLAS. New York: Privately printed, 1952.

Zeisler, Ernest Bloomfield. BAKER STREET CHRONOLOGY: COMMENTARIES ON THE SACRED WRITINGS OF DR. JOHN H. WATSON. Chicago: Alexander J. Isaacs, 1953.

THE ADVENTURES OF SHERLOCK HOLMES

Abrams, Ian Neil. "The Triple-W Conundrum and the Spousal Nomenclature Riddle: Some Notes Towards an Inclusive Solution." *Sherlockian Meddler* 9, No. 2 (June 1981): 30–32.

Adams, Robert Winthrop, "John H. Watson, M.D., Characterologist." *Baker Street Journal* 4, No. 2 (Apr. 1954): 81–92.

Akers, Arthur K. "Who Was Mrs. Watson's First Husband?" *Baker Street Journal* 10, No. 1 (Jan. 1960): 35–36.

Alberstat, Mark J. "Was Holmes Ancestor of a Certain Boxer?" *Canadian Holmes* 6, No. 4 (Summer 1983): 32–33. (Letters to CH).

Altick, Richard D. "Mr. Sherlock Holmes and Dr. Samuel Johnson." In 221B: STUDIES IN SHERLOCK HOLMES, edited by Vincent Starrett, 109–128. New York: The Macmillan Company, 1940.

Anderson, Poul. "In the Island of Uffa." In WEST BY ONE AND BY ONE: AN ANTHOLOGY OF IRREGULAR WRITINGS. Scowrers and Molly Maguires of San Francisco and the Trained Cormorants of Los Angeles County, 125–132. San Francisco: Privately printed, 1965.

———. "The James Quotient." *Baker Street Journal* 15, No. 3 (Sept. 1965): 154–158.

Andrew, Clifton R. "What Happened to Watson's Married Life After June 14, 1889?" *Baker Street Journal*, Christmas Annual (1958): 42–44.

Andrews, C. R. "What Kind of Shenanigans Went on at St. Monica's?" *Baker Street Journal*, Christmas Annual (1956): 42–45.

Arenfalk, Poul. "Mysteries in 'The Man with the Twisted Lip,' " *Irregular Report* 2, No. 5 (March 1962): 1–4.

Asher, Richard. "Holmes and the Fair Sex." *Sherlock Holmes Journal* 2, No. 3 (Summer 1955): 15–22.

Ashton, Ralph A. "The Fourth Occupant, or the Room with the Twisted Tongue." *Baker Street Journal* 11, No. 1 (March 1961): 38–40.

Aton, Elizabeth Henckler. "Five Orange Pips—A Family Affair?" *Wheelwrightings* 13, No. 2 (Sept. 1990): 29–33.

Austin, Bliss. A BAKER STREET CHRISTMAS STOCKING. Westfield, N.J.: Hydraulic Press, 1955.

———. "Thumbing His Way to Fame." *Baker Street Journal* [O.S.] 1, No. 4 (Oct. 1946): 424–432.

———. "What Son Was Watson? A Case of Identity." In A BAKER STREET FOUR-WHEELER, edited by Edgar W. Smith, 43–53. Maplewood, N.J., and New York: The Pamphlet House, 1944.

Bailey, L. W. "Scandal Behind the 'Scandal.' " *Sherlock Holmes Journal* 9, No. 3 (Winter 1969): 82–85.

Ball, John. "The Practical Art of Baritsu, the Japanese Wrestling System; With Some Observations on Its Use by Mr. Sherlock Holmes." *Baker Street Journal* 14, No. 1 (March 1964): 31–36.

Ball, John, Jr. "Early Days in Baker Street." *Baker Street Journal* 5, No. 4 (Oct. 1955): 211–219.

Ballew, William. "Two-Gun Watson? Or 'The Curious Incident of The Bull Dog in the Medical Bag.' " *Holmes and Watson Report* 1, No. 2 (May 1997): 31–34.

Barnes, W. J. "Saxe-Coburg Square—A New Identification," *Sherlock Holmes Journal* 2, No. 3 (Summer 1955): 31–34.

Barzun, Jacques. "A Note on John Clay's Education." *Baker Street Journal* 31, No. 1 (March 1981): 22–23.

Beckmeyer, Doyle W. "Valuable Sherlockian Hunting-Ground." In ILLUSTRIOUS CLIENT'S THIRD CASE-BOOK, edited by J. N. Williamson and H. B. Williams, 111–115. Indianapolis, Ind.: The Illustrious Clients, 1953.

Beirle, John D. "The Curious Incident of the Drive Through Middlesex and Surrey." *Baker Street Journal* 7, No. 4 (Oct. 1957): 216–219.

Bell, H. W. "Three Identifications: Lauriston Gardens, Upper Swandam Lane, Saxe-Coburg Square." In 221B: STUDIES IN SHERLOCK HOLMES, edited by Vincent Starrett, 59–67.

Bengis, Nathan L. "A Scandal in Baker Street." *Baker Street Journal* [O. S.] 2, No. 2 (Apr. 1947): 145–157 and No. 3 (July 1947): 311–321.

———. "Sherlock Stays After School." In ILLUSTRIOUS CLIENT'S SECOND CASE-BOOK, edited by J. N. Williamson, 72–78. Indianapolis, Ind.: The Illustrious Clients, 1949.

Bergman, Ted. "The Case of the City and Suburban Bank." *Baker Street Cab Lantern* (July 1963): 27.

Berman, Ruth. "James Watson." *Baker Street Journal* 22, No. 4 (Dec. 1972): 237–241.

———. "On Docketing a Hebrew Rabbi." *Baker Street Journal* 10, No. 2 (Apr. 1960): 80–82.

———. "Uffa's Midnight Visitor." *Baker Street Journal* 33, No. 1 (March 1983): 7–8.

Bett, W. H. "New Light on Dundas." *Sherlock Holmes Journal* 11, No. 4 (Autumn 1974): 134–135.

Betzner, Ray. "Whatever Happened to Baby Rucastle?" *Agony Column* 4, No. 2 (Apr. 1986): 4 (Thesis No. 4).

Bigelow, S. Tupper. "Barred-Tail Geese." *Sherlock Holmes Journal* 6, No. 4 (Spring 1964): 108–109.

———. "Misprision of Felony and Sherlock Holmes." *Sherlock Holmes Journal* 5, No. 3 (Winter 1961): 68–70.

———. "Sherlock Holmes and Misprision of Felony." *Baker Street Journal* 8, No. 3 (July 1958): 139–146.

———. "Sherlock Holmes Was No Burglar." *Baker Street Journal*, Christmas Annual (1958): 26–37.

———. "The Blue Enigma." *Baker Street Journal* 11, No. 4 (Dec. 1961): 203–214.

———. "Two Canonical Problems Solved." *Baker Street Journal*, Christmas Annual (1959): 261–271.

———. "Was It Baxter?" *Sherlock Holmes Journal* 7, No. 4 (Spring 1966): 125–126.

Blackburn, Julian. "Identity of King of Bohemia." *Baker Street Journal* 21, No. 2 (June 1971): 114–116.

Blake, S. F. "Sherlock Holmes's Dressing Gown(s)." *Baker Street Journal* 10, No. 2 (Apr. 1960): 86–89.

———. "Sherlock Holmes and the Italian Cipher." *Baker Street Journal* 9, No. 1 (Jan. 1959): 14–20.

Blakeney, T. S. "Case for Identification—In Bohemia." *Sherlock Holmes Journal* 3, No. 2 (Winter 1956): 15–16.

———. "Some Disjecta Membra." *Sherlock Holmes Journal* 4, No. 3 (Winter 1959): 101–103.

———. "Thoughts on *The Sign of Four*." *Sherlock Holmes Journal* 3, No. 4 (Summer 1958): 6–8.

Blau, Peter. "The Matter Is a Perfectly Trivial One . . ." In MORE LEAVES FROM THE COPPER BEECHES, 167–174. Lititz, Pa.: Sutter House, 1976.

Blaustein, Albert P. "Sherlock Holmes As a Lawyer." *Baker Street Journal* [O. S.] 3, No. 3 (1948): 306–308.

Blegen, Theodore C. "These Were Hidden Fires, Indeed!" In EXPLORING SHERLOCK HOLMES, edited by E. W. McDiarmid and Theodore C. Blegen, 9–26. La Crosse, Wisc: Sumac Press, 1957.

Boswell, Rolfe. "A Connecticut Yankee in Support of Sir Arthur." *Baker Street Journal* [O. S.] 2, No. 2 (1947): 119–127.

———. "Dr. Roylott's Wily Filip: With a Proem on Veneration of Vipers." *Baker Street Journal* [O. S.] 1, No. 3 (July 1946): 307–311.

———. " 'In Uffish Thought.' " *Baker Street Journal* [O. S.] 1, No. 1 (Jan. 1946): 21–24.

———. "Sarasate, Sherlock and Shaw," *Baker Street Journal* 2, No. 1 (Jan. 1952): 22–29.

Boucher, Anthony. "Records of Baker Street." *Baker Street Journal* [O. S.] 4, No. 1 (1949): 97–104.

Boucher, Anthony, and Denis Green. "Amateur Mendicant Society." Broadcast by Basil Rathbone and Nigel Bruce on Apr. 2, 1945. "Novelized" by Ken Greenwald, "Case of the Amateur Mendicant Society," 45–58. In LOST ADVENTURES OF SHERLOCK HOLMES. New York: Mallard Press, 1989.

———. "The Camberwell Poisoners." Broadcast on Feb. 18, 1946. "Novelized" by Ken Greenwald in LOST ADVENTURES OF SHERLOCK HOLMES. 145–159.

———. "The Island of Uffa." Radio script broadcast on December 11, 1944.

Bousquet, Robert J. "Sherlock Holmes—Linguist." In INTERIM REPORT 1993: THE BOSCOMBE VALLEY MYSTERY REVISITED, 40–42. Hampshire, England: Franco-Midland Hardware Co., 1993.

Brend, Gavin, "From Maiwand to Marylebone." *Sherlock Holmes Journal* 1, No. 3 (June 1953): 40–44.

———. "Jabez Muses." *Baker Street Journal* 3, No. 3 (July 1953): 169.

———. "The Five Orange Pips." *Sherlock Holmes Journal* 2, No. 3 (Summer 1955): 2.

———. "The Route of the Blue Carbuncle." *Sherlock Holmes Journal* 2, No. 4 (Winter 1955): 2–6.

Brodie, Robert N. " 'Take a Wire, Like a Good Fellow': The Telegraph in the Canon." *Baker Street Journal* 41, No. 3 (Sept. 1991): 148–152.

Brody, Howard. "The Commonplace Murder of Mary Sutherland." *Baker Street Miscellanea* 23 (Fall 1980): 1–3.

Brooks, Clive. "The Adventure of the Amateur Mendicants." In SHERLOCK HOLMES REVISITED, VOL. 2: MORE UNCHRONICLED ADVENTURES, 103–126. Hampshire, England: SpyGlass Crime, 1990.

Brown, John W. SHERLOCK HOLMES IN STREATHAM. London: Local History Publications, 1993.

Brundage, Paul H. "In Defense of Irene Adler." *Baker Street Journal* 31, No. 4 (Dec. 1981): 234–238.

Bryan-Brown, F. D., "Some Thoughts on 'The Speckled Band.' " *Sherlock Holmes Journal* 10, No. 3 (Winter 1971): 89–92.

Buchholtz, James. "A Tremor at the Edge of the Web." *Baker Street Journal* 8, No. 1 (Jan. 1958): 5–9.

Burnham, Ernest C., Jr., "The Tattooed Fish in *The Red-Headed League*." *Baker Street Journal* 12, No. 4 (Dec. 1962): 219–222.

Burr, Robert C. "But What About the Blood, Holmes?" *Baker Street Journal* 39, No. 2 (June 1989): 75, 78.

———. "The Long Consultation." *Wheelwrightings* 8, No. 2 (Sept. 1985): 26–28.

Butler, Anthony R. "Sherlock Holmes as a Chemist." *Sherlock Holmes Journal* 12, Nos. 3 & 4 (Summer 1976): 81–82.

Calamai, Peter. "Headlines and Deadlines: How Sherlock Holmes Used the Press." In SHERLOCK HOLMES: VICTORIAN SLEUTH TO MODERN HERO, edited by Charles R. Putney, Joseph A. Cutshall King, and Sally Sugarman, 25–36. Lanham, Md., and London: Scarecrow Press, Inc., 1996.

Campbell, Patrick J. "Sherlock Holmes and the Simultaneous Equations." *Canadian Holmes* 15, No. 2 (Winter 1991): 11–15.

Carr, John Dickson, and Adrian Conan Doyle. "The Adventure of the Gold Hunter." In EXPLOITS OF SHERLOCK HOLMES, 30–53. London: John Murray, 1954.

Chambers, Patrick T. "The Strangest Snake in the World." *Wheelwrightings* 10, No. 3 (Jan. 1988): 25–28.

Chaney, Warren H. "Sherlock Holmes in Texas." *Pip's Log* 1, No. 1 (Nov. 3, 1980): 5–7.

Chorley, Jennifer. "An Amazing Epistle—Fact or Fiction?" *Baker Street Journal* 15, No. 3 (Sept. 1965): 165–166.

———. "Some Diggings Down Under." *Sherlock Holmes Journal* 6, No. 2 (Spring 1963): 49–51.

Christ, Jay Finley. "James Boswell and the Island of Uffa." *Baker Street Journal* [O. S.] 1, No. 1 (Jan. 1946): 24–27.

———. "Problems in *A Scandal in Bohemia*." *Baker Street Gasogene* 1, No. 2 (1961). Reprinted in REFLECTIONS ON A SCANDAL IN BOHEMIA, 53–62. New York: Magico Magazine, 1986.

———. "Sherlock Backs a Turkey." In SHERLOCKIAN STUDIES, edited by Robert A. Cutter, 23. Jackson Heights, N.Y.: The Baker Street, 1947.

———. "Thumbs Up Thumbs Down," *Sherlock Holmes Journal* 2, No. 1 (July 1954): 41–42.

Christie, Winifred M. "On the Remarkable Explorations of Sigerson." *Sherlock Holmes Journal* 1, No. 2 (Sept. 1952): 39–44.

Clapp, Roger T. "The Curious Problem of the Railway Timetables." In THE SECOND CAB: FIFTEEN SHERLOCKIAN ESSAYS, ONE SONNET, AND A QUIZ, edited by James Keddie, Jr., 34–38. Boston: The Speckled Band, 1944.

Clark, Benjamin S. "Was There More to Watson Than Met the Private Eye?" *Baker Street Journal* 19, No. 4 (Dec. 1969): 216–219.

———. "The Horsham Fiasco." *Baker Street Journal* 1, No. 1 (Jan. 1951): 4–8.

Clark, John D. "King of Bohemia?" *Baker Street Journal* 15, No. 3 (Sept. 1965): 142—146.

Clark, Michael. "Who Was Mrs. Turner?" *Devon County Chronicle* 12, No. 3 (March 1976): 6.

Clarke, Richard W. "Certain Ladies of Baker Street." *Baker Street Journal* 2, No. 1 (Jan. 1952): 34–38.

———. "On the Nomenclature of Watson's Ships." *Baker Street Journal* [O. S.] 1, No. 2 (1946): 119–121.

———. "The Story I Like Best." *Baker Street Journal* [O. S.] 3, No. 2 (1948): 188–190.

Clarkson, Paul S. "Scandalous Case of Identity." *Baker Street Journal* 19, No. 4 (Dec. 1969): 230–234.

Cold, Jørgen. "What Did Sherlock Holmes Drink?" In ILLUSTRIOUS CLIENT'S THIRD CASE-BOOK, edited by J. N. Williamson and H. B. Williams, 91–96.

Cole, Eleanor S. "Holmes, Watson and the K-9's." *Baker Street Journal* 1, No. 1 (Jan. 1951): 25–29.

Collins, Howard. "Ex Libris Sherlock Holmes." In PROFILE BY GASLIGHT, edited by Edgar B. Smith, 26–39. New York: Simon and Schuster, 1944.

Coltart, J. S. "The Watsons." *The Fortnightly Review* 129 (May 1931): 650–657.

Cornell, Philip. "A Fresh Bite at The Speckled Band." *Passengers' Log* 2, No. 1 (Oct. 1998): 8–12.

Crosland, Donna. "A Conclusion to the Identity of 'Mrs. Turner.'" *Sherlockian Meddler* 10, No. 3 (1985): 23–24.

Cross, Melvin. "The Lantern of Sherlock Holmes." *Baker Street Journal* [O. S.] 1, No. 4 (1946): 433–442.

Cumings, Thayer. "Great Holmes Sale." In SEVEN ON SHERLOCK. Privately printed, 1968.

Curjel, Harald. " 'Rent-a-Crowd' in 1888." *Baker Street Journal* 27, No. 3 (Sept. 1977): 138–140.

———. "Sherlock Holmes and the Pecking Order: A Study in Social Attitudes." *Sherlock Holmes Journal* 14, Nos. 3 and 4 (Summer 1980): 91–93.

———. "Some Further Thoughts on Canonical Weaponry." *Sherlock Holmes Journal* 15, No. 3 (Winter 1981): 82–84.

Daish, W. G. "Ponderings on Pitfalls." *Sherlock Holmes Journal* 5, No. 4 (Summer 1962): 118–119.

Dalton, Patsy. "Canon Fodder." *Sherlock Holmes Journal* 11, No. 4 (Autumn 1974): 112–117.

Dandrew, Thomas A. "Mrs. Turner?" *Baker Street Journal* 29, No. 2 (June 1979): 84–89.

Darak, Greg. "But Why Dissolve the League?" *Baker Street Journal* 39, No. 2 (June 1989): 108–109.

———. "The Date of *The Red-Headed League*." *Baker Street Journal* 41, No. 4 (Dec. 1991): 235–236.

Darkbloom, Vivian [Nabokov, Vladimir]. "Holmes Is Where the Heart Is, or Tooth-Tooth, Tootsie." *Baker Street Miscellanea* 6 (June 1976): 9–14.

De Stefano, James J. "On the Defence of Dr. Watson Regarding Mrs. Turner." *Baker Street Journal* 29, No. 2 (June 1979): 90–91.

DePaw, David P. "The Original Pistol of John H. Watson, M.D., Late of 221B Baker Street, London." *Baker Street Chronicle* 1, No. 5 (Nov. 1981): 3–4.

Deschamps, Peter. "Another Look to the Lady." *Prescott's Press* 1, No. 2 (July 1978): 42–45.

Dickensheet, Dean W. "A Last Word for Irene Adler." *Shades of Sherlock* 2, No. 2 (Dec. 1967): 5.

———. "On a Polychromatic Paradox." *Vermissa Daily Herald* 3, No. 3 (Jan. 1982): 3.

Dickensheet, Dean W. and Shirley. "The Profession of Henry Baker: A Minor Exercise in Application of Method." *Pontine Dossier Annual* 1, No. 1 (1970): 36–40.

Dobson, A. W. "Arms and the Man." *Sherlock Holmes Journal* 8, No. 1 (Winter 1966): 20–23.

Doheney, Teresa, and Brian Scrivener. "Happily Ever After." In INTERIM REPORT 1993: THE BOSCOMBE VALLEY CONTRACT REVIEWED, 36–39. Hampshire, England: Franco-Midland Hardware Company, 1993.

Donegall, Lord. "Editorial Notes [Watson and Bradshaw]." *Sherlock Holmes Journal* 5, No. 2 (Spring 1961): 35–36.

———. "The Horological Holmes." *Sherlock Holmes Journal* 8, No. 4 (Summer 1968): 120–122.

Dorian, N. Currier. " 'A Bad Lot,' " *Baker Street Journal* 6, No. 1 (Jan. 1956): 51–57.

Doyle, Arthur Conan. ADVENTURE OF THE ENGINEER'S THUMB. Edited and annotated by Philip Weller. Lee-on-the-Solent, Hampshire: Sherlock Publications, 1995. The Company Canon.

———. ADVENTURES OF SHERLOCK HOLMES. Edited and with an introduction by Richard Lancelyn Green. Oxford and New York: Oxford University Press, 1994.

———. ANGELS OF DARKNESS. Unpublished. Described in John Dickson Carr, LIFE OF SIR ARTHUR CONAN DOYLE. New York: Harper & Brothers, 1949. Subsequently published as *Angels of Darkness, A Drama in Three Acts*. New York: Baker Street Irregulars, 2001.

E.J.C. and Robertson, Allen. "Commuting a Felony." *Baker Street Journal* 3, No. 3 (1948): 309–316.

Eaton, Herbert. "King of Bohemia Unmasked." *Vermissa Herald* 3, No. 1 (Jan. 1969): 2–6.

Ellison, Charles O. "The Chemical Corner." In SHERLOCK HOLMES AND HIS CREATOR, edited by Trevor Hall, 30–38. London: Gerald O. Duckworth Ltd., 1978.

Erickson, Carl T. "Royal Blood and Feet of Clay." *Baker Street Journal* 4, No. 2 (Apr. 1954): 98–99.

Fagin, Vernon. "Sherlock Holmes, Lewis Carroll, Victorian Photography, and That Scandal in Bohemia." *Baker Street Journal* 30, No. 3 (Sept. 1980): 158–159, 162–165.

Fay, Arthur D. "Ships in the Canon." *Baker Street Journal* 17, No. 1 (March 1967): 3–8.

Felstead, S. Theodore. SHADES OF SCOTLAND YARD: STORIES GRAVE AND GAY OF THE WORLD'S GREATEST DETECTIVE FORCE. New York: Roy Publishers, n.d.

Fenton, Irving M. "An Analysis of the Crimes and Near-Crimes at Appledore Towers in the Light of the English Criminal Law." *Baker Street Journal* 6, No. 2 (Apr. 1956): 69–74.

Fisher, Charles. "Sherlock Holmes and Jack the Ripper." In LEAVES FROM THE COPPER BEECHES, edited by Ames Johnston, Thomas Hart, Henry A. Shalet, and H. W. Starr, 18–32. Philadelphia: Sons of the Copper Beeches, 1959.

Folsom, Henry T. "Seventeen Out of Twenty-Three." *Baker Street Journal* 14, No. 1 (March 1964): 24–26.

Foss, Lt.-Col. T. F., and J. M. Linsenmeyer, J.D. "Look to the Lady." *Baker Street Journal* 27, No. 2 (June 1977): 79–85.

Foss, T. F. Letter. *Baker Street Journal* 28, No. 4 (Dec. 1978): 227.

Foss, Thomas Frederick. "The Bounder and the Bigamist." *Baker Street Journal* 34, No. 1 (March 1984): 8–11.

———. "But Whose Royal Blood?" *Baker Street Journal* 22, No. 1 (March 1972): 29–35.

———. "A Minor Matter of Bigamy." *Sherlock Holmes Journal* 13, No. 2 (Summer 1977): 45–46.

———. "No Dope-Ridden Don." *Baker Street Journal* 28, No. 1 (March 1978): 26–27.

Foster, R. W. "The Curious Incident of the Snake in the Night Time." In MORE LEAVES FROM THE COPPER BEECHES, edited by H. W. Starr, James G. Jewell, Carl Anderson, and William Miller, 59–62. Lititz, Pa.: Sutter House, 1976.

Foster, Richard. "The Slippery Mr. Moulton, the Brazen Hatty Doran, and the Elusive Mr. Doran," *Baker Street Journal* 24, No. 4 (Dec. 1974): 215–217.

Foxwell, E., and T. C. Farrar. EXPRESS TRAINS, ENGLISH AND FOREIGN. London: Smith, Elder & Co., 1889.

Francis, Henry G., editor-in-chief. THE OFFICIAL ENCYCLOPEDIA OF BRIDGE. Memphis, Tenn.: American Contract Bridge League, 1994.

Francis, Thomas J. "Watson a Name?" *Quarter£y $tatement* 10, No. 1 (Feb. 1989): 11–13.

Fréchette, V. D., and J. R. Varner. "The Beryl Coronet—Genuine or Counterfeit?" *Baker Street Journal* 22, No. 1 (March 1972): 26–28, 42.

Fune, Joseph. A PAPER: OF TOBACCO. TREATING OF THE RISE, PROGRESS, PLEASURES, AND ADVANTAGES OF SMOKING. London: Chapman and Hall, 1839.

Fusco, Andrew G. "The Case Against Mr. Holmes." In BEYOND BAKER STREET: A SHERLOCKIAN ANTHOLOGY, edited and annotated by Michael Harrison, 95–108. Indianapolis, Ind., and New York: The Bobbs-Merrill Company, Inc., 1976.

Galerstein, David H. "The Granada Series and 'The Red Headed League.' " *Wheelwrightings* 12, No. 2 (Sept. 1989): 18–20.

———. "The Real Loot." *Baker Street Miscellanea* 60 (Winter 1989): 19–21.

———. "Turner-McCarthy." *Baker Street Journal* 34, No. 4 (Dec. 1984): 244.

Gallivan, Kevin J. J. "Murder on the Half-Shell, or What 'A Woman'?" *Covert Notes* (N. S.) 2, No. 3 (Sept. 1979): 10–19.

George, Isaac S. "Violet the Hunter." *Baker Street Journal* [O. S.] 4, No. 1 (Jan. 1949): 29–37.

George, Marian M. A JOURNEY TO ENGLAND AND WALES. Chicago: A. Flanagan Company, 1901.

Gill, William H. "Some Notable Sherlockian Buildings." *Sherlock Holmes Journal* 4, No. 4 (Spring 1960): 124–126.

Gillies, Joseph H. "Where is Eyford?" *Baker Street Journal* 19, No. 4 (Dec. 1969): 213–215.

Girand, E. V. "On the Antiquity of Scandal in Bohemia." *Baker Street Journal* 23, No. 3 (Sept. 1973): 162–169.

Girand, John. "Frank Moulton's Arizona Adventures." *Baker Street Journal* 19, No. 4 (Dec. 1969): 206–212.

Goodman, Charles. "The Dental Holmes." *Baker Street Journal* [O. S.] 2, No. 4 (Oct. 1947): 381–393.

Goslin, Verner. "Further Identifications." *Sherlock Holmes Journal* 9, No. 4 (Summer 1970): 144.

———. "The Extraordinary Story of the Red-Headed Copier." *Sherlock Holmes Journal* 10, No. 2 (Winter 1971): 77–78.

Green, Richard Lancelyn. "The Shameful Secret of Stoke Moran." *Musgrave Papers* 9 (1996): 64–68.

Grosbayne, Benjamin. "Sherlock Holmes—Musician." *Baker Street Journal* [O. S.] 3, No. 1 (1948): 47–57.

Hall, John. "And Now?—Ballarat." In INTERIM REPORT 1993: THE BOSCOMBE VALLEY CONTRACT REVIEWED, 17–19. Hampshire, England: Franco-Midland Hardware Company, 1993.

———. "Whatever Her Sins Are." *Musgrave Papers*, 9th Issue (1996): 81–91.

Hall, Trevor. "The Early Years of Sherlock Holmes." In SHERLOCK HOLMES: TEN LITERARY STUDIES. 18–35. New York: St. Martin's Press, 1969.

———. "The Love Life of Sherlock Holmes." In SHERLOCK HOLMES: TEN LITERARY STUDIES, 132–147. New York: St. Martin's Press, 1969.

Hall, William S. "The True and Proper Coat of Arms of Mr. Sherlock Holmes: With Also the Coats of Arms of John H. Watson, M.D., and James Moriarty, Sc.D." In PROFILE BY GASLIGHT, edited by Edgar W. Smith, 114–124.

Hammer, David L. "Scandal in Bulgaria (or, Who Was That Masked Man?)" *Sherlock Holmes Journal* 18, No. 3 (Winter 1987): 81–84.

———. "Then I Thought of You, Mr. Holmes." *Baker Street Miscellanea* 66 (Summer 1991): 7–11.

———. "Who Was That Gentleman?" In STUDIES IN SCARLET. Dubuque, Iowa: Gasogene Press, 1989.

Harbottle, S. T. L. "Sherlock Holmes and the Law." *Sherlock Holmes Journal* 1, No. 3 (June 1953): 7–10.

Harkison, Judy. " 'A Chorus of Groans,' Notes Sherlock Holmes." *Smithsonian* 18, No. 6 (Sept. 1987): 196.

Harrington, Hugh T. "A Quite Exceptional Woman." *Canadian Holmes* 15, No. 3 (Spring 1992): 9–10.

———. "The Most Overdressed Man in the Canon." *Wheelwrightings* 13, No. 3 (Jan. 1991): 30–31.

Harris, Robert G. "It's Not Always 1957." *Baker Street Journal* 8, No. 1 (Jan. 1958): 29–32.

Harrison, Michael. "Sherlock Holmes and the King of Bohemia: The Solution of a Royal Mystery." In BEYOND BAKER STREET: A SHERLOCKIAN ANTHOLOGY, edited and annotated by Michael Harrison, 137–172. Indianapolis and New York: The Bobbs-Merrill Co., 1976.

———. "The Blue Book of the Holmeses: A Genealogical Note, as an Appendix to the Saga." *Baker Street Journal* 14, No. 2 (June 1964): 81–83.

Hart, Archibald. "The Effects of Trades Upon Hands." *Baker Street Journal* [O. S.] 3, No. 4 (Oct. 1948): 418–420.

Haugen, David N. "James! James??" *Beaten's Christmas Annual* 5 (1987): 11–12.

Hearn, Otis. "Undertones of *Boscombe Valley*." *Baker Street Journal* 28, No. 1 (March 1978): 36–40.

Heldenbrand, Page. "Sherlock Holmes in Disguise." *Baker Street Journal* [O. S.] 1, No. 3 (July 1946): 318–322.

Herzog, Evelyn A. "Royal House of Europe Revisited." *Baker Street Journal* 31, No. 3 (Sept. 1981): 175–176.

———. "The Case of the Superfluous Sleuth." *Baker Street Miscellanea* 10 (June 1977): 1–3.

Hicks, John L. "No Fire Without Some Smoke." *Baker Street Journal* 5, No. 1 (Jan. 1955): 27–33.

Hill, Sandy. "*The* Woman." In Murderess Ink: The Better Half of the Mystery, perpetrated by Dilys Winn, 227–228. New York: Workman Publishing, 1979.

Hoff, Ebbe Curtis. "The Adventure of John and Mary." *Baker Street Journal* 9, No. 3 (July 1959): 136–152.

Hoffer, Phil. "Julia Stoner as the First 'Woman.' " *Baker Street Journal* 29, No. 2 (June 1979): 106–108.

Hoffman, Banesh. "Red Faces and 'The Red-Headed League.' " In Beyond Baker Street: A Sherlockian Anthology, edited by Michael Harrison, 175–185.

Hollyer, Cameron. Importance of Knowing Sherlock, by Mr. W. H. Toronto, Ontario: Privately printed, 1971.

Holmes, Bruce. "Affair of the Purloined Plot." *Canadian Holmes* 14, No. 3 (Spring 1991): 19, 21.

Holroyd, James Edward. "The Egg Spoon [On the Cheetah as Watch-Dog]." *Sherlock Holmes Journal* 2, No. 3 (Summer 1955): 14.

———. "The Egg Spoon." *Sherlock Holmes Journal* 1, No. 1 (1952): 24–26.

———. "The Egg-Spoon." *Sherlock Holmes Journal* 2, No. 4 (Winter 1955): 26–27.

Holstein, Leon S. "Inspector G. Lestrade." *Baker Street Journal* 8, No. 2 (Apr. 1958): 78–84.

———"7. Knowledge of Chemistry—Profound." *Baker Street Journal* 4, No. 1 (Jan. 1954): 44–49.

Howard, Aija. "He Remains: The Man." *Devon County Chronicle* 16, No. 2 (Feb. 1980): 3–4, 7.

Howland, Charles Berry. "The Sense of Humor of Violet Hunter." In More Leaves from the Copper Beeches, edited by H. W. Starr, et al., 109–114. Lititz, PA: Sutter House, 1976.

Hughes, Robert. The Fatal Shore. New York: Random House, 1986.

Hunt, T. B., and H. W. Starr. "What Happened to Mary Morstan?" *Baker Street Journal* [O.S.] 2, No. 3 (1947): 237–246.

Hyder, William. "The Blue Carbuncle: Loose Ends & Moral Ambiguities." *Musgrave Papers* 9 (1996): 57–63.

———. "Religious Figures in the Canon." In From Baltimore to Baker Street, 163–180. Toronto: Metropolitan Reference Library, 1995.

————. "Sherlock Holmes as Musician." In FROM BALTIMORE TO BAKER STREET, 21–46.

————. "Titles in the Canon." In FROM BALTIMORE TO BAKER STREET, 141–162.

————. "Watson's Education and Medical Career." In FROM BALTIMORE TO BAKER STREET, 46–65.

Iraldi, James C. "The Other Geese." *Baker Street Journal* 4, No. 3 (July 1954): 156–159.

Jackson, Michael. AMERICAN EXPRESS POCKET GUIDE TO LONDON. New York: Simon and Schuster, 1981.

James, Garry. "Shooting the Guns of Sherlock Holmes." *Handguns for Sport and Defense* 5, No. 10 (Oct. 1991): 70–75.

Jenkins, William D. "The Beryl Coronet: Who Wore It?" *Baker Street Miscellanea* 59 (Fall 1989): 24–25.

Johnson, Frederic A. "Sherlock Holmes, The Criminal?" *Baker Street Journal* 10, No. 3 (July 1960): 172–174.

Johnson, Hugh. VINTAGE: THE STORY OF WINE. New York, London: Simon and Schuster, 1989.

Johnson, Karen L. "The Myopic Maiden." *Columbine's New-Fangled Banner* 1 (May 1983): 7–9.

Johnson, Roger. "Baker Street Bizarre." *Sherlock Holmes Journal* 15, No. 2 (Summer 1981): 49–51.

————. "I came to Baker-street by the Underground." *Sherlock Holmes Railway Journal* 2 (1994): 21–34.

Jones, Kelvin I. "Scandal in 'A Scandal in Bohemia': Who Was That Lady I Saw That Prince With?" *Canadian Holmes* 5, No. 4 (Summer 1982): 12–18.

Kasson, Philip. "The True Blue: A Case of Identification." *Baker Street Journal* 11, No. 4 (Dec. 1961): 200–202.

Katz, Robert S. "Mary Morstan Moriarty." *Baker Street Journal* 27, No. 1 (March 1977): 22–23.

————. "A Study in Landladies." *Baker Street Journal* 38, No. 2 (June 1988): 92–93.

Kean, Michael H. "Holmes Knew." *Grimpen Mire Gazette* 4, No. 2 (Christmas 1984): 10.

Keefauver, Brad. "A Consideration of the Camberwell Poisoning Case." *Wheelwrightings* 9, No. 2 (Sept. 1986): 13–16.

————. "Domesticity in Disguise." *Plugs & Dottles* 147 (Dec. 1990): 4–5, 7.

Kennedy, Bruce. "Blind Man's Bluff." *Baker Street Journal* 23, No. 1 (March 1973): 46–47.

————. "Mrs. Turner of Baker Street." *Baker Street Pages* 21 (March 1967): 2.

————. "The Victorian Flashlight: Sherlock Holmes and Dark Lanterns." *Baker Street Journal* 30, No. 3 (Sept. 1980): 141–143.

King, Daniel P. "On the Armoury in Baker Street." *Baker Street Journal* 24, No. 1 (March 1974): 15–19.

Klauber, Lawrence M. "The Truth About the Speckled Band." *Baker Street Journal* [O. S.] 3, No. 2 (Apr. 1948): 149–157.

Klinefelter, Walter. "The Writings of Sherlock Holmes." *Baker Street Journal* [O. S.] 1, No. 4 (Oct. 1946): 409–416.

Klinger, Leslie S. "The Crimes of Sherlock Holmes." *Sherlock Holmes Review* 5, No 1 (1997): 27–30.

———. "The Dating of *The Five Orange Pips*." *Baker Street Journal* 45, No. 2 (June 1995): 70–79.

———. "Layout of a 'Most Desirable Residence.' " *Shoso-In Bulletin* 6 (1996): 78–81.

———. "The Writings of Sherlock Holmes." *Baker Street West 1* 3, No. 1 (Jan. 1997): 23–26.

Kramer, Fred. "A Revealing Buffet on Baker Street." *Baker Street Journal* 41, No. 3 (Sept. 1991): 158–161.

Krone, Karen A. "On the Distinction Between the Characteristics of Various Typewriters." *The Dispatch Box* (Long Beach) 7 (Oct. 31, 1984): 10–11.

Lai, Rick. "Dr. Roylott's Correspondent." *Wheelwrightings* 7, No. 2 (Sept. 1984): 19–25.

Lanza, Kenneth. "Scandal in Bensonhurst." *Baker Street Miscellanea* 65 (Apr. 1991): 21–24.

Lanzalotti, John A. "Saxe-Coburg Square." *Baker Street Journal* 41, No. 4 (Dec. 1991): 207–211.

Lawson, Douglas. "The Speckled Band—What Is It?" *Baker Street Journal* 4, No. 1 (Jan. 1954): 12–20.

Leavitt, Robert Keith. "Annie Oakley in Baker Street." In PROFILE BY GASLIGHT, edited by Edgar W. Smith, 230–242. New York: Simon & Schuster, 1944.

———. "Nummi in Arca, or The Fiscal Holmes." In 221B: STUDIES IN SHERLOCK HOLMES, edited by Vincent Starrett, 16–36. New York: Macmillan Co., 1940.

———. "The Preposterously Paired Performances of the Preacher's Portrait." *Baker Street Journal* [O. S.] 3, No. 4 (1948): 404–417.

Lellenberg, Jon L. "The Sherlockian Baedeker: IX. The Alpha Inn." *Baker Street Miscellanea* 16 (Dec. 1978): 19–22.

Linsenmeyer, John. "The Spurious Squires." *Baker Street Journal* 23, No. 1 (March 1973): 11–17.

Lithner, Klas. "On Holmes's Mission for the King of Scandinavia." *Baker Street Miscellanea* 43 (Autumn 1985): 25–27.

Lockwood, John. "A Study in White." *Sherlock Holmes Journal* 11, No. 3 (Winter 1973): 91–93.

Longfellow, Esther. "The Distaff Side of Baker Street." *Baker Street Journal* [O. S.] 1, No. 1 (Jan. 1946): 9–13.

Lovisi, Gary. THE LOSS OF THE BRITISH BARK SOPHY ANDERSON. Brooklyn: Gryphon Books, 1992.

Macdonell, A. G. "Mr. Moriarty." In BAKER STREET STUDIES, edited by H. W. Bell, 161–175. London: Constable & Co. Ltd., 1934.

Mackenzie, J. B. "Sherlock Holmes' Plots and Strategy." In THE GREEN BAG. Boston: The Boston Book Co., 1902; reprinted in *Baker Street Journal*, Christmas Annual (1956): 56–61.

Mackenzie, Stanley. "The Engineer's Thumb." In "The Engineer's Thumb Symposium." *Sherlock Holmes Journal* 5, No. 4 (Summer 1962): 107–112.

Mappen, Marc. "Jerseyana." *New York Times*, July 8, 1990, New Jersey section, p. 17.

Martin, Alastair. "Lola and Irene, Heavenly Twins." *Baker Street Journal* 22, No. 4 (Dec. 1972): 242–244.

McClure, Michael W. "The Final Red-Headed Problem." In COMMANDING VIEWS FROM THE EMPTY HOUSE, edited by William R. Cochran and Gordon R. Speck, 37–42. Indianapolis: Gasogene Books, 1996.

McCullam, William, "A Singular Occurrence at a Fashionable Wedding." *Baker Street Journal* 22, No. 4 (Dec. 1972), 226–231.

McDade, Thomas M. "Heads and Holmes." *Baker Street Journal* 11, No. 2 (Sept. 1961): 162–166.

McGee, Tom. "Reflections on *The Beryl Coronet*." *Baker Street Journal* 39, No. 4 (Dec. 1989): 214–218.

McLauchlin, Russell. "What Price Baker Street?" *Baker Street Journal* 2, No. 2 (Apr. 1952): 65–70.

McNeil, Ian. "An Engineer's Thoughts on 'The Engineer's Thumb.' " In "The Engineer's Thumb Symposium." *Sherlock Holmes Journal* 5, No. 4 (Summer 1962): 107–112.

McWilliams, Debra. "The Pocket Petrarch." *Baker Street Journal* 39, No. 1 (March 1989): 7–12.

Merriman, Charles O. "A Tourist Guide to the London of Sherlock Holmes," Walk No. 2. *Sherlock Holmes Journal* 10, No. 2 (Summer 1971): 54–56.

Merritt, Russell L. "Finances in Baker Street." *Baker Street Journal* 8, No. 4 (Oct. 1958): 238–240.

Meyer, Charles A. "British Firearms at Maiwand." *News from the Diggings* 10, No. 1 (March 1989): 1–4.

Meyer, Charles. "*Scandal in Bohemia*—Revisited." *Baker Street Miscellanea* 62 (Summer 1990): 31–35.

Meyers, Don. "Sherlock's London." *Wigmore Street Post Office* 7 (Summer 1996): 3–4.

Michell, Humfrey. "The Sartorial Sherlock Holmes." In A BAKER STREET FOUR-WHEELER, edited by Edgar W. Smith, 31–36. Maplewood, NJ, and New York: Pamphlet House, 1944. Footnote 6 is an "Editor's Note," which states: "Mr.

Christopher Morley, reader extraordinary for *The Pamphlet House*, saw in this reference an opportunity he had awaited for many years to deliver himself on the subject of dressing gowns."

Michell, J. H. and Humfrey. "Sherlock Holmes the Chemist." *Baker Street Journal* [O. S.] 1, No. 3 (1946): 245–252.

Milburn, Martin. "The Official Forces in 'The Boscombe Valley Mystery.' " In ANNUAL REPORT 1993: THE BOSCOMBE VALLEY CONTRACT. Hampshire, England: Franco-Midland Hardware Company, 1993.

Mills, D.D. Elden H. "Another Controversy?" *Sherlock Holmes Journal* 12, No. 1 (Spring 1975): 36.

Montgomery, James. "Art in the Blood." In ART IN THE BLOOD, AND WHAT IS THIS THING CALLED MUSIC? (OR BODY AND SOUL), n.p. Philadelphia: Privately printed, 1950.

Moore, David. "The Errant Holmes." *Hurlstone Papers* 1, No. 5 (July 1977): 7–12.

Morehead, Alfred H., Richard L. Frey, and Geoffrey Mott-Smith. THE NEW COMPLETE HOYLE. Garden City, N.Y.: Garden City Books, 1964.

Morley, Christopher. "The Blue Carbuncle, or the Season of Forgiveness." In ADVENTURE OF THE BLUE CARBUNCLE, edited by Edgar W. Smith, 9–16. New York: Baker Street Irregulars, Inc., 1948.

———. "Clinical Notes by a Resident Patient." In PROFILE BY GASLIGHT, edited by Edgar W. Smith, 48–59. New York: Simon & Schuster, 1944.

———. "Clinical Notes by a Resident Patient." *Baker Street Journal* [O. S.] 1, No. 1 (1946): 33–38.

———. "In the Island of Uffa." *Baker Street Journal* 1, No. 2 (Apr. 1951): 56–58.

Morley, Christopher, writing as "Jane Nightwork." "Dr. Watson's Secret." In 221B: STUDIES IN SHERLOCK HOLMES, edited by Vincent Starrett, 46–53. New York: Macmillan Co., 1940.

Morley, Felix. "How The Child Got into the Chimney." *Baker Street Journal*, Christmas Annual (1958): 7–9.

———. "The Significance of the Second Stain." In PROFILE BY GASLIGHT, edited by Edgar W. Smith, 243–259. New York: Simon & Schuster, 1944.

Morley, Frank V. "I Am Puzzled About Saxe-Coburg Square." *Baker Street Journal* 5, No. 3 (July 1955): 139–141.

Morrow, L. A. "The Game Is . . ." *Baker Street Journal* 7, No. 1 (Jan. 1957): 32–38.

Mortimore, Roger. "Hiss!" *Baker Street News* 2, No. 1 (1985): 2–3.

Nathan, Hartley R., and Clifford S. Goldfarb. "Sherlock Holmes: The Jewish Connection." *Canadian Holmes* 9, No. 3 (Spring 1986): 5–13.

Needleman, Lionel. "Unravelling *The Speckled Band*." *Baker Street Journal* 34, No. 3 (Sept. 1984): 139–149.

Nevers, Kevin. "Considering the Speckled Band." *Notes from a Notorious Card Club* 1, No. 1 (1976): 2–3.

"A Night with the Thames Police." *Strand Magazine*, Feb. 1891.

Nordon, Pierre. CONAN DOYLE. Translated from the French by Frances Partridge. London: John Murray, 1966.

Offord, Lenore Glen. "The Brief Adventure of Mr. Turner." *Baker Street Journal* [O.S.] 1, No. 3 (July 1946): 253–259.

————. "About Miss Mary Sutherland." *Serpentine Muse* 6, No. 3 (Winter 1983): 18–21.

Oglesbee, Frank W. "Marksmanship on the Moor." *Baker Street Miscellanea* 30 (Summer 1982): 22–27.

Oldberg, Richard. "A Fundamentalist View of the Canon." *Baker Street Journal* 30, No. 1 (March 1980): 32–34.

Olding, Alan C. "An Alternate Conclusion for 'The Speckled Band.' " *Prescott's Press* (N. S.) No. 3 (Sept. 1989): 13–14.

————. "Ballarat Revisited." *News from the Diggings* 9, No. 2 (June 1988): 5–6. Reprinted in INTERIM REPORT 1993: THE BOSCOMBE VALLEY CONTRACT REVIEWED, edited by Philip Weller, 14–16. Hampshire, England: Franco-Midland Hardware Company, 1993.

————. "The Madness of Colonel Warburton." *Notes from the Diggings* 3, No. 1 (March 1982): 2–5.

————. " 'The Smith-Mortimer Succession Case,' 'The Tankerville Club Scandal,' 'The Famous Card Scandal of the Nonpareil Club.' " *News from the Diggings* 13, No. 3 (Sept. 1992): 1–4.

Olney, Clarke. "The Literacy of Sherlock Holmes." *Sherlock Holmes Journal* 2, No. 4 (Winter 1955): 9–15.

Palmer, Stephen G., III. "Sherlock Holmes and the Law." In SHERLOCK HOLMES: MASTER DETECTIVE, edited by Theodore C. Blegen and E. W. McDiarmid, 36–44. La Crosse, Wisc.: Norwegian Explorers, 1952.

Pasley, Robert S. "The Truth About Doctors' Commons." *Canadian Holmes* 13, No. 4 (Summer 1990): 20–22.

Pattrick, Robert R. "Moriarty Was There." *Baker Street Journal*, Christmas Annual (1958): 45–53.

————. "The Case of the Superfluous Landlady." *Baker Street Journal* 3, No. 4 (Oct. 1953): 241–243.

Pearson, Roberta. "A Scandal in Kent." *Serpentine Muse* 6, No. 1 (Summer 1981): 4–12.

"Peculiarities of Workmen." *Tit-Bits*, Jan. 10, 1891.

Peller, Rivkah. "Of the Drinking Habits of Snakes." *Varieties of Ash* 1 (Jan. 1991): 31–34.

Pennell, Vernon. "A Résumé of the Medical Life of John H. Watson, M.D., Late of the Army Medical Department." *Sherlock Holmes Journal* 3, No. 2 (Winter 1956): 6–11.

Peterson, Svend. "When the Game Was Not Afoot." *Baker Street Journal* [O. S.] 4, No. 1 (1949): 59–71.

Pike, Langdale (Christ, Jay Finley). SHERLOCK'S ANNIVERSARIES. New York: Crowborough Private Press, 1961.

Playfair, Giles. "John and James." *Baker Street Journal* [O. S.] 1, No. 3 (July 1946): 271–276.

"Portraits of Celebrities at Different Times of Their Lives." *Strand Magazine* III (1892): 275.

Pratt, Fletcher. "The Gastronomic Holmes." *Baker Street Journal* 2, No. 2 (Apr. 1952): 94–99.

———. "Very Little Murder." *Baker Street Journal* 5, No. 2 (Apr. 1955): 69–76.

Prestige, Colin. "Problem of Pope's Court." *Sherlock Holmes Journal* 1, No. 3 (June 1953): 27–28.

———. "South London Adventures." *Sherlock Holmes Journal* 3, No. 3 (Autumn 1957): 5–8.

Price, Edmund T. "The Singular Adventure of the Grice Patersons in the Island of Uffa and the Loss of the British Barque 'Sophy Anderson.' " *Baker Street Journal*, Christmas Annual (1959): 302–310.

Rabe, W. T., "An Engineer's Tom Thumb," *Baker Street Journal* 19, No. 4 (Dec. 1969), 220–221.

Randall, David A., "On the First Book Publication of 'The Red-headed League' and 'The Boscombe Valley Mystery,' " *Baker Street Journal* [O. S.] 2, No. 4 (Oct. 1947), 491–496.

Randall, Warren, "Leapin' Lizards: An Irregular and Unnatural History of the Speckled Band." *Prescott's Press* (N. S.) 3 (Sept. 1989): 25–29.

" 'The Red-Headed League' Reviewed." *Sherlock Holmes Journal* 2, No. 1 (July 1954): 29–34.

Redmond, Christopher. "Art in the Blood: Two Canonical Relatives. II. 'The History of My Unhappy Brother.' " *Baker Street Journal* 15, No. 2 (June 1965): 87–89.

———. "From the Commonplace Book." *Canadian Holmes* 5, No. 3 (1982): 27.

———. "In Praise of *The Boscombe Valley Mystery*." *Baker Street Journal* 31, No. 3 (Sept. 1981): 170–174.

———. "Irene Adler Identified." *Canadian Holmes* 7, No. 2 (Dec. 1983): 10.

———. THE TIN DISPATCH-BOX: A COMPENDIUM OF THE UNPUBLISHED CASES OF MR. SHERLOCK HOLMES. Lawrence, Kan.: Privately printed, 1965.

Redmond, Donald A. "Azure Three Caltrops or St. Simon." *Baker Street Miscellanea* 30 (Summer 1982): 17–21.

———. "Choosy Beggars: The Amateur Mendicant Society." *Baker Street Miscellanea* 33 (Spring 1983): 13–16.

———. "Ship Ahoy, Captain Basil." *Baker Street Journal* 36, No. 4 (Dec. 1986): 223–230.

————. "Some Chemical Problems in the Canon." *Baker Street Journal* 14, No. 3 (Sept. 1964): 145–152.

Rhode, Franklin, "Palmer and Pritchard Were Among the Heads of Their Profession: Pt. 1, William Palmer, the Sporting Surgeon of Rugeley." *Baker Street Journal* 17, No 2 (June 1967): 70–74.

————. "Palmer and Pritchard Were Among the Heads of Their Profession: Pt. 2., Edward Pritchard, the Satyr of Sauchiehall Street." *Baker Street Journal* 18, No. 1 (March 1968): 39–43.

Rice, Rev. Otis R. "Clergymen in the Canon." *Baker Street Journal* 4, No. 3 (July 1954): 133–143.

Rice, Susan. "The Amature [*sic*] Mendicants." *Serpentine Muse* 8, No. 4 (Spring 1990): 6–10.

Rich, Mary Ellen. "The Uffan Way." *Serpentine Muse* 12, No. 1 (Summer 1993): 18–24.

Ridgeway, Jerry. "Upon the Size of Cabinets." *Sherlockian Musings* 11, No. 2 (1986): 9.

Roberts, A. C., and Gene A. Leeb, "First You See It, Then You Don't: Another Scandal in Bohemia." *Baker Street Journal* 27, No. 1 (March 1977): 44–45.

Rodell, Marie F. "Living on Baker Street." *Baker Street Journal* [O. S.] 2, No. 1 (1947): 35–37.

Rosenblatt, Julia Carlson, and Frederic H. Sonnenschmidt. DINING WITH SHERLOCK HOLMES. Indianapolis and New York: The Bobbs-Merrill Company, 1976.

Rosenblum, Morris. "Anticipating Sherlock Holmes, or A Grecian Irene Adler and the Fire Trick." *Baker Street Journal* 2, No. 3 (July 1952): 135.

————. "Foreign Language Quotations in the Canon." *Baker Street Journal* [O. S.] 3, No. 4 (Oct. 1948): 425–434.

————. "The Horatian Spirit in Holmes." In ILLUSTRIOUS CLIENT'S THIRD CASEBOOK, edited by J. N. Williamson and H. B. Williams, 119–126. Indianapolis: The Illustrious Clients, 1953. Revised edition, New York: Magico Magazine, 1984, 97–102.

————. Letter quoted in "From the Editor's Commonplace Book." *Baker Street Journal* [O. S.] 2, No. 4 (1947): 438–439.

————. "Some Latin Byways in the Canon." *Baker Street Journal* 1, No. 1 (1948): 15–20.

Russell, Clarke. "Three in Charge." Reprinted in *Baker Street Journal* [O. S.] 3, No. 3 (1948): 341–357.

Ryan, Harold. "Sherlock and Francesco." *Sherlock Holmes Journal* 12, No. 2 (Winter 1975): 47–48.

Sayers, Dorothy L. "Dr. Watson's Christian Name." In PROFILE BY GASLIGHT, edited by Edgar W. Smith, 180–186. New York; Simon & Schuster, 1944.

Sayers, Dorothy L. UNPOPULAR OPINIONS. London: Victor Gollancz Ltd., 1946.

Sayle, Jane. "Francesco Petrarch (1304–1374)." *Baker Street Pillar Box* 12 (Oct. 1992): 25–27.

Scarlett, E. P. "The Medica Murderer." *Buffalo Chips* 5, No. 10 (Jan. 1989): n.p.

Scheideman, Warren. "The Unexpected Case of Colonel Warburton." *Sherlock Holmes Journal* 13, No. 2 (Summer 1977): 38–40.

Schenck, Remsen Ten Eyck. "Baker Street Fables." *Baker Street Journal* 2, No. 2 (Apr. 1952): 85–92.

———. "The Effect of Trades Upon the Body." *Baker Street Journal* 3, No. 1 (Jan. 1953): 31–36.

Scholefield, C. E. "Red-Headed Clients' Conundrums." *Sherlock Holmes Journal* 10, No. 2 (Winter 1971): 74–76.

Scholefield, Charles. "Knowledge of Literature—Nil?: Hafiz." *Sherlock Holmes Journal* 11, No. 3 (Winter 1973): 80–81.

Scholten, Paul, M.D. "The Connoisseurship of Sherlock Holmes with Observations on the Place of Brandy in Victorian Medical Therapeutics." *Baker Street Miscellanea* 54 (Summer 1988): 1–7.

Schutz, Robert. "Half-Sister; No Mystery." *Baker Street Gasogene* 1, No. 2 (1961): 14–15.

Schwartz, Joel. "Holmes's Three Continents." *Prescott's Press* (N. S.) 6 (June 1990): 27–28.

Schweickert, William P. "A Child in the Chimney." *Prescott's Press* 3, No. 2 (1980): 6–11; reprinted in *Baker Street Journal* 35, No. 2 (June 1985): 102–104.

———. "A Question of Barometric Pressure." *Baker Street Journal* 30, No. 4 (Dec. 1980): 243–244.

———. "Thumb Thing Strange," *Prescott's Press* 2, No. 1 (1979): 12–15.

Sewell, Gordon. "Holmes and Watson in the South Country." *Sherlock Holmes Journal* 3, No. 3 (Autumn 1957): 10–12.

Shackleford, Lee. "The Hunter and the Hunted." *Camden House Journal* 8, No. 11 (Nov. 1986): 2–3.

Shalet, Stephen A. "Cannons in the Canon." In MORE LEAVES FROM THE COPPER BEECHES, 93–98. Lititz, PA: Sutter House, 1976.

Shaw, John Bennett. "An Adventure Within 'The Adventure of the Noble Bachelor.' " *Sherlock Holmes Journal* 9, No. 1 (Winter 1968): 21–23.

Shearn, A. L. "The Street and the Detective." *Baker Street Journal*, Christmas Annual (1957): 50–54.

Sherbrooke-Walker, R. D. "Holmes, Watson and Tobacco." *Sherlock Holmes Journal* 1, No. 2 (Sept. 1952): 7–12.

"Sherlock Holmes Examination Paper," *Tit-Bits* (Dec. 16, 1893).

Shreffler, Phillip A. "In the Island of Staffa." *Morning Post* 3, No. 1 (Feb. 1982): 6–7.

———. "Was Watson Color-Blind?" *Devon County Chronicle* 8, Nos. 4–5 (Sept. 1972): 3–6.

Simmons, George. "Sherlock Holmes—The Inner Man," *Baker Street Journal* [O. S.] 2, No. 2 (Apr. 1947): 129–135.

———. "Was Watson Color-Blind?" *Devon County Chronicle* 8, Nos. 4–5 (Sept. 1972): 3–6.

Simon, André L., ed. WINES OF THE WORLD. New York: McGraw-Hill Book Company, 1967.

Simpson, A. Carson. "It Must Have Been Two Other Fellows." In LEAVES FROM THE COPPER BEECHES, 41–53. Narbeth, PA: Livingston Pub. Co., 1959.

———. NUMISMATICS IN THE CANON, PT. I: FULL THIRTY THOUSAND MARKS OF ENGLISH COIN. Philadelphia, Pa.: International Printing Company, 1957.

———. NUMISMATICS IN THE CANON, PT. II: A VERY TREASURY OF COINS OF DIVERS REALM. Philadelphia, Pa.: International Printing Company, 1958.

———. NUMISMATICS IN THE CANON, PART III: SMALL TITLES AND ORDERS. Philadelphia, Pa.: Privately printed, 1959.

———. "Scandal in Genealogy." In MORE LEAVES FROM THE COPPER BEECHES, 97–107. Lititz, PA: Sutter House, 1976.

———. "Whose Was It? Conjectures on a Coronet." *Baker Street Journal*, Christmas Annual (1957): 9–17.

Simpson, Helen. "Medical Career and Capacities of Dr. J. H. Watson." BAKER STREET STUDIES, edited by H. W. Bell, 35–62. London: Constable & Co., 1934.

Smith, Edgar W. "From the Editor's Commonplace Book." *Baker Street Journal* 1, No. 1 (Jan. 1951): 40.

———. "A Scandal in Identity." PROFILE BY GASLIGHT, edited by Edgar W. Smith, 262–273. New York: Simon & Schuster, 1944.

Sohl, John P. "Sherlock Holmes's Knowledge of the Goose." *Honker* 1, No. 2 (Dec. 1977): 3–8.

Speck, Gordon R. "Lady Frances and the Camberwell Connection." *Wheelwrightings* 10, No . 2 (Sept. 1987): 15–17.

———. "Sherlock Holmes: An Augustan in a Romantic World." *Baker Street Miscellanea* 30 (Summer 1982): 29–31.

Squire, William. "Regarding the Identity of Bisulphate of Baryta." *Baker Street Journal* 24, No. 1 (March 1974): 22, 30.

Starrett, Vincent. "The Singular Adventures of Martha Hudson." In BAKER STREET STUDIES, edited by H. W. Bell, 87–130. London: Constable & Co., 1934.

Stix, Thomas L. "Concerning 'The Red-Headed League.'" *Baker Street Journal* 4, No. 2 (Apr. 1954): 93–99.

———. "Sherlock Holmes Impeached (I)." *Baker Street Journal* 15, No. 2 (June 1965): 75–76.

———. "Un-Christmaslike Thoughts on 'The Blue Carbuncle.'" *Baker Street Journal* 11, No. 4 (Dec. 1961): 218–220.

Sundholm, Göran. "Vem van Kungen av Böhmen?" *Baker Street Cab Lantern* No. 7 (1969): 17–20.

Suszynski, James, " 'Don't Call Us, We'll Call You.' " *Baker Street Miscellanea* 54 (Summer 1988): 13–15.

Swift, Wayne B. "On the Sinister Affair of the Darkbloom Paper." *Baker Street Miscellanea* 8 (Dec. 1976): 1–4.

Symons, Julian. PORTRAIT OF AN ARTIST: CONAN DOYLE. London: Whizzard Press,1979.

The Red-Headed League. Granada Television Production. Developed for television by John Hawkesworth. ITV Network, Sunday, September 22, 1985. The *Adventures of Sherlock Holmes*. Second Series, No. 5.

Thomas, Charles J. "The Mysterious Coventry Factory." *Baker Street Journal* 28, No. 2 (June 1978): 92–95.

Thomson, June. "Case of the Amateur Mendicants." In SECRET FILES OF SHERLOCK HOLMES, 39–69. London: Constable & Company, Limited, 1990.

———. "Case of the Camberwell Poisoning." In SECRET CHRONICLES OF SHERLOCK HOLMES, 141–167. London: Constable & Company Limited, 1992.

Torese, Dante M. "Firearms in the Canon: The Guns of Sherlock Holmes and John H. Watson." *Baker Street Journal* 42, No. 3 (Sept. 1992): 154–157.

Townsend, C. E. C. "The Bar of Gold." *Sherlock Holmes Journal* 2, No. 1 (July 1954): 25–28.

Tracy, Jack. "In Search of Uffa." *Holmesian Observer* 2, No. 3 (June 1972): 16–17.

Upton, Jean. "The Conundrum of the Coif." *The Ritual* 12 (Autumn 1993): 10–12.

Utechin, Nicholas. "Some Remarkable Wines." *Baker Street Journal* 27, No. 3 (Sept. 1977): 142–145.

Vatza, Edward J. "Adventure of the Yankee Diva." *Baker Street Journal* 42, No. 3 (Sept. 1992): 135–138.

———. "In Search of Irene Adler." *Confederate Chronicles* 5 (Aug. 1983): 7, 15.

———. "What Did Watson Mean by the *Late* Irene Adler?" *Canonfire* 1, No. 3 (Oct. 1983): 1–2.

"De Vergissing van Sherlock Holmes" [Sherlock Holmes's Error]. PANORAMA (Amsterdam) 51 (Dec. 12–18, 1970): 52–53.

Waggoner, Larry. "The Final Solution." *Devon County Chronicle* 14, Nos. 4–5 (Oct. 1978): 3–6.

Walsh, B. D. J. "Sherlock Holmes and the Railways." *Sherlock Holmes Journal* 9, No. 2 (Summer 1969), 40–48. Reprinted in *Sherlock Holmes Railway Journal* 1 (1993): 5–22.

Walsh, William J. "Upon the Identity of Bisulphate of Baryta." *Baker Street Journal* 20, No. 2 (June 1970): 110–111.

Warrack, Guy. SHERLOCK HOLMES AND MUSIC. London: Faber and Faber Limited, 1947.

Waterhouse, William C. "The Case of the Persian Proverb." *Baker Street Journal* 40, No. 3 (Sept. 1990): 135–136.

Waters, Frank. "Upon the Probable Number of Cases of Mr. Sherlock Holmes." *Baker Street Journal* 3, No. 1 (Jan. 1953): 25–28.

Welch, George W. "The Terai Planter." *Baker Street Journal* 6, No. 1 (Jan. 1956): 36–39.

Weller, Philip. "A Relative Question." In INTERIM REPORT 1991: THE FINAL PROBLEM CONTRACT REVIEWED, 33–34. Hornsea, England: Franco-Midland Hardware Company, 1991.

———. "Boscombe Byways." In INTERIM REPORT 1993: THE BOSCOMBE VALLEY CONTRACT REVIEWED, 7–11. Hampshire, England: Franco-Midland Company, 1993.

———. "Ramble Round Ross: Some Geographical Considerations." In ANNUAL REPORT 1993: THE BOSCOMBE VALLEY CONTRACT, 17–20. Hampshire, England: Franco-Midland Company, 1993.

Wellman, Manly Wade. "The Great Man's Great Son." *Baker Street Journal* [O. S.] 1, No. 3 (1946): 326–336.

———. "A New Scandal in Bohemia." *Baker Street Journal* [O. S.] 2, No. 1 (1947): 90.

———. "Scoundrels in Bohemia." *Baker Street Journal* 4, No. 4 (Oct. 1954): 232–238.

———. "Two Southern Exposures of Sherlock Holmes." *Baker Street Journal* [O. S.] 2, No. 4 (1947): 422–426.

White, Kathryn. "Gothic Elements of 'The Speckled Band.' " In THE CASE FILES OF SHERLOCK HOLMES: THE SPECKLED BAND, edited by Christopher and Barbara Roden, 113–118. Ashcroft, British Columbia: Calabash Press, 1997.

White, William Braid. "Dr. Watson and the Peerage." *Baker Street Journal* [O. S.] 2, No. 1 (1947): 18–23.

Whitlam, Carol. "The Noble Bachelor." *Musgrave Papers* 9 (1996): 75–80.

Wigglesworth, Belden. "The Amoral Mr. Holmes." In CANON FODDER, edited by Charles O. Grey, 101–107. Little Rock, Ark.: The Arkansas Valley Investors, Ltd., 1976.

Williams, Howard B. "Half-Sister; Half Mystery." *Baker Street Journal* 8, No. 2 (Apr. 1958): 100–103.

———. "Then Falls Thy Shadow." In ILLUSTRIOUS CLIENT'S CASE-BOOK, edited by J. N. Williamson and H. B. Williams, 50–53. Indianapolis, Ind.: The Illustrious Clients, 1948.

Williamson, J. N. "The Sad Case of Young Stamford." *Baker Street Journal* [O. S.] 3, No. 4 (Oct. 1948): 449–451.

———. "A Scandal in 'A Scandal in Bohemia.' " *Baker Street Journal* 1, No. 4 (Oct. 1951): 141–143.

Wilson, Alan. "Where Was the 'Bar of Gold?' " *Sherlock Holmes Journal* 6, No. 3 (Winter 1963): 84–85.

Winkworth, Stephen. ROOM TWO MORE GUNS: THE INTRIGUING HISTORY OF THE PERSONAL COLUMN OF THE TIMES. London: George Allen & Unwin, 1986.

Wolf, John B. "Another Incubus in the Saddle." In EXPLORING SHERLOCK HOLMES, edited by E. W. McDiarmid & Theodore C. Blegen, 66–81. La Crosse, Wisc.: Sumac Press, 1957.

Wolff, Julian. "Adventuress of Sherlock Holmes: Some Observations Upon the Identification of Irene." *Baker Street Journal* 7, No. 1 (Jan. 1957): 29–31.

———. "King of Bohemia." In PRACTICAL HANDBOOK OF SHERLOCKIAN HERALDRY, compiled by Julian Wolff, 22–33. New York: Privately printed, 1955.

Yates, Donald. "An Illumination of the 'John/James' Question." *Baker Street Miscellanea* 38 (Summer 1984): 23–24, 28.

Zeisler, Ernest Bloomfield. "A Pigment of the Imagination." *Sherlock Holmes Journal* 5, No. 2 (Spring 1961): 50–52.

THE MEMOIRS OF SHERLOCK HOLMES

Adams, Stephen, "Holmes: A Student of London?" *Sherlock Holmes Journal* 2, No. 4 (Winter 1955): 17–18.

Aikin, Bruce. "A Study in 'Dull, Dirty Crimson.' " *Covert Notes* [N. S.] 2, No. 1 (March 1979): 14–17.

Aldrich, Frederick A. "Holmes's Litmus Test." *Canadian Holmes* 9, No. 4 (Summer 1986): 14–15.

Anderson, Poul and Karen. "The Curious Behaviour of the Ritual in the Daytime." *Baker Street Journal*, Christmas Annual (1960): 304–311.

Andrew, Clifton R., "A Rejoinder to Professor Hill." *Baker Street Journal* 5, No. 3 (July 1955): 154–156.

———. "Who Is Who, and When in the Gloria Scott." In ILLUSTRIOUS CLIENT'S CASE-BOOK, edited by J. N. Williamson and H. B. Williams, 30–32. Indianapolis: The Illustrious Clients, 1948.

Asher, Richard. "Holmes and the Fair Sex." *Sherlock Holmes Journal* 2, No. 3 (Summer 1955): 15–22.

———. "Malingering." *Sherlock Holmes Journal* 4, No. 2 (Spring 1959): 54–58.

Ball, John, Jr. "The Twenty-Three Deductions." *Baker Street Journal* 8, No. 4 (Oct. 1958): 234–237.

Barrett, William G. "The Diogenes Club." *Sherlock Holmes Journal* 9, No. 2 (Summer 1969): 53–55.

Barzun, Jacques. "Sherlock Holmes' Will—A Forgery." *Baker Street Journal* 6, No. 2 (Apr. 1956): 75–79.

Beerman, Herman. "Malingering What Hath Man Wrought!" In More Leaves from the Copper Beeches, 181–192. Lititz, PA: Sutter House, 1976.

Bengis, Nathan L. "Sherlock Holmes' Will." *London Mystery Magazine*, June 1955. Reprinted in *Baker Street Journal* 6, No. 2 (Apr. 1956): 80–81.

———. "What Was the Month?" *Baker Street Journal* 7, No. 4 (Oct. 1957): 204–214.

———. "Where There's a Will, There's a Pay." *Baker Street Journal* 6, No. 4 (Oct. 1956): 226–232.

———. "Whose Was It?" *Baker Street Journal* 3, No. 2 (Apr. 1953): 69–76.

Bengtsson, Hans-Uno. " 'And the Calculation Is a Simple One.' " *Baker Street Journal* 39, No. 4 (Dec. 1989): 232–236.

Bigelow, S. Tupper. "Identifying the Diogenes Club: An Armchair Exercise." *Baker Street Journal* 18, No. 2 (June 1968): 67–73.

———. "Silver Blaze: The Master Vindicated." *Baker Street Journal* 15, No. 2 (June 1965): 79–82.

Blakeney, T. S. "The Location of 'The Three Students.' " *Sherlock Holmes Journal* 4, No. 1 (Winter 1958): 14.

Boswell, Rolfe. "On 'The Adventure of the Tired Captain.' " *Baker Street Journal* [O.S.] 2, No. 2 (Apr. 1947): 160–162.

Boucher, Anthony. "Was the Later Holmes an Imposter?" In Profile by Gaslight, edited by Edgar W. Smith, 60–70. New York: Simon & Schuster, 1944.

Bower, Anthony J. "The Journey by Holmes and Watson from Winchester to London in a Pullman Car?" *Sherlock Holmes Railway Journal* 1 (1993): 23–25.

Brend, Gavin. "The Black Boy's Visit to Hurlstone." *Baker Street Journal* 3, No. 4 (Oct. 1953): 217–224.

———. "From the Horse's Mouth." *Sherlock Holmes Journal* 1, No. 4 (Dec. 1959): 39–40.

———. "Was Sherlock Holmes at Westminster?" *Sherlock Holmes Journal* 2, No. 1 (July 1954): 39–41.

Bristowe, W. S. "Oxford or Cambridge?" *Sherlock Holmes Journal* 4, No. 2 (Spring 1959): 75–76.

———. "The Truth About Moriarty." In Seventeen Steps to 221B, edited by James E. Holroyd, 144–160. London: Allen and Unwin, 1967.

———. "What a Terrible Criminal He Would Have Made." *Sherlock Holmes Journal* 5, No. 1 (Winter 1960): 6–14.

Brody, Howard. "The Commonplace Murder of Mary Sutherland." *Baker Street Miscellanea* 23, (Fall 1980):1–3.

———. "On the Use of Nitrite of Amyl in Catalepsy." *Baker Street Journal* 26, No. 4 (Dec. 1976): 206–208.

Bryan-Brown, Frederick. "Sherlockian Schools and Schoolmasters." *Sherlock Holmes Journal* 3, No. 1 (Summer 1956): 2–7.

Buchholtz, James. "A Tremor at the Edge of the Web." *Baker Street Journal* 8, No. 1 (Jan. 1958): 5–9.

Burnham, Ernest C., Jr. "The Tattooed Fish in *The Red-Headed League.*" *Baker Street Journal* 12, No. 4 (Dec. 1962): 219–222.

Burr, Howard E. "Stuart Brows Encircled, or Tudor Loins Embraced?" *Baker Street Journal* 35, No. 3 (Sept. 1985): 161–169.

Burr, Robert C. "Prosit! . . . Salut! . . . Here's Mud in Your Eye: Sherlock Holmes and Alcohol." In SHERLOCK HOLMES: VINTAGE AND SPIRITED, edited and introduced by Michael H. Kean, 20–27. New York: Magico Magazine, 1994.

Buxton, Edward. "He Solved the Case and Won the Race." In THE THIRD CAB, 39–41. Boston: The Speckled Band, 1960.

Byerly, Ann and Christopher. "The Musgrave Ritual—Solved." *Baker Street Journal* 27, No. 2 (June 1977): 96–103.

Callaway, J. S. "Mycroft and Her Majesty's Invisible Government." *Baker Street Journal* 24, No. 2 (June 1974): 72–76.

Caplan, Richard M. "Sherlock Holmes and 'Brain Fever.' " *Perspectives in Biology and Medicine* 30, No. 3 (Spring 1987): 433–439.

Chorley, Jennifer. " 'Briarbrae' Revisited." *Sherlock Holmes Journal* 6, No. 2 (Spring 1963): 56–57.

Christ, Jay Finley. "The Case of the Chinaman's Chance." *Chicago Tribune*, Nov. 18, 1946. Reprinted in FINCH'S FINAL FLING, n.p. New York and Copenhagen: Candlelight Press, 1963.

———. IRREGULAR CHRONOLOGY OF BAKER STREET—FRAGMENTS. Ann Arbor, Mich.: The Fanlight House, 1947.

———. "Musgrave Mathematics." In ILLUSTRIOUS CLIENT'S CASE-BOOK, edited by J. N. Williamson and H. B. Williams, 14–19. Indianapolis: The Illustrious Clients, 1948.

———. "Sherlock Pulls a Fast One." In FLASHES BY FANLIGHT, 11. Ann Arbor, Mich.: The Fanlight Press, 1946.

———. "Silver Blaze: An Identification As of 1893 A.D." *Baker Street Journal* [O.S.] 4, No. 1 (1948): 12–15.

Christie, Mrs. Winifred M. "On the Remarkable Explorations of Sigerson." *Sherlock Holmes Journal* 1, No. 2 (Sept. 1952): 39–44.

Christie, Mrs. Winifred. "Sherlock Holmes and Graphology." *Sherlock Holmes Journal* 2, No. 4 (Winter 1955): 28–31.

Chujoy, Anatole. "The Only Second Stain." *Baker Street Journal* 4, No. 3 (July 1954): 165–168.

Clapp, Roger T. "The Curious Problem of the Railway Timetables." In THE SECOND CAB, edited by James Keddie, Jr., 34–38. Boston: Privately printed, 1947.

Clark, Benjamin S. "The Final Problem." *Baker Street Journal* 16, No. 2 (June 1966): 68–69.

Clark, Edward F., Jr. "Brag and Bounce." *Baker Street Journal* 33, No. 2 (June 1983): 75–78.

———. "Study of an Untold Tale." *Baker Street Journal* 13, No. 4 (Dec. 1963): 217–228.

Clarke, Richard W. "On the Nomenclature of Watson's Ships." *Baker Street Journal* [O. S.] 1, No. 2 (1946): 119–121.

Cochran, Leonard. "Sherlock Holmes and Logic: The Education of a Genius." *Baker Street Journal* 17, No. 1 (March 1967): 15–19.

Cochran, William. " 'Ah, There You Lay Your Finger Upon the One Point . . .' " *Wheelwrightings* 8, No. 3 (Jan. 1986): 14–17.

Connors, Joseph B. "Holmes and the Oxford Manner." In CULTIVATING SHERLOCK HOLMES, edited by Bryce L. Crawford, Jr., and Joseph B. Connors, 39–47. La Crosse, Wisc.: Sumac Press, for the Norwegian Explorers, 1978.

Cooke, Catherine. "A Certain Gracious Railway Station." *Sherlock Holmes Railway Journal*, 2 (1994): 37–42.

Cooper, Anthony G. "Browsings in Birmingham." *Sherlock Holmes Journal* 4, No. 4 (Spring 1960): 140.

Coules, Bert. " 'There Was Something Strange in All This': A Ramble Round Some Final Problems." *Musgrave Papers* 4 (1991): 31–37.

Cox, J. Randolph. "Mycroft Holmes: Private Detective." *Baker Street Journal* 6, No. 4 (Oct. 1956): 197–200.

Crawford, Bryce, Jr., and R. C. Moore. "The Final Problem—Where?" In EXPLORING SHERLOCK HOLMES, edited by E. W. McDiarmid and Theodore C. Blegen, 82–87. La Crosse, WI: Sumac Press, 1957.

Crosson, Frederick J. "Geopolitics and Reichenbach Falls." *Baker Street Journal* 31, No. 1 (March 1981): 6–9.

Cuccia, Alle. "An Essay Loosely Inspired by Silver Blaze." *Prescott's Press* [N. S.] 2 (June 1989): 7–9.

Cumings, Thayer. " 'Don't Write—Telegraph!' " In BEST OF THE PIPS, 87–96. New York: Five Orange Pips of Westchester County, 1955.

Curjel, Harald. "Death by Anoxia." *Baker Street Journal* 28, No. 3 (Sept. 1978): 152–156.

———. "Some Thoughts on the Case of 'Silver Blaze.' " *Sherlock Holmes Journal* 13, No. 2 (Summer 1977): 36–38.

Dandrew, Thomas A. "The Early Holmes' Love Life, or What Was Really Going on Between Sherlock and the Trevors?" *Naval Signals* 22 (March 26, 1985): 12–13.

Dardess, John, M.D., " 'It Will Just Cover That Bare Space on the Wall.' " *Baker Street Journal* 20, No. 2 (June 1970), 103–109.

———. "On the Dating of *The Valley of Fear*." *Baker Street Journal* [O. S.] 3, No. 4 (Oct. 1948): 481–482.

Davies, Bernard. "Canonical Connections." *Sherlock Holmes Journal* 5, No. 2 (Spring 1961): 37–41.

———. "Vacations and Stations." *Sherlock Holmes Journal* 17, No. 2 (Summer 1985): 43–48 (Pt. I); 17, No. 3 (Winter 1985): 74–78 (Pt. II).

Davis, Elmer. "On the Emotional Geology of Baker Street." In 221B: STUDIES IN SHERLOCK HOLMES, edited by Vincent Starrett, 37–47. New York: Macmillan Co., 1940.

———. "The Real Sherlock Holmes." THE LATER ADVENTURES OF SHERLOCK HOLMES, Vol. 1. New York: Limited Edition Club, 1952.

Dennison, Patrick. "Brussels in a Day?" In THE FINAL PROBLEM CONTRACT, edited by Philip Weller, 14–17. Hornsea, England: Franco-Midland Hardware Company, 1991.

Dern, John A. "A Moment of Prayer." *Baker Street Journal* 42, No. 4 (Dec. 1992): 231–232.

Ditzler, Kirk. "The Game Is Up: 'The Gloria Scott' Revisited." *Wheelwrightings* 4, No. 2 (Sept. 1981): 9–11.

Donegall, Lord. "Baker Street and Beyond." *The New Strand* 1, No. 9 (Aug. 1962): 1048–1050.

Dorn, William S. "Mycroft Holmes: An Enigma No More." *Sherlock Holmes Journal* 13, No. 2 (Summer 1977): 59–62.

Doyle, Arthur Conan. ADVENTURE OF THE STOCKBROKER'S CLERK. Edited and annotated by Philip Weller. Lee-on-the-Solent, England: Sherlock Publications, 1995.

———. MEMOIRS OF SHERLOCK HOLMES. Edited with an Introduction by Christopher Roden. Oxford and New York: Oxford University Press, 1993.

Drazen, Patrick E. "Next Stop, Norbury: Reflections on *The Yellow Face*." *Baker Street Journal* 29, No. 1 (March 1979): 16–20.

Dudley, W. E. "Dr. Holmes, I Presume." *Baker Street Journal* 24, No. 4 (Dec. 1974): 218–220.

———. "Dr. Watson's Triple Play." *Baker Street Journal* 23, No. 1 (March 1973): 22–27.

Elwin, Verrier. "College Life of Sherlock Holmes." In MOTLEY, 157–163. Bombay: Orient Longmans Ltd., 1954.

Evans, Webster. "Sherlock Holmes and Sport." *Sherlock Holmes Journal* 2, No. 3 (Summer 1955): 35–42.

Ewen, Greg, and Brad Keefauver. "Shooting Holes in More Than the Wall: New Thoughts on the 'V.R.' " *Wheelwrightings* 11, No. 1 (May 1988): 26–29.

Farrell, Stephen. "A Treatise upon Sherlockian Firearms." *Sherlock Holmes Journal* 23, No. 3 (Winter 1995): 88–89.

Fletcher, George. "The New York Connection: Holmes and Hargreave." *Baker Street Journal* 42, No. 4 (Dec. 1992): 214–220.

Foss, Thomas Frederick. "Colonel James Barclay." *Baker Street Journal* 20, No. 4 (Dec. 1970): 231–233.

———. "The Press and Holmes." *Baker Street Journal* 18, No. 4 (Dec. 1968): 214–219.

Fox, Lyttleton. "Mycroft Recomputed." *Baker Street Journal* 19, No. 1 (March 1969): 4–11.

Frisbie, James P. "But There Goes the Bell . . ." *Baker Street Journal* 7, No. 2 (Apr. 1957): 74–77.

Fusco, Andrew G. " 'Or Some Written Memorandum Thereof . . .' " *Baker Street Journal* 22, No. 2 (June 1972): 114–119.

Galbraith, A. S. "The Real Moriarty." *Baker Street Journal*, Christmas Annual (1957): 55–62.

Galerstein, David H. "When Did He Do It?" *Canadian Holmes* 15, No. 2 (Winter 1991): 10.

Gill, William H. "Some Notable Sherlockian Buildings." *Sherlock Holmes Journal* 4, No. 4 (Spring 1960): 124–126.

Gore-Booth, Paul H. "The Journeys of Sherlock Holmes: A Topical Monograph." *Baker Street Journal* [O. S.] 3, No. 1 (1948): 159–168.

Goslin, Vernon. "The Singular Stockbroker's Clerk." *Sherlock Holmes Journal* 8, No. 3 (Winter 1967): 90–93.

Grasse, Marvin. "Who Killed Holmes?" *Atlantic Monthly*, June, 1955, 88–90.

Grazebrook, O. F. STUDIES IN SHERLOCK HOLMES, I: OXFORD OR CAMBRIDGE. London: Privately printed, 1949.

Green, Roger Lancelyn. " 'At the University': Some Thoughts on the Academic Experience of Mr. Sherlock Holmes." *Sherlock Holmes Journal* 9, No. 4 (Summer 1970): 123–125.

Greenwood, E. P. "Some Random Thoughts on Railway Journeys by Holmes and Watson." *Sherlock Holmes Journal* 1, No. 3 (June 1953): 19–21.

Griffith, Adrian N. "Some Observations on Sherlock Holmes and Dr. Watson at Bart's." *St. Bartholomew's Hospital Journal* 55, No. 12 (Dec. 1951): 273–274. Reprinted in *Commonplace Book* 2, Nos. 7–8 (Winter-Spring 1966): 142–147.

Hall, John. "What Was the Month?" THE CASE FILES OF SHERLOCK HOLMES: THE MUSGRAVE RITUAL, edited by Christopher and Barbara Roden, 29–36. Penyffordd, Chester: Calabash Press, 1996.

Hall, Trevor. "The Documents in the Case." In SHERLOCK HOLMES: TEN LITERARY STUDIES, 109–122. New York: St. Martin's Press, 1969.

———. "A Note on Sherlock Holmes's Schooling." In SHERLOCK HOLMES: TEN LITERARY STUDIES, 36–43. New York: St. Martin's Press, 1969.

———. "Sherlock Holmes's University and College." In SHERLOCK HOLMES: TEN LITERARY STUDIES, 56–85. New York: St. Martin's Press, 1969.

———. "Thomas Stearns Eliot and Sherlock Holmes." SHERLOCK HOLMES AND HIS CREATOR, 45–54. London: Gerald Duckworth & Co. Ltd., 1978.

Hammer, David L. "A Psychological Study of Mr. Sherlock Holmes in the Year 1891." *Canadian Holmes* 11, No. 3 (Spring 1988): 5–11. Reprinted in expanded form as "The Psychosis," in THE BEFORE-BREAKFAST PIPE OF MR. SHERLOCK HOLMES, 132–149. Dubuque, Iowa: Gasogene Press, Ltd., 1995.

Hammond, Roland, M.D."The Attempted Mayhem of 'Silver Blaze.' " *Baker Street Journal* [O.S.] 1, No. 2 (1946): 157–161.

Harris, Bruce. "The Real Crook in *The Crooked Man*." *Baker Street Journal* 43, No. 2 (June 1993): 96.

Harrison, Michael. "Baker Street Harrisonia #5." *Baker Street Miscellanea* 64 (Winter 1990): 13–20.

———. I, SHERLOCK HOLMES. New York: E. P. Dutton, 1977.

Hart, Archibald. "The Effect of Trades upon Hands." *Baker Street Journal* [O. S.] 3, No. 4 (1948): 318–320.

Harville, Jack. "The Musgrave Ritual: An Alternate Solution." *Baker Street Journal* 30, No. 4 (Dec. 1980): 201–203.

Hathaway, John. "Another Case of Identity." *Vermissa Herald* 7, No. 2 (Apr. 1973): 7–8.

Haynes, George C. " 'What the Law Had Gained the Stage Had Lost.' " *Baker Street Journal*, Christmas Annual (1960): 301–303.

Heldenbrand, Page. "The Duplicity of Sherlock Holmes." In TWO BAKER STREET AKRONISMS, 7–11. Summit, N.J.: Pamphlet House, 1945. Also contains "The Strange Case of Colonel Moran," by C. R. Andrew.

———. "On an Obscure Nervous Page." *Baker Street Journal* 4, No. 3 (1954): 154–155.

Hench, Philip. "Of Violence at Meiringen." In EXPLORING SHERLOCK HOLMES, edited by E. W. McDiarmid and Theodore C. Blegen, 97–120. La Crosse, WI: Sumac Press, 1957.

Hicks, John L. "No Fire Without Some Smoke." *Baker Street Journal* 5, No. 1 (Jan. 1955): 27–33.

Hill, Pope R., Sr. "The Final Problem." *Baker Street Journal* 5, No. 3 (July 1955): 149–153.

Hinrich, D. "Munsters v. Mallows." *Sherlock Holmes Journal* 6, No. 4 (Spring 1964): 131.

———. "The Royal Mallows, 1854–1888." *Sherlock Holmes Journal* 6, No. 1 (Winter 1962): 20–22.

Hobb, Alexander Moore. "The Sport of Kings." *Baker Street Journal* 23, No. 2 (June 1973): 81–86.

Hoff, Ebbe Curtis. "The Adventure of John and Mary." *Baker Street Journal* 9, No. 3 (July 1959): 136–152.

Hogan, John C. "Sherlock Holmes—Was He a 'Playboy'?" *Baker Street Journal* 16, No. 2 (June 1966): 101–107.

"Holmes, Mycroft." Letter to the SUNDAY TIMES, April 8, 1951. Reprinted in THE SHERLOCK HOLMES SCRAPBOOK, edited by Peter Haining, 74. New York: Clarkson N. Potter, 1974.

Holstein, L. S. "The Puzzle of Reigate." *Baker Street Journal* 2, No. 4 (Oct. 1952): 221–225.

Hook, D. Marcus. "More on the Railway Journeys." *Baker Street Journal* [O. S.] 3, No. 2 (Apr. 1948): 228–229.

Hoskison, Peter. "Delicate Case of Mr. S. Holmes and His University Home." *Cambridge Evening News*, Jan. 5, 1974.

Howard, Robin, and Hugh Willison. "The Nature of Catalepsy and the Model for Percy Trevelyan." *Sherlock Holmes Journal* 20, No. 4 (Summer 1992): 128–130.

Huber, Christine. "The Demise of the 'Gloria Scott'." *Columbine's New-Fangled Banner* 3 (1984): 3–4.

Huber, Christine, and Karen L. Johnson. "Two Scenarios for 'The Naval Treaty.'" *Columbine's New-Fangled Banner* 4 (1984): 1–4.

Hughes, Robert. THE FATAL SHORE. New York: Random House, 1986.

Hyder, William. "Sherlock Holmes as Musician." In FROM BALTIMORE TO BAKER STREET, 21–44. Toronto: Metropolitan Reference Library, 1995.

Hyslop, John. "Sherlock Holmes and the Press." *Sherlock Holmes Journal* 4, No. 1 (Winter 1958): 4–8.

Jackson, Steven. "Holmes and Bertillonage." *Sherlock Holmes Journal* 23, No. 1 (Winter 1996): 17–20.

Jaffee, Irving L. "The Final Problem." ELEMENTARY MY DEAR WATSON, 13–15. Brooklyn, N.Y.: Theo. Gauss Sons, 1965.

Jaffee, Mary. "Yes, Dear Little Medea, There Was and Is a Professor Moriarty." *Baker Street Journal* 27, No. 1 (March 1977): 33–35.

James, Garry. "Shooting the Guns of Sherlock Holmes." *Handguns for Sport and Defense* 5, No. 10 (Oct. 1991): 70–75.

Johnson, C. Arnold. "An East Wind." *Baker Street Journal* 31, No. 1 (March 1981): 10–13.

Jones, Bob. SHERLOCK HOLMES, THE GOLFER. Monterey, Calif.: Angel Press, 1981.

———. SHERLOCK HOLMES SAVED GOLF. Monterey, Calif.: Angel Press, 1986.

Jones, Kelvin I. "A Villa Called Lachine." *Wheelwrightings* 7, No. 3 (Jan. 1985): 5–9.

Jordan, Anne. "'My Note to You Was Absolutely Genuine.'" In ANNUAL REPORT 1991: THE FINAL PROBLEM CONTRACT, edited by Philip Weller, 43–45. Hampshire, England: Sherlock Publications, 1991.

———. "Was Holmes a Cab Driver?" *The Ritual* 11 (Spring 1993): 6–11.

Jossi, Otto. MEIRINGEN AND ITS ENVIRONS. Zurich: Art Institut. Orell Fussli, 1907.

Kaiser, Thomas E. "Baritsu, Some Further Notes." *Baker Street Journal* 29, No. 1 (March 1979): 35–36.

Kallis, Stephen, A., Jr. "Reigate Revisited." *Baker Street Journal* 14, No. 1 (March 1964): 37–38.

Kaser, Michael C. "Sherlock Holmes on the Continent." *Baker Street Journal* 6, No. 1 (Jan. 1956): 19–24.

Kaye, Marvin. THE HISTRIONIC HOLMES. Culver City, Calif.: Luther Norris, 1971.

Keddie, James, Sr. Letter originally appearing in *Saturday Review of Literature*, June 27, 1936. Reprinted as "Gasogene, Coal Scuttle, Persian Slipper," in BEST OF THE CABS, 32–34. Boston: Stoke Moran Publishers,1980.

Keefauver, Brad. "In the Beginning: Money-Making on Montague Street." *Quarter£y $tatement* 5, No. 3 (Aug. 1984): 33–36.

———. "One We May Have Heard Before." *Camden House Journal* 9, No. 1 (Jan. 1987): 2–3.

———. "Oxford, Cambridge or . . . ? The Final Answer." *Afghanistanzas* 6, No. 5 (Nov. 1982): 8–10; and 6, No. 6 (Dec. 1982): 11–13.

Kennedy, Bruce. "Alma Mater, or Two Unexplained Years." *Baker Street Journal* 19, No. 3 (Sept. 1969): 158–160.

———. "Problems with 'The Final Problem.' " *Prescott's Press* 4, No. 1 (Jan. 1982): 29–33.

———. "A Tribute, Though Not Necessarily Glowing, to the Napoleon of Crime." *Prescott's Press* 3, No. 2 (1980): 15–17.

———. " 'Whose Was It?' " *Baker Street Journal* 26, No. 2 (June 1976): 79–80.

King, Daniel P. "On the Armoury in Baker Street." *Baker Street Journal* 24, No. 1 (March 1974): 15–19.

Klinger, Leslie S. "From Prussia With Love: Contemplating *The Naval Treaty*," *Musgrave Papers*, 11 (Summer 1998): 93–101.

———. "Layout of 'A Most Desirable Residence.' " *Shoso-In Bulletin* 6 (1996): 78–81.

———."The Writings of Sherlock Holmes." *Baker Street West 1* 3, No. 1 (Jan. 1997): 23–26.

Knox, Ronald A. "The Mystery of Mycroft." In BAKER STREET STUDIES, edited by H. W. Bell, 133–157. London: Constable & Co., 1934.

———. "Studies in the Literature of Sherlock Holmes." In ESSAYS IN SATIRE, 145–178. London: Sheed and Ward, 1928.

Lachtman, Howard. "Straightening Out the Crooked Man." *Baker Street Journal* 31, No. 1 (March 1981): 39.

Lai, Rick. "Mycroft's Avenger." *Wheelwrightings* 12, No. 2 (Sept. 1989): 16–17.

———. "Victor Trevor and the Sinister Savant." *Wheelwrightings* 8, No. 1 (May 1985): 18–21.

Lawfield, Matthew, "The Musgrave Ritual." *Sherlock Holmes Journal* 15, No. 2 (Summer 1981): 40–43.

Leavitt, Robert Keith. "Annie Oakley in Baker Street." In PROFILE BY GASLIGHT, edited by Edgar W. Smith, 230–242. New York: Simon & Schuster, 1944.

———. "Nummi in Arca or The Fiscal Holmes." In 221B: STUDIES IN SHERLOCK HOLMES, edited by Vincent Starrett, 16–36. New York: Macmillan Co., 1940.

Lellenberg, Jon L. "The Early Holmes: Alone in Bloomsbury." In A TOUCH OF THE CLASS, edited by Michael H. Kean, 55–66. Wilmette, Ill.: The Pondicherry Press, 1981.

———. "A Novel Treatise." *Baker Street Journal* 23, No. 1 (March 1973): 6–10.

———. "Revised Treatise." *Baker Street Journal* 33, No. 2 (June 1983): 100.

Leonard, William. "Re: Vampires." *Baker Street Journal*, Christmas Annual (1957): 20–25.

Levin, Alfred A. "Reichenbach Revisited." *Varieties of Ash* 1, No. 1 (June 1991): 29–50.

———. Unpublished manuscript annotating "The Final Problem." In the files of the editor.

Linsenmeyer, John. "Sherlock Holmes's University—Oxford or Cambridge?" *Baker Street Journal* 39, No. 2 (June 1989): 71–74.

Lithner, Klas. "On Holmes's Mission for the King of Scandinavia." *Baker Street Miscellanea* 43 (Autumn 1985): 25–27.

MacDonnell, A. G. "Mr. Moriarty." BAKER STREET STUDIES, edited by H. W. Bell, 159–175. London: Constable & Co., 1934.

Mackenzie, Armine D. "The Case of the Illustrious Predecessor." *Baker Street Gasogene* 1, No. 2 (1961): 29–31.

Mackey, Ann M. "The Secret of the Initial Problem, or Observations & Postulations." *Prescott's Press* (N. S.) 5 (March 1990): 27–30.

MacNaghten, Sir H. "The Education of Holmes." *Sunday Times*, Aug. 26, 1934. Reproduced in SHERLOCK HOLMES SCRAPBOOK, edited by Peter Haining, 42. New York: Clarkson N. Potter, 1974.

Mallalieu, J. P. W. "Shady Mr. Holmes." *Spectator*, Feb. 27, 1953, 247.

Marino, Joseph R. "A Question of Disguise." In ANNUAL REPORT 1991: FINAL PROBLEM CONTRACT, edited by Philip Weller, 46–48. Hampshire, England: Sherlock Publications, 1991.

Maxfield, David K. "Was Teddy an Ichneumon?" *Baker Street Journal* 29, No. 3 (Sept. 1979): 167–168.

McCallister, David R. "The Black Barrister Who Baffled Baker Street." *Wheelwrightings* 14, No. 1 (May 1991): 28–33.

———. "The Old School of the Old Schoolfellows—Watson and Phelps: The Case for Winchester College." *Baker Street Journal* 41, No. 3 (Sept. 1991): 135–141.

McClune, Michael C. and William P. Schweikert. "A Crooked Story." *Prescott's Press* [N. S.] 11 (Sept. 1991): 12–14, 23.

McClure, Michael W. "The Final Red-Headed Problem." In COMMANDING VIEWS

FROM THE EMPTY HOUSE, edited by William R. Cochran and Gordon R. Speck, 37–42. Indianapolis: Gasogene Books, 1997.

McDade, Thomas M. "Heads and Holmes." *Baker Street Journal* 11, No. 2 (Sept. 1961): 162–166.

McDiarmid, E. W. "Professor Sherlock Holmes, Ph.D." In EXPLORING SHERLOCK HOLMES, edited by E. W. McDiarmid and Theodore C. Blegen, 27–41. La Crosse, WI: Sumac Press, 1957.

McKee, Wilbur K. "The Son of a Certain Gracious Lady." *Baker Street Journal* 8, No. 3 (July 1958): 133–138.

McLaren, R. M. "Doctor Watson–Punter or Speculator?" *Sherlock Holmes Journal* 1, No. 1 (May 1952): 8–10.

McLauchlin, Russell. Letter. *Baker Street Journal* [O. S.] 1, No. 4 (Oct. 1946): 475–476.

Meaker, Samuel R., M.D. "Watson Medicus." In THE THIRD CAB, 26–36. Boston: Privately published, 1960.

Medawar, Tony. "The Final Solution." *Sherlock Holmes Journal* 20, No. 4 (Summer 1992): 118–121.

Meers, Michael A. "Holmes and Watson Travelling Through Switzerland." In ANNUAL REPORT 1991: THE FINAL PROBLEM CONTRACT, edited by Philip Weller, 20–22. Hampshire, England; Sherlock Publications, 1991.

Merrill, Edward A. "The Case of the Missing Calendar." *Baker Street Journal* 21, No. 3 (Sept. 1971): 132–139.

———. "FOR THE SAKE OF THE TRUST": SHERLOCK HOLMES AND THE MUSGRAVE RITUAL. Bloomington, Ind.: Gaslight Publications, 1982.

———. "Holmes and Brunton: Civil Engineers." *Baker Street Journal* 20, No. 1 (March 1970): 39–47.

———. "Hurlstone Revisited." *Baker Street Journal* 24, No. 4 (Dec. 1974): 221–231.

———. "Letters to Baker Street." *Baker Street Journal* 20, No. 4 (Dec. 1970): 243.

———. "Letters to Baker Street." *Baker Street Journal* 22, No. 1 (March 1972): 46–48.

Merriman, C. O. "In Clubland." *Sherlock Holmes Journal* 7, No. 1 (Winter 1964): 29–30.

———. "Unfair to Mycroft," *Sherlock Holmes Journal* 1, No. 4 (Dec. 1953), 41–42.

Metcalfe, N. P. "Oxford or Cambridge or Both?" *Baker Street Journal*, Christmas Annual (1956): 7–14.

Meyer, Charles A. "The Curious Incident of the Doctor in the Night-time." *Baker Street Journal* 38, No. 2 (June 1988): 92–93.

———. "Speculations Upon the Identity of the Royal Mallows." *Sherlock Holmes Journal* 23, No. 3 (Winter 1995): 86–87.

Meyer, Nicholas. THE SEVEN-PER-CENT SOLUTION. New York: E. P. Dutton & Co., Inc., 1974.

Michell, J. H. and Humfrey. "Sherlock Holmes the Chemist." *Baker Street Journal* [O. S.] 1, No. 3 (1946): 245–252.

Mihalakis, Athene. "A Rose by Any Other Name." *Baker Street West 1* 3, No. 3 (Sept. 1997): 21–24.

Milner, Richard. "Sherlock Holmes and the Mystery of the Red Rose." *Baker Street Journal* 37, No. 3 (Sept. 1987): 162–164.

Mitchelson, Austin. THE BAKER STREET IRREGULAR: THE UNAUTHORIZED BIOGRAPHY OF SHERLOCK HOLMES. Essex, England: Ian Henry Publications, 1994.

Montgomery, James. "Meiringen Musings." In SHOTS FROM THE CANON, 9. Philadelphia: Privately printed, 1953.

Morgan, F. E. "Sherlock Holmes and Foreign Affairs." *Sherlock Holmes Journal* 11, No. 1 (Winter 1972): 28–29.

Moriarty, Daniel. "The Peculiar Persecution of Professor Moriarty." *Baker Street Journal* 10, No. 1 (March 1960): 15–34.

Morley, Christopher. "Dr. Watson's Secret." In 221B: STUDIES IN SHERLOCK HOLMES, edited by Vincent Starrett, 45–53. New York: Macmillan Co., 1940.

———. "In Memoriam Sherlock Holmes." In Doyle, Arthur Conan, COMPLETE SHERLOCK HOLMES, vii–xiv. New York: Doubleday, Doran & Co., 1930.

———. "Sherlock Holmes Returns." *The Courier* 39, No. 5 (Dec. 1962): 66–67.

———. "Sherlock Holmes Revisits Cambridge." *Baker Street Journal* [O.S.] 3, No. 3 (July 1948): 295–299.

———. "Was Sherlock Holmes an American?" In 221B: STUDIES IN SHERLOCK HOLMES, edited by Vincent Starrett, 5–16. New York: Macmillan Co., 1940.

Mortimore, Roger. "Lying Dectective." *Baker Street News* 1, No. 2 (1984): 2–3.

———. "That Is to Say, Mr. Holmes." *Baker Street Pillar Box* 13 (1993): 13–16.

Moss, Robert A. "Sherlock Holmes's College at Oxford." *Baker Street Journal* 29, No. 1 (March 1979): 25–27.

Nathan, Hartley R. *The Naval Treaty*: The Holdhurst-Harrison Connection." *Baker Street Journal* 31, No. 3 (Summer 1981): 147–154.

Neblett, William. SHERLOCK'S LOGIC. New York: Dorset Press, 1985.

Nevill, Ralph. LONDON CLUBS: THEIR HISTORY AND TREASURES. London: Chatto & Windus, 1911.

Newton, G. B. "The Date of *The Valley of Fear*." *Sherlock Holmes Journal* 2, No. 4 (Winter 1955): 38–42.

Olding, Alan C. "Transportation Problems." *Sherlock Holmes Journal* 13, No. 2 (Summer 1977): 64.

Otten, Eric H. "Who Was Mycroft? or The Truth Behind the Myth." In THE NOBLE BACHELORS' RED-COVERED VOLUME, edited by Philip A. Shreffler, 20–22. St. Louis: Birchmoor Press, 1974.

Pasley, Robert S. "*The Greek Interpreter* Interpreted: A Revisionist Essay." *Baker Street Journal* 35, No. 2 (June 1985): 106–111.

————. "The Return of Moriarty." *Baker Street Journal* 28, No. 3 (Sept. 1978): 161–163.

Pelger, David. "Vamberry or Vambery, A Possible Identification." *Baker Street Journal* 43, No. 4 (Dec. 1993): 204–207.

Perceval, William. "Sherlock Holmes and Air-Guns." *Sherlock Holmes Journal* 6, No. 1 (Winter 1962): 15–16.

Perry, Milton F. "The Body Beside the Tracks, or The True *Adventures of Sherlock Holmes* in Kansas City." *Baker Street Miscellanea* 6 (June 1976): 1–5.

Pitts, Zasu. "Mrs. Hudson Speaks." *Baker Street Journal* [O. S.] 2, No. 3 (1947): 328–331.

Portugal, Eustace. "The Holmes-Moriarty Duel." *Commonplace Book* 4, No. 16 (Fall 1968): 310–312.

Potter, Beverly Baer. "Thoughts on *The Yellow Face*." *Baker Street Journal* 24, No. 3 (Sept. 1974): 164–165, 167.

Pratt, Fletcher. "Holmes and the Royal Navy." In THE SECOND CAB, edited by James Keddie, 65–69. Boston: Privately printed, 1947.

Prunet, Bernard. "The Final Problem: A Study in Railways." *Sherlock Holmes Railway Journal* 3 (1995): 26–33.

Quayle, Edward. "Suffer the Little Children . . ." *Baker Street Journal* 3, No. 4 (1948): 463–470.

Rand, Stuart C. "What Sherlock Didn't Know." *Baker Street Journal* 1, No. 3 (July 1951): 83–88.

Randall, David A. A CATALOG OF ORIGINAL MANUSCRIPTS, AND FIRST AND OTHER IMPORTANT EDITIONS OF THE TALES OF SHERLOCK HOLMES, AS WRITTEN BY SIR ARTHUR CONAN DOYLE, TOGETHER WITH IMPORTANT BIOGRAPHIES, PASTICHES, ARTICLES, *ETC.*, AND A FEW EXTRAORDINARY ASSOCIATION AND UNIQUE ITEMS. New York: The Scribner Book Store, 1943.

Ranild, Svend. "The Thomas Hogram Letters." *Sherlock Holmes Journal* 20, No. 2 (Summer 1991): 54–57.

Redfearn, Auberon. "A Game At Which Two Can Play: A Reichenbach Rumination." *Musgrave Papers* 4 (1991): 27–30.

Redmond, Chris. "An Identification of Colonel Warburton." *Shades of Sherlock*, 3 (Feb. 1967): 5–6.

Redmond, Donald A. "The Armchair Still Misplaced." *Baker Street Journal* 22, No. 2 (June 1972): 78–80.

————. "Norbury Again but Why Whisper?" *Medical Bulletin* 11, No. 1 (Spring 1985): 5–8.

————. "Some Pretty Cases from the Tin Box." *Sherlock Holmes Journal* 12, No. 1 (Spring 1975): 3–9.

————. "Vamberry the Wine Merchant." *Sherlock Holmes Journal* 12, Nos. 3–4 (Summer 1976): 76–77.

Reeler, Kenneth Clark. "Well Then, About That Chasm . . ." *Holmesian Observer* 1, No. 5 (July 1971): 3–6; 1, No. 6 (Aug. 1971): 5–7; 1, No. 7 (Sept. 1971): 3–4.

Rendell, Vernon. "The Limitations of Sherlock Holmes." BAKER STREET STUDIES, edited by H. W. Bell, 63–84. London: Constable & Co., 1934.

Rice, Rev. Otis G. "Clergymen in the Canon." *Baker Street Journal* 4, No. 3 (July 1954):133–143.

Richards, E. Butler. "Musgrave Musings." *Baker Street Miscellanea* 17 (March 1979): 16–19.

Roberts, S. C. "The Music of Baker Street." *Baker Street Journal* [O. S.] 2, No. 4 (1947): 429–432.

———. "The Personality of Sherlock Holmes." *Sherlock Holmes Journal* 1, No. 1 (May 1952): 2–7.

———. "Sherlock Holmes and the Fair Sex." In BAKER STREET STUDIES, edited by H. W. Bell, 177–201. London: Constable & Co., 1934.

Robinson, Robert E. "The Beddington Plot." *Baker Street Miscellanea* 44 (Winter 1985): 25–29.

Rodin, Alvin E., and Jack D. Key, "Sherlock Holmes's Use of Imagination and the Case of the Unperturbed Dog." *Canadian Holmes* 13, No. 4 (Summer 1990): 3–7.

Rosenberger, Edgar S. "On the Railway Journals of Sherlock Holmes." *Baker Street Journal* [O.S.] 2, No. 2 (1947): 175–179.

Rosenblum, Morris. "Foreign Language Quotations in the Canon." *Baker Street Journal* [O. S.] 3, No. 4 (1948): 425–434.

———. "The Horatian Spirit in Holmes." ILLUSTRIOUS CLIENT'S THIRD CASE-BOOK, edited by J. N. Williamson and H. B. Williams, 97–102. Indianapolis: The Illustrious Clients, 1953.

———. "Some Latin Byways in the Canon." *Baker Street Journal* [O. S.] 3, No. 1 (1948): 15–20.

Rouby, Jason. "A Confidential Communication." *Baker Street Journal* 15, No. 4 (Dec. 1965): 224–226.

Saunders, Alan. "The Return of Porlock." In ANNUAL REPORT 1991: THE FINAL PROBLEM CONTRACT, edited by Philip Weller, 35–38. Hampshire, England: Sherlock Publications, 1991.

Sayers, Dorothy L. "Holmes' College Career." BAKER STREET STUDIES, edited by H. W. Bell, 1–34. London: Constable & Co., 1934.

Scheideman, J. W. "Economic Cares and Cabs: A Dialogue About Mycroft." *Baker Street Journal* 25, No. 1 (March 1975): 23–24, 27.

———. "Edward, Artfully Disguised as Mycroft Holmes." *Vermissa Herald* 8, No. 3 (Sept. 1974): 2–6, 9.

Schutz, Robert H. A BIBLIOGRAPHY OF THE IDENTIFICATION OF HOLMES'S COLLEGE AND UNIVERSITY. Pittsburgh, Pa.: Arnsworth Castle Business Index, 1961.

————. "Some Problems in 'The Yellow Face.' " *Baker Street Journal* 12, No. 1 (March 1962): 31.

Scott, Alison M. "Organizing the Brain Attic: Indexing the Commonplace Books of Sherlock Holmes." *Baker Street Journal* 44, No. 4 (Dec. 1994): 199–203.

Sellars, Crighton. "Dr. Watson and the British Army." *Baker Street Journal* [O. S.] 2, No. 3 (July 1947): 332–341.

Shalet, Stephen A. "Cannons in the Canon." In More Leaves from the Copper Beeches, 93–98. Lititz, PA: Sutter House, 1976.

Shanks, John. "You Have Been to University I Perceive." *Three Pipe Problem* 2 (Aug. 1979): 10–16.

"Sherlock Holmes and Railways." *Sherlock Holmes Journal* 9, No. 2 (Summer 1969): 40–48. Reprinted in *Sherlock Holmes Railway Journal* 1 (1993): 5–22.

Shreffler, Philip A. "Taking Col. Ross's Breath Away." *Prescott's Press* [N.S.] 6 (June 1990): 15–18.

Silverstein, Albert and Myrna. "Concerning the Extraordinary Events at the Reichenbach Falls." *Baker Street Journal* 20, No. 1 (March 1970): 21–29.

Simmons, George. "Sherlock Holmes—The Inner Man." *Baker Street Journal* [O. S.] 2, No. 2 (1947): 129–35.

Simms, Bartlett, D. "Another Look at the Diogenes Club." *Camden House Journal* 10, No. 9 (Sept. 1988): 2–3.

Simpson, A. Carson. "The Curious Incident of the Missing Corpse." *Baker Street Journal* 4, No. 1 (Jan. 1954): 24–34.

————. I'm Off to Philadelphia in the Morning. Philadelphia: International Printing Company, 1960.

Sitwell, Maj. Gen. H. D. W. "Some Notes on St. Edward's Crown and the Musgrave Ritual." *Baker Street Journal* 3, No. 2 (Apr. 1953): 77–82.

Skottowe, Philip F. "Sherlock Holmes and the Stage." *Sherlock Holmes Journal* 7, No. 3 (Winter 1965): 73–77.

Small, C. Russell. " 'The Curious Incident,' or From Homer to Holmes." *Baker Street Journal* 2, No. 4 (Oct. 1952): 229–230.

Smith, Edgar W. "From the Editor's Commonplace Book." *Baker Street Journal* [O. S.] 1, No. 2 (1946): 187–194.

Smith, Red. "The Nefarious Holmes." *New York Herald Tribune*, Jan. 13, 1953, 24; Jan. 14, 1953, 26.

Snyder, Eileen. "*The Yellow Face*—A Problem in Genetics." *Baker Street Journal* 24, No. 4 (March 1974): 232–236.

Speck, Gordon R. "Holmes, Heroics, Hiatus: A Man to Match Swiss Mountains." In Commanding Views from the Empty House, edited by William R. Cochran and Gordon R. Speck, 111–113. Indianapolis: Gasogene Books, 1997.

Stavert, Geoffrey S. "Case of the Straw Basher's Hatband." *Sherlock Holmes Journal* 13, No. 4 (Autumn 1978): 122–123.

Stephens, Charles B. "The Birlstone Hoax." *Baker Street Journal* [O. S.] 4, No. 1 (Jan. 1949): 5–11.

———. "Silas Brown, or, Who Shot Desborough's Bolt?" *Baker Street Journal* [O.S.] 2, No. 3 (1947): 257–261.

Stern, Madeleine B. THE GAME'S A HEAD. Rockville Centre, N.Y.: Paulette Greene, 1983.

Stix, Thomas L. "Casual Comments on *The Crooked Man*." *Baker Street Journal* 12, No. 2 (June 1962): 99–100.

———. "The Reigate Puzzler." *Baker Street Journal* 13, No. 2 (June 1963): 93–95.

———. "Sherlock Holmes Impeached (II: *Silver Blaze*)." *Baker Street Journal* 15, No. 2 (June 1965): 76–78.

———. "The Yellow Face." *Baker Street Journal* 24, No. 3 (Sept. 1974): 166–167.

———. "We Ask the Questions!" *Baker Street Journal* 17, No. 3 (Sept. 1967): 149–151.

Swanson, Martin J. "Graphologists in the Canon." *Baker Street Journal* 12, No. 2 (June 1962): 73–80.

Swift, Francine M., and Wayne B. Swift. "Winchester Races." In THE TRI-METALLIC QUESTION, edited by Peter Horrocks, 19–23. London: Sherlock Holmes Society of London, 1991.

Swift, Francine M. "Grave Musings." In A TOUCH OF THE CLASS, edited by Michael H. Kean, 75–84. Wilmette, IL: Pondicherry Press, 1981.

———. "Why the Dog Did Nothing in the Night-Time." *Serpentine Muse* 13, No. 2 (Spring 1997): 13–14.

Swift, Wayne B. "Silver Blaze—A Corrected Identification." *Baker Street Journal* 41, No. 1 (March 1991): 25–36.

Swift, Wayne B. and Francine M. "Burghclere (the Railway Stop for 'King's Pyland') and Kingsclere (King's Pyland)." *Sherlock Holmes Journal* 22, No. 4 (Summer 1996): 126–128.

———. "Locations on Dartmoor Related to Silver Blaze." In HOUND AND HORSE, A DARTMOOR COMMONPLACE BOOK, edited by Shirley Purves, 59–63. Sherlock Holmes Society of London, 1992.

Thomas, Charles J. "Interpreting the Greek Interpreter." *Sherlock Holmes Journal* 13, No. 3 (Spring 1978): 81–83.

Thurbon, William T. "Education of Sherlock Holmes—A Footnote." *Baker Street Miscellanea* 7 (Sept. 1976): 11–12.

Tooley, M. W. "Was Musgrave One of Three Men?" *Sherlock Holmes Journal* 14, No. 2 (Winter 1979: 41–43.

Torese, Dante M. "Firearms in the Canon: The Guns of Sherlock Holmes and John H. Watson." *Baker Street Journal* 42, No. 3 (Sept. 1992): 154–157.

———. "Some Musings on 'The Final Problem.' " *Prescott's Press* [N. S.] 16 (Dec. 1992): 7–8.

Trapp, David James. "Holmes the Graphologist." *Baker Street Journal* 31, No. 1 (March 1981): 20–21.

Utechin, Nicholas, "Hurlstone and the Ritual." *Baker Street Journal* 21, No. 3 (Sept. 1971), 140–142.

———. "The Importance of 'The Final Problem.' " *Sherlock Holmes Journal* 20, No. 2 (Summer 1991): 41.

———. "Letters to Baker Street." *Baker Street Journal* 22, No. 1 (March 1972): 48–49.

———. SHERLOCK HOLMES AT OXFORD. Oxford: Robert Dugdale, 1977.

———. " 'This Charming Town.' " *Baker Street Journal* 26, No. 3 (Sept. 1976): 135–140.

Van Liere, Edward J. "Sherlock Holmes and Doctor Watson, Perennial Athletes." In A DOCTOR ENJOYS SHERLOCK HOLMES, 117–126. New York, Washington, and Hollywood: Vantage Press, 1959.

Waggoner, Larry. "The Unknown Moriarty." *Baker Street Journal* 28 No. 3 (Sept. 1978): 165–167.

Wall, Rev. Wayne. "The Satanic Motif in Moriarty." *Baker Street Journal* 27, No. 1 (March 1977): 27–32.

Walsh, B. D. J. "Sherlock Holmes and Railways." *Sherlock Holmes Journal* 9, No. 2 (Summer 1969): 40–48. Reprinted in *Sherlock Holmes Railway Journal* 1 (1993): 5–22.

Walters, Lee R. "The Great Experiment." *Baker Street Journal* 38, No. 2 (June 1988): 94–95.

Warner, Richard S. "A Chronological Look at *The Resident Patient*." *Baker Street Journal* 34, No. 2 (June 1984): 93–95.

Warrack, Guy. "Passed to You, Admiralty Intelligence." *Sherlock Holmes Journal* 4, No. 2 (Spring 1959): 79–80.

Weber, John. "The Locale of 'Silver Blaze'—Some Tentative Identifications." *Sherlock Holmes Journal* 19, No. 3 (Winter 1989): 73–75.

Webster, H. T. "Observations of Sherlock Holmes as an Athlete and Sportsman." *Baker Street Journal* [O. S.] 3, No. 1 (1948): 24–31.

Wehrle, Lou. "Transvestism in the Canon." In MORE LEAVES FROM THE COPPER BEECHES, 41–46. Lititz, PA: Sutter House, 1976.

Welch, George W. "The Terai Planter." *Baker Street Journal* 6, No. 1 (Jan. 1956): 35–39.

———. "The 'Silver Blaze' Formula." *Sherlock Holmes Journal* 3, No. 1 (Summer 1956): 19.

Weller, Philip. "A Baker Street Dozen—Some Singular Railway Connections in the Canon." *Sherlock Holmes Railway Journal* 1 (1993): 40–44.

———. "A Relative Question: Another Case of Identity." In INTERIM REPORT 1991: FINAL PROBLEM CONTRACT REVIEWED, edited by Philip Weller, 33–35. Hampshire, England: Sherlock Publications, 1991.

———. "A Thoroughbred Case: The Strengths and Weaknesses of Silver Blaze," *The Ritual* 19 (Spring 1997): 30–33.

Wellman, Manly Wade. "The Great Man's Great Son." *Baker Street Journal* [O. S.] 1, No. 3 (1946): 326–336.

———. "Two Southern Exposures of Sherlock Holmes." *Baker Street Journal* [O. S.] 2, No. 4 (1947): 422–426.

Williams, H. B. "Dating 'The Yellow Face.' " In CLIENT'S CASE-NOTES, edited by Brian R. MacDonald, 24–25. Indianapolis, Ind.: The Illustrious Clients, 1983.

———. "Pleasure in Pictures." *Baker Street Journal* 13, No. 4 (Dec. 1963): 232–235.

Williamson, Jerry Neal. " 'There Was Something Very Strange.' " *Baker Street Journal* 12, No. 4 (Dec. 1962): 201–209.

Wills-Wood, Christopher. "The Missing Inventor: A Historical Hypothesis." In INTERIM REPORT 1991: FINAL PROBLEM CONTRACT REVIEWED, edited by Philip Weller, 23–25. Hampshire, England: Sherlock Publications, 1991.

Wilson, Evan M. "Sherlock Holmes and the Indian Mutiny: Or, Where and What Was Bhurtee?—An Identification." *Baker Street Journal* 28, No. 1 (March 1978): 22–23.

———. "Sherlock Holmes in Eastern Asia: the Thirty-Six Steps, or Vambery Again." *Baker Street Journal* 33, No. 2 (June 1983): 86–88.

———. "Vambery, the So-Called Wine Merchant, or the Dervish of Windsor Castle." *Baker Street Journal* 32, No. 3 (Sept. 1982): 140–142.

Winn, Dilys. "The Butler." In MURDER INK, perpetrated by Dilys Winn: 287–289. New York: Workman Publishing, 1977.

Wolff, Julian, M.D. "The Dynamics of the Binomial Theorem." *Baker Street Journal* 13, No. 4 (Dec. 1963): 199–200.

Woods, Carol P. "The Curious Matter of the Congratulatory Telegrams." *Baker Street Journal* 42, No. 1 (March 1992): 16–17.

Zeisler, Ernest B. "Some Observations Upon *Silver Blaze*." *Baker Street Journal* 11, No. 4 (Dec. 1961): 238–240.

Zunic, Jim. "The First Greek Interpreter." *Baker Street Journal* 28, No. 3 (Sept. 1978): 157–158, 167.

THE RETURN OF SHERLOCK HOLMES

Adams, Rev. Stephen. "Holmes: A Student of London?" *Sherlock Holmes Journal* 2, No. 4 (Winter 1955): 17–18.

Alberstat, Mark. "The Wicked Colonel's Canadian Connection." *Canadian Holmes* 11, No. 2 (Christmas 1987): 31–32, 37.

Allen, Frank A. D. "Witchcraft in Baker Street." In BEYOND BAKER STREET, edited and annotated by Michael Harrison, 1–11. Indianapolis: Bobbs-Merrill Company, 1976.

Anderson, Poul. "Sherlock Holmes, Explorer." *Beeman's Christmas Annual* (1984): 2–4.

Andrew, C. R. "Don't Sell Holmes's Memory Short." *Baker Street Journal* 4, No. 4 (Oct. 1954): 219–222.

Andrew, Clifton R. "The Closed Window Mystery In *The Dancing Men.*" *Baker Street Journal* 11, No. 3 (Sept. 1961): 178–179.

Armstrong, Walter P., Jr. "The Truth About Sherlock Holmes." *Baker Street Journal* [O. S.] 1, No. 4 (1946): 391–401.

Aronson, Marvin E., M.D. "The Case of the Norwood Builder." *Baker Street Journal* 15, No. 1 (March 1965): 22–24.

Asher, Dr. Richard. "Holmes and the Fair Sex." *Sherlock Holmes Journal* 2, No. 3 (Summer 1955): 15–22.

Austin, Bliss. A BAKER STREET CHRISTMAS STOCKING. Westfield, N.J.: Hydraulic Press,1955. Reprinted in Bliss Austin, AUSTIN'S SHERLOCKIAN STUDIES: THE COLLECTED ANNUALS, 15–20. New York: Magico Magazine, 1986.

———. "Two Bibliographical Footnotes. "*Baker Street Journal* 4, No. 1 (Jan. 1954): 41–43.

Bailey, L. W. "The Dark Lady of Appledore Towers." *Sherlock Holmes Journal* 4, No. 4 (Spring 1960): 43–45.

Baker Street Miscellanea Editors. "The 'The Second Stain' Second Handwriting—Identified." *Baker Street Miscellanea* 16 (Dec. 1978): 12–14.

Baring-Gould, William S. "I Have My Eye on a Suite in Baker Street." In ANNOTATED SHERLOCK HOLMES, 85–102. New York: Clarkson N. Potter, 1967.

Bartholomew, J. G. BARTHOLOMEW'S HANDY REFERENCE ATLAS OF LONDON & SUBURBS. Geographical Institute, Edinburgh: John Bartholomew & Co., 1908.

Barzun, Jacques. "A Few Trifling Paragraphs." *Baker Street Journal* 21, No. 4 (Dec. 1971): 224–225.

Batory, Dana Martin. "Hiatus in Paradise." *Megavore: The Journal of Popular Fiction* 11 (Oct. 1, 1980): 29–33.

———. "Tut, Tut, Sherlock!" *Baker Street Miscellanea* 31 (Autumn 1982): 22–24, 32.

Baum, Christopher F. "The Twice-Stained Treaty." *Baker Street Journal* 32, No. 3 (Sept.1982): 146–148.

Beckett, David. "The Tosca." *Baker Street Journal* 25, No. 2 (June 1973): 119–121.

Bell, H. W. "Three Identifications: Two Localities in 'The Six Napoleons,' the Drive to Thaddeus Sholto's House, Birlstone Manor." In PROFILE BY GASLIGHT, edited by Edgar W. Smith, 283–289. New York: Simon & Schuster, 1944.

Bengis, Nathan, Colin Prestige, Cornelis Helling, Sydney C. Roberts, A. M. Robertson, James Edward Holroyd, and Lord Donegall. "Literary Osmosis."

Sherlock Holmes Journal 4, No. 4 (Spring 1960): 138–139; 5, No. 1 (Winter 1960): 27–28.

Bengtsson, Hans-Uno, ". . . det djup till vilket persiljan sjönk . . ." *Sherlockiana* 36, Nos. 2–3 (1991): 16–17 (rate of sinking graphed).

———. "A Norwegian Named Sigerson." *Baker Street Journal* 37, No. 3 (Sept. 1987): 148–152.

Bensky, Jerold M. " 'Sigerson'—What Is in a Name?" *Baker Street Journal* 23, No. 1 (March 1973): 28–31.

Berdan, M. S. "A Suggested Two-Thirds of *The Missing Three-Quarter.*" *Baker Street Journal* 38, No. 3 (Sept. 1988): 151–155.

Berdan, Marshall S. "The Great Derbyshire Duke-Out." *Baker Street Journal* 39, No. 2 (June 1989): 81–95.

Bergquist, John E. "Holmes, Watson and Wine." In CULTIVATING SHERLOCK HOLMES, edited by Bryce L. Crawford, Jr., and Joseph B. Connors, 48–55. La Cross, WI: Sumac Press, 1978.

Berl, Col. E. Ennalls. "Sherlock Holmes and the Telephone." *Baker Street Journal* 3, No. 4 (Oct. 1953): 197–210.

Bett, Wingate. "Watson's Second Marriage." *Sherlock Holmes Journal* 3, No. 1 (Winter 1956): 21–22.

Bigelow, S. Tupper. "Fingerprints and Sherlock Holmes." *Baker Street Journal* 17, No. 3 (Sept. 1967): 131–135.

———. "Hallamshire Revisited." *Baker Street Journal* 13, No. 2 (June 1963): 87–90.

———. "The Hoof-Marks in 'The Priory School.' " *Baker Street Journal* 12, No. 3 (Sept. 1962): 169–174.

———. "Those Five Volumes." *Baker Street Journal* 11, No. 1 (March 1961): 31–37.

———. "Two Canonical Problems Solved." *Baker Street Journal*, Christmas Annual (1959): 261–271.

———. "Was It Attempted Murder?" *Baker Street Journal* 14, No. 2 (June 1964): 99–106.

Bird, Tony. "Sidelights on Thucydides." In A STUDY IN DARK BLUE: SHERLOCK HOLMES AND OXFORD, edited by Margaret Bird, 93–94. London: Sherlock Holmes Society of London, 1994.

Blake, S. F. "Sherlock Holmes's Dressing Gown(s)." *Baker Street Journal* 10, No. 2 (Apr. 1960): 86–89.

Blakeney, T. S. "Disjecta Membra." *Baker Street Journal* 25, No. 3 (Sept. 1975): 142–143.

———. "The Location of 'The Three Students.' " *Sherlock Holmes Journal* 4, No. 1 (Winter 1958): 14.

———. "Some Disjecta Membra." *Sherlock Holmes Journal* 4, No. 3 (Winter 1959): 101–103.

————. "Thoughts on 'The Priory School.' " *Holmesian Observer Annual*, 1971, 26–28, kindly transcribed for this editor by Steven Clarkson.

Bolitho, Hector, and Derek Peel. WITHOUT THE CITY WALL: AN ADVENTURE IN LONDON STREET-NAMES, NORTH OF THE RIVER. London: John Murray, 1952.

Boswell, Rolfe. "On 'The Adventure of the Tired Captain.' " *Baker Street Journal* [O. S.] 2, No. 2 (Apr. 1947): 160–162.

Boucher, Anthony. "Ballade of the Later Holmes." *Baker Street Journal* [O. S.] 1, No. 1 (Jan. 1946): 44.

————. Quoted in "From the Editor's Commonplace Book." *Baker Street Journal* [O.S.] 2, No. 1 (1947): 60–61.

————. "Was the Later Holmes an Imposter?" In PROFILE BY GASLIGHT, edited by Edgar W. Smith, 60–70. New York: Simon & Schuster, 1944.

Bousquet, Robert J. "The Vocabulary of Abe Slaney." In INTERIM REPORT 1997: THE DANCING MEN CONTRACT REVIEWED, with editor's notes by Philip Weller, 17–21. Hampshire, England: Franco Midland Hardware Company, 1997.

Brend, Gavin. "Charles Augustus Milverton: The Date." *Sherlock Holmes Journal* 6, No. 3 (Winter 1963): 74–76.

Bristowe, W. S. "Oxford or Cambridge?" *Sherlock Holmes Journal* 4, No. 2 (Spring 1959): 75–76.

Bristowe, W. S. "The Three Students in Limelight, Electric Light and Daylight." *Sherlock Holmes Journal* 3, No. 2 (Winter 1956): 2–5.

Broadbent, Michael. THE NEW GREAT VINTAGE WINE BOOK. New York: Alfred A. Knopf, 1991.

Brody, Howard. "That Trip to Norway." *Baker Street Miscellanea* 6 (June 1976): 15–17.

————. "The First Most Interesting Object." *Baker Street Journal* 28, No. 1 (March 1978): 28–31.

————. "Who Was Dr. Leslie Armstrong?" *Baker Street Miscellanea* 8 (Dec. 1976): 9–10.

Brown, David. "Mary Fraser of Adelaide." *Baker Street Journal* 35, No. 3 (Sept. 1985): 147–152.

Bryan-Brown, Frederick. "Sherlockian Schools and Schoolmasters." *Sherlock Holmes Journal* 3, No. 1 (Summer 1956): 2–7.

Buddle, Judy L. "Playing Your Cards As Best You Can." *Baker Street Journal* 41, No. 2 (June 1991): 97–99.

Cantor, Murray A. "A Reconstruction of the Norwood Builder." *Prescott's Press* [N. S.], 10 (June 1991): 9–11.

Carlson, Ron. " 'A High-at-us.' " *Feathers from the Nest* 5, No, 2 (Apr. 1975): 5.

Chambers, Robert S. "The Journey to a Lost Horizon." *Baker Street Journal* 26, No. 4 (Dec. 1976): 229–230.

Chorley, Jennifer. "Some Diggings Down Under." *Sherlock Holmes Journal* 6, No. 2 (Spring 1963): 49–51.

Christ, Jay Finley. "The Later Holmes An Imposter: A Sequel." *Baker Street Gasogene* 1, No. 1 (1961): 21–33.

Chujoy, Anatole. "The Only Second Stain." *Baker Street Journal* 4, No. 3 (July 1954): 165–168.

Clapp, Roger T. "The Curious Problem of the Railway Timetables." In THE SECOND CAB, edited by James Keddie, Jr., 34–38. Boston: Privately printed, 1947.

Clarke, Richard W. "On the Nomenclature of Watson's Ships." *Baker Street Journal* [O. S.] 1, No. 2 (1946): 119–121.

Clarkson, Steve. Letter. *Baker Street Journal* 30, No. 1 (March 1980): 43.

Cochran, Leonard. "The Adventure of the Empty Boast, or What Was the Real Motive for the Murder of Ronald Adair?" *Baker Street Journal* 22, No. 2 (Sept. 1972): 168–171.

Cochran, William R. "The Disappearance of the First Mrs. Watson." *Wheelwrightings* 9, No. 1 (May 1986): 22–24.

———. "The Magic Wine Bottle." *Wheelwrightings* 9, No. 2 (Sept. 1986): 21–23.

———. "Rummaging Through the Empty House." *Baker Street Journal* 30, No. 4 (Dec. 1980): 212–215.

Coffin, James A. "The Adventure of Black Peter: A Murder, A Killing, or A Suicide?" *Baker Street Journal* 43, No. 1 (March 1993): 20–24.

Cole, Eleanor S. "Holmes, Watson and the K-9's." *Baker Street Journal* 1, No. 1 (Jan. 1951): 25–29.

Coleman, Peter. "Sherlock Holmes and the Bicycle." In ANNUAL REPORT 1990: THE PRIORY SCHOOL CONTRACT, edited by Philip Weller, 13–16. Doncaster, England: Franco-Midland Hardware Company, 1990.

Collins, Dennis A. "Tracing 221B: A New Solution." *Sherlock Holmes Journal* 20, No. 2 (Summer 1991): 60–63.

Collins, William P. "Two Theatre-Goers Homeward Bound." *Baker Street Miscellanea* 44 (Winter 1985): 30–32.

Crocker, Stephen F. "Pseudepigraphical Matter in the Holmesian Canon." *Baker Street Journal* 2, No. 3 (July 1952): 158–164.

Cross, Melvin. "The Lantern of Sherlock Holmes." *Baker Street Journal* [O. S.] 1, No. 4 (1946): 433–442.

Dahlinger, Susan. "The Adventures of a Hated Rival." *Shades of Sherlock* 16 (July 1970): 4–5.

Davies, Bernard. A RAMBLE THROUGH THE RAGGED SHAW AND OTHER STUDIES AT THE PRIORY SCHOOL, DERBYSHIRE. Edited by Heather Owen. London: Sherlock Holmes Society of London, 1985.

———. "Back Yards of Baker Street." *Sherlock Holmes Journal* 4, No. 3 (Winter

1959): 83–88. Reprinted in SEVENTEEN STEPS TO 221B: A COLLECTION OF SHERLOCKIAN PIECES BY ENGLISH WRITERS, edited by James Edward Holroyd, 167–178. London: George Allen & Unwin Ltd., 1967.

———. "Holdernesse: A Ducal Double." *Baker Street Miscellanea* 46 (Summer 1986): 1–11, and 47 (Autumn 1986): 3–11.

———. "The Mews of Marylebone." *Sherlock Holmes Journal* 6, No. 1 (Winter 1962): 6–10.

———. "Three Distressed Gentlewomen." In A GAGGLE OF GOVERNESSES, edited by Pamela Bruxner, 2–30. London: Sherlock Holmes Society of London, 1997.

Davis, Elmer. Introduction to THE RETURN OF SHERLOCK HOLMES. In THE LATER ADVENTURES OF SHERLOCK HOLMES, Vol. 1, edited by Edgar W. Smith, v–xxi. New York: Limited Editions Club, 1952.

Dickensheet, Dean W. "On a Polychromatic Paradox." *Vermissa Daily Herald* 3, No. 3 (Jan. 1982): 3.

Dodd, Patricia. "Communicating in Code." *Sherlockian Muse* 3, No. 2 (Summer 1977): 6–8, 11.

Donegall, Lord. "April 1891–April 1894." *The New Strand* 1, No. 6 (May 1962): 678–680. Reprinted in SEVENTEEN STEPS TO 221B, edited by James Edward Holroyd, 161–166. London: George Allen & Unwin Ltd., 1967.

———. "The Blanched Soldier, The Devil's Foot, and The Solitary Cyclist." *New Strand Magazine* 18 (Winter 1964). Reproduced in BAKER STREET AND BEYOND, 91–95. London: Westminster Libraries and Sherlock Holmes Society of London, 1993.

Doyle, Arthur Conan. ADVENTURE OF THE PRIORY SCHOOL: A FACSIMILE OF THE ORIGINAL MANUSCRIPT IN THE MARVIN P. EPSTEIN SHERLOCK HOLMES COLLECTION. Santa Barbara: Santa Teresa Press, 1985.

———. THE COMPANY CANON: THE ADVENTURE OF THE DANCING MEN. Edited and annotated by Philip Weller. Lee-on-the-Solent, Hampshire: Sherlock Publications, 1995.

———. THE COMPANY CANON: THE ADVENTURE OF THE EMPTY HOUSE. Edited and annotated by Philip Weller. Lee-on-the-Solent, Hampshire: Sherlock Publications, 1994.

———. THE RETURN OF SHERLOCK HOLMES. Edited by Richard Lancelyn Green. Oxford and New York: Oxford University Press, 1993.

———. "B.24." In ROUND THE FIRE STORIES. London: George Bell and Sons, 1908.

Drazen, Patrick E. "The Greater Vehicle: Holmes in Tibet." *Baker Street Journal* 26, No. 4 (Dec. 1976): 220–226.

———. "Who Was That Private Detective I Saw You With?" *Camden House Journal* 2, No. 5 (May 1980): 2–6.

Dudley, William E. "Some Persecutions Are More Peculiar Than Others." *HP* 1, No. 7 (March 1979): 8–11.

———. THE UNTOLD SHERLOCK HOLMES. New York: Hansom Press, 1983.

Durgin, Cyrus. "The Speckled Band 1956." In THE THIRD CAB, 12–16. Boston: Privately printed, 1960.

Earle, Ralph, II "The Curious Incident of the Avoidance of Probate, with Some Reflections on the Premature Senility of Colonel Sebastian Moran." *Baker Street Journal* 17, No. 3 (Sept. 1967): 144–147.

Eckrich, Joe. "The Death and Resurrection of Sherlock Holmes." *Camden House Journal* 8, No. 12 (Dec. 1986): 2–3.

Elie, Rudolph. "The Battle of Charing Cross." THE THIRD CAB, 17–25. Boston: Privately printed, 1960.

Evans, Webster. "Sherlock Holmes and Sport." *Sherlock Holmes Journal* 2, No. 3 (Summer 1955): 35–42.

Fage-Pedersen, Anders. A CASE OF IDENTITY. *Bilag til* [Supplement to] *Sherlockiana* 8, Nos. 1–2 (1963): 7.

Farmer, J. S., and W. E. Henley. DICTIONARY OF SLANG. New York: George Routledge & Sons, 1912.

Farmer, Philip José. "A Case of a Case of Identity Recased, or The Grey Eyes Have It." Addendum 2 to TARZAN ALIVE, 215–248. Garden City, N.Y.: Doubleday & Co., 1972.

Feinberg, Samuel. "The Dented Idol—Undented." *Baker Street Journal* 24, No. 3 (Sept. 1974): 174–180.

Fenton, Irving M. "An Analysis of the Crimes and Near-Crimes at Appledore Towers in the Light of the English Criminal Law." *Baker Street Journal* 6, No. 2 (Apr. 1956): 69–74.

Fisher, Charles. "A Challenge from Baker Street." In LEAVES FROM THE COPPER BEECHES, 15–32. Narberth, PA: Livingston Pub. Co., 1959.

Fistell, Ira. "Notes on the Death of Cardinal Tosca." *Notorious Canary-Trainers Manual* 1, No. 4 (Fall 1975): 5–6.

Fleischauer, William E. "Who Was Huret?" *Baker Street Journal* 21, No. 3 (Sept. 1971): 163–168.

Foss, T. Frederick. "But That Is Another Story." *Baker Street Journal* 25, No. 2 (June 1975): 68–70.

———. "The Missing Years." *Sherlock Holmes Journal* 9, No. 3 (Winter 1969): 86–87.

Foster, S. G. exec. ed. AUSTRALIANS: A HISTORICAL LIBRARY. Sydney: Fairfax, Syme & Weldon Associates, 1987.

Galbraith, A. D. "The Real Moriarty." *Baker Street Journal*, Christmas Annual (1957): 55–62.

Galerstein, David H. "The Dented Idol." *Baker Street Journal* 21, No. 4 (Dec. 1971): 226–231.

———. "I Have the Right to Private Judgment." *Baker Street Journal* 24, No. 3 (Sept. 1974): 168–173.

———. "A Man with a Maid in Appledore Towers." *Canadian Holmes* 7, No. 4 (Summer 1984): 21–22.

———. "Who Killed the Villain? Not Lady X, Anyway." *Canadian Holmes* 4, No. 2 (Christmas 1980): 11 [n.p.].

Gardner, George K. "What Sherlock Did Know." *Baker Street Journal* 1, No. 3 (July 1951): 89–90.

Gejrot, Tomas. "Var Sherlock Holmes patient hos Sigmund Freud?" [Was Sherlock Holmes a patient of Sigmund Freud's?]. *Observanda Medica Ferrosan* [Malmö, Sweden] 2 (1988): 61.

Gomme, G. Laurence. LONDON IN THE REIGN OF VICTORIA (1837–1897). Chicago and New York: Herbert S. Stone & Company, 1898.

Goodman, Charles, D.D.S. "The Dental Holmes." In PROFILE BY GASLIGHT, edited by Edgar W. Smith, 85–97. New York: Simon & Schuster, 1944.

Gore-Booth, Paul H. "The Journeys of Sherlock Holmes: A Topical Monograph." *Baker Street Journal* [O. S.] 3, No. 1 (1948): 159–168.

Grandia, Rick. " 'I had to cycle to the Station.' " In A GAGGLE OF GOVERNESSES, edited by Pamela Bruxner, 30–32. London: Sherlock Holmes Society of London, 1997.

Green, Richard Lancelyn. "On Tour with Sigerson." *Sherlock Holmes Journal* 14, No. 1 (Spring 1979): 24–26.

Green, Roger Lancelyn. "Dr. Watson's First Critic." *Sherlock Holmes Journal* 3, No. 4 (Summer 1958): 8–9.

Greengold, Al. "That Green and Gold Monster." *Baker Street Journal* 40, No. 3 (Sept. 1990): 161–162.

Greenwood, E. P. "Some Random Thoughts on Railway Journeys by Holmes and Watson." *Sherlock Holmes Journal* 1, No. 3 (June 1953): 19–21.

Haddon-MacRoberts, M. "The Mystery of the Missing Bicycles." *Baker Street Journal* 31, No. 3 (Sept. 1981): 135–144.

———. "On Determining the Direction of Travel of a Bicycle from Its Tracks." *Baker Street Journal* 33, No. 3 (Sept. 1983): 144–145.

Halén, Harry. "Sherlock Holmes Venäjällä" [Sherlock Holmes in Russia]. *Bibliophilos* [Helsinki] 2 (1973): 57–61.

Hall, Trevor H. "A Note on *The Priory School*." In SHERLOCK HOLMES: TEN LITERARY STUDIES, 123–131. New York: St. Martin's Press, 1969.

———. "Sherlock Holmes's University and College." In SHERLOCK HOLMES: TEN LITERARY STUDIES, 56–85. New York: St. Martin's Press, 1969.

Harbottle, S. T. L. "Sherlock Holmes and the Law." *Sherlock Holmes Journal* 1, No. 3 (June 1953): 7–10.

Harrington, Hugh T. "Anna the Nihilist, Detective." *Plugs & Dottles*, 146 (Nov. 1990): 7.

Harris, Bruce. "Did Sherlock Holmes Kill Charles Augustus Milverton?" *Baker Street Journal* 32, No. 1 (March 1982): 45–47.

Harrison, Michael. I, SHERLOCK HOLMES: MEMOIRS OF MR. SHERLOCK HOLMES, OM, LATE CONSULTING PRIVATE DETECTIVE-IN-ORDINARY TO THEIR MAJESTIES QUEEN VICTORIA, KING EDWARD VII, AND KING GEORGE V. New York: E. P. Dutton, 1977.

Hilton, Isabel. THE SEARCH FOR THE PANCHEN LAMA. New York: W. W. Norton, 2000.

Hodgson, Ralph. Letter to Christopher Morley. Reprinted in "Clinical Notes by a Resident Patient," *Baker Street Journal* [O. S.] 1, No. 4 (1946): 404–406.

Hoff, Ebbe Curtis. "The Adventure of John and Mary." *Baker Street Journal* 9, No. 3 (July 1959): 136–152.

Hoffmann, Banesh. "A Reverent Comment on *The Second Stain*." *Baker Street Journal* 13, No. 2 (June 1963): 91–92.

Holly, Raymond L. "Europeans in Lhasa in 1891." *Baker Street Journal* 30, No. 3 (Sept. 1980): 151–157.

———. "A Laboratory at Montpelier." *Camden House Journal* 6, No. 6 (June 1984): 2.

Holmes, Bruce. "Defending Sherlock Holmes's Credibility." *Baker Street Journal* 39, No. 4 (Dec. 1989): 238.

Holmes, Marcella. "Sherlock Holmes and the Prime Minister." *Baker Street Journal* 5, No. 1 (Jan. 1955): 34–39.

Holroyd, James Edward. "The Egg-Spoon." *Sherlock Holmes Journal* 8, No. 2 (Spring 1967): 59.

———. "On the Route to Appledore Towers." *Sherlock Holmes Journal* 2, No. 1 (July 1954): 17.

———. "221 Baker Street." *Cornhill Magazine* 987 (Summer 1951): 244–254. Reprinted in BAKER STREET BY-WAYS, 53–67. London: George Allen & Unwin Ltd., 1959.

———. "Solutions by Numbers." In BAKER STREET BY-WAYS, 68–74. London: George Allen & Unwin Ltd., 1959.

Hyder, William, ed. "*The Napoleon Bust Business Again*." New York: The Baker Street Irregulars (2003).

Hyder, William. "Parsley and Butter: The Abernetty Business." *Baker Street Journal* 44, No. 3 (Sept. 1994): 152–160.

———. "The Root of the Matter." *Baker Street Miscellanea* 72 (Winter 1992): 33–34.

Hyman, Ian, and Peter Gilmore. "Tracking Down Sherlock Holmes." *Sparks: A Magazine for the Staff of Marks & Spencer*, Autumn 1972, 10–11.

Hyslop, James T. "The Master Adds a Postscript (An Extract from the Files of John H. Watson, M.D.)." *Baker Street Journal* [O. S.] 2, No. 2 (Apr. 1947): 113–118.

———. "Sherlock Holmes and the Press." *Sherlock Holmes Journal* 4, No. 1 (Winter 1958): 4–8.

Iacono, Paul O. "The True Location of 221B." *Baker Street Journal* 31, No. 2 (Sept. 1981): 161–168.

Iraldi, James C. "The Victorian Gondola." *Baker Street Journal* 1, No. 3 (July 1951): 99–103.

Iriarte, Antonio. "Sherlock Holmes and *The Strand Magazine*." In INTERIM REPORT 1994: EMPTY HOUSE CONTRACT REVIEWED, edited by Philip Weller, 14–19. Hampshire England: Franco-Midland Hardware Company, 1994.

Isen, B. George. "Holmes's Part in the Adventure of the Second Stain: A Third Stain, or a Carefully Guarded Account?" In MORE LEAVES FROM THE COPPER BEECHES, 35–40. Lititz, PA: Sutter House. 1976.

Jackson, Alan A. LONDON'S TERMINI. Newton Abbot: David & Charles, 1969.

Jaeck, Kathrin. "Turn Around, Turn Around." *Wheelwrightings* 11, No. 3 (Jan. 1989): 15–17.

Jenkins, William D. "A Peculiar Persecution." *Baker Street Journal* 14, No. 1 (March 1964): 45–53.

———. "This Case of the Ferrers Documents." *Scandal Sheet* 2, No. 4 (Oct. 1976): 6–7.

Jewell, Donald Girard. A CANONICAL DOG'S LIFE: A MONOGRAPH ON CANINES IN THE TIME OF SHERLOCK HOLMES. Westminster: Pinchin Lane Press,1993.

Johnson, C. Arnold. "An East Wind." *Baker Street Journal* 31, No. 1 (March 1981): 10–13.

———. "Lord Iddesleigh?" *Devon County Chronicle* 16, No. 3 (May 1980): 3–4.

Jones, Kelvin I. "The Chronology of 'The Abbey Grange.' " *Wheelwrightings* 10, No. 1 (May 1987): 19–21.

———. "The Ferrers Documents Case." *Pip's Log* 1, No. 3 (Dec. 25, 1981): n.p.

———. "The Mystery of Camden Place." *Camden House Journal* 5, No. 4 (Apr. 1983): 2–7.

———. "The Professor and the Pterodactyl: An Untold Tale of Dr. Watson." *Sherlock Holmes Journal* 8, No. 1 (Winter 1966): 14–16.

———. SHERLOCK HOLMES AND THE KENT RAILWAYS. New York: Magico Magazine, 1987.

———. "Yoxley Old Place." *Baker Street Chronicle* 3, No. 2 (March-Apr. 1983): 8–9.

Jordan, Anne. "I am a Poor Man." In INTERIM REPORT 1990: THE PRIORY SCHOOL CONTRACT REVIEWED, edited by Philip Weller, 12–13. Doncaster, England: Franco-Midland Hardware Company, 1990.

Judson, Ralph. "The Mystery of Baritsu: A Sidelight Upon Sherlock Holmes's Accomplishments." *Baker Street Journal*, Christmas Annual (1958): 10–16.

Kamil, Irving. "The Priory School Map: A Re-Examination." *Baker Street Journal* 34, No. 1 (March 1984): 12–16.

———. "The Search for Oscar Meunier." *Baker Street Journal* 38, No. 4 (Dec. 1988): 209–214.

———. "Sherlock Holmes and the Easter Island Script." *Baker Street Journal* 30, No. 1 (March 1980): 39–42.

Katz, Robert S. "John H. Watson, M.D.: The Non-Surgical Surgeon." *Baker Street Journal* 38, No. 4 (Dec. 1988): 223–225.

Kaye, Marvin. The Histrionic Holmes: An Analysis and Dissertation on the Impersonatory Genius of Sherlock Holmes. Culver City, Calif.: Luther Norris, 1971.

Keller, Robert. "Sherlock Holmes: A Spectra?" *Baker Street Journal* 25, No. 3 (Sept. 1975): 160–161, 167.

Kennedy, Bruce. "The Victorian Flashlight: Sherlock Holmes and Dark Lanterns." *Baker Street Journal* 30, No. 3 (Sept. 1980): 141–143.

Kernish, Robert. "The Curious Case of the Second Stain." *Baker Street Journal* 16, No. 3 (Sept. 1966): 173–174.

Kierman, Ray. "A Shocking Affair." *Baker Street Journal* 2, No. 2 (Apr. 1952): 103–107. Reprinted as " 'It Is a Curious Little Problem.' " *Baker Street Journal*, Christmas Annual (1957): 26–30.

Kimball, Elliot. "The Milverton Mess." *Sherlock Holmes Journal* 5, No. 4 (Spring 1962): 100–102.

Klinger, Leslie S. "Art in Whose Blood?" *The Ritual* 21 (Spring 1998): 3–7.

———. "Layout of a 'Most Desirable Residence.' " *Shoso-In Bulletin* 6 (1996): 78–81.

———. "Watson's Final Accounts?" *New Baker Street Pillar Box* 22 (Spring 1995): 15–16, and editor's response, 16–17.

———. "The Writings of Sherlock Holmes." *Baker Street West 1* 3, No. 1 (Jan. 1997): 23–26.

Klinger, Leslie S., and Timothy Bourke. What Game Was Afoot in The Red-Headed League? Beverly Hills: Daypark Press, 1997.

Knox, Ronald A. "Mystery of Mycroft." Baker Street Studies, edited by H. W. Bell, 131–158. London: Constable & Co., 1934.

———. "Studies in the Literature of Sherlock Holmes." In Essays in Satire, 145–175. London: Sheed and Ward, 1928.

Koelle, John B. "Random Thoughts on *The Dancing Men*." *Baker Street Journal* 16, No. 1 (March 1966): 18–20.

Konhauser, Joseph D. E., Dan Velleman, and Stan Wagon. Which Way Did the Bicycle Go? . . . and Other Intriguing Mathematical Mysteries. Mathematical Association of America, 1996.

Lai, Rick. "Flashman and Colonel Moran." *Wheelwrightings* 12, No. 3 (Jan. 1990): 16–18.

Leavitt, Robert K. "Nummi in Arca, or the Fiscal Holmes." In 221B: STUDIES IN SHERLOCK HOLMES, edited by Vincent Starrett, 16–36. New York: Macmillan Co., 1940.

Lellenberg, Jon L. "Revised Treatise." *Baker Street Journal* 33, No. 2 (June 1983): 100.

Levitt, Mark E. "The Vatican File." *Prescott's Press* [N. S] 7 (Sept. 1990): 7–10. Reprinted in *Baker Street Journal* 41, No. 4 (Dec.1991): 212–214.

Linsenmeyer, John. "Sherlock Holmes's University—Oxford or Cambridge?" *Baker Street Journal* 39, No. 2 (June 1989): 71–74.

Lohmann, Charles P., III. "Horace and Jonathan." *Holmeswork* 10 (Jan. 1983): 1–5.

London Stock Exchange. A HISTORY OF THE LONDON STOCK EXCHANGE. London: Privately printed, 1996.

Loper, Rev. Brant. "The Blackguard Parson Who Married Violet—He Must Have Been Mad." *Canadian Holmes* 5, No. 3 (Spring 1982): 9–11.

Luman, Richard. "The Second Hand in *The Second Stain*." *Baker Street Journal* 28, No. 3 (Sept. 1978): 133–136, 140.

Mallalieu, J. P. W. "Shady Mr. Holmes." *The Spectator*, Feb. 27, 1953, 247. Reproduced in *Commonplace Book* 2, Nos. 5–6 (Summer-Fall 1965): 89. Also reproduced in A SHERLOCK HOLMES COMPENDIUM, edited by Peter Haining, 181–184. London: W. H. Allen, 1980.

Malloy, Michael P. "Notes on the Identity of Milverton's Murderer." *Baker Street Journal* 27, No. 4 (Dec. 1977): 198–200.

Margolin, Jerry. "Take Neither the First, Nor the Second . . ." *Baker Street Journal* 25, No. 4 (Dec. 1975): 231–233.

Matusiba, Naoki. "The Connection with Lloyd's and Sherlock Holmes." *Studies of the Nippon Sherlock Holmes Club* 3, No.1 (May 1992): 88–104. Text in Japanese.

Maun, Ian. "Remarkable Sign." *Sherlock Holmes Journal* 9, No. 2 (Summer 1969): 69.

McComas, Stanley. "Lhove at Lhassa." *Baker Street Journal* 1, No. 2 (Apr. 1951): 43–51.

McCormack, George J. "A Second Look at *The Second Stain*." *Baker Street Journal* 42, No. 1 (March 1992), 38–41.

McGaw, Lisa. "Some Trifling Notes on Sherlock Holmes and Ornithology." *Baker Street Journal* 10, No. 4 (Oct. 1960): 231–234.

McPharlin, Paul. "221B Baker Street: Certain Physical Details." *Baker Street Journal* [O. S] 2, No. 2 (Apr. 1947): 180–194.

Merrell, David W. "An 'Unwonted Tidiness': Reichenbach Revealed." *Baker Street Journal* 52, No. 2 (Summer 2002): 14–22.

Merriman, Charles O. "In Search of Sherlock Holmes." *Sherlock Holmes Journal* 8, No. 1 (Winter 1966): 7–12.

Merritt, Russell L. "Re: The Adventure of the Worst Man in London." *Baker Street Journal*, Christmas Annual (1959): 296–301.

Metcalfe, N. P. "Oxford or Cambridge or Both?" *Baker Street Journal*, Christmas Annual (1956): 7–14.

Meyer, Charles A. "Lady Eva's Secret Revealed." *Baker Street Journal* 38, No. 3 (Sept. 1988): 168–170.

———. "The Proper Dress for Solitary Cyclists." *Naval Signals* 29 (Oct. 1992): 19–20.

———. "The Second Most Dangerous Man in London." *Baker Street Miscellanea* (Autumn 1988): 16–24.

Michell, Humfrey. "Letter to Baker Street." *Baker Street Journal* [O. S.] 3, No. 2 (Apr. 1948): 230–231.

Montgomery, James. Sidelights on Sherlock. Privately printed, 1951.

Moorman, Ed. "A Short But Interesting Visit." *Baker Street Journal* 43, No. 1 (March 1993): 16–19.

Morehead, Alfred H., Richard L. Frey, and Geoffrey Mott-Smith. The New Complete Hoyle. Garden City, N.Y.: Garden City Books (1964).

Morgan, F. E. "Sherlock Holmes and Foreign Affairs." *Sherlock Holmes Journal* 11, No. 1 (Winter 1972): 28–29.

Morley, Christopher. "Clinical Notes by a Resident Patient." In Profile by Gaslight, edited by Edgar W. Smith, 48–59. New York, Simon & Schuster, 1994.

———. "Clinical Notes by a Resident Patient." *Baker Street Journal* [O. S.] 2, No. 2 (Apr. 1947): 138–143.

———. "Clinical Notes by a Resident Patient." *Baker Street Journal* [O. S.] 3, No. 1 (Jan. 1948): 41–42. On John Hector McFarland's Inability to Get Back from Lower Norwood.

———. "Clinical Notes by a Resident Patient." *Baker Street Journal* 1, No. 2 (Apr. 1951): 55–59.

———. "Report from Baker Street." *New York Times Book Review*, Nov. 27, 1949. Reprinted in *Commonplace Book* 3, No. 9 ((Summer 1966): 182.

Morley, Felix. "The Significance of the Second Stain." In Profile by Gaslight, edited by Edgar W. Smith, 243–259. New York, Simon & Schuster, 1994.

Morris, Sir Harold. "Sherlock Holmes." In Back View, 48–56. London: Peter Davies, 1960.

Morton, Humphrey. "A Long Drive to Hampstead." *Sherlock Holmes Journal* 5, No. 1 (Winter 1960): 22–23.

———. "A Milvertonian Identification." *Sherlock Holmes Journal* 6, No. 1 (Winter 1962): 14–15.

Naganuma, Kohki. "Holmes and Communication." *Baker Street Journal* 21, No. 1 (March 1971): 14–21.

Needleman, Lionel. "A Practical handbook of Canonical Gardens." *Canadian Holmes* 7, No. 4 (Summer 1984): 3–6.

Nelson, James. "Sherlock and the Sherpas." *Baker Street Journal* 7, No. 3 (July 1957): 161–164.

Ober, Harry. "Comments on Watson's 'The Adventure of the Dancing Men.' " In THE FOURTH CAB, 55–56. Boston: Stoke Moran Publishers, 1976.

Olding, Alan C. "Holmes in Terra Australis Incognita—Incognito." *Sherlock Holmes Journal* 13, No. 2 (Summer 1977): 42–43.

———. " 'The Smith-Mortimer Succession Case,' 'The Tankerville Club Scandal,' 'The Famous Card Scandal of the Nonpareil Club.' " *News from the Diggings* 13, No. 3 (Sept. 1992): 1–4.

———. "The Solitary Cyclist Rings a Little Bell." *News from the Diggings* 10, No. 4 (Dec. 1989): 3–4.

Olney, Professor Clarke. "The Literacy of Sherlock Holmes." *Sherlock Holmes Journal* 2, No. 4 (Winter 1955): 9–15.

Pasley, Robert S. "Breaking the Entail." *Baker Street Journal* 39, No. 2 (June 1989): 96–98.

Peck, Andrew Jay. "The Solitary Man-Uscript." *Baker Street Journal* 22, No. 2 (June 1972): 71–73.

———. "Touch of a Vanished Hand." *Sherlock Holmes Journal* 11, No. 2 (Summer 1973): 71.

Perceval, William. "Sherlock Holmes and Air-Guns." *Sherlock Holmes Journal* 6, No. 1 (Winter 1962): 15–16.

Petersen, Svend. SHERLOCK HOLMES ALMANAC. Washington, D.C.: Privately printed, 1956.

Plimental, William E. Letter. *Baker Street Journal* 5, No. 2 (Apr. 1955): 121.

Potter, H. C. "The Case of the Unrequited Innocents." *Baker Street Journal* 27, No. 2 (June 1977): 88–92.

Pratt, Fletcher. "Holmes and the Royal Navy." In THE SECOND CAB, edited by James Keddie, Jr., 65–69. Boston: Privately printed, 1947.

———. "The Secret Message of the Dancing Men." In PROFILE BY GASLIGHT, edited by Edgar W. Smith, 274–282. New York: Simon & Schuster, 1944.

Prestige, Colin. "Agents of Evil." *Baker Street Journal* 5, No. 3 (July 1955): 144–147.

Randall, David A. "The Adventure of the Notorious Forger." *Baker Street Journal* [O. S.] 1, No. 4 (1946): 371–377.

Randall, Warren. "A Silliness at the Empty House." *Prescott's Press* [N. S.], Souvenir Edition (Dec. 1988): 8–10.

Redmond, Chris. "Doyle's Idea of a Duke: Who Holdernesse Was." *Canadian Holmes* 7, No. 2 (Dec. 1983): 27–29.

———. "Somewhere in Norway." *Sherlock Holmes Review* 2, No. 2 (1989): 87–89.

Redmond, Chris, and Ursula Moran. "Second Thoughts on 'The Three Students,'" *Sherlock Holmes Journal* 16, No. 4 (Summer 1984): 106–109.

Redmond, Donald A. "Double 'L'—Why in the Empty House?" *Baker Street Regular* 1, No. 3 (Apr. 1979): 5–6.

———. "Lord Bellinger—Who Else?" *Baker Street Miscellanea* 3 (Sept. 1975): 1–3.

———. "The Palimpsest and the Forgeries." *Baker Street Journal* 34, No. 3 (Sept. 1984): 159–165.

———. "La Tosca! Encore! Encore!" *Baker Street Miscellanea* 8 (Dec. 1976): 17–18.

———. "Ship Ahoy, Captain Basil." *Baker Street Journal* 36, No. 4 (Dec. 1986): 223–230.

———. "Some Chemical Problems in the Canon." *Baker Street Journal* 14, No. 3 (Sept. 1964): 145–152.

Rendall, Vernon. "The Limitations of Sherlock Holmes." In BAKER STREET STUDIES, edited by H. W. Bell. 63–84. London: Constable & Co., 1934.

———. THE LONDON NIGHTS OF BELSIZE. London: John Lane, 1917. A portion is reproduced as "Belsize as a Commentator: Sherlock Holmes," in INCUNABULAR SHERLOCK HOLMES, edited by Edgar W. Smith, 75–92. Morristown, NJ: Baker Street Irregulars, Inc., 1958.

Rice, Rev. Otis R. "Clergymen in the Canon." *Baker Street Journal* 4, No. 3 (July 1954): 133–143.

Richards, Anthony. "On The Right Track." In INTERIM REPORT 1990: THE PRIORY SCHOOL CONTRACT REVIEWED, edited by Philip Weller, 3–4. Doncaster, England: Franco-Midland Hardware Company, 1990.

Risley, Randall. "*The Adventure of the Missing Three-Quarter*: Rugby and a Date for the Adventure." *Camden House Journal* 3, No. 7 (July 1981): 2–3.

Roberts, Aubrey C. "The Real Second Stain: A Tarnished Idol." *Baker Street Journal* 32, No. 4 (Dec. 1982): 227–229.

Roberts, David. "About This Wilson and His Canaries." In MORE LEAVES FROM THE COPPER BEECHES, 161–165. Litiz, PA: Sutter House, 1976.

Robertson, Allen. "Baker Street, Beecher and Borden." *Baker Street Journal* 3, No. 1 (Jan. 1953): 44–47.

Roche, Robert F. "The Worst Man in London: Who Shot Him? And When?" *Baker Street Journal* 25, No. 1 (March 1975): 25–27.

Rolfe, W. J. A SATCHEL GUIDE FOR THE VACATION TOURIST IN EUROPE. Boston and New York: Houghton Mifflin Company, 1910.

Rosenblatt, Albert M. "Divorce, Canonical Style: Checkmate." *Baker Street Journal* 35, No. 1 (March 1985): 15–18.

Rosenblum, Morris. "Hafiz and Horace, Huxtable and Holmes." *Baker Street Journal* [O. S.] 1, No. 3 (July 1946): 261–269.

————. "Some Latin Byways in the Canon." *Baker Street Journal* [O. S.] 3, No. 1 (Jan. 1948): 15–20.

Rossi, John P. "The Characters in *The Second Stain*." *Baker Street Journal* 23, No. 1 (March 1973): 4–5.

Sanderson, Shirley. "Another Case of Identity." *Sherlock Holmes Journal* 6, No. 3 (Winter 1963): 86–87.

Sare, Michael J. "The Compleat Recovery of the Cipher of Abe Slaney." *News from the Diggings* 9, No. 3 (Sept. 1988): 1–7. Reprinted in *Sherlock Holmes Journal* 19, No. 3 (Winter 1989): 76–80.

Sarjeant, William A. S. "Mackleton Revisited and Found in the Peaks." *Canadian Holmes* 10, No. 4 (Summer 1987): 22–27.

Saunders, Alan. "Absurd Hieroglyphics: The Coded Messages in "The Dancing Men." In ANNUAL REPORT 1997: THE DANCING MEN CONTRACT, edited by Philip Weller, 15–24. Hampshire, England: Franco-Midland Hardware Company, 1997.

Sayers, Dorothy L., "Holmes's College Career." In UNPOPULAR OPINIONS, 134–147. London: Victor Gollancz Ltd., 1946.

Sayers, Dorothy L., ed. OMNIBUS OF CRIME. New York: Payson and Clarke Ltd., 1929.

Schenck, Remsen Ten Eyck. "Baker Street Fables." *Baker Street Journal* 2, No. 2 (Apr. 1952): 85–93.

————. Letter. *Baker Street Journal* [O. S.] 4, No. 1 (Jan. 1949): 95–96.

Schonberg, Harold C. "Sherlock and Malocchio!" *New York Times*, May 12, 1968, Section II, 17. Reprinted in *Commonplace Book* 4, No. 15 (Aug. 1968): 288.

Schultz, Robert S. "The Ballistics of the Empty House." *Baker Street Journal* [O. S.] 2, No. 4 (1947): 373–378.

Schwartz, Richard S. "Three Students in Search of a Scholar." *Baker Street Journal*, Christmas Annual (1957): 45–49.

Sellars, Crighton. "Dr. Watson and the British Army." *Baker Street Journal* [O. S.] 2, No. 3 (July 1947): 332–341.

Sequeira, Christopher G. C. "Sherlock Holmes versus Jack the Ripper. Part 2, 'No Stranger to the Knife: By Whose Hands the Deeds Were Done.'" *Passengers' Log* 1, No. 3 (May 1998): 31–35.

Shearn, A. L. "The Street and the Detective." *Baker Street Journal*, Christmas Annual (1957): 50–54.

Sherbrooke-Walker, Ronald. "Clothes Canonical." *Sherlock Holmes Journal* 6, No. 4 (Spring 1964): 104–108.

Short, Ernest H. "221B Baker Street: Where Sherlock Holmes Lived." *Baker Street Journal* [O. S.] 4, No. 1 (Jan. 1949): 48, 50–52.

Shulman, David. "The Origin of The Dancing Men." *Baker Street Journal* 23, No. 1 (March 1973): 19–21.

Simpson, A. Carson. Letter. *Baker Street Journal* 5, No. 3 (July 1955): 187.

———. SHERLOCK HOLMES'S WANDERJAHRE. PART I: FANGET AN! Philadelphia: International Printing Company, 1953.

———. SHERLOCK HOLMES'S WANDERJAHRE. PART II: POST HUC NEC ERGO PROPTER HUC GABETQUE. Philadelphia: International Printing Company, 1954.

———. SHERLOCK HOLMES'S WANDERJAHRE. PART III, IN FERNEM LAND, UNNAHBAR EUREN SCHRITTEN. Philadelphia: International Printing Company, 1955.

Simpson, Helen. "Medical Career and Capacities of Dr. J. H. Watson." In BAKER STREET STUDIES, edited by H. W. Bell, 35–61. London: Constable & Co., 1934.

Sisson, Jon Borden. "Dr. Handy's Wild-Eyed Man." *Baker Street Journal* 20, No. 3 (Sept. 1970), 170–179.

Skene Melvin, David. "Sailing the Butterboat into Uncharted Seas." *Baker Street Journal* 26, No. 4 (Dec. 1976): 233–234.

Smith, Edgar W. "Dr. Watson and the Great Censorship." *Baker Street Journal* 2, No. 3 (July 1952): 138–151.

———. "Sherlock Holmes and the Great Hiatus." *Baker Street Journal* [O. S.] 1, No. 3 (July 1946): 277–285.

Smith, Red. "Dear Me, Mr. Holmes." *New York Herald Tribune*, Jan. 14, 1953, 26. Reprinted in VIEWS OF SPORT, 188–191. New York: Alfred A. Knopf, 1954, and *Commonplace Book* 1, No. 1 (Summer 1964): 10–11.

———. "The Nefarious Holmes." *New York Herald Tribune*, Jan. 13, 1953, 24. Reprinted in *Commonplace Book* 1, No. 1 (Summer 1964): 10–11.

Smith, William. "Studies on The Dancing Men." *Baker Street Journal* 19, No. 2 (June 1969): 79–84.

Sommerlad, Uwe. "The Second Most Dangerous Man in London?" In INTERIM REPORT 1994: THE EMPTY HOUSE CONTRACT REVIEWED, 33–35. Hampshire, England: Franco-Midland Hardware Company, 1994.

Sovine, J. W., M.D. "The Toxicanon." *Baker Street Journal* 8, No. 2 (Apr. 1958): 107–112.

Speck, Gordon, R. " ' . . . And a Week Later I Was in Florence.' " *Baker Street Miscellanea* 38 (Summer 1984): 25–28.

———. "The Provenance of Parker, the Garroter." *Camden House Journal* 10, No. 5 (May 1988): 3–4.

Starr, H.W. "*The Abbey Grange*, or Who Used Eustace?" *Baker Street Journal* 21, No. 4 (Dec. 1971): 215–220, 223.

Stavert, Geoffrey. "In the Wheelmarks of Violet Smith." *Sherlock Holmes Journal* 17, No. 4 (Summer 1986): 110–112.

Stix, Thomas L. "A Few Irreverent Remarks on *The Second Stain*." *Sherlock Holmes Journal* 6, No. 1 (Winter 1962): 19–20.

———. "A Little Dirt on *The Empty House*." *Baker Street Journal* 14, No. 2 (June 1954): 93–95.

Stowe, Thomas D. "More About Tires in *The Priory School.*" *Baker Street Journal* 16, No. 4 (Dec. 1966): 219–221.

Sutherland-Bruce, D. "The Von Herder Air-Rifle." *News from the Diggings* 3, No. 3 (Sept. 1982): 1–2.

Swift, Francine Morris. "The Depths to Which *What* Will Sink?" *Sherlockian Muse* 5, No. 4 (Spring 1981): 4–8.

Symons, T. H. B. "Some Notes on the Sixth Duke of Holdernesse." *Baker Street Journal* 9, No. 1 (Jan. 1959): 5–9.

Thornton, John P. and Susan M. "The Adventure of the Elusive Boundary Line: An Account of the Master's Encounter with Destiny in Central Asia." *Little Bookshop at the Corner of Church Street Journal* (1987): 1–12.

Torese, Dante M. "Firearms in the Canon: *The Adventure of the Dancing Men.*" *Baker Street Journal* 41, No. 1 (March 1991): 39–43.

Trudeau, Noah André. "The Second Most Dangerous Man in London—Dangerous to Whom?" *Baker Street Journal* 22, No. 2 (June 1972): 104–106, 119.

Utechin, Nicholas. "The Colonel of the Matter: The Early Career of Colonel Sebastian Moran." In BEYOND BAKER STREET, edited by Michael Harrison, 283–294. Indianapolis: Bobbs-Merrill Company, 1976.

———. "Some Remarkable Wines." *Baker Street Journal* 27, No. 3 (Sept. 1977): 142–145.

———. "The Tree That Wasn't." *Baker Street Journal* 22, No. 4 (Dec. 1972), 245–249.

Vaill, C. B. H. "Quick, Watson, the Needle!" *Baker Street Journal* [O. S.] 1, No. 4 (1946): 445–448.

Van Liere, Edward J. A DOCTOR ENJOYS SHERLOCK HOLMES. New York, Washington, Hollywood: Vantage Press, 1959.

VanValkenburgh, Norman J. "The Old Shikari." *Baker Street Journal* 31, No. 1 (March 1981): 14–19.

Varriano, Sue. "*Abbey Grange.*" *The Trigger Wire* 2, No. 2 (1980): 3–5.

Wagley, Philip Franklin, M.D. "A Lingering Mystery About the Norwood Affair." *Baker Street Journal* 22, No. 1 (Sept. 1972): 166–167.

Waldeck, John. "Windows on Baker Street." *Mycroft's Messenger* 27–28 (Oct.-Dec. 1981): 24–25. Expanded in TAILS OF THE GIANT RATS: SHERLOCKIAN MUSINGS BY THE GIANT RATS OF MASSILLON, edited by Hugh T. Harrington and Roy K. Preece, Jr., 50–56. Massillon, Ohio: The Village Bookshelf, 1990.

Ware, J. R. PASSING ENGLISH OF THE VICTORIAN ERA. New York: George Routledge & Sons [1909].

Warner, Richard. "The Scorcher and the Lady." *Baker Street Journal* 31, No. 3 (Sept. 1981): 145–147.

Warshauer, Richard. " 'My Friend, Wilson Hargreave,' " *Baker Street Journal* 23, No. 2 (June 1973): 113–115.

Waxenberg, Michael. "The Will of The Norwood Builder." *Baker Street Journal* 42, No. 1 (March 1992): 34–37.

Weiss, Jay, D.M.D., "Holmes as a Patient." *Baker Street Journal* 13, No. 2 (June 1963): 96–98.

Weller, Philip. "A Further Return to Mackleton: Some Considerations of 'On The Right Track,' " In INTERIM REPORT 1990: THE PRIORY SCHOOL CONTRACT REVIEWED, 5–8. Doncaster, England: Franco-Midland Hardware Company, 1990.

———. "The Geography of the Priory School." In ANNUAL REPORT 1990: THE PRIORY SCHOOL CONTRACT, 5–9. Doncaster, England: Franco-Midland Hardware Company, 1990.

———. "The Norfolk Dance Hall and Other Locations: The Geography of 'The Dancing Men.' " In ANNUAL REPORT 1997: THE DANCING MEN CONTRACT, 29–42. Doncaster, England: Franco-Midland Hardware Company, 1990.

———. "The Priority of The Priory School." *Baker Street Journal* 41, No. 4 (Dec. 1991): 203–206.

———. SHERLOCK HOLMES AND AIR-GUNS. Lee-on-the-Solent, Hampshire, England: Sherlock Publications (1995).

Wellman, Manly Wade. 'The Great Man's Great Son: An Inquiry into the Most Private Life of Mr. Sherlock Holmes." *Baker Street Journal* [O. S.] 1, No. 3 (July 1946): 326–336.

———. "Scoundrels in Bohemia." *Baker Street Journal* 4, No. 4 (Oct. 1954): 232–238.

White, Peter. "Who Dunnit: A Look at *The Second Stain.*" *Camden House Journal* 11, No. 1 (Jan. 1989): 2–3.

Whitlam, Carol M. "Holmes and Agatha." *Shoso-In Bulletin* 4 (Summer 1994): 94–95.

Whitlam, Carol. "Researching the Coal-Tar Derivatives." *Musgrave Papers* 1 (1988): 30–33.

Wigglesworth, Belden. "The French Background of Sherlock Holmes: Aspects and Possibilities." In THE SECOND CAB, edited by James Keddie, Jr. 39–45. Boston: Privately printed, 1947.

Wilde, Percival. "The Bust in the Window." *Baker Street Journal* [O. S.] 3, No. 3 (July 1948): 300–305.

———. DESIGN FOR MURDER. New York: Random House, 1941.

Williams, H. B. "A Non-Canonical Clue." In ILLUSTRIOUS CLIENT'S THIRD CASE-BOOK, edited by J. N. Williamson and H. B. Williams, 94–99. Indianapolis: Illustrious Clients, 1953.

Williamson, Jerry Neal. "The Sad Case of Young Stamford." *Baker Street Journal* [O. S.] 3, No. 4 (Oct. 1948): 449–451.

Wilson, Alan. " 'Son of Escott.' " *Baker Street Journal* 10, No. 3 (July 1960): 161–163.

Wilson, Evan M. "Sherlock Holmes and Diplomacy, or the Not So Singular Contents of the European Secretary's Dispatch-Box." *Baker Street Journal* 24, No. 2 (Jun 1974): 94–98.

Woodhead, Ed S. "In Defense of Dr. Watson." *Baker Street Journal* [O. S.] 1, No. 4 (1946): 417–422.

Woods, Carol Paul. "The Statement of Obadiah Wilson." *Baker Street Journal* 34, No. 4 (Dec. 1984): 221–223.

Yates, Donald A. "On the Dating of *The Dancing Men*." *Baker Street Journal* 42, No. 4 (Dec. 1992): 221–223.

Young, Francis Albert. "Upon the Identification of Cardinal Tosca." *Baker Street Journal* 4, No. 2 (June 1964): 80.

Yuichi, Hirayama. "The More Deeply Sunk Impression." *Nezire Zanmai International* 1 (Sept. 1991): 5–10.

Yuichi, Hirayama, and John Hall. SOME KNOWLEDGE OF BARITSU: AN INVESTIGATION OF THE JAPANESE SYSTEM OF WRESTLING USED BY MR. SHERLOCK HOLMES. Huddersfield, England: Northern Musgraves, 1996.

HIS LAST BOW

Allen, F. A., M.P.S. "Devilish Drugs, Part One." *May and Baker Pharmaceutical Bulletin*, Dec. 1956. Reprinted in *Sherlock Holmes Journal* 3, No. 13 (Autumn 1957): 12–14.

Anderson, Verner. "Radix Pedis Diabolis: A Speculative Identification." *Sherlock Holmes Journal* 12, No. 2 (Winter 1975): 54–55.

Armstrong, Walter P., Jr. "The Truth About Sherlock Holmes." *Baker Street Journal* [O. S.] 1, No. 4 (Oct. 1946): 391–401.

Asher, Richard. "Malingering." *Sherlock Holmes Journal* 4, No. 2 (Spring 1959): 54–58.

Asimov, Isaac. "The Problem of the Blundering Chemist." *Science Digest* 88 (1980), 8–17.

Beckemeyer, Doyle W. "The Irregular Holmes." *Baker Street Journal* 2, No. 1 (Jan. 1952): 18–20.

Beerman, Herman. "Malingering What Hath Man Wrought!" In MORE LEAVES FROM THE COPPER BEECHES, 181–192. Litiz, PA: Sutter House, 1976.

Bell, H. W. SHERLOCK HOLMES AND DR. WATSON: THE CHRONOLOGY OF THEIR ADVENTURES. London: Constable & Co., 1932.

Bengis, Nathan L. "Sidney Johnson—Suspect." *Sherlock Holmes Journal* 2, No. 3 (Summer 1955): 24.

———. "Take a Bow, Dr. Watson." *Baker Street Journal* 8, No. 4 (Oct. 1958): 218–229.

Benton, John L. "Dr. Watson's Automobile." *Baker Street Journal* 39, No. 2 (June 1989): 79–80.

———. "That Weird Kitchen at Wisteria Lodge." *Sherlockian Meddler* 10, No. 3 (1985): 7–9.

Berdan, Marshall S. "Watson and Shaw: Subtle Echoes in the Canon." *Baker Street Journal* 39, No. 4 (Dec. 1989): 206–208.

Bigelow, S. Tupper. "Sherlock Holmes Was No Burglar." *Baker Street Journal*, Christmas Annual (1958): 26–37.

Blake, S. F. "Sherlock Holmes and the Italian Cipher." *Baker Street Journal* 9, No. 1 (Jan. 1959): 14–20.

Blau, Peter. " 'It Is An Old Manuscript.' " *Baker Street Miscellanea* 14 (June 1978): 18–20.

Blaustein, Albert P. "Sherlock Holmes: Was Conan Doyle's Famed Detective a Lawyer?" *American Bar Association Journal* 34, No. 6 (June 1948): 473–474. Reprinted as "Sherlock Holmes as a Lawyer." *Baker Street Journal* [O. S] 3, No. 3 (July 1948): 306–308.

Bonn, Ronald S. "The Problem of the Postulated Doctor." *Baker Street Journal* 14, No. 1 (March 1964): 14–21.

———. "*Radix Pedis Diaboli*." *Baker Street Journal* 18, No. 2 (June 1968): 90–93.

Boswell, Rolfe. "Squaring 'The Red Circle.' " *Baker Street Journal* 1, No. 3 (July 1951): 113–114.

Boucher, Anthony. "Introduction to Arthur Conan Doyle," THE FINAL ADVENTURES OF SHERLOCK HOLMES, Vol. I, edited by Edgar W. Smith, v-xviii. New York: Limited Editions Club, 1952.

Bruxner, Pamela. Introduction to THE CORNISH HORROR, edited by Pamela Bruxner, i. London: Sherlock Holmes Society of London, 1998.

———. "Some Devilish Locations." *Sherlock Holmes Journal* 18, No. 4 (Summer 1988): 114–118.

Butler, Allen H. "The Airship as Holmes's 'Warship of the Future.' " *Canadian Holmes* 15, No. 2 (Winter 1991): 32–36.

———. "Automobiles in *His Last Bow*." *Baker Street Journal* 38, No. 1 (March 1988): 29–31.

Callaway, J. S., U.S.N. "An Enquiry into the Identity of the Bruce-Partington Submarine," *Baker Street Journal* 21, No. 3 (Sept. 1971): 151–153.

Chorley, Jennifer. "1896–1964, 'The Wheel Has Come Full Circle.' " *Sherlock Holmes Journal* 6, No. 3 (Winter 1963): 89–90.

Clark, Benjamin S. "Mycroft, Come Back: All is Forgiven." *Baker Street Journal* 21, No. 3 (Sept. 1971): 169–174.

Clark, Benjamin, Jr. "Holmes on the Range." *Baker Street Journal* 3, No. 2 (Apr. 1953): 91–97.

Clark, Edward F., Jr. "*Wisteria Lodge* Revisited (A Model Cop, a Model Laundry Item, and a Not-So-Model Culinary Artist)." *Baker Street Journal* 31, No. 1 (March 1981): 24–31.

Collie, Sir John, M.D., J.P. MALINGERING AND FEIGNED SICKNESS. London: Edward Arnold, 1913.

Cooper, Peter, F.P.S. "The Devil's Foot: An Excursion into Holmesian Toxicology." *Pharmaceutical Journal* 197 (Dec. 1966): 657–658. Reprinted in *Sherlock Holmes Journal* 8, No. 2 (Spring 1967): 59–61, and *Baker Street Journal* 18, No. 2 (June 1968): 94–96.

Coppola, Joseph A. "Submarine Technology and the Bruce-Partington Adventures." *Baker Street Journal* 43, No. 3 (Sept. 1993): 146–151.

Crelling, Jack. "The Mystery of the Bruce-Partington Plans." *Camden House Journal* 10, No. 6 (June 1988): 2–3.

Cross, Melvin. "The Lantern of Sherlock Holmes." *Baker Street Journal* [O. S.] 1, No. 4 (Oct. 1946): 433–442.

Crump, Norman. "Inner or Outer Rail?" *Sherlock Holmes Journal* 1, No. 1 (May 1952): 16–23.

Cummings, Thayer. "A Check on Lady Frances." *Baker Street Journal* 5, No. 3 (July 1955): 133–138. Reprinted in Cummings, Thayer, SEVEN ON SHERLOCK, 23–26. New York: Privately printed, 1968.

Curjel, Harald. "The Site of Von Bork's House." *Sherlock Holmes Journal* 11, No. 1 (Winter 1972): 26–28.

Dahlinger, S. E. "Of Mites and Men." CASE FILES OF SHERLOCK HOLMES: THE DYING DETECTIVE, edited by Christopher and Barbara Roden, 41–52. Ashcroft, B.C.: Calabash Press, 1998.

Davies, Bernard. "The Ancient Cornish Language." In THE CORNISH HORROR, edited by Pamela Bruxner, 21–33. London: Sherlock Holmes Society of London, 1997.

———. "Ever-Decreasing Circles: A Slight Case of Railway Mania." *Sherlock Holmes Railway Journal*, 3 (1995): 5–25.

———. "Three Distressed Gentlewomen." A GAGGLE OF GOVERNESSES, edited by Pamela Bruxner, 1–29. London: Sherlock Holmes Society of London, 1997.

Davies, David Stuart. "Why Did He Use Watson?" In CASE FILES OF SHERLOCK HOLMES: THE DYING DETECTIVE, edited by Christopher and Barbara Roden, 83–89. Ashcroft, B.C.: Calabash Press, 1998.

Davis, Norman M. "The Adventure of the American Interlude." *Baker Street Journal* 33, No. 1 (March 1983): 10–16.

Decarie, Graeme. "The Singular Case of *His Last Bow*." *Canadian Holmes* 15, No. 3 (Spring 1992): 32–34.

Dickensheet, Dean W. "On the Victorian Reticence of John H. Watson, M.D.," *Baker Street Miscellanea* 22 (Summer 1980): 16–19, 38.

Dietz, Henry A. "Murillo and San Pedro: An Excursion in Identification." *Baker Street Journal* 39, No. 3 (Sept. 1989): 153–168.

Doyle, Arthur Conan. ADVENTURE OF THE DEVIL'S FOOT. Edited and annotated by Philip Weller. Lee-on-the-Solent, Hampshire: Sherlock Publications, 1995.

———. ADVENTURE OF THE DYING DETECTIVE. London: Westminster Libraries and the Arthur Conan Doyle Society, 1991.

———. DISAPPEARANCE OF LADY FRANCES CARFAX. Edited and annotated by Philip Weller. Lee-on-the-Solent, Hampshire: Franco-Midland Hardware Company, 1995.

———. HIS LAST BOW: SOME REMINISCENCES OF SHERLOCK HOLMES. Edited with an Introduction by Owen Dudley Edwards. Oxford and New York: Oxford University Press, 1993.

———. THE LATER ADVENTURES OF SHERLOCK HOLMES. New York: Limited Editions Club, 1952. Introduction by Rex Stout, reproduced in INTRODUCING SHERLOCK HOLMES, edited by Edgar W. Smith, v–xi. Morristown, N.J.: Baker Street Irregulars, 1959.

———. A VISIT TO THREE FRONTS. London, New York, and Toronto: Hodder and Stoughton, 1916.

Doyle, Steven, writing as Spencer C. Kennedy. "*Adventure of the Red Circle*: An Examination of the Original Manuscript." *Sherlock Holmes Review* 1, No. 1 (1986): 8–9.

Drazen, Patrick. "That Old Black Magic." *Camden House Journal* 2, No. 3 (March 1980): 2–3.

Ehrenkranz, N. Joel. "A. Conan Doyle, Sherlock Holmes, and Murder by Tropical Infection." *Review of Infectious Diseases* 9, No. 1 (Jan.-Feb. 1987): 222–225.

Ennis, Robert S. "Devil's Foot or Angel Dust?" *Baker Street Journal* 42, No. 2 (June 1992): 89–92.

"Exotic Diseases." *The Practitioner* 222 (Apr. 1979): 442.

Fetherston, Sonia. "The Illuminated Man: Reflections on the Butler Staples." In CASE FILES OF SHERLOCK HOLMES: THE DYING DETECTIVE, edited by Christopher and Barbara Roden, 99–106. See above.

Foss, Lt. Colonel T. Frederick. "Doctor, Why Clobber the Colonels?" *Sherlock Holmes Journal* 12, Nos. 3 & 4 (Summer 1976): 82–83.

———. "The Farsighted Herr Von Bork." *Baker Street Journal* 30, No. 4 (Dec. 1980): 220–222.

Fraser, Cathy. "A Singular Set of People: The Characters in 'Wisteria Lodge.' " In ANNUAL REPORT 1992: THE WISTERIA LODGE CONTRACT, edited by Philip Weller, 7–10. Hampshire, England: Franco-Midland Hardware Company, 1992.

Fusco, Andrew G. "The Case Against Mr. Holmes." In BEYOND BAKER STREET, edited and annotated by Michael Harrison, 95–108. Indianapolis: Bobbs-Merrill Company, 1976.

Galerstein, David H. "A Solution to the Long Island Cave Mystery." *Baker Street Journal* 33, No. 4 (Dec. 1983): 233–234.

Geisser, Markus. "Pferdestärken im Canon." *Reichenbach Journal* 6 (Winter/Spring 1994).

Gore-Booth, Paul, ed. "The Bruce-Partington Keys." *Sherlock Holmes Journal* 2, No. 2 (Dec. 1954): 14–15.

Griffin, Daniel. "Emilia Lucca's Story." *Baker Street Journal* 15, No. 2 (June 1965): 97–102.

Grosbayne, Benjamin. "Sherlock Holmes—Musician." *Baker Street Journal* [O. S.] 3, No. 1 (Jan. 1948): 47–57.

Groves, Derham. "The Reason Behind the Reasoning." *Sherlock Holmes Journal* 12, No. 2 (Winter 1975): 67.

Hall, John. "His Payments Were Princely." In CASE FILES OF SHERLOCK HOLMES: THE DYING DETECTIVE, edited by Christopher and Barbara Roden, 90–97. Ashcroft, B.C.: Calabash Press, 1998.

Hall, Trevor H. "The Late Mr. Sherlock Holmes." In THE LATE MR. SHERLOCK HOLMES AND OTHER LITERARY STUDIES, 108–129. London: Gerald Duckworth & Co. Ltd., 1971.

———. "Sherlock Holmes, Madness and Music." In SHERLOCK HOLMES: TEN LITERARY STUDIES, 86–92. New York: St. Martin's Press.

Hammer, David L. "Sherlock Holmes: Secret Agent." *Baker Street Journal* 36, No. 4 (Dec. 1986): 231–234.

———. "The Twenty-Second Man." *Baker Street Journal* 38, No. 1 (March 1988): 18–22.

Harkinson, Judy. " 'A Chorus of Groans,' Notes Sherlock Holmes." *Smithsonian* 18, No. 6 (Sept. 1987): 196.

Hayes, Stephen. "There Was More Than One Rat in Sumatra." *Baker Street Journal* 24, No. 3 (Sept. 1974): 154–157.

Hayne, Donald, quoted in "The Editor's Commonplace Book." *Baker Street Journal* [O. S.] 1, No. 2 (Apr. 1946): 189–190.

Heldenbrand, Page. "A Ghostly Watson?" *Baker Street Journal* [O. S.] 3, No. 4 (Oct. 1948): 482–483.

Helling, Cornelis. "The True Author of 'His Last Bow' and 'The Mazarin Stone.' " *Sherlock Holmes Journal* 7, No. 4 (Spring 1966): 123–124.

Hogan, John V. L. "An Unsolved Puzzle in the Writings." *Baker Street Journal* 3, No. 3 (July 1953): 173–174.

Inman, Charles G. "Are There Really No Caves on Long Island?" *Baker Street Journal* 41, No. 4 (Dec. 1991): 218–219.

Iriarte, Antonio. "Spanish Silver and Spanish Eyes?" In ANNUAL REPORT 1996: THE LADY CONTRACT, edited by Philip Weller, 36–39. Hampshire, England: Franco-Midland Hardware Company, 1996.

James, Geoffrey. "Sherlock Holmes at the Marne." *Baker Street Journal* 38, No. 1 (March 1988): 25–28.

Jenkins, Walter S. "Tsutsugamushi to You, Dr. Ober." *Baker Street Journal* 18, No. 2 (June 1968): 84.

Jones, Bob. "A Missed Clue in *The Devil's Foot*." *Baker Street Journal* 41, No. 4 (Dec. 1991): 215–217.

Jordan, Anne. "Outward Appearances Can Be Deceptive." In ANNUAL REPORT 1992: THE WISTERIA LODGE CONTRACT, edited by Philip Weller, 22–23. Hampshire, England: Franco-Midland Hardware Company, 1992.

Kane, Alex. "A Question of Misogyny?" In INTERIM REPORT 1996: THE LADY CONTRACT REVIEWED, edited by Philip Weller, 19. Hampshire: Franco-Midland Hardware Company, 1996.

Kaser, Michael. "A Solution to 'Lady Frances Carfax.'" *Baker Street Journal* 9, No. 2 (Apr. 1959): 85–87.

Kass, David. "The Long Island Cave Mystery—Solved." *Baker Street Journal* 35, No. 1 (March 1985): 27–28.

Katz, Robert S. "It Is Horribly Contagious." *Baker Street Miscellanea* 59 (Fall 1989): 21–23.

Kean, Michael H. "The Politics of Defense." *Baker Street Journal* 43, No. 4 (Dec. 1993): 249.

———. WHO WAS BRUCE-PARTINGTON. Shelburne, Ontario: Battered Silicon Dispatch Box, 1998.

Klinger, Leslie S. "On Sherlock Holmes's Money." *New Baker Street Pillar Box* 22 (Spring 1995): 26–29.

Kluge, Mary Ann. "Looking Back at the 'Dying Detective.'" *Camden House Journal* 7, No. 7 (July 1985): 2.

Knox, Ronald A. "The Mystery of Mycroft." In BAKER STREET STUDIES, edited by H. W. Bell, 133–157. London: Constable & Co., 1934.

Koelle, George B. "The Poisons in the Canon." In LEAVES FROM THE COPPER BEECHES, edited by Ames Johnson, et al., 91–96. Narberth, PA: Livingston Pub. Co., 1959.

L'Etang, Hugh. "Some Observations on the Black Formosa Corruption and Tapanuli Fever." *Sherlock Holmes Journal* 4, No. 2 (Spring 1959): 58–60.

Lai, Rick. "The Savage Reversion." *Golden Perils* 6, No. 4 (May 1986): 22–25.

———. "The Tiger of Haiti." *Wheelwrightings* 8, No. 3 (Jan. 1986): 18–24.

Layng, Charles. "Watson's War with the Army." *Baker Street Journal* 2, No. 2 (Apr. 1952): 73–80.

Lellenberg, Jon L. "The *Magnum Opus* of His Latter Years." *Baker Street Journal* 37, No. 2 (June 1987): 71–74.

———. "'Touch Him Where You Would He Was False.'" *Baker Street Journal* 38, No. 1 (March 1988): 23–24.

Lithner, Klas. "San Pedro Revisited." *Baker Street Miscellanea* 50 (Summer 1987): 27–30.

Michaud, Rosemary. "All in Your Hands, Mr. Holmes." *Shoso-In Bulletin* 8 (Summer 1998): 162–168.

Michell, Humfrey. "Lady Frances Carfax Reappears." *Baker Street Journal* [O. S.] 2, No. 4 (Oct. 1947): 472.

———. "The Sartorial Sherlock Holmes." In A BAKER STREET FOUR-WHEELER, edited by Edgar W. Smith, 31–36. Maplewood, NJ, and New York: Pamphlet House, 1944.

Morley, Christopher. "Was Sherlock Holmes an American?" In 221B: STUDIES IN SHERLOCK HOLMES, edited by Vincent Starrett, 5–15. New York: Macmillan Co., 1940.

Morley, Felix. "The Significance of the Second Stain." In PROFILE BY GASLIGHT. edited by Edgar W. Smith, 243–259. New York: Simon & Schuster, 1944.

Morrow, Daniel. "What Were the Technical Papers, Mycroft?" *Scandal Sheet*, Jan. 1971, 2–4.

Nydell, Margaret (Omar), ed. "On the Chaldean Influences in Cornish." *Baker Street Journal* 45, No. 1 (March 1993): 24–30.

Ober, William B. "Conan Doyle's Dying Detective: Problem in Differential Diagnosis." *New York State Journal of Medicine* 67, No. 15 (Aug. 1967): 2141–2145.

Officer, Harvey. "Sherlock Holmes and Music." In 221B: STUDIES IN SHERLOCK HOLMES, edited by Vincent Starrett, 71–73. New York: Macmillan Co., 1940.

Olney, Professor Clarke. "The Literacy of Sherlock Holmes." *Sherlock Holmes Journal* 2, No. 4 (Winter 1955): 9–15.

Pachter, Josh. "Come Now, Gentlemen!" *Baker Street Journal* 20, No. 3 (Sept. 1970): 168–169.

Pratt, Fletcher. "Holmes and the Royal Navy." In THE SECOND CAB, edited by James Keddie, Jr., 65–69. Boston: Privately printed, 1947.

Purves, Shirley. "The Tin-Mining Tregennis Family." In THE CORNISH HORROR, edited by Pamela Bruxner, 35–37. London: Sherlock Holmes Society of London, 1997.

Purvis, Mark Hunter. "Was Holy Peters the Only Villain?" In ANNUAL REPORT 1996: THE LADY CONTRACT, edited by Philip Weller, 11–13. Hampshire, England: Franco-Midland Hardware Company, 1996.

Rannie, J. Alan. "The Railway Journeys of Mr. Sherlock Holmes." *Railway Magazine* 126 (May 1935): 316–321. Reprinted in *Sherlock Holmes Railway Journal* 5 (1997): 5–19.

Ravin, James G., M.D. "The Devil's-Foot Root Identified: Eserine." *Baker Street Journal* 32, No. 4 (Dec. 1982): 199–202.

Raymond, Trevor. "Quarter Days: St. Jean Baptiste Day." *Canadian Holmes* 16, No.

4 (1993): 1–4. Reprinted in CANADIAN HOLMES: THE FIRST TWENTY-FIVE YEARS, edited by Christopher Redmond, 193–198.

Redmond, Chris. "The Crime of Culverton Smith." *Wheelwrightings* 11, No. 1 (May 1988): 9–12.

Reed, John Shelton. "A Note on 'The Long Island Cave Mystery' Mystery." *Baker Street Journal* 19, No. 2 (June 1969): 112–113.

Rice, Rev. Otis R. "Clergymen in the Canon." *Baker Street Journal* 4, No. 3 (July 1954): 133–143.

Roden, Christopher. "A Study in Manuscript." In THE CASE FILES OF SHERLOCK HOLMES: THE DYING DETECTIVE, edited by Christopher and Barbara Roden, 137–144. Ashcroft, B.C.: Calabash Press, 1998.

Saxe, Stephen. "Tregennis and Poe." *Baker Street Journal* [O. S.] 1, No. 1 (Jan. 1946): 90–91.

Schulte, Heinz. "Sherlock Holmes and Foreign Spies." *Sherlock Holmes Journal* 20, No. 1 (Winter 1990): 27–29.

Schweickert, William P. "More Light on *Wisteria Lodge*." *Canadian Holmes* 12, No. 2 (Winter 1988): 19–20.

Sellars, Mrs. Crighton. "Altamont." *Baker Street Journal* [O. S.] 3, No. 1 (Jan. 1948): 59.

———. Letter. *Baker Street Journal* [O. S.] 4, No. 1 (Jan. 1949): 54–56.

Sewell, Gordon. "Holmes and Watson in the South Country." *Southern Daily Echo*, October 2, 1957. Reprinted in *Sherlock Holmes Journal* 3, No. 3 (Autumn 1957): 10–12.

Simon, André L., ed. WINES OF THE WORLD. New York, Toronto, London and Sydney: McGraw-Hill Book Company, 1967.

Smith, David P. "A Re-Examination of Sherlock Holmes at the Marne." *Baker Street Journal* 38, No. 4 (Dec. 1988): 206–208.

Smith, Edgar W. "Adventure of the Veiled Author." *Baker Street Journal* [O. S.] 1, No. 2 (Apr. 1946): 129–135.

———. "Dr. Watson and the Great Censorship." *Baker Street Journal* 2, No. 3 (July 1952): 138–151.

———. "On the Forms of Address." *Baker Street Journal* 9, No. 3 (July 1959): 131–132.

Smyth, Ian. "Not Where—But Why?" In SUNDAY IN SUSSEX, edited by Pamela Bruxner, n.p. London: Sherlock Holmes Society of London, 1993.

Solberg, Andrew L. "The Intertwining Chronologies of *The Illustrious Client* and *The Red Circle*." *Baker Street Journal* 44, No. 1 (March 1994): 28–32.

Speck, Gordon R. "Götterdämmerung and the 'New Woman': Twilight and Dawn in a Hazy Red Circle." *Camden House Journal* 12, No. 7 (July 1990): 2–3.

———. "Spy and Counterspy." *Camden House Journal* 5, No. 9 (Sept. 1983): 2–3.

Stacpoole-Ryding, Richard. "Undertaking Villainy." In INTERIM REPORT 1996:

THE LADY CONTRACT REVIEWED, edited by Philip Weller, 13–15. Hampshire, England: Franco-Midland Hardware Company, 1996.

Stajic, Marina, Ph.D. "However Improbable . . . ," In THE CORNISH HORROR, edited by Pamela Bruxner, 13–17. London: Sherlock Holmes Society of London, 1997.

Starrett, Vincent. "Explanation." In 221B: STUDIES IN SHERLOCK HOLMES, xi-xvi. New York: Macmillan Co., 1940.

———. "The Singular Adventures of Martha Hudson." In BAKER STREET STUDIES, edited by H. W. Bell, 85–130. London: Constable & Co., 1934.

Staubach, Edward R. "The Polyphonic Motets of Lassus." *Baker Street Journal* 44, No. 3 (Sept. 1994): 169–172.

———. "Taking Issue with Mr. Warrack." *Baker Street Journal* 48, No. 3 (Sept. 1998): 19–25.

Stevens, Cindy. "The Location of San Pedro." In ANNUAL REPORT 1992: THE WISTERIA LODGE CONTRACT, edited by Philip Weller, 47–49. Hampshire, England: Franco-Midland Hardware Company, 1992.

Swanson, Martin J. "Authorship Question." *Sherlock Holmes Journal* 5, No. 3 (Winter 1961): 94.

Thomas, Charles. MR. HOLMES IN CORNWALL, by "Percy Trevelyan." Redruth, Cornwall: Penwith Books, 1980.

Tracy, Jack. "Nota Pedis Diaboli." *Baker Street Journal* 25, No. 2 (June 1975): 101–104.

Tyler, Varro E., Jr. "The Physiological Properties and Chemical Constituents of Some Habit-Forming Plants: Devil's Foot Root, Radix Pedis Diaboli." *Lloydia* 29, No. 4 (Dec. 1966): 291–292. Referred to in *Sherlock Holmes Journal* 8, No. 2 (Spring 1967): 61, as a "letter to the *Pharmaceutical Journal*."

Ulrich, William. "Notes After an Evening in the Cave." *Prescott's Press* [N. S.] 15 (Sept. 1992): 7–8.

Wait, Richard. "The Case of the Neophyte and the Motet." In THE SECOND CAB, edited by James Keddie, Jr. . 70–72. Boston: Privately printed, 1947.

Walbridge, Earle F. "The Care and Feeding of Sherlock Holmes." In 221B: STUDIES IN SHERLOCK HOLMES, edited by Vincent Starrett, 54–68. New York: Macmillan Co., 1940.

Weber, John. "A Carfax Excursus." In INTERIM REPORT 1996: THE LADY CONTRACT REVIEWED, edited by Philip Weller, 8–10. Hampshire, England: Franco-Midland Hardware Company, 1996.

Weller, Philip. "The Lady Is Abroad," In INTERIM REPORT 1996: THE LADY CONTRACT REVIEWED, edited by Philip Weller, 3–6. Hampshire, England: Franco-Midland Hardware Company, 1996.

———. "The Lady Is at Home." In INTERIM REPORT 1996: THE LADY CONTRACT

REVIEWED, edited by Philip Weller, 43–50. Hampshire, England: Franco-Midland Hardware Company, 1996.

———. "Wistful Locations." In INTERIM REPORT 1992: THE WISTERIA LODGE CONTRACT REVIEWED, edited by Philip Weller, 10–13. Hampshire, England: Franco-Midland Hardware Company, 1992.

Weller, Philip, ed. ANNUAL REPORT 2000: THE DEVIL'S FOOT CONTRACT. Hampshire, England: Franco-Midland Hardware Company, 2000.

Wesson, Sheldon. "Light Upon the Candle." *Baker Street Journal* 38, No. 4 (Dec. 1988): 238–239.

White, William Braid. "Dr. Watson and the Peerage." *Baker Street Journal* [O. S.] 2, No. 1 (Jan. 1947): 18–23.

Wigglesworth, Belden. "The Road from Skibbareen." *Baker Street Journal* 7, No. 4 (Oct. 1957): 36–38.

Wills-Wood, Chris. "Disappearances and Revolutionaries: Some Considerations of the Plot of 'Wisteria Lodge.' " In ANNUAL REPORT 1992: THE WISTERIA LODGE CONTRACT, edited by Philip Weller, 3–6. Hampshire, England: Franco-Midland Hardware Company, 1992.

Wilson, Evan M. "Sherlock Holmes and Latin America: An Identification and Some Lovely Ladies." *Baker Street Journal* 22, No. 3 (Sept. 1972): 148–152.

Wolff, Julian. "I Have My Eye on a Suite in Baker Street." *Baker Street Journal* [O.S.] 1, No. 3 (July 1946): 296–299.

Wood, Peter H. "An Automatic Self-Adjusting Solution: Bruce-Partington Dives Again." *Baker Street Journal* 34, No. 3 (Sept. 1984): 166–172.

Wood, Willis B. "Sherlock in Kansas." In THE SECOND CAB, edited by James Keddie, Jr., 78–81. Boston: Privately printed, 1947.

Yates, Donald A. "A Final Illumination of the Lucca Code." *Baker Street Journal* 6, No. 3 (July 1956): 146–151.

THE CASE-BOOK OF SHERLOCK HOLMES

Adams, Rev. Stephen. "Holmes: A Student of London?" *Sherlock Holmes Journal* 2, No. 4 (Winter 1955): 17–18.

Aldrich, Dr. Frederick A. "The Great Jellyfish Which Killed Macpherson Lives Off Newfoundland," *Canadian Holmes* 4, No. 2 (Christmas 1980): n.p.

Alessandri, Tom. " 'My Own Chronicler': The Ageing Holmes." *Baker Street Journal* 28, No. 1 (March 1978): 44–45.

Alexander, Arthur M. HOT ON THE SCENT: A VISITOR'S GUIDE TO THE LONDON OF SHERLOCK HOLMES. Ashcroft, British Columbia: Calabash Press, 1999.

Allen, F. A., M.P.S. "Devilish Drugs, Part One." *Sherlock Holmes Journal* 3, No. 3

(Autumn 1957): 12–14. Reprinted from the May and Baker *Pharmaceutical Bulletin*, Dec. 1956.

Altick, Richard D. "Mr. Sherlock Holmes and Dr. Samuel Johnson." IN 221B: STUDIES IN SHERLOCK HOLMES, edited by Vincent Starrett, 109–120. New York: Macmillan Co., 1940.

Anderson, Poul. "Creeping in Samford." *Baker Street Journal* 49, No. 2 (June 1999): 40–45.

Andrew, Clifton. "My Old Friend Charlie Peace." *Sherlock Holmes Journal* 4, No. 4 (Spring 1960): 118–119.

———. "Sherlock Holmes on the Turf." In A BAKER STREET FOUR-WHEELER, edited by Edgar W. Smith, 38–42. Maplewood, NJ, and New York: Pamphlet House, 1944.

———. "That Scotland Yarder, Gregson—What a Help(?) He Was." In ILLUSTRIOUS CLIENT'S SECOND CASE-BOOK, edited by J. N. Williamson, 35–38. Indianapolis: Illustrious Clients, 1949.

Asher, Dr. Richard. "Holmes and the Fair Sex." *Sherlock Holmes Journal* 2, No. 3 (Summer 1955): 15–22.

Austin, Bliss. "Three Footnotes to 'Adventure of the Illustrious Client,'" In ILLUSTRIOUS CLIENT'S THIRD CASE-BOOK, edited by J. N. Williamson and H. B. Williams, 89–92. Indianapolis: Illustrious Clients, 1953.

———. "Thumbing His Way to Fame." *Baker Street Journal* [O. S.] 1, No. 4 (Oct. 1946): 424–432.

Ball, John. "The Pastiche in the Canon." In MORE LEAVES FROM THE COPPER BEECHES, 175–180. See above.

Batory, Dana Martin. "The Tail of the Sumatran Rat." *Baker Street Miscellanea* 26 (Summer 1981): 6–7, 10.

Beam, Thelma. "Emsworth's Illness Was Conversion Hysteria." *Canadian Holmes* 9, No. 1 (Autumn 1985): 7–9. Reprinted as "The Hysteria of Godfrey Emsworth" in CANADIAN HOLMES: THE FIRST TWENTY-FIVE YEARS, edited by Christopher Redmond, 116–118. Ashcroft, B.C.: Calabash Press, 1997.

Bengis, Nathan L. "Sherlock Stays After School." In ILLUSTRIOUS CLIENT'S SECOND CASE-BOOK, edited by J. N. Williamson, 72–78. Indianapolis: Illustrious Clients, 1949.

———. "Smothered Mate." *Baker Street Journal* 10, No. 4 (Oct. 1960): 216–220

Bengtsson, Hans-Uno. " 'It Needs Careful Handling.' " *Baker Street Journal* 44, No. 2 (June 1994): 82–90. Reprinted from *Trepiporsproblem och bagateller* [Three-pipe problem and trifling matters]. (In Swedish, 1993).

Bentley, E. C. THOSE DAYS. London: Constable & Co., Ltd., 1940.

Berg, Stanton O. "The Firearms-Safeties of Sherlockian-Victorian London," Part II. *Association of Firearm and Tool Mark Examiners (AFTE) Journal* 30, No. 4 (Fall 1998): 601–613.

Bigelow, S. Tupper. "Sherlock Holmes and Chess." *Sherlock Holmes Journal* 4, No. 1 (Winter 1958): 12–14.

———. "Sherlock Holmes Was No Burglar." *Baker Street Journal*, Christmas Annual (1958): 26–37

Blau, Peter E. "In Memoriam: Muzaffar Ad-Din." *Baker Street Journal* 24, No. 3 (Sept. 1974): 141–145.

———. "It Is an Old Manuscript: The Adventure of the Second Chip." *Baker Street Miscellanea* 26 (Summer 1981): 8–10.

Bogomoletz, Wladimir V. "The Case of the Two Coptic Patriarchs: A Reappraisal." *Baker Street Journal* 52, No. 2 (Summer 2002): 5–13.

Bond, Scott. "The 'Dreadful' Adventures of Charlie Peace." In A TOUCH OF THE CLASS, edited by Michael Kean, 9–15. Wilmette, IL: Pondicherry Press, 1981.

Boswell, Rolfe. Letter. Reported in "From the Editor's Commonplace Book." *Baker Street Journal* [O. S.] 2, No. 2 (Apr. 1947): 161–162.

Boucher, Anthony. "Prolegomena to a Holmesian Discography." *Baker Street Journal* 1, No. 2 (Apr. 1946): 229–231.

———. "The Records of Baker Street." *Baker Street Journal* [O. S.] 4, No. 1 (Jan. 1949): 97–104.

Bristowe, W. S. "The Giant Rat of Sumatra." *Sherlock Holmes Journal* 11, No. 4 (Autumn 1974): 136–137.

Brodie, Robert N. "A Prospect of Mincing Lane." *Wheelwrightings* 13, No. 2 (Sept. 1990): 15–16.

Brown, Richard. "Rejuvenation Therapy: Historical Background to *The Creeping Man*." *Canadian Holmes* 9, No. 2 (Winter 1985): 9–15.

Bryan-Brown, Frederick. "Sherlockian Schools and Schoolmasters." *Sherlock Holmes Journal* 3, No. 1 (Summer 1956): 2–7.

Byerly, Ann. "The Case of the Second Door." *Camden House Journal* 2, No. 11 (Nov. 1980): 3–5.

Cantor, Murray A. "The Eternal Feminine Rides Again." *Baker Street Miscellanea* 70 (Summer 1992): 25–27.

———. "Unintentional (?) Inconsistencies in 'The Illustrious Client.'" *Baker Street Miscellanea* 59 (Fall 1989): 34–37.

Caplan, Richard M., M.D. "The Curious Circumstance of the Missing Brother." *Baker Street Journal* 34, No. 3 (Sept. 1984): 136–138.

Chizar, David, Rozella B. Smith, and Lorna Simonsen. "Another Perspective on *The Adventure of the Mazarin Stone*." *Baker Street Journal* 26, No. 4 (Dec. 1976): 213–216.

Chorley, Jennifer. "Goodly Volumes . . ." *Sherlock Holmes Journal* 7, No. 4 (Spring 1966): 18–19.

Cirone, Nino. "Watson: Victorian Pirate." In THE WINNING ESSAYS: THE DR. JOHN H. WATSON ANNUAL PRIZE ESSAY COMPETITION, 2001, 2–14. Hertfordshire, England: Friends of Dr. Watson, 2002.

Clarke, Richard W. "On the Nomenclature of Watson's Ships." *Baker Street Journal* [O. S] 1, No. 2 (Apr. 1946): 119–121.

Cochran, William. "Re: The Shoscombe Spaniels." *Wheelwrightings* 13, No. 1 (May 1990): 28–30.

Cold, Jørgen. "What Did Sherlock Holmes Drink?" In ILLUSTRIOUS CLIENT'S THIRD CASE-BOOK, edited by J. N. Williamson and H. B. Williams, 110–118. Indianapolis: Illustrious Clients, 1953.

Cole, Eleanor S. "Holmes, Watson and the K-9's." *Baker Street Journal* 1, No. 1 (Jan. 1951): 25–29.

Cole, James A. "Maud Bellamy." *Baker Street Journal* 29, No. 2 (June 1979): 71–72.

Collins, William P. "Norbury and Steve Dixie: Holmes and Victorian Racial Attitudes." *Baker Street Journal* 27, No. 3 (Sept. 1977): 149–152.

Cooke, Catherine. "An Appeal on Behalf of the Jellyfish." In SUNDAY IN SUSSEX, edited by Pamela Bruxner, n.p. London: Sherlock Holmes Society of London, 1993.

———. " 'The Singular Facts Connected with Professor Presbury.' " In THE DARK IS LIGHT ENOUGH, edited by Jonathan McCafferty, 14–15. London: Sherlock Holmes Society of London, 1989.

Cooper, A. G. "Holmesian Humour." *Sherlock Holmes Journal* 6, No. 4 (Spring 1964): 109–113.

Cross, Leslie. "Sherlock Holmes, Writer: An Unsolved Case." *Baker Street Journal* 14, No. 1 (March 1964): 39–42.

Cypser, Darlene. "Barker, The Hated Rival." *Baker Street Journal* 35, No. 4 (Dec. 1985): 211–212.

Dandrew, Thomas. "The Love Life of That Creep Professor Presbury." *Naval Signals* 31 (June 1993): 3–5.

Darak, Greg. "Perfect Crime in 'The Blanched Soldier.' " *Baker Street Journal* 47, No. 4 (Dec. 1997): 26–29.

Davies, Bernard. "The Members for Berkshire." In FETLOCKS, FEMURS AND PHALANGES, edited by Pamela Bruxner, 3–32. London: Sherlock Holmes Society of London, 1995.

———. "South Down Solo." In SUNDAY IN SUSSEX, edited by Pamela Bruxner, n.p. London: Sherlock Holmes Society of London, 1993.

———. "Three Distressed Gentlewomen." In A GAGGLE OF GOVERNESSES, edited by Pamela Bruxner, 2–29. London: Sherlock Holmes Society of London, 1998.

Davis, Elmer. "On the Emotional Geology of Baker Street." In 221B: STUDIES IN SHERLOCK HOLMES, edited by Vincent Starrett, 37–46. New York: Macmillan Co., 1940.

Dickensheet, Dean W. and Shirley J. "A Remarkable Invention." *Baker Street Journal* 14, No. 4 (Dec. 1964): 208–215.

Donegall, Lord. "The Blanched Soldier, The Devil's Foot, and The Solitary Cyclist." *Sherlock Holmes Journal* 7, No. 1 (Winter 1964): 13–16.

Donnelson, Gar. "PLEASE GIVE THE YARD A CALL, WATSON." Lincoln, Neb.: Privately printed, 1986.

Dow, Jeff and Wanda. "Langurtin." *Baker Street Journal* 47, No. 3 (Sept. 1997): 32–34.

Doyle, Arthur Conan. ADVENTURE OF THE LION'S MANE. Facsimile of the manuscript. London: Westminster Libraries and Sherlock Holmes Society, 1992.

———. THE CASE-BOOK OF SHERLOCK HOLMES. Edited, with an introduction, by W. W. Robson. Oxford and New York: Oxford University Press, 1993.

———. THE CROWN DIAMOND, OR AN EVENING WITH SHERLOCK HOLMES. New York: Privately printed for the Baskerrette Press, 1958.

———. THE PROBLEM OF THOR BRIDGE. Edited and annotated by Philip Weller. Lee-on-the-Solent, Hampshire: Sherlock Publications, n. d.

———. Preface to SHERLOCK HOLMES: THE COMPLETE SHORT STORIES. London: John Murray, 1928.

Dudley, W. E. "Dr. Watson's Triple Play." *Baker Street Journal* 23, No. 1 (March 1973): 22–27.

———. "*The Mazarin Stone* and *The Empty House*." *Baker Street Journal* 27, No. 4 (Dec. 1977): 209–212.

———. "Who Was Neil Gibson?" *Baker Street Journal* 25, No. 3 (Sept. 1975): 173–176.

Duke, Michael. " 'My Summer Quarters.' " *Passengers' Log* 3, No. 4, and 4, No. 1 (Aug. and Oct. 2000): 47–50.

Eckrich, Joseph J. "Holmes and the Blanched Soldier." *Wheelwrightings* 11, No. 3 (Jan. 1989): 25–26.

Farmer, Philip José. DOC SAVAGE: HIS APOCALYPTIC LIFE. Garden City, N.Y.: Doubleday & Co., 1973.

Farrell, Stephen. "A Shot Towards the Light." In THE TRI-METALLIC QUESTION, edited by Peter Horrocks, 53–54. London: Sherlock Holmes Society of London, 1991.

Faurot, R. M. " 'Cut Out the Poetry, Watson.' " *Baker Street Journal* 30, No. 2 (June 1980): 77–82.

Feinberg, Samuel. "Will the Real Carina Please Stand Up?" *Baker Street Journal* 26, No. 2 (June 1976): 81–90.

Fenton, Irving. "On Friendship." *Baker Street Journal* 9, No. 1 (Jan. 1959): 23–25.

Fiedler, Judith. "In Memoriam—Baron Adelbert Gruner, 1860–1913." In THE ILLUSTRIOUS CLIENT'S SECOND CASE-BOOK, edited by J. N. Williamson, 79–82. Indianapolis: Illustrious Clients, 1949.

Folsom, Henry T. " 'My Biblical Knowledge is a Trifle Rusty! . . .' " *Baker Street Journal* 15, No. 3 (Dec. 1965): 174–182.

———. "Seventeen Out of Twenty-Three." *Baker Street Journal* 14, No. 1 (March 1964), 24–26.

Galbraith, A. S. "The Real Moriarty." *Baker Street Journal*, Christmas Annual (1957): 55–62.

Galerstein, David. " 'I Have the Right to Private Judgement.' " *Baker Street Journal* 24, No. 3 (Sept. 1974): 168–173.

Gore-Booth, Paul H. "The Journeys of Sherlock Holmes: A Topical Monograph." *Baker Street Journal* [O. S.] 3, No. 2 (Apr. 1948): 159–168.

Graham, R. P. "The Unknown Worm." *Baker Street Journal* [O. S.] 2, No. 2 (Apr. 1947): 212.

———. "Carina or Karina?" An Old Mystery Resolved." *Sherlock Holmes Journal* 22, No. 2 (Summer 1995): 47–48.

Green, Roger Lancelyn. " 'At the University': Some Thoughts on the Academic Experiences of Mr. Sherlock Holmes." *Sherlock Holmes Journal* 9, No. 4 (Summer 1970): 123–124.

Grosbayne, Benjamin. "Sherlock Holmes—Musician." *Baker Street Journal* [O. S.] 3, No. 1 (Jan. 1948): 47–57.

Haddon-MacRoberts, M. "The Mystery of the Third Plaster Skull." *Sherlock Holmes Journal* 16, No. 4 (Summer 1984): 113.

Hahn, Robert W. "Recount, Please, Mr. Holmes." *Baker Street Journal* 26, No. 4 (Dec. 1976): 209–212.

Hall, Trevor H. "The Book-Collector." In THE LATE MR. SHERLOCK HOLMES AND OTHER LITERARY STUDIES, 23–39.

———. "A College Friendship?" In SHERLOCK HOLMES: TEN LITERARY STUDIES, 93–108. New York: St. Martin's Press, 1970.

———. "Conan Doyle and Spiritualism." In SHERLOCK HOLMES AND HIS CREATOR, 91–143. London: Gerald Duckworth & Co., Ltd., 1978.

———. "Dr. Watson's Marriages." THE LATE MR. SHERLOCK HOLMES AND OTHER LITERARY STUDIES, 40–63. New York: St. Martin's Press, 1971.

———. "The Early Years of Sherlock Holmes." In SHERLOCK HOLMES: TEN LITERARY STUDIES, 18–35. New York: St. Martin's Press, 1970.

———. "The Erudition of Sherlock Holmes." In SHERLOCK HOLMES: TEN LITERARY STUDIES, 44–55. New York: St. Martin's Press, 1970.

———. "The Late Mr. Sherlock Holmes." In THE LATE MR. SHERLOCK HOLMES AND OTHER LITERARY STUDIES, 108–129. New York: St. Martin's Press, 1971.

———. "A Note on *The Priory School*." In SHERLOCK HOLMES: TEN LITERARY STUDIES, 123–141. New York: St. Martin's Press, 1970.

———. "The Problem of the Unpublished Cases." In THE LATE MR. SHERLOCK HOLMES & OTHER LITERARY STUDIES, 86–107. New York: St. Martin's Press, 1971.

———. "Sherlock Holmes: Ascetic or Gourmet?" In THE LATE MR. SHERLOCK

HOLMES & OTHER LITERARY STUDIES. London, 13–22. New York: St. Martin's Press, 1971.

———. "Sherlock Holmes's University and College." In SHERLOCK HOLMES: TEN LITERARY STUDIES, 56–85. New York: St. Martin's Press, 1970.

Hammer, David L. "A Second Case of Identity." *Baker Street Miscellanea* 43 (Autumn 1985): 21–24.

Hanson, C. W., Jr. "Some Remarks upon Watson's Absence from 'The Adventure of the Blanched Soldier,' or Hansen's Disease Revisited." In MORE LEAVES FROM THE COPPER BEECHES, 151–160. Lititz, PA: Sutter House, 1976.

Harbottle, S. T. L. " 'My Charges are on a Fixed Scale . . . '?" *Sherlock Holmes Journal* 2, No. 1 (July 1954): 22–24.

Hardenbrook, Don, writing as Gaston Corday Huret III. "The Laughter of Sherlock Holmes." *Shoso-In Bulletin* 7 (1997): 182–187.

Haynes, George. "The Last Mrs. Watson." *Sherlock Holmes Journal* 6, No. 2 (Spring 1963): 53.

Healy, Grant. "The Observance of Trifles—7. Langdale Pike." *Sherlockian* 1, No. 3 (Sept. 1987): 40–42.

Hedgpeth, Joel. "Re-Examination of the Adventure of the Lion's Mane." *Baker Street Journal* [O. S.] 3, No. 3 (July 1948): 285–294.

———. "Who Was Isadora Persano ? Or, A Poet's (?) Revenge." In WEST BY ONE AND BY ONE, edited by Poul Anderson, 44–50. San Francisco: Privately printed, 1965.

Heifetz, Carl L. "Regarding the True Ætiology of the Skin-Lightening Syndrome in 'The Adventure of the Blanched Soldier.' " *Holmes and Watson Report* 1, No. 7 (March 1998): 42–48.

Heldenbrand, Page. "A Ghostly Watson?" *Baker Street Journal* [O. S.] 3, No. 4 (Oct. 1948): 482–483.

Herzog, Evelyn. "Eugenia Ronder." *Baker Street Journal* 29, No. 2 (June 1979): 72.

Hicks, John L. "No Fire Without Some Smoke." *Baker Street Journal* 5, No. 1 (Jan. 1955): 27–33.

Higgins, W. W. "Some Further Notes on the Garridebs." *Plugs & Dottles*, No. 154 (July 1991): 4–5.

Hinrich, Derek. "The Politician, the Lighthouse and the Trained Cormorant: An Hypothesis." *Sherlock Holmes Journal* 21, No. 1 (Winter 1992): 22–23.

Holland, Glenn. "A Left-Handed Defence of 'The Three Gables.' " *Baker Street Pages* 48 (March 1969): 2–4.

Holly, Raymond L. "A Pythagorean Theory." *Baker Street Journal* 37, No. 2 (June 1987): 81–86.

———. "The Three Real Garridebs." *Baker Street Miscellanea* 50 (Summer 1987): 23–26.

———. "Where Was Abbas Parva?" *Camden House Journal* 3, No. 4 (Apr. 1981): 2.

———. "Windows, Doors, and the Bridge of Fools." *Camden House Journal* 12, No. 9 (Sept. 1990): 2–3.

Hollyer, Cameron. "Murk IV Meets Watson the Benedict." *Canadian Holmes* 7, No. 1 (Autumn 1983): 5–11. Reprinted as "How Many Wives Did Watson Wed? A Study in Computation," in CANADIAN HOLMES: THE FIRST TWENTY-FIVE YEARS, edited by Christopher Redmond, 69–73. Ashcroft, B.C.: Calabash Press, 1997.

Holstein, Leon S. " '7. Knowledge of Chemistry-Profound,' " *Baker Street Journal* 4, No. 1 (Jan. 1954): 44–49.

Hunt, A. Godfrey. "An Essex Adventure." *Sherlock Holmes Journal* 21, No. 1 (Winter 1992): 15–20.

Hunter-Purvis, Mark. "The Real Problem of Thor Bridge." In ANNUAL REPORT 1995: THE THOR BRIDGE CONTRACT, edited by Philip Weller, 9–12. Hampshire, England: Franco-Midland Hardware Company, 1995.

Hyder, William. "The Martha Myth." *Baker Street Journal* 41, No. 1 (March 1991): 9–19. Revised and expanded, "The Martha Myth," in FROM BALTIMORE TO BAKER STREET, 126–140. Toronto: Metropolitan Toronto Reference Library, 1995.

Inman, Charles G. "Roy: Russian or Irish?" *Baker Street Journal* 43, No. 1 (March 1993): 7–8.

Jackson, Robert, M.D. "Sir James Saunders: A Case of Identity." Paper presented at the Fourth Annual Meeting of the Sir James Saunders Society in Dallas, Tex., Dec. 5, 1977, noted in Thomsen, Robert J., "Holmes's Service for Sir James Saunders."

James, Garry. "Shooting the Guns of Sherlock Holmes." *Handguns for Sport & Defence* 5, No. 10 (Oct. 1991): 70–75.

James, Garry, and Scott MacMillan. "The Guns of Sherlock Holmes." *Guns & Ammo* 19, No. 4 (Apr. 1975): 50–53, 83.

Jewell, Donald Girard. A TROUT IN THE MILK: A MONOGRAPH ON FISH AND FISHING IN THE TIME OF SHERLOCK HOLMES. Westminster, Md.: Pinchin Lane Press, 1991.

Johnson, C. Arnold. "A Well-Known Criminal Investigator." *Mycroft's Messenger* 8 (Aug. 1978): 4–5.

Johnson, Roger. "Boats and Bathing Cots." In SUNDAY IN SUSSEX, edited by Pamela Bruxner, n.p. London: Sherlock Holmes Society of London, 1993.

Jones, Bob. " 'It Was From the Carlton Club.' " *Baker Street Journal* 33, No. 1 (March 1983): 19–22.

Jones, Kelvin I. THE CARFAX SYNDROME: BEING A STUDY IN VAMPIRISM IN THE CANON. New York: Magico Magazine, 1984.

———. "A Talent for Crime." *Wheelwrightings* 4, No. 3 (Jan. 1982): 23–27.

Kaser, Michael C. "Sherlock Holmes on the Continent." *Baker Street Journal* 6, No. 1 (Jan. 1956): 19–24.

Katz, Robert S. "John H. Watson, M.D.: The Non-Surgical Surgeon." *Baker Street Journal* 38, No. 4 (Dec. 1988): 223–225.

Keefauver, Brad. "He Must Have Been Lucky at Cards: One More Look at Watson's Wives." *Wheelwrightings* 10, No. 2 (Sept. 1987): 5–14.

———. "Why There Are No Garridebs." *Plugs & Dottles* 153 (June 1991): 4–5.

———. "The Worm Unknown." *Camden House Journal* 9, No. 3 (March 1987): 2–3.

Kelly, Norman. "Sotheby's & Christie's: Fact or Fiction." *Wheelwrightings* 4, No. 2 (Sept. 1981): 8–9.

Klinefelter. Walter. EX LIBRIS A. CONAN DOYLE: SHERLOCK HOLMES. Chicago: Black Cat Press, 1938.

Klinger, Leslie S. "Art in Whose Blood?" *The Ritual* 21 (Spring 1998): 3–7.

———. "Layout of a 'Most Desirable Residence.'" *Shoso-In Bulletin* 6 (1996): 78–81.

———. "Paging Through the Canon." *Wigmore Street Post Office Journal* 12 (Summer 1998): 12–14.

Kluge, Mary Ann. "Combing the Lion's Mane." *Camden House Journal* 5, No. 7 (July 1983): n.p.

Kobayashi, Tsukasa, and Akane Higashiyama. "The Original Holmes." *Baker Street Journal* 38, No. 3 (Sept. 1988): 135–143.

Koelle, George B. "The Poisons of the Canon." In LEAVES FROM THE COPPER BEECHES, 91–96. See above.

Kozinn, Sondra D. "Dog Gonnit." *Baker Street Journal* 43, No. 2 (June 1993): 120.

Kupferberg, Herbert. "Adventure of the Bodiless Virtuoso." *Baker Street Journal* 14, No. 4 (Dec. 1964): 201–207. Reprinted from *High Fidelity Magazine*, May 1958.

Lachtman, Howard. "Vigor: A Case for Identity." *Baker Street Journal* 27, No. 1 (March 1977): 37–40.

Lai, Rick. "Lowenstein's Other Client." *Wheelwrightings* 7, No. 3 (Jan. 1985): 10–14.

Lauterbach, Charles E., and Edward S. Lauterbach. "The Man Who Seldom Laughed." *Baker Street Journal* Christmas Annual No. 5 (1960): 265–271.

Lavazzi, Charles. "Sherlock Holmes, High-Fidelity Pioneer or, The Advent of a Shure Thing." *Baker Street Journal* 39, No. 1 (March 1989): 36–38.

Leavitt, Robert Keith. "Annie Oakley in Baker Street." In PROFILE BY GASLIGHT, edited by Edgar W. Smith, 230–242. New York: Simon & Schuster, 1944.

———. "Who Was Cecil Forrester?" *Baker Street Journal* [O. S.] 1, No. 2 (Apr. 1946): 201–205.

Leonard, Patrick J., Sr. "Thor Bridge—A Mystery Remains." *Prescott's Press* [N. S.] 11 (Sept. 1991): 16–20.

Leonard, William. "Re: Vampires." *Baker Street Journal*, Christmas Annual (1957): 20–25.

Levine, Arthur L. "Lowenstein's Other Creeper." *Baker Street Journal* 6, No. 1 (Jan. 1956): 30–33.

Mackler, Allen. "Carina: An Identification." *Baker Street Miscellanea* 3, (Sept. 1975): 4–5.

Malloy, Michael P. "Tobacco Amblyopia and Holmes." *Baker Street Journal* 26, No. 2 (June 1976): 94–98, 117.

Marshall, Guy. "The Horrendous Hiatus of Vanderbilt and the Yeggman." *Sherlock Holmes Journal* 15, No. 1 (Winter 1980): 21–24.

Mason, Bill. "Dead? Not Hardly." *Holmes & Watson Report* 5, No. 3 (July 2001): 30–36.

McCafferty, Jonathan. "Where Thor Art Thou?" In The Tri-Metallic Question, edited by Peter Horrocks, 46–49. London: Sherlock Holmes Society of London, 1991.

———. "Will The Creeping Man Stand Up?" In The Dark is Light Enough, edited by Jonathan McCafferty, 33–34. London: Sherlock Holmes Society of London, 1989.

McCallister, David R. "Sherlock Holmes's 'Hated Rivals.'" *Baker Street Miscellanea* 72 (Winter 1992): 14–18.

McCauley, Gordon. "On Barker, the Rival." *Canadian Holmes* 7, No. 3 (Spring, 1984): 22–23.

McGinley, E. W. The Firearms of Sherlock Holmes. Syracuse, N.Y.: Privately printed, 1994.

McLaren, R. M. "Doctor Watson—Punter or Speculator?" *Sherlock Holmes Journal* 1, No. 1 (May 1952): 8–10.

McLauchlin, Russell. "Apocryphal?" *Baker Street Journal* [O. S.] 1, No. 4 (Oct. 1946): 475–476.

Meaker, Samuel R., M.D., M.R.C.S. "Watson Medicus." In The Third Cab, 26–37. Boston: Privately printed, 1960.

Merriman, Charles O. "In Search of Sherlock Holmes." *Sherlock Holmes Journal* 8, No. 1 (Winter 1966): 7–12.

Metcalfe, N. P. "Oxford or Cambridge or Both?" *Baker Street Journal*, Christmas Annual (1956): 7–14.

Metcalfe, Percy. "Holmes's University Career—A Reassessment." *Sherlock Holmes Journal* 9, No. 4 (Summer 1970): 125–130.

Meyer, Charles A. "A Footnote to the Adventure of the Retired Colourman." *Baker Street Miscellanea* 54 (Summer 1988): 25–26.

———. "The Haven: Lewisham's Answer to Chicago's 'Murder Castle.'" *Baker Street Miscellanea* 58 (Summer 1989): 29–32.

———. "The Real Creeps in 'The Adventure of the Creeping Man.'" *Naval Signals* 30 (March 1993): 3–8.

———. "The Rehabilitation of the Creeping Man." *Baker Street Miscellanea* 69 (Spring 1992): 23–26.

Michell, Humfrey. Letter. *Baker Street Journal* 4, No. 3 (July 1954): 197–198.

Miller, William G. "The Mystery of the Indelible Pencil." *Baker Street Journal* 21, No. 3 (Sept. 1971): 175–176.

Monahan, Eric. BANKING AND FINANCE IN THE CANON. Paignton, Devon: Parallel Publications, 1997.

Montgomery, James. "Man or Mountain." In SHOTS FROM THE CANON, 5. Philadelphia: Privately printed, 1953.

Morley, Christopher. "Clinical Notes by a Resident Patient." *Baker Street Journal* [O. S.] 1, No. 4 (Oct. 1946): 404–408.

———. "Clinical Notes by a Resident Patient." *Baker Street Journal* [O. S.] 2, No. 2 (June 1947): 141.

———. "Clinical Notes by a Resident Patient." *Baker Street Journal* 4, No. 3 (July 1954): 152–153.

———. "Watson à la Mode." *Baker Street Journal* [O. S.] 1, No. 1 (Jan. 1946): 15–20.

Morrow, Daniel. "Barker of Baker Street." *Scandal Sheet* 1, No. 3 (Apr. 1972): 2–3.

Newton, G. B. "Billy the Page." *Sherlock Holmes Journal* 2, No. 3 (Summer 1955): 7–10.

———. "Concerning the Authorship of 'The Mazarin Stone.'" *Sherlock Holmes Journal* 4, No. 2 (Spring 1959): 52–54.

Niver, Harold. "The Dracula Legend and the Sussex Vampire." *Calabash* 4 (Sept. 1983): 1–14.

Norland, James J., M.D. "A Little White Error." *The Formulary* 8 (June 2000): 32–35.

Oates, Jonathan. "Sherlock Holmes in Lee and Lewisham." *Sherlock Holmes Journal* 24, No. 1 (Winter 1998), 6–13.

O'Brien, Thomas F. "Re: Vampires, Again." *Baker Street Journal* 37, No. 3 (Sept. 1987): 154–158.

Palmer, Stuart. "Notes on Certain Evidences of Caniphobia in Mr. Sherlock Holmes and His Associates." *Baker Street Journal* 5, No. 4 (Oct. 1955): 197–204.

"Penang Lawyer, A." "The Name's the Same." *Sherlock Holmes Review* 2, No. 1 (July 1954): 11–13.

Pennell, Vernon. "A Resumé of the Medical Life of John H. Watson, M.D., Late of the Army Medical Department." *Sherlock Holmes Journal* 3, No. 2 (Winter 1956): 6–11.

Petersen, Svend. "When The Game Was Not Afoot." *Baker Street Journal* [O. S.] 4, No. 1: 59–71.

Pond, Walter. "A Pleas for Respect for the Canon with Some Observations on *The Three Gables*." *Baker Street Journal* 28, No. 1 (March 1978): 41–42.

Porter, Philip. "The Inns and Outs of Cambridge." In THE DARK IS LIGHT ENOUGH, edited by Jonathan McCafferty, 16–17. London: Sherlock Holmes Society of London, 1989.

Potter, H. C. "The Veiled Lodger Revisited." *Baker Street Journal* 22, No. 3 (Sept. 1972): 158–166.

Prager, J. C., and Albert Silverstein. "Lowenstein of Prague: The Most Maligned Man in the Canon." *Baker Street Journal* 23, No. 4 (Dec. 1973): 220–227.

Radford, John. "The Strange Flight of Sherlock Holmes." *Musgrave Papers* 4 (1991): 21–26.

Ramamurthy, T. V. "The Case of the Awkward Pencil." *Sherlock Holmes Journal* 1, No. 4 (Dec. 1953): 41–42.

Ravin, James G. "Wainwright Was No Mean Artist." *Baker Street Journal* 37, No. 1 (March 1987): 37–40.

Redmond, Christopher. "Disease Grips Him After Night in Strange Bed: Notes on *The Blanched Soldier*," *Canadian Holmes* 8, No. 3 (Spring 1985): 15–17.

———. "The Prosthesis Fixation of Dr. John H. Watson (Or: Stop, You're Pulling My Wooden Leg!)." *Canadian Holmes* 5, No. 2 (Christmas 1981): 15–19.

———. "Still Sits the Cormorant." *Sherlock Holmes Journal* 11, No. 2 (Summer 1973): 58–63.

———. "Where He Got a Name: The Man Lived in Canada." *Canadian Holmes* 5, No. 1 (Autumn 1981): 2–3.

Reed, Linda J. "A Private Matter." *Wheelwrightings* 9, No. 1 (May 1986): 18–20.

Rendall, Vernon. "The Limitations of Sherlock Holmes." In BAKER STREET STUDIES, edited by H. W. Bell. London, 63–84. London: Constable & Co., 1934.

Rhode, Franklin. "Langdale Pike and Steve Dixie: Two Cases of Identity." *Baker Street Journal* 20, No. 1 (March 1970): 17–20.

———. " 'My Old Friend Charlie Peace.' " *Baker Street Journal* 16, No. 2 (June 1966): 77–80.

Rosenblatt, Julia C. "The Secret Love of Sherlock Holmes." *Baker Street Miscellanea* 5 (March 1976): 1–7.

Rosenblum, Morris. "The Horatian Spirit in Holmes." In ILLUSTRIOUS CLIENT'S THIRD CASE-BOOK, edited by J. N. Williamson and H. B. Williams, 119–126. Indianapolis: Illustrious Clients, 1953.

Rothman, Steven. "How Come a Bull Ring?: A Brief Investigation." *Baker Street Journal* 35, No. 3 (Sept. 1985): 170–171.

Ryan, Alan, ed. THE PENGUIN BOOK OF VAMPIRE STORIES. New York: Doubleday & Company, Inc., 1987; Penguin Books, 1988.

Saltzman, Shulamit. "The Other Watson." *Baker Street Journal* 28, No. 1 (March 1978): 6–9.

Sayers, Dorothy L. "Dr. Watson, Widower." UNPOPULAR OPINIONS, 152–167. London: Victor Gollancz, 1946.

Scheideman, J. W. "On Behalf of an Anonymous Gentleman." *Baker Street Journal* 28, No. 3 (Sept. 1978): 137–140.

———. "The Tension Between Fact and Fancy: Re: A Letter to Sherlock Holmes from Morrison, Morrison & Dodd." *Vermissa Herald* 8, No. 2 (Apr. 1974): 2–3.

Schenck, Remsen Ten Eyck. "Baker Street Fables." *Baker Street Journal* 2, No. 2 (Apr. 1952): 85–92.

Schutz, Robert H. "My Old Friend . . . ?" *Baker Street Journal*, Christmas Annual (1960): 286–288.

Sellars, Crighton. "Dr. Watson and the British Army." *Baker Street Journal* [O. S.] 2, No. 3 (July 1947): 332–336.

Shepherd, Walter. "Barker, Not Holmes." *Sherlock Holmes Journal* 13, No. 2 (Summer 1977): 63–64.

Shreffler, Philip A. "Moriarty: A Life Study." *Baker Street Journal* 23, No. 2 (June 1973): 92–96.

Silberman, Carl M., M.D. "A Short Monograph on *The Blanched Soldier.*" *Baker Street Journal* 23, No. 3 (Sept. 1973): 152–155.

Silverstein, Albert, ed. "The Cornish Horrors Descend on *Thor Bridge.*" *Baker Street Journal* 30, No. 3 (Sept. 1980): 136–140.

Singleton, Paul. "Notes on The Creeping Man." *Prescott's Press* [N.S.] 11 (Sept. 1991): 10–11.

Simpson, Helen. "Medical Career and Capacities of Dr. J. H. Watson." In BAKER STREET STUDIES, edited by H. W. Bell, 35–61. London: Constable & Co., 1934.

Smith, E. B., and H. Beerman. "Sherlock Holmes and Dermatology." *International Journal of Dermatology* 16 (1977): 433–438.

Smith, Edgar W. "From the Editor's Commonplace Book." *Baker Street Journal* 2, No. 2 (Apr. 1952): 115–120.

———. "The Other Giant." *Baker Street Journal* 1, No. 3 (July 1951): 81–82.

Smith, Francis. "The Only Selfish Action I Can Recall." *Sherlock Holmes Journal* 9, No. 4 (Summer 1970): 134–135.

Sovine, J. W., M.D. "The Toxicanon." *Baker Street Journal* 8, No. 2 (Apr. 1958): 107–112.

Speck, Gordon R. "The Adventure of the Sussex Vampire: Hoax, Jokes, and Hubris." *Baker Street Miscellanea* 32 (Winter 1982): 7–9, 24.

Starr, H. W. "Some New Light on Watson." *Baker Street Journal* [O. S.] 1, No. 1 (March 1946): 55–63.

Stavert, Geoffrey. "I Thought I Thor Thor Bridge." In THE TRI-METALLIC QUESTION, edited by Peter Horrocks, 42–45. London: Sherlock Holmes Society of London, 1991.

Stern, Madelaine. "Sherlock Holmes: Rare-Book Collector: A Study in Book Detection." *The Papers of the Bibliographical Society of America* 97 (1953): 133–155.

Stoker, Bram. DRACULA. New York: Signet, 1992.

Swanson, Martin J. "Graphologists in the Canon." *Baker Street Journal* 12, No. 2 (June 1962): 73–80.

Swift, Francine and Wayne. " 'He has the name of being a Dangerous Man': Inquiries into the Identity of Sir Robert Norberton." In FETLOCKS, FEMURS AND PHALANGES, edited by Pamela Bruxner, 47–49. London: Sherlock Holmes Society of London, 1995.

———. "Shoscombe Prince." *Baker Street Journal* 45, No. 3 (Sept. 1995): 147–156.

Swift, Wayne B. "The Great Yellow Diamond." *Baker Street Journal* 29, No. 1 (March 1979): 21–24.

Thomsen, Robert J. "Holmes's Service for Sir James Saunders." *Baker Street Journal* 41, No. 4 (Dec. 1991): 230–234.

Torese, Dante M. "Firearms in the Canon: The Guns of Sherlock Holmes and John H. Watson." *Baker Street Journal* 42, No. 3 (Sept. 1992): 154–157.

Utechin, Nicholas. SHERLOCK HOLMES AT OXFORD. 2nd. ed. Oxford: Robert Dugdale, 1981.

Van Zanten, Rob, and Liz Evans. "A Foregone Conclusion." *News from the Diggings* 9, No. 4 (Dec. 1988): 4.

Walwyn, Brett. "The Truth About Gruner." *Canadian Holmes* 8, No. 3 (Spring 1985): 3–4.

Warner, Richard S. "To Simpson—A Canonical Hero." *Baker Street Journal* 32, No. 1 (March 1982): 16–18.

Webb, Keith E. "Baron Grunner [*sic*] Receives an Answer." *Shoso-In Bulletin* 3 (Aug. 1993): 6–7.

Weber, John. "Summer's Lease." *The Musgrave Papers* 12 (1999): 52–66.

Webster, H. T. "Observations on Sherlock Holmes as an Athlete and Sportsman." *Baker Street Journal* [O. S.] 3, No. 1 (Jan. 1948): 24–31.

Weller, Philip. SHERLOCK HOLMES AND AIR-GUNS. Hampshire, England: Sherlock Publications, 1995.

———. "Over the Alps with Holmes." In THE TRI-METALLIC QUESTION, edited by Peter Horrocks, 50–52. London: Sherlock Holmes Society of London, 1991.

———. "Watson's Pocket Cannon." In ANNUAL REPORT 1995: THE THOR BRIDGE CONTRACT REVIEWED, 29–36. Hampshire, England: Franco-Midland Hardware Company, 1995.

Wetherbee, Winthrop. "The Third Continent: Further Light on Dr. Watson." *Baker Street Journal* 2, No. 3 (July 1952): 124–134.

Whitaker, Joseph, ed. WHITAKER'S ALMANACK, 1900. London: J. Whitaker & Sons Ltd.

Williamson, J. N. "The Latest Treatise on Pathology." *Baker Street Journal* 6, No. 4 (Oct. 1956): 208–214.

Wincor, Richard. "The Sherlock Holmes Opening." *Baker Street Journal* 15, No. 2 (June 1965): 92–94.

Wolff, Julian. "Remember the Mane?" *Baker Street Journal* [O. S.] 3, No. 4 (Oct. 1948): 471–473.

Wood, Willis B. "Sherlock in Kansas." In THE SECOND CAB, edited by James Keddie, Jr., 78–81. Boston: Privately printed, 1947.

Woollcott, Alexander. "The Baker Street Irregulars." In LONG, LONG AGO, 172–175. New York: The Viking Press, 1943.

Wortman, B. Dean. "The Two-Author Theory of *The Blanched Soldier*." *Baker Street Journal* 38, No. 3 (Sept. 1988): 158–159.

Yuichi, Hirayama, and Mizuochi Masako. "Another Solution of *The Lion's Mane*." *Nezire Zanmai International* 2 (1992): 22–25.

NOTES FOR SCHOLARS

T HERE ARE SIGNIFICANT differences between this edition and Baring-Gould's classic *Annotated Sherlock Holmes*. Baring-Gould emphasised the "chronology" of the stories—the dates on which the events recounted in the stories actually occurred—and devoted a significant portion of his notes to that topic. Sherlockian "chronologisation" is a complex science, and I have not intended to belittle the efforts of the chronologists by summarising and relegating their work to an appendix following the text. However, to point out all of the "clues" used by various chronologists in reaching their conclusions would have multiplied the notes exceedingly. Students of the techniques of devising a chronology are advised to read Andrew Jay Peck's introduction to *The Date Being—?: A Compendium of Chronological Data*, available in an expanded and revised edition by Judge Peck and this editor.

There are at least three starting points for a modern textual analysis of each story: the *Strand Magazine* version, the original English book version, and the original American book version, which have surprising differences. Also important to any student of the text are the *Oxford Sherlock Holmes*, edited generally by Owen Dudley Edwards, and the Heritage (Limited Editions Club) edition of the Canon, edited by Edgar W. Smith. Both purport to present "definitive" text, the former with notes. My own version of the text relies most heavily on the English book text of the stories, under the theory that these versions received the most careful review from the author. However, "careful" review is a relative term, and numerous textual problems exist. In my notes, I have indicated significant variations among the sources.

While an examination of the original manuscript of the story, to review changes made by the author before submission for publication, would be very valuable, of the 56 stories, only 37 manuscripts are extant, and all but 13 are in the hands of private collectors, unavailable to students. Five of the manuscripts have been published in facsimile, "The Priory School," "The Dying Detective," "The Lion's Mane," "Shoscombe Old Place," and "The Six Napoleons." Scholars have examined a few manuscripts *in situ* and published their notes, and I have taken advantage of those available resources. In an apparent scholarly "first," I was also able to compare a typescript of the author's manuscript of "The Six Napoleons" to the published version and note significant changes made *after* submission of the manuscript.

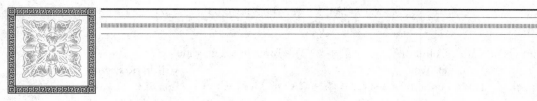

Active Sherlockian Societies*

Geographical†

The Sydney Passengers

AU NS Sydney

Bill Barnes
19 Malvern Avenue
Manly, N.S.W. 2095
AUSTRALIA

The Sherlock Holmes Society of Australia

AU SA Adelaide

Alan C. Olding
P.O. Box 13
Stirling, S.A. 5152
AUSTRALIA

The Elementary Victorians

AU VI Melbourne

Steve Duke
P.O. Box 340
Reservoir, Vic. 3073
AUSTRALIA

The Sherlock Holmes Society of Melbourne

AU VI Melbourne

Michael Duke
3 Gillies Street
Hampton, Vic. 3188
AUSTRALIA

Japan Sherlock Holmes Club
(Midland Branch, Melbourne Office)

AU VI Sandringham

Shin-ichi Enomoto
19/122 Beach Road
Sandringham, Vic.
3191
AUSTRALIA

The Sherlock Holmes Society of Western Australia

AU WA Perth

Douglas Sutherland-
Bruce
P.O. Box 554
Mundaring, W.A. 6073
AUSTRALIA

The 221Bees

BE Lummen

Ivo Dekoning
Goeslaerstraat 45
3560 Lummen
BELGIUM

The Singular Society of the Baker Street Dozen

CA AB Calgary

Charles Prepolec
3805 Marlborough
Drive NE #D-308
Calgary, AB T2A 5M4
CANADA

The C.P.R. Stockholder's Society

CA AB Edmonton

Barry Patchett
2015 104-A Street
Edmonton, AB T7J 5A6
CANADA

The Binomial Theorists of Nanaimo

CA BC Nanaimo

W. E. Ricker
3052 Hammond Bay Road
Nanaimo, BC V9T 1E2
CANADA

*Thanks to Peter E. Blau for the compilation of all of the scion societies. For updates, the reader is referred to http://members.cox.net/sherlock1/Sherlocktron.html.

†The letters beneath the society name indicate the postal codes for country, state or province, and the full name of the primary city.

The Stormy Petrels of British Columbia
Peter H. Wood
CA BC Vancouver   1525 Pendrell Street #201
Vancouver, BC V6G 1S6
CANADA

The Great Herd of Bisons of the Fertile Plains
Ihor Mayba
CA MB Winnipeg   6 Melness Bay
Winnipeg, MB R2K 2T5
CANADA

The Halifax Spence Munros
Mark J. Alberstat
CA NS Halifax   5 Lorraine Street
Dartmouth, NS B3A 2B9
CANADA

The Whodunit Society
Michael Shumacher
CA ON London   95 Ridout Street
South London,
ON N6C 3X3
CANADA

Capital Holmes
Sheila Vaudrey
CA ON Ottawa   215 Chandler
Ottawa, ON K2C 0G3
CANADA

The Bootmakers of Toronto
Edwin Van der Flaes
CA ON Toronto   47 Manor Road West
Toronto, ON M5P 1E6
CANADA

The Midland Electric Company
Bob Coghill
CA ON Toronto   65 Coe Hill Drive #2
Toronto, ON M6S 3E2
CANADA

The Bimetallic Question
Wilfrid de Freitas
CA QC Montreal   Box 883
Stock Exchange Tower
Montreal, QC H4Z 1K2
CANADA

Regina's Irregulars
Brian S. Brodie
CA SK Regina   2720 Thornton Avenue
Regina, SK S4S 1J1
CANADA

The Casebook of Saskatoon
William A. S. Sarjeant
CA SK Saskatoon   Department of Geological
Sciences
University of Saskatchewan
Saskatoon, SK S7N 5E2
CANADA

Ceska spolecnost Sherlocka Holmese
(The Czech Sherlock Holmes Society)
Ales Kolodrubec
CZ Prague   130 00 Praha 3
Milesovska 1   CZECH REPUBLIC

The A. C. Doyle & Sherlock Holmes Society of
Copenhagen
Michael Morton
DE Copenhagen   DK-2620 Albertslund
Loevens Kvarter 4 A   DENMARK

Sherlock Holmes Klubben i Danmark
(The Danish Baker Street Irregulars)
Bjarne Nielsen
DE Copenhagen   Sherlock Holmes Museet,
Algade 3
DK-4500 Nykobing
Sjaelland
DENMARK

The Great Greenland Expedition Society
Bjarne Nielsen
DE Nykobing
Sjaelland
Sherlock Holmes Museet,
Algade 3
DK-4500 Nykobing
Sjaelland
DENMARK

The Copenhagen Speckled Gang
Mia Stampe
DK Copenhagen
(scion of S.H. Klubben)
Hellebaekgade 19 (3.tv.)
2000 Copenhagen N
DENMARK

La Societe Sherlock Holmes de France
Thierry Saint-Joanis
FR Paris
26 avenue de la
Republique
75011 Paris
FRANCE

Les Evades de Dartmoor
François Hoff
FR Strasbourg
19 rue de Marechal Joffre
F-67000 Strasbourg
FRANCE

Le Cercle Litteraire de l'Escarboucle Bleue
Jean-Paul Cabot
FR Toulouse
Ecole Chateau d'Ancely
4 allee du Vivarais
31300 Toulouse
FRANCE

221b: Deutscher-Sherlock-Holmes-Club
Olaf H. Maurer
GE Ludwigshafen
P.O. Box 150314
67028 Ludwigshafen am
Rhein
GERMANY

The Sherlock Holmes Society of India
Ramesh C. Madan
IN New Delhi
Hill View Apartments #B-33
Vasant Vihar, New Delhi
110057
INDIA

The Sherlock Holmes Society of Jerusalem
Moshe Nalick
IS Jerusalem
Kiryat Telshe-Stone 114/3
D.N. Harei Yehuda
ISRAEL

Uno Studio in Holmes
Francesco Leprai
IT Florence
Via Aurelia Antica 268
58046 Marina di Grosseto
(GR)
ITALY

The Japan Sherlock Holmes Club
(Marronier Branch)
Kumeo Nakajima
JA Ashikaga
(scion of JSHC)
8-1 Tsukiya-cho
Ashikaga City, Tochigi 326
JAPAN

The Saitama-Chiba Union
Fujiko Ohata
JA Chiba
(scion of JSHC)
1-23-11 Goko
Matsudo-shi, Chiba 270
JAPAN

The Doshisha University Sherlock Holmes Club
Ai Masugi
JA Doshisha University
(scion of JSHC)
16 Ohmiya-ichinoicho
Kita-ku, Kyoto 603
JAPAN

The Japan Sherlock Holmes Club (Fukuoka Branch)
Shigehide Hayashi
JA Fukuoka
(scion of JSHC)
4-38-10 Hibaru, Minami-ku
Fukuoka-shi, Fukuoka 815
JAPAN

The Society of the Three Schoolgirls

JA Hiroshima
(scion of JSHC)

Kakuko Harada
7-24 Eba-Honmachi,
   Naka-ku
Hiroshima-shi, Hiroshima
   730-0833
JAPAN

The Gacho Club

JA Ibaraki
(scion of JSHC)

Yukari Iijima
1-2-47 Namiki
Tsuchiura-shi, Ibaraki 300
JAPAN

The Japan Sherlock Holmes Club
(Kamakura Branch)

JA Kanagawa
(scion of JSHC)

Izumi Hirabayashi
1-16-20-216 Shichirigahama
Kamakura-shi, Kanagawa
   248-0026
JAPAN

The Gloria Scott

JA Kobe
(scion of JSHC)

Tomoji Ohta
5-3-1 Shimosawa-dori,
   Hyogo-ku
Kobe-shi, Hyogo 652
JAPAN

The Bohemian Club

JA Kumamoto
(scion of JSHC)

Yuko Maeda
1974-7 Asouda,
   Shimizu-machi
Kumamoto-shi,
   Kumamoto 860
JAPAN

The Japan Sherlock Holmes Club
(Midland Branch)

JA Nagoya
(scion of JSHC)

Yasuki Kawasaki
1-3-3-C-2 Ikeshita,
   Chikusa-ku
Nogoya-shi, Aichi 464-0067
JAPAN

The Red Circle of Niigata

JA Niigata
(scion of JSHC)

Yukio Yamazaki
1-24-14 Uchino-nishi
Niigata-shi, Niigata 950-21
JAPAN

The Adventure of the Empty House Club

JA Okayama
(scion of JSHC)

Sadako Saito
1941-1 Ugaki, Mizu-cho
Mizu-gun, Okayama 709-21
JAPAN

The Japan Sherlock Holmes Club
(Western Area Branch)

JA Osaka
 (scion of JSHC)

Saburo Hiraga
3-6-24 Ueno-higashi
Toyonaka-shi, Osaka 560
JAPAN

The Silver Blaze Society

JA Saitama
 (scion of JSHC)

Yoshiki Miyasaka
2-130-3-307 Suno-cho
Omiya-shi, Saitama 330
JAPAN

The Sendai Holmesian Society

JA Sendai City
 (scion of JSHC)

Masayuki Kikuchi
3-24-3 Katsura, Izumi-ku
Sendai-shi, Miyagi 981-31
JAPAN

The Japan Sherlock Holmes Club

JA Tokyo

Tsukasa Kobayashi
Ohizumi-machi 2-55-8
Nerima-ku, Tokyo 178
JAPAN

The Japanese Cabinet

JA Tokyo

Yuichi Hirayama
2-10-12 Kamirenjaku,
   Mitaka-shi
Tokyo 181-0012
JAPAN

The Men with the Twisted Konjo
          Yuichi Hirayama
JA Tokyo   2-10-12 Kamirenjaku,
          Mitaka-shi
          Tokyo 181-0012
          JAPAN

The Baritsu Society of Japan
          Kiyoshi Tanaka
JA Tokyo   8-7 Baba-cho, Isogo-ku
(scion of JSHC)   Yokohama City,
          Kanagawa 235
          JAPAN

The Black-Headed League
          Masamichi Higurashi
JA Tokyo   3-13-7-305 Nishikubo
(scion of JSHC)   Musashino, Tokyo 180
          JAPAN

The Tokyo Nonpareil Club
          Ryoichi Ando
JA Tokyo   1-14-1-412 Kamoi,
(scion of JSHC)   Midori-ku
          Yokohama-shi, Kanagawa
          226
          JAPAN

The Seventeen Steppes
          Loudmila Konkova
KY Osh   Kurmanjan-Datka Str 271
          Osh Oblast Library, Soros
          Res. Ctr.
          KYRGYZSTAN 714000

The Antipodean Holmesian Society
          Ted Nye
NZ Dunedin   51 Irvine Road, the Cove
          Dunedin
          NEW ZEALAND

Os Naufragos do Norah Creina
[The Norah Creina Castaways]
          Joel Lima
PO Lisbon   Largo do Mastro 29-3,
          Porta D
          1100 Lisboa
          PORTUGAL

The Ural Holmesian Society
          Alexander Shaburov
RU Ekaterinburg Ul. Cherepanova 4-334
          Ekaterinburg 620034
          RUSSIA

Circulo Holmes
          Joan Proubasta
SP Barcelona Camelies 83, 1.o 3.a
          08024 Barcelona
          SPAIN

The Amateur Mendicant Society of Madrid
          Miguel Gonzalez Pedel
SP Madrid   Modesto Lafuente 18 (6B)
          28010 Madrid
          SPAIN

The Swedish Pathological Society
          Joakim Eklund
SWE Goteborg Bogatan 37-A
          S-412 72 Goteborg
          SWEDEN

The Baskerville Hall Club of Sweden
          Anders Wiggstrom
SWE Stockholm Byggmastarvagen 29
          S-168 32 Bromma
          SWEDEN

The Fierce Badgers in Ystad
          Lars Jannedal
SWE Ystad   Hagermansgatan 16
          S-261 32 Ystad
          SWEDEN

Societe d'etudes holmesiennes de la Suisse
romande

	Vincent P. Delay
SWI Lausanne	Chemin de la Chaumiere 1
	CH-1010 Lausanne
	SWITZERLAND

The Reichenbach Irregulars

	Roger Biemann
SWI Meiringen	Dammstrasse 61
	CH-8702 Zollikon b/Zurich
	SWITZERLAND

The Abbey Grangers of Chislehurst

	Colin Prestige
UK EN Chislehurst	22 Pelham Court,
	145 Fulham Road
	London SW3 6SH
	ENGLAND

The Cardboard Boxers of Croydon

	Andrew A. P. Butler
UK EN Croydon	8 Park Hill Road
	Croydon, Surrey CR0 5NA
	ENGLAND

The Baskerville Hounds

	Philip Weller
UK EN Dartmoor	6 Bramham Moor, Hill Head
	Fareham, Hampshire
	PO14 3RU
	ENGLAND

The Poor Folk Upon the Moors

	Clare Taylor
UK EN Dartmoor/	2 Lynbridge Court,
Exeter/Totnes	Chapel Street
	Tavistock, Devonshire
	PL19 8DU
	ENGLAND

The Franco-Midland Hardware Company

	Philip Weller
UK EN Doncaster	6 Bramham Moor,
(West Midlands)	Hill Head
	Fareham, Hampshire
	PO14 3RU
	ENGLAND

The Priory Scholars of Leicester

	Philip Weller
UK EN Leicester	6 Bramham Moor,
(East Midlands)	Hill Head
	Fareham, Hampshire
	PO14 3RU
	ENGLAND

The Sherlock Holmes International Society

	John Aidiniantz
UK EN London	The Sherlock Holmes
	Museum
	221b Baker Street
	London NW1 6XE,
	ENGLAND

The Sherlock Holmes Society of London

	Bob Ellis
UK EN London	13 Crofton Avenue
	Orpington, Kent BR6 8DU
	ENGLAND

The Merton Lodgers

	Brian F. Scrivener
UK EN London	94 Reigate Avenue
(Merton)	Sutton, Surrey SM1 3JJ
	ENGLAND

The Glades of the New Forest

	Emma Barrow
UK EN New Forest	87 East Avenue
(Hampshire)	Bournemouth, Dorset
	BH3 7BJ
	ENGLAND

The East Anglian Dancing Men (and Women)
Geoff Budd
UK EN Norwich
28 Bissley Drive
(East Anglia)
Maidenhead, Berks.
SL6 3U2
ENGLAND

The Fratton Lodgers
Ian Smyth
UK EN Portsmouth
31 Sandfield Crescent
Cowplain, Hampshire
ENGLAND

The Retired Colourmen of Essex
Jolyon Hunt
UK EN
21 Mount Avenue
Southend-on-Sea
Westcliff-on-Sea, Essex
SS0 8PS
ENGLAND

The Head Llamas
Alan and Catherine Saunders
UK EN Staines
12 Booth Drive, Laleham
(Surrey/Middlesex)
Staines, Middlesex
TW18 1PR
ENGLAND

The Northern Musgraves
John Addy
UK EN York
23 East Street, Lightcliffe
Halifax, W. Yorks. HX3 8TU
ENGLAND

The Crew of the S.S. May Day
Oscar Ross
UK NI Belfast
19 Ardcarn Way
Belfast BT5 7RP,
Northern Ireland
UNITED KINGDOM

The Genius Loci
Lee Eric Shackleford
US AL Birmingham
Box 55704
Birmingham, AL
35255-5704

The Arkansas Valley Investors, Ltd.
Jason Rouby
US AR Little Rock
11 McKinley Circle
Little Rock, AR
72207-6333

Harding Brothers of High Street
Paul D. Haynie
US AR Searcy
Box 12247
Harding University
Searcy, AR 72149-0001

The Desert Beekeepers
Doris and Richard Dale
US AZ Fountain Hills
Box 18635
Fountain Hills, AZ
85269-8635

The Family of Col. Moran
Gordon H. Palmer
US CA Agoura
111 Apache Circle
Thousand Oaks, CA
91362-3210

The Loungers and Idlers of the Empire
Edna Jukofsky
US CA Arcadia
5316 Huddart Avenue
Arcadia, CA 91006-5953

The Diogenes Club of the Monterey Peninsula
Michael H. Kean
US CA Carmel-
3040 Sloat Road
by-the-Sea
Pebble Beach, CA
93953-2837

The Goose Club of the Alpha Inn [California]
John P. Sohl
US CA Culver City   20446 Orey Place
Winnetka, CA 91306-4246

Bow Street Runners
Fred H. Holt
US CA Fresno   350 Minnewawa Avenue
#133
Clovis, CA 93612-0958

The Wax Vestas of the Dartmoor Professor
Michael J. Brady
US CA La Puente   8551 California Avenue
Whittier, CA 90605-1518

The Trained Cormorants of Long Beach, California
Jim Coffin
US CA Long Beach   6570 East Paseo Alcazaa
Anaheim Hills, CA
92807-4910

The Curious Collectors of Baker Street
Jerry and Chrys Kegley
US CA Los Angeles   110 El Nido Avenue #41
Pasadena, CA 91107-4442

The Wisteria-Hysteria
Marilyn Genaro
US CA Los Angeles   19944-A Sherman Way
Winnetka, CA 91306-3606

The Knights of the Gnomon
Richard R. Rutter
US CA Redwood City   Rock Creek Court
Redwood City, CA
94602-4051

The Napa Valley Napoleons of S.H.
Donald A. Yates
US CA Saint Helena   555 Canon Park Drive
Saint Helena, CA
94574-9726

The Christopher Morley Whiskey & Sodality Club
Steven E. Whiting
US CA San Diego   9528 Miramar Road #180
San Diego, CA 92126-4599

The Grimpen Admirers of Sherlock Holmes
Steven E. Whiting
US CA San Diego   9528 Miramar Road #180
San Diego, CA 92126-4599

The Noble West Enders
Jim Ferreira
US CA San Francisco   573 Oriole Avenue
Livermore, CA 94550-2684

The Persian Slipper Club of San Francisco
Raymond A. de Groat
US CA San Francisco   19147 Crest Avenue
Castro Valley, CA
94546-2816

The Scowrers and Molly Maguires of San Francisco
Jim Ferreira
US CA San Francisco   753 Oriole Avenue
Livermore, CA 94550-2684

The Tigers of San Pedro
John Farrell
US CA San Pedro   25314 Woodward Avenue
Lomita, CA 90717-2250

The Pips of Orange County
Robert A. Dunning
US CA Santa Ana   2025 Martha Lane
Santa Ana, CA 92706-3219

The Scion of the Green Dragon
Mary Ellen and
US CA Santa Maria   Walt Daugherty
1305 Mira Flores Drive
Santa Maria, CA 93455-5609

The Legends of the West Country

Howard Lachtman

US CA Stockton 926 West Mendocino Avenue

Stockton, CA 95204-3024

The Cardboard Boxers of Susanville

William Ballew

US CA Susanville Box 1954

Susanville, CA 96130-1954

The Blustering Gales from the South-West

Paula Salo

US CA Torrance 4421 Pacific Coast Highway #E-112

Torrance, CA 90505-5646

Dr. Watson's Neglected Patients

Mark G. Langston

US CO Denver 1143 South Monaco Parkway

Denver, CO 80224-1809

The Winter Assizes at Norwich

Charles A. Adams

US CT Bozrah 60 River Road

East Haddam, CT 06423-1403

The Men on the Tor

Harold E. Niver

US CT East Haddam Baskerville Hall

29 Woodhaven Road

Rocky Hill, CT 06067-1045

The Yale Sherlock Holmes Society

David F. Musto

US CT New Haven Box 207900

New Haven, CT 06520-7900

The Red Circle of Washington, D.C.

Peter E. Blau

US DC Washington 7103 Endicott Ct.

Bethesda, MD 20817-4401

The Salon Pistols of Gainesville

Robert Zuczek

US FL Gainesville 3942 N.W. 65th Avenue

Gainesville, FL 32653-8368

The Tropical Deerstalkers

Robert S. Ennis

US FL Miami 3455 Stallion Lane

Weston, FL 33331-3035

Sherlock Holmes' Dumber Brothers

Richard Bryer

US FL North 2026 Gray Court
Fort Myers Fort Myers, FL 33903-6436

The Pleasant Places of Florida

Carl L. Heifetz

US FL Saint 1220 Winding Willow Drive
Petersburg New Port Richey, FL 34655-7120

The House of Stuart: The Sherlockian Society of the Treasure Coast

Mr. S. Holmes

US FL Stuart Box 221

Palm City, FL 34990-0221

The Plant Plotters

Ann Evelyn Morris

US FL Tampa1 2524 Lovers Lane

Riverview, FL 33569-6813

The Confederates of Wisteria Lodge

Mary Leonard

US GA Atlanta Mycroft Manor

1265 Willow Park Way

Cumming, GA 30041-7911

The Keepers of the Bullpup

Ira Block

US GA Madison 406 Pine Street

Madison, GA 30650-1614

The Andaman Islanders
          Marcia Eveland
US HI Honolulu   94-444 Hokuili Street
          Mililani, HI 96789-2309

The Priory School Dropouts
          B. Dean Wortman
US IA Ames   223 Lynn Avenue
          Ames, IA 50014-7166

The Younger Stamfords
          Richard M. Caplan
US IA Iowa City   708 Greenwood Drive
          Iowa City, IA 52246-2124

The Iowa Valley of Fear
          Paul A. Tambrino
US IA Marshalltown 3702 South Center Street
          Marshalltown, IA
             50158-4760

The Camford Scholars
          Elizabeth A. Burns
US IL Bloomington- R.R. 3, Box 221
Normal   Clinton, IL 61727-9300

The Double-Barrelled Tiger Cubs
          John F. Wyman
US IL Champaign-   508 West Elm Street
Urbana   Urbana, IL 61801-3134

The Chester Baskerville Society
          Michael W. McClure
US IL Chester   1415 Swanwick Street
          Chester, IL 62233-1317

Altamont's Agents of Chicago
          John N. Wilson
US IL Chicago   11837 West 118th Street
          Palos Park, IL 60464-1401

Colonel Sebastian Moran's Secret Gun Club
          Elliott M. Black
US IL Chicago   2511 Windsor Lane
          Northbrook, IL 60062-7040

The Criterion Bar Association
          Susan Z. Diamond
US IL Chicago   16W603 3rd Avenue
          Bensenville, IL 60106-2327

The Dedicated Associates of Lomax
          Richard A. Myhre
US IL Chicago   1319 Poplar Court
          Homewood, IL 60430-4221

The Hounds of the Baskerville [*sic*]
          Robert J. Mangler
US IL Chicago   103 Broadway Avenue
          Wilmette, IL 60091-3462

Hugo's Companions
          Wayne Siatt
US IL Chicago   2310 West Burlington
          Avenue
          Downers Grove, IL
             60515-2444

Sherlockians by Invitation Only Society (SBIOS)
          Donald B. Izban
US IL Chicago   Streamwood Manor
          213 Ivy Court
          Streamwood, IL
             60107-2200

The Solar Pons Breakfast Club
          Bernadette Donze
US IL Chicago   7224 South Kidwell Road
          Downers Grove, IL
             60516-3766

The Sons of Baker Street
          Wayne B. Siatt
US IL Chicago   2310 West Burlington
          Avenue
          Downers Grove, IL
             60515-2444

The STUD Sherlockian Society
Allan T. Devitt
US IL Chicago   16W603 3rd Avenue
Bensenville, IL 60106-2327

The Torists International, S.S.
Claudine Kastner
US IL Chicago   810 Burning Bush Lane
Mount Prospect, IL
60056-1957

The Scotland Yarders
Susan Richman
US IL Chicago   472 Burton Avenue
(North Shore)   Highland Park, IL
60035-4939

The South Downers
Kenn Czarnecki
US IL Chicago 16701 Olcott Avenue
Heights   Tinley Park, IL 60477-2453

The Occupants of the Empty House
William R. Cochran
US IL Du Quoin   517 North Vine Street
Du Quoin, IL 62832-2047

The Fellowship of the Fallen Elm
Tom Tully
US IL Elmhurst   303 East Harrison Street
Elmhurst, IL 60126-5374

Watson's Bull Pups of Elmhurst
James Cunningham
US IL Elmhurst   266 Grace Avenue
Elmhurst, IL 60126-3170

The Pinkertons of the Fox River Valley
Barton A. Eberman
US IL Geneva   405 South 1st Street
Geneva, IL 60134-2707

The Baker Street Pages
Tim O'Connor
US IL Kankakee River 6015 West Route 115
Valley   Herscher, IL 60941-6139

The Hansoms of John Clayton
Robert C. Burr
US IL Peoria   4010 Devon Lane
Peoria, IL 61614-7109

The Alpha Public House Goose Club
John Bowen
US IL Roodhouse   109 East Prairie Street
Roodhouse, IL 62082-1135

The Little Knot of Roughs
Ellen Yocom
US IL Waverly Junior 420 West Tremont Street
High School   Waverly, IL 62692-9527

The Friends of Baron Gruner
Brian R. MacDonald
US IN Batesville   7801 North 700-W
Fairland, IN 46126-9544

The Hated Rivals on the Surrey Shore
William A. Barton
US IN Indianapolis Box 26290
Indianapolis, IN
46226-0290

The Illustrious Clients of Indianapolis
Mark Gagen
US IN Indianapolis 7649 Meadow Ridge Drive
Fishers, IN 46038-2220

The Retired Colourmen
Michael F. Whelan
US IN Indianapolis Sussex Downs
7938 Mill Stream Circle
Indianapolis, IN
46278-2105

The Society of the Solitary Cyclists
Virginia J. K. Young
US IN South Bend   230 East Dayton Street
South Bend, IN 46613-2423

Mapleton Stables at Louisville
Larry DeKay
US KY Louisville   Box 43546
Louisville, KY 40253-0546

The Silver Blazers
Ralph Hall
US KY Louisville   2906 Wallingford Court
Louisville, KY 40218-2363

The Mystik Krewe of Sherlock Holmes
Robin C. Leckbee
US LA New Orleansc   868 Shadow Oak Lane
Mandeville, LA 70471-1248

The Speckled Band of Boston
Richard M. Olken
US MA Boston   200 Hyslop Road
Brookline, MA 02445-5724

The Bull-Terrier Club
W. Scott Monty
US MA Boston   1836 Columbia Road #2
(Boston University)   Boston, MA 02127-4342

The Friends of Irene Adler
Daniel Posnansky
US MA Cambridge   Box 380768
Cambridge, MA
02238-0768

Dr. Watson's Stethoscope
Frank Medlar
US MA Chestnut Hill   Bapst Library
(Boston College)   Boston College
Chestnut Hill, MA 02167

A Sherlockian Connection: The Berkshires
Mrs. Henry J. Arbour
US MA North Adams   1201 Notch Road
North Adams, MA
01247-3632

Society of the Naval Treaty
Lynn Whitall
US MD Annapolis   562 Maynadier Lane
Crownsville, MD
21032-2136

The Carlton Club
Karen Lane
US MD Baltimore   837 Bear Cabin Drive
Forest Hill, MD
21050-2732

The Six Napoleons of Baltimore
William Hyder
US MD Baltimore   5488 Cedar Lane #C-3
Columbia, MD 21044-1374

The Denizens of the Bar of Gold
Art Renkwitz
US MD Easton   1908 Pig Neck Road
Cambridge, MD
21613-3644

Watson's Tin Box
Paul Churchill
US MD Ellicott City   2118 Carroll Dale Road
Eldersburg, MD
21784-7033

The Arcadia Mixture
Frederick C. Page, Jr.
US MI Ann Arbor   1354 Ardmoor Avenue
Ann Arbor, MI 48103-5348

The Amateur Mendicant Society
Raymond Mandziuk
US MI Detroit   23825 Scott Drive
Farmington Hills, MI
48336-2853

The Greek Interpreters of East Lansing
  Shari Conroy
US MI East Landing 4440 Beeman Road
  Williamston, MI
  48895-9607

The Ribston-Pippins
  Regina S. Stinson
US MI Royal Oak 715 Amelia Avenue
  Royal Oak, MI 48073-2756

The Lady Frances Carfax Society
  Linda J. Reed
US MN Minneapolis 2809 Fremont Avenue
  South #211
  Minneapolis, MN
  55408-2036

Martha Hudson's Cronies
  Julia Carraher
US MN Minneapolis 4242 Stevens Avenue
  South #2
  Minneapolis, MN
  55409-2004

The Norwegian Explorers of Minnesota
  Julie A. McKuras
US MN Minneapolis 111 Elmer L. Andersen
  Library
  University of Minnesota
  Minneapolis, MN 55455

The Great Alkali Plainsmen of Greater Kansas City
  Stan Carmack
US MO Kansas City 2393 N.W. Summerfield
  Drive
  Lee's Summit, MO
  64081-1923

The Harpooners of the Sea Unicorn
  Michael E. Bragg
US MO St. Charles Box 256
  Saint Charles, MO
  63302-0256

The Jefferson Hopes of St. Louis
  Michael Waxenberg
US MO St. Louis 7353 Princeton Avenue
  Saint Louis, MO
  63130-2923

The Noble Bachelors of St. Louis
  Randall Getz
US MO St. Louis 7456 Cornell Avenue
  University City, MO
  63130-2914

The Parallel Case of St. Louis
  Joseph J. Eckrich
US MO St. Louis 914 Oakmoor Drive
  Fenton, MO 63026-7008

The Men of the Abbey Grange
  Edwin L. Childers, Jr.
US MO Warrensburg 506 Hancock Avenue
  Warrensburg, MO
  64093-1432

The Altamontanans of Great Falls
  Mona Morstein
US MT Great Falls 3420 9th Street NE
  Great Falls, MT
  59404-1260

The Maiwand Jezails
  Richard D. Lesh
US NE Omaha 205 Lory Street
and Lincoln1 Fort Collins, CO
  80524-3905

Cox & Co. of New England
  Robert F. Fritsch
US NH Penacook Box 3003
  Nashua, NH 03061-3003

The Capers of Sherlock Holmes
  Susan Cohen
US NJ Cape May 877 West Hand Avenue
  Cape May Court House, NJ
  08210-1865

Mrs. Hudson's Cliffdwellers of Cliffside Park, New Jersey

	Henry W. Boote
US NJ Cliffside Park	184 Central Avenue
	Old Tappan, NJ
	07675-7360

The Red-Headed League of Jersey

	Peter Christianson
US NJ Flemington	4175 Milords Lane
	Doylestown, PA 18901-9662

The Epilogues of Sherlock Holmes

	Robert S. Katz
US NJ Morristown	11 Van Beuren Road
	Morristown, NJ 07960-7008

The Delaware Valley of Fear

	James P. Suszynski
US NJ Mount Holly	Box 404
	Hainesport, NJ 08036-0404

The Goose Club of the Alpha Inn of Princeton University

	Thomas Drucker
US NJ Princeton	304 South Hanover Street
	Carlisle, PA 17013-3938

The Gila Lizards of the Arid and Repulsive Desert

	Marilynne McKay
US NM Albuquerque	6434 Rio Grande
	Boulevard NW
	Albuquerque, NM
	87107-5631

The Sloane Rangers

	Trisha Stanton
US NM Las Cruces	639 South San Pedro Street
	Las Cruces, NM
	88001-3630

The Brothers Three of Moriarty

	Caroline Bryan
US NM Santa Fe	Box 57057
	Albuquerque, NM
	87187-7057

The Shawlockians

	Bill Dunning
US NM Santa Fe	1 Herrada Terrace
	Santa Fe, NM 87505-8207

The Mexborough Lodgers

	John D. Whitehouse
US NV Las Vegas	6334 Cranberry Lane
	Las Vegas, NV 89156-5923

The Jarveys of the Metropolis

	Paul and Jenny McFarlane
US NV Reno	10180 Deadwood Drive
	Reno, NV 89506-8541

Dr. Watson's Holmestead

	Alfred N. Weiner
US NY Binghamton	4105 Marietta Drive
(Broome County)	Vestal, NY 13850-4032

The Montague Street Lodgers of Brooklyn

	Thom Utecht
US NY Brooklyn	1676 East 55th Street
	Brooklyn, NY 11234-3906

An Irish Secret Society at Buffalo

	Bruce D. Aikin
US NY Buffalo	Box 26
	Newfane, NY 14108-0026

Round the Fire

	Dolores Rossi Script
US NY Buffalo	887 West Ferry Street
	Buffalo, NY 14209-1409

The Hudson Valley Sciontists

US NY Dutchess
County

Nancy C. Alden
Box 365, 7 High Street
Staatsburg-on-Hudson, NY
12580-0365

The Consulting Detectives

US NY East Meadow

Herbert M. Levy
Box 197
East Meadow, NY
11554-0197

The Three Garridebs

US NY Eastchester

Dante M. Torrese
11 Chestnut Street
Ardsley, NY 10502-1001

The Long Island Cave Sleuths

US NY Floral Park

Beverly Halm
Hillside Junior High
School 172
8114 257th Street
Floral Park, NY 11004-1499

The Delaware Deerstalkers

US NY Hancock

Leonard E. Sienko, Jr.
12 East Main Street
Hancock, NY 13783-1128

The Baker Street Underground

US NY Ithaca

Andrew Jay Peck
185 West End Avenue,
#11-F
New York, NY 10023-5544

The Keepers of the Segregated Queen

US NY Lockport

Fred J. Serafin
127 Grant Street
Lockport, NY 14094-5032

The Beryl Coronet Society of the United Nations

US NY New York

Leonor Maia-Sampaio
415 East 52nd Street, #1-DC
New York, NY 10022-6466

The Isle of Uffa Chowder and Marching Society

US NY New York

Susan Rice
125 Washington Place, #2-E
New York, NY 10014-3838

The Lucca Gang

US NY New York

Ted Friedman
115 Lenox Avenue
Demarest, NJ 07267-2112

The Priory Scholars

US NY New York

William Nadel
235 West 71st Street
New York, NY 10023-3705

The Retired Colour People of Metropolitan
New York

US NY New York

David H. Galerstein
49 Stonewyck Place
Monroe Township, NJ
08831-2671

The Young Sherlockians of New York

US NY New York

Mohamad Bazzi
8008 35th Avenue, #5-F
Jackson Heights, NY
11372-4934

The Federal Street Irregulars of Saratoga Springs

US NY Saratoga
Springs

A. T. Retzlaff
Box 982
Saratoga Springs, NY
12866-0897

Altamont's Agents

US NY Schenectady

Thomas A. Dandrew II
375 Langley Road
Amsterdam, NY
12010-7915

Watson's Tin Dispatchers

US NY Staten Island

Francine and Dick Kitts
35 Van Cortlandt Avenue
Staten Island, NY
10301-4019

The Long Island Cave Dwellers
Helen E. Heinrich
US NY Stony Brook   7 Palfrey Street
Stony Brook, NY
11790-2611

The Mycroft Holmes Society of Syracuse
Carol Cavalluzzi
US NY Syracuse   108 Marvin Road
Syracuse, NY 13207-2243

The Students of Deduction
Stephen Imburgia
US NY Webster   1055 Klem Road
Webster, NY 14580-8628

The Inverness Capers
Michael Senuta
US OH Akron   881 Columbine Drive
Barberton, OH 44203-4320

The Tankerville Club
Paul D. Herbert
US OH Cincinnati   734 Alpine Drive
Milford, OH 45150-1401

The Addleton Barrowists of Circleville, Ohio
P. Thomas Harker
US OH Circleville   404 South Washington
Street
Circleville, OH 43113-1716

Mrs. Hudson's Lodgers
The Stetaks
US OH Cleveland   15529 Diagonal Road
La Grange, OH 44050-9531

Mycroft's Isolated Companions
Dwight J. McDonald
US OH Cleveland   1711 Cypress Avenue
Cleveland, OH 44109-4409

The Clients of Sherlock Holmes
Sherry Rose-Bond
US OH Columbus   5471 Riverport Drive
Columbus, OH

The Agra Treasurers
Tom McElfresh
US OH Dayton   Box 2604
Covington, KY 41012-2604

The Darlington Substitutes
Martin Arbagi
US OH Dayton   History Department
Wright State University
Dayton, OH 45435-0001

The Giant Rats of Massillon
Roy K. Preece, Jr.
US OH Massillon   The Village Bookshelf
746 Amherst Road NE
Massillon, OH 44646-8506

The Stormy Petrels of Maumee Bay
Mark J. McGovern
US OH Toledo   3033 Sherbrooke Road
Toledo, OH 43606-3772

The Afghanistan Perceivers of Oklahoma
Vic Lahti
US OK Tulsa   8515 East 64th Street
Tulsa, OK 74133-7634

The Noble and Most Singular Order of the Blue
Carbuncle
Tammy Vale
US OR Portland   4505 N.E. 24th Avenue
Portland, OR 97211-6418

The Vamberry Wine Merchants
Drucilla Weiland
US OR Portland   6173 S.W. Washington Court
Lake Oswego, OR
97035-4565

The Brooks of Carlisle

US PA Carlisle

Thomas Drucker
304 South Hanover Street
Carlisle, PA 17013-3838

The E. Hopkins Trust Company

US PA Lebanon

Jeff Decker
R.D. 3, Box 7631
Racehorse Drive
Jonestown, PA 17038-9227

The Bitches of the Copper Beeches

US PA Philadelphia

K. Jeanne O. Jewell
1012 Waltham Road
Berwyn, PA 19312-2225

The Sons of the Copper Beeches

US PA Philadelphia

Gideon D. Hill III
644 Bridle Road
Glenside, PA 19038-2004

The Fifth Northumberland Fusiliers

US PA Pittsburgh

William H. Conway
2330 Bensonia Avenue
Pittsburgh, PA 15216-3444

The Royal Berkshire Regiment

US PA Pittsburgh

Eric Minde
1471 Beechwood Boulevard
Pittsburgh, PA 15217-1326

Boss McGinty's Bird Watchers

US PA Wilkes-Barre

Frederick C. Sauls
Department of Chemistry
King's College
Wilkes-Barre, PA
18711-0802

The Residents of York College

US PA York

David M. Hershey
1708 West Market Street
York, PA 17404-5419

The White Rose Irregulars of York

US PA York-
Harrisburg area

Larry D. Williams
1304 Forrest Drive
New Cumberland, PA
17070-1326

The Cornish Horrors

US RI Kingston

Jan C. Prager
57 West Park Lane
Kingston, RI 02881-1798

The Hansom Wheels

US SC Columbia

Myrtle Robinson
6117 Lakeshore Drive
Columbia, SC 29206-4331

The Knights of Shag

US SC Greenville

C. A. Lewis, Sr.
Box 9041
Greenville, SC 29604-9041

The Survivors of the Gloria Scott

US SC Greenville

David J. Milner
Box 515
Taylors, SC 29687-0515

The Strand's Sherlockians

US SC Myrtle Beach

Randy Howell
304 Saint Andrews Lane
Myrtle Beach, SC
29757-6306

The Sign of the Four Faces

US SD Sioux Falls

Cary J. Wencil
5009 South Caraway Drive
Sioux Falls, SD 57108-2822

The Baker Street Volunteers

US TN Knoxville

Stefanie Kate Hawks
P.O. Box 9486
Knoxville, TN 37940-9486

The Giant Rats of Sumatra

Robert A. Lanier

US TN Memphis   635 West Drive

Memphis, TN 38112-1728

The Fresh Rashers of Nashville

Bill Mason

US TN Nashville   2367 Lights Chapel Road

Greenbrier, TN 37073-4926

The Nashville Scholars of the Three Pipe Problem

Gael B. Stahl

US TN Nashville   1763 Needmore Road

Old Hickory, TN

37138-1126

The Waterloo Station

Carolyn Hoehn

US TX Austin   11208 Amethyst Trail

Austin, TX 78750-1425

The Crew of the Barque "Lone Star"

Donald J. Hobbs

US TX Dallas   2100 Elm Creek Lane

Flower Mound, TX

75028-4680

The Diogenes Club of Dallas

Jim Webb

US TX Dallas   3811 Wooded Creek Drive

Dallas, TX 75244-4751

The Maniac Collectors

Don Hobbs

US TX Dallas   2100 Elm Creek Lane

Flower Mound, TX

75028-4680

The John Openshaw Society

Thomas L. Harman

US TX Houston   University of Houston/

Clear Lake

2700 Bay Area Blvd.

(Box 161)

Houston, TX 77058-1098

The Strange Old Book Collectors

Ben Fairbank

US TX San Antonio   Box 15075

San Antonio, TX

78212-8275

The Country of the Saints

Kevin John

US UT Brigham City   637 North 200 West

Brigham City, UT

84302-1415

The Avenging Angels

Heidi-Marie Mason

US UT Salt Lake City   1207 East 8320 South

Sandy, UT 84094-1337

The Game Is Afoot

Richard R. Morrison, Jr.

US VA Charlottesville   144 Woodlake Drive

Charlottesville, VA

22901-1342

The Cremona Fiddlers of Williamsburg

David F. Morrill

US VA Williamsburg   17 James Square

Williamsburg, VA

23185-3346

The Goose Club of the Alpha Inn [Vermont]

William E. Wicker

US VT Burlington   17 Birchwood Drive

Colchester, VT 05446-3616

The Baker Street Breakfast Club

Sally Sugarman

US VT Shaftsbury   Box 407

Shaftsbury, VT 05262-0407

The Loungers and Idlers

Janet Bailey

US WA Bainbridge   4320 Old Mill Road NE

Island   Bainbridge Island, WA

98110-3128

Dr. Whatcom's Sherlockian Society
Bobbie Hurst
US WA Bellingham   1225 East Sunset Drive
(Whatcom County)   #609
Bellingham, WA
98226-3597

The Sherlock Holmes League
Michael Meaney
US WA Seattle   4094 West Lake Sammish
Parkway SE
Bellevue, WA 98008-5938

The Sound of the Baskervilles
David N. Haugen
US WA Seattle   3606 Harborcrest Court NW
Gig Harbor, WA
98332-8981

The Conductors of Aldersgate Street Station
Fred Zensen
US WA Vancouver   15103 N.E. 27th Avenue
Vancouver, WA 98686-1524

The Thor Bridge Fishers
Alan J. Block
US WI Beloit   1419 Chapin Street
Beloit, WI 53511-5601

The Notorious Canary-Trainers
Thomas M. Boykoff
US WI Madison   222 Randolph Drive #303
Madison, WI 53717-1647

The Bagatelle Card Club
Daniel P. King
US WI Milwaukee   5125 North Cumberland
Boulevard
Whitefish Bay, WI
53217-5747

Randall's Gang
Paul B. Smedegaard
US WI Racine   Crabapple Cottage
929 Lathrop Avenue
Racine, WI 53405-2339

The Merripit House Guests
Ed Christenson
US WI Sheboygan   1545 Villa Park Drive
Oshkosh, WI 54904-8273

The Norwood Building Inspectors
Richard Hartman
US WV Charleston   305 Highland Avenue
South Charleston, WV
25303-1911

The Scion of the Four
Andrew G. Fusco
US WV Morgantown   2400 Cranberry Square
Morgantown, WV
26505-9209

PROFESSIONAL

The Baker Street Bar Association
David R. McCallister
lawyers   8142 Quail Hollow
Boulevard
Wesley Chapel, FL
33544-2021

The Black Pearl of the Borgias
Dolores (Dee) Script
poetry/writing/   887 West Ferry Street
lecturing   Buffalo, NY 14209-1409

The Blanched Soldiers of NOAH

dermatologists

Marshall L. Blankenship
1555 Astor Street #12-NE
Chicago, IL 60610-5756

The Board-School Beacons

educational research
and psychometry

Michael H. Kean
3040 Sloat Road
Pebble Beach, CA
93953-2837

The Bruce-Partington Planners Within the Military-Industrial Complex

national security

Jon L. Lellenberg
3133 Connecticut Avenue
NW #827
Washington, DC
20008-5110

Clerks of the Assizes

court clerks felony
trial court

James Motylenski
537 Christie Street
South Hempstead, NY
11550-8004

The Forensic Faces of Sherlock Holmes

forensic science

Marina Stajic
425 East 51st Street, #4-A
New York, NY 10022-6465

Holmes in Scale

model craftsmen and
artists

William C. Thomas
3308 North 4th Street
Broken Arrow, OK
74012-8267

Moriarty's Mathematicians

mathematics majors

John R. Clark
Box 821
Lowell, AR 72745-0821

The Norwood Fire Brigade

fire service

Capt. Randall Getz
Hazelwood Fire
    Department
6800 Howdershell Road
Hazelwood, MO 63042

The Old Soldiers of Baker Street of the Two Saults (Old SOB's)

military Sherlockians

John S. Rabe
1742 Grevelia Street #I
South Pasadena, CA
91030-2734

The Old Soldiers of Baker Street, Detachment 221B (Flying Column)

military and ex-
military Sherlockians

Col. Ted Schulz
The Pontine Pines
461 Forest Highlands
Flagstaff, AZ 86001-8428

The Practical, But Limited, Geologists

geology

Peter E. Blau
7103 Endicott Ct.
Bethesda, MD 20817-4401

The Red Lamp League

medicine

Edmond C. Noll
Box 4322
North Hollywood, CA
91617-0322

The Sherlockian Oenophiles Tasting Society (S.O.T.S.)

alcoholic Sherlockians

Maribeau Briggs
853 Lexington Avenue, #4-A
New York, NY 10021-6639

The Sir James Saunders Society

dermatology

Don E. Hazelrigg
15 Victoria Drive
Newburgh, IN 47630-1500

Some Freaks of Atavism

historians
Bullitt Lowry
Department of History
Box 13735, North Texas
Station
Denton, TX 76203

Stimson & Co.

funeral directors
Michael W. McClure
1415 Swanwick Street
Chester, IL 62233-1317

The Sub-Librarians Scion of The Baker Street
Irregulars in the American Library Association

librarians
Marsha L. Pollak
1318 Mildred Avenue
San Jose, CA 95125-3855

The Trifling Monographers

practitioners of
public relations
Graham Sudbury
Box 506
Taos, NM 87571-0506

OTHER

The 140

tobacco-smoking
Sherlockians
John F. Farrell
25314 Woodward Avenue
Lomita, CA 90717-2250

The 140 Varieties of Tobacco Ash

privately-banded cigar
dinners
Steven T. Doyle
540 West Sycamore Street
Zionsville, IN 46077-1755

221b Baker Street/Los Angeles

study of the sitting-
room at 221b
Chuck Kovacic
9337 Sophia Avenue
North Hills, CA 91343-2820

The Adventuresses of Sherlock Holmes

women's special-
interest group
Evelyn A. Herzog
360 West 21st Street, #5-A
New York, NY 10011-3310

alt.fan.holmes (Usenet/Internet)

computerized
newsgroup
Chuck Lavazzi
Internet: clavazzi@nyx.cs.
du.edu
WWIVnet: 3@3456

The American Exchange

members of Franco-
Midland Hardware Co.
Robert M. Carter
Box 762
Fort Montgomery, NY
10922-0762

The American Firm

giving large-print
books to adult homes
Edward S. Smith Jr.
Box 353
Williston Park, NY
11596-0353

The Apocryphal Calabash

pipe-smoking
Sherlockians
Wayne B. Anderson
Box 250
Lake Hughes, CA
93532-0250

The Arthur Conan Doyle Study Group

members of Franco-
Midland Hardware Co.
Mark Chadderton
20 Delhi Road
Bournemouth, Dorset
BH9 2SS
ENGLAND

The Baker Street Branch Lines

Holmesian railways
Philip Weller
6 Bramham Moor,
Hill Head
Fareham, Hampshire
PO14 3RU
ENGLAND

The Baker Street Builders

builders of full-scale | Chuck Kovacic
9337 Sophia Avenue
North Hills, CA 91343-2820

The Baker Street Constables (Fans of Jeremy Brett)

a Jeremy Brett fan
club | Kathleen L. Hinck
55 Eighth Street
North Arlington, NJ
07031-4754

The Baker Street E-regulars

computerized
(electronic mailing list) | <jsielke@pobox.com>
John L. Sielke
1353 Samuel Drive
Vineland, NJ 08360-4471

The Baker Street Irregulars

American national
Sherlockian society | Michael F. Whelan
Sussex Downs
7938 Mill Stream Circle
Indianapolis, IN
46278-2105

The Baker Street Juniors

young Sherlockians
(scion of JSHC) | Sho Nakanishi
3-15-19 Sen-nin-cho
Hachioji-shi, Tokyo 193
JAPAN

The Baker Street Ladies

(scion of The
Japan Sherlock
Holmes Club) | Yumiko Shigaki
1-27-9-B Fukazawa
Setagaya-ku, Tokyo 158
JAPAN

The Baker Street Streakers, Irregular!

streaking!! | Henry W. Gould
1239 College Avenue
Morgantown, WV
26505-5124

The BBC (Baskerville Bash Committee)

annual dinner
during birthday
weekend | Paula J. Perry
346 East 87th Street, #4-A
New York, NY 10128-4844

The Belles of Saint Monica

midwestern
Sherlockian women | Ruthann H. Stetak
15529 Diagonal Road
La Grange, OH 44050-9531

The Billy Club

Bills and Williams
(named/Investitured) | Bill Vande Water
697 Greenbelt Parkway
West
Holbrook, NY 11741-4216

The Birdy Edwards Society

19th-century
detective literature | J. Randolph Cox
Box 226
Dundas, MN 55019-0226

The Boulevard Assassins

social but secretive | Huret, the Boulevard
Assassin
11 Greenway North
Albany, NY 12208-1803

The BrettFretts

a Jeremy Brett fan
club | Ashley Lynn Decker
R.R. 1, Box 205
Graysville, PA 15337-9331

The Brown Bagatelle Club

Afghanistan Perceivers
discussion group | Vic Lahti
5815 East 64th Street
Tulsa, OK 74133-7634

C.A.L.A.B.A.S.H. (Convivial Attendant Liaisons Among B.S.I. and Adventuresses of Sherlock Holmes)

honoring the third
buy-law of the B.S.I. | Paul B. Smedegaard
Crabapple Cottage
929 Lathrop Avenue
Racine, WI 53405-2339

Cartwright's Companions

sub-scion of Chester
Baskerville Society

Michael W. McClure
1415 Swanwick Street
Chester, IL 62233-1317

A Case of Identifiers

preserving
photographs of
Sherlockians

Bill Vande Water
697 Greenbelt Parkway
West
Holbrook, NY 11741-4216

The Central Press Syndicate

Afghanistan Perceivers
discussion group

Vic Lahti
5815 East 64th Street
Tulsa, OK 74133-7634

Le cercle des eleves de Harry Dixon

honorary society

Gerard Dole
10 rue de Buci
75006 Paris
FRANCE

The Clients of Adrian Mulliner

Wodehouseans of
BSI—Sherlockians
of TWS

Jon L. Lellenberg
3133 Connecticut Avenue
NW #827
Washington, DC
20008-5110

The Companions of Jefferson Hope

S'ian who have had
aortic aneurisms

Robert E. Robinson
6117 Lakeshore Drive
Columbia, SC 29206-4331

The Conan Doyle (Crowborough) Establishment

information on ACD
and tours of his home

Brian Pugh
20 Clare Road
Lewes, Sussex BN7 1PN
ENGLAND

The Conk-Singleton Forgers

free-and-easy
Sherlockians

Morris Owen
67 Cremorne Road, Unit 2
Cremorne Point, N.S.W.
2090
AUSTRALIA

The Consorts of the Kings of Scandinavia

consorts of the Kings
of Scandinavia

Marina Stajic
425 East 51st Street, #4-A
New York, NY 10022-6465

The Constabulary

S'ian students of
British police history

John B. Taylor
Box 804
Midlothian, TX 76065-0804

The Dead-Headed League

a geo-academic society

Paul David Rivadue
Garden City High School
Garden City, NY
11530-1499

The Diogenes Club of Gothenburg

Sherlock Holmes
literature

Lennart Engstrom
Vastes Gata 60
S-421 53 V. Frolunda
Gothenburg, SWEDEN

The Dog in the Night-time

individualistic and
quietly alert

Wendell Cochran
4351 S.W. Willow Street
Seattle, WA 98136-1769

The Edmonton Deerstalker

members elected by
membership
committee

Peter H. Wood
1525 Pendrell Street #201
Vancouver, BC V6G 1S6
CANADA

The Excelsior Guild

honor society of
The Baker Street Pages

Tim O'Connor
6015 West Route 115
Herscher, IL 60941-6139

The Five Orange Pips

Sherlockian scholarship

Albert M. Rosenblatt
300 Freedom Road
Poughkeepsie, NY
12569-5431

The Frenzied Hands

Sherlockian
percussionists

Jim Coffin
6570 East Paseo Alcazaa
Anaheim Hill, CA
92807-4910

The Friends of Dr. Watson

medical aspects
of the Canon

Richard J. Stacpoole-
Ryding
14 Western Close
Letchworth, Herts.
SD6 4SZ
ENGLAND

The Friends of Mrs. Hudson

Canonical dining
and cooking

Francine M. Swift
Sumatra Lodge,
Wigmore Street
4622 Morgan Drive
Chevy Chase, MD
20815-5315

Gerard's Hussars

members of Franco-
Midland Hardware Co.

Brian W. Pugh
20 Clare Road
Lewes, Sussex BN7 1PN
ENGLAND

The Goose Club

performing Sherlockian
puppet shows

Maki Koizumi
2-1-1-615 Mutsu-ura
Kanazawa-ku, Yokohama
236
JAPAN

The Grand-Hounds of the Internet
computerized
Sherlockian
grandparents

Sandy Kozinn
Internet: skozinn@
worldnet.att.net

The Great Hiatus

corresponding about
foreign translations

John Farrell
25314 Woodward Avenue
Lomita, CA 90717-2250

Greuze tomo-no-kai

artists in the Canon
(scion of JSHC)

Takahiko Endo
3-12 Takahata, Hino-shi
Tokyo 191-0031
JAPAN

The H. W.
people whose
initials are H. W.

Helen Wesson
729 Waterway
Venice, FL 34285-2935

The High Tors

a correspondence
society

Larry Waggoner
1649 Yarbro Lane
Paducah, KY 42003-0283

His Last Miaow

Sherlockians who
have lived with cats

Marina Stajic
425 East 51st Street #4-A
New York, NY 10022-6465

The Holmes Peak Preservation Society
promotion and
protection of Holmes
Peak

Dick Warner
3168 South Rockford Drive
Tulsa, OK 74105-2129

Holmes' Unofficial Force

a correspondence
society

Sandra Buck
R.R. 1, Box 2090
Morrill, ME 04952-9729

Holmesian Studies Special Interest Group

American Mensa
special-interest group

Michael J. Halm
2062 Yoast Avenue
Cincinnati, OH 45225-1480

Hounds of the Internet

computerized
(electronic mailing list)

<sclarkson@home.com>
Steve Clarkson
9213 Winding Way
Ellicott City, MD
21043-6445

The Hugh Boone Society

sub-scion of The
Red-Headed League

Ann Byerly Marlowe
10324 Castlehedge Terrace
Silver Spring, MD
20902-6807

The Ineffable Twaddlers

sub-scion of The
Illustrious Clients

Pat Ward
5119 Turtle Creek Court #5
Indianapolis, IN
46227-1855

The Inner Brotherhood of the Holy Four

Holmes & Watson
and Gilbert & Sullivan

Colin Prestige
22 Pelham Court,
145 Fulham Road
London SW3 6SH
ENGLAND

The Intelligent Corresponders

an e-mail
correspondence society

Tabitha Smith
Internet: saralockh@aol.com

Irregular Special Railway Company

Holmesians interested
in railways

Antony Richards
170 Woodland Road
Sawston, Cambridge
CB2 4DX
ENGLAND

J-Holmes

an Internet society
(scion of JSHC)

Kei-ichi Narita
2243 Chugenji
Niigata-shi, Niigata
950-2251
JAPAN

The James Phillimore Society

conjuring and the
Canon

Maribeau Briggs
46 East 29th Street, #3-F
New York, NY 10016-7904

The Jeremy Brett Society of France

admirers of Jeremy
Brett

Severine Rubin
Le clos de l'Arc (entree 5)
Avenue Gaston Berger
13090 Aix-en-Provence
FRANCE

The Last Dog Hung Post-Prandial Club

closing up watering
holes after meetings

Paul B. Smedegaard
Crabapple Cottage
929 Lathrop Avenue
Racine, WI 53405-2339

The Literary Shortcomings

for writers of
Sherlockian literature

Rosemary Michaud
43 Grove Street
Randolph, MA 02368-2964

The Maiwand Survivors Society

walking-wounded
Sherlockians

Murray, c/o Swift
Sumatra Lodge on
Wigmore Street
4622 Morgan Drive
Chevy Chase, MD
20815-5315

The Master's Masons

members of the
Masons

Ron Fish
Box 4
Circleville, NY 10919-0004

The Meiringen Meringues

Sherlockian visitors to
Meiringen

Vivian M. Heisler-Castel
1616 Redwood Avenue
Langhorne, PA 19047-2026

The Messengers from Porlock

truly ephemeral;
studied Porlock

Graham Sudbury
8/7/93 Box 506
Taos, NM 87571-0506

The Midwest Scion of the Four

a travelling barber-
shop quartette

Joseph J. Eckrich
914 Oakmoor Drive
Fenton, MO 63026-7008

The Mini-Tonga Scion Society
Trish and Jay Pearlman
collectors of   1656 East 19th Street, #2-E
Sherlockian miniatures Brooklyn, NY 11229-1317

The Mongooses of Henry Wood
Mattias Bostrom
a correspondence   Domherrevagen 12
society   S-178 39 Ekero
                       SWEDEN

The Montague Street Incorrigibles
Brad Keefauver
a correspondence   4009 Chelsea Place
society   Peoria, IL 61614-7201

The Mrs. Turner Thames Club Breakfasters
Donald A. Yates
annual breakfast   555 Canon Park Drive
during birthday   Saint Helena, CA
weekend   94574-9726

The Napoleons of Crime
Uwe Sommerlad
members of Franco-   Rodelheimer Landstrasse
Midland Hardware Co.   32
                       D-60487 Frankfurt am Main
                       GERMANY

Nishichikuma-Shobou Co. Mag.
Kokage Midorikawa
publishing parodies   Nishino 6321-648, Kaida
and pastiches   Kiso-gun, Nagano-ken
                       JAPAN

The Occupants of the Full House
Jean Upton
correspondence society 41 Sandford Road
(visits welcomed)   Chelmsford, Essex
                       CM2 6DE
                       ENGLAND

The One Fixed Point Society for Two-Dimensional
Sherlockians
William R. Cochran
replicas of S'ians   517 North Vine Street
who won't leave home   Du Quoin, IL 61832-2047

"One of One-Forty"
Elizabeth J. Ash
a correspondence   111 South 9th Street, #101
society   La Crosse, WI 54601-4186

The Oxbridge Scholars
Donald G. Jewell
Canonical scholarship 4685 Geeting Road
                       Westminster, MD
                       21158-1720

The Page Boys of 221B
Robert G. Allison-
young Sherlockians   Gallimore
                       Route II
                       18920 Quivira Road
                       Spring Hill, KS 66083-8989

The Persian Slipper of the Ribston-Pippins
Sam Stinson
pipe-smoking subscion 715 Amelia Avenue
of Ribston-Pippins   Royal Oak, MI 48073-2756

The Phoenician Tin Traders Ladies and
Gentlemen's International Corresponding Society
John D. Whitehouse
language of the Canon 6334 Cranberry Lane
and the S'ian era   Las Vegas, NV 89115-5923

The Practical Preservers of Sherlockiana
Mary Schroeder
a national   3131 Russell Boulevard
philanthropic society Saint Louis, MO
                       63104-1538

The Praed Street Irregulars
George A. Vanderburgh
American national   Box 204
Pontine society   Shelburne, ON L0N 1S0
                       CANADA

The Protective Order of the Persian Slipper

Steve W. Schaefer

pure fun 606 North Main Street
Madison, GA 30650-1442

The Quaker Street Irregulars

John Ruyle

supporters of 521 Vincente Avenue
Turlock Loams Berkeley, CA 94707-1521

The Red-Headed League

Ann Byerly Marlowe

red-headed 10324 Castlehedge Terrace
Sherlockians Silver Spring, MD
20902-5807

The Reichenbach Falls Lemming Society

Sherlockians who Brad Keefauver
attend the Media 4009 Chelsea Place
WestCon Peoria, IL 61614-7201

The Reichenbach Rangers

Darlene Logan

academic (New Mexico 111 West Mathews Street
Military Institute) Roswell, NM 88201-5723

The Reichenbachian Cliff-Divers

Kendall J. Pagan

cliff-diving c/o The Lascarian Press
Sherlockians 4010 Devon Lane
Peoria, IL 61614-7109

The Retired Colonels

George Vanderburgh

people interested Box 204
in Holmes and Doyle Shelburne, ON L0N 1S0
CANADA

The Sacred Six

Bill Vande Water

Sherlockian inner 697 Greenbelt Parkway
circle West
Holbrook, NY 11741-4216

The Scandalous Bohemians

David Richardson

an America Online Internet: mfrankland@
chat-room group aol.com

The Scrimshanders of the Harpooners of the Sea
Unicorn

John T. Foster

sub-scion/Harpooners Box 256
of the Sea Unicorn Saint Charles, MO
63302-0256

Sergeant of Marines

Elementary, my Francis J. Carroll, Jr.
dear Simpson— 712 Prospect Place
Gung Ho!!! Bellmore, NY 11710-4520

The Seven Passengers

Larry DeKay

study of Solar Pons Box 43546
Louisville, KY 40253-0546

The Shadows of the Elm

Caroline Bryan

a correspondence Box 57057
society (young S'ians) Albuquerque, NM
87187-7057

Sherlock Holmes Lapel Pin Society

Ralph Hall

collectors of 2906 Wallingford Court
Sherlockian lapel pins Louisville, KY 40218-2363

The Sherlock Holmes Research Committee (Japan)

Saburo Hiraga

publ. "Studies of the 3-6-24 Ueno-higashi
Nippon S.H. Club" Toyonaka-shi, Osaka 560
JAPAN

The Sherlock Holmes Wireless Society

Ron Fish

licensed amateur Box 4
radio operators Circleville, NY 10919-0004

Sherlock Holmes' Chinese Society
Sherlockian studies
(in Chinese)
Henry P. Cheng
P.O. Box 1, Canal Street
Station
New York, NY 10013-0001

Sherlock Holmes' Varied Correspondents (sic)
a correspondence
society (audiocassette)
Desmond Tyler
162 Leybridge Court,
Eltham Road
London SE12 8TL
ENGLAND

Sherlock's Haven BBS
computerized bulletin
board
(300/1200/2400/9600/19200
N-8-1 516-433-1843)
Steven L. Gardner
19 Hanover Place, #106
Hicksville, NY 11801-5103

Sherlockians Keen to Inhibit and Rectify
Mendacious Identifications of Sherlock Holmes
(SKIRMISH)
gently pursues the
premise of its name
Graham Sudbury
Box 506
Taos, NM 87571-0506

Sherlocktron
Internet Website
<members.home.net/
sherlock1/
Sherlocktron.html>
Willis G. Frick
513 Via Presa
San Clemente, CA
92672-9474

The Singular Society of the Friends of Algar
Holmes' relationship
with the police
Peter Williams
18 Gorsey Lane, Litherland
Liverpool L21 0DH
ENGLAND

The Sinister Ballarat Gang
dedicated to left-
handed Sherlockiana
Kevin J. Reed
672 Prospect Avenue
Long Beach, CA
90814-1814

The Slurred Accounts of the Bribed Auditors
insurance/auditors/
accountants
Paul H. Brundage
2632 Central Court
Union City, CA 94587-2128

The Society for the Immense Knowledge of
Sensational Literature (SIKSL)
a correspondence
society
Drew Thomas
5 Pheasant Court
Flanders, NJ 07836-9506

The Solar Pons Society of London
British scion of Praed
Street Irregulars
Roger Johnson
41 Sandford Road
Chelmsford, Essex
CM2 6DE
ENGLAND

The Solitary Cyclists of Sweden
honorary Swedish
society
Ted Bergman
Salgstigen 35
S-181 62 Lidingo
SWEDEN

The Solitary Sherlockian
a correspondence
society
Candace Drimmer
Compania Continental
Mexico
Andres Bello No. 10 Piso 5
Mexico CP 11560
MEXICO

The Strangers' Room
unofficial consulting
scion
Andrew Joffe
340 East 63rd Street, #4-A
New York, NY 10021-7716

The Three Garish Debs
a playful society
Barbara Roscoe
7101 Mardel Avenue
Saint Louis, MO
63109-1124

The Timekeepers of Morton and Waylight

science fiction/
psychic/time travel

John D. Whitehouse
6334 Cranberry Lane
Las Vegas, NV 89156-5923

The Trained Cormorants of Gifu

visitors to cormorant
fishing at Gifu

Helen Wesson
729 Waterway
Venice, FL 34285-2935

Traveling Companions of a Decrepit Italian Priest

traveling Sherlockians

Cornelia Ingersoll
5840 Cameron Run
Terrace #913
Alexandria, VA 22303-2701

The Two Thurstons

pool hustlers

Bjarne Nielsen
Sherlock Holmes Museet,
Algade 3
DK-4500 Nykobing
Sjaelland
DENMARK

The Unequalled Bag of Tigers

cats who are
companions to
Sherlockians

Pat Ward
5199 Turtle Creek Court, #5
Indianapolis, IN
46227-1855

Victorian Gamers Afoot!

gamers (role-playing
or board)

Bill Barton
Box 26290
Indianapolis, IN
46226-0290

The Voices of the Whispering Knights

scion of The Praed
Street Irregulars

Frances Van Antwerp
73 East Park Street
Westerville, OH
43081-2301

Von Herder Airguns, Ltd.

a correspondence
society

Michael Ross
Postfach 42 06 70
50900 Koln
GERMANY

Watson's Erroneous Deductions

just good
Sherlockian friends

Richard J. Kitts
35 Van Cortlandt Avenue
Staten Island, NY
10301-4019

The Watsonians

admirers of
Dr. Watson

Susan Z. Diamond
16W603 3rd Avenue
Bensenville, IL 60106-2327

WelcomeHolmes
computerized
(electronic mailing
list)

<jimhawkins@thehawk.net>
Jim Hawkins
644 Vivian Drive
Nashville, TN 37211-5935

The Wigmore Street Post Office

users of the Prodigy
computer service

(Prodigy ID KVJT07B)
Melanie J. Hughes
2664 Sam Hardwick
Boulevard
Jacksonville, FL
32246-3850

The William Gillette Memorial Luncheon

annual luncheon
during birthday
weekend

Susan Rice
125 Washington Place, #2-E
New York, NY 10014-3838

Wilson's Basement Dwellers

correspondence about
Sherlockian humor

Caroline Bryan
Box 57057
Albuquerque, NM
87187-7057

Yottsu-no-shomei-sha [The Sign of Four Co.]
Tatsuo Saneyoshi
parodies and pastiches 3068-5, Naruse Machida
Tokyo 194
JAPAN

THE SHERLOCKIAN WEB

Sherlockian websites and Internet resources abound. A detailed survey is available online, in John Bergquist's splendid "Sherlockian Resources on the Internet: A Survey" (July 2003): www.tc.umn.edu/~bergq003/holmes/. The following is a selected list.

GENERAL

- Chris Redmond's www.sherlockian.net, a jumping-off point for nearly everything Sherlockian appearing on the web
- Sherlocktron, another collection of links, including Peter Blau's invaluable lists of Baker Street Irregular investitures, information about the location of Canonical manuscripts, and other items: http://members.cox.net/sherlock1/Sherlock tron.html
- DeWaal's *Universal Sherlock Holmes* bibliography online (and searchable): http://special.lib.umn.edu/rare/ush/ush.html
- The official website of the Sherlock Holmes Society of London, with some material from the always-superb *Sherlock Holmes Journal*: www.sherlock holmes.org.uk
- The official website of the Baker Street Irregulars: www.bakerstreetjournal.com

ARTHUR CONAN DOYLE

- The official website of the Arthur Conan Doyle Society: www.ash-tree.bc.ca/acdsocy.html
- *New York Times* obituary: www.nytimes.com/learning/general/onthisday/bday/0522 .html
- The award-winning www.siracd.com, which includes material on Spiritualism
- The website of the Friends of the Arthur Conan Doyle Collection, at the Toronto Metropolitan Library: www.acdfriends.org

- A succinct exposition of the tangled subject of ownership of the Conan Doyle copyrights for the Sherlock Holmes tales: www.sherlockian.net/acd/copyright .html
- An essential checklist of Conan Doyle's manuscripts, including facsimiles, created by Randall Stock: http://members.aol.com/shbest/ref/rfms.htm

SHERLOCK HOLMES AND JOHN H. WATSON

- The thorny subject of chronologies, and why they disagree, is tackled by Peter H. Wood, in his essay "The Leading Problems of Chronology": www.sher lockian.net/world/chronology.html.
- A site with text versions of the cases complete with most of the Sidney Paget illustrations is Michael Sherman's 221B Baker Street at http://221bakerstreet. org. Many cases also are presented in Palm DOC and/or Adobe Acrobat format.
- A compendium of the work of many different illustrators of the Canon is the Pinotheca Holmesiana, www.bakerstreet221b.de/gallery.htm.
- A concordance of the Canon is available at http://mrmoon.com/moonfind/ holmes/index.mv, allowing the user to search by keyword and quickly find the tales in which the keyword appears, in context.
- Continuing under construction is the Sherlock Holmes Atlas at http:// roofie.evo.org/sherlock/sherlock_atlas.html, which locates many geographical references in the Canon.

VICTORIAN RESOURCES

- Scholarly resources for Victorian research are linked at http://victorianresearch .org.
- A superb, searchable compendium of Victorian resources, contemporary literature, and commentary is the Victorian Dictionary at www.victorianlondon.org.
- The Victorian Web, a doorway to current Victorian scholarship, is at http://65 .107.211.206/victorian/victov.html.
- Danish Sherlockian Mia Stampe's "Exquisite Victorian Links" is an excellent collection of the range of Victorian information on the Internet, including history, costuming, customs, and antiques: http://www.gfy.ku.dk/~ams/sh/victorian .html.

DISCUSSIONS

- Any person seriously interested in the Canon can subscribe to the Hounds of the Internet, an e-mail mailing list with over 500 members. Send a message to list serv@listserv.kent.edu. Leave the subject line blank and type "subscribe hounds-1 <Your Name>" in the body. Many leading Sherlockian scholars post to the list. Anyone can read digests of the current week's messages on www.bcpl .lib.md.us/~lmoskowi/hounds/hounds.html, and users can choose between regular (individual messages) or digest (a packet of messages) mode.
- Most widely accessible is the newsgroup alt.fan.holmes. The quality of the discussion is not at the level of erudition as the Hounds of the Internet, but the chat is available using any standard newsgroup reader (such as that built into Netscape Navigator™).

Lastly, my own website, www.annotatedsherlockholmes.com, contains several articles I've written on abstruse aspects of Sherlock Holmes and Dr. Watson, as well as news about this volume and its successor, book signings and other events, a sample of my forthcoming book in the SHERLOCK HOLMES REFERENCE LIBRARY, links to some of my other books, and an e-mail link to me.

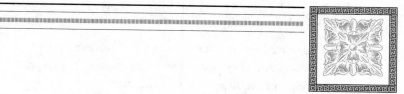

ACKNOWLEDGEMENTS

T HE EVOLUTION OF the volumes has been a long one, and there are many who helped me along the way. Christopher Roden provided early discouraging words that led me to the right path, and he has been a friend ever since. Steven Doyle and Mark Gagen edited and published the SHERLOCK HOLMES REFERENCE LIBRARY, from which these volumes grew, and invested in the results when no one else was interested. Michael Dirda introduced me to my publisher and was "mid-wife" to these volumes—I hope that his hopes have been fulfilled.

My Sherlockian mentors Otto Penzler, Alan Olding, Jon Lellenberg, Peter Blau, Don Pollock, Nicholas Meyer, David Stuart Davies, Julie Rosenblatt, Chris Redmond, and Bernard Davies helped me in countless ways. Jerry Wachs, Al Rosenblatt, Catherine Cooke, Dick Sveum, Peter Calamai, Philip Weller, Hirayama Yuichi, Bill Barnes, Dan Stashower, Costa Rossakis, and Bob Katz, to mention only a few, have been generous with their friendship. Nicholas Utechin and especially Steve Rothman, editors of the world's leading Sherlockian journals, have been immensely supportive of my work from the beginning. Kinsprit Susan Dahlinger kindly read parts of this book in draft and gave me critical insights. Jerry Margolin, the world's greatest collector of original Sherlock Holmes art, was a great help with the illustrations, including loans of precious items. Mike Whelan generously took vacation time to read and correct the introduction and was always available for wise counsel and friendship. George Vanderburgh helped me get started with scans of relevant text, and Bill Cochran kindly made the work of Newt and Lillian Williams available to me. John Sohl and John Farrell, fellow members of the Goose Club of the Alpha Inn of Santa Monica first pointed me in scholarly directions. Countless other Sherlockians made contributions on research topics, which I have attempted to acknowledge *in situ*. My dear friend and occasional co-author Andy Peck gave general and constant support as well as specific suggestions.

This edition could not have been produced without the help of Ronald L. DeWaal's *Universal Sherlock Holmes*, Jack Tracy's *Encyclopedia Sherlockiana*, Steve Clarkson's *Canonical Compendium*, and scores of other handbooks, reference works, indexes, and collections. Each of those essential reference works is the product of many, many hours of patient research and labour by pioneers who went largely unrewarded. My own work on the Holmes canon has made me bow down in admiration to those scholars who came before me, especially those who laboured before computers and such specialised reference works existed. This work is an attempt to stand on the shoulders of those giants.

The W. W. Norton team has been incredible. My editor Robert Weil's immediate enthusiasm for the project, thoughtful criticisms, careful pruning, and constant cheerleading gave the work its present shape. It was a great delight (and relief) to find that Bob so closely shared my vision for these volumes. Patricia Chui got down into the trenches of the notes and made an enormous contribution, constantly suggesting new topics to annotate and then doing the initial spade work. Other Norton colleagues—Brendan Curry and Tom Mayer, who shepherded the materials through publication; Julia Druskin, production manager, who unblinkingly handled the daunting task of reproducing hundreds of illustrations; Jo Anne Metsch, who created the stunning design of both volumes; Chin-Yee Lai, who brilliantly designed the cover; Eleen Cheung, who painstakingly oversaw the design of the jackets; Nancy Palmquist, managing editor; Bill Rusin, sales director—all earned my immense gratitude and admiration. Louise Brockett and Rachel Salzman brought unbounded energy to the publicity and promotion of the project. Special thanks to Drake McFeely, president, and Jeannie Luciano, publisher, whose belief in the project made it all possible.

Megan Underwood, Camille McDuffie, and Lynn Goldberg at Goldberg McDuffie & Co. put immense effort and great inspiration into finding ways to bring this work to the attention of readers and reviewers and made the publicity process memorable, enjoyable, and rewarding for a first-timer.

My law partner Bob Kopple has been an unstinting cheerleader for the entire project from the beginning. My agent Don Maass was tireless and undaunted by numerous obstacles. My friend and attorney Jonathan Kirsch, who combines a brilliant law career with an astonishing quantity of biblical scholarship, not only provided essential help but is my constant rôle model.

My dear friend Barbara Roisman Cooper put in countless hours checking and correcting countless footnotes, and she has earned my deepest gratitude. Her husband Marty also contributed sage advice about publicity and put up with numerous Sherlockian events. Bob and Mallory Kroner, and Mike and Donna Sedgwick all warmed me with their friendship and smiled tolerantly at my constant ramblings on Sherlock Holmes.

My family has been understanding to a fault, and my children Matt, Wendy, Stacy, Evan, and Amanda have given me uncritical love. My parents, Jack and Lenore, taught me to love books and people; sadly, neither survived to see this work published.

Lastly, and most of all, *the* woman, my beloved wife Sharon: She gave me the impetus to begin this work; she gave me her own time, listening, reading, collating, checking, proofreading, and commenting; she allowed me to steal hundreds of weekend and evening hours from her and our family; and she gave me her unstinting friendship and love throughout. Without her, this work would not exist.